THE BEST OF

O
HENRY

THE BEST OF

O HENRY

OVER 100 STORIES
INCLUDING THE GIFT OF THE MAGI
AND THE FURNISHED ROOM

MALLARD
PRESS

An Imprint of BDD Promotional Book Company, Inc.
666 Fifth Avenue
New York, NY 10103

MALLARD
PRESS

Cabbages and Kings was first published in 1904
Roads of Destiny was first published in 1903
Whirligigs was first published in 1903
Heart of the West was first published in 1907
The Four Million was first published in 1906

This edition published in the United States of America in 1989 by
MALLARD PRESS
An Imprint of BDD Promotional Book Company, Inc.
666 Fifth Avenue
New York, NY 10103

'Mallard Press and its accompanying design and logo are trademarks
of BDD Promotional Book Company, Inc.'

By arrangement with The Octopus Group Limited

ISBN 0 792 45008 6

Printed and bound in the United Kingdom by William Clowes Ltd, Beccles.

CONTENTS

Introduction

WILLIAM SYDNEY PORTER (later known throughout the literary world by the pseudonym O. Henry) was born on 11 September 1862 in Greensboro, North Carolina. He was never close to his father, a family doctor with an interest verging on obsession in the theory of perpetual motion, and when his mother died of tuberculosis in 1865, Bill Porter was left a virtual orphan.

With little formal education, Bill had to rely on an aunt who ran a private school to provide him with reading material and encourage his story-writing. By the age of fifteen, however, he was at work in his uncle's drugstore in Greensboro, where he remained for the next five years. At 20, the pale, anaemic-looking youth travelled to Texas to work on a sheep farm. Despite his diffident manner, he was rapidly accepted by the cowboys, betraying at this early stage a capacity to win the confidence of people from walks of life far removed from his own – a quality that was to stand him in good stead in acquiring material for his stories. Young Porter was fascinated by his colleagues' accounts of the exploits of cattle rustlers and desperadoes, his ingenious imagination converting their anecdotes at a later date into such memorable tales as 'The Pimienta Pancakes' and 'Art and the Bronco'.

In 1884, the young man moved to Austin, Texas, embarking on a period of successive personal and professional failures and tragedies. Having met and fallen in love with a young Texan girl, Bill Porter was married soon after his move to the city. But their early happiness was soon overshadowed by the young bride's inherited illness and the death of their first child at under a year old. The couple's second child, Margaret, however, survived to maturity, enjoying her father's eventual rise to fame and fortune.

During this difficult time, Porter struggled to support his ailing family on the proceeds of his job as a draftsman at the General Land Office. Here he gained something of a reputation as a cartoonist, using every spare moment of his day to make caricature sketches of his colleagues. Encouraged by their admiration and yielding to his long-nurtured desire to write, Porter embarked on an ill-starred venture. In 1894 he launched a comic weekly magazine, *The Rolling Stone*, which folded after only a few issues.

Disheartened and in debt, Bill took a job as a teller at the First National Bank in Austin. What followed next is shrouded in mystery, but it seems that discrepancies amounting to just under $1,000 were discovered in the young man's accounts and he was dismissed, pending federal investigations. The Porter family moved to Houston, where Bill took a job as a journalist on the local paper, the *Post*.

It was nearly a year later, in 1896, that a warrant was issued for Bill's arrest on charges of embezzlement. Preferring to take his chances elsewhere, he left his young family and fled to New Orleans and thence to Mexico. For two years, he lived among the drifters and profiteers of this legendary refuge of renegades and fugitives. Subsequent rumour has it that he lived off the proceeds of a bank robbery, but, whatever the truth of the matter, he continued to support his family from over the border until news of his wife's rapidly declining health drew him back to Texas in 1898. She died soon afterwards, but not before seeing her husband indicted, tried and imprisoned for three years in the Ohio Federal Penitentiary.

Showing considerable courage in adversity and determination to build something positive out of his apparent ruin (characteristics reflected in many of his fictional creations, from downtrodden New York waitress Tildy to unlikely romantic Dry Valley Johnson), Porter turned his prison term to advantage. A model prisoner, he was popular with warders and fellow inmates alike. From the latter he gleaned valuable insights into the more engaging of criminal minds, employed later in his portrayal of the con men and petty thieves of collections such as *The Gentle Grafter*. From one of the prison staff, a certain Orrin Henry, Porter borrowed the famous pseudonym behind whose anonymity he was to launch his meteoric rise to success in the field of popular fiction.

O. Henry's first published stories, 'Whistling Dick's Christmas Stocking' and 'Georgia's Ruling', appeared in minor periodicals in 1899 and 1900 respectively. On his release from prison, O. Henry established himself in a shabby bedsitting-room in Pittsburgh, writing like a maniac and besieging New York editors and publishers with story upon story. The editor of *Ainslee's* magazine recognized a unique and innovative talent in the mysterious author from Ohio and offered to guarantee him an income if he would come to New York City. In 1902, therefore, O. Henry arrived in town. At once he was bowled over by his impressions of urban life, whose downtrodden masses, bar-flies and hucksters figure so largely in his best-known stories. He soon developed a liking (continued long after affluence and success might have been expected to induce a more comfort-oriented lifestyle) for pacing the streets late at night, studying faces, observing with a remarkable eye every tiny detail of workaday city life. As he later declared: 'I've got some of my best yarns from park benches, lamp posts and newspaper stands. . . . There are stories in everything.'

Thus began one of the most extraordinary careers in literary history. In the space of only eight years, this unknown and unlikely figure had established himself as America's most popular short story writer. Readers were captivated by his natural wit, human warmth and sympathy and the authentic dialect used in his evocations of drama lurking just beneath the surface of everyday life. His character sketches, drawn with the precision and economy of a cartoonist, and his dexterous plotting were unlike anything previously written and retain their uniquely irresistible appeal to this day.

Throughout his short prolific career, O. Henry continued to write for journals and magazines. By 1904, however, his reputation was such that he was encouraged to publish a collection of his stories. This appeared, to great acclaim, the same year. Drawing from his experiences in Mexico, *Cabbages and Kings* depicts life in a fictional 'volatile republic' of Central America peopled by wealthy speculators, colourful señoritas, blundering detectives and political intriguers. It is a lazy-paced world of irony, swindle and adventure, set against an exotic background and already the offbeat, surprise endings that were to become O. Henry's trademark, are apparent.

In the next, perhaps his most famous collection, *The Four Million*, published in 1906, the stories explore the swarming main streets and back alleys of New York, revealing with insight and compassionate humour the trials and foibles of an almost unlimited range of social types. This volume includes probably O. Henry's finest tale, 'The Gift of the Magi', a poignant story of impecunious love, sacrifice and irony at Christmas time.

Over the next four years, O. Henry's output of stories was little short of superhuman. In 1907 appeared *The Trimmed Lamp*, closely followed by *Heart of the West*, a collection of anecdotes set largely in Texas in which his inventive genius transformed the cowboys' tales told to him nearly 20 years earlier into such hilarious *tours de force* as 'The Pimienta Pancakes'. More tales of urban life were published in *The Voice of the City* in 1908, while in *Roads of Destiny* (1909), besides the quota of villainous outlaws, drifters and braggarts, he broadened his scope to include a Quixote-like fantasy set in Northern France. One of the stories from this volume, 'A Retrieved Reformation', was adapted for the stage and became the hit of the 1910 season under the title *Alias Jimmy Valentine*. Having refused to do the adaptation himself, O. Henry – never renowned for his financial know-how and shunning unwanted publicity – sold the dramatisation rights for a mere $500, thereby missing out on the $100,000 worth of royalties earned by the smash hit. *Options*, *Strictly Business* and *Whirligigs* appeared between the end of 1909 and the middle of 1910, the latter being a further collection of tales of office and business life, exploring the absurdities, coincidences and dramas of working existence in a furious whirl of hilarity and paradox.

O. Henry had remarried and moved back to the mid-West at the height of his success. The strain of constant pressure and the tension and excitement of city life had proved a drain on his physical resources and, when he returned to the city in 1910 he was immediately struck down with pneumonia at the Caledonian Hotel and died in hospital two days later at the age of 48. Three further volumes of short stories were published after his death, *Rolling Stones*, *Waifs and Strays* and *The Gentle Grafter*. The last of these, composed mainly of yarns about cool-headed sharp-dressing trickster Jeff Peters, was based on anecdotes heard during O. Henry's spell in prison. Among his most amusing volumes, these stories of con and counter-con are narrated in the persona of the eminently believable Peters, revealing at its best O. Henry's unique gift for authentic characterisation through dialogue.

The anonymity of style which is such a feature of O. Henry's writing appears to have been mirrored in the life of the man himself. Little is known of his personal life. He appears to have avoided friendship, although those who did know him have testified to his kindly and considerate nature. One such acquaintance described him as 'a childlike individual, absolutely without guile, and at times utterly helpless'. This courteous, self-deprecating character is now one of the legends of New York. His stories evoke all the glamour and loneliness of that glittering city in the age of the roué and the two-cent cup of coffee – an age now past. But the spirit of understanding, humour and wistful wisdom that shines through the stories of O. Henry is timeless, as compelling today as it ever was.

THE PROEM

by the Carpenter

THEY WILL TELL YOU IN ANCHURIA that President Miraflores, of that volatile republic, died by his own hand in the coast town of Coralio, that he had reached thus far in flight from the inconveniences of an imminent revolution, and that one hundred thousand dollars, government funds, which he carried with him in an American leather valise as a souvenir of his tempestuous administration, was never afterward recovered.

For a *real*, a boy will show you his grave. It is back of the town near a little bridge that spans a mangrove swamp. A plain slab of wood stands at its head. Some one has burned upon the headstone with a hot iron this inscription:

RAMON ANGEL DE LAS CRUZES

Y MIRAFLORES

PRESIDENTE DE LA REPUBLICA

DE ANCHURIA

QUE SEA SU JUEZ DIOS

It is characteristic of this buoyant people that they pursue no man beyond the grave. 'Let God be his judge!' – Even with the hundred thousand unfound, though greatly coveted, the hue and cry went no further than that.

To the stranger or the guest the people of Coralio will relate the story of the tragic end of their former president; how he strove to escape from the country with the public funds and also with Doña Isabel Guilbert, the young American opera singer; and how, being apprehended by members of the opposing political party in Coralio, he shot himself through the head rather than give up the funds, and, in consequence, the Señorita Guilbert. They will relate further that Doña Isabel, her adventurous bark of fortune shoaled by the simultaneous loss of her distinguished admirer and the souvenir hundred thousand, dropped anchor on this stagnant coast, awaiting a rising tide.

They say, in Coralio, that she found a prompt and prosperous tide in the form of Frank Goodwin, an American resident of the town, an investor who had grown wealthy by dealing in the products of the country – a banana king, a rubber prince, a sarsaparilla, indigo, and mahogany baron. The Señorita Guilbert, you will be told, married Señor Goodwin one month after the president's death, thus, in the very moment when Fortune had ceased to smile, wresting from her a gift greater than the prize withdrawn.

Of the American, Don Frank Goodwin, and of his wife the natives have nothing but good to say. Don Frank has lived among them for years, and has compelled their respect. His lady is easily queen of what social life the sober coast affords. The wife of the governor of the district, herself, who was of the proud Castilian family of Monteleon y Dolorosa de los Santos y Mendez, feels honored to unfold her napkin with olive-hued, ringed hands at the table of Señora Goodwin. Were you to refer (with your northern prejudices) to the vivacious past of Mrs. Goodwin when her audacious and gleeful abandon in light opera captured the mature president's fancy, or to her share in that statesman's downfall and malfeasance, the Latin shrug of the shoulder would be your only answer and rebuttal. What prejudices there were in Coralio concerning Señora Goodwin seemed now to be in her favor, whatever they had been in the past.

It would seem that the story is ended, instead of begun; that the close of tragedy and the climax of a romance have covered the ground of interest; but, to the more curious reader it shall be some slight instruction to trace the close threads that underlie the ingenuous web of circumstances.

The headpiece bearing the name of President Miraflores is daily scrubbed with soap-bark and sand. An old half-breed Indian tends the grave with fidelity and the dawdling minuteness of inherited sloth. He chops down the weeds and ever-springing grass with his machete, he plucks ants and scorpions and beetles from it with his horny fingers, and sprinkles its turf with water from the plaza fountain. There is no grave anywhere so well kept and ordered.

Only by following out the underlying threads will it be made clear why the old Indian, Galvez, is secretly paid to keep green the grave of President Miraflores by one who never saw that unfortunate statesman in life or in death, and why that one was wont to walk in the twilight, casting from a distance looks of gentle sadness upon that unhonored mound.

Elsewhere than at Coralio one learns of the impetuous career of Isabel Guilbert. New Orleans gave her birth and the mingled French and Spanish creole nature that tinctured her life with such turbulence and warmth. She had little education, but a knowledge of men and motives that seemed to have come by instinct. Far beyond the common woman was she endowed with intrepid rashness, with a love for the pursuit of adventure to the brink of danger, and with desire for the pleasures of life. Her spirit was one to chafe under any curb; she was Eve after the fall, but before the bitterness of it was felt. She wore life as a rose in her bosom.

Of the legion of men who had been at her feet it was said that but one was so fortunate as to engage her fancy. To President Miraflores, the brilliant but unstable ruler of Anchuria, she yielded the key to her resolute heart. How, then, do we find her (as the Coralians would have told you) the wife of Frank Goodwin, and happily living a life of dull and dreamy inaction?

The underlying threads reach far, stretching across the sea. Following them out it will be made plain why 'Shorty' O'Day, of the Columbia Detective Agency, resigned his position. And, for a lighter pastime, it shall be a duty and a pleasing sport to wander with Momus beneath the tropic stars where Melpomene once stalked austere. Now to cause laughter to echo from those lavish jungles and frowning crags where formerly rang the cries of pirates' victims; to lay aside pike and cutlass and attack with quip and jollity; to draw one saving titter of mirth from the rusty casque of Romance – this were pleasant to do in the shade of the lemon-trees on that coast that is curved like lips set for smiling.

For there are yet tales of the Spanish Main. That segment of continent washed by the tempestuous Caribbean, and presenting to the sea a formidable border of tropical jungle topped by the overweening Cordilleras, is still begirt by mystery and romance. In past times buccaneers and revolutionists roused the echoes of its cliffs, and the condor wheeled perpetually above where, in the green groves, they made food for him with their matchlocks and toledos.

Taken and retaken by sea rovers, by adverse powers and by sudden uprising of rebellious factions, the historic 300 miles of adventurous coast has scarcely known for hundreds of years whom rightly to call its master. Pizarro, Balboa, Sir Francis Drake, and Bolivar did what they could to make it a part of Christendom. Sir John Morgan, Lafitte, and other eminent swashbucklers bombarded and pounded it in the name of Abaddon.

The game still goes on. The guns of the rovers are silenced; but the tintype man, the enlarged photograph brigand, the kodaking tourist and the scouts of the gentle brigade of fakirs have found it out, and carry on the work. The hucksters of Germany, France, and Sicily now bag its small change across their counters. Gentleman adventurers throng the waiting-rooms of its rulers with proposals for railways and concessions. The little *opéra-bouffe* nations play at government and intrigue until some day a big, silent gunboat glides into the offing and warns them not to break their toys. And with these changes comes also the small adventurer, with empty pockets to fill, light of heart, busy-brained – the modern fairy prince, bearing an alarm clock with which, more surely than by the sentimental kiss, to awaken the beautiful tropics from their centuries' sleep. Generally he wears a shamrock, which he matches pridefully against the extravagant palms; and it is he who has driven Melpomene to the wings, and set Comedy to dancing before the footlights of the Southern Cross.

So, there is a little tale to tell of many things. Perhaps to the promiscuous ear of the Walrus it shall come with most avail; for in it there are indeed shoes and ships and sealing-wax and cabbage-palms and presidents instead of kings.

Add to these a little love and counterplotting, and scatter everywhere throughout the maze a trail of tropical dollars – dollars warmed no more by the torrid sun than by the hot palms of the scouts of Fortune – and, after all, here seems to be Life, itself, with talk enough to weary the most garrulous of Walruses.

FOX-IN-THE-MORNING'

CORALIO RECLINED, IN THE MID-DAY HEAT, like some vacuous beauty lounging in a guarded harem. The town lay at the sea's edge on a strip of alluvial coast. It was set like a little pearl in an emerald band. Behind it, and seeming almost to topple, imminent, above it, rose the sea-following range of the Cordilleras. In front the sea was spread, a smiling jailer, but even more incorruptible than the frowning mountains. The waves swished along the smooth beach; the parrots screamed in the orange and ceiba-trees; the palms waved their limber fronds foolishly like an awkward chorus at the prima donna's cue to enter.

Suddenly the town was full of excitement. A native boy dashed down a grass-grown street, shrieking: '*Busca el Señor* Goodwin. *Ha venido un telegrama por él!*'

The word passed quickly. Telegrams do not often come to anyone in Coralio. The cry of Señor Goodwin was taken up by a dozen officious voices. The main street running parallel to the beach became populated with those who desired to expedite the delivery of the despatch. Knots of women with complexions varying from palest olive to deepest brown gathered at street corners and plaintively carolled: 'Un telegrama por Señor Goodwin!' The comandante, Don Señor el Coronel Encarnación Rios, who was loyal to the Ins and suspected Goodwin's devotion to the Outs, hissed: 'Aha!' and wrote in his secret memorandum book the accusive fact the Señor Goodwin had on that momentous date received a telegram.

In the midst of the hullabaloo a man stepped to the door of a small wooden building and looked out. Above the door was a sign that read 'Keogh and Clancy' – a nomenclature that seemed not to be indigenous to that tropical soil. The man in the door was Billy Keogh, scout of fortune and progress and latter-day rover of the Spanish Main. Tintypes and photographs were the weapons with which Keogh and Clancy were at that time assailing the hopeless shores. Outside the shop were set two large frames filled with specimens of their art and skill.

Keogh leaned in the doorway, his bold and humorous countenance wearing a look of interest at the unusual influx of life and sound into the street. When the meaning of the disturbance became clear to him he placed a hand beside his mouth and shouted: 'Hey! Frank!' in such a robustious voice that the feeble clamor of the natives was drowned and silenced.

Fifty yards away, on the seaward side of the street, stood the abode of the consul for the United States. Out from the door of this building tumbled Goodwin at the call. He had been smoking with Willard Geddie, the consul, on the back porch of the consulate, which was conceded to be the coolest spot in Coralio.

'Hurry up,' shouted Keogh. 'There's a riot in town on account of a telegram that's come for you. You want to be careful about these things, my boy. It won't do to trifle with the feelings of the public this way. You'll be getting a pink note some day with violet scent on it; and then the country'll be steeped in the throes of a revolution.'

Goodwin had strolled up the street and met the boy with the message. The ox-eyed women gazed at him with shy admiration, for his type drew them. He was big, blond, and jauntily dressed in white linen, with buckskin zapatos. His manner was courtly, with a sort of kindly truculence in it tempered by a merciful eye. When the telegram had been delivered, and the bearer of it dismissed with a gratuity, the relieved populace returned to the contiguities of shade from which curiosity had drawn it – the women to their baking in the mud ovens under the orange-trees, or to the interminable combing of their long, straight hair; the men to their cigarettes and gossip in the cantinas.

Goodwin sat on Keogh's doorstep and read his telegram. It was from Bob Englehart, an American, who lived in San Mateo, the capital city of Anchuria, eighty miles in the interior. Englehart was a gold miner, an ardent revolutionist and 'good people.' That he was a man of resource and imagination was proven by the telegram he had sent. It had been his task to send a confidential message to his friend in Coralio. This could not have been accomplished in either Spanish or English, for the eye politic in Anchuria was an active one. The Ins and the Outs were perpetually on their guard. But Englehart was a diplomatist. There existed but one code upon which he might make requisition with promise of safety – the great and potent code of Slang. So, here is the message that slipped, unconstrued, through the fingers of curious officials, and came to the eye of Goodwin:

His Nibs skedaddled yesterday per jack-rabbit line with all the coin in the kitty and the bundle of muslin he's spoony about. The boodle is six figures short. Our crowd in good shape, but we need the spondulicks. You collar it. The main guy and the dry goods are headed for the briny. You know what to do.

Bob

This screed, remarkable as it was, had no mystery for Goodwin. He was the most successful of the small advance-guard of speculative Americans that had invaded Anchuria, and he had not reached that enviable pinnacle without having well exercised the arts of foresight and deduction. He had taken up political intrigue as a matter of business. He was acute enough to wield a certain influence among the leading schemers, and he was prosperous enough to be able to purchase the respect of the petty office-holders. There was always a revolutionary party; and to it he had always allied himself; for the adherents of a new administration received the rewards of their labors. There was now a Liberal party seeking to overturn President Miraflores. If the wheel successfully revolved, Goodwin stood to win a concession to 30,000 manzanas of the finest coffee lands in the interior. Certain incidents in the recent career of President Miraflores had excited a shrewd suspicion in Goodwin's mind that the government was near a dissolution from another cause than that of a revolution, and now Englehart's telegram had come as a corroboration of his wisdom.

The telegram, which had remained unintelligible to the Anchurian linguists who had applied to it in vain their knowledge of Spanish and elemental English, conveyed a stimulating piece of news to Goodwin's understanding. It informed him that the president of the republic had decamped from the capital city with the contents of the treasury. Furthermore, that he was accompanied in his flight by that winning adventuress Isabel Guilbert, the opera singer, whose troupe of performers had been entertained by the president at San Mateo during the past month on a scale less modest than that with which royal visitors are often content. The reference to the 'jack-rabbit line' could mean nothing else than the mule-back system of transport that prevailed between Coralio and the capital. The hint that the 'boodle' was 'six figures short' made the condition of the national treasury lamentably clear. Also it was convincingly true that the ingoing party – its way now made a pacific one – would need the 'spondulicks.' Unless its pledges should be fulfilled, and the spoils held for the delectation of the victors, precarious indeed would be the position of the new government. Therefore it was exceeding necessary to 'collar the main guy,' and recapture the sinews of war and government.

Goodwin handed the message to Keogh.

'Read that, Billy,' he said. 'It's from Bob Englehart. Can you manage the cipher?'

Keogh sat in the other half of the doorway, and carefully perused the telegram.

' 'Tis not a cipher,' he said, finally. ' 'Tis what they call literature, and that's a system of language put in the mouths of people that they've never been introduced to by writers of imagination. The magazines invented it, but I never knew before that President Norvin Green had stamped it with the seal of his approval. 'Tis now no longer literature, but language. The dictionaries tried, but they couldn't make it go for anything but dialect. Sure, now that the Western Union indorses it, it won't be long till a race of people will spring up that speaks it.'

'You're running too much to philology, Billy,' said Goodwin. 'Do you make out the meaning of it?'

'Sure,' replied the philosopher of Fortune. 'All languages come easy to the man who must know 'em. I've even failed to misunderstand an order to evacuate in classical Chinese when it was backed up by the muzzle of a breech-loader. This little literary essay I hold in my hands means a game of Fox-in-the-Morning. Ever play that, Frank, when you was a kid?'

'I think so,' said Goodwin, laughing. 'You join hands all 'round, and —'

'You do not,' interrupted Keogh. 'You've got a fine sporting game mixed up in your head with "All Around the Rosebush." The spirit of "Fox-in-the-Morning" is opposed to the holding of hands. I'll tell you how it's played. This president man and his companion in play, they stand up over in San Mateo, ready for the run, and shout: "Fox-in-the-Morning!" Me and you, standing here, we say: "Goose and the Gander!" They say: "How many miles is it to London town?" We say: "Only a few, if your legs are long enough. How many comes out?" They say: "More than you're able to catch." And then the game commences.'

'I catch the idea,' said Goodwin. 'It won't do to let the goose and gander slip through our fingers, Billy; their feathers are too valuable. Our crowd is prepared and able to step into the shoes of the government at once; but with the treasury empty we'd stay in power about as long as a tenderfoot would stick on an untamed bronco. We must play the fox on every foot of the coast to prevent their getting out of the country.'

'By the mule-back schedule,' said Keogh, 'it's five days down from San Mateo. We've got plenty of time to set out outposts. There's only three places on the coast where they can hope to sail from – here and Solitas and Alazan. They're the only points we'll have to guard. It's as easy as a chess problem – fox to play, and mate in three moves. Oh, goosey, goosey, gander, whither do you wander? By the blessing of the literary telegraph the boodle of this benighted fatherland shall be preserved to the honest political party that is seeking to overthrow it.'

The situation had been justly outlined by Keogh. The down trail from the capital was at all times a weary road to travel. A jiggety-joggety journey it was; ice-cold and hot, wet and dry. The trail climbed appalling mountains, wound like a rotten string about the brows of breathless precipices, plunged through chilling snow-fed streams, and wriggled like a snake through sunless forests teeming with menacing insect and animal life. After descending to the foothills it turned to a trident, the central prong ending at Alazan. Another branched off to Coralio; the third penetrated to Solitas. Between the sea and the foothills stretched the five miles breadth of alluvial coast. Here was the flora of the tropics in its rankest and most prodigal growth. Spaces here and there had been wrested from the jungle and planted with bananas and cane and orange groves. The rest was a riot of wild vegetation, the home of monkeys, tapirs, jaguars, alligators and prodigious reptiles and insects.

Where no road was cut a serpent could scarcely make its way through the tangle of vines and creepers. Across the treacherous mangrove swamps few things without wings could safely pass. Therefore the fugitives could hope to reach the coast only by one of the routes named.

'Keep the matter quiet, Billy,' advised Goodwin. 'We don't want the Ins to know that the president is in flight. I suppose Bob's information is something of a scoop in the capital as yet. Otherwise he would not have tried to make his message a confidential one; and besides, everybody would have heard the news. I'm going around now to see Dr. Zavalla, and start a man up the trail to cut the telegraph wire.'

As Goodwin rose, Keogh threw his hat upon the grass by the door and expelled a tremendous sigh.

'What's the trouble, Billy?' asked Goodwin, pausing. 'That's the first time I ever heard you sigh.'

' 'Tis the last,' said Keogh. 'With that sorrowful puff of wind I resign myself to a life of praiseworthy but harassing honesty. What are tin-types, if you please, to the opportunities of the great and hilarious class of ganders and geese? Not that I would be a president, Frank – and the boodle he's got is too big for me to handle – but in some ways I feel my conscience hurting me for addicting myself to photographing a nation instead of running away with it. Frank, did you ever see the "bundle of muslin" that His Excellency has wrapped up and carried off?'

'Isabel Guilbert?' said Goodwin, laughing. 'No, I never did. From what I've heard of her, though, I imagine that she wouldn't stick at anything to carry her point. Don't get romantic, Billy. Sometimes I begin to fear that there's Irish blood in your ancestry.'

'I never saw her either,' went on Keogh; 'but they say she's got all the ladies of mythology, sculpture, and fiction reduced to chromos. They say she can look at a man once, and he'll turn monkey and climb trees to pick cocoanuts for her. Think of that president man with Lord knows how many hundreds of thousands of dollars in one hand, and this muslin siren in the other, galloping down hill on a sympathetic mule amid song-birds and flowers! And here is Billy Keogh, because he is virtuous, condemned to the unprofitable swindle of slandering the faces of missing links on tin for an honest living! 'Tis an injustice of nature.'

'Cheer up,' said Goodwin. 'You are a pretty poor fox to be envying a gander. Maybe the enchanting Guilbert will take a fancy to you and your tintypes after we impoverish her royal escort.'

'She could do worse,' reflected Keogh; 'but she won't. 'Tis not a tintype gallery, but the gallery of the gods that she's fitted to adorn. She's a very wicked lady, and the president man is in luck. But I hear Clancy swearing in the back room for having to do all the work.' And Keogh plunged for the rear of the 'gallery,' whistling gaily in a spontaneous way that belied his recent sigh over the questionable good luck of the flying president.

Goodwin turned from the main street into a much narrower one that intersected it at a right angle.

These side streets were covered by a growth of thick, rank grass, which was kept to a navigable shortness by the machetes of the police. Stone sidewalks, little more than a ledge in width, ran along the base of the mean and monotonous adobe houses. At the outskirts of the village these streets dwindled to nothing; and here were set the palm-thatched huts of the Caribs and the poorer natives, and the shabby cabins of negroes from Jamaica and the West India islands. A few structures raised their heads above the red-tiled roofs of the one-story houses – the bell tower of the *Calaboza*, the Hotel de los Estranjeros, the residence of the Vesuvius Fruit Company's agent, the store and residence of Bernard Brannigan, a ruined cathedral in which Columbus had once set foot, and, most imposing of all, the Casa Morena – the summer 'White House' of the President of Anchuria. On the principal street running along the beach – the Broadway of Coralio – were the larger stores, the government *bodega* and post-office, the *cuartel*, the rum-shops and the market place.

On his way Goodwin passed the house of Bernard Brannigan. It was a modern wooden building, two stories in height. The ground floor was occupied by Brannigan's store, the upper one contained the living apartments. A wide cool porch ran around the house half way up its outer walls. A handsome, vivacious girl neatly dressed in flowing white leaned over the railing and smiled down upon Goodwin. She was no darker than many an Andalusian of high descent, and she sparkled and glowed like a tropical moonlight.

'Good evening, Miss Paula,' said Goodwin, taking off his hat, with his ready smile. There was little difference in his manner whether he addressed women or men. Everybody in Coralio like to receive the salutation of the big American.

'Is there any news, Mr. Goodwin? Please don't say no. Isn't it warm? I feel just like Mariana in her moated grange – or was it a range? – it's hot enough.'

'No, there's no news to tell, I believe,' said Goodwin, with a mischievous look in his eye, 'except that old Geddie is getting grumpier and crosser every day. If something doesn't happen to relieve his mind I'll have to quit smoking on his back porch – and there's no other place available that is cool enough.'

'He isn't grumpy,' said Paula Brannigan, impulsively, 'when he –'

But she ceased suddenly, and drew back with a deepening color; for her mother had been a *mestizo* lady, and the Spanish blood had brought to Paula a certain shyness that was an adornment to the other half of her demonstrative nature.

THE LOTUS AND THE BOTTLE

WILLARD GEDDIE, CONSUL FOR the United States in Coralio, was working leisurely on his yearly report. Goodwin, who had strolled in as he did daily for a smoke on the much coveted porch, had found him so absorbed in his work that he departed after roundly abusing the consul for his lack of hospitality.

'I shall complain to the civil service department,' said Goodwin; – 'or is it a department? – perhaps it's only a theory. One gets neither civility nor service from you. You won't talk; and you won't set out anything to drink. What kind of a way is that of representing your government?'

Goodwin strolled out and across to the hotel to see if he could bully the quarantine doctor into a game on Coralio's solitary billiard table. His plans were completed for the interception of the fugitives from the capital; and now it was but a waiting game that he had to play.

The consul was interested in his report. He was only twenty-four; and he had not been in Coralio long enough for his enthusiasm to cool in the heat of the tropics – a paradox that may be allowed between Cancer and Capricorn.

So many thousand bunches of bananas, so many thousand oranges and cocoanuts, so many ounces of gold dust, pounds of rubber, coffee, indigo and sarsaparilla – actually, exports were twenty per cent. greater than for the previous year!

A little thrill of satisfaction ran through the consul. Perhaps, he thought, the State Department, upon reading his introduction, would notice – and then he leaned back in his chair and laughed. He was getting as bad as the others. For the moment he had forgotten that Coralio was an insignificant town in an insignificant republic lying along the by-ways of a second-rate sea. He thought of Gregg, the quarantine doctor, who subscribed from the London *Lancet*, expecting to find it quoting his reports to the home Board of Health concerning the yellow fever germ. The consul knew that not one in fifty of his acquaintances in the States had ever heard of Coralio. He knew that two men, at any rate, would have to read his report – some underling in the State Department and a compositor in the Public Printing Office. Perhaps the typesticker would note the increase of commerce in Coralio, and speak of it, over the cheese and beer, to a friend.

He had just written: 'Most unaccountable is the supineness of the large exporters in the United States in permitting the French and German houses to practically control the trade interests of this rich and productive country' – when he heard the hoarse notes of a steamer's siren.

Geddie laid down his pen and gathered his Panama hat and umbrella. By the sound he knew it to be the *Valhalla*, one of the line of fruit vessels plying for the Vesuvius Company. Down to niños of five years, everyone in Coralio could name you each incoming steamer by the note of her siren.

The consul sauntered by a roundabout, shaded way to the beach. By reason of long practice he gauged his stroll so accurately that by the time he arrived on the sandy shore the boat of the customs officials was rowing back from the steamer, which had been boarded and inspected according to the laws of Anchuria.

There is no harbor at Coralio. Vessels of the draught of the *Valhalla* must ride at anchor a mile from shore. When they take on fruit it is conveyed on lighters and freighter sloops. At Solitas, where there was a fine harbor, ships of many kinds were to be seen, but in the roadstead off Coralio scarcely any save the fruiters paused. Now and then a tramp coaster, or a mysterious brig from Spain, or a saucy French barque would hang innocently for a few days in the offing. Then the custom-house crew would become doubly vigilant and wary. At night a sloop or two would be making strange trips in and out along the shore; and in the morning the stock of Three-Star Hennessey, wines and drygoods in Coralio would be found vastly increased. It has also been said that the customs officials jingled more silver in the pockets of their red-striped trousers, and that the record books showed no increase in import duties received.

The customs boat and the *Valhalla* gig reached the shore at the same time. When they grounded in the shallow water there was still five yards of rolling surf between them and dry sand. Then half-clothed Caribs dashed into the water, and brought in on their backs the *Valhalla's* purser and the little native officials in their cotton undershirts, blue trousers with red stripes, and flapping straw hats.

At college Geddie had been a treasure as a first-baseman. He now closed his umbrella, stuck it upright in the sand, and stooped, with his hands resting upon his knees. The purser, burlesquing the pitchers' contortions, hurled at the consul the heavy roll of newspapers, tied with a string, that the steamer always brought for him. Geddie leaped high and caught the roll with a sounding 'thwack.' The loungers on the beach – about a third of the population of the town – laughed and applauded delightedly. Every week they expected to see that roll of papers delivered and received in the same manner, and they were never disappointed. Innovations did not flourish in Coralio.

The consul re-hoisted his umbrella and walked back to the consulate.

This home of a great nation's representative was a wooden structure of two rooms, with a native-built gallery of poles, bamboo and nipa palm running on three sides of it. One room was the official apartment, furnished chastely with a flat-top desk, a hammock, and three uncomfortable cane-seated chairs. Engravings of the first and latest president of the country represented hung against the wall. The other room was the consul's living apartment.

It was eleven o'clock when he returned from the beach, and therefore breakfast time. Chanca, the Carib woman who cooked for him, was just serving the meal on the side of the gallery facing the sea – a spot famous as the coolest in Coralio. The breakfast consisted of shark's fin soup, stew of land crabs, breadfruit, a boiled iguana steak, aguacates, a freshly cut pineapple, claret and coffee.

Geddie took his seat and unrolled with luxurious laziness his bundle of newspapers. Here in Coralio for two days or longer he would read of goings-on in the world very much as we of the world read those whimsical contributions to inexact science that assume to portray the doings of the Martians. After he had finished with the papers they would be sent on the rounds of the other English-speaking residents of the town.

The paper that came first to his hand was one of those bulky mattresses of printed stuff upon which the readers of certain New York journals are supposed to take their Sabbath literary nap. Opening this the consul rested it upon the table, supporting its weight with the aid of the back of a chair. Then he partook of his meal deliberately, turning the leaves from time to time and glancing half idly at the contents.

Presently he was struck by something familiar to him in a picture – a half-page, badly printed reproduction of a photograph of a vessel. Languidly interested, he leaned for a nearer scrutiny and a view of the florid headlines of the column next to the picture.

Yes, he was not mistaken. The engraving was of the eight-hundred-ton yacht *Idalia*, belonging to 'that prince of good fellows, Midas of the money market, and society's pink of perfection, J. Ward Tolliver.'

Slowly sipping his black coffee, Geddie read the column of print. Following a listed statement of Mr. Tolliver's real estate and bonds, came a description of the yacht's furnishings, and then the grain of news no bigger than a mustard seed. Mr. Tolliver, with a party of favored guests, would sail the next day on a six weeks' cruise along the Central American and South

American coasts and among the Bahama Islands. Among the guests were Mrs. Cumberland Payne and Miss Ida Payne, of Norfolk.

The writer, with the fatuous presumption that was demanded of him by his readers, had concocted a romance suited to their palates. He bracketed the names of Miss Payne and Mr. Tolliver until he had well-nigh read the marriage ceremony over them. He played coyly and insinuatingly upon the strings of 'on dit' and 'Madame Rumor' and 'a little bird' and 'no one would be surprised,' and ended with congratulations.

Geddie, having finished his breakfast, took his papers to the edge of the gallery, and sat there in his favorite steamer chair with his feet on the bamboo railing. He lighted a cigar, and looked out upon the sea. He felt a glow of satisfaction at finding he was so little disturbed by what he had read. He told himself that he had conquered the distress that had sent him, a voluntary exile, to this far land of the lotus. He could never forget Ida, of course; but there was no longer any pain in thinking about her. When they had had that misunderstanding and quarrel he had impulsively sought his consulship with the desire to retaliate upon her by detaching himself from her world and presence. He had succeeded thoroughly in that. During the twelve months of his life in Coralio no word had passed between them, though he had sometimes heard of her through the dilatory correspondence with the few friends to whom he still wrote. Still he could not repress a little thrill of satisfaction at knowing that she had not yet married Tolliver or any one else. But evidently Tolliver had not yet abandoned hope.

Well, it made no difference to him now. He had eaten of the lotus. He was happy and content in this land of perpetual afternoon. Those old days of life in the States seemed like an irritating dream. He hoped Ida would be as happy as he was. The climate as balmy as that of distant Avalon; the fetterless idyllic round of enchanted days; the life among this indolent, romantic people – a life full of music, flowers, and low laughter; the influence of the imminent sea and mountains, and the many shapes of love and magic and beauty that bloomed in the white tropic nights – with all he was more than content. Also, there was Paula Brannigan.

Geddie intended to marry Paula – if, of course, she would consent; but he felt rather sure that she would do that. Somehow, he kept postponing his proposal. Several times he had been quite near to it; but a mysterious something always held him back. Perhaps it was only the unconscious, instinctive conviction that the act would sever the last tie that bound him to his old world.

He could be very happy with Paula. Few of the native girls could be compared with her. She had attended a convent school in New Orleans for two years; and when she chose to display her accomplishments no one could detect any difference between her and the girls of Norfolk and Manhattan. But it was delicious to see her at home dressed, as she sometimes was, in the native costume, with bare shoulders and flowing sleeves.

Bernard Brannigan was the great merchant of Coralio. Besides his store, he maintained a train of pack mules, and carried on a lively trade with the interior towns and villages. He had married a native lady of high Castilian descent but with a tinge of Indian brown showing through her olive cheek. The union of the Irish and the Spanish had produced, as it so often has, an offshoot of rare beauty and variety. They were very excellent people indeed, and the upper story of their house was ready to be placed at the service of Geddie and Paula as soon as he should make up his mind to speak about it.

By the time two hours were whiled away the consul tired of reading. The papers lay scattered about him on the gallery. Reclining there, he gazed dreamily out upon an Eden. A clump of banana plants interposed their broad shields between him and the sun. The gentle slope from the consulate to the sea was covered with the dark-green foliage of lemon-trees and orange-trees just bursting into bloom. A lagoon pierced the land like a dark jagged crystal, and above it a pale ceiba-tree rose almost to the clouds. The waving cocoanut palms on the beach flared their decorative green leaves against the slate of an almost quiescent sea. His senses were cognizant of brilliant scarlet and ochres amid the vert of the coppice, of odors of fruit and bloom and the smoke from Chanca's clay oven under the calabash-tree; of the treble laughter of the native women in their huts, the song of the robin, the salt taste of the breeze, the diminuendo of the faint surf running along the shore – and, gradually, of a white speck, growing to a blur, that introduced itself upon the drab prospect of the sea.

Lazily interested, he watched this blue increase until it became the *Idalia* steaming at full speed, coming down the coast. Without changing his position he kept his eyes upon the beautiful white yacht as she drew swiftly near and came opposite to Coralio. Then, sitting upright, he saw her float steadily past and on. Scarcely a mile of sea had separated her from the shore. He had seen the frequent flash of her polished brass work and the stripes of her deck-awnings – so much, and no more. Like a ship on a magic lantern slide the *Idalia* had crossed the illuminated circle of the consul's little world, and was gone. Save for the tiny cloud of smoke that was left hanging over the brim of the sea, she might have been an immaterial thing, a chimera of his idle brain.

Geddie went into his office and sat down to dawdle over his report. If the reading of the article in the paper had left him unshaken, this silent passing of the *Idalia* had done for him still more. It had brought the calm and peace of a situation from which all uncertainty had been erased. He knew that men sometimes hope without being aware of it. Now, since she had come two thousand miles and had passed without a sign, not even his unconscious self need cling to the past any longer.

After dinner, when the sun was low behind the mountains, Geddie walked on the little strip of beach under the cocoanuts. The wind was blowing mildly landward, and the surface of the sea was rippled by tiny wavelets.

A miniature breaker, spreading with a soft 'swish' upon the sand, brought with it something round and shiny that rolled back again as the wave receded. The next influx beached it clear, and Geddie picked it up. The thing was a long-necked wine bottle of colorless glass. The cork had been driven in tightly to the level of the mouth, and the end covered with dark-red sealing-wax. The bottle contained only what seemed to be a sheet of paper, much curled from the manipulation it had undergone while being inserted. In the sealing-wax was the impression of a seal – probably of a signet-ring, bearing the initials of a monogram; but the impression had been hastily made, and the letters were past anything more certain than a shrewd conjecture. Ida Payne had always worn a signet-ring in preference to any other finger decoration. Geddie thought he could make out the familiar 'I P'; and a queer sensation of disquietude went over him. More personal and intimate was this reminder of her than had been the sight of the vessel she was doubtless on. He walked back to his house, and set the bottle on his desk.

Throwing off his hat and coat, and lighting a lamp – for the night had crowded precipitately upon the brief twilight – he began to examine his piece of sea salvage.

By holding the bottle near the light and turning it judiciously, he made out that it contained a double sheet of note-paper filled with close writing; further, that the paper was of the same size and shade as that always used by Ida; and that, to the best of his belief, the handwriting was hers. The imperfect glass of the bottle so distorted the rays of light that he could read no word of the writing; but certain capital letters, of which he caught comprehensive glimpses, were Ida's, he felt sure.

There was a little smile both of perplexity and amusement in Geddie's eyes as he set the bottle down, and laid three cigars side by side on his desk. He fetched his steamer chair from the gallery, and stretched himself comfortably. He would smoke those three cigars while considering the problem.

For it amounted to a problem. He almost wished that he had not found the bottle; but the bottle was there. Why should it have drifted in from the sea, whence come so many disquieting things, to disturb his peace?

In this dreamy land, where time seemed so redundant, he had fallen into the habit of bestowing much thought upon even trifling matters.

He began to speculate upon many fanciful theories concerning the story of the bottle, rejecting each in turn.

Ships in danger of wreck or disablement sometimes cast forth such precarious messengers calling for aid. But he had seen the *Idalia* not three hours before, safe and speeding. Suppose the crew had mutinied and imprisoned the passengers below, and the message was one begging for succor! But, premising such an improbable outrage, would the agitated captives have taken the pains to fill four pages of note-paper with carefully penned arguments to their rescue?

Thus by elimination he soon rid the matter of the more unlikely theories, and was reduced – though aversely – to the less assailable one that the bottle contained a message to himself. Ida knew he was in Coralio; she must have launched the bottle while the yacht was passing and the wind blowing fairly toward the shore.

As soon as Geddie reached this conclusion a wrinkle came between his brows and a stubborn look settled around his mouth. He sat looking out through the doorway at the gigantic fire-flies traversing the quiet streets.

If this was a message to him from Ida, what could it mean save an overture toward a reconciliation? And if that, why had she not used the safe methods of the post instead of this uncertain and even flippant means of communication? A note in an empty bottle, cast into the sea! There was something light and frivolous about it, if not actually contemptuous.

The thought stirred his pride and subdued whatever emotions had been resurrected by the finding of the bottle.

Geddie put on his coat and hat and walked out. He followed a street that led him along the border of the little plaza where a band was playing and people were rambling, care-free and indolent. Some timorous *señoritas* scurrying past with fire-flies tangled in the jetty braids of their hair glanced at him with shy, flattering eyes. The air was languorous with the scent of jasmin and orange-blossoms.

The consul stayed his steps at the house of Bernard Brannigan. Paula was swinging in a hammock on the gallery. She rose from it like a bird from its nest. The color came to her cheek at the sound of Geddie's voice.

He was charmed at the sight of her costume – a flounced muslin dress, with a little jacket of white flannel, all made with neatness and style. He suggested a stroll, and they walked out to the old Indian well on the hill road. They sat on the curb, and there Geddie made the expected but long-deferred speech. Certain though he had been that she would not say him nay, he was thrilled with joy at the completeness and sweetness of her surrender. Here was surely a heart made for love and steadfastness. Here was no caprice or questionings or captious standards of convention.

When Geddie kissed Paula at her door that night he was happier than he had ever been before. 'Here in this hollow lotus land, ever to live and lie reclined' seemed to him, as it has seemed to many mariners, the best as well as the easiest. His future would be an ideal one. He had attained a Paradise without a serpent. His Eve would be indeed a part of him, unbeguiled, and therefore more beguiling. He had made his decision tonight, and his heart was full of serene, assured content.

Geddie went back to his house whistling that finest and saddest love song, 'La Golondrina.' At the door his tame monkey leaped down from his shelf, chattering briskly. The consul turned to his desk to get him some nuts he usually kept there. Reaching in the half-darkness, his hand struck against the bottle. He started as if he had touched the cold rotundity of a serpent.

He had forgotten that the bottle was there.

He lighted the lamp and fed the monkey. Then, very deliberately, he lighted a cigar and took the bottle in his hand and walked down the path to the beach.

There was a moon and the sea was glorious. The breeze had shifted, as it did each evening, and was now rushing steadily seaward.

Stepping to the water's edge, Geddie hurled the unopened bottle far out into the sea. It disappeared for a moment, and then shot upward twice its length. Geddie stood still, watching it. The moonlight was so bright that he could see it bobbing up and down with the little waves. Slowly it receded from the shore, flashing and turning as it went. The wind was carrying it out to sea. Soon it became a mere speck, doubtfully discerned at irregular intervals; and then the mystery of it was swallowed up by the greater mystery of the ocean. Geddie stood still upon the beach, smoking and looking out upon the water.

'Simon! – Oh, Simon! – wake up there, Simon!' bawled a sonorous voice at the edge of the water.

Old Simon Cruz was a half-breed fisherman and smuggler who lived in a hut on the beach. Out of his earliest nap Simon was thus awakened.

He slipped on his shoes and went outside. Just landing from one of the *Valhalla's* boats was the third mate of that vessel, who was an acquaintance of Simon's, and three sailors from the fruiter.

'Go up, Simon,' called the mate, 'and find Dr. Gregg or Mr. Goodwin or anybody that's a friend to Mr. Geddie, and bring 'em here at once.'

'Saints of the skies!' said Simon, sleepily, 'nothing has happened to Mr. Geddie?'

'He's under that tarpauling,' said the mate, pointing to the boat, 'and he's rather more than half drowned. We seen him from the steamer nearly a mile out from shore, swimmin' like mad after a bottle that was floatin' in the water outward bound. We lowered the gig and started for him. He nearly had his hand on the bottle, when he gave out and went under. We pulled him out in time to save him, maybe; but the doctor is the one to decide that.'

'A bottle?' said the old man, rubbing his eyes. He was not yet fully awake. 'Where is the bottle?'

'Driftin' along out there some'eres,' said the mate, jerking his thumb toward the sea. 'Get on with you, Simon.'

SMITH

GOODWIN AND THE ARDENT PATRIOT, Zavalla, took all the precautions that their foresight could contrive to prevent the escape of President Miraflores and his companion. They sent trusted messengers up the coast to Solitas and Alazan to warn the local leaders of the flight, and to instruct them to patrol the water line and arrest the fugitives at all hazards should they reveal themselves in that territory. After this was done there remained only to cover the district about Coralio and await the coming of the quarry. The nets were well spread. The roads were so few, the opportunities for embarkation so limited, and the two or three probable points of exit so well guarded that it would be strange indeed if there should slip through the meshes so much of the country's dignity, romance, and collateral. The president would, without doubt, move as secretly as possible and endeavor to board a vessel by stealth from some secluded point along the shore.

On the fourth day after the receipt of Englehart's telegram the *Karlsefin*, a Norwegian steamer chartered by the New Orleans fruit trade, anchored off Coralio with three hoarse toots of her siren. The *Karlsefin* was not one of the line operated by the Vesuvius Fruit Company. She was something of a dilettante, doing odd jobs for a company that was scarcely important enough to figure as a rival to the Vesuvius. The movements of the *Karlsefin* were dependent upon the state of the market. Sometimes she would ply steadily between the Spanish Main and New Orleans in the regular transport of fruit; next she would be making erratic trips to Mobile or Charleston, or even as far north as New York, according to the distribution of the fruit supply.

Goodwin lounged upon the beach with the usual crowd of idlers that had gathered to view the steamer. Now that President Miraflores might be expected to reach the borders of his adjured country at any time, the orders were to keep a strict and unrelenting watch. Every vessel that approached the shores might now be considered a possible means of escape for the fugitives; and an eye was kept even on the sloops and dories that belonged to the sea-going contingent of Coralio. Goodwin and Zavalla moved everywhere, but without ostentation, watching the loopholes of escape.

The customs officials crowded importantly into their boat and rowed out to the *Karlsefin*. A boat from the steamer landed her purser with his papers, and took out the quarantine doctor with his green umbrella and clinical thermometer. Next a swarm of Caribs began to load upon lighters the thousands of bunches of bananas heaped upon the shore and row them out to the steamer. The *Karlsefin* had no passenger list, and was soon done with the attention of the authorities. The purser declared that the steamer would remain at anchor until morning, taking on her fruit during the night. The *Karlsefin* had come, he said, from New York, to which port her latest load of oranges and cocoanuts had been conveyed. Two or three of the freighter sloops were engaged to assist in the work, for the captain was anxious to make a quick return in order to reap the advantage offered by a certain dearth of fruit in the States.

About four o'clock in the afternoon another of those marine monsters, not very familiar in those waters, hove in sight, following the fateful *Idalia* – a graceful steam yacht, painted a light buff, clean-cut as a steel engraving. The beautiful vessel hovered off shore, seesawing the waves as lightly as a duck in a rain barrel. A swift boat manned by a crew in uniform came ashore, and a stocky-built man leaped to the sands.

The new-comer seemed to turn a disapproving eye upon the rather motley congregation of native Anchurians, and made his way at once toward Goodwin, who was the most conspicuously Anglo-Saxon figure present. Goodwin greeted him with courtesy.

Conversation developed that the newly landed one was named Smith, and that he had come in a yacht. A meagre biography, truly; for the yacht was most apparent; and the 'Smith' not beyond a reasonable guess before the revelation. Yet to the eye of Goodwin, who had seen several things, there was a discrepancy between Smith and his yacht. A bullet-headed man Smith was, with an oblique, dead eye and the moustache of a cocktail-mixer. And unless he had shifted costumes before putting off for shore he had affronted the deck of his correct vessel clad in a pearl-gray derby, a gay plaid suit and vaudeville neckwear. Men owning pleasure yachts generally harmonize better with them.

Smith looked business, but he was no advertiser. He commented upon the scenery, remarking upon its fidelity to the pictures in the geography; and then inquired for the United States consul. Goodwin pointed out the starred-and-striped bunting hanging above the little consulate, which was concealed behind the orange-trees.

'Mr. Geddie, the consul, will be sure to be there,' said Goodwin. 'He was very nearly drowned a few days ago while taking a swim in the sea, and the doctor has ordered him to remain indoors for some time.'

Smith plowed his way through the sand to the consulate, his haberdashery creating violent discord against the smooth tropical blues and greens.

Geddie was lounging in his hammock, somewhat pale of face and languid in pose. On that night when the *Valhalla's* boat had brought him ashore apparently drenched to death by the sea, Dr. Gregg and his other friends had toiled for hours to preserve the little spark of life that remained to him. The bottle, with its impotent message, was gone out to sea, and the problem that it had provoked was reduced to a simple sum in addition – one and one make two, by the rule of arithmetic; one by the rule of romance.

There is a quaint old theory that man may have two souls – a peripheral one which serves ordinarily, and a central one which is stirred only at certain times, but then with activity and vigor. While under the domination of the former a man will shave, vote, pay taxes, give money to his family, buy subscription books and comport himself on the average plan. But let the central soul suddenly become dominant, and he may, in the twinkling of an eye, turn upon the partner of his joys with furious execration; he may change his politics while you could snap your fingers; he may deal out deadly insult to his dearest friend; he may get him, instanter, to a monastery or a dance hall; he may elope, or hang himself – or he may write a song or poem, or kiss his wife unasked, or give his funds to the search of a microbe. Then the peripheral soul will return; and we have our safe, sane citizen again. It is but the revolt of the Ego against Order; and its effect is to shake up the atoms only that they may settle where they belong.

Geddie's revulsion had been a mild one – no more than a swim in a summer sea after so inglorious an object as a drifting bottle. And now he was himself again. Upon his desk, ready for the post, was a letter to his government tendering his resignation as consul, to be effective as soon as another could be appointed in his place. For Bernard Brannigan, who never did things in a half-way manner, was to take Geddie at once for a partner in his very profitable and various enterprises; and Paula was happily engaged in plans for refurnishing and decorating the upper story of the Brannigan house.

The consul rose from his hammock when he saw the conspicuous stranger in his door.

'Keep your seat, old man,' said the visitor, with an airy wave of his large hand. 'My name's Smith; and I've come in a yacht. You are the consul – is that right? A big, cool guy on the beach directed me here. Thought I'd pay my respects to the flag.'

'Sit down,' said Geddie. 'I've been admiring your craft ever since it came in sight. Looks like a fast sailer. What's her tonnage?'

'Search me!' said Smith. 'I don't know what she weighs in at. But she's got a tidy gait. The *Rambler* – that's her name – don't take the dust of anything afloat. This is my first trip on her. I'm taking a squint along this coast just to get an idea of the countries where the rubber and red pepper and revolutions come from. I had no idea there was so much scenery down here. Why, Central Park ain't in it with this neck of the woods. I'm from New York. They get monkeys, and cocoanuts, and parrots down here – is that right?'

'We have them all,' said Geddie. 'I'm quite sure that our fauna and flora would take a prize over Central Park.'

'Maybe they would,' admitted Smith, cheerfully. 'I haven't seen them yet. But I guess you've got us skinned on the animal and vegetation question. You don't have much travel here, do you?'

'Travel?' queried the consul. 'I suppose you mean passengers on the steamers. No; very few people land in Coralio. An investor now and then – tourists and sight-seers generally go further down the coast to one of the larger towns where there is a harbor.'

'I see a ship out there loading up with bananas,' said Smith. 'Any passengers come on her?'

'That's the *Karlsefin*,' said the consul. 'She's a tramp fruiter – made her last trip to New York, I believe. No; she brought no passengers. I saw her boat come ashore, and there was no one. About the only exciting recreation we have here is watching steamers when they arrive; and a passenger on one of them generally causes the whole town to turn out. If you are going to remain in Coralio a while, Mr. Smith, I'll be glad to take you around to meet some people. There are four or five American chaps that are good to know, besides the native high-fliers.'

'Thanks,' said the yachtsman, 'but I wouldn't put you to the trouble. I'd like to meet the guys you speak of, but I won't be here long enough to do much knocking around. That cool gent on the beach spoke of a doctor; can you tell me where I could find him? The *Rambler* ain't quite as steady on her feet as a Broadway hotel; and a fellow gets a touch of seasickness now and then. Thought I'd strike the croaker for a handful of the little sugar pills, in case I need 'em.'

'You will be apt to find Dr. Gregg at the hotel,' said the consul. 'You can see it from the door – it's that two-story building with the balcony, where the orange-trees are.'

The Hotel de los Estranjeros was a dreary hostelry, in great disuse both by strangers and friends. It stood at a corner of the Street of the Holy Sepulchre. A grove of small orange-trees crowded against one side of it, enclosed by a low, rock wall over which a tall man might easily step. The house was of plastered adobe, stained a hundred shades of color by the salt breeze and the sun. Upon its upper balcony opened a central door and two windows containing broad jalousies instead of sashes.

The lower floor communicated by two doorways with the narrow, rock-paved sidewalk. The *pulperia* – or drinking shop – of the proprietress, Madama Timotea Ortiz, occupied the ground floor. On the bottles of brandy, *anisada*, Scotch 'smoke' and inexpensive wines behind the little counter the dust lay thick save where the fingers of infrequent customers had left irregular prints. The upper story contained four or five guest-rooms which were rarely put to their destined use. Sometimes a fruit-grower, riding in from his plantation to confer with his agent, would pass a melancholy night in the dismal upper story; sometimes a minor native official on some trifling government quest would have his pomp and majesty awed by Madama's sepulchral hospitality. But Madama sat behind her bar content, nor desiring to quarrel with Fate. If any one required meat, drink, or lodging at the Hotel de los Estranjeros they had but to come, and be served. *Está bueno*. If they came not, why, then, they came not. *Está bueno*.

As the exceptional yachtsman was making his way down the precarious sidewalk of the Street of the Holy Sepulchre, the solitary permanent guest of that decaying hotel sat at its door, enjoying the breeze from the sea.

Dr. Gregg, the quarantine physician, was a man of fifty or sixty, with a florid face and the longest beard between Topeka and Terra del Fuego. He held his position by virtue of an appointment by the Board of Health of a seaport city in one of the Southern states. That city feared the ancient enemy of every Southern seaport – the yellow fever – and it was the duty of Dr. Gregg to examine crew and passengers of every vessel leaving Coralio for preliminary symptoms. The duties were light, and the salary, for one who lived in Coralio, ample. Surplus time there was in plenty; and the good doctor added to his gains by a large private practice among the residents of the coast. The fact that he did not know ten words of Spanish was no obstacle; a pulse could be felt and a fee collected without one being a linguist. Add to the description the facts that the doctor had a story to tell concerning the operation of trepanning which no listener had ever allowed him to conclude, and that he believed in brandy as a prophylactic; and the special points of interest possessed by Dr. Gregg will have become exhausted.

The doctor had dragged a chair to the sidewalk. He was coatless, and he leaned back against the wall and smoked, while he stroked his beard. Surprise came into his pale blue eyes when he caught sight of Smith in his unusual and prismatic clothes.

'You're Dr. Gregg – is that right?' said Smith, feeling the dog's head pin in his tie. 'The constable – I mean the consul, told me you hung out at this caravansary. My name's Smith; and I came in a yacht. Taking a cruise around, looking at the monkeys and pineapple trees. Come inside and have a drink, Doc. This café looks on the blink, but I guess it can set out something wet.'

'I will join you, sir, in just a taste of brandy,' said Dr. Gregg, rising quickly 'I find that as a prophylactic a little brandy is almost a necessity in this climate.'

As they turned to enter the *pulperia* a native man, barefoot, glided noiselessly up and addressed the doctor in Spanish. He was yellowish-brown, like an over-ripe lemon; he wore a cotton shirt and ragged linen trousers girded by a leather belt. His face was like an animal's, live and wary, but without promise of much intelligence. This man jabbered with animation and so much seriousness that it seemed a pity that his words were to be wasted.

Dr. Gregg felt his pulse.

'You sick?' he inquired.

'*Mi mujer está enferma en la casa,*' said the man, thus endeavoring to convey the news, in the only language open to him, that his wife lay ill in her palm-thatched hut.

The doctor drew a handful of capsules filled with a white powder from his trousers pocket. He counted out ten of them into the native's hand, and held up his forefinger impressively.

'Take one,' said the doctor, 'every two hours.' He then held up two fingers, shaking them emphatically before the native's face. Next he pulled out his watch and ran his finger round its dial twice. Again the two fingers confronted the patient's nose. 'Two – two – two hours,' repeated the doctor.

'*Si Señor,*' said the native, sadly.

He pulled a cheap silver watch from his own pocket and laid it in the doctor's hand. 'Me bring,' said he, struggling painfully with his scant English, 'other watchy to-morrow.' Then he departed downheartedly with his capsules.

'A very ignorant race of people, sir,' said the doctor, as he slipped the watch into his pocket. 'He seems to have mistaken my directions for taking the physic for the fee. However, it is all right. He owes me an account, anyway. The chances are that he won't bring the other watch. You can't depend on anything they promise you. About that drink, now? How did you come to Coralio, Mr. Smith? I was not aware that any boats except the *Karlsefin* had arrived for some days.'

The two leaned against the deserted bar; and Madama set out a bottle without waiting for the doctor's order. There was no dust on it.

After they had drank twice Smith said:

'You say there were no passengers on the *Karlsefin*, Doc? Are you sure about that? It seems to me I heard somebody down on the beach say that there was one or two aboard.'

'They were mistaken, sir. I myself went out and put all hands through a medical examination, as usual. The *Karlsefin* sails as soon as she gets her bananas loaded, which will be about daylight in the morning, and she got everything ready this afternoon. No, sir, there was no passenger list. Like that Three-Star? A French schooner landed two slooploads of it a month ago. If any customs duties on it went to the distinguished republic of Anchuria you may have my hat. If you won't have another, come out and let's sit in the cool a while. It isn't often we exiles get a chance to talk with somebody from the outside world.

The doctor brought out another chair to the sidewalk for his new acquaintance. The two seated themselves.

'You are a man of the world,' said Dr. Gregg; 'a man of travel and experience. Your decision in a manner of ethics and, no doubt, on the points of equity, ability, and professional probity should be of value. I would be glad if you will listen to the history of a case that I think stands unique in medical annals.

'About nine years ago, while I was engaged in the practice of medicine in my native city, I was called to treat a case of contusion of the skull. I made the diagnosis that a splinter of bone was pressing upon the brain, and that the surgical operation known as trepanning was required. However, as the patient was a gentleman of wealth and position, I called in for consultation Dr. — '

Smith rose from his chair, and laid a hand, soft with apology, upon the doctor's shirt sleeve.

'Say, Doc,' he said, solemnly, 'I want to hear that story. You've got me interested; and I don't want to miss the rest of it. I know it's a loola by the way it begins; and I want to tell it at the next meeting of the Barney O'Flynn Association, if you don't mind. But I've got one or two matters to attend to first. If I get 'em attended to in time I'll come right back and hear you spiel the rest before bedtime – is that right?'

'By all means,' said the doctor, 'get your business attended to, and then return. I shall wait up for you. You see, one of the most prominent physicians at the consultation diagnosed the trouble as a blood clot; another said it was an abscess, but I — '

'Don't tell me now, Doc. Don't spoil the story. Wait till I come back. I want to hear it as it runs off the reel – is that right?'

The mountains reached up their bulky shoulders to receive the level gallop of Apollo's homing steeds, the day died in the lagoons and in the shadowed banana groves and in the mangrove swamps, where the great blue crabs were beginning to crawl to land for their nightly ramble. And it died, at last, upon the highest peaks. Then the brief twilight, ephemeral as the flight of a moth, came and went; the Southern Cross peeped with its topmost eye above a row of palms, and the fire-flies heralded with their torches the approach of soft-footed night.

In the offing the *Karlsefin* swayed at anchor, her lights seeming to penetrate the water to countless fathoms with their shimmering, lanceolate reflections. The Caribs were busy loading her by means of the great lighters heaped full from the piles of fruit ranged upon the shore.

On the sandy beach, with his back against a cocoanut-tree and the stubs of many cigars lying around him, Smith sat waiting, never relaxing his sharp gaze in the direction of the steamer.

The incongruous yachtsman had concentrated his interest upon the innocent fruiter. Twice had he been assured that no passengers had come to Coralio on board of her. And yet, with a persistence not to be attributed to an idling voyager, he had appealed the case to the higher court of his own eye-sight. Surprisingly like some gay-coated lizard, he crouched at the foot of the cocoanut palm, and with the beady, shifting eyes of the selfsame reptile, sustained his espionage on the *Karlsefin*.

On the white sands a whiter gig belonging to the yacht was drawn up, guarded by one of the white-ducked crew. Not far away in a *pulperia* on the shore-following Calle Grande three other sailors swaggered with their cues around Coralio's solitary billiard-table. The boat lay there as if under orders to be ready for use at any moment. There was in the atmosphere a hint of expectation, of waiting for something to occur, which was foreign to the air of Coralio.

Like some passing bird of brilliant plumage, Smith alights on this palmy shore but to preen his wings for an instant and then to fly away upon silent pinions. When morning dawned there was no Smith, no waiting gig, no yacht in the offing. Smith left no intimation of his mission there, no footprints to show where he had followed the trail of his mystery on the sands of Coralio that night. He came; he spake his strange jargon of the asphalt and the cafés; he sat under the cocoanut-tree, and vanished. The next morning Coralio, Smithless, ate its fried plantain and said: 'The man of pictured clothing went himself away.' With the *siesta* the incident passed, yawning, into history.

So, for a time, must Smith pass behind the scenes of the play. He comes no more to Coralio nor to Dr. Gregg, who sits in vain, wagging his redundant beard, waiting to enrich his derelict audience with his moving tale of trepanning and jealousy.

But prosperously to the lucidity of these loose pages, Smith shall flutter among them again. In the nick of time he shall come to tell us why he strewed so many anxious cigar stumps around the cocoanut palm that night. This he must do; for, when he sailed away before the dawn in his yacht *Rambler*, he carried with him the answer to a riddle so big and preposterous that few in Anchuria had ventured even to propound it.

CAUGHT

THE PLANS FOR THE DETENTION of the flying President Miraflores and his companion at the coast line seemed hardly likely to fail. Dr. Zavalla himself had gone to the port of Alazan to establish a guard at that point. At Coralio the Liberal patriot Varras could be depended upon to keep close watch. Goodwin held himself responsible for the district about Coralio.

The news of the president's flight had been disclosed to no one in the coast towns save trusted members of the ambitious political party that was desirous of succeeding to power. The telegraph wire running from San Mateo to the coast had been cut far up on the mountain trail by an emissary of Zavalla's. Long before this could be repaired and word received along it from the capital the fugitives would have reached the coast and the question of escape or capture been solved.

Goodwin had stationed armed sentinels at frequent intervals along the shore for a mile in each direction from Coralio. They were instructed to keep a vigilant lookout during the night to prevent Miraflores from attempting to embark stealthily by means of some boat or sloop found by chance at the water's edge. A dozen patrols walked the streets of Coralio unsuspected, ready to intercept the truant official should he show himself there.

Goodwin was very well convinced that no precautions had been overlooked. He strolled about the streets that bore such high-sounding names and were but narrow, grass-covered lanes, lending his own aid to the vigil that had been intrusted to him by Bob Englehart.

The town had begun the tepid round of its nightly diversions. A few leisurely dandies, clad in white duck, with flowing neckties, and winging slim bamboo canes, threaded the grassy by-ways toward the houses of their favored señoritas. Those who wooed the art of music dragged tirelessly at whining concertinas, or fingered lugubrious guitars at doors and windows. An occasional soldier from the *cuartel*, with flapping straw hat, without coat or shoes, hurried by, balancing his long gun like a lance in one hand. From every density of the foliage the giant tree frogs sounded their loud and irritating clatter. Further out, where the by-ways perished at the brink of the jungle, the guttural cries of marauding baboons and the coughing of the alligators in the black estuaries fractured the vain silence of the wood.

By ten o'clock the streets were deserted. The oil lamps that had burned, a sickly yellow, at random corners, had been extinguished by some economical civic agent. Coralio lay sleeping calmly between toppling mountains and encroaching sea like a stolen babe in the arms of its abductors. Somewhere over in that tropical darkness – perhaps already threading the profundities of the alluvial lowlands – the high adventurer and his mate were moving toward land's end. The game of Fox-in-the-Morning should be coming soon to its close.

Goodwin, at his deliberate gait, passed the long, low *cuartel* where Coralio's contingent of Anchuria's military force slumbered, with its bare toes pointed heavenward. There was a law that no civilian might come so near the headquarters of that citadel of war after nine o'clock, but Goodwin was always forgetting the minor statutes.

'*Quièn vive?*' shrieked the sentinel, wrestling prodigiously with his lengthy musket.

'*Americano,*' growled Goodwin, without turning his head, and passed on, unhalted.

To the right he turned, and to the left up the street that ultimately reached the Plaza Nacional. When within the toss of a cigar stump from the intersecting Street of the Holy Sepulchre, he stopped suddenly in the pathway.

He saw the form of a tall man, clothed in black and carrying a large valise, hurry down the cross-street in the direction of the beach. And Goodwin's second glance made him aware of a woman at the man's elbow on the farther side, who seemed to urge forward, if not even to assist, her companion in their swift but silent progress. They were no Coralians, those two.

Goodwin followed at increased speed, but without any of the artful tactics that are so dear to the heart of the sleuth. The American was too broad to feel the instinct of the detective. He stood as an agent for the people of Anchuria, and but for political reasons he would have demanded then and there the money. It was the design of his party to secure the imperilled fund, to restore it to the treasury of the country, and to declare itself in power without bloodshed or resistance.

The couple halted at the door of the Hotel de los Estranjeros, and the man struck upon the wood with the impatience of one unused to his entry being stayed. Madama was long in response; but after a time her light showed, the door was opened, and the guests housed.

Goodwin stood in the quiet street, lighting another cigar. In two minutes a faint gleam began to show between the slats of the jalousies in the upper story of the hotel. 'They have engaged rooms,' said Goodwin to himself. 'So, then, their arrangements for sailing have yet to be made.'

At that moment there came along one Estebán Delgado, a barber, an enemy to existing government, a jovial plotter against stagnation in any form. This barber was one of Coralio's saddest dogs, often remaining out of doors as late as eleven, post meridian. He was a partisan Liberal; and he greeted Goodwin with flatulent importance as a brother in the cause. But he had something important to tell.

'What think you, Don Frank!' he cried, in the universal tone of the conspirator. 'I have to-night shaved *la barba* – what you call the 'weeskers' of the *Presidente* himself, of this countree! Consider! He sent for me to come. In the poor *casita* of an old woman he awaited me – in a verree leetle house in a dark place. *Carramba!* – el Señor Presidente to make himself thus secret and obscured! I think he desired not to be known – but, *carajo!* can you shave a man and not see his face? This gold piece he gave me, and said it was to be all quite still. I think, Don Frank, there is what you call a chip over the bug.'

'Have you ever seen President Miraflores before?' asked Goodwin.

'But once,' answered Estebán. 'He is tall; and he had weeskers verree black and sufficient.'

'Was any one else present when you shaved him?'

'An old Indian woman, Señor, that belonged with the *casa*, and one señorita – a ladee of so much beautee! – *ah Dios!*'

'All right, Estebán,' said Goodwin. 'It's very lucky that you happened along with your tonsorial information. The new administration will be likely to remember you for this.'

Then in a few words he made the barber acquainted with the crisis into which the affairs of the nation had culminated, and instructed him to remain outside, keeping watch upon the two sides of the hotel that looked upon the street, and observing whether any one should attempt to leave the house by any door or window. Goodwin himself went to the door through which the guests had entered, opened it and stepped inside.

Madama had returned downstairs from her journey above to see after the comfort of her lodgers. Her candle stood upon the bar. She was about to take a thimbleful of rum as a solace for having her rest disturbed. She looked up without surprise or alarm as her third caller entered.

'Ah! it is the Señor Goodwin. Not often does he honor my poor house by his presence.'

'I must come oftener,' said Goodwin, with the Goodwin smile. 'I hear that your cognac is the best between Belize to the north and Rio to the south. Set out the bottle, Madama, and let us have the proof in *un vasito* for each of us.'

'My *aguardiente*,' said Madama, with pride, 'is the best. It grows, in beautiful bottles, in the dark places among the banana-trees. *Si, Señor*. Only at midnight can they be picked by sailor-men who bring them, before daylight comes, to your back door. Good *aguardiente* is a verree difficult fruit to handle, Señor Goodwin.'

Smuggling, in Coralio, was much nearer than competition to being the life of trade. One spoke of it slyly, yet with a certain conceit, when it had been well accomplished.

'You have guests in the house to-night,' said Goodwin, laying a silver dollar upon the counter.

'Why not?' said Madama, counting the change. 'Two; but the smallest while finished to arrive. One señor, not quite old, and one señorita of sufficient handsomeness. To their rooms they have ascended, not desiring the to-eat nor the to-drink. Two rooms – *Número* 9 and *Número* 10.'

'I was expecting that gentleman and that lady,' said Goodwin. 'I have important *negocios* that must be transacted. Will you allow me to see them?'

'Why not?' sighed Madama, placidly. 'Why should not Señor Goodwin ascend and speak to his friends? *Está bueno*. Room *Número* 9 and room *Número* 10.'

Goodwin loosened in his coat pocket the American revolver that he carried, and ascended the steep, dark stairway.

In the hallway above, the saffron light from a hanging lamp allowed him to select the gaudy numbers on the doors. He turned the knob of Number 9, entered and closed the door behind him.

If that was Isabel Guilbert seated by the table in that poorly furnished room, report had failed to do her charms justice. She rested her head upon one hand. Extreme fatigue was signified in every line of her figure; and upon her countenance a deep perplexity was written. Her eyes were gray-irised, and of that mould that seems to have belonged to the orbs of all the famous queens of hearts. Their whites were singularly clear and brilliant, concealed above the irises by heavy horizontal lids, and showing a snowy line below them. Such eyes denote great nobility, vigor, and, if you can conceive of it, a most venerous selfishness. She looked up when the American entered with an expression of surprised inquiry, but without alarm.

Goodwin took off his hat and seated himself, with his characteristic deliberate ease, upon a corner of the table. He held a lighted cigar between his fingers. He took this familiar course because he was sure that preliminaries would be wasted upon Miss Guilbert. He knew her history, and the small part that the conventions had played in it.

'Good evening,' he said. 'Now, madame, let us come to business at once. You will observe that I mention no names, but I know who is in the next room, and what he carries in that valise. That is the point which brings me here. I have come to dictate terms of surrender.'

The lady neither moved nor replied, but steadily regarded the cigar in Goodwin's hand.

'We,' continued the dictator, thoughtfully regarding the neat buckskin shoe on his gently swinging foot – 'I speak for a considerable majority of the people – demand the return of the stolen funds belonging to them. Our terms go very little further than that. They are very simple. As an accredited spokesman, I promise that our interference will cease if they are accepted. Give up the money, and you and your companion will be permitted to proceed wherever you will. In fact, assistance will be given you in the matter of securing a passage by any outgoing vessel you may choose. It is on my personal responsibility that I add congratulations to the gentleman in Number 10 upon his taste in feminine charms.'

Returning his cigar to his mouth, Goodwin observed her, and saw that her eyes followed it and rested upon it with icy and significant concentration. Apparently she had not heard a word he had said. He understood, tossed the cigar out the window, and, with an amused laugh, slid from the table to his feet.

'That is better,' said the lady. 'It makes it possible for me to listen to you. For a second lesson in good manners, you might now tell me by whom I am being insulted.'

'I am sorry,' said Goodwin, leaning one hand on the table, 'that my time is too brief for devoting much of it to a course of etiquette. Come, now; I appeal to your good sense. You have shown yourself, in more than one instance, to be well aware of what is to your advantage. This is an occasion that demands the exercise of your undoubted intelligence. There is no mystery here. I am Frank Goodwin; and I have come for the money. I entered this room at a venture. Had I entered the other I would have had it before now. Do you want it in words? The gentleman in Number 10 has betrayed a great trust. He has robbed his people of a large sum, and it is I who will prevent their losing it. I do not say who that gentleman is; but if I should be forced to see him and he should prove to be a certain high official of the republic, it will be my duty to arrest him. The house is guarded. I am offering you liberal terms. It is not absolutely necessary that I confer personally with the gentleman in the next room. Bring me the valise containing the money, and we will call the affair ended.'

The lady arose from her chair, and stood for a moment, thinking deeply.

'Do you live here, Mr. Goodwin?' she asked, presently.

'Yes.'

'What is your authority for this intrusion?'

'I am an instrument of the republic. I was advised by wire of the movements of the – gentleman in Number 10.'

'May I ask you two or three questions? I believe you to be a man more apt to be truthful than – timid. What sort of a town is this – Coralio, I think they call it?'

'Not much of a town,' said Goodwin, smiling. 'A banana town, as they run. Grass huts, 'dobes, five or six two-story houses, accommodations limited, population half-breed Spanish and Indian, Caribs and blackamoors. No sidewalks to speak of, no amusements. Rather unmoral. That's an offhand sketch, of course.'

'Are there any inducements, say in a social or in a business way, for people to reside here?'

'Oh, yes,' answered Goodwin, smiling broadly. 'There are no afternoon teas, no hand-organs, no department stores – and there is no extradition treaty.'

'He told me,' went on the lady, speaking as if to herself, and with a light frown, 'that there were towns on this coast of beauty and importance; that there was a pleasing social order – especially an American colony of cultured residents.'

'There is an American colony,' said Goodwin, gazing at her in some wonder. 'Some of the members are all right. Some are fugitives from justice from the States. I recall two exiled bank presidents, one army paymaster under a cloud, a couple of manslayers, and a widow – arsenic, I believe, was the suspicion in her case. I myself complete the colony, but, as yet, I have not distinguished myself by any particular crime.'

'Do not lose hope,' said the lady, dryly; 'I see nothing in your actions to-night to guarantee your further obscurity. Some mistake has been made; I do not know just where. But *him* you shall not disturb to-night. The journey has fatigued him so that he has fallen asleep, I think, in his clothes. You talk of stolen money! I do not understand you. Some mistake has been made. I will convince you. Remain where you are and I will bring you the valise that you seem to covet so, and show it to you.'

She moved toward the closed door that connected the two rooms, but stopped, and half turned and bestowed upon Goodwin a grave searching look that ended in a quizzical smile.

'You force my door,' she said, 'and you follow your ruffianly behavior with the basest accusations; and yet' – she hesitated, as if to reconsider what she was about to say – 'and yet – it is a puzzling thing – I am sure there has been some mistake.'

She took a step toward the door, but Goodwin stayed her by a light touch upon her arm. I have said before that women turned to look at him in the streets. He was the viking sort of man, big, good-looking, and with an air of kindly truculence. She was dark and proud, glowing or pale as her mood moved her. I do not know if Eve were light or dark, but if such a woman had stood in the garden I know that the apple would have been eaten. This woman was to be Goodwin's fate, and he did not know it; but he must have felt the first throes of destiny, for, as he faced her, the knowledge of what report named her turned bitter in his throat.

'If there has been any mistake,' he said, hotly, 'it was yours. I do not blame the man who has lost his country, his honor, and is about to lose the poor consolation of his stolen riches as much as I blame you, for, by Heaven! I can very well see how he was brought to it. I can understand, and pity him. It is such women as you that strew this degraded coast with wretched exiles, that make men forget their trusts, that drag—'

The lady interrupted him with a weary gesture.

'There is no need to continue your insults,' she said, coldly, 'I do not understand what you are saying, nor do I know what mad blunder you are making; but if the inspection of the contents of a gentleman's portmanteau will rid me of you, let us delay it no longer.'

She passed quickly and noiselessly into the other room, and returned with the heavy leather valise, which she handed to the American with an air of patient contempt.

Goodwin set the valise quickly upon the table and began to unfasten the straps. The lady stood by, with an expression of infinite scorn and weariness upon her face.

The valise opened wide to a powerful, sidelong wrench. Goodwin dragged out two or three articles of clothing, exposing the bulk of its contents – package after package of tightly packed United States bank and treasury notes of large denomination. Reckoning from the high figures written upon the paper bands that bound them, the total must have come closely upon the hundred thousand mark.

Goodwin glanced swiftly at the woman, and saw, with surprise and a thrill of pleasure that he wondered at, that she had experienced an unmistakable shock. Her eyes grew wide, she gasped, and leaned heavily against the table. She had been ignorant, then, he inferred, that her companion had looted the government treasury. But why, he angrily asked himself, should he be so well pleased to think this wandering and unscrupulous singer not so black as report had painted her?

A noise in the other room startled them both. The door swung open, and a tall, elderly, dark complexioned man, recently shaven, hurried into the room.

All the pictures of President Miraflores represent him as the possessor of a luxuriant supply of dark and carefully tended whiskers; but the story of the barber, Estebán, had prepared Goodwin for the change.

The man stumbled in from the dark room, his eyes blinking at the lamplight, and heavy from sleep.

'What does this mean?' he demanded in excellent English, with a keen and perturbed look at the American – 'robbery?'

'Very near it,' answered Goodwin. 'But I rather think I'm in time to prevent it. I represent the people to whom this money belongs and I have come to convey it back to them.' He thrust his hand into a pocket of his loose linen coat.

The other man's hand went quickly behind him.

'Don't draw,' called Goodwin, sharply; 'I've got you covered from my pocket.'

The lady stepped forward, and laid one hand upon the shoulder of her hesitating companion. She pointed to the table. 'Tell me the truth – the truth,' she said, in a low voice. 'Whose money is that?'

The man did not answer. He gave a deep, long-drawn sigh, leaned and kissed her on the forehead, stepped back into the other room and closed the door.

Goodwin foresaw his purpose, and jumped for the door, but the report of the pistol echoed as his hand touched the knob. A heavy fall followed, and some one swept him aside and struggled into the room of the fallen man.

A desolation, thought Goodwin, greater than that derived from the loss of cavalier and gold must have been in the heart of the enchantress to have wrung from her, in that moment, the cry of one turning to the all-forgiving, all-comforting earthly consoler – to have made her call out from that bloody and dishonored room – 'Oh, mother, mother, mother!'

But there was an alarm outside. The barber, Estebán, at the sound of the shot, had raised his voice; and the shot itself had aroused half the town. A pattering of feet came up the street, and official orders rang out on the still air. Goodwin had a duty to perform. Circumstances had made him the custodian of his adopted country's treasure. Swiftly cramming the money into the valise, he closed it, leaned far out of the window and dropped it into a thick orange-tree in the little inclosure below.

They will tell you in Coralio, as they delight in telling the stranger, of the conclusion of that tragic flight. They will tell you how the upholders of the law came apace when the alarm was sounded – the *Comandante* in red slippers and a jacket like a head waiter's and girded sword, the soldiers with their interminable guns, followed by outnumbering officers struggling into their gold lace and epaulettes; the bare-footed policemen (the only capables in the lot), and ruffled citizens of every hue and description.

They say that the countenance of the dead man was marred sadly by the effects of the shot, but he was identified as the fallen president by both Goodwin and the barber Estebán. On the next morning messages began to come over the mended telegraph wire; and the story of the flight from the capital was given out to the public. In San Mateo the revolutionary party had seized the sceptre of government, without opposition, and the *vivas* of the mercurial populace quickly effaced the interest belonging to the unfortunate Miraflores.

They will relate to you how the new government sifted the towns and raked the roads to find the valise containing Anchuria's surplus capital, which the president was known to have carried with him, but all in vain. In Coralio Señor Goodwin himself led the searching party which combed that town as carefully as a woman combs her hair; but the money was not found.

So they buried the dead man, without honors, back of the town near the little bridge that spans the mangrove swamp; and for a *real* a boy will show you his grave. They say that the old woman in whose hut the barber shaved the president placed the wooden slab at his head, and burned the inscription upon it with a hot iron.

You will hear also that Señor Goodwin, like a tower of strength, shielded Doña Isabel Guilbert through those subsequent distressful days; and that his scruples as to her past career (if he had any) vanished; and her adventuresome waywardness (if she had any) left her, and they were wedded and were happy.

The American built a home on a little foot hill near the town. It is a conglomerate structure of native woods that, exported, would be worth a fortune, and of brick, palm, glass, bamboo and adobe. There is a paradise of nature about it; and something of the same sort within. The natives speak of its interior with hands uplifted in admiration. There are floors polished like mirrors and covered with hand-woven Indian rugs of silk fibre, tall ornaments and pictures, musical instruments and papered walls – 'figure-it-to-yourself!' they exclaim.

But they cannot tell you in Coralio (as you shall learn) what became of the money that Frank Goodwin dropped into the orange-tree. But that shall come later; for the palms are fluttering in the breeze, bidding us to sport and gaiety.

CUPID'S EXILE NUMBER TWO

THE UNITED STATES OF AMERICA, after looking over its stock of consular timber, selected Mr. John De Graffenreid Atwood, of Dalesburg, Alabama, for a successor to Willard Geddie, resigned.

Without prejudice to Mr. Atwood, it will have to be acknowledged that, in this instance, it was the man who sought the office. As with the self-banished Geddie, it was nothing less than the artful smiles of lovely women that had driven Johnny Atwood to the desperate expedient of accepting office under a despised Federal Government so that he might go far, far away and never see again the false, fair face that had wrecked his young life. The consulship at Coralio seemed to offer a retreat sufficiently removed and romantic enough to inject the necessary drama into the pastoral scenes of Dalesburg life.

It was while playing the part of Cupid's exile that Johnny added his handiwork to the long list of casualties along the Spanish Main by his famous manipulation of the shoe market, and his unparalleled feat of elevating the most despised and useless weed in his own country from obscurity to be a valuable product in international commerce.

The trouble began, as trouble often begins instead of ending, with a romance. In Dalesburg there was a man named Elijah Hemstetter, who kept a general store. His family consisted of one daughter called Rosine, a name that atoned much for 'Hemstetter.' This young woman was possessed of plentiful attractions, so that the young men of the community were agitated in their bosoms. Among the more agitated was Johnny, the son of Judge Atwood, who lived in the big colonial mansion on the edge of Dalesburg.

It would seem that the desirable Rosine should have been pleased to return the affection of an Atwood, a name honored all over the state long before and since the war. It does seem that she should have gladly consented to have been led into that stately but rather empty colonial mansion. But not so. There was a cloud on the horizon, a threatening, cumulus cloud, in the shape of a lively and shrewd young farmer in the neighborhood who dared to enter the lists as a rival to the high-born Atwood.

One night Johnny propounded to Rosine a question that is considered of much importance by the young of the human species. The accessories were all there – moonlight, oleanders, magnolias, the mockbird's song. Whether or not the shadow of Pinkney Dawson, the prosperous young farmer, came between them on that occasion is not known; but Rosine's answer was unfavorable. Mr. John De Graffenreid Atwood bowed till his hat touched the lawn grass, and went away with his head high, but with a sore wound in his pedigree and heart. A Hemstetter refuse an Atwood! Zounds!

Among other accidents of that year was a Democratic president. Judge Atwood was a warhorse of Democracy. Johnny persuaded him to set the wheels moving for some foreign appointment. He would go away – away. Perhaps in years to come Rosine would think how true, how faithful his love had been, and would drop a tear – maybe in the cream she would be skimming for Pink Dawson's breakfast.

The wheels of politics revolved; and Johnny was appointed consul to Coralio. Just before leaving he dropped in at Hemstetter's to say good-bye. There was a queer, pinkish look about Rosine's eyes; and had the two been alone, the United States might have had to cast about for another consul. But Pink Dawson was there, of course, talking about his 400-acre orchard, and the three-mile alfalfa tract, and the 200-acre pasture. So Johnny shook hands with Rosine as coolly as if he were only going to run up to Montgomery for a couple of days. They had the royal manner when they chose, those Atwoods.

'If you happen to strike anything in the way of a good investment down there, Johnny,' said Pink Dawson, 'just let me know, will you? I reckon I could lay my hands on a few extra thousands 'most any time for a profitable deal.'

'Certainly, Pink,' said Johnny, pleasantly. 'If I strike anything of the sort I'll let you in with pleasure.'

So Johnny went down to Mobile and took a fruit steamer for the coast of Anchuria.

When the new consul arrived in Coralio the strangeness of the scenes diverted him much. He was only twenty-two; and the grief of youth is not worn like a garment as it is by older men. It has its seasons when it reigns; and then it is unseated for a time by the assertion of the keen senses.

Billy Keogh and Johnny seemed to conceive a mutual friendship at once. Keogh took the new consul about town and presented him to the handful of Americans and the smaller number of French and Germans who made up the 'foreign' contingent. And then, of course, he had to be more formally introduced to the native officials, and have his credentials transmitted through an interpreter.

There was something about the young Southerner that the sophisticated Keogh liked. His manner was simple almost to boyishness; but he possessed the cool carelessness of a man of far greater age and experience. Neither uniforms nor titles, red tape nor foreign languages, mountains nor sea weighed upon his spirits. He was heir to all the ages, an Atwood, of Dalesburg; and you might know every thought conceived in his bosom.

Geddie came down to the consulate to explain the duties and workings of the office. He and Keogh tried to interest the new consul in their description of the work that his government expected him to perform.

'It's all right,' said Johnny from the hammock that he had set up as the official reclining place. 'If anything turns up that has to be done I'll let you fellows do it. You can't expect a Democrat to work during his first term of holding office.'

'You might look over these headings' suggested Geddie, 'of the different lines of exports you will have to keep account of. The fruit is classified; and there are the valuable woods, coffee, rubber —'

'That last account sounds all right,' interrupted Mr. Atwood. 'Sounds as if it could be stretched. I want to buy a new flag, a monkey, a guitar and a barrel of pineapples. Will that rubber account stretch over 'em?'

'That's merely statistics,' said Geddie, smiling. 'The expense account is what you want. It is supposed to have a slight elasticity. The "stationery" items are sometimes carelessly audited by the State Department.'

'We're wasting our time,' said Keogh. 'This man was born to hold office. He penetrates to the root of the art at one step of his eagle eye. The true genius of government shows its hand in every word of his speech.'

'I didn't take this job with any intention of working,' explained Johnny, lazily. 'I wanted to go somewhere in the world where they didn't talk about farms. There are none here, are there?'

'Not the kind you are acquainted with,' answered the ex-consul. 'There is no such art here as agriculture. There never was a plow or a reaper within the boundaries of Anchuria.'

'This is the country for me,' murmured the consul and immediately he fell asleep.

The cheerful tintypist pursued his intimacy with Johnny in spite of open charges that he did so to obtain a preëmption on a seat in the coveted spot, the rear gallery of the consulate. But whether his designs were selfish or purely friendly, Keogh achieved that desirable privilege. Few were the nights on which the two could not be found reposing there in the sea breeze, with their heels on the railing, and the cigars and brandy conveniently near.

One evening they had sat thus, mainly silent, for their talk had dwindled before the stilling influence of an unusual night.

There was a great, full moon; and the sea was mother-of-pearl. Almost every sound was hushed, for the air was but faintly stirring; and the town lay panting, waiting for the night to cool. Off-shore lay the fruit steamer *Andador*, of the Vesuvius line, full-laden and scheduled to sail at six in the morning. There were no loiterers on the beach. So bright was the moonlight that the two men could see the small pebbles shining on the beach where the gentle surf wetted them.

Then down the coast, tacking close to shore, slowly swam a little sloop, white-winged like some snowy sea fowl. Its course lay within twenty points of the wind's eye; so it veered in and out again in long slow strokes like the movements of a graceful skater.

Again the tactics of its crew brought it close in shore, this time nearly opposite the consulate; and then there blew from the sloop clear and surprising notes as if from a horn of elfland. A fairy bugle it might have been, sweet and silvery and unexpected, playing with spirit the familiar air of 'Home, Sweet Home.'

It was a scene set for the land of the lotus. The authority of the sea and the tropics, the mystery that attends unknown sails, and the prestige of drifting music on moonlit waters gave it an anodynous charm. Johnny Atwood felt it, and thought of Dalesburg; but as soon as Keogh's mind had arrived at a theory concerning the peripatetic solo he sprang to the railing, and his ear-rending yawp fractured the silence of Coralio like a cannon shot.

'Mel-lin-ger a-hoy!'

The sloop was now on its outward track; but from it came a clear, answering hail:

'Good-bye, Billy . . . going home – bye!'

The *Andador* was the sloop's destination. No doubt some passenger with a sailing permit from some up-the-coast point had come down in this sloop to catch the regular fruit steamer on its return trip. Like a coquettish pigeon the little boat tacked on its eccentric way until at last its white sail was lost to sight against the larger bulk of the fruiter's side.

'That's old H. P. Mellinger,' explained Keogh, dropping back into his chair. 'He's going back to New York. He was private secretary of the late hot-foot president of this grocery and fruit stand that they call a country. His job's over now; and I guess old Mellinger is glad.'

'Why does he disappear to music, like Zo-zo, the magic queen?' asked Johnny. 'Just to show 'em that he doesn't care?'

'That noise you heard is a phonograph,' said Keogh. 'I sold him that. Mellinger had a graft in this country that was the only thing of its kind in the world. The tooting machine saved it for him once, and he always carried it around with him afterward.'

'Tell me about it,' demanded Johnny, betraying interest.

'I'm no disseminator of narratives,' said Keogh. 'I can use language for purposes of speech; but when I attempt a discourse the words come out as they will, and they may make sense when they strike the atmosphere, or they may not.'

'I want to hear about that graft,' persisted Johnny. 'You've got no right to refuse. I've told you all about every man, woman and hitching post in Dalesburg.'

'You shall hear it,' said Keogh. 'I said my instincts of narrative were perplexed. Don't you believe it. It's an art I've acquired along with many other of the graces and sciences.'

THE PHONOGRAPH AND THE GRAFT

'WHAT WAS THIS GRAFT?' asked Johnny, with the impatience of the great public to whom tales are told.

' 'Tis contrary to art and philosophy to give you the information,' said Keogh, calmly. 'The art of narrative consists in concealing from your audience everything it wants to know until after you expose your favorite opinions on topics foreign to the subject. A good story is like a bitter pill with the sugar coating inside of it. I will begin, if you please, with a horoscope located in the Cherokee Nation; and end with a moral tune on the phonograph.

'Me and Henry Horsecollar brought the first phonograph to this country. Henry was a quarter-breed, quarter-back Cherokee, educated East in the idioms of football, and West in contraband whisky, and a gentleman, the same as you and me. He was easy and romping in his ways; a man about six foot, with a kind of rubber-tire movement. Yes, he was a little man about five foot five, or five foot eleven. He was what you would call a medium tall man of average smallness. Henry had quit college once, and the Muscogee jail three times – the last-named institution on account of introducing and selling whisky in the territories. Henry Horsecollar never let any cigar stores come up and stand behind him. He didn't belong to that tribe of Indians.

'Henry and me met at Texarkana, and figured out this phonograph scheme. He had $360 which came to him out of a land allotment in the reservation. I had run down from Little Rock on account of a distressful scene I had witnessed on the street there. A man stood on a box and passed around some gold watches, screw case, stem-winders, Elgin movement, very elegant. Twenty bucks they cost you over the counter. At three dollars the crowd fought for the tickets. The man happened to find a valise full of them handy, and he passed them out like putting hot biscuits on a plate. The backs were hard to unscrew, but the crowd put its ear to the case, and they ticked mollifying and agreeable. Three of these watches were genuine tickers; the rest were only kickers. He? Why, empty cases with one of them horny black bugs that fly around electric lights in 'em. Them bugs kick off minutes and seconds industrious and beautiful. So, this man I was speaking of cleaned up $288; and then he went away, because he knew that when it came time to wind watches in Little Rock an entomologist would be needed, and he wasn't one.

'So, as I say, Henry had $360, and I had $288. The idea of introducing the phonograph to South America was Henry's; but I took to it freely, being fond of machinery of all kinds.

' "The Latin races," says Henry, explaining easily in the idioms he learned at college, "are peculiarly adapted to be victims of the phonograph. They have the artistic temperament. They yearn for music and color and gaiety. They give wampum to the hand-organ man and the four-legged chicken in the tent when they're months behind with the grocery and the bread-fruit tree."

' "Then," says I, "we'll export canned music to the Latins; but I'm mindful of Mr. Julius Caesar's account of 'em where he says: '*Omnia Gallia in tres partes divisa est';* which is the same as to say, 'We will need all of our gall in devising means to tree them parties.' "

'I hated to make a show of education; but I was disinclined to be overdone in syntax by a mere Indian, a member of a race to which we owe nothing except the land on which the United States is situated.

'We bought a fine phonograph in Texarkana – one of the best make – and half a trunkful of records. We packed up, and took the T. and P. for New Orleans. From that celebrated centre of molasses and disfranchised coon songs we took a steamer for South America.

'We landed at Solitas, forty miles up the coast from here. 'Twas a palatable enough place to look at. The houses were clean and white; and to look at 'em stuck around among the scenery they reminded you of hard-boiled eggs served with lettuce. There was a block of skyscraper mountains in the suburbs; and they kept pretty quiet, like they had crept up there and were watching the town. And the sea was remarking "Sh-sh-sh" on the beach; and now and then a ripe cocoanut would drop kerblip in the sand; and that was all there was doing. Yes, I judge that town was considerably on the quiet. I judge that after Gabriel quits blowing his horn, and the car starts, with Philadelphia swinging to the last strap, and Pine Gully, Arkansas, hanging onto the rear step, this town of Solitas will wake up and ask if anybody spoke.

'The captain went ashore with us, and agreed to conduct what he seemed to like to call the obsequies. He introduced Henry and me to the United States Consul, and a roan man, the head of the Department of Mercenary and Licentious Dispositions, the way it read upon his sign.

' "I touch here a week again from to-day," says the captain.

' "By that time," we told him, "we'll be amassing wealth in the interior towns with our galvanized prima donna and correct imitations of Sousa's band excavating a march from a tin mine."

' "Ye'll not," says the captain. "Ye'll be hypnotized. Any gentleman in the audience who kindly steps upon the stage and looks this country in the eye will be converted to the hypothesis that he's but a fly in the Elgin creamery. Ye'll be standing knee deep in the surf waiting for me, and your machine for making Hamburger steak out of the hitherto respected art of music will be playing 'There's no place like home.' "

'Henry skinned a twenty off his roll, and received from the Bureau of Mercenary Dispositions a paper bearing a red seal and a dialect story, and no change.

'Then we got the consul full of red wine, and struck him for a horoscope. He was a thin, youngish kind of a man, I should say past fifty, sort of French-Irish in his affections, and puffed up with disconsolation. Yes, he was a flattened kind of a man, in whom drink lay stagnant, inclined to corpulence and misery. Yes, I think he was a kind of a Dutchman, being very sad and genial in his ways.

' "The marvellous invention,' he says, "entitled the phonograph, has never invaded these shores. The people have never heard it. They would not believe it if they should. Simple-hearted children of nature, progress has never condemned them to accept the work of a can-opener as an overture, and rag-time might incite them to a bloody revolution. But you can try the experiment. The best chance you have is that the populace may not wake up when you play. There's two ways," says the consul, "they may take it.

They may become inebriated with attention, like an Atlanta colonel listening to "Marching Through Georgia," or they will get excited and transpose the key of the music with an axe and yourselves into a dungeon. In the latter case," says the consul, "I'll do my duty by cabling to the State Department, and I'll wrap the Stars and Stripes around you when you come to be shot, and threaten them with the vengeance of the greatest gold export and financial reserve nation on earth. The flag is full of bullet holes now," says the consul, "made in that way. Twice before," says the consul, "I have cabled our government for a couple of gunboats to protect American citizens. The first time the Department sent me a pair of gum boots. The other time was when a man named Pease was going to be executed here. They referred that appeal to the Secretary of Agriculture. Let us now disturb the señor behind the bar for a subsequence of the red wine."

'Thus soliloquized the consul of Solitas to me and Henry Horsecollar.

'But, notwithstanding, we hired a room that afternoon in the Calle de los Angeles, the main street that runs along the shore, and put our trunks there. 'Twas a good-sized room, dark and cheerful, but small. 'Twas on a various street, diversified by houses and conservatory plants. The peasantry of the city passed to and fro on the fine pasturage between the sidewalks. 'Twas, for the world, like an open chorus when the Royal Kafoozlum is about to enter.

'We were rubbing the dust off the machine and getting fixed to start business the next day, when a big, fine-looking white man in white clothes stopped at the door and looked in. We extended the invitations, and he walked inside and sized us up. He was chewing a long cigar, and wrinkling his eyes, meditative, like a girl trying to decide which dress to wear to the party.

' "New York?" he says to me finally.

' "Originally, and from time to time," I says. "Hasn't it rubbed off yet?"

' "It's simple," says he, "when you know how. It's the fit of the vest. They don't cut vests right anywhere else. Coats, maybe, but not vests."

'The white man looks at Henry Horsecollar and hesitates.

' "Injun," says Henry; "tame Injun."

' "Mellinger," says the man – "Homer P. Mellinger. Boys, you're confiscated. You're babies in the wood without a chaperon or referee, and it's my duty to start you going. I'll knock out the props and launch you proper in the pellucid waters of this tropical mud puddle. You'll have to be christened, and if you'll come with me I'll break a bottle of wine across your bows, according to Hoyle."

'Well, for two days Homer P. Mellinger did the honors. That man cut ice in Anchuria. He was It. He was the Royal Kafoozlum. If me and Henry was babes in the wood, he was a Robin Redbreast from the topmost bough. Him and me and Henry Horsecollar locked arms, and toted that phonograph around, and had wassail and diversions. Everywhere we found doors open we went inside and set the machine going, and Mellinger called upon the people to observe the artful music and his two lifelong friends, the Señores Americanos. The opera chorus was agitated with esteem, and followed us from house to house. There was a different kind of drink to be had with every tune. The natives had acquirements of a pleasant thing in the way of a drink that gums itself to the recollection. They chop off the end of a green cocoanut, and pour in on the juice of it French brandy and other adjuvants. We had them and other things.

'Mine and Henry's money was counterfeit. Everything was on Homer P. Mellinger. That man could find rolls of bills concealed in places on his person where Hermann the Wizard couldn't have conjured out a rabbit or an omelette. He could have founded universities, and made orchid collections, and then had enough left to purchase the colored vote of his country. Henry and me wondered what his graft was. One evening he told us.

' "Boys," said he, "I've deceived you. You think I'm a painted butterfly; but in fact I'm the hardest worked man in this country. Ten years ago I landed on its shores; and two years ago on the point of its jaw. Yes, I guess I can get the decision over this ginger cake commonwealth at the end of any round I choose. I'll confide in you because you are my countrymen and guests, even if you have assaulted my adopted shores with the worst system of noises ever set to music.

' "My job is private secretary to the president of this republic; and my duties are running it. I'm not headlined in the bills, but I'm the mustard in the salad dressing just the same. There isn't a law goes before Congress, there isn't a concession granted, there isn't an import duty levied but what H. P. Mellinger he cooks and seasons it. In the front office I fill the president's inkstand and search visiting statesmen for dirks and dynamite; but in the back room I dictate the policy of the government. You'd never guess in the world how I got my pull. It's the only graft of its kind on earth. I'll put you wise. You remember the old top-liner in the copy book – 'Honesty is the Best Policy'? That's it. I'm working honesty for a graft. I'm the only honest man in the republic. The government knows it; the people know it; the boodlers know it; the foreign investors know it. I make the government keep its faith. If a man is promised a job he gets it. If outside capital buys a concession it gets the goods. I run a monopoly of square dealing here. There's no competition. If Colonel Diogenes were to flash his lantern in this precinct he'd have my address inside of two minutes. There isn't big money in it, but it's a sure thing, and lets a man sleep of nights."

'Thus Homer P. Mellinger made oration to me and Henry Horsecollar. And, later, he divested himself of this remark:

' "Boys, I'm to hold a *soirée* this evening with a gang of leading citizens, and I want your assistance. You bring the musical corn sheller and give the affair the outside appearance of a function. There's important business on hand, but it mustn't show. I can talk to you people. I've been pained for years on account of not having anybody to blow off and brag to. I get homesick sometimes, and I'd swap the entire prequisites of office for just one hour to have a stein and a caviare sandwich somewhere on Thirty-fourth Street, and stand and watch the street cars go by, and smell the peanut roaster at old Giuseppe's fruit stand."

' "Yes," said I, "there's fine caviare at Billy Renfrow's café, corner of Thirty-fourth and—"

' "God knows it, interrupts Mellinger, "and if you'd told me you knew Billy Renfrow I'd have invented tons of ways of making you happy. Billy was my side-kicker in New York. There is a man who never knew what crooked was. Here I am working Honesty for a graft, but that man loses money on it. Carrambos! I get sick at times of this country. Everything's rotten. From the executive down to the coffee pickers, they're plotting to down each other and skin their friends. If a mule driver takes off his hat to an official, that man figures it out that he's a popular idol, and sets his pegs to stir up a revolution and upset the administration. It's one of my little chores as private secretary to smell out these revolutions and affix the kibosh before they break out and scratch the paint off the government property. That's why I'm down here now in this mildewed coast town. The governor of the district and his crew are plotting to uprise. I've got every one of their names, and they're invited to listen to the phonograph to-night, compliments of H. P. M. That's the way I'll get them in a bunch, and things are on the programme to happen to them.''

'We three were sitting at table in the cantina of the Purified Saints. Mellinger poured out wine, and was looking some worried; I was thinking.

' "They're a sharp crowd,'' he says, kind of fretful. "They're capitalized by a foreign syndicate after rubber, and they're loaded to the muzzle for bribing. I'm sick,'' goes on Mellinger, "of comic opera. I want to smell East River and wear suspenders again. At times I feel like throwing up my job, but I'm d — n fool enough to be sort of proud of it. 'There's Mellinger,' they say here. '*Por Dios!* you can't touch him with a million.' I'd like to take that record back and show it to Billy Renfrow some day; and that tightens my grip whenever I see a fat thing that I could corral just by winding one eye – and losing my graft. By —, they can't monkey with me. They know it. What money I get I make honest and spend it. Some day I'll make a pile and go back and eat caviare with Billy. To-night I'll show you how to handle a bunch of corruptionists. I'll show them what Mellinger, private secretary, means when you spell it with the cotton and tissue paper off.''

'Mellinger appears shaky, and breaks his glass against the neck of the bottle.

'I says to myself, "White man, if I'm not mistaken there's been a bait laid out where the tail of your eye could see it.''

'That night, according to arrangements, me and Henry took the phonograph to a room in a 'dobe house in a dirty side street, where the grass was knee high. 'Twas a long room, lit with smoky oil lamps. There was plenty of chairs, and a table at the back end. We set the phonograph on the table. Mellinger was there, walking up and down, disturbed in his predicaments. He chewed cigars and spat 'em out, and he bit the thumb nail of his left hand.

'By and by the invitations to the musicale came sliding in by pairs and threes and spade flushes. Their color was of a diversity, running from a three-days' smoked meerschaum to a patent-leather polish. They were as polite as wax, being devastated with enjoyments to give Señor Mellinger the good evenings. I understood their Spanish talk – I ran a pumping engine two years in a Mexican silver mine, and had it pat – but I never let on.

'Maybe fifty of 'em had come, and was seated, when in slid the king bee, the governor of the district. Mellinger met him at the door, and escorted him to the grand stand. When I saw that Latin man I knew that Mellinger, private secretary, had all the dances on his card taken. That was a big, squashy man, the color of a rubber overshoe, and he had an eye like a head waiter's.

'Mellinger explained, fluent, in the Castilian idioms, that his soul was disconcerted with joy at introducing to his respected friends America's greatest invention, the wonder of the age. Henry got the cue and run on an elegant brass-band record and the festivities became initiated. The governor man had a bit of English under his hat, and when the music was choked off he says:

' "Ver-r-ree fine. *Gr-r-r-racias*, the American gentlemen, the so esplendeed moosic as to playee."

'The table was a long one, and Henry and me sat at the end of it next the wall. The governor sat at the other end. Homer P. Mellinger stood at the side of it. I was just wondering how Mellinger was going to handle his crowd, when the home talent suddenly opened the services.

'That governor man was suitable for uprisings and policies. I judge he was a ready kind of man, who took his own time. Yes, he was full of attention and immediateness. He leaned his hands on the table and imposed his face toward the secretary man.

' "Do the American señores understand Spanish?" he asks in his native accents.

' "They do not," says Mellinger.

' "Then listen," goes on the Latin man, prompt. "The musics are of sufficient prettiness, but not of necessity. Let us speak of business. I well know why we are here, since I observe my compatriots. You had a whisper yesterday, Señor Mellinger, of our proposals. To-night we will speak out. We know that you stand in the president's favor, and we know your influence. The government will be changed. We know the worth of your services. We esteem your friendship and aid so much that" – Mellinger raises his hand, but the governor man bottles him up. "Do not speak until I have done."

'The governor man then draws a package wrapped in paper from his pocket, and lays it on the table by Mellinger's hand.

' "In that you will find fifty thousand dollars in money of your country. You can do nothing against us, but you can be worth that for us. Go back to the capital and obey our instructions. Take that money now. We trust you. You will find with it a paper giving in detail the work you will be expected to do for us. Do not have the unwiseness of refuse."

'The governor man paused, with his eyes fixed on Mellinger, full of expressions and observances. I looked at Mellinger, and was glad Billy Renfrow couldn't see him then. The sweat was popping out on his forehead, and he stood dumb, tapping the little package with the ends of his fingers. The colorado-maduro gang was after his graft. He had only to change his politics, and stuff five fingers in his inside pocket.

'Henry whispers to me and wants the pause in the programme interpreted. I whisper back: "H. P. is up against a bribe, senator's size, and the coons have got him going." I saw Mellinger's hand moving closer to the package. "He's weakening," I whispered to Henry. "We'll remind him," says Henry, "of the peanut-roaster on Thirty-fourth Street, New York."

'Henry stooped down and got a record from the basketful we'd brought, slid it in the phonograph, and started her off. It was a cornet solo, very neat and beautiful, and the name of it was "Home, Sweet Home." Not one of them fifty-odd men in the room moved while it was playing, and the governor man kept his eyes steady on Mellinger. I saw Mellinger's head go up little by little, and his hand came creeping away from the package. Not until the last note sounded did anybody stir. And then Homer P. Mellinger takes up the bundle of boodle and slams it in the governor man's face.

' "That's my answer," says Mellinger, private secretary, "and there'll be another in the morning. I have proofs of conspiracy against every man of you. The show is over, gentlemen."

' "There's one more act," puts in the governor man. "You are a servant,

I believe, employed by the president to copy letters and answer raps at the door. I am governor here. *Señores*, I call upon you in the name of the cause to seize this man.''

'That brindled gang of conspirators shoved back their chairs and advanced in force. I could see where Mellinger had made a mistake in massing his enemy so as to make a grand-stand play. I think he made another one, too; but we can pass that, Mellinger's idea of a graft and mine being different, according to estimations and points of view.

'There was only one window and door in that room, and they were in the front end. Here was fifty-odd Latin men coming in a bunch to obstruct the legislation of Mellinger. You may say there were three of us, for me and Henry, simultaneous, declared New York City and the Cherokee Nation in sympathy with the weaker party.

'Then it was that Henry Horsecollar rose to a point of disorder and intervened, showing, admirable, the advantages of education as applied to the American Indian's natural intellect and native refinement. He stood up and smoothed back his hair on each side with his hands as you have seen little girls do when they play.

' "Get behind me, both of you," says Henry.

' "What's it to be, chief?" I asked.

' "I'm going to buck centre," says Henry, in his football idioms. "There isn't a tackle in the lot of them. Follow me close, and rush the game."

'Then that cultured Red Man exhaled an arrangement of sounds with his mouth that made the Latin aggregation pause, with thoughtfulness and hesitations. The matter of his proclamation seemed to be a co-operation of the Carlisle war-whoop with the Cherokee college yell. He went at the chocolate team like a bean out of a little boy's nigger shooter. His right elbow laid out the governor man on the gridiron, and he made a lane the length of the crowd so wide that a woman could have carried a step-ladder through it without striking against anything. All Mellinger and me had to do was to follow.

'It took us just three minutes to get out of that street around to military headquarters, where Mellinger had things his own way. A colonel and a battalion of bare-toed infantry turned out and went back to the scene of the musicale with us, but the conspirator gang was gone. But we recaptured the phonograph with honors of war, and marched back to the *cuartel* with it playing "All Coons Look Al ke t> Me."

'The next day Mellinger takes me and Henry to one side, and begins to shed tens and twenties.

' "I want to buy that phonograph," says he. "I liked that last tune it played at the *soirée*."

' "This is more money than the machine is worth," says I.

' " 'Tis government expense money," says Mellinger. "The government pays for it, and it's getting the tune-grinder cheap."

'Me and Henry knew that pretty well. We knew that it had saved Homer P. Mellinger's graft when he was on the point of losing it; but we never let him know we knew it.

' "Now you boys better slide off further down the coast for a while," says Mellinger, "till I get the screws put on these fellows here. If you don't they'll give you trouble. And if you ever happen to see Billy Renfrow again before

I do, tell him I'm coming back to New York as soon as I can make a stake – honest.''

'Me and Henry laid low until the day the steamer came back. When we saw the captain's boat on the beach we went down and stood in the edge of the water. The captain grinned when he saw us.

' "I told you you'd be waiting," he says. "Where's the Hamburger machine?"

' "It stays behind," I says, "to play 'Home, Sweet Home.' "

' "I told you so," says the captain again. "Climb in the boat."

'And that,' said Keogh, 'is the way me and Henry Horsecollar introduced the phonograph into this country. Henry went back to the States, but I've been rummaging around in the tropics ever since. They say Mellinger never travelled a mile after that without his phonograph. I guess it kept him reminded about his graft whenever he saw the siren voice of the boodler tip him the wink with a bribe in its hand.'

'I suppose he's taking it home with him as a souvenir,' remarked the consul.

'Not as a souvenir,' said Keogh. 'He'll need two of 'em in New York, running day and night.'

MONEY MAZE

THE NEW ADMINISTRATION of Anchuria entered upon its duties and privileges with enthusiasm. Its first act was to send an agent to Coralio with imperative orders to recover, if possible, the sum of money ravished from the treasury by the ill-fated Miraflores.

Colonel Emilio Falcon, the private secretary of Losada, the new president, was despatched from the capital upon this important mission.

The position of private secretary to a tropical president is a responsible one. He must be a diplomat, a spy, a ruler of men, a body-guard to his chief, and a smeller-out of plots and nascent revolutions. Often he is the power behind the throne, the dictator of policy; and a president chooses him with a dozen times the care with which he selects a matrimonial mate.

Colonel Falcon, a handsome and urbane gentleman of Castilian courtesy and débonair manners, came to Coralio with the task before him of striking upon the cold trail of the lost money. There he conferred with the military authorities, who had received instructions to cooperate with him in the search.

Colonel Falcon established his headquarters in one of the rooms of the Casa Morena. Here for a week he held informal sittings – much as if he were a kind of unified grand jury – and summoned before him all those whose testimony might illumine the financial tragedy that had accompanied the less momentous one of the late president's death.

Two or three who were thus examined, among whom was the barber Estebán, declared that they had identified the body of the president before its burial.

'Of a truth,' testified Estebán before the mighty secretary, 'it was he, the president. Consider! – how could I shave a man and not see his face? He sent for me to shave him in a small house. He had a beard very black and thick.

Had I ever seen the president before? Why not? I saw him once ride forth in
a carriage from the *vapor* in Solitas. When I shaved him he gave me a gold
piece, and said there was to be no talk. But I am a Liberal – I am devoted to
my country – and I spake of these things to Señor Goodwin.'

'It is known,' said Colonel Falcon, smoothly, 'that the late President took
with him an American leather valise, containing a large amount of money.
Did you see that?'

'*De veras* – no,' Estebán answered. 'The light in the little house was but
a small lamp by which I could scarcely see to shave the President. Such a
thing there may have been, but I did not see it. No. Also in the room was
a young lady – a señorita of much beauty – that I could see even in so small
a light. But the money, señor, or the thing in which it was carried – that I
did not see.'

The *comandante* and other officers gave testimony that they had been
awakened and alarmed by the noise of a pistol-shot in the Hotel de los
Estranjeros. Hurrying thither to protect the peace and dignity of the republic,
they found a man lying dead, with a pistol clutched in his hand. Beside him
was a young woman, weeping sorely. Señor Goodwin was also in the room
when they entered it. But of the valise of money they saw nothing.

Madame Timotea Ortiz, the proprietress of the hotel in which the game
of Fox-in-the-Morning had been played out, told of the coming of the two
guests to her house.

'To my house they came,' said she – 'one *señor*, not quite old, and one
señorita of sufficient handsomeness. They desired not to eat or to drink – not
even of my *aguardiente*, which is the best. To their rooms they ascended –
Número Nueve and *Número Diez*. Later came Señor Goodwin, who ascended
to speak with them. Then I heard a great noise like that of a *canon*, and they
said that the *pobre Presidente* had shot himself. *Está bueno*. I saw nothing of
money or of the thing you call *veliz* that you say he carried it in.'

Colonel Falcon soon came to the reasonable conclusion that if any one in
Coralio could furnish a clue to the vanished money, Frank Goodwin must
be the man. But the wise secretary pursued a different course in seeking
information from the American. Goodwin was a powerful friend to the new
administration, and one who was not to be carelessly dealt with in respect
to either his honesty or his courage. Even the private secretary of His
Excellency hesitated to have this rubber prince and mahogany baron haled
before him as a common citizen of Anchuria. So he sent Goodwin a flowery
epistle, each word-petal dripping with honey, requesting the favor of an
interview. Goodwin replied with an invitation to dinner at his own house.

Before the hour named the American walked over to the Casa Morena,
and greeted his guest frankly and friendly. Then the two strolled, in the cool
of the afternoon, to Goodwin's home in the environs.

The American left Colonel Falcon in a big, cool, shadowed room with a
floor of inlaid and polished woods that any millionaire in the States would
have envied, excusing himself for a few minutes. He crossed a *patio*, shaded
with deftly arranged awnings and plants, and entered a long room looking
upon the sea in the opposite wing of the house. The broad jalousies were
opened wide, and the ocean breeze flowed in through the room, an invisible
current of coolness and health. Goodwin's wife sat near one of the windows,
making a water-color sketch of the afternoon seascape.

Here was a woman who looked to be happy. And more – she looked to be content. Had a poet been inspired to pen just similes concerning her favor, he would have likened her full, clear eyes, with their white-encircled, gray irises, to moonflowers. With none of the goddesses whose traditional charms have become coldly classic would the discerning rhymester have compared her. She was purely Paradisaic, not Olympian. If you can imagine Eve, after the eviction, beguiling the flaming warriors and serenely re-entering the Garden, you will have her. Just so human, and still so harmonious with Eden seemed Mrs. Goodwin.

When her husband entered she looked up, and her lips curved and parted; her eyelids fluttered twice or thrice – a movement remindful (Poesy forgive us!) of the tail-wagging of a faithful dog and a little ripple went through her like the commotion set up in a weeping willow by a puff of wind. Thus she ever acknowledged his coming, were it twenty times a day. If they who sometimes sat over their wine in Coralio, reshaping old, diverting stories of the madcap career of Isabel Guilbert, could have seen the wife of Frank Goodwin that afternoon in the estimable aura of her happy wifehood, they might have disbelieved, or have agreed to forget, those graphic annals of the life of the one for whom their president gave up his country and his honor.

'I have brought a guest to dinner,' said Goodwin. 'One Colonel Falcon, from San Mateo. He is come on government business. I do not think you will care to see him, so I prescribe for you one of those convenient and indisputable feminine headaches.'

'He has come to inquire about the lost money, has he not?' asked Mrs. Goodwin, going on with her sketch.

'A good guess!' acknowledged Goodwin. 'He has been holding an inquisition among the natives for three days. I am next on his list of witnesses, but as he feels shy about dragging one of Uncle Sam's subjects before him, he consents to give it the outward appearance of a social function. He will apply the torture over my own wine and provender.'

'Has he found any one who saw the valise of money?'

'Not a soul. Even Madame Ortiz, whose eyes are so sharp for the sight of a revenue official, does not remember that there was any baggage.'

Mrs. Goodwin laid down her brush and sighed.

'I am so sorry, Frank,' she said, 'that they are giving you so much trouble about the money. But we can't let them know about it, can we?'

'Not without doing our intelligence a great injustice,' said Goodwin, with a smile and a shrug that he had picked up from the natives. '*Americano*, though I am, they would have me in the *calaboza* in half an hour if they knew we had appropriated that valise. No; we must appear as ignorant about the money as the other ignoramuses in Coralio.'

'Do you think that this man they have sent suspects you?' she asked, with a little pucker of her brows.

'He'd better not,' said the American, carelessly. 'It's lucky that no one caught a sight of the valise except myself. As I was in the rooms when the shot was fired, it is not surprising that they should want to investigate my part in the affair rather closely. But there's no cause for alarm. This colonel is down on the list of events for a good dinner, with a dessert of American "bluff" that will end the matter, I think.'

Mrs. Goodwin rose and walked to the window. Goodwin followed and stood by her side. She leaned to him, and rested in the protection of his strength, as she had always rested since that dark night on which he had first made himself her tower of refuge. Thus they stood for a little while.

Straight through the lavish growth of tropical branch and leaf and vine that confronted them had been cunningly trimmed a vista, that ended at the cleared environs of Coralio, on the banks of the mangrove swamp. At the other end of the aërial tunnel they could see the grave and wooden headpiece that bore the name of the unhappy President Miraflores. From this window when the rains forbade the open, and from the green and shady slopes of Goodwin's fruitful lands when the skies were smiling, his wife was wont to look upon that grave with a gentle sadness that was now scarcely a mar to her happiness.

'I loved him so, Frank!' she said, 'even after that terrible flight and its awful ending. And you have been so good to me, and have made me so happy. It has all grown into such a strange puzzle. If they were to find out that we got the money do you think they would force you to make the amount good to the government?'

'They would undoubtedly try,' answered Goodwin. 'You are right about its being a puzzle. And it must remain a puzzle to Falcon and all his countrymen until it solves itself. You and I, who know more than any one else, only know half of the solution. We must not let even a hint about this money get abroad. Let them come to the theory that the president concealed it in the mountains during his journey, or that he found means to ship it out of the country before he reached Coralio. I don't think that Falcon suspects me. He is making a close investigation, according to his orders, but he will find out nothing.'

Thus they spake together. Had any one overheard or overseen them as they discussed the lost funds of Anchuria there would have been a second puzzle presented. For upon the faces and in the bearing of each of them was visible (if countenances are to be believed) Saxon honesty and pride and honorable thoughts. In Goodwin's steady eyes and firm lineaments, moulded into material shape by the inward spirit of kindness and generosity and courage, there was nothing reconcilable with his words.

As for his wife, physiognomy championed her even in the face of their accusive talk. Nobility was in her guise; purity was in her glance. The devotion that she manifested had not even the appearance of that feeling that now and then inspires a woman to share the guilt of her partner out of the pathetic greatness of her love. No, there was a discrepancy here between what the eye would have seen and the ear have heard.

Dinner was served to Goodwin and his guest in the *patio*, under cool foliage and flowers. The American begged the illustrious secretary to excuse the absence of Mrs. Goodwin, who was suffering, he said, from a headache brought on by a slight *calentura*.

After the meal they lingered, according to the custom, over their coffee and cigars. Colonel Falcon, with true Castilian delicacy, waited for his host to open the question that they had met to discuss. He had not long to wait. As soon as the cigars were lighted, the American cleared the way by inquiring whether the secretary's investigations in the town had furnished him with any clue to the lost funds.

'I have found no one yet,' admitted Colonel Falcon, 'who even had sight of the valise or the money. Yet I have persisted. It has been proven in the capital that President Miraflores set out from San Mateo with one hundred thousand dollars belonging to the government, accompanied by *Señorita* Isabel Guilbert, the opera singer. The Government, officially and personally, is loath to believe,' concluded Colonel Falcon, with a smile, 'that our last president's tastes would have permitted him to abandon on the route, as excess baggage, either of the desirable articles with which his flight was burdened.'

'I suppose you would like to hear what I have to say about the affairs,' said Goodwin, coming directly to the point. 'It will not require many words.

'On that night, with others of our friends here, I was keeping a look-out for the President, having been notified of his flight by a telegram in our national cipher from Englehart, one of our leaders in the capital. About ten o'clock that night I saw a man and a woman hurrying along the streets. They went to the Hotel de los Estranjeros, and engaged rooms. I followed them upstairs, leaving Estebán, who had come up, to watch outside. The barber had told me that he had shaved the beard from the President's face that night therefore I was prepared, when I entered the rooms, to find him with a smooth face. When I apprehended him in the name of the people he drew a pistol and shot himself instantly. In a few minutes many officers and citizens were on the spot. I suppose you have been informed of the subsequent facts.'

Goodwin paused. Losada's agent maintained an attitude of waiting, as if he expected a continuance.

'And now,' went on the American, looking steadily into the eyes of the other man, and giving each word a deliberate emphasis, 'you will oblige me by attending carefully to what I have to add. I saw no valise or receptacle of any kind, or any money belonging to the Republic of Anchuria. If President Miraflores decamped with any funds belonging to the treasury of this country, or to himself, or to any one else, I saw no trace of it in the house or elsewhere, at that time or at any other. Does that statement cover the ground of the inquiry you wished to make of me?'

Colonel Falcon bowed, and described a fluent curve with his cigar. His duty was performed. Goodwin was not to be disputed. He was a loyal supporter of the government, and enjoyed the full confidence of the new president. His rectitude had been the capital that had brought him fortune in Anchuria, just as it had formed the lucrative 'graft' of Mellinger, the secretary of Miraflores.

'I thank you, *Señor* Goodwin,' said Falcon, 'for speaking plainly. Your word will be sufficient for the President. But *Señor* Goodwin, I am instructed to pursue every clue that presents itself in this matter. There is one that I have not yet touched upon. Our friends in France, *señor*, have a saying, *"Cherchez la femme,"* when there is a mystery without a clue. But here we do not have to search. The woman who accompanied the late president in his flight must surely—'

'I must interrupt you there,' interposed Goodwin. 'It is true that when I entered the hotel for the purpose of intercepting President Miraflores I found a lady there. I must beg of you to remember that that lady is now my wife. I speak for her as I do for myself. She knows nothing of the fate of the valise or of the money that you are seeking. You will say to his excellency that I guarantee her innocence. I do not need to add to you, Colonel Falcon, that I do not care to have her questioned or disturbed.'

Colonel Falcon bowed again.

'*Por supuesto*, no!' he cried. And to indicate that the inquiry was ended he added: 'And now, *señor*, let me beg of you to show me that sea view from your *galería* of which you spoke. I am a lover of the sea.'

In the early evening Goodwin walked back to the town with his guest, leaving him at the corner of the Calle Grande. As he was returning homeward one 'Beelzebub' Blythe, with the air of a courtier and the outward aspect of a scarecrow, pounced upon him hopefully from the door of a *pulpería*.

Blythe had been re-christened 'Beelzebub' as an acknowledgment of the greatness of his fall. Once in some distant Paradise Lost, he had fore-gathered with the angels of the earth. But Fate had hurled him headlong down to the tropics, where flamed in his bosom a fire that was seldom quenched. In Coralio they called him a beachcomber; but he was, in reality, a categorical idealist who strove to anamorphosize the dull verities of life by the means of brandy and rum. As Beelzebub, himself, might have held in his clutch with unwitting tenacity his harp or crown during his tremendous fall, so his namesake had clung to his gold-rimmed eye-glasses as the only souvenir of his lost estate. These he wore with impressiveness and distinction while he combed beaches and extracted toll from his friends. By some mysterious means he kept his drink-reddened face always smoothly shaven. For the rest he sponged gracefully upon whomsoever he could for enough to keep him pretty drunk, and sheltered from the rains and night dews.

'Hallo, Goodwin!' called the derelict, airily. 'I was hoping I'd strike you. I wanted to see you particularly. Suppose we go where we can talk. Of course you know there's a chap down here looking up the money old Miraflores lost.'

'Yes,' said Goodwin, 'I've been talking with him. Let's go into Espada's place. I can spare you ten minutes.'

They went into the *pulpería* and sat at a little table upon stools with rawhide tops.

'Have a drink?' said Goodwin.

'They can't bring it too quickly,' said Blythe. 'I've been in a drought ever since morning. Hi – *muchacho! – el aguardiente por acá.*'

'Now, what do you want to see me about?' asked Goodwin, when the drinks were before them.

'Confound it, old man,' drawled Blythe, 'why do you spoil a golden moment like this with business? I wanted to see you – well, this has the preference.' He gulped down his brandy, and gazed longingly into the empty glass.

'Have another?' suggested Goodwin.

'Between gentlemen,' said the fallen angel, 'I don't quite like your use of that word "another." It isn't quite delicate. But the concrete idea that the word represents is not displeasing.'

The glasses were refilled. Blythe sipped blissfully from his, as he began to enter the state of a true idealist.

'I must trot along in a minute or two,' hinted Goodwin. 'Was there anything in particular?'

Blythe did not reply at once.

'Old Losada would make it a hot country,' he remarked at length, 'for the man who swiped that gripsack of treasury boodle, don't you think?'

'Undoubtedly, he would,' agreed Goodwin calmly, as he rose leisurely to his feet. 'I'll be running over to the house now, old man, Mrs. Goodwin is alone. There was nothing important you had to say, was there?'

'That's all,' said Blythe. 'Unless you wouldn't mind sending in another drink from the bar as you go out. Old Espada has closed my account to profit and loss. And pay for the lot, will you, like a good fellow?'

'All right,' said Goodwin. *'Buenas noches.'*

'Beelzebub' Blythe lingered over his cups, polishing his eyeglasses with a disreputable handkerchief.

'I thought I could do it, but I couldn't,' he muttered to himself after a time. 'A gentleman can't blackmail the man that he drinks with.'

THE ADMIRAL

SPILLED MILK DRAWS FEW TEARS from an Anchurian administration. Many are its lacteal sources; and the clocks' hands point forever to milking time. Even the rich cream skimmed from the treasury by the bewitched Miraflores did not cause the newly installed patriots to waste time in unprofitable regrets. The government philosophically set about supplying the deficiency by increasing the import duties and by 'suggesting' to wealthy private citizens that contributions according to their means would be considered patriotic and in order. Prosperity was expected to attend the reign of Losada, the new president. The ousted office-holders and military favorites organized a new 'Liberal' party, and began to lay their plans for a resuccession. Thus the game on Anchurian politics began, like a Chinese comedy, to unwind slowly its serial length. Here and there Mirth peeps for an instant from the wings and illumines the florid lines.

A dozen quarts of champagne in conjunction with an informal sitting of the president and his cabinet led to the establishment of the navy and the appointment of Felipe Carrera as its admiral.

Next to the champagne the credit of the appointment belongs to Don Sabas Placido, the newly confirmed Minister of War.

The President had requested a convention of his cabinet for the discussion of questions politic and for the transaction of certain routine matters of state. The session had been signally tedious; the business and the wine prodigiously dry. A sudden, prankish humor of Don Sabas, impelling him to the deed, spiced the grave affairs of state with a whiff of agreeable playfulness.

In the dilatory order of business had come a bulletin from the coast department of Orilla del Mar reporting the seizure by the custom-house officers at the town of Coralio of the sloop *Estrella del Noche* and her cargo of dry goods, patent medicines, granulated sugar and three-star brandy. Also six Martini rifles and a barrel of American whisky. Caught in the act of smuggling, the sloop with its cargo was now, according to law, the property of the republic.

The Collector of Customs, in making his report, departed from the conventional forms so far as to suggest that the confiscated vessel be converted to the use of the government. The prize was the first capture to the credit of the department in ten years. The collector took opportunity to pat his department on the back.

It often happened that government officers required transportation from point to point along the coast, and means were usually lacking. Furthermore, the sloop could be manned by a royal crew and employed as a coast-guard to discourage the pernicious art of smuggling. The collector also ventured to nominate one to whom the charge of the boat could be safely intrusted – a young man of Coralio, Felipe Carrera – not, be it understood, one of extreme wisdom, but loyal and the best sailor along the coast.

It was upon this hint that the Minister of War acted, executing a rare piece of drollery that so enlivened the tedium of executive session.

In the constitution of this small, maritime banana republic was a forgotten section that provided for the maintenance of a navy. This provision – with many other wiser ones – had lain inert since the establishment of the republic. Anchuria had no navy and had no use for one. It was characteristic of Don Sabas – a man at once merry, learned, whimsical and audacious – that he should have disturbed the dust of this musty and sleeping statute to increase the humor of the world by so much as a smile from his indulgent colleagues.

With delightful mock seriousness the Minister of War proposed the creation of a navy. He argued its need and the glories it might achieve with such gay and witty zeal that the travesty overcame with its humor even the swart dignity of President Losada himself.

The champagne was bubbling trickily in the veins of the mercurial statesmen. It was not the custom of the grave governors of Anchuria to enliven their sessions with a beverage so apt to cast a veil of disparagement over sober affairs. The wine had been a thoughtful compliment tendered by the agent of the Vesuvius Fruit Company as a token of amicable relations – and certain consummated deals – between that company and the republic of Anchuria.

The jest was carried to its end. A formidable, official document was prepared, encrusted with chromatic seals and jaunty with fluttering ribbons, bearing the florid signatures of state. This commission conferred upon el Señor Don Felipe Carrera the title of Flag Admiral of the Republic of Anchuria. Thus within the space of a few minutes and the dominion of a dozen 'extra dry,' the country took its place among the naval powers of the world, and Felipe Carrera became entitled to a salute of nineteen guns whenever he might enter port.

The southern races are lacking in that particular kind of humor that finds entertainment in the defects and misfortunes bestowed by Nature. Owing to this defect in their constitution they are not moved to laughter (as are their northern brothers) by the spectacle of the deformed, the feeble-minded or the insane.

Felipe Carrera was sent upon earth with but half his wits. Therefore, the people of Coralio called him 'El pobrecito loco' – 'the poor little crazed one' – saying that God had sent but half of him to earth, retaining the other half.

A sombre youth, glowering, and speaking only at the rarest times, Felipe was but negatively 'loco.' On shore he generally refused all conversation. He seemed to know that he was badly handicapped on land, where so many kinds of understanding are needed; but on the water his only talent set him equal with most men. Few sailors whom God had carefully and completely made could handle a sailboat as well. Five points nearer the wind than even the best of them he could sail his sloop. When the elements raged and set other men to cowering, the deficiencies of Felipe seemed of little importance.

He was a perfect sailor, if an imperfect man. He owned no boat, but worked among the crews of the schooners and sloops that skimmed the coast, trading and freighting fruit out to the steamers where there was no harbor. It was through his famous skill and boldness on the sea, as well as for the pity felt for his mental imperfections, that he was recommended by the collector as a suitable custodian of the captured sloop.

When the outcome of Don Sabas' little pleasantry arrived in the form of the imposing and preposterous commission, the collector smiled. He had not expected such prompt and overwhelming response to his recommendation. He despatched a *muchacho* at once to fetch the future admiral.

The collector waited in his official quarters. His office was in the Calle Grande, and the sea breezes hummed through its windows all day. The collector, in white linen and canvas shoes, philandered with papers on an antique desk. A parrot, perched on a pen rack, seasoned the official tedium with a fire of choice Castilian imprecations. Two rooms opened into the collector's. In one the clerical force of young men of variegated complexions transacted with glitter and parade their several duties. Through the open door of the other room could be seen a bronze babe, guiltless of clothing, that rollicked upon the floor. In a grass hammock a thin woman, tinted a pale lemon, played a guitar and swung contentedly in the breeze. Thus surrounded by the routine of his high duties and the visible tokens of agreeable domesticity, the collector's heart was further made happy by the power placed in his hands to brighten the fortunes of the 'innocent' Felipe.

Felipe came and stood before the collector. He was a lad of twenty, not ill-favored in looks, but with an expression of distant and pondering vacuity. He wore white cotton trousers, down the seams of which he had sewed red stripes with some vague aim at military decoration. A flimsy blue shirt fell open at his throat; his feet were bare; he held in his hand the cheapest of straw hats from the States.

'Señor Carrera,' said the collector, gravely, producing the showy commission, 'I have sent for you at the President's bidding. This document that I present to you confers upon you the title of Admiral of this great republic, and gives you absolute command of the naval forces and fleet of our country. You may think, friend Felipe, that we have no navy – but yes! The sloop the *Estrella del Noche*, that my brave men captured from the coast smugglers, is to be placed under your command. The boat is to be devoted to the services of your country. You will be ready at all times to convey officials of the government to points along the coast where they may be obliged to visit. You will also act as a coast-guard to prevent, as far as you may be able, the crime of smuggling. You will uphold the honor and prestige of your country at sea, and endeavor to place Anchuria among the proudest naval powers of the world. These are your instructions as the Minister of War desires me to convey them to you. *Por Dios!* I do not know how all this is to be accomplished, for not one word did his letter contain in respect to a crew or to the expenses of this navy. Perhaps you are to provide a crew yourself, Señor Admiral – I do not know – but it is a very high honor that has descended upon you. I now hand you your commission. When you are ready for the boat I will give orders that she shall be made over into your charge. That is as far as my instructions go.'

Felipe took the commission that the collector handed to him. He gazed through the open window at the sea for a moment, with his customary expression of deep but vain pondering. Then he turned without having spoken a word, and walked swiftly away through the hot sand of the street.

'*Pobrecito loco!*' sighed the collector; and the parrot on the pen racks screeched 'Loco! – loco! – loco!'

The next morning a strange procession filed through the streets to the collector's office. At its head was the admiral of the navy. Somewhere Felipe had raked together a pitiful semblance of a military uniform – a pair of red trousers, a dingy blue short jacket heavily ornamented with gold braid, and an old fatigue cap that must have been cast away by one of the British soldiers in Belize and brought away by Felipe on one of his coasting voyages. Buckled around his waist was an ancient ship's cutlass contributed to his equipment by Pedro Lafitte, the baker, who proudly asserted its inheritance from his ancestor, the illustrious buccaneer. At the admiral's heels tagged his newly shipped crew – three grinning, glossy, black Caribs, bare to the waist, the sand spurting in showers from the spring of their naked feet.

Briefly and with dignity Felipe demanded his vessel of the collector. And now a fresh honor awaited him. The collector's wife, who played the guitar and read novels in the hammock all day, had more than a little romance in her placid yellow bosom. She had found in an old book an engraving of a flag that purported to be the naval flag of Anchuria. Perhaps it had so been designed by the founders of the nation; but, as no navy had ever been established, oblivion had claimed the flag. Laboriously with her own hands she had made a flag after the pattern – a red cross upon a blue-and-white ground. She presented it to Felipe with these words: 'Brave sailor, this flag is of your country. Be true, and defend it with your life. Go you with God.'

For the first time since his appointment the admiral showed a flicker of emotion. He took the silken emblem, and passed his hand reverently over its surface. 'I am the admiral,' he said to the collector's lady. Being on land he could bring himself to no more exuberant expression of sentiment. At sea with the flag at the masthead of his navy, some more eloquent exposition of feelings might be forthcoming.

Abruptly the admiral departed with his crew. For the next three days they were busy giving the *Estrella del Noche* a new coat of white paint trimmed with blue. And then Felipe further adorned himself by fastening a handful of brilliant parrot's plumes in his cap. Again he tramped with his faithful crew to the collector's office and formally notified him that the sloop's name had been changed to *El Nacional*.

During the next few months the navy had its troubles. Even an admiral is perplexed to know what to do without any orders. But none came. Neither did any salaries. *El Nacional* swung idly at anchor.

When Felipe's little store of money was exhausted he went to the collector and raised the question of finances.

'Salaries!' exclaimed the collector, with hands raised; '*Valgame Dios!* not one *centavo* of my own pay have I received for the last seven months. The pay of an admiral, do you ask? *Quién sabe?* Should it be less than three thousand *pesos? Mira!* you will see a revolution in this country very soon. A good sign of it is when the government calls all the time for *pesos, pesos, pesos,* and pays none out.'

Felipe left the collector's office with a look almost of content on his sombre face. A revolution would mean fighting, and then the government would need his services. It was rather humiliating to be an admiral without anything to do, and have a hungry crew at your heels begging for *reales* to buy plantains and tobacco with.

When he returned to where his happy-go-lucky Caribs were waiting they sprang up and saluted, as he had drilled them to do.

'Come, *muchachos*,' said the admiral; 'it seems that the government is poor. It had no money to give us. We will earn what we need to live upon. Thus will we serve our country. Soon' – his heavy eyes almost lighted up – 'it may gladly call upon us for help.'

Thereafter *El Nacional* turned out with the other coast craft and became a wage-earner. She worked with the lighters freighting bananas and oranges out to the fruit steamers that could not approach nearer than a mile from the shore. Surely a self-supporting navy deserves red letters in the budget of any nation.

After earning enough at freighting to keep himself and his crew in provisions for a week Felipe would anchor the navy and hang about the little telegraph office, looking like one of the chorus of an insolvent comic opera troupe beseiging the manager's den. A hope for orders from the capital was always in his heart. That his services as admiral had never been called into requirement hurt his pride and patriotism. At every call he would inquire, gravely and expectantly, for despatches. The operator would pretend to make a search, and then reply:

'Not yet, it seems, *Señor el Almirante – poco tiempo!*'

Outside in the shade of the lime-trees the crew chewed sugar cane or slumbered, well content to serve a country that was contented with so little service.

One day in the early summer the revolution predicted by the collector flamed out suddenly. It had long been smoldering. At the first note of alarm the admiral of the navy force and fleet made all sail for a larger port on the coast of a neighboring republic, where he traded a hastily collected cargo of fruit for its value in cartridges for the five Martini rifles, the only guns that the navy could boast. Then to the telegraph office sped the admiral. Sprawling in his favorite corner, in his fast-decaying uniform, with his prodigious sabre distributed between his red legs, he waited for the long-delayed, but now soon expected, orders.

'Not yet, *Señor el Almirante*,' the telegraph clerk would call to him – '*poco tiempo!*'

At the answer the admiral would plump himself down with a great rattling of scabbard to await the infrequent tick of the little instrument on the table.

'They will come,' would be his unshaken reply; 'I am the admiral.'

THE FLAG PARAMOUNT

AT THE HEAD OF THE INSURGENT PARTY appeared that Hector and learned Theban of the southern republic, Don Sabas Placido. A traveller, a soldier, a poet, a scientist, a statesman, and a connoisseur – the wonder was that he could content himself with the petty, remote life of his native country.

'It is a whim of Placido's,' said a friend who knew him well, 'to take up political intrigue. It is not otherwise than as if he had come upon a new -tempo in music, a new bacillus in the air, a new scent, or rhyme, or explosive.

He will squeeze this revolution dry of sensations, and a week afterward will forget it, skimming the seas of the world in his brigantine to add to his already world-famous collections. Collections of what? *Por Dios!* of everything from postage stamps to prehistoric stone idols.'

But, for a mere dilettante, the aesthetic Placido seemed to be creating a lively row. The people admired him; they were fascinated by his brilliancy and flattered by his taking an interest in so small a thing as his native country. They rallied to the call of his lieutenants in the capital, where (somewhat contrary to arrangements) the army remained faithful to the government. There was also lively skirmishing in the coast towns. It was rumored that the revolution was aided by the Vesuvius Fruit Company, the power that forever stood with chiding smile and uplifted finger to keep Anchuria in the class of good children. Two of its steamers, the *Traveler* and the *Salvador*, were known to have conveyed insurgent troops from point to point along the coast.

As yet there had been no actual uprising in Coralio. Military law prevailed, and the ferment was bottled for the time. And then came the word that everywhere the revolutionists were encountering defeat. In the capital the president's forces triumphed; and there was a rumor that the leaders of the revolt had been forced to fly, hotly pursued.

In the little telegraph office at Coralio there was always a gathering of officials and loyal citizens, awaiting news from the seat of government. One morning the telegraph key began clicking, and presently the operator called, loudly: 'One telegram for *el Almirante*, Don Señor Felipe Carrera!'

There was a shuffling sound, a great rattling of tin scabbard, and the admiral, prompt at his spot of waiting, leaped across the room to receive it.

The message was handed to him. Slowly spelling it out, he found it to be his first official order – thus running:

—

Proceed immediately with your vessel to mouth of Rio Ruiz; transport beef and provisions to barracks at Alforan.

                                        Martinez, General

Small glory, to be sure, in this, his country's first call. But it had called, and joy surged in the admiral's breast. He drew his cutlass belt to another buckle hole, roused his dozing crew, and in a quarter of an hour *El Nacional* was tacking swiftly down coast in a stiff landward breeze.

The Rio Ruiz is a small river, emptying into the sea ten miles below Coralio. That portion of the coast is wild and solitary. Through a gorge in the Cordilleras rushes the Rio Ruiz, cold and bubbling, to glide, at last, with breadth and leisure, through an alluvial morass into the sea.

In two hours *El Nacional* entered the river's mouth. The banks were crowded with a disposition of formidable trees. The sumptuous undergrowth of the tropics overflowed the land, and drowned itself in the fallow waters. Silently the sloop entered there, and met a deeper silence. Brilliant with greens and ochres and floral scarlets, the umbrageous mouth of the Rio Ruiz furnished no sound or movement save of the sea-going water as it purled against the prow of the vessel. Small chance there seemed of wresting beef or provisions from that empty solitude.

The admiral decided to cast anchor, and, at the chain's rattle, the forest was stimulated to instant and resounding uproar. The mouth of the Rio Ruiz had only been taking a morning nap. Parrots and baboons screeched and barked in the trees; a whirring and a hissing and a booming marked the awakening of animal life; a dark blue bulk was visible for an instant, as a startled tapir fought his way through the vines.

The navy, under orders, hung in the mouth of the little river for hours. The crew served the dinner of shark's fin soup, plantains, crab gumbo and sour wine. The admiral, with a three-foot telescope, closely scanned the impervious foliage fifty yards away.

It was nearly sunset when a reverberating 'hallo-o-o!' came from the forest to their left. It was answered; and three men, mounted upon mules, crashed through the tropic tangle to within a dozen yards of the river's bank. There they dismounted; and one, unbuckling his belt, struck each mule a violent blow with his sword scabbard, so that they, with a fling of heels, dashed back again into the forest.

Those were strange-looking men to be conveying beef and provisions. One was a large and exceedingly active man, of striking presence. He was of the purest Spanish type, with curling, gray-besprinkled, dark hair, blue, sparkling eyes, and the pronounced air of a *caballero grande*. The other two were small, brown-faced men, wearing white military uniforms, high riding boots and swords. The clothes of all were drenched, bespattered and rent by the thicket. Some stress of circumstance must have driven them, *diable à quatre*, through flood, mire and jungle.

'O-hê! Señor Almirante,' called the large man. 'Send to us your boat.'

The dory was lowered, and Felipe, with one of the Caribs, rowed toward the left bank.

The large man stood near the water's brink, waist deep in the curling vines. As he gazed upon the scarecrow figure in the stern of the dory a sprightly interest beamed upon his mobile face.

Months of wageless and thankless service had dimmed the admiral's splendor. His red trousers were patched and ragged. Most of the bright buttons and yellow braid were gone from his jacket. The visor of his cap was torn, and depended almost to his eyes. The admiral's feet were bare.

'Dear admiral,' cried the large man, and his voice was like a blast from a horn, 'I kiss your hands. I knew we could build upon your fidelity. You had our despatch – from General Martinez. A little nearer with your boat, dear Admiral. Upon these devils of shifting vines we stand with the smallest security.'

Felipe regarded him with a stolid face.

'Provisions and beef for the barracks at Alforan,' he quoted.

'No fault of the butchers, *Almirante mio*, that the beef awaits you not. But you are come in time to save the cattle. Get us aboard your vessel, señor, at once. You first, *caballeros – à priesa!* Come back for me. The boat is too small.'

The dory conveyed the two officers to the sloop, and returned for the large man.

'Have you so gross a thing as food, good admiral?' he cried, when aboard. 'And, perhaps, coffee? Beef and provisions! *Nombre de Dios!* a little longer and we could have eaten one of those mules that you, Colonel Rafael, saluted so feelingly with your sword scabbard at parting. Let us have food; and then we will sail – for the barracks at Alforan – no?'

The Caribs prepared a meal, to which the three passengers of *El Nacional* set themselves with famished delight. About sunset, as was its custom, the breeze veered and swept back from the mountains, cool and steady, bringing a taste of the stagnant lagoons and mangrove swamps that guttered the lowlands. The mainsail of the sloop was hoisted and swelled to it, and at that moment they heard shouts and a waxing clamor from the bosky profundities of the shore.

'The butchers, my dear admiral,' said the large man, smiling, 'too late for the slaughter.'

Further than his orders to his crew, the admiral was saying nothing. The topsail and jib were spread, and the sloop glided out of the estuary. The large man and his companions had bestowed themselves with what comfort they could about the bare deck. Belike, the thing big in their minds had been their departure from that critical shore; and now that the hazard was so far reduced their thoughts were loosed to the consideration of further deliverance. But when they saw the sloop turn and fly up coast again they relaxed, satisfied with the course the admiral had taken.

The large man sat at ease, his spirited blue eye engaged in the contemplation of the navy's commander. He was trying to estimate this sombre and fantastic lad, whose impenetrable stolidity puzzled him. Himself a fugitive, his life sought, and chafing under the smart of defeat and failure, it was characteristic of him to transfer instantly his interest to the study of a thing new to him. It was like him, too, to have conceived and risked all upon this last desperate and madcap scheme – this message to a poor crazed *fanático* cruising about with his grotesque uniform and his farcical title. But his companions had been at their wit's end; escape had seemed incredible; and now he was pleased with the success of the plan they had called crack-brained and precarious.

The brief tropic twilight seemed to slide swiftly into the pearly splendor of a moonlight night. And now the lights of Coralio appeared, distributed against the darkening shore to their right. The admiral stood, silent, at the tiller; the Caribs, like black panthers, held the sheets, leaping noiselessly at his short commands. The three passengers were watching intently the sea before them, and when at length they came in sight of the bulk of a steamer lying a mile out from the town, with her lights radiating deep into the water, they held a sudden voluble and close-headed converse. The sloop was speeding as if to strike midway between ship and shore.

The large man suddenly separated from his companions and approached the scarecrow at the helm.

'My dear admiral,' he said, 'the government has been exceedingly remiss. I feel all the shame for it that only its ignorance of your devoted service has prevented it from sustaining. An inexcusable oversight has been made. A vessel, a uniform and a crew worthy of your fidelity shall be furnished you. But just now, dear admiral, there is business of moment afoot. The steamer lying there is the *Salvador*. I and my friends desire to be conveyed to her, where we are sent on the government's business. Do us the favor to shape your course accordingly.'

Without replying, the admiral gave a sharp command, and put the tiller hard to port. *El Nacional* swerved, and headed straight as an arrow's course for the shore.

'Do me the favor,' said the large man, a trifle restively, 'to acknowledge, at least, that you catch the sound of my words.' It was possible that the fellow might be lacking in senses as well as intellect.

The admiral emitted a croaking, harsh laugh, and spake.

'They will stand you,' he said, 'with your face to a wall and shoot you dead. That is the way they kill traitors. I knew you when you stepped into my boat. I have seen your picture in a book. You are Sabas Placido, traitor to your country. With your face to a wall. So, you will die. I am the admiral, and I will take you to them. With your face to a wall. Yes.'

Don Sabas half turned and waved his hand, with a ringing laugh, toward his fellow fugitives. 'To you, *caballeros*, I have related the history of that session when we issued that O! so ridiculous commission. Of a truth our jest has been turned against us. Behold the Frankenstein's monster we have created!'

Don Sabas glanced toward the shore. The lights of Coralio were drawing near. He could see the beach, the warehouse of the *Bodega Nacional*, the long, low *cuartel* occupied by the soldiers, and, behind that, gleaming in the moonlight, a stretch of high adobe wall. He had seen men stood with their faces to that wall and shot dead.

Again he addressed the extravagant figure at the helm.

'It is true,' he said, 'that I am fleeing the country. But, receive the assurance that I care very little for that. Courts and camps everywhere are open to Sabas Placido. *Vaya!* what is this molehill of a republic – this pig's head of a country – to a man like me? I am a *paisano* of everywhere. In Rome, in London, in Paris, in Vienna, you will hear them say: "Welcome back, Don Sabas." Come! – *tonto* – baboon of a boy – admiral, whatever you call yourself, turn your boat. Put us on board the *Salvador*, and here is your pay – five hundred *pesos* in money of the *Estados Unidos* — more than your lying government will pay you in twenty years.'

Don Sabas pressed a plump purse against the youth's hand. The admiral gave no heed to the words or the movement. Braced against the helm, he was holding the sloop dead on her shoreward course. His dull face was lit almost to intelligence by some inward conceit that seemed to afford him joy, and found utterance in another parrot-like cackle.

'That is why they do it,' he said – 'so that you will not see the guns. They fire – boom! – and you fall dead. With your face to the wall. Yes.'

The admiral called a sudden order to his crew. The lithe, silent Caribs made fast the sheets they held, and slipped down the hatchway into the hold of the sloop. When the last one had disappeared, Don Sabas, like a big, brown leopard, leaped forward, closed and fastened the hatch and stood, smiling.

'No rifles, if you please, dear admiral,' he said. 'It was a whimsey of mine once to compile a dictionary of the Carib *lengua*. So, I understood your order. Perhaps now you will — '

He cut short his words, for he heard the dull 'swish' of iron scraping along tin. The admiral had drawn the cutlass of Pedro Lafitte, and was darting upon him. The blade descended, and it was only by a display of surprising agility that the large man escaped, with only a bruised shoulder, the glancing weapon. He was drawing his pistol as he sprang, and the next instant he shot the admiral down.

Don Sabas stooped over him, and rose again.

'In the heart,' he said briefly. '*Señores*, the navy is abolished.'

Colonel Rafael sprang to the helm, and the other officer hastened to loose

the mainsail sheets. The boom swung round; *El Nacional* veered and began
to tack industriously for the *Salvador*.

'Strike that flag, *señor*,' called Colonel Rafael. 'Our friends on the steamer
will wonder why we are sailing under it.'

'Well said,' cried Don Sabas. Advancing to the mast he lowered the flag
to the deck, where lay its too loyal supporter. Thus ended the Minister of
War's little piece of after-dinner drollery, and by the same hand that began
it.

Suddenly Don Sabas gave a great cry of joy, and ran down the slanting
deck to the side of Colonel Rafael. Across his arm he carried the flag of the
extinguished navy.

'*Mire! mire! señor*. Ah, *Dios*! Already can I hear that great bear of an
Oestreicher shout, "*Du hast mein herz gebrochen!*" *Mire*! Of my friend, Herr
Grunitz, of Vienna, you have heard me relate. That man has travelled to
Ceylon for an orchid – to Patagonia for a headdress – to Benares for a slipper
– to Mozambique for a spearhead to add to his famous collections. Thou
knowest, also, *amigo* Rafael, that I have been a gather of curios. My collection
of battle flags of the world's navies was the most complete in existence until
last year. Then Herr Grunitz secured two, O! such rare specimens. One of
a Barbary state, and one of the Makarooroos, a tribe on the west coast of
Africa. I have not those, but they can be procured. But this flag, *señor* – do
you know now what it is? Name of God! Do you know? See that red cross
upon the blue-and-white ground! You never saw it before? *Seguarmente no*.
It is the naval flag of your country. *Mire!* This rotten tub we stand upon is
its navy – that dead cockatoo lying there was its commander – that stroke
of cutlass and single pistol shot a sea battle. All a piece of absurd foolery, I
grant you – but authentic. There has never been another flag like this, and
there never will be another. No. It is unique in the whole world. Yes. Think
of what that means to a collector of flags! Do you know, *Coronel mío*, how
many golden crowns Herr Grunitz would give for this flag? Ten thousand,
likely. Well, a hundred thousand would not buy it. Beautiful flag! Only flag!
Little devil of a most heaven-born flag! *O-hê!* old grumbler beyond the ocean.
Wait till Don Sabas comes again to the Königin Strasse. He will let you kneel
and touch the folds of it with one finger. *O-hê!* old spectacled ransacker of
the world!'

Forgotten was the impotent revolution, the danger, the loss, the gall of
defeat. Possessed solely by the inordinate and unparalleled passion of the
collector, he strode up and down the little deck, clasping to his breast with
one hand the paragon of a flag. He snapped his fingers triumphantly toward
the east. He shouted the paean to his prize in trumpet tones, as though he
would make old Grunitz hear in his musty den beyond the sea.

They were waiting, on the *Salvador*, to welcome them. The sloop came
close alongside the steamer where her sides were sliced almost to the lower
deck for the loading of fruit. The sailors of the *Salvador* grappled and held
her there.

Captain McLeod leaned over the side.

'Well, *señor*, the jig is up, I'm told.'

'The jig is up?' Don Sabas looked perplexed for a moment. 'That revolution
– ah, yes!' With a shrug of his shoulders he dismissed the matter.

The captain learned of the escape and the imprisoned crew.

'Caribs?' he said; 'no harm in them.' He slipped down into the sloop and kicked loose the hasp of the hatch. The black fellows came tumbling up, sweating but grinning.

'Hey! black boys!' said the captain, in a dialet of his own; 'you sabe, catchy boat and vamos back same place quick.'

They saw him point to themselves, the sloop and Coralio. 'Yas, yas!' they cried, with broader grins and many nods.

The four – Don Sabas, the two officers and the captain – moved to quit the sloop. Don Sabas lagged a little behind, looking at the still form of the late admiral, sprawled in his paltry trappings.

'*Pobrecito loco*,' he said softly.

He was a brilliant cosmopolite and a *cognoscente* of high rank; but, after all, he was of the same race and blood and instinct as this people. Even as the simple *paisanos* of Coralio had said it, so said Don Sabas. Without a smile, he looked, and said, 'That poor little crazed one!'

Stooping he raised the limp shoulders, drew the priceless and induplicable flag under them and over the breast, pinning it there with the diamond star of the Order of San Carlos that he took from the collar of his own coat.

He followed after the others, and stood with them upon the deck of the *Salvador*. The sailors that steadied *El Nacional* shoved her off. The jabbering Caribs hauled away at the rigging; the sloop headed for the shore.

And Herr Grunitz's collection of naval flags was still the finest in the world.

THE SHAMROCK AND THE PALM

ONE NIGHT WHEN THERE WAS NO BREEZE, and Coralio seemed closer than ever to the gratings of Avernus, five men were grouped about the door of the photograph establishment of Keogh and Clancy. Thus, in all the scorched and exotic places of the earth, Caucasians meet when the day's work is done to preserve the fullness of the heritage by the aspersion of alien things.

Johnny Atwood lay stretched upon the grass in the undress uniform of a Carib, and prated feebly of the cool water to be had in the cucumberwood pumps of Dalesburg. Dr. Gregg, through the prestige of his whiskers and as a bribe against the relation of his imminent professional tales, was conceded the hammock that was swung between the door jamb and a calabash-tree. Keogh had moved out upon the grass a little table that held the instrument for burnishing completed photographs. He was the only busy one of the group. Industriously from between the cylinders of the burnisher rolled the finished depictments of Coralio's citizens. Blanchard, the French mining engineer, in his cool linen viewed the smoke of his cigarette through his calm glasses, impervious to the heat. Clancy sat on the steps, smoking his short pipe. His mood was the gossip's; the others were reduced, by the humidity, to the state of disability desirable in an audience.

Clancy was an American with an Irish diathesis and cosmopolitan proclivities. Many businesses had claimed him, but not for long. The roadster's blood was in his veins. The voice of the tintype was but one of the many callings that had wooed him upon so many roads. Sometimes he could be persuaded to oral construction of his voyages into the informal and egregious. To-night there were symptoms of divulgement in him.

' 'Tis elegant weather for filibusterin',' he volunteered. 'It reminds me of the time I struggled to liberate a nation from the poisonous breath of a tyrant's clutch. 'Twas hard work. 'Tis strainin' to the back and makes corns on the hands.'

'I didn't know you had ever lent your sword to an oppressed people,' murmured Atwood, from the grass.

'I did,' said Clancy; 'and they turned it into a plowshare.'

'What country was so fortunate as to secure your aid?' airily inquired Blanchard.

'Where's Kamchatka?' asked Clancy, with seeming irrelevance.

'Why, off Siberia somewhere in the Arctic regions,' somebody answered, doubtfully.

'I thought that was the cold one,' said Clancy, with a satisfied nod. 'I'm always gettin' the two names mixed. 'Twas Guatemala, then – the hot one – I've been filibusterin' with. Ye'll find that country on the map. 'Tis in the district known as the tropics. By the foresight of Providence, it lies on the coast so the geography man could run the names of the towns off into the water. They're an inch long, small type, composed of Spanish dialects, and, 'tis my opinion, of the same system of syntax that blew up the *Maine*. Yes, 'twas that country I sailed against, single-handed, and endeavored to liberate it from a tyrannical government with a single-barreled pickaxe, unloaded at that. Ye don't understand, of course. 'Tis a statement demandin' elucidation and apologies.

' 'Twas in New Orleans one morning about the first of June; I was standin' down on the wharf, lookin' about at the ships in the river. There was a little steamer moored right opposite me that seemed about ready to sail. The funnels of it were throwin' out smoke, and a gang of roustabouts were carryin' aboard a pile of boxes that was stacked up on the wharf. The boxes were about two feet square, and somethin' like four feet long, and they seemed to be pretty heavy.

'I walked over, careless, to the stack of boxes. I saw one of them had been broken in handlin'. 'Twas curiosity made me pull up the loose top and look inside. The box was packed full of Winchester rifles. "So, so," says I to myself; "somebody's gettin' a twist on the neutrality laws. Somebody's aidin' with munitions of war. I wonder where the popguns are goin'?"

'I heard somebody cough, and I turned around. There stood a little, round, fat man with a brown face and white clothes, a first-class-looking little man, with a four-karat diamond on his finger and his eye full of interrogations and respects. I judged he was a kind of foreigner – may be from Russia or Japan or the archipelagoes.

' "Hist!" says the round man, full of concealments and confidences. "Will the señor respect the discoveryments he had made, that the mans on the ship shall not be acquaint? The señor will be a gentleman that shall not expose one thing that by accident occur."

' "Monseer," says I – for I judged him to be a kind of Frenchman – "receive my most exasperated assurances that your secret is safe with James Clancy. Furthermore, I will go so far as to remark, Veev la Liberty – veev it good and strong. Whenever you hear of a Clancy obstructin' the abolishment of existin' governments you may notify me by return mail."

' "The señor is good," says the dark, fat man, smilin' under his black mustache. "Wish you to come aboard my ship and drink of wine a glass."

'Bein' a Clancy, in two minutes me and the foreigner man were seated at a table in the cabin of the steamer, with a bottle between us. I could hear the heavy boxes bein' dumped into the hold. I judged that cargo must consist of at least 2,000 Winchesters. Me and the brown man drank the bottle of stuff, and he called the steward to bring another. When you amalgamate a Clancy with the contents of a bottle you practically instigate secession. I had heard a good deal about these revolutions in them tropical localities, and I began to want a hand in it.

' "You goin' to stir things up in your country ain't you, monseer?" says I, with a wink to let him know I was on.

' "Yes, yes," said the little man, pounding his fist on the table. "A change of the greatest will occur. Too long have the people been oppressed with the promises and the never-to-happen things to become. The great work it shall be carry on. Yes. Our forces shall in the capital city strike of the soonest. *Carrambos!*"

' "*Carrambos* is the word," says I, beginning to invest myself with enthusiasm and more wine, "likewise veeva, as I said before. May the shamrock of old – I mean the banana-vine or the pie-plant, or whatever the imperial emblem may be of your down-trodden country, wave forever."

' "A thousand thank-yous," says the round man, "for your emission of amicable utterances. What our cause needs of the very most is mans who will work do, to lift it along. Oh, for one thousands strong, good mans to aid the General De Vega that he shall to his country bring those success and glory! It is hard – oh, so hard to find good mans to help in the work."

' "Monseer," says I, leanin' over the table and graspin' his hand, "I don't know where your country is, but me heart bleeds for it. The heart of a Clancy was never deaf to the sight of an oppressed people. The family is filibusters by birth, and foreigners by trade. If you can use James Clancy's arms and his blood in denudin' your shores of the tyrant's yoke they're yours to command."

'General De Vega was overcome with joy to confiscate my condolence of his conspiracies and predicaments. He tried to embrace me across the table, but his fatness, and the wine that had been in the bottles, prevented. Thus was I welcomed into the ranks of filibustery. Then the general man told me his country had the name of Guatemala, and was the greatest nation laved by any ocean whatever anywhere. He looked at me with tears in his eyes, and from time to time he would emit the remark, "Ah! big, strong, brave mans! That is what my country need."

'General De Vega, as was the name by which he denounced himself, brought out a document for me to sign, which I did, makin' a fine flourish and curlycue with the tail of the "y."

' "Your passage-money," says the general, business-like, "shall from your pay be deduct."

' " 'Twill not," says I, haughty. "I'll pay my own passage." A hundred and eighty dollars I had in my inside pocket, and 'twas no common filibuster I was goin' to be, filibusterin' for me board and clothes.

'The steamer was to sail in two hours, and I went ashore to get some things together I'd need. When I came aboard I showed the general with pride the outfit. 'Twas a fine Chinchilla overcoat, Arctic over-shoes, fur cap and earmuffs, with elegant fleece-lined gloves and woolen muffler.

' "*Carrambos!*" says the little general. "What clothes are these that shall go to the tropic?" And then the little spalpeen laughs, and he calls the captain, and the captain calls the purser, and they pipe up the chief engineer, and the whole gang leans against the cabin and laughs at Clancy's wardrobe for Guatemala.

'I reflects a bit, serious, and asks the general again to denominate the terms by which his country is called. He tells me, and I see then that 'twas the t'other one, Kamchatka, I had in mind. Since then I've had difficulty in separatin' the two nations in name, climate, and geographic disposition.

'I paid my passage – twenty-four dollars, first cabin – and ate at table with the officer crowd. Down on the lower deck was a gang of second-class passengers, about forty of them, seemin' to be Dagoes and the like. I wondered what so many of them were goin' along for.

'Well, then, in three days we sailed alongside that Guatemala. 'Twas a blue country, and not yellow as 'tis miscolored on the map. We landed at a town on the coast, where a train of cars was waitin' for us on a dinky little railroad. The boxes on the steamer were brought ashore and loaded on the cars. The gang of Dagoes got aboard, too, the general and me in the front car. Yes, me and General De Vega headed the revolution, as it pulled out of the seaport town. That train travelled about as fast as a policeman goin' to a riot. It penetrated the most conspicuous lot of fuzzy scenery ever seen outside a geography. We run some forty miles in seven hours, and the train stopped. There was no more railroad. 'Twas a sort of camp in a damp gorge full of wildness and melancholies. They was gradin' and choppin' out the forests ahead to continue the road. "Here," says I to myself, "is the romantic haunt of the revolutionists. Here will Clancy, by the virtue that is in a superior race and the inculcation of Fenian tactics, strike a tremendous blow for liberty."

'They unloaded the boxes from the train and begun to knock the tops off. From the first one that was open I saw General De Vega take the Winchester rifles and pass them around to a squad of morbid soldiery. The other boxes was opened next, and, believe me or not, divil another gun was to be seen. Every other box in the load was full of pickaxes and spades.

'And then – sorrow be upon them tropics – the proud Clancy and the dishonored Dagoes, each one of them, had to shoulder a pick or a spade, and march away to work on that dirty little railroad. Yes, 'twas that the Dagoes shipped for, and 'twas that the filibusterin' Clancy signed for, though unbeknownst to himself at the time. In after days I found out about it. It seems 'twas hard to get hands to work on that road. The intelligent natives of the country was too lazy to work. Indeed the saints know, 'twas unnecessary. By stretchin' out one hand, they could seize the most delicate and costly fruits of the earth, and, by stretchin' out the other, they could sleep for days at a time without hearin' a seven-o'clock whistle or the footsteps of the rent man upon the stairs. So, regular, the steamers travelled to the United States to seduce labor. Usually the imported spade-slingers died in two or three months from eatin' the over-ripe water and breathin' the violent tropical scenery. Wherefore they made them sign contracts for a year, when they hired them, and put an armed guard over the poor divils to keep them from runnin' away.

' 'Twas thus I was double-crossed by the tropics through a family failin' of goin' out of the way to hunt disturbances.

'They gave me a pick, and I took it, meditatin' an insurrection on the spot; but there was the guards handlin' the Winchesters careless, and I come to the conclusion that discretion was the best part of filibusterin'. There was about a hundred of us in the gang startin' out to work, and the word was given to move. I steps out of the ranks and goes up to that General De Vega man, who was smokin' a cigar and gazin' upon the scene with satisfactions and glory. He smiles at me polite and devilish. "Plenty work," says he, "for big, strong mans in Guatemala. Yes. T'irty dollars in the month. Good pay. Ah, yes. You strong, brave man. Bimeby we push those railroad in the capital very quick. They want you go work now. *Adios*, strong mans."

' "Monseer," says I, lingerin', "will you tell a poor little Irishman this: When I set foot on your cockroachy steamer, and breathed liberal and revolutionary sentiments into your sour wine, did you think I was conspirin' to sling a pick on your contemptuous little railroad? And when you answered me with patriotic recitations, humping up the star-spangled cause of liberty, did you have meditations of reducin' me to the ranks of the stump-grubbin' Dagoes in the chain-gangs of your vile and grovelin' country?"

'The general man expanded his rotundity and laughed considerable. Yes, he laughed very long and loud, and I, Clancy, stood and waited.

' "Comical mans!" he shouts, at last. "So you will kill me from the laughing. Yes; it is hard to find the brave, strong mans to aid my country. Revolutions? Did I speak of r-r-revolutions? Not one word. I say, big, strong mans is need in Guatemala. So. The mistake is of you. You have looked in those one box containing those gun for the guard. You think all boxes is contain gun? No.

' "There is not war in Guatemala. But work? Yes. Good. T'irty dollar in the month. You shall shoulder one pickaxe, señor, and dig for the liberty and prosperity of Guatemala. Off to your work. The guard waits for you."

' "Little, fat poodle dog of a brown man," says I, quiet, but full of indignations and discomforts, "things shall happen to you. Maybe not right away, but as soon as J. Clancy can formulate somethin' in the way of repartee."

'The boss of the gang orders us to work. I tramps off with the Dagoes, and I hears the distinguished patriot and kidnapper laughin' hearty as we go.

' 'Tis a sorrowful fact, for eight weeks I built railroads for that misbehavin' country. I filibustered twelve hours a day with a heavy pick and a spade, choppin' away the luxurious landscape that grew upon the right of way. We worked in swamps that smelled like there was a leak in the gas mains, trampin' down a fine assortment of the most expensive hot-house plants and vegetables. The scene was tropical beyond the wildest imagination of the geography man. The trees was all sky-scrapers; the under-brush was full of needles and pins; there was monkeys jumpin' around and crocodiles and pink-tailed mockin'-birds, and ye stood knee-deep in the rotten water and grabbed roots for the liberation of Guatemala. Of nights we would build smudges in camp to discourage the mosquitoes, and sit in the smoke, with the guards pacin' all around us. There was two hundred men workin' on the road – mostly Dagoes, nigger-men, Spanish-men and Swedes. Three or four were Irish.

'One old man named Halloran – a man of Hibernian entitlements and discretions, explained it to me. He had been workin' on the road a year. Most of them died in less than six months. He was dried up to gristle and bone and shook with chills every third night.

' "When you first come," says he, "ye think ye'll leave right away. But they hold out your first month's pay for your passage over, and by that time the tropics has its grip on ye. Ye're surrounded by a ragin' forest full of disreputable beasts – lions and baboons and anacondas – waitin' to devour ye. The sun strikes ye hard, and melts the marrow in your bones. Ye get similar to the lettuce-eaters the poetry-book speaks about. Ye forget the elevated sintiments of life, such as patriotism, revenge, disturbances of the peace and the dacint love of a clane shirt. Ye do your work, and ye swallow the kerosene ile and rubber pipestems dished up to ye by the Dago cook for food. Ye light your pipeful, and say to yoursilf, 'Nixt week I'll break away,' and ye go to sleep and call yersilf a liar, for ye know ye'll never do it."

' "Who is this general man," asks I, "that calls himself De Vega?"

' " 'Tis the man," says Halloran, "who is tryin' to complete the finishin' of the railroad. 'Twas the project of a private corporation, but it was busted, and then the government took it up. De Vegy is a big politician, and wants to be president. The people want the railroad completed, as they're taxed mighty on account of it. The De Vegy man is pushin' it along as a campaign move."

' " 'Tis not my way," says I, "to make threats against any man, but there's an account to be settled between the railroad man and James O'Dowd Clancy."

' " 'Twas that way I thought, mesilf, at first," Halloran says, with a big sigh, "until I got to be a lettuce-eater. The fault's wid these tropics. They rejuices a man's system. 'Tis a land, as the poet says, 'Where it always seems to be after dinner.' I does me work and smokes me pipe and sleeps. There's little else in life, anyway. Ye'll get that way yersilf, mighty soon. Don't be harborin' any sintiments at all, Clancy."

' "I can't help it," says I; "I'm full of 'em. I enlisted in the revolutionary army of this dark country in good faith to fight for its liberty, honors and silver candlesticks; instead of which I am set to amputatin' its scenery and grubbin' its roots. 'Tis the general man will have to pay for it."

'Two months I worked on that railroad before I found a chance to get away. One day a gang of us was sent back to the end of the completed line to fetch some picks that had been sent down to Port Barrios to be sharpened. They were brought on a hand-car, and I noticed, when I started away, that the car was left there on the track.

'That night, about twelve, I woke up Halloran and told him my scheme.

' "Run away?" says Halloran. "Good Lord, Clancy, do ye mean it? Why, I ain't got the nerve. It's too chilly, and I ain't slept enough. Run away? I told you, Clancy, I've eat the lettuce. I've lost my grip. 'Tis the tropics that's done it. 'Tis like the poet says: 'Forgotten are our friends that we have left behind; in the hollow lettuce-land we will live and lay reclined.' You better go on, Clancy, I'll stay, I guess. It's too early and cold, and I'm sleepy."

'So I had to leave Halloran. I dressed quiet, and slipped out of the tent we were in. When the guard came along I knocked him over, like a ninepin, with a green cocoanut I had, and made for the railroad. I got on that hand-car and made it fly. 'Twas yet a while before daybreak when I saw the lights of Port Barrios about a mile away. I stopped the hand-car there and walked to the town. I stepped inside the corporations of that town with care and hesitations. I was not afraid of the army of Guatemala, but me soul quaked at the prospect of a hand-to-hand struggle with its employment bureau. 'Tis a country that hires its help easy and keeps 'em long. Sure I can fancy Missis

America and Missis Guatemala passin' a bit of gossip some fine, still night across the mountains. "Oh, dear," says Missis America, "and it's a lot of trouble I'm havin' ag'in with the help, señora, ma'am." "Laws, now!" says Missis Guatemala, "you don't say so, ma'am! Now, mine never think of leavin' me – te-he! ma'am," snickers Missis Guatemala.

'I was wonderin' how I was goin' to move away from them tropics without bein' hired again. Dark as it was, I could see a steamer ridin' in the harbor, with smoke emergin' from her stacks. I turned down a little grass street that run down to the water. On the beach I found a little brown nigger-man just about to shove off in a skiff.

' "Hold on, Sambo," says I, "savve English?"

' "Heap plenty yes," says he, with a pleasant grin.

' "What steamer is that?" I asks him, "and where is it going? And what's the news, and the good word and the time of day?"

' "That steamer the *Conchita*," said the brown man, affable and easy, rollin' a cigarette. "Him come from New Orleans for load banana. Him got load last night. I think him sail in one, two hour. Verree nice day we shall be goin' to have. You hear some talkee 'bout big battle, maybe so? You think catchee General De Vega, señor? Yes? No?"

' "How's that, Sambo?" says I. "Big battle? What battle? Who wants catchee General De Vega? I've been up at my old gold mines in the interior for a couple of months, and haven't heard any news."

' "Oh," says the nigger-man, proud to speak the English, "verree great revolution in Guatemala one week ago. General De Vega, him try be president. Him raise armee – one – five – ten thousand mans for fight at the government. Those on government send five – forty – hundred thousand soldiers to suppress revolution. They fight big battle yesterday at Lomagrande – that about nineteen or fifty mile in the mountain. That government soldier wheep General De Vega – oh, most bad. Five hundred – nine hundred – two thousand of his mans is kill. That revolution is smash suppress – bust – very quick. General De Vega, him r-r-run away fast on one big mule. Yes, *carrambos!* The general, him r-r-run away, and his armee is kill. That government soldier, they try to find General De Vega verree much. They want catchee him for shoot. You think they catchee that general, señor?"

' "Saints grant it!" says I. ' 'Twould be the judgment of Providence for settin' the warlike talent of a Clancy to gradin' the tropics with a pick and shovel. But 'tis not so much a question of insurrections now, me little man, as 'tis of the hired-man problem. 'Tis anxious I am to resign a situation of responsibility and trust with the white wings department of your great and degraded country. Row me in your little boat out to that steamer, and I'll give ye five dollars – sinker pacers – sinker pacers," says I, reducin' the offer to the language and denomination of the tropic dialects.

' "*Cinco pesos*," repeats the little man. "Five dollee, you give?"

' 'Twas not such a bad little man. He had hesitations at first, sayin' that passengers leaving the country had to have papers and passports, but at last he took me out alongside the steamer.

'Day was just breakin' as we struck her, and there wasn't a soul to be seen on board. The water was very still, and the nigger-man gave me a lift from the boat, and I climbed onto the steamer where her side was sliced to the deck for loadin' fruit. The hatches was open, and I looked down and saw the cargo of bananas that filled the hold to within six feet of the top. I thinks to

myself, "Clancy, you better go as a stowaway. It's safer. The steamer men
might hand you back to the employment bureau. The tropic'll get you,
Clancy, if you don't watch out."

'So I jumps down easy among the bananas and digs out a hole to hide in
among the bunches. In an hour or so I could hear the engines goin', and feel
the steamer rockin', and I knew we were off to sea. They left the hatches
open for ventilation, and pretty soon it was light enough in the hold to see
fairly well. I got to feelin' a bit hungry, and thought I'd have a light fruit
lunch, by way of refreshment. I creeped out of the hole I'd made and stood
up straight. Just then I saw another man crawl up about ten feet away and
reach out and skin a banana and stuff it into his mouth. 'Twas a dirty man,
black-faced and ragged and disgraceful of aspect. Yes, the man was a ringer
for the pictures of the fat Weary Willie in the funny papers. I looked again,
and saw it was my general man – De Vega, the great revolutionist, mule-
rider and pick-axe importer. When he saw me the general hesitated with his
mouth filled with banana and his eyes the size of cocoanuts.

' "Hist!" I says. "Not a word, or they'll put us off and make us walk. 'Veev
la Liberty!' " I adds, copperin' the sentiment by shovin' a banana into the
source of it. I was certain the general wouldn't recognize me. The nefarious
work of the tropics had left me lookin' different. There was half an inch of
roan whiskers coverin' me face, and me costume was a pair of blue overalls
and a red shirt.

' "How you come in the ship, señor?" asked the general as soon as he could
speak.

' "By the back door – whist!" says I. " 'Twas a glorious blow for liberty we
struck," I continues; "but we was overpowered by numbers. Let us accept
our defeat like brave men and eat another banana."

' "Were you in the cause of liberty fightin', señor?" says the general,
sheddin' tears on the cargo.

' "To the last," say I. ' 'Twas I led the last desperate charge against the
minions of the tyrant. But it made them mad, and we was forced to retreat.
'Twas I, general, procured the mule upon which you escaped. Could you give
that ripe bunch a little boost this way, general? It's a bit out of my reach.
Thanks."

' "Say you so, brave patriot?" said the general, again weepin'. "Ah, *Dios!*
And I have not the means to reward your devotion. Barely did I my life
bring away. *Carrambos!* what a devil's animal was that mule, señor! Like
ships in one storm was I dashed about. The skin on myself was ripped away
with the thorns and vines. Upon the bark of a hundred trees did that beast
of the infernal bump, and cause outrage to the legs of mine. In the night to
Port Barrios I came. I dispossess myself of that mountain of mule and hasten
along the water shore. I find a little boat to be tied. I launch myself and row
to the steamer. I cannot see any mans on board, so I climbed one rope which
hang at the side. I then myself hid in the bananas. Surely, I say, if the ship
captains view me, they shall throw me again to those Guatemala. Those
things are not good. Guatemala will shoot General De Vega. Therefore, I am
hide and remain silent. Life itself is glorious. Liberty, it is pretty good; but
so good as life I do not think."

'Three days, as I said, was the trip to New Orleans. The general man and
me got to be cronies of the deepest dye. Bananas we ate until they were
distasteful to the sight and an eyesore to the palate, but to bananas alone was

the bill of fare reduced. At night I crawls out, careful, on the lower deck, and gets a bucket of fresh water.

'That General De Vega was a man inhabited by an engorgement of words and sentences. He added to the monotony of the voyage by divestin' himself of conversation. He believed I was a revolutionist of his own party, there bein', as he told me, a good many Americans and other foreigners in its ranks. 'Twas a braggart and a conceited little gabbler it was, though he considered himself a hero. 'Twas on himself he wasted all his regrets at the failin' of his plot. Not a word did the little balloon have to say about the other misbehavin' idiots that had been shot, or run themselves to death in his revolution.

'The second day out he was feelin' pretty braggy and uppish for a stowed-away conspirator that owed his existence to a mule and stolen bananas. He was tellin' me about the great railroad he had been buildin', and he relates what he calls a comic incident about a fool Irishman he inveigled from New Orleans to sling a pick on his little morgue of a narrow-gauge line. 'Twas sorrowful to hear the little, dirty general tell the opprobrious story of how he put salt upon the tail of that reckless and silly bird, Clancy. Laugh, he did, hearty and long. He shook with laughin', the black-faced rebel and outcast, standin' neck-deep in bananas, without friends or country.

' "Ah, señor," he snickers, "to the death you would have laughed at that drollest Irish. I say to him: 'Strong, big mans is need very much in Guatemala.' 'I will blows strike for your down-pressed country,' he say. 'That shall you do,' I tell him. Ah! it was an Irish so comic. He sees one box break upon the wharf that contain for the guard a few gun. He think there is gun in all the box. But that is all pick-axe. Yes, Ah! señor, could you the face of that Irish have seen when they set him to the work!"

' 'Twas thus the ex-boss of the employment bureau contributed to the tedium of the trip with merry jests and anecdote. But now and then he would weep upon the bananas and make oration about the lost cause of liberty and the mule.

' 'Twas a pleasant sound when the steamer bumped against the pier in New Orleans. Pretty soon we heard the pat-a-pat of hundreds of bare feet, and the Dago gang that unloads the fruit jumped on the deck and down into the hold. Me and the general worked a while at passin' up the bunches, and they thought we were part of the gang. After about an hour we managed to slip off the steamer onto the wharf.

' 'Twas a great honor on the hands of an obscure Clancy, havin' the entertainment of the representative of a great foreign filibusterin' power. I first bought for the general and myself many long drinks and things to eat that were not bananas. The general man trotted along at my side, leavin' all the arrangements to me. I led him up to Lafayette Square and set him on a bench in the little park. Cigarettes I had bought for him, and he humped himself down on the seat like a little fat, contented hobo. I look him over as he sets there, and what I see pleases me. Brown by nature and instinct, he is now brindled with dirt and dust. Praise to the mule, his clothes is mostly strings and flaps. Yes, the looks of the general man is agreeable to Clancy.

'I ask him, delicate, if, by any chance, he brought away anybody's money with him from Guatemala. He sighs and bumps his shoulders against the bench. Not a cent. All right. Maybe, he tells me, some of his friends in the tropic outfit will send him funds later. The general was as clear a case of no visible means as I ever saw.

'I told him not to move from the bench, and then I went up to the corner of Poydras and Carondelet. Along there is O'Hara's beat. In five minutes along comes O'Hara, a big, fine man, red-faced, with shinin' buttons, swingin' his club. 'Twould be a fine thing for Guatemala to move into O'Hara's precinct. 'Twould be a fine bit of recreation for Danny to suppress revolutions and uprisin's once or twice a week with his club.

' "Is 5046 workin' yet, Danny?" says I, walkin' up to him.

' "Overtime," says O'Hara, lookin' over me suspicious. "Want some of it?"

'Fifty-forty-six is the celebrated city ordinance authorizin' arrest, conviction, and imprisonment of persons that succeed in concealin' their crimes from the police.

' "Don't ye know Jimmy Clancy?" says I. "Ye pink-gilled monster." So, when O'Hara recognized me beneath the scandalous exterior bestowed upon me by the tropics, I backed him into a doorway and told him what I wanted, and why I wanted it. "All right, Jimmy," says O'Hara. "Go back and hold the bench. I'll be along in ten minutes."

'In that time O'Hara strolled through Lafayette Square and spied two Weary Willies disgracin' one of the benches. In ten minutes more J. Clancy and General De Vega, late candidate for the presidency of Guatemala, was in the station house. The general is badly frightened, and calls upon me to proclaim his distinguishments and rank.

' "The man," says I to the police, "used to be a railroad man. He's on the bum now. 'Tis a little bughouse he is, on account of losin' his job."

' "*Carrambos!*" says the general, fizzin' like a little soda-water fountain, "you fought, señor, with my forces in my native country. Why do you say the lies? You shall say I am the General De Vega, one soldier, one *caballero—*"

' "Railroader," says I again. "On the hog. No good. Been livin' for three days on stolen bananas. Look at him. Ain't that enough?"

'Twenty-five dollars or sixty days, was what the recorder gave the general. He didn't have a cent, so he took the time. They let me go, as I knew they would, for I had money to show, and O'Hara spoke for me. Yes; sixty days he got. 'Twas just so long that I slung a pick for the great country of Kam – Guatemala.'

Clancy paused. The bright starlight showed a reminiscent look of happy content on his seasoned features. Keogh learned in his chair and gave his partner a slap on his thinly-clad back that sounded like the crack of the surf on the sand.

'Tell 'em, you divil,' he chuckled, 'how you got even with the tropical general in the way of agricultural maneuvrings.'

'Havin' no money,' concluded Clancy, with unction, 'they set him to work his fine out with a gang from the parish prison clearing Ursulines Street. Around the corner was a saloon decorated genially with electric fans and cool merchandise. I made that me headquarters, and every fifteen minutes I'd walk around and take a look at the little man filibusterin' with a rake and shovel. 'Twas just such a hot broth of a day as this has been. And I'd call at him "Hey, monseer!" and he'd look at me black, with the damp showin' though his shirt in places.

' "Fat, strong mans," says I to General De Vega, "is needed in New Orleans. Yes. To carry on the good work. Carrambos! Erin go bragh!" '

BREAKFAST IN CORALIO WAS at eleven. Therefore the people did not go to market early. The little wooden market-house stood on a patch of short-trimmed grass, under the vivid green foliage of a bread-fruit tree.

Thither one morning the venders leisurely convened, bringing their wares with them. A porch or platform six feet wide encircled the building, shaded from the mid-morning sun by the projecting, grass-thatched roof. Upon this platform the venders were wont to display their goods – newly-killed beef, fish, crabs, fruit of the country, cassava, eggs, *dulces* and high, tottering stacks of native tortillas as large around as the sombrero of a Spanish grandee.

But on this morning they whose stations lay on the seaward side of the market-house, instead of spreading their merchandise formed themselves into a softly jabbering and gesticulating group. For there upon their space of the platform was sprawled, asleep, the unbeautiful figure of 'Beelzebub' Blythe. He lay upon a ragged strip of cocoa matting, more than ever a fallen angel in appearance. His suit of coarse flax, soiled, bursting at the seams, crumpled into a thousand diversified wrinkles and creases, inclosed him absurdly, like the garb of some effigy that had been stuffed in sport and thrown there after indignity had been wrought upon it. But firmly upon the high bridge of his nose reposed his gold-rimmed glasses, the surviving badge of his ancient glory.

The sun's rays, reflecting quiveringly from the rippling sea upon his face, and the voices of the marketmen woke 'Beelzebub' Blythe. He sat up, blinking, and leaned his back against the wall of the market. Drawing a blighted silk handkerchief from his pocket, he assiduously rubbed and burnished his glasses. And while doing this he became aware that his bedroom had been invaded, and that polite brown and yellow men were beseeching him to vacate in favor of their market stuff.

If the señor would have the goodness – a thousand pardons for bringing to him molestation – but soon would come the *compradores* for the day's provisions – surely they had ten thousand regrets at disturbing him!

In this manner they expanded to him the intimation that he must clear out and cease to clog the wheels of trade.

Blythe stepped from the platform with the air of a prince leaving his canopied couch. He never quite lost that air, even at the lowest point of his fall. It is clear that the college of good breeding does not necessarily maintain a chair of morals within its walls.

Blythe shook out his wry clothing, and moved slowly up the Calle Grande through the hot sand. He moved without a destination in his mind. The little town was languidly stirring to its daily life. Golden-skinned babies tumbled over one another in the grass. The sea breeze brought him appetite, but nothing to satisfy it. Throughout Coralio were its morning odors – those from the heavily fragrant tropical flowers and from the bread baking in the outdoor ovens of clay and the pervading smoke of their fires. When the smoke cleared, the crystal air, with some of the efficacy of faith, seemed to remove the mountains almost to the sea, bringing them so near that one might count the scarred glades on their wooded sides. The light-footed Caribs were swiftly gliding to their tasks at the waterside. Already along the bosky trails from the banana groves files of horses were slowly moving, concealed, except for their nodding heads and plodding legs, by the bunches of green-golden fruit heaped upon their backs. On doorsills sat women combing their long, black hair and calling, one to another, across the narrow thoroughfares. Peace reigned in Coralio – arid and bald peace; but still peace.

On that bright morning when Nature seemed to be offering the lotus on the Dawn's golden platter 'Beelzebub' Blythe had reached rock bottom. Further descent seemed impossible. That last night's slumber in a public place had done for him. As long as he had had a roof to cover him there had remained, unbridged, the space that separates a gentleman from the beasts of the jungle and the fowls of the air. But now he was little more than a whimpering oyster led to be devoured on the sands of a Southern sea by the artful walrus, Circumstance, and the implacable carpenter, Fate.

To Blythe money was now but a memory. He had drained his friends of all that their good-fellowship had to offer; then he had squeezed them to the last drop of their generosity; and at the last, Aaron-like, he had smitten the rock of their hardening bosoms for the scattering, ignoble drops of Charity itself.

He had exhausted his credit to the last *real*. With the minute keenness of the shameless sponger he was aware of every source in Coralio from which a glass of rum, a meal, or a piece of silver could be wheedled. Marshalling each such source in his mind, he considered it with all the thoroughness and penetration that hunger and thirst lent him for the task. All his optimism failed to thresh a grain of hope from the chaff of his postulations. He had played out the game. That one night in the open had shaken his nerves. Until then there had been left to him at least a few grounds upon which he could base his unblushing demands upon his neighbors' stores. Now he must beg instead of borrowing. The most brazen sophistry could not dignify by the name of 'loan' the coin contemptuously flung to a beach-comber who slept on the bare boards of the public market.

But on this morning no beggar would have more thankfully received a charitable coin, for the demon thirst had him by the throat – the drunkard's matutinal thirst that requires to be slaked at each morning station on the road to Tophet.

Blythe walked slowly up the street, keeping a watchful eye for any miracle that might drop manna upon him in his wilderness. As he passed the popular eating house of Madama Vasquez, Madama's boarders were just sitting down to freshly-baked bread, **aguacates**, pines and delicious coffee that sent forth odorous guarantee of its quality upon the breeze. Madama was serving; she turned her shy, stolid, melancholy gaze for a moment out the window; she saw Blythe, and her expression turned more shy and embarrassed. 'Beelzebub' owed her twenty *pesos*. He bowed as he had once bowed to less embarrassed dames to whom he owed nothing, and passed on.

Merchants and their clerks were throwing open the solid wooden doors of their shops. Polite but cool were the glances they cast upon Blythe as he lounged tentatively by with the remains of his old jaunty air; for they were his creditors almost without exception.

At the little fountain in the *plaza* he made an apology for a toilet with his wetted handkerchief. Across the open square filed the dolorous line of friends of the prisoners in the *calaboza*, bearing the morning meal of the immured.

The food in their hands aroused small longing in Blythe. It was drink that his soul craved, or money to buy it.

In the streets he met many with whom he had been friends and equals, and whose patience and liberality he had gradually exhausted. Willard Geddie and Paula cantered past him with the coolest of nods, returning from their daily horseback ride along the old Indian road. Keogh passed him at another corner, whistling cheerfully and bearing a prize of newly-laid eggs for the breakfast of himself and Clancy. The jovial scout of Fortune was one of Blythe's victims who had plunged his hand oftenest into his pocket to aid him. But now it seemed that Keogh, too, had fortified himself against further invasions. His curt greeting and the ominous light in his full gray eye quickened the steps of 'Beelzebub,' whom desperation had almost incited to attempt an additional 'loan.'

Three drinking shops the forlorn one next visited in succession. In all of these his money, his credit, and his welcome had long since been spent; but Blythe felt that he would have fawned in the dust at the feet of an enemy that morning for one draught of *aguardiente*. In two of the *pulperías* his courageous petition for drink was met with a refusal so polite that it stung worse than abuse. The third establishment had acquired something of American methods; and here he was seized bodily and cast out upon his hands and knees.

This physical indignity caused a singular change in the man. As he picked himself up and walked away, an expression of absolute relief came upon his features. The specious and conciliatory smile that had been graven there was succeeded by a look of calm and sinister resolve. 'Beelzebub' had been floundering in the sea of improbity, holding by a slender life-line to the respectable world that had cast him overboard. He must have left that with this ultimate shock the line had snapped, and have experienced the welcome ease of the drowning swimmer who has ceased to struggle.

Blythe walked to the next corner and stood there while he brushed the sand from his garments and repolished his glasses.

'I've got to do it – oh, I've got to do it,' he told himself, aloud. 'If I had a quart of rum I believe I could stave it off yet – for a little while. But there's no more rum for – 'Beelzebub,' as they call me. By the flames of Tartarus! If I'm to sit at the right hand of Satan somebody has got to pay the court expenses. You'll have to pony up, Mr. Frank Goodwin. You're a good fellow; but a gentleman must draw the line at being kicked into the gutter. Blackmail isn't a pretty word, but it's the next station on the road I'm travelling.'

With purpose in his steps Blythe now moved rapidly through the town by way of its landward environs. He passed through the squalid quarters of the improvident negroes and on beyond the picturesque shacks of the poorer *mestizos*. From many points along his course he could see, through the umbrageous glades, the house of Frank Goodwin on its wooded hill. And as he crossed the little bridge over the lagoon he saw the old Indian, Galvez, scrubbing at the wooden slab that bore the name of Miraflores. Beyond the lagoon the lands of Goodwin began to slope gently upward. A grassy road, shaded by a munificent and diverse array of tropical flora, wound from the edge of an outlying banana grove to the dwelling. Blythe took this road with long and purposeful strides.

Goodwin was seated on his coolest gallery, dictating letters to his secretary, a sallow and capable native youth. The household adhered to the American plan of breakfast; and that meal had been a thing of the past for the better part of an hour.

The castaway walked to the steps, and flourished a hand.

'Good morning, Blythe,' said Goodwin, looking up. 'Come in and have a chair. Anything I can do for you?'

'I want to speak to you in private.'

Goodwin nodded at his secretary, who strolled out under a mango tree and lit a cigarette. Blythe took the chair that he had left vacant.

'I want some money,' he began, doggedly.

'I'm sorry,' said Goodwin, with equal directness, 'but you can't have any. You're drinking yourself to death, Blythe. Your friends have done all they could to help you to brace up. You won't help yourself. There's no use furnishing you with money to ruin yourself with any longer.'

'Dear man,' said Blythe, tilting back his chair, 'it isn't a question of social economy now. It's past that. I like you, Goodwin; and I've come to stick a knife between your ribs. I was kicked out of Espada's saloon this morning; and Society owes me reparation for my wounded feelings.'

'I didn't kick you out.'

'No; but in a general way you represent Society; and in a particular way you represent my last chance. I've had to come down to it, old man – I tried to do it a month ago when Losada's man was here turning things over; but I couldn't do it then. Now it's different. I want a thousand dollars, Goodwin; and you have to give it to me.'

'Only last week,' said Goodwin, with a smile, 'a silver dollar was all you were asking for.'

'An evidence,' said Blythe, flippantly, 'that I was still virtuous – though under heavy pressure. The wages of sin should be something higher than a *peso* worth forty-eight cents. Let's talk business. I am the villain in the third act; and I must have my merited, if only temporary, triumph. I saw you collar the late president's valiseful of boodle. Oh, I know it's blackmail; but I'm liberal about the price. I know I'm a cheap villain – one of the regular sawmill-drama kind – but you're one of my particular friends, and I don't want to stick you hard.'

'Suppose you go into the details,' suggested Goodwin, calmly arranging his letters on the table.

'All right,' said 'Beelzebub.' 'I like the way you take it. I despise histrionics; so you will please prepare yourself for the facts without any red fire, calcium or grace notes on the saxophone.

'On the night that His Fly-by-night Excellency arrived in town I was very drunk. You will excuse the pride with which I state that fact; but it was quite a feat for me to attain that desirable state. Somebody had left a cot out under the orange trees in the yard of Madama Ortiz's hotel. I stepped over the wall, laid down upon it, and fell asleep. I was awakened by an orange that dropped from the tree upon my nose; and I laid there for awhile cursing Sir Isaac Newton, or whoever it was that invented gravitation, for not confining his theory to apples.

'And then along came Mr. Miraflores and his true-love with the treasury in a valise, and went into the hotel. Next you hove in sight, and held a pow-wow with the tonsorial artist who insisted upon talking shop after hours. I tried to slumber again; but once more my rest was disturbed – this time by the noise of the popgun that went off upstairs. Then that valise came crashing down into an orange tree just above my head; and I arose from my couch, not knowing when it might begin to rain Saratoga trunks. When the army and the constabulary began to arrive, with their medals and decorations hastily pinned to their pajamas, and their snickersnees drawn, I crawled into the welcome shadow of a banana plant. I remained there for an hour, by which time the excitement and the people had cleared away. And then, my dear Goodwin – excuse me – I saw you sneak back and pluck that ripe and juicy valise from the orange tree. I followed you, and saw you take it to your own house. A hundred-thousand-dollar crop from one orange tree in a season about breaks the record of the fruit-growing industry.

'Being a gentleman at that time, of course, I never mentioned the incident to any one. But this morning I was kicked out of a saloon, my code of honor is all out at the elbows, and I'd sell my mother's prayer-book for three fingers of *aguardiente*. I'm not putting on the screws hard. It ought to be worth a thousand to you for me to have slept on that cot through the whole business without waking up and seeing anything.'

Goodwin opened two more letters, and made memoranda in pencil on them. Then he called 'Manuel!' to his secretary, who came, spryly.

'The *Ariel* – when does she sail?' asked Goodwin.

'Señor,' answered the youth, 'at three this afternoon. She drops downcoast to Punta Soledad to complete her cargo of fruit. From there she sails for New Orleans without delay.'

'*Bueno!*' said Goodwin. 'These letters may wait yet awhile.'

The secretary returned to his cigarette under the mango tree.

'In round numbers,' said Goodwin, facing Blythe squarely, 'how much money do you owe in this town, not including the sums you have "borrowed" from me?'

'Five hundred – at a rough guess,' answered Blythe, lightly.

'Go somewhere in the town and draw up a schedule of your debts,' said Goodwin. 'Come back here in two hours, and I will send Manuel with the money to pay them. I will also have a decent outfit of clothing ready for you. You will sail on the *Ariel* at three. Manuel will accompany you as far as the deck of the steamer. There he will hand you one thousand dollars in cash. I suppose that we needn't discuss what you will be expected to do in return.'

'Oh, I understand,' piped Blythe, cheerily. 'I was asleep all the time on the cot under Madama Ortiz's orange trees; and I shake off the dust of Coralio forever. I'll play fair. No more of the lotus for me. Your proposition is O.K. You're a good fellow, Goodwin; and I let you off light. I'll agree to everything. But in the meantime – I've a devil of a thirst on, old man –'

'Not a *centavo*,' said Goodwin, firmly, 'until you are on board the *Ariel*. You would be drunk in thirty minutes if you had money now.'

But he noticed the blood-streaked eyeballs, the relaxed form, and the shaking hands of 'Beelzebub'; and he stepped into the dining room through the low window, and brought out a glass and a decanter of brandy.

'Take a bracer, anyway, before you go,' he proposed, even as a man to the friend whom he entertains.

'Beelzebub' Blythe's eyes glistened at the sight of the solace for which his soul burned. To-day for the first time his poisoned nerves had been denied their steadying dose; and their retort was a mounting torment. He grasped the decanter and rattled its crystal mouth against the glass in his trembling hand. He flushed the glass, and then stood erect, holding it aloft for an instant. For one fleeting moment he held his head above the drowning waves of his abyss. He nodded easily at Goodwin, raised his brimming glass and murmured a 'health' that men had used in his ancient Paradise Lost. And then so suddenly that he spilled the brandy over his hand, he set down his glass, untasted.

'In two hours,' his dry lips muttered to Goodwin, as he marched down the steps and turned his face toward the town.

In the edge of the cool banana grove 'Beelzebub' halted, and snapped the tongue of his belt buckle into another hole.

'I couldn't do it,' he explained, feverishly, to the waving banana fronds. 'I wanted to, but I couldn't. A gentleman can't drink with the man that he blackmails.'

SHOES

JOHN DE GRAFFENREID ATWOOD ate of the lotus, root, stem, and flower. The tropics gobbled him up. He plunged enthusiastically into his work, which was to try to forget Rosine.

Now, they who dine on the lotus rarely consume it plain. There is a sauce *au diable* that goes with it; and the distillers are the chefs who prepare it. And on Johnny's menu card it read 'brandy.' With a bottle between them, he and Billy Keogh would sit on the porch of the little consulate at night and roar out great, indecorous songs, until the natives, slipping hastily past, would shrug a shoulder and mutter things to themselves about the '*Americanos diablos.*'

One day Johnny's *mozo* brought the mail and dumped it on the table. Johnny leaned from his hammock, and fingered the four or five letters dejectedly. Keogh was sitting on the edge of the table chopping lazily with a paper knife at the legs of a centipede that was crawling among the stationery. Johnny was in that phase of lotus-eating when all the world tastes bitter in one's mouth.

'Same old thing!' he complained. 'Fool people writing for information about the country. They want to know all about raising fruit, and how to make a fortune without work. Half of 'em don't even send stamps for a reply. They think a consul hasn't anything to do but write letters. Slit those envelopes for me, old man, and see what they want. I'm feeling too rocky to move.'

Keogh, acclimated beyond all possibility of ill-humor, drew his chair to the table with smiling compliance on his rose-pink countenance, and began to slit open the letters. Four of them were from citizens in various parts of the United States who seemed to regard the consul at Coralio as a cyclopaedia of information. They asked long lists of questions, numerically arranged, about the climate, products, possibilities, laws, business chances, and statistics of the country in which the consul had the honor of representing his own government.

'Write 'em, please, Billy,' said that inert official 'just a line, referring them to the latest consular report. Tell 'em the State Department will be delighted to furnish the literary gems. Sign my name. Don't let your pen scratch, Billy; it'll keep me awake.'

'Don't snore,' said Keogh, amiably, 'and I'll do your work for you. You need a corps of assistants, anyhow. Don't see how you ever get out a report. Wake up a minute! – here's one more letter – it's from your own town, too – Dalesburg.'

'That so?' murmured Johnny, showing a mild obligatory interest. 'What's it about?'

'Postmaster writes,' explained Keogh. 'Says a citizen of the town wants some facts and advice from you. Says the citizen has an idea in his head of coming down where you are and opening a shoe store. Wants to know if you think the business would pay. Says he's heard of the boom along this coast, and wants to get in on the ground floor.'

In spite of the heat and his bad temper, Johnny's hammock swayed with his laughter. Keogh laughed too; and the pet monkey on the top shelf of the bookcase chattered in shrill sympathy with the ironical reception of the letter from Dalesburg.

'Great bunions!' exclaimed the consul. 'Shoe store! What'll they ask about next, I wonder? Overcoat factory, I reckon. Say, Billy – of our 3,000 citizens, how many do you suppose ever had a pair of shoes?'

Keogh reflected judicially.

'Let's see – there's you and me and—'

'Not me,' said Johnny, promptly and incorrectly, holding up a foot encased in a disreputable deerskin *zapato*. 'I haven't been a victim to shoes in months.'

'But you've got 'em, though,' went on Keogh. 'And there's Goodwin and Blanchard and Geddie and old Lutz and Doc Gregg and that Italian that's agent for the banana company, and there's old Delgado – no; he wears sandals. And, oh, yes; there's Madama Ortiz, "what kapes the hotel" – she had a pair of red slippers at the *baile* the other night. And Miss Pasa, her daughter, that went to school in the States – she brought back some civilized notions in the way of footgear. And there's the *comandante's* sister that dresses up her feet on feast-days – and Mrs. Geddie, who wears a two with a Castilian instep – and that's about all the ladies. Let's see – don't some of the soldiers at the *cuartel* – no that's so; they're allowed shoes only when on the march. In barracks they turn their little toeses out to grass.'

' 'Bout right,' agreed the consul. 'Not over twenty out of the three thousand ever felt leather on their walking arrangements. Oh, yes; Coralio is just the town for an enterprising shoe store – that doesn't want to part with its goods. Wonder if old Patterson is trying to jolly me! He always was full of things he called jokes. Write him a letter, Billy. I'll dictate it. We'll jolly him back a few.'

Keogh dipped his pen, and wrote at Johnny's dictation. With many pauses, filled in with smoke and sundry travellings of the bottle and glasses, the following reply to the Dalesburg communication was perpetrated:

Mr. Obadiah Patterson,
    Dalesburg, Ala.

Dear Sir: In reply to your favor of July 2d, I have the honor to inform you that, according to my opinion, there is no place on the habitable globe that presents to the eye stronger evidence of the need of a first-class shoe store than does the town of Coralio. There are 3,000 inhabitants in the place, and not a single shoe store! The situation speaks for itself. This coast is rapidly becoming the goal of enterprising business men, but the shoe business is one that has been sadly overlooked or neglected.

In fact, there are a considerable number of our citizens actually without shoes at present.

Besides the want above mentioned, there is also a crying need for a brewery, a college of higher mathematics, a coal yard, and a clean and intellectual Punch and Judy show. I have the honor to be, sir,

> Your Obt. Servant,
> John de Graffenreid Atwood,
> *U.S. Consul at Coralio.*

P.S. – Hello! Uncle Obadiah. How's the old burg racking along? What would the government do without you and me? Look out for a green-headed parrot and a bunch of bananas soon, from your old friend

> Johnny

'I throw in that postscript,' explained the consul, 'so Uncle Obadiah won't take offence at the official tone of the letter! Now, Billy, you get that correspondence fixed up, and send Pancho to the post-office with it. The *Ariadne* takes the mail out to-morrow if they make up that load of fruit to-day.'

The night programme in Coralio never varied. The recreations of the people were soporific and flat. They wandered about, barefoot and aimless, speaking lowly and smoking cigar or cigarette. Looking down on the dimly lighted ways one seemed to see a threading maze of brunette ghosts tangled with a procession of insane fire-flies. In some houses the thrumming of lugubrious guitars added to the depression of the *triste* night. Giant tree-frogs rattled in the foliage as loudly as the end man's 'bones' in a minstrel troupe. By nine o'clock the streets were almost deserted.

Not at the consulate was there often a change of bill. Keogh would come there nightly, for Coralio's one cool place with the little seaward porch of that official residence.

The brandy would be kept moving; and before midnight sentiment would begin to stir in the heart of the self-exiled consul. Then he would relate to Keogh the story of his ended romance. Each night Keogh would listen patiently to the tale, and be ready with untiring sympathy.

'But don't you think for a minute' – thus Johnny would always conclude his woeful narrative – 'that I'm grieving about that girl, Billy. I've forgotten her. She never enters my mind. If she were to enter that door right now, my pulse wouldn't gain a beat. That's all over long ago.'

'Don't I know it?' Keogh would answer. 'Of course you've forgotten her. Proper thing to do. Wasn't quite O.K. of her to listen to the knocks that – er – Dink Pawson kept giving you.'

'Pink Dawson!' – a world of contempt would be in Johnny's tones – 'Poor white trash! That's what he was. Had five hundred acres of farming land, though; and that counted. Maybe I'll have a chance to get back at him some day. The Dawsons weren't anybody. Everybody in Alabama knows the Atwoods. Say, Billy – did you know my mother was a De Graffenreid?'

'Why, no,' Keogh would say; 'is that so?' He had heard it some three hundred times.

'Fact. The De Graffenreids of Hancock County. But I never think of that girl any more, do I, Billy?'

'Not for a minute, my boy,' would be the last sounds heard by the conqueror of Cupid.

At this point Johnny would fall into a gentle slumber, and Keogh would saunter out to his own shack under the calabash tree at the edge of the plaza.

In a day or two the letter from the Dalesburg postmaster and its answer had been forgotten by the Coralio exiles. But on the 26th day of July the fruit of the reply appeared upon the tree of events.

The *Andador*, a fruit steamer that visited Coralio regularly, drew into the offing and anchored. The beach was lined with spectators while the quarantine doctor and the custom-house crew rowed out to attend to their duties.

An hour later Billy Keogh lounged into the consulate, clean and cool in his linen clothes, and grinning like a pleased shark.

'Guess what?' he said to Johnny, lounging in his hammock.

'Too hot to guess,' said Johnny, lazily.

'Your shoe-store man's come,' said Keogh, rolling the sweet morsel on his tongue, 'with a stock of goods big enough to supply the continent as far down as Terra del Fuego. They're carting his cases over to the custom-house now. Six barges full they brought ashore and have paddled back for the rest. Oh, ye saints in glory! won't there be regalements in the air when he gets onto the joke and has an interview with Mr. Consul? It'll be worth nine years in the tropics just to witness that one joyful moment.'

Keogh loved to take his mirth easily. He selected a clean place on the matting and lay upon the floor. The walls shook with his enjoyment. Johnny turned half over and blinked.

'Don't tell me,' he said, 'that anybody was fool enough to take that letter seriously.'

'Four-thousand-dollar stock of goods!' gasped Keogh, in ecstasy. 'Talk about coals to Newcastle! Why didn't he take a ship-load of palm-leaf fans to Spitzbergen while he was about it? Saw the old codger on the beach. You ought to have been there when he put on his specs and squinted at the five hundred or so barefooted citizens standing around.'

'Are you telling the truth, Billy?' asked the consul, weakly.

'Am I? You ought to see the buncoed gentleman's daughter he brought along. Looks! She makes the brick-dust señoritas here look like tar-babies.'

'Go on,' said Johnny, 'if you can stop that asinine giggling. I hate to see a grown man make a laughing hyena of himself.'

'Name is Hemstetter,' went on Keogh. 'He's a – Hello! what's the matter now?'

Johnny's moccasined feet struck the floor with a thud as he wriggled out of his hammock.

'Get up, you idiot,' he said, sternly, 'or I'll brain you with this inkstand. That's Rosine and her father. Gad! what a drivelling idiot old Patterson is! Get up, here, Billy Keogh, and help me. What the devil are we going to do? Has all the world gone crazy?'

Keogh rose and dusted himself. He managed to regain a decorous demeanor.

'Situation has got to be met, Johnny,' he said, with some success at seriousness. 'I didn't think about its being your girl until you spoke. First thing to do is to get them comfortable quarters. You go down and face the music, and I'll trot out to Goodwin's and see if Mrs. Goodwin won't take them in. They've got the decentest house in town.'

'Bless you, Billy!' said the consul. 'I knew you wouldn't desert me. The world's bound to come to an end, but maybe we can stave it off for a day or two.'

Keogh hoisted his umbrella and set out for Goodwin's house. Johnny put on his coat and hat. He picked up the brandy bottle, but set it down again without drinking, and marched bravely down to the beach.

In the shade of the custom-house walls he found Mr. Hemstetter and Rosine surrounded by a mass of gaping citizens. The customs officers were ducking and scraping, while the captain of the *Andador* interpreted the business of the new arrivals. Rosine looked healthy and very much alive. She was gazing at the strange scenes around her with amused interest. There was a faint blush upon her round cheek as she greeted her old admirer. Mr. Hemstetter shook hands with Johnny in a very friendly way. He was an oldish, impractical man – one of that numerous class of erratic business men who are forever dissatisfied, and seeking a change.

'I am very glad to see you, John – may I call you John?' he said. 'Let me thank you for your prompt answer to our postmaster's letter of inquiry. He volunteered to write to you on my behalf. I was looking about for something different in the way of a business in which the profits would be greater. I had noticed in the papers that this coast was receiving much attention from investors. I am extremely grateful for your advice to come. I sold out everything that I possess, and invested the proceeds in as fine a stock of shoes as could be bought in the North. You have a picturesque town here, John. I hope business will be as good as your letter justifies me in expecting.'

Johnny's agony was abbreviated by the arrival of Keogh, who hurried up with the news that Mrs. Goodwin would be much pleased to place rooms at the disposal of Mr. Hemstetter and his daughter. So there Mr. Hemstetter and Rosine were at once conducted and left to recuperate from the fatigue of the voyage, while Johnny went down to see that the cases of shoes were safely stored in the customs warehouse pending their examination by the officials. Keogh, grinning like a shark, skirmished about to find Goodwin, to instruct him not to expose to Mr. Hemstetter the true state of Coralio as a shoe market until Johnny hd been given a chance to redeem the situation, if such a thing were possible.

That night the consul and Keogh held a desperate consultation on the breezy porch of the consulate.

'Send 'em back home,' began Keogh, reading Johnny's thoughts.

'I would,' said Johnny, after a little silence; 'but I've been lying to you, Billy.'

'All right about that,' said Keogh, affably.

'I've told you hundreds of times,' said Johnny, slowly, 'that I had forgotten that girl, haven't I?'

'About three hundred and seventy-five,' admitted the monument of patience.

'I lied,' repeated the consul, 'every time. I never forget her for one minute. I was an obstinate ass for running away just because she said "No" once. And I was too proud a fool to go back. I talked with Rosine a few minutes this evening up at Goodwin's. I found out one thing. You remember that farmer fellow who was always after her?'

'Dink Pawson?' said Keogh.

'Pink Dawson. Well, he wasn't a hill of beans to her. She says she didn't believe a word of the things he told her about me. But I'm sewed up now, Billy. That tomfool letter we sent ruined whatever chance I had left. She'll despise me when she finds out that her old father has been made the victim of a joke that a decent school boy wouldn't have been guilty of. Shoes! Why he couldn't sell twenty pairs of shoes in Coralio if he kept store here for twenty years. You put a pair of shoes on one of these Caribs or Spanish brown boys and what'd he do? Stand on his head and squeal until he'd kicked 'em off. None of 'em ever wore shoes and they never will. If I send 'em back home I'll have to tell the whole story, and what'll she think of me? I want that girl worse than ever, Billy, and now when she's in reach I've lost her forever because I tried to be funny when the thermometer was at 102.'

'Keep cheerful,' said the optimistic Keogh. 'And let 'em open the store. I've been busy myself this afternoon. We can stir up a temporary boom in foot-gear anyhow. I'll buy six pairs when the doors open. I've been around and seen all the fellows and explained the catastrophe. They'll all buy shoes like they were centipedes. Frank Goodwin will take cases of 'em. The Geddies want about eleven pairs between 'em. Clancy is going to invest the savings of weeks, and even old Doc Gregg wants three pairs of alligator-hide slippers if they've got any tens. Blanchard got a look at Miss Hemstetter; and as he's a Frenchman, no less than a dozen pairs will do for him.'

'A dozen customers,' said Johnny, 'for a $4,000 stock of shoes! It won't work. There's a big problem here to figure out. You go home, Billy, and leave me alone. I've got to work at it all by myself. Take that bottle of Three-star along with you – no, sir; not another ounce of booze for the United States consul. I'll sit here to-night and pull out the think stop. If there's a soft place on this proposition anywhere I'll land on it. If there isn't there'll be another wreck to the credit of the gorgeous tropics.'

Keogh left, feeling that he could be of no use. Johnny laid a handful of cigars on a table and stretchd himself in a steamer chair. When the sudden daylight broke, silvering the harbor ripples, he was still sitting there. Then he got up, whistling a little tune, and took his bath.

At nine o'clock he walked down to the dingy little cable office and hung for half an hour over a blank. The result of his application was the following message, which he signed and had transmitted at a cost of $33:

To Pinkney Dawson,
    Dalesburg, Ala.

    Draft for $100 comes to you next mail. Ship me immediately 500 pounds stiff, dry cockleburrs. New use here in arts. Market price twenty cents pound. Further orders likely. Rush.

SHIPS

WITHIN A WEEK A SUITABLE building had been secured in the Calle Grande, and Mr. Hemstetter's stock of shoes arranged upon their shelves. The rent of the store was moderate; and the stock made a fine showing of neat white boxes, attractively displayed.

Johnny's friends stood by him loyally. On the first day Keogh strolled into the store in a casual kind of way about once every hour, and bought shoes. After he had purchased a pair each of extension soles, congress gaiters, button kids, low-quartered calfs, dancing pumps, rubber boots, tans of various hues, tennis shoes and flowered slippers, he sought out Johnny to be prompted as to names of other kinds that he might inquire for. The other English-speaking residents also played their parts nobly by buying often and liberally. Keogh was grand marshal, and made them distribute their patronage, thus keeping up a fair run of custom for several days.

Mr. Hemstetter was gratified by the amount of business done thus far; but expressed surprise that the natives were so backward with their custom.

'Oh, they're awfully shy,' explained Johnny, as he wiped his forehead nervously. 'They'll get the habit pretty soon. They'll come with a rush when they do come.'

One afternoon Keogh dropped into the consul's office, chewing an unlighted cigar thoughtfully.

'Got anything up your sleeve?' he inquired of Johnny. 'If you have it's about time to show it. If you can borrow some gent's hat in the audience, and make a lot of customers for an idle stock of shoes come out on it, you'd better spiel. The boys have all laid in enough foot-wear to last 'em ten years; and there's nothing doing in the shoe store but dolcy far nienty. I just came by there. Your venerable victim was standing in the door, gazing through his specs at the bare toes passing by his emporium. The natives here have got the true artistic temperament. Me and Clancy took eighteen tin-types this morning in two hours. There's been but one pair of shoes sold all day. Blanchard went in and bought a pair of fur-lined house-slippers because he thought he saw Miss Hemstetter go into the store. I saw him throw the slippers into the lagoon afterwards.'

'There's a Mobile fruit steamer coming in to-morrow or next day,' said Johnny. 'We can't do anything until then.'

'What are you going to do – try to create a demand?'

'Political economy isn't your strong point,' said the consul, impudently. 'You can't create a demand. But you can create a necessity for a demand. That's what I am going to do.'

Two weeks after the consul sent his cable, a fruit steamer brought him a huge, mysterious brown bale of some unknown commodity. Johnny's influence with the custom-house people was sufficiently strong for him to get the goods turned over to him without the usual inspection. He had the bale taken to the consulate and snugly stowed in the back room.

That night he ripped open a corner of it and took out a handful of the cockleburrs. He examined them with the care with which a warrior examines his arms before he goes forth to battle for his lady-love and life. The burrs were the ripe August product, as hard as filberts, and bristling with spines as tough and sharp as needles. Johnny whistled softly a little tune, and went out to find Billy Keogh.

Later in the night, when Coralio was steeped in slumber, he and Billy went forth into the deserted streets with their coats bulging like balloons. All up and down the Calle Grande they went, sowing the sharp burrs carefully in the sand, along the narrow sidewalks, in every foot of grass between the silent houses. And then they took the side streets and byways, missing none. No place where the foot of man, woman or child might fall was slighted. Many trips they made to and from the prickly hoard. And then, nearly at the dawn, they laid themselves down to rest calmly, as great generals do after planning a victory according to the revised tactics, and slept, knowing that they had sowed with the accuracy of Satan sowing tares and the perseverance of Paul planting.

With the rising sun came the purveyors of fruits and meats, and arranged their wares in and around the little market-house. At one end of the town near the seashore the market-house stood; and the sowing of the burrs had not been carried that far. The dealers waited long past the hour when their sales usually began. None came to buy. '*Qué hay?*' they began to exclaim, one to another.

At their accustomed time, from every 'dobe and palm hut and grass-thatched shack and dim *patio* glided women – black women, brown women, lemon-colored women, women dun and yellow and tawny. They were the marketers starting to purchase the family supply of cassava, plantains, meat, fowls, and tortillas. Décolleté they were and bare-armed and bare-footed, with a single skirt reaching below the knee. Stolid and ox-eyed, they stepped from their doorways into the narrow paths or upon the soft grass of the streets.

The first to emerge uttered ambiguous squeals, and raised one foot quickly. Another step and they sat down, with shrill cries of alarm, to pick at the new and painful insects that had stung them upon the feet. '*Qué picadores diablos!*' they screeched to one another across the narrow ways. Some tried the grass instead of the paths, but there they were also stung and bitten by the strange little prickly balls. They plumped down in the grass, and added their lamentations to those of their sisters in the sandy paths. All through the town was heard the plaint of the feminine jabber. The venders in the market still wondered why no customers came.

Then men, lords of the earth, came forth. They, too, began to hop, to dance, to limp, and to curse. They stood stranded and foolish, or stooped to pluck at the scourge that attacked their feet and ankles. Some loudly proclaimed the pest to be poisonous spiders of an unknown species.

And then the children ran out for their morning romp. And now to the uproar was added the howls of limping infants and cockleburred childhood. Every minute the advancing day brought forth fresh victims.

Doña Maria Castillas y Buenventura de las Casas stepped from her honored doorway, as was her daily custom, to procure fresh bread from the *panadería* across the street. She was clad in a skirt of flowered yellow satin, a chemise of ruffled linen, and wore a purple mantilla from the looms of Spain. Her lemon-tinted feet, alas! were bare. Her progress was majestic, for were not her ancestors hidalgos of Aragon? Three steps she made across the velvety grass, and set her aristocratic sole upon a bunch of Johnny's burrs. Doña Maria Castillas y Buenventura de las Casas emitted a yowl even as a wildcat. Turning about, she fell upon hands and knees, and crawled – ay, like a beast of the field she crawled back to her honorable door-sill.

Don Señor Ildefonso Federico Valdazar, *Juez de la Paz*, weighing twenty stone, attempted to convey his bulk to the *pulpería* at the corner of the plaza in order to assuage his matutinal thirst. The first plunge of his unshod foot into the cool grass struck a concealed mine. Don Ildefonso fell like a crumpled cathedral, crying out that he had been fatally bitten by a deadly scorpion. Everywhere were the shoeless citizens hopping, stumbling, limping, and

picking from their feet the venomous insects that had come in a single night
to harass them.

The first to perceive the remedy was Estebán Delgado, the barber, a man
of travel and education. Sitting upon a stone, he plucked burrs from his toes,
and made oration:

'Behold, my friend, these bugs of the devil! I know them well. They soar
through the skies in swarms like pigeons. These are the dead ones that fell
during the night. In Yucatan I have seen them as large as oranges. Yes! There
they hiss like serpents, and have wings like bats. It is the shoes – the shoes
that one needs! *Zapatos – zapatos para mi!*'

Estebán hobbled to Mr. Hemstetter's store, and bought shoes. Coming out,
he swaggered down the street with impunity, reviling loudly the bugs of the
devil. The suffering ones sat up or stood upon one foot and beheld the
immune barber. Men, women, and children took up the cry: *'Zapatos!
zapatos!'*

The necessity for the demand had been created. The demand followed.
That day Mr. Hemstetter sold three hundred pairs of shoes.

'It is really surprising,' he said to Johnny, who came up in the evening to
help him straighten out the stock, 'how trade is picking up. Yesterday I made
but three sales.'

'I told you they'd whoop things up when they got started,' said the consul.

'I think I shall order a dozen more cases of goods, to keep the stock up,'
said Mr. Hemstetter, beaming through his spectacles.

'I wouldn't send in any orders yet,' advised Johnny. 'Wait till you see how
the trade holds up.'

Each night Johnny and Keogh sowed the crop that grew dollars by day.
And the end of ten days two-thirds of the stock of shoes had been sold and
the stock of cockleburrs was exhausted. Johnny cabled to Pink Dawson for
another 500 pounds, paying twenty cents per pound as before. Mr. Hemstetter
carefully made up an order for $1,500 worth of shoes from Northern firms.
Johnny hung about the store until this order was ready for the mail, and
succeeded in destroying it before it reached the post office.

That night he took Rosine under the mango tree by Goodwin's porch, and
confessed everything. She looked him in the eye, and said: 'You are a very
wicked man. Father and I will go back home. You say it was a joke? I think
it is a very serious matter.'

But at the end of half an hour's argument the conversation had been
turned upon a different subject. The two were considering the respective
merits of pale blue and pink wall paper with which the old colonial mansion
of the Atwoods in Dalesburg was to be decorated after the wedding.

On the next morning Johnny confessed to Mr. Hemstetter. The shoe
merchant put on his spectacles, and said through them: 'You strike me as
being a most extraordinary young scamp. If I had not managed this enterprise
with good business judgment my entire stock of goods might have been a
complete loss. Now how do you propose to dispose of the rest of it?'

When the second invoice of cockleburrs arrived Johnny loaded them and
the remainder of the shoes into a schooner, and sailed down the coast to
Alazan.

There, in the same dark and diabolical manner, he repeated his success;
and came back with a bag of money and not so much as a shoestring.

And then he besought his great Uncle of the waving goatee and starred vest to accept his resignation, for the lotus no longer lured him. He hankered for the spinach and cress of Dalesburg.

The services of Mr. William Terence Keogh as acting consul, *pro tem.*, were suggested and accepted, and Johnny sailed with the Hemstetters back to his native shores.

Keogh slipped into the sinecure of the American consulship with the ease that never left him even in such high places. The tintype establishment was soon to become a thing of the past, although its deadly work along the peaceful and helpless Spanish Main was never effaced. The restless partners were about to be off again, scouting ahead of the slow ranks of Fortune. But now they would take different ways. There were rumors of a promising uprising in Peru; and thither the martial Clancy would turn his adventurous steps. As for Keogh, he was figuring in his mind and on quires of Government letter-heads a scheme that dwarfed the art of misrepresenting the human countenance upon tin.

'What suits me,' Keogh used to say, 'in the way of a business proposition is something diversified that looks like a longer shot than it is – something in the way of a genteel graft that isn't worked enough for the correspondence schools to be teaching it by mail. I take the long end; but I like to have at least as good a chance to win as a man learning to play poker on an ocean steamer, or running for governor of Texas on the Republican ticket. And when I cash in my winnings, I don't want to find any widows' and orphans' chips in my stack.'

The grass-grown globe was the green table on which Keogh gambled. The games he played were of his own invention. He was no grubber after the diffident dollar. Nor did he care to follow it with horn and hounds. Rather he loved to coax it with egregious and brilliant flies from its habitat in the waters of strange streams. Yet Keogh was a business man; and his schemes, in spite of their singularity, were as solidly set as the plans of a building contractor. In Arthur's time Sir William Keogh would have been a Knight of the Round Table. In these modern days he rides abroad, seeking the Graft instead of the Grail.

Three days after Johnny's departure, two small schooners appeared off Coralio. After some delay a boat put off from one of them, and brought a sunburned young man ashore. This young man had a shrewd and calculating eye; and he gazed with amazement at the strange things that he saw. He found on the beach some one who directed him to the consul's office; and thither he made his way at a nervous gait.

Keogh was sprawled in the official chair, drawing caricatures of his uncle's head on an official pad of paper. He looked up at his visitor.

'Where's Johnny Atwood?' inquired the sunburned young man, in a business tone.

'Gone,' said Keogh, working carefully at Uncle Sam's necktie.

'That's just like him,' remarked the nut-brown one, leaning against the table. 'He always was a fellow to gallivant around instead of 'tending to business. Will he be in soon?'

'Don't think so,' said Keogh, after a fair amount of deliberation.

'I s'pose he's out at some of his tomfoolery,' conjectured the visitor, in a tone of virtuous conviction. 'Johnny never would stick to anything long enough to succeed. I wonder how he manages to run his business here, and never be 'round to look after it.'

'I'm looking after the business just now,' admitted the *pro tem*. consul.

'Are you – then, say! – where's the factory?'

'What factory?' asked Keogh, with a mildly polite interest.

'Why, the factory where they use them cockleburrs. Lord knows what they use 'em for, anyway! I've got the basements of both them ships out there loaded with 'em. I'll give you a bargain in this lot. I've had every man, woman, and child around Dalesburg that wasn't busy pickin' 'em for a month. I hired these ships to bring 'em over. Everybody thought I was crazy. Now, you can have this lot for fifteen cents a pound, delivered on land. And if you want more I guess old Alabam' can come up to the demand. Johnny told me when he left home that if he struck anything down here that there was any money in he'd let me in on it. Shall I drive the ships in and hitch?'

A look of supreme, almost incredulous, delight dawned in Keogh's ruddy countenance. He dropped his pencil. His eyes turned upon the sunburned young man with joy in them mingled with fear lest his ecstasy should prove a dream.

'For God's sake, tell me,' said Keogh, earnestly, 'are you Dink Pawson?'

'My name is Pinkney Dawson,' said the cornerer of the cockleburr market.

Billy Keogh slid rapturously and gently from his chair to his favorite strip of matting on the floor.

There were not many sounds in Coralio on that sultry afternoon. Among those that were may be mentioned a noise of enraptured and unrighteous laughter from a prostrate Irish-American, while a sunburned young man, with a shrewd eye, looked on him with wonder and amazement. Also the 'tramp, tramp, tramp' of many well-shod feet in the streets outside. Also the lonesome wash of the waves that beat along the historic shores of the Spanish Main.

MASTERS OF ARTS

A TWO-INCH STUB OF A BLUE pencil was the wand with which Keogh performed the preliminary acts of his magic. So, with this he covered paper with diagrams and figures while he waited for the United States of America to send down to Coralio a successor to Atwood, resigned.

The new scheme that his mind had conceived, his stout heart indorsed, and his blue pencil corroborated, was laid around the characteristics and human frailties of the new president of Anchuria. These characteristics, and the situation out of which Keogh hoped to wrest a golden tribute, deserve chronicling contributive to the clear order of events.

President Losada – many called him Dictator – was a man whose genius would have made him conspicuous even among Anglo-Saxons, had not that genius been intermixed with other traits that were petty and subversive. He had some of the lofty patriotism of Washington (the man he most admired), the force of Napoleon, and much of the wisdom of the sages. These characteristics might have justified him in the assumption of the title of 'The Illustrious Liberator,' had they not been accompanied by a stupendous and amazing vanity that kept him in the less worthy ranks of the dictators.

Yet he did his country great service. With a mighty grasp he shook it nearly free from the shackles of ignorance and sloth and the vermin that fed upon it, and all but made it a power in the council of nations. He established schools and hospitals, built roads, bridges, railroads and palaces, and bestowed generous subsidies upon the arts and sciences. He was the absolute despot and the idol of his people. The wealth of the country poured into his hands. Other presidents had been rapacious without reason. Losada amassed enormous wealth, but his people had their share of the benefits.

The joint in his armor was his insatiate passion for monuments and tokens commemorating his glory. In every town he caused to be erected statues of himself bearing legends in praise of his greatness. In the walls of every public edifice, tablets were fixed reciting his splendor and the gratitude of his subjects. His statuettes and portraits were scattered throughout the land in every house and hut. One of the sycophants in his court painted him as St. John, with a halo and a train of attendants in full uniform. Losada saw nothing incongruous in this picture, and had it hung in a church in the capital. He ordered from a French sculptor a marble group including himself with Napoleon, Alexander the Great, and one or two others whom he deemed worthy of the honor.

He ransacked Europe for decorations, employing policy, money and intrigue to cajole the orders he coveted from kings and rulers. On state occasions his breast was covered from shoulder to shoulder with crosses, stars, golden roses, medals and ribbons. It was said that the man who could contrive for him a new decoration, or invent some new method of extolling his greatness, might plunge a hand deep into the treasury.

This was the man upon whom Billy Keogh had his eye. The gentle buccaneer had observed the rain of favors that fell upon those who ministered to the president's vanities, and he did not deem it his duty to hoist his umbrella against the scattering drops of liquid fortune.

In a few weeks the new consul arrived, releasing Keogh from his temporary duties. He was a young man fresh from college, who lived for botany alone. The consulate at Coralio gave him the opportunity to study tropical flora. He wore smoked glasses, and carried a green umbrella. He filled the cool, back porch of the consulate with plants and specimens so that space for a bottle and chair was not to be found. Keogh gazed on him sadly, but without rancour, and began to pack his gripsack. For his new plot against stagnation along the Spanish Main required of him a voyage overseas.

Soon came the *Karlsefin* again – she of the trampish habits – gleaning a cargo of cocoanuts for a speculative descent upon the New York market. Keogh was booked for a passage on the return trip.

'Yes, I'm going to New York,' he explained to the group of his countrymen that had gathered on the beach to see him off. 'But I'll be back before you miss me. I've undertaken the art education of this piebald country, and I'm not the man to desert it while it's in the early throes of tintypes.'

With this mysterious declaration of his intentions Keogh boarded the *Karlsefin*.

Ten days later, shivering, with the collar of his thin coat turned high, he burst into the studio of Carolus White at the top of a tall building in Tenth Street, New York City.

Carolus White was smoking a cigarette and frying sausages over an oil stove. He was only twenty-three, and had noble theories about art.

'Billy Keogh!' exclaimed White, extending the hand that was not busy with the frying pan. 'From what part of the uncivilized world, I wonder!'

'Hello, Carry,' said Keogh, dragging forward a stool, and holding his fingers close to the stove. 'I'm glad I found you so soon. I've been looking for you all day in the directories and art galleries. The free-lunch man on the corner told me where you were, quick. I was sure you'd be painting pictures yet.'

Keogh glanced about the studio with the shrewd eye of a connoisseur in business.

'Yes, you can do it,' he declared, with many gentle nods of his head. 'That big one in the corner with the angels and green clouds and bandwagon is just the sort of thing we want. What would you call that, Carry – scene from Coney Island, ain't it?'

'That,' said White, 'I had intended to call "The Translation of Elijah," but you may be nearer right than I am.'

'Name doesn't matter,' said Keogh, largely; 'it's the frame and the varieties of paint that does the trick. Now, I can tell you in a minute what I want. I've come on a little voyage of two thousand miles to take you in with me on a scheme. I thought of you as soon as the scheme showed itself to me. How would you like to go back with me and paint a picture? Ninety days for the trip, and five thousand dollars for the job.'

'Cereal food or hair-tonic posters?' asked White.

'It isn't an ad.'

'What kind of a picture is it to be?'

'It's a long story,' said Keogh.

'Go ahead with it. If you don't mind, while you talk I'll just keep my eye on these sausages. Let 'em get one shade deeper than a Vandyke brown and you spoil 'em.'

Keogh explained his project. They were to return to Coralio, where White was to pose as a distinguished American portrait painter who was touring in the tropics as a relaxation from his arduous and remunerative professional labors. It was not an unreasonable hope, even to those who had trod in the beaten paths of business, that an artist with so much prestige might secure a commission to perpetuate upon canvas the lineaments of the president, and secure a share of the *pesos* that were raining upon the caterers to his weaknesses.

Keogh had set his price at ten thousand dollars. Artists had been paid more for portraits. He and White were to share the expenses of the trip, and divide the possible profits. Thus he laid the scheme before White, whom he had known in the West before one declared for Art and the other became a Bedouin.

Before long the two machinators abandoned the rigor of the bare studio for a snug corner of a café. There they sat far into the night, with old envelopes and Keogh's stub of blue pencil between them.

At twelve o'clock White doubled up in his chair, with his chin on his fist, and shut his eyes at the unbeautiful wall-paper.

'I'll go with you, Billy,' he said, in the quiet tones of decision. 'I've got two or three hundred saved up for sausages and rent; and I'll take the chance with you. Five thousand! It will give me two years in Paris and one in Italy. I'll begin to pack to-morrow.'

'You'll begin in ten minutes,' said Keogh. 'It's to-morrow now. The *Karlsefin* starts back at four P.M. Come on to your painting shop, and I'll help you.'

For five months in the year Coralio is the Newport of Anchuria. Then only does the town possess life. From November to March it is practically the seat of the government. The president with his official family sojourns there; and society follows him. The pleasure-loving people make the season one long holiday of amusement and rejoicing. *Fiestas*, balls, games, sea bathing, processions and small theatres contribute to their enjoyment. The famous Swiss band from the capital plays in the little plaza every evening, while the fourteen carriages and vehicles in the town circle in funereal but complacent procession. Indians from the interior mountains, looking like prehistoric stone idols, come down to peddle their handiwork in the streets. The people throng the narrow ways, a chattering, happy, careless stream of buoyant humanity. Preposterous children rigged out with the shortest of ballet skirts and gilt wings, howl, underfoot, among the effervescent crowds. Especially is the arrival of the presidential party, at the opening of the season, attended with pomp, show and patriotic demonstrations of enthusiasm and delight.

When Keogh and White reached their destination, on the return trip of the *Karlsefin*, the gay winter season was well begun. As they stepped upon the beach they could hear the band playing in the plaza. The village maidens, with fire-flies already fixed in their dark locks, were gliding, barefoot and coy-eyed, along the paths. Dandies in white linen, swinging their canes, were beginning their seductive strolls. The air was full of human essence, of artificial enticement, of coquetry, indolence, pleasure – the man-made sense of existence.

The first two or three days after their arrival were spent in preliminaries. Keogh escorted the artist about town, introducing him to the little circle of English-speaking residents and pulling whatever wires he could to effect the spreading of White's fame as a painter. And then Keogh planned a more spectacular demonstration of the idea he wished to keep before the public.

He and White engaged rooms in the Hotel de los Estranjeros. The two were clad in new suits of immaculate duck, with American straw hats, and carried canes of remarkable uniqueness and inutility. Few caballeros in Coralio – even the gorgeously uniformed officers of the Anchurian army – were as conspicuous for ease and elegance of demeanor as Keogh and his friend, the great American painter, Señor White.

White set up his easel on the beach and made striking sketches of the mountain and sea views. The native population formed at his rear in a vast, chattering semicircle to watch his work. Keogh, with his care for details, had arranged for himself a pose which he carried out with fidelity. His rôle was that of friend to the great artist, a man of affairs and leisure. The visible emblem of his position was a pocket camera.

'For branding the man who owns it,' said he, 'a genteel dilettante with a bank account and an easy conscience, a steam-yacht ain't in it with a camera. You see a man doing nothing but loafing around making snapshots, and you know right away he reads up well in "Bradstreet." You notice these old millionaire boys – soon as they get through taking everything else in sight they go to taking photographs. People are more impressed by a kodak than they are by a title or a four-carat scarf-pin.' So Keogh strolled blandly about Coralio, snapping the scenery and the shrinking señoritas, while White posed conspicuously in the higher regions of art.

Two weeks after their arrival, the scheme began to bear fruit. An aide-de-camp of the president drove to the hotel in a dashing victoria. The president desired that Señor White come to the Casa Morena for an informal interview.

Keogh gripped his pipe tightly between his teeth. 'Not a cent less than ten thousand,' he said to the artist – 'remember the price. And in gold or its equivalent – don't let him stick you with this bargain-counter stuff they call money here.'

'Perhaps it isn't that he wants,' said White.

'Get out!' said Keogh, with splendid confidence. 'I know what he wants. He wants his picture painted by the celebrated young American painter and filibuster now sojourning in this down-trodden country. Off you go.'

The victoria sped away with the artist. Keogh walked up and down, puffing great clouds of smoke from his pipe, and waited. In an hour the victoria swept again to the door of the hotel, deposited White, and vanished. The artist dashed up the stairs, three at a step. Keogh stopped smoking, and became a silent interrogation point.

'Landed,' exclaimed White, with his boyish face flushed with elation. 'Billy, you are a wonder. He wants a picture. I'll tell you all about it. By Heavens! that dictator chap is a corker! He's a dictator clear down to his finger-ends. He's a kind of combination of Julius Caesar, Lucifer and Chauncey Depew done in sepia. Polite and grim – that's his way. The room I saw him in was about ten acres big, and looked like a Mississippi steamboat with its gilding and mirrors and white paint. He talks English better than I can ever hope to. The matter of the price came up. I mentioned ten thousand. I expected him to call the guard and have me taken out and shot. He didn't move an eyelash. He just waved one of his chestnut hands in a careless way, and said, "Whatever you say." I am to go back to-morrow and discuss with him the details of the picture.'

Keogh hung his head. Self-abasement was easy to read in his downcast countenance.

'I'm failing, Carry,' he said, sorrowfully. 'I'm not fit to handle these man's-size schemes any longer. Peddling oranges in a push-cart is about the suitable graft for me. When I said ten thousand, I swear I thought I had sized up that brown man's limit to within two cents. He'd have melted down for fifteen thousand just as easy. Say – Carry – you'll see the old man Keogh safe in some nice, quiet idiot asylum, won't you, if he makes a break like that again?'

The Casa Morena, although only one story in height, was a building of brown stone, luxurious as a palace in its interior. It stood on a low hill in a walled garden of splendid tropical flora at the upper edge of Coralio. The next day the president's carriage came again for the artist. Keogh went out for a walk along the beach, where he and his 'picture-box' were now familiar sights. When he returned to the hotel White was sitting in a steamer-chair on the balcony.

'Well,' said Keogh, 'did you and His Nibs decide on the kind of chromo he wants?'

White got up and walked back and forth on the balcony a few times. Then he stopped and laughed strangely. His face was flushed, and his eyes were bright with a kind of angry amusement.

'Look here, Billy,' he said, somewhat roughly, 'when you first came to me in my studio and mentioned a picture, I thought you wanted a Smashed Oats or a Hair Tonic poster painted on a range of mountains or the side of a continent. Well, either of those jobs would have been Art in its highest form compared to the one you've steered me against. I can't paint that picture, Billy. You've got to let me out. Let me try to tell you what that barbarian wants. He had it all planned out and even a sketch made of his idea. The old boy doesn't draw badly at all. But, ye goddesses of Art! listen to the monstrosity he expects me to paint. He wants himself in the centre of the canvas, of course. He is to be painted as Jupiter sitting on Olympus, with the clouds at his feet. At one side of him stands George Washington, in full regimentals, with his hand on the president's shoulder. An angel with outstretched wings hovers overhead, and is placing a laurel wreath on the president's head, crowning him – Queen of the May, I suppose. In the background is to be cannon, more angels and soldiers. The man who would paint that picture would have to have the soul of a dog, and would deserve to go down into oblivion without even a tin can tied to his tail to sound his memory.'

Little beads of moisture crept out all over Billy Keogh's brow. The stub of his blue pencil had not figured out a contingency like this. The machinery of his plan had run with flattering smoothness until now. He dragged another chair upon the balcony, and got White back to his heat. He lit his pipe with apparent calm.

'Now, sonny,' he said, with gentle grimness, 'you and me will have an Art to Art talk. You've got your art and I've got mine. Yours is the real Pierian stuff that turns up its nose at bock-beer signs and oleographs of the Old Mill. Mine's the art of Business. This was my scheme, and it worked out like two-and-two. Paint that president man as Old King Cole, or Venus, or a landscape, or a fresco, or a bunch of lilies, or anything he thinks he looks like. But get the paint on the canvas and collect the spoils. You wouldn't throw me down, Carry, at this stage of the game. Think of that ten thousand.'

'I can't help thinking of it,' said White, 'and that's what hurts. I'm tempted to throw every ideal I ever had down in the mire, and steep my soul in infamy by painting that picture. That five thousand meant three years of foreign study to me, and I'd almost sell my soul for that.'

'Now it ain't as bad as that,' said Keogh, soothingly. 'It's a business proposition. It's so much paint and time against money. I don't fall in with your idea that that picture would so everlastingly jolt the art side of the question. George Washington was all right, you know, and nobody could say a word against the angel. I don't think so bad of that group. If you was to give Jupiter a pair of epaulets and a sword, and kind of work the clouds around to look like a blackberry patch, it wouldn't make such a bad battle scene. Why, if we hadn't already settled on the price, he ought to pay an extra thousand for Washington, and the angel ought to raise it five hundred.'

'You don't understand, Billy,' said White, with an uneasy laugh. 'Some of us fellows who try to paint have big notions about Art. I wanted to paint a picture some day that people would stand before and forget that it was made of paint. I wanted it to creep into them like a bar of music and mushroom there like a soft bullet. And I wanted 'em to go away and ask, "What else has he done?" And I didn't want 'em to find a thing; not a portrait nor a magazine cover nor an illustration nor a drawing of a girl – nothing but *the* picture. That's why I've lived on fried sausages, and tried to keep true to myself. I persuaded myself to do this portrait for the chance it might give to me to study abroad. But this howling, screaming caricature! Good Lord! can't you see how it is?'

'Sure,' said Keogh, as tenderly as he would have spoken to a child, and he laid a long fore-finger on White's knee. 'I see. It's bad to have your art all slugged up like that. I know. You wanted to paint a big thing like the panorama of the battle of Gettysburg. But let me kalsomine you a little mental sketch to consider. Up to date we're out $385.50 on this scheme. Our capital took every cent both of us could raise. We've got about enough left to get back to New York on. I need my share of that ten thousand. I want to work a copper deal in Idaho, and make a hundred thousand. That's the business end of the thing. Come down off your art perch, Carry, and let's land that hatful of dollars.'

'Billy,' said White, with an effort, 'I'll try. I won't say I'll do it, but I'll try. I'll go at it, and put it through if I can.'

'That's business,' said Keogh heartily. 'Good boy! Now, here's another thing – rush that picture – crowd it through as quick as you can. Get a couple of boys to help you mix the paint if necessary. I've picked up some pointers around town. The people here are beginning to get sick of Mr. President. They say he's been too free with concessions; and they accuse him of trying to make a dicker with England to sell out the country. We want that picture done and paid for before there's any row.'

In the great *patio* of Casa Morena, the president caused to be stretched a huge canvas. Under this White set up his temporary studio. For two hours each day the great man sat to him.

White worked faithfully. But, as the work progressed, he had seasons of bitter scorn, of infinite self-contempt, of sullen gloom and sardonic gaiety. Keogh, with the patience of a great general, soothed, coaxed, argued – kept him at the picture.

At the end of a month White announced that the picture was completed – Jupiter, Washington, angels, clouds, cannon and all. His face was pale and his mouth drawn straight when he told Keogh. He said the president was much pleased with it. It was to be hung in the National Gallery of Statesmen and Heroes. The artist had been requested to return to Casa Morena on the following day to receive payment. At the appointed time he left the hotel, silent under his friend's joyful talk of their success.

An hour later he walked into the room where Keogh was waiting, threw his hat on the floor, and sat upon the table.

'Billy,' he said, in strained and laboring tones, 'I've a little money out West in a small business that my brother is running. It's what I've been living on while I've been studying art. I'll draw out my share and pay you back what you've lost on this scheme.'

'Lost!' exclaimed Keogh, jumping up. 'Didn't you get paid for the picture?'

'Yes, I got paid,' said White. 'But just now there isn't any picture, and there isn't any pay. If you care to hear about it, here are the edifying details. The president and I were looking at the painting. His secretary brought a bank draft on New York for ten thousand dollars and handed it to me. The moment I touched it I went wild. I tore it into little pieces and threw them on the floor. A workman was repainting the pillars inside the *patio*. A bucket of his paint happened to be convenient. I picked up his brush and slapped a quart of blue paint all over that ten-thousand-dollar nightmare. I bowed, and walked out. The president didn't move or speak. That was one time he was taken by surprise. It's tough on you, Billy, but I couldn't help it.'

There seemed to be excitement in Coralio. Outside there was a confused, rising murmur pierced by high-pitched cries. '*Abajo el traidor – Muerte al traidor!*' were the words they seemed to form.

'Listen to that!' exclaimed White, bitterly: 'I know that much Spanish. They're shouting, "Down with the traitor!" I heard them before. I felt that they meant me. I was a traitor to Art. The picture had to go.'

' "Down with the blank fool" would have suited your case better,' said Keogh with fiery emphasis. 'You tear up ten thousand dollars like an old rag because the way you've spread on five dollars' worth of paint hurts your conscience. Next time I pick a side-partner in a scheme the man has got to go before a notary and swear he never even heard the word "ideal" mentioned.'

Keogh strode from the room, white-hot. White paid little attention to his resentment. The scorn of Billy Keogh seemed a trifling thing beside the greater self-scorn he had escaped.

In Coralio the excitement waxed. An outburst was imminent. The cause of this demonstration of displeasure was the presence in the town of a big, pink-cheeked Englishman, who, it was said, was an agent of his government come to clinch the bargain by which the president placed his people in the hands of a foreign power. It was charged that not only had he given away priceless concessions, but that the public debt was to be transferred into the hands of the English, and the custom-houses turned over to them as a guarantee. The long-enduring people had determined to make their protest felt.

On that night, in Coralio and in other towns, their ire found vent. Yelling mobs, mercurial but dangerous, roamed the streets. They overthrew the great bronze statue of the president that stood in the centre of the plaza, and hacked it to shapeless pieces. They tore from public buildings the tablets set there proclaiming the glory of the 'Illustrious Liberator.' His pictures in the government office were demolished. The mobs even attacked the Casa Morena, but were driven away by the military, which remained faithful to the executive. All the night terror reigned.

The greatness of Losada was shown by the fact that by noon the next day order was restored, and he was still absolute. He issued proclamations denying positively that any negotiations of any kind had been entered into with England. Sir Stafford Vaughn, the pink-cheeked Englishman, also declared in placards and in public print that his presence there had no international significance. He was a traveller without guile. In fact (so he stated), he had not even spoken with the president or been in his presence since his arrival.

During this disturbance, White was preparing for his homeward voyage in the steamship that was to sail within two or three days. About noon, Keogh, the restless, took his camera out with the hope of speeding the lagging hours. The town was now as quiet as if peace had never departed from her perch on the red-tiled roofs.

About the middle of the afternoon, Keogh hurried back to the hotel with something decidedly special in his air. He retired to the little room where he developed his pictures.

Later on he came out to White on the balcony, with a luminous, grim, predatory smile on his face.

'Do you know what that is?' he asked, holding up a 4 x 5 photograph mounted on cardboard.

'Snap-shot of a señorita sitting in the sand – alliteration unintentional,' guessed White, lazily.

'Wrong,' said Keogh with shining eyes. 'It's a slung-shot. It's a can of dynamite. It's a gold mine. It's a sight-draft on your president man for twenty thousand dollars – yes, sir – twenty thousand this time, and no spoiling the picture. No ethics of art in the way. Art! You with your smelly little tubes! I've got you skinned to death with a kodak. Take a look at that.'

White took the picture in his hand, and gave a long whistle.

'Jove,' he exclaimed, 'but wouldn't that stir up a row in town if you let it be seen. How in the world did you get it, Billy?'

'You know that high wall around the president man's back garden? I was up there trying to get a bird's-eye of the town. I happened to notice a chink in the wall where a stone and a lot of plaster had slid out. Thinks I, I'll take a peep through to see how Mr. President's cabbages are growing. The first thing I saw was him and this Sir Englishman sitting at a little table about twenty feet away. They had the table all spread over with documents, and they were hobnobbing over them as thick as two pirates. 'Twas a nice corner of the garden, all private and shady with palms and orange trees, and they had a pail of champagne set by handy in the grass. I knew then was the time for me to make my big hit in Art. So I raised the machine up to the crack, and pressed the button. Just as I do so them old boys shook hands on the deal – you see they took that way in the picture.'

Keogh put on his coat and hat.

'What are you going to do with it?' asked White.

'Me,' said Keogh in a hurt tone, 'why, I'm going to tie a pink ribbon to it and hang it on the what-not, of course. I'm surprised at you. But while I'm out you just try to figure out what gingercake potentate would be most likely to want to buy this work of art for his private collection – just to keep it out of circulation.'

The sunset was reddening the tops of the cocoanut palms when Billy Keogh came back from Casa Morena. He nodded to the artist's questioning gaze; and lay down on a cot with his hands under the back of his head.

'I saw him. He paid the money like a little man. They didn't want to let me in at first. I told 'em it was important. Yes, that president man is on the plenty-able list. He's got a beautiful business system about the way he uses his brains. All I had to do was to hold up the photograph so he could see it, and name the price. He just smiled, and walked over to a safe and got the cash. Twenty one-thousand-dollar brand-new United States Treasury notes he laid on the table, like I'd pay out a dollar and a quarter. Fine notes, too – they crackled with a sound like burning the brush off a ten-acre lot.'

'Let's try the feel of one,' said White, curiously. 'I never saw a thousand-dollar bill.' Keogh did not immediately respond.

'Carry,' he said, in an absent-minded way, 'you think a heap of your art, don't you?'

'More,' said White, frankly, 'than has been for the financial good of myself and my friends.'

'I thought you were a fool the other day,' went on Keogh, quietly, 'and I'm not sure now that you wasn't. But if you was, so am I. I've been in some funny deals, Carry, but I've always managed to scramble fair, and match my brains and capital against the other fellow's. But when it comes to – well, when you've got the other fellow cinched, and the screws on him, and he's got to put up – why, it don't strike me as being a man's game. They've got a name for it, you know; it's – confound you, don't you understand? A fellow feels – it's something like that blamed art of yours – he – well, I tore that photograph up and laid the pieces on that stack of money and shoved the whole business back across the table. "Excuse me, Mr. Losada," I said, "but I guess I've made a mistake in the price. You get the photo for nothing." Now, Carry, you get out the pencil, and we'll do some more figuring. I'd like to save enough out of our capital for you to have some fried sausages in your joint when you get back to New York.'

DICKY

THERE IS LITTLE CONSECUTIVENESS along the Spanish Main. Things happen there intermittently. Even Time seems to hang his scythe daily on the branch of an orange tree while he takes a siesta and a cigarette.

After the ineffectual revolt against the administration of President Losada, the country settled again into quiet toleration of the abuses with which he had been charged. In Coralio old political enemies went arm-in-arm, lightly eschewing for the time all differences of opinion.

The failure of the art expedition did not stretch the cat-footed Keogh upon his back. The ups and downs of Fortune made smooth travelling for his nimble steps. His blue pencil stub was at work again before the smoke of the steamer on which White sailed had cleared away from the horizon. He had but to speak a word to Geddie to find his credit negotiable for whatever goods he wanted from the store of Brannigan & Company. On the same day on which White arrived in New York, Keogh, at the rear of a train of five pack mules loaded with hardware and cutlery, set his face toward the grim, interior mountains. There the Indian tribes wash gold dust from the auriferous streams; and when a market is brought to them trading is brisk and *muy bueno* in the Cordilleras.

In Coralio Time folded his wings and paced wearily along his drowsy path. They who had most cheered the torpid hours were gone. Clancy had sailed on a Spanish barque for Colon, contemplating a cut across the isthmus and then a further voyage to end at Calao, where the fighting was said to be on. Geddie, whose quiet and genial nature had once served to mitigate the frequent dull reaction of lotus eating, was now a homeman, happy with his bright orchid, Paula, and never even dreaming of or regretting the unsolved, sealed and monogrammed Bottle whose contents, now inconsiderable, were held safely in the keeping of the sea.

Well may the Walrus, most discerning and eclectic of beasts, place sealing-wax midway on his programme of topics that fall pertinent and diverting upon the ear.

Atwood was gone – he of the hospitable back porch and ingenuous cunning. Dr. Gregg, with his trepanning story smouldering within him, was a whiskered volcano, always showing signs of imminent eruption, and was not to be considered in the ranks of those who might contribute to the amelioration of ennui. The new consul's note chimed with the sad sea waves and the violent tropical greens – he had not a bar of Scheherazade or of the Round Table in his lute. Goodwin was employed with large projects: what time he was loosed from them found him at his home, where he loved to be. Therefore it will be seen that there was a dearth of fellowship and entertainment among the foreign contingent of Coralio.

And then Dicky Maloney dropped down from the clouds upon the town, and amused it.

Nobody knew where Dicky Maloney hailed from or how he reached Coralio. He appeared there one day; and that was all. He afterward said that he came on the fruit steamer *Thor*; but an inspection of the *Thor's* passenger list of that date was found to be Maloneyless. Curiosity, however, soon perished; and Dicky took his place among the odd fish cast up by the Caribbean.

He was an active, devil-may-care, rollicking fellow with an engaging gray eye, the most irresistible grin, a rather dark or much sunburned complexion, and a head of the fieriest red hair ever seen in that country. Speaking the Spanish language as well as he spoke English, and seeming always to have plenty of silver in his pockets, it was not long before he was a welcome companion whithersoever he went. He had an extreme fondness for *vino blanco*, and gained the reputation of being able to drink more of it than any three men in town. Everybody called him 'Dicky'; everybody cheered up at the sight of him – especially the natives, to whom his marvellous red hair and his free-and-easy style were a constant delight and envy. Wherever you went in the town you would soon see Dicky or hear his genial laugh, and find around him a group of admirers who appreciated him both for his good nature and the white wine he was always so ready to buy.

A considerable amount of speculation was had concerning the object of his sojourn there, until one day he silenced this by opening a small shop for the sale of tobacco, *dulces* and the handiwork of the interior Indians – fibre-and-silk-woven goods, deerskin *zapatos* and basketwork of *tule* reeds. Even then he did not change his habits; for he was drinking and playing cards half the day and night with the *comandante*, the collector of customs, the *Jefe Político* and other gay dogs among the native officials.

One day Dicky saw Pasa, the daughter of Madama Ortiz, sitting in the side-door of the Hotel de los Estranjeros. He stopped in his tracks, still, for the first time in Coralio; and then he sped, swift as a deer, to find Vasquez, a gilded native youth, to present him.

The young men had named Pasa '*La Santita Naranjadita.*' *Naranjadita* is a Spanish word for a certain color that you must go to more trouble to describe in English. By saying 'The little saint, tinted the most beautiful delicate-slightly-orange-golden,' you will approximate the description of Madama Ortiz's daughter.

La Madama Ortiz sold rum in addition to other liquors. Now, you must know that the rum expiates whatever opprobrium attends upon the other commodities. For rum-making, mind you, is a government monopoly; and to keep a government dispensary assures respectability if not pre-eminence. Moreover, the saddest of precisions could find no fault with the conduct of the shop. Customers drank there in the lowest of spirits and fearsomely, as in the shadow of the dead; for Madama's ancient and vaunted lineage counteracted even the rum's behest to be merry. For, was she not of the

Iglesias, who landed with Pizarro? And had not her deceased husband been *comisionado de caminos y puentes* for the district?

In the evenings Pasa sat by the window in the room next to the one where they drank, and strummed dreamily upon her guitar. And then, by twos and threes, would come visiting young caballeros and occupy the prim line of chairs set against the wall of this room. They were there to besiege the heart of *'La Santita.'* Their method (which is not proof against intelligent competition) consisted of expanding the chest, looking valorous, and consuming a gross of two of cigarettes. Even saints delicately oranged prefer to be wooed differently.

Doña Pasa would tide over the vast chasms of nicotinized silence with music from her guitar, while she wondered if the romances she had read about gallant and more – more contiguous cavaliers were all lies. At somewhat regular intervals Madama would glide in from the dispensary with a sort of drought-suggesting gleam in her eye, and there would be a rustling of stiffly-starched white trousers as one of the caballeros would propose an adjournment to the bar.

That Dicky Maloney would, sooner or later, explore this field was a thing to be foreseen. There were few doors in Coralio into which his red head had not been poked.

In an incredibly short space of time after his first sight of her he was there, seated close beside her rocking chair. There were no back-against-the-wall poses in Dicky's theory of wooing. His plan of subjection was an attack at close range. To carry the fortress with one concentrated, ardent, eloquent, irresistible *escalade* – that was Dicky's way.

Pasa was descended from the proudest Spanish families in the country. Moreover, she had had unusual advantages. Two years in a New Orleans school had elevated her ambitions and fitted her for a fate above the ordinary maidens of her native land. And yet here she succumbed to the first red-haired scamp with a glib tongue and a charming smile that came along and courted her properly.

Very soon Dicky took her to the little church in the corner of the plaza, and 'Mrs. Maloney' was added to her string of distinguished names.

And it was her fate to sit, with her patient, saintly eyes and figure like a bisque Psyche, behind the sequestered counter of the little shop, while Dicky drank and philandered with his frivolous acquaintances.

The women, with their naturally fine instinct, saw a chance for vivisection, and delicately taunted her with his habits. She turned upon them in a beautiful, steady gaze of sorrowful contempt.

'You meat-cows,' she said, in her level, crystal-clear tones; 'you know nothing of a man. Your men are *maromeros*. They are fit only to roll cigarettes in the shade until the sun strikes and shrivels them up. They drone in your hammocks and you comb their hair and feed them with fresh fruit. My man is no such blood. Let him drink of the wine. When he has taken sufficient of it to drown one of your *flaccitos* he will come home to me more of a man than one thousand of your *pobrecitos*. *My* hair he smooths and braids; to me he sings; he himself removes my *zapatos*, and there, there, upon each instep leaves a kiss. He holds – Oh, you will never understand! Blind ones who have never known a *man*.'

Sometimes mysterious things happened at night about Dicky's shop. While the front of it was dark, in the little room back of it Dicky and a few of his friends would sit about a table carrying on some kind of very quiet *negocios* until quite late. Finally he would let them out the front door very carefully, and go upstairs to his little saint. These visitors were generally conspirator-like men with dark clothes and hats. Of course, these dark doings were noticed after a while, and talked about.

Dicky seemed to care nothing at all for the society of the alien residents of the town. He avoided Goodwin, and his skilful escape from the trepanning story of Dr. Gregg is still referred to, in Coralio, as a masterpiece of lightning diplomacy.

Many letters arrived, addressed to 'Mr. Dicky Maloney,' or 'Señor Dickee Maloney,' to the considerable pride of Pasa. That so many people should desire to write to him only confirmed her own suspicion that the light from his red head shone around the world. As to their contents she never felt curiosity. There was a wife for you!

The one mistake Dicky made in Coralio was to run out of money at the wrong time. Where his money came from was a puzzle, for the sales of his shop were next to nothing, but that source failed, and at a peculiarly unfortunate time. It was when the *comandante*, Don Señor el Coronel Encarnatión Rios, looked upon the little saint seated in the shop and felt his heart go pitapat.

The *comandante*, who was versed in all the intricate arts of gallantry, first delicately hinted at his sentiments by donning his dress uniform and strutting up and down fiercely before her window. Pasa, glancing demurely with her saintly eyes, instantly perceived his resemblance to her parrot, Chichi, and was diverted to the extent of a smile. The *comandante* saw the smile, which was not intended for him. Convinced of an impression made, he entered the shop, confidently, and advanced to open compliment. Pasa froze; he pranced; she flamed royally; he was charmed to injudicious persistence; she commanded him to leave the shop; he tried to capture her hand, – and Dicky entered, smiling broadly, full of white wine and the devil.

He spent five minutes in punishing the *comandante* scientifically and carefully, so that the pain might be prolonged as far as possible. At the end of that time he pitched the rash wooer out the door upon the stones of the street, senseless.

A barefooted policeman who had been watching the affair from across the street blew a whistle. A squad of four soldiers came running from the *cuartel* around the corner. When they saw that the offender was Dicky, they stopped, and blew more whistles, which brought out reinforcements of eight. Deeming the odds against them sufficiently reduced, the military advanced upon the disturber.

Dicky, being thoroughly imbued with the martial spirit, stooped and drew the *comandante's* sword, which was girded about him, and charged his foe. He chased the standing army four squares, playfully prodding its squealing rear and hacking at its ginger-colored heels.

But he was not so successful with the civic authorities. Six muscular, nimble policemen overpowered him and conveyed him, triumphantly but warily, to jail. 'El Diablo Colorado' they dubbed him, and derided the military for its defeat.

Dicky, with the rest of the prisoners, could look out through the barred door at the grass of the little plaza, at a row of orange trees and the red tile roofs and 'dobe walls of a line of insignificant stores.

At sunset along a path across this plaza came a melancholy procession of sad-faced women bearing plantains, casaba, bread and fruit – each coming with food to some wretch behind those bars to whom she still clung and furnished the means of life. Twice a day – morning and evening – they were permitted to come. Water was furnished to her compulsory guests by the republic, but no food.

That evening Dicky's name was called by the sentry, and he stepped before the bars of the door. There stood his little saint, a black mantilla draped about her head and shoulders, her face like glorified melancholy, her clear eyes gazing longingly at him as if they might draw him between the bars to her. She brought a chicken, some oranges, *dulces* and a loaf of white bread. A soldier inspected the food, and passed it in to Dicky. Pasa spoke calmly as she always did, briefly, in her thrilling, flute-like tones. 'Angel of my life,' she said, 'let it not be long that thou art away from me. Thou knowest that life is not a thing to be endured with thou not at my side. Tell me if I can do aught to this matter. If not, I will wait – a little while. I come again in the morning.'

Dicky, with his shoes removed so as not to disturb his fellow prisoners, tramped the floor of the jail half the night condemning his lack of money and the cause of it – whatever that might have been. He knew very well that money would have brought his release at once.

For two days succeeding Pasa came at the appointed times and brought him food. He eagerly inquired each time if a letter or package had come for him, and she mournfully shook her head.

On the morning of the third day she brought only a small loaf of bread. There were dark circles under her eyes. She seemed as calm as ever.

'By jingo,' said Dicky, who seemed to speak English or Spanish as the whim seized him, 'this is dry provender, *muchachita*. Is this the best you can dig up for a fellow?'

Pasa looked at him as a mother looks at a beloved but capricious babe.

'Think better of it,' she said, in a low voice; 'since for the next meal there will be nothing. The last *centavo* is spent.' She pressed close against the grating.

'Sell the goods in the shop – take anything for them.'

'Have I not tried? Did I not offer them for one-tenth their cost? Not even one *peso* would any one give. There is not one *real* in this town to assist Dickee Malonee.'

Dicky clenched his teeth grimly. 'That's the *comandante*,' he growled. 'He's responsible for that sentiment. Wait, oh, wait till the cards are all out.'

Pasa lowered her voice to almost a whisper. 'And, listen, heart of my heart,' she said, 'I have endeavored to be brave, but I cannot live without thee. Three days now —'

Dicky caught a faint gleam of steel from the folds of her mantilla. For once she looked in his face and saw it without a smile, stern, menacing and purposeful. Then he suddenly raised his hand and his smile came back like a gleam of sunshine. The hoarse signal of an incoming steamer's siren sounded in the harbor. Dicky called to the sentry who was pacing before the door. 'What steamer comes?'

'The *Catarina*.'

'Of the Vesuvius line?'

'Without doubt, of that line.'

'Go you, *picarilla*,' said Dicky joyously to Pasa, 'to the American consul. Tell him I wish to speak with him. See that he comes at once. And look you! let me see a different look in those eyes, for I promise your head shall rest upon this arm to-night.'

It was an hour before the consul came. He held his green umbrella under his arm, and mopped his forehead impatiently.

'Now, see here, Maloney,' he began, captiously, 'you fellows seem to think you can cut up any kind of row, and expect me to pull you out of it. I'm neither the War Department nor a gold mine. This country has its laws, you know, and there's one against pounding the senses out of the regular army. You Irish are forever getting into trouble. I don't see what I can do. Any thing like tobacco, now, to make you comfortable – or newspapers–'

'Son of Eli,' interrupted Dicky, gravely, 'you haven't changed an iota. That is almost a duplicate of the speech you made when old Koen's donkeys and geese got into the chapel loft, and the culprits wanted to hide in your room.'

'Oh, heavens!' exclaimed the consul, hurriedly adjusting his spectacles. 'Are you a Yale man, too? Were you in that crowd? I don't seem to remember any one with red – any one named Maloney. Such a lot of collegemen seem to have misused their advantages. One of the best mathematicians of the class of '91 is selling lottery tickets in Belize. A Cornell man dropped off here last month. He was second steward on a guano boat. I'll write to the department if you like, Maloney. Or if there's any tobacco, or newspa–'

'There's nothing,' interrupted Dicky, shortly, 'but this. You go tell the captain of the *Catarina* that Dicky Maloney wants to see him as soon as he can conveniently come. Tell him where I am. Hurry. That's all.'

The consul, glad to be let off so easily, hurried away. The captain of the *Catarina*, a stout man, Sicilian born, soon appeared, shoving, with little ceremony, through the guards to the jail door. The Vesuvius Fruit Company had a habit of doing things that way in Anchuria.

'I am exceedingly sorry – exceedingly sorry,' said the captain, 'to see this occur. I place myself at your service, Mr. Maloney. What you need shall be furnished. Whatever you say shall be done.'

Dicky looked at him unsmilingly. His red hair could not detract from his attitude of severe dignity as he stood, tall and calm, with his now grim mouth forming a horizontal line.

'Captain De Lucco, I believe I still have funds in the hands of your company – ample and personal funds. I ordered a remittance last week. The money has not arrived. You know what is needed in this game. Money and money and more money. Why has it not been sent?'

'By the *Cristóbal*,' replied De Lucco, gesticulating, 'it was despatched. Where is the *Cristóbal*? Off Cape Antonio I spoke her with a broken shaft. A tramp coaster was towing her back to New Orleans. I brought money ashore thinking your need for it might not withstand delay. In this envelope is one thousand dollars. There is more if you need it, Mr. Maloney.'

'For the present it will suffice,' said Dicky, softening as he crinkled the envelope and looked down at the half-inch thickness of smooth dingy bills.

'The long green!' he said, gently, with a new reverence in his gaze. 'Is there anything it will not buy, Captain?'

'I had three friends,' replied De Lucco, who was a bit of a philosopher, 'who had money. One of them speculated in stocks and made ten million; another is in heaven, and the third married a poor girl whom he loved.'

'The answer, then,' said Dicky, 'is held by the Almighty, Wall Street and Cupid. So, the question remains.'

'This,' queried the captain, including Dicky's surroundings in a significant gesture of his hand, 'is it – it is not – it is not connected with the business of your little shop? There is no failure in your plans?'

'No, no,' said Dicky. 'This is merely the result of a little private affair of mine, a digression from the regular line of business. They say for a complete life a man must know poverty, love, and war. But they don't go well together, *capitán mío*. No, there is no failure in my business. The little shop is doing very well.'

When the captain had departed Dicky called the sergeant of the jail and asked:

'Am I *preso* by the military or the civil authority?'

'Surely there is no martial law in effect now, señor.'

'*Bueno*. Now go or send to the alcalde, the *Juez de la Paz* and the *Jefe de los Policios*. Tell them I am prepared at once to satisfy the demands of justice.' A folded bill of the 'long green' slid into the sergeant's hands.

Then Dicky's smile came back again, for he knew that the hours of his captivity were numbered; and he hummed, in time with the sentry's tread:

'They're hanging men and women now,
For lacking of the green.'

So, that night Dicky sat by the window of the room over his shop and his little saint sat close by, working at something silken and dainty. Dicky was thoughtful and grave. His red hair was in an unusual state of disorder. Pasa's fingers often ached to smooth and arrange it, but Dicky would never allow it. He was poring, to-night, over a great litter of maps and books and papers on his table until that perpendicular line came between his brows that always distressed Pasa. Presently she went and brought his hat, and stood with it until he looked up, inquiringly.

'It is sad for you here,' she explained. 'Go out and drink *vino blanco*. Come back when you get that smile you used to wear. That is what I wish to see.'

Dicky laughed and threw down his paper. 'The *vino blanco* stage is past. It has served its turn. Perhaps, after all, there was less entered my mouth and more my ears than people thought. But, there will be no more maps or frowns to-night. I promise you that. Come.'

They sat upon a reed *silleta* at the window and watched the quivering gleams from the lights of the *Catarina* reflected in the harbor.

Presently Pasa rippled out one of her infrequent chirrups of audible laughter.

'I was thinking,' she began, anticipating Dicky's question, 'of the foolish things girls have in their minds. Because I went to school in the States I used to have ambitions. Nothing less than to be the president's wife would satisfy me. And, look, thou red picaroon, to what obscure fate thou hast stolen me!'

'Don't give up hope,' said Dicky, smiling. 'More than one Irishman has been the ruler of a South American country. There was a dictator of Chili named O'Higgins. Why not a President Maloney, of Anchuria? Say the word, *santita mía*, and we'll make the race.'

'No, no, no, thou red-haired, reckless one!' sighed Pasa; 'I am content' – she laid her head against his arm – 'here.'

ROUGE ET NOIR

IT HAS BEEN INDICATED THAT disaffection followed the elevation of Losada to the presidency. This feeling continued to grow. Throughout the entire republic there seemed to be a spirit of silent, sullen discontent. Even the old Liberal party to which Goodwin, Zavalla and other patriots had lent their aid was disappointed. Losada had failed to become a popular idol. Fresh taxes, fresh import duties and, more than all, his tolerance of the outrageous oppression of citizens by the military had rendered him the most obnoxious president since the despicable Alforan. The majority of his own cabinet were out of sympathy with him. The army, which he had courted by giving it license to tyrannize, had been his main, and thus far adequate support.

But the most impolitic of the administration's moves had been when it antagonized the Vesuvius Fruit Company, an organization plying twelve steamers and with cash and capital somewhat larger than Anchuria's surplus and debt combined.

Reasonably an established concern like the Vesuvius would become irritated at having a small, retail republic with no rating at all attempt to squeeze it. So when the government proxies applied for a subsidy they encountered a polite refusal. The president at once retaliated by clapping an export duty of one *real* per bunch of bananas – a thing unprecedented in fruit-growing countries. The Vesuvius Company had invested large sums in wharves and plantations along the Anchuria coast, their agents had erected fine homes in the towns where they had their headquarters, and heretofore had worked with the republic in good-will and with advantage to both. It would lose an immense sum if compelled to move out. The selling price of bananas from Vera Cruz to Trinidad was three *reals* per bunch. This new duty of one *real* would have ruined the fruit growers in Anchuria and have seriously discommoded the Vesuvius Company had it declined to pay it. But for some reason, the Vesuvius continued to buy Anchuria fruit, paying four *reals* for it; and not suffering the growers to bear the loss.

This apparent victory deceived His Excellency; and he began to hunger for more of it. He sent an emissary to request a conference with a representative of the fruit company. The Vesuvius sent Mr. Franzoni, a little, stout, cheerful man, always cool, and whistling airs from Verdi's operas. Señor Espiritión, of the office of the Minister of Finance, attempted the sandbagging in behalf of Anchuria. The meeting took place in the cabin of the *Salvador*, of the Vesuvius line.

Señor Espiritión opened negotiations by announcing that the government contemplated the building of a railroad to skirt the alluvial coast lands. After touching upon the benefits such a road would confer upon the interests of the Vesuvius, he reached the definite suggestion that a contribution to the road's expenses of, say, fifty thousand *pesos* would not be more than an equivalent to benefits received.

Mr. Franzoni denied that his company would receive any benefits from a contemplated road. As its representative he must decline to contribute fifty thousand *pesos*. But he would assume the responsibility of offering twenty-five.

Did Señor Espiritión understand Señor Franzoni to mean twenty-five thousand *pesos?*

By no means. Twenty-five *pesos*. And in silver; not in gold.

'Your offer insults my government,' cried Señor Espiritión, rising with indignation.

'Then,' said Mr. Franzoni, in warning tone, *'we will change it.'*

The offer was never changed. Could Mr. Franzoni have meant the government?

This was the state of affairs in Anchuria when the winter season opened at Coralio at the end of the second year of Losada's administration. So, when the government and society made its annual exodus to the sea-shore it was evident that the presidential advent would not be celebrated by unlimited rejoicing. The tenth of November was the day set for the entrance into Coralio of the gay company from the capital. A narrow-gauge railroad runs twenty miles into the interior from Solitas. The government party travels by carriage from San Mateo to this road's terminal point, and proceeds by train to Solitas. From here they march in grand procession to Coralio where, on the day of their coming, festivities and ceremonies abound. But this season saw an ominous dawning of the tenth of November.

Although the rainy season was over, the day seemed to hark back to reeking June. A fine drizzle of rain fell all during the forenoon. The procession entered Coralio amid a strange silence.

President Losada was an elderly man, grizzly bearded, with a considerable ratio of Indian blood revealed in his cinnamon complexion. His carriage headed the procession, surrounded and guarded by Captain Cruz and his famous troop of one hundred light horse *'El Ciento Huilando.'* Colonel Rocas followed, with a regiment of the regular army.

The president's sharp, beady eyes glanced about him for the expected demonstration of welcome; but he faced a stolid, indifferent array of citizens. Sightseers the Anchurians are by birth and habit, and they turned out to their last able-bodied unit to witness the scene; but they maintained an accusive silence. They crowded the streets to the very wheel ruts; they covered the red tile roofs to the eaves, but there was never a *'viva'* from them. No wreaths of palm and lemon branches or gorgeous strings of paper roses hung from the windows and balconies as was the custom. There was an apathy, a dull, dissenting disapprobation, that was the more ominous because it puzzled. No one feared an outburst, a revolt of the discontents, for they had no leader. The president and those loyal to him had never even heard whispered a name among them capable of crystallizing the dissatisfaction into opposition. No, there could be no danger. The people always procured a new idol before they destroyed an old one.

At length, after a prodigious galloping and curvetting of red-sashed majors, gold-laced colonels and epauletted generals, the procession formed for its annual progress down the Calle Grande to the Casa Morena, where the ceremony of welcome to the visiting president always took place.

The Swiss band led the line of march. After it pranced the local *comandante*, mounted, and a detachment of his troops. Next came a carriage with four members of the cabinet, conspicuous among them the Minister of War, old General Pilar, with his white moustache and his soldierly bearing. Then the president's vehicle, containing also the Ministers of Finance and State; and surrounded by Captain Cruz's light horse formed in a close double file of fours. Following them, the rest of the officials of state, the judges and distinguished military and social ornaments of public and private life.

As the band struck up, and the movement began, like a bird of ill-omen the *Valhalla*, the swiftest steamship of the Vesuvius line, glided into the harbor in plain view of the president and his train. Of course, there was nothing menacing about its arrival – a business firm does not go to war with a nation – but it reminded Señor Espirítión and others in those carriages that the Vesuvius Fruit Company was undoubtedly carrying something up its sleeve for them.

By the time the van of the procession had reached the government building, Captain Cronin, of the *Valhalla*, and Mr. Vincenti, member of the Vesuvius Company, had landed and were pushing their way, bluff, hearty, and nonchalant, through the crowd on the narrow sidewalk. Clad in white linen, big, debonair, with an air of good-humored authority, they made conspicuous figures among the dark mass of unimposing Anchurians, as they penetrated to within a few yards of the steps of the Casa Morena. Looking easily above the heads of the crowd, they perceived another that towered above the undersized natives. It was the fiery poll of Dicky Maloney against the wall close by the lower step and his broad, seductive grin showed that he recognized their presence.

Dicky had attired himself becomingly for the festive occasion in a well-fitting black suit. Pasa was close by his side, her head covered with the ubiquitous black mantilla.

Mr. Vincenti looked at her attentively.

'Botticelli's Madonna,' he remarked, gravely. 'I wonder when she got into the game. I don't like his getting tangled with the women. I hoped he would keep away from them.'

Captain Cronin's laugh almost drew attention from the parade.

'With that head of hair! Keep away from the women! And a Maloney! Hasn't he got a license? But, nonsense aside, what do you think of the prospects? It's a species of filibustering out of my line.'

Vincenti glanced again at Dicky's head and smiled.

'*Rouge et noir*,' he said. 'There you have it. Make your play, gentlemen. Our money is on the red.'

'The lad's game,' said Cronin, with a commending look at the tall, easy figure by the steps. 'But 'tis all like fly-by-night theatricals to me. The talk's bigger than the stage; there's a smell of gasoline in the air, and they're their own audience and scene-shifters.'

They ceased talking, for General Pilar had descended from the first carriage and had taken his stand upon the top step of Casa Morena. As the oldest member of the cabinet, custom had decreed that he should make the address of welcome, presenting the keys of the official residence to the president at its close.

General Pilar was one of the most distinguished citizens of the republic. Hero of three wars and innumerable revolutions, he was an honored guest at European courts and camps. An eloquent speaker and a friend to the people, he represented the highest type of the Anchurians.

Holding in his hand the gilt keys of Casa Morena, he began his address in a historical form, touching upon each administration and the advance of civilization and prosperity from the first striving after liberty down to present times. Arriving at the régime of President Losada, at which point, according to precedent, he should have delivered a eulogy upon its wise conduct and the happiness of the people, General Pilar paused. Then he silently held up the bunch of keys high above his head, with his eyes closely regarding it. The ribbon with which they were bound fluttered in the breeze.

'It still blows,' cried the speaker, exultantly. 'Citizens of Anchuria, give thanks to the saints this night that our air is still free.'

Thus disposing of Losada's administration, he abruptly reverted to that of Olivarra, Anchuria's most popular ruler. Olivarra had been assassinated nine years before while in the prime of life and usefulness. A faction of the Liberal party led by Losada himself had been accused of the deed. Whether guilty or not, it was eight years before the ambitious and scheming Losada had gained his goal.

Upon this theme General Pilar's eloquence was loosed. He drew the picture of the beneficent Olivarra with a loving hand. He reminded the people of the peace, the security, and the happiness they had enjoyed during that period. He recalled in vivid detail and with significant contrast the last winter sojourn of President Olivarra in Coralio, when his appearance at their fiestas was the signal for thundering *vivas* of love and approbation.

The first public expression of sentiment from the people that day followed. A low, sustained murmur went among them like the surf rolling along the shore.

'Ten dollars to a dinner at the Saint Charles,' remarked Mr. Vincenti, 'that *rouge* wins.'

'I never bet against my own interests,' said Captain Cronin, lighting a cigar. 'Long-winded old boy, for his age. What's he talking about?'

'My Spanish,' replied Vincenti, 'runs about ten words to the minute; he is something around two hundred. Whatever he's saying, he's getting them warmed up.'

'Friends and brothers,' General Pilar was saying, 'could I reach out my hand this day across the lamentable silence of the grave to Olivarra "the Good," to the ruler who was one of you, whose tears fell when you sorrowed, and whose smile followed your joy – I would bring him back to you, but – Olivarra is dead – dead at the hands of a craven assassin!'

The speaker turned and gazed boldly into the carriage of the president. His arm remained extended aloft as if to sustain his peroration. The president was listening, aghast, at this remarkable address of welcome. He was sunk back upon his seat, trembling with rage and dumb surprise, his dark hands tightly gripping the carriage cushions.

Half rising, he extended one arm toward the speaker, and shouted a harsh command at Captain Cruz. The leader of the 'Flying Hundred' sat his horse, immovable, with folded arms, giving no sign of having heard. Losada sank back again, his dark features distinctly paling.

'Who says that Olivarra is dead' suddenly cried the speaker, his voice, old as he was, sounding like a battle trumpet. 'His body lies in the grave, but to the people he loved he has bequeathed his spirit – yes, more – his learning, his courage, his kindness – yes, more – his youth, his image – people of Anchuria, have you forgotten Ramon, the son of Olivarra?'

Cronin and Vincenti, watching closely, saw Dicky Maloney suddenly raise his hat, tear off his shock of red hair, leap up the steps and stand at the side of General Pilar. The Minister of War laid his arm across the young man's shoulders. All who had known President Olivarra saw again his same lion-like pose, the same frank, undaunted expression, the same high forehead with the peculiar line of the clustering, crisp black hair.

General Pilar was an experienced orator. He seized the moment of breathless silence that preceded the storm.

'Citizens of Anchuria,' he trumpeted, holding aloft the keys to Casa Morena, 'I am here to deliver these keys – the keys to your homes and liberty – to your chosen president. Shall I deliver them to Enrico Olivarra's assassin, or to his son?'

'Olivarra! Olivarra!' the crowd shrieked and howled. All vociferated the magic name – men, women, children and the parrots.

And the enthusiasm was not confined to the blood of the plebs. Colonel Rocas ascended the steps and laid his sword theatrically at young Ramon Olivarra's feet. Four members of the cabinet embraced him. Captain Cruz gave a command, and twenty of *El Ciento Huilando* dismounted and arranged themselves in a cordon about the steps of Casa Morena.

But Ramon Olivarra seized that moment to prove himself a born genius and politician. He waved those soldiers aside, and descended the steps to the street. There, without losing his dignity or the distinguished elegance that the loss of his red hair brought him, he took the proletariat to his bosom – the barefooted, the dirty, Indians, Caribs, babies, beggars, old, young, saints, soldiers and sinners – he missed none of them.

While this act of the drama was being presented, the scene shifters had been busy at the duties that had been assigned to them. Two of Cruz's dragoons had seized the bridle reins of Losada's horses; others formed a close guard around the carriage; and they galloped off with the tyrant and his two unpopular Ministers. No doubt a place had been prepared for them. There are a number of well-barred stone apartments in Coralio.

'*Rouge* wins,' said Mr. Vincenti, calmly lighting another cigar.

Captain Cronin had been intently watching the vicinity of the stone steps for some time.

'Good boy!' he exclaimed suddenly, as if relieved. 'I wondered if he was going to forget his Kathleen Mavourneen.'

Young Olivarra had reascended the steps and spoken a few words to General Pilar. Then that distinguished veteran descended to the ground and approached Pasa, who still stood, wonder-eyed, where Dicky had left her. With his plumed hat in his hand, and his medals and decorations shining on his breast, the general spoke to her and gave her his arms, and they went up the stone steps of the Casa Morena together. And then Ramon Olivarra stepped forward and took both her hands before all the people.

And while the cheering was breaking out afresh everywhere, Captain Cronin and Mr. Vincenti turned and walked back toward the shore where the gig was waiting for them.

'There'll be another "*presidente proclamada*" in the morning,' said Mr. Vincenti, musingly. 'As a rule they are not as reliable as the elected ones, but this youngster seems to have some good stuff in him. He planned and manoeuvred the entire campaign. Olivarra's widow, you know, was wealthy. After her husband was assassinated she went to the States, and educated her son at Yale. The Vesuvius Company hunted him up, and backed him in the little game.'

'It's a glorious thing,' said Cronin, half jestingly, 'to be able to discharge a government, and insert one of your own choosing, in these days.'

'Oh, it is only a matter of business,' said Vincenti, stopping and offering the stump of his cigar to a monkey that swung down from a lime tree; 'and that is what moves the world of to-day. That extra *real* on the price of bananas had to go. We took the shortest way of removing it.'

TWO RECALLS

THERE REMAIN THREE DUTIES to be performed before the curtain falls upon the patched comedy. Two have been promised; the third is no less obligatory.

It was set forth in the programme of this tropic vaudeville that it would be made known why Shorty O'Day, of the Columbia Detective Agency, lost his position. Also that Smith should come again to tell us what mystery he followed that night on the shores of Anchuria when he strewed so many cigar stumps around the cocoanut palm during his lonely night vigil on the beach. These things were promised; but a bigger thing yet remains to be accomplished – the clearing up of a seeming wrong that has been done according to the array of chronicled facts (truthfully set forth) that have been presented. And one voice, speaking, shall do these three things.

Two men sat on a stringer of a North River pier in the City of New York. A steamer from the tropics had begun to unload bananas and oranges on the pier. Now and then a banana or two would fall from an overripe bunch, and one of the two men would shamble forward, seize the fruit and return to share it with his companion.

One of the men was in the ultimate stage of deterioration. As far as rain and wind and sun could wreck the garments he wore, it had been done. In his person the ravages of drink were as plainly visible. And yet, upon his high-bridged, rubicund nose was jauntily perched a pair of shining and flawless gold-rimmed glasses.

The other man was not so far gone upon the descending Highway of the Incompetents. Truly, the flower of his manhood had gone to seed – seed that, perhaps, no soil might sprout. But there were still cross-cuts along where he travelled through which he might yet regain the pathway of usefulness without disturbing the slumbering Miracles. This man was short and compactly built. He had an oblique, dead eye, like that of a sting-ray, and the moustache of a cocktail mixer. We know the eye and the moustache; we know that Smith of the luxurious yacht, the gorgeous raiment, the mysterious mission, the magic disappearance, has come again, though shorn of the accessories of his former state.

At his third banana, the man with the nose glasses spat it from him with a shudder.

'Deuce take all fruit!' he remarked, in a patrician tone of disgust. 'I lived for two years where these things grow. The memory of their taste lingers with you. The oranges are not so bad. Just see if you can gather a couple of them, O'Day, when the next broken crate comes up.'

'Did you live down with the monkeys?' asked the other, made tepidly garrulous by the sunshine and the alleviating meal of juicy fruit. 'I was down there, once myself. But only for a few hours. That was when I was with the Columbia Detective Agency. The monkey people did me up. I'd have my job yet if it hadn't been for them. I'll tell you about it.

'One day the chief sent a note around to the office that read; "Send O'Day here at once for a big piece of business." I was the crack detective of the agency at that time. They always handed me the big jobs. The address the chief wrote from was down in the Wall Street district.

'When I got there I found him in a private office with a lot of directors who were looking pretty fuzzy. They stated the case. The president of the Republic Insurance Company had skipped with about a tenth of a million dollars in cash. The directors wanted him back pretty bad, but they wanted the money worse. They said they needed it. They had traced the old gent's movements to where he boarded a tramp fruit steamer bound for South America that same morning with his daughter and a big gripsack – all the family he had.

'One of the directors had his steam yacht coaled and with steam up, ready for the trip; and he turned her over to me, cart blongsh. In four hours I was on board of her, and hot on the trail of the fruit tub. I had a pretty good idea where old Wahrfield – that was his name, J. Churchill Wahrfield – would head for. At that time we had a treaty with about every foreign country except Belgium and that banana republic Anchuria. There wasn't a photo of old Wahrfield to be had in New York – he had been foxy there – but I had his description. And besides, the lady with him would be a dead-give-away anywhere. She was one of the high-flyers in Society – not the kind that have their pictures in the Sunday papers – but the real sort that open chrysanthemum shows and christen battleships.

'Well, sir, we never got a sight of that fruit tub on the road. The ocean is a pretty big place; and I guess we took different paths across it. But we kept going toward this Anchuria, where the fruiter was bound for.

'We struck the monkey coast one afternoon about four. There was a ratty-looking steamer off shore taking on bananas. The monkeys were loading her up with big barges. It might be the one the old man had taken, and it might not. I went ashore to look around. The scenery was pretty good. I never saw any finer on the New York stage. I struck an American on shore, a big, cool chap, standing around with the monkeys. He showed me the consul's office. The consul was a nice young fellow. He said the fruiter was the *Karlsefin*, running generally to New Orleans, but took her last cargo to New York. Then I was sure my people were on board, although everybody told me that no passengers had landed. I didn't think they would land until after dark, for they might have been shy about it on account of seeing that yacht of mine hanging around. So, all I had to do was to wait and nab 'em when they came ashore. I couldn't arrest old Wahrfield without extradition papers, but my play was to get the cash. They generally give up if you strike 'em when they're tired and rattled and short on nerve.

'After dark I sat under a cocoanut tree on the beach for a while, and then I walked around and investigated that town some, and it was enough to give you the lions. If a man could stay in New York and be honest, he'd better do it than to hit that monkey town with a million.

'Dinky little mud houses; grass over your shoe tops in the streets; ladies in low-neck-and-short-sleeves walking around smoking cigars; tree frogs rattling like a hose cart going to a ten blow; big mountains dropping gravel in the back yards; and the sea licking the paint off in front – no, sir – a man had better be in God's country living on free lunch than there.

'The main street ran along the beach, and I walked down it, and then

turned up a kind of lane where the houses were made of poles and straw. I
wanted to see what the monkeys did when they weren't climbing cocoanut
trees. The very first shack I looked in I saw my people. They must have
come ashore while I was promenading. A man about fifty, smooth face,
heavy eyebrows, dressed in black broadcloth, looking like he was just about
to say, "Can any little boy in the Sunday School answer that?" He was
freezing on to a grip that weighed like a dozen gold bricks, and a swell girl
– a regular peach, with a Fifth Avenue cut – was sitting on a wooden chair.
An old black woman was fixing some coffee and beans on a table. The light
they had came from a lantern hung on a nail. I went and stood in the door,
and they looked at me, and I said:

' "Mr. Wahrfield, you are my prisoner. I hope, for the lady's sake, you
will take the matter sensibly. You know why I want you."

' "Who are you?" says the old gent.

' "O'Day," says I, "of the Columbia Detective Agency. And now, sir, let
me give you a piece of good advice. You go back and take your medicine like
a man. Hand 'em back the boodle; and maybe they'll let you off light. Go
back easy, and I'll put in a word for you. I'll give you five minutes to decide."
I pulled out my watch and waited.

'Then the young lady chipped in. She was one of the genuine high-
steppers. You could tell by the way her clothes fit and the style she had that
Fifth Avenue was made for her.

' "Come inside," she says. "Don't stand in the door and disturb the whole
street with that suit of clothes. Now, what is it you want?"

' "Three minutes gone," I said. "I'll tell you again while the other two
tick off."

' "You'll admit being the president of the Republic, won't you?"

' "I am," says he.

' "Well, then," says I, "it ought to be plain to you. Wanted, in New York,
J. Churchill Wahrfield, president of the Republic Insurance Company.

' "Also the funds belonging to said company, now in that grip, in the
unlawful possession of said J. Churchill Wahrfield."

' "Oh-h-h-h!" says the young lady, as if she was thinking, "you want to
take us back to New York?"

' "To take Mr. Wahrfield. There's no charge against you, miss. There'll be
no objection, of course, to your returning with your father."

'Of a sudden the girl gave a tiny scream and grabbed the old boy around
the neck. "Oh, father, father!" she says, kind of contralto, "can this be true?
Have you taken money that is not yours? Speak, father!" It made you shiver
to hear the tremolo stop she put on her voice.

'The old boy looked pretty bughouse when she first grappled him, but she
went on, whispering in his ear and patting his off shoulder till he stood still,
but sweating a little.

'She got him to one side and they talked together a minute, and then he
put on some gold eyeglasses and walked up and handed me the grip.

' "Mr. Detective," he says, talking a little broken. "I conclude to return
with you. I have finished to discover that life on this desolate and displeased
coast would be worse than to die, itself. I will go back and hurl myself upon
the mercy of the Republic Company. Have you brought a sheep?"

' "Sheep!" says I; "I haven't a single—"

' "Ship," cut in the young lady. "Don't get funny. Father is of German birth, and doesn't speak perfect English. How did you come?"

'The girl was all broke up. She had a handkerchief to her face, and kept saying every little bit, "Oh, father, father!" She walked up to me and laid her lily-white hand on the clothes that had pained her at first. I told her I came in a private yacht.

' "Mr. O'Day," she says. "Oh, take us away from this horrid country at once. Can you! Will you! Say you will."

' "I'll try," I said, concealing the fact that I was dying to get them on salt water before they could change their mind.

'One thing they both kicked against was going through the town to the boat landing. Said they dreaded publicity, and now that they were going to return, they had a hope that the thing might yet be kept out of the papers. They swore they wouldn't go unless I got them out to the yacht without any one knowing it, so I agreed to humor them.

'The sailors who rowed me ashore were playing billiards in a barroom near the water, waiting for orders, and I proposed to have them take the boat down the beach half a mile or so, and take us up there. How to get them word was the question, for I couldn't leave the grip with the prisoner, and I couldn't take it with me, not knowing but what the monkeys might stick me up.

'The young lady says the old colored woman would take them a note. I sat down and wrote it, and gave it to the dame with plain directions what to do, and she grins like a baboon and shakes her head.

'Then Mr. Wahrfield handed her a string of foreign dialect, and she nods her head and says, "See, señor," maybe fifty times, and lights out with the note. "Old Augusta only understands German," said Miss Wahrfield, smiling at me. "We stopped in her house to ask where we could find lodging, and she insisted upon our having coffee. She tells us she was raised in a German family in San Domingo."

' "Very likely," I said. "But you can search me for German words, except *nix verstay* and *noch einst*. I would have called that 'See, señor' French, though, on a gamble."

'Well, we three make a sneak around the edge of town so as not to be seen. We got tangled in vines and ferns and the banana bushes and tropical scenery a good deal. The monkey suburbs was as wild as places in Central Park. We came out on the beach a good half mile below. A brown chap was lying asleep under a cocoanut tree, with a ten-foot musket beside him. Mr. Wahrfield takes up the gun and pitches it into the sea. "The coast is guarded," he says. "Rebellion and plots ripen like fruit." He pointed to the sleeping man, who never stirred. "Thus," he says, "they perform trusts. Children!"

'I saw our boat coming, and I struck a match and lit a piece of newspaper to show them where we were. In thirty minutes we were on board the yacht.

'The first thing, Mr. Wahrfield and his daughter and I took the grip into the owner's cabin, opened it up and took an inventory. There was one hundred and five thousand dollars, United States treasury notes, in it, beside a lot of diamond jewelry and a couple of hundred Havana cigars. I gave the old man the cigars and a receipt for the rest of the lot, as agent for the company, and locked the stuff up in my private quarters.

'I never had a pleasanter trip than that one. After we got to sea the young lady turned out to be the jolliest ever. The very first time we sat down to dinner, and the steward filled her glass with champagne – that director's yacht was a regular floating Waldorf-Astoria – she winks at me and says, "What's the use to borrow trouble, Mr. Fly Cop? Here's hoping you may live to eat the hen that scratches on your grave." There was a piano on board, and she sat down to it and sung better than you give up two cases to hear plenty times. She knew about nine operas clear through. She was sure enough *bon ton* and swell. She wasn't one of the "among others present" kind; she belonged on the special mention list!

'The old man, too, perked up amazingly on the way. He passed the cigars, and says to me once, quite chipper, out of a cloud of smoke, "Mr. O'Day, somehow I think the Republic Company will not give me the much trouble. Guard well the gripvalise of the money, Mr. O'Day, for that it must be returned to them that it belongs when we finish to arrive."

'When we landed in New York I 'phoned to the chief to meet us in that director's office. We got in a cab and went there. I carried the grip, and we walked in, and I was pleased to see that the chief had got together that same old crowd of moneybugs with pink faces and white vests to see us march in. I set the grip on the table. "There's the money," I said.

' "And your prisoner?" said the chief.

'I pointed to Mr. Wahrfield, and he stepped forward and says:

' "The honor of a word with you, sir, to explain."

'He and the chief went into another room and stayed ten minutes. When they came back the chief looked as black as a ton of coal.

' "Did this gentleman," he says to me, "have this valise in his possession when you first saw him?"

' "He did," said I.

'The chief took up the grip and handed it to the prisoner with a bow, and says to the director crowd: "Do any of you recognize this gentleman?"

'They all shook their pink faces.

' "Allow me to present," he goes on, "Señor Miraflores, president of the Republic of Anchuria. The señor has generously consented to overlook this outrageous blunder, on condition that we undertake to secure him against the annoyance of public comment. It is a concession on his part to overlook an insult for which he might claim international redress. I think we can gratefully promise him secrecy in the matter.'

'They gave him a pink nod all round.

' "O'Day," he says to me. "As a private detective you're wasted. In a war where kidnapping governments is in the rules you'd be invaluable. Come down to the office at eleven."

'I knew what that meant.

' "So that's the president of the monkeys," says I. "Well, why couldn't he have said so?"

'Wouldn't it jar you?'

THE VITAGRAPHOSCOPE

VAUDEVILLE IS INTRINSICALLY episodic and discontinuous. Its audiences do not demand dénouements. Sufficient unto each 'turn' is the evil thereof. No one cares how many romances the singing comédienne may have had if she can capably sustain the limelight and a high note or two. The audiences reck not if the performing dogs get to the pound the moment they have jumped through their last hoop. They do not desire bulletins about the possible injuries received by the comic bicyclist who retires head-first from the stage in a crash of (property) china-ware. Neither do they consider that their seat coupons entitle them to be instructed whether or not there is a sentiment between the lady solo banjoist and the Irish monologist.

Therefore let us have no lifting of the curtain upon a tableau of the united lovers, backgrounded by defeated villainy and derogated by the comic, osculating maid and butler, thrown in as a sop to the Cerberi of the fifty-cent seats.

But our programme ends with a brief 'turn' or two; and then to the exits. Whoever sits the show out may find, if he will, the slender thread that binds together, though ever so slightly, the story that, perhaps, only the Walrus will understand.

Extracts from a letter from the first vice-president of the Republic Insurance Company, of New York City, to Frank Goodwin, of Coralio, Republic of Anchuria.

My Dear Mr. Goodwin: – Your communication per Messrs. Howland and Fourchet, of New Orleans, has reached us. Also their draft on N. Y. for $100,000, the amount abstracted from the funds of this company by the late J. Churchill Wahrfield, its former president. . . . The officers and directors unite in requesting me to express to you their sincere esteem and thanks for your prompt and much appreciated return of the entire missing sum within two weeks from the time of its disappearance. . . . Can assure you that the matter will not be allowed to receive the least publicity. . . . Regret exceedingly the distressing death of Mr. Wahrfield by his own hand, but. . . . Congratulations on your marriage to Miss Wahrfield . . . many charms, winning manners, noble and womanly nature and envied position in the best metropolitan society. . . .

Cordially yours,
Lucius E. Applegate
First Vice-President the Republic Insurance Company

The Vitagraphoscope (Moving Pictures)

The Last Sausage

SCENE – *An Artist's Studio*. The artist, a young man of prepossessing appearance, sits in a dejected attitude, amid a litter of sketches, with his head resting upon his hand. An oil stove stands on a pine box in the centre of the studio.

The artist rises, tightens his waist belt to another hole, and lights the stove. He goes to a tin bread box, half-hidden by a screen, takes out a solitary link of sausage, turns the box up-side-down to show that there is no more, and chucks the sausage into a frying-pan, which he sets upon the stove. The flame of the stove goes out, showing that there is no more oil. The artist, in evident despair, seizes the sausage, in a sudden access of rage, and hurls it violently from him. At the same time a door opens, and a man who enters receives the sausage forcibly against his nose. He seems to cry out; and is observed to make a dance step or two, vigorously. The newcomer is a ruddy-faced, active, keen-looking man, apparently of Irish ancestry. Next he is observed to laugh immoderately; he kicks over the stove; he claps the artist (who is vainly striving to grasp his hand) vehemently upon the back. Then he goes through a pantomime which to the sufficiently intelligent spectator reveals that he has acquired large sums of money by trading pot-metal hatches and razors to the Indians of the Cordillera Mountains for gold dust. He draws a roll of money as large as a small loaf of bread from his pocket, and waves it above his head, while at the same time he makes pantomime of drinking from a glass. The artist hurriedly secures his hat, and the two leave the studio together.

The Writing on the Sands

SCENE – *The Beach at Nice.* A woman, beautiful, still young, exquisitely clothed, complacent, poised, reclines near the water, idly scrawling letters in the sand with the staff of her silken parasol. The beauty of her face is audacious; her languid pose is one that you feel to be impermanent – you wait, expectant, for her to spring or glide or crawl, like a panther that has unaccountably become stock-still. She idly scrawls in the sand; and the word that she always writes is 'Isabel.' A man sits a few yards away. You can see that they are companions, even if no longer comrades. His face is dark and smooth, and almost inscrutable – but not quite. The two speak little together. The man also scratches on the sand with his cane. And the word that he writes is 'Anchuria.' And then he looks out where the Mediterranean and the sky intermingle with death in his gaze.

The Wilderness and Thou

SCENE – *The Borders of a Gentleman's Estate in a Tropical Land.* An old Indian, with a mahogany-colored face, is trimming the grass on a grave by a mangrove swamp. Presently he rises to his feet and walks slowly toward a grove that is shaded by the gathering, brief twilight. In the edge of the grove stands a man who is stalwart, with a kind and courteous air, and a woman of a serene and clear-cut loveliness. When the old Indian comes up to them the man drops money in his hand. The grave-tender, with the stolid pride of his race, takes it as his due, and goes his way. The two in the edge of the grove turn back along the dim pathway, and walk close, close – for, after all, what is the world at its best but a little round field of the moving pictures with two walking together in it?

CURTAIN

ROADS OF DESTINY

I go to seek on many roads
   What is to be.
True heart and strong, with love to light—
Will they not bear me in the fight
To order, shun or wield or mould
   My Destiny?

UNPUBLISHED POEMS OF DAVID MIGNOT

THE SONG WAS OVER. The words were David's; the air, one of the countryside. The company about the inn table applauded heartily, for the young poet paid for the wine. Only the notary, M. Papineau, shook his head a little at the lines, for he was a man of books, and he had not drunk with the rest.

David went out into the village street, where the night air drove the wine vapor from his head. And then he remembered that he and Yvonne had quarrelled that day, and that he had resolved to leave his home that night to seek fame and honor in the great world outside.

'When my poems are on every man's tongue,' he told himself, in a fine exhilaration, 'she will, perhaps, think of the hard words she spoke this day.'

Except the roysterers in the tavern, the village folk were abed. David crept softly into his room in the shed of his father's cottage and made a bundle of his small store of clothing. With this upon a staff, he set his face outward upon the road that ran from Vernoy.

He passed his father's herd of sheep huddled in their nightly pen – the sheep he herded daily, leaving them to scatter while he wrote verses on scraps of paper. He saw a light yet shining in Yvonne's window, and a weakness shook his purpose of a sudden. Perhaps that light meant that she rued, sleepless, her anger, and that morning might— But, no! His decision was made. Vernoy was no place for him. Not one soul there could share his thoughts. Out along that road lay his fate and his future.

Three leagues across the dim, moonlit champaign ran the road, straight as a plowman's furrow. It was believed in the village that the road ran to Paris, at least; and this name the poet whispered often to himself as he walked. Never so far from Vernoy had David travelled before.

THE LEFT BRANCH *Three leagues, then, the road ran, and turned into a puzzle. It joined with another and a larger road at right angles. David stood, uncertain, for a while, and then took the road to the left.*

Upon this more important highway were, imprinted in the dust, wheel tracks left by the recent passage of some vehicle. Some half an hour later these traces were verified by the sight of a ponderous carriage mired in a little brook at the bottom of a steep hill. The driver and postilions were shouting and tugging at the horses' bridles. On the road at one side stood a huge black-clothed man and a slender lady wrapped in a long, light cloak.

David saw the lack of skill in the efforts of the servants. He quietly assumed control of the work. He directed the outriders to cease their clamor at the horses and to exercise their strength upon the wheels. The driver alone urged the animals with his familiar voice; David himself heaved a powerful shoulder at the rear of the carriage, and with one harmonious tug the great vehicle rolled up on solid ground. The outriders climbed to their places.

David stood for a moment upon one foot. The huge gentleman waved a hand. 'You will enter the carriage,' he said, in a voice large, like himself, but smoothed by art and habit. Obedience belonged in the path of such a voice. Brief as was the young poet's hesitation, it was cut shorter still by a renewal of the command. David's foot went to the step. In the darkness he perceived dimly the form of the lady upon the rear seat. He was about to seat himself opposite, when the voice again swayed him to its will. 'You will sit at the lady's side.'

The gentleman swung his great weight to the forward seat. The carriage proceeded up the hill. The lady was shrunk, silent, into her corner. David could not estimate whether she was old or young, but a delicate, mild perfume from her clothes stirred his poet's fancy to the belief that there was loveliness beneath the mystery. Here was an adventure such as he had often imagined. But as yet he held no key to it, for no word was spoken while he sat with his impenetrable companions.

In an hour's time David perceived through the window that the vehicle traversed the street of some town. Then it stopped in front of a closed and darkened house, and a postilion alighted to hammer impatiently upon the door. A latticed window above flew wide and a night-capped head popped out.

'Who are ye that disturb honest folk at this time of night? My house is closed. 'Tis too late for profitable travellers to be abroad. Cease knocking at my door, and be off.'

'Open!' spluttered the postilion, loudly; 'open for Monseigneur the Marquis de Beaupertuys.'

'Ah!' cried the voice above. 'Ten thousand pardons, my lord. I did not know – the hour is so late – at once shall the door be opened, and the house placed at my lord's disposal.'

Inside was heard the clink of chair and bar, and the door was flung open. Shivering with chill and apprehension, the landlord of the Silver Flagon stood, half clad, candle in hand, upon the threshold.

David followed the marquis out of the carriage. 'Assist the lady,' he was ordered. The poet obeyed. He felt her small hand tremble as he guided her descent. 'Into the house,' was the next command.

The room was the long dining-hall of the tavern. A great oak table ran down its length. The huge gentleman seated himself in a chair at the nearer end. The lady sank into another against the wall, with an air of great weariness. David stood, considering how best he might now take his leave and continue upon his way.

'My lord,' said the landlord, bowing to the floor, 'h-had I ex-expected this honor, entertainment would have been ready. T-t-there is wine and cold fowl and m-m-maybe—'

'Candles,' said the marquis, spreading the fingers of one plump white hand in a gesture he had.

'Y-yes, my lord.' He fetched half a dozen candles, lighted them, and set them upon the table.

'If monsieur would, perhaps, deign to taste a certain Burgundy – there is a cask –'

'Candles,' said monsieur, spreading his fingers.

'Assuredly – quickly – I fly, my lord.'

A dozen more lighted candles shone in the hall. The great bulk of the marquis overflowed his chair. He was dressed in fine black from head to foot save for the snowy ruffles at his wrist and throat. Even the hilt and scabbard of his sword were black. His expression was one of sneering pride. The ends of an upturned moustache reached nearly to his mocking eyes.

The lady sat motionless, and now David perceived that she was young, and possessed a pathetic and appealing beauty. He was startled from the contemplation of her forlorn loveliness by the booming voice of the marquis.

'What is your name and pursuit?'

'David Mignot. I am a poet.'

The moustache of the marquis curled nearer to his eyes.

'How do you live?'

'I am also a shepherd; I guarded my father's flock,' David answered, with his head high, but a flush upon his cheek.

'Then listen, master shepherd and poet, to the fortune you have blundered upon to-night. This lady is my niece, Mademoiselle Lucie de Varennes. She is of noble descent and is possessed of ten thousand francs a year in her own right. As to her charms, you have but to observe for yourself. If the inventory pleases your shepherd's heart, she becomes your wife at a word. Do not interrupt me. To-night I conveyed her to the château of the Comte de Villemaur, to whom her hand had been promised. Guests were present; the priest was waiting; her marriage to one eligible in rank and fortune was ready to be accomplished. At the altar this demoiselle, so meek and dutiful, turned upon me like a leopardess, charged me with cruelty and crimes, and broke, before the gaping priest, the troth I had plighted for her. I swore there and then, by ten thousand devils, that she should marry the first man we met after leaving the château, be he prince, charcoal-burner, or thief. You, shepherd, are the first. Mademoiselle must be wed this night. If not you, then another. You have ten minutes in which to make your decision. Do not vex me with words or questions. Ten minutes, shepherd; and they are speeding.'

The marquis drummed loudly with his white fingers upon the table. He sank into a veiled attitude of waiting. It was as if some great house had shut its doors and windows against approach. David would have spoken, but the huge man's bearing stopped his tongue. Instead, he stood by the lady's chair and bowed.

'Mademoiselle,' he said, and he marvelled to find his words flowing easily before so much elegance and beauty. 'You have heard me say I was a shepherd. I have also had the fancy, at times, that I am a poet. If it be the test of a poet to adore and cherish the beautiful, that fancy is now strengthened. Can I serve you in any way, mademoiselle?'

The young woman looked up at him with eyes dry and mournful. His frank, glowing face, made serious by the gravity of the adventure, his strong, straight figure and the liquid sympathy in his blue eyes, perhaps, also, her imminent need of long-denied help and kindness, thawed her to sudden tears.

'Monsieur', she said, in low tones, 'you look to be true and kind. He is my uncle, the brother of my father, and my only relative. He loved my mother, and he hates me because I am like her. He has made my life one long terror. I am afraid of his very looks, and never before dared to disobey him. But to-night he would have married me to a man three times my age. You will forgive me for bringing this vexation upon you, monsieur. You will, of course, decline this mad act he tries to force upon you. But let me thank you for your generous words, at least. I have had none spoken to me in so long.'

There was now something more than generosity in the poet's eyes. Poet he must have been, for Yvonne was forgotten; this fine, new loveliness held him with its freshness and grace. The subtle perfume from her filled him with strange emotions. His tender look fell warmly upon her. She leaned to it, thirstily.

'Ten minutes,' said David, 'is given me in which to do what I would devote years to achieve. I will not say I pity you, mademoiselle; it would not be true – I love you. I cannot ask love from you yet, but let me rescue you from this cruel man, and, in time, love may come. I think I have a future, I will not always be a shepherd. For the present I will cherish you with all my heart and make your life less sad. Will you trust your fate to me, mademoiselle?'

'Ah, you would sacrifice yourself from pity!'

'From love. The time is almost up, mademoiselle.'

'You will regret it, and despise me.'

'I will live only to make you happy, and myself worthy of you.'

Her fine small hand crept into his from beneath her cloak.

'I will trust you,' she breathed, 'with my life. And – and love – may not be so far off as you think. Tell him. Once away from the power of his eyes I may forget.'

David went and stood before the marquis. The black figure stirred, and the mocking eyes glanced at the great hall clock.

'Two minutes to spare. A shepherd requires eight minutes to decide whether he will accept a bride of beauty and income! Speak up, shepherd, do you consent to become mademoiselle's husband?'

'Mademoiselle,' said David, standing proudly, 'has done me the honor to yield to my request that she become my wife.'

'Well said!' said the marquis. 'You have yet the making of a courtier in you, master shepherd. Mademoiselle could have drawn a worse prize, after all. And now to be done with the affair as quick as the Church and the devil will allow!'

He struck the table soundly with his sword hilt. The landlord came, knee-shaking, bringing more candles in the hope of anticipating the great lord's whims. 'Fetch a priest,' said the marquis, 'a priest; do you understand? In ten minutes have a priest here, or – '

The landlord dropped his candles and flew.

The priest came heavy-eyed and ruffled. He made David Mignot and Lucie de Varennes man and wife, pocketed a gold piece that the marquis tossed him, and shuffled out again into the night.

'Wine,' ordered the marquis, spreading his ominous fingers at the host.

'Fill glasses,' he said, when it was brought. He stood up at the head of the table in the candlelight, a black mountain of venom and conceit, with something like the memory of an old love turned to poison in his eye, as it fell upon his niece.

'Monsieur Mignot,' he said, raising his wine-glass, 'drink after I say this to you: You have taken to be your wife one who will make your life a foul and wretched thing. The blood in her is an inheritance running black lies and red ruin. She will bring you shame and anxiety. The devil that descended to her is there in her eyes and skin and mouth that stoop even to beguile a peasant. There is your promise, monsieur poet, for a happy life. Drink your wine. At last, mademoiselle, I am rid of you.'

The marquis drank. A little grievous cry, as if from a sudden wound, came from the girl's lips. David, with his glass in his hand, stepped forward three paces and faced the marquis. There was little of a shepherd in his bearing.

'Just now,' he said calmly, 'you did me the honor to call me "monsieur." May I hope, therefore, that my marriage to mademoiselle has placed me somewhat nearer to you in – let us say, reflected rank – has given me the right to stand more as an equal to monseigneur in a certain little piece of business I have in my mind?'

'You may hope, shepherd,' sneered the marquis.

'Then,' said David, dashing his glass of wine into the contemptuous eyes that mocked him, 'perhaps you will condescend to fight me.'

The fury of the great lord outbroke in one sudden curse like a blast from a horn. He tore his sword from its black sheath; he called to the hovering landlord: 'A sword there, for this lout!' He turned to the lady, with a laugh that chilled her heart, and said: 'You put much labor upon me, madame. It seems I must find you a husband and make you a widow in the same night.'

'I know not sword-play,' said David. He flushed to make the confession before his lady.

' "I know not sword-play," ' mimicked the marquis. 'Shall we fight like peasants with oaken cudgels? *Hola!* François, my pistols!'

A postilion brought two shining great pistols ornamented with carven silver from the carriage holsters. The marquis tossed one upon the table near David's hand. 'To the other end of the table,' he cried; 'even a shepherd may pull a trigger. Few of them attain the honor to die by the weapon of a De Beaupertuys.'

The shepherd and the marquis faced each other from the ends of the long table. The landlord, in an ague of terror, clutched the air and stammered: 'M-M-Monseigneur, for the love of Christ! not in my house! – do not spill blood – it will ruin my custom —' The look of the marquis, threatening him, paralyzed his tongue.

'Coward,' cried the lord of Beaupertuys, 'cease chattering your teeth long enough to give the word for us, if you can.'

Mine host's knees smote the floor. He was without a vocabulary. Even sounds were beyond him. Still, by gestures he seemed to beseech peace in the name of his house and custom.

'I will give the word,' said the lady, in a clear voice. She went up to David and kissed him sweetly. Her eyes were sparkling bright, and color had come to her cheek. She stood against the wall, and the two men levelled their pistols for her count.

'*Un – deux – trois!*'

The two reports came so nearly together that the candles flickered but once. The marquis stood, smiling, the fingers of his left hand resting, outspread, upon the end of the table. David remained erect, and turned his head very slowly, searching for his wife with his eyes. Then, as a garment falls from where it is hung, he sank, crumpled, upon the floor.

With a little cry of terror and despair, the widowed maid ran and stooped above him. She found his wound, and then looked up with her old look of pale melancholy. 'Through his heart,' she whispered. 'Oh, his heart!'

'Come,' boomed the great voice of the marquis, 'out with you to the carriage! Daybreak shall not find you on my hands. Wed you shall be again, and to a living husband, this night. The next we come upon, my lady, highwayman or peasant. If the road yields no other, then the churl that opens my gates. Out with you to the carriage!'

The marquis, implacable and huge, the lady wrapped again in the mystery of her cloak, the postilion bearing the weapons – all moved out to the waiting carriage. The sound of its ponderous wheels rolling away echoed through the slumbering village. In the hall of the Silver Flagon the distracted landlord wrung his hands above the slain poet's body, while the flames of the four and twenty candles danced and flickered on the table.

THE RIGHT BRANCH *Three leagues, then, the road ran, and turned into a puzzle. It joined with another and a larger road at right angles. David stood, uncertain, for a while, and then took the road to the right.*

Whither it led he knew not, but he was resolved to leave Vernoy far behind that night. He travelled a league and then passed a large château which showed testimony of recent entertainment. Lights shone from every window; from the great stone gateway ran a tracery of wheel tracks drawn in the dust by the vehicles of the guests.

Three leagues farther and David was weary. He rested and slept for a while on a bed of pine boughs at the roadside. Then up and on again along the unknown way.

Thus for five days he travelled the great road, sleeping upon Nature's balsamic beds or in peasants' ricks, eating of their black, hospitable bread, drinking from streams or the willing cup of the goat-herd.

At length he crossed a great bridge and set his foot within the smiling city that has crushed or crowned more poets than all the rest of the world. His breath came quickly as Paris sang to him in a little undertone her vital chant of greeting – the hum of voice and foot and wheel.

High up under the eaves of an old house in the Rue Conti, David paid for lodging, and set himself, in a wooden chair, to his poems. The street, once sheltering citizens of import and consequence, was now given over to those who ever follow in the wake of decline.

The houses were tall and still possessed of a ruined dignity, but many of them were empty save for dust and the spider. By night there was the clash of steel and the cries of brawlers straying restlessly from inn to inn. Where once gentility abode was now but a rancid and rude incontinence. But here David found housing commensurate to his scant purse. Daylight and candle-light found him at pen and paper.

One afternoon he was returning from a foraging trip to the lower world, with bread and curds and a bottle of thin wine. Halfway up his dark stairway he met – or rather came upon, for she rested on the stair – a young woman of a beauty that should balk even the justice of a poet's imagination. A loose, dark cloak, flung open, showed a rich gown beneath. Her eyes changed swiftly with every little shade of thought. Within one moment they would be round and artless like a child's, and long and cozening like a gypsy's. One hand raised her gown, undraping a nude shoe, high-heeled, with its ribbons dangling, untied. So heavenly she was, so unfitted to stoop, so qualified to charm and command! Perhaps she had seen David coming, and had waited for his help there.

Ah, would monsieur pardon that she occupied the stairway, but the shoe! – the naughty shoe! Alas! it would not remain tied. Ah! if monsieur *would* be so gracious!

The poet's fingers trembled as he tied the contrary ribbons. Then he would have fled from the danger of her presence, but the eyes grew long and cozening, like a gypsy's, and held him. He leaned against the balustrade, clutching his bottle of sour wine.

'You have been so good,' she said, smiling. 'Does monsieur, perhaps, live in the house?'

'Yes, madame. I – I think so, madame.'

'Perhaps in the third story, then?'

'No, madame; higher up.'

The lady fluttered her fingers with the least possible gesture of impatience.

'Pardon. Certainly I am not discreet in asking. Monsieur will forgive me? It is surely not becoming that I should inquire where he lodges.'

'Madame, do not say so. I live in the—'

'No, no, no; do not tell me. Now I see that I erred. But I cannot lose the interest I feel in this house and all that is in it. Once it was my home. Often I come here but to dream of those happy days again. Will you let that be my excuse?'

'Let me tell you, then, for you need no excuse,' stammered the poet. 'I live in the top floor – the small room where the stairs turn.'

'In the front room?' asked the lady, turning her head sidewise.

'The rear, madame.'

The lady sighed, as if with relief.

'I will detain you no longer, then, monsieur,' she said, employing the round and artless eye. 'Take good care of my house. Alas! only the memories of it are mine now. Adieu, and accept my thanks for your courtesy.'

She was gone, leaving but a smile and a trace of sweet perfume. David climbed the stairs as one in slumber. But he awoke from it, and the smile and the perfume lingered with him and never afterward did either seem quite to leave him. This lady of whom he knew nothing drove him to lyrics of eyes, chansons of swiftly conceived love, odes to curling hair, and sonnets to slippers on slender feet.

Poet he must have been, for Yvonne was forgotten; this fine, new loveliness held him with its freshness and grace. The subtle perfume about her filled him with strange emotions.

On a certain night three persons were gathered about a table in a room on the third floor of the same house. Three chairs and the table and a lighted candle upon it was all the furniture. One of the persons was a huge man, dressed in black. His expression was one of sneering pride. The ends of his upturned moustache reached nearly to his mocking eyes. Another was a lady, young and beautiful, with eyes that could be round and artless, like a child's, or long and cozening, like a gypsy's, but were now keen and ambitious, like any other conspirator's. The third was a man of action, a combatant, a bold and impatient executive, breathing fire and steel. He was addressed by the others as Captain Desrolles.

This man struck the table with his fist, and said, with controlled violence:
'To-night. To-night as he goes to midnight mass. I am tired of the plotting that gets nowhere. I am sick of signals and ciphers and secret meetings and such *baragouin*. Let us be honest traitors. If France is to be rid of him, let us kill in the open, and not hunt with snares and traps. To-night, I say. I back my words. My hand will do the deed. To-night, as he goes to mass.'

The lady turned upon him a cordial look. Woman, however wedded to plots, must ever thus bow to rash courage. The big man stroked his upturned moustache.

'Dear captain,' he said, in a great voice, softened by habit, 'this time I agree with you. Nothing is to be gained by waiting. Enough of the palace guards belong to us to make the endeavor a safe one.'

'To-night,' repeated Captain Desrolles, again striking the table. 'You have heard me, marquis; my hand will do the deed.'

'But now,' said the huge man, softly, 'comes a question. Word must be sent to our partisans in the palace, and a signal agreed upon. Our stanchest men must accompany the royal carriage. At this hour what messenger can penetrate so far as the south doorway? Ribout is stationed there; once a message is placed in his hands, all will go well.'

'I will send the message,' said the lady.

'You, countess?' said the marquis, raising his eyebrows. 'Your devotion is great, we know, but—'

'Listen!' exclaimed the lady, rising and resting her hands upon the table; 'in a garret of this house lives a youth from the provinces as guileless and tender as the lambs he tended there. I have met him twice or thrice upon the stairs. I questioned him, fearing that he might dwell too near the room in which we are accustomed to meet. He is mine, if I will. He writes poems in his garret, and I think he dreams of me. He will do what I say. He shall take the message to the palace.'

The marquis rose from his chair and bowed. 'You did not permit me to finish my sentence, countess,' he said. 'I would have said: "Your devotion is great, but your wit and charm are infinitely greater." '

While the conspirators were thus engaged, David was polishing some lines addressed to his *amorette d'escalier*. He heard a timorous knock at his door, and opened it, with a great throb, to behold her there, panting as one in straits, with eyes wide open and artless, like a child's.

'Monsieur,' she breathed, 'I come to you in distress. I believe you to be good and true, and I know of no other help. How I flew through the streets among the swaggering men! Monsieur, my mother is dying. My uncle is a captain of guards in the palace of the king. Some one must fly to bring him. May I hope—'

'Mademoiselle,' interrupted David, his eyes shining with the desire to do her service, 'your hopes shall be my wings. Tell me how I may reach him.'

The lady thrust a sealed paper into his hand.

'Go to the south gate – the south gate, mind – and say to the guards there, "The falcon has left his nest." They will pass you, and you will go to the south entrance to the palace. Repeat the words, and give this letter to the man who will reply "Let him strike when he will." This is the password, monsieur, entrusted to me by my uncle, for now when the country is disturbed and men plot against the king's life, no one without it can gain entrance to the palace grounds after nightfall. If you will, monsieur, take him this letter so that my mother may see him before she closes her eyes.'

'Give it me,' said David, eagerly. 'But shall I let you return home through the streets alone so late? I—'

'No, no – fly. Each moment is like a precious jewel. Some time,' said the lady, with eyes long and cozening, like a gypsy's, 'I will try to thank you for your goodness.'

The poet thrust the letter into his breast, and bounded down the stairway. The lady, when he was gone, returned to the room below.

The eloquent eyebrows of the marquis interrogated her.

'He is gone,' she said, 'as fleet and stupid as one of his own sheep, to deliver it.'

The table shook again from the batter of Captain Desrolles's fist.

'Sacred name!' he cried; 'I have left my pistols behind! I can trust no others.'

'Take this,' said the marquis, drawing from beneath his cloak a shining, great weapon, ornamented with carven silver. 'There are none truer. But guard it closely, for it bears my arms and crest, and already I am suspected. Me, I must put many leagues between myself and Paris this night. To-morrow must find me in my château. After you, dear countess.'

The marquis puffed out the candle. The lady, well cloaked, and the two gentlemen softly descended the stairway and flowed into the crowd that roamed along the narrow pavements of the Rue Conti.

David sped. At the south gate of the king's residence a halberd was laid to his breast, but he turned its point with the words: 'The falcon has left his nest.'

'Pass, brother,' said the guard, 'and go quickly.'

On the south steps of the palace they moved to seize him, but again the *mot de passe* charmed the watchers. One among them stepped forward and began: 'Let him strike—' But a flurry among the guards told of a surprise. A man of keen look and soldierly stride suddenly pressed through them and seized the letter which David held in his hand. 'Come with me,' he said, and led him inside the great hall. Then he tore open the letter and read it. He beckoned to a man uniformed as an officer of musketeers, who was passing. 'Captain Tetreau, you will have the guards at the south entrance and the south gate arrested and confined. Place men known to be loyal in their places.' To David he said: 'Come with me.'

He conducted him through a corridor and an anteroom into a spacious chamber, where a melancholy man, sombrely dressed, sat brooding in a great leather-covered chair. To that man he said:

'Sire, I have told you that the palace is as full of traitors and spies as a sewer is of rats. You have thought, sire, that it was my fancy. This man penetrated to your very door by their connivance. He bore a letter which I have intercepted. I have brought him here that your majesty may no longer think my zeal excessive.'

'I will question him,' said the king, stirring in his chair. He looked at David with heavy eyes dulled by an opaque film. The poet bent his knee.

'From where do you come?' asked the king.

'From the village of Vernoy, in the province of Eure-et-Loir, sire.'

'What do you follow in Paris?'

'I – I would be a poet, sire.'

'What did you in Vernoy?'

'I minded my father's flock of sheep.'

The king stirred again, and the film lifted from his eyes.

'Ah! in the fields?'

'Yes, sire.'

'You lived in the fields; you went out in the cool of the morning and lay among the hedges in the grass. The flock distributed itself upon the hillside; you drank of the living stream; you ate your sweet brown bread in the shade; and you listened, doubtless, to blackbirds piping in the grove. Is not that so, shepherd?'

'It is, sire,' answered David, with a sigh; 'and to the bees at the flowers, and, maybe, to the grape gatherers singing on the hill.'

'Yes, yes,' said the king, impatiently; 'maybe to them; but surely to the blackbirds. They whistled often, in the grove, did they not?'

'Nowhere, sire, so sweetly as in Eure-et-Loir. I have endeavored to express their song in some verses that I have written.'

'Can you repeat those verses?' asked the king eagerly. 'A long time ago I listened to the blackbirds. It would be something better than a kingdom if one could rightly construe their song. And at night you drove the sheep to the fold and then sat, in peace and tranquillity, to your pleasant bread. Can you repeat those verses, shepherd?'

'They run this way, sire,' said David, with respectful ardor:

> 'Lazy shepherd, see you lambkins
>   Skip, ecstatic, on the mead;
> See the firs dance in the breezes,
>   Hear Pan blowing at his reed.
>
> 'Hear us calling from the tree-tops,
>   See us swoop upon your flock;
> Yield us wool to make our nests warm
>   In the branches of the—'

'If you please your majesty,' interrupted a harsh voice, 'I will ask a question or two of this rhymester. There is little time to spare. I crave pardon, sire, if my anxiety for your safety offends.'

'The loyalty,' said the king, 'of the Duke d'Aumale is too well proven to give offence.' He sank into his chair, and the film came again over his eyes.

'First,' said the duke, 'I will read you the letter he brought:

'To-night is the anniversary of the dauphin's death. If he goes, as is his custom, to midnight mass to pray for the soul of his son, the falcon will strike, at the corner of the Rue Esplanade. If this be his intention, set a red light in the upper room at the southwest corner of the palace, that the falcon may take heed.'

'Peasant,' said the duke, sternly, 'you have heard these words. Who gave you this message to bring?'

'My lord duke,' said David, sincerely, 'I will tell you. A lady gave it me. She said her mother was ill, and that this writing would fetch her uncle to her bedside. I do not know the meaning of the letter, but I will swear that she is beautiful and good.'

'Describe the woman,' commanded the duke, 'and how you came to be her dupe.'

'Describe her!' said David with a tender smile. 'You would command words to perform miracles. Well, she is made of sunshine and deep shade. She is slender, like the alders, and moves with their grace. Her eyes change while you gaze into them; now round, and then half shut as the sun peeps between two clouds. When she comes, heaven is all about her; when she leaves, there is chaos and a scent of hawthorn blossoms. She came to me in the Rue Conti, number twenty-nine.'

'It is the house,' said the duke, turning to the king, 'that we have been watching. Thanks to the poet's tongue, we have a picture of the infamous Countess Quebedaux.'

'Sire and my lord duke,' said David, earnestly, 'I hope my poor words have done no injustice. I have looked into that lady's eyes. I will stake my life that she is an angel, letter or no letter.'

The duke looked at him steadily. 'I will put you to the proof,' he said, slowly. 'Dressed as the king, you shall, yourself, attend mass in his carriage at midnight. Do you accept the test?'

David smiled. 'I have looked into her eyes,' he said. 'I had my proof there. Take yours how you will.'

Half an hour before twelve the Duke d'Aumale, with his own hands, set a red lamp in a southwest window of the palace. At ten minutes to the hour, David, leaning on his arm, dressed as the king, from top to toe, with his head bowed in his cloak, walked slowly from the royal apartments to the waiting carriage. The duke assisted him inside and closed the door. The carriage whirled away along its route to the cathedral.

On the *qui vive* in a house at the corner of the Rue Esplanade was Captain Tetreau with twenty men, ready to pounce upon the conspirators when they should appear.

But it seemed that, for some reason, the plotters had slightly altered their plans. When the royal carriage had reached the Rue Christopher, one square nearer than the Rue Esplanade, forth from it burst Captain Desrolles, with his band of would-be regicides, and assailed the equipage. The guards upon the carriage, though surprised at the premature attack, descended and fought valiantly. The noise of conflict attracted the force of Captain Tetreau, and they came pelting down the street to the rescue. But, in the meantime, the desperate Desrolles had torn open the door of the king's carriage, thrust his weapon against the body of the dark figure inside, and fired.

Now, with loyal reinforcements at hand, the street rang with cries and the rasp of steel, but the frightened horses had dashed away. Upon the cushions lay the dead body of the poor mock king and poet, slain by a ball from the pistol of Monseigneur, the Marquis de Beaupertuys.

THE MAIN ROAD *Three leagues, then, the road ran, and turned into a puzzle. It joined with another and a larger road at right angles. David stood, uncertain, for a while, and then sat himself to rest upon its side.*

Whither those roads led he knew not. Either way there seemed to lie a great world full of chance and peril. And then, sitting there, his eye fell upon a bright star, one that he and Yvonne had named for theirs. That set him thinking of Yvonne, and he wondered if he had not been too hasty. Why should he leave her and his home because a few hot words had come between them? Was love so brittle a thing that jealousy, the very proof of it, could break it? Mornings always brought a cure for the little heartaches of evening. There was yet time for him to return home without any one in the sweetly sleeping village of Vernoy being the wiser. His heart was Yvonne's; there where he had lived always he could write his poems and find his happiness.

David rose, and shook off his unrest and the wild mood that had tempted him. He set his face steadfastly back along the road he had come. By the time he had retravelled the road to Vernoy, his desire to rove was gone. He passed the sheepfold, and the sheep scurried, with a drumming flutter, at his late footsteps, warming his heart by the homely sound. He crept without noise into his little room and lay there, thankful that his feet had escaped the distress of new roads that night.

How well he knew woman's heart! The next evening Yvonne was at the well in the road where the young congregated in order that the *curé* might have business. The corner of her eye was engaged in a search for David, albeit her set mouth seemed unrelenting. He saw the look; braved the mouth, drew from it a recantation and, later, a kiss as they walked homeward together.

Three months afterward they were married. David's father was shrewd and prosperous. He gave them a wedding that was heard of three leagues away. Both the young people were favorites in the village. There was a procession in the streets, a dance on the green; they had the marionettes and a tumbler out from Dreux to delight the guests.

Then a year, and David's father died. The sheep and the cottage descended to him. He already had the seemliest wife in the village. Yvonne's milk pails and her brass kettles were bright – *ouf!* they blinded you in the sun when you passed that way. But you must keep your eyes upon her yard, for flower beds were so neat and gay they restored to you your sight. And you might hear her sing, aye, as far as the double chestnut tree above Père Gruneau's blacksmith forge.

But a day came when David drew out paper from a long-shut drawer, and began to bite the end of a pencil. Spring had come again and touched his heart. Poet he must have been, for now Yvonne was well-nigh forgotten. This fine new loveliness of earth held him with its witchery and grace. The perfume from her woods and meadows stirred him strangely. Daily had he gone forth with his flock, and brought it safe at night. But now he stretched himself under the hedge and pieced words together on his bits of paper. The sheep strayed, and the wolves, perceiving that difficult poems make easy mutton, ventured from the woods and stole his lambs.

David's stock of poems grew larger and his flock smaller. Yvonne's nose and temper waxed sharp and her talk blunt. Her pans and kettles grew dull, but her eyes had caught their flash. She pointed out to the poet that his neglect was reducing the flock and bringing woe upon the household. David hired a boy to guard the sheep, locked himself in the little room in the top of the cottage, and wrote more poems. The boy, being a poet by nature, but not furnished with an outlet in the way of writing, spent his time in slumber. The wolves lost no time in discovering that poetry and sleep are practically the same; so the flock steadily grew smaller. Yvonne's ill temper increased at an equal rate. Sometimes she would stand in the yard and rail at David through his high window. Then you could hear her as far as the double chestnut tree above Père Gruneau's blacksmith forge.

M. Papineau, the kind, wise, meddling old notary, saw this, as he saw everything at which his nose pointed. He went to David, fortified himself with a great pinch of snuff, and said:

'Friend Mignot, I affixed the seal upon the marriage certificate of your father. It would distress me to be obliged to attest a paper signifying the bankruptcy of his son. But that is what you are coming to. I speak as an old friend. Now, listen to what I have to say. You have your heart set, I perceive, upon poetry. At Dreux, I have a friend, one Monsieur Bril — Georges Bril. He lives in a little cleared space in a houseful of books. He is a learned man; he visits Paris each year; he himself has written books. He will tell you when the catacombs were made, how they found out the names of the stars, and why the plover has a long bill. The meaning and the form of poetry is to him as intelligent as the baa of a sheep is to you. I will give you a letter to him, and you shall take him your poems and let him read them. Then you will know if you shall write more, or give your attention to your wife and business.'

'Write the letter,' said David. 'I am sorry you did not speak of this sooner.'

At sunrise the next morning he was on the road to Dreux with the precious roll of poems under his arm. At noon he wiped the dust from his feet at the door of Monsieur Bril. That learned man broke the seal of M. Papineau's letter, and sucked up its contents through his gleaming spectacles as the sun draws water. He took David inside to his study and sat him down upon a little island beat upon by a sea of books.

Monsieur Bril had a conscience. He flinched not even at a mass of manuscript the thickness of a finger length and rolled to an incorrigible curve. He broke the back of the roll against his knee and began to read. He slighted nothing; he bored into the lump as a worm into a nut, seeking for a kernel.

Meanwhile, David sat, marooned, trembling in the spray of so much literature. It roared in his ears. He held no chart or compass for voyaging in that sea. Half the world, he thought, must be writing books.

Monsieur Bril bored to the last page of the poems. Then he took off his spectacles and wiped them with his handkerchief.

'My old friend, Papineau, is well?' he asked.

'In the best of health,' said David.

'How many sheep have you, Monsieur Mignot?'

'Three hundred and nine, when I counted them yesterday. The flock has had ill fortune. To that number it has decreased from eight hundred and fifty.'

'You have a wife and a home, and lived in comfort. The sheep brought you plenty. You went into the fields with them and lived in the keen air and ate the sweet bread of contentment. You had but to be vigilant and recline there upon nature's breast, listening to the whistle of the blackbirds in the grove. Am I right thus far?'

'It was so,' said David.

'I have read all your verses,' continued Monsieur Bril, his eyes wandering about his sea of books as if he conned the horizon for a sail. 'Look yonder, through that window, Monsieur Mignot; tell me what you see in that tree.'

'I see a crow,' said David, looking.

'There is a bird,' said Monsieur Bril, 'that shall assist me where I am disposed to shirk a duty. You know that bird, Monsieur Mignot; he is the philosopher of the air. He is happy through submission to his lot. None so merry or full-crawed as he with his whimsical eye and rollicking step. The fields yield him what he desires. He never grieves that his plumage is not gay, like the oriole's. And you have heard, Monsieur Mignot, the notes that nature has given him? Is the nightingale any happier, do you think?'

David rose to his feet. The crow cawed harshly from his tree.

'I thank you, Monsieur Bril,' he said, slowly. 'There was not, then, one nightingale note among all those croaks.?'

'I could not have missed it,' said Monsieur Bril, with a sigh. 'I read every word. Live your poetry, man; do not try to write it any more.'

'I thank you,' said David, again. 'And now I will be going back to my sheep.'

'If you would dine with me,' said the man of books, 'and overlook the smart of it, I will give you reasons at length.'

'No,' said the poet, 'I must be back in the fields cawing at my sheep.'

Back along the road to Vernoy he trudged with his poems under his arm. When he reached his village he turned into the shop of one Zeigler, a Jew out of Armenia, who sold anything that came to his hand.

'Friend,' said David, 'wolves from the forest harass my sheep on the hills. I must purchase firearms to protect them. What have you?'

'A bad day, this, for me, friend Mignot,' said Zeigler, spreading his hands, 'for I perceive that I must sell you a weapon that will not fetch a tenth of its value. Only last week I bought from a peddler a wagon full of goods that he procured at a sale by a *commissionaire* of the crown. The sale was of the château and belongings of a great lord – I know not his title – who has been banished for conspiracy against the king. There are some choice firearms in the lot. This pistol – oh, a weapon fit for a prince! – it shall be only forty francs to you, friend Mignot – if I lose ten by the sale. But perhaps an arquebuse —'

'This will do,' said David, throwing the money on the counter. 'Is it charged?'

'I will charge it,' said Zeigler. 'And, for ten francs more, add a store of powder and ball.'

David laid his pistol under his coat and walked to his cottage. Yvonne was not there. Of late she had taken to gadding much among the neighbors. But a fire was glowing in the kitchen stove. David opened the door of it and thrust his poems in upon the coals. As they blazed up they made a singing, harsh sound in the flue.

'The song of the crow!' said the poet.

He went up to his attic room and closed the door. So quiet was the village that a score of people heard the roar of the great pistol. They flocked thither, and up the stairs where the smoke, issuing, drew their notice.

The man laid the body of the poet upon his bed, awkwardly arranging it to conceal the torn plumage of the poor black crow. The women chattered in a luxury of zealous pity. Some of them ran to tell Yvonne.

M. Papineau, whose nose had brought him there among the first, picked up the weapon and ran his eye over its silver mountings with a mingled air of connoisseurship and grief.

'The arms,' he explained, aside, to the *curé*, 'and crest of Monseigneur, the Marquis de Beaupertuys.'

THE GUARDIAN OF THE ACCOLADE

NOT THE LEAST IMPORTANT of the force of the Weymouth Bank was Uncle Bushrod. Sixty years had Uncle Bushrod given of faithful service to the house of Weymouth as chattel, servitor, and friend. Of the color of the mahogany bank furniture was Uncle Bushrod – thus dark was he externally; white as the uninked pages of the bank ledgers was his soul. Eminently pleasing to Uncle Bushrod would the comparison have been; for to him the only institution in existence worth considering was the Weymouth Bank, of which he was something between porter and generalissimo-in-charge.

Weymouth lay, dreamy and umbrageous, among the low foothills along the brow of a Southern valley. Three banks there were in Weymouthville. Two were hopeless, misguided enterprises, lacking the presence and prestige of a Weymouth to give them glory. The third was The Bank, managed by the Weymouths – and Uncle Bushrod. In the old Weymouth homestead – the red brick, white-porticoed mansion, the first to your right as you crossed Elder Creek, coming into town – lived Mr. Robert Weymouth (the president of the bank), his widowed daughter, Mrs. Vesey – called 'Miss Letty' by every one – and her two children, Nan and Guy. There, also in a cottage on the grounds, resided Uncle Bushrod and Aunt Malindy, his wife. Mr. William Weymouth (the cashier of the bank) lived in a modern, fine house on the principal avenue.

Mr. Robert was a large, stout man, sixty-two years of age, with a smooth, plump face, long iron-gray hair and fiery blue eyes. He was high-tempered, kind, and generous, with a youthful smile and a formidable, stern voice that did not always mean what it sounded like. Mr. William was a milder man, correct in deportment and absorbed in business. The Weymouths formed The Family of Weymouthville, and were looked up to, as was their right of heritage.

Uncle Bushrod was the bank's trusted porter, messenger, vassal, and guardian. He carried a key to the vault, just as Mr. Robert and Mr. William did. Sometimes there was ten, fifteen, or twenty thousand dollars in sacked silver stacked on the vault floor. It was safe with Uncle Bushrod. He was a Weymouth in heart, honesty, and pride.

Of late Uncle Bushrod had not been without worry. It was on account of Marse Robert. For nearly a year Mr. Robert had been known to indulge in too much drink. Not enough, understand, to become tipsy, but the habit was getting a hold upon him, and every one was beginning to notice it. Half a dozen times a day he would leave the bank and step around to the Merchants' and Planters' Hotel to take a drink. Mr. Robert's usual keen judgment and business capacity became a little impaired. Mr. William, a Weymouth, but not so rich in experience, tried to dam the inevitable backflow of the tide, but with incomplete success. The deposits in the Weymouth Bank dropped from six figures to five. Past-due paper began to accumulate, owing to injudicious loans. No one cared to address Mr. Robert on the subject of temperance. Many of his friends said that the cause of it had been the death of his wife some two years before. Others hesitated on account of Mr. Robert's quick temper, which was extremely apt to resent personal interference of such a nature. Miss Letty and the children noticed the change and grieved about it. Uncle Bushrod also worried, but he was one of those who would not have dared to remonstrate, although he and Marse Robert had been raised almost as companions. But there was a heavier shock coming to Uncle Bushrod than that caused by the bank president's toddies and juleps.

Mr. Robert had a passion for fishing, which he usually indulged whenever the season and business permitted. One day, when reports had been coming in relating to the bass and perch, he announced his intention of making a two- or three-days' visit to the lakes. He was going down, he said, to Reedy Lake with Judge Archinard, an old friend.

Now, Uncle Bushrod was treasurer of the Sons and Daughters of the Burning Bush. Every association he belonged to made him treasurer without hesitation. He stood AA1 in colored circles. He was understood among them to be Mr. Bushrod Weymouth, of the Weymouth Bank.

The night following the day on which Mr. Robert mentioned his intended fishing-trip the old man woke up and rose from his bed at twelve o'clock, declaring he must go down to the bank and fetch the pass-book of the Sons and Daughters, which he had forgotten to bring home. The bookkeeper had balanced it for him that day, put the cancelled checks in it, and snapped two elastic bands around it. He put but one band around other pass-books.

Aunt Malindy objected to the mission at so late an hour, denouncing it as foolish and unnecessary, but Uncle Bushrod was not to be deflected from duty.

'I done told Sister Adaline Hoskins,' he said, 'to come by here for dat book to-morrow mawnin' at sebin o'clock, for to kar' it to de meetin' of de bo'd of 'rangements, and dat book gwine to be here when she come.'

So, Uncle Bushrod put on his old brown suit, got his thick hickory stick, and meandered through the almost deserted streets of Weymouthville. He entered the bank, unlocking the side door, and found the pass-book where he had left it in the little back room used for private consultations, where he always hung his coat. Looking about casually, he saw that everything was as he had left it, and was about to start for home when he was brought to a standstill by the sudden rattle of a key in the front door. Some one came quickly in, closed the door softly, and entered the counting-room through the door in the iron railing.

That division of the bank's space was connected with the back room by a narrow passage-way, now in deep darkness.

Uncle Bushrod, firmly gripping his hickory stick, tiptoed gently up this passage until he could see the midnight intruder into the sacred precincts of the Weymouth Bank. One dim gas-jet burned there, but even in its nebulous light he perceived at once that the prowler was the banks' president.

Wondering, fearful, undecided what to do, the old colored man stood motionless in the gloomy strip of hallway, and waited developments.

The vault, with its big iron door, was opposite him. Inside that was the safe, holding the papers of value, the gold and currency of the bank. On the floor of the vault was, perhaps, eighteen thousand dollars in silver.

The president took his key from his pocket, opened the vault and went inside, nearly closing the door behind him. Uncle Bushrod saw, through the narrow aperture, the flicker of a candle. In a minute or two – it seemed an hour to the watcher – Mr. Robert came out, bringing with him a large hand-satchel, handling it in a careful but hurried manner, as if fearful that he might be observed. With one hand he closed and locked the vault door.

With a reluctant theory forming itself beneath his wool, Uncle Bushrod waited and watched, shaking in his concealing shadow.

Mr. Robert set the satchel softly upon a desk, and turned his coat collar up about his neck and ears. He was dressed in a rough suit of gray, as if for travelling. He glanced with frowning intentness at the big office clock above the burning gas-jet, and then looked lingeringly about the bank – lingeringly and fondly, Uncle Bushrod thought, as one who bids farewell to dear and familiar scenes.

Now he caught up his burden again and moved promptly and softly out of the bank by the way he had come locking the front door behind him.

For a minute or longer Uncle Bushrod was as stone in his tracks. Had that midnight rifler of safes and vaults been any other on earth than the man he was, the old retainer would have rushed upon him and struck to save the Weymouth property. But now the watcher's soul was tortured by the poignant dread of something worse than mere robbery. He was seized by an accusing terror that said the Weymouth name and the Weymouth honor was about to be lost. Marse Robert robbing the bank! What else could it mean? The hour of the night, the stealthy visit to the vault, the satchel brought forth full and with expedition and silence, the prowler's rough dress, his solicitous reading of the clock, and noiseless departure – what else could it mean?

And then to the turmoil of Uncle Bushrod's thoughts came the corroborating recollection of preceding events – Mr. Robert's increasing intemperance and consequent many moods of royal high spirits and stern tempers; the casual talk he had heard in the bank of the decrease in business and difficulty in collecting loans. What else could it all mean but that Mr. Robert Weymouth was an absconder – was about to fly with the bank's remaining funds, leaving Mr. William, Miss Letty, little Nan, Guy, and Uncle Bushrod to bear the disgrace?

During one minute Uncle Bushrod considered these things, and then he awoke to sudden determination and action.

'Lawd! Lawd!' he moaned aloud, as he hobbled hastily toward the side door. 'Sech a come-off after all dese here years of big doin's and fine doin's. Scan'lous sights upon de yearth when de Weymouth fambly done turn out robbers and 'bezzlers! Time for Uncle Bushrod to clean out somebody's chicken-coop and eben matters up. Oh, Lawd! Marse Robert, you ain't gwine do dat. 'N Miss Letty an' dem chillum so proud and talkin' "Weymouth, Weymouth," all de time! I'm gwine to stop you ef I can. 'Spec you shoot Mr. Nigger's head off ef he fool wid you, but I'm gwine stop you ef I can.'

Uncle Bushrod, aided by his hickory stick, impeded by his rheumatism, hurried down the street toward the railroad station, where the two lines touching Weymouthville met. As he had expected and feared, he saw there Mr. Robert, standing in the shadow of the building, waiting for the train. He held the satchel in his hand.

When Uncle Bushrod came within twenty yards of the bank president, standing like a huge, gray ghost by the station wall, sudden perturbation seized him. The rashness and audacity of the thing he had come to do struck him fully. He would have been happy could he have turned and fled from the possibilities of the famous Weymouth wrath. But again he saw, in his fancy, the white reproachful face of Miss Letty, and the distressed looks of Nan and Guy, should he fail in his duty and they questioned him as to his stewardship.

Braced by the thought, he approached in a straight line, clearing his throat and pounding with his stick so that he might be early recognized. Thus he might avoid the likely danger of too suddenly surprising the sometimes hasty Robert.

'Is that you, Bushrod?' called the clamant, clear voice of the gray ghost.

'Yes, suh, Marse Robert.'

'What the devil are you doing out at this time of night?'

For the first time in his life, Uncle Bushrod told Marse Robert a falsehood. He could not repress it. He would have to circumlocute a little. His nerve was not equal to a direct attack.

'I done been down, suh, to see ol' Aunt M'ria Patterson. She taken sick in de night, and I kyar'ed her a bottle of M'lindy's medercine. Yes, suh.'

'Humph!' said Robert. 'You better get home out of the night air. It's damp. You'll hardly be worth killing to-morrow on account of your rheumatism. Think it'll be a clear day, Bushrod?'

'I 'low it will, suh. De sun sot red las' night.'

Mr. Robert lit a cigar in the shadow, and the smoke looked like his gray ghost expanding and escaping into the night air. Somehow, Uncle Bushrod could barely force his reluctant tongue to the dreadful subject. He stood, awkward, shambling, with his feet upon the gravel and fumbling with his stick. But then, afar off – three miles away, at the Jimtown switch – he heard the faint whistle of the coming train, the one that was to transport the Weymouth name into the regions of dishonor and shame. All fear left him. He took off his hat and faced the chief of the clan he served, the great, royal, kind, lofty, terrible Weymouth, – he bearded him there at the brink of the awful thing that was about to happen.

'Marse Robert,' he began, his voice quavering a little with the stress of his feelings, 'you 'member de day dey-all rode de tunnament at Oak Lawn? De day, suh, dat you win in de ridin', and you crown Miss Lucy de queen?'

'Tournament?' said Mr. Robert, taking his cigar from his mouth, 'Yes, I remember very well the – but what the deuce are you talking about tournaments here at midnight for? Go 'long home, Bushrod. I believe you're sleepwalking.'

'Miss Lucy tetch you on de shoulder,' continued the old man, never heeding, 'wid a s'ord, and say: "I mek you a knight, Suh Robert – rise up, pure and fearless and widout reproach." Dat what Miss Lucy say. Dat's been a long time ago, but me nor you ain't forgot it. And den dar's another time we ain't forgot – de time when Miss Lucy lay on her las' bed. She sent for Uncle Bushrod, and she say: "Uncle Bushrod, when I die, I want you to take good care of Mr. Robert. Seem like" – so Miss Lucy say – "he listen to you mo' dan to anybody else. He apt to be mighty fractious sometimes, and maybe he cuss you when you try to 'suade him but he need somebody what understand him to be 'round wid him. He am like a little child sometimes" – so Miss Lucy say, wid her eyes shinin' in her po', thin face – "but he always been" – dem was her words – "my knight, pure and fearless and widout reproach." '

Mr. Robert began to mask, as was his habit, a tendency to softheartedness with a spurious anger.

'You – you old windbag!' he growled through a cloud of swirling cigar smoke. 'I believe you are crazy. I told you to go home, Bushrod. Miss Lucy said that, did she? Well, we haven't kept the scutcheon very clear. Two years ago last week, wasn't it, Bushrod, when she died? Confound it! Are you going to stand there all night gabbing like a coffee-colored gander?'

The train whistled again. Now it was at the water tank, a mile away.

'Marse Robert,' said Uncle Bushrod, laying his hand on the satchel that the banker held. 'For Gawd's sake, don't take dis wid you. I knows what's in it. I knows where you got it in de bank. Don' kyar it wid you. Dey's big trouble in dat valise for Miss Lucy and Miss Lucy's child's chillun. Hit's bound to destroy de name of Weymouth and bow dem dat own it wid shame and triberlation. Marse Robert, you can kill dis ole nigger ef you will, but don't take away dis 'ere' valise. If I ever crosses over de Jordan, what I gwine to say to Miss Lucy when she ax me: "Uncle Bushrod, wharfo' didn' you take good care of Mr. Robert?" '

Mr. Robert Weymouth threw away his cigar and shook free one arm with that peculiar gesture that always preceded his outbursts of irascibility. Uncle Bushrod bowed his head to the expected storm, but he did not flinch. If the house of Weymouth was to fall, he would fall with it. The banker spoke, and Uncle Bushrod blinked with surprise. The storm was there, but it was suppressed to the quietness of a summer breeze.

'Bushrod,' said Mr. Robert, in a lower voice than he usually employed, 'you have overstepped all bounds. You have presumed upon the leniency with which you have been treated to meddle unpardonably. So you know what is in this satchel! Your long and faithful service is some excuse, but – go home, Bushrod – not another word!'

But Bushrod grasped the satchel with a firmer hand. The headlight of the train was lightening the shadows about the station. The roar was increasing, and folks were stirring about at the track side.

'Marse Robert, gimme dis 'er' valise. I got a right, suh, to talk to you dis 'ere' way. I slaved for you and 'tended to you from a child up. I went th'ough de war as yo' body-servant tell we whipped de Yankees and sent 'em back to de No'th. I was at yo' weddin', and I was n' fur away when yo' Miss Letty was bawn. And Miss Letty's chillun, dey watches to-day for Uncle Bushrod when he comes home ever' evenin'. I been a' Weymouth, all 'cept in color and entitlements. Both of us is old, Marse Robert. 'Tain't goin' to be long tell we gwine to see Miss Lucy and has to give an account of our doin's. De ole nigger man won't be 'spected to say much mo' dan he done all he could by de fambly dat owned him. But de Weymouths, dey must say dey been livin' pure and fearless and widout reproach. Gimme dis valise, Marse Robert – I'm gwine to hab it. I'm gwine to take it back to the bank and lock it up in de vault. I'm gwine to do Miss Lucy's biddin'. Turn 'er loose, Marse Robert.'

The train was standing at the station. Some men were pushing trucks along the side. Two or three sleepy passengers got off and wandered away into the night. The conductor stepped to the gravel, swung his lantern and called: 'Hello, Frank!' at some one invisible. The bell clanged, the brakes hissed, the conductor drawled: 'All aboard!'

Mr. Robert released his hold on the satchel. Uncle Bushrod hugged it to his breast with both arms, as a lover clasps his first beloved.

'Take it back with you, Bushrod,' said Mr. Robert, thrusting his hands into his pockets. 'And let the subject drop – now mind! You've said quite enough. I'm going to take this train. Tell Mr. William I will be back on Saturday. Good-night.'

The banker climbed the steps of the moving train and disappeared in a coach. Uncle Bushrod stood motionless, still embracing the precious satchel. His eyes were closed and his lips were moving in thanks to the Master above for the salvation of the Weymouth honor. He knew Mr. Robert would return when he said he would. The Weymouths never lied. Nor now, thank the Lord! could it be said that they embezzled the money in banks.

Then awake to the necessity for further guardianship of Weymouth trust funds, the old man started for the bank with the redeemed satchel.

Three hours from Weymouthville, in the gray dawn, Mr. Robert alighted from the train at a lonely flag-station. Dimly he could see the figure of a man waiting on the platform and the shape of a spring-wagon, team and driver. Half a dozen lengthy bamboo fishing-poles projected from the wagon's rear.

'You're here, Bob,' said Judge Archinard, Mr. Robert's old friend and schoolmate. 'It's going to be a royal day for fishing. I thought you said – why, didn't you bring along the stuff?'

The president of the Weymouth Bank took off his hat and rumpled his gray locks.

'Well, Ben, to tell the truth, there's an infernally presumptuous old nigger belonging in my family that broke up the arrangement. He came down to the depot and vetoed the whole proceeding. He means all right, and – well, I reckon he is right. Somehow, he found out what I had along – though I hid it in the bank vault and sneaked it out at midnight. I reckon he has noticed that I've been indulging a little more than a gentleman should, and he laid for me with some reaching arguments.

'I'm going to quit drinking,' Mr. Robert concluded. 'I've come to the conclusion that a man can't keep it up and be quite what he'd like to be – "pure and fearless and without reproach" – that's the way old Bushrod quoted it.'

'Well, I'll have to admit,' said the judge, thoughtfully, as they climbed into the wagon, 'that the old darkey's argument can't conscientiously be overruled.'

'Still,' said Mr. Robert, with a ghost of a sigh, 'there was two quarts of the finest old silk-velvet Bourbon in that satchel you ever wet your lips with.'

THE DISCOUNTERS OF MONEY

THE SPECTACLE OF THE MONEY-CALIPHS of the present day going about Bagdad-on-the-Subway trying to relieve the wants of the people is enough to make the great Al Raschid turn Haroun in his grave. If not so, then the assertion should do so, the real caliph having been a wit and a scholar and therefore a hater of puns.

How properly to alleviate the troubles of the poor is one of the greatest troubles of the rich. But one thing agreed upon by all professional philan-thropists is that you must never hand over any cash to your subject. The poor are notoriously temperamental; and when they get money they exhibit a strong tendency to spend it for stuffed olives and enlarged crayon portraits instead of giving it to the instalment man.

And still, old Haroun had some advantages as an eleemosynarian. He took around with him on his rambles his vizier, Giafar (a vizier is a composite of a chauffeur, a secretary of state, and a night-and-day bank), and old Uncle Mesrour, his executioner, who toted a snickersnee. With this entourage a caliphing tour could hardly fail to be successful. Have you noticed lately any newspaper articles headed, 'What Shall We Do With Our Ex-Presidents?' Well, now, suppose that Mr. Carnegie should engage *him* and Joe Gans to go about assisting in the distribution of free libraries? Do you suppose any town would have the hardihood to refuse one? That caliphalous combination would cause two libraries to grow where there had been only one set of E. P. Roe's works before.

But, as I said, the money-caliphs are handicapped. They have the idea that earth has no sorrow that dough cannot heal; and they rely upon it solely. Al Raschid administered justice, rewarded the deserving, and punished whomsoever he disliked on the spot. He was the originator of the short-story contest. Whenever he succored any chance pick-up in the bazaars he always made the succoree tell the sad story of his life. If the narrative lacked construction, style, and *esprit* he commanded his vizier to dole him out a couple of thousand ten-dollar notes of the First National Bank of the Bosphorus, or else gave him a soft job as Keeper of the Bird Seed for the Bulbuls in the Imperial Gardens. If the story was a cracker-jack, he had Mesrour, the executioner, whack off his head. The report that Haroun Al Raschid is yet alive and is editing the magazine that your grandmother used to subscribe for lacks confirmation.

And now follows the Story of the Millionaire, the Inefficacious Increment, and the Babes Drawn from the Wood.

Young Howard Pilkins, the millionaire, got his money ornithologically. He was a shrewd judge of storks, and got in on the ground floor at the residence of his immediate ancestors, the Pilkins Brewing Company. For his mother was a partner in the business. Finally old man Pilkins died from a torpid liver, and then Mrs. Pilkins died from worry on account of torpid delivery-wagons – and there you have young Howard Pilkins with 4,000,000, and a good fellow at that. He was an agreeable, modestly arrogant young man, who implicitly believed that money could buy anything that the world had to offer. And Bagdad-on-the-Subway for a long time did everything possible to encourage his belief.

But the Rat-trap caught him at last; he heard the spring snap, and found his heart in a wire cage regarding a piece of cheese whose other name was Alice von der Ruysling.

The Von der Ruyslings still live in that little square about which so much has been said, and in which so little had been done. To-day you hear of Mr. Tilden's underground passage, and you hear of Mr. Gould's elevated passage, and that about ends the noise in the world made by Gramercy Square. But once it was different. The Von der Ruyslings live there yet, and they received *the first key ever made to Gramercy Park.*

You shall have no description of Alice v. d. R. Just call up in your mind the picture of your own Maggie or Vera or Beatrice, straighten her nose, soften her voice, tone her down and then tone her up, make her beautiful and unattainable – and you have a faint dry-point etching of Alice. The family owned a crumbly brick house and a coachman named Joseph in a coat of many colors, and a horse so old that he claimed to belong to the order of the Perissodactyla, and had toes instead of hoofs. In the year 1898 the family had to buy a new set of harness for the Perissodactyl. Before using it they made Joseph smear it over with a mixture of ashes and soot. It was the Von der Ruysling family that bought the territory between the Bowery and East River and Rivington Street and the Statue of Liberty, in the year 1649, from an Indian chief for a quart of passementerie and a pair of Turkey-red portières designed for a Harlem flat. I have always admired that Indian's perspicacity and good taste. All this is merely to convince you that the Von der Ruyslings were exactly the kind of poor aristocrats that turn down their noses at people who have money. Oh, well, I don't mean that; I mean people who have *just* money.

One evening Pilkins went down to the red brick house in Gramercy Square, and made what he thought was a proposal to Alice v. d. R. Alice, with her nose turned down, and thinking of his money, considered it a proposition, and refused it and him. Pilkins, summoning all his resources as any good general would have done, made an indiscreet reference to the advantages that his money would provide. That settled it. The lady turned so cold that Walter Wellman himself would have waited until spring to make a dash for her in a dog-sled.

But Pilkins was something of a sport himself. You can't fool all the millionaires every time the ball drops on the Western Union Building.

'If, at any time,' he said to A. v. d. R., 'you feel that you would like to reconsider your answer, send me a rose like that.'

Pilkins audaciously touched a Jacque rose that she wore loosely in her hair.

'Very well,' said she. 'And when I do, you will understand by it that either you or I have learned something new about the purchasing power of money. You've been spoiled, my friend. No, I don't think I could marry you. Tomorrow I will send you back the presents you have given me.'

'Presents!' said Pilkins in surprise. 'I never gave you a present in my life. I would like to see a full-length portrait of the man that you would take a present from. Why, you never would let me send you flowers or candy or even art calendars.'

'You've forgotten,' said Alice v. d. R., with a little smile. 'It was a long time ago when our families were neighbors. You were seven, and I was trundling my doll on the sidewalk. You gave me a little gray, hairy kitten, with shoe-buttony eyes. Its head came off and it was full of candy. You paid five cents for it – you told me so. I haven't the candy to return to you – I hadn't developed a conscience at three, so I ate it. But I have the kitten yet, and I will wrap it up neatly to-night and send it to you tomorrow.'

Beneath the lightness of Alice v. d. R.'s talk the steadfastness of her rejection showed firm and plain. So there was nothing left for him but to leave the crumbly red brick house, and be off with his abhorred millions.

On his way back, Pilkins walked through Madison Square. The hour hand on the clock hung about eight; the air was stingingly cool, but not at the freezing point. The dim little square seemed like a great, cold, unroofed room, with its four walls of houses, spangled with thousands of insufficient lights. Only a few loiterers huddled here and there on the benches.

But suddenly Pilkins came upon a youth sitting brave, and, as if conflicting with summer sultriness, coatless, his white shirt-sleeves conspicuous in the light from the globe of an electric. Close at his side was a girl, smiling, dreamy, happy. Around her shoulders was, palpably, the missing coat of the cold-defying youth. It appeared to be a modern panorama of the Babes in the Wood, revised and brought up to date, with the exception that the robins hadn't turned up yet with the protecting leaves.

With delight the money-caliphs view a situation that they think is relievable while you wait.

Pilkins sat on the bench, one seat removed from the youth. He glanced cautiously and saw (as men do see; and women – oh! never can) that they were of the same order.

Pilkins leaned over after a short time and spoke to the youth, who answered smilingly, and courteously. From general topics the conversation concentrated to the bed-rock of grim personalities. But Pilkins did it as delicately and heartily as any caliph could have done. And when it came to the point, the youth turned to him soft-voiced and with his undiminished smile.

'I don't want to seem unappreciative, old man,' he said, with a youth's somewhat too-early spontaneity of address, 'but, you see, I can't accept anything from a stranger. I know you're all right, and I'm tremendously obliged, but I couldn't think of borrowing from anybody. You see, I'm Marcus Clayton – the Claytons of Roanoke County, Virginia, you know. The young lady is Miss Eva Bedford – I reckon you've heard of the Bedfords. She's seventeen and one of the Bedfords of Bedford County. We've eloped from home to get married, and we wanted to see New York. We got in this afternoon. Somebody got my pocketbook in the ferry-boat, and I had only three cents in change outside of it. I'll get some work somewhere to-morrow, and we'll get married.'

'But, I say, old man,' said Pilkins, in confidential low tones, 'you can't keep the lady out here in the cold all night. Now, as for hotels—'

'I told you,' said the youth, with a broader smile, 'that I didn't have but three cents. Besides, if I had a thousand, we'd have to wait here until morning. You can understand that, of course. I'm much obliged, but I can't take any of your money. Miss Bedford and I have lived an outdoor life, and we don't mind a little cold. I'll get work of some kind to-morrow. We've got a paper bag of cakes and chocolates, and we'll get along all right.'

'Listen,' said the millionaire, impressively. 'My name is Pilkins, and I'm worth several million dollars. I happen to have in my pockets about $800 or $900 in cash. Don't you think you are drawing it rather fine when you decline to accept as much of it as will make you and the young lady comfortable at least for the night?'

'I can't say, sir, that I do think so,' said Clayton of Roanoke County. 'I've been raised to look at such things differently. But I'm mightily obliged to you, just the same.'

'Then you force me to say good-night,' said the millionaire.

Twice that day had his money been scorned by simple ones to whom his dollars had appeared as but tin tobacco-tags. He was no worshipper of the actual minted coin or stamped paper, but he had always believed in its almost unlimited power to purchase.

Pilkins walked away rapidly, and then turned abruptly and returned to the bench where the young couple sat. He took off his hat and began to speak. The girl looked at him with the same sprightly glowing interest that she had been giving to the lights and statuary and sky-reaching buildings that made the old square seem so far away from Bedford County.

'Mr. – er – Roanoke,' said Pilkins, 'I admire your – your indepen – your idiocy so much that I'm going to appeal to your chivalry. I believe that's what you Southerners call it when you keep a lady sitting outdoors on a bench on a cold night just to keep your old, out-of-date pride going. Now, I've a friend – a lady – whom I have known all my life – who lives a few blocks from here – with her parents and sisters and aunts, and all that kind of endorsement, of course. I am sure this young lady would be happy and pleased to put up – that is, to have Miss – er – Bedford give her the pleasure of having her as a guest for the night. Don't you think, Mr. Roanoke, of – er – Virginia, that you could unbend your prejudices that far?'

Clayton of Roanoke rose and held out his hand.

'Old man,' he said. 'Miss Bedford will be much pleased to accept the hospitality of the lady you refer to.'

He formally introduced Mr. Pilkins to Miss Bedford. The girl looked at him sweetly and comfortably. 'It's a lovely evening, Mr. Pilkins – don't you think so?' she said slowly.

Pilkins conducted them to the crumbly red brick house of the Von der Ruyslings. His card brought Alice downstairs wondering. The runaways were sent into the drawing-room, while Pilkins told Alice all about it in the hall.

'Of course, I will take her in,' said Alice. 'Haven't those Southern girls a thoroughbred air? Of course, she will stay here. You will look after Mr. Clayton, of course.'

'Will I?' said Pilkins, delighted. 'Oh, yes, I'll look after him! As a citizen of New York, and therefore a part owner of its public parks, I'm going to extend to him the hospitality of Madison Square tonight. He's going to sit there on a bench till morning. There's no use arguing with him. Isn't he wonderful? I'm glad you'll look after the little lady, Alice. I tell you those Babes in the Wood made my – that is, er – made Wall Street and the Bank of England look like penny arcades.'

Miss Von der Ruysling whisked Miss Bedford of Bedford County up to restful regions upstairs. When she came down, she put an oblong small pasteboard box into Pilkins' hands.

'Your present,' she said, 'that I am returning to you.'

'Oh, yes, I remember,' said Pilkins, with a sigh, 'the woolly kitten.'

He left Clayton on a park bench, and shook hands with him heartily.

'After I get work,' said the youth, 'I'll look you up. Your address is on your card, isn't it? Thanks. Well, good-night. I'm awfully obliged to you for your kindness. No, thanks, I don't smoke. Good-night.'

In his room, Pilkins opened the box and took out the staring, funny kitten, long ago ravaged of his candy and minus one shoe-button eye. Pilkins looked at it sorrowfully.

'After all,' he said, 'I don't believe that just money alone will—'

And then he gave a shout and dug into the bottom of the box for something else that had been the kitten's resting-place – a crushed but red, red, fragrant, glorious, promising Jacqueminot rose.

THE ENCHANTED PROFILE

THERE ARE FEW CALIPHESSES. Women are Scheherazades by birth, predilection, instinct, and arrangement of the vocal cords. The thousand and one stories are being told every day by hundreds of thousands of viziers' daughters to their respective sultans. But the bow-string will get some of 'em yet if they don't watch out.

I heard a story, though, of one Lady Caliph. It isn't precisely an Arabian Nights story, because it brings in Cinderella, who flourished her dishrag in another epoch and country. So, if you don't mind the mixed dates (which seem to give it an Eastern flavor, after all), we'll get along.

In New York there is an old, old hotel. You have seen woodcuts of it in the magazines. It was built – let's see – at a time when there was nothing above Fourteenth Street except the old Indian trail to Boston and Hammerstein's office. Soon the old hostelry will be torn down. And, as the stout walls are riven apart and the bricks go roaring down the chutes, crowds of citizens will gather at the nearest corners and weep over the destruction of a dear old landmark. Civic pride is strong in New Bagdad; and the wettest weeper and the loudest howler against the iconoclasts will be the man (originally from Terre Haute) whose fond memories of the old hotel are limited to his having been kicked out from its free-lunch counter in 1873.

At the hotel always stopped Mrs. Maggie Brown. Mrs. Brown was a bony woman of sixty, dressed in the rustiest black, and carrying a handbag made, apparently, from the hide of the original animal that Adam decided to call an alligator. She always occupied a small parlor and bedroom at the top of the hotel at a rental of two dollars per day. And always, while she was there, each day came hurrying to see her many men, sharp-faced, anxious-looking, with only seconds to spare. For Maggie Brown was said to be the third richest woman in the world; and these solicitous gentlemen were only the city's wealthiest brokers and business men seeking trifling loans of half a dozen millions or so from the dingy old lady with the prehistoric handbag.

The stenographer and typewriter of the Acropolis Hotel (there! I've let the name of it out!) was Miss Ida Bates. She was a holdover from the Greek classics. There wasn't a flaw in her looks. Some old-timer in paying his regards to a lady said: 'To have loved her was a liberal education.' Well, even to have looked over the black hair and neat white shirtwaist of Miss Bates was equal to a full course in any correspondence school in the country. She sometimes did a little typewriting for me and, as she refused to take the money in advance, she came to look upon me as something of a friend and protégé. She had unfailing kindliness and good nature; and not even a whitelead drummer or a fur importer had ever dared to cross the dead line of good behavior in her presence. The entire force of the Acropolis, from the owner, who lived in Vienna, down to the head porter, who had been bedridden for sixteen years, would have sprung to her defence in a moment.

One day I walked past Miss Bates's little sanctum Remingtorium, and saw in her place a black-haired unit – unmistakably a person – pounding with each of her forefingers upon the keys. Musing on the mutability of temporal affairs, I passed on. The next day I went on a two weeks' vacation. Returning,

I strolled through the lobby of the Acropolis, and saw, with a little warm glow of auld lang syne, Miss Bates, as Grecian and kind and flawless as ever, just putting the cover on her machine. The hour for closing had come; but she asked me in to sit for a few minutes in the dictation chair. Miss Bates explained her absence and return to the Acropolis Hotel in words identical with or similar to these following:

'Well, Man, how are the stories coming?'

'Pretty regularly,' said I. 'About equal to their going.'

'I'm sorry,' said she. 'Good typewriting is the main thing in a story. You've missed me, haven't you?'

'No one,' said I, 'whom I have ever known knows as well as you do how to space properly belt buckles, semicolons, hotel guests, and hairpins. But you've been away too. I saw a package of peppermint-pepsin in your place the other day.'

'I was going to tell you about it,' said Miss Bates, 'if you hadn't interrupted me.

'Of course, you know about Maggie Brown, who stops here. Well, she's worth $40,000,000. She lives in Jersey in a ten-dollar flat. She's always got more cash on hand than half a dozen business candidates for vice-president. I don't know whether she carries it in her stocking or not, but I know she's mighty popular down in the part of the town where they worship the golden calf.

'Well, about two weeks ago, Mrs. Brown stops at the door and rubbers at me for ten minutes. I'm sitting with my side to her, striking off some manifold copies of a copper-mine proposition for a nice old man from Tonopah. But I always see everything all around me. When I'm hard at work I can see things through my side-combs; and I can leave one button unbuttoned in the back of my shirtwaist and see who's behind me. I didn't look around, because I make from eighteen to twenty dollars a week, and I didn't have to.

'That evening at knocking-off time she sends for me to come up to her apartment. I expected to have to typewrite about two thousand words of notes-of-hand, liens, and contracts, with a ten-cent tip in sight; but I went. Well, Man, I was certainly surprised. Old Maggie Brown had turned human.

' "Child," says she, "you're the most beautiful creature I ever saw in my life. I want you to quit your work and come and live with me. I've no kith or kin," says she, "except a husband and a son or two, and I hold no communication with any of 'em. They're extravagant burdens on a hard-working woman. I want you to be a daughter to me. They say I'm stingy and mean, and the papers print lies about my doing my own cooking and washing. It's a lie," she goes on. "I put my washing out, except the handkerchiefs and stockings and petticoats and collars, and light stuff like that. I've got forty million dollars in cash and stocks and bonds that are as negotiable as Standard Oil, preferred, at a church fair. I'm a lonely old woman and I need companionship. You're the most beautiful human being I ever saw," says she. "Will you come and live with me? I'll show 'em whether I can spend money or not" she says.

'Well, Man, what would you have done? Of course, I fell to it. And, to tell you the truth, I began to like old Maggie. It wasn't all on account of the forty millions and what she could do for me. I was kind of lonesome in the world, too. Everybody's got to have somebody they can explain to about the pain in their left shoulder and how fast patent-leather shoes wear out when they begin to crack. And you can't talk about such things to men you meet in hotels – they're looking for just such openings.

'So I gave up my job in the hotel and went with Mrs. Brown. I certainly seemed to have a mash on her. She'd look at me for half an hour at a time when I was sitting, reading, or looking at the magazines.

'One time I says to her: "Do I remind you of some deceased relative or friend of your childhood, Mrs. Brown? I've noticed you give me a pretty good optical inspection from time to time."

' "You have a face," she says, "exactly like a dear friend of mine – the best friend I ever had. But I like you for yourself, child, too," she says.

'And say, Man, what do you suppose she did? Loosened up like a Marcel wave in the surf at Coney. She took me to a swell dressmaker and gave her *à la carte* to fit me out – money no object. They were rush orders, and madame locked the front door and put the whole force to work.

'Then we moved to – where do you think? – no; guess again – that's right – the Hotel Bonton. We had a six-room apartment; and it cost $100 a day. I saw the bill. I began to love that old lady.

'And then, Man, when my dresses began to come in – oh, I won't tell you about 'em! you couldn't understand. And I began to call her Aunt Maggie. You've read about Cinderella, of course. Well, what Cinderella said when the prince fitted that 3½ A on her foot was a hard-luck story compared to the things I told myself.

'Then Aunt Maggie says she is going to give me a coming-out banquet in the Bonton that'll make moving Vans of all the old Dutch families on Fifth Avenue.

' "I've been out before, Aunt Maggie," says I. "But I'll come out again. But you know," says I, "that this is one of the swellest hotels in the city. And you know – pardon me – that it's hard to get a bunch of notables together unless you've trained for it."

' "Don't fret about that, child," says Aunt Maggie. "I don't send out invitations – I issue orders. I'll have fifty guests here that couldn't be brought together again at any reception unless it were given by King Edward or William Travers Jerome. They are men, of course, and all of 'em either owe me money or intend to. Some of their wives won't come, but a good many will."

'Well, I wish you could have been at that banquet. The dinner service was all gold and cut glass. There were about forty men and eight ladies present besides Aunt Maggie and I. You'd never have known the third richest woman in the world. She had on a new black silk dress with so much passementerie on it that it sounded exactly like a hailstorm I heard once when I was staying all night with a girl that lived on a top-floor studio.

'And my dress! – say, Man, I can't waste the words on you. It was all hand-made lace – where there was any of it at all – and it cost $300. I saw the bill. The men were all baldheaded or white-sidewhiskered, and they kept up a running fire of light repartee about 3 per cent., and Bryan and the cotton crop.

'On the left of me was something that talked like a banker, and on my right was a young fellow who said he was a newspaper artist. He was the only – well, I was going to tell you.

'After the dinner was over Mrs. Brown and I went up to the apartment.

We had to squeeze our way through a mob of reporters all the way through the halls. That's one of the things money does for you. Say, do you happen to know a newspaper artist named Lathrop – a tall man with nice eyes and an easy way of talking? No, I don't remember what paper he works on. Well, all right.

'When we got upstairs Mrs. Brown telephones for the bill right away. It came, and it was $600. I saw the bill. Aunt Maggie fainted. I got her on a lounge and opened the bead-work.

' "Child," says she, when she got back to the world, "what was it? A raise of rent or an income-tax?"

' "Just a little dinner," says I. "Nothing to worry about – hardly a drop in the bucket-shop. Sit up and take notice – a dispossess notice, if there's no other kind."

'But, say, Man, do you know what Aunt Maggie did? She got cold feet! She hustled me out of that Hotel Bonton at nine the next morning. We went to a rooming-house on the lower West Side. She rented one room that had water on the floor below and light on the floor above. After we got moved all you could see in the room was about $1,500 worth of new swell dresses and a one-burner gas-stove.

'Aunt Maggie had had a sudden attack of the hedges. I guess everybody has got to go on a spree once in their life. A man spends his on highballs, and a woman gets woozy on clothes. But with forty million dollars – say! I'd like to have a picture of – but, speaking of pictures, did you ever run across a newspaper artist named Lathrop – a tall – oh, I asked you that before, didn't I? He was mighty nice to me at the dinner. His voice just suited me. I guess he must have thought I was to inherit some of Aunt Maggie's money.

'Well, Mr. Man, three days of that light-housekeeping was plenty for me. Aunt Maggie was affectionate as ever. She'd hardly let me get out of her sight. But let me tell you. She was a hedger from Hedgersville, Hedger County. Seventy-five cents a day was the limit she set. We cooked our own meals in the room. There I was, with a thousand dollars' worth of the latest things in clothes, doing stunts over a one-burner gas-stove.

'As I say, on the third day I flew the coop. I couldn't stand for throwing together a fifteen-cent kidney stew while wearing, at the same time, a $150 house-dress, with Valenciennes lace insertion. So I goes into the closet and puts on the cheapest dress Mrs. Brown had bought for me – it's the one I've got on now – not so bad for $75, is it? I'd left all my own clothes in my sister's flat in Brooklyn.

' "Mrs. Brown, formerly 'Aunt Maggie,' " says I to her, "I am going to extend my feet alternately, one after the other, in such a manner and direction that this tenement will recede from me in the quickest possible time. I am no worshipper of money," says I, "but there are some things I can't stand. I can stand the fabulous monster that I've read about that blows hot birds and cold bottles with the same breath. But I can't stand a quitter," says I. "They say you've got forty million dollars – well, you'll never have any less. And I was beginning to like you, too," says I.

'Well, the late Aunt Maggie kicks till the tears flow. She offers to move into a swell room with a two-burner stove and running water.

' "I've spent an awful lot of money, child," says she. "We'll have to economize for a while. You're the most beautiful creature I ever laid eyes on," she says, "and I don't want you to leave me."

'Well, you see me, don't you? I walked straight to the Acropolis and asked for my job back, and I got it. How did you say your writings were getting along? I know you've lost out some by not having me to typewrite 'em. Do you ever have 'em illustrated? And, by the way, did you ever happen to know a newspaper artist – oh, shut up! I know I asked you before. I wonder what paper he works on? It's funny, but I couldn't help thinking that he wasn't thinking about the money he might have been thinking I was thinking I'd get from old Maggie Brown. If I only knew some of the newspaper editors I'd – '

The sound of an easy footstep came from the doorway. Ida Bates saw who it was with her back-hair comb. I saw her turn pink, perfect statue that she was – a miracle that I share with Pygmalion only.

'Am I excusable?' she said to me – adorable petitioner that she became. 'It's – it's Mr. Lathrop. I wonder if it really wasn't the money – I wonder, if after all, he – '

Of course, I was invited to the wedding. After the ceremony I dragged Lathrop aside.

'You an artist,' said I, 'and haven't figured out why Maggie Brown conceived such a strong liking for Miss Bates – that was? Let me show you.'

The bride wore a simple white dress as beautifully draped as the costumes of the ancient Greeks. I took some leaves from one of the decorative wreaths in the little parlor, and made a chaplet of them, and placed them on née Bates' shining chestnut hair, and made her turn her profile to her husband.

'By jingo!' said he. 'Isn't Ida's head a dead ringer for the lady's head on the silver dollar?'

'NEXT TO READING MATTER'

HE COMPELLED MY INTEREST as he stepped from the ferry at Desbrosses Street. He had the air of being familiar with hemispheres and worlds, of entering New York as the lord of a demesne who revisited it after years of absence. But I thought that, with all his air, he had never before set foot on the slippery cobblestones of the City of Too Many Caliphs.

He wore loose clothes of strange bluish drab color, and a conservative, round Panama hat without the cock-a-loop indentations and cants with which Northern fanciers disfigure the tropic head-gear. Moreover, he was the homeliest man I have ever seen. His ugliness was less repellent than startling – arising from a sort of Lincolnian ruggedness and irregularity of feature that spellbound you with wonder and dismay. So may have looked afrites or the shapes metamorphosed from the vapor of the fisherman's vase. As he afterward told me, his name was Judson Tate; and he may as well be called so at once. He wore his green silk tie through a topaz ring; and he carried a cane made of the vertebrae of a shark.

Judson Tate accosted me with some large and casual inquiries about the city's streets and hotels, in the manner of one who had but for the moment forgotten the trifling details. I could think of no reason for dispraising my own quiet hotel in the downtown district; so the mid-morning of the night found us already victualed and drinked (at my expense), and ready to be chaired and tobaccoed in a quiet corner of the lobby.

There was something on Judson Tate's mind, and, such as it was, he tried
to convey it to me. Already he had accepted me as his friend; and when I
looked at his great, snuff-brown first-mate's hand, with which he brought
emphasis to his periods, within six inches of my nose, I wondered if, by any
chance, he was as sudden in conceiving enmity against strangers.

When this man began to talk I perceived in him a certain power. His
voice was a persuasive instrument, upon which he played with a somewhat
specious but effective art. He did not try to make you forget his ugliness; he
flaunted it in your face and made it part of the charm of his speech. Shutting
your eyes, you would have trailed after this rat-catcher's pipes at least to the
walls of Hamelin. Beyond that you would have had to be more childish to
follow. But let him play his own tune to the words set down, so that if all
is too dull, the art of music may bear the blame.

'Women,' said Judson Tate, 'are mysterious creatures.'

My spirits sank. I was not there to listen to such a world-old hypothesis
– to such a time-worn, long-ago-refuted, bald, feeble, illogical, vicious, patent
sophistry – to an ancient, baseless, wearisome, ragged, unfounded, insidious
falsehood originated by women themselves, and by them insinuated, foisted,
thrust, spread, and ingeniously promulgated into the ears of mankind by
underhanded, secret, and deceptive methods, for the purpose of argumenting,
furthering, and reinforcing their own charms and designs.

'Oh, I don't know!' said I, vernacularly.

'Have you ever heard of Oratama?' he asked.

'Possibly,' I answered. 'I seem to recall a toe dancer – or a suburban addition
– or was it a perfume? – of some such name.'

'It is a town,' said Judson Tate, 'on the coast of a foreign country of which
you know nothing and could understand less. It is a country governed by a
dictator and controlled by revolutions and insubordination. It was there that
a great life-drama was played, with Judson Tate, the homeliest man in
America, and Fergus McMahan, the handsomest adventurer in history or
fiction, and Señorita Anabela Zamora, the beautiful daughter of the alcalde
of Oratama, as chief actors. And, another thing – nowhere else on the globe
except in the department of Trienta y tres in Uruguay does the *chuchula*
plant grow. The products of the country I speak of are valuable woods,
dye-stuffs, gold, rubber, ivory, and cocoa.'

'I was not aware,' said I, 'that South America produced any ivory.'

'There you are twice mistaken,' said Judson Tate, distributing the words
over at least an octave of his wonderful voice. 'I did not say that the country
I spoke of was in South America – I must be careful, my dear man; I have
been in politics there, you know. But, even so – I have played chess against
its president with a set carved from the nasal bones of the tapir – one of our
native specimens of the order of *perissodactyle ungulates* inhabiting the
Cordilleras – which was as pretty ivory as you would care to see.

'But it was of romance and adventure and the ways of women that I was
going to tell you, and not of zoölogical animals.

'For fifteen years I was the ruling power behind old Sancho Benavides, the
Royal High Thumbscrew of the republic. You've seen his picture in the
papers – a mushy black man with whiskers like the notes on a Swiss
music-box cylinder, and a scroll in his right hand like the ones they write
births on in the family Bible. Well, that chocolate potentate used to be the
biggest item of interest anywhere between the color line and the parallels of

latitude. It was three throws, horses, whether he was to wind up in the Hall of Fame or the Bureau of Combustibles. He'd have been sure called the Roosevelt of the Southern Continent if it hadn't been that Grover Cleveland was President at the time. He'd hold office a couple of terms, then he'd sit out for a hand – always after appointing his own successor for the interims.

'But it was not Benavides, the Liberator, who was making all this fame for himself. Not him. It was Judson Tate. Benavides was only the chip over the bug. I gave him the tip when to declare war and increase import duties and wear his state trousers. But that wasn't what I wanted to tell you. How did I get to be It? I'll tell you. Because I'm the most gifted talker that ever made vocal sounds since Adam first opened his eyes, pushed aside the smelling-salts, and asked: "Where am I?"

'As you observe, I am about the ugliest man you ever saw outside the gallery of photographs of the New England early Christian Scientists. So, at an early age, I perceived that what I lacked in looks I must make up in eloquence. That I've done. I get what I go after. As the back-stop and still small voice of old Benavides I made all the great historical powers-behind-the-throne, such as Talleyrand, Mrs. de Pompadour, and Loeb, look as small as the minority report of a Duma. I could talk nations into or out of debt, harangue armies to sleep in the battlefield, reduce insurrections, inflammations, taxes, appropriations or surpluses with a few words, and call up the dogs of war or the dove of peace with the same bird-like whistle. Beauty and epaulettes and curly moustaches and Grecian profiles in other men were never in my way. When people first look at me they shudder. Unless they are in the last stages of *angina pectoris* they are mine in ten minutes after I begin to talk. Women and men – I win 'em as they come. Now, you wouldn' think women would fancy a man with a face like mine, would you?'

'Oh, yes, Mr. Tate,' said I. 'History is bright and fiction dull with homely men who have charmed women. There seems—'

'Pardon me,' interrupted Judson Tate, 'but you don't quite understand. You have yet to hear my story.

'Fergus McMahan was a friend of mine in the capital. For a handsome man I'll admit he was the duty-free merchandise. He had blond curls and laughing blue eyes and was featured regular. They said he was a ringer for the statue they call Herr Mees, the god of speech, and eloquence resting in some museum in Rome. Some German anarchist, I suppose. They are always resting and talking.

'But Fergus was no talker. He was brought up with the idea that to be beautiful was to make good. His conversation was about as edifying as listening to a leak dropping in a tin dish-pan at the head of the bed when you want to go to sleep. But he and me got to be friends – maybe because we was so opposite, don't you think? Looking at the Hallowe'en mask that I call my face when I'm shaving seemed to give Fergus pleasure; and I'm sure that whenever I heard the feeble output of throat noises that he called conversation I felt contented to be a gargoyle with a silver tongue.

'One time I found it necessary to go down to this coast town of Oratama to straighten out a lot of political unrest and chop off a few heads in the customs and military departments. Fergus, who owned the ice and sulphur-match concessions of the republic, says he'll keep me company.

'So, in a jangle of mule-train bells, we gallops into Oratama, and the town belonged to us as much as Long Island Sound doesn't belong to Japan when T. R. is at Oyster Bay. I say us; but I mean me. Everybody for four nations, two oceans, one bay and isthmus, and five archipelagoes around had heard of Judson Tate. Gentleman adventurer, they called me. I had been written up in five columns of the yellow journals, 40,000 words (with marginal decorations) in a monthly magazine, and a stickful on the twelfth page of the New York *Times*. If the beauty of Fergus McMahan gained any part of our reception in Oratama, I'll eat the price-tag in my Panama. It was me that they hung out paper flowers and palm branches for. I am not a jealous man; I am stating facts. The people were Nebuchadnezzars; they bit the grass before me; there was no dust in the town for them to bite. They bowed down to Judson Tate. They knew that I was the power behind Sancho Benavides. A word from me was more to them than a whole deckle-edged library from East Aurora in sectional bookcases was from anybody else. And yet there are people who spend hours fixing their faces – rubbing in cold cream and massaging the muscles (always toward the eyes) and taking in the slack with tincture of benzoin and electrolyzing moles – to what end? Looking handsome. Oh, what a mistake! It's the larynx that the beauty doctors ought to work on. It's words more than warts, talk more than talcum, palaver more than power, blarney more than bloom that counts – the phonograph instead of the photograph. But I was going to tell you.

'The local Astors put me and Fergus up at the Centipede Club, a frame building built on posts sunk in the surf. The tide's only nine inches. The Little Big High Low Jack-in-the-game of the town came around and kowtowed. Oh, it wasn't to Herr Mees. They had heard about Judson Tate.

'One afternoon me and Fergus McMahan was sitting on the seaward gallery of the Centipede, drinking iced rum and talking.

' "Judson," says Fergus, "there's an angel in Oratama."

' "So long," says I, "as it ain't Gabriel, why talk as if you had heard a trump blow?"

' "It's the Señorita Anabela Zamora," says Fergus. "She's – she's – she's as lovely as – as hell!"

' "Bravo!" says I, laughing heartily. "You have a true lover's eloquence to paint the beauties of your inamorata. You remind me," says I, "of Faust's wooing of Marguerite – that is, if he wooed her after he went down the trap-door of the stage."

' "Judson," says Fergus, "you know you are as beautiless as a rhinoceros. You can't have any interest in women. I'm awfully gone on Miss Anabela. And that's why I'm telling you."

' "Oh, *seguramente*," say I. "I know I have a front elevation like an Aztec god that guards a buried treasure that never did exist in Jefferson County, Yucatan. But there are compensations. For instance, I am It in this country as far as the eye can reach, and then a few perches and poles. And again," says I, "when I engage people in a set-to of oral, vocal, and laryngeal utterances, I do not usually confine my side of the argument to what may be likened to a cheap phonographic reproduction of the ravings of a jellyfish."

' "Oh, I know," says Fergus, amiable, "that I'm not handy at small talk. Or large, either. That's why I'm telling you. I want you to help me."

' "How can I do it?" I asked.

' "I have subsidized," says Fergus, "the services of Señorita Anabela's duenna, whose name is Francesca. You have a reputation in this country, Judson," says Fergus, "of being a great man and a hero."

' "I have," says I. "And I deserve it."

' "And I," says Fergus, "am the best-looking man between the Arctic circle and Antarctic ice pack."

' "With limitations," says I, "as to physiognomy and geography, I freely concede you to be."

' "Between the two of us," says Fergus, "we ought to land the Señorita Anabela Zamora. The lady, as you know, is of an old Spanish family, and further than looking at her driving in the family *carruaje* of afternoons around the plaza, or catching a glimpse of her through a barred window of evenings, she is as unapproachable as a star."

' "Land her for which one of us?" says I.

‐' "For me, of course," says Fergus. "You've never seen her. Now, I've had Francesca point me out to her as being you on several occasions. When she sees me on the plaza, she thinks she's looking at Don Judson Tate, the greatest hero, statesman, and romantic figure in the country. With your reputation and my looks combined in one man, how can she resist him? She's heard all about your thrilling history, of course. And she's seen me. Can any woman want more?" asks Fergus McMahan.

' "Can she do with less?" I ask. "How can we separate our mutual attractions, and how shall we apportion the proceeds?"

'Then Fergus tells me his scheme.

'The house of the alcalde, Don Luis Zamora, he says, has a *patio*, of course – a kind of inner courtyard opening from the street. In an angle of it is his daughter's window – as dark a place as you could find. And what do you think he wants me to do? Why, knowing my freedom, charm, and skilfulness of tongue, he proposes that I go into the *patio* at midnight, when the hobgoblin face of me cannot be seen, and make love to her for him – for the pretty man that she has just seen on the plaza, thinking him to be Don Judson Tate.

'Why shouldn't I do it for him – for my friend, Fergus McMahan? For him to ask me was a compliment – an acknowledgment of his own short-comings.

' "You little, lily-white, fine-haired, high polished piece of dumb sculpture," says I, "I'll help you. Make your arrangements and get me in the dark outside her window and my stream of conversation opened up with the moonlight tremolo stop turned on, and she's yours."

' "Keep your face hid, Jud," says Fergus. "For heaven's sake, keep your face hid. I'm a friend of yours in all kinds of sentiment, but this is a business deal. If I could talk I wouldn't ask you. But seeing me and listening to you I don't see why she can't be landed."

' "By you?" says I.

' "By me," says Fergus.

'Well, Fergus and the duenna, Francesca, attended to the details. And one night they fetched me a long black cloak with a high collar, and led me to the house at midnight. I stood by the window in the *patio* until I heard a voice as soft and sweet as an angel's whisper on the other side of the bars. I could see only a faint, white-clad shape inside; and, true to Fergus, I pulled the collar of my cloak high up, for it was July in the wet season, and the nights were chilly. And, smothering a laugh as I thought of the tongue-tied Fergus, I began to talk.

'Well, sir, I talked an hour at the Señorita Anabela. I say "at" because it was not "with." Now and then she would say: "Oh, Señor," or "Now, ain't you foolin'?" or "I know you don't mean that," and such things as women will when they are being rightly courted. Both of us knew English and Spanish; so in two languages I tried to win the heart of the lady for my friend Fergus. But for the bars to the window I could have done it in one. At the end of the hour she dismissed me and gave me a big, red rose. I handed it over to Fergus when I got home.

'For three weeks every third or fourth night I impersonated my friend in the *patio* at the window of Señorita Anabela. At last she admitted that her heart was mine, and spoke of having seen me every afternoon when she drove in the plaza. It was Fergus she had seen, of course. But it was my talk that won her. Suppose Fergus had gone there and tried to make a hit in the dark with his beauty all invisible, and not a word to say for himself!

'On the last night she promised to be mine – that is, Fergus's. And she put her hand between the bars for me to kiss. I bestowed the kiss and took the news to Fergus.

' "You might have left that for me to do," says he.

' "That'll be your job hereafter," says I. "Keep on doing that and don't try to talk. Maybe after she thinks she's in love she won't notice the difference between real conversation and the inarticulate sort of droning that you give forth."

'Now, I had never seen Señorita Anabela. So, the next day Fergus asks me to walk with him through the plaza and view the daily promenade and exhibition of Oratama society, a sight that had no interest for me. But I went; and children and dogs took to the banana groves and mangrove swamps as soon as they had a look at my face.

' "Here she comes," said Fergus, twirling his moustache – "the one in white, in the open carriage with the black horse."

'I looked and felt the ground rock under my feet. For Señorita Anabela Zamora was the most beautiful woman in the world, and the only one from that moment on, so far as Judson Tate was concerned. I saw at a glance that I must be hers and she mine forever. I thought of my face and nearly fainted; and then I thought of my other talents and stood upright again. And I had been wooing her for three weeks for another man!"

'As Señorita Anabela's carriage rolled slowly past, she gave Fergus a long, soft glance from the corners of her night-black eyes, a glance that would have sent Judson Tate up into heaven in a rubber-tired chariot. But she never looked at me. And that handsome man only ruffles his curls and smirks and prances like a lady-killer at my side.

' "What do you think of her, Judson?" asks Fergus, with an air.

' "This much," says I. 'She is to be Mrs. Judson Tate. I am no man to play tricks on a friend. So take your warning."

'I thought Fergus would die laughing.

' "Well, well, well," said he, "you old dough-face! Struck too, are you? That's great! But you're too late. Francesca tells me that Anabela talks of nothing but me, day and night. Of course, I'm awfully obliged to you for making that chin-music to her of evenings. But, do you know, I've an idea that I could have done it as well myself."

' "Mrs. Judson Tate," says I. "Don't forget the name. You've had the use of my tongue to go with your good looks, my boy. You can't lend me your looks; but hereafter my tongue is my own. Keep your mind on the name that's to be on the visiting cards two inches by three and a half – 'Mrs. Judson Tate.' That's all."

' "All right," says Fergus, laughing again. "I've talked with her father, the alcalde, and he's willing. He's to give a *baile* to-morrow evening in his new warehouse. If you were a dancing man, Jud, I'd expect you around to meet the future Mrs. McMahan."

'But on the next evening, when the music was playing loudest at the Alcalde Zamora's *baile*, into the room steps Judson Tate in new white linen clothes as if he were the biggest man in the whole nation, which he was.

'Some of the musicians jumped off the key when they saw my face, and one or two of the timidest señoritas let out a screech or two. But up prances the alcalde and almost wipes the dust off my shoes with his forehead. No mere good looks could have won me that sensational entrance.

' "I hear much, Señor Zamora," says I, "of the charm of your daughter. It would give me great pleasure to be presented to her."

'There were about six dozen willow rocking-chairs, with pink tidies tied on to them, arranged against the walls. In one of them sat Señorita Anabela in white Swiss and red slippers, with pearls and fire flies in her hair. Fergus was at the other end of the room trying to break away from two maroons and a claybank girl.

'The alcalde leads me up to Anabela and presents me. When she took the first look at my face she dropped her fan and nearly turned her chair over from the shock. But I'm used to that.

'I sat down by her and began to talk. When she heard me speak she jumped, and her eyes got as big as alligator pears. She couldn't strike a balance between the tones of my voice and the face I carried. But I kept on talking in the key of C, which is the ladies' key; and presently she sat still in her chair and a dreamy look came into her eyes. She was coming my way. She knew of Judson Tate, and what a big man he was, and the big things he had done; and that was in my favor. But, of course, it was some shock to her to find out that I was not the pretty man that had been pointed out to her as the great Judson. And then I took the Spanish language, which is better than English for certain purposes, and played on it like a harp of a thousand strings. I ranged from the second G below the staff up to F-sharp above it. I set my voice to poetry, art, romance, flowers, and moonlight. I repeated some of the verses that I had murmured to her in the dark at her window; and I knew from a sudden soft sparkle in her eye that she recognized in my voice the tones of her midnight mysterious wooer.

'Anyhow, I had Fergus McMahan going. Oh, the vocal is the true art – no doubt about that. Handsome is as handsome palavers. That's the renovated proverb.

'I took Señorita Anabela for a walk in the lemon grove while Fergus, disfiguring himself with an ugly frown, was waltzing with the claybank girl. Before we returned I had permission to come to her window in the *patio* the next evening at midnight and talk some more.

'Oh, it was easy enough. In two weeks Anabela was engaged to me, and Fergus was out. He took it calm, for a handsome man, and told me he wasn't going to give in.

' "Talk may be all right in its place, Judson," he says to me, "although I've never thought it worth cultivating. But," says he, "to expect mere words to back up successfully a face like yours in a lady's good graces is like expecting a man to make a square meal on the ringing of a dinner-bell."

'But I haven't begun on the story I was going to tell you yet.

'One day I took a long ride in the hot sunshine, and then took a bath in the cold waters of a lagoon on the edge of the town before I'd cooled off.

'That evening after dark I called at the alcalde's to see Anabela. I was calling regular every evening then, and we were to be married in a month. She was looking like a bulbul, a gazelle, and a tea-rose, and her eyes were as soft and bright as two quarts of cream skimmed off from the Milky Way. She looked at my rugged features without any expression of fear or repugnance. Indeed, I fancied that I saw a look of deep admiration and affection, such as she had cast at Fergus on the plaza.

'I sat down, and opened my mouth to tell Anabela what she loved to hear – that she was a trust, monopolizing all the loveliness of earth. I opened my mouth, and instead of the usual vibrating words of love and compliment, there came forth a faint wheeze such as a baby with croup might emit. Not a word – not a syllable – not an intelligible sound. I had caught cold in my laryngeal regions when I took my injudicious bath.

'For two hours I sat trying to entertain Anabela. She talked a certain amount, but it was perfunctory and diluted. The nearest approach I made to speech was to formulate a sound like a clam trying to sing "A Life on the Ocean Wave" at low tide. It seemed that Anabela's eyes did not rest upon me as often as usual. I had nothing with which to charm her ears. We looked at pictures and she played the guitar occasionally, very badly. When I left, her parting manner seemed cool – or at least thoughtful.

'This happened for five evenings consecutively.

'On the sixth day she ran away with Fergus McMahan.

'It was known that they fled in a sailing yacht bound for Belize. I was only eight hours behind them in a small steam launch belonging to the Revenue Department.

'Before I sailed, I rushed into the botica of old Manuel Iquito, a half-breed Indian druggist. I could not speak, but I pointed to my throat and made a sound like escaping steam. He began to yawn. In an hour, according to the customs of the country, I would have been waited on. I reached across the counter, seized him by the throat, and pointed again to my own. He yawned once more, and thrust into my hand a small bottle containing a black liquid.

' "Take one small spoonful every two hours," says he.

'I threw him a dollar and skinned for the steamer.

'I steamed into the harbor at Belize thirteen seconds behind the yacht that Anabela and Fergus were on. They started for the shore in a dory just as my skiff was lowered over the side. I tried to order my sailormen to row faster, but the sounds died in my larynx before they came to the light. Then I thought of old Iquito's medicine, and I got out his bottle and took a swallow of it.

'The two boats landed at the same moment. I walked straight up to Anabela and Fergus. Her eyes rested upon me for an instant; then she turned them, full of feeling and confidence, upon Fergus. I knew I could not speak, but I was desperate. In speech lay my only hope. I could not stand beside Fergus and challenge comparison in the way of beauty. Purely involuntarily, my larynx and epiglottis attempted to reproduce the sounds that my mind was calling upon my vocal organs to send forth.

'To my intense surprise and delight the words rolled forth beautifully clear, resonant, exquisitely modulated, full of power, expression, and long-repressed emotion.

' "Señorita Anabela," says I, "may I speak with you aside for a moment?"

'You don't want details about that, do you? Thanks. The old eloquence had come back all right. I led her under a cocoanut palm and put my old verbal spell on her again.

' "Judson," says she, "when you are talking to me I can hear nothing else – I can see nothing else – there is nothing and nobody·else in the world for me."

'Well, that's about all of the story. Anabela went back to Oratama in the steamer with me. I never heard what became of Fergus. I never saw him any more. Anabela is now Mrs. Judson Tate. Has my story bored you much?'

'No,' said I. 'I am always interested in psychological studies. A human heart – and especially a woman's – is a wonderful thing to contemplate.'

'It is,' said Judson Tate. 'And so are the trachea and the bronchial tubes of man. And the larynx, too. Did you ever make a study of the windpipe?'

'Never,' said I. 'But I have taken much pleasure in your story. May I ask after Mrs. Tate, and inquire of her present health and whereabouts.'

'Oh, sure,' said Judson Tate. 'We are living in Bergen Avenue, Jersey City. The climate down in Oratama didn't suit Mrs. T. I don't suppose you ever dissected the arytenoid cartilages of the epiglottis, did you?'

'Why, no,' said I, 'I am no surgeon.'

'Pardon me,' said Judson Tate, 'but every man should know enough of anatomy and therapeutics to safeguard his own health. A sudden cold may set up capillary bronchitis or inflammation of the pulmonary vesicles which may result in a serious affection of the vocal organs.'

'Perhaps so,' said I, with some impatience; 'but that is neither here nor there. Speaking of the strange manifestations of the affection of women, I—'

'Yes, yes,' interrupted Judson Tate, 'they have peculiar ways. But, as I was going to tell you: when I went back to Oratama I found out from Manuel Iquito what was in that mixture he gave me for my lost voice. I told you how quick it cured me. He made that stuff from the *chuchula* plant. Now, look here.'

Judson Tate drew an oblong white pasteboard box from his pocket.

'For any cough,' he said, 'or cold, or hoarseness, or bronchial affection whatsoever, I have here the greatest remedy in the world. You see the formula printed on the box. Each tablet contains licorice, 2 grains; balsam tolu, 1/10 grain; oil of anise, 1/20 minim; oil of tar, 1/60 minim; oleo-resin of cubebs, 1/60 minim; fluid extract of *chuchula*, 1/10 minim.

'I am in New York,' went on Judson Tate, 'for the purpose of organizing a company to market the greatest remedy for throat affections ever discovered. At present I am introducing the lozenges in a small way. I have here a box containing four dozen, which I am selling for the small sum of fifty cents. If you are suffering—'

I got up and went away without a word. I walked slowly up to the little park near my hotel, leaving Judson Tate alone with his conscience. My feelings were lacerated. He had poured gently upon me a story that I might have used. There was a little of the breath of life in it, and some of the synthetic atmosphere that passes, when cunningly tinkered, in the marts. And, at the last it had proven to be a commercial pill, coated with the sugar of fiction. The worst of it was that I could not offer it for sale. Advertising departments and counting-rooms look down upon me. And it would never do for the literary. Therefore I sat upon a bench with other disappointed ones until my eyelids drooped.

I went to my room, and, as my custom is, read for an hour stories in my favorite magazines. This was to get my mind back to art again.

And as I read each story, I threw the magazines sadly and hopelessly, one by one, upon the floor. Each author, without one exception to bring balm to my heart, wrote liltingly and sprightly a story of some particular make of motor-car that seemed to control the sparking plug of his genius.

And when the last one was hurled from me I took heart.

'If readers can swallow so many proprietary automobiles,' I said to myself, 'they ought not to strain at one of Tate's Compound Magic Chuchula Bronchial Lozenges.'

And so if you see this story in print you will understand that business is business, and that if Arts gets very far ahead of Commerce, she will have to get up and hustle.

I may as well add, to make a clean job of it, that you can't buy the *chuchula* plant in the drug stores.

ART AND THE BRONCO

OUT OF THE WILDERNESS HAD COME a painter. Genius, whose coronations alone are democratic, had woven a chaplet of chaparral for the brow of Lonny Briscoe. Art, whose divine woven expression flows impartially from the fingertips of a cowboy or a dilettante emperor, had chosen for a medium the Boy Artist of the San Saba. The outcome, seven feet by twelve of besmeared canvas, stood, gilt-framed, in the lobby of the Capitol.

The legislature was in session; the capital city of that great Western state was enjoying the season of activity and profit that the congregation of the solons bestowed. The boarding houses were corralling the easy dollars of the gamesome lawmakers. The greatest state in the West, an empire in area and resources, had arisen and repudiated the old libel or barbarism, lawbreaking, and bloodshed. Order reigned within her borders. Life and property were as safe there, sir, as anywhere among the corrupt cities of the effete East. Pillow-shams, churches, strawberry feasts and *habeas corpus* flourished. With impunity might the tenderfoot ventilate his 'stovepipe' or his theories of culture. The arts and sciences receive nurture and subsidy. And, therefore, it behooved the legislature of this great state to make appropriation for the purchase of Lonny Briscoe's immortal painting.

Rarely has the San Saba country contributed to the spread of the fine arts. Its sons have excelled in the soldier graces, in the throw of the lariat, the manipulation of the esteemed .45, the intrepidity of the one-card draw, and the nocturnal stimulation of towns from undue lethargy; but, hitherto, it had not been famed as a stronghold of aesthetics. Lonny Briscoe's brush had removed that disability. Here, among the limestone rocks, the succulent cactus, and the drought-parched grass of that arid valley, had been born the Boy Artist. Why he came to woo art is beyond postulation. Beyond doubt, some spore of the afflatus must have sprung up within him in spite of the desert soil of San Saba. The tricksy spirit of creation must have incited him to attempted expression and then have sat hilarious among the white-hot sands of the valley, watching its mischievous work. For Lonny's picture, viewed as a thing of art, was something to have driven away dull care from the bosoms of the critics.

The painting – one might almost say panorama – was designed to portray a typical Western scene, interest culminating in a central animal figure, that of a stampeding steer, life-size, wild-eyed, fiery, breaking away in a mad rush from the herd that, close-ridden by a typical cow puncher, occupied a position somewhat in the right background of the picture. The landscape presented fitting and faithful accessories. Chaparral, mesquite, and pear were distributed in just proportions. A Spanish dagger-plant, with its waxen blossoms in a creamy aggregation as large as a water-bucket, contributed floral beauty and variety. The distance was undulating prairie, bisected by stretches of the intermittent streams peculiar to the region lined with the rich green of live-oak and water-elm. A richly mottled rattlesnake lay coiled beneath a pale green clump of prickly pear in the foreground. A third of the canvas was ultramarine and lake white – the typical Western sky and the flying clouds, rainless and feathery.

Between two plastered pillars in the commodious hallway near the door of the chamber of representatives stood the painting. Citizens and law-makers passed there by twos and groups and sometimes crowds to gaze upon it. Many – perhaps a majority of them – had lived the prairie life and recalled easily the familiar scene. Old cattlemen stood, reminiscent and candidly pleased, chatting with brothers of former camps and trails of the days it brought back to mind. Art critics were few in the town, and there was heard none of that jargon of color, perspective, and feeling such as the East loves to use as a curb and a rod to the pretensions of the artist. 'Twas a great picture, most of them agreed, admiring the gilt frame – larger than any they had ever seen.

Senator Kinney was the picture's champion and sponsor. It was he who so often stepped forward and asserted, with the voice of a bronco buster, that it would be a lasting blot, sir, upon the name of this great state if it should decline to recognize in a proper manner the genius that had so brilliantly transferred to imperishable canvas a scene so typical of the great sources of our state's wealth and prosperity, land – and – er – live-stock.

Senator Kinney represented a section of the state in the extreme West – 400 miles from the San Saba country – but the true lover of art is not limited by metes and bounds. Nor was Senator Mullens, representing the San Saba country, lukewarm in his belief that the state should purchase the painting of his constituent. He was advised that the San Saba country was unanimous in its admiration of the great painting by one of its own denizens. Hundreds of connoisseurs had straddled their broncos and ridden miles to view it before its removal to the capital. Senator Mullens desired reëlection, and he knew the importance of the San Saba vote. He also knew that with the help of Senator Kinney – who was a power in the legislature – the thing could be put through. Now, Senator Kinney had an irrigation bill that he wanted passed for the benefit of his own section, and he knew Senator Mullens could render him valuable aid and information, the San Saba country already enjoying the benefits of similar legislation. With these interests happily dovetailed, wonder at the sudden interest in art at the state capital must, necessarily, be small. Few artists have uncovered their first picture to the world under happier auspices than did Lonny Briscoe.

Senators Kinney and Mullens came to an understanding in the matter of irrigation and art while partaking of long drinks in the café of the Empire Hotel.

'H'm!' said Senator Kinney, 'I don't know. I'm no art critic, but it seems to me the thing won't work. It looks like the worst kind of a chromo to me. I don't want to cast any reflections upon the artistic talent of your constituent, Senator, but I, myself, wouldn't give six bits for the picture – without the frame. How are you going to cram a thing like that down the throat of a legislature that kicks about a little item in the expense bill of six hundred and eighty-one dollars for rubber erasers for only one term? It's wasting time. I'd like to help you, Mullens, but they'd laugh us out of the Senate chamber if we were to try it.'

'But you don't get the point,' said Senator Mullens, in his deliberate tones, tapping Kinney's glass with his long forefinger. 'I have my own doubts as to what the picture is intended to represent, a bullfight or a Japanese allegory, but I want this legislature to make an appropriation to purchase. Of course, the subject of the picture should have been in the state historical line, but it's too late to have the paint scraped off and changed. The state won't miss the money and the picture can be stowed away in a lumber-room where it won't annoy any one. Now, here's the point to work on, leaving art to look after itself – the chap that painted the picture is the grandson of Lucien Briscoe.'

'Say it again,' said Kinney, leaning his head thoughtfully. 'Of the old, original Lucien Briscoe?'

'Of him. "The man who," you know. The man who carved the state out of the wilderness. The man who settled the Indians. The man who cleaned out the horse thieves. The man who refused the crown. The state's favorite son. Do you see the point now?'

'Wrap up the picture,' said Kinney. 'It's as good as sold. Why didn't you say that at first, instead of philandering along about art. I'll resign my seat in the Senate and go back to chain-carrying for the county surveyor the day I can't make this state buy a picture calcimined by a grandson of Lucien Briscoe. Did you ever hear of a special appropriation for the purchase of a home for the daughter of One-Eyed Smothers? Well, that went through like a motion to adjourn, and old One-Eyed never killed half as many Indians as Briscoe did. About what figure had you and the calciminer agreed upon to sandbag the treasury for?'

'I thought,' said Mullens, 'that maybe five hundred —'

'Five hundred!' interrupted Kinney, as he hammered on his glass for a lead pencil and looked around for a waiter. 'Only five hundred for a red steer on the hoof delivered by a grandson of Lucien Briscoe! Where's your state pride, man? Two thousand is what it'll be. You'll introduce the bill and I'll get up on the floor of the Senate and wave the scalp of every Indian old Lucien ever murdered. Let's see, there was something else proud and foolish he did, wasn't there? Oh, yes; he declined all emoluments and benefits he was entitled to. Refused his head-right and veteran donation certificates. Could have been governor, but wouldn't. Declined a pension. Now's the state's chance to pay up. It'll have to take the picture, but then it deserves some punishment for keeping the Briscoe family waiting so long. We'll bring this thing up about the middle of the month, after the tax bill is settled. Now, Mullens, you send over, as soon as you can, and get me the figures on the cost of those irrigation ditches and the statistics about the increased production per acre. I'm going to need you when that bill of mine comes up. I reckon we'll be able to pull along pretty well together this session and maybe others to come, eh, Senator?'

Thus did fortune elect to smile upon the Boy Artist of the San Saba. Fate had already done her share when she arranged his atoms in the cosmogony of creation as the grandson of Lucien Briscoe.

The original Briscoe had been a pioneer both as to territorial occupation and in certain acts prompted by a great and simple heart. He had been one of the first settlers and crusaders against the wild forces of nature, the savage and the shallow politician. His name and memory were revered equally with any upon the list comprising Houston, Boone, Crockett, Clark, and Green. He had lived simply, independently, and unvexed by ambition. Even a less shrewd man than Senator Kinney could have prophesied that his state would hasten to honor and reward his grandson, come out of the chaparral at even so late a day.

And so, before the great picture by the door of the chamber of representatives at frequent times for many days could be found the breezy, robust form of Senator Kinney and be heard his clarion voice reciting the past deeds of Lucien Briscoe in connection with the handiwork of his grandson. Senator Mullens's work was more subdued in sight and sound, but directed along identical lines.

Then, as the day for the introduction of the bill for appropriation draws nigh, up from the San Saba country rides Lonny Briscoe and a loyal lobby of cowpunchers, bronco-back, to boost the cause of art and glorify the name of friendship, for Lonny is one of them, a knight of stirrup and chaparreras, as handy with the lariat and .45 as he is with brush and palette.

On a March afternoon the lobby dashed with a whoop, into town. The cowpunchers had adjusted their garb suitable from that prescribed for the range to the more conventional requirements of town. They had conceded their leather chaparreras and transferred their six-shooters and belts from their persons to the horns of their saddles. Among them rode Lonny, a youth of twenty-three, brown, solemn-faced, ingenuous, bowlegged, reticent, bestriding Hot Tamales, the most sagacious cow pony west of the Mississippi. Senator Mullens had informed him of the bright prospects of the situation; had even mentioned – so great was his confidence in the capable Kinney – the price that the state would, in all likelihood, pay. It seemed to Lonny that fame and fortune were in his hands. Certainly, a spark of the divine fire was in the little brown centaur's breast, for he was counting the two thousand dollars as but a means to future development of his talent. Some day he would paint a picture even greater than this – one, say, twelve feet by twenty, full of scope and atmosphere and action.

During the three days that yet intervened before the coming of the date fixed for the introduction of the bill, the centaur lobby did valiant service. Coatless, spurred, weather-tanned, full of enthusiasm expressed in bizarre terms, they loafed in front of the painting with tireless zeal. Reasoning not unshrewdly, they estimated that their comments upon its fidelity to nature would be received as expert evidence. Loudly they praised the skill of the painter whenever there were ears near to which such evidence might be profitably addressed. Lem Perry, the leader of the claque, had a somewhat set speech, being uninventive in the construction of new phrases.

'Look at the two-year-old, now,' he would say, waving a cinnamon-brown hand toward the salient point of the picture. 'Why, dang my hide, the critter's alive. I can jest her him "lumpety-lump," a-cuttin' away from the herd, pretendin' he's skeered. He's a mean scamp, that there steer. Look at his eyes a-wallin' and his tail a-wavin'. He's true and nat'ral to life. He's jest hankerin' fur a cow pony to round him up and send him scootin' back to the bunch. Dang my hide! jest look at that tail of his'n a-wavin'. Never knowed a steer to wave his tail any other way, dang my hide ef I did.'

Jud Shelby, while admitting the excellence of the steer, resolutely confined himself to open admiration of the landscape, to the end that the entire picture receive its meed of praise.

'That piece of range,' he declared, 'is a dead ringer for Dead Hoss Valley. Same grass, same lay of the land, same old Whipper-will Creek skallyhootin' in and out of them motts of timber. Them buzzards on the left is circlin' 'round over Sam Kildrake's old paint hoss that killed hisself overdrinkin' on a hot day. You can't see the hoss for that mott of ellums on the creek, but he's thar. Anybody that was goin' to look for Dead Hoss Valley and come across this picture, why, he's jest light off'n his bronco and hunt a place to camp.'

Skinny Rogers, wedded to comedy, conceived a complimentary little piece of acting that never failed to make an impression. Edging quite near to the picture, he would suddenly, at favorable moments, emit a piercing and awful 'Yi-yi!' leap high and away, coming down with a great stamp of heels and whirring of rowels upon the stone-flagged floor.

'Jeeming Christopher!' – so ran his lines – 'thought that rattler was a gin-u-ine one. Ding baste my skin if I didn't. Seemed to me I heard him rattle. Look at the blamed, unconverted insect a-layin' under that pear. Little more, and somebody would a-been snake-bit.'

With these artful dodges, contributed by Lonny's faithful coterie, with the sonorous Kinney perpetually sounding the picture's merits, and with the solvent prestige of the pioneer Briscoe covering it like a precious varnish, it seemed that the San Saba country could not fail to add a reputation as an art centre to its well-known superiority in steer-roping contests and achievements with the precarious busted flush. Thus was created for the picture an atmosphere, due rather to externals than to the artist's brush, but through it the people seemed to gaze with more admiration. There was a magic in the name of Briscoe that counted high against faulty technique and crude coloring. The old Indian fighter and wolf slayer would have smiled grimly in his happy hunting grounds had he known that his dilettante ghost was thus figuring as an art patron two generations after his uninspired existence.

Came the day when the Senate was expected to pass the bill of Senator Mullens appropriating two thousand dollars for the purchase of the picture. The gallery of the Senate chamber was early pre-empted by Lonny and the San Saba lobby. In the front row of chairs they sat, wild-haired, self-conscious, jingling, creaking, and rattling, subdued by the majesty of the council hall.

The bill was introduced, went to the second reading, and then Senator Mullens spoke for it dryly, tediously, and at length. Senator Kinney then arose, and the welkin seized the bell-rope preparatory to ring. Oratory was at that time a living thing; the world had not quite come to measure its questions by geometry and the multiplication table. It was the day of the silver tongue, the sweeping gesture, the decorative apostrophe, the moving peroration.

The Senator spoke. The San Saba contingent sat, breathing hard, in the gallery, its disordered hair hanging down to its eyes, its sixteen-ounce hats shifted restlessly from knee to knee. Below, the distinguished Senators either lounged at their desks with the abandon of proven statesmanship or maintained correct attitudes indicative of a first term.

Senator Kinney spoke for an hour. History was his theme – history mitigated by patriotism and sentiment. He referred casually to the picture in the outer hall – it was unnecessary, he said, to dilate upon its merits – the Senators had seen for themselves. The painter of the picture was the grandson of Lucien Briscoe. Then came the word-pictures of Briscoe's life set forth in thrilling colors. His rude and venturesome life, his simple-minded love for the commonwealth he helped to upbuild, his contempt for rewards and praise, his extreme and sturdy independence, and the great services he had rendered the state. The subject of the oration was Lucien Briscoe; the painting stood in the background serving simply as a means, now happily brought forward, through which the state might bestow a tardy recompense upon the descendant of its favorite son. Frequent enthusiastic applause from the Senators testified to the well reception of the sentiment.

The bill passed without an opposing vote. To-morrow it would be taken up by the House. Already was it fixed to glide through that body on rubber tires, Blandford, Grayson, and Plummer, all wheel-horses and orators, and provided with plentiful memoranda concerning the deeds of pioneer Briscoe, had agreed to furnish the motive power.

The San Saba lobby and its *protégé* stumbled awkwardly down the stairs and out into the Capitol yard. Then they herded closely and gave one yell of triumph. But one of them – Buck-Kneed Summers it was – hit the key with the thoughtful remark:

'She cut the mustard,' he said, 'all right. I reckon they're goin' to buy Lon's steer. I ain't right much on the parlyment'ry but I gather that's what the signs added up. But she seems to me, Lonny, the argyment ran principal to grandfather, instead of paint. It's reasonable calculatin' that you want to be glad you got the Briscoe brand on you, my son.'

That remark clinched in Lonny's mind an unpleasant, vague suspicion to the same effect. His reticence increased, and he gathered grass from the ground, chewing it pensively. The picture as a picture had been humiliatingly absent from the Senator's arguments. The painter had been held up as a grandson, pure and simple. While this was gratifying on certain lines, it made art look little and slab-sided. The Boy Artist was thinking.

The hotel Lonny stopped at was near the Capitol. It was near to the one o'clock dinner hour when the appropriation had been passed by the Senate. The hotel clerk told Lonny that a famous artist from New York had arrived in town that day and was in the hotel. He was on his way westward to New Mexico to study the effect of sunlight upon the ancient walls of the Zuñis. Modern stone reflects light. Those ancient building materials absorb it. The artist wanted this effect in a picture he was painting and was travelling two thousand miles to get it.

Lonny sought this man out after dinner and told his story. The artist was an unhealthy man, kept alive by genius and indifference to life. He went with Lonny to the Capitol and stood there before the picture. The artist pulled his beard and looked unhappy.

'Should like to have your sentiments,' said Lonny, 'just as they run out of the pen.'

'It's the way they'll come,' said the painter man. 'I took three different kinds of medicine before dinner – by the tablespoonful. The taste still lingers. I am primed for telling the truth. You want to know if the picture is, or if it isn't?'

'Right,' said Lonny. 'Is it wool or cotton? Should I paint some more or cut it out and ride herd a-plenty?'

'I heard a rumor during pie,' said the artist, 'that the state is about to pay you two thousand dollars for this picture.'

'It's passed the Senate,' said Lonny, 'and the House rounds it up to-morrow.'

'That's lucky,' said the pale man. 'Do you carry a rabbit's foot?'

'No,' said Lonny, 'but it seems I had a grandfather. He's considerable mixed up in the color scheme. It took me a year to paint that picture. Is she entirely awful or not? Some says, now, that that steer's tail ain't badly drawed. They think it's proportioned nice. Tell me.'

The artist glanced at Lonny's wiry figure and nut-brown skin. Something stirred him to a passing irritation.

'For Art's sake, son,' he said fractiously, 'don't spend any more money for paint. It isn't a picture at all. It's a gun. You hold up the state with it, if you like, and get your two thousand, but don't get in front of any more canvas. Live under it. Buy a couple of hundred ponies with the money – I'm told they're that cheap – and ride, ride, ride. Fill your lungs and eat and sleep and be happy. No more pictures. You look healthy. That's genius. Cultivate it.' He looked at his watch. 'Twenty minutes to three. Four capsules and one tablet at three. That's all you wanted to know, isn't it?'

At three o'clock the cowpunchers rode up for Lonny, bringing Hot Tamales, saddled. Traditions must be observed. To celebrate the passage of the bill by the Senate the gang must ride wildly through the town, creating uproar and excitement. Liquor must be partaken of, the suburbs shot up, and the glory of the San Saba country vociferously proclaimed. A part of the programme had been carried out in the saloons on the way up.

Lonny mounted Hot Tamales, the accomplished little beast prancing with fire and intelligence. He was glad to feel Lonny's bowlegged grip against his ribs again. Lonny was his friend, and he was willing to do things for him.

'Come on, boys,' said Lonny, urging Hot Tamales into a gallop with his knees. With a whoop, the inspired lobby tore after him through the dust. Lonny led his cohorts straight for the Capitol. With a wild yell, the gang indorsed his now evident intention of riding into it. Hooray for San Saba!

Up the six broad, limestone steps clattered the broncos of the cowpunchers. Into the resounding hallway they pattered, scattering in dismay those passing on foot. Lonny, in the lead, shoved Hot Tamales direct for the great picture. At that hour a downpouring, soft light from the second-story windows bathed the big canvas. Against the darker background of the hall the painting stood out with valuable effect. In spite of the defects of the art you could almost fancy that you gazed out upon a landscape. You might well flinch a step from the convincing figure of the life-sized steer stampeding across the grass. Perhaps it thus seemed to Hot Tamales. The scene was in his line. Perhaps he only obeyed the will of his rider. His ears pricked up; he snorted. Lonny leaned forward in the saddle and elevated his elbows, wing-like. Thus signals the cowpuncher to his steed to launch himself full speed ahead. Did Hot Tamales fancy he saw a steer, red and cavorting, that should be headed off and driven back to herd? There was a fierce clatter of hoofs, a rush, a gathering of steely flank muscles, a leap to the jerk of the bridle rein, and Hot Tamales, with Lonny bending low in the saddle to dodge the top of the frame, ripped through the great canvas like a shell from a mortar, leaving the cloth hanging in ragged shreds about a monstrous hole.

Quickly Lonny pulled up his pony, and rounded the pillars. Spectators came running, too astounded to add speech to the commotion. The sergeant-at-arms of the House came forth, frowned, looked ominous, and then grinned. Many of the legislators crowded out to observe the tumult. Lonny's cowpunchers were stricken to silent horror by his mad deed.

Senator Kinney happened to be among the earliest to emerge. Before he could speak Lonny leaned in his saddle as Hot Tamales pranced, pointed his quirt at the Senator, and said, calmly:

'That was a fine speech you made to-day, mister, but you might as well let up on that 'propriation business. I ain't askin' the state to give me nothin'. I thought I had a picture to sell to it, but it wasn't one. You said a heap of things about Grandfather Briscoe that makes me kind of proud I'm his grandson. Well, the Briscoes ain't takin' presents from the state yet. Anybody can have the frame that wants it. Hit her up, boys.'

Away scuttled the San Saba delegation out of the hall, down the steps, along the dusty street.

Halfway to the San Saba country they camped that night. At bed-time Lonny stole away from the campfire and sought Hot Tamales, placidly eating grass at the end of his stake rope. Lonny hung upon his neck, and his art aspirations went forth forever in one long, regretful sigh. But as he thus made renunciation his breath formed a word or two.

'You was the only one, Tamales, what seen anything in it. It *did* look like a steer, didn't it, old hoss?'

PHOEBE

'YOU ARE A MAN OF MANY novel adventures and varied enterprises,' I said to Captain Patricio Maloné. 'Do you believe that the possible element of good luck or bad luck – if there is such a thing as luck – has influenced your career or persisted for or against you to such an extent that you were forced to attribute results to the operation of the aforesaid good luck or bad luck?'

This question (of almost the dull insolence of legal phraseology) was put while we sat in Rousselin's little red-tiled café near Congo Square in New Orleans.

Brown-faced, white-hatted, finger-ringed captains of adventure came often to Rousselin's for the cognac. They came from sea and land, and were chary of relating the things they had seen – not because they were more wonderful than the fantasies of the Ananiases of print, but because they were so different. And I was a perpetual wedding-guest, always striving to cast my buttonhole over the finger of one of these mariners of fortune. This Captain Maloné was a Hiberno-Iberian creole who had gone to and fro in the earth and walked up and down in it. He looked like any other well-dressed man of thirty-five whom you might meet, except that he was hopelessly weather-tanned, and wore on his chain an ancient ivory-and-gold Peruvian charm against evil, which has nothing at all to do with his story.

'My answer to your question,' said the captain, smiling, 'will be to tell you the story of Bad-Luck Kearny. That is, if you don't mind hearing it.'

My reply was to pound on the table for Rousselin.

'Strolling along Tchoupitoulas Street one night,' began Captain Maloné, 'I noticed, without especially taxing my interest, a small man walking rapidly toward me. He stepped upon a wooden cellar door, crashed through it, and disappeared. I rescued him from a heap of soft coal below. He dusted himself briskly, swearing fluently in a mechanical tone, as an underpaid actor recites the gipsy's curse. Gratitude and the dust in his throat seemed to call for fluids to clear them away. His desire for liquidation was expressed so heartily that I went with him to a café down the street where we had some vile vermouth and bitters.

'Looking across that little table I had my first clear sight of Francis Kearny. He was about five feet seven, but as tough as a cypress knee. His hair was darkest red, his mouth such a mere slit that you wondered how the flood of his words came rushing from it. His eyes were the brightest and lightest blue and the hopefullest that I ever saw. He gave the double impression that he was at bay and that you had better not crowd him further.

' "Just in from a gold-hunting expedition on the coast of Costa Rica," he explained. "Second mate of a banana steamer told me the natives were panning out enough from the beach sands to buy all the rum, red calico, and parlor melodeons in the world. The day I got there a syndicate named Incorporated Jones gets a government concession to all minerals from a given point. For a next choice I take coast fever and count green and blue lizards for six weeks in a grass hut. I had to be notified when I was well, for the reptiles were actually there. Then I shipped back as third cook on a Norwegian tramp that blew up her boiler two miles below Quarantine. I was due to bust through that cellar door here to-night, so I hurried the rest of the way up the river, roustabouting on a lower coast packet that made a landing for every fisherman that wanted a plug of tobacco. And now I'm here for what comes next. And it'll be along, it'll be along," said this queer Mr. Kearny; "it'll be along on the beams of my bright but not very particular star."

'From the first the personality of Kearny charmed me. I saw in him the bold heart, the restless nature, and the valiant front against the buffets of fate that make his countrymen such valuable comrades in risk and adventure. And just then I was wanting such men. Moored at a fruit company's pier I had a 500-ton steamer ready to sail the next day with a cargo of sugar, lumber, and corrugated iron for a port in – well, let us call the country Esperando – it has not been long ago, and the name of Patricio Maloné is still spoken there when its unsettled politics are discussed. Beneath the sugar and iron were packed a thousand Winchester rifles. In Aguas Frias, the capital, Don Rafael Valdevia, Minister of War, Esperando's greatest-hearted and most able patriot, awaited my coming. No doubt you have heard, with a smile, of the insignificant wars and uprisings in those little tropic republics. They make but a faint clamor against the din of great nations' battles; but down there, under all the ridiculous uniforms and petty diplomacy and senseless countermarching and intrigue, are to be found statesmen and patriots. Don

Rafael Valdevia was one. His great ambition was to raise Esperando into peace and honest prosperity and the respect of the serious nations. So he waited for my rifles in Aguas Frias. But one would think I am trying to win a recruit in you! No; it was Francis Kearny I wanted. And so I told him, speaking long over our execrable vermouth, breathing the stifling odor from garlic and tarpaulins, which, as you know, is the distinctive flavor of cafés in the lower slant of our city. I spoke of the tyrant President Cruz and the burdens that his greed and insolent cruelty laid upon the people. And at that Kearny's tears flowed. And then I dried them with a picture of the fat rewards that would be ours when the oppressor should be overthrown and the wise and generous Valdevia in his seat. Then Kearny leaped to his feet and wrung my hand with the strength of a roustabout. He was mine, he said, till the last minion of the hated despot was hurled from the highest peaks of the Cordilleras into the sea.

'I paid the score and we went out. Near the door Kearny's elbow overturned an upright glass showcase, smashing it into little bits. I paid the storekeeper the price he asked.

' "Come to my hotel for the night," I said to Kearny. "We sail to-morrow at noon."

'He agreed; but on the sidewalk he fell to cursing again in the dull, monotonous, glib way that he had done when I pulled him out of the coal cellar.

' "Captain," said he, "before we go any further, it's no more than fair to tell you that I'm known from Baffin's Bay to Tierra del Fuego as 'Bad-Luck' Kearny. And I'm It. Everything I get into goes up in the air except a balloon. Every bet I ever made I lost except when I coppered it. Every boat I ever sailed on sank except the submarines. Everything I was ever interested in went to pieces except a patent bombshell that I invented. Everything I ever took hold of and tried to run I ran into the ground except when I tried to plough. And that's why they call me Bad-Luck Kearny. I thought I'd tell you."

' "Bad-luck," said I, "or what goes by the name, may now and then tangle the affairs of any man. But if it persists beyond the estimate of what we may call the 'averages' there must be a cause for it."

' "There is," said Kearny, emphatically, "and when we walk another square I will show it to you."

'Surprised, I kept by his side until we came to Canal Street and out into the middle of its great width.

'Kearny seized me by an arm and pointed a tragic fore-finger at a rather brilliant star that shone steadily about thirty degrees over the horizon.

' "That's Saturn," said he, "the star that presides over bad luck and evil and disappointment and nothing doing and trouble. I was born under that star. Every move I make, up bobs Saturn and blocks it. He's the hoodoo planet of the heavens. They say he's 73,000 miles in diameter and no solider body than split-pea soup, and he's got as many disreputable and malignant rings as Chicago. Now, what kind of a star is that to be born under?"

'I asked Kearny where he had obtained all this astonishing knowledge.

' "From Azrath, the great astrologer of Cleveland, Ohio," said he. "That man looked at a glass ball and told me my name before I'd taken a chair. He prophesied the date of my birth and death before I'd said a word. And then he cast my horoscope, and the sidereal system socked me in the solar plexus.

It was bad luck for Francis Kearny from A to Izard and for his friends that were implicated with him. For that I gave up ten dollars. This Azrath was sorry, but he respected his profession too much to read the heavens wrong for any man. It was night time, and he showed me which Saturn was, and how to find it in different balconies and longitudes.

' "But Saturn wasn't all. He was only the man higher up. He furnishes so much bad luck that they allow him a gang of deputy sparklers to help hand it out. They're circulating and revolving and hanging around the main supply all the time, each one throwing the hoodoo on his own particular district.

' "You see that ugly little red star about eight inches above and to the right of Saturn?" Kearny asked me. "Well, that's her. That's Phoebe. She's got me in charge. 'By the day of your birth,' says Azrath to me, 'your life is subjected to the influence of Saturn. By the hour and minute of it you must dwell under the sway and direct authority of Phoebe, the ninth satellite.' So said this Azrath." Kearny shook his fist viciously skyward. "Curse her, she's done her work well," said he. "Ever since I was astrologized, bad luck has followed me like my shadow, as I told you. And for many years before. Now, Captain, I've told you my handicap as a man should. If you're afraid this evil star of mine might cripple your scheme, leave me out of it."

'I reassured Kearny as well as I could. I told him that for the time we would banish both astrology and astronomy from our heads. The manifest valor and enthusiasm of the man drew me. "Let us see what a little courage and diligence will do against bad luck," I said. "We will sail to-morrow for Esperando."

'Fifty miles down the Mississippi our steamer broke her rudder. We sent for a tug to tow us back and lost three days. When we struck the blue waters of the Gulf, all the storm clouds of the Atlantic seemed to have concentrated above us. We thought surely to sweeten those leaping waves with our sugar, and to stack our arms and lumber on the floor of the Mexican Gulf.

'Kearny did not seek to cast off one iota of the burden of our danger from the shoulders of his fatal horoscope. He weathered every storm on deck, smoking a black pipe, to keep which alight rain and sea-water seemed but as oil. And he shook his fist at the black clouds behind which his baleful star winked its unseen eye. When the skies cleared one evening, he reviled his malignant guardian with grim humor.

' "On watch, aren't you, you red-headed vixen? Out making it hot for little Francis Kearny and his friends, according to Hoyle. Twinkle, twinkle, little devil! You're a lady, aren't you – dogging a man with bad luck just because he happened to be born while your boss was floorwalker. Get busy and sink the ship, you one-eyed banshee. Phoebe! H'm! Sounds as mild as a milkmaid. You can't judge a woman by her name. Why couldn't I have had a man star? I can't make the remarks to Phoebe that I could to a man. Oh, Phoebe, you be – blasted!"

'For eight days gales and squalls and water-spouts beat us from our course. Five days only should have landed us in Esperando. Our Jonah swallowed the bad credit of it with appealing frankness; but that scarcely lessened the hardships our cause was made to suffer.

'At last one afternoon we steamed into the calm estuary of the little Rio Escondido. Three miles up this we crept, feeling for the shallow channel between the low banks that were crowded to the edge with gigantic trees and riotous vegetation. Then our whistle gave a little toot, and in five minutes we heard a shout and Carlos – my brave Carlos Quintana – crashed through the tangled vines waving his cap madly for joy.

'A hundred yards away was his camp, where three hundred chosen patriots of Esperando were awaiting our coming. For a month Carlos had been drilling them there in the tactics of war, and filling them with the spirit of revolution and liberty.

' "My Captain – *compadre mío!*" shouted Carlos, while yet my boat was being lowered. "You should see them in the drill by *companies* – in the column wheel – in the march by fours – they are superb! Also in the manual of arms – but, alas! performed only with sticks of bamboo. The guns, *captain* – say that you have brought the guns!'

' "A thousand Winchesters, Carlos," I called to him. "And two Gatlings."

' "*Válgame Dios!*" he cried, throwing his cap in the air. "We shall sweep the world!"

'At that moment Kearny tumbled from the steamer's side into the river. He could not swim, so the crew threw him a rope and drew him back aboard. I caught his eye and his look of pathetic but still bright and undaunted consciousness of his guilty luck. I told myself that although he might be a man to shun, he was also one to be admired.

'I gave orders to the sailing-master that the arms, ammunition, and provisions were to be landed at once. That was easy in the steamer's boats, except for the two Gatling guns. For their transportation ashore we carried a stout flatboat, brought for the purpose in the steamer's hold.

'In the meantime I walked with Carlos to the camp and made the soldiers a little speech in Spanish, which they received with enthusiasm; and then I had some wine and a cigarette in Carlos's tent. Later we walked back to the river to see how the unloading was being conducted.

'The small arms and provisions were already ashore, and the petty officers had squads of men conveying them to camp. One Gatling had been safely landed; the other was just being hoisted over the side of the vessel as we arrived. I noticed Kearny darting about on board, seeming to have the ambition of ten men, and to be doing the work of five. I think his zeal bubbled over when he saw Carlos and me. A rope's end was swinging loose from some part of the tackle. Kearny leaped impetuously and caught it. There was a crackle and a hiss and a smoke of scorching hemp, and the Gatling dropped straight as a plummet through the bottom of the flatboat and buried itself in twenty feet of water and five feet of river mud.

'I turned my back on the scene. I heard Carlos's loud cries as if from some extreme grief too poignant for words. I heard the complaining murmur of the crew and the maledictions of Torres, the sailing-master – I could not bear to look.

'By night some degree of order had been restored in camp. Military rules were not drawn strictly, and the men were grouped about the fires of their several messes, playing games of chance, singing their native songs, or discussing with voluble animation the contingencies of our march upon the capital.

'To my tent, which had been pitched for me close to that of my chief lieutenant, came Kearny, indomitable, smiling, bright-eyed, bearing no traces of the buffets of his evil star. Rather was his aspect that of a heroic martyr whose tribulations were so high-sourced and glorious that he even took a splendor and a prestige from them.

' "Well, Captain," said he, "I guess you realize that Bad-Luck Kearny is still on deck. It was a shame, now, about that gun. She only needed to be slewed two inches to clear the rail; and that's why I grabbed that rope's end. Who'd have thought that a sailor – even a Sicilian lubber on a banana coaster – would have fastened a line in a bow-knot? Don't think I'm trying to dodge the responsibility, Captain. It's my luck."

' "There are men, Kearny," said I, gravely, "who pass through life blaming upon luck and chance the mistakes that result from their own faults and incompetency. I do not say that you are such a man. But if all your mishaps are traceable to that tiny star, the sooner we endow our colleges with chairs of moral astronomy, the better."

' "It isn't the size of the star that counts," said Kearny; "it's the quality. Just the way it is with women. That's why they gave the biggest planets masculine names, and the little stars feminine ones – to even things up when it comes to getting their work in. Suppose they had called my star Agamemnon or Bill McCarty or something like that instead of Phoebe. Every time one of those old boys touched their calamity button and sent me down one of their wireless pieces of bad luck, I could talk back and tell 'em what I thought of 'em in suitable terms. But you can't address such remarks to a Phoebe."

' "It pleases you to make a joke of it, Kearny," said I, without smiling. "But it is no joke to me to think of my Gatling mired in the river ooze."

' "As to that," said Kearny, abandoning his light mood at once, "I have already done what I could. I have had some experience in hoisting stone in quarries. Torres and I have already spliced three hawsers and stretched them from the steamer's stern to a tree on shore. We will rig a tackle and have the gun on terra firma before noon to-morrow."

'One could not remain long at outs with Bad-Luck Kearny.

' "Once more," said I to him, "we will waive this question of luck. Have you ever had experience in drilling raw troops?"

' "I was first sergeant and drill-master,' said Kearny, "in the Chilean army for one year. And captain of artillery for another."

' "What became of your command?" I asked.

' "Shot down to a man," said Kearny, "during the revolutions against Balmaceda."

'Somehow the misfortunes of the evil-starred one seemed to turn to me their comedy side. I lay back upon my goat's-hide cot and laughed until the woods echoed. Kearny grinned. "I told you how it was," he said.

' "To-morrow," I said, "I shall detail one hundred men under your command for manual-of-arms drill and company evolutions. You will rank as lieutenant. Now, for God's sake, Kearny," I urged him, "try to combat this superstition if it is one. Bad luck may be like any other visitor – preferring to stop where it is expected. Get your mind off stars. Look upon Esperando as your planet of good fortune."

' "I thank you, Captain," said Kearny quietly. "I will try to make it the best handicap I ever ran."

'By noon the next day the submerged Gatling was rescued, as Kearny had promised. Then Carlos and Manuel Ortiz and Kearny (my lieutenants) distributed Winchesters among the troops and put them through an incessant rifle drill. We fired no shots, blank or solid, for of all coasts Esperando is the stillest; and we had no desire to sound any warnings in the ear of that corrupt government until they should carry with them the message of Liberty and the downfall of Oppression.

'In the afternoon came a mule-rider bearing a written message to me from Don Rafael Valdevia in the capital, Aguas Frias.

'Whenever that man's name comes to my lips, words of tribute to his greatness, his noble simplicity, and his conspicuous genius follow irrepressibly. He was a traveller, a student of peoples and governments, a master of sciences, a poet, an orator, a leader, a soldier, a critic of the world's campaigns and the idol of the people of Esperando. I had been honored by his friendship for years. It was I who first turned his mind to the thought that he should leave for his monument a new Esperando – a country freed from the rule of unscrupulous tyrants, and a people made happy and prosperous by wise and impartial legislation. When he had consented he threw himself into the cause with the undivided zeal with which he endowed all of his acts. The coffers of his fortune were opened to those of us to whom were entrusted the secret moves of the game. His popularity was already so great that he had practically forced President Cruz to offer him the portfolio of Minister of War.

'The time, Don Rafael said in his letter, was ripe. Success, he prophesied, was certain. The people were beginning to clamor publicly against Cruz's misrule. Bands of citizens in the capital were even going about of nights hurling stones at public buildings and expressing their dissatisfaction. A bronze statue of President Cruz in the Botanical Gardens had been lassoed about the neck and overthrown. It only remained for me to arrive with my force and my thousand rifles, and for himself to come forward and proclaim himself the people's savior, to overthrow Cruz in a single day. There would be but a half-hearted resistance from the six hundred government troops stationed in the capital. The country was ours. He presumed that by this time my steamer had arrived at Quintana's camp. He proposed the eighteenth of July for the attack. That would give us six days in which to strike camp and march to Aguas Frias. In the meantime Don Rafael remained my good friend and *compadre en la causa de la libertad*.

'On the morning of the 14th we began our march toward the sea-following range of mountains, over the sixty-mile trail to the capital. Our small arms and provisions were laden on pack mules. Twenty men harnessed to each Gatling gun rolled them smoothly along the flat, alluvial lowlands. Our troops, well shod and well fed, moved with alacrity and heartiness. I and my three lieutenants were mounted on the tough mountain ponies of the country.

'A mile out of camp one of the pack mules, becoming stubborn, broke away from the train and plunged from the path into the thicket. The alert Kearny spurred quickly after it and intercepted its flight. Rising in his stirrups, he released one foot and bestowed upon the mutinous animal a hearty kick. The mule tottered and fell with a crash broadside upon the ground. As we gathered around it, it walled its great eyes almost humanly toward Kearny and expired. That was bad; but worse, to our minds, was the concomitant disaster. Part of the mule's burden had been one hundred pounds of the finest coffee to be had in the tropics. The bag burst and spilled the priceless brown mass of the ground berries among the dense vines and weeds of the swampy land. *Mala suerte!* When you take away from an Esperandan his coffee, you abstract his patriotism and 50 per cent. of his value as a soldier.

The men began to rake up the precious stuff; but I beckoned Kearny back along the trail where they would not hear. The limit had been reached.

'I took from my pocket a wallet of money and drew out some bills.

' "Mr. Kearny," said I, "here are some funds belonging to Don Rafael Valdevia, which I am expending in his cause. I know of no better service it can buy for him than this. Here is one hundred dollars. Luck or no luck, we part company here. Star or no star, calamity seems to travel by your side. You will return to the steamer. She touches at Amotapa to discharge her lumber and iron, and then puts back to New Orleans. Hand this note to the sailing-master, who will give you passage." I wrote on a leaf torn from my book, and placed it and the money in Kearny's hand.

' "Good-bye," I said, extending my own. "It is not that I am displeased with you; but there is no place in this expedition for – let us say, the Señorita Phoebe." I said this with a smile, trying to smooth the thing for him. "May you have better luck, *compañero*."

'Kearny took the money and the paper.

' "It was just a little touch," said he, "just a little lift with the toe of my boot – but what's the odds? – that blamed mule would have died if I had only dusted his ribs with a powder puff. It was my luck. Well, Captain, I would have liked to be in that little fight with you over in Aguas Frias. Success to the cause. *Adiós!*"

'He turned around and set off down the trail without looking back. The unfortunate mule's pack-saddle was transferred to Kearny's pony, and we again took up the march.

'Four days we journeyed over the foot-hills and mountains, fording icy torrents, winding around the crumbling brows of ragged peaks, creeping along the rocky flanges that overlooked awful precipices, crawling breathlessly over tottering bridges that crossed bottomless chasms.

'On the evening of the seventeenth we camped by a little stream on the bare hills five miles from Aguas Frias. At daybreak we were to take up the march again.

'At midnight I was standing outside my tent inhaling the fresh cold air. The stars were shining bright in the cloudless sky, giving the heavens their proper aspect of illimitable depth in distance when viewed from the vague darkness of the blotted earth. Almost at its zenith was the planet Saturn; and with a half-smile I observed the sinister red sparkle of his malignant attendant – the demon star of Kearny's ill luck. And then my thoughts strayed across the hills to the scene of our coming triumph where the heroic and noble Don Rafael awaited our coming to set a new and shining star in the firmament of nations.

'I heard a slight rustling in the deep grass to my right. I turned and saw Kearny coming toward me. He was ragged and dew-drenched and limping. His hat and one boot were gone. About one foot he had tied some makeshift of cloth and grass. But his manner as he approached was that of a man who knows his own virtues well enough to be superior to rebuffs.

' "Well, sir," I said, staring at him coldly, "if there is anything in persistence, I see no reason why you should not succeed in wrecking and ruining us yet."

' "I kept half a day's journey behind," said Kearny fishing out a stone from the covering of his lame foot, "so the bad luck wouldn't touch you. I couldn't help it, Captain; I wanted to be in on this game. It was a pretty tough trip, especially in the department of the commissary. In the low grounds there were always bananas and oranges. Higher up it was worse; but your men left a good deal of goat meat hanging on the bushes in the camps. Here's your hundred dollars. You're nearly there now, Captain. Let me in on the scrapping to-morrow."

' "Not for a hundred times a hundred would I have the tiniest thing go wrong with my plans now," I said, "whether caused by evil planets or the blunders of mere man. But yonder is Augas Frias, five miles away, and a clear road. I am of the mind to defy Saturn and all his satellites to spoil our success now. At any rate, I will not turn away to-night as weary a traveller and as good a soldier as you are, Lieutenant Kearny. Manuel Ortiz's tent is there by the brightest fire. Rout him out and tell him to supply you with food and blankets and clothes. We march again at daybreak."

'Kearny thanked me briefly but feeling and moved away.

'He had gone scarcely a dozen steps when a sudden flash of bright light illumined the surrounding hills; a sinister, growing, hissing sound like escaping steam filled my ears. Then followed a roar as of distant thunder, which grew louder every instant. This terrifying noise culminated in a tremendous explosion, which seemed to rock the hills as an earthquake would; the illumination waxed to a glare so fierce that I clapped my hands to my eyes to save them. I thought the end of the world had come. I could think of no natural phenomenon that would explain it. My wits were staggering. The deafening explosion trailed off into the rumbling roar that had preceded it; and through this I heard the frightened shouts of my troops as they stumbled from their resting places and rushed wildly about. Also I heard the harsh tones of Kearny's voice crying: "They'll blame it on me, of course, and what the devil it is, it's not Francis Kearny that can give you an answer."

'I opened my eyes. The hills were still there, dark and solid. It had not been, then, a volcano or an earthquake. I looked up at the sky and saw a comet-like trail crossing the zenith and extending westward – a fiery trail waning fainter and narrower each moment.

' "A meteor!" I called aloud. "A meteor has fallen. There is no danger."

'And then all other sounds were drowned by a great shout from Kearny's throat. He had raised both hands above his head and was standing tiptoe.

' "PHOEBE'S GONE!" he cried, with all his lungs. "She's busted and gone to hell. Look, Captain, the little red-headed hoodoo has blown herself to smithereens. She found Kearny too tough to handle, and she puffed up with spite and meanness till her boiler blew up. It'll be Bad-Luck Kearny no more. Oh, let us by joyful!

' "Humpty Dumpty sat on a wall;
Humpty busted, and that'll be all!"

'I looked up, wondering, and picked out Saturn in his place. But the small red twinkling luminary in his vicinity, which Kearny had pointed out to me as his evil star, had vanished. I had seen it there but half an hour before; there was no doubt that one of those awful and mysterious spasms of nature had hurled it from the heavens.

'I clapped Kearny on the shoulder.

' "Little man," said I, "let this clear the way for you. It appears that astrology has failed to subdue you. Your horoscope must be cast anew with pluck and loyalty for controlling stars. I play you to win. Now, get to your tent, and sleep. Daybreak is the word."

'At nine o'clock on the morning of the eighteenth of July I rode into Aguas Frias with Kearny at my side. In his clean linen suit and with his military poise and keen eye he was a model of a fighting adventurer. I had visions of him riding as commander of President Valdevia's bodyguard when the plums of the new republic should begin to fall.

'Carlos followed with the troops and supplies. He was to halt in a wood outside the town and remain concealed there until he received the word to advance.

'Kearny and I rode down the Calle Ancha toward the *residencia* of Don Rafael at the other side of the town. As we passed the superb white buildings of the University of Esperando, I saw at an open window the gleaming spectacles and bald head of Herr Bergowitz, professor of the natural sciences and friend of Don Rafael and of me and of the cause. He waved his hand to me, with his broad, bland smile.

'There was no excitement apparent in Aguas Frias. The people went about leisurely as at all times; the market was thronged with bareheaded women buying fruit and *carne*; we heard the twang and tinkle of string bands in the patios of the *cantinas*. We could see that it was a waiting game that Don Rafael was playing.

'His *residencia* was a large but low building around a great courtyard in grounds crowded with ornamental trees and tropic shrubs. At his door an old woman who came informed us that Don Rafael had not yet risen.

' "Tell him," said I, "that Captain Maloné and a friend wish to see him at once. Perhaps he has overslept.'

'She came back looking frightened.

' "I have called," she said, "and rung his bell many times, but he does not answer.'

'I knew where his sleeping-room was. Kearny and I pushed by her and went to it. I put my shoulder against the thin door and forced it open.

'In an armchair by a great table covered with maps and books sat Don Rafael with his eyes closed. I touched his hand. He had been dead many hours. On his head above one ear was a wound caused by a heavy blow. It had ceased to bleed long before.

'I made the old woman call a *mozo*, and dispatched him in haste to fetch Herr Bergowitz.

'He came, and we stood about as if we were half stunned by the awful shock. Thus can the letting of a few drops of blood from one man's veins drain the life of a nation.

'Presently Herr Bergowitz stooped and picked up a darkish stone the size of an orange which he saw under the table. He examined it closely through his great glasses with the eye of science.

' "A fragment," said he, "of detonating meteor. The most remarkable one in twenty years exploded above this city a little after midnight this morning."

'The professor looked quickly up at the ceiling. We saw the blue sky through a hole the size of an orange nearly above Don Rafael's chair.

'I heard a familiar sound, and turned. Kearny had thrown himself on the floor and was babbling his compendium of bitter, blood-freezing curses against the star of his evil luck.

'Undoubtedly Phoebe had been feminine. Even when hurtling on her way to fiery dissolution and everlasting doom, the last word had been hers.'

Captain Maloné was not unskilled in narrative. He knew the point where a story should end. I sat reveling in his effective conclusion when he aroused me by continuing:

'Of course,' said, he 'our schemes were at an end. There was no one to take Don Rafael's place. Our little army melted away like dew before the sun.

'One day after I had returned to New Orleans I related this story to a friend who holds a professorship in Tulane University.

'When I had finished he laughed and asked whether I had any knowledge of Kearny's luck afterward. I told him no, that I had seen him no more; but that when he left me, he had expressed confidence that his future would be successful now that his unlucky star had been overthrown.

' "No doubt," said the professor, "he is happier not to know one fact. If he derives his bad luck from Phoebe, the ninth satellite of Saturn, that malicious lady is still engaged in overlooking his career. The star close to Saturn that he imagined to be her was near that planet simply by the chance of its orbit – probably at different times he has regarded many other stars that happened to be in Saturn's neighborhood as his evil one. The real Phoebe is visible only through a very good telescope."

'About a year afterward,' continued Captain Maloné, 'I was walking down a street that crossed the Poydras Market. An immensely stout, pink-faced lady in black satin crowded me from the narrow sidewalk with a frown. Behind her trailed a little man laden to the gunwhales with bundles and bags of goods and vegetables.

'It was Kearny – but changed. I stopped and shook one of his hands, which still clung to a bag of garlic and red peppers.

' "How is the luck old *compañero*?" I asked him. I had not the heart to tell him the truth about his star.

' "Well," said he, "I am married, as you may guess."

' "Francis!" called the big lady, in deep tones, "are you going to stop in the street talking all day?"

' "I am coming, Phoebe dear," said Kearny hastening after her.'

Captain Maloné ceased again.

'After all, do you believe in luck?' I asked.

'Do you?' answered the captain, with his ambiguous smile shaded by the brim of his soft straw hat.

A DOUBLE-DYED DECEIVER

THE TROUBLE BEGAN IN LAREDO. It was the Llano Kid's fault, for he should have confined his habit of manslaughter to Mexicans. But the Kid was past twenty; and to have only Mexicans to one's credit at twenty is to blush unseen on the Rio Grande border.

It happened in old Justo Valdo's gambling house. There was a poker game at which sat players who were not all friends, as happens often where men ride in from afar to shoot Folly as she gallops. There was a row over so small a matter as a pair of queens; and when the smoke had cleared away it was found that the Kid had committed an indiscretion, and his adversary had been guilty of a blunder. For, the unfortunate combatant, instead of being a Greaser, was a high-blooded youth from the cow ranches, of about the Kid's own age and possessed of friends and champions. His blunder in missing the Kid's right ear only a sixteenth of an inch when he pulled his gun did not lessen the indiscretion of the better marksman.

The Kid, not being equipped with a retinue, nor bountifully supplied with personal admirers and supporters – on account of a rather umbrageous reputation, even for the border – considered it not incompatible with his indisputable gameness to perform that judicious tractional act known as 'pulling his freight.'

Quickly the avengers gathered and sought him. Three of them overtook him within a rod of the station. The Kid turned and showed his teeth in that brilliant but mirthless smile that usually preceded his deeds of insolence and violence, and his pursuers fell back without making it necessary for him even to reach for his weapon.

But in this affair the Kid had not felt the grim thirst for encounter that usually urged him on to battle. It had been a purely chance row, born of the cards and certain epithets impossible for a gentleman to brook that had passed between the two. The Kid had rather liked the slim, haughty, brown-faced young chap whom his bullet had cut off in the first pride of manhood. And now he wanted no more blood. He wanted to get away and have a good long sleep somewhere in the sun on the mesquite grass with his handkerchief over his face. Even a Mexican might have crossed his path in safety while he was in this mood.

The Kid openly boarded the north-bound passenger train that departed five minutes later. But at Webb, a few miles out, where it was flagged to take on a traveller, he abandoned that manner of escape. There were telegraph stations ahead; and the Kid looked askance at electricity and steam. Saddle and spur were his rocks of safety.

The man whom he had shot was a stranger to him. But the Kid knew that he was of the Coralitos outfit from Hidalgo; and that the punchers from that ranch were more relentless and vengeful than Kentucky feudists when wrong or harm was done to one of them. So, with the wisdom that has characterized many great fighters, the Kid decided to pile up as many leagues as possible of chaparral and pear between himself and the retaliation of the Coralitos bunch.

Near the station was a store; and near the store, scattered among the mesquite and elms, stood the saddled horses of the customers. Most of them waited, half asleep, with sagging limbs and drooping heads. But one, a long-legged roan with a curved neck, snorted and pawed the turf. Him the Kid mounted, gripped with his knees, and slapped gently with the owner's own quirt.

If the slaying of the temerarious card-player had cast a cloud over the Kid's standing as a good and true citizen, this last act of his veiled his figure in the darkest shadows of disrepute. On the Rio Grande border if you take a man's life you sometimes take trash; but if you take his horse, you take a thing the loss of which renders him poor, indeed, and which enriches you not – if you are caught. For the Kid there was no turning back now.

With the springing roan under him he felt little care or uneasiness. After a five-mile gallop he drew into the plainsman's jogging trot, and rode north-eastward toward the Nueces River bottoms. He knew the country well

- its most tortuous and obscure trails through the great wilderness of brush and pear, and its camps and lonesome ranches where one might find safe entertainment. Always he bore to the east; for the Kid had never seen the ocean, and he had a fancy to lay his hand upon the mane of the great Gulf, the gamesome colt of the greater waters.

So after three days he stood on the shore at Corpus Christi, and looked out across the gentle ripples of a quiet sea.

Captain Boone, of the schooner *Flyaway*, stood near his skiff, which one of his crew was guarding in the surf. When ready to sail he had discovered that one of the necessaries of life, in the parallelogrammatic shape of plug tobacco, had been forgotten. A sailor had been dispatched for the missing cargo. Meanwhile the captain paced the sands, chewing profanely at his pocket store.

A slim, wiry youth in high-heeled boots came down to the water's edge. His face was boyish, but with a premature severity that hinted at a man's experience. His complexion was naturally dark; and the sun and wind of an outdoor life had burned it to a coffee-brown. His hair was as black and straight as an Indian's; his face had not yet been upturned to the humiliation of a razor; his eyes were a cold and steady blue. He carried his left arm somewhat away from his body, for pearlhandled .45s are frowned upon by town marshals, and are a little bulky when packed in the left armhole of one's vest. He looked beyond Captain Boone at the gulf with the impersonal and expressionless dignity of a Chinese emperor.

'Thinkin' of buyin' that 'ar gulf, buddy?' asked the captain, made sarcastic by his narrow escape from the tobaccoless voyage.

'Why, no,' said the Kid gently, 'I reckon not. I never saw it before. I was just looking at it. Not thinking of selling it, are you?'

'Not this trip,' said the captain. 'I'll send it to you C.O.D. when I get back to Buenas Tierras. Here comes that capstan-footed lubber with the chewin'. I ought to've weighed anchor an hour ago.'

'Is that your ship out there?' asked the Kid.

'Why, yes,' answered the captain, 'if you want to call a schooner a ship, and I don't mind lyin'. But you better say Miller and Gonzales, owners, and ordinary plain, Billy-be-damned old Samuel K. Boone, skipper.'

'Where are you going to?' asked the refugee.

'Buenas Tierras, coast of South America – I forget what they called the country the last time I was there. Cargo – lumber, corrugated iron, and machetes.'

'What kind of a country is it?' asked the Kid – 'hot or cold?'

'Warmish, buddy,' said the captain. 'But a regular Paradise Lost for elegance of scenery and be-yooty of geography. Ye're wakened every morning by the sweet singin' of red birds with seven purple tails, and the sighin' of breezes in the posies and roses. And the inhabitants never work, for they can reach out and pick steamer baskets of the choicest hothouse fruit without gettin' out of bed. And there's no Sunday and no ice and no rent and no troubles and no use and no nothin'. It's a great country for a man to go to sleep with, and wait for somethin' to turn up. The bananys and oranges and hurricanes and pincapples that ye eat comes from there.'

'That sounds to me!' said the Kid, at last betraying interest. 'What'll the expressage be to take me out there with you?'

'Twenty-four dollars,' said Captain Boone; 'grub and transportation. Second cabin. I haven't got a first cabin.'

'You've got my company,' said the Kid, pulling out a buckskin bag.

With three hundred dollars he had gone to Laredo for his regular 'blowout.' The duel in Valdos's had cut short his season of hilarity, but it had left him with nearly $200 for aid in the flight that it had made necessary.

'All right, buddy,' said the captain. 'I hope your ma won't blame me for this little childish escapade of yours.' He beckoned to one of the boat's crew. 'Let Sanchez lift you out to the skiff so you won't get your feet wet.'

Thacker, the United States consul at Buenas Tierras, was not yet drunk. It was only eleven o'clock; and he never arrived at his desired state of beatitude – a state where he sang ancient maudlin vaudeville songs and pelted his screaming parrot with banana peels – until the middle of the afternoon. So, when he looked up from his hammock at the sound of a slight cough, and saw the Kid standing in the door of the consulate, he was still in a condition to extend the hospitality and courtesy due from the representative of a great nation. 'Don't disturb yourself,' said the Kid easily. 'I just dropped in. They told me it was customary to light at your camp before starting in to round up the town. I just came in on a ship from Texas.'

'Glad to see you, Mr. – ,' said the consul.

The Kid laughed.

'Sprague Dalton,' he said. 'It sounds funny to me to hear it. I'm called the Llano Kid in the Rio Grande country.'

'I'm Thacker,' said the consul. 'Take that cane-bottom chair. Now if you've come to invest, you want somebody to advise you. These dingies will cheat you out of the gold in your teeth if you don't understand their ways. Try a cigar?'

'Much obliged,' said the Kid, 'but if it wasn't for my corn shucks and the little bag in my back pocket I couldn't live a minute.' He took out his 'makings,' and rolled a cigarette.

'They speak Spanish here,' said the consul. 'You'll need an interpreter. If there's anything I can do, why, I'd be delighted. If you're buying fruit lands or looking for a concession of any sort, you'll want somebody who knows the ropes to look out for you.'

'I speak Spanish,' said the Kid, 'abut nine times better than I do English. Everybody speaks it on the range where I come from. And I'm not in the market for anything.'

'You speak Spanish?' said Thacker, thoughtfully. He regarded the Kid absorbedly.

'You look like a Spaniard, too,' he continued. 'And you're from Texas. And you can't be more than twenty or twenty-one. I wonder if you've got any nerve.'

'You got a deal of some kind to put through?' asked the Texan, with unexpected shrewdness.

'Are you open to a proposition?' said Thacker.

'What's the use to deny it?' said the Kid. 'I got into a little gun frolic down in Laredo, and plugged a white man. There wasn't any Mexican handy. And I come down to your parrot-and-money range just for to smell the morning-glories and marigolds. Now, do you *sabe*?'

Thacker got up and closed the door.

'Let me see your hand,' he said.

He took the Kid's left hand, and examined the back of it closely.

'I can do it,' he said, excitedly. 'Your flesh is as hard as wood and as healthy as a baby's. It will heal in a week.'

'If it's a fist fight you want to back me for,' said the Kid, 'don't put your money up yet. Make it gun work, and I'll keep you company. But no bare-handed scrapping, like ladies at a tea-party, for me.'

'It's easier than that,' said Thacker. 'Just step here, will you?'

Through the window he pointed to a two-story white-stuccoed house with wide galleries rising amid the deep-green tropical foliage on a wooden hill that sloped gently from the sea.

'In that house,' said Thacker, 'a fine old Castilian gentleman and his wife are yearning to gather you into their arms and fill your pockets with money. Old Santos Urique lives there. He owns half the gold-mines in the country.'

'You haven't been eating loco weed, have you?' asked the Kid.

'Sit down again,' said Thacker, 'and I'll tell you. Twelve years ago they lost a kid. No, he didn't die – although most of 'em here do from drinking the surface water. He was a wild little devil, even if he wasn't but eight years old. Everybody knows about it. Some Americans who were through here prospecting for gold had letters to Señor Urique, and the boy who was a favorite with them. They filled his head with big stories about the States; and about a month after they left, the kid disappeared, too. He was supposed to have stowed himself away among the banana bunches on a fruit steamer, and gone to New Orleans. He was seen once afterward in Texas, it was thought, but they never heard anything more of him. Old Urique has spent thousands of dollars having him looked for. The madam was broken up worst of all. The kid was her life. She wears mourning yet. But they say she believes he'll come back to her some day, and never gives up hope. On the back of the boy's left hand was tattooed a flying eagle carrying a spear in his claws. That's old Urique's coat of arms or something that he inherited in Spain.'

The Kid raised his left hand slowly and gazed at it curiously.

'That's it,' said Thacker, reaching behind the official desk for his bottle of smuggled brandy. 'You're not so slow. I can do it. What was I consul at Sandakan for? I never knew till now. In a week I'll have the eagle bird with the frog-sticker blended in so you'd think you were born with it. I brought a set of the needles and ink just because I was sure you'd drop in some day, Mr. Dalton.'

'Oh, hell,' said the Kid. 'I thought I told you my name!'

'All right, "Kid," then. It won't be that long. How does "Señorito Urique" sound, for a change?'

'I never played son any that I remember of,' said the Kid. 'If I had any parents to mention they went over the divide about the time I gave my first bleat. What is the plan of your round-up?'

Thacker leaned back against the wall and held his glass up to the light.

'We've come now,' said he, 'to the question of how far you're willing to go in a little matter of the sort.'

'I told you why I came down here,' said the Kid simply.

'A good answer,' said the consul. 'But you won't have to go that far. Here's the scheme. After I get the trade-mark tattooed on your hand I'll notify old Urique. In the meantime I'll furnish you with all of the family history I can find out, so you can be studying up points to talk about. You've got the looks, you speak the Spanish, you know the facts, you can tell about Texas, you've got the tattoo mark. When I notify them that the rightful heir has returned and is waiting to know whether he will be received and pardoned what will happen? They'll simply rush down here and fall on your neck, and the curtain goes down for refreshments and a stroll in the lobby.'

'I'm waiting,' said the Kid. 'I haven't had my saddle off in your camp long, pardner, and I never met you before; but if you intend to let it go at a parental blessing, why, I'm mistaken in my man, that's all.'

'Thanks,' said the consul. 'I haven't met anybody in a long time that keeps up with an argument as well as you do. The rest of it is simple. If they take you in only for a while it's long enough. Don't give 'em time to hunt up the strawberry mark on your left shoulder. Old Urique keeps anywhere from $50,000 to $100,000 in his house all the time in a little safe that you could open with a shoe buttoner. Get it. My skill as a tattooer is worth half the boodle. We go halves and catch a tramp steamer for Rio Janeiro. Let the United States go to pieces if it can't get along without my services. *Qué dice, señor?'*

'It sounds to me!' said the Kid, nodding his head. 'I'm out for the dust.'

'All right, then,' said Thacker. 'You'll have to keep close until we get the bird on you. You can live in the back room here. I do my own cooking, and I'll make you as comfortable as a parsimonious government will allow me.'

Thacker had set the time at a week, but it was two weeks before the design that he patiently tattooed upon the Kid's hand was to his notion. And then Thacker called a *muchacho*, and dispatched this note to the intended victim:

El Señor Don Santos Urique,
    La Casa Blanca,
My Dear Sir:
    I beg permission to inform you that there is in my house as a temporary guest a young man who arrived in Buenas Tierras from the United States some days ago. Without wishing to excite any hopes that may not be realized, I think there is a possibility of his being your long-absent son. It might be well for you to call and see him. If he is, it is my opinion that his intention was to return to his home, but upon arriving here, his courage failed him from doubts as to how he would be received. Your true servant,

                                        Thompson Thacker

Half an hour afterward – quick time for Buenas Tierras – Señor Urique's ancient landau drove to the consul's door, with the bare-footed coachman beating and shouting at the team of fat, awkward horses.

A tall man with a white moustache alighted, and assisted to the ground a lady who was dressed and veiled in unrelieved black.

The two hastened inside, and were met by Thacker with his best diplomatic bow. By his desk stood a slender young man with clear-cut, sunbrowned features and smoothly brushed black hair.

Señora Urique threw back her heavy veil with a quick gesture. She was past middle age, and her hair was beginning to silver, but her full, proud figure and clear olive skin retained traces of the beauty peculiar to the Basque province. But, once you had seen her eyes, and comprehended the great sadness that was revealed in their deep shadows and hopeless expression, you saw that the woman lived only in some memory.

She bent upon the young man a long look of the most agonized questioning. Then her great black eyes turned, and her gaze rested upon his left hand. And then with a sob, not loud, but seeming to shake the room, she cried 'Hijo mío!' and caught the Llano Kid to her heart.

A month afterward the Kid came to the consulate in response to a message sent by Thacker.

He looked the young Spanish caballero. His clothes were imported, and the wiles of the jewellers had not been spent upon him in vain. A more than respectable diamond shone on his finger as he rolled a shuck cigarette.

'What's doing?' asked Thacker.

'Nothing much,' said the Kid calmly. 'I eat my first iguana steak to-day. They're them big lizards, you *sabe*? I reckon, though, that frijoles and side bacon would do me about as well. Do you care for iguanas, Thacker?'

'No, nor for some other kinds of reptiles,' said Thacker.

It was three in the afternoon, and in another hour he would be in his state of beatitude.

'It's time you were making good, sonny,' he went on, with an ugly look on his reddened face. 'You're not playing up to me square. You've been the prodigal son for four weeks now, and you could have had veal for every meal on a gold dish if you'd wanted it. Now, Mr. Kid, do you think it's right to leave me out so long on a husk diet? What's the trouble? Don't you get your filial eyes on anything that looks like cash in the Casa Blanca? Don't tell me you don't. Everybody knows where old Urique keeps his stuff. It's U.S. currency, too; he don't accept anything else. What's doing? Don't say "nothing" this time.'

'Why, sure,' said the Kid, admiring his diamond, 'there's plenty of money up there. I'm no judge of collateral in bunches, but I will undertake for to say that I've seen the rise of $50,000 at a time in that tin grub box that my adopted father calls his safe. And he lets me carry the key sometimes just to show me that he knows I'm the real little Francisco that strayed from the herd a long time ago.'

'Well, what are you waiting for?' asked Thacker angrily. 'Don't you forget that I can upset your apple-cart any day I want to. If old Urique knew you were an impostor, what sort of things would happen to you? Oh, you don't know this country, Mr. Texas Kid. The laws here have got mustard spread between 'em. These people here'd stretch you out like a frog that had been stepped on, and give you about fifty sticks at every corner of the plaza. And they'd wear every stick out, too. What was left of you they'd feed to alligators.'

'I might as well tell you now, pardner,' said the Kid, sliding down low on his steamer chair, 'that things are going to stay just as they are. They're about right now.'

'What do you mean?' asked Thacker, rattling the bottom of his glass on his desk.

'The scheme's off,' said the Kid. 'And whenever you have the pleasure of speaking to me address me as Don Francisco Urique. I'll guarantee I'll answer to it. We'll let Colonel Urique keep his money. His little tin safe is as good as the time-locker in the First National Bank of Laredo as far as you and me are concerned.'

'You're going to throw me down, then, are you?' said the consul.

'Sure,' said the Kid, cheerfully. 'Throw you down. That's it. And now I'll tell you why. The first night I was up at the colonel's house they introduced me to a bedroom. No blankets on the floor – a real room, with a bed and things in it. And before I was asleep, in comes this artificial mother of mine and tucks in the covers. "Panchito," she says, "my little lost one, God has brought you back to me. I bless His name forever." It was that, or some truck like that, she said. And down comes a drop or two of rain and hits me on the nose. And all that stuck by me, Mr. Thacker. And it's been that way ever since. And it's got to stay that way. Don't you think that it's for what's in it for me, either, that I say so. If you have any such ideas keep 'em to yourself. I haven't had much truck with women in my life, and no mothers to speak of, but here's a lady that we've got to keep fooled. Once she stood it; twice she won't. I'm a low-down wolf, and the devil may have sent me on this trail instead of God, but I'll travel it to the end. And now, don't forget that I'm Don Francisco Urique whenever you happen to mention my name.'

'I'll expose you to-day, you – you double-eyed traitor,' stammered Thacker.

The Kid arose and, without violence, took Thacker by the throat with a hand of steel, and shoved him slowly into a corner. Then he drew from under his left arm his pearl-handled .45 and poked the cold muzzle of it against the consul's mouth.

'I told you why I come here,' he said, with his old freezing smile. 'If I leave here, you'll be the reason. Never forget it, pardner. Now, what is my name?'

'Er – Don Francisco Urique,' gasped Thacker.

From outside came a sound of wheels, and the shouting of someone, and the sharp thwacks of a wooden whipstock upon the backs of fat horses.

The Kid put up his gun, and walked toward the door. But he turned again and came back to the trembling Thacker, and held up his left hand with its back toward the consul.

'There's one more reason,' he said, slowly, 'why things have got to stand as they are. The fellow I killed in Laredo had one of them same pictures on his left hand.'

Outside, the ancient landau of Don Santos Urique rattled to the door. The coachman ceased his bellowing. Señora Urique, in a voluminous gay gown of white lace and flying ribbons, leaned forward with a happy look in her great soft eyes.

'Are you within, dear son?' she called, in the rippling Castilian.

'*Madre mía, yo vengo* [mother, I come],' answered the young Don Francisco Urique.

THE PASSING OF BLACK EAGLE

FOR SOME MONTHS OF A CERTAIN year a grim bandit infested the Texas border along the Rio Grande. Peculiarly striking to the optic nerve was this notorious marauder. His personality secured him the title of 'Black Eagle, the Terror of the Border.' Many fearsome tales are on record concerning the doings of him and his followers. Suddenly, in the space of a single minute, Black Eagle vanished from earth. He was never heard of again. His own band never even guessed the mystery of his disappearance. The border ranches and settlements feared he would come again to ride and ravage the mesquite flats. He never will. It is to disclose the fate of Black Eagle that this narrative is written.

The initial movement of the story is furnished by the foot of a bartender in St. Louis. His discerning eye fell upon the form of Chicken Ruggles as he pecked with avidity at the free lunch. Chicken was a 'hobo.' He had a long nose like the bill of a fowl, an inordinate appetite for poultry, and a habit of gratifying it without expense, which accounts for the name given him by his fellow vagrants.

Physicians agree that the partaking of liquids at meal times is not a healthy practice. The hygiene of the saloon promulgates the opposite. Chicken had neglected to purchase a drink to accompany his meal. The bartender rounded the counter, caught the injudicious diner by the ear with a lemon squeezer, led him to the door and kicked him into the street.

Thus the mind of Chicken was brought to realize the signs of coming winter. The night was cold; the stars shone with unkindly brilliancy; people were hurrying along the streets in two egotistic, jostling streams. Men had donned their overcoats, and Chicken knew to an exact percentage the increased difficulty of coaxing dimes from those buttoned-in vest pockets. The time had come for his annual exodus to the South.

A little boy, five or six years old, stood looking with covetous eyes in a confectioner's window. In one small hand he held an empty two-ounce vial; in the other he grasped tightly something flat and round, with a shining milled edge. The scene presented a field of operations commensurate to Chicken's talents and daring. After sweeping the horizon to make sure that no official tug was cruising near, he insidiously accosted his prey. The boy, having been early taught by his household to regard altruistic advances with extreme suspicion, received the overtures coldly.

Then Chicken knew that he must make one of those desperate, nerve-shattering plunges into speculation that fortune sometimes requires of those who would win her favor. Five cents was his capital, and this he must risk against the chance of winning what lay within the close grasp of the youngster's chubby hand. It was a fearful lottery, Chicken knew. But he must accomplish his end by strategy, since he had a wholesome terror of plundering infants by force. Once, in a park, driven by hunger, he had committed an onslaught upon a bottle of peptonized infant's food in the possession of an occupant of a baby carriage. The outraged infant had so promptly opened its mouth and pressed the button that communicated with the welkin that help arrived, and Chicken did his thirty days in a snug coop. Wherefore he was, as he said, 'leary of kids.'

Beginning artfully to question the boy concerning his choice of sweets, he gradually drew out the information he wanted. Mamma said he was to ask the drug-store man for ten cents' worth of paregoric in the bottle; he was to keep his hand shut tight over the dollar; he must not stop to talk to any one in the street; he must ask the drug-store man to wrap up the change and put it in the pocket of his trousers. Indeed, they had pockets – two of them! And he liked chocolate creams best.

Chicken went into the store and turned plunger. He invested his entire capital in C.A.N.D.Y. stocks, simply to pave the way to the greater risk following.

He gave the sweets to the youngster, and had the satisfaction of perceiving that confidence was established. After that it was easy to obtain leadership of the expedition, to take the investment by the hand and lead it to a nice drug store he knew of in the same block. There Chicken, with a parental air, passed over the dollar and called for the medicine, while the boy crunched his candy, glad to be relieved of the responsibility of the purchase. And then the successful investor searching his pockets, found an overcoat button – the extent of his winter trousseau – and, wrapping it carefully, placed the ostensible change in the pocket of confiding juvenility. Setting the youngster's face homeward, and patting him benevolently on the back – for Chicken's heart was as soft as those of his feathered namesakes – the speculator quit the market with a profit of 1,700 per cent. on his invested capital.

Two hours later an Iron Mountain freight engine pulled out of the railroad yards, Texas bound, with a string of empties. In one of the cattle cars, half buried in excelsior, Chicken lay at ease. Beside him in his nest was a quart bottle of very poor whisky and a paper bag of bread and cheese. Mr. Ruggles, in his private car, was on his trip south for the winter season.

For a week that car was trundled southward, shifted, laid over, and manipulated after the manner of rolling stock, but Chicken stuck to it, leaving it only at necessary times to satisfy his hunger and thirst. He knew it must go down to the cattle country, and San Antonio, in the heart of it, was his goal. There the air was salubrious and mild; the people indulgent and long-suffering. The bartenders there would not kick him. If he should eat too long or too often at one place they would swear at him as if by rote and without heat. They swore so drawlingly, and they rarely paused short of their full vocabulary, which was copious, so that Chicken had often gulped a good meal during the process of the vituperative prohibition. The season there was always spring-like; the plazas were pleasant at night, with music and gaiety: except during the slight and infrequent cold snaps, one could sleep comfortably out of doors in case the interiors should develop inhospitality.

At Texarkana his car was switched to the I. and G.N. Then still southward it trailed until, at length, it crawled across the Colorado bridge at Austin, and lined out, straight as an arrow, for the run to San Antonio.

When the freight halted at that town Chicken was fast asleep. In ten minutes the train was off again for Laredo, the end of the road. Those empty cattle cars were for distribution along the line at points from which the ranches shipped their stock.

When Chicken awoke his car was stationary. Looking out between the slats he saw it was a bright, moonlit night. Scrambling out, he saw his car with three others abandoned on a little siding in a wild and lonesome country. A cattle pen and chute stood on one side of the track. The railroad bisected a vast, dim ocean of prairie, in the midst of which Chicken, with his futile rolling stock, was as completely stranded as was Robinson with his land-locked boat.

A white post stood near the rails. Going up to it, Chicken read the letters at the top, S.A. 90. Laredo was nearly as far to the south. He was almost a hundred miles from any town. Coyotes began to yelp in the mysterious sea around him. Chicken felt lonesome. He had lived in Boston without an education, in Chicago without nerve, in Philadelphia without a sleeping place, in New York without a pull, and in Pittsburg sober, and yet he had never felt so lonely as now.

Suddenly through the intense silence, he heard the whicker of a horse. The sound came from the side of the track toward the east, and Chicken began to explore timorously in that direction. He stepped high along the mat of curly mesquite grass, for he was afraid of everything there might be in this wilderness – snakes, rats, brigands, centipedes, mirages, cowboys, fandangoes, tarantulas, tamales – he had read of them in the story papers. Rounding a clump of prickly pear that reared high its fantastic and menacing array of rounded heads, he was struck to shivering terror by a snort and a thunderous plunge, as the horse, himself startled, bounded away some fifty yards, and then resumed his grazing. But here was the one thing in the desert that Chicken did not fear. He had been reared on a farm; he had handled horses, understood them, and could ride.

Approaching slowly and speaking soothingly, he followed the animal, which, after its first flight, seemed gentle enough, and secured the end of the twenty-foot lariat that dragged after him in the grass. It required him but a few moments to contrive the rope into an ingenious nose-bridle, after the style of the Mexican *borsal*. In another he was upon the horse's back and off at a splendid lope, giving the animal free choice of direction. 'He will take me somewhere,' said Chicken to himself.

It would have been a thing of joy, that untrammelled gallop over the moonlit prairie, even to Chicken, who loathed exertion, but that his mood was not for it. His head ached, a growing thirst was upon him; the 'somewhere' whither his lucky mount might convey him was full of dismal peradventure.

And now he noted that the horse moved to a definite goal. Where the prairie lay smooth he kept his course straight as an arrow's toward the east. Deflected by hill or arroyo or impracticable spinous brakes, he quickly flowed again into the current, charted by his unerring instinct. At last, upon the side of a gentle rise, he suddenly subsided to a complacent walk. A stone's cast away stood a little mott of coma trees; beneath it a *jacal* such as the Mexicans erect – a one-room house of upright poles daubed with clay and roofed with grass or tule reeds. An experienced eye would have estimated the spot as the headquarters of a small sheep ranch. In the moonlight the ground in the nearby corral showed pulverized to a level smoothness by the hoofs of the sheep. Everywhere was carelessly distributed the paraphernalia of the place – ropes, bridles, saddles, sheep pelts, wool sacks, feed troughs, and camp litter. The barrel of drinking water stood in the end of the two-horse wagon near the door. The harness was piled, promiscuous, upon the wagon tongue, soaking up the dew.

Chicken slipped to earth, and tied the horse to a tree. He halloed again and again, but the house remained quiet. The door stood open, and he entered cautiously. The light was sufficient for him to see that no one was at home. He struck a match and lighted a lamp that stood on a table. The room was that of a bachelor ranchman who was content with the necessaries of life. Chicken rummaged intelligently until he found what he had hardly dared hope for – a small brown jug that still contained something near a quart of his desire.

Half an hour later, Chicken – now a gamecock of hostile aspect – emerged from the house with unsteady steps. He had drawn upon the absent ranchman's equipment to replace his own ragged attire. He wore a suit of coarse brown ducking, the coat being a sort of rakish bolero, jaunty to a degree. Boots he had donned, and spurs that whirred with every lurching step. Buckled around him was a belt full of cartridges with a big six-shooter in each of its two holsters.

Prowling about, he found blankets, a saddle and bridle with which he caparisoned his steed. Again mounting, he rode swiftly away, singing a loud and tuneless song.

Bud King's band of desperadoes, outlaws and horse and cattle thieves were in camp at a secluded spot on the bank of the Frio. Their depredations in the Rio Grande country, while no bolder than usual, had been advertised more extensively, and Captain Kinney's company of rangers had been ordered down to look after them. Consequently, Bud King, who was a wise general, instead of cutting out a hot trail for the upholders of the law, as his men wished to do, retired for the time to the prickly fastnesses of the Frio valley.

Though the move was a prudent one, and not incompatible with Bud's well-known courage, it raised dissension among the members of the band. In fact, while they thus lay ingloriously *perdu* in the brush, the question of Bud King's fitness for the leadership was argued, with closed doors, as it were, by his followers. Never before had Bud's skill or efficiency been brought to criticism; but his glory was waning (and such is glory's fate) in the light of a newer star. The sentiment of the band was crystallizing into the opinion that Black Eagle could lead them with more luster, profit, and distinction.

This Black Eagle – sub-titled the 'Terror of the Border' – had been a member of the gang about three months.

One night they were in camp on the San Miguel water-hole a solitary horseman on the regulation fiery steed dashed in among them. The newcomer was of portentous and devastating aspect. A beak-like nose with a predatory curve projected above a mass of bristling, blue-black whiskers. His eye was cavernous and fierce. He was spurred, sombreroed, booted, garnished with revolvers, abundantly drunk, and very much unafraid. Few people in the country drained by the Rio Bravo would have cared thus to invade alone the camp of Bud King. But this fell bird swooped fearlessly upon them and demanded to be fed.

Hospitality in the prairie country is not limited. Even if your enemy pass your way you must feed him before you shoot him. You must empty your larder into him before you empty your lead. So the stranger of undeclared intentions was set down to a mighty feast.

A talkative bird he was, full of most marvellous loud tales and exploits, and speaking a language at times obscure but never colorless. He was a new sensation to Bud King's men, who rarely encountered new types. They hung, delighted, upon his vainglorious boasting, the spicy strangeness of his lingo, his contemptuous familiarity with life, the world, and remote places, and the extravagant frankness with which he conveyed his sentiments.

To their guest the band of outlaws seemed to be nothing more than a congregation of country bumpkins whom he was 'stringing for grub' just as he would have told his stories at the back door of a farmhouse to wheedle a meal. And, indeed, his ignorance was not without excuse, for the 'bad man' of the Southwest does not run to extremes. Those brigands might justly have been taken for a little party of peaceable rustics assembled for a fish-fry or pecan gathering. Gentle of manner, slouching of gait, soft-voiced, unpicturesquely clothed; not one of them presented to the eye any witness of the desperate records they had earned.

For two days the glittering stranger within the camp was feasted. Then, by common consent, he was invited to become a member of the band. He consented, presenting for enrolment the prodigious name of 'Captain Montressor.' This was immediately overruled by the band, and 'Piggy' substituted as a compliment to the awful and insatiate appetite of its owner.

Thus did the Texas border receive the most spectacular brigand that ever rode its chaparral.

For the next three months Bud King conducted business as usual, escaping encounters with law officers and being content with reasonable profits. The band ran off some very good companies of horses from the ranges, and a few bunches of fine cattle which they got safely across the Rio Grande and disposed of to fair advantage. Often the band would ride into the little villages and Mexican settlements, terrorizing the inhabitants and plundering for the provisions and ammunition they needed. It was during these bloodless raids that Piggy's ferocious aspect and frightful voice gained him a renown more widespread and glorious than those other gentle-voiced and sad-faced desperadoes could have acquired in a lifetime.

The Mexicans, most apt in nomenclature, first called him The Black Eagle, and used to frighten the babes by threatening them with tales of the dreadful robber who carried off little children in his great beak. Soon the name extended, and Black Eagle, the Terror of the Border, became a recognized factor in exaggerated newspaper reports and ranch gossip.

The country from the Nueces to the Rio Grande was a wild but fertile stretch, given over to the sheep and cattle ranches. Range was free; the inhabitants were few; the law was mainly a letter, and the pirates met with little opposition until the flaunting and garish Piggy gave the band undue advertisement. Then Kinney's ranger company headed for those precincts, and Bud King knew that it meant grim and sudden war or else temporary retirement. Regarding the risk to be unnecessary, he drew off his band to an almost inaccessible spot on the bank of the Frio. Wherefore, as has been said, dissatisfaction arose among the members, and impeachment proceedings against Bud were premeditated, with Black Eagle in high favor for the succession. Bud King was not unaware of the sentiment, and he called aside Cactus Taylor, his trusted lieutenant, to discuss it.

'If the boys,' said Bud, 'ain't satisfied with me, I'm willin' to step out. They're buckin' against my way of handlin' 'em. And 'specially because I concludes to hit the brush while Sam Kinney is ridin' the line. I saves 'em from bein' shot or sent up on a state contract, and they up and says I'm no good.'

'It ain't so much that,' explained Cactus, 'as it is they're plum locoed about

Piggy. They want them whiskers and that nose of his to split the wind at the head of the column.'

'There's somethin' mighty seldom about Piggy,' declared Bud, musingly. 'I never yet see anything on the hoof that he exactly grades up with. He can shore holler a plenty, and he straddles a hoss from where you laid the chunk. But he ain't never been smoked yet. You know, Cactus, we ain't had a row since he's been with us. Piggy's all right for skearin' the greaser kids and layin' waste a cross-roads store. I reckon he's the finest canned oyster buccaneer and cheese pirate that ever was, but how's his appetite for fightin'? I've knowed some citizens you'd think was starvin' for trouble get a bad case of dyspepsy the first dose of lead they had to take.'

'He talks all spraddled out,' said Cactus, ' 'bout the rookuses he's been in. He claims to have saw the elephant and hearn the owl.'

'I know,' replied Bud, using the cow-puncher's expressive phrase of skepticism, 'but it sounds to me!'

This conversation was held one night in camp while the other members of the band – eight in number – were sprawling around the fire, lingering over their supper. When Bud and Cactus ceased talking they heard Piggy's formidable voice holding forth to the others as usual while he was engaged in checking, though never satisfying, his ravening appetite.

'Wat's de use,' he was saying, 'of chasin' little red cowses and hosses 'round for t'ousands of miles? Dere ain't nuttin' in it. Gallopin' t'rough dese bushes and briers, and gettin' a t'irst dat a brewery couldn't put out, and missin' meals! Say! You know what I'd do if I was main finger of dis bunch? I'd stick up a train. I'd blow de express car and make hard dollars where you guys get wind. Youse makes me tired. Dis sook-cow kind of cheap sport gives me a pain.'

Later on, a deputation waited on Bud. They stood on one leg, chewed mesquite twigs and circumlocuted, for they hated to hurt his feelings. Bud foresaw their business, and made it easy for them. Bigger risks and larger profits was what they wanted.

The suggestion of Piggy's about holding up a train had fired their imagination and increased their admiration for the dash and boldness of the instigator. They were such simple, artless, and custom-bound bushrangers that they had never before thought of extending their habits beyond the running off of live-stock and the shooting of such of their acquaintances as ventured to interfere.

Bud acted 'on the level,' agreeing to take a subordinate place in the gang until Black Eagle should have been given a trial as leader.

After a great deal of consultation, studying of time-tables and discussion of the country's topography, the time and place for carrying out their new enterprise was decided upon. At that time there was a feedstuff famine in Mexico and a cattle famine in certain parts of the United States, and there was a brisk international trade. Much money was being shipped along the railroads that connected the two republics. It was agreed that the most promising place for the contemplated robbery was at Espina, a little station on the I. and G.N., about forty miles north of Laredo. The train stopped there one minute; the country around was wild and unsettled; the station consisted of but one house in which the agent lived.

Black Eagle's band set out, riding by night. Arriving in the vicinity of Espina they rested their horses all day in a thicket a few miles distant.

The train was due at Espina at 10.30 p.m. They could rob the train and be well over the Mexican border with their booty by daylight the next morning.

To do Black Eagle justice, he exhibited no signs of flinching from the responsible honors that had been conferred upon him.

He assigned his men to their respective posts with discretion, and coached them carefully as to their duties. On each side of the track four of the band were to lie concealed in the chaparral. Gotch-Ear Rodgers was to stick up the station agent. Bronco Charlie was to remain with the horses, holding them in readiness. At a spot where it was calculated the engine would be when the train stopped, Bud King was to lie hidden on one side, and Black Eagle himself on the other. The two would get the drop on the engineer and fireman, force them to descend and proceed to the rear. Then the express car would be looted, and the escape made. No one was to move until Black Eagle gave the signal by firing his revolver. The plan was perfect.

At ten minutes to train time every man was at his post, effectually concealed by the thick chaparral that grew almost to the rails. The night was dark and lowering, with a fine drizzle falling from the flying gulf clouds. Black Eagle crouched behind a bush within five yards of the track. Two six-shooters were belted around him. Occasionally he drew a large black bottle from his pocket and raised it to his mouth.

A star appeared far down the track which soon waxed into the headlight of the approaching train. It came on with an increasing roar; the engine bore down upon the ambushing desperadoes with a glare and a shriek like some avenging monster come to deliver them to justice. Black Eagle flattened himself upon the ground. The engine, contrary to their calculations, instead of stopping between him and Bud King's place of concealment, passed fully forty yards farther before it came to a stand.

The bandit leader rose to his feet and peered around the bush. His men all lay quiet, awaiting the signal. Immediately opposite Black Eagle was a thing that drew his attention. Instead of being a regular passenger train, it was a mixed one. Before him stood a box car, the door of which, by some means, had been left slightly open. Black Eagle went up to it and pushed the door farther open. An odor came forth – a damp, rancid, familiar, musty, intoxicating, beloved odor stirring strongly at old memories of happy days and travels. Black Eagle sniffed at the witching smell as the returned wanderer smells of the rose that twines his boyhood's cottage home. Nostalgia seized him. He put his hand inside. Excelsior – dry, springy, curly, soft, enticing, covered the floor. Outside the drizzle had turned to a chilling rain.

The train bell clanged. The bandit chief unbuckled his belt and cast it, with its revolvers, upon the ground. His spurs followed quickly, and his broad sombrero. Black Eagle was moulting. The train started with a rattling jerk. The ex-Terror of the Border scrambled into the box car and closed the door. Stretched luxuriously upon the excelsior, with the black bottle clasped closely to his breast, his eyes closed, and a foolish, happy smile upon his terrible features Chicken Ruggles started upon his return trip.

Undisturbed, with the band of desperate bandits lying motionless, awaiting the signal to attack, the train pulled out from Espina. As its speed increased, and the black masses of chaparral went whizzing past on either side, the express messenger, lighting his pipe, looked through his window and remarked, feelingly:

'What a jim-dandy place for a hold-up!'

A RETRIEVED REFORMATION

A GUARD CAME TO THE PRISON shoe-shop, where Jimmy Valentine was assiduously stitching uppers, and escorted him to the front office. There the warden handed Jimmy his pardon, which had been signed that morning by the governor. Jimmy took it in a tired kind of way. He had served nearly ten months of a four-year sentence. He had expected to stay only about three months, at the longest. When a man with as many friends on the outside as Jimmy Valentine had is received in the 'stir' it is hardly worth while to cut his hair.

'Now, Valentine,' said the warden, 'you'll go out in the morning. Brace up, and make a man of yourself. You're not a bad fellow at heart. Stop cracking safes, and live straight.'

'Me?' said Jimmy, in surprise. 'Why, I never cracked a safe in my life.'

'Oh, no,' laughed the warden. 'Of course not. Let's see, now. How was it you happened to get sent up on that Springfield job? Was it because you wouldn't prove an alibi for fear of compromising somebody in extremely high-toned society? Or was it simply a case of a mean old jury that had it in for you? It's always one or the other with you innocent victims.'

'Me?' said Jimmy, still blankly virtuous. 'Why, warden, I never was in Springfield in my life!'

'Take him back, Cronin,' smiled the warden, 'and fix him up with outgoing clothes. Unlock him at seven in the morning, and let him come to the bull-pen. Better think over my advice, Valentine.'

At a quarter past seven on the next morning Jimmy stood in the warden's outer office. He had on a suit of the villainously fitting, ready-made clothes and a pair of stiff, squeaky shoes that the state furnishes to its discharged compulsory guests.

The clerk handed him a railroad ticket and the five-dollar bill with which the law expected him to rehabilitate himself into good citizenship and prosperity. The warden gave him a cigar, and shook hands. Valentine, 9762, was chronicled on the books 'Pardoned by Governor,' and Mr. James Valentine walked out into the sunshine.

Disregarding the song of the birds, the waving green trees, and the smell of the flowers, Jimmy headed straight for a restaurant. There he tasted the first sweet joys of liberty in the shape of a broiled chicken and a bottle of white wine – followed by a cigar a grade better than the one the warden had given him. From there he proceeded leisurely to the depot. He tossed a quarter into the hat of a blind man sitting by the door, and boarded his train. Three hours set him down in a little town near the state line. He went to the café of one Mike Dolan and shook hands with Mike, who was alone behind the bar.

'Sorry we couldn't make it sooner, Jimmy, me boy,' said Mike. 'But we had that protest from Springfield to buck against, and the governor nearly balked. Feeling all right?'

'Fine,' said Jimmy. 'Got my key?'

He got his key and went upstairs, unlocking the door of a room at the rear. Everything was just as he had left it. There on the floor was still Ben Price's collar-button that had been torn from that eminent detective's shirt-band when they had overpowered Jimmy to arrest him.

Pulling out from the wall a folding-bed, Jimmy slid back a panel in the wall and dragged out a dust-covered suitcase. He opened this and gazed fondly at the finest set of burglar's tools in the East. It was a complete set, made of specially tempered steel, the latest designs in drills, punches, braces and bits, jemmies, clamps, and augers, with two or three novelties invented by Jimmy himself, in which he took pride. Over nine hundred dollars they had cost him to have made at—, a place where they make such things for the profession.

In half an hour Jimmy went downstairs and through the café. He was now dressed in tasteful and well-fitting clothes, and carried his dusted and cleaned suitcase in his hand.

'Got anything on?' asked Mike Dolan, genially.

'Me?' said Jimmy, in a puzzled tone. 'I don't understand. I'm representing the New York Amalgamated Short Snap Biscuit Cracker and Frazzled Wheat Company.'

This statement delighted Mike to such an extent that Jimmy had to take a seltzer-and-milk on the spot. He never touched 'hard' drinks.

A week after the release of Valentine, 9762, there was a neat job of safe-burglary done in Richmond, Indiana, with no clue to the author. A scant eight hundred dollars was all that was secured. Two weeks after that a patented, improved, burglar-proof safe in Logansport was opened like a cheese to the tune of fifteen hundred dollars, currency; securities and silver untouched. That began to interest the rogue-catchers. Then an old-fashioned bank-safe in Jefferson City became active and threw out of its crater an eruption of bank-notes, amounting to five thousand dollars. The losses were now high enough to bring the matter up into Ben Price's class of work. By comparing notes, a remarkable similarity in the methods of the burglaries was noticed. Ben Price investigated the scenes of the robberies, and was heard to remark:

'That's Dandy Jim Valentine's autograph. He's resumed business. Look at that combination knob – jerked out as easy as pulling up a radish in wet weather. He's got the only clamps that can do it. And look how clean those tumblers were punched out! Jimmy never has to drill but one hole. Yes, I guess I want Mr. Valentine. He'll do his bit next time without any short-time or clemency foolishness.'

Ben Price knew Jimmy's habits. He had learned them while working up the Springfield case. Long jumps, quick get-aways, no confederates, and a taste for good society – these ways had helped Mr. Valentine to become noted as a successful dodger of retribution. It was given out that Ben Price had taken up the trail of the elusive cracksman, and other people with burglar-proof safes felt more at ease.

One afternoon Jimmy Valentine and his suitcase climbed out of the mail-hack in Elmore, a little town five miles off the railroad down in the black-jack country of Arkansas. Jimmy, looking like an athletic young senior just home from college, went down the board sidewalk toward the hotel.

A young lady crossed the street, passed him at the corner and entered a door over which was the sign 'The Elmore Bank.' Jimmy Valentine looked into her eyes, forgot what he was, and became another man. She lowered her eyes and colored slightly. Young men of Jimmy's style and looks were scarce in Elmore.

Jimmy collared a boy that was loafing on the steps of the bank as if he were one of the stock-holders, and began to ask him questions about the town, feeding him dimes at intervals. By and by the young lady came out, looking royally unconscious of the young man with the suitcase, and went her way.

'Isn't that young lady Miss Polly Simpson?' asked Jimmy, with specious guile.

'Naw,' said the boy. 'She's Annabel Adams. Her pa owns this bank. What'd you come to Elmore for? Is that a gold watch-chain? I'm going to get a bulldog. Got any more dimes?'

Jimmy went to the Planter's Hotel, registered as Ralph D. Spencer, and engaged a room. He leaned on the desk and declared his platform to the clerk. He said he had come to Elmore to look for a location to go into business. How was the shoe business, now, in the town? He had thought of the shoe business. Was there an opening?

The clerk was impressed by the clothes and manner of Jimmy. He, himself, was something of a pattern of fashion to the thinly gilded youth of Elmore, but he now perceived his shortcomings. While trying to figure out Jimmy's manner of tying his four-in-hand he cordially gave information.

Yes, there ought to be a good opening in the shoe line. There wasn't an exclusive shoe-store in the place. The dry-goods and general stores handled them. Business in all lines was fairly good. Hoped Mr. Spencer would decide to locate in Elmore. He would find it a pleasant town to live in, and the people very sociable.

Mr. Spencer thought he would stop over in the town a few days and look over the situation. No, the clerk needn't call the boy. He would carry up his suitcase, himself; it was rather heavy.

Mr. Ralph Spencer, the phoenix that arose from Jimmy Valentine's ashes – ashes left by the flame of a sudden and alternative attack of love – remained in Elmore, and prospered. He opened a shoe-store and secured a good run of trade.

Socially he was also a success, and made many friends. And he accomplished the wish of his heart. He met Miss Annabel Adams, and became more and more captivated by her charms.

At the end of a year the situation of Mr. Ralph Spencer was this: he had won the respect of the community, his shoe-store was flourishing, and he and Annabel were engaged to be married in two weeks. Mr. Adams, the typical, plodding, country banker, approved of Spencer. Annabel's pride in him almost equalled her affection. He was as much at home in the family of Mr. Adams and that of Annabel's married sister as if he were already a member.

One day Jimmy sat down in his room and wrote this letter, which he mailed to the safe address of one of his old friends in St. Louis:

Dear Old Pal:

I want you to be at Sullivan's place, in Little Rock, next Wednesday night at nine o'clock. I want you to wind up some little matters for me. And, also, I want to make you a present of my kit of tools. I know you'll be glad to get them – you couldn't duplicate the lot for a thousand dollars. Say, Billy, I've quit the old business – a year ago. I've got a nice store. I'm making an honest living, and I'm going to marry the finest girl on earth two weeks from now. It's the only life, Billy – the straight one. I wouldn't touch a dollar of another man's money now for a million. After I get married I'm going to sell out and go West, where there won't be so much danger of having old scores brought up against me. I tell you, Billy, she's an angel. She believes in me; and I wouldn't do another crooked thing for the whole world. Be sure to be at Sully's, for I must see you. I'll bring along the tools with me.

Your old friend,
Jimmy

On the Monday night after Jimmy wrote this letter, Ben Price jogged unobtrusively into Elmore in a livery buggy. He lounged about town in his quiet way until he found out what he wanted to know. From the drug-store across the street from Spencer's shoe-store he got a good look at Ralph D. Spencer.

'Going to marry the banker's daughter are you, Jimmy?' said Ben to himself, softly. 'Well, I don't know!'

The next morning Jimmy took breakfast at the Adamses. He was going to Little Rock that day to order his wedding-suit and buy something nice for Annabel. That would be the first time he had left town since he came to Elmore. It had been more than a year now since those last professional 'jobs,' and he thought he could safely venture out.

After breakfast quite a family party went down town together – Mr. Adams, Annabel, Jimmy, and Annabel's married sister with her two little girls, aged five and nine. They came by the hotel where Jimmy still boarded, and he ran up to his room and brought along his suitcase. Then they went on to the bank. There stood Jimmy's horse and buggy and Dolph Gibson, who was going to drive him over to the railroad station.

All went inside the high, carved oak railings into the banking-room – Jimmy included, for Mr. Adams's future son-in-law was welcome anywhere. The clerks were pleased to be greeted by the good-looking, agreeable young man who was going to marry Miss Annabel. Jimmy set his suitcase down. Annabel, whose heart was bubbling with happiness and lively youth, put on Jimmy's hat and picked up the suitcase. 'Wouldn't I make a nice drummer?' said Annabel. 'My! Ralph, how heavy it is. Feels like it was full of gold bricks.'

'Lot of nickel-plated shoe-horns in there,' said Jimmy, cooly, 'that I'm going to return. Thought I'd save express charges by taking them up. I'm getting awfully economical.'

The Elmore Bank had just put in a new safe and vault. Mr. Adams was very proud of it, and insisted on an inspection by every one. The vault was a small one, but it had a new patented door. It fastened with three solid steel bolts thrown simultaneously with a single handle, and had a time-lock. Mr. Adams beamingly explained its workings to Mr. Spencer, who showed a courteous but not too intelligent interest. The two children, May and Agatha, were delighted by the shining metal and funny clock and knobs.

While they were thus engaged Ben Price sauntered in and leaned on his elbow, looking casually inside between the railings. He told the teller that he didn't want anything; he was just waiting for a man he knew.

Suddenly there was a scream or two from the women, and a commotion. Unperceived by the elders, May, the nine-year-old girl, in a spirit of play, had shut Agatha in the vault. She had then shot the bolts and turned the knob of the combination as she had seen Mr. Adams do.

The old banker sprang to the handle and tugged at it for a moment. 'The door can't be opened,' he groaned. 'The clock hasn't been wound nor the combination set.'

Agatha's mother screamed again, hysterically.

'Hush!' said Mr. Adams, raising his trembling hand. 'All be quiet for a moment, Agatha!' he called as loudly as he could. 'Listen to me.' During the following silence they could just hear the faint sound of the child wildly shrieking in the dark vault in a panic of terror.

'My precious darling!' wailed the mother. 'She will die of fright! Open the door! Oh, break it open! Can't you men do something?'

'There isn't a man nearer than Little Rock who can open that door,' said Mr. Adams, in a shaky voice. 'My God! Spencer, what shall we do? That child – she can't stand it long in there. There isn't enough air, and, besides, she'll go into convulsions from fright.'

Agatha's mother, frantic now, beat the door of the vault with her hands. Somebody wildly suggested dynamite. Annabel turned to Jimmy, her large eyes full of anguish, but not yet despairing. To a woman nothing seems quite impossible to the powers of the man she worships.

'Can't you do something, Ralph – *try*, won't you?'

He looked at her with a queer, soft smile on his lips and in his keen eyes.

'Annabel,' he said, 'give me that rose you are wearing, will you?'

Hardly believing that she heard him aright, she unpinned the bud from the bosom of her dress, and placed it in his hand. Jimmy stuffed it into his vest-pocket, threw off his coat and pulled up his shirt-sleeves. With that act Ralph D. Spencer passed away and Jimmy Valentine took his place.

'Get away from the door, all of you,' he commanded, shortly.

He set his suitcase on the table, and opened it out flat. From that time on he seemed to be unconscious of the presence of any one else. He laid out the shining, queer implements swiftly and orderly, whistling softly to himself as he always did when at work. In a deep silence and immovable, the others watched him as if under a spell.

In a minute Jimmy's pet drill was biting smoothly into the steel door. In ten minutes – breaking his own burglarious record – he threw back the bolts and opened the door.

Agatha, almost collapsed, but safe, was gathered into her mother's arms. Jimmy Valentine put on his coat, and walked outside the railings toward the front door. As he went he thought he heard a far-away voice that he once knew call 'Ralph!' But he never hesitated.

At the door a big man stood somewhat in his way.

'Hello, Ben!' said Jimmy, still with his strange smile. 'Got around at last, have you? Well, let's go. I don't know that it makes much difference, now.'

And then Ben Price acted rather strangely.

'Guess you're mistaken, Mr. Spencer,' he said. 'Don't believe I recognize you. Your buggy's waiting for you, ain't it?'

And Ben Price turned and strolled down the street.

CHERCHEZ LA FEMME

ROBBINS, REPORTER FOR THE *Picayune*, and Dumars, of *L'Abeille* – the old French newspaper that has buzzed for nearly a century – were good friends, well proven by years of ups and downs together. They were seated where they had a habit of meeting – in the little, Creole-haunted café of Madame Tibault, in Dumaine Street. If you know the place, you will experience a thrill of pleasure in recalling it to mind. It is small and dark, with six little polished tables, at which you may sit and drink the best coffee in New Orleans, and concoctions of absinthe equal to Sazerac's best. Madame Tibault, fat and indulgent, presides at the desk, and takes your money. Nicolette and Mémé, Madame's nieces, in charming bib aprons, bring the desirable beverages.

Dumars, with true Creole luxury, was sipping his absinthe, with half-closed eyes, in a swirl of cigarette smoke. Robbins was looking over the morning *Pic.*, detecting, as young reporters will, the gross blunders in the make-up, and the envious blue-pencilling his own stuff had received. This item, in the advertising columns, caught his eye, and with an exclamation of sudden interest he read it aloud to his friend.

> PUBLIC AUCTION. - At three o'clock this afternoon there will be sold to the highest bidder all the common property of the Little Sisters of Samaria, at the home of the Sisterhood, in Bonhomme Street. The sale will dispose of the building, ground, and the complete furnishings of the house and chapel, without reserve.

This notice stirred the two friends to a reminiscent talk concerning an episode in their journalistic career that had occurred about two years before. They recalled the incidents, went over the old theories, and discussed it anew from the different perspective time had brought.

There were no other customers in the café. Madame's fine ear had caught the line of their talk, and she came over to their table – for had it not been her lost money – her vanished twenty thousand dollars – that had set the whole matter going?

The three took up the long-abandoned mystery, threshing over the old, dry chaff of it. It was in the chapel of this house of the Little Sisters of Samaria that Robbins and Dumars had stood during that eager, fruitless news search of theirs, and looked upon the gilded statue of the Virgin.

'Thass so, boys,' said Madame, summing up. 'Thass ver' wicked man, M'sieur Morin. Everybody shall be cert' he steal those money I plaze in his hand to keep safe. Yes. He's foun' spend that money, somehow.' Madame turned a broad and comprehensive smile upon Dumars. 'I ond'stand you, M'sieur Dumars, those day you come ask me fo' tell ev'ything I know 'bout M'sieur Morin. Ah! yes, I know most time when those men lose money you say "*Cherchez la femme*" – there is somewhere the woman. But not for M'sieur Morin. No, boys. Before he shall die, he is like one saint. You might's well, M'sieur Dumars, go try find those money in those statue of Virgin Mary that M'sieur Morin present at those *p'tite sœurs*, as try find one *femme*.'

At Madame Tibault's last words, Robbins started slightly and cast a keen sidelong glance at Dumars. The Creole sat, unmoved, dreamily watching the spirals of his cigarette smoke.

It was then nine o'clock in the morning and, a few minutes later, the two friends separated, going different ways to their day's duties. And now follows the brief story of Madame Tibault's vanished thousands:

New Orleans will readily recall to mind the circumstances attendant upon the death of Mr. Gaspard Morin, in that city. Mr. Morin was an artistic goldsmith and jeweller in the old French Quarter, and a man held in the highest esteem. He belonged to one of the oldest French families, and was of some distinction as an antiquary and historian. He was a bachelor, about fifty years of age. He lived in quiet comfort, at one of those rare old hostelries in Royal Street. He was found in his rooms, one morning, dead from unknown causes.

When his affairs came to be looked into, it was found that he was practically insolvent, his stock of goods and personal property barely – but nearly enough to free him from censure – covering his liabilities. Following came the disclosure that he had been intrusted with the sum of twenty thousand dollars by a former upper servant in the Morin family, one Madame Tibault, which she had received as a legacy from relatives in France.

The most searching scrutiny by friends and the legal authorities failed to reveal the disposition of the money. It had vanished, and left no trace. Some weeks before his death, Mr. Morin had drawn the entire amount, in gold coin, from the bank where it had been placed while he looked about (he told Madame Tibault) for a safe investment. Therefore, Mr. Morin's memory seemed doomed to bear the cloud of dishonesty, while Madame was, of course, disconsolate.

Then it was that Robbins and Dumars, representing their respective journals, began one of those pertinacious private investigations which, of late years, the press has adopted as a means to glory and the satisfaction of public curiosity.

'Cherchez la femme,' said Dumars.

'That's the ticket!' agreed Robbins. 'All roads lead to the eternal feminine. We will find the woman.'

They exhausted the knowledge of the staff of Mr. Morin's hotel, from the bellboy down to the proprietor. They gently, but inflexibly, pumped the family of the deceased as far as his cousins twice removed. They artfully sounded the employees of the late jeweller, and dogged his customers for information concerning his habits. Like bloodhounds they traced every step of the supposed defaulter, as nearly as might be, for years along the limited and monotonous paths he had trodden.

At the end of their labors, Mr. Morin stood, an immaculate man. Not one weakness that might be served up as a criminal tendency, not one deviation from the path of rectitude, not even a hint of a predilection for the opposite sex, was found to be placed to his debit. His life had been as regular and austere as a monk's; his habits, simple and unconcealed. Generous, charitable, and a model in propriety, was the verdict of all who knew him.

'What, now?' asked Robbins, fingering his empty notebook.

'Cherchez la femme,' said Dumars, lighting a cigarette. 'Try Lady Bellairs.'

This piece of femininity was the race-track of the season. Being feminine, she was erratic in her gaits, and there were a few heavy losers about town who had believed she could be true. The reporters applied for information.

Mr. Morin? Certainly not. He was never ever a spectator at the races. Not that kind of a man. Surprised the gentlemen should ask.

'Shall we throw it up?' suggested Robbins, 'and let the puzzle department have a try?'

'*Cherchez la femme*,' hummed Dumars, reaching for a match. 'Try the Little Sisters of What-d'-you-call-'em.'

It had developed, during the investigation, that Mr. Morin had held this benevolent order in particular favor. He had contributed liberally toward its support and had chosen its chapel as his favorite place of private worship. It was said that he went there daily to make his devotions at the altar. Indeed, toward the last of his life his whole mind seemed to have fixed itself upon religious matters, perhaps to the detriment of his worldly affairs.

Thither went Robbins and Dumars, and were admitted through the narrow doorway in the blank stone wall that frowned upon Bonhomme Street. An old woman was sweeping the chapel. She told them that Sister Félicité, the head of the order, was then at prayer at the altar in the alcove. In a few moments she would emerge. Heavy, black curtains screened the alcove. They waited.

Soon the curtains were disturbed, and Sister Félicité came forth. She was tall, tragic, bony, and plain-featured, dressed in the black gown and severe bonnet of the sisterhood.

Robbins, a good rough-and-tumble reporter, but lacking the delicate touch, began to speak.

They represented the press. The lady had, no doubt, heard of the Morin affair. It was necessary, in justice to that gentleman's memory, to probe the mystery of the lost money. It was known that he had come often to this chapel. Any information, now, concerning Mr. Morin's habits, tastes, the friends he had, and so on, would be of value in doing him posthumous justice.

Sister Félicité had heard. Whatever she knew would be willingly told, but it was very little. Monsieur Morin had been a good friend to the order, sometimes contributing as much as a hundred dollars. The sisterhood was an independent one, depending entirely upon private contributions for the means to carry on its charitable work. Mr. Morin had presented the chapel with silver candlesticks and an altar cloth. He came every day to worship in the chapel, sometimes remaining for an hour. He was a devout Catholic, consecrated to holiness. Yes, and also in the alcove was a statue of the Virgin that he had himself modeled, cast, and presented to the order. Oh, it was cruel to cast a doubt upon so good a man!

Robbins was also profoundly grieved at the imputation. But, until it was found what Mr. Morin had done with Madame Tibault's money, he feared the tongue of slander would not be stilled. Sometimes – in fact, very often – in affairs of the kind there was – er – as the saying goes – er – a lady in the case. In absolute confidence, now – if – perhaps—

Sister Félicité's large eyes regarded him solemnly.

'There was one woman,' she said, slowly, 'to whom he bowed – whom he gave his heart.'

Robbins fumbled rapturously for his pencil.

'Behold the woman!' said Sister Félicité, suddenly, in deep tones.

She reached a long arm and swept aside the curtain of the alcove. In there was a shrine, lit to a glow of soft color by the light pouring through a stained-glass window. Within a deep niche in the bare stone wall stood an image of the Virgin Mary, the color of pure gold.

Dumars, a conventional Catholic, succumbed to the dramatic in the act. He bowed his head for an instant and made the sign of the cross. The somewhat abashed Robbins, murmuring an indistinct apology, backed awkwardly away. Sister Félicité drew back the curtain, and the reporters departed.

On the narrow stone sidewalk of Bonhomme Street, Robbins turned to Dumars, with unworthy sarcasm.

'Well, what next? Churchy law fem?'

'Absinthe,' said Dumars.

With the history of the missing money thus partially related, some conjecture may be formed of the sudden idea that Madame Tibault's words seemed to have suggested to Robbins's brain.

Was it so wild a surmise – that the religious fanatic had offered up his wealth – or, rather, Madame Tibault's – in the shape of a material symbol of his consuming devotion? Stranger things have been done in the name of worship. Was it not possible that the lost thousands were molded into the lustrous image? That the goldsmith had formed it of the pure and precious metal, and set it there, through some hope of a perhaps disordered brain to propitiate the saints and pave the way to his own selfish glory?

That afternoon, at five minutes to three, Robbins entered the chapel door of the Little Sisters of Samaria. He saw, in the dim light, a crowd of perhaps a hundred people gathered to attend the sale. Most of them were members of various religious orders, priests and churchmen, come to purchase the paraphernalia of the chapel, lest they fall into desecrating hands. Others were business men and agents come to bid upon the realty. A clerical-looking brother had volunteered to wield the hammer, bringing to the office of auctioneer the anomaly of choice diction and dignity of manner.

A few of the minor articles were sold, and then two assistants brought forward the image of the Virgin.

Robbins started the bidding at ten dollars. A stout man, in an ecclesiastical garb, went to fifteen. A voice from another part of the crowd raised to twenty. The three bid alternately, raising by bids of five, until the offer was fifty dollars. Then the stout man dropped out, and Robbins, as a sort of *coup de main*, went to a hundred.

'One hundred and fifty,' said the other voice.

'Two hundred,' bid Robbins, boldly.

'Two-fifty,' called his competitor, promptly.

The reporter hesitated for the space of a lightning flash, estimating how much he could borrow from the boys in the office, and screw from the business manager from his next month's salary.

'Three hundred,' he offered.

'Three-fifty,' spoke up the other, in a louder voice – a voice that sent Robbins diving suddenly through the crowd in its direction, to catch Dumars, its owner, ferociously by the collar.

'You unconverted idiot!' hissed Robbins, close to his ear – 'pool!'

'Agreed!' said Dumars, coolly. 'I couldn't raise three hundred and fifty dollars with a search-warrant, but I can stand half. What you come bidding against me for?'

'I thought I was the only fool in the crowd,' explained Robbins.

No one else bidding, the statue was knocked down to the syndicate at their last offer. Dumars remained with the prize, while Robbins hurried forth to wring from the resources and credit of both the prize. He soon returned with the money, and the two musketeers loaded their precious package into a carriage and drove with it to Dumars's room, in old Chartres Street, near by. They lugged it, covered with a cloth, up the stairs, and deposited it on a table. A hundred pounds it weighed, if an ounce, and at that estimate, according to their calculation, if their daring theory were correct, it stood there, worth twenty thousand golden dollars.

Robbins removed the covering, and opened his pocket-knife.

'*Sacré!*' muttered Dumars, shuddering. 'It is the Mother of Christ. What would you do?'

'Shut up, Judas!' said Robbins, coldly. 'It's too late for you to be saved now.'

With a firm hand, he clipped a slice from the shoulder of the image. The cut showed a dull, grayish metal, with a thin coating of gold leaf.

'Lead!' announced Robbins, hurling his knife to the floor – 'gilded!'

'To the devil with it!' said Dumars forgetting his scruples. 'I must have a drink.'

Together they walked moodily to the café of Madame Tibault, two squares away.

It seemed that Madame's mind had been stirred that day to fresh recollections of the past services of the two young men in her behalf.

'You mustn't sit by those table,' she interposed, as they were about to drop into their accustomed seats. 'Thass so, boys. But no. I mek you come at this room, like my *très bons amis*. Yes. I goin' mek for you myself one *anisette* and one *café royale* ver' fine. Ah! I lak treat my fren' nize. Yes. Plis come in this way.'

Madame led them into the little back room, into which she sometimes invited the especially favored of her customers. In two comfortable armchairs, by a big window that opened upon the courtyard, she placed them, with a low table between. Bustling hospitably about, she began to prepare the promised refreshments.

It was the first time the reporters had been honored with admission to the sacred precincts. The room was in dusky twilight, flecked with gleams of the polished fine woods and burnished glass and metal that the Creoles love. From the little courtyard a tiny fountain sent in an insinuating sound of trickling waters, to which a banana plant by the window kept time with its tremulous leaves.

Robbins, an investigator by nature, sent a curious glance roving about the room. From some barbaric ancestor, Madame had inherited a *penchant* for the crude in decoration.

. The walls were adorned with cheap lithographs – florid libels upon nature, addressed to the taste of the *bourgeoisie* – birthday cards, garish newspaper supplements, and specimens of art-advertising calculated to reduce the optic nerve to stunned submission. A patch of something unintelligible in the midst of the more candid display puzzled Robbins, and he rose and took a step nearer, to interrogate it at closer range. Then he leaned weakly against the wall, and called out:

'Madame Tibault! Oh, madame! Since when – oh! since when have you been in the habit of papering your walls with five thousand dollar United States four per cent. gold bonds? Tell me – is this a Grimm's fairy tale, or should I consult an oculist?'

At his words, Madame Tibault and Dumars approached.

'H'what you say?' said Madame, cheerily. 'H'what you say, M'sieur Robbin'? *Bon!* Ah those nize li'l peezes papier! One tam I think those wa't you call calendair, wiz ze l'l day of mont' below. But, no. Those wall is broke in those plaze, M'sieur Robbin', and I plaze those li'l peezes papier to conceal ze crack. I did think the couleur harm'nize so well with the wall papier. Where I get them from? Ah, yes, I remem' ver' well. One day M'sieur Morin, he come at my house – thass 'bout one mont' before he shall die – thass 'long 'bout tam he promise fo' inves' those money fo' me. M'sieur Morin, he leave those li'l peezes papier in those table, and say ver' much 'bout money thass hard for me to ond'stan. *Mais* I never see those money again. Thass ver' wicked man, M'sieur Morin. H'what you call those peezes papier, M'sieur Robbin' – *bon!*'

Robbins explained.

'There's your twenty thousand dollars, with coupons attached,' he said, running his thumb around the edge of the four bonds. 'Better get an expert to peel them off for you. Mister Morin was all right. I'm going out to get my ears trimmed.'

He dragged Dumars by the arm into the outer room. Madame was screaming for Nicolette and Mémé to come and observe the fortune returned to her by M'sieur Morin, the best of men, that saint in glory.

'Marsy,' said Robbins. 'I'm going on a jamboree. For three days the esteemed *Pic.* will have to get along without my valuable services. I advise you to join me. Now, that green stuff you drink is no good. It stimulates thought. What we want to do is to forget to remember. I'll introduce you to the only lady in this case that is guaranteed to produce the desired results. Her name is Belle of Kentucky, twelve-year-old Bourbon. In quarts. How does the idea strike you?'

'*Allons!*' said Dumars. '*Cherchez la femme.*'

FRIENDS IN SAN ROSARIO

THE WEST-BOUND STOPPED at San Rosario on time at 8.20 A.M. A man with a thick black-leather wallet under his arm left the train and walked rapidly up the main street of the town. There were other passengers who also got off at San Rosario, but they either slouched limberly over to the railroad eating-house or the Silver Dollar saloon, or joined the groups of idlers about the station.

Indecision had no part in the movements of the man with the wallet. He was short in stature, but strongly built, with very light, closely trimmed hair, smooth, determined face, and aggressive, gold-rimmed nose glasses. He was well dressed in the prevailing Eastern style. His air denoted a quiet but conscious reserve force, if not actual authority.

After walking a distance of three squares he came to the center of the town's business area. Here another street of importance crossed the main one, forming the hub of San Rosario's life and commerce. Upon one corner stood the post office. Upon another Rebensky's Clothing Emporium. The other two diagonally opposing corners were occupied by the town's two banks, the First National and the Stockmen's National. Into the First National Bank of San Rosario the newcomer walked, never slowing his brisk step until he stood at the cashier's window. The bank opened for business at nine, and the working force was already assembled, each member preparing his department for the day's business. The cashier was examining the mail when he noticed the stranger standing at his window.

'Bank doesn't open 'til nine,' he remarked, curtly, but without feeling. He had had to make that statement so often to early birds since San Rosario adopted city banking hours.

'I am well aware of that,' said the other man, in cool, brittle tones. 'Will you kindly receive my card?'

The cashier drew the small, spotless parallelogram inside the bars of his wicket, and read:

J. F. C. NETTLEWICK
NATIONAL BANK EXAMINER

'Oh – er – will you walk around inside, Mr. – er – Nettlewick. Your first visit – didn't know your business, of course. Walk right around, please.'

The examiner was quickly inside the sacred precincts of the bank, where he was ponderously introduced to each employee in turn by Mr. Edlinger, the cashier – a middle-aged gentleman of deliberation, discretion, and method.

'I was kind of expecting Sam Turner round again, pretty soon,' said Mr. Edlinger. 'Sam's been examining us now for about four years. I guess you'll find us all right, though considering the tightness in business. Not overly much money on hand, but able to stand the storms, sir, stand the storms.'

'Mr. Turner and I have been ordered by the Comptroller to exchange districts,' said the examiner, in his decisive, formal tones. 'He is covering my old territory in southern Illinois and Indiana. I will take the cash first, please.'

Perry Dorsey, the teller, was already arranging his cash on the counter for the examiner's inspection. He knew it was right to a cent, and he had nothing to fear, but he was nervous and flustered. So was every man in the bank. There was something so icy and swift, so impersonal and uncompromising about this man that his very presence seemed an accusation. He looked to be a man who would never make nor overlook an error.

Mr. Nettlewick first seized the currency, and with a rapid, almost juggling motion, counted it by packages. Then he spun the sponge cup toward him and verified the count by bills. His thin, white fingers flew like some expert musician's upon the keys of a piano. He dumped the gold upon the counter with a crash, and the coins whined and sang as they skimmed across the marble slab from the tips of his nimble digits. The air was full of fractional currency when he came to the halves and quarters. He counted the last nickel and dime. He had the scales brought, and he weighed every sack of silver in the vault. He questioned Dorsey concerning each of the cash memoranda – certain checks, charge slips, etc., carried over from the previous day's work – with unimpeachable courtesy, yet with something so mysteriously momentous in his frigid manner, that the teller was reduced to pink cheeks and a stammering tongue.

This newly imported examiner was so different from Sam Turner. It had been Sam's way to enter the bank with a shout, pass the cigars, and tell the latest stories he had picked up on his rounds. His customary greeting to Dorsey had been, 'Hello, Perry! Haven't skipped out with the boodle yet, I see.' Turner's way of counting the cash had been different too. He would finger the packages of bills in a tired kind of way, and then go into the vault and kick over a few sacks of silver, and the thing was done. Halves and quarters and dimes? Not for Sam Turner. 'No chicken feed for me,' he would say when they were set before him. 'I'm not in the agricultural department.' But, then, Turner was a Texan, an old friend of the bank's president, and had known Dorsey since he was a baby.

While the examiner was counting the cash, Major Thomas B. Kingman – known to every one as 'Major Tom' – the president of the First National, drove up to the side door with his old dun horse and buggy, and came inside. He saw the examiner busy with the money, and, going into the little 'pony corral,' as he called it, in which his desk was railed off, he began to look over his letters.

Earlier, a little incident had occurred that even the sharp eyes of the examiner had failed to notice. When he had begun his work at the cash counter, Mr. Edlinger had winked significantly at Roy Wilson, the youthful bank messenger, and nodded his head slightly toward the front door. Roy understood, got his hat and walked leisurely out, with his collector's book under his arm. Once outside, he made a beeline for the Stockmen's National. That bank was also getting ready to open. No customers had, as yet, presented themselves.

'Say, you people!' cried Roy, with the familiarity of youth and long acquaintance, 'you want to get a move on you. There's a new bank examiner over at the First, and he's a stem-winder. He's counting nickels on Perry, and he's got the whole outfit bluffed. Mr. Edlinger gave me the tip to let you know.'

Mr. Buckley, president of the Stockmen's National – a stout, elderly man, looking like a farmer dressed for Sunday – heard Roy from his private office at the rear and called him.

'Has Major Kingman come down to the bank yet?' he asked of the boy.

'Yes, sir, he was just driving up as I left,' said Roy.

'I want you to take him a note. Put it into his own hands as soon as you get back.'

Mr. Buckley sat down and began to write.

Roy returned and handed to Major Kingman the envelope containing the note. The major read it, folded it, and slipped it into his vest pocket. He leaned back in his chair for a few moments as if he were meditating deeply, and then rose and went into the vault. He came out with the bulky, old-fashioned leather note case stamped on the back in gilt letters, 'Bills Discounted.' In this were the notes due the bank with their attached securities, and the major, in his rough way, dumped the lot upon his desk and began to sort them over.

By this time Nettlewick had finished his count of the cash. His pencil fluttered like a swallow over the sheet of paper on which he had set his figures. He opened his black wallet, which seemed to be also a kind of secret memorandum book, made a few rapid figures in it, wheeled and transfixed

Dorsey with the glare of his spectacles. That look seemed to say: 'You're safe this time, but—'

'Cash all correct,' snapped the examiner. He made a dash for the individual bookkeeper, and, for a few minutes there was a fluttering of ledger leaves and a sailing of balance sheets through the air.

'How often do you balance your pass-books?' he demanded, suddenly.

'Er – once a month,' faltered the individual bookkeeper, wondering how many years they would give him.

'All right,' said the examiner, turning and charging upon the general bookkeeper, who had the statements of his foreign banks and their reconcilement memoranda ready. Everything there was found to be all right. Then the stub book of the certificates of deposit. Flutter – flutter – zip – zip – check! All right, list of over-drafts, please. Thanks. H'm-m. Unsigned bills of the bank next. All right.

Then came the cashier's turn, and easy-going Mr. Edlinger rubbed his nose and polished his glasses nervously under the quick fire of questions concerning the circulation, undivided profits, bank real estate, and stock ownership.

Presently Nettlewick was aware of a big man towering above him at his elbow – a man sixty years of age, rugged and hale, with a rough, grizzled beard, a mass of gray hair, and a pair of penetrating blue eyes that confronted the formidable glasses of the examiner without a flicker.

'Er – Major Kingman, our president – er – Mr. Nettlewick,' said the cashier.

Two men of very different types shook hands. One was a finished product of the world of straight lines, conventional methods, and formal affairs. The other was something freer, wider, and nearer to nature. Tom Kingman had not been cut to any pattern. He had been mule-driver, cowboy, ranger, soldier, sheriff, prospector and cattleman. Now, when he was bank president, his old comrades from the prairies, of the saddle, tent, and trail, found no change in him. He had made his fortune when Texas cattle were at the high tide of value, and had organized the First National Bank of San Rosario. In spite of his largeness of heart and sometimes unwise generosity toward his old friends, the bank had prospered, for Major Tom Kingman knew men as well as he knew cattle. Of late years the cattle business had known a depression, and the major's bank was one of the few whose losses had not been great.

'And now,' said the examiner, briskly, pulling out his watch, 'the last thing is the loans. We will take them up now, if you please.'

He had gone through the First National at almost record-breaking speed – but thoroughly, as he did everything. The running order of the bank was smooth and clean, and that had facilitated his work. There was but one other bank in the town. He received from the Government a fee of twenty-five dollars for each bank that he examined. He should be able to go over those loans and discounts in half an hour. If so, he could examine the other bank immediately afterward, and catch the 11.45, the only other train that day in the direction he was working. Otherwise, he would have to spend the night and Sunday in this uninteresting Western town. That was why Mr. Nettlewick was rushing matters.

'Come with me, sir,' said Major Kingman, in his deep voice, that united the Southern drawl with the rhythmic twang of the West. 'We will go over them together. Nobody in the bank knows those notes as I do. Some of 'em

THE BEST OF O. HENRY

are a little wobbly on their legs, and some are mavericks without extra many brands on their backs, but they'll 'most all pay out at the round-up.'

The two sat down at the president's desk. First, the examiner went through the notes at lightning speed, and added up their total, finding it to agree with the amount of loans carried on the book of daily balances. Next, he took up the larger loans, inquiring scrupulously into the condition of their endorsers or securities. The new examiner's mind seemed to course and turn and make unexpected dashes hither and thither like a bloodhound seeking a trail. Finally he pushed aside all the notes except a few, which he arranged in a neat pile before him, and began a dry, formal little speech.

'I find, sir, the condition of your bank to be very good, considering the poor crops and the depression in the cattle interests of your state. The clerical work seems to be done accurately and punctually. Your past-due paper is moderate in amount, and promises only a small loss. I would recommend the calling in of your large loans, and the making of only sixty and ninety day or call loans until general business revives. And now, there is one thing more, and I will have finished with the bank. Here are six notes aggregating something like $40,000. They are secured, according to their faces, by various stocks, bonds, shares, etc., to the value of $70,000. Those securities are missing from the notes to which they should be attached. I suppose you have them in the safe or vault. You will permit me to examine them.'

Major Tom's light-blue eyes turned unflinchingly toward the examiner.

'No, sir,' he said, in a low but steady tone; 'those securities are neither in the safe nor the vault. I have taken them. You may hold me personally responsible for their absence.'

Nettlewick felt a slight thrill. He had not expected this. He had struck a momentous trail when the hunt was drawing to a close.

'Ah!' said the examiner. He waited a moment, and then continued: 'May I ask you to explain more definitely?'

'The securities were taken by me,' repeated the major. 'It was not for my own use, but to save an old friend in trouble. Come in here, sir, and we'll talk it over.'

He led the examiner into the bank's private office at the rear, and closed the door. There was a desk, and a table, and half-a-dozen leather-covered chairs. On the wall was the mounted head of a Texas steer with horns five feet from tip to tip. Opposite hung the major's old cavalry saber that he had carried at Shiloh and Fort Pillow.

Placing a chair for Nettlewick, the major seated himself by the window, from which he could see the post-office and the carved limestone front of the Stockmen's National. He did not speak at once, and Nettlewick felt, perhaps, that the ice should be broken by something so near its own temperature as the voice of official warning.

'Your statement,' he began, 'since you have failed to modify it, amounts, as you must know, to a very serious thing. You are aware, also, of what my duty must compel me to do. I shall have to go before the United States Commissioner and make — '

'I know, I know,' said Major Tom, with a wave of his hand. 'You don't suppose I'd run a bank without being posted on national banking laws and the revised statutes! Do your duty. I'm not asking any favors. But I spoke of my friend. I did want you to hear me tell about Bob.'

Nettlewick settled himself in his chair. There would be no leaving San

Rosario for him that day. He would have to telegraph to the Comptroller of the Currency; he would have to swear out a warrant before the United States Commissioner for the arrest of Major Kingman; perhaps he would be ordered to close the bank on account of the loss of the securities. It was not the first crime the examiner had unearthed. Once or twice the terrible upheaval of human emotions that his investigations had loosed had almost caused a ripple in his official calm. He had seen bank men kneel and plead and cry like women for a chance – an hour's time – the overlooking of a single error. One cashier had shot himself at his desk before him. None of them had taken it with the dignity and coolness of this stern old Westerner. Nettlewick felt that he owed it to him at least to listen if he wished to talk. With his elbow on the arm of his chair, and his square chin resting upon the fingers of his right hand, the bank examiner waited to hear the confession of the president of the First National Bank of San Rosario.

'When a man's your friend,' began Major Tom, somewhat didactically, 'for forty years, and tried by water, fire, earth, and cyclones, when you can do him a little favor you feel like doing it.'

('Embezzle for him $70,000 worth of securities,' thought the examiner.)

'We were cowboys together, Bob and I,' continued the major, speaking slowly, and deliberately, and musingly, as if his thoughts were rather with the past than the critical present, 'and we prospected together for gold and silver over Arizona, New Mexico, and a good part of California. We were both in the war of sixty-one, but in different commands. We've fought Indians and horse thieves side by side; we've starved for weeks in a cabin in the Arizona mountains, buried twenty feet deep in snow; we've ridden herd together when the wind blew so hard the lightning couldn't strike – well, Bob and I have been through some rough spells since the first time we met in the branding camp of the old Anchor-Bar ranch. And during that time we've found it necessary more than once to help each other out of tight places. In those days it was expected of a man to stick to his friend, and he didn't ask any credit for it. Probably next day you'd need him to get at your back and help stand off a band of Apaches, or put a tourniquet on your leg above a rattlesnake bite and ride for whisky. So, after all, it was give and take, and if you didn't stand square with your pardner, why, you might be shy one when you needed him. But Bob was a man who was willing to go further than that. He never played a limit.

'Twenty years ago I was sheriff of this county and I made Bob my chief deputy. That was before the boom in cattle when we both made our stake. I was sheriff and collector, and it was a big thing for me then. I was married, and we had a boy and a girl – a four and a six year old. There was a comfortable house next to the courthouse, furnished by the county, rent free, and I was saving some money. Bob did most of the office work. Both of us had seen rough times and plenty of rustling and danger, and I tell you it was great to hear the rain and sleet dashing against the windows of nights, and be warm and safe and comfortable, and know you could get up in the morning and be shaved and have folks call you "mister." And then, I had the finest wife and kids that ever struck the range, and my old friend with me enjoying the first fruits of prosperity and white shirts, and I guess I was happy. Yes, I was happy about that time.'

The major sighed and glanced casually out of the window. The bank examiner changed his position, and leaned his chin upon his other hand.

'One winter,' continued the major, 'the money for the county taxes came pouring in so fast that I didn't have time to take the stuff to the bank for a week. I just shoved the checks into a cigar box and the money into a sack, and locked them in the big safe that belonged in the sheriff's office.

'I had been overworked that week, and was about sick, anyway. My nerves were out of order, and my sleep at night didn't seem to rest me. The doctor had some scientific name for it, and I was taking medicine. And so, added to the rest, I went to bed at night with that money on my mind. Not that there was much need of being worried, for the safe was a good one, and nobody but Bob and I knew the combination. On Friday night there was about $6,500 in cash in the bag. On Saturday morning I went to the office as usual. The safe was locked, and Bob was writing at his desk. I opened the safe, and the money was gone. I called Bob, and roused everybody in the courthouse to announce the robbery. It struck me that Bob took it pretty quiet, considering how much it reflected upon both him and me.

'Two days went by and we never got a clew. It couldn't have been burglars, for the safe had been opened by the combination in the proper way. People must have begun to talk, for one afternoon in comes Alice – that's my wife – and the boy and girl, and Alice stamps her foot, and her eyes flash, and she cries out, "The lying wretches – Tom, Tom!" and I catch her in a faint, and bring her 'round little by little, and she lays her head down and cries for the first time since she took Tom Kingman's name and fortunes. And Jack and Zilla – the youngsters – they were always wild as tiger's cubs to rush at Bob and climb all over him whenever they were allowed to come to the courthouse – they stood and kicked their little shoes, and herded together like scared partridges. They were having their first trip down into the shadows of life. Bob was working at his desk, and he got up and went out without a word. The grand jury was in session then, and the next morning Bob went before them and confessed that he stole the money. He said he lost it in a poker game. In fifteen minutes they had found a true bill and sent me the warrant to arrest the man with whom I'd been closer than a thousand brothers for many a year.

'I did it, and then I said to Bob, pointing: "There's my house, and here's my office, and up there's Maine, and out that way is California, and over there is Florida – and that's your range 'til court meets. You're in my charge, and I take the responsibility. You be here when you're wanted.'

' "Thanks, Tom," he said, kind of carelessly; "I was sort of hoping you wouldn't lock me up. Court meets next Monday, so, if you don't object, I'll just loaf around the office until then. I've got one favor to ask, if it isn't too much. If you'd let the kids come out in the yard once in a while and have a romp I'd like it."

' "Why not?" I answered him. "They're welcome, and so are you. And come to my house the same as ever." You see, Mr. Nettlewick, you can't make a friend of a thief, but neither can you make a thief of a friend, all at once.'

The examiner made no answer. At that moment was heard the shrill whistle of a locomotive pulling into the depot. That was the train on the little, narrow-gauge road that struck into San Rosario from the south. The major cocked his ear and listened for a moment, and looked at his watch. The narrow-gauge was in on time – 10.35. The major continued.

'So Bob hung around the office, reading the papers and smoking. I put another deputy to work in his place, and, after a while, the first excitement of the case wore off.

'One day when we were alone in the office Bob came over to where I was sitting. He was looking sort of grim and blue – the same look he used to get when he'd been up watching for Indians all night or herd-riding.

' "Tom,' says he, "it's harder than standing off redskins; it's harder than lying in the lava desert forty miles from water; but I'm going to stick it out to the end. You know that's been my style. But if you'd tip me the smallest kind of a sign – if you'd just say, 'Bob I understand,' why, it would make it lots easier."

'I was surprised. "I don't know what you mean, Bob," I said. "Of course, you know that I'd do anything under the sun to help you that I could. But you've got me guessing."

'"All right, Tom," was all he said, and he went back to his newspaper and lit another cigar.

'It was the night before the court met when I found out what he meant. I went to bed that night with the same old, light-headed, nervous feeling come back upon me. I dropped off to sleep about midnight. When I woke I was standing half dressed in one of the courthouse corridors. Bob was holding one of my arms, our family doctor the other and Alice was shaking me and half crying. She had sent for the doctor without my knowing it, and when he came they had found me out of bed and missing, and had begun a search.

' "Sleep-walking," said the doctor.

'All of us went back to the house, and the doctor told us some remarkable stories about the strange things people had done while in that condition. I was feeling rather chilly after my trip out, and, as my wife was out of the room at the time, I pulled upon the door of an old wardrobe that stood in the room and dragged out a big quilt I had seen in there. With it tumbled out the bag of money for stealing which Bob was to be tried – and convicted – in the morning.

' "How the jumping rattlesnakes did that get there?" I yelled, and all hands must have seen how surprised I was. Bob knew in a flash.

'"You darned old snoozer," he said, with the old-time look on his face, "I saw you put it there. I watched you open the safe and take it out, and I followed you. I looked through the window and saw you hide it in that wardrobe."

' "Then, you blankety-blank, flop-eared, sheep-headed coyote, what did you say you took it for?"

' "Because," said Bob, simply, "I didn't know you were asleep."

'I saw him glance toward the door of the room where Jack and Zilla were, and I knew then what it meant to be a man's friend from Bob's point of view.'

Major Tom paused, and again directed his glance out of the window. He saw someone in the Stockmen's National Bank reach and draw a yellow shade down the whole length of its plate-glass, big front window, although the position of the sun did not seem to warrant such a defensive movement against its rays.

Nettlewick sat up straight in his chair. He had listened patiently, but without consuming interest, to the major's story. It had impressed him as irrelevant to the situation, and it could certainly have no effect upon the consequences. Those Western people, he thought, had an exaggerated sentimentality. They were not business-like. They needed to be protected from their friends. Evidently the major had concluded. And what he had said amounted to nothing.

'May I ask,' said the examiner, 'if you have anything further to say that bears directly upon the question of those abstracted securities?'

'Abstracted securities, sir!' Major Tom turned suddenly in his chair, his blue eyes flashing upon the examiner. 'What do you mean, sir?'

He drew from his coat pocket a batch of folded papers held together by a rubber band, tossed them into Nettlewick's hands, and rose to his feet.

'You'll find those securities there, sir, every stock, bond, and share of 'em. I took them from the notes while you were counting the cash. Examine and compare them for yourself.'

The major led the way back into the banking room. The examiner, astounded, perplexed, nettled, at sea, followed. He felt that he had been made the victim of something that was not exactly a hoax, but that left him in the shoes of one who had been played upon, used, and then discarded, without even an inkling of the game. Perhaps, also, his official position had been irreverently juggled with. But there was nothing he could take hold of. An official report of the matter would be an absurdity. And, somehow, he felt that he would never know anything more about the matter than he did then.

Frigidly, mechanically, Nettlewick examined the securities, found them to tally with the notes, gathered his black wallet, and rose to depart.

'I will say,' he protested, turning the indignant glare of his glasses upon Major Kingman, 'that your statements – your misleading statements, which you have not condescended to explain – do not appear to be quite the thing, regarded either as business or humor. I do not understand such motives or actions.'

Major Tom looked down at him serenely and not unkindly.

'Son,' he said, 'there are plenty of things in the chaparral, and on the prairies, and up the cañons that you don't understand. But I want to thank you for listening to a garrulous old man's prosy story. We old Texans love to talk about our adventures and our old comrades, and the home folks have long ago learned to run when we begin with "Once upon a time," so we have to spin our yarns to the stranger within our gates.'

The major smiled, but the examiner only bowed coldly, and abruptly quitted the bank. They saw him travel diagonally across the street in a straight line and enter the Stockmen's National Bank.

Major Tom sat down at his desk and drew from his vest pocket the note Roy had given him. He had read it once, but hurriedly, and now, with something like a twinkle in his eyes, he read it again. These were the words he read:

Dear Tom:

I hear there's one of Uncle Sam's greyhounds going through you, and that means that we'll catch him inside of a couple of hours, maybe. Now, I want you to do something for me. We've got just $2,200 in the bank, and the law requires that we have $20,000. I let Ross and Fisher have $18,000 late yesterday afternoon to buy up that Gibson bunch of cattle. They'll realize $40,000 in less than thirty days on the transaction, but that won't make my cash on hand look any prettier to that bank examiner. Now, I can't show him those notes, for they're just plain notes of hand without any security in sight, but you know very well that Pink Ross and Jim Fisher are two of the finest white men God ever made, and they'll do the square thing. You remember Jim Fisher – he was the one who shot that faro dealer in El Paso. I wired Sam Bradshaw's bank to send me $20,000, and it will get in on the narrow-gauge at 10.35. You can't let a bank examiner in to count $2,200 and close your doors. Tom, you hold that examiner. Hold him. Hold him if you have to rope him and sit on his head. Watch our front window after the narrow-gauge gets in, and when we've got the cash inside we'll pull down the shade for a signal. Don't turn him loose till then. I'm counting on you, Tom.

> Your Old Pard,
> Bob Buckley,
> *Prest. Stockmen's National*

The major began to tear the note into small pieces and throw them into his waste basket. He gave a satisfied little chuckle as he did so.

'Confounded old reckless cowpuncher!' he growled, contentedly, 'that pays him some on account for what he tried to do for me in the sheriff's office twenty years ago.'

THE FOURTH IN SALVADOR

ON A SUMMER'S DAY, while the city was rocking with the din and red uproar of patriotism, Billy Casparis told me this story.

In his way, Billy is Ulysses, Jr. Like Satan, he comes from going to and fro upon the earth and walking up and down in it. To-morrow morning while you are cracking your breakfast egg he may be off with his little alligator grip to boom a town site in the middle of Lake Okeechobee or to trade horses with the Patagonians.

We sat at a little, round table, and between us were glasses holding big lumps of ice, and above us leaned an artificial palm. And because our scene was set with the properties of the one they recalled to his mind, Billy was stirred to narrative.

'It reminds me,' said he, 'of a Fourth I helped to celebrate down in Salvador. 'Twas while I was running an ice factory down there, after I unloaded that silver mine I had in Colorado. I had what they called a "conditional concession." They made me put up a thousand dollars cash forfeit that I would make ice continuously for six months. If I did that I could draw down my ante. If I failed to do so the government took the pot. So the inspectors kept dropping in, trying to catch me without the goods.

'One day when the thermometer was at 110, the clock at half-past one, and the calendar at July third, two of the little, brown, oily nosers in red trousers slid in to make an inspection. Now, the factory hadn't turned out a pound of ice in three weeks, for a couple of reasons. The Salvador heathen wouldn't buy it; they said it made things cold they put it in. And I couldn't make any more, because I was broke. All I was holding on for was to get down my thousand so I could leave the country. The six months would be up on the sixth of July.

'Well, I showed 'em all the ice I had. I raised the lid of a darkish vat, and there was an elegant 100-pound block of ice, beautiful and convincing to the eye. I was about to close down the lid again when one of those brunette sleuths flops down on his red knees and lays a slanderous and violent hand on my guarantee of good faith. And in two minutes more they had dragged out on the floor that fine chunk of molded glass that had cost me fifty dollars to have shipped down from Frisco.

' 'Ice-y?' says the fellow that played me the dishonorable trick; "verree warm ice-y. Yes. The day is that hot, señor. Yes. Maybeso it is of desirableness to leave him out to get the cool. Yes."

' "Yes," says I, "yes," for I knew they had me. "Touching's believing, ain't it, boys? Now there's some might say the seats of your trousers are sky blue, but 'tis my opinion they are red. Let's apply the tests of the laying on of hands and feet." And so I hoisted both those inspectors out of the door on the toe of my shoe, and sat down to cool off on my block of disreputable glass.

'And, as I live without oats, while I sat there, homesick for money. and without a cent to my ambition, there came on the breeze the most beautiful smell my nose had entered for a year. God knows where it came from in that backyard of a country – it was a bouquet of soaked lemon peel, cigar stumps, and stale beer – exactly the smell of Goldbrick Charley's place on Fourteenth Street where I used to play pinochle of afternoons with the third-rate actors. And that smell drove my troubles through me and clinched 'em at the back. I began to long for my country and feel sentiments about it; and I said words about Salvador that you wouldn't think could come legitimate out of an ice factory.

'And while I was sitting there, down through the blazing sunshine in his clean, white clothes comes Maximilian Jones, an American interested in rubber and rosewood.

' "Great carrambos!" says I, when he stepped in, for I was in a bad temper, "didn't I have catastrophes enough? I know what you want. You want to tell me that story again about Johnny Ammiger and the widow on the train. You've told it nine times already this month."

' "It must be the heat," says Jones, stopping in the door, amazed. "Poor Billy. He's got bugs. Sitting on ice, and calling his best friends pseudonyms. Hi! – *muchaco!*" Jones called my force of employees, who was sitting in the sun, playing with his toes, and told him to put on his trousers and run for the doctor.

' "Come back," says I. "Sit down, Maxy, and forget it. 'Tis not ice you see, nor a lunatic upon it. 'Tis only an exile full of homesickness sitting on a lump of glass that's just cost him a thousand dollars. Now, what was it Johnny said to the widow first? I'd like to hear it again, Maxy – honest. Don't mind what I said."

'Maximilian Jones and I sat down and talked. He was about as sick of the country as I was, for the grafters were squeezing him for half the profits of his rosewood and rubber. Down in the bottom of a tank of water I had a dozen bottles of sticky Frisco beer; and I fished these up, and we fell to talking about home and the flag and Hail Columbia and home-fried potatoes; and the drivel we contributed would have sickened any man enjoying those blessings. But at that time we were out of 'em. You can't appreciate home till you've left it, money till it's spent, your wife till she's joined a woman's club, nor Old Glory till you see it hanging on a broomstick on the shanty of a consul in a foreign town.

'And sitting there me and Maximilian Jones, scratching at our prickly heat and kicking at the lizards on the floor, became afflicted with a dose of patriotism and affection for our country. There was me, Billy Casparis, reduced from a capitalist to a pauper by over-addiction to my glass (in the lump), declares my trouble off for the present and myself to be an uncrowned sovereign of the greatest country on earth. And Maximilian Jones pours out whole drug stores of his wrath on oligarchies and potentates in red trousers and calico shoes. And we issues a declaration of interference in which we guarantee that the fourth day of July shall be celebrated in Salvador with all the kinds of salutes, explosions, honors of war, oratory, and liquids known to tradition. Yes, neither me nor Jones breathed with soul so dead. There shall be rucuses in Salvador, we say, and the monkeys had better climb the tallest cocoanut trees and the fire department get out its red slashes and two tin buckets.

'About this time into the factory steps a native man incriminated by the name of General Mary Esperanza Dingo. He was some pumpkin both in politics and color, and the friend of me and Jones. He was full of politeness and a kind of intelligence, having picked up the latter and managed to preserve the former during a two years' residence in Philadelphia studying medicine. For a Salvadorian he was not such a calamitous little man, though he always would play jack, queen, king, ace, deuce for a straight.

'General Mary sits with us and has a bottle. While he was in the States he had acquired a synopsis of the English language and the art of admiring our institutions. By and by the General gets up and tiptoes to the doors and windows and other stage entrances, remarking "Hist!" at each one. They all do that in Salvador before they ask for a drink of water or the time of day, being conspirators from the cradle and matinée idols by proclamation.

' "Hist!" says General Dingo again, and then he lays his chest on the table quite like Gaspard the Miser. "Good friends, señores, to-morrow will be the great day of Liberty and Independence. The hearts of Americans and Salvadorians should beat together. Of your history and your great Washington I know. Is it not so?"

'Now, me and Jones thought that nice of the General to remember when the Fourth came. It made us feel good. He must have heard the news going round in Philadelphia about that disturbance we had with England.

' "Yes," says me and Maxy together, "we knew it. We were talking about it when you came in. And you can bet your bottom concession that there'll be fuss and feathers in the air to-morrow. We are few in numbers, but the welkin may as well reach out to push the button, for it's got to ring."

' "I, too, shall assist," says the General, thumping his collar-bone. "I, too, am on the side of Liberty. Noble Americans, we will make the day one to be never forgotten."

' "For us American whisky," says Jones – "none of your Scotch smoke or anisada or Three Star Hennessey to-morrow. We'll borrow the consul's flag; old man Billfinger shall make orations, and we'll have a barbecue on the plaza."

' "Fireworks," says I, "will be scarce; but we'll have all the cartridges in the shops for our guns. I've got two navy sixes I brought from Denver."

' "There is one cannon," said the General; "one big cannon that will go 'BOOM!' And three hundred men with rifles to shoot."

' "Oh, say!" says Jones, "Generalissimo, you're the real silk elastic. We'll make it a joint international celebration. Please, General, get a white horse and a blue sash and be grand marshal."

' "With my sword," says the General, rolling his eyes, "I shall ride at the head of the brave men who gather in the name of Liberty."

' "And you might," we suggest, "see the commandante and advise him that we are going to prize things up a bit. We Americans, you know, are accustomed to using municipal regulations for gun wadding when we line up to help the eagle scream. He might suspend the rules for one day. We don't want to get in the calaboose for spanking his soldiers if they get in our way, do you see?"

' "Hist!" says General Mary. "The commandante is with us, heart and soul. He will aid us. He is one of us."

'We made all the arrangements that afternoon. There was a buck coon from Georgia in Salvador who had drifted down there from a busted-up colored colony that had been started on some possumless land in Mexico. As soon as he heard us say "barbecue" he wept for joy and groveled on the ground. He dug his trench on the plaza, and got half a beef on the coals for an all-night roast. Me and Maxy went to see the rest of the Americans in the town and they all sizzled like a seidlitz with joy at the idea of solemnizing an old-time Fourth.

'There were six of us all together – Martin Dillard, a coffee planter; Henry Barnes, a railroad man; old man Billfinger, an educated tintype taker; me and Jonesy, and Jerry, the boss of the barbecue. There was also an Englishman in town named Sterrett, who was there to write a book on Domestic Architecture of the Insect World. We felt some bashfulness about inviting a Britisher to help crow over his own country, but we decided to risk it, out of our personal regard for him.

'We found Sterrett in pajamas working at his manuscript with a bottle of brandy for a paper weight.

' "Englishman," says Jones, "let us interrupt your disquisition on bug houses for a moment. To-morrow is the Fourth of July. We don't want to hurt your feelings, but we're going to commemorate the day when we licked you by a little refined debauchery and nonsense – something that can be heard about five miles off. If you are broad-gauged enough to taste whisky at your own wake, we'd be pleased to have you join us."

' "Do you know," says Sterrett, setting his glasses on his nose, "I like your cheek in asking me if I'll join you; blast me if I don't. You might have known I would, without asking. Not as a traitor to my own country, but for the intrinsic joy of a blooming row."

'On the morning of the Fourth I woke up in that old shanty of an ice factory feeling sore. I looked around at the wreck of all I possessed, and my heart was full of bile. From where I lay on my cot I could look through the window and see the consul's old ragged Stars and Stripes hanging over his shack. "You're all kinds of a fool, Billy Casparis," I says to myself; "and of all your crimes against sense it does look like this idea of celebrating the Fourth should receive the award of demerit. Your business is busted up, your

thousand dollars is gone into the kitty of this corrupt country on that last
bluff you made, you've got just fifteen Chili dollars left, worthy forty-six
cents each at bedtime last night and steadily going down. To-day you'll blow
in your last cent hurrahing for that flag, and tomorrow you'll be living on
bananas from the stalk and screwing your drinks out of your friends. What's
the flag done for you? While you were under it you worked for what you
got. You wore your finger nails down skinning suckers, and salting mines,
and driving bears and alligators off your town lot additions. How much does
patriotism count for on deposit when the little man with the green eye-shade
in the savings-bank adds up your book? Suppose you were to get pinched
over here in this irreligious country for some little crime or other, and
appealed to your country for protection – what would it do for you? Turn
your appeal over to a committee of one railroad man, an army officer, a
member of each labour union, and a colored man to investigate whether any
of your ancestors were ever related to a cousin of Mark Hanna, and then file
the papers in the Smithsonian Institution until after the next election. That's
the kind of a sidetrack the Stars and Stripes would switch you on to."

'You can see that I was feeling like an indigo plant; but after I washed my
face in some cool water, and got out my navys and ammunition, and started
up to the Saloon of the Immaculate Saints where we were to meet, I felt
better. And when I saw those other American boys come swaggering into
the trysting place – cool, easy, conspicuous fellows, ready to risk any kind
of a one-card draw, or to fight grizzlies, fire, or extradition, I began to feel
glad I was one of 'em. So, I says to myself again: "Billy, you've got fifteen
dollars and a country left this morning – blow in the dollars and blow up the
town as an American gentleman should on Independence Day."

'It is my recollection that we began the day along conventional lines. The
six of us – for Sterrett was along – made progress among the cantinas divesting
the bars as we went of all strong drink bearing American labels. We kept
informing the atmosphere as to the glory and preëminence of the United
States and its ability to subdue, out-jump, and eradicate the other nations of
the earth. And, as the findings of American labels grew more plentiful, we
became more contaminated with patriotism. Maximilian Jones hopes that
our late foe, Mr. Sterrett, will not take offense at our enthusiasm. He sets
down his bottle and shakes Sterrett's hand. "As white man to white man,"
says he, "denude our uproar of the slightest taint of personality. Excuse us
for Bunker Hill, Patrick Henry, and Waldorf Astor, and such grievances as
might lie between us as nations."

' "Fellow hoodlums," says Sterrett, "on behalf of the Queen I ask you to
cheese it. It is an honor to be a guest at disturbing the peace under the
American flag. Let us chant the passionate strains of 'Yankee Doodle' while
the señor behind the bar mitigates the occasion with another round of
cochineal and aqua fortis."

'Old Man Billfinger, being charged with a kind of rhetoric, makes speeches
every time we stop. We explained to such citizens as we happened to step
on that we were celebrating the dawn of our private brand of liberty, and to
please enter such inhumanities as we might commit on the list of unavoidable
casualties.

'About eleven o'clock our bulletins read: "A considerable rise in temperature, accompanied by thirst and other alarming symptoms." We hooked
arms and stretched our line across the narrow streets, all of us armed with

THE BEST OF O. HENRY   215

Winchesters and navys for purposes of noise and without malice. We stopped
on a street corner and fired a dozen or so rounds, and began a serial assortment
of United States whoops and yells, probably the first ever heard in that town.
    'When we made that noise things began to liven up. We heard a pattering
up a side street, and here came General Mary Esperanza Dingo on a white
horse with a couple of hundred brown boys following him in red undershirts
and bare feet, dragging guns ten feet long. Jones and me had forgot all about
General Mary and his promise to help us celebrate. We fired another salute
and gave another yell, while the General shook hands with us and waved his
sword.
    ' "Oh, General," shouts Jones, "this is great. This will be a real pleasure
to the eagle. Get down and have a drink."
    ' "Drink?" says the general. "No. There is no time to drink. Viva la
Libertad!"
    ' "Don't forget E Pluribus Unum!" says Henry Barnes.
    ' "Viva it good and strong," says I. "Likewise viva George Washington.
God save the Union, and," I says, bowing to Sterrett, "don't discard the
Queen."
    ' "Thanks," says Sterrett. "The next round's mine. All in to the bar Army,
too."
    'But we were deprived of Sterrett's treat by a lot of gunshot several squares
away, which General Dingo seemed to think he ought to look after. He
spurred his old white plug up that way, and the soldiers scuttled along after
him.
    ' "Mary is a real tropical bird," says Jones. "He's turned out the infantry
to help us do honor to the Fourth. We'll get that cannon he spoke of after
a while and fire some window-breakers with it. But just now I want some of
that barbecued beef. Let us on to the plaza."
    'There we found the meat gloriously done, and Jerry waiting, anxious. We
sat around on the grass, and got hunks of it on our tin plates. Maximilian
Jones, always made tender-hearted by drink, cried some because George
Washington couldn't be there to enjoy the day. "There was a man I love,
Billy," he says, weeping on my shoulder. "Poor George! To think he's gone,
and missed the fireworks. A little more salt, please, Jerry."
    'From what we could hear, General Dingo seemed to be kindly contributing
some noise while we feasted. There were guns going off around town, and
pretty soon we heard that cannon go "BOOM!" just as he said it would. And
then men began to skim along the edge of the plaza, dodging in among the
orange trees and houses. We certainly had things stirred up in Salvador. We
felt proud of the occasion and grateful to General Dingo. Sterrett was about
to take a bite off a juice piece of rib when a bullet took it away from his
mouth.
    ' "Somebody's celebrating with ball cartridges," says he, reaching for
another piece. "Little over-zealous for a non-resident patriot, isn't it?"
    ' "Don't mind it," I says to him. "'Twas an accident. They happen, you
know, on the Fourth. After one reading of the Declaration of Independence
in New York I've known the S. R. O. sign to be hung out at all the hospitals
and police stations."
    'But then Jerry gives a howl and jumps up with one hand clapped to the
back of his leg where another bullet has acted over-zealous. And then comes
a quantity of yells, and round a corner and across the plaza gallops General

Mary Esperanza Dingo embracing the neck of his horse, with his men running behind him, mostly dropping their guns by way of discharging ballast. And chasing 'em all is a company of feverish little warriors wearing blue trousers and caps.

' "Assistance, *amigos*," the General shouts, trying to stop his horse. "Assistance, in the name of Liberty!"

' "That's the Compañía Azul, the President's bodyguard," says Jones. "What a shame! They've jumped on poor old Mary just because he was helping us to celebrate. Come on, boys, it's our Fourth; – do we let that little squad of A.D.T.'s break it up?"

' "I vote No," says Martin Dillard, gathering his Winchester. "It's the privilege of an American citizen to drink, drill, dress up, and be dreadful on the Fourth of July, no matter whose country he's in."

' "Fellow citizens!" says old man Billfinger, "In the darkest hour of Freedom's birth, when our brave forefathers promulgated the principles of undying liberty, they never expected that a bunch of blue jays like that should be allowed to bust up an anniversary. Let us preserve and protect the Constitution."

'We made it unanimous, and then we gathered our guns and assaulted the blue troops in force. We fired over their heads, and then charged 'em with a yell, and they broke and ran. We were irritated at having our barbecue disturbed, and we chased 'em a quarter of a mile. Some of 'em we caught and kicked hard. The General rallied his troops and joined in the chase. Finally they scattered in a thick banana grove, and we couldn't flush a single one. So we sat down and rested.

'If I were to be put, severe, through the third degree, I wouldn't be able to tell much about the rest of the day. I mind that we pervaded the town considerable, calling upon the people to bring out more armies for us to destroy. I remember seeing a crowd somewhere, and a tall man that wasn't Billfinger making a Fourth of July speech from a balcony. And that was about all.

'Somebody must have hauled the old ice factory up to where I was, and put it around me, for there's where I was when I woke up the next morning. As soon as I could recollect my name and address I got up and held an inquest. My last cent was gone. I was all in.

'And then a neat black carriage drives to the door, and out steps General Dingo and a bay man in a silk hat and tan shoes.

' "Yes," says I to myself, "I see it now. You're the Chief de Policeos and High Lord Chamberlain of the Calaboosum; and you want Billy Casparis for excess of patriotism and assault with intent. All right. Might as well be in jail, anyhow."

'But it seems that General Mary is smiling, and the bay man shakes my hand, and speaks in the American dialect.

' "General Dingo has informed me, Señor Casparis, of your gallant service in our cause. I desire to thank you with my person. The bravery of you and the other *señores Americanos* turned the struggle for liberty in our favor. Our party triumphed. The terrible battle will live forever in history."

' "Battle?" says I; "what battle?" and I ran my mind back along history, trying to think.

' "Señor Casparis is modest," says General Dingo. "He led his brave *compadres* into the thickest of the fearful conflict. Yes. Without their aid the revolution would have failed."

' "Why, now," says I, "don't tell me there was a revolution yesterday. That was only a Fourth of—"

'But right there I abbreviated. It seemed to me it might be best.

' "After the terrible struggle," says the bay man, "President Bolano was forced to fly. To-day Caballo is President by proclamation. Ah, yes. Beneath the new administration I am the head of the Department of Mercantile Concessions. On my file I find one report, Señor Casparis, that you have not made ice in accord with your contract." And here the bay man smiles at me, 'cute.

' "Oh, well," says I, "I guess the report's straight. I know they caught me. That's all there is to it."

' "Do not say so," says the bay man. He pulls off a glove and goes over and lays his hand on that chunk of glass.

' "Ice," says he, nodding his head, solemn.

'General Dingo also steps over and feels of it.

' "Ice," says the General; "I'll swear to it."

' "If Señor Casparis," says the bay man, "will present himself to the treasury on the sixth day of this month he will receive back the thousand dollars he did deposit as a forfeit. *Adiós, señor*."

'The General and the bay man bowed themselves out, and I bowed as often as they did.

'And when the carriage rolls away through the sand I bows once more, deeper than ever, till my hat touches the ground. But this time 'twas not intended for them. For, over their heads, I saw the old flag fluttering in the breeze above the consul's roof; and 'twas to it I made my profoundest salute.'

THE EMANCIPATION OF BILLY

IN THE OLD, OLD, SQUARE-PORTICOED mansion, with the wry window-shutters and the paint peeling off in discolored flakes lived one of the last of the war governors.

The South has forgotten the enmity of the great conflict, but it refuses to abandon its old traditions and idols. In 'Governor' Pemberton, as he was still fondly called, the inhabitants of Elmville saw the relic of their state's ancient greatness and glory. In his day he had been a man large in the eye of his country. His state had pressed upon him every honor within its gift. And now when he was old, and enjoying a richly merited repose outside the swift current of public affairs, his townsmen loved to do him reverence for the sake of the past.

The Governor's decaying 'mansion' stood upon the main street of Elmville within a few feet of its rickety paling-fence. Every morning the Governor would descend the steps with extreme care and deliberation – on account of his rheumatism – and then the click of his gold-headed cane would be heard as he slowly proceeded up the rugged brick sidewalk. He was now nearly seventy-eight, but he had grown old gracefully and beautifully. His rather long, smooth hair and flowing, parted whiskers were snow-white. His full-skirted frock-coat was always buttoned snugly about his tall, spare figure. He wore a high, well-kept silk hat – known as a 'plug' in Elmville – and nearly always gloves. His manners were punctilious, and somewhat overcharged with courtesy.

The Governor's walks up Lee Avenue, the principal street, developed in their course into a sort of memorial, triumphant procession. Everyone he met saluted him with a profound respect. Many would remove their hats. Those who were honored with his personal friendship would pause to shake hands, and then you would see exemplified the genuine *beau idéal* Southern courtesy.

Upon reaching the corner of the second square from the mansion, the Governor would pause. Another street crossed the avenue there, and traffic, to the extent of several farmers' wagons and a peddler's cart or two, would rage about the junction. Then the falcon eye of General Deffenbaugh would perceive the situation, and the General would hasten, with ponderous solicitude, from his office in the First National Bank building to the assistance of his old friend.

When the two exchanged greetings the decay of modern manners would become accusingly apparent. The General's bulky and commanding figure would bend lissomely at a point where you would have regarded its ability to do so with incredulity. The Governor's cherished rheumatism would be compelled, for the moment, to give way before a genuflexion brought down from the days of the cavaliers. The Governor would take the General's arm and be piloted safely between the haywagons and the sprinkling-cart to the other side of the street. Proceeding to the post-office in the care of his friend, the esteemed statesman would there hold an informal levée among the citizens who were come for their morning mail. Here, gathering two or three prominent in law, politics, or family, the pageant would make a stately progress along the Avenue, stopping at the Palace Hotel where, perhaps, would be found upon the register the name of some guest deemed worthy of an introduction to the state's venerable and illustrious son. If any such were found, an hour or two would be spent in recalling the faded glories of the Governor's long-vanished administration.

On the return march the General would invariably suggest that, His Excellency being no doubt fatigued, it would be wise to recuperate for a few minutes at the Drug Emporium of Mr. Appleby R. Fentress (an elegant gentleman, sir – one of the Catham County Fentresses – so many of our best-blooded families have had to go into trade, sir, since the war).

Mr. Appleby R. Fentress was a connoisseur in fatigue. Indeed, if he had not been, his memory alone should have enabled him to prescribe, for the majestic invasion of his pharmacy was a casual happening that had surprised him almost daily for years. Mr. Fentress knew the formula of, and possessed the skill to compound, a certain potion antagonistic to fatigue, the salient ingredient of which he described (no doubt in pharmaceutical terms) as 'genuine old hand-made Clover Leaf '59, Private Stock.'

Nor did the ceremony of administering the potion ever vary. Mr. Fentress would first compound two of the celebrated mixtures – one for the Governor, and the other for the General to 'sample.' Then the Governor would make this little speech in his high, piping, quavering voice:

'No, sir – not one drop until you have prepared one for yourself and joined us, Mr. Fentress. Your father, sir, was one of my most valued supporters and friends during My Administration, and any mark of esteem I can confer upon his son is not only a pleasure but a duty, sir.'

Blushing with delight at the royal condescension, the druggist would obey, and all would drink to the General's toast: 'The prosperity of our grand old state, gentlemen – the memory of her glorious past – the health of her Favorite Son.'

Some one of the Old Guard was always at hand to escort the Governor home. Sometimes the General's business duties denied him the privilege, and then Judge Bloomfield or Colonel Titus, or one of the Ashford County Slaughters would be on hand to perform the rite.

Such were the observances attendant upon the Governor's morning stroll to the post-office. How much more magnificent, impressive, and spectacular, then, was the scene at public functions when the General would lead forth the silver-haired relic of former greatness, like some rare and fragile waxwork figure, and trumpet his pristine eminence to his fellow citizens!

General Deffenbaugh was the Voice of Elmville. Some said he was Elmville. At any rate, he had no competitor as the Mouthpiece. He owned enough stock in the *Daily Banner* to dictate its utterance, enough shares in the First National Bank to be the referee of its loans, and a war record that left him without a rival for first place at barbecues, school commencements, and Decoration Days. Besides these acquirements he was possessed with endowments. His personality was inspiring and triumphant. Undisputed sway had molded him to the likeness of a fatted Roman emperor. The tones of his voice were not otherwise than clarion. To say that the General was public spirited would fall short of doing him justice. He had spirit enough for a dozen publics. And as a sure foundation for it all, he had a heart that was big and stanch. Yes; General Deffenbaugh was Elmville.

One little incident that usually occurred during the Governor's morning walk has had its chronicling delayed by more important matters. The procession was accustomed to halt before a small brick office on the Avenue, fronted by a short flight of steep wooden steps. A modest tin sign over the door bore the words: 'Wm. B. Pemberton: Attorney-at-Law.'

Looking inside, the General would roar: 'Hello, Billy, my boy.' The less distinguished members of the escort would call: 'Morning, Billy.' The Governor would pipe: 'Good-morning, William.'

Then a patient-looking little man with hair turning gray along the temples would come down the steps and shake hands with each one of the party. All Elmville shook hands when it met.

The formalities concluded, the little man would go back to his table, heaped with law books and papers, while the procession would proceed.

Billy Pemberton was, as his sign declared, a lawyer, by profession. By occupation and common consent he was the Son of his Father. This was the shadow in which Billy lived, the pit out of which he had unsuccessfully striven for years to climb and, he had come to believe, the grave in which his ambitions were destined to be buried. Filial respect and duty he paid beyond the habit of most sons, but he aspired to be known and appraised by his own deeds and worth.

After many years of tireless labor he had become known in certain quarters far from Elmville as a master of the principles of the law. Twice he had gone to Washington and argued cases before the highest tribunal with such acute logic and learning that the silken gowns on the bench had rustled from the force of it. His income from his practice had grown until he was able to support his father, in the old family mansion (which neither of them would have thought of abandoning, rickety as it was) in the comfort and almost the luxury of the old extravagant days. Yet, he remained to Elmville as only 'Billy' Pemberton, the son of our distinguished and honored fellow-townsman, 'ex-Governor Pemberton.' Thus was he introduced at public gatherings where he sometimes spoke, haltingly and prosily, for his talents were too serious and deep for extempore brilliancy; thus was he presented to strangers and to the lawyers who made the circuit of the courts; and so the *Daily Banner* referred to him in print. To be 'the son of' was his doom. Whatever he should accomplish would have to be sacrificed upon the altar of this magnificent but fatal parental precedence.

The peculiarity and the saddest thing about Billy's ambition was that the only world he thirsted to conquer was Elmville. His nature was diffident and unassuming. National or State honors might have oppressed him. But, above all things, he hungered for the appreciation of the friends among whom he had been born and raised. He would not have plucked one leaf from the garlands that were so lavishly bestowed upon his father, he merely rebelled against having his own wreaths woven from those dried and self-same branches. But Elmville 'Billied' and 'sonned' him to his concealed but lasting chagrin, until at length he grew more reserved and formal and studious than ever.

There came a morning when Billy found among his mail a letter from a very high source, tendering him the appointment to an important judicial position in the new island possessions of our country. The honor was a distinguished one, for the entire nation had discussed the probable recipients of these positions, and had agreed that the situation demanded only men of the highest character, ripe learning, and evenly balanced mind.

Billy could not subdue a certain exultation at this token of the success of his long and arduous labors, but, at the same time, a whimsical smile lingered around his mouth, for he foresaw in which Elmville would place the credit. 'We congratulate Governor Pemberton upon the mark of appreciation conferred upon his son' – 'Elmville rejoices with our honored citizen, Governor Pemberton, at his son's success' – 'Put her there Billy!' – 'Judge Billy Pemberton, sir; son of our State's war hero and the people's pride!' – these were the phrases, printed and oral, conjured up by Billy's prophetic fancy. Grandson of his State, and stepchild of Elmville – thus had fate fixed his kinship to the body politic.

Billy lived with his father in the old mansion. The two and an elderly lady – a distant relative – comprised the family. Perhaps, though, old Jeff, the Governor's ancient colored body-servant, should be included. Without doubt, he would have claimed the honor. There were other servants, but Thomas Jefferson Pemberton, sah, was a member of 'de fambly.'

Jeff was the one Elmvillian who gave to Billy the gold of approval unmixed with the alloy of paternalism. To him 'Mars William' was the greatest man in Talbot County. Beaten upon though he was by the shining light that emanates from an ex-war governor, and loyal as he remained to the old *régime*, his faith and admiration were Billy's. As valet to a hero, and a member of the family, he may have had superior opportunities for judging.

Jeff was the first one to whom Billy revealed the news. When he reached home for supper Jeff took his 'plug' hat and smoothed it before hanging it upon the hall-rack.

'Dar now!' said the old man: 'I knowed it was er comin', I knowed it was gwine ter happen. Er Judge, you says, Mars William? Dem Yankees done made you er judge? It's high time, sah, dey was doin' somep'n to make up for dey rescality endurin' de war. I boun' dey holds a confab and says: 'Le's make Mars William Pemberton er judge, and dat'll settle it.' Does you have to go away down to dem Fillypines, Mars William, or kin you judge 'em from here?'

'I'd have to live there most of the time of course,' said Billy.

'I wonder what de Gubnor gwine say 'bout dat,' speculated Jeff.

Billy wondered too.

After supper, when the two sat in the library, according to their habit, the Governor smoking his clay pipe and Billy his cigar, the son dutifully confessed to having been tendered the appointment.

For a long time the Governor sat, smoking, without making any comment. Billy reclined in his favorite rocker, waiting, perhaps still flushed with satisfaction over the tender that had come to him, unsolicited, in his dingy little office, above the heads of the intriguing, time-serving, clamorous multitude.

At last the Governor spoke; and, though his words were seemingly irrelevant, they were to the point. His voice had a note of martyrdom running through its senile quaver.

'My rheumatism has been growing steadily worse these past months, William.'

'I am sorry, Father,' said Billy, gently.

'And I am nearly seventy-eight. I am getting to be an old man. I can recall the names of but two or three who were in public life during My Administration. What did you say is the nature of this position that is offered you, William?'

'A Federal judgeship, Father. I believe it is considered to be a somewhat flattering tender. It is outside of politics and wire-pulling, you know.'

'No doubt, no doubt. Few of the Pembertons have engaged in professional life for nearly a century. None of them have ever held Federal positions. They have been landowners, slave-owners, and planters on a large scale. One or two of the Derwents – your mother's family – were in the law. Have you decided to accept this appointment, William?'

'I am thinking it over,' said Billy, slowly, regarding the ash of his cigar.

'You have been a good son to me,' continued the Governor, stirring his pipe with the handle of a penholder.

'I've been your son all my life,' said Billy, darkly.

'I am often gratified,' piped the Governor, betraying a touch of complacency, 'by being congratulated upon having a son with such sound and sterling qualities. Especially in this, our native town, is your name linked with mine in the talk of our citizens.'

'I never knew anyone to forget the vinculum,' murmured Billy, unintelligibly.

'Whatever prestige,' pursued the parent, 'I may be possessed of, by virtue of my name and services to the state, has been yours to draw upon freely. I have not hesitated to exert it in your behalf whenever opportunity offered. And you have deserved it, William. You've been the best of sons. And now this appointment comes to take you away from me. I have but a few years left to live. I am almost dependent upon others now, even in walking and dressing. What would I do without you, my son?'

The Governor's pipe dropped to the floor. A tear trickled from his eye. His voice had risen, and crumbled to a weakling falsetto, and ceased. He was an old, old man about to be bereft of the son that cherished him.

Billy rose, and laid his hand upon the Governor's shoulder.

'Don't worry, father,' he said, cheerfully. 'I'm not going to accept. Elmville is good enough for me. I'll write to-night and decline it.'

At the next interchange of devoirs between the Governor and General Deffenbaugh on Lee Avenue, His Excellency, with a comfortable air of self-satisfaction, spoke of the appointment that had been tendered to Billy.

The General whistled.

'That's a plum for Billy,' he shouted. 'Who'd have thought that Billy – but, confound it, it's been in him all the time. It's a boost for Elmville. It'll send real estate up. It's an honor to our state. It's a compliment to the South. We've all been blind about Billy. When does he leave? We must have a reception. Great Gatlings! that job's eight thousand a year! There's been a car-load of lead-pencils worn to stubs figuring on those appointments. Think of it! Our little, wood-sawing, mealy-mouthed Billy! Angel unawares doesn't begin to express it. Elmville is disgraced forever unless she lines up in a hurry for ratification and apology.'

The venerable Moloch smiled fatuously. He carried the fire with which to consume all these tributes to Billy, the smoke of which would ascend as an incense to himself.

'William,' said the Governor, with modest pride, 'has declined the appointment. He refuses to leave me in my old age. He is a good son.'

The General swung around and laid a large forefinger upon the bosom of his friend. Much of the General's success had been due to his dexterity in establishing swift lines of communication between cause and effect.

'Governor,' he said, with a keen look in his big, ox-like eyes, 'you've been complaining to Billy about your rheumatism.'

'My dear General,' replied the Governor, stiffly, 'my son is forty-two. He is quite capable of deciding such questions for himself. And I, as his parent, feel it my duty to state that your remark about – er – rheumatism is a mighty poor shot from a very small bore, sir, aimed at a purely personal and private affliction.'

'If you will allow me,' retorted the General, 'you've afflicted the public with it for some time; and 'twas no small bore, at that.'

This first tiff between the two old comrades might have grown into something more serious but for the fortunate interruption caused by the ostentatious approach of Colonel Titus and another one of the court retinue from the right county, to whom the General confided the coddled statesman and went his way.

After Billy had so effectually entombed his ambitions, and taken the veil, so to speak, in a sonnery, he was surprised to discover how much lighter of heart and happier he felt. He realized what a long, restless struggle he had maintained, and how much he had lost by failing to cull the simple but wholesome pleasures by the way. His heart warmed now to Elmville and the friends who had refused to set him upon a pedestal. It was better, he began to think, to be 'Billy' and his father's son, and to be hailed familiarly by cheery neighbors and grown-up playmates, than to be 'Your Honor,' and sit among strangers, hearing, maybe, through the arguments of learned counsel, that old man's feeble voice crying: 'What would I do without you, my son?'

Billy began to surprise his acquaintances by whistling as he walked up the street; others he astounded by slapping them disrespectfully upon their backs and raking up old anecdotes he had not had the time to recollect for years. Though he hammered away at his law cases as thoroughly as ever, he found more time for relaxation and the company of his friends. Some of the younger set were actually after him to join the golf club. A striking proof of his abandonment to obscurity was his adoption of a most undignified, rakish little soft hat, reserving the 'plug' for Sundays and state occasions. Billy was beginning to enjoy Elmville, though that irreverent burgh had neglected to crown him with bay and myrtle.

All the while uneventful peace pervaded Elmville. The Governor continued to make his triumphal parades to the post-office with the General as chief marshal, for the slight squall that had rippled their friendship had, to all indications, been forgotten by both.

But one day Elmville woke to sudden excitement. The news had come that a touring presidential party would honor Elmville by a twenty-minute stop. The Executive had promised a five-minute address from the balcony of the Palace Hotel.

Elmville arose as one man – that man being, of course, General Deffenbaugh – to receive becomingly the chieftain of all the clans. The train with the tiny Stars and Stripes fluttering from the engine pilot arrived. Elmville had done her best. There were bands, flowers, carriages, uniforms, banners, and committees without end. High-school girls in white frocks impeded the steps of the party with roses strewn nervously in bunches. The chieftain had seen it all before – scores of times. He could have pictured it exactly in advance, from the Blue-and-Gray speech down to the smallest rosebud. Yet his kindly smile of interest greeted Elmville's display as if it had been the only and original.

In the upper rotunda of the Palace Hotel the town's most illustrious were assembled for the honor of being presented to the distinguished guests previous to the expected address. Outside, Elmville's inglorious but patriotic masses filled the streets.

Here, in the hotel General Deffenbaugh was holding in reserve Elmville's trump card. Elmville knew; for the trump was a fixed one, and its lead consecrated by archaic custom.

At the proper moment Governor Pemberton, beautifully venerable, magnificently antique, tall, paramount, stepped forward upon the arm of the General.

Elmville watched and harked with bated breath. Never until now – when a Northern President of the United States should clasp hands with ex-war-Governor Pemberton – would the breach be entirely closed – would the country be made one and indivisible – no North, not much South, very little East, and no West to speak of. So Elmville excitedly scraped kalsomine from the walls of the Palace Hotel with its Sunday best, and waited for the Voice to speak.

And Billy! We had nearly forgotten Billy. He was cast for Son, and he waited patiently for his cue. He carried his 'plug' in his hand, and felt serene. He admired his father's striking air and pose. After all, it was a great deal to be son of a man who could so gallantly hold the position of a cynosure for three generations.

General Deffenbaugh cleared his throat. Elmville opened its mouth, and squirmed. The chieftain with the kindly, fateful face was holding out his hand, smiling. Ex-war-Governor Pemberton extended his own across the chasm. But what was this the General was saying?

'Mr. President, allow me to present to you one who has the honor to be the father of our foremost distinguished citizen, learned and honored jurist, beloved townsman, and model Southern gentleman – the Honorable William B. Pemberton.'

THE ENCHANTED KISS

BUT A CLERK IN THE CUT-RATE Drug Store was Samuel Tansey, yet his slender frame was a pad that enfolded the passion of Romeo, the gloom of Lara, the romance of D'Artagnan, and the desperate inspiration of Melnotte. Pity, then, that he had been denied expression, that he was doomed to the burden of utter timidity and diffidence, that Fate had set him tongue-tied and scarlet before the muslin-clad angels whom he adored and vainly longed to rescue, clasp, comfort, and subdue.

The clock's hands were pointing close upon the hour of ten while Tansey was playing billiards with a number of his friends. On alternate evenings he was released from duty at the store after seven o'clock. Even among his fellow men Tansey was timorous and constrained. In his imagination he had done valiant deeds and performed acts of distinguished gallantry; but in fact he was a shallow youth of twenty-three, with an over-modest demeanor and scant vocabulary.

When the clock struck ten, Tansey hastily laid down his cue and struck sharply upon the show-case with a coin for the attendant to come and receive the pay for his score.

'What's your hurry, Tansey?' called one. 'Got another engagement?'

'Tansey got an engagement!' echoed another. 'Not on your life. Tansey's got to get home at ten by Mother Peek's orders.'

'It's no such thing,' chimed in a pale youth, taking a large cigar from his mouth; 'Tansey's afraid to be late because Miss Katie might come downstairs to unlock the door, and kiss him in the hall.'

This delicate piece of raillery sent a fiery tingle into Tansey's blood, for the indictment was true – barring the kiss. That was a thing to dream of; to wildly hope for; but too remote and sacred a thing to think of lightly.

Casting a cold and contemptuous look at the speaker – a punishment commensurate with his own diffident spirit – Tansey left the room, descending the stairs into the street.

For two years he had silently adored Miss Peek, worshipping her from a spiritual distance through which her attractions took on stellar brightness and mystery. Mrs. Peek kept a few choice boarders, among whom was Tansey. The other young men romped with Katie, chased her with crickets in their fingers, and 'jollied' her with an irreverent freedom that turned Tansey's heart into cold lead in his bosom. The signs of his adoration were few – a tremulous 'Good morning,' stealthy glances at her during meals, and occasionally (Oh, rapture!) a blushing, delirious game of cribbage with her in the parlor on some rare evening when a miraculous lack of engagement kept her at home. Kiss him in the hall! Aye, he feared it, but it was an ecstatic fear such as Elijah must have felt when the chariot lifted him into the unknown.

But to-night the gibes of his associates had stung him to a feeling of forward, lawless mutiny; a defiant, challenging, atavistic recklessness. Spirit of corsair, adventurer, lover, poet, Bohemian, possessed him. The stars he saw above him seemed no more unattainable, no less high, than the favor of Miss Peek or the fearsome sweetness of her delectable lips. His fate seemed to him strangely dramatic and pathetic, and to call for a solace consonant with its extremity. A saloon was near by, and to this he flitted, called for absinthe – beyond doubt the drink most adequate to his mood – the tipple of the roué, the abandoned, the vainly sighing lover.

Once he drank of it, and again, and then again until he felt a strange, exalted sense of non-participation in worldly affairs pervade him. Tansey was no drinker; his consumption of three absinthe anisettes within almost as few minutes proclaimed his unproficiency in the art; Tansey was merely flooding with unproven liquor his sorrows; which record and tradition alleged to be drownable.

Coming out upon the sidewalk, he snapped his fingers defiantly in the direction of the Peek homestead, turned the other way, and voyaged, Columbus-like, into the wilds of an enchanted street. Nor is the figure exorbitant, for, beyond his store the foot of Tansey had scarcely been set for years – store and boarding-house; between these ports he was chartered to run, and contrary currents had rarely deflected his prow.

Tansey aimlessly protracted his walk, and, whether it was his unfamiliarity with the district, his recent accession of audacious errantry, or the sophistical whisper of a certain green-eyed fairy, he came to last to tread a shuttered, blank, and echoing thoroughfare, dark and unpeopled. And, suddenly, this way came to an end (as many streets do in the Spanish-built, archaic town of San Antone), butting its head against an imminent, high, brick wall. No – the street still lived! To the right and to the left it breathed through slender tubes of exit – narrow, somnolent ravines, cobble paved and unlighted. Accommodating a rise in the street to the right was reared a phantom flight of five luminous steps of limestone, flanked by a wall of the same height and of the same material.

Upon one of these steps Tansey seated himself and bethought him of his love, and how she might never know she was his love. And of Mother Peek, fat, vigilant and kind; not unpleased, Tansey thought, that he and Katie should play cribbage in the parlor together. For the Cut-rate had not cut his salary, which, sordidly speaking, ranked him star boarder at the Peeks'. And he thought of Captain Peek, Katie's father, a man he dreaded and abhorred; a genteel loafer and spendthrift, battening upon the labor of his women-folk; a very queer fish, and, according to repute, not of the freshest.

The night had turned chill and foggy. The heart of the town, with its noises, was left behind. Reflected from the high vapors, its distant lights were manifest in quivering, cone-shaped streamers, in questionable blushes of unnamed colors, in unstable, ghostly waves of far, electric flashes. Now that the darkness was become more friendly, the wall against which the street splintered developed a stone coping topped with an armature of spikes.

Beyond it loomed what appeared to be the acute angles of mountain peaks, pierced here and there by little lambent parallelograms. Considering this vista, Tansey at length persuaded himself that the seeming mountains were, in fact, the convent of Santa Mercedes, with which ancient and bulky pile he was better familiar from different coigns of view. A pleasant noise of singing in his ears reënforced his opinion. High, sweet, holy carolling, far and harmonious and uprising, as of sanctified nuns at their responses. At what hour did the Sisters sing? He tried to think – was it six, eight, twelve? Tansey leaned his back against the limestone wall and wondered. Strange things followed. The air was full of white, fluttering pigeons that circled about, and settled upon the convent wall. The wall blossomed with a quantity of shining green eyes that blinked and peered at him from the solid masonry. A pink, classic nymph came from an excavation in the cavernous road and danced, barefoot and airy, upon the ragged flints. The sky was traversed by a company of beribboned cats, marching in stupendous, aërial procession. The noise of singing grew louder; an illumination of unseasonable fireflies danced past, and strange whispers came out of the dark without meaning or excuse.

Without amazement Tansey took note of these phenomena. He was on some new plane of understanding, though his mind seemed to him clear and, indeed, happily tranquil.

A desire for movement and exploration seized him: he rose and turned into the black gash of street to his right. For a time the high wall formed one of its boundaries, but farther on, two rows of black-windowed houses closed it in.

Here was the city's quarter once given over to the Spaniard. Here were still his forbidding abodes of concrete and adobe, standing cold and indomitable against the century. From the murky fissure, the eye saw, flung against the sky, the tangled filigree of his Moorish balconies. Through stone archways breaths of dead, vault-chilled air coughed upon him; his feet struck jingling iron rings in staples stone-buried for half a cycle. Along these paltry avenues had swaggered the arrogant Don, had caracoled and serenaded and blustered while the tomahawk and the pioneer's rifle were already uplifted to expel him from a continent. And Tansey, stumbling through this old-world dust, looked up, dark as it was, and saw Andalusian beauties glimmering on the balconies. Some of them were laughing and listening to the goblin music that still followed; others harked fearfully through the night, trying to catch the hoof beats of caballeros whose last echoes from those stones had died away a century ago. Those women were silent, but Tansey heard the jangle of horseless bridle-bits, the whirr of riderless rowels, and, now and then, a muttered malediction in a foreign tongue. But he was not frightened. Shadows, nor shadows of sound could daunt him. Afraid? No. Afraid of Mother Peek? Afraid to face the girl of his heart? Afraid of tipsy Captain Peek? Nay! nor of these apparitions, nor of that spectral singing that always pursued him. Singing! He would show them! He lifted up a strong and untuneful voice:

'When you hear them bells go tingalingJing,'

serving notice upon those mysterious agencies that if it should come to a face-to-face encounter

'There'll be a hot time
In the old town
To-night!'

How long Tansey consumed in treading this haunted byway was not clear to him, but in time he emerged into a more commodious avenue. When within a few yards of the corner he perceived, through a window, that a small confectionery of mean appearance was set in the angle. His same glance that estimated its meagre equipment, its cheap soda-water fountain and stock of tobacco and sweets, took cognizance of Captain Peek within lighting a cigar at a swinging gaslight.

As Tansey rounded the corner Captain Peek came out, and they met *vis-à-vis*. An exultant joy filled Tansey when he found himself sustaining the encounter with implicit courage. Peek, indeed! He raised his hand, and snapped his fingers loudly.

It was Peek himself who quailed guiltily before the valiant mien of the drug clerk. Sharp surprise and a palpable fear bourgeoned upon the Captain's face. And, verily, that face was one to rather call up such expressions upon the faces of others. The face of a libidinous heathen idol, small eyed, with carven folds in the heavy jowls, and a consuming, pagan license in its expression. In the gutter just beyond the store Tansey saw a closed carriage standing with its back toward him and a motionless driver perched in his place.

'Why, it's Tansey!' exclaimed Captain Peek. 'How are you, Tansey? H-have a cigar, Tansey?'

'Why, it's Peek!' cried Tansey, jubilant at his own temerity. 'What devilry are you up to now, Peek? Back streets and a closed carriage! Fie! Peek!'

'There's no one in the carriage,' said the Captain, smoothly.

'Everybody out of it is in luck,' continued Tansey, aggressively. 'I'd love for you to know, Peek, that I'm not stuck on you. You're a bottle-nosed scoundrel.'

'Why, the little rat's drunk!' cried the Captain, joyfully; 'only drunk, and I thought he was on! Go home, Tansey, and quit bothering grown persons on the street.'

But just then a white-clad figure sprang out of the carriage, and a shrill voice – Katie's voice – sliced the air: 'Sam! Sam! – help me, Sam!'

Tansey sprang toward her, but Captain Peek interposed his bulky form. Wonder of wonders! the whilom spiritless youth struck out with his right, and the hulking Captain went over in a swearing heap. Tansey flew to Katie, and took her in his arms like a conquering knight. She raised her face, and he kissed her – violets! electricity! caramels! champagne! Here was the attainment of a dream that brought no disenchantment.

'Oh, Sam,' cried Katie, when she could, 'I knew you would come to rescue me. What do you suppose the mean things were going to do with me?'

'Have your picture taken,' said Tansey, wondering at the foolishness of his remark.

'No, they were going to eat me. I heard them talking about it.'

'Eat you!' said Tansey, after pondering a moment. 'That can't be; there's no plates.'

But a sudden noise warned him to turn. Down upon him were bearing the Captain and a monstrous long-bearded dwarf in a spangled cloak and red trunk-hose. The dwarf leaped twenty feet and clutched him. The Captain seized Katie and hurled her, shrieking, back into the carriage, himself followed, and the vehicle dashed away. The dwarf lifted Tansey high above his head and ran with him into the store. Holding him with one hand, he raised the lid of an enormous chest half filled with cakes of ice, flung Tansey inside, and closed down the cover.

The force of the fall must have been great, for Tansey lost consciousness. When his faculties revived his first sensation was one of severe cold along his back and limbs. Opening his eyes he found himself to be seated upon the lime-stone steps still facing the wall and convent of Santa Mercedes. His first thought was of the ecstatic kiss from Katie. The outrageous villainy of Captain Peek, the unnatural mystery of the situation, his preposterous conflict with the dwarf – these things roused and angered him, but left no impression of the unreal.

'I'll go back there to-morrow,' he grumbled aloud, 'and knock the head off that comic-opera squab. Running out and picking up perfect strangers, and shoving them into cold storage!'

But the kiss remained uppermost in his mind. 'I might have done that long ago,' he mused. 'She liked it, too. She called me "Sam" four times. I'll not go up that street again. Too much scrapping. Guess I'll move down the other way. Wonder what she meant by saying they were going to eat her!'

Tansey began to feel sleepy, but after a while he decided to move along again. This time he ventured into the street to his left. It ran level for a distance, and then dipped gently downward, opening into a vast, dim, barren space – the old Military Plaza. To his left, some hundred yards distant, he saw a cluster of flickering lights along the Plaza's border. He knew the locality at once.

Huddled within narrow confines were the remnants of the once-famous purveyors of the celebrated Mexican national cookery. A few years before, their nightly encampments upon the historic Alamo Plaza, in the heart of the city, had been a carnival, a saturnalia that was renowned throughout the land. Then the caterers numbered hundreds; the patrons thousands. Drawn by the coquettish *señoritas*, the music of the weird Spanish minstrels, and the strange piquant Mexican dishes served at a hundred competing tables, crowds thronged the Alamo Plaza all night. Travellers, rancheros, family parties, gay gasconading rounders, sight-seers and prowlers of polyglot, owlish San Antone mingled there at the centre of the city's fun and frolic. The popping of corks, pistols, and questions; the glitter of eyes, jewels, and daggers; the ring of laughter and coin – these were the order of the night.

But now no longer. To some half-dozen tents, fires, and tables had dwindled the picturesque festival, and these had been relegated to an ancient disused plaza.

Often had Tansey strolled down to these stands at night to partake of the delectable *chili-con-carne*, a dish evolved by the genius of Mexico, composed of delicate meats, minced with aromatic herbs and the poignant *chili colorado* – a compound full of singular savor and a fiery zest delightful to the Southron's palate.

The titillating odor of this concoction came now, on the breeze, to the nostrils of Tansey, awakening in him hunger for it. As he turned in that direction he saw a carriage dash up to the Mexicans' tents out of the gloom of the Plaza. Some figures moved back and forward in the uncertain light of the lanterns, and then the carriage was driven swiftly away.

Tansey approached, and sat at one of the tables covered with gaudy oilcloth. Traffic was dull at the moment. A few half-grown boys noisily fared at another table; the Mexicans hung listless and phlegmatic about their wares. And it was still. The night hum of the city crowded to the wall of dark buildings surrounding the Plaza, and subsided to an indefinite buzz through which sharply perforated the crackle of the languid fires and the rattle of fork and spoon. A sedative wind blew from the southeast. The starless firmament pressed down upon the earth like a leaden cover.

In all that quiet Tansey turned his head suddenly, and saw, without disquietude, a troop of spectral horsemen deploy into the Plaza and charge a luminous line of infantry that advanced to sustain the shock. He saw the fierce flame of cannon and small arms, but heard no sound. The careless victuallers lounged vacantly, not deigning to view the conflict. Tansey mildly wondered to what nations these mute combatants might belong; turned his back to them and ordered his *chili* and coffee from the Mexican woman who advanced to serve him. The woman was old and careworn; her face was lined like the rind of a cantaloupe. She fetched the viands from a vessel set by the smouldering fire, and then retired to a tent, dark within, that stood near by.

Presently Tansey heard a turmoil in the tent; a wailing, broken-hearted pleading in the harmonious Spanish tongue, and then two figures tumbled out into the light of the lanterns. One was the old woman; the other was a man clothed with a sumptuous and flashing splendor. The woman seemed to clutch and beseech from him something against his will. The man broke from her and struck her brutally back into the tent, where she lay, whimpering and invisible. Observing Tansey, he walked rapidly to the table where he sat. Tansey recognized him to be Ramon Torres, a Mexican, the proprietor of the stand he was patronizing.

Torres was a handsome, nearly full-blooded descendant of the Spanish, seemingly about thirty years of age, and of a haughty, but extremely courteous demeanor. To-night he was dressed with signal magnificence. His costume was that of a triumphant *matador*, made of purple velvet almost hidden by jeweled embroidery. Diamonds of enormous size flashed upon his garb and his hands. He reached for a chair, and, seating himself at the opposite side of the table, began to roll a finical cigarette.

'Ah, Meester Tansee,' he said, with a sultry fire in his silky, black eye, 'I give myself pleasure to see you this evening. Meester Tansee, you have many times come to eat at my table. I theenk you a safe man – a verree good friend. How much would it please you to leeve forever?'

'Not come back any more?' inquired Tansey.

'No; not leave – *leeve*; the not-to-die.'

'I would call that,' said Tansey, 'a snap.'

Torres leaned his elbows upon the table, swallowed a mouthful of smoke, and spake – each word being projected in a little puff of gray.

'How old do you theenk I am, Meester Tansee?'

'Oh, twenty-eight or thirty.'

'Thees day,' said the Mexican 'ees my birthday. I am four hundred and three years of old to-day.'

'Another proof,' said Tansey, airily, 'of the healthfulness of our climate.'

'Eet is not the air. I am to relate to you a secret of verree fine value. Listen me, Meester Tansee. At the age of twenty-three I arrive in Mexico from Spain. When? In the year fifteen hundred nineteen, with the *soldados* of Hernando Cortez. I come to thees country seventeen fifteen. I saw your Alamo reduced. It was like yesterday to me. Three hundred ninety-six year ago I learn the secret always to leeve. Look at these clothes I wear – at these *diamantes*. Do you theenk I buy them with the money I make with selling the *chili-con-carne*, Meester Tansee?'

'I should think not,' said Tansey, promptly. Torres laughed loudly.

'*Válgame Dios!* but I do. But it not the kind you eating now. I make a deeferent kind, the eating of which makes men to always leeve. What do you think! One thousand people I supply – *diez pesos* each one pays me the month. You see! ten thousand *pesos* everee month! *Qué diablos!* how not I wear the fine *ropo!* You see that old woman try to hold me back a little while ago? That ees my wife. When I marry her she is young – seventeen years – *bonita*—. Like the rest she ees become old and – what you say! – tough? I am the same – young all the time. To-night I resolve to dress myself and find another wife befitting my age. This old woman try to sc-r-ratch my face. Ha! Ha! Meester Tansee – same way they do *entre los Americanos*.'

'And this health-food you spoke of?' said Tansey.

'Hear me,' said Torres, leaning over the table until he lay flat upon it; 'eet is the *chili-con-carne* made not from the beef or the chicken, but from the flesh of the *señorita* – young and tender. That ees the secret. Everee month you must eat it, having care to do so before the moon is full, and you will not die any times. See how I trust you, friend Tansee! To-night I have bought one young ladee – veree pretty – so *fina, gorda, blandita!* To-morrow the *chili* will be ready. *Ahora si!* One thousand dollars I pay for thees young ladee. From the *Americano* I have bought – a veree tip-top man – *el Capitan Peek* – *Qué es, Señor?*'

For Tansey had sprung to his feet, upsetting the chair. The words of Katie reverberated in his ears: 'They're going to eat me, Sam.' This, then, was the monstrous fate to which she had been delivered by her unnatural parent. The carriage he had seen drive up from the Plaza was Captain Peek's. Where was Katie? Perhaps already—

Before he could decide what to do a loud scream came from the tent. The old Mexican woman ran out, a flashing knife in her hand. 'I have released her,' she cried. 'You shall kill no more. They will hang you – *ingrato – encantador!*'

Torres, with a hissing exclamation, sprang at her.

'Ramoncito!' she shrieked; 'once you loved me.'

The Mexican's arm raised and descended. 'You are old,' he cried; and she fell and lay motionless.

Another scream; the flaps of the tent were flung aside, and there stood Katie, white with fear, her wrists still bound with a cruel cord.

'Sam!' she cried, 'save me again!'

Tansey rounded the table, and flung himself, with superb nerve, upon the Mexican. Just then a clangor began; the clocks of the city were tolling the midnight hour. Tansey clutched at Torres and, for a moment, felt in his grasp the crunch of velvet and the cold facets of the glittering gems. The next instant, the bedecked caballero turned in his hands to a shrunken, leather-visaged, white-bearded, old, old screaming mummy, sandalled, ragged, four hundred and three. The Mexican woman was crawling to her feet, and laughing. She shook her brown hand in the face of the whining *viejo*.

'Go, now,' she cried, 'and seek your señorita. It was I, Ramoncito, who brought you to this. Within each moon you eat of the life-giving *chili*. It was I that kept the wrong time for you. You should have eaten *yesterday* instead of *to-morrow*. It is too late. Off with you, *hombre!* You are too old for me!'

'This,' decided Tansey, releasing his hold of the graybeard, 'is a private family matter concerning age, and no business of mine.'

With one of the table knives he hastened to saw asunder the fetters of the fair captive; and then, for the second time that night he kissed Katie Peek – tasted again the sweetness, the wonder, the thrill of it, attained once more the maximum of his incessant dreams.

The next instant an icy blade was driven deep between his shoulders; he felt his blood slowly congeal; heard the senile cackle of the perennial Spaniard; saw the Plaza rise and reel till the zenith crashed into the horizon – and knew no more.

When Tansey opened his eyes again he was sitting upon those self-same steps gazing upon the dark bulk of the sleeping convent. In the middle of his back was still the acute, chilling pain. How had he been conveyed back there again? He got stiffly to his feet and stretched his cramped limbs. Supporting himself against the stonework he revolved in his mind the extravagant adventures that had befallen him each time he had strayed from the steps that night. In reviewing them certain features strained his credulity. Had he really met Captain Peek or Katie or the unparalleled Mexican in his wanderings – had he really encountered them under commonplace conditions and his over-stimulated brain had supplied the incongruities? However that might be, a sudden, elating thought caused him an intense joy. Nearly all of us have, at some point in our lives – either to excuse our own stupidity or placate our consciences – promulgated some theory of fatalism. We have set up an intelligent Fate that works by codes and signals. Tansey had done likewise; and now he read, through the night's incidents, the finger-prints of destiny. Each excursion that he had made had led to the one paramount finale – to Katie and that kiss, which survived and grew strong and intoxicating in his memory. Clearly, Fate was holding up to him the mirror that night, calling him to observe what awaited him at the end of whichever road he might take. He immediately turned, and hurried homeward.

Clothed in an elaborate, pale blue wrapper, cut to fit, Miss Katie Peek reclined in an arm-chair before a waning fire in her room. Her little, bare feet were thrust into house-shoes rimmed with swan's down. By the light of a small lamp she was attacking the society news of the latest Sunday paper. Some happy substance, seemingly indestructible, was being rhythmically crushed between her small white teeth. Miss Katie read of functions and furbelows, but she kept a vigilant ear for outside sounds and a frequent eye upon the clock over the mantel. At every footstep upon the asphalt sidewalk her smooth, round chin would cease for a moment its regular rise and fall, and a frown of listening would pucker her pretty brows.

At last she heard the latch of the iron gate click. She sprang up, tripped swiftly to the mirror, where she made a few of those feminine, flickering passes at her front hair and throat which are warranted to hypnotize the approaching guest.

The door-bell rang. Miss Katie, in her haste, turned the blaze of the lamp lower instead of higher, and hastened noiselessly downstairs into the hall. She turned the key, the door opened, and Mr. Tansey side-stepped in.

'Why, the i-de-a!' exclaimed Miss Katie, 'is this you, Mr. Tansey? It's after midnight. Aren't you ashamed to wake me up at such an hour to let you in? You're just *awful!*'

'I was late,' said Tansey, brilliantly.

'I should think you were! Ma was awfully worried about you. When you weren't in by ten, that hateful Tom McGill said you were out calling on another – said you were out calling on some young lady. I just despise Mr. McGill. Well, I'm not going to scold you any more, Mr. Tansey, if it *is* a little late – Oh! I turned it the wrong way!'

Miss Katie gave a little scream. Absent-mindedly she had turned the blaze of the lamp entirely out instead of higher. It was very dark.

Tansey heard a musical, soft giggle, and breathed an entrancing odor of heliotrope. A groping light hand touched his arm.

'How awkward I was! Can you find your way – Sam?'

'I – I think I have a match, Miss K-Katie.'

A scratching sound; a flame; a glow of light held at arm's length by the recreant follower of Destiny illuminating a tableau which shall end the ignominious chronicle – a maid with unkissed, curling, contemptuous lips slowly lifting the lamp chimney and allowing the wick to ignite; then waving a scornful and abjuring hand toward the staircase – the unhappy Tansey erstwhile champion in the prophetic lists of fortune, ingloriously ascending to his just and certain doom, while (let us imagine) half within the wings stands the imminent figure of Fate jerking wildly at the wrong strings, and mixing things up in her usual able manner.

A DEPARTMENTAL CASE

IN TEXAS YOU MAY TRAVEL a thousand miles in a straight line. If your course is a crooked one, it is likely that both the distance and your rate of speed may be vastly increased. Clouds there sail serenely against the wind. The whip-poorwill delivers its disconsolate cry with the notes exactly reversed from those of the Northern brother. Given a drought and a subsequently lively rain, and lo! from a glazed and stony soil will spring in a single night blossomed lilies, miraculously fair. Tom Green County was once the standard of measurement. I have forgotten how many New Jerseys and Rhode Islands it was that could have been stowed away and lost in its chaparral. But the legislative axe has slashed Tom Green into a handful of counties hardly larger than European kingdoms. The legislature convenes at Austin, near the centre of the state; and, while the representative from Rio Grande country is gathering his palm leaf fan and his linen duster to set out for the capital, the Pan-handle solon winds his muffler above his well-buttoned overcoat and kicks the snow from his well-greased boots ready for the same journey. All this merely to hint that the big ex-republic of the Southwest forms a sizable star on the flag, and to prepare for the corollary that things sometimes happen there uncut to pattern and unfettered by metes and bounds.

The Commissioner of Insurance, Statistics, and History of the State of

Texas was an official of no very great or very small importance. The past tense is used, for now he is Commissioner of Insurance alone. Statistics and history are no longer proper nouns in the government records.

In the year 188–, the governor appointed Luke Coonrod Standifer to be head of this department. Standifer was then fifty-five years of age, and a Texan to the core. His father had been one of the state's earliest settlers and pioneers. Standifer himself had served the commonwealth as Indian fighter, soldier, ranger and legislator. Much learning he did not claim, but he had drunk pretty deep of the spring of experience.

If other grounds were less abundant, Texas should be well up in the lists of glory as the grateful republic. For both as republic and state, it has busily heaped honors and solid rewards upon its sons who rescued it from the wilderness.

Wherefore and therefore, Luke Coonrod Standifer, son of Ezra Standifer, ex-Terry ranger, simon-pure democrat, and lucky dweller in an unrepresented portion of the politico-geographical map, was appointed Commissioner of Insurance, Statistics, and History.

Standifer accepted the honor with some doubt as to the nature of the office he was to fill and his capacity for filling it – but he accepted, and by wire. He immediately set out from the little country town where he maintained (and was scarcely maintained by) a somnolent and unfruitful office of surveying and map-drawing. Before departing, he had looked under the I's, S's, and H's in the 'Encyclopaedia Britannica' what information and preparation toward his official duties that those weighty volumes afforded.

A few weeks of incumbency diminished the new commissioner's awe of the great and important office he had been called upon to conduct. An increasing familiarity with its workings soon restored him to his accustomed placid course of life. In his office was an old spectacled clerk – a consecrated, informed, able machine, who held his desk regardless of changes of administrative heads. Old Kauffman instructed his new chief gradually in the knowledge of the department without seeming to do so, and kept the wheels revolving without the slip of a cog.

Indeed, the Department of Insurance, Statistics, and History carried no great heft of the burden of state. Its main work was the regulating of the business done in the state by foreign insurance companies, and the letter of the law was its guide. As for statistics – well, you wrote letters to country officers, and scissored other people's reports, and each year you got out a report of your own about the corn crop and the cotton crop and pecans and pigs and black and white population, and a great many columns of figures headed 'bushels' and 'acres' and 'square miles,' etc. – and there you were. History? The branch was purely a receptive one. Old ladies interested in the science bothered you some with long reports of proceedings of their historical societies. Some twenty or thirty people would write you each year that they had secured Sam Houston's pocket-knife or Santa Ana's whisky-flask or Davy Crockett's rifle – all absolutely authenticated – and demanded legislative appropriation to purchase. Most of the work in the history branch went into pigeonholes.

One sizzling August afternoon the commissioner reclined in his office chair, with his feet upon the long, official table covered with green billiard cloth. The commissioner was smoking a cigar, and dreamily regarding the quivering landscape framed by the window that looked upon the treeless capitol grounds. Perhaps he was thinking of the rough and ready life he had led, of the old days of breathless adventure and movement, of the comrades who now trod other paths or had ceased to tread any, of the changes civilization and peace had brought, and, maybe, complacently, of the snug and comfortable camp pitched for him under the dome of the capitol of the state that had not forgotten his services.

The business of the department was lax. Insurance was easy. Statistics were not in demand. History was dead. Old Kauffman, the efficient and perpetual clerk, had requested an infrequent half-holiday, incited to the unusual dissipation by the joy of having successfully twisted the tail of a Connecticut insurance company that was trying to do business contrary to the edicts of the great Lone Star State.

The office was very still. A few subdued noises trickled in through the open door from the other departments – a dull tinkling crash from the treasurer's office adjoining, as a clerk tossed a bag of silver to the floor of the vault – the vague intermittent clatter of a dilatory typewriter – a dull tapping from the state geologist's quarters as if some woodpecker had flown in to bore for his prey in the cool of the massive building – and then a faint rustle, and the light shuffling of the well-worn shoes along the hall, the sounds ceasing at the door toward which the commissioner's lethargic back was presented. Following this, the sound of a gentle voice speaking words unintelligible to the commissioner's somewhat dormant comprehension, but giving evidence of bewilderment and hesitation.

The voice was feminine; the commissioner was of the race of cavaliers who make salaam before the trail of a skirt without considering the quality of its cloth.

There stood in the door a faded woman, one of the numerous sisterhood of the unhappy. She was dressed all in black – poverty's perpetual mourning for lost joys. Her face had the contours of twenty and the lines of forty. She may have lived that intervening score of years in a twelve-month. There was about her yet an aurum of indignant, unappeased, protesting youth that shone faintly through the premature veil of unearned decline.

'I beg your pardon, ma'am,' said the commissioner, gaining his feet to the accompaniment of a great creaking and sliding of his chair.

'Are you the governor, sir?' asked the vision of melancholy.

The commissioner hesitated at the end of his best bow, with his hand in the bosom of his double-breasted 'frock.' Truth at last conquered.

'Well, no ma'am. I am not the governor. I have the honor to be Commissioner of Insurance, Statistics, and History. Is there anything, ma'am, I can do for you? Won't you have a chair, ma'am?'

The lady subsided into the chair handed her, probably from purely physical reasons. She wielded a cheap fan – last token of gentility to be abandoned. Her clothing seemed to indicate a reduction almost to extreme poverty. She looked at the man who was not the governor, and saw kindliness and simplicity and a rugged, unadorned courtliness emanating from a countenance tanned, and toughened by forty years of outdoor life. Also, she saw that his eyes were clear and strong and blue. Just as they had been when he used them to skim the horizon for raiding Kiowas and Sioux. His mouth was as set and firm as it had been on that day when he bearded the old Lion Sam Houston himself, and defied him during that season when secession was the theme. Now, in bearing and dress, Luke Coonrod Standifer endeavored to do credit to the important arts and sciences of Insurance, Statistics, and History. He had abandoned the careless dress of his country home. Now, his broad-brimmed black slouch hat, and his long-tailed 'frock' made him not the least imposing of the official family, even if his office was reckoned to stand at the tail of the list.

'You wanted to see the governor, ma'am?' asked the commissioner, with a deferential manner he always used toward the fair sex.

'I hardly know,' said the lady, hesitatingly. 'I suppose so.' And then, suddenly drawn by the sympathetic look of the other, she poured forth the story of her need.

It was a story so common that the public has come to look at its monotony instead of its pity. The old tale of an unhappy married life – made so by a brutal, conscienceless husband, a robber, a spendthrift, a moral coward, and a bully, who failed to provide even the means of the barest existence. Yes, he had come down in the scale so low as to strike her. It happened only the day before – there was the bruise on one temple – she had offended his highness by asking for a little money to live on. And yet she must needs, womanlike, append a plea for her tyrant – he was drinking; he had rarely abused her thus when sober.

'I thought,' mourned this pale sister of sorrow, 'that maybe the state might be willing to give me some relief. I've heard of such things being done for the families of old settlers. I've heard tell that the state used to give land to the men who fought for it against Mexico, and settled up the country, and helped drive out the Indians. My father did all of that, and he never received anything. He never would take it. I thought the governor would be the one to see, and that's why I came. If Father was entitled to anything, they might let it come to me.'

'It's possible, ma'am,' said Standifer, 'that such might be the case. But 'most all the veterans and settlers got their land certificates issued and located long ago. Still, we can look that up in the land office and be sure. Your father's name, now, was—'

'Amos Colvin, sir.'

'Good Lord!' exclaimed Standifer, rising and unbuttoning his tight coat, excitedly. 'Are you Amos Colvin's daughter? Why, ma'am, Amos Colvin and me were thicker than two hoss thieves for more than ten years! We fought Kiowas, drove cattle, and rangered side by side nearly all over Texas. I remember seeing you once before now. You were a kid, about seven, a-riding a little yellow pony up and down. Amos and me stopped at your home for a little grub when we were trailing that band of Mexican cattle thieves down through Karnes and Bee. Great tarantulas! and you're Amos Colvin's little girl! Did you ever hear your father mention Luke Standifer – just kind of casually – as if he'd met me once or twice?'

A little pale smile flitted across the lady's white face.

'It seems to me,' she said, 'that I don't remember hearing him talk about much else. Every day there was some story he had to tell about what he and you had done. Mighty near the last thing I heard him tell was about the time when the Indians wounded him, and you crawled out to him through the grass, with a canteen of water while they—'

'Yes, yes – well – oh, that wasn't anything,' said Standifer, 'hemming' loudly and buttoning his coat again briskly. 'And now, ma'am, who was the infernal skunk – I beg your pardon, ma'am – who was the gentleman you married?'

'Benton Sharp.'

The commissioner plumped down again into his chair with a groan. This gentle, sad little woman in the rusty black gown the daughter of his oldest friend, the wife of Benton Sharp! Benton Sharp, one of the most noted 'bad' men in that part of the state – a man who had been a cattle thief, an outlaw, a desperado, and was now a gambler, a swaggering bully, who plied his trade in the larger frontier towns, relying upon his record and the quickness of his gun play to maintain his supremacy. Seldom did anyone take the risk of going 'up against' Benton Sharp. Even the law officers were content to let him make his own terms of peace. Sharp was a ready and an accurate shot, and as lucky as a brand-new penny at coming clear of scrapes. Standifer wondered how this pillaging eagle ever came to be mated with Amos Colvin's little dove and expressed his wonder.

Mrs. Sharp sighed.

'You see, Mr. Standifer, we didn't know anything about him, and he can be very pleasant and kind when he wants to. We lived down in the little town of Goliad. Benton came riding down that way and stopped there a while. I reckon I was some better looking then than I am now. He was good to me for a whole year after we were married. He insured his life for me for five thousand dollars. But for the last six months he has done everything but kill me. I often wish he had done that, too. He got out of money for a while, and abused me shamefully for not having anything he could spend. Then Father died and left me the little home in Goliad. My husband made me sell that and turned me out into the world. I've barely been able to live, for I'm not strong enough to work. Lately, I heard he was making money in San Antonio, so I went there, and found him, and asked for a little help. This,' touching the livid bruise on her temple, 'is what he gave me. So I came on to Austin to see the governor. I once heard Father say that there was some land or a pension coming to him from the state that he never would ask for.'

Luke Standifer rose to his feet, and pushed his chair back. He looked rather perplexedly around the big office with its handsome furniture.

'It's a long trail to follow,' he said, slowly, 'trying to get back dues from the government. There's red tape and lawyers and rulings and evidences and courts to keep you waiting. I'm not certain,' continued the commissioner, with a profoundly meditative frown, 'whether this department that I'm the boss of has any jurisdiction or not. It's only Insurance, Statistics, and History, ma'am, and it don't sound as if it would cover the case. But sometimes a saddle blanket can be made to stretch. You keep your seat, just for a few minutes, ma'am, till I step into the next room and see about it.'

The state treasurer was seated within his massive, complicated railings, reading a newspaper. Business for the day was about over. The clerks lolled at their desks, awaiting the closing hour. The Commissioner of Insurance, Statistics, and History entered, and leaned in at the window.

The treasurer, a little, brisk old man, with snow-white moustache and beard, jumped up youthfully and came forward to greet Standifer. They were friends of old.

'Uncle Frank,' said the commissioner, using the familiar name by which the historic treasurer was addressed by every Texan, 'how much money have you got on hand?'

The treasurer named the sum of the last balance down to the odd cents – something more than a million dollars.

The commissioner whistled lowly, and his eyes grew hopefully bright.

'You know, or else you've heard of, Amos Colvin, Uncle Frank?'

'Knew him well,' said the treasurer, promptly. 'A good man. A valuable citizen. One of the settlers in the Southwest.'

'His daughter,' said Standifer, 'is sitting in my office. She's penniless. She's married to Benton Sharp, a coyote and a murderer. He's reduced her to want and broken her heart. Her father helped build up this state, and it's the state's turn to help his child. A couple of thousand dollars will buy back her home and let her live in peace. The State of Texas can't afford to refuse it. Give me the money, Uncle Frank, and I'll give it to her right away. We'll fix up the red-tape business afterward.'

The treasurer looked a little bewildered.

'Why, Standifer,' he said, 'you know I can't pay a cent out of the treasury without a warrant from the comptroller. I can't disburse a dollar without a voucher to show for it.'

The commissioner betrayed a slight impatience.

'I'll give you a voucher,' he declared. 'What's this job they've given me for? Am I just a knot on a mesquite stump? Can't my office stand for it? Charge it up to Insurance and the other two sideshows. Don't Statistics show that Amos Colvin came to this state when it was in the hands of Greasers and rattlesnakes and Comanches, and fought day and night to make a white man's country of it? Don't they show that Amos Colvin's daughter is brought to ruin by a villain who's trying to pull down what you and I and old Texans shed our blood to build up? Don't History show that the Lone Star State never yet failed to grant relief to the suffering and oppressed children of the men who made her the grandest commonwealth in the Union? If Statistics and History don't bear out the claim of Amos Colvin's child I'll ask the next legislature to abolish my office. Come, now, Uncle Frank, let her have the money. I'll sign the papers officially, if you say so; and then if the governor or the comptroller or the janitor or anybody else makes a kick, by the Lord I'll refer the matter to the people, and see if they won't indorse the act.'

The treasurer looked sympathetic but shocked. The commissioner's voice had grown louder as he rounded off the sentences that, however praiseworthy they might be in sentiment, reflected somewhat upon the capacity of the head of a more or less important department of state. The clerks were beginning to listen.

'Now, Standifer,' said the treasurer, soothingly, 'you know I'd like to help in this matter, but stop and think a moment, please. Every cent in the treasury is expended only by appropriation made by the legislature, and drawn out by checks issued by the comptroller. I can't control the use of a cent of it. Neither can you. Your department isn't disbursive – it isn't even administrative – it's purely clerical. The only way for the lady to obtain relief is to petition the legislature, and—'

'To the devil with the legislature,' said Standifer, turning away.

The treasurer called him back.

'I'd be glad, Standifer, to contribute a hundred dollars personally toward the immediate expenses of Colvin's daughter.' He reached for his pocketbook.

'Never mind, Uncle Frank,' said the commissioner, in a softer tone. 'There's no need of that. She hasn't asked for anything of that sort yet. Besides, her case is in my hands. I see now what a little rag-tag, bob-tail, gotch-eared department I've been put in charge of. It seems to be about as important as an almanac or a hotel register. But while I'm running it, it won't turn away any daughters of Amos Colvin without stretching its jurisdiction to cover, if possible. You want to keep your eye on the Department of Insurance, Statistics, and History.'

The commissioner returned to his office, looking thoughtful. He opened and closed an inkstand on his desk many times with extreme and undue attention before he spoke. 'Why don't you get a divorce?' he asked, suddenly.

'I haven't the money to pay for it,' answered the lady.

'Just at present,' announced the commissioner, in a formal tone, 'the powers of my department appear to be considerably stringhalted. Statistics seem to be overdrawn at the bank, and History isn't good for a square meal. But you've come to the right place, ma'am. The department will see you through. Where did you say your husband is, ma'am?'

'He was in San Antonio yesterday. He is living there now.'

Suddenly the commissioner abandoned his official air. He took the faded little woman's hands in his, and spoke in the old voice he used on the trail and around campfires.

'Your name's Amanda, isn't it?'

'Yes, sir.'

'I thought so. I've heard your dad say it often enough. Well, Amanda, here's your father's best friend, the head of a big office in the state government, that's going to help you out of your troubles. And here's the old bush-whacker and cowpuncher that your father has helped out of scrapes time and time again wants to ask you a question. Amanda, have you got enough money to run you for the next two or three days?'

Mrs. Sharp's white face flushed the least bit.

'Plenty, sir – for a few days.'

'All right, then, ma'am. Now you go back where you are stopping here, and you come to the office again the day after to-morrow at four o'clock in the afternoon. Very likely by that time there will be something definite to report to you.' The commissioner hesitated, and looked a trifle embarrassed. 'You said your husband had insured his life for $5,000. Do you know whether the premiums have been kept paid upon it or not?'

'He paid for a whole year in advance about five months ago,' said Mrs. Sharp. 'I have the policy and receipts in my trunk.'

'Oh, that's all right, then,' said Standifer. 'It's best to look after things of that sort. Some day they may come in handy.'

Mrs. Sharp departed, and soon afterward Luke Standifer went down to the little hotel where he boarded and looked up the railroad time-table in the daily paper. Half an hour later he removed his coat and vest, and strapped a peculiarly constructed pistol holster across his shoulders, leaving the receptacle close under his left armpit. Into the holster he shoved a short-barreled .44-calibre revolver. Putting on his clothes again, he strolled down to the station and caught the five-twenty afternoon train for San Antonio.

The San Antonio *Express* of the following morning contained this sensational piece of news:

BENTON SHARP MEETS HIS MATCH

THE MOST NOTED DESPERADO IN SOUTHWEST TEXAS SHOT TO DEATH IN THE
GOLD FRONT RESTAURANT – PROMINENT. STATE OFFICIAL SUCCESSFULLY
DEFENDS HIMSELF AGAINST THE NOTED BULLY – MAGNIFICENT EXHIBITION OF
QUICK GUN PLAY.

Last night about eleven o'clock Benton Sharp, with two other men, entered
the Gold Front Restaurant and seated themselves at a table. Sharp had been
drinking, and was loud and boisterous, as he always was when under the
influence of liquor. Five minutes after the party was seated a tall, well-
dressed, elderly gentleman entered the restaurant. Few present recognized
the Honorable Luke Standifer, the recently appointed Commissioner of
Insurance, Statistics, and History.

Going over to the same side where Sharp was, Mr. Standifer prepared to
take a seat at the next table. In hanging his hat upon one of the hooks along
the wall he let it fall upon Sharp's head. Sharp turned, being in an especially
ugly humor, and cursed the other roundly. Mr. Standifer apologized calmly
for the accident, but Sharp continued his vituperations. Mr. Standifer was
observed to draw near and speak a few sentences to the desperado in so low
a tone that no one else caught the words. Sharp sprang up, wild with rage.
In the meantime Mr. Standifer had stepped some yards away, and was
standing quietly with his arms folded across the breast of his loosely hanging
coat.

With that impetuous and deadly rapidity that made Sharp so dreaded, he
reached for the gun he always carried in his hip pocket – a movement that
has preceded the death of at least a dozen men at his hands. Quick as the
motion was, the bystanders assert that it was met by the most beautiful
exhibition of lightning gun-pulling ever witnessed in the Southwest. As
Sharp's pistol was being raised – and the act was really quicker than the eye
could follow – a glittering .44 appeared as if by some conjuring trick in the
right hand of Mr. Standifer, who, without a perceptible movement of his
arm, shot Benton Sharp through the heart. It seems that the new Commissioner of Insurance, Statistics, and History has been an old-time Indian fighter
and ranger for many years, which accounts for the happy knack he has of
handling a .44.

It is not believed that Mr. Standifer will be put to any inconvenience
beyond a necessary formal hearing to-day, as all the witnesses who were
present unite in declaring that the deed was done in self-defense.

When Mrs. Sharp appeared at the office of the commissioner, according to
appointment, she found that gentleman calmly eating a golden russet apple.
He greeted her without embarrassment and without hesitation at approaching
the subject that was the topic of the day.

'I had to do it, ma'am,' he said, simply, 'or get it myself. Mr. Kauffman,'
he added, turning to the old clerk, 'please look up the records of the Security
Life Insurance Company and see if they are all right.'

'No need to look,' grunted Kauffman, who had everything in his head.
'It's all O.K. They pay all losses within ten days.'

Mrs. Sharp soon rose to depart. She had arranged to remain in town until
the policy was paid. The commissioner did not detain her. She was a woman,

and he did not know just what to say to her at present. Rest and time would bring her what she needed.

But, as she was leaving, Luke Standifer indulged himself in an official remark:

'The Department of Insurance, Statistics, and History, ma'am, has done the best it could with your case. 'Twas a case hard to cover according to red tape. Statistics failed, and History missed fire, but, if I may be permitted to say it, we came out particularly strong on Insurance.'

THE RENAISSANCE AT CHARLEROI

GRANDEMONT CHARLES WAS a little Creole gentleman, aged thirty-four, with a bald spot on the top of his head and the manners of a prince. By day he was a clerk in a cotton broker's office in one of those cold, rancid mountains of oozy brick, down near the levee in New Orleans. By night, in his three-story-high *chambre garnie* in the old French Quarter he was again the last male descendant of the Charles family, that noble house that had lorded it in France, and had pushed its way smiling, rapiered, and courtly into Louisiana's early and brilliant days. Of late years the Charleses had subsided into the more republican but scarcely less royally carried magnificence and ease of plantation life along the Mississippi. Perhaps Grandemont was even Marquis de Brassé. There was that title in the family. But a marquis on seventy-five dollars per month! *Vraiment!* Still, it has been done on less.

Grandemont had saved out of his salary the sum of six hundred dollars. Enough, you would say, for any man to marry on. So, after a silence of two years on that subject, he reopened the most hazardous question to Mlle. Adèle Fauquier, riding down to Meade d'Or, her father's plantation. Her answer was the same that it had been any time during the last ten years: 'First find my brother, Monsieur Charles.'

This time he had stood before her, perhaps discouraged by a love so long and hopeless, being dependent upon a contingency so unreasonable, and demanded to be told in simple words whether she loved him or no.

Adèle looked at him steadily out of her gray eyes that betrayed no secrets and answered, a little more softly:

'Grandemont, you have no right to ask that question unless you can do what I ask of you. Either bring back brother Victor to us or the proof that he died.'

Somehow, though five times thus rejected, his heart was not so heavy when he left. She had not denied that she loved. Upon what shallow waters can the bark of passion remain afloat! Or, shall we play the doctrinaire, and hint that at thirty-four the tides of life are calmer and cognizant of many sources instead of but one – as at four-and-twenty?

Victor Fauquier would never be found. In those early days of his disappearance there was money to the Charles name, and Grandemont had spent the dollars as if they were picayunes in trying to find the lost youth. Even then he had had small hope of success, for the Mississippi gives up a victim from its oily tangles only at the whim of its malign will.

A thousand times had Grandemont conned in his mind the scene of Victor's disappearance. And, at each time that Adèle had set her stubborn but pitiful alternative against his suit, still clearer it repeated itself in his brain.

The boy had been the family favorite: daring, winning, reckless. His unwise fancy had been captured by a girl on the plantation – the daughter of an overseer. Victor's family was in ignorance of the intrigue, as far as it had gone. To save them the inevitable pain that his course promised, Grandemont strove to prevent it. Omnipotent money smoothed the way. The overseer and his daughter left, between a sunset and dawn, for an undesignated bourne. Grandemont was confident that this stroke would bring the boy to reason. He rode over to Meade d'Or to talk with him. The two strolled out of the house and grounds, crossed the road, and, mounting the levee, walked its broad path while they conversed. A thundercloud was hanging, imminent, above, but, as yet, no rain fell. At Grandemont's disclosure of his interference in the clandestine romance, Victor attacked him, in a wild and sudden fury. Grandemont, though of slight frame, possessed muscles of iron. He caught the wrists amid a shower of blows descending upon him, bent the lad backward and stretched him upon the levee path. In a little while the gust of passion was spent, and he was allowed to rise. Calm now, but a powder mine where he had been but a whiff of the tantrums, Victor extended his hand toward the dwelling house of Meade d'Or.

'You and they,' he cried, 'have conspired to destroy my happiness. None of you shall ever look upon my face again.'

Turning, he ran swiftly down the levee, disappearing in the darkness, Grandemont followed as well as he could, calling to him, but in vain. For longer than an hour he pursued the search. Descending the side of the levee, he penetrated the rank density of weeds and willows that undergrew the trees until the river's edge, shouting Victor's name. There was never an answer, though once he thought he heard a bubbling scream from the dun waters sliding past. Then the storm broke, and he returned to the house drenched and dejected.

There he explained the boy's absence sufficiently, he thought, not speaking of the tangle that had led to it, for he hoped that Victor would return as soon as his anger had cooled. Afterward, when the threat was made good and they saw his face no more, he found it difficult to alter his explanations of that night, and there clung a certain mystery to the boy's reasons for vanishing as well as to the manner of it.

It was on that night that Grandemont first perceived a new and singular expression in Adèle's eyes whenever she looked at him. And through the years following that expression was always there. He could not read it, for it was born of a thought she would never otherwise reveal.

Perhaps, if he had known that Adèle had stood at the gate on that unlucky night, where she had followed, lingering to await the return of her brother and lover, wondering why they had chosen so tempestuous an hour and so black a spot to hold converse – if he had known that a sudden flash of lightning had revealed to her sight that short, sharp struggle as Victor was sinking under his hands, he might have explained everything, and she—

I know not what she would have done. But one thing is clear – there was something besides her brother's disappearance between Grandemont's pleadings for her hand and Adèle's 'yes.' Ten years had passed, and what she had seen during the space of that lightning flash remained an indelible picture. She had loved her brother, but was she holding out for the solution of that mystery or for the 'Truth'! Women have been known to reverence it, even as an abstract principle. It is said there have been a few who, in the matter of their affections, have considered a life to be a small thing as compared with a lie. That I do not know. But, I wonder, had Grandemont cast himself at her feet crying that his hand had sent Victor to the bottom of that inscrutable river, and that he could no longer sully his love with a lie, I wonder if – I wonder what she would have done!

But, Grandemont Charles, Arcadian little gentleman, never guessed the meaning of that look in Adèle's eyes; and from his last bootless payment of his devoirs he rode away as rich as ever in honor and love, but poor in hope.

That was in September. It was during the first winter month that Grandemont conceived his idea of the *renaissance*. Since Adèle would never be his, and wealth without her were useless trumpery, why need he add to that hoard of slowly harvested dollars? Why should he even retain that hoard?

Hundreds were the cigarettes he consumed over his claret, sitting at the little polished tables in the Royal street cafés while thinking over his plan. By and by he had it perfect. It would cost, beyond doubt, all the money he had, but – *le jeu vaut la chandelle* – for some hours he would be once more a Charles of Charleroi. Once again should the nineteenth of January, that most significant day in the fortunes of the house of Charles, be fittingly observed. On that date the French king had seated a Charles by his side at table; on that date Armand Charles, Marquis de Brassé, landed, like a brilliant meteor, in New Orleans; it was the date of his mother's wedding; of Grandemont's birth. Since Grandemont could remember until the breaking up of the family that anniversary had been the synonym for feasting, hospitality, and proud commemoration.

Charleroi was the old family plantation, lying some twenty miles down the river. Years ago the estate had been sold to discharge the debts of its too-bountiful owners. Once again it had changed hands, and now the must and mildew of litigation had settled upon it. A question of heirship was in the courts, and the dwelling house of Charleroi, unless the tales told of ghostly powdered and laced Charleses haunting its unechoing chambers were true, stood uninhabited.

Grandemont found the solicitor in chancery who held the keys pending the decision. He proved to be an old friend of the family. Grandemont explained briefly that he desired to rent the house for two or three days. He wanted to give a dinner at his old home to a few friends. That was all.

'Take it for a week – a month, if you will,' said the solicitor; 'but do not speak to me of rental.' With a sigh he concluded: 'The dinners I have eaten under that roof, *mon fils!*'

There came to many of the old-established dealers in furniture, china, silverware, decorations, and household fittings at their stores on Canal, Chartres, St. Charles and Royal streets, a quiet young man with a little bald spot on the top of his head, distinguished manners, and the eye of a *connoisseur*, who explained what he wanted. To hire the complete and elegant equipment of a dining-room, hall, reception-room, and cloakrooms. The goods were to be packed and sent, by boat, to the Charleroi landing, and would be returned within three or four days. All damage or loss to be promptly paid for.

Many of those old merchants knew Grandemont by sight, and the Charleses of old by association. Some of them were of Creole stock and felt a thrill of responsive sympathy with the magnificently indiscreet design of this impoverished clerk who would revive but for a moment the ancient flame of glory with the fuel of his savings.

'Choose what you want,' they said to him. 'Handle everything carefully. See that the damage bill is kept low, and the charges for the loan will not oppress you.'

To the wine merchants next; and here a doleful slice was lopped from the six hundred. It was an exquisite pleasure to Grandemont once more to pick among the precious vintages. The champagne bins lured him like the abodes of sirens, but these he was forced to pass. With his six hundred he stood before them as a child with a penny stands before a French doll. But he bought with taste and discretion of other wines – Chablis, Moselle, Château d'Or, Hochheimer, and port of right age and pedigree.

The matter of the cuisine gave him some studious hours until he suddenly recollected André – André, their old *chef* – the most sublime master of French Creole cookery in the Mississippi Valley. Perhaps he was yet somewhere about the plantation. The solicitor had told him that the place was still being cultivated, in accordance with a compromise agreement between the litigants.

On the next Sunday after the thought Grandemont rode, horseback, down to Charleroi. The big, square house with its two long ells looked blank and cheerless with its closed shutters and doors.

The shrubbery in the yard was ragged and riotous. Fallen leaves from the grove littered the walks and porches. Turning down the lane at the side of the house, Grandemont rode on to the quarters of the plantation hands. He found the workers streaming back from church, careless, happy, and bedecked in gay yellows, reds, and blues.

Yes, André was still there; his wool a little grayer, his mouth as wide; his laughter as ready as ever. Grandemont told him of his plan, and the old *chef* swayed with pride and delight. With a sigh of relief, knowing that he need have no further concern until the serving of that dinner was announced, he placed in André's hands a liberal sum for the cost of it, giving *carte blanche* for its creation.

Among the blacks were also a number of the old house servants. Absalom, the former major domo, and a half-dozen of the younger men, once waiters and attachés of the kitchen, pantry, and other domestic departments, crowded around to meet *'M'shi Grande.'* Absalom guaranteed to marshal, of these, a corps of assistants that would perform with credit the serving of the dinner.

After distributing a liberal largesse among the faithful, Grandemont rode back to town well pleased. There were many other smaller details to think of and provide for, but eventually the scheme was complete, and now there remained only the issuance of the invitations to his guests.

Along the river within the scope of a score of miles dwelt some half-dozen families with whose princely hospitality that of the Charleses had been contemporaneous. They were the proudest and most august of the old régime. Their small circle had been a brilliant one; their social relations close and warm; their houses full of rare welcome and discriminating bounty. Those friends, said Grandemont, should once more, if never again, sit at Charleroi on a nineteenth of January to celebrate the festal day of his house.

Grandemont had his cards of invitation engraved. They were expensive, but beautiful. In one particular their good taste might have been disputed;

but the Creole allowed himself that one feather in the cap of his fugacious splendor. Might he not be allowed, for the one day of the *renaissance*, to be 'Grandemont du Puy Charles, of Charleroi'? He sent the invitations out early in January so that the guests might not fail to receive due notice.

At eight o'clock in the morning of the nineteenth, the lower coast steamboat *River Belle* gingerly approached the long unused landing at Charleroi. The bridge was lowered, and a swarm of the plantation hands streamed along the rotting pier, bearing ashore a strange assortment of freight. Great shapeless bundles and bales and packets swathed in cloths and bound with ropes; tubs and urns of palms, evergreens, and tropical flowers; tables, mirrors, chairs, couches, carpets, and pictures – all carefully bound and padded against the dangers of transit.

Grandemont was among them, the busiest there. To the safe conveyance of certain large hampers eloquent with printed cautions to delicate handling he gave his superintendence, for they contained the fragile china and glassware. The dropping of one of those hampers would have cost him more than he could have saved in a year.

The last article unloaded, the *River Belle* backed off and continued her course down stream. In less than an hour everything had been conveyed to the house. And came then Absalom's task, directing the placing of the furniture and wares. There was plenty of help, for that day was always a holiday in Charleroi, and the Negroes did not suffer the old traditions to lapse. Almost the entire population of the quarters volunteered their aid. A score of piccaninnies were sweeping at the leaves in the yard. In the big kitchen at the rear André was lording it with his old-time magnificence over his numerous sub-cooks and scullions. Shutters were flung wide; dust spun in clouds; the house echoed to voices and the tread of busy feet. The prince had come again, and Charleroi woke from its long sleep.

The full moon, as she rose across the river that night and peeped above the levee, saw a sight that had been long missing from her orbit. The old plantation house shed a soft and alluring radiance from every window. Of its two-score rooms only four had been refurnished – the large reception chamber, the dining hall, and two smaller rooms for the convenience of the expected guests. But lighted wax candles were set in the windows of every room.

The dining hall was the *chef-d'oeuvre*. The long table, set with twenty-five covers, sparkled like a winter landscape with its snowy napery and china and the icy gleam of crystal. The chaste beauty of the room had required small adornment. The polished floor burned to a glowing ruby with the reflection of candlelight. The rich wainscoting reached halfway to the ceiling. Along and above this had been set the relieving lightness of a few water-colour sketches of fruit and flower.

The reception chamber was fitted in a simple but elegant style. Its arrangement suggested nothing of the fact that on the morrow the rooms would again be cleared and abandoned to the dust and the spider. The entrance hall was imposing with palms and ferns and the light of an immense candelabrum.

At seven o'clock Grandemont, in evening dress, with pearls – a family passion – in his spotless linen, emerged from somewhere. The invitations had specified eight as the dining hour. He drew an armchair upon the porch, and sat there, smoking cigarettes and half dreaming.

The moon was an hour high. Fifty yards back from the gate stood the house, under its noble grove. The road ran in front, and then came the grass-grown levee and the insatiate river beyond. Just above the levee top a tiny red light was creeping down and a tiny green one was creeping up. Then the passing steamers saluted, and the hoarse din startled the drowsy silence of the melancholy lowlands. The stillness returned, save for the little voices of the night – the owl's recitative, the capriccio of the crickets, the concerto of the frogs in the grass. The piccaninnies and the dawdlers from the quarters had been dismissed to their confines, and the mêlée of the day was reduced to an orderly and intelligent silence. The six colored waiters, in their white jackets, paced, cat-footed, about the table, pretending to arrange where all was beyond betterment. Absalom, in black and shining pumps, posed, superior, here and there where the lights set off his grandeur. And Grandemont rested in his chair, waiting for his guests.

He must have drifted into a dream – and an extravagant one – for he was master of Charleroi and Adèle was his wife. She was coming out to him now; he could hear her steps; he could feel her hand upon his shoulder—

'Pardon moi, M'shi Grande' – it was Absalom's hand touching him, it was Absalom's voice, speaking the patois of the blacks – 'but it is eight o'clock.'

Eight o'clock. Grandemont sprang up. In the moonlight he could see the row of hitching-posts outside the gate. Long ago the horses of the guests should have stood there. They were vacant.

A chanted roar of indignation, a just, waxing bellow of affront and dishonored genius came from André's kitchen, filling the house with rhythmic protest. The beautiful dinner, the pearl of a dinner, the little excellent superb jewel of a dinner! But one moment more of waiting and not even the thousand thunders of black pigs of the quarters would touch it!

'They are a little late,' said Grandemont, calmly. 'They will come soon. Tell André to hold back dinner. And ask him if, by some chance, a bull from the pastures has broken, roaring, into the house.'

He seated himself again to his cigarettes. Though he had said it, he scarcely believed Charleroi would entertain company that night. For the first time in history the invitation of a Charles had been ignored. So simple in courtesy and honor was Grandemont and, perhaps, so serenely confident in the prestige of his name, that the most likely reasons for his vacant board did not occur to him.

Charleroi stood by a road traveled daily by people from those plantations whither his invitations had gone. No doubt even on the day before the sudden reanimation of the old house they had driven past and observed the evidences of long desertion and decay. They had looked at the corpse of Charleroi and then at Grandemont's invitations, and, though the puzzle or tasteless hoax or whatever the thing meant left them perplexed, they would not seek its solution by the folly of a visit to that deserted house.

The moon was now above the grove, and the yard was pied with deep shadows save where they lightened in the tender glow of outpouring candlelight. A crisp breeze from the river hinted at the possibility of frost when the night should have become older. The grass at one side of the steps was specked with the white stubs of Grandemont's cigarettes. The cotton-broker's clerk sat in his chair with the smoke spiralling above him. I doubt that he once thought of the little fortune he had so impotently squandered. Perhaps it was compensation enough for him to sit thus at Charleroi for a

few retrieved hours. Idly his mind wandered in and out many fanciful paths
of memory. He smiled to himself as a paraphrased line of Scripture strayed
into his mind: 'A certain *poor* man made a feast.'

He heard the sound of Absalom coughing a note of summons. Grandemont
stirred. This time he had not been asleep – only drowsing.

'Nine o'clock, *M'shi Grande*,' said Absalom in the uninflected voice of a
good servant who states a fact unqualified by personal opinion.

Grandemont rose to his feet. In their time all the Charleses had been
proven, and they were gallant losers.

'Serve dinner,' he said, calmly. And then he checked Absalom's movement
to obey, for something clicked the gate latch and was coming down the walk
towards the house. Something that shuffled its feet and muttered to itself as
it came. It stopped in the current of light at the foot of the steps and spake,
in the universal whine of the gadding mendicant.

'Kind sir, could you spare a poor, hungry man, out of luck, a little to eat?
And to sleep in the corner of a shed? For' – the thing concluded, irrelevantly
– 'I can sleep now. There are no mountains to dance reels in the night; and
the copper kettles are all scoured bright. The iron band is still around my
ankle, and a link, if it is your desire I should be chained.'

It set a foot upon the step and drew up the rags that hung upon the limb.
Above the distorted shoe, caked with dust of a hundred leagues, they saw the
link and the iron band. The clothes of the tramp were wrecked to piebald tatters
by sun and rain and wear. A mat of brown, tangled hair and beard covered his
head and face, out of which his eyes stared distractedly. Grandemont noticed
that he carried in one hand a white, square card.

'What is that?' he asked.

'I picked it up, sir, at the side of the road.' The vagabond handed the card
to Grandemont. 'Just a little to eat, sir. A little parched corn, a *tortilla*, or a
handful of beans. Goat's meat I cannot eat. When I cut their throats they cry
like children.'

Grandemont held up the card. It was one of his own invitations to dinner.
No doubt someone had cast it away from a passing carriage after comparing
it with the tenantless house at Charleroi.

'From the hedges and highways bid them come,' he said to himself, softly
smiling. And then Absalom: 'Send Louis to me.'

Louis, once his own body-servant, came promptly, in his white jacket.

'This gentleman,' said Grandemont, 'will dine with me. Furnish him with
bath and clothes. In twenty minutes have him ready and dinner served.'

Louis approached the disreputable guest with the suavity due to a visitor
to Charleroi, and spirited him away to inner regions.

Promptly, in twenty minutes, Absalom announced dinner, and, a moment
later, the guest was ushered into the dining hall where Grandemont waited,
standing, at the head of the table. The attentions of Louis had transformed
the stranger into something resembling the polite animal. Clean linen and
an old evening suit that had been sent down from town to clothe a waiter
had worked a miracle with his exterior. Brush and comb had partially subdued
the wild disorder of his hair. Now he might have passed for no more
extravagant a thing than one of those *poseurs* in art and music who affect
such oddity of guise. The man's countenance and demeanor, as he approached
the table, exhibited nothing of the awkwardness or confusion to be expected
from his Arabian Nights change. He allowed Absalom to seat him at

Grandemont's right hand with the manner of one thus accustomed to be waited upon.

'It grieves me,' said Grandemont, 'to be obliged to exchange names with a guest. My own name is Charles.'

'In the mountains,' said the wayfarer, 'they call me Gringo. Along the roads they call me Jack.'

'I prefer the latter,' said Grandemont. 'A glass of wine with you, Mr. Jack.'

Course after course was served by the supernumerous waiters. Grandemont, inspired by the results of André's exquisite skill in cookery and his own in the selection of wines, became the model host, talkative, witty, and genial. The guest was fitful in conversation. His mind seemed to be sustaining a succession of waves of dementia followed by intervals of comparative lucidity. There was the glassy brightness of recent fever in his eyes. A long course of it must have been the cause of his emaciation and weakness, his distracted mind, and the dull pallor that showed even through the tan of wind and sun.

'Charles,' he said to Grandemont – for thus he seemed to interpret his name – 'you never saw the mountains dance, did you?'

'No, Mr. Jack,' answered Grandemont, gravely, 'the spectacle has been denied me. But, I assure you, I can understand it must be a diverting sight. The big ones, you know, white with snow on the tops, waltzing – décolleté, we may say.'

'You first scour the kettles,' said Mr. Jack, leaning toward him excitedly, 'to cook the beans in the morning, and you lie down on a blanket and keep quite still. Then they come out and dance for you. You would go out and dance with them but you are chained every night to the centre pole of the hut. You believe the mountains dance, don't you, Charlie?'

'I contradict no traveler's tales,' said Grandemont, with a smile.

Mr. Jack laughed loudly. He dropped his voice to a confidential whisper.

'You are a fool to believe it,' he went on. 'They don't really dance. It's the fever in your head. It's the hard work and the bad water that does it. You are sick for weeks and there is no medicine. The fever comes on every evening, and then you are as strong as two men. One night the compañía are lying drunk with mescal. They have brought back sacks of silver dollars from a ride, and they drink to celebrate. In the night you file the chain in two and go down the mountain. You walk for miles – hundreds of them. By and by the mountains are all gone, and you come to the prairies. They do not dance at night; they are merciful, and you sleep. Then you come to the river, and it says things to you. You follow it down, down, but you can't find what you are looking for.'

Mr. Jack leaned back in his chair, and his eyes slowly closed. The food and wine had steeped him in a deep calm. The tense strain had been smoothed from his face. The languor of repletion was claiming him. Drowsily he spoke again.

'It's bad manners – I know – to go to sleep – at table – but – that was – such a good dinner – Grande, old fellow.'

Grande! The owner of the name started and set down his glass. How should this wretched tatterdemalion whom he had invited, Caliph-like, to sit at his feast know his name?

Not at first, but soon, little by little, the suspicion, wild and unreasonable as it was, stole into his brain. He drew out his watch with hands that almost balked him by their trembling, and opened the back case. There was a picture there – a photograph fixed to the inner side.

Rising, Grandemont shook Mr. Jack by the shoulder. The weary guest opened his eyes. Grandemont held the watch.

'Look at this picture, Mr. Jack. Have you ever—'

'My sister Adèle!'

The vagrant's voice rang loud and sudden through the room. He started to his feet, but Grandemont's arms were about him, and Grandemont was calling him 'Victor! – Victor Fauquier! *Merci, merci, mon Dieu!'*

Too far overcome by sleep and fatigue was the lost one to talk that night. Days afterward, when the tropic *calentura* had cooled in his veins, the disordered fragments he had spoken were completed in shape and sequence. He told the story of his angry flight, of toils and calamities on sea and shore, of his ebbing and flowing fortune in southern lands, and of his latest peril when, held a captive, he served menially in a stronghold of bandits in the Sonora Mountains of Mexico. And of the fever that seized him there and his escape and delirium, during which he strayed, perhaps led by some marvelous instinct, back to the river on whose bank he had been born. And of the proud and stubborn thing in his blood that had kept him silent through all those years, clouding the honor of one, though he knew it not, and keeping apart two loving hearts. 'What a thing is love!' you may say. And if I grant it, you shall say, with me: 'What a thing is pride!'

On a couch in the reception chamber Victor lay, with a dawning understanding in his heavy eyes and peace in his softened countenance. Absalom was preparing a lounge for the transient master of Charleroi, who, to-morrow, would be again the clerk of a cotton broker, but also—

'To-morrow,' Grandemont was saying, as he stood by the couch of his guest, speaking the words with his face shining as must have shone the face of Elijah's charioteer when he announced the glories of that heavenly journey – 'To-morrow I will take you to Her.'

ON BEHALF OF THE MANAGEMENT

THIS IS THE STORY OF THE MAN manager, and how he held his own until the very last paragraph.

I had it from Sully Magoon, viva voce. The words are indeed his; and if they do not constitute truthful fiction my memory should be taxed with the blame.

It is not deemed amiss to point out, in the beginning, the stress that is laid upon the masculinity of the manager. For, according to Sully, the term when applied to the feminine division of mankind has precisely an opposite meaning. The woman manager (he says) economizes, saves, oppresses her household with bargains and contrivances, and looks sourly upon any pence that are cast to the fiddler for even a single jig-step on life's arid march. Wherefore her menfolk call her blessed and praise her; and then sneak out the back door to see the Gilhooly Sisters do a buck-and-wing dance.

Now, the man manager (I still quote Sully) is a Caesar without a Brutus. He is an autocrat without responsibility, a player who imperils no stake of his own. His office is to enact, to reverberate, to boom, to expand, to out-coruscate – profitably, if he can. Bill-paying and growing gray hairs over results belong to his principals. It is his to guide the risk, to be the Apotheosis of Front, the three-tailed Bashaw of Bluff, the Essential Oil of Razzle-Dazzle.

We sat at luncheon, and Sully Magoon told me. I asked for particulars.

'My old friend Denver Galloway was a born manager,' said Sully. 'He first saw the light of day in New York at three years of age. He was born in Pittsburgh, but his parents moved East the third summer afterward.

'When Denver grew up, he went into the managing business. At the age of eight he managed a news-stand for the Dago that owned it. After that he was manager at different times of a skating-rink, a livery-stable, a policy game, a restaurant, a dancing academy, a walking match, a burlesque company, a drygoods store, a dozen hotels and summer resorts, an insurance company, and a district leader's campaign. That campaign, when Coughlin was elected on the East Side, gave Denver a boost. It got him a job as manager of a Broadway hotel, and for a while he managed Senator O'Grady's campaign in the nineteenth.

'Denver was a New Yorker all over. I think he was out of the city just twice before the time I'm going to tell you about. Once he went rabbit-shooting in Yonkers. The other time I met him just landing from a North River ferry. "Been out West on a big trip, Sully, old boy," said he: "Gad! Sully, I had no idea we had such a big country. It's immense. Never conceived of the magnificence of the West before. It's gorgeous and glorious and infinite. Makes the East seem cramped and little. It's a grand thing to travel and get an idea of the extent and resources of our country."

'I'd made several little runs out to California and down to Mexico and up through Alaska, so I sits down with Denver for a chat about the things he saw.

' "Took in the Yosemite, out there, of course?" I asks.

' "Well – no," says Denver, "I don't think so. At least, I don't recollect it. You see, I only had three days, and I didn't get any farther west than Youngstown, Ohio."

'About two years ago I dropped into New York with a little fly-paper proposition about a Tennessee mica mine that I wanted to spread out in a nice, sunny window, in the hopes of catching a few. I was coming out of a printing-shop one afternoon with a batch of fine, sticky prospectuses when I ran against Denver coming around a corner. I never saw him looking so much like a tiger-lily. He was as beautiful and new as a trellis of sweet peas, and as rollicking as a clarinet solo. We shook hands, and he asked me what I was doing, and I gave him the outlines of the scandal I was trying to create in mica.

' "Pooh, pooh! for your mica," says Denver. "Don't you know better, Sully, then to bump up against the coffers of little old New York with anything as transparent as mica? Now, you come with me over to the Hotel Brunswick. You're just the man I was hoping for. I've got something there in sepia and curled hair that I want you to look at."

' "You putting up at the Brunswick?" I asks.

' "Not a cent," says Denver, cheerful. "The syndicate that owns the hotel puts up. I'm manager."

'The Brunswick wasn't one of them Broadway pot-houses all full of palms and hyphens and flowers and costumes – kind of a mixture of lawns and laundries. It was on one of the East Side avenues; but it was a solid, old-time caravansary such as the Mayor of Skaneateles or the Governor of Missouri might stop at. Eight stories high it stalked up, with new striped awnings, and the electric had it as light as day.

' "I've been manager here for a year," says Denver, as we drew nigh. "When I took charge," says he, "nobody nor nothing ever stopped at the Brunswick. The clock over the clerk's desk used to run for weeks without winding. A man fell dead with heart-disease on the sidewalk in front of it one day, and when they went to pick him up he was two blocks away. I figures out a scheme to catch the West Indies and South American trade. I persuaded the owners to invest a few more thousands, and I put every cent of it in electric light, cayenne pepper, gold-leaf, and garlic. I got a Spanish-speaking force of employees and a string band; and there was talk going around of a cockfight in the basement every Sunday. Maybe I didn't catch the nut-brown gang! From Havana to Patagonia the Don Señors knew about the Brunswick. We get the high-fliers from Cuba and Mexico and the couple of Americas farther south; and they've simply got the boodle to bombard every bullfinch in the bush with." ¸

'When we get to the hotel, Denver stops me at the door.

' "There's a little liver-colored man," says he, "sitting in a big leather chair to your right, inside. You sit down and watch him for a few minutes, and then tell me what you think."

'I took a chair, while Denver circulates around in the big rotunda. The room was about full of curly-headed Cubans and South American brunettes of different shades; and the atmosphere was international with cigarette smoke, lit up by diamond rings and edged off with a whisper of garlic.

'That Denver Galloway was sure a relief to the eye. Six feet two he was, red-headed, and pink-gilled as a sun-perch. And the air he had! Court of Saint James, Chauncey Olcott, Kentucky colonels, Count of Monte Cristo, grand opera – all these things he reminded you of when he was doing the honors. When he raised his finger the hotel porters and bell-boys skated across the floor like cockroaches, and even the clerk behind the desk looked as meek and unimportant as Andy Carnegie.

'Denver passed around, shaking hands with his guests, and saying over the two or three Spanish words he knew until it was like a coronation rehearsal or a Bryan barbecue in Texas.

'I watched the little man he told me to. 'Twas a little foreign person in a double-breasted frock-coat, trying to touch the floor with his toes. He was the color of vici kid, and his whiskers was like excelsior made out of mahogany wood. He breathed hard, and he never once took his eyes off of Denver. There was a look of admiration and respect on his face like you see on a boy that's following a champion baseball team, or the Kaiser William looking at himself in a glass.

'After Denver goes his rounds he takes me into his private office.

' "What's your report on the dingy I told you to watch?" he asks. ¸

' "Well," says I, "if you was as big a man as he takes you to be, nine rooms and bath in the Hall of Fame, rent free till 1 October, would be about your size."

' "You've caught the idea," says Denver. "I've given him the wizard grip and the cabalistic eye. The glamor that emanates from yours truly has enveloped him like a North River fog. He seems to think that Señor Galloway is the man who. I guess they don't raise 74-inch sorrel-tops with romping ways down in his precinct. Now, Sully," goes on Denver, "if you was asked, what would you take the little man to be?"

' "Why," says I, "the barber around the corner or, if he's royal, the king of the boot-blacks."

' "Never judge by looks," says Denver; "he's the dark-horse candidate for president of a South American republic."

' "Well," says I, "he didn't look quite that bad to me."

'Then Denver draws his chair up close and gives out his scheme.

' "Sully," says he, with seriousness and levity, "I've been a manager of one thing and another for over twenty years. That's what I was cut out for – to have somebody else to put up the money and look after the repairs and the police and taxes while I run the business. I never had a dollar of my own invested in my life. I wouldn't know how it felt to have the dealer rake in a coin of mine. But I can handle other people's stuff and manage other people's enterprises. I've had an ambition to get hold of something big – something higher than hotels and lumber-yards and local politics. I want to be manager of something way up – like a railroad or a diamond trust or an automobile factory. Now here comes this little man from the tropics with just what I want, and he's offered me the job."

' "What job?" I asks. "Is he going to revive the Georgia Minstrels or open a cigar store?"

' "He's no 'coon," says Denver, severe. "He's General Rompiro – General Josey Alfonso Sapolio Jew-Ann Rompiro – he has his cards printed by a news-ticker. He's the real thing, Sully, and he wants me to manage his campaign – he wants Denver C. Galloway for a president-maker. Think of that, Sully! Old Denver romping down to the tropics, plucking lotos-flowers and pineapples with one hand and making presidents with the other! Won't it make Uncle Mark Hanna mad? And I want you to go too, Sully. You can help me more than any man I know. I've been herding that brown man for a month in the hotel so he wouldn't stray down around Fourteenth Street and get roped in by that crowd of refugee tamale-eaters down there. And he's landed, and D. C. G. is manager of General J. A. S. J. Rompiro's presidential campaign in the great republic of – what's its name?"

'Denver gets down an atlas from a shelf, and we have a look at the afflicted country. 'Twas a dark blue one, on the west coast, about the size of a special delivery stamp.

' "From what the General tells me," says Denver, "and from what I can gather from the encyclopaedia and by conversing with the janitor of the Astor Library, it'll be as easy to handle the vote of that country as it would be for Tammany to get a man named Geoghan appointed on the White Wings force."

' "Why don't General Rumptyro stay at home," said I, "and manage his own canvass?"

' "You don't understand South American politics," says Denver, getting out the cigars. "It's this way. General Rompiro had the misfortune of becoming a popular idol. He distinguished himself by leading the army in pursuit of a couple of sailors who had stolen the plaza – or the carramba, or something belonging to the government. The people called him a hero and the government got jealous. The president sends for the chief of the Department of Public Edifices. 'Fine me a nice, clean adobe wall,' says he, 'and stand Señor Rompiro up against it. Then call out a file of soldiers and – then let him be up against it.' Something," goes on Denver, "like the way they've treated Hobson and Carrie Nation in our country. So the General had to flee. But he was thoughtful enough to bring along his roll. He's got sinews of war enough to buy a battleship and float her off in the christening fluid."

' "What chance has he got to be president?"

' "Wasn't I just giving you his rating?" says Denver. "His country is one of the few in South America where the presidents are elected by popular ballot. The General can't go there just now. It hurts to be shot against a wall. He needs a campaign manager to go down and whoop things up for him – to get the boys in line and the new two-dollar bills afloat and the babies kissed and the machine in running order. Sully, I don't want to brag, but you remember how I brought Coughlin under the wire for leader of the nineteenth? Ours was the banner district. Don't you suppose I know how to manage a little monkey-cage of a country like that? Why, with the dough the General's willing to turn loose I could put two more coats of Japan varnish on him and have him elected Governor of Georgia. New York has got the finest lot of campaign managers in the world, Sully, and you give me a feeling of hauteur when you cast doubts on my ability to handle the political situation in a country so small that they have to print the names of the towns in the appendix and footnotes."

'I argued with Denver some. I told him that politics down in that tropical atmosphere was bound to be different from the nineteenth district; but I might just as well have been a Congressman from North Dakota trying to get an appropriation for a lighthouse and a coast survey. Denver Galloway had ambitions in the manager line, and what I said didn't amount to as much as a fig-leaf at the National Dressmakers' Convention. "I'll give you three days to cogitate about going," says Denver; "and I'll introduce you to General Rompiro to-morrow, so you can get his ideas drawn right from the rose wood."

'I put on my best reception-to-Booker-Washington manner the next day and tapped the distinguished rubber-plant for what he knew.

'General Rompiro wasn't so gloomy inside as he appeared on the surface. He was polite enough; and he exuded a number of sounds that made a fair stagger at arranging themselves into language. It was English he aimed at, and when his system of syntax reached your mind it wasn't past you to understand it. If you took a college professor's magazine essay and a Chinese laundryman's explanation of a lost shirt and jumbled 'em together, you'd have about what the General handed you out for conversation. He told me all about his bleeding country, and what they were trying to do for it before the doctor came. But he mostly talked of Denver C. Galloway.

' "Ah, señor," says he, "that is the most fine of mans. Never I have seen one man so magnifico, so gr-r-rand, so conformable to make done things so swiftly by other mans. He shall make other mans do the acts and himself to order and regulate, until we arrive at seeing accomplishments of a suddenly. Oh, yes, señor. In my countree there is not such mans of so beegness, so good talk, so compliments, so strongness of sense and such. Ah, that Señor Galloway!"

' "Yes," says I, "old Denver is the boy you want. He's managed every kind of business here except filibustering, and he might as well complete the list."

'Before the three days was up I decided to join Denver in his campaign. Denver got three months' vacation from his hotel owners. For a week we lived in a room with the General, and got all the pointers about his country that we could interpret from the noises he made. When we got ready to start, Denver had a pocket full of memorandums, and letters from the General to his friends, and a list of names and addresses of loyal politicians who would help along the boom of the exiled popular idol. Besides these liabilities we carried assets to the amount of $20,000 in assorted United States currency. General Rompiro looked like a burnt effigy, but he was Br'er Fox himself when it came to the real science of politics.

' "Here is moneys," says the General, "of a small amount. There is more with me – moocho more. Plentee moneys shall you be supplied, Señor Galloway. More I shall send you at all times that you need. I shall desire to pay feefty – hundred thousand pesos, if necessario, to be elect. How no? Sacramento! If that I am president and do not make one meelion dolla in the one year you shall keek me on that side! – *válgame Dios!'*

'Denver got a Cuban cigar-maker to fix up a little cipher code with English and Spanish words, and gave the General a copy, so we could cable him bulletins about the election, or for more money, and then we were ready to start. General Rompiro escorted us to the steamer. On the pier he hugged Denver around the waist and sobbed. "Noble mans," says he, "General Rompiro propels into you his confidence and trust. Go, in the hands of the saints to do the work for your friend. *Viva la libertad!"*

' "Sure," says Denver. "And viva la liberality an' la soaperino and hoch der land of the lotus and the vote us. Don't worry, General. We'll have you elected as sure as bananas grow upside down."

' "Make pictures on me," pleads the General – "make pictures on me for money as it is needful."

' "Does he want to be tattooed, would you think?" asks Denver, wrinkling up his eyes.

' "Stupid!" says I. "He wants you to draw on him for election expenses. It'll be worse than tattooing. More like an autopsy."

'Me and Denver steamed down to Panama, and then hiked across the Isthmus, and then by steamer again down to the town of Espiritu on the coast of the General's country.

'That was a town to send J. Howard Payne to the growler. I'll tell you how you could make one like it. Take a lot of Filipino huts and a couple of hundred brick-kilns and arrange 'em in squares in a cemetery. Cart down all the conservatory plants in the Astor and Vanderbilt greenhouses, and stick 'em about wherever there's room. Turn all the Bellevue patients and the barbers' convention and the Tuskegee school loose in the streets, and run the thermometer up to 120 in the shade. Set a fringe of the Rocky Mountains around the rear, let in rain, and set the whole business on Rockaway Beach in the middle of January – and you'd have a good imitation of Espiritu.

'It took me and Denver about a week to get acclimated. Denver sent out the letters the General had given him, and notified the rest of the gang that there was something doing at the captain's office. We set up headquarters in an old 'dobe house on a side street where the grass was waist high. The election was only four weeks off; but there wasn't any excitement. The home candidate for president was named Roadrickeys. This town of Espiritu wasn't the capital any more than Cleveland, Ohio, is the capital of the United States, but it was the political centre where they cooked up revolutions, and made up the slates.

'At the end of the week Denver says the machine is started running.

' "Sully,' says he, "we've got a walkover. Just because General Rompiro ain't Don Juan-on-the-spot the other crowd ain't at work. They're as full of apathy as a territorial delegate during the chaplain's prayer. Now we want to introduce a little hot stuff in the way of campaigning, and we'll surprise 'em at the polls."

' "How are you going to go about it?" I asks.

' "Why, the usual way," says Denver, surprised. "We'll get the orators on our side out every night to make speeches in .the native lingo, and have torch-light parades under the shade of the palms, and free drinks, and buy up all the brass bands, of course, and – well, I'll turn the baby-kissing over to you, Sully – I've seen a lot of 'em."

' "What else?" says I.

' "Why, you know," says Denver. "We get the heelers out with the crackly two-spots, and coal-tickets, and orders for groceries, and have a couple of picnics out under the banyan trees, and dances in the Firemen's Hall – and the usual things. But first of all, Sully, I'm going to have the biggest clam-bake down on the beach that was ever seen south of the tropic of Capricorn. I figured that out from the start. We'll stuff the whole town and the jungle folk for miles around with clams. That's the first thing on the programme. Suppose you go out now, and make the arrangements for that. I want to look over the estimates the General made of the vote in the coast districts."

'I had learned some Spanish in Mexico, so I goes out, as Denver says, and in fifteen minutes I come back to headquarters.

' "If there ever was a clam in this country nobody ever saw it," I says.

' "Great sky-rockets!" says Denver, with his mouth and eyes open. "No clams? How in the – who ever saw a country without clams? What kind of a – how's an election to be pulled off without a clam-bake, I'd like to know? Are you sure there's no clams, Sully?"

' "Not even a can," says I.

' "Then for God's sake go out and try to find out what the people here do eat. We've got to fill 'em up with grub of some kind."

'I went out again. Sully was manager. In half an hour I gets back.

' "They eat," says I, "tortillas, cassava, carne de chivo, arroz con pello, aquacates, zapates, yucca, and huevos fritos."

' "A man that would eat them things" says Denver getting a little mad, "ought to have his vote challenged."

'In a few more days the campaign managers from the other towns came sliding into Espiritu. Our headquarters was a busy place. We had an inter-preter, and ice-water, and drinks, and cigars, and Denver flashed the General's roll so often that it got so small you couldn't have bought a Republican vote in Ohio with it.

'And then Denver cabled to General Rompiro for ten thousand dollars more and got it.

'There were a number of Americans in Espiritu, but they were all in business or grafts of some kind, and wouldn't take any hand in politics, which was sensible enough. But they showed me and Denver a fine time, and fixed us up so we could get decent things to eat and drink. There was one American, named Hicks, used to come and loaf at the headquarters. Hicks had had fourteen years of Espiritu. He was six feet four and weighed in at 135. Cocoa was his line; and coast fever and the climate had taken all the life out of him. They said he hadn't smiled in eight years. His face was three feet long, and it never moved except when he opened it to take quinine. He used to sit in our headquarters and kill fleas and talk sarcastic.

' "I don't take much interest in politics," says Hicks, one day, "but I'd like you to tell me what you're trying to do down here, Galloway?"

' "We're boosting General Rompiro, of course," says Denver. "We're going to put him in the presidential chair. I'm his manager."

' "Well," says Hicks, "if I was you I'd be a little slower about it. You've got a long time ahead of you, you know."

' "Not any longer than I need," says Denver.

'Denver went ahead and worked things smooth. He dealt out money on the quiet to his lieutenants, and they were always coming after it. There was free drinks for everybody in town, and bands playing every night, and fireworks, and there was a lot of heelers going around buying up votes day and night for the new style of politics in Espiritu, and everybody liked it.

'The day set for the election was 4 November. On the night before Denver and me were smoking our pipes in headquarters, and in comes Hicks and unjoints himself, and sits in a chair, mournful. Denver is cheerful and confident. "Rompiro will win in a romp," says he. "We'll carry the country by 10,000. It's all over but the vivas. To-morrow will tell the tale."

' "What's going to happen to-morrow?" asks Hicks.

' "Why, the presidential election, of course," says Denver.

' "Say," says Hicks, looking kind of funny. "Didn't anybody tell you fellows that the election was held a week before you came? Congress changed the date to July 27. Roadrickeys was elected by 17,000. I thought you was booming old Rompiro for next term, two years from now. Wondered if you was going to keep such a hot lick that long."

'I dropped my pipe on the floor. Denver bit the stem off of his. Neither of us said anything.

'And then I heard a sound like somebody ripping a clapboard off of a barn-roof. 'Twas Hicks laughing for the first time in eight years.'

Sully Magoon paused while the waiter poured us black coffee.

'You friend was, indeed, something of a manager,' I said.

'Wait a minute,' said Sully, 'I haven't given you any idea of what he could do yet. That's all to come.

'When we got back to New York there was General Rompiro waiting for us on the pier. He was dancing like a cinnamon bear, all impatient for the news, for Denver had just cabled him when we would arrive and nothing more.

' "Am I elect?" he shouts. "Am I elect, friend of mine? Is it that mine country have demand General Rompiro for the president? The last dollar of mine have I sent you that last time. It is necessario that I am elect. I have no more money. Am I elect, Señor Galloway?"

'Denver turns to me.

' "Leave me with old Rompey, Sully," he says. "I've got to break it to him gently. 'Twould be indecent for other eyes to witness the operation. This is the time, Sully," says he, "when old Denver has got to make good as a jollier and a silver-tongued sorcerer, or else give up all the medals he's earned."

'A couple of days later I went around to the hotel. There was Denver in his old place looking like a hero of two historical novels, and telling 'em what a fine time he's had down on his orange plantation in Florida.

' "Did you fix things up with the General?" I ask him.

' "Did I?" says Denver. "Come and see."

'He takes me by the arm and walks me to the dining-room door. There was a little chocolate-brown fat man in a dress suit, with his face shining with joy as he swelled himself and skipped about the floor. Danged if Denver hadn't made General Rompiro head waiter of the Hotel Brunswick!'

'Is Mr. Galloway still in the managing business?' I asked, as Mr. Magoon ceased.

Sully shook his head.

'Denver married an auburn-haired widow that owns a big hotel in Harlem. He just helps around the place.'

WHISTLING DICK'S CHRISTMAS STOCKING

IT WAS WITH MUCH CAUTION that Whistling Dick slid back the door of the box-car, for Article 5716, City Ordinances, authorized (perhaps unconstitutionally) arrest on suspicion, and he was familiar of old with this ordinance. So, before climbing out, he surveyed the field with all the care of a good general.

He saw no change since his last visit to this big, almsgiving, long-suffering city of the South, the cold weather paradise of the tramps. The levee where his freight-car stood was pimpled with dark bulks of merchandise. The breeze reeked with the well-remembered, sickening smell of the old tarpaulins that covered bales and barrels. The dun river slipped along among the shipping with an oily gurgle. Far down toward Chalmette he could see the great bend in the stream, outlined by the row of electric lights. Across the river Algiers lay, a long, irregular blot, made darker by the dawn which lightened the sky beyond. An industrious tug or two, coming for some early sailing ship, gave a few appalling toots, that seemed to be the signal for breaking day. The Italian luggers were creeping nearer their landing, laden with early vegetables and shellfish. A vague roar, subterranean in quality, from dray wheels and street cars, began to make itself heard and felt; and the ferryboats, the Mary Anns of water craft, stirred sullenly to their menial morning tasks.

Whistling Dick's red hair popped suddenly back into the car. A sight too imposing and magnificent for his gaze had been added to the scene. A vast, incomparable policeman rounded a pile of rice sacks and stood within twenty yards of the car. The daily miracle of the dawn, now being performed above Algiers, received the flattering attention of this specimen of municipal official splendor. He gazed with unbiased dignity at the faintly glowing colors until, at last, he turned to them his broad back, as if convinced that legal interference was not needed, and the sunrise might proceed unchecked. So he turned his face to the rice bags, and, drawing a flat flask from an inside pocket, he placed it to his lips and regarded the firmament.

Whistling Dick, professional tramp, possessed a half-friendly acquaintance with this officer. They had met several times before on the levee at night, for the officer, himself a lover of music, had been attracted by the exquisite whistling of the shiftless vagabond. Still, he did not care, under the present circumstances, to renew the acquaintance. There is a difference between meeting a policeman upon a lonely wharf and whistling a few operatic airs with him, and being caught by him crawling out of a freight-car. So Dick waited, as even a New Orleans policeman must move on some time – perhaps it is a retributive law of nature – and before long 'Big Fritz' majestically disappeared between the trains of cars.

Whistling Dick waited as long as his judgment advised, and then slid swiftly to the ground. Assuming as far as possible the air of an honest laborer who seeks his daily toil, he moved across the network of railway lines, with the intention of making his way by quiet Girod Street to a certain bench in Lafayette Square, where, according to appointment, he hoped to rejoin a pal known as 'Slick,' this adventurous pilgrim having preceded him by one day in a cattle-car into which a loose slat had enticed him.

As Whistling Dick picked his way where night still lingered among the big, reeking, musty warehouses, he gave way to the habit that had won for him his title. Subdued, yet clear, with each note as true and liquid as a bobolink's, his whistle tinkled about the dim, cold mountains of brick like drops of rain falling into a hidden pool. He followed an air, but it swam mistily into a swirling current of improvisation. You could cull out the trill of mountain brooks, the staccato of green rushes shivering above the chilly lagoons, the pipe of sleepy birds.

Rounding a corner, the whistler collided with a mountain of blue and brass.

'So,' observed the mountain calmly, 'you are already pack. Und dere vill not pe frost before two veeks yet! Und you haf forgotten how to vistle. Dere was a valse note in dot last bar.'

'Watcher know about it?' said Whistling Dick, with tentative familiarity; 'you wit yer little Gherman-band nixcumrous chunes. Watcher know about music? Pick yer ears, and listen agin. Here's de way I whistled it – see?'

He puckered his lips, but the big policeman held up his hand.

'Shtop,' he said, 'und learn der right way. Und learn also dot a rolling shtone can't vistle for a cent.'

Big Fritz's heavy moustache rounded into a circle, and from its depths came a sound deep and mellow as that from a flute. He repeated a few bars of the air the tramp had been whistling. The rendition was cold, but correct, and he emphasized the note he had taken exception to.

'Dot p is p natural, and not p vlat. Py der vay, you petter pe glad I meet you. Von hour later, und I vould haf to put you in a gage to vistle mit der chail pirds. Der orders are to bull all der pums after sunrise.'

'To which?'

'To bull der pums – eferybody mitout fisible means. Dirty days is der price, or fifteen tollars.'

'Is dat straight, or a game you givin' me?'

'It's der pest tip you efer had. I gif it to you pecause I pelief you are not so bad as der rest. Und pecause you can vistle "Der Freischütz" bezzer dan I myself gan. Don't run against any more bolicemans aroundt der corners, but go away from town a few tays. Goot-pye.'

So Madame Orleans had at last grown weary of the strange and ruffled brood that came yearly to nestle beneath her charitable pinions.

After the big policeman had departed, Whistling Dick stood for an irresolute minute, feeling all the outraged indignation of a delinquent tenant who is ordered to vacate his premises. He had pictured to himself a day of dreamful ease when he should have joined his pal; a day of lounging on the wharf, munching the bananas and cocoanuts scattered in unloading the fruit steamers; and then a feast along the free-lunch counters from which the easy-going owners were too good-natured or too generous to drive him away, and afterward a pipe in one of the little flowery parks and a snooze in some shady corner of the wharf. But here was a stern order to exile, and one that he knew must be obeyed. So, with a wary eye open for the gleam of brass buttons, he began to retreat toward a rural refuge. A few days in the country need not necessarily prove disastrous. Beyond the possibility of a slight nip of frost, there was no formidable evil to be looked for.

However, it was with a depressed spirit that Whistling Dick passed the old French market on his chosen route down the river. For safety's sake he still presented to the world his portrayal of the part of the worthy artisan on his way to labor. A stall-keeper in the market, undeceived, hailed him by the generic name of his ilk, and 'Jack' halted, taken by surprise. The vendor, melted by this proof of his own acuteness, bestowed a foot of Frankfurter and half a loaf, and thus the problem of breakfast was solved.

When the streets, from topographical reasons, began to shun the river bank the exile mounted to the top of the levee, and on its well-trodden path pursued his way. The suburban eye regarded him with cold suspicion, individuals reflected the stern spirit of the city's heartless edict. He missed the seclusion of the crowded town and the safety he could always find in the multitude.

At Chalmette, six miles upon his desultory way, there suddenly menaced him a vast and bewildering industry. A new port was being established; the dock was being built, compresses were going up; picks and shovels and barrows struck at him like serpents from every side. An arrogant foreman bore down upon him, estimating his muscles with the eye of a recruiting-sergeant. Brown men and black men all about him were toiling away. He fled in terror.

By noon he had reached the country of the plantations, the great, sad, silent levels bordering the mighty river. He overlooked fields of sugarcane so vast that their farthest limits melted into the sky. The sugar-making season was well advanced, and the cutters were at work; the wagons creaked drearily after them; the Negro teamsters inspired the mules to greater speed with mellow and sonorous imprecations. Dark-green groves, blurred by the blue of distance, showed where the plantation-houses stood. The tall chimneys of the sugar-mills caught the eye miles distant, like lighthouses at sea.

At a certain point Whistling Dick's unerring nose caught the scent of frying fish. Like a pointer to a quail, he made his way down the levee side straight to the camp of a credulous and ancient fisherman, whom he charmed with song and story, so that he dined like an admiral, and then like a philosopher annihilated the worst three hours of the day by a nap under the trees.

When he awoke and again continued his hegira, a frosty sparkle in the air succeeded the drowsy warmth of the day, and as this portent of a chilly night translated itself to the brain of Sir Peregrine, he lengthened his stride and bethought him of shelter. He traveled a road that faithfully followed the convolutions of the levee, running along its base, but whither he knew not. Bushes and rank grass crowded it to the wheel ruts, and out of this ambuscade pests of the lowlands swarmed after him, humming a keen vicious soprano. And as the night grew nearer, although colder, the whine of the mosquitoes became a greedy, petulant snarl that shut out all other sounds. To his right, against the heavens, he saw a green light moving, and, accompanying it, the masts and funnels of a big incoming steamer, moving as upon a screen at a magic-lantern show. And there were mysterious marshes at his left, out of which came queer gurgling cries and a choked croaking. The whistling vagrant struck up a merry warble to offset these melancholy influences, and it is likely that never before, since Pan himself jiggered it on his reeds, had such sounds been heard in those depressing solitudes.

A distant clatter in the rear quickly developed into the swift beat of horses' hoofs, and Whistling Dick stepped aside into the dew-wet grass to clear the track. Turning his head, he saw approaching a fine team of stylish grays drawing a double surrey. A stout man with a white moustache occupied the front seat, giving all his attention to the rigid lines in his hands. Behind him sat a placid, middle-aged lady and a brilliant-looking girl hardly arrived at young ladyhood. The lap-robe had slipped partly from the knees of the gentleman driving, and Whistling Dick saw two stout canvas bags between his feet – bags such as, while loafing in cities,.he had seen warily transferred between express wagons and bank doors. The remaining space in the vehicle was filled with parcels of various sizes and shapes.

As the surrey swept even with the sidetracked tramp, the bright-eyed girl, seized by some merry, madcap impulse, leaned out toward him with a sweet, dazzling smile, and cried, 'Mer-ry Christ-mas!' in a shrill, plaintive treble.

Such a thing had not often happened to Whistling Dick, and he felt handicapped in devising the correct response. But lacking time for reflection, he let his instinct decide, and snatching off his battered derby, he rapidly extended it at arm's length, and drew it back with a continuous motion, and shouted a loud, but ceremonious, 'Ah, there!' after the flying surrey.

The sudden movement of the girl had caused one of the parcels to become unwrapped, and something limp and black fell from it into the road. The tramp picked it up and found it to be a new black silk stocking, long and fine and slender. It crunched crisply, and yet with a luxurious softness, between his fingers.

'Ther bloomin' little skeezicks!' said Whistling Dick, with a broad grin bisecting his freckled face. 'Wot d'yer think of dat, now! Mer-ry Chris-mus! Sounded like a cuckoo clock, dat's what she did. Dem guys is swells, too, bet yer life, an' der old 'un stacks dem sacks of dough down under his trotters like dey was common as dried apples. Been shoppin' fer Chrismus, and de kid's lost one of her new socks w'ot she was goin' to hold up Santy wid. De bloomin' little skeezicks! Wit' her "Mer-ry Chris-mus!" W'ot 'd yer t'ink! Same as to say, "Hello, Jack, how goes it!" and as swell as Fift' Av'noo, and as easy as a blowout in Cincinnat".'

Whistling Dick folded the stocking carefully and stuffed it into his pocket.

It was nearly two hours later when he came upon signs of habitation. The buildings of an extensive plantation were brought into view by a turn in the road. He easily selected the planter's residence in a large square building with two wings, with numerous good-sized, well-lighted windows, and broad verandas running around its full extent. It was set upon a smooth lawn, which was faintly lit by the far-reaching rays of the lamps within. A noble grove surrounded it, and old-fashioned shrubbery grew thickly about the walls and fences. The quarters of the hands and the mill buildings were situated at a distance in the rear.

The road was now enclosed on each side by a fence, and presently, as Whistling Dick drew nearer the houses, he suddenly stopped and sniffed the air.

'If dere ain't a hobo stew cookin' somewhere in dis immediate precinct,' he said to himself, 'me nose has quit tellin' de trut'.'

Without hesitation he climbed the fence to windward. He found himself in an apparently disused lot, where piles of old bricks were stacked, and rejected, decaying lumber. In a corner he saw the faint glow of a fire that had become little more than a bed of living coals, and he thought he could see some dim human forms sitting or lying about it. He drew nearer, and by the light of a little blaze that suddenly flared up he saw plainly the fat figure of a ragged man in an old brown sweater and cap.

'Dat man,' said Whistling Dick to himself softly, 'is a dead ringer for Boston Harry. I'll try him wit' de high sign.'

He whistled one or two bars of a rag-time melody, and the air was immediately taken up, and then quickly ended with a peculiar run. The first whistler walked confidently up to the fire. The fat man looked up and spake in a loud, asthmatic wheeze:

'Gents, the unexpected but welcome addition to our circle is Mr. Whistling Dick, an old friend of mine for whom I fully vouches. The waiter will lay another cover at once. Mr. W. D. will join us at supper, during which function he will enlighten us in regard to the circumstances that give us the pleasure of his company.'

'Chewin' de stuffin' out'n de dictionary, as usual, Boston,' said Whistling Dick; 'but t'anks all de same for de invitashun. I guess I finds meeself here about de same way as yous guys. A cop gimme de tip dis mornin'. Yous workin' on dis farm?'

'A guest,' said Boston sternly, 'shouldn't never insult his entertainers until he's filled up wid grub. 'Tain't good business sense. Workin'!' – but I will restrain myself. We five – me, Deaf Pete, Blinky, Goggles, and Indiana Tom – got put on to this scheme of Noo Orleans to work visiting gentlemen upon her dirty streets, and we hit the road last evening just as the tender hues of twilight had flopped down upon the daisies and things. Blinky, pass the empty oyster-can at your left to the empty gentleman at your right.'

For the next ten minutes the gang of roadsters paid their undivided attention to the supper. In an old five-gallon kerosene can they had cooked a stew of potatoes, meat, and onions which they partook of from smaller cans they had found scattered about the vacant lot.

Whistling Dick had known Boston Harry of old, and knew him to be one of the shrewdest and most successful of his brotherhood. He looked like a prosperous stock-drover or a solid merchant from some country village. He was stout and hale, with a ruddy, always smoothly shaven face. His clothes were strong and neat, and he gave special attention to his decent-appearing shoes. During the past ten years he had acquired a reputation for working a larger number of successfully managed confidence games than any of his acquaintances, and he had not a day's work to be counted against him. It was rumored among his associates that he had saved a considerable amount of money. The four other men were fair specimens of the slinking, ill-clad, noisome genus who carried their labels of 'suspicious' in plain view.

After the bottom of the large can had been scraped, and pipes lit at the coals, two of the men called Boston aside and spake with him lowly and mysteriously. He nodded decisively, and then said aloud to Whistling Dick:

'Listen, sonny, to some plain talky-talk. We five are on a lay. I've guaranteed you to be square, and you're to come in on the profits equal with the boys, and you've got to help. Two hundred hands on this plantation are expecting to be paid a week's wages to-morrow morning. To-morrow's Christmas, and they want to lay off. Says the boss: "Work from five to nine in the morning to get a train load of sugar off, and I'll pay every man cash down for the week and a day extra." They say: "Hooray for the boss! It goes." He drives to Noo Orleans to-day, and fetches back the cold dollars. Two thousand and seventy-four fifty is the amount. I got the figures from a man who talks too much, who got 'em from the book-keeper. The boss of this plantation thinks he's going to pay this wealth to the hands. He's got it down wrong; he's going to pay it to us. It's going to stay in the leisure class, where it belongs. Now, half of this haul goes to me, and the other half the rest of you may divide. Why the difference? I represent the brains. It's my scheme. Here's the way we're going to get it. There's some company at supper in the house, but they'll leave about nine. They've just happened in for an hour or so. If they don't go pretty soon, we'll work the scheme anyhow. We want all night to get away good with the dollars. They're heavy. About nine o'clock Deaf Pete and Blinky'll go down the road about a quarter beyond the house, and set fire to a big cane-field there that the cutters haven't touched yet. The wind's just right to have it roaring in two minutes. The alarm'll be given, and every man Jack about the place will be down there in ten minutes, fighting fire. That'll leave the money sacks and the women alone in the house for us to handle. You've heard cane burn? Well, there's mighty few women who can screech loud enough to be heard above its crackling. The thing's dead safe. The only danger is in being caught before we can get far enough away with the money. Now, if you—'

'Boston,' interrupted Whistling Dick, rising to his feet, 't'anks for de grub yous fellers has given me, but I'll be movin' on now.'

'What do you mean?' asked Boston, also rising.

'W'y, you can count me outer dis deal. You oughter know that. I'm on de bum all right enough, but dat other t'ing don't go wit' me. Burglary is no good. I'll say good night and many t'anks fer—'

Whistling Dick had moved away a few steps as he spoke, but he stopped very suddenly. Boston had him covered with a short revolver of roomy calibre.

'Take your seat,' said the tramp leader. 'I'd feel mighty proud of myself if I let you go and spoil the game. You'll stick right in this camp until we finish the job. The end of that brick pile is your limit. You go two inches beyond that, and I'll have to shoot. Better take it easy, now.'

'It's my way of doin',' said Whistling Dick. 'Easy goes. You can depresss de muzzle of dat twelve-incher, and run 'em back on de trucks. I remains, as de newspapers say, "in yer midst." '

'All right,' said Boston, lowering his piece, as the other returned and took his seat again on a projecting plank in a pile of timber. 'Don't try to leave; that's all. I wouldn't miss this chance even if I had to shoot an old acquaintance to make it go. I don't want to hurt anybody specially, but this thousand dollars I'm going to get will fix me for fair. I'm going to drop the road, and start a saloon in a little town I know about. I'm tired of being kicked around.'

Boston Harry took from his pocket a cheap silver watch and held it near the fire.

'It's a quarter to nine,' he said. 'Pete, you and Blinky start. Go down the road past the house and fire the cane in a dozen places. Then strike for the levee, and come back on it, instead of the road, so you won't meet anybody. By the time you get back the men will all be striking out for the fire, and we'll break for the house and collar the dollars. Everybody cough up what matches he's got.'

The two surly tramps made a collection of all the matches in the party, Whistling Dick contributing his quota with propitiatory alacrity, and then they departed in the dim starlight in the direction of the road.

Of the three remaining vagrants, two, Goggles and Indiana Tom, reclined lazily upon convenient lumber and regarded Whistling Dick with undisguised disfavor. Boston, observing that the dissenting recruit was disposed to remain peaceably, relaxed a little of his vigilance. Whistling Dick arose presently and strolled leisurely up and down keeping carefully within the territory assigned him.

'Dis planter chap,' he said, pausing before Boston Harry, 'w'ot makes yer t'ink he's got de tin in de house wit' 'im?'

'I'm advised of the facts in the case,' said Boston. 'He drove to Noo Orleans and got it, I say, to-day. Want to change your mind now and come in?'

'Naw, I was just askin'. Wot kind o' team did de boss drive?'

'Pair of grays.'

'Double surrey?'

'Women folks along?'

'Wife and kid. Say, what morning paper are you trying to pump news for?'

'I was just conversin' to pass de time away. I guess dat team passed me in de road dis evenin'. Dat's all.'

As Whistling Dick put his hands into his pockets and continued his curtailed beat up and down by the fire, he felt the silk stocking he had picked up in the road.

'Ther bloomin' little skeezicks,' he muttered, with a grin.

As he walked up and down he could see, through a sort of natural opening or lane among the trees, the planter's residence some seventy-five yards distant. The side of the house toward him exhibited spacious, well-lighted windows through which a soft radiance streamed, illuminating the broad veranda and some extent of the lawn beneath.

'What's that you said?' asked Boston, sharply.

'Oh, nuttin' 't all,' said Whistling Dick, lounging carelessly and kicking meditatively at a little stone on the ground.

'Just as easy,' continued the warbling vagrant softly to himself, 'an' sociable an' swell, an' sassy, wit' her "Mer-ry Chris-mus." Wot d'yer t'ink, now!'

Dinner, two hours late, was being served in the Bellemeade plantation dining-room.

The dining-room and all its appurtenances spoke of an old régime that was here continued rather than suggested to the memory. The plate was rich to the extent that its age and quaintness alone saved it from being showy; there were interesting names signed in the corners of the pictures on the walls; the viands were of the kind that bring a shine into the eyes of gourmets. The service was swift, silent, lavish, as in the days when the waiters were assets like the plate. The names by which the planter's family and their visitors addressed one another were historic in the annals of two nations. Their manners and conversation had that most difficult kind of ease – the kind that still preserves punctilio. The planter himself seemed to be the dynamo that generated the larger portion of the gaiety and wit. The younger ones at the board found it more than difficult to turn back on him his guns of raillery and banter. It is true, the young men attempted to storm his works repeatedly, incited by the hope of gaining the approbation of their fair companions; but even when they sped a well-aimed shaft, the planter forced them to feel defeat by the tremendous discomfiting thunder of the laughter with which he accompanied his retorts. At the head of the table, serene, matronly, benevolent, reigned the mistress of the house, placing here and there the right smile, the right word, the encouraging glance.

The talk of the party was too desultory, too evanescent to follow, but at last they came to the subject of the tramp nuisance, one that had of late vexed the plantations for many miles around. The planter seized the occasion to direct his good-natured fire of raillery at the mistress, accusing her of encouraging the plague. 'They swarm up and down the river every winter,' he said. 'They overrun New Orleans, and we catch the surplus, which is generally the worst part. And, a day or two ago, Madame New Orleans, suddenly discovering that she can't go shopping without brushing her skirts against great rows of the vagabonds sunning themselves on the banquettes, says to the police, "Catch 'em all," and the police catch a dozen or two, and the remaining three or four thousand overflow up and down the levees, and madame there' – pointing tragically with the carving-knife at her – 'feeds them. They won't work, they defy my overseers, and they make friends with my dogs; and you, madame, feed them before my eyes, and intimidate me when I would interfere. Tell us, please, how many to-day did you thus incite to future laziness and depredation?'

'Six, I think,' said madame, with a reflective smile; 'but you know two of them offered to work, for you heard them yourself.'

The planter's disconcerting laugh rang out again.

'Yes, at their own trades. And one was an artificial-flower maker, and the other a glass-blower. Oh, they were looking for work! Not a hand would they consent to lift to labor of any other kind.'

'And another one,' continued the soft-hearted mistress, 'used quite good language. It was really extraordinary for one of his class. And he carried a watch. And had lived in Boston. I don't believe they are all bad. They have always seemed to me to rather lack development. I always look upon them as children with whom wisdom has remained at a stand-still while whiskers have continued to grow. We passed one this evening as we were driving home who had a face as good as it was incompetent. He was whistling the intermezzo from "Cavalleria" and blowing the spirit of Mascagni himself into it.'

A bright-eyed young girl who sat at the left of the mistress leaned over and said in a confidential undertone:

'I wonder, Mamma, if that tramp we passed on the road found my stocking, and do you think he will hang it up to-night? Now I can hang up but one. Do you know why I wanted a new pair of silk stockings when I have plenty? Well, old Aunt Judy says, if you hang up two that have never been worn, Santa Claus will fill one with good things, and Monsieur Pambe will place in the other payment for all the words you have spoken – good or bad – on the day before Christmas. That's why I've been unusually nice and polite to everyone to-day. Monsieur Pambe, you know, is a witch gentleman! he—'

The words of the young girl were interrupted by a startling thing.

Like the wraith of some burned-out shooting star, a black streak came crashing through the window-pane and upon the table, where it shivered into fragments a dozen pieces of crystal and china ware, and then glanced between the heads of the guests to the wall, imprinting therein a deep, round indentation, at which, to-day, the visitor to Bellemeade marvels as he gazes upon it and listens to this tale as it is told.

The women screamed in many keys, and the men sprang to their feet, and would have laid their hands upon their swords had not the verities of chronology forbidden.

The planter was the first to act; he sprang to the intruding missile and held it up to view.

'By Jupiter!' he cried. 'A meteoric shower of hosiery! Has communication at last been established with Mars?'

'I should say – ahem! – Venus,' ventured a young gentleman visitor, looking hopefully for approbation toward the unresponsive young-lady visitors.

The planter held at arm's length the unceremonious visitor – a long dangling black stocking. 'It's loaded,' he announced.

As he spoke he reversed the stocking, holding it by the toe, and down from it dropped a roundish stone, wrapped about by a piece of yellowish paper. 'Now for the first interstellar message of the century!' he cried; and nodding to the company, who had crowded about him, he adjusted his glasses with provoking deliberation, and examined it closely. When he finished he had changed from the jolly host to the practical, decisive man of business. He immediately struck a bell, and said to the silent-footed mulatoo man who responded: 'Go and tell Mr. Wesley to get Reeves and Maurice and about ten stout hands they can rely upon, and come to the hall door at once. Tell him to have the men arm themselves, and bring plenty of ropes and plough lines. Tell him to hurry.' And then he read aloud from the paper these words:

To the Gent of de Hous:
    Dere is five tuff hoboes xcept meself in the vaken lot near de road war de old brick piles is. Dey got me stuck up wid a gun see and I taken dis means of comunikaten. 2 of der lads is gone down to set fire to de cain field below de house and when yous fellers goes to turn de hoes on it de hole gang is goin to rob de house of de money too gotto pay off wit say git a move on ye say de kid dropt dis sock in der rode tel her mery crismus de same as she told me. Ketch de bums down de rode first and den sen a relefe core to get me out of soke youres truly,
                                                    Whistlen Dick

There was some quiet, but rapid, maneuvering at Bellemeade during the ensuring half hour, which ended in five disgusted and sullen tramps being captured and locked securely in an out-house pending the coming of the morning and retribution. For another result, the visiting young gentlemen had secured the unqualified worship of the visiting young ladies by their distinguished and heroic conduct. For still another, behold Whistling Dick, the hero, seated at the planter's table, feasting upon viands his experience had never before included, and waited upon by admiring femininity in shapes of such beauty and 'swellness' that even his ever-full mouth could scarcely prevent him from whistling. He was made to disclose in detail his adventure with the evil gang of Boston Harry, and how he cunningly wrote the note and wrapped it around the stone and placed it in the toe of the stocking, and, watching his chance, sent it silently, with a wonderful centrifugal momentum, like a comet, at one of the big lighted windows of the dining-room.

The planter vowed that the wanderer should wander no more; that his was a goodness and an honesty that should be rewarded, and that a debt of gratitude had been made that must be paid; for had he not saved them from a doubtless imminent loss, and maybe a greater calamity? He assured Whistling Dick that he might consider himself a charge upon the honor of Bellemeade; that a position suited to his powers would be found for him at once, and hinted that the way would be heartily smoothed for him to rise to as high places of emolument and trust as the plantation afforded.

But now, they said, he must be weary, and the immediate thing to consider was rest and sleep. So the mistress spoke to a servant, and Whistling Dick was conducted to a room in the wing of the house occupied by the servants. To this room, in a few minutes, was brought a portable tin bathtub filled with water, which was placed on a piece of oiled cloth upon the floor. There the vagrant was left to pass the night.

By the light of the candle he examined the room. A bed, with the covers neatly turned back, revealed snowy pillows and sheets. A worn, but clean, red carpet covered the floor. There was a dresser with a beveled mirror, a washstand with a flowered bowl and pitcher; the two or three chairs were softly upholstered. A little table held books, papers, and a day-old cluster of roses in a jar. There were towels on a rack and soap in a white dish.

Whistling Dick set his candle on a chair and placed his hat carefully under the table. After satisfying what we must suppose to have been his curiosity by a sober scrutiny, he removed his coat, folded it, and laid it upon the floor, near the wall, as far as possible from the unused bathtub. Taking his coat for a pillow, he stretched himself luxuriously upon the carpet.

When, on Christmas morning, the first streaks of dawn broke above the marshes, Whistling Dick awoke and reached instinctively for his hat. Then he remembered that the skirts of Fortune had swept him into their folds on the night previous, and he went to the window and raised it, to let the fresh breath of the morning cool his brow and fix the yet dream-like memory of his good luck within his brain.

As he stood there, certain dread and ominous sounds pierced the fearful hollow of his ear.

The force of plantation workers, eager to complete the shortened task allotted to them, were all astir. The mighty din of the ogre Labor shook the earth, and the poor tattered and forever disguised Prince in search of his fortune held tight to the window-sill even in the enchanted castle, and trembled.

Already from the bosom of the mill came the thunder of rolling barrels of sugar, and (prison-like sounds) there was a great rattling of chains as the mules were harried with stimulant imprecations to their places by the wagon-tongues. A little vicious 'dummy' engine, with a train of flat cars in tow, stewed and fumed on the plantation tap of the narrow-gauge railroad, and a toiling, hurrying, hallooing stream of workers were dimly seen in the half darkness loading the train with the weekly output of sugar. Here was a poem, an epic – nay, a tragedy – with work, the curse of the world, for its theme.

The December air was frosty, but the sweat broke out upon Whistling Dick's face. He thrust his head out of the window and looked down. Fifteen feet below him, against the wall of the house, he could make out that a border of flowers grew, and by that token he overhung a bed of soft earth.

Softly as a burglar goes, he clambered out upon the sill, lowered himself until he hung by his hands alone, and then dropped safely. No one seemed to be about upon this side of the house. He dodged low and skimmed swiftly across the yard to the low fence. It was an easy matter to vault this, for a terror urged him such as lifts the gazelle over the thorn bush when the lion pursues. A crash through the dew-drenched weeds on the roadside, a clutching, slippery rush up the grassy side of the levee to the footpath at the summit, and – he was free!

The east was blushing and brightening. The wind, himself a vagrant rover, saluted his brother upon the cheek. Some wild geese, high above, gave cry. A rabbit skipped along the path before him, free to turn to the right or to the left as his mood should send him. The river slid past, and certainly no one could tell the ultimate abiding place of its waters.

A small, ruffled, brown-breasted bird, sitting upon a dogwood sapling, began a soft, throaty, tender little piping in praise of the dew which entices foolish worms from their holes; but suddenly he stopped, and sat with his head turned sidewise, listening.

From the path along the levee there burst forth a jubilant, stirring, buoyant, thrilling whistle, loud and keen and clear as the cleanest notes of the piccolo. The soaring sound rippled and trilled and arpeggioed as the songs of wild birds do not; but had a wild free grace that, in a way, reminded the small brown bird of something familiar, but exactly what he could not tell. There was in it the bird call, or reveille, that all birds know; but a great waste of lavish, unmeaning things that art had added and arranged, besides, and that were quite puzzling and strange; and the little brown bird sat with his head on one side until the sound died away in the distance.

The little bird did not know that the part of that strange warbling that he understood was just what kept the warbler without his breakfast; but he knew very well that the part he did not understand did not concern him, so he gave a little flutter of his wings and swooped down like a brown bullet upon a big fat worm that was wriggling along the levee path.

THE HALBERDIER OF THE LITTLE RHEINSCHLOSS

GO SOMETIMES INTO THE *BIERHALLE* and restaurant called Old Munich. Not long ago it was a resort of interesting Bohemians, but now only artists and musicians and literary folk frequent it. But the Pilsener is yet good, and I take some diversion from the conversation of Waiter No. 18.

For many years the customers of Old Munich have accepted the place as a faithful copy from the ancient German town. The big hall with its smoky rafters, rows of imported steins, portrait of Goethe, and verses painted on the walls – translated into German from the original of tʰe Cincinnati poets – seems atmospherically correct when viewed through the bottom of a glass.

But not long ago the proprietors added the room above, called it the Little Rheinschloss, and built in a stairway. Up there was an imitation stone parapet, ivy-covered, and the walls were painted to represent depth and distance, with the Rhine winding at the base of the vineyarded slopes, and the castle of Ehrenbreitstein looming directly opposite the entrance. Of course there were tables and chairs; and you could have beer and food brought you, as you naturally would on top of a castle on the Rhine.

I went into Old Munich one afternoon when there were few customers, and sat at my usual table near the stairway. I was shocked and almost displeased to perceive that the glass cigar-case by the orchestra stand had been smashed to smithereens. I did not like things to happen in Old Munich. Nothing had ever happened there before.

Waiter No. 18 came and breathed on my neck. I was his by right of discovery. Eighteen's brain was built like a corral. It was full of ideas which, when he opened the gate, came huddling out like a flock of sheep that might get together afterward or might not. I did not shine as a shepherd. As a type Eighteen fitted nowhere. I did not find out if he had a nationality, family, creed, grievance, hobby, soul, preference, home or vote. He only came always to my table and, as long as his leisure would permit, let words flutter from him like swallows leaving a barn at daylight.

'How did the cigar-case come to be broken, Eighteen?' I asked, with a certain feeling of personal grievance.

'I can tell you about that, sir,' said he, resting his foot on the chair next to mine. 'Did you ever have anybody hand you a double handful of good luck while both your hands was full of bad luck, and stop to notice how your fingers behaved?'

'No riddles, Eighteen,' said I. 'Leave out palmistry and manicuring.'

'You remember,' said Eighteen, 'the guy in the hammered brass Prince Albert and the oroide gold pants and the amalgamated copper hat, that carried the combination meat-axe, ice-pick, and liberty-pole, and used to stand on the first landing as you go up to the Little Rindslosh?'

'Why, yes,' said I. 'The halberdier. I never noticed him particularly. I remember I thought he was only a suit of armor. He had a perfect poise.'

'He had more than that,' said Eighteen. 'He was me friend. He was an advertisement. The boss hired him to stand on the stairs for a kind of scenery to show there was something doing in the has-been line upstairs. What did you call him – a what kind of beer?'

'A halberdier,' said I. 'That was an ancient man-at-arms of many hundred years ago.'

'Some mistake,' said Eighteen. 'This one wasn't that old. He wasn't over twenty-three or four.

'It was the boss's idea, rigging a man up in an ante-bellum suit of tin-ware and standing him on the landing of the slosh. He bought the goods at a Fourth Avenue antique store, and hung a sign out: "Able-bodied hal – halberdier wanted. Costume furnished."

'The same morning a young man with wrecked good clothes and a hungry look comes in, bringing the sign with him. I was filling the mustard-pots at my station.

' "I'm it," says he, "whatever it is. But I never halberdiered in a restaurant. Put me on. Is it a mesquerade?"

' "I hear talk in the kitchen of a fishball," says I.

' "Bully for you, Eighteen," says he. "You and I'll get on. Show me the boss's desk."

'Well, the boss tries the Harveyized pajamas on him, and they fitted him like the scales on a baked redsnapper, and he gets the job. You've seen what it is – he stood straight up in the corner of the first landing with his halberd to his shoulder, looking right ahead and guarding the Portugals of the castle. The boss is nutty about having the true Old-World flavor to his joint. "Halberdiers goes with Rindsloshes," says he, "just as rats goes with ratskellers and white cotton stockings with Tyrolean villages." The boss is a kind of a antiologist, and is all posted upon data and such information.

'From 8 p.m. to two in the morning was the Halberdier's hours. He got two meals with us help and a dollar a night. I eat with him at the table. He liked me. He never told his name. He was traveling impromptu, like kings, I guess. The first time at supper I says to him, "Have some more of the spuds, Mr. Frelinghuysen," "Oh, don't be so formal, and offish, Eighteen," says he. "Call me Hal – that's short for halberdier." "Oh, don't think I wanted to pry for names," says I. "I know all about the dizzy fall from wealth and greatness. We've got a count washing dishes in the kitchen; and the third bartender used to be a Pullman conductor. And they *work*, Sir Percival," says I, sarcastic.

' "Eighteen," says he, "as a friendly devil in a cabbage-scented hell, would you mind cutting up this piece of steak for me? I don't say that it's got more muscle than I have, but—" And then he shows me the insides of his hands. They were blistered and cut and corned and swelled up till they looked like a couple of flank steaks criss-crossed with a knife – the kind the butchers hide and take home, knowing what is the best.

' "Shoveling coal," says he, "and piling bricks and loading drays. But they gave out, and I had to resign. I was born for a halberdier, and I've been educated for twenty-four years to fill the position. Now, quit knocking my profession, and pass along a lot more of that ham. I'm holding the closing exercises," says he, "of a forty-eight-hour fast."

'The second night he was on the job he walks down from his corner to the cigar-case and calls for cigarettes. The customers at the tables all snicker out loud to show their acquaintance with history. The boss is on.

' "An' – let's see – oh, yes – "An anarchism," says the boss. "Cigarettes was not made at the time when halberdiers was invented."

' "The ones you sell was," says Sir Percival. "Caporal wins from chronology by the length of a cork tip." So he gets 'em and lights one, and puts the box in his brass helmet and goes back to patrolling the Rindslosh.

'He made a big hit, 'specially with the ladies. Some of 'em would poke him with their fingers to see if he was real or only a kind of a stuffed figure they burn in elegy. And when he'd move they'd squeak, in his halberdashery. He slept at $2 a week in a hall-room on Third Avenue. He invited me up there one night. He had a little book on the washstand that he read instead of shopping in the saloons after hours. "I'm onto that," says I, "from reading about it in novels. All the heroes on the bum carry the little book. It's either Tantalus or Liver or Horace, and it's printed in Latin, and you're a college man. And I wouldn't be surprised," says I, "if you wasn't educated, too." But it was only the batting averages of the League for the last ten years.

'One night, about half-past eleven, there comes in a party of these highrollers that are always hunting up new places to eat in and poke fun at. There was a swell girl in a 40 H.-P. auto tan coat and veil, and a fat old man with white side-whiskers, and a young chap that couldn't keep his feet off the tail of the girl's coat, and an oldish lady that looked upon life as immoral and unnecessary. "How perfectly delightful," they says, "to sup in a slosh." Up the stairs they go; and in half a minute back down comes the girl, her skirts swishing like the waves on the beach. She stops on the landing and looks our halberdier in the eye.

' "You!" she says, with a smile that reminded me of lemon sherbet. I was waiting upstairs in the slosh, then, and I was right down here by the door, putting some vinegar and cayenne into an empty bottle of tabasco, and I heard all they said.

' "I," says Sir Percival, without moving. "I'm only local color. Are my haurberk, helmet, and halberd on straight?"

' "Is there an explanation to this?" says she. "Is it a practical joke such as men play in those Griddle-cake and Lamb Clubs? I'm afraid I don't see the point. I heard, vaguely, that you were away. For three months I – we have not seen you or heard from you."

' "I'm halberdiering for my living," says the statue. "I'm working," says he. "I don't suppose you know what work means."

' "Have you – have you lost your money?" she asks.

'Sir Percival studies a minute.

' "I am poorer," says he, "than the poorest sandwich man on the streets – if I don't earn my living."

' "You call this work?" says she. "I thought a man worked with his hands or his head instead of becoming a mountebank."

' "The calling of a halberdier," says he, "is an ancient and honorable one. Sometimes," says he, "the man-at-arms at the door has saved the castle while the plumed knights were cake-walking in the banquet-halls above."

' "I see you're not ashamed," says she, "of your peculiar tastes. I wonder, though, that the manhood I used to think I saw in you didn't prompt you to draw water or hew wood instead of publicly flaunting your ignominy in this disgraceful masquerade."

'Sir Percival kind of rattles his armor and says: "Helen, will you suspend sentence in this matter for just a little while? You don't understand," says he. 'I've got to hold this job down a bit longer."

' "You like being a harlequin – or halberdier, as you call it?" says she.

' "I wouldn't get thrown out of the job just now," says he, with a grin, "to be appointed Minister to the Court of St. James's."

'And then the 40 H.-P. girl's eyes sparkled as hard as diamonds.

' "Very well," says she. "You shall have full run of your serving-man's tastes this night." And she swims over to the boss's desk and gives him a smile that knocks the specks off his nose.

' "I think your Rindslosh," says she, "is as beautiful as a dream. It is a little slice of the Old World set down in New York. We shall have a nice supper up there; but if you will grant us one favor the illusion will be perfect – give us your halberdier to wait on our table."

'That hit the boss's antiology hobby just right. "Sure," says he, "dot vill

be fine. Und der orchestra shall blay 'Die Wacht am Rhein' all der time."
And he goes over and tells the halberdier to go upstairs and hustle the grub
at the swells' table.

' "I'm on the job," says Sir Percival, taking off his helmet and hanging it
on his halberd and leaning 'em in the corner. The girl goes up and takes her
seat and I see her jaw squared tight under her smile. "We're going to be
waited on by a real halberdier," says she, "one who is proud of his profession.
Isn't it sweet?"

' "Ripping," says the swell young man. "Much prefer a waiter," says the
fat old gent. "I hope he doesn't come from a cheap museum," says the old
lady; "he might have microbes in his costume."

'Before he goes to the table, Sir Percival takes me by the arm. "Eighteen,"
says he, "I've got to pull off this job without a blunder. You coach me straight
or I'll take that halberd and make hash out of you." And then he goes up to
the table with his coat of mail on and a napkin over his arm and waits for
the order.

' "Why, it's Deering!" says the young swell. "Hello, old man. What the —"

' "Beg pardon, sir," interrupts the halberdier, "I'm waiting on the table."

'The old man looks at him grim, like a Boston bull. "So, Deering," he says,
"you're at work yet."

' "Yes, sir," says Sir Percival, quiet and gentlemanly as I could have been
myself, "for almost three months, now." "You haven't been discharged
during the time?" asks the old man. "Not once, sir," says he, "though I've
had to change my work several times."

' "Waiter," orders the girl, short and sharp, "another napkin." He brings
her one, respectful.

'I never saw more devil, if I may say it, stirred up in a lady. There was two
bright red spots on her cheeks, and her eyes looked exactly like a wildcat's
I'd seen in the zoo. Her foot kept slapping the floor all the time.

' "Waiter," she orders, "bring me filtered water without ice. Bring me a
foot-stool. Take away this empty salt-cellar." She kept him on the jump. She
was sure giving the halberdier his.

'There wasn't but a few customers up in the slosh at that time, so I hung
out near the door so I could help Sir Percival serve.

'He got along fine with the olives and celery and the bluepoints. That was
easy. And then the consommé came up the dumb-waiter all in one big silver
tureen. Instead of serving it from the side-table he picks it up between his
hands and starts to the dining-table with it. When nearly there he drops the
tureen smash on the floor, and the soup soaks all the lower part of that girl's
swell silk dress.

' "Stupid – incompetent," says she, giving him a look. "Standing in a
corner with a halberd seems to be your mission in life."

' "Pardon me, lady," says he. "It was just a little bit hotter than blazes. I
couldn't help it."

'The old man pulls out a memorandum book and hunts in it. "The 25th
of April, Deering," says he. "I know it," says Sir Percival. "And ten minutes
to twelve o'clock," says the old man. "By Jupiter! you haven't won yet." And
he pounds the table with his fist and yells to me: "Waiter, call the manager
at once – tell him to hurry here as fast as he can." I go after the boss, and
old Brockmann hikes up to the slosh on the jump.

' "I want this man discharged at once," roars the old guy. "Look what he's done. Ruined my daughter's dress. It cost at least $600. Discharge this awkward lout at once or I'll sue you for the price of it."

' "Dis is bad pizness," says the boss. "Six hundred dollars is much. I reckon I vill half to—"

' "Wait a minute, Herr Brockmann," says Sir Percival, easy and smiling. But he was worked up under his tin suitings; I could see that. And then he made the finest, neatest little speech I ever listened to. I can't give you the words, of course. He give the millionaires a lovely roast in a sarcastic way, describing their automobiles and opera-boxes and diamonds; and then he got around to the working-classes and the kind of grub they eat and the long hours they work – and all that sort of stuff – bunkum, of course. "The restless rich," says he, "never content with their luxuries, always prowling among the haunts of the poor and humble, amusing themselves with the imperfections and misfortunes of their fellow men and women. And even here, Herr Brockmann," he says, "in this beautiful Rindslosh, a grand and enlightening reproduction of Old-World history and architecture, they come to disturb its symmetry and picturesqueness by demanding in their arrogance that the halberdier of the castle wait upon their table! I have faithfully and conscientiously," says he, "performed my duties as a halberdier. I know nothing of a waiter's duties. It was the insolent whim of these transient, pampered aristocrats that I should be detailed to serve them food. Must I be blamed – must I be deprived of the means of a livelihood," he goes on, "on account of an accident that was the result of their own presumption and haughtiness? But what hurt me more than all," says Sir Percival, "is the desecration that has been done to this splendid Rindslosh – the confiscation of its halberdier to serve menially at the banquet board."

'Even I could see that this stuff was piffle; but it caught the boss.

' "Mein Gott," says he, "you vas right. Ein halberdier have not got der right to dish up soup. Him I vill not discharge. Have anoder waiter if you like, and let mein halberdier go back and stand mit his halberd. But, gentlemen," he says, pointing to the old man, "you go ahead and sue mit der dress. Sue me for $600 or $6,000. I stand der suit." And the boss puffs off downstairs. Old Brockmann was an all-right Dutchman.

'Just then the clock strikes twelve, and the old guy laughs loud. "You win, Deering," says he. "Let me explain to all," he goes on. "Some time ago Mr. Deering asked me for something that I did not want to give him." (I looks at the girl, and she turns as red as a pickled beet.) "I told him," says the old guy, "if he would earn his own living for three months without once being discharged for incompetence, I would give him what he wanted. It seems that the time was up at twelve o'clock to-night. I came near fetching you, though, Deering, on that soup question," says the old boy, standing up and grabbing Sir Percival's hand.

'The halberdier lets out a yell and jumps three feet high.

' "Look out for those hands," says he, and he holds 'em up. You never saw such hands except on a laborer in a limestone quarry.

' "Heavens, boy!" says old side-whiskers, "what have you been doing to 'em?"

' "Oh," says Sir Percival, "little chores like hauling coal and excavating rock till they went back on me. And when I couldn't hold a pick or a whip I took up halberdiering to give 'em a rest. Tureens full of hot soup don't seem to be a particular soothing treatment."

'I would have bet on that girl. That high-tempered kind always go as far the other way, according to my experience. She whizzes round the table like a cyclone and catches both his hands in hers. "Poor hands – dear hands," she sings out, and sheds tears on 'em and holds 'em close to her bosom. Well, sir, with all that Rindslosh scenery it was just like a play. And the halberdier sits down at the table at the girl's side, and I served the rest of the supper. And that was about all, except that when they left he shed his hardware store and went with 'em.'

I dislike to be side-tracked from an original proposition.

'But you haven't told me, Eighteen,' said I, 'how the cigar-case came to be broken.'

'Oh, that was last night,' said Eighteen. 'Sir Percival and the girl drove up in a cream-colored motor-car, and had dinner in the Rindslosh. "The same table, Billy," I heard her say as they went up. I waited on 'em. We've got a new halberdier now, a bow-legged guy with a face like a sheep. As they came downstairs Sir Percival passes him a ten-case note. The new halberdier drops his halberd, and it falls on the cigar-case. That's how that happened.'

TWO RENEGADES

IN THE GATE CITY OF THE SOUTH the Confederate Veterans were reuniting; and I stood to see them march, beneath the tangled flags of the great conflict, to the hall of their oratory and commemoration.

While the irregular and halting line was passing I made onslaught upon it and dragged forth from the ranks my friend Barnard O'Keefe, who had no right to be there. For he was a Northerner born and bred; and what should he be doing hallooing for the Stars and Bars among those gray and moribund veterans? And why should he be trudging, with his shining, martial, humorous, broad face, among those warriors of a previous and alien generation?

I say I dragged him forth, and held him till the last hickory leg and waving goatee had stumbled past. And then I hustled him out of the crowd into a cool interior; for the Gate City was stirred that day, and the hand-organs wisely eliminated 'Marching Through Georgia' from their repertories.

'Now, what devilry are you up to?' I asked of O'Keefe when there were a table and things in glasses between us.

O'Keefe wiped his heated face and instigated a commotion among the floating ice in his glass before he chose to answer.

'I am assisting at the wake,' said he, 'of the only nation on earth that ever did me a good turn. As one gentleman to another, I am ratifying and celebrating the foreign policy of the late Jefferson Davis, as fine a statesman as ever settled the financial question of a country. Equal ratio – that was his platform – a barrel of money for a barrel of flour – a pair of $20 bills for a pair of boots – a hatful of currency for a new hat – say, ain't that simple compared with W.J.B.'s little old oxidized plank?'

'What talk is this?' I asked. 'Your financial digression is merely a subterfuge. Why were you marching in the ranks of the Confederate Veterans?'

'Because, my lad,' answered O'Keefe, 'the Confederate Government in its might and power interposed to protect and defend Barnard O'Keefe against immediate and dangerous assassination at the hands of a bloodthirsty foreign country after the United States of America had overruled his appeal for protection, and had instructed Private Secretary Cortelyou to reduce his estimate of the Republican majority for 1905 by one vote.'

'Come, Barney,' said I, 'the Confederate States of America has been out of existence nearly forty years. You do not look older yourself. When was it that the deceased government exerted its foreign policy in your behalf?'

'Four months ago,' said O'Keefe, promptly. 'The infamous foreign power I alluded to is still staggering from the official blow dealt it by Mr. Davis's contraband aggregation of states. That's why you see me cake-walking with the ex-rebs to the illegitimate tune about 'simmonseels and cotton. I vote for the Great Father in Washington, but I am not going back on Mars' Jeff. You say the Confederacy has been dead forty years? Well, if it hadn't been for it, I'd have been breathing today with soul so dead I couldn't have whispered a single cussword about my native land. The O'Keefes are not overburdened with ingratitude.'

I must have looked bewildered. 'The war was over,' I said vacantly, 'in—' O'Keefe laughed loudly, scattering my thoughts.

'Ask old Doc Millikin if the war is over!' he shouted, hugely diverted. 'Oh, no! Doc hasn't surrendered yet. And the Confederate States! Well, I just told you they bucked officially and solidly and nationally against a foreign government four months ago and kept me from being shot. Old Jeff's country stepped in and brought me off under its wing while Roosevelt was having a gunboat painted and waiting for the National Campaign Committee to look up whether I had ever scratched the ticket.'

'Isn't there a story in this, Barney?' I asked.

'No,' said O'Keefe; 'but I'll give you the facts. You know I went down to Panama when this irritation about a canal began. I thought I'd get in on the ground floor. I did, and had to sleep on it, and drink water with little zoos in it; so, of course, I got the Chagres fever. That was in a little town called San Juan on the coast.

'After I got the fever hard enough to kill a Port-au-Prince nigger, I had a relapse in the shape of Doc Millikin.

'There was a doctor to attend a sick man! If Doc Millikin had your case, he made the terrors of death seem like an invitation to a donkey-party. He had the bedside manners of a Piute medicine-man and the soothing presence of a dray loaded with iron bridge-girders. When he laid his hand on your fevered brow you felt like Cap John Smith just before Pocahontas went his bail.

'Well, this old medical outrage floated down to my shack when I sent for him. He was built like a shad, and his eyebrows was black, and his white whiskers trickled down from his chin like milk coming out of a sprinkling-pot. He had a nigger boy along carrying an old tomato-can full of calomel, and a saw.

'Doc felt my pulse, and then he began to mess up some calomel with an agricultural implement that belonged to the trowel class.

' "I don't want any death-mask made yet, Doc," I says, "nor my liver put in a plaster-of-paris cast. I'm sick; and it's medicine I need, not frescoing."

' "You're a blame Yankee, ain't you?" asked Doc, going on mixing up his Portland cement.

' "I'm from the North," says I, "but I'm a plain man, and don't care for mural decorations. When you get the Isthmus all asphalted over with that boll-weevil prescription, would you mind giving me a dose of painkiller, or a little strychnine on toast to case up this feeling of unhealthiness that I have got?"

' "They was all sassy, just like you," says old Doc, "but we lowered their temperature considerable. Yes, sir, I reckon we sent a good many of ye over to old *mortuis nisi bonum*. Look at Antietam and Bull Run and Seven Pines and around Nashville! There never was a battle where we didn't lick ye unless you was ten to our one. I knew you were a blame Yankee the minute I laid eyes on you."

' "Don't reopen the chasm, Doc," I begs him. "Any Yankeeness I may have is geographical; and, as far as I am concerned a Southerner is as good as a Filipino any day. I'm feeling too bad to argue. Let's have secession without misrepresentation, if you say so; but what I need is more laudanum and less Lundy's Lane. If you're mixing that compound gefloxide of gefloxicum for me, please fill my ears with it before you get around to the battle of Gettysburg, for there is a subject full of talk."

'By this time Doc Millikin had thrown up a line of fortifications on square pieces of paper; and he says to me: "Yank, take one of these powders every two hours. They won't kill you. I'll be around again about sundown to see if you're alive."

'Old Doc's powders knocked the chagres. I stayed in San Juan, and got to knowing him better. He was from Mississippi, and the red-hottest Southerner that ever smelled mint. He made Stonewall Jackson and R. E. Lee look like Abolitionists. He had a family somewhere down near Yazoo City; but he stayed away from the States on account of an uncontrollable liking he had for the absence of a Yankee government. Him and me got as thick personally as the Emperor of Russia and the dove of peace, but sectionally we didn't amalgamate.

' 'Twas a beautiful system of medical practice introduced by old Doc into that isthmus of land. He'd take that bracket-saw and the mild chloride and his hypodermic, and treat anything from yellow fever to a personal friend.

'Besides his other liabilities Doc could play a flute for a minute or two. He was guilty of two tunes – "Dixie" and another one that was mighty close to the "Suwanee River" – you might say one of its tributaries. He used to come down and sit with me while I was getting well, and aggrieve his flute and say unreconstructed things about the North. You'd have thought the smoke from the first gun at Fort Sumter was still floating around in the air.

'You know that was about the time they staged them property revolutions down there, that wound up in the fifth act with the thrilling canal scene where Uncle Sam has nine curtain-calls holding Miss Panama by the hand, while the bloodhounds keep Senator Morgan treed up in a cocoanut-palm.

'That's the way it wound up; but at first it seemed as if Colombia was going to make Panama look like one of the $3.98 kind, with dents made in it in the factory, like they wear at North Beach fish fries. For mine, I played the straw-hat crowd to win; and they gave me a colonel's commission over a brigade of twenty-seven men in the left wing and second joint of the insurgent army.

'The Colombian troops were awfully rude to us. One day when I had my brigade in a sandy spot, with its shoes off doing a battalion drill by squads, the Government army rushed from behind a bush at us, acting as noisy and disagreeable as they could.

'My troops enfiladed, left-faced, and left the spot. After enticing the enemy for three miles or so we struck a brier-patch and had to sit down. When we were ordered to throw up our toes and surrender we obeyed. Five of my best staff-officers fell, suffering extremely with stone-bruised heels.

'Then and there those Colombians took your friend Barney, sir, stripped him of the insignia of his rank, consisting of a pair of brass knuckles and a canteen of rum, and dragged him before a military court. The presiding general went through the usual legal formalities that sometimes cause a case to hang on the calendar of a South American military court as long as ten minutes. He asked me my age, and then sentenced me to be shot.

'They woke up the court interpreter, an American named Jenks, who was in the rum business and vice versa, and told him to translate the verdict.

'Jenks stretched himself and took a morphine tablet.

' "You've got to back up against th' 'dobe, old man,' says he to me. 'Three weeks, I believe, you get. Haven't got a chew of fine-cut on you, have you?"

' "Translate that again, with foot notes and a glossary," says I. "I don't know whether I'm discharged, condemned, or handed over to the Gerry Society."

' "Oh," says Jenks, "don't you understand? You're to be stood up against a 'dobe wall and shot in two or three weeks – three, I think, they said."

' "Would you mind asking 'em which?" says I. "A week don't amount to much after you are dead, but it seems a real nice long spell while you are alive."

' "It's two weeks," says the interpreter, after inquiring in Spanish of the court. "Shall I ask 'em again?"

' "Let be," says I. "Let's have a stationary verdict. If I keep on appealing this way they'll have me shot about ten days before I was captured. No, I haven't got any fine-cut."

'They sends me over to the *calaboza* with a detachment of colored postal-telegraph boys carrying Enfield rifles, and I am locked up in a kind of brick bakery. The temperature in there was just about the kind mentioned in the cooking recipes that call for a quick oven.

'Then I gives a silver dollar to one of the guards to send for the United States consul. He comes around in pajamas with a pair of glasses on his nose and a dozen or two inside of him.

' "I'm to be shot in two weeks," says I. "And although I've made a memorandum of it, I don't seem to get it off my mind. You want to call up Uncle Sam on the cable as quick as you can and get him all worked up about it. Have 'em send the *Kentucky* and the *Kearsage* and the *Oregon* down right away. That'll be about enough battleships; but it wouldn't hurt to have a couple of cruisers and a torpedo-boat destroyer, too. And – say, if Dewey isn't busy, better have him come along on the fastest one of the fleet."

' "Now, see here, O'Keefe," says the consul, getting the best of a hiccup, "what do you want to bother the State Department about this matter for?"

' "Didn't you hear me?" says I; "I'm to be shot in two weeks. Did you think I said I was going to a lawn-party? And it wouldn't hurt if Roosevelt could get the Japs to send down the *Yellowyamstiskookum* or the *Ogotosingsing* or some other first-class cruiser to help. It would make me feel safer."

' "Now, what you want," says the consul, "is not to get excited. I'll send you over some chewing tobacco and some banana fritters when I go back. The United States can't interfere in this. You know you were caught insurging against the government, and you're subject to the laws of this country. Tell you the truth, I've had an intimation from the State Department – unofficially, of course – that whenever a soldier of fortune demands a fleet of gunboats in a case of revolutionary *katzenjammer*, I should cut the cable, give him all the tobacco he wants, and after he's shot take his clothes, if they fit me, for part payment of my salary."

' "Consul," says I to him, "this is a serious question. You are representing Uncle Sam. This ain't any little international tomfoolery, like a universal peace congress or the christening of the *Shamrock IV*. I'm an American citizen and I demand protection. I demand the Mosquito fleet, and Schley, and the Atlantic squadron, and Bob Evans, and General E. Byrd Grubb, and two or three protocols. What are you going to do about it?"

' "Nothing doing," says the consul.

' "Be off with you, then," says I, out of patience with him, "and send me Doc Millikin. Ask Doc to come and see me."

'Doc comes and looks through the bars at me, surrounded by dirty soldiers, with even my shoes and canteen confiscated, and he looks mightily pleased.

' "Hello, Yank," says he, "getting a little taste of Johnson's Island, now, ain't ye?"

' "Doc," says I, "I've just had an interview with the U.S. consul. I gather from his remarks that I might just as well have been caught selling suspenders in Kishineff under the name of Rosenstein as to be in my present condition. It seems that the only maritime aid I am to receive from the United States is some navy-plug to chew. Doc," says I, "can't you suspend hostilities on the slavery question long enough to do something for me?"

' "It ain't been my habit," Doc Millikin answers, "to do any painless dentistry when I find a Yank cutting an eyetooth. So the Stars and Stripes ain't landing any marines to shell the huts of the Colombian cannibals, hey? Oh, say, can you see by the dawn's early light the star-spangled banner has fluked in the fight? What's the matter with the War Department, hey? It's a great thing to be a citizen of a gold-standard nation, ain't it?"

' "Rub it in, Doc, all you want," says I. "I guess we're weak on foreign policy."

' "For a Yank," says Doc, putting on his specs and talking more mild, "you ain't so bad. If you had come from below the line I reckon I would have liked you right smart. Now since your country has gone back on you, you have to come to the old doctor whose cotton you burned and whose mules you stole and whose niggers you freed to help you. Ain't that so, Yank?"

' "It is," says I heartily, "and let's have a diagnosis of the case right away, for in two weeks' time all you can do is to hold an autopsy and I don't want to be amputated if I can help it."

' "Now," says Doc, business-like, "it's easy enough for you to get out of this scrape. Money'll do it. You've got to pay a long string of 'em from General Pomposo down to this anthropoid ape guarding your door. About $10,000 will do the trick. Have you got the money?"

' "Me?" says I. "I've got one Chili dollar, two *real* pieces, and a *medio*."

' "Then if you've any last words, utter 'em," says that old reb. "The roster of your financial budget sounds quite much to me like the noise of a requiem."

' "Change the treatment," says I. "I admit that I'm short. Call a consultation or use radium or smuggle me in some saws or something."

' "Yank," says Doc Millikin, 'I've a good notion to help you. There's only one government in the world that can get you out of this difficulty; and that's the Confederate States of America, the grandest nation that ever existed."

'Just as you said to me I says to Doc; "Why, the Confederacy ain't a nation. It's been absolved forty years ago."

' "That's a campaign lie," says Doc. "She's running along as solid as the Roman Empire. She's the only hope you've got. Now, you being a Yank, have got to go through with some preliminary obsequies before you can get official aid. You've got to take the oath of allegiance to the Confederate Government. Then I'll guarantee she does all she can for you. What do you say, Yank? – it's your last chance."

' "If you're fooling with me, Doc," I answered, "you're no better than the United States. But as you say it's the last chance, hurry up and swear me. I always did like corn whisky and 'possum anyhow. I believe I'm half Southerner by nature. I'm willing to try the Ku Klux in place of the khaki. Get brisk."

'Doc Millikin thinks awhile, and then he offers me this oath of allegiance to take without any kind of a chaser:

' "I, Barnard O'Keefe, Yank, being of sound body but a Republican mind, hereby swear to transfer my fealty, respect, and allegiance to the Confederate States of America, and the Government thereof, in consideration of said government, through its official acts and powers, obtaining my freedom and release from confinement and sentence of death brought about by the exuberance of my Irish proclivities and my general pizenness as a Yank."

'I repeated these words after Doc, but they seemed to me a kind of hocus-pocus; and I don't believe any life-insurance company in the country would have issued me a policy on the strength of 'em.

'Doc went away saying he would communicate with his government immediately.

'Say – you can imagine how I felt – me to be shot in two weeks and my only hope for help being a government that's been dead so long that it isn't even remembered except on Decoration Day and when Joe Wheeler signs the voucher for his pay-check. But it was all there was in sight; and somehow I thought Doc Millikin had something up his old alpaca sleeve that wasn't all foolishness.

'Around to the jail comes old Doc again in about a week. I was fleabitten, a mite sarcastic, and fundamentally hungry.

' "Any Confederate ironclads in the offing?" I asks. "Do you notice any sounds resembling the approach of Jeb Stewart's cavalry overland or Stonewall Jackson sneaking up in the rear? If you do, I wish you'd say so."

' "It's too soon yet for help to come," says Doc.

' "The sooner the better," says I. "I don't care if it gets in fully fifteen minutes before I am shot; and if you happen to lay eyes on Beauregard or Albert Sidney Johnson or any of the relief corps, wig-wag 'em to hike along."

' "There's been no answer received yet," says Doc.

' "Don't forget," says I, "that there's only four days more. I don't know how you propose to work this thing, Doc," I says to him; "but it seems to me I'd sleep better if you had got a government that was alive and on the map – like Afghanistan or Great Britain, or old man Kruger's kingdom, to take this matter up. I don't mean any disrespect to your Confederate States, but

I can't help feeling that my chances of being pulled out of this scrape was decidedly weakened when General Lee surrendered."

' "It's your only chance," said Doc; "don't quarrel with it. What did your own country do for you?"

'It was only two days before the morning I was to be shot when Doc Millikin came around again.

' "All right, Yank," says he. "Help's come. The Confederate States of America is going to apply for your release. The representative of the government arrived on a fruit-steamer last night."

' "Bully!" says I – "bully for you, Doc! I suppose it's marines with a Gatling. I'm going to love your country all I can for this."

' "Negotiations," says old Doc, "will be opened between the two governments at once. You will know later on to-day if they are successful."

'About four in in the afternoon a soldier in red trousers brings a paper round to the jail, and they unlocks the door and I walks out. The guard at the door bows and I bows, and I steps into the grass and wades around to Doc Millikin's shack.

'Doc was sitting in his hammock playing "Dixie," soft and low and out of tune, on his flute. I interrupted him at "Look away! look away!" and shook his hand for five minutes.

' "I never thought," says Doc, taking a chew fretfully, "that I'd ever try to save any blame Yank's life. But, Mr. O'Keefe, I don't see but what you are entitled to be considered part human, anyhow. I never thought Yanks had any of the rudiments of decorum and laudability about them. I reckon I might have been too aggregative in my tabulation. But it ain't me you want to thank – it's the Confederate States of America."

' "And I'm much obliged to 'em," says I. "It's a poor man that wouldn't be patriotic with a country that's saved his life. I'll drink to the Stars and Bars whenever there's a flag-staff and a glass convenient. But where," says I, "are the rescuing troops? If there was a gun fired or a shell burst, I didn't hear it."

'Doc Millikin raises up and points out the window with his flute at the banana-steamer loading with fruit.

' "Yank," says he, "there's a steamer that's going to sail in the morning. If I was you, I'd sail on it. The Confederate Government's done all it can for you. There wasn't a gun fired. The negotiations was carried on secretly between the two nations by the purser of that steamer. I got him to do it because I didn't want to appear in it. Twelve thousand dollars was paid to the officials in bribes to let you go."

' "Man!" says I, sitting down hard – "twelve thousand – how will I ever – who could have – where did the money come from?"

' "Yazoo City," says Doc Millikin; "I've got a little bit saved up there. Two barrels full. It looks good to these Colombians. 'Twas Confederate money, every dollar of it. Now do you see why you'd better leave before they try to pass some of it on an expert?"

' "I do," says I.

' "Now, let's hear you give the password," says Doc Millikin.

' "Hurrah for Jeff Davis!" says I.

' "Correct," says Doc. "And let me tell you something. The next tune I learn on my flute is going to be 'Yankee Doodle.' I reckon there's some Yanks that are not so pizen. Or, if you was me, would you try 'The Red, White, and Blue'?" '

THE LONESOME ROAD

BROWN AS A COFFEE-BERRY, rugged, pistoled, spurred, wary, indefeasible, I saw my old friend, Deputy-Marshal Buck Caperton, stumble, with jingling rowels, into a chair in the marshal's outer office.

And because the courthouse was almost deserted at that hour, and because Buck would sometimes relate to me things that were out of print, I followed him in and tricked him into talk through knowledge of a weakness he had. For, cigarettes rolled with sweet corn husk were as honey to Buck's palate; and though he could finger the trigger of a forty-five with skill and suddenness, he never could learn to roll a cigarette.

It was through no fault of mine (for I rolled the cigarettes tight and smooth), but the upshot of some whim of his own, that instead of to an Odyssey of the chaparral, I listened to – a dissertation upon matrimony! This from Buck Caperton! But I maintain that the cigarettes were impeccable, and crave absolution for myself.

'We just brought in Jim and Bud Granberry,' said Buck. 'Train robbing, you know. Held up the Aransas Pass last month. We caught 'em in the Twenty-Mile pear flat, south of the Nueces.'

'Have much trouble coralling them?' I asked, for here was the meat that my hunger for epics craved.

'Some,' said Buck; and then, during a little pause, his thoughts stampeded off the trail. 'It's kind of queer about women,' he went on, 'and the place they're supposed to occupy in botany. If I was asked to classify them I'd say they was a human loco weed. Ever see a bronc that had been chewing loco? Ride him up to a puddle of water two feet wide, and he'll give a snort and fall back on you. It looks as big as the Mississippi River to him. Next trip he'd walk into a cañon a thousand feet deep thinking it was a prairie-dog hole. Same way with a married man.

'I was thinking of Perry Rountree, that used to be my sidekicker before he committed matrimony. In them days me and Perry hated disturbances of any kind. We roamed around considerable, stirring up the echoes and making 'em attend to business. Why, when me and Perry wanted to have some fun in a town it was a picnic for the census takers. They just counted the marshal's posse that it took to subdue us, and there was your population. But then there came along this Mariana Good-night girl and looked at Perry sideways, and he was all bridle-wise and saddle-broke before you could skin a yearling.

'I wasn't even asked to the wedding. I reckon the bride had my pedigree and the front elevation of my habits all mapped out, and she decided that Perry would trot better in double harness without any unconverted mustang like Buck Caperton whickering around on the matrimonial range. So it was six months before I saw Perry again.

'One day I was passing on the edge of town, and I see something like a man in a little yard by a little house with a sprinkling-pot squirting water on a rosebush. Seemed to me, I'd seen something like it before, and I stopped at the gate, trying to figure out its brands. 'Twas not Perry Rountree, but 'twas the kind of a curdled jellyfish matrimony had made out of him.

'Homicide was what that Mariana had perpetrated. He was looking well enough, but he had on a white collar and shoes, and you could tell in a minute that he'd speak polite and pay taxes and stick his little finger out while drinking, just like a sheep man or a citizen. Great skyrockets! but I hated to see Perry all corrupted and Willie-ized like that.

'He came out to the gate and shook hands; and I says, with scorn, and speaking like a paroquet with the pip: "Beg pardon – Mr. Rountree, I believe. Seems to me I sagatiated in your associations once, if I am not mistaken."

' "Oh, go to the devil, Buck," says Perry, polite, as I was afraid he'd be.

' "Well, then," says I, "you poor, contaminated adjunct of a sprinkling-pot and degraded household pet, what did you go and do it for? Look at you, all decent and unriotous, and only fit to sit on juries and mend the wood-house door. You was a man once. I have hostility for all such acts. Why don't you go in the house and count the tidies or set the clock, and not stand out here in the atmosphere? A jackrabbit might come along and bite you."

' "Now, Buck," says Perry, speaking mild, and some sorrowful, "you don't understand. A married man has got to be different. He feels different from a tough old cloudburst like you. It's sinful to waste time pulling up towns just to look at their roots, and playing faro and looking upon red liquor, and such restless policies as them."

' "There was a time," I says, and I expect I sighed when I mentioned it, "when a certain domesticated little Mary's lamb I could name was some instructed himself in the line of pernicious sprightliness. I never expected, Perry, to see you reduced down from a full-grown pestilence to such a frivolous fraction of a man. Why," says I, "you've got a necktie on; and you speak a senseless kind of indoor drivel, that reminds me of a storekeeper or a lady. You look to me like you might tote an umbrella and wear suspenders, and go home of nights."

' "The little woman," says Perry, "has made some improvements, I believe. You can't understand, Buck. I haven't been away from the house at night since we was married."

'We talked on a while, me and Perry, and, as sure as I live, that man interrupted me in the middle of my talk to tell me about six tomato plants he had growing in his garden. Shoved his agricultural degradation right up under my nose while I was telling him about the fun we had tarring and feathering that faro dealer at California Pete's layout! But by and by Perry shows a flicker of sense.

' "Buck," says he, "I'll have to admit that it is a little dull at times. Not that I'm not perfectly happy with the little woman, but a man seems to require some excitement now and then. Now, I'll tell you: Mariana's gone visiting this afternoon, and she won't be home till seven o'clock. That's the limit for both of us – seven o'clock. Neither of us ever stays out a minute after that time unless we are together. Now, I'm glad you came along, Buck," says Perry, "for I'm feeling just like having one more rip-roaring razoo with you for the sake of old times. What you say to us putting in the afternoon having fun? – I'd like it fine," says Perry.

'I slapped that old captive range-rider half across his little garden.

' "Get your hat, you old dried-up alligator," I shouts, "you ain't dead yet. You're part human, anyhow, if you did get all bogged up in matrimony.

We'll take this town to pieces, and see what makes it tick. We'll make all kinds of profligate demands upon the science of cork pulling. You'll grow horns yet, old muley cow," says I, punching Perry in the ribs, "if you trot around on the trail of vice with your Uncle Buck."

' "I'll have to be home by seven, you know," says Perry again.

' "Oh, yes," says I, winking to myself, for I knew the kind of seven o'clocks Perry Rountree got back by after he once got to passing repartee with the bartenders.

'We goes down to the Gray Mule saloon – that old 'dobe building by the depot.

' "Give it a name," says I, as soon as we got one hoof on the footrest.

' "Sarsaparilla," says Perry.

You could have knocked me down with a lemon peeling.

' "Insult me as much as you want to," I says to Perry, "but don't startle the bartender. He may have heart-disease. Come on, now; your tongue got twisted. The tall glasses," I orders, "and the bottle in the left hand corner of the ice-chest."

' "Sarsaparilla," repeats Perry, and then his eyes get animated, and I sees he's got some great scheme in his mind he wants to emit.

' "Buck," he says, all interested, "I'll tell you what! I want to make this a red-letter day. I've been keeping close at home, and I want to turn myself a-loose. We'll have the highest old time you ever saw. We'll go in the back room here and play checkers till half-past six."

'I leaned against the bar, and I says to Gotch-eared Mike, who was on watch:

' "For God's sake don't mention this. You know what Perry used to be. He's had the fever, and the doctor says we must humor him."

' "Give us the checker-board and the men, Mike," says Perry. "Come on, Buck, I'm just wild to have some excitement."

'I went in the back room with Perry. Before we closed the door, I says to Mike:

' "Don't ever let it straggle out from under your hat that you seen Buck Caperton fraternal with sarsaparilla or *persona grata* with a checker-board, or I'll make a swallow-fork in your other ear."

'I locked the door and me and Perry played checkers. To see that poor old humiliated piece of household bric-à-bric sitting there and sniggering out loud whenever he jumped a man, and all obnoxious with animation when he got into my king row, would have made a sheep-dog sick with mortification. Him that was once satisfied only when he was pegging six boards at keno or giving the faro dealers nervous prostration – to see him pushing them checkers about like Sally Louisa at a school-children's party – why, I was all smothered up with mortification.

'And I sits there playing the black men, all sweating for fear somebody I knew would find it out. And I thinks to myself some about this marrying business, and how it seems to be the same kind of a game as that Mrs. Delilah played. She give her old man a hair cut, and everybody knows what a man's head looks like after a woman cuts his hair. And then when the Pharisees came around to guy him he was so 'shamed he went to work and kicked the whole house down on top of the whole outfit. "Them married men," thinks I, "lose all their spirit and instinct for riot and foolishness. They won't drink, they won't buck the tiger, they won't even fight. What do they want to go and stay married for?" I asks myself.

'But Perry seems to be having hilarity in considerable quantities.

' "Buck old hoss," says he, "isn't this just the hell-roaring time we ever had in our lives? I don't know when I've been stirred up so. You see, I've been sticking pretty close to home since I married, and I haven't been on a spree in a long time."

' "Spree!" Yes, that's what he called it. Playing checkers in the back room of the Gray Mule! I suppose it did seem to him a little immoral and nearer to a prolonged debauch than standing over six tomato plants with a sprinkling pot.

'Every little bit Perry looks at his watch and says:

' "I got to be home, you know, Buck, at seven."

' "All right," I'd say. "Romp along and move. This here excitement's killing me. If I don't reform some, and loosen up the strain of this checkered dissipation I won't have a nerve left."

'It might have been half-past six when commotions began to go on outside in the street. We heard a yelling and a six-shootering, and a lot of galloping and maneuvers.

' "What's that?" I wonders.

' "Oh, some nonsense outside," says Perry. "It's your move. We just got time to play this game."

' "I'll just take a peep through the window," says I, "and see. You can't expect a mere mortal to stand the excitement of having a king jumped and listen to an unidentified conflict going on at the same time."

'The Gray Mule saloon was one of them old Spanish 'dobe buildings, and the back room only had two little windows a foot wide, with iron bars in 'em. I looked out one, and I see the cause of the rucus.

'There was the Trimble gang – ten of 'em – the worst outfit of desperadoes and horse-thieves in Texas, coming up the street shooting right and left. They was coming right straight for the Gray Mule. Then they got past the range of my sight, but we heard 'em ride up to the front door, and then they socked the place full of lead. We heard the big looking-glass behind the bar knocked all to pieces and the bottles crashing. We could see Gotch-eared Mike in his apron running across the plaza like a coyote, with the bullets puffing up the dust all around him. Then the gang went to work in the saloon, drinking what they wanted and smashing what they didn't.

'Me and Perry both knew that gang and they knew us. The year before Perry married, him and me was in the same ranger company – and we fought that outfit down on the San Miguel, and brought back Ben Trimble and two others for murder.

' "We can't get out," says I. "We'll have to stay in here till they leave."

Perry looked at his watch.

' "Twenty-five to seven," says he. "We can finish that game. I got two men on you. It's your move, Buck. I got to be home at seven, you know."

'We sat down and went on playing. The Trimble gang had a rough-house for sure. They were getting good and drunk. They'd drink a while and holler a while, and then they'd shoot up a few bottles and glasses. Two or three times they came and tried to open our door. Ham Gossett, the town marshal, had a posse in the houses and stores across the street, and was trying to bag a Trimble or two through the windows.

'I lost that game of checkers. I'm free in saying that I lost three kings that I might have saved if I had been corralled in a more peaceful pasture. But that drivelling married man sat there and cackled when he won a man like an unintelligent hen picking up a grain of corn.

'When the game was over Perry gets up and looks at his watch.

' "I've had a glorious time, Buck," says he, "but I'll have to be going now. It's a quarter to seven, and I got to be home by seven, you know."

'I thought he was joking.

' "They'll clear out or be dead drunk in half an hour or an hour," says I. "You ain't that tired of being married that you want to commit any more sudden suicide, are you?" says I, giving him the laugh.

' "One time," says Perry, "I was half an hour late getting home. I met Mariana on the street looking for me. If you could have seen her, Buck – but you don't understand. She knows what a wild kind of a snoozer I've been, and she's afraid something will happen. I'll never be late getting home again. I'll say good-bye to you now, Buck."

'I got between him and the door.

' "Married man," says I, "I know you was christened a fool the minute the preacher tangled you up, but don't you never sometimes think one little think on a human basis? There's ten of that gang in there, and they're pizen with whisky and desire for murder. They'll drink you up like a bottle of booze before you get halfway to the door. Be intelligent, now, and use at least wild-hog sense. Sit down and wait till we have some chance to get out without being carried in baskets."

' "I got to be home by seven, Buck," repeats this hen-pecked thing of little wisdom, like an unthinking poll parrot. "Mariana," says he, " 'll be looking out for me." And he reaches down and pulls a leg out of the checker table. "I'll go through this Trimble outfit," says he, "like a cottontail through a brush corral. I'm not pestered any more with a desire to engage in rucuses, but I got to be home by seven. You lock the door after me, Buck. And don't forget – I won three out them five games. I'd play longer, but Mariana—"

' "Hush up, you old locoed road rummer," I interrupts. "Did you ever notice your Uncle Buck locking doors against trouble? I'm not married," says I, "but I'm as big a d—n fool as any Mormon. One from four leaves three," says I, and I gathers out another leg of the table. "We'll get home by seven," says I, "whether it's the heavenly one or the other. May I see you home?" says I, "you sarsaparilla-drinking, checker-playing glutton for death and destruction."

'We opened the door easy, and then stampeded for the front. Part of the gang was lined up at the bar; part of 'em was passing over the drinks, and two or three was peeping out the door and window taking shots at the marshal's crowd. The room was so full of smoke we got halfway to the front door before they noticed us. Then I heard Berry Trimble's voice somewhere yell out:

' "How'd that Buck Caperton get in here?" and he skinned the side of my neck with a bullet. I reckon he felt bad over that miss, for Berry's the best shot south of the Southern Pacific Railroad. But the smoke in the saloon was some too thick for good shooting.

'Me and Perry smashed over two of the gang with our table legs, which didn't miss like the guns did, and as we run out the door I grabbed a

Winchester from a fellow who was watching the outside, and I turned and regulated the account of Mr. Berry.

'Me and Perry got out and around the corner all right. I never much expected to get out, but I wasn't going to be intimidated by that married man. According to Perry's idea, checkers was the event of the day, but if I am any judge of gentle recreations that little table-leg parade through the Gray Mule saloon deserved the head-lines in the bill of particulars.

' "Walk fast," says Perry, "it's two minutes to seven, and I got to be home by—"

' "Oh, shut up," says I. "I had an appointment as chief performer at an inquest at seven, and I'm not kicking about not keeping it."

'I had to pass by Perry's little house. His Mariana was standing at the gate. We got there at five minutes past seven. She had on a blue wrapper, and her hair was pulled back smooth like little girls do when they want to look grown-folksy. She didn't see us till we got close, and saw Perry, and a kind of look scooted around over her face – danged if I can describe it. I heard her breathe long, just like a cow when you turn her calf in the lot, and she says: "You're late, Perry."

' "Five minutes," says Perry, cheerful. "Me and old Buck was having a game of checkers."

'Perry introduces me to Mariana, and they ask me to come in. No, sir-ee. I'd had enough truck with married folks for that day. I says I'll be going along, and that I've spent a very pleasant afternoon with my old partner – "especially," says I, just to jostle Perry, "during that game when the table legs came all loose." But I'd promised him not to let her know anything.

'I've been worrying over that business ever since it happened,' continued Buck. 'There's one thing about it that's got me all twisted up, and I can't figure it out.'

'What was that?' I asked, as I rolled and handed Buck the last cigarette.

'Why, I'll tell you: When I saw the look that little woman give Perry when she turned round and saw him coming back to the ranch safe – why was it I got the idea all in a minute that that look of hers was worth more than the whole caboodle of us – sarsaparilla, checkers, and all, and that the d—n fool in the game wasn't named Perry Rountree at all?'

THE WORLD AND THE DOOR

A FAVORITE DODGE TO GET your story read by the public is to assert that it is true, and then add that Truth is stranger than Fiction. I do not know if the yarn I am anxious for you to read is true; but the Spanish purser of the fruit steamer *El Carrero* swore to me by the shrine of Santa Guadalupe that he had the facts from the U.S. vice-consul at La Paz – a person who could not possibly have been cognizant of half of them.

As for the adage quoted above, I take pleasure in puncturing it by affirming that I read in a purely fictional story the other day the line:

' "Be it so," said the policeman.' Nothing so strange has yet cropped out in Truth.

When H. Ferguson Hedges, millionaire promoter, investor, and man-about-New-York, turned his thoughts upon matters convivial, and word of it went 'down the line,' bouncers took a precautionary turn at the Indian clubs, waiters put ironstone china on his favorite tables, cab drivers crowded close to the curbstone in front of all-night cafés, and careful cashiers in his regular haunts charged up a few bottles to his account by way of preface and introduction.

As a money power a one-millionaire is of small account in a city where the man who cuts your slice of beef behind the free-lunch counter rides to work in his own automobile. But Hedges spent his money as lavishly, loudly, and showily as though he were only a clerk squandering a week's wages. And, after all, the bartender takes no interest in your reserve fund. He would rather look you up on his cash register than in Bradstreet.

On the evening that the material allegation of facts begins, Hedges was bidding dull care begone in the company of five or six good fellows – acquaintances and friends who had gathered in his wake.

Among them were two younger men – Ralph Merriam, a broker, and Wade, his friend.

Two deep-sea cabmen were chartered. At Columbus Circle they hove to long enough to revile the statue of the great navigator, unpatriotically rebuking him for having voyaged in search of land instead of liquids. Midnight overtook the party marooned in the rear of a cheap café far uptown.

Hedges was arrogant, overriding, and quarrelsome. He was burly and tough, iron-gray but vigorous, 'good' for the rest of the night. There was a dispute – about nothing that matters – and the five-fingered words were passed – the words that represent the glove cast into the lists. Merriam played the rôle of the verbal Hotspur.

Hedges rose quickly, seized his chair, swung it once and smashed wildly down at Merriam's head. Merriam dodged, drew a small revolver and shot Hedges in the chest. The leading roysterer stumbled, fell in a wry heap, and lay still.

Wade, a commuter, had formed that habit of promptness. He juggled Merriam out a side door, walked him to the corner, ran him a block and caught a hansom. They rode five minutes and then got out on a dark corner and dismissed the cab. Across the street the lights of a small saloon betrayed its hectic hospitality.

'Go in the back room of that saloon,' said Wade, 'and wait. I'll go find out what's doing and let you know. You may take two drinks while I am gone – no more.'

At ten minutes to one o'clock Wade returned.

'Brace up, old chap,' he said. 'The ambulance got there just as I did. The doctor says he's dead. You may have one more drink. You let me run this thing for you. You've got to skip. I don't believe a chair is legally a deadly weapon. You've got to make tracks, that's all there is to it.'

Merriam complained of the cold querulously, and asked for another drink. 'Did you notice what big veins he had on the back of his hands?' he said. 'I never could stand – I never could—'

'Take one more,' said Wade, 'and then come on. I'll see you through.'

Wade kept his promise so well that at eleven o'clock the next morning Merriam, with a new suit case full of new clothes and hair-brushes, stepped quietly on board a little 500-ton fruit steamer at an East River pier. The vessel had brought the season's first cargo of limes from Port Limon, and was homeward bound. Merriam had his bank balance of $2,800 in his pocket in large bills, and brief instructions to pile up as much water as he could between himself and New York. There was no time for anything more.

From Port Limon Merriam worked down the coast by schooner and sloop to Colon, thence across the isthmus to Panama, where he caught a tramp bound for Callao and such intermediate ports as might tempt the discursive skipper from his course.

It was at La Paz that Merriam decided to land – La Paz the Beautiful, a little harborless town smothered in a living green ribbon that banded the foot of a cloud-piercing mountain. Here the little steamer stopped to tread water while the captain's dory took him ashore that he might feel the pulse of the cocoanut market. Merriam went too, with his suit case, and remained.

Kalb, the vice-consul, a Graeco-Armenian citizen of the United States, born in Hesse-Darmstadt, and educated in Cincinnati ward primaries, considered all Americans his brothers and bankers. He attached himself to Merriam's elbow, introduced him to every one in La Paz who wore shoes, borrowed ten dollars and went back to his hammock.

There was a little wooden hotel in the edge of a banana grove, facing the sea, that catered to the tastes of the few foreigners that had dropped out of the world into the *triste* Peruvian town. At Kalb's introductory: 'Shake hands with—,' he had obediently exchanged manual salutations with a German doctor, one French and two Italian merchants, and three or four Americans who were spoken of as gold men, rubber men, mahogany men – anything but men of living tissue.

After dinner Merriam sat in a corner of the broad front *galería* with Bibb, a Vermonter interested in hydraulic mining, and smoked and drank Scotch 'smoke.' The moonlit sea, spreading infinitely before him, seemed to separate him beyond all apprehension from his old life. The horrid tragedy in which he had played such a disastrous part now began, for the first time since he stole on board the fruiter, a wretched fugitive, to lose its sharper outlines. Distance lent assuagement to his view. Bibb had opened the flood-gates of a stream of long-dammed discourse, overjoyed to have captured an audience that had not suffered under a hundred repetitions of his views and theories.

'One year more,' said Bibb, 'and I'll go back to God's country. Oh, I know it's pretty here, and you get *dolce far niente* handed to you in chunks, but this country wasn't made for a white man to live in. You've got to have to plug through snow now and then, and see a game of baseball and wear a stiff collar and have a policeman cuss you. Still, La Paz is a good sort of a pipe-dreamy old hole. And Mrs. Conant is here. When any of us feels particularly like jumping into the sea we rush around to her house and propose. It's nicer to be rejected by Mrs. Conant than it is to be drowned. And they say drowning is a delightful sensation.'

'Many like her here?' asked Merriam.

'Not anywhere,' said Bibb, with a comfortable sigh. 'She's the only white woman in La Paz. The rest range from a dappled dun to the color of a b-flat piano key. She's been here a year. Comes from – well, you know how a woman can talk – ask 'em to say "string" and they'll say "crow's foot" or "cat's cradle." Sometimes you'd think she was from Oshkosh, and again from Jacksonville, Florida, and the next day from Cape Cod.'

'Mystery?' ventured Merriam.

'M – well, she looks it; but her talk's translucent enough. But that's a woman. I suppose if the Sphinx were to begin talking she'd merely say: "Goodness me! more visitors coming for dinner, and nothing to eat but the sand which is here." But you won't think about that when you meet her, Merriam. You'll propose to her too.'

To make a hard story soft, Merriam did meet her and propose to her. He found her to be a woman in black with hair the color of a bronze turkey's wings, and mysterious, *remembering* eyes that – well, that looked as if she might have been a trained nurse looking on when Eve was created. Her words and manner, though, were translucent, as Bibb had said. She spoke, vaguely, of friends in California and some of the lower parishes in Louisiana. The tropical climate and indolent life suited her; she had thought of buying an orange grove later on; La Paz, all in all, charmed her.

Merriam's courtship of the Sphinx lasted three months, although he did not know that he was courting her. He was using her as an antidote for remorse, until he found, too late, that he had acquired the habit. During that time he had received no news from home. Wade did not know where he was; and he was not sure of Wade's exact address, and was afraid to write. He thought he had better let matters rest as they were for a while.

One afternoon he and Mrs. Conant hired two ponies and rode out along the mountain trail as far as the little cold river that came tumbling down the foothills. There they stopped for a drink, and Merriam spoke his piece – he proposed, as Bibb had prophesied.

Mrs. Conant gave him one glance of brilliant tenderness, and then her face took on such a strange, haggard look that Merriam was shaken out of his intoxication and back to his senses.

'I beg your pardon, Florence,' he said, releasing her hand; 'but I'll have to hedge on part of what I said. I can't ask you to marry me, of course. I killed a man in New York – a man who was my friend – shot him down – in quite a cowardly manner, I understand. Of course, the drinking didn't excuse it. Well, I couldn't resist having my say; and I'll always mean it. I'm here as a fugitive from justice, and – I suppose that ends our acquaintance.'

Mrs. Conant plucked little leaves assiduously from the low-hanging branch of a lime tree.

'I suppose so,' she said, in low and oddly uneven tones; 'but that depends upon you. I'll be as honest as you were. I poisoned my husband. I am a self-made widow. A man cannot love a murderess. So I suppose that ends our acquaintance.'

She looked up at him slowly. His face turned a little pale, and he stared at her blankly, like a deaf-and-dumb man who was wondering what it was all about.

She took a swift step toward him, with stiffened arms and eyes blazing.

'Don't look at me like that!' she cried, as though she were in acute pain. 'Curse me, or turn your back on me, but don't look that way. Am I a woman to be beaten? If I could show you – here on my arms, and on my back are scars – and it has been more than a year – scars that he made in his brutal rages. A holy nun would have risen and struck the fiend down. Yes, I killed him. The foul and horrible words that he hurled at me that last day are repeated in my ears every night when I sleep. And then came his blows, and the end of my endurance. I got the poison that afternoon. It was his custom to drink every night in the library before going to bed a hot punch made of rum and wine. Only from my fair hands would be receive it – because he knew that the fumes of spirits always sickened me. That night when the maid brought it to me I sent her downstairs on an errand. Before taking him his drink I went to my little private cabinet and poured into it more than a teaspoonful of tincture of aconite – enough to kill three men, so I had learned. I had drawn $6,000 that I had in bank, and with that and a few things in a satchel I left the house without any one seeing me. As I passed the library I heard him stagger up and fall heavily on a couch. I took a night train for New Orleans, and from there I sailed to the Bermudas. I finally cast anchor in La Paz. And now what have you to say? Can you open your mouth?'

Merriam came back to life.

'Florence,' he said, earnestly, 'I want you. I don't care what you've done. If the world—'

'Ralph,' she interrupted, almost with a scream, 'be my world!'

Her eyes melted; she relaxed magnificently and swayed toward Merriam so suddenly that he had to jump to catch her.

Dear me! in such scenes how the talk runs into artificial prose. But it can't be helped. It's the subconscious smell of the footlights' smoke that's in all of us. Stir the depths of your cook's soul sufficiently and she will discourse in Bulwer-Lyttonese.

Merriam and Mrs. Conant were very happy. He announced their engagement at the Hotel Orilla del Mar. Eight foreigners and four native Astors pounded his back and shouted insincere congratulations at him. Pedrito, the Castilian-mannered barkeep, was goaded to extra duty until his agility would have turned a Boston cherry-phosphate clerk a pale lilac with envy.

They were both very happy. According to the strange mathematics of the god of mutual affinity, the shadows that clouded their pasts when united became only half as dense instead of darker. They shut the world out and bolted the doors. Each was the other's world. Mrs. Conant lived again. The remembering look left her eyes. Merriam was with her every moment that was possible. On a little plateau under a grove of palms and calabash trees they were going to build a fairy bungalow. They were to be married in two months. Many hours of the day they had their heads together over the house plans. Their joint capital would set up a business in fruit or woods that would yield a comfortable support. 'Good-night, my world,' would say Mrs. Conant every evening when Merriam left her for his hotel. They were very happy. Their love had, circumstantially, that element of melancholy in it that it seems to require to attain its supremest elevation. And it seemed that their mutual great misfortune or sin was a bond that nothing could sever.

One day a steamer hove in the offing. Bare-legged and bare-shouldered La Paz scampered down to the beach, for the arrival of a steamer was their loop-the-loop, circus, Emancipation Day, and four-o'clock tea.

When the steamer was near enough, wise ones proclaimed that she was the *Pájaro*, bound up-coast from Callao to Panama.

The *Pájaro* put on brakes a mile off shore. Soon a boat came bobbing shoreward. Merriam strolled down on the beach to look on. In the shallow water the Carib sailors sprang out and dragged the boat with a mighty rush to the firm shingle. Out climbed the purser, the captain, and two passengers ploughing their way through the deep sand toward the hotel. Merriam glanced toward them with the mild interest due to strangers. There was something familiar to him in the walk of one of the passengers. He looked again, and his blood seemed to turn to strawberry ice cream in his veins. Burly, arrogant, debonair as ever, H. Ferguson Hedges, the man he had killed, was coming toward him ten feet away.

When Hedges saw Merriam his face flushed a dark red. Then he shouted in his old, bluff way: 'Hello, Merriam. Glad to see you. Didn't expect to find you out here. Quinby, this is my old friend Merriam, of New York – Merriam, Mr. Quinby.'

Merriam gave Hedges and then Quinby an ice-cold hand.

'Br-r-r!' said Hedges. 'But you've got a frappéed flipper! Man, you're not well. You're as yellow as a Chinaman. Malarial here? Steer us to a bar if there is such a thing, and let's take a prophylactic.'

Merriam, still half comatose, led them toward the Hotel Orilla del Mar.

'Quinby and I,' explained Hedges, puffing through the slippery sand, 'are looking out along the coast for some investments. We've just come up from Concepción and Valparaiso and Lima. The captain of this subsidized ferry boat told us there was some good picking around here in silver mines. So we got off. Now, where is that café, Merriam? Oh, in this portable soda-water pavilion?'

Leaving Quinby at the bar, Hedges drew Merriam aside.

'Now, what does this mean?' he said, with gruff kindness. 'Are you sulking about that fool row we had?'

'I thought,' stammered Merriam – 'I heard – they told me you were – that I had—'

'Well, you didn't, and I'm not,' said Hedges. 'That fool young ambulance surgeon told Wade I was a candidate for a coffin just because I'd got tired and quit breathing. I laid up in a private hospital for a month; but here I am, kicking as hard as ever. Wade and I tried to find you, but couldn't. Now, Merriam, shake hands and forget it all. I was as much to blame as you were; and the shot really did me good – I came out of the hospital as healthy and fit as a cab horse. Come on; that drink's waiting.'

'Old man,' said Merriam, brokenly, 'I don't know how to thank you – I – well, you know—'

'Oh, forget it,' boomed Hedges. 'Quinby'll die of thirst if we don't join him.'

Bibb was sitting on the shady side of the gallery waiting for the eleven-o'clock breakfast. Presently Merriam came out and joined him. His eye was strangely bright.

'Bibb, my boy,' said he, slowly waving his hand, 'do you see those mountains and that sea and sky and sunshine? – they're mine, Bibbsy – all mine.'

'You go in,' said Bibb, 'and take eight grains of quinine, right away. It won't do in this climate for a man to get to thinking he's Rockefeller, or James O'Neill either.'

Inside, the purser was untying a great roll of newspapers, many of them weeks old, gathered in the lower ports by the *Pájaro* to be distributed at casual stopping-places. Thus do the beneficent voyagers scatter news and entertainment among the prisoners of sea and mountains.

Tío Pancho, the hotel proprietor, set his great silver-rimmed *anteojos* upon his nose and divided the papers into a number of smaller rolls. A barefooted *muchacho* dashed in, desiring the post of messenger.

'*Vien venido,*' said Tío Pancho. 'This to Señora Conant; that to el Doctor S-S-Schlegel – *Dios!* what a name to say! that to Señor Davis – one for Don Alberto. These two for the *Casa de Huéspedes, Numero 6, en la calle de las Buenas Gracias.* And say to them all, *muchacho,* that the *Pájaro* sails for Panama at three this afternoon. If any have letters to send by the post, let them come quickly, that they may first pass through the *correo.*'

Mrs. Conant received her roll of newspapers at four o'clock. The boy was late in delivering them, because he had been deflected from his duty by an iguana that crossed his path and to which he immediately gave chase. But it made no hardship, for she had no letters to send.

She was idling in a hammock in the *patio* of the house that she occupied, half awake, half happily dreaming of the paradise that she and Merriam had created out of the wrecks of their pasts. She was content now for the horizon of that shimmering sea to be the horizon of her life. They had shut out the world and closed the door.

Merriam was coming to her house at seven, after his dinner at the hotel. She would put on a white dress and an apricot-colored lace mantilla, and they would walk an hour under the cocoanut palms by the lagoon. She smiled contentedly, and chose a paper at random from the roll the boy had brought.

At first the words of a certain headline of a Sunday newspaper meant nothing to her; they conveyed only a visualized sense of familiarity. The largest type ran thus: 'Lloyd B. Conant secures divorce.' And then the sub headings: 'Well-known Saint Louis paint manufacturer wins suit, pleading one year's absence of wife.' 'Her mysterious disappearance recalled.' 'Nothing has been heard of her since.'

Twisting herself quickly out of the hammock, Mrs. Conant's eye soon traversed the half-column of the *Recall.* It ended thus: 'It will be remembered that Mrs. Conant disappeared one evening in March of last year. It was freely rumored that her marriage with Lloyd B. Conant resulted in much unhap-piness. Stories were not wanting to the effect that his cruelty toward his wife had more than once taken the form of physical abuse. After her departure a full bottle of tincture of aconite, a deadly poison, was found in a small medicine cabinet in her bedroom. This might have been an indication that she meditated suicide. It is supposed that she abandoned such an intention if she possessed it, and left her home instead.'

Mrs. Conant slowly dropped the paper, and sat on a chair, clasping her hands tightly.

'Let me think – O God! – let me think,' she whispered. 'I took the bottle with me . . . I threw it out of the window of the train . . . I — . . . there was another bottle in the cabinet . . . there were two, side by side – the aconite – and the valerian that I took when I could not sleep . . . If they found the aconite bottle full, why – but, he is alive, of course – I gave him a harmless dose of valerian . . . I am not a murderess in fact . . . Ralph, I – O God, don't let this be a dream!'

She went into the part of the house that she rented from the old Peruvian man and his wife, shut the door, and walked up and down her room swiftly and feverishly for half an hour. Merriam's photograph stood in a frame on a table. She picked it up, looked at it with a smile of exquisite tenderness, and – dropped four tears on it. And Merriam only twenty rods away! Then she stood still for ten minutes, looking into space. She looked into space through a slowly opening door. On her side of the door was the building material for a castle of Romance – love, an Arcady of waving palms, a lullaby of waves on the shore of a haven of rest, respite, peace, a lotus land of dreamy ease and security – a life of poetry and heart's ease and refuge. Romanticist, will you tell me what Mrs. Conant saw on the other side of the door? You cannot? – that is, you will not? Very well; then listen.

She saw herself go into a department store and buy five spools of silk thread and three yards of gingham to make an apron for the cook. 'Shall I charge it, ma'am' asks the clerk. As she walked out a lady whom she met greeted her cordially. 'Oh, where did you get the pattern for those sleeves, dear Mrs. Conant?' she said. At the corner a policeman helped her across the street and touched his helmet. 'Any callers?' she asked the maid when she reached home. 'Mrs. Waldron,' answered the maid, 'and the two Misses Jenkinson.' 'Very well,' she said. 'You may bring me a cup of tea, Maggie.'

Mrs. Conant went to the door and called Angela, the old Peruvian woman. 'If Mateo is there send him to me.' Mateo, a half-breed, shuffling and old but efficient, came.

'Is there a steamer or a vessel of any kind leaving this coast to-night or to-morrow that I can get passage on?' she asked.

Mateo considered.

'At Punta Reina, thirty miles down the coast, señora,' he answered, 'there is a small steamer loading with cinchona and dyewoods. She sails for San Francisco to-morrow at sunrise. So says my brother, who arrived in his sloop to-day, passing by Punta Reina.'

'You must take me in that sloop to the steamer to-night. Will you do that?'

'Perhaps —' Mateo shrugged a suggestive shoulder. Mrs. Conant took a handful of money from a drawer and gave it to him.

'Get the sloop ready behind the little point of land below the town,' she ordered. 'Get sailors, and be ready to sail at six o'clock. In half an hour bring a cart partly filled with straw into the *patio* here, and take my trunk to the sloop. There is more money yet. Now, hurry.'

For one time Mateo walked away without shuffling his feet.

'Angela,' cried Mrs. Conant, almost fiercely, 'come and help me pack. I am going away. Out with this trunk. My clothes first. Stir yourself. Those dark dresses first. Hurry.'

From the first she did not waver from her decision. Her view was clear and final. Her door had opened and let the world in. Her love for Merriam was not lessened; but it now appeared a hopeless and unrealizable thing. The visions of their future that had seemed so blissful and complete had vanished. She tried to assure herself that her renunciation was rather for his sake than for her own. Now that she was cleared of her burden – at least, technically – would not his own weigh too heavily upon him? If she should cling to him, would not the difference forever silently mar and corrode their happiness? Thus she reasoned; but there were a thousand little voices calling to her that she could feel rather than hear, like the hum of distant, powerful machinery – the little voices of the world, that, when raised in unison, can send their insistent call through the thickest door.

Once, while packing, a brief shadow of the lotus dream came back to her. She held Merriam's picture to her heart with one hand, while she threw a pair of shoes into the trunk with her other.

At six o'clock Mateo returned and reported the sloop ready. He and his brother lifted the trunk into the cart, covered it with straw, and conveyed it to the point of embarkation. From there they transferred it on board in the sloop's dory. Then Mateo returned for additional orders.

Mrs. Conant was ready. She had settled all business matters with Angela, and was impatiently waiting. She wore a long, loose black-silk duster that she often walked about in when the evenings were chilly. On her head was a small round hat, and over it the apricot-colored lace mantilla.

Dusk had quickly followed the short twilight. Mateo led her by dark and grass-grown streets toward the point behind which the sloop was anchored. On turning a corner they beheld the Hotel Orilla del Mar three streets away, nebulously aglow with its array of kerosene lamps.

Mrs. Conant paused, with streaming eyes. 'I must, *I must* see him once before I go,' she murmured in anguish. But even then she did not falter in her decision. Quickly she invented a plan by which she might speak to him, and yet make her departure without his knowing. She would walk past the hotel, ask some one to call him out, and talk a few moments on some trivial excuse, leaving him expecting to see her at her home at seven.

She unpinned her hat and gave it to Mateo. 'Keep this, and wait here till I come,' she ordered. Then she draped the mantilla over her head as she usually did when walking after sunset, and went straight to the Orilla del Mar.

She was glad to see the bulky, white-clad figure of Tío Pancho standing alone on the gallery.

'Tío Pancho,' she said, with a charming smile, 'may I trouble you to ask Mr. Merriam to come out for just a few moments that I may speak with him?'

Tío Pancho bowed as an elephant bows.

'*Buenas tardes*, Señora Conant,' he said, as a cavalier talks. And then he went on, less at his ease:

'But does not the señora know that Señor Merriam sailed on the *Pájaro* for Panama at three o'clock of this afternoon?'

THE THEORY AND THE HOUND

NOT MANY DAYS AGO MY OLD FRIEND from the tropics, J. P. Bridger, United States consul on the island of Ratona, was in the city. We had wassail and jubilee and saw the Flatiron building, and missed seeing the Bronxless menagerie by about a couple of nights. And then, at the ebb tide, we were walking up a street that parallels and parodies Broadway.

A woman with a comely and mundane countenance passed us, holding in leash a wheezing, vicious, waddling brute of a yellow pug. The dog entangled himself with Bridger's legs and mumbled his ankles in a snarling, peevish, sulky bite. Bridger, with a happy smile kicked the breath out of the brute; the woman showered us with a quick rain of well-conceived adjectives that left us in no doubt as to our place in her opinion, and we passed on. Ten yards farther an old woman with disordered white hair and her bankbook tucked well hidden beneath her tattered shawl begged. Bridger stopped and disinterred for her a quarter from his holiday waistcoat.

On the next corner a quarter of a ton of well-clothed man with a rice-powdered, fat, white jowl, stood holding the chain of a devil-born bulldog whose forelegs were strangers by the length of a dachshund. A little woman in a last-season's hat confronted him and wept, which was plainly all she could do, while he cursed her in low, sweet, practised tones.

Bridger smiled again – strictly to himself – and this time he took out a little memorandum book and made a note of it. This he had no right to do without due explanation, and I said so.

'It's a new theory,' said Bridger, 'that I picked up down in Ratona. I've been gathering support for it as I knock about. The world isn't ripe for it yet, but – well, I'll tell you; and then you run your mind back along the people you've known and see what you make of it.'

And so I cornered Bridger in a place where they have artificial palms and wine; and he told me the story which is here in my words and on his responsibility.

One afternoon at three o'clock, on the island of Ratona, a boy raced along the beach screaming, '*Pájaro*, ahoy!'

Thus he made known the keenness of his hearing and the justice of his discrimination in pitch.

He who first heard and made oral proclamation concerning the toot of an approaching steamer's whistle, and correctly named the steamer, was a small hero in Ratona – until the next steamer came. Wherefore, there was rivalry among the barefoot youth of Ratona, and many fell victims to the softly blown conch shells of sloops which, as they enter harbor, sound surprisingly like a distant steamer's signal. And some could name you the vessel when its call, in your duller ears, sounded no louder than the sigh of the wind through the branches of the cocoanut palms.

But to-day he who proclaimed the *Pájaro* gained his honors. Ratona bent its ear to listen; and soon the deep-tongued blast grew louder and nearer, and at length Ratona saw above the line of palms on the low 'point' the two black funnels of the fruiter slowly creeping toward the mouth of the harbor.

You must know that Ratona is an island twenty miles off the south of a

South American republic. It is a port of that republic; and it sleeps sweetly in a smiling sea, toiling not nor spinning; fed by the abundant tropics where all things 'ripen, cease and fall toward the grave.'

Eight hundred people dream life away in a green-embowered village that follows the horseshoe curve of its bijou harbor. They are mostly Spanish and Indian mestizos, with a shading of San Domingo Negroes, a lightening of pure-blood Spanish officials, and a slight leavening of the froth of three or four pioneering white races. No steamers touch at Ratona save the fruit steamers which take on their banana inspectors there on their way to the coast. They leave Sunday newspapers, ice, quinine, bacon, watermelons, and vaccine matter at the island and that is about all the touch Ratona gets with the world.

The *Pájaro* paused at the mouth of the harbor, rolling heavily in the swell that sent the whitecaps racing beyond the smooth water inside. Already two dories from the village – one conveying fruit inspectors, the other going for what it could get – were halfway out to the steamer.

The inspector's dory was taken on board with them, and the *Pájaro* steamed away for the mainland for its load of fruit.

The other boat returned to Ratona bearing a contribution from the *Pájaro's* store of ice, the usual roll of newspapers, and one passenger – Taylor Plunkett, sheriff of Chatham County, Kentucky.

Bridger, the United States consul at Ratona, was cleaning his rifle in the official shanty under a bread-fruit tree twenty yards from the water of the harbor. The consul occupied a place somewhat near the tail of his political party's procession. The music of the band wagon sounded very faintly to him in the distance. The plums of office went to others. Bridger's share of the spoils – the consulship at Ratona – was little more than a prune – a dried prune from the boarding-house department of the public crib. But $900 yearly was opulence in Ratona. Besides, Bridger had contracted a passion for shooting alligators in the lagoons near his consulate, and he was not unhappy.

He looked up from a careful inspection of his rifle lock and saw a broad man filling his doorway. A broad, noiseless, slow-moving man sunburned almost to the brown of Vandyke. A man of forty-five, neatly clothed in homespun, with scanty light hair, a close-clipped brown-and-gray beard and pale-blue eyes expressing mildness and simplicity.

'You are Mr. Bridger, the consul,' said the broad man. 'They directed me here. Can you tell me what those big bunches of things like gourds are in those trees that look like feather dusters along the edge of the water?'

'Take that chair,' said the consul, reoiling his cleaning rag. 'No, the other one – that bamboo thing won't hold you. Why, they're cocoanuts – green cocoanuts. The shell of 'em is always a light green before they're ripe.'

'Much obliged,' said the other man, sitting down carefully. 'I didn't quite like to tell the folks at home they were olives unless I was sure about it. My name is Plunkett. I'm sheriff of Chatham County, Kentucky. I've got extradition papers in my pocket authorizing the arrest of a man on this island. They've been signed by the President of this country, and they're in correct shape. The man's name is Wade Williams. He's in the cocoanut raising business. What he's wanted for is the murder of his wife two years ago. Where can I find him?'

The consul squinted an eye and looked through his rifle barrel.

'There's nobody on the island who calls himself "Williams," ' he remarked.

'Didn't suppose there was,' said Plunkett mildly. 'He'll do by any other name.'

'Besides myself,' said Bridger, 'there are only two Americans on Ratona – Bob Reeves and Henry Morgan.'

'The man I want sells cocoanuts,' suggested Plunkett.

'You see the cocoanut walk extending up to the point?' said the consul, waving his hand toward the open door. 'That belongs to Bob Reeves. Henry Morgan owns half the trees to loo'ard on the island.'

'One month ago,' said the sheriff, 'Wade Williams wrote a confidential letter to a man in Chatham County, telling him where he was and how he was getting along. The letter was lost; and the person that found it gave it away. They sent me after him, and I've got the papers. I reckon he's one of your cocoanut men for certain.'

'You've got his picture, of course,' said Bridger. 'It might be Reeves or Morgan, but I'd hate to think it. They're both as fine fellows as you'd meet in an all-day auto ride.'

'No,' doubtfully answered Plunkett; 'there wasn't any picture of Williams to be had. And I never saw him myself. I've been sheriff only a year. But I've got a pretty accurate description of him. About 5 feet 11; dark hair and eyes; nose inclined to be Roman; heavy about the shoulders; strong, white teeth, with none missing; laughs a good deal, talkative; drinks considerably but never to intoxication; looks you square in the eye when talking; age thirty-five. Which one of your men does that description fit?'

The consul grinned broadly.

'I'll tell you what you do,' he said, laying down his rifle and slipping on his dingy black alpaca coat. 'You come along, Mr. Plunkett, and I'll take you up to see the boys. If you can tell which one of 'em your description fits better than it does the other you have the advantage of me.'

Bridger conducted the sheriff out and along the hard beach close to which the tiny houses of the village were distributed. Immediately back of the town rose sudden, small, thickly wooded hills. Up one of these, by means of steps cut in the hard clay, the consul led Plunkett. On the very verge of an eminence was perched a two-room wooden cottage with a thatched roof. A Carib woman was washing clothes outside. The consul ushered the sheriff to the door of the room that overlooked the harbor.

Two men were in the room, about to sit down, in their shirt sleeves, to a table spread for dinner. They bore little resemblance one to the other in detail; but the general description given by Plunkett could have been justly applied to either. In height, color of hair, shape of nose, build, and manners each of them tallied with it. They were fair types of jovial, ready-witted, broad-gauged Americans who had gravitated together for companionship in an alien land.

'Hello, Bridger!' they called in unison at sight of the consul. 'Come and have dinner with us!' And then they noticed Plunkett at his heels, and came forward with hospitable curiosity.

'Gentlemen,' said the consul, his voice taking an unaccustomed formality, 'this is Mr. Plunkett. Mr. Plunkett – Mr. Reeves and Mr. Morgan.'

The cocoanut barons greeted the newcomer joyously. Reeves seemed about an inch taller than Morgan, but his laugh was not quite as loud. Morgan's eyes were deep brown; Reeves's were black. Reeves was the host and busied himself with fetching other chairs and calling to the Carib woman for supplemental table ware. It was explained that Morgan lived in a bamboo shack to 'loo'ard,' but that every day the two friends dined together. Plunkett stood still during the preparations, looking about mildly with his pale-blue eyes. Bridger looked apologetic and uneasy.

At length two other covers were laid and the company was assigned to places. Reeves and Morgan stood side by side across the table from the visitors. Reeves nodded genially as a signal for all to seat themselves. And then suddenly Plunkett raised his hand with a gesture of authority. He was looking straight between Reeves and Morgan.

'Wade Williams,' he said quietly, 'you are under arrest for murder.'

Reeves and Morgan instantly exchanged a quick, bright glance, the quality of which was interrogation, with a seasoning of surprise. Then, simultaneously they turned to the speaker with a puzzled and frank deprecation in their gaze.

'Can't say that we understand you, Mr. Plunkett,' said Morgan, cheerfully. 'Did you say "Williams"?'

'What's the joke, Bridgy?' asked Reeves, turning to the consul with a smile.

Before Bridger could answer, Plunkett spoke again.

'I'll explain,' he said, quietly. 'One of you don't need any explanation, but this is for the other one. One of you is Wade Williams of Chatham County, Kentucky. You murdered your wife on May 5, two years ago, after ill-treating and abusing her continually for five years. I have the proper papers in my pocket for taking you back with me, and you are going. We will return on the fruit steamer that comes back by this island to-morrow to leave its inspectors. I acknowledge, gentlemen, that I'm not quite sure which one of you is Williams. But Wade Williams goes back to Chatham County to-morrow. I want you to understand that.'

A great sound of merry laughter from Morgan and Reeves went out over the still harbor. Two or three fishermen in the fleet of sloops anchored there looked up at the house of the *diablos Americanos* on the hill and wondered.

'My dear Mr. Plunkett,' cried Morgan, conquering his mirth, 'the dinner is getting cold. Let us sit down and eat. I am anxious to get my spoon into that shark-fin soup. Business afterward.'

'Sit down, gentlemen, if you please,' added Reeves, pleasantly. 'I am sure Mr. Plunkett will not object. Perhaps a little time may be of advantage to him in identifying – the gentleman he wishes to arrest.'

'No objections, I'm sure,' said Plunkett, dropping into his chair heavily. 'I'm hungry myself. I didn't want to accept the hospitality of you folks without giving you notice; that's all.'

Reeves set bottles and glasses on the table.

'There's cognac,' he said, 'and anisada, and Scotch "smoke," and rye. Take your choice.'

Bridger chose rye, Reeves poured three fingers of Scotch for himself, Morgan took the same. The sheriff, against much protestation, filled his glass from the water bottle.

'Here's to the appetite,' said Reeves, raising his glass, 'of Mr. Williams!' Morgan's laugh and his drink encountering sent him into a choking-splutter. All began to pay attention to the dinner, which was well cooked and palatable.

'Williams!' called Plunkett, suddenly and sharply.

All looked up wonderingly. Reeves found the sheriff's mild eye resting upon him. He flushed a little.

'See here,' he said, with some asperity, 'my name's Reeves, and I don't want you to — ' But the comedy of the thing came to his rescue and he ended with a laugh.

'I suppose, Mr. Plunkett,' said Morgan, carefully seasoning an alligator pear, 'that you are aware of the fact that you will import a good deal of trouble for yourself into Kentucky if you take back the wrong man – that is, of course, if you take anybody back?'

'Thank you for the salt,' said the sheriff. 'Oh, I'll take somebody back. It'll be one of you two gentlemen. Yes, I know I'll get stuck for damages if I make a mistake. But I'm going to try to get the right man.'

'I'll tell you what you do,' said Morgan, leaning forward with a jolly twinkle in his eyes. 'You take me. I'll go without any trouble. The cocoanut business hasn't panned out well this year, and I'd like to make some extra money out of your bondsmen.'

'That's not fair,' chimed in Reeves. 'I got only $16 a thousand for my last shipment. Take me, Mr. Plunkett.'

'I'll take Wade Williams,' said the sheriff, patiently, 'or I'll come pretty close to it.'

'It's like dining with a ghost,' remarked Morgan, with a pretended shiver. 'The ghost of a murderer, too! Will somebody pass the tooth-picks to the shade of the naughty Mr. Williams?'

Plunkett seemed as unconcerned as if he were dining at his own table in Chatham County. He was a gallant trencherman, and the strange tropic viands tickled his palate. Heavy, commonplace, almost slothful in his movements, he appeared to be devoid of all the cunning and watchfulness of the sleuth. He even ceased to observe, with any sharpness or attempted discrimination, the two men, one of whom he had undertaken with surprising self-confidence to drag away upon the serious charge of wife-murder. Here, indeed, was a problem set before him that if wrongly solved would have amounted to his serious discomfiture, yet there he sat puzzling his soul (to all appearances) over the novel flavor of a broiled iguana cutlet.

The consul felt a decided discomfort. Reeves and Morgan were his friends and pals; yet the sheriff from Kentucky had a certain right to his official aid and moral support. So Bridger sat the silentest around the board and tried to estimate the peculiar situation. His conclusion was that both Reeves and Morgan, quickwitted, as he knew them to be, had conceived at the moment of Plunkett's disclosure of his mission – and in the brief space of a lightning flash – the idea that the other might be the guilty Williams; and that each of them had decided in that moment loyally to protect his comrade against the doom that threatened him. This was the consul's theory, and if he had been a bookmaker at a race of wits for life and liberty he would have offered heavy odds against the plodding sheriff from Chatham County, Kentucky.

When the meal was concluded the Carib woman came and removed the dishes and cloth. Reeves strewed the table with excellent cigars, and Plunkett, with the others, lighted one of these with evident gratification.

'I may be dull,' said Morgan, with a grin and a wink at Bridger; 'but I want to know if I am. Now, I say this is all a joke of Mr. Plunkett's concocted to frighten two babes-in-the-woods. Is this Williamson to be taken seriously or not?'

' "Williams,"' corrected Plunkett, gravely. 'I never got off any jokes in my life. I know I wouldn't travel 2,000 miles to get off a poor one as this would be if I didn't take Wade Williams back with me. Gentlemen!' continued the sheriff, now letting his mild eyes travel impartially from one of the company to another, 'see if you can find any joke in this case. Wade Williams is listening to the words I utter now; but out of politeness I will speak of him as a third person. For five years he made his wife lead the life of a dog – No; I'll take that back. No dog in Kentucky was ever treated as she was. He spent the money that she brought him – spent it at races, at the card table, and on horses and hunting. He was a good fellow to his friends, but a cold, sullen demon at home. He wound up the five years of neglect by striking her with his closed hand – a hand as hard as a stone – when she was ill and weak from suffering. She died the next day; and he skipped. That's all there is to it. It's enough. I never saw Williams; but I knew his wife. I'm not a man to tell half. She and I were keeping company when she met him. She went to Louisville on a visit and saw him there. I'll admit that he spoilt my chances in no time. I lived then on the edge of the Cumberland Mountains. I was elected sheriff of Chatham County a year after Wade Williams killed his wife. My official duty sends me out here after him; but I'll admit that there's personal feeling, too. And he's going back with me. Mr. – er – Reeves, will you pass me a match?'

'Awfully imprudent of Williams,' said Morgan, putting his feet up against the wall, 'to strike a Kentucky lady. Seems to me I've heard they were scrappers.'

'Bad, bad Williams,' said Reeves, pouring out more 'Scotch.'

The two men spoke lightly, but the consul saw and felt the tension and the carefulness in their actions and words. 'Good old fellows,' he said to himself; 'they're both all right. Each of 'em is standing by the other like a little brick church.'

And then a dog walked into the room where they sat – a black-and-tan hound, long-eared, lazy, confident of welcome.

Plunkett turned his head and looked at the animal, which halted, confidently, within a few feet of his chair.

Suddenly the sheriff, with a deep-mouthed oath, left his seat and bestowed upon the dog a vicious and heavy kick, with his ponderous shoe.

The hound, heart-broken, astonished, with flapping ears and in-curved tail, uttered a piercing yelp of pain and surprise.

Reeves and the consul remained in their chairs, saying nothing, but astonished at the unexpected show of intolerance from the easy-going man from Chatham County.

But Morgan, with a suddenly purpling face, leaped to his feet and raised a threatening arm above the guest.

'You – brute!' he shouted, passionately; 'why did you do that?'

Quickly the amenities returned, Plunkett muttered some indistinct apology and regained his seat. Morgan with a decided effort controlled his indignation and also returned to his chair.

And then Plunkett, with the spring of a tiger, leaped around the corner of the table and snapped handcuffs on the paralyzed Morgan's wrists.

'Hound-lover and woman-killer!' he cried; 'get ready to meet your God.'

When Bridger had finished I asked him:

'Did he get the right man?'

'He did,' said the consul.

'And how did he know?' I inquired, being in a kind of bewilderment.

'When he put Morgan in the dory,' answered Bridger, 'the next day to take him aboard the *Pájaro*, this man Plunkett stopped to shake hands with me and I asked him the same question.

' "Mr. Bridger," said he. "I'm a Kentuckian, and I've seen a great deal of both men and animals. And I never yet saw a man that was overfond of horses and dogs but what was cruel to women." '

THE HYPOTHESES OF FAILURE

LAWYER GOOCH BESTOWED HIS undivided attention upon the engrossing arts of his profession. But one flight of fancy did he allow his mind to entertain. He was fond of likening his suite of office rooms to the bottom of a ship. The rooms were three in number, with a door opening from one to another. These doors could also be closed.

'Ships,' Lawyer Gooch would say, 'are constructed for safety, with separate, water-tight compartments in their bottoms. If one compartment springs a leak it fills with water; but the good ship goes on unhurt. Were it not for the separating bulkheads one leak would sink the vessel. Now it often happens that while I am occupied with clients, other clients with conflicting interests call. With the assistance of Archibald – an office boy with a future – I cause the dangerous influx to be diverted into separate compartments, while I sound with my legal plummet the depth of each. If necessary, they may be baled into the hallway and permitted to escape by way of the stairs, which we may term the lee scuppers. Thus the good ship of business is kept afloat; whereas if the element that supports her were allowed to mingle freely in her hold we might be swamped – ha, ha, ha!'

The law is dry. Good jokes are few. Surely it might be permitted Lawyer Gooch to mitigate the bore of briefs, the tedium of torts and the prosiness of processes with even so light a levy upon the good property of humor.

Lawyer Gooch's practice leaned largely to the settlement of marital infelicities. Did matrimony languish through complications, he mediated, soothed, and arbitrated. Did it suffer from implications, he readjusted, defended, and championed. Did it arrive at the extremity of duplications, he always got light sentences for his clients.

But not always was Lawyer Gooch the keen, armed, wily belligerent, ready with his two-edged sword to lop off the shackles of Hymen. He had been known to build up instead of demolishing, to reunite instead of severing, to lead erring and foolish ones back into the fold instead of scattering the flock. Often had he by his eloquent and moving appeals sent husband and wife, weeping, back into each other's arms. Frequently he had coached childhood so successfully that, at the psychological moment (and at a given signal), the plaintive pipe of 'Papa, won't you tum home adain to me and muvver?' had won the day and upheld the pillars of a tottering home.

Unprejudiced persons admitted that Lawyer Gooch received as big fees from these reyoked clients as would have been paid him had the cases been contested in court. Prejudiced ones intimated that his fees were doubled, because the penitent couples always came back later for the divorce, anyhow.

There came a season in June when the legal ship of Lawyer Gooch (to borrow his own figure) was nearly becalmed. The divorce mill grinds slowly in June. It is the month of Cupid and Hymen.

Lawyer Gooch, then, sat idle in the middle room of his clientless suite. A small anteroom connected – or rather separated – this apartment from the hallway. Here was stationed Archibald, who wrested from visitors their cards or oral nomenclature which he bore to his master while they waited.

Suddenly, on this day, there came a great knocking at the outermost door.

Archibald, opening it, was thrust aside as superfluous by the visitor, who without due reverence at once penetrated to the office of Lawyer Gooch and threw himself with good-natured insolence into a comfortable chair facing that gentleman.

'You are Phineas C. Gooch, attorney-at-law?' said the visitor, his tone of voice and inflection making his words at once a question, an assertion, and an accusation.

Before committing himself by a reply, the lawyer estimated his possible client in one of his brief but shrewd and calculating glances.

The man was of the emphatic type – large-sized, active, bold and debonair in demeanor, vain beyond a doubt, slightly swaggering, ready and at ease. He was well clothed, but with a shade too much ornateness. He was seeking a lawyer; but if that fact would seem to saddle him with troubles they were not patent in his beaming eye and courageous air.

'My name is Gooch,' at length the lawyer admitted. Upon pressure he would also have confessed to the Phineas C. But he did not consider it good practice to volunteer information. 'I did not receive your card,' he continued, by way of rebuke, 'so I—'

'I know you didn't,' remarked the visitor, coolly; 'and you won't just yet. Light up?' He threw a leg over an arm of his chair, and tossed a handful of rich-hued cigars upon the table. Lawyer Gooch knew the brand. He thawed just enough to accept the invitation to smoke.

'You are a divorce lawyer,' said the cardless visitor. This time there was no interrogation in his voice. Nor did his words constitute a simple assertion. They formed a charge – a denunciation – as one would say to a dog: 'You are a dog.' Lawyer Gooch was silent under the imputation.

'You handle,' continued the visitor, 'all the various ramifications of busted-up connubiality. You are a surgeon, we might say, who extracts Cupid's darts when he shoots 'em into the wrong parties. You furnish patent, incandescent lights for premises where the torch of Hymen has burned so low you can't light a cigar at it. Am I right, Mr. Gooch?'

'I have undertaken cases,' said the lawyer, guardedly, 'in the line to which your figurative speech seems to refer. Do you wish to consult me professionally, Mr. —' The lawyer paused, with significance.

'Not yet,' said the other, with an arch wave of his cigar, 'not just yet. Let us approach the subject with the caution that should have been used in the original act that makes this pow-wow necessary. There exists a matrimonial jumble to be straightened out. But before I give you names I want your honest – well, anyhow, your professional opinion on the merits of the mix-up. I want you to size up the catastrophe – abstractly – you understand? I'm Mr. Nobody; and I've got a story to tell you. Then you say what's what. Do you get my wireless?'

'You want to state a hypothetical case?' suggested Lawyer Gooch.

'That's the word I was after. "Apothecary" was the best shot I could make at it in my mind. The hypothetical goes. I'll state the case. Suppose there's a woman – a deuced fine-looking woman – who has run away from her husband and home? She's badly mashed on another man who went to her town to work up some real estate business. Now, we may as well call this woman's husband Thomas R. Billings, for that's his name. I'm giving you straight tips on the cognomens. The Lothario chap is Henry K. Jessup. The Billingses lived in a little town called Susanville – a good many miles from here. Now, Jessup leaves Susanville two weeks ago. The next day Mrs. Billings follows him. She's dead gone on this man Jessup; you can bet your law library on that.'

Lawyer Gooch's client said this with such unctuous satisfaction that even the callous lawyer experienced a slight ripple of repulsion. He now saw clearly in his fatuous visitor the conceit of the lady-killer, the egoistic complacency of the successful trifler.

'Now,' continued the visitor, 'suppose this Mr. Billings wasn't happy at home? We'll say she and her husband didn't gee worth a cent. They've got incompatibility to burn. The things she likes, Billings wouldn't have as a gift with trading-stamps. It's Tabby and Rover with them all the time. She's an educated woman in science and culture, and she reads things out loud at meetings. Billings is not on. He don't appreciate progress and obelisks and ethics, and things of that sort. Old Billings is simply a blink when it comes to such things. The lady is out and out above his class. Now, lawyer, don't it look like a fair equalization of rights and wrongs that a woman like that should be allowed to throw down Billings and take the man that can appreciate her?'

'Incompatibility,' said Lawyer Gooch, 'is undoubtedly the source of much marital discord and unhappiness. Where it is positively proved, divorce would seem to be the equitable remedy. Are you – excuse me – is this man Jessup one to whom the lady may safely trust her future?'

'Oh, you can bet on Jessup,' said the client, with a confident wag of his head. 'Jessup's all right. He'll do the square thing. Why, he left Susanville just to keep people from talking about Mrs. Billings. But she followed him up, and now, of course, he'll stick to her. When she gets a divorce, all legal and proper, Jessup will do the proper thing.'

'And now,' said Lawyer Gooch, 'continuing the hypothesis, if you prefer, and supposing that my services should be desired in the case, what—'

The client rose impulsively to his feet.

'Oh, dang the hypothetical business,' he exclaimed, impatiently. 'Let's let her drop, and get down to straight talk. You ought to know who I am by this time. I want that woman to have her divorce. I'll pay for it. The day you set Mrs. Billings free I'll pay you five hundred dollars.'

Lawyer Gooch's client banged his fist upon the table to punctuate his generosity.

'If that is the case—' began the lawyer.

'Lady to see you, sir,' bawled Archibald, bouncing in from his anteroom. He had orders to always announce immediately any client that might come. There was no sense in turning business away.

Lawyer Gooch took client number one by the arm and led him suavely into one of the adjoining rooms. 'Favor me by remaining here a few minutes, sir,' said he. 'I will return and resume our consultation with the least possible delay. I am rather expecting a visit from a very wealthy old lady in connection with a will. I will not keep you waiting long.'

The breezy gentleman seated himself with obliging acquiescence, and took up a magazine. The lawyer returned to the middle office, carefully closing behind him the connecting door.

'Show the lady in, Archibald,' he said to the office boy, who was awaiting the order.

A tall lady, of commanding presence and sternly handsome, entered the room. She wore robes – robes; not clothes – ample and fluent. In her eye could be perceived the lambent flame of genius and soul. In her hand was a green bag of the capacity of a bushel, and an umbrella that also seemed to wear a robe, ample and fluent. She accepted a chair.

'Are you Mr. Phineas C. Gooch, the lawyer?' she asked, in formal and unconciliatory tones.

'I am,' answered Lawyer Gooch, without circumlocution. He never circumlocuted when dealing with a woman. Women circumlocute. Time is wasted when both sides in debate employ the same tactics.

'As a lawyer, sir,' began the lady, 'You may have acquired some knowledge of the human heart. Do you believe that the pusillanimous and petty conventions of our artificial social life should stand as an obstacle in the way of a noble and affectionate heart when it finds its true mate among the miserable and worthless wretches in the world that are called men?'

'Madam,' said Lawyer Gooch, in the tone that he used in curbing his female clients, 'this is an office for conducting the practices of law. I am a lawyer, not a philosopher, nor the editor of an "Answers to the Lovelorn" column of a newspaper. I have other clients waiting. I will ask you kindly to come to the point.'

'Well, you needn't get so stiff around the gills about it,' said the lady, with a snap of her luminous eyes and a startling gyration of her umbrella. 'Business is what I've come for. I want your opinion in the matter of a suit for a divorce, as the vulgar would call it, but which is really only the readjustment of the false and ignoble conditions that the shortsighted laws of man have interposed between a loving—'

'I beg your pardon, madam,' interrupted Lawyer Gooch, with some impatience, 'for reminding you again that this is a law office. Perhaps Mrs. Wilcox—'

'Mrs. Wilcox is all right,' cut in the lady, with a hint of asperity, 'And so are Tolstoi, and Mrs. Gertrude Atherton, and Omar Khayyam, and Mr. Edward Bok. I've read 'em all. I would like to discuss with you the divine right of the soul as opposed to the freedom-destroying restrictions of a bigoted and narrow-minded society. But I will proceed to business. I would prefer to lay the matter before you in an impersonal way until you pass upon its merits. That is to describe it as a supposable instance, without—'

'You wish to state a hypothetical case?' said Lawyer Gooch.

'I was going to say that,' said the lady, sharply. 'Now, suppose there is a woman who is all soul and heart and aspirations for a complete existence. This woman has a husband who is far below her in intellect, in taste – in everything. Bah! he is a brute. He despises literature. He sneers at the lofty thoughts of the world's great thinkers. He thinks only of real estate and such sordid things. He is no mate for a woman with soul. We will say that this unfortunate wife one day meets with her ideal – a man with brain and heart and force. She loves him. Although this man feels the thrill of a new-found affinity he is too noble, too honorable to declare himself. He flies from the presence of his beloved. She flies after him, trampling, with superb indifference, upon the fetters with which an unenlightened social system would bind her. Now, what will a divorce cost? Eliza Ann Timmins, the poetess of Sycamore Gap, got one for three hundred and forty dollars. Can I – I mean can this lady I speak of get one that cheap?'

'Madam,' said Lawyer Gooch, 'your last two or three sentences delight me with their intelligence and clearness. Can we not now abandon the hypothetical and come down to names and business?'

'I should say so,' exclaimed the lady, adopting the practical with admirable readiness. 'Thomas R. Billings is the name of the low brute who stands between the happiness of his legal – his legal, but not his spiritual – wife and Henry K. Jessup, the noble man whom nature intended for her mate. I,' concluded the client, with an air of dramatic revelation, 'am Mrs. Billings!'

'Gentleman to see you, sir,' shouted Archibald, invading the room almost at a handspring. Lawyer Gooch arose from his chair.

'Mrs Billings,' he said, courteously, 'allow me to conduct you into the adjoining office apartment for a few minutes. I am expecting a very wealthy old gentleman on business connected with a will. In a very short while I will join you, and continue our consultation.'

With his accustomed chivalrous manner, Lawyer Gooch ushered his soulful client into the remaining unoccupied room, and came out, closing the door with circumspection.

The next visitor introduced by Archibald was a thin, nervous, irritable-looking man of middle age, with a worried and apprehensive expression of countenance. He carried in one hand a small satchel, which he set down upon the floor beside the chair which the lawyer placed for him. His clothing was of good quality, but it was worn without regard to neatness or style, and appeared to be covered with the dust of travel.

You make a specialty of divorce cases,' he said, in an agitated but businesslike tone.

'I may say,' began Lawyer Gooch, 'that my practice has not altogether avoided –'

, 'I know you do,' interrupted client number three. 'You needn't tell me. I've heard all about you. I have a case to lay before you without necessarily disclosing any connection that I might have with it – that is –'

'You wish,' said Lawyer Gooch, 'to state a hypothetical case.'

'You may call it that. I am a plain man of business. I will be as brief as possible. We will first take up the hypothetical woman. We will say she is married uncongenially. In many ways she is a superior woman. Physically she is considered to be handsome. She is devoted to what she calls literature – poetry and prose, and such stuff. Her husband is a plain man in the business walks of life. Their home has not been happy, although the husband has tried to make it so. Some time ago a man – a stranger – came to the peaceful town in which they lived and engaged in some real estate operations. This woman met him, and became unaccountably infatuated with him. Her attentions became so open that the man felt the community to be no safe place for him, so he left it. She abandoned husband and home, and followed him. She forsook her home, where she was provided with every comfort, to follow this man who had inspired her with such a strange affection. Is there anything more to be deplored,' concluded the client, in a trembling voice, 'than the wrecking of a home by a woman's uncalculating folly?'

Lawyer Gooch delivered the cautious opinion that there was not.

'This man she has gone to join,' resumed the visitor, 'is not the man to make her happy. It is a wild and foolish self-deception that makes her think he will. Her husband, in spite of their many disagreements, is the only one capable of dealing with her sensitive and peculiar nature. But this she does not realize now.'

'Would you consider a divorce the logical cure in the case you present?' asked Lawyer Gooch, who felt that the conversation was wandering too far from the field of business.

'A divorce!' exclaimed the client, feelingly – almost tearfully. 'No, no – not that. I have read, Mr. Gooch, of many instances where your sympathy and kindly interest led you to act as a mediator between estranged husband and wife, and brought them together again. Let us drop the hypothetical case – I need conceal no longer that it is I who am the sufferer in this said affair – the names you shall have – Thomas R. Billings and Wife – and Henry K. Jessup, the man with whom she is infatuated.'

Client number three laid his hand upon Mr. Gooch's arm. Deep emotion was written upon his careworn face. 'For Heaven's sake,' he said fervently, 'help me in this hour of trouble. Seek out Mrs. Billings, and persuade her to abandon this distressing pursuit of her lamentable folly. Tell her, Mr. Gooch, that her husband is willing to receive her back to his heart and home – promise her anything that will induce her to return. I have heard of your success in these matters. Mrs. Billings cannot be very far away. I am worn out with travel and weariness. Twice during the pursuit I saw her, but various circumstances prevented our having an interview. Will you undertake this mission for me, Mr. Gooch, and earn my everlasting gratitude?'

'It is true,' said Lawyer Gooch, frowning slightly at the other's last words, but immediately calling up an expression of virtuous benevolence, 'that on a number of occasions I have been successful in persuading couples who sought the severing of their matrimonial bonds to think better of their rash intentions and return to their homes reconciled. But I assure you that the work is often exceedingly difficult. The amount of argument, perseverance, and, if I may be allowed to say it, eloquence that it requires would astonish you. But this is a case in which my sympathies would be wholly enlisted. I feel deeply for you sir, and I would be most happy to see husband and wife reunited. But my time,' concluded the lawyer, looking at his watch as if suddenly reminded of the fact, 'is valuable.'

'I am aware of that,' said the client, 'and if you will take the case and persuade Mrs. Billings to return home and leave the man alone that she is following – on that day I will pay you the sum of one thousand dollars. I have made a little money in real estate during the recent boom in Susanville, and I will not begrudge that amount.'

'Retain your seat for a few moments, please,' said Lawyer Gooch, arising and again consulting his watch. 'I have another client waiting in an adjoining room whom I had very nearly forgotten. I will return in the briefest possible space.'

The situation was now one that fully satisfied Lawyer Gooch's love of intricacy and complication. He revelled in cases that presented such subtle problems and possibilities. It pleased him to think that he was master of the happiness and fate of the three individuals who sat, unconscious of one another's presence, within his reach. His old figure of the ship glided into his mind. But now the figure failed, for to have filled every compartment of an actual vessel would have been to endanger her safety; while here, with his compartments full, his ship of affairs could but sail on to the advantageous port of a fine, fat fee. The thing for him to do, of course, was to wring the best bargain he could from some one of his anxious cargo.

First he called to the office boy: 'Lock the outer door, Archibald, and admit no one.' Then he moved, with long, silent strides, into the room in which client number one waited. That gentleman sat, patiently scanning the pictures in the magazine, with a cigar in his mouth and his feet upon a table.

'Well,' he remarked, cheerfully, as the lawyer entered, 'have you made up your mind? Does five hundred dollars go for getting the fair lady a divorce?'

'You mean that as a retainer?' asked Lawyer Gooch, softly interrogative.

'Hey? No; for the whole job. It's enough, ain't it?'

'My fee,' said Lawyer Gooch, 'would be one thousand five hundred dollars. Five hundred dollars down, and the remainder upon issuance of the divorce.'

A loud whistle came from client number one. His feet descended to the floor.

'Guess we can't close the deal,' he said, arising. 'I cleaned up five hundred dollars in a little real estate dicker down in Susanville. I'd do anything I could to free the lady, but it outsizes my pile.'

'Could you stand one thousand two hundred dollars?' asked the lawyer, insinuatingly.

'Five hundred is my limit, I tell you. Guess I'll have to hunt up a cheaper lawyer.' The client put on his hat.

'Out this way, please,' said Lawyer Gooch, opening the door that led into the hallway.

As the gentleman flowed out of the compartment and down the stairs, Lawyer Gooch smiled to himself. 'Exit Mr. Jessup,' he murmured, as he fingered the Henry Clay tuft of hair at his ear. 'And now for the forsaken husband.' He returned to the middle office, and assumed a businesslike manner.

'I understand,' he said to client number three, 'that you agree to pay one thousand dollars if I bring about, or am instrumental in bringing about, the return of Mrs. Billings to her home, and her abandonment of her infatuated pursuit of the man for whom she has conceived such a violent fancy. Also that the case is now unreservedly in my hands on that basis. Is that correct?'

'Entirely,' said the other, eagerly. 'And I can produce the cash any time at two hours' notice.'

Lawyer Gooch stood up at his full height. His thin figure seemed to expand. His thumbs sought the armholes of his vest. Upon his face was a look of sympathetic benignity that he always wore during such undertakings.

'Then, sir,' he said, in kindly tones, 'I think I can promise you an early relief from your troubles. I have that much confidence in my powers of argument and persuasion, in the natural impules of the human heart towards good, and in the strong influence of a husband's unfaltering love. Mrs. Billings, sir, is here – in that room—' the lawyer's long arm pointed to the door. 'I will call her in at at once; and our united pleadings—'

Lawyer Gooch paused, for client number three had leaped from his chair as if propelled by steel springs, and clutched at his satchel.

'What the devil,' he exclaimed, harshly, 'do you mean? That woman in there! I thought I shook her off forty miles back.'

He ran to the open window, looked out below, and threw one leg over the sill.

'Stop!' cried Lawyer Gooch, in amazement. 'What would you do? Come, Mr. Billings, and face your erring but innocent wife. Our combined entreaties cannot fail to—'

'Billings!' shouted the now thoroughly moved client; 'I'll Billings you, you old idiot!'

Turning, he hurled his satchel with fury at the lawyer's head. It struck that astounded peacemaker between the eyes, causing him to stagger backward a pace or two. When Lawyer Gooch recovered his wits he saw that his client had disappeared. Rushing to the window, he leaned out, and saw the recreant gathering himself up from the top of a shed upon which he had dropped from the second-story window. Without stopping to collect his hat he then plunged downward the remaining ten feet to the alley, up which he flew with prodigious celerity until the surrounding building swallowed him up from view.

Lawyer Gooch passed his hand tremblingly across his brow. It was an habitual act with him, serving to clear his thoughts. Perhaps also it now seemed to soothe the spot where a very hard alligator-hide satchel had struck.

The satchel lay upon the floor, wide open, with its contents spilled about. Mechanically Lawyer Gooch stooped to gather up the articles. The first was a collar; and the omniscient eye of the man of law perceived, wonderingly, the initials H. K. J. marked upon it. Then came a comb, a brush, a folded map and a piece of soap. Lastly, a handful of old business letters, addressed – every one of them – to 'Henry K. Jessup, Esq.'

Lawyer Gooch closed the satchel, and set it upon the table. He hesitated for a moment, and then put on his hat and walked into the office boy's anteroom.

'Archibald,' he said mildly, as he opened the hall door, 'I am going to the Supreme Court rooms. In five minutes you may step into the inner office, and inform the lady who is waiting there that' – here Lawyer Gooch made use of the vernacular – 'that there's nothing doing.'

CALLOWAY'S CODE

THE NEW YORK ENTERPRISE sent H. B. Calloway as special correspondent to the Russo-Japanese-Portsmouth war.

For two months Calloway hung about Yokohama and Tokio, shaking dice with the other correspondents for drinks of 'rickshaws – oh, no, that's something to ride in; anyhow, he wasn't earning the salary that his paper was paying him. But that was not Calloway's fault. The little brown men who held the strings of Fate between their fingers were not ready for the readers of the Enterprise to season their breakfast bacon and eggs with the battles of the descendants of the gods.

But soon the column of correspondents that were to go out with the First Army tightened their field-glass belts and went down to the Yalu with Kuroki. Calloway was one of these.

Now, this is no history of the battle of Yalu River. That has been told in detail by the correspondents who gazed at the shrapnel smoke rings from a distance of three miles. But, for justice's sake, let it be understood that the Japanese commander prohibited a nearer view.

Calloway's feat was accomplished before the battle. What he did was to furnish the *Enterprise* with the biggest beat of the war. That paper published exclusively and in detail the news of the attack on the lines of the Russian General Zassulitch on the same day that it was made. No other paper printed a word about it for two days afterward, except a London paper, whose account was absolutely incorrect and untrue.

Calloway did this in face of the fact that General Kuroki was making his moves and laying his plans with the profoundest secrecy as far as the world outside his camps was concerned. The correspondents were forbidden to send out any news whatever of his plans; and every message that was allowed on the wires was censored with rigid severity.

The correspondent for the London paper handed in a cablegram describing Kuroki's plans; but as it was wrong from beginning to end the censor grinned and let it go through.

So, there they were – Kuroki on one side of the Yalu with forty-two thousand infantry, five thousand cavalry, and one hundred and twenty-four guns. On the other side Zassulitch waited for him with only twenty-three thousand men, and with a long stretch of river to guard. And Calloway had got hold of some important inside information that he knew would bring the *Enterprise* staff around a cablegram as thick as flies around a Park Row lemonade stand. If he could only get that message past the censor – the new censor who had arrived and taken his post that day!

Calloway did the obviously proper thing. He lit his pipe and sat down on a gun carriage to think it over. And there we must leave him; for the rest of the story belongs to Vesey, a sixteen-dollar-a-week reporter on the *Enterprise*.

Calloway's cablegram was handed to the managing editor at four o'clock in the afternoon. He read it three times; and then drew a pocket mirror from a pigeon-hole in his desk, and looked at his reflection carefully. Then he went over to the desk of Boyd, his assistant (he usually called Boyd when he wanted him), and laid the cablegram before him.

'It's from Calloway,' he said. 'See what you make of it.'

The message was dated at Wi-ju, and these were the words of it:

Foregone preconcerted rash witching goes muffled rumor mine dark silent unfortunate richmond existing great hotly brute select mooted parlous beggars ye angel incontrovertible.

Boyd read it twice.

'It's either a cipher or a sunstroke,' said he.

'Ever hear of anything like a code in the office – a secret code?' asked the m. e., who had held his desk for only two years. Managing editors come and go.

'None except the vernacular that the lady specials write in,' said Boyd. 'Couldn't be an acrostic, could it?'

'I thought of that,' said the m. e., 'but the beginning letters contain only four vowels. It must be a code of some sort.'

'Try 'em in groups,' suggested Boyd. 'Let's see – "Rash witching goes" not with me it doesn't. "Muffled rumor mine" – must have an underground wire. "Dark silent unfortunate richmond" – no reason why he should knock that town so hard. "Existing great hotly" – no, it doesn't pan out. I'll call Scott.'

The city editor came in a hurry, and tried his luck. A city editor must know something about everything; so Scott knew a little about cipher-writing.

'It may be what is called an inverted alphabet cipher,' said he. 'I'll try that. "R" seems to be the oftenest used initial letter, with the exception of "m." Assuming "r" to mean "e," the most frequently used vowel, we transpose the letters – so.'

Scott worked rapidly with his pencil for two minutes; and then showed the first word according to his reading – the word 'Scejtzez.'

'Great!' cried Boyd. 'It's a charade. My first is a Russian General. Go on, Scott.'

'No, that won't work,' said the city editor. 'It's undoubtedly a code. It's impossible to read it without the key. Has the office ever used a cipher code?'

'Just what I was asking,' said the m. e. 'Hustle everybody up that ought to know. We must get at it some way. Calloway has evidently got hold of something big, and the censor has put the screws on, or he wouldn't have cabled in a lot of chop suey like this.'

Throughout the office of the *Enterprise* a dragnet was sent, hauling in such members of the staff as would be likely to know of a code, past or present, by reason of their wisdom, information, natural intelligence, or length of servitude. They got together in a group in the city room, with the m. e. in the centre. No one had heard of a code. All began to explain to the head investigator that newspapers never use a code, anyhow – that is, a cipher code. Of course the Associated Press stuff is a sort of code – an abbreviation, rather – but—

The m. e. knew all that, and said so. He asked each man how long he had worked on the paper. Not one of them had drawn pay from an *Enterprise* envelope for longer than six years. Calloway had been on the paper twelve years.

'Try old Heffelbauer,' said the m. e. 'He was here when Park Row was a potato patch.'

Heffelbauer was an institution. He was half janitor, half handyman about the office, and half watchman – thus becoming the peer of thirteen and one-half tailors. Sent for, he came, radiating his nationality.

'Heffelbauer,' said the m. e., 'did you ever hear of a code belonging to the office a long time ago – a private code? You know what a code is, don't you?'

'Yah,' said Heffelbauer. 'Sure I know vat a code is. Yah, apout dwelf or fifteen year ago der office had a code. Der reborters in der city-room haf it here.'

'Ah!' said the m. e. 'We're getting on the trail now. Where was it kept, Heffelbauer? What do you know about it?'

'Somedimes,' said the retainer, 'dey keep it in der little room behind der library room.'

'Can you find it?' asked the m. e., eagerly. 'Do you know where it is?'

'Mein Gott!' said Heffelbauer. 'How long you dink a code live? Der

reborters call him a maskeet. But von day he butt mit his head der editor,
und—'

'Oh, he's talking about a goat,' said Boyd. 'Get out, Heffelbauer.'

Again discomfited, the concerted wit and resource of the *Enterprise* huddled
around Calloway's puzzle, considering its mysterious words in vain.

Then Vesey came in.

Vesey was the youngest reporter. He had a thirty-two-inch chest and wore
a number fourteen collar; but his bright Scotch plaid suit gave him presence
and conferred no obscurity upon his whereabouts. He wore his hat in such
a position that people followed him about to see him take it off, convinced
that it must be hung upon a peg driven into the back of his head. He was
never without an immense, knotted, hard-wood cane with a German-silver
tip on its crooked handle. Vesey was the best photograph hustler in the office.
Scott said it was because no living human being could resist the personal
triumph it was to hand his picture over to Vesey. Vesey always wrote his
own news stories, except the big ones, which were sent to the rewrite men.
Add to this fact that among the inhabitants, temples, and groves of the earth
nothing existed that could abash Vesey, and his dim sketch is concluded.

Vesey butted into the circle of cipher readers very much as Heffelbauer's
'code' would have done, and asked what was up. Some one explained, with
the touch of half-familiar condescension that they always used toward him.
Vesey reached out and took the cablegram from the m. e.'s hand. Under the
protection of some special Providence, he was always doing appalling things
like that, and coming off unscathed.

'It's a code,' said Vesey. 'Anybody got the key?'

'The office has no code,' said Boyd, reaching for the message. Vesey held
to it.

'Then old Calloway expects us to read it, anyhow,' said he. 'He's up a tree,
or something, and he's made this up so as to get it by the censor. It's up to
us. Gee! I wish they had sent me, too. Say – we can't afford to fall down on
our end of it. "Foregone, preconcerted rash, witching" – h'm.'

Vesey sat down on a table corner and began to whistle softly, frowning at
the cablegram.

'Let's have it, please,' said the m. e. 'We've got to get to work on it.'

'I believe I've got a line on it,' said Vesey. 'Give me ten minutes.'

He walked to his desk, threw his hat into a waste-basket, spread out flat
on his chest like a gorgeous lizard, and started his pencil going. The wit and
wisdom of the *Enterprise* remained in a loose group, and smiled at one
another, nodding their heads toward Vesey. Then they began to exchange
their theories about the cipher.

It took Vesey exactly fifteen minutes. He brought to the m. e. a pad with
the code-key written on it.

'I felt the swing of it as soon as I saw it,' said Vesey. 'Hurrah for old
Calloway! He's done the Japs and every paper in town that prints literature
instead of news. Take a look at that.'

Thus had Vesey set forth the reading of the code:

Foregone–conclusion	Existing–conditions
Preconcerted–arrangement	Great–White Way
Rash–act	Hotly–contested
Witching–hour of midnight	Brute–force

Goes–without saying   Select–few
Muffled–report   Mooted–question
Rumor–hath it   Parlous–times
Mine–host   Beggars–description
Dark–horse   Ye–correspondent
Silent–majority   Angel–unawares
Unfortunate–pedestrians[1]   Incontrovertible–fact
Richmond–in the field

'It's simply newspaper English,' explained Vesey. 'I've been reporting on the *Enterprise* long enough to know it by heart. Old Calloway gives us the cue word, and we use the word that naturally follows it just as we use 'em in the paper. Read it over, and you'll see how pat they drop into their places. Now, here's the message he intended us to get.'
Vesey handed out another sheet of paper.

Concluded arrangement to act at hour of midnight without saying. Report hath it that a large body of cavalry and an overwhelming force of infantry will be thrown into the field. Conditions white. Way contested by only a small force. Question the *Times* description. Its correspondent is unaware of the facts.

'Great stuff!' cried Boyd, excitedly. 'Kuroki crosses the Yalu tonight and attacks. Oh, we won't do a thing to the sheets that make up with Addison's essays, real estate transfers, and bowling scores!'
'Mr. Vesey,' said the m. e., with his jollying-which-you-should-regard-as-a-favor manner, 'you have cast a serious reflection upon the literary standards of the paper that employs you. You have also assisted materially in giving us the biggest 'beat' of the year. I will let you know in a day or two whether you are to be discharged or retained at larger salary. Somebody send Ames to me.'
Ames was the king-pin, the snowy-petalled marguerite, the star-bright looloo of the rewrite men. He saw attempted murder in the pains of green-apple colic, cyclones in the summer zephyr, lost children in every top-spinning urchin, an uprising of the down-trodden masses in every hurling of a derelict potato at a passing automobile. When not rewriting, Ames sat on the porch of his Brooklyn villa playing checkers with his ten-year-old son.
Ames and the 'war editor' shut themselves in a room. There was a map in there stuck full of little pins that represented armies and divisions. Their fingers had been itching for days to move those pins along the crooked line of the Yalu. They did so now; and in words of fire Ames translated Calloway's brief message into a front page masterpiece that set the world talking. He told of the secret councils of the Japanese officers; gave Kuroki's flaming speeches in full; counted the cavalry and infantry to a man and a horse; described the quick and silent building of the bridge at Suikauchen, across which the Mikado's legions were hurled upon the surprised Zassulitch,

[1]Mr. Vesey afterward explained that the logical journalistic complement of the word 'unfortunate' was once the word 'victim.' But, since the automobile became so popular, the correct following word is now 'pedestrians.' Of course, in Calloway's code it meant infantry.

whose troops were widely scattered along the river. And the battle! – well, you know what Ames can do with a battle if you give him just one smell of smoke for a foundation. And in the same story, with seemingly supernatural knowledge, he gleefully scored the most profound and ponderous paper in England for the false and misleading account of the intended movements of the Japanese First Army printed in its issue of *the same date*.

Only one error was made; and that was the fault of the cable operator at Wi-ju. Calloway pointed it out after he come back. The word 'great' in his code should have been 'gage' and its complemental words 'of battle.' But it went to Ames 'conditions white,' and of course he took that to mean snow. His description of the Japanese army struggling through the snowstorm, blinded by whirling flakes, was thrillingly vivid. The artists turned out some effective illustrations that made a hit as pictures of the artillery dragging their guns through the drifts. But, as the attack was made on the first day of May, the 'conditions white' excited some amusement. But it made no difference to the *Enterprise*, anyway.

It was wonderful. And Calloway was wonderful in having made the new censor believe that his jargon of words meant no more than a complaint of the dearth of news and a petition for more expense money. And Vesey was wonderful. And most wonderful of all are words, and how they make friends one with another, being oft associated, until not even obituary notices them do part.

On the second day following, the city editor halted at Vesey's desk where the reporter was writing the story of a man who had broken his leg by falling into a coal-hole – Ames having failed to find a murder motive in it.

'The old man says your salary is to be raised to twenty a week,' said Scott.

'All right,' said Vesey. 'Every little helps. Say – Mr. Scott, which would you say – "We can state without fear of successful contradiction," or, "On the whole it can be safely asserted"?'

A MATTER OF MEAN ELEVATION

ONE WINTER THE ALCAZAR OPERA Company of New Orleans made a speculative trip along the Mexican, Central American, and South American coasts. The venture proved a most successful one. The music-loving, impressionable Spanish-Americans deluged the company with dollars and 'vivas.' The manager waxed plump and amiable. But for the prohibitive climate he would have put forth the distinctive flower of his prosperity – the overcoat of fur, braided, frogged, and opulent. Almost was he persuaded to raise the salaries of his company. But with a mighty effort he conquered the impulse toward such an unprofitable effervescence of joy.

At Macuto, on the coast of Venezuela, the company scored its greatest success. Imagine Coney Island translated into Spanish and you will comprehend Macuto. The fashionable season is from November to March. Down from La Guayra and Caracas and Valencia and other interior towns flock the people for their holiday season. There are bathing and fiestas and bull fights and scandal. And then the people have a passion for music that the bands in the plaza and on the sea beach stir but do not satisfy. The coming of the

Alcazar Opera Company aroused the utmost ardor and zeal among the pleasure seekers.

The illustrious Guzman Blanco, President and Dictator of Venezuela, sojourned in Macuto with his court for the season. That potent ruler – who himself paid a subsidy of 40,000 pesos each year to grand opera in Caracas – ordered one of the government warehouses to be cleared for a temporary theatre. A stage was quickly constructed and rough wooden benches made for the audience. Private boxes were added for the use of the President and the notables of the army and Government.

The company remained in Macuto for two weeks. Each performance filled the house as closely as it could be packed. Then the music-mad people fought for room in the open doors and windows, and crowded about, hundreds deep on the outside. Those audiences formed a brilliantly diversified patch of color. The hue of their faces ranged from the clear olive of the pure-blood Spaniards down through the yellow and brown shades of the mestizos to the coal-black Carib and the Jamaica Negro. Scattered among them were little groups of Indians with faces like stone idols, wrapped in gaudy fibre-woven blankets – Indians down from the mountain states of Zamora and Los Andes and Miranda to trade their gold dust in the coast towns.

The spell cast upon these denizens of the interior fastnesses was remarkable. They sat in petrified ecstasy, conspicuous among the excitable Macutians, who wildly strove with tongue and hand to give evidence of their delight. Only once did the sombre rapture of these aboriginals find expression. During the rendition of 'Faust,' Guzman Blanco, extravagantly pleased by the 'Jewel Song,' cast upon the stage a purse of gold pieces. Other distinguished citizens followed his lead to the extent of whatever loose coin they had convenient, while some of the fair and fashionable señoras were moved, in imitation, to fling a jewel or a ring or two at the feet of the Marguerite – who was, according to the bills, Mlle Nina Giraud. Then from different parts of the house rose sundry of the stolid hillmen and cast upon the stage little brown and dun bags that fell with soft 'thumps' and did not rebound. It was, no doubt, pleasure at the tribute to her art that caused Mlle Giraud's eyes to shine so brightly when she opened these little deerskin bags in her dressing room and found them to contain pure gold dust. If so, the pleasure was rightly hers, for her voice in song, pure, strong, and thrilling with the feeling of the emotional artist, deserved the tribute that it earned.

But the triumph of the Alcazar Opera Company is not the theme: it but leans upon and colors it. There happened in Macuto a tragic thing, an unsolvable mystery, that sobered for a time the gaiety of the happy season.

One evening between the short twilight and the time when she should have whirled upon the stage in the red and black of the ardent Carmen, Mlle Nina Giraud disappeared from the sight and ken of 6,000 pairs of eyes and as many minds in Macuto. There was the usual turmoil and hurrying to seek her. Messengers flew to the little French-kept hotel where she stayed; others of the company hastened here or there where she might be lingering in some *tienda* or unduly prolonging her bath upon the beach. All search was fruitless. Mademoiselle had vanished.

Half an hour passed, and she did not appear. The dictator, unused to the caprices of prime donne, became impatient. He sent an aide from his box to say to the manager that if the curtain did not at once rise he would immediately hale the entire company to the calabosa, though it would desolate his heart, indeed, to be compelled to such an act. Birds in Macuto could be made to sing.

The manager abandoned hope, for the time, of Mlle Giraud. A member of the chorus, who had dreamed hopelessly for years of the blessed opportunity, quickly Carmenized herself and the opera went on.

Afterward, when the lost cantatrice appeared not, the aid of the authorities was invoked. The President at once set the army, the police, and all citizens to the search. Not one clue to Mlle Giraud's disappearance was found. The Alcazar left to fill engagements farther down the coast.

On the way back the steamer stopped at Macuto and the manager made anxious inquiry. Not a trace of the lady had been discovered. The Alcazar could do no more. The personal belongings of the missing lady were stored in the hotel against her possible later reappearance and the opera company continued upon its homeward voyage to New Orleans.

On the *camino real* along the beach the two saddle mules and the four pack mules of Señor Don Johnny Armstrong stood, patiently awaiting the crack of the whip of the *arriero*, Luis. That would be the signal for the start on another long journey into the mountains. The pack mules were loaded with a varied assortment of hardware and cutlery. These articles Don Johnny traded to the interior Indians for the gold dust that they washed from the Andean streams and stored in quills and bags against his coming. It was a profitable business, and Señor Armstrong expected soon to be able to purchase the coffee plantation that he coveted.

Armstrong stood on the narrow sidewalk, exchanging garbled Spanish with old Peralto, the rich native merchant who had just charged him four prices for half a gross of pot-metal hatchets, and abridged English with Rucker, the little German who was Consul for the United States.

'Take with you, señor,' said Peralto, 'the blessings of the saints upon your journey.'

'Better try quinine,' growled Rucker through his pipe. 'Take two grains every night. And don't make your trip too long, Johnny, because we haf needs of you. It is ein villainous game dot Melville play of whist, and dere is no oder substitute. *Auf wiedersehen*, und keep your eyes dot mule's ear between when you on der edge of der brecipices ride.'

The bells of Luis's mule jingled and the pack train filed after the warning note. Armstrong waved a good-bye and took his place at the trail of the procession. Up the narrow street they turned, and passed the two-story wooden Hotel Inglés where Ives and Dawson and Richards and the rest of the chaps were dawdling on the broad piazza, reading week-old newspapers. They crowded to the railing and shouted many friendly and wise and foolish farewells after him. Across the plaza they trotted slowly past the bronze statue of Guzman Blanco, within its fence of bayoneted rifles captured from revolutionists, and out of the town between the rows of thatched huts swarming with the unclothed youth of Macuto. They plunged into the damp coolness of banana groves at length to emerge upon a bright stream, where brown women in scant raiment laundered clothes destructively upon the rocks. Then the pack train, fording the stream, attacked the sudden ascent, and bade adieu to such civilization as the coast afforded.

For weeks Armstrong, guided by Luis, followed his regular route among the mountains. After he had collected an arroba of the precious metal, winning a profit of nearly $5,000, the heads of the lightened mules were

turned down-trail again. Where the head of the Guarico River springs from
a great gash in the mountainside, Luis halted the train.

'Half a day's journey from here, Señor,' said he, 'is the village of Tacuzama,
which we have never visited. I think many ounces of gold may be procured
there. It is worth the trial.'

Armstrong concurred, and they turned again upward toward Tacuzama.
The trail was abrupt and precipitous, mounting through a dense forest. As
night fell, dark and gloomy, Luis once more halted. Before them was a black
chasm, bisecting the path as far as they could see.

Luis dismounted. 'There should be a bridge,' he called, and ran along the
cleft a distance. 'It is here,' he cried, and remounting, led the way. In a few
moments Armstrong heard a sound as though a thunderous drum were
beating somewhere in the dark. It was the falling of the mules' hoofs upon
the bridge made of strong hides lashed to poles and stretched across the
chasm. Half a mile further was Tacuzama. The village was a congregation
of rock and mud huts set in that profundity of an obscure wood. As they
rode in a sound inconsistent with that brooding solitude met their ears. From
a long, low mud hut that they were nearing rose the glorious voice of a
woman in song. The words were English, the air familiar to Armstrong's
memory, but not to his musical knowledge.

He slipped from his mule and stole to a narrow window in one end of the
house. Peering cautiously inside, he saw, within three feet of him, a woman
of marvellous, imposing beauty, clothed in a splendid loose robe of leopard
skins. The hut was packed close to the small space in which she stood with
the squatting figures of Indians.

The woman finished her song and seated herself close to the little window,
as if grateful for the unpolluted air that entered it. When she had ceased
several of the audience rose and cast little softly falling bags at her feet. A
harsh murmur – no doubt a barbarous kind of applause and comment – went
through the grim assembly.

Armstrong was used to seizing opportunities promptly. Taking advantage
of the noise he called to the women in a low but distinct voice: 'Do not turn
your head this way, but listen. I am an American. If you need assistance tell
me how I can render it. Answer as briefly as you can.'

The woman was worthy of his boldness. Only by a sudden flush of her
pale cheek did she acknowledge understanding of his words. Then she spoke,
scarcely moving her lips.

'I am held a prisoner by these Indians. God knows I need help. In two
hours come to the little hut twenty yards toward the mountainside. There
will be a light and a red curtain in the window. There is always a guard at
the door whom you will have to overcome. For the love of heaven, do not
fail to come.'

The story seems to shrink from adventure and rescue and mystery. The
theme is one too gentle for those brave and quickening tones. And yet it
reaches as far back as time itself. It has been named 'environment,' which
is a weak a word as any to express the unnamable kinship of man to nature,
that queer fraternity that causes stones and trees and salt water and clouds
to play upon our emotions. Why are we made serious and solemn and
sublime by mountain heights, grave and contemplative by an abundance of
overhanging trees, reduced to inconstancy and monkey capers by the ripples
on a sandy beach? Did the protoplasm – but enough. The chemists are

looking into the matter, and before long they will have all life in the table of the symbols.

Briefly, then, in order to confine the story within scientific bounds, John Armstrong went to the hut, choked the Indian guard and carried away Mlle Giraud. With her was also conveyed a number of pounds of gold dust she had collected during her six months' forced engagement in Tacuzama. The Carabobo Indians are easily the most enthusiastic lovers of music between the equator and the French Opera House in New Orleans. They are also strong believers that the advice of Emerson was good when he said: 'The thing thou wantest, O discontented man – take it, and pay the price.' A number of them had attended the performance of the Alcazar Opera Company in Macuto, and found Mlle Giraud's style and technique satisfactory. They wanted her, so they took her one evening suddenly and without any fuss. They treated her with much consideration, exacting only one song recital each day. She was quite pleased at being rescued by Mr. Armstrong. So much for mystery and adventure. Now to resume the theory of the protoplasm.

John Armstrong and Mlle Giraud rode among the Andean peaks, enveloped in their greatness and sublimity. The mightiest cousins, furthest removed, in Nature's great family became conscious of the tie. Among those huge piles of primordial upheaval, amid those gigantic silences and elongated fields of distance the littlenesses of men are precipitated as one chemical throws down a sediment from another. They moved reverently, as in a temple. Their souls were uplifted in unison with the stately heights. They traveled in a zone of majesty and peace.

To Armstrong the woman seemed almost a holy thing. Yet bathed in the white, still dignity of her martyrdom that purified her earthly beauty and gave out, it seemed, an aura of transcendent loveliness, in those first hours of companionship she drew from him an adoration that was half human love, half the worship of a descended goddess.

Never yet since her rescue had she smiled. Over her dress she still wore the robe of leopard skins, for the mountain air was cold. She looked to be some splendid princess belonging to those wild and awesome altitudes. The spirit of the region chimed with hers. Her eyes were always turned upon the somber cliffs, the blue gorges, and the snow-clad turrets, looking a sublime melancholy equal to their own. At times on the journey she sang thrilling te deums and misereres that struck the true note of the hills, and made their route seem like a solemn march down a cathedral aisle. The rescued one spoke but seldom, her mood partaking of the hush of nature that surrounded them. Armstrong looked upon her as an angel. He could not bring himself to the sacrilege of attempting to woo her as other women may be wooed.

On the third day they had descended as far as the *tierra templada*, the zone of the table lands and foot hills. The mountains were receding in their rear, but still towered, exhibiting yet impressively their formidable heads. Here they met signs of man. They saw the white houses of coffee plantations gleam across the clearings. They struck into a road where they met travelers and pack-mules. Cattle were grazing on the slopes. They passed a little village where the round-eyed *niños* shrieked and called at sight of them.

Mlle Giraud laid aside her leopard-skin robe. It seemed to be a trifle incongruous now. In the mountains it had appeared fitting and natural. And if Armstrong was not mistaken she laid aside with it something of the high dignity of her demeanor. As the country became more populous and significant of comfortable life he saw, with a feeling of joy, that the exalted princess and priestess of the Andean peaks was changing to a woman – an earth woman, but no less enticing. A little color crept to the surface of her marble cheek. She arranged the conventional dress that the removal of the robe now disclosed with the solicitous touch of one who is conscious of the eyes of others. She smoothed the careless sweep of her hair. A mundane interest, long latent in the chilling atmosphere of the ascetic peaks, showed in her eyes.

This thaw in his divinity sent Armstrong's heart going faster. So might an Arctic explorer thrill at his first ken of green fields and liquescent waters. They were on a lower plane of earth and life and were succumbing to its peculiar, subtle influence. The austerity of the hills no longer thinned the air they breathed. About them was the breath of fruit and corn and builded homes, the comfortable smell of smoke and warm earth and the consolations man has placed between himself and the dust of his brother earth from which he sprung. While traversing those awful mountains, Mlle Giraud had seemed to be wrapped in their spirit of reverent reserve. Was this that same woman – now palpitating, warm, eager, throbbing with conscious life and charm, feminine to her fingertips? Pondering over this, Armstrong felt certain misgivings intrude upon his thoughts. He wished he could stop there with this changing creature, descending no farther. Here was the elevation and environment to which her nature seemed to respond with its best. He feared to go down upon the man-dominated levels. Would her spirit not yield still further in that artificial zone to which they were descending?

Now from a little plateau they saw the sea flash at the edge of the green lowlands. Mlle Giraud gave a little, catching sigh.

'Oh, look, Mr. Armstrong, there is the sea! Isn't it lovely? I'm so tired of mountains.' She heaved a pretty shoulder in a gesture of repugnance. 'Those horrid Indians! Just think of what I suffered! Although I suppose I attained my ambition of becoming a stellar attraction, I wouldn't care to repeat the engagement. It was very nice of you to bring me away. Tell me, Mr. Armstrong – honestly, now – do I look such an awful, awful fright? I haven't looked into a mirror, you know, for months.'

Armstrong made answer according to his changed moods. Also he laid his hand upon hers as it rested upon the horn of her saddle. Luis was at the head of the pack train and could not see. She allowed it to remain there, and her eyes smiled frankly into his.

Then at sundown they dropped upon the coast level under the palms and lemons among the vivid greens and scarlets and ochres of the *tierra caliente*. They rode into Macuto, and saw the line of volatile bathers frolicking in the surf. The mountains were very far away.

Mlle Giraud's eyes were shining with a joy that could not have existed under the chaperonage of the mountain-tops. There were other spirits calling to her – nymphs of the orange groves, pixies from the chattering surfs, imps, born of the music, the perfumes, colors and the insinuating presence of humanity. She laughed aloud, musically, at a sudden thought.

'Won't there be a sensation?' she called to Armstrong. 'Don't I wish I had an engagement just now, though! What a picnic the press agent would have! "Held a prisoner by a band of savage Indians subdued by the spell of her wonderful voice" – wouldn't that make great stuff? But I guess I quit the game winner, anyhow – there ought to be a couple of thousand dollars in that sack of gold dust I collected as encores, don't you think?'

He left her at the door of the little Hotel de Buen Descansar, where she had stopped before. Two hours later he returned to the hotel. He glanced in at the open door of the little combined reception room and café.

Half a dozen of Macuto's representative social and official *caballeros* were distributed about the room. Señor Villablanca, the wealthy rubber concessionist, reposed his fat figure on two chairs, with an emollient smile beaming upon his chocolate-colored face. Guilbert, the French mining engineer, leered through his polished nose-glasses. Colonel Mendez, of the regular army, in gold-laced uniform and fatuous grin, was busily extracting corks from champagne bottles. Other patterns of Macutian gallantry and fashion pranced and posed. The air was hazy with cigarette smoke. Wine dripped upon the floor.

Perched upon a table in the centre of the room in an attitude of easy pre-eminence was Mlle Giraud. A chic costume of white lawn and cherry ribbons supplanted her traveling garb. There was a suggestion of lace, and a frill or two, with a discreet, small implication of hand-embroidered pink hosiery. Upon her lap rested a guitar. In her face was the light of resurrection, the peace of elysium attained through fire and suffering. She was singing to a lively accompaniment a little song:

'When you see de big round moon
Comin' up like a balloon,
Dis nigger skips fur to kiss de lips
Of his stylish, black-faced coon.'

The singer caught sight of Armstrong.

'Hi! there, Johnny,' she called; 'I've been expecting you for an hour. What kept you? Gee! but these smoked guys are the slowest you ever saw. They ain't on, at all. Come along in, and I'll make this coffee-colored old sport with the gold epaulettes open one for you right off the ice.'

'Thank you,' said Armstrong; 'not just now, I believe. I've several things to attend to.'

He walked out and down the street, and met Rucker coming up from the Consulate.

'Play you a game of billiards,' said Armstrong. 'I want something to take the taste of the sea level out of my mouth.'

'GIRL'

IN GILT LETTERS ON THE ground glass of the door of room No. 962 were the words: 'Robbins & Hartley, Brokers.' The clerks had gone. It was past five, and with the solid tramp of a drove of prize Percherons, scrub-women were invading the cloud-capped twenty-story office building. A puff of red-hot air flavored with lemon peelings, soft-coal smoke, and train oil came in through the half-open windows.

Robbins, fifty, something of an overweight beau, and addicted to first nights and hotel palm-rooms, pretended to be envious of his partner's commuter's joys.

'Going to be something doing in the humidity line to-night,' he said. 'You out-of-town chaps will be the people, with your katydids and moonlight and long drinks and things out on the front porch.'

Hartley, twenty-nine, serious, thin, good-looking, nervous, sighed and frowned a little.

'Yes,' said he, 'we always have cool nights in Floralhurst especially in the winter.'

A man with an air of mystery came in the door and went up to Hartley.

'I've found where she lives,' he announced in the portentous half-whisper that makes the detective at work a marked being to his fellow men.

Hartley scowled him into a state of dramatic silence and quietude. But by that time Robbins had got his cane and set his tie pin to his liking, and with a debonair nod went out to his metropolitan amusements.

'Here is the address,' said the detective in a natural tone, being deprived of an audience to foil.

Hartley took the leaf torn out of the sleuth's dingy memorandum book. On it were pencilled the words 'Vivienne Arlington, No. 341 East — th Street, care of Mrs. McComus.'

'Moved there a week ago,' said the detective. 'Now, if you want any shadowing done, Mr. Hartley, I can do you as fine a job in that line as anybody in the city. It will be only $7 a day and expenses. Can send in a daily type-written report, covering —'

'You needn't go on,' interrupted the broker. 'It isn't a case of that kind. I merely wanted the address. How much shall I pay you?'

'One day's work,' said the sleuth. 'A tenner will cover it.'

Hartley paid the man and dismissed him. Then he left the office and boarded a Broadway car. At the first large crosstown artery of travel he took an eastbound car that deposited him in a decaying avenue, whose ancient structures once sheltered the pride and glory of the town.

Walking a few squares, he came to the building that he sought. It was a new flat-house, bearing carved upon its cheap stone portal its sonorous name, 'The Vallambrosa.' Fire-escapes zigzagged down its front – these laden with household goods, drying clothes, and squalling children evicted by the midsummer heat. Here and there a pale rubber plant peeped from the miscellaneous mass as if wondering to what kingdom it belonged – vegetable, animal, or artificial.

Hartley pressed the 'McComus' button. The door latch clicked spasmodically – now hospitably, now doubtfully, as though in anxiety whether it might be admitting friends or duns. Hartley entered and began to climb the stairs after the manner of those who seek their friends in city flathouses – which is the manner of a boy who climbs an apple-tree, stopping when he comes upon what he wants.

On the fourth floor he saw Vivienne standing in an open door. She invited him inside, with a nod and a bright, genuine smile. She placed a chair for him near a window, and poised herself gracefully upon the edge of one of those Jekyll-and-Hyde pieces of furniture that are masked and mysteriously hooded, unguessable bulks by day and inquisitorial racks of torture by night.

Hartley cast a quick, critical, appreciative glance at her before speaking, and told himself that his taste in choosing had been flawless.

Vivienne was about twenty-one. She was of the purest Saxon type. Her hair was a ruddy golden, each filament of the neatly gathered mass shining with its own lustre and delicate graduation of color. In perfect harmony were her ivory-clear complexion and deep sea-blue eyes that looked upon the world with the ingenuous calmness of a mermaid or the pixie of an undiscovered mountain stream. Her frame was strong and yet possessed the grace of absolute naturalness. And yet with all her Northern clearness and frankness of line and coloring, there seemed to be something of the tropics in her – something of languor in the droop of her pose, of love of ease in her ingenuous complacency of satisfaction and comfort in the mere act of breathing – something that seemed to claim for her a right as a perfect work of nature to exist and be admired equally with a rare flower or some beautiful, milk-white dove among its sober-hued companions.

She was dressed in a white waist and dark skirt – the discreet masquerade of goose-girl and duchess.

'Vivienne,' said Hartley, looking at her pleadingly, 'you did not answer my last letter. It was only by nearly a week's search that I found where you had moved to. Why have you kept me in suspense when you knew how anxiously I was waiting to see you and hear from you?'

The girl looked out the window dreamily.

'Mr. Hartley,' she said hesitatingly, 'I hardly know what to say to you. I realize all the advantages of your offer, and sometimes I feel sure that I could be contented with you. But, again, I am doubtful. I was born a city girl, and I am afraid to bind myself to a quiet suburban life.'

'My dear girl,' said Hartley, ardently, 'have I not told you that you shall have everything that your heart can desire that is in my power to give you? You shall come to the city for the theatres, for shopping, and to visit your friends as often as you care to. You can trust me, can you not?'

'To the fullest,' she said, turning her frank eyes upon him with a smile. 'I know you are the kindest of men, and that the girl you get will be a lucky one. I learned all about you when I was at the Montgomerys'.'

'Ah!' exclaimed Hartley, with a tender, reminiscent light in his eye; 'I remember well the evening I first saw you at the Montgomerys'. Mrs. Montgomery was sounding your praises to me all the evening. And she hardly did you justice. I shall never forget that supper. Come, Vivienne, promise me. I want you. You'll never regret coming with me. No one else will ever give you as pleasant a home.'

The girl sighed and looked down at her folded hands.

A sudden jealous suspicion seized Hartley.

'Tell me, Vivienne,' he asked, regarding her keenly, 'is there another – is there some one else?'

A rosy flush crept slowly over her fair cheeks and neck.

'You shouldn't ask that, Mr. Hartley,' she said, in some confusion. 'But I will tell you. There is one other – but he has no right – I have promised him nothing.'

'His name?' demanded Hartley, sternly.

'Townsend.'

'Rafford Townsend!' exclaimed Hartley, with a grim tightening of his jaw. 'How did that man come to know you? After all I've done for him—'

'His auto has just stopped below,' said Vivienne, bending over the window-sill. 'He's coming for his answer. Oh, I don't know what to do!'

The bell in the flat kitchen whirred. Vivienne hurried to press the latch button.

'Stay here,' said Hartley. 'I will meet him in the hall.'

Townsend, looking like a Spanish grandee in his light tweeds, Panama hat, and curling black mustache, came up the stairs three at a time. He stopped at sight of Hartley and looked foolish.

'Go back,' said Hartley, firmly, pointing downstairs with his forefinger.

'Hullo!' said Townsend, feigning surprise. 'What's up? What are you doing here, old man?'

'Go back,' repeated Hartley, inflexibly. 'The Law of the Jungle. Do you want the Pack to tear you to pieces? The kill is mine.'

'I came here to see a plumber about the bathroom connections,' said Townsend, bravely.

'All right,' said Hartley. 'You shall have that lying plaster to stick upon your traitorous soul. But, go back.'

Townsend went downstairs, leaving a bitter word to be wafted up the draught of the stair-case. Hartley went back to his wooing.

'Vivienne,' said he, masterfully. 'I have got to have you. I will take no more refusals or dilly-dallying.'

'When do you want me?' she asked.

'Now. As soon as you can get ready.'

She stood calmly before him and looked him in the eye.

'Do you think for one moment,' she said, 'that I would enter your home while Héloïse is there?'

Hartley cringed as if from an unexpected blow. He folded his arms and paced the carpet once or twice.

'She shall go,' he declared, grimly. Drops stood upon his brow. 'Why should I let that woman make my life miserable? Never have I seen one day of freedom from trouble since I have known her. You are right, Vivienne. Héloïse must be sent away before I can take you home. But she shall go. I have decided. I will turn her from my doors.'

'When will you do this?' asked the girl.

Hartley clinched his teeth and bent his brows together.

'To-night,' he said, resolutely. 'I will send her away to-night.'

'Then,' said Vivienne, 'my answer is "yes." Come for me when you will.'

She looked into his eyes with a sweet, sincere light in her own. Hartley could scarcely believe that her surrender was true, it was so swift and complete.

'Promise me,' he said, feelingly, 'on your word and honor.'

'On my word and honor,' repeated Vivienne, softly.

At the door he turned and gazed at her happily, but yet as one who scarcely trusts the foundations of his joy.

'To-morrow,' he said, with a forefinger of reminder uplifted.

'To-morrow,' she repeated with a smile of truth and candor.

In an hour and forty minutes Hartley stepped off the train at Floralhurst. A brisk walk of ten minutes brought him to the gate of a handsome two-story cottage set upon a wide and well-tended lawn. Halfway to the house he was met by a woman with jet-black braided hair and flowing white summer gown, who half strangled him without apparent cause.

When they stepped into the hall she said:

'Mamma's here. The auto is coming for her in half an hour. She came to dinner, but there's no dinner.'

'I've something to tell you,' said Hartley. 'I thought to break it to you gently, but since your mother is here we may as well out with it.'

He stooped and whispered something at her ear.

His wife screamed. Her mother came running into the hall. The dark-haired woman screamed again – the joyful scream of a well-beloved and petted woman.

'Oh, mamma!' she cried, ecstatically, 'what do you think? Vivienne is coming to cook for us! She is the one that stayed with the Montgomerys a whole year. And now, Billy, dear,' she concluded, 'you must go right down into the kitchen and discharge Héloïse. She has been drunk again the whole day long.'

SOCIOLOGY IN SERGE AND STRAW

THE SEASON OF IRRESPONSIBILITY is at hand. Come, let us twine round our brow wreaths of poison ivy (that is for idiocy), and wander hand in hand with sociology in the summer fields.

Likely as not the world is flat. The wise men have tried to prove that it is round, with indifferent success. They pointed out to us a ship going to sea, and bade us observe that, at length, the convexity of the earth hid from our view all but the vessel's topmast. But we picked up a telescope and looked, and saw the decks and hull again. Then the wise men said: 'Oh, pshaw! anyhow, the variation of the intersection of the equator and the ecliptic proves it.' We could not see this through our telescope, so we remained silent. But it stands to reason that, if the world were round, the queues of Chinamen would stand straight up from their heads instead of hanging down their backs, as travelers assure us they do.

Another hot-weather corroboration of the flat theory is the fact that all of life, as we know it, moves in little, unavailing circles. More justly than to anything else, it can be likened to the game of baseball. Crack! we hit the ball, and away we go. If we earn a run (in life we call it success) we get back to the home plate and sit upon a bench. If we are thrown out, we walk back to the home plate – and sit upon a bench.

The circumnavigators of the alleged globe may have sailed the rim of a watery circle back to the same port again. The truly great return at the high tide of their attainments to the simplicity of a child. The billionaire sits down at his mahogany to his bowl of bread and milk. When you reach the end of your career, just take down the sign 'Goal' and look at the other side of it. You will find 'Beginning Point' there. It has been reversed while you were going around the track.

But this is humor, and must be stopped. Let us get back to the serious questions that arise whenever sociology turns summer boarder. You are invited to consider the scene of the story – wild, Atlantic waves, thundering against a wooded and rock-bound shore – in the Greater City of New York.

The town of Fishampton, on the south shore of Long Island, is noted for its clam fritters and the summer residence of the Van Plushvelts.

The Van Plushvelts have a hundred million dollars, and their name is a household word with tradesmen and photographers.

On the fifteenth of June the Van Plushvelts boarded up the front door of their city house, carefully deposited their cat on the sidewalk, instructed the caretaker not to allow it to eat any of the ivy on the walls, and whizzed away in a 40-horse-power to Fishampton to stray alone in the shade – Amaryllis not being in their class. If you are a subscriber to the *Toadies' Magazine*, you have often— You say you are not? Well, you buy it at a news-stand, thinking that the news-dealer is not wise to you. But he knows about it all. HE knows – HE knows! I say that you have often seen in the *Toadies' Magazine* pictures of the Van Plushvelts' summer home; so it will not be described here. Our business is with young Haywood Van Plushvelt, sixteen years old, heir to the century of millions, darling of the financial gods, and great grandson of Peter Van Plushvelt, former owner of a particularly fine cabbage patch that has been ruined by an intrusive lot of downtown skyscrapers.

One afternoon young Haywood Van Plushvelt strolled out between the granite gate posts of 'Dolce far Niente' – that's what they called the place; and it was an improvement on dolce far Rockaway, I can tell you.

Haywood walked down into the village. He was human, after all, and his prospective millions weighed upon him. Wealth had wreaked upon him its direfullest. He was the product of private tutors. Even under his first hobby-horse had tan bark been strewn. He had been born with a gold spoon, lobster fork, and fish-set in his mouth. For which I hope, later, to submit justification, I must ask your consideration of his haberdashery and tailoring.

Young Fortunatus was dressed in a neat suit of dark blue serge, a neat white straw hat, neat low-cut tan shoes, linen of the well-known 'immaculate' trade mark, a neat, narrow four-in-hand tie, and carried a slender, neat, bamboo cane.

Down Persimmon Street (there's never tree north of Hagerstown, Md.) came from the village 'Smoky' Dodson, fifteen and a half, worst boy in Fishampton. 'Smoky' was dressed in a ragged red sweater, wrecked and weather-worn golf cap, run-over shoes, and trousers of the 'serviceable' brand. Dust, clinging to the moisture induced by free exercise, darkened wide areas of his face. 'Smoky' carried a baseball bat, and a league ball that advertised itself in the rotundity of his trousers pocket. Haywood stopped and passed the time of day.

'Going to play ball?' he asked.

'Smoky's' eyes and countenance confronted him with a frank blue-and-freckled scrutiny.

'Me?' he said, with deadly mildness; 'sure not. Can't you see I've got a divin' suit on? I'm goin' up in a submarine balloon to catch butterflies with a two-inch auger.'

'Excuse me,' said Haywood, with the insulting politeness of his caste, 'for mistaking you for a gentleman. I might have known better.'

'How might you have known better if you thought I was one?' said 'Smoky,' unconsciously a logician.

'By your appearance,' said Haywood. 'No gentleman is dirty, ragged, and a liar.'

'Smoky' hooted once like a ferry-boat, spat on his hand, got a firm grip on his baseball bat and then dropped it against the fence.

'Say,' said he, 'I knows you. You're the pup that belongs in that swell private summer sanitarium for city guys over there. I seen you come out of the gate. You can't bluff nobody because you're rich. And because you got on swell clothes. Arabella! Yah!'

'Ragamuffin!' said Haywood.

'Smoky' picked up a fence-rail splinter and laid it on his shoulder.

'Dare you to knock it off,' he challenged.

'I wouldn't soil my hands with you,' said the aristocrat.

' 'Fraid,' said 'Smoky' concisely. 'Youse city ducks ain't got the sand. I kin lick you with one hand.'

'I don't wish to have any trouble with you,' said Haywood. 'I asked you a civil question; and you replied like a – like a – a cad.'

'Wot's a cad?' asked 'Smoky.'

'A cad is a disagreeable person,' answered Haywood, 'who lacks manners and doesn't know his place. They sometimes play baseball.'

'I can tell you what a mollycoddle is,' said 'Smoky.' 'It's a monkey dressed up by its mother and sent out to pick daisies on the lawn.'

'When you have the honor to refer to the members of my family,' said Haywood, with some dim ideas of a code in his mind, 'you'd better leave the ladies out of your remarks.'

'Ho! ladies!' mocked the rude one. 'I say ladies! I know what them rich women in the city does. They drink cocktails and swear and give parties to gorillas. The papers say so.'

Then Haywood knew that it must be. He took off his coat, folded it neatly and laid it on the roadside grass, placed his hat upon it and began to unknot his blue silk tie.

'Hadn't yer better ring fer your maid, Arabella?' taunted 'Smoky.' 'Wot yer going to do – go to bed?'

'I'm going to give you a good trouncing,' said the hero. He did not hesitate, although the enemy was far beneath him socially. He remembered that his father once thrashed a cabman, and the papers gave it two columns, first page. And the *Toadies' Magazine* had a special article on Upper Cuts by the Upper Classes, and ran new pictures of the Van Plushvelt country seat, at Fishampton.

'Wot's trouncing?' asked 'Smoky,' suspiciously. 'I don't want your old clothes. I'm no – oh, you mean to scrap! My, my! I won't do a thing to mamma's pet. Criminy! I'd hate to be a hand-laundered thing like you.'

'Smoky' waited with some awkwardness for his adversary to prepare for battle. His own decks were always clear for action. When he should spit upon the palm of his terrible right it was equivalent to 'You may fire now, Gridley.'

The hated patrician advanced, with his shirt sleeves neatly rolled up. 'Smoky' waited, in an attitude of ease, expecting the affair to be conducted according to Fishampton's rules of war. These allowed combat to be prefaced by stigma, recrimination, epithet, abuse, and insult gradually increasing in emphasis and degree. After a round of these 'you're anothers' would come the chip knocked from the shoulder, or the advance across the 'dare' line drawn with a toe on the ground. Next light taps given and taken, these also increasing in force until finally the blood was up and fists going at their best.

But Haywood did not know Fishampton's rules. *Noblesse oblige* kept a faint smile on his face as he walked slowly up to 'Smoky' and said:

'Going to play ball?'

'Smoky' quickly understood this to be a putting of the previous question, giving him the chance to make a practical apology by answering it with civility and relevance.

'Listen this time,' said he. 'I'm goin' skatin' on the river. Don't you see me automobile with Chinese lanterns on it standin' and waitin' for me?'

Haywood knocked him down.

'Smoky' felt wronged. To thus deprive him of preliminary wrangle and objurgation was to send an armored knight full tilt against a crashing lance without permitting him first to caracole around the list to the flourish of trumpets. But he scrambled up and fell upon his foe, head, feet, and fists.

The fight lasted one round of an hour and ten minutes. It was lengthened until it was more like a war or a family feud than a fight. Haywood had learned some of the science of boxing and wrestling from his tutors, but these he discarded for the more instinctive methods of battle handed down by the cave-dwelling Van Plushvelts.

So, when he found himself, during the mêlée, seated upon the kicking and roaring 'Smoky's' chest, he improved the opportunity by vigorously kneading handfuls of sand and soil into his adversary's ears, eyes, and mouth, and when 'Smoky' got the proper leg hold and 'turned' him, he fastened both hands in the Plushvelt hair and pounded the Plushvelt head against the lap of mother earth. Of course, the strife was not incessantly active. There were seasons when one sat upon the other, holding him down while each blew like a grampus, spat out the more inconveniently large sections of gravel and earth, and strove to subdue the spirit of his opponent with a frightful and soul-paralyzing glare.

At last, it seemed that in the language of the ring, their efforts lacked steam. They broke away, and each disappeared in a cloud as he brushed away the dust of the conflict. As soon as his breath permitted, Haywood walked close to 'Smoky' and said:

'Going to play ball?'

'Smoky' looked pensively at the sky, at his bat lying on the ground, and at the 'leaguer' rounding his pocket.

'Sure,' he said off-handedly. 'The "Yellowjackets" play the "Long Islands." I'm cap'n of the "Long Islands." '

'I guess I didn't mean to say you were ragged,' said Haywood. 'But you are dirty, you know.'

'Sure,' said 'Smoky.' 'Yer get that way knockin' around. Say, I don't believe them New York papers about ladies drinkin' and havin' monkeys dinin' at the table with 'em. I guess they're lies, like they print about people eatin' out of silver plates, and ownin' dogs that cost $100.'

'Certainly,' said Haywood. 'What do you play on your team?'

'Ketcher. Ever play any?'

'Never in my life,' said Haywood. 'I've never known any fellows except one or two of my cousins.'

'Jer like to learn? We're goin' to have a practice game before the match. Wanter come along? I'll put yer in left-field, and yer won't be long ketchin' on.'

'I'd like it bully,' said Haywood. 'I've always wanted to play baseball.'

The ladies' maids of New York and the families of Western mine owners with social ambitions will remember well the sensation that was created by the report that the young multi-millionaire, Haywood Van Plushvelt, was playing ball with the village youths of Fishampton. It was conceded that the millennium of democracy had come. Reporters and photographers swarmed to the island. The papers printed half-page pictures of him as short-stop stopping a hot grounder. The *Toadies' Magazine* got out a Bat and Ball number that covered the subject historically, beginning with the vampire bat and ending with the Patriarchs' ball – illustrated with interior views of the Van Plushvelt country seat. Ministers, educators, and sociologists everywhere hailed the event as the tocsin call that proclaimed the universal brotherhood of man.

One afternoon I was reclining under the trees near the shore at Fishampton in the esteemed company of an eminent, bald-headed young sociologist. By way of note it may be inserted that all sociologists are more or less bald, and exactly thirty-two. Look 'em over.

The sociologist was citing the Van Plushvelt case as the most important 'uplift' symptom of a generation and as an excuse for his own existence.

Immediately before us were the village baseball grounds. And now came the sportive youth of Fishampton and distributed themselves, shouting, about the diamond.

'There,' said the sociologist, pointing, 'there is young Plushvelt.'

I raised myself (so far a cosycophant with Mary Ann) and gazed.

Young Van Plushvelt sat upon the ground. He was dressed in a ragged red sweater, wrecked and weather-worn golf cap, run-over shoes, and trousers of the 'serviceable' brand. Dust, clinging to the moisture induced by free exercise, darkened the wide areas of his face.

'That is he,' repeated the socioligist. If he had said 'him' I could have been less vindictive.

On a bench, with an air, sat the young millionaire's chum.

He was dressed in a neat suit of dark blue serge, a neat white straw hat, neat low-cut tan shoes, linen of the well-known 'immaculate' trade mark, a neat, narrow four-in-hand tie, and carried a slender, neat bamboo cane.

I laughed loudly and vulgarly.

'What you want to do,' said I to the sociologist, 'is to establish a reformatory for the Logical Vicious Circle. Or else I've got wheels. It looks to me as if things are running round and round in circles instead of getting anywhere.'

'What do you mean?' asked the man of progress.

'Why, look what he has done to "Smoky," ' I replied.

'You will always be a fool,' said my friend, the sociologist, getting up and walking away.

THE RANSOM OF RED CHIEF

IT LOOKED LIKE A GOOD THING, but wait till I tell you. We were down South, in Alabama – Bill Driscoll and myself – when this kidnapping idea struck us. It was, as Bill afterward expressed it, 'during a moment of temporary mental apparition'; but we didn't find that out till later.

There was a town down there, as flat as a flannel-cake, and called Summit, of course. It contained inhabitants of as undeleterious and self-satisfied a class of peasantry as ever clustered around a Maypole.

Bill and me had a joint capital of about six hundred dollars, and we needed just two thousand dollars more to pull off a fraudulent town-lot scheme in Western Illinois with. We talked it over on the front steps of the hotel. Philoprogenitoveness, says we, is strong in semi-rural communities; therefore, and for other reasons, a kidnapping project ought to do better there than in the radius of newspapers that send reporters out in plain clothes to stir up talk about such things. We knew that Summit couldn't get after us with anything stronger than constables and, maybe, some lackadaisical blood-hounds and a diatribe or two in the *Weekly Farmers' Budget*. So, it looked good.

We selected for our victim the only child of a prominent citizen named Ebenezer Dorset. The father was respectable and tight, a mortgage fancier and a stern, upright collection-plate passer and forecloser. The kid was a boy of ten, with bas-relief freckles, and hair the color of the cover of the magazine you buy at the news-stand when you want to catch a train. Bill and me figured that Ebenezer would melt down for a ransom of two thousand dollars to a cent. But wait till I tell you.

About two miles from Summit was a little mountain, covered with a dense cedar brake. On the rear elevation of this mountain was a cave. There we stored provisions.

One evening after sundown, we drove in a buggy past old Dorset's house. The kid was in the street, throwing rocks at a kitten on the opposite fence.

'Hey, little boy!' says Bill, 'would you like to have a bag of candy and a nice ride?'

The boy catches Bill neatly in the eye with a piece of brick.

'That will cost the old man an extra five hundred dollars,' says Bill, climbing over the wheel.

That boy put up a fight like a welter-weight cinnamon bear; but, at last, we got him down in the bottom of the buggy and drove away. We took him up to the cave, and I hitched the horse in the cedar brake. After dark I drove the buggy to the little village, three miles away, where we had hired it, and walked back to the mountain.

Bill was pasting court-plaster over the scratches and bruises on his features. There was a fire burning behind the big rock at the entrance of the cave, and the boy was watching a pot of boiling coffee, with two buzzard tail-feathers stuck in his red hair. He points a stick at me when I come up, and says:

'Ha! cursed paleface, do you dare to enter the camp of Red Chief, the terror of the plains?'

'He's all right now,' says Bill, rolling up his trousers and examining some bruises on his shins. 'We're playing Indian. We're making Buffalo Bill's show look like magic-lantern views of Palestine in the town hall. I'm Old Hank, the Trapper, Red Chief's captive, and I'm to be scalped at daybreak. By Geronimo! that kid can kick hard.'

Yes, sir, that boy seemed to be having the time of his life. The fun of camping out in a cave had made him forget that he was a captive himself. He immediately christened me Snake-eye, the Spy, and announced that, when his braves returned from the warpath, I was to be broiled at the stake at the rising of the sun.

Then we had supper; and he filled his mouth full of bacon and bread and gravy, and began to talk. He made a during-dinner speech something like this:

'I like this fine. I never camped out before; but I had a pet 'possum once, and I was nine last birthday. I hate to go to school. Rats ate up sixteen of Jimmy Talbot's aunt's speckled hen's eggs. Are there any real Indians in these woods? I want some more gravy. Does the trees moving make the wind blow? We had five puppies. What makes your nose so red, Hank? My father has lots of money. Are the stars hot? I whipped Ed Walker twice, Saturday. I don't like girls. You dassent catch toads unless with a string. Do oxen make any noise? Why are oranges round? Have you got beds to sleep on in this cave? Amos Murray has got six toes. A parrot can talk, but a monkey or a fish can't. How many does it take to make twelve?'

Every few minutes he would remember that he was a pesky redskin, and pick up his stick rifle and tiptoe to the mouth of the cave to rubber for the scouts of the hated paleface. Now and then he would let out a war-whoop that made Old Hank the Trapper shiver. That boy had Bill terrorized from the start.

'Red Chief,' says I to the kid, 'would you like to go home?'

'Aw, what for?' says he. 'I don't have any fun at home. I hate to go to school. I like to camp out. You won't take me back home again, Snake-eye, will you?'

'Not right away,' says I. 'We'll stay here in the cave awhile.'

'All right!' says he. 'That'll be fine. I never had such fun in all my life.'

We went to bed about eleven o'clock. We spread down some wide blankets and quilts and put Red Chief between us. We weren't afraid he'd run away. He kept us awake for three hours, jumping up and reaching for his rifle and screeching: 'Hist! pard,' in mine and Bill's ears, as the fancied crackle of a twig or the rustle of a leaf revealed to his young imagination the stealthy approach of the outlaw band. At last, I fell into a troubled sleep, and dreamed that I had been kidnapped and chained to a tree by a ferocious pirate with red hair.

Just at daybreak, I was awakened by a series of awful screams from Bill. They weren't yells, or howls, or shouts, or whoops, or yawps, such as you'd expect from a manly set of vocal organs – they were simply indecent, terrifying, humiliating screams, such as women emit when they see ghosts or caterpillars. It's an awful thing to hear a strong, desperate, fat man scream incontinently in a cave at daybreak.

I jumped up to see what the matter was. Red Chief was sitting on Bill's chest, with one hand twined in Bill's hair. In the other he had the sharp case-knife we used for slicing bacon; and he was industriously and realistically trying to take Bill's scalp, according to the sentence that had been pronounced upon him the evening before.

I got the knife away from the kid and made him lie down again. But, from that moment, Bill's spirit was broken. He laid down on his side of the bed, but he never closed an eye again in sleep as long as that boy was with us. I dozed off for a while, but along toward sun-up I remembered that Red Chief had said I was to be burned at the stake at the rising of the sun. I wasn't nervous or afraid; but I sat up and lit my pipe and leaned against a rock.

'What you getting up so soon for, Sam?' asked Bill.

'Me?' says I. 'Oh, I got a kind of pain in my shoulder. I thought sitting up would rest it.'

'You're a liar!' says Bill. 'You're afraid. You was to be burned at sun-rise, and you was afraid he'd do it. And he would, too, if he could find a match.

Ain't it awful, Sam? Do you think anybody will pay out money to get a little imp like that back home?'

'Sure,' said I. 'A rowdy kid like that is just the kind that parents dote on. Now, you and the Chief get up and cook breakfast, while I go up on the top of this mountain and reconnoitre.'

I went up on the peak of the little mountain and ran my eye over the contiguous vicinity. Over towards Summit I expected to see the sturdy yeomanry of the village armed with scythes and pitchforks beating the countryside for the dastardly kidnappers. But what I saw was a peaceful landscape dotted with one man ploughing with a dun mule. Nobody was dragging the creek; no couriers dashed hither and yon, bringing tidings of no news to the distracted parents. There was a sylvan attitude of somnolent sleepiness pervading that section of the external outward surface of Alabama that lay exposed to my view. 'Perhaps,' says I to myself, 'it has not yet been discovered that the wolves have borne away the tender lambkin from the fold. Heaven help the wolves!' says I, and I went down the mountain to breakfast.

When I got to the cave I found Bill backed up against the side of it, breathing hard, and the boy threatening to smash him with a rock half as big as a cocoanut.

'He put a red-hot boiled potato down my back,' explained Bill, 'and then mashed it with his foot; and I boxed his ears. Have you got a gun about you, Sam?'

I took the rock away from the boy and kind of patched up the argument. 'I'll fix you,' says the kid to Bill. 'No man ever yet struck the Red Chief but he got paid for it. You better beware!'

After breakfast the kid takes a piece of leather with strings wrapped around it out of his pocket and goes outside the cave unwinding it.

'What's he up to now?' says Bill, anxiously. 'You don't think he'll run away, do you, Sam?'

'No fear of it,' says I. 'He don't seem to be much of a home body. But we've got to fix up some plan about the ransom. There don't seem to be much excitement around Summit on account of his disappearance; but maybe they haven't realized yet that he's gone. His folks may think he's spending the night with Aunt Jane or one of the neighbors. Anyhow, he'll be missed to-day. To-night we must get a message to his father demanding the two thousand dollars for his return.'

Just then we heard a kind of war-whoop, such as David might have emitted when he knocked out the champion Goliath. It was a sling that Red Chief had pulled out of his pocket, and he was whirling it around his head.

I dodged, and heard a heavy thud and a kind of a sigh from Bill, like a horse gives out when you take his saddle off. A niggerhead rock the size of an egg had caught Bill just behind his left ear. He loosened himself all over and fell in the fire across the frying pan of hot water for washing the dishes. I dragged him out and poured cold water on his head for half an hour.

By and by, Bill sits up and feels behind his ear and says: 'Sam, do you know who my favorite Biblical character is?'

'Take it easy,' says I. 'You'll come to your senses presently.'

'King Herod,' says he. 'You won't go away and leave me here alone, will you, Sam?'

I went out and caught that boy and shook him until his freckles rattled.

'If you don't behave,' says I, 'I'll take you straight home. Now, are you going to be good, or not?'

'I was only funning,' says he, sullenly. 'I didn't mean to hurt Old Hank. But what did he hit me for? I'll behave, Snake-eye, if you won't send me home, and if you'll let me play the Black Scout to-day.'

'I don't know the game,' says I. 'That's for you and Mr. Bill to decide. He's your playmate for the day. I'm going away for a while, on business. Now, you come in and make friends with him and say you are sorry for hurting him, or home you go, at once.'

I made him and Bill shake hands, and then I took Bill aside and told him I was going to Poplar Grove, a little village three miles from the cave, and find out what I could about how the kidnapping had been regarded in Summit. Also, I thought it best to send a peremptory letter to old man Dorset that day, demanding the ransom and dictating how it should be paid.

'You know, Sam,' says Bill, 'I've stood by you without batting an eye in earthquakes, fire and flood – in poker games, dynamite outrages, police raids, train robberies, and cyclones. I never lost my nerve yet till we kidnapped that two-legged skyrocket of a kid. He's got me going. You won't leave me long with him, will you, Sam?'

'I'll be back some time this afternoon,' says I. 'You must keep the boy amused and quiet till I return. And now we'll write the letter to old Dorset.'

Bill and I got paper and pencil and worked on the letter while Red Chief, with a blanket wrapped around him, strutted up and down, guarding the mouth of the cave. Bill begged me tearfully to make the ransom fifteen hundred dollars instead of two thousand. 'I ain't attempting,' says he, 'to decry the celebrated moral aspect of parental affection, but we're dealing with humans, and it ain't human for anybody to give up two thousand dollars for that forty-pound chunk of freckled wildcat. I'm willing to take a chance at fifteen hundred dollars. You can charge the difference up to me.'

So, to relieve Bill, I acceded, and we collaborated a letter that ran this way:

Ebenezer Dorset, Esq.:

We have your boy concealed in a place far from Summit. It is useless for you or the most skilful detectives to attempt to find him. Absolutely, the only terms on which you can have him restored to you are these: We demand fifteen hundred dollars in large bills for his return; the money to be left at midnight to-night at the same spot and in the same box as your reply – as hereinafter described. If you agree to these terms, send your answer in writing by a solitary messenger to-night at half-past eight o'clock. After crossing Owl Creek on the road to Poplar Grove, there are three large trees about a hundred yards apart, close to the fence of the wheat field on the right-hand side. At the bottom of the fence-post, opposite the third tree, will be found a small pasteboard box.

The messenger will place the answer in this box and return immediately to Summit.

If you attempt any treachery or fail to comply with our demand as stated, you will never see your boy again.

If you pay the money as demanded, he will be returned to you safe and well within three hours. These terms are final, and if you do not accede to them no further communication will be attempted.

Two Desperate Men

I addressed this letter to Dorset, and put it in my pocket. As I was about to start, the kid comes up to me and says:

'Aw, Snake-eye, you said I could play the Black Scout while you was gone.'

'Play it, of course,' says I. 'Mr. Bill will play with you. What kind of a game is it?'

'I'm the Black Scout,' says Red Chief, 'and I have to ride to the stockade to warn the settlers that the Indians are coming. I'm tired of playing Indian myself. I want to be the Black Scout.'

'All right,' says I. 'It sounds harmless to me. I guess Mr. Bill will help you foil the pesky savages.'

'What am I to do?' asks Bill, looking at the kid suspiciously.

'You are the hoss,' says Black Scout. 'Get down on your hands and knees. How can I ride to the stockade without a hoss?'

'You'd better keep him interested,' said I, 'till we get the scheme going. Loosen up.'

'Bill gets down on his all fours, and a look comes in his eye like a rabbit's when you catch it in a trap.

'How far is it to the stockade, kid?' he asks, in a husky manner of voice.

'Ninety miles,' says the Black Scout. 'And you have to hump yourself to get there on time. Whoa, now!'

The Black Scout jumps on Bill's back and digs his heels in his side.

'For Heaven's sake,' says Bill, 'hurry back, Sam, as soon as you can. I wish we hadn't made the ransom more than a thousand. Say, you quit kicking me or I'll get up and warm you good.'

I walked over to Poplar Grove and sat around the post-office and store, talking with the chaw-bacons that came in to trade. One whiskerando says that he hears Summit is all upset on account of Elder Ebenezer Dorset's boy having been lost or stolen. That was all I wanted to know. I bought some smoking tobacco, referred casually to the price of black-eyed peas, posted my letter surreptitiously, and came away. The postmaster said the mail-carrier would come by in an hour to take the mail to Summit.

When I got back to the cave Bill and the boy were not to be found. I explored the vicinity of the cave, and risked a yodel or two, but there was no response.

So I lighted my pipe and sat down on a mossy bank to await developments.

In about half an hour I heard the bushes rustle, and Bill wabbled out into the little glade in front of the cave. Behind him was the kid, stepping softly like a scout, with a broad grin on his face. Bill stopped, took off his hat, and wiped his face with a red handkerchief. The kid stopped about eight feet behind him.

'Sam,' says Bill, 'I suppose you'll think I'm a renegade, but I couldn't help it. I'm a grown person with masculine proclivities and habits of self-defense, but there is a time when all systems of egotism and predominance fail. The boy is gone. I sent him home. All is off. There was martyrs in old times,' goes on Bill, 'that suffered death rather than give up the particular graft they enjoyed. None of 'em ever was subjugated to such supernatural tortures as I have been. I tried to be faithful to our articles of depredation; but there came a limit.'

'What's the trouble, Bill?' I asks him.

'I was rode,' says Bill, 'the ninety miles to the stockade, not barring an inch. Then, when the settlers was rescued, I was given oats. Sand ain't a palatable substitute. And then, for an hour I had to try to explain to him why there was nothin' in holes, how a road can run both ways, and what makes the grass green. I tell you, Sam, a human can only stand so much. I takes him by the neck of his clothes and drags him down the mountain. On the way he kicks my legs black and blue from the knees down; and I've got to have two or three bites on my thumb and hand cauterized.

'But he's gone' – continues Bill – 'gone home. I showed him the road to Summit and kicked him about eight feet nearer there at one kick. I'm sorry we lose the ransom; but it was either that or Bill Driscoll to the mad-house.'

Bill is puffing and blowing, but there is a look of ineffable peace and growing content on his rose-pink features.

'Bill,' says I, 'there isn't any heart disease in your family, is there?'

'No,' says Bill, 'nothing chronic except malaria and accidents. Why?'

'Then you might turn around,' says I, 'and have a look behind you.'

Bill turns and sees the boy, and loses his complexion and sits down plump on the ground and begins to pluck aimlessly at grass and little sticks. For an hour I was afraid of his mind. And then I told him that my scheme was to put the whole job through immediately and that we would get the ransom and be off with it by midnight if old Dorset fell in with our proposition. So Bill braced up enough to give the kid a weak sort of a smile and a promise to play the Russian in a Japanese war with him as soon as he felt a little better.

I had a scheme for collecting that ransom without danger of being caught by counterplots that ought to commend itself to professional kidnappers. The tree under which the answer was to be left – and the money later on – was close to the road fence with big, bare fields on all sides. If a gang of constables should be watching for any one to come for the note, they could see him a long way off crossing the fields or in the road. But no, siree! At half-past eight I was up in that tree as well hidden as a tree toad, waiting for the messenger to arrive.

Exactly on time, a half-grown boy rides up the road on a bicycle, locates the pasteboard box at the foot of the fence-post, slips a folded piece of paper into it, and pedals away again back toward Summit.

I waited an hour and then concluded the thing was square. I slid down the tree, got the note, slipped along the fence till I struck the woods, and was back at the cave in another half an hour. I opened the note, got near the lantern, and read it to Bill. It was written with a pen in a crabbed hand, and the sum and substance of it was this:

Two Desperate Men.

Gentlemen: I received your letter to-day by post, in regard to the ransom you ask for the return of my son. I think you are a little high in your demands, and I hereby make you a counter-proposition, which I am inclined to believe you will accept. You bring Johnny home and pay me two hundred and fifty dollars in cash, and I agree to take him off your hands. You had better come at night, for the neighbors believe he is lost, and I couldn't be responsible for what they would do to anybody they saw bringing him back. Very respectfully,

Ebenezer Dorset

'Great pirates of Penzance,' says I; 'of all the impudent—'

But I glanced at Bill, and hesitated. He had the most appealing look in his eyes I ever saw on the face of a dumb or a talking brute.

'Sam,' says he, 'what's two hundred and fifty dollars, after all? We've got the money. One more night of this kid will send me to a bed in Bedlam. Besides being a thorough gentleman, I think Mr. Dorset is a spendthrift for making us such a liberal offer. You ain't going to let the chance go, are you?'

'Tell you the truth, Bill,' says I, 'this little he ewe lamb has somewhat got on my nerves too. We'll take him home, pay the ransom, and make our getaway.'

We took him home that night. We got him to go by telling him that his father had bought a silver-mounted rifle and a pair of moccasins for him, and we were to hunt bears the next day.

It was just twelve o'clock when we knocked at Ebenezer's front door. Just at the moment when I should have been abstracting the fifteen hundred dollars from the box under the tree, according to the original proposition, Bill was counting out two hundred and fifty dollars into Dorset's hand.

When the kid found out we were going to leave him at home he started up a howl like a calliope and fastened himself as tight as a leech to Bill's leg. His father peeled him away gradually, like a porous plaster.

'How long can you hold him?' asks Bill.

'I'm not as strong as I used to be,' says old Dorset, 'but I think I can promise you ten minutes.'

'Enough,' says Bill. 'In ten minutes I shall cross the Central, Southern, and Middle Western States, and be legging it trippingly for the Canadian border.'

And, as dark as it was, and as fat as Bill was, and as good a runner as I am, he was a good mile and a half out of Summit before I could catch up with him.

THE MARRY MONTH OF MAY

PRITHEE, SMITE THE POET IN the eye when he would sing to you praises of the month of May. It is a month presided over by the spirits of mischief and madness. Pixies and flibbertigibbets haunt the budding woods; Puck and his train of midgets are busy in town and country.

In May Nature holds up at us a chiding finger, bidding us remember that we are not gods, but overconceited members of her own great family. She reminds us that we are brothers to the chowder-doomed clam and the donkey; lineal scions of the pansy and the chimpanzee, and but cousins-german to the cooing doves, the quacking ducks, and the house-maids and policemen in the parks.

In May Cupid shoots blindfolded – millionaires marry stenographers; wise professors woo white-aproned gum-chewers behind quick-lunch counters; schoolma'ams make big bad boys remain after school; lads with ladders steal lightly over lawns where Juliet waits in her trellised window with her telescope packed; young couples out for a walk come home married; old chaps put on white spats and promenade near the Normal School; even married men, grown unwontedly tender and sentimental, whack their spouses on the back and growl: 'How goes it, old girl?'

This May, who is no goddess, but Circe, masquerading at the dance given in honor of the fair débutante, Summer, puts the kibosh on us all.

Old Mr. Coulson groaned a little, and then sat up straight in his invalid's chair. He had the gout very bad in one foot, a house near Gramercy Park, half a million dollars, and a daughter. And he had a housekeeper. Mrs. Widdup. The fact and the name deserve a sentence each. They have it.

When May poked Mr. Coulson he became elder brother to the turtle-dove. In the window near which he sat were boxes of jonquils, of hyacinths, geraniums, and pansies. The breeze brought their odor into the room. Immediately there was a well-contested round between the breath of the flowers and the able and active effluvium from gout liniment. The liniment won easily; but not before the flowers got an uppercut to old Mr. Coulson's nose. The deadly work of the implacable, false enchantress May was done.

Across the park to the olfactories of Mr. Coulson came other unmistakable, characteristic, copyrighted smells of spring that belong to the-big-city-above-the-Subway, alone. The smells of hot asphalt, underground caverns, gasoline, patchouli, orange peel, sewer gas, Albany grabs, Egyptian cigarettes, mortar and the undried ink on newspapers. The inblowing air was sweet and mild. Sparrows wrangled happily everywhere outdoors. Never trust May.

Mr. Coulson twisted the ends of his white mustache, cursed his foot, and pounded a bell on the table by his side.

In came Mrs. Widdup. She was comely to the eye, fair, flustered, forty, and foxy.

'Higgins is out, sir,' she said, with a smile suggestive of vibratory massage. 'He went to post a letter. Can I do anything for you, sir?'

'It's time for my aconite,' said old Mr. Coulson. 'Drop it for me. The bottle's there. Three drops. In water. D— that is, confound Higgins! There's nobody in this house cares if I die here in this chair for want of attention.'

Mrs. Widdup sighed deeply.

'Don't be saying that, sir,' she said. 'There's them that would care more than any one knows. Thirteen drops you said, sir?'

'Three,' said old man Coulson.

He took his dose and then Mrs. Widdup's hand. She blushed. Oh, yes, it can be done. Just hold your breath and compress the diaphragm.

'Mrs. Widdup,' said Mr. Coulson, 'the springtime's full upon us.'

'Ain't that right?' said Mrs. Widdup. 'The air's real warm. And there's bock-beer signs on every corner. And the park's all yaller and pink and blue with flowers; and I have such shooting pains up my legs and body.'

' "In the spring," ' quoted Mr. Coulson, curling his mustache, ' "a y— that is, a man's – fancy lightly turns to thoughts of love." '

'Lawsy, now!' exclaimed Mrs. Widdup; 'ain't that right? Seems like it's in the air.'

' "In the spring," ' continued old Mr. Coulson, ' "a livelier iris shines upon the burnished dove." '

'They do be lively, the Irish,' sighed Mrs. Widdup, pensively.

'Mrs. Widdup,' said Mr. Coulson, making a face at a twinge of his gouty foot, 'this would be a lonesome house without you. I'm an – that is, I'm an elderly man – but I'm worth a comfortable lot of money. If half a million dollars' worth of Government bonds and the true affection of a heart that, though no longer beating with the first ardor of youth, can still throb with genuine—'

The loud noise of an overturned chair near the portières of the adjoining room interrupted the venerable and scarcely suspecting victim of May.

In stalked Miss Van Meeker Constantia Coulson, bony, durable, tall, high-nosed, frigid, well-bred, thirty-five, in-the-neighborhood-of-Gramercy-Parkish. She put up a lorgnette. Mrs. Widdup hastily stooped and arranged the bandages on Mr. Coulson's gouty foot.

'I thought Higgins was with you,' said Miss Van Meeker Constantia.

'Higgins went out,' explained her father, 'and Mrs. Widdup answered the bell. That is better now, Mrs. Widdup, thank you. No; there is nothing else I require.'

The housekeeper retired, pink under the cool, inquiring stare of Miss Coulson.

'This spring weather is lovely, isn't it, daughter?' said the old man, consciously conscious.

'That's just it,' replied Miss Van Meeker Constantia Coulson, somewhat obscurely. 'When does Mrs. Widdup start on her vacation, papa?'

'I believe she said a week from to-day,' said Mr. Coulson.

Miss Van Meeker Constantia stood for a minute at the window gazing toward the little park, flooded with the mellow afternoon sunlight. With the eye of a botanist she viewed the flowers – most potent weapons of insidious May. With the cool pulses of a virgin of Cologne she withstood the attack of the ethereal mildness. The arrows of the pleasant sunshine fell back, frostbitten, from the cold panoply of her unthrilled bosom. The odor of the flowers waked no soft sentiments in the unexplored recesses of her dormant heart. The chirp of the sparrows gave her a pain. She mocked at May.

But although Miss Coulson was proof against the season, she was keen enough to estimate its power. She knew that elderly men and thick-waisted women jumped as educated fleas in the ridiculous train of May, the merry mocker of the months. She had heard of foolish old gentlemen marrying their housekeepers before. What a humiliating thing, after all, was this feeling called love!

The next morning at 8 o'clock, when the iceman called, the cook told him that Miss Coulson wanted to see him in the basement.

'Well, ain't I the Olcott and Depew; not mentioning the first name at all?' said the iceman, admiringly, of himself.

As a concession he rolled his sleeves down, dropped his icehooks on a syringa and went back. When Miss Van Meeker Constantia Coulson addressed him he took off his hat.

'There is a rear entrance to this basement,' said Miss Coulson, 'which can be reached by driving into the vacant lot next door, where they are excavating for a building. I want you to bring in that way within two hours 1,000 pounds of ice. You may have to bring another man or two to help you. I will show you where I want it placed. I also want 1,000 pounds a day delivered the same way for the next four days. Your company may charge the ice on our regular bill. This is for your extra trouble.'

Miss Coulson tendered a ten-dollar bill. The iceman bowed, and held his hat in his two hands behind him.

'Now if you'll excuse me, lady. It'll be a pleasure to fix things up for you any way you please.'

Alas for May!

About noon Mr. Coulson knocked two glasses off his table, broke the spring of his bell, and yelled for Higgins at the same time.

'Bring an axe,' commanded Mr. Coulson, sardonically, 'or send out for a quart of prussic acid, or have a policeman come in and shoot me. I'd rather that than be frozen to death.'

'It does seem to be getting cold, sir,' said Higgins. 'I hadn't noticed it before I'll close the window, sir.'

'Do,' said Mr. Coulson. 'They call this spring, do they? If it keeps up long I'll go back to Palm Beach. House feels like a morgue.'

Later Miss Coulson dutifully came in to inquire how the gout was progressing.

' 'Stantia,' said the old man, 'how is the weather outdoors?'

'Bright,' answered Miss Coulson, 'but chilly.'

'Feels like the dead of winter to me,' said Mr. Coulson.

'An instance,' said Constantia, gazing abstractedly out of the window, 'of "winter lingering in the lap of spring," though the metaphor is not in the most refined taste.'

A little later she walked down by the side of the little park and on westward to Broadway to accomplish a little shopping.

A little later than that Mrs. Widdup entered the invalid's room.

'Did you ring, sir?' she asked, dimpling in many places. 'I asked Higgins to go to the drug store, and I thought I heard your bell.'

'I did not,' said Mr. Coulson.

'I'm afraid,' said Mrs. Widdup, 'I interrupted you, sir, yesterday when you were about to say something.'

'How comes it, Mrs. Widdup,' said old man Coulson, sternly, 'that I find it so cold in this house?'

'Cold, sir?' said the housekeeper, 'why, now, since you speak of it it do seem cold in this room. But outdoors it's as warm and fine as June, sir. And how this weather do seem to make one's heart jump out of one's shirt waist, sir. And the ivy all leaved out on the side of the house, and the hand-organs playing, and the children dancing on the sidewalk – 'tis a great time for speaking out what's in the heart. You were saying yesterday, sir—'

'Woman!' roared Mr. Coulson; 'you are a fool. I pay you to take care of this house. I am freezing to death in my own room, and you come in and drivel to me about ivy and hand-organs. Get me an overcoat at once. See that all doors and windows are closed below. An old, fat, irresponsible, one-sided object like you pratling about springtime and flowers in the middle of winter! When Higgins comes back, tell him to bring me a hot rum punch. And now get out!'

But who shall shame the bright face of May? Rogue though she be and disturber of sane men's peace, no wise virgin's cunning nor cold storage shall make her bow her head in the bright galaxy of months.

Oh, yes, the story was not quite finished.

A night passed, and Higgins helped old man Coulson in the morning to his chair by the window. The cold of the room was gone. Heavenly odors and fragrant mildness entered.

In hurried Mrs. Widdup, and stood by his chair. Mr. Coulson reached his bony hand and grasped her plump one.

'Mrs. Widdup,' he said, 'this house would be no home without you. I have half a million dollars. If that and the true affection of a heart no longer in its youthful prime, but still not cold could—'

'I found out what made it cold,' said Mrs. Widdup, leaning against his chair. "Twas ice – tons of it – in the basement and in the furnace room, everywhere. I shut off the registers that it was coming through into your room, Mr. Coulson, poor soul! And now it's May-time again.'

'A true heart,' went on old man Coulson, a little wanderingly, 'that the springtime has brought to life again, and – but what will my daughter say, Mrs. Widdup?'

'Never fear, sir,' said Mrs. Widdup, cheerfully, 'Miss Coulson, she ran away with the iceman last night, sir!'

A TECHNICAL ERROR

I NEVER CARED ESPECIALLY for feuds, believing them to be even more over-rated products of our country than grapefruit, scrapple, or honeymoons. Nevertheless, if I may be allowed, I will tell you of an Indian Territory feud of which I was press-agent, camp-follower, and inaccessory during the fact.

I was on a visit to Sam Durkee's ranch, where I had a great time falling off unmanicured ponies and waving my bare hand at the lower jaws of wolves about two miles away. Sam was a hardened person of about twenty-five, with a reputation for going home in the dark with perfect equanimity, though often with reluctance.

Over in the Creek Nation was a family bearing the name of Tatum. I was told that the Durkees and Tatums had been feuding for years. Several of each family had bitten the grass, and it was expected that more Nebuchadnezzars would follow. A younger generation of each family was growing up, and the grass was keeping pace with them. But I gathered that they had fought fairly; that they had not lain in cornfields and aimed at the division of their enemies' suspenders in the back – partly, perhaps, because there were no cornfields, and nobody wore more than one suspender. Nor had any woman or child of either house ever been harmed. In those days – and you will find it so yet – their women were safe.

Sam Durkee had a girl. (If it were an all-fiction magazine that I expected to sell this story to, I should say, 'Mr. Durkee rejoiced in a fiancée.') Her name was Ella Baynes. They appeared to be devoted to each other, and to have perfect confidence in each other, as all couples do who are and have or aren't and haven't. She was tolerably pretty, with a heavy mass of brown hair that helped her along. He introduced me to her, which seemed not to lessen her preference for him; so I reasoned that they were surely soul-mates.

Miss Baynes lived in Kingfisher, twenty miles from the ranch. Sam lived on a gallop between the two places.

One day there came to kingfisher a courageous young man, rather small, with smooth face and regular features. He made many inquiries about the business of the town, and especially of the inhabitants cognominally. He said he was from Muscogee, and he looked it, with his yellow shoes and crocheted four-in-hand. I met him once when I rode in for the mail. He said his name was Beverly Travers, which seemed rather improbable.

There were active times on the ranch just then, and Sam was too busy to

go to town often. As an incompetent and generally worthless guest, it
devolved upon me to ride in for little things such as post cards, barrels of
flours, baking-powder, smoking-tobacco, and – letters from Ella.

One day, when I was messenger for half a gross of cigarette papers and a
couple of wagon tires, I saw the alleged Beverly Travers in a yellow-wheeled
buggy with Ella Baynes, driving about town as ostentatiously as the black,
waxy mud would permit. I knew that this information would bring no balm
of Gilead to Sam's soul, so I refrained from including it in the news of the
city that I retailed on my return. But on the next afternoon an elongated
ex-cowboy of the name of Simmons, an old-time pal of Sam's, who kept a
feed store in Kingfisher, rode out to the ranch and rolled and burned many
cigarettes before he would talk. When he did make oration, his words were
these:

'Say, Sam, there's been a description of a galoot miscallin' himself Bevel-
edged Travels impairing the atmospheric air of Kingfisher for the past two
weeks. You know who he was? He was not otherwise that Ben Tatum, from
the Creek Nation, son of old Gopher Tatum that your Uncle Newt shot last
February. You know what he done this morning? He killed your brother
Lester – shot him in the co't-house yard.'

I wondered if Sam had heard. He pulled a twig from a mesquite bush,
chewed it gravely, and said:

'He did, did he? He killed Lester?'

'The same,' said Simmons. 'And he did more. He run away with your girl,
the same as to say Miss Ella Baynes, I thought you might like to know, so
I rode out to impart the information.'

'I am much obliged, Jim,' said Sam, taking the chewed twig from his
mouth. 'Yes, I'm glad you rode out. Yes, I'm right glad.'

'Well, I'll be ridin' back, I reckon. That boy I left in the feed store don't
know hay from oats. He shot Lester in the *back*.'

'Shot him in the back?'

'Yes, while he was hitchin' his hoss.'

'I'm much obliged, Jim.'

'I kind of thought you'd like to know as soon as you could.'

'Come in and have some coffee before you ride back, Jim?'

'Why, no, I reckon not; I must get back to the store.'

'And you say—'

'Yes, Sam. Everybody seen 'em drive away together in a buckboard, with
a big bundle, like clothes, tied up in the back of it. He was drivin' the team
he brought over with him from Muscogee. They'll be hard to overtake right
away.'

'And which—'

'I was goin' to tell you. They left on the Guthrie road; but there's no
tellin' which forks they'll take – you know that.'

'All right, Jim; much obliged.'

'You're welcome, Sam.'

Simmons rolled a cigarette and stabbed his pony with both heels. Twenty
yards away he reined up and called back:

'You don't want no – assistance, as you might say?'

'Not any, thanks.'

'I didn't think you would. Well, so long!'

Sam took out and opened a bone-handled pocket-knife and scraped a dried piece of mud from his left boot. I thought at first he was going to swear a vendetta on the blade of it, or recite 'The Gipsy's Curse.' The few feuds I had ever seen or read about usually opened that way. This one seemed to be presented with a new treatment. Thus offered on the stage, it would have been hissed off, and one of Belasco's thrilling melodramas demanded instead.

'I wonder,' said Sam, with a profoundly thoughtful expression, 'if the cook has any cold beans left over!'

He called Wash, the Negro cook, and finding that he had some, ordered him to heat up the pot and make some strong coffee. Then we went into Sam's private room, where he slept, and kept his armory, dogs, and the saddles of his favorite mounts. He took three or four six-shooters out of a bookcase and began to look them over, whistling 'The Cowboy's Lament' abstractedly. Afterward he ordered the two best horses on the ranch saddled and tied to the hitching-post.

Now, in the feud business, in all sections of the country, I have observed that in one particular there is a delicate but strict etiquette belonging. You must not mention the word or refer to the subject in the presence of a feudist. It would be more reprehensible than commenting upon the mole on the chin of your rich aunt. I found, later on, that there is another unwritten rule, but I think that belongs solely to the West.

It yet lacked two hours to supper-time; but in twenty minutes Sam and I were plunging deep into the reheated beans, hot coffee, and cold beef.

'Nothing like a good meal before a long ride,' said Sam. 'Eat hearty.'

I had a sudden suspicion.

'Why did you have two horses saddled?' I asked.

'One, two – one, two,' said Sam. 'You can count, can't you?'

His mathematics carried with it a momentary qualm and a lesson. The thought had not occurred to him that the thought could possibly occur to me not to ride at his side on that red road to revenge and justice. It was the higher calculus. I was booked for the trail. I began to eat more beans.

In an hour we set forth at a steady gallop eastward. Our horses were Kentucky-bred, strengthened by the mesquite grass of the west. Ben Tatum's steeds may have been swifter, and he had a good lead; but if he had heard the punctual thuds of the hoofs of those trailers of ours, born in the heart of fuedland, he might have felt that retribution was creeping up on the hoof-prints of his dapper nags.

I knew that Ben Tatum's card to play was flight – flight until he came within the safer territory of his own henchmen and supporters. He knew that the man pursuing him would follow the trail to any end where it might lead.

During the ride Sam talked of the prospect for rain, of the price of beef, and of the musical glasses. You would have thought he had never had a brother or a sweetheart or any enemy on earth. There are some subjects too big even for the words in the 'Unabridged.' Knowing this phase of the feud code, but not having practised it sufficiently, I overdid the thing by telling some slightly funny anecdotes. Sam laughed at exactly the right place – laughed with his mouth. When I caught sight of his mouth, I wished I had been blessed with enough sense of humor to have suppressed those anecdotes.

Our first sight of them we had in Guthrie. Tired and hungry, we stumbled, unwashed, into a little yellow-pine hotel and sat at a table. In the opposite corner we saw the fugitives. They were bent upon their meal, but looked around at times uneasily.

The girl was dressed in brown – one of these smooth, half-shiny, silky-looking affairs with lace collar and cuffs, and what I believe they call an accordion-pleated skirt. She wore a thick brown veil down to her nose, and a broad-brimmed straw hat with some kind of feathers adorning it. The man wore plain, dark clothes, and his hair was trimmed very short. He was such a man as you might see anywhere.

There they were – the murderer and the woman he had stolen. There we were – the rightful avenger, according to the code, and the supernumerary who writes these words.

For one time, at least, in the heart of the supernumerary there rose the killing instinct. For one moment he joined the force of combatants – orally.

'What are you waiting for, Sam?' I said in a whisper. 'Let him have it now!'

Sam gave a melancholy sigh.

'You don't understand; but *he* does,' he said. '*He* knows. Mr. Tenderfoot, there's a rule out here among white men in the Nation that you can't shoot a man when he's with a woman. I never knew it to be broke yet. You *can't* do it. You've got to get him in a gang or by himself. That's why. He knows it, too. We all know. So, that's Mr. Ben Tatum! One of the "pretty men"! I'll cut him out of the herd before they leave the hotel, and regulate his account!'

After supper the flying pair disappeared quickly. Although Sam haunted lobby and stairway and halls half the night, in some mysterious way the fugitives eluded him; and in the morning the veiled lady in the brown dress with the accordion-pleated skirt and the dapper young man with the close-clipped hair, and the buckboard with the prancing nags, were gone.

It is a monotonous story, that of the ride; so it shall be curtailed. Once again we overtook them on a road. We were about fifty yards behind. They turned in the buckboard and looked at us; then drove on without whipping up their horses. Their safety no longer lay in speed. Ben Tatum knew. He knew that the only rock of safety left to him was the code. There is no doubt that, had he been alone, the matter would have been settled quickly with Sam Durkee in the usual way; but he had something at his side that kept still the trigger-finger of both. It seemed likely that he was no coward.

So, you may perceive that woman, on occasions, may postpone instead of precipitating conflict between man and man. But not willingly or consciously. She is oblivious of codes.

Five miles farther, we came upon the future great Western city of Chandler. The horses of pursuers and pursued were starved and weary. There was one hotel that offered danger to man and entertainment to beast; so the four of us met again in the dining room at the ringing of a bell so resonant and large that it had cracked the welkin long ago. The dining room was not as large as the one at Guthrie.

Just as we were eating apple pie – how Ben Davises and tragedy impinge upon each other! – I noticed Sam looking with keen intentness at our quarry where they were seated at a table across the room. The girl still wore the brown dress with lace collar and cuffs, and the veil drawn down to her nose. The man bent over his plate, with his close-cropped head held low.

'There's a code,' I heard Sam say, either to me or to himself, 'that won't

let you shoot a man in the company of a woman; but, by thunder, there ain't
one to keep you from killing a woman in the company of a man!'

And, quicker than my mind could follow his argument, he whipped a
Colt's automatic from under his left arm and pumped six bullets into the
body that the brown dress covered – the brown dress with the lace collar and
cuffs and the accordion-pleated skirt.

The young person in the dark sack suit, from whose head and from whose
life a woman's glory had been clipped, laid her head on her arms stretched
upon the table; while people came running to raise Ben Tatum from the
floor in his feminine masquerade that had given Sam the opportunity to set
aside, technically, the obligations of the code.

SUITE HOMES AND THEIR ROMANCE

FEW YOUNG COUPLES IN THE Big-City-of-Bluff began their married existence with
greater promise of happiness than did Mr. and Mrs. Claude Turpin. They
felt no especial animosity toward each other; they were comfortably established in a handsome apartment house that had a name and accommodations
like those of a sleeping-car; they were living as expensively as the couple on
the next floor above who had twice their income; and their marriage had
occurred on a wager, a ferry-boat, and first acquaintance, thus securing a
sensational newspaper notice of their names attached to pictures of the Queen
of Roumania and M. Santos-Dumont.

Turpin's income was $200 per month. On pay day, after calculating the
amounts due for rent, instalments on furniture and piano, gas, and bills owed
to the florist, confectioner, milliner, tailor, wine merchant, and cab company,
the Turpins would find that they still had $200 left to spend. How to do this
is one of the secrets of metropolitan life.

The domestic life of the Turpins was a beautiful picture to see. But you
couldn't gaze upon it as you could at an oleography of 'Don't Wake Grandma,'
or 'Brooklyn by Moonlight.'

You had to blink when you looked at it and you heard a fizzing sound just
like the machine with a 'scope' at the end of it. Yes; there wasn't much
repose about the picture of the Turpins' domestic life. It was something like
'Spearing Salmon in the Columbia River,' or 'Japanese Artillery in Action.'

Every day was just like another; as the days are in New York. In the
morning Turpin would take bromo-seltzer, his pocket change from under
the clock, his hat, no breakfast, and his departure for the office. At noon
Mrs. Turpin would get out of bed and humor, put on a kimono, airs, and the
water to boil for coffee.

Turpin lunched downtown. He came home at 6 to dress for dinner. They
always dined out. They strayed from the chop-house to chop-sueydom, from
terrace to table d'hôte, from rathskeller to roadhouse, from café to casino,
from Maria's to the Martha Washington. Such is domestic life in the great
city. Your vine is the mistletoe; your fig tree bears dates. Your household
gods are Mercury and John Howard Payne. For the wedding march you now
hear only 'Come with the Gypsy Bride.' You rarely dine at the same place
twice in succession. You tire of the food; and, besides, you want to give them
time for the question of that souvenir silver sugar bowl to blow over.

The Turpins were therefore happy. They made many warm and delightful friends, some of whom they remembered the next day. Their home life was an ideal one, according to the rules and regulations of the Book of Bluff.

There came a time when it dawned upon Turpin that his wife was getting away with too much money. If you belong to the near-swell class in the Big City, and your income is $200 per month, and you find at the end of the month, after looking over the bills for current expenses, that you, yourself, have spent $150, you very naturally wonder what has become of the other $50. So you suspect your wife. And perhaps you give her a hint that something needs explanation.

'I say, Vivien,' said Turpin, one afternoon when they were enjoying in rapt silence the peace and quiet of their cozy apartment, 'you've been creating a hiatus big enough for a dog to crawl through in this month's honorarium. You haven't been paying your dressmaker anything on account, have you?'

There was a moment's silence. No sounds could be heard except the breathing of the fox terrier, and the subdued, monotonous sizzling of Vivien's fulvous locks against the insensate curling irons. Claude Turpin, sitting upon a pillow that he had thoughtfully placed upon the convolutions of the apartment sofa, narrowly watched the riante, lovely face of his wife.

'Claudie, dear,' said she, touching her finger to her ruby tongue and testing the unresponsive curling irons, 'you do me an injustice. Mme. Toinette has not seen a cent of mine since the day you paid your tailor ten dollars on account.'

Turpin's suspicions were allayed for the time. But one day soon there came an anonymous letter to him that read:

Watch your wife. She is blowing in your money secretly. I was a sufferer just as you are. The place is No. 345 Blank Street. A word to the wise, etc.
A Man Who Knows

Turpin took this letter to the captain of police of the precinct that he lived in.

'My precinct is as clean as a hound's tooth,' said the captain. 'The lid's shut down as close there as it is over the eye of a Williamsburg girl when she's kissed at a party. But if you think there's anything queer at the address, I'll go there with ye.'

On the next afternoon at 3, Turpin and the captain crept softly up the stairs of No. 345 Blank Street. A dozen plain-clothes men, dressed in full police uniforms, so as to allay suspicion, waited in the hall below.

At the top of the stairs was a door, which was found to be locked. The captain took a key from his pocket and unlocked it. The two men entered.

They found themselves in a large room, occupied by twenty or twenty-five elegantly clothed ladies. Racing charts hung against the walls, a ticker clicked in one corner; with a telephone receiver to his ear a man was calling out the various positions of the horses in a very exciting race. The occupants of the room looked up at the intruders; but, as if reassured by the sight of the captain's uniform, they reverted their attention to the man at the telephone.

'You see,' said the captain to Turpin, 'the value of an anonymous letter!

No high-minded and self-respecting gentleman should consider one worthy
of notice. Is your wife among this assembly, Mr. Turpin?'

'She is not,' said Turpin.

'And if she was,' continued the captain, 'would she be within the reach
of the tongue of slander? These ladies constitute a Browning Society. They
meet to discuss the meaning of the great poet. The telephone is connected
with Boston, whence the parent society transmits frequently its interpretations of the poems. Be ashamed of yer suspicions, Mr. Turpin.'

'Go soak your shield,' said Turpin. 'Vivien knows how to take care of
herself in a pool-room. She's not dropping anything on the ponies. There
must be something queer going on here.'

'Nothing but Browning,' said the captain. 'Hear that?'

'Thanatopsis by a nose,' drawled the man at the telephone.

'That's not Browning; that's Longfellow,' said Turpin, who sometimes read
books.

'Back to the pasture!' exclaimed the captain. 'Longfellow made the
pacing-to-wagon record of 7.53 'way back in 1868.'

'I believe there's something queer about this joint,' repeated Turpin.

'I don't see it,' said the captain.

'I know it looks like a pool-room, all right,' persisted Turpin, 'but that's
all a blind. Vivien has been dropping a lot of coin somewhere. I believe
there's some underhanded work going on here.'

A number of racing sheets were tacked close together, covering a large
space on one of the walls. Turpin, suspicious, tore several of them down. A
door, previously hidden, was revealed. Turpin placed an ear to the crack and
listened intently. He heard the soft hum of many voices, low and guarded
laughter, and a sharp, metallic clicking and scraping as if from a multitude
of tiny but busy objects.

'My God! It is as I feared!' whispered Turpin to himself. 'Summon your
men at once!' he called to the captain. 'She is in there, I know.'

At the blowing of the captain's whistle the uniformed plain-clothes men
rushed up the stairs into the pool-room. When they saw the betting paraphernalia distributed around they halted, surprised and puzzled to know
why they had been summoned.

But the captain pointed to the locked door and bade them break it down.
In a few moments they demolished it with the axes they carried. Into the
other room sprang Claude Turpin, with the captain at his heels.

The scene was one that lingered long in Turpin's mind. Nearly a score of
women – women expensively and fashionably clothed, many beautiful and
of refined appearance – had been seated at little marble-topped tables. When
the police burst open the door they shrieked and ran here and there like
gayly plumed birds that had been disturbed in a tropical grove. Some became
hysterical; one or two fainted; several knelt at the feet of the officers and
besought them for mercy on account of their families and social position.

A man who had been seated behind a desk had seized a roll of currency
as large as the ankle of a Paradise Roof Gardens chorus girl and jumped out
of the window. Half a dozen attendants huddled at one end of the room,
breathless from fear.

Upon the tables remained the damning and incontrovertible evidences of
the guilt of the habituées of that sinister room – dish after dish heaped high

with ice cream, and surrounded by stacks of empty ones, scraped to the last spoonful.

'Ladies,' said the captain to his weeping circle of prisoners, 'I'll not hold any of yez. Some of yez I recognize as having fine houses and good standing in the community, with hard-working husbands and childer at home. But I'll read ye a bit of a lecture before ye go. In the next room there's a 20-to-1 shot just dropped in under the wire three lengths ahead of the field. Is this the way ye waste your husbands' money instead of helping earn it? Home wid yez! The lid's on the ice-cream freezer in this precinct.'

Claude Turpin's wife was among the patrons of the raided room. He led her to their apartment in stern silence. There she wept so remorsefully and besought his forgiveness so pleadingly that he forgot his just anger, and soon he gathered his penitent golden-haired Vivien in his arms and forgave her.

'Darling,' she murmured, half sobbingly, as the moonlight drifted through the open window, glorifying her sweet, upturned face, 'I know I done wrong. I will never touch ice cream again. I forgot you were not a millionaire. I used to go there every day. But to-day I felt some strange, sad presentiment of evil, and I was not myself. I ate only eleven saucers.'

'Say no more,' said Claude, gently, as he fondly caressed her waving curls.

'And you are sure that you fully forgive me?' asked Vivien, gazing at him entreatingly with dewy eyes of heavenly blue.

'Almost sure, little one,' answered Claude, stooping and lightly touching her snowy forehead with his lips. 'I'll let you know later on. I've got a month's salary down on Vanilla to win the three-year-old steeplechase to-morrow; and if the ice-cream hunch is to the good you are It again – see?'

THE WHIRLIGIG OF LIFE

JUSTICE-OF-THE-PEACE BENAJA Widdup sat in the door of his office smoking his elder-stem pipe. Halfway to the Zenith the Cumberland range rose blue-gray in the afternoon haze. A speckled hen swaggered down the main street of the 'settlement,' cackling foolishly.

Up the road came a sound of creaking axles, and then a slow cloud of dust, and then a bull-cart bearing Ransie Bilbro and his wife. The cart stopped at the Justice's door, and the two climbed down. Ransie was a narrow six feet of sallow brown skin and yellow hair. The imperturbability of the mountains hung upon him like a suit of armor. The woman was calicoed, angled, snuff-brushed, and weary with unknown desires. Through it all gleamed a faint protest of cheated youth unconscious of its loss.

The Justice of the Peace slipped his feet into his shoes, for the sake of dignity, and moved to let them enter.

'We-all,' said the woman, in a voice like the wind blowing through pine boughs, 'wants a divo'ce.' She looked at Ransie to see if he noted any flaw or ambiguity or evasion or partiality or self-partisanship in her statement of their business.

'A divo'ce,' repeated Ransie, with a solemn nod. 'We-all can't git along together nohow. It's lonesome enough fur to live in the mount'ins when a man and a woman keers fur one another. But when she's a-spittin' like a

wildcat or a-sullenin' like a hoot-owl in the cabin, a man ain't got no call to
live with her.'

'When he's a no-'count varmint,' said the woman, without any special
warmth, 'a-traipsin' along of scalawags and moonshiners and a-layin' on his
back pizen 'ith co'n whiskey, and a-pesterin' folks with a pack o' hungry,
triflin' houn's to feed!'

'When she keeps a-throwin skillet lids,' came Ransie's antiphony, 'and
slings b'ilin' water on the best coon-dog in the Cumberlands, and sets herself
again' cookin' a man's victuals, and keeps him awake o' nights accusin' him
of a sight of doin's!'

'When he's al'ays a-fightin' the revenues, and gits a hard name in the
mount'ins fur a mean man, who's gwine to be able fur to sleep o' nights?'

The Justice of the Peace stirred deliberately to his duties. He placed his
one chair and a wooden stool for his petitioners. He opened his book of
statutes on the table and scanned the index. Presently he wiped his spectacles
and shifted his inkstand.

'The law and the statutes,' said he, 'air silent on the subjeck of divo'ce as
fur as the jurisdiction of this co't air concerned. But, accordin' to equity and
the Constitution and the golden rule, it's a bad barg'in that can't run both
ways. If a justice of the peace can marry a couple, it's plain that he is bound
to be able to divo'ce 'em. This here office will issue a decree of divo'ce and
abide by the decision of the Supreme Co't to hold it good.'

Ransie Bilbro drew a small tobacco-bag from his trousers pocket. Out of
this he shook upon the table a five-dollar note. 'Sold a b'arskin and two foxes
fur that,' he remarked. 'It's all the money we got.'

'The regular price of a divo'ce in this co't,' said the Justice, 'air five dollars.'
He stuffed the bill into the pocket of his homespun vest with a deceptive air
of indifference. With much bodily toil and mental travail he wrote the
decree upon half a sheet of foolscap, and then copied it upon the other.
Ransie Bilbro and his wife listened to his reading of the document that was
to give them freedom:

Know all men by these presents that Ransie Bilbro and his wife, Ariela
Bilbro, this day personally appeared before me and promises that hereinafter
they will neither love, honor, nor obey each other, neither for better nor
worse, being of sound mind and body, and accept summons for divorce
according to the peace and dignity of the State. Herein fail not, so help you
God. Benaja Widdup, justice of the peace in and for the county of Piedmont,
State of Tennessee.

The Justice was about to hand one of the documents to Ransie. The voice of
Ariela delayed the transfer. Both men looked at her. Their dull masculinity
was confronted by something sudden and unexpected in the woman.

'Judge, don't you give him that air paper yit. 'Tain't all settled, nohow. I
got to have my rights first. I got to have my ali-money. 'Tain't no kind of a
way to do fur a man to divo'ce his wife 'thout her havin' a cent fur to do
with. I'm a-layin' off to be a-goin' up to brother Ed's up on Hogback Mount'in.
I'm bound fur to hev a pa'r of shoes and some snuff and things besides. Ef
Rance kin affo'd a divo'ce, let him pay me ali-money.'

Ransie Bilbro was stricken to dumb perplexity. There had been no previous
hint of alimony. Women were always bringing up startling and unlooked for
issues.

Justice Benaja Widdup felt that the point demanded judicial decision. The authorities were also silent on the subject of alimony. But the woman's feet were bare. The trail to Hogback Mountain was steep and flinty.

'Ariela Bilbro,' he asked, in official tones, 'how much did you 'low would be good and sufficient ali-money in the case befo' the co't?'

'I 'lowed,' she answered, 'fur the shoes and all, to say five dollars. That ain't much fur ali-money, but I reckon that'll git me up to brother Ed's.'

'The amount,' said the Justice, 'air not onreasonable. Ransie Bilbro, you air ordered by the co't to pay the plaintiff the sum of five dollars befo' the decree of divo'ce air issued.'

'I hain't no mo' money,' breathed Ransie, heavily. 'I done paid you all I had.'

'Otherwise,' said the Justice, looking severely over his spectacles, 'you air in contempt of co't.'

'I reckon if you gimme till to-morrow,' pleaded the husband, 'I mout be able to rake or scrape it up somewhars. I never looked for to be a-payin' no ali-money.'

'The case air adjourned,' said Benaja Widdup, 'till to-morrow, when you-all will present yo'selves and obey the order of the co't. Followin' of which the decrees of divo'ce will be delivered.' He sat down in the door and began to loosen a shoestring.

'We mout as well go down to Uncle Ziah's,' decided Ransie, 'and spend the night.' He climbed into the cart on one side, and Ariela climbed in on the other. Obeying the flat of his rope, the little red bull slowly came around on a tack, and the cart crawled away in the nimbus arising from its wheels.

Justice-of-the-peace Benaja Widdup smoked his elder-stem pipe. Late in the afternoon he got his weekly paper, and read it until the twilight dimmed its lines. Then he lit the tallow candle on his table, and read until the moon rose, marking the time for supper. He lived in the double log cabin on the slope near the girdled poplar. Going home to supper he crossed a little branch darkened by a laurel thicket. The dark figure of a man stepped from the laurels and pointed a rifle at his breast. His hat was pulled down low, and something covered most of his face.

'I want yo' money,' said the figure, ' 'thout any talk. I'm gettin' nervous, and my finger's a-wabblin on this here trigger.'

'I've only got f-f-five dollars,' said the Justice, producing it from his vest pocket.

'Roll it up,' came the order, 'and stick it in the end of this here gun-bar'l.'

The bill was crisp and new. Even fingers that were clumsy and trembling found little difficulty in making a spill of it and inserting it (this with less ease) into the muzzle of the rifle.

'Now I reckon you kin be goin' along,' said the robber.

The Justice lingered not on his way.

The next day came the little red bull, drawing the cart to the office door. Justice Benaja Widdup had his shoes on, for he was expecting the visit. In his presence Ransie Bilbro handed to his wife a five-dollar bill. The official's eye sharply viewed it. It seemed to curl up as though it had been rolled and inserted into the end of a gun-barrel. But the Justice refrained from comment. It is true that other bills might be inclined to curl. He handed each one a decree of divorce. Each stood awkwardly silent, slowly folding the guarantee of freedom. The woman cast a shy glance full of constraint at Ransie.

'I reckon you'll be goin' back up to the cabin,' she said, 'along 'ith the bull-cart. There's bread in the tin box settin' on the shelf. I put the bacon in the bilin'-pot to keep the hounds from gettin' it. Don't forget to wind the clock to-night.'

'You air a-goin' to your brother Ed's?' asked Ransie, with fine unconcern.

'I was 'lowin' to get along up thar afore night. I ain't sayin' as they'll pester theyselves any to make me welcome, but I hain't nowhar else fur to go. It's a right smart ways, and I reckon I better be goin'. I'll be a-sayin' good-bye, Ranse – that is, if you keer fur to say so.'

'I don't know as anybody's a hound dog,' said Ransie, in a martyr's voice, 'fur to not want to say good-bye – 'less you air so anxious to git away that you don't want me to say it.'

Ariela was silent. She folded the five-dollar bill and her decree carefully, and placed them in the bosom of her dress. Benaja Widdup watched the money disappear with mournful eyes behind his spectacles.

And then with his next words he achieved rank (as his thoughts ran) with either the great crowd of the world's sympathizers or the little crowd of its great financiers.

'Be kind o' lonesome in the old cabin to-night, Ransie,' she said.

Ransie Bilbro stared out at the Cumberlands, clear blue now in the sunlight. He did not look at Ariela.

'I 'low it might be lonesome,' he said; 'but when folks gits mad and wants a divo'ce, you can't make folks stay.'

'There's others wanted a divo'ce,' said Ariela, speaking to the wooden stool. 'Besides, nobody don't want nobody to stay.'

'Nobody never said they didn't.'

'Nobody never said they did. I reckon I better start on now to brother Ed's.'

'Nobody can't wind that old clock.'

'Want me to go along 'ith you in the cart and wind it fur you, Ranse?'

The mountaineer's countenance was proof against emotion. But he reached out a big hand and enclosed Ariela's thin brown one. Her soul peeped out once through her impassive face, hallowing it.

'Them hounds sha'n't pester you no more,' said Ransie. 'I reckon I been mean and low down. You wind that clock, Ariela.'

'My heart hit's in that cabin, Ranse,' she whispered, 'along 'ith you. I ain't a-goin' to git mad no more. Le's be startin', Ranse, so's we kin git home by sundown.'

Justice-of-the-peace Benaja Widdup interposed as they started for the door, forgetting his presence.

'In the name of the State of Tennessee,' he said, 'I forbid you-all to be a-defyin' of its laws and statutes. This co't is mo' than willin' and full of joy to see the clouds of discord and misunderstandin' rollin' away from two lovin' hearts, but it air the duty of the co't to p'eserve the morals and integrity of the State. The co't reminds you that you air no longer man and wife, but air divo'ced by regular decree, and as such air not entitled to the benefits and 'purtenances of the mattermonal estate.'

Ariela caught Ransie's arm. Did those words mean that she must lose him now when they had just learned the lesson of life?

'But the co't air prepared,' went on the Justice, 'fur to remove the disabilities set up by the decree of divo'ce. The co't air on hand to perform the solemn ceremony of marri'ge, thus fixin' things up and enablin' the parties in the case to resume the honor'ble and elevatin' state of mattermony which they desires. The fee fur performin' said ceremony will be, in this case, to wit, five dollars.'

Ariela caught the gleam of promise in his words. Swiftly her hand went to her bosom. Freely as an alighting dove the bill fluttered to the Justice's table. Her sallow cheek colored as she stood hand in hand with Ransie and listened to the reuniting words.

Ransie helped her into the cart, and climbed in beside her. The little red bull turned once more, and they set out, hand-clasped, for the mountains.

Justice-of-the-peace Benaja Widdup sat in his door and took off his shoes. Once again he fingered the bill tucked down in his vest pocket. Once again he smoked his elder-stem pipe. Once again the speckled hen swaggered down the main street of the 'settlement,' cackling foolishly.

A SACRIFICE HIT

THE EDITOR OF THE *HEARTHSTONE MAGAZINE* has his own ideas about the selection of manuscript for his publication. His theory is no secret; in fact, he will expound it to you willingly sitting at his mahogany desk, smiling benignantly and tapping his knee gently with his gold-rimmed eye-glasses.

'The *Hearthstone*,' he will say, 'does not employ a staff of readers. We obtain opinions of the manuscripts submitted to us directly from types of the various classes of our readers.'

That is the editor's theory; and this is the way he carries it out:

When a batch of MSS. is received the editor stuffs every one of his pockets full of them and distributes them as he goes about during the day. The office employees, the hall porter, the janitor, the elevator man, messenger boys, the waiters at the café where the editor has luncheon, the man at the news-stand where he buys his evening paper, the grocer and the milkman, the guard on the 5:30 uptown elevated train, the ticket-chopper at Sixty —th street, the cook and maid at his home – these are the readers who pass upon MSS. sent in to the *Hearthstone Magazine*. If his pockets are not entirely emptied by the time he reaches the bosom of his family the remaining ones are handed over to his wife to read after the baby goes to sleep. A few days later the editor gathers in the MSS. during his regular rounds and considers the verdict of his assorted readers.

This system of making up a magazine has been very successful; and the circulation, paced by the advertising rates, is making a wonderful record of speed.

The *Hearthstone* Company also publishes books, and its imprint is to be found on several successful works – all recommended, says the editor, by the *Hearthstone's* army of volunteer readers. Now and then (according to talkative members of the editorial staff) the *Hearthstone* has allowed manuscripts to slip through its fingers on the advice of its heterogeneous readers, that afterward proved to be famous sellers when brought out by other houses.

For instance (the gossips say), 'The Rise and Fall of Silas Latham' was unfavorably passed upon by the elevator-man; the office-boy unanimously rejected 'The Boss'; 'In the Bishop's Carriage' was contemptuously looked upon by the street-car conductor; 'The Deliverance' was turned down by a clerk in the subscription department whose wife's mother had just begun a two month's visit at his home; 'The Queen's Quair' came back from the janitor with the comment: 'So is the book.'

But nevertheless the *Hearthstone* adheres to its theory and system, and it will never lack volunteer readers; for each one of the widely scattered staff, from the young lady stenographer in the editorial office to the man who shovels in coal (whose adverse decision lost to the *Hearthstone* Company the manuscript of 'The Under World'), has expectations of becoming editor of the magazine some day.

This method of the *Hearthstone* was well known to Allen Slayton when he wrote his novelette entitled 'Love Is All.' Slayton had hung about the editorial offices of all the magazines so persistently that he was acquainted with the inner workings of every one in Gotham.

He knew not only that the editor of the *Hearthstone* handed his MSS. around among different types of people for reading, but that the stories of sentimental love-interest went to Miss Puffkin, the editor's stenographer. Another of the editor's peculiar customs was to conceal invariably the name of the writer from his readers of MSS. so that a glittering name might not influence the sincerity of their reports.

Slayton made 'Love Is All' the effort of his life. He gave it six months of the best work of his heart and brain. It was a pure love-story, fine, elevated, romantic, passionate – a prose poem that set the divine blessing of love (I am transposing from the manuscript) high above all earthly gifts and honors, and listed it in the catalogue of heaven's choicest rewards. Slayton's literary ambition was intense. He would have sacrificed all other worldly possessions to have gained fame in his chosen art. He would almost have cut off his right hand, or have offered himself to the knife of the appendicitis fancier to have realized his dream of seeing one of his efforts published in the *Hearthstone*.

Slayton finished 'Love Is All,' and took it to the *Hearthstone* in person. The office of the magazine was in a large, conglomerate building, presided under by a janitor.

As the writer stepped inside the door on his way to the elevator a potato masher flew through the hall, wrecking Slayton's hat, and smashing the glass of the door. Closely following in the wake of the utensil flew the janitor, a bulky, unwholesome man, suspenderless and sordid, panic-stricken and breathless. A frowsy, fat woman with flying hair followed the missile. The janitor's foot slipped on the tiled floor, he fell in a heap with an exclamation of despair. The woman pounced upon him and seized his hair. The man bellowed lustily.

Her vengeance wreaked, the virago rose and stalked, triumphant as Minerva, back to some cryptic domestic retreat at the rear. The janitor got to his feet, blown and humiliated.

'This is married life,' he said to Slayton with a certain bruised humor. 'That's the girl I used to lay awake of nights thinking about. Sorry about your hat, mister. Say, don't snitch to the tenants about this, will yer? I don't want to lose me job.'

Slayton took the elevator at the end of the hall and went up to the offices of the *Hearthstone*. He left the MS. of 'Love Is All' with the editor, who agreed to give him an answer as to its availability at the end of the week.

Slayton formulated his great winning scheme on his way down. It struck him with one brilliant flash, and he could not refrain from admiring his own genius in conceiving the idea. That very night he set about carrying it into execution.

Miss Puffkin, the *Hearthstone* stenographer, boarded in the same house with the author. She was an oldish, thin, exclusive, languishing, sentimental maid; and Slayton had been introduced to her some time before.

The writer's daring and self-sacrificing project was this; he knew that the editor of the *Hearthstone* relied strongly upon Miss Puffkin's judgment in the manuscript of romantic and sentimental fiction. Her taste represented the immense average of mediocre women who devour novels and stories of that type. The central idea and keynote of 'Love Is All' was love at first sight – the enrapturing, irresistible, soul-thrilling feeling that compels a man or a women to recognize his or her spirit-mate as soon as heart speaks to heart. Suppose he should impress this divine truth upon Miss Puffkin personally! – would she not surely indorse her new and rapturous sensations by recommending highly to the editor of the *Hearthstone* the novelette 'Love Is All'?

Slayton thought so. And that night he took Miss Puffkin to the theatre. The next night he made vehement love to her in the dim parlor of the boarding-house. He quoted freely from 'Love Is All'; and he wound up with Miss Puffkin's head on his shoulder, and visions of literary fame dancing in his head.

But Slayton did not stop at love-making. This, he said to himself, was the turning point of his life; and, like a true sportsman, he 'went the limit.' On Thursday night he and Miss Puffkin walked over to the Big Church in the Middle of the Block and were married.

Brave Slayton! Chateaubriand died in a garret, Byron courted a widow, Keats starved to death, Poe mixed his drinks, De Quincey hit the pipe, Ade lived in Chicago, James kept on doing it, Dickens wore white socks, De Maupassant wore a strait-jacket, Tom Watson became a Populist, Jeremiah wept, all these authors did these things, for the sake of literature, but thou didst cap them all; thou marriedst a wife for to carve for thyself a niche in the temple of fame!

On Friday morning Mrs. Slayton said she would go over to the *Hearthstone* office, hand in one or two manuscripts that the editor had given her to read, and resign her position as stenographer.

'Was there anything – er – that – er – you particularly fancied in the stories you are going to turn in?' asked Slayton with a thumping heart.

'There was one – a novelette, that I liked so much,' said his wife. 'I haven't read anything in years that I thought was half as nice and true to life.'

That afternoon Slayton hurried down to the *Hearthstone* office. He felt that his reward was close at hand. With a novelette in the *Hearthstone*, literary reputation would soon be his.

The office boy met him at the railing in the outer office. It was not for unsuccessful authors to hold personal colloquy with the editor except at rare intervals.

Slayton, hugging himself internally, was nursing in his heart the exquisite hope of being able to crush the office boy with his forthcoming success.

He inquired concerning his novelette. The office boy went into the sacred precincts and brought forth a large envelope, thick with more than the bulk of a thousand checks.

'The boss told me to tell you he's sorry,' said the boy, 'but your manuscript ain't available for the magazine.'

Slayton stood dazed. 'Can you tell me,' he stammered, 'whether or no Miss Puff – that is my – I mean Miss Puffkin – handed in a novelette this morning that she had been asked to read?'

'Sure she did,' answered the office boy, wisely. 'I heard the old man say that Miss Puffkin said it was a daisy. The name of it was, "Married for the Mazuma, or a Working Girl's Triumph."

'Say, you!' said the office boy, confidentially, 'your name's Slayton, ain't it? I guess I mixed cases on you without meanin' to do it. The boss gave me some manuscript to hand around the other day and I got the ones for Miss Puffkin and the janitor mixed. I guess it's all right, though.'

And then Slayton looked closer and saw on the cover of his manuscript, under the title 'Love Is All,' the janitor's comment scribbled with a piece of charcoal:

'The – you say!'

THE ROADS WE TAKE

TWENTY MILES WEST OF TUCSON the 'Sunset Express' stopped at a tank to take on water. Besides the aqueous addition the engine of that famous flyer acquired some other things that were not good for it.

While the fireman was lowering the feeding hose, Bob Tidball, 'Shark' Dodson, and a quarter-bred Creek Indian called John Big Dog climbed on the engine and showed the engineer three round orifices in pieces of ordnance that they carried. These orifices so impressed the engineer with their possibilities that he raised both hands in a gesture such as accompanies the ejaculation 'Do tell!'

At the crisp command of Shark Dodson, who was leader of the attacking force, the engineer descended to the ground and uncoupled the engine and tender. Then John Big Dog, perched upon the coal, sportively held two guns upon the engine driver and the fireman, and suggested that they run the engine fifty yards away and there await further orders.

Shark Dodson and Bob Tidball, scorning to put such low-grade ore as the passengers through the mill, struck out for the rich pocket of the express car. They found the messenger serene in the belief that the 'Sunset Express' was taking on nothing more stimulating and dangerous than aqua pura. While Bob was knocking this idea out of his head with the butt-end of his six-shooter Shark Dodson was already dosing the express-car safe with dynamite.

The safe exploded to the tune of $30,000, all gold and currency. The passengers thrust their heads casually out of the windows to look for the thunder-cloud. The conductor jerked at the bell rope, which sagged down loose and unresisting, at his tug. Shark Dodson and Bob Tidball, with their booty in a stout canvas bag, tumbled out of the express car and ran awkwardly in their high-heeled boots to the engine.

The engineer, sullenly angry but wise, ran the engine, according to orders, rapidly away from the inert train. But before this was accomplished the express messenger, recovered from Bob Tidball's persuader to neutrality, jumped out of his car with a Winchester rifle and took a trick in the game. Mr. John Big Dog, sitting on the coal tender, unwittingly made a wrong lead by giving an imitation of a target, and the messenger trumped him. With a ball exactly between his shoulder blades the Creek chevalier of industry rolled off to the ground, thus increasing the share of his comrades in the loot by one-sixth each.

Two miles from the tank the engineer was ordered to stop.

The robbers waved a defiant adieu and plunged down the steep slope into the thick woods that lined the track. Five minutes of crashing through a thicket of chaparral brought them to open woods, where the three horses were tied to low-hanging branches. One was waiting for John Big Dog, who would never ride by night or day again. This animal the robbers divested of saddle and bridle and set free. They mounted the other two with the bag across one pommel, and rode fast and with discretion through the forest and up a primeval, lonely gorge. Here the animal that bore Bob Tidball slipped on a mossy boulder and broke a foreleg. They shot him through the head at once and sat down to hold a council of flight. Made secure for the present by the tortuous trail they had traveled, the question of time was no longer so big. Many miles and hours lay between them and the spryest posse that could follow. Shark Dodson's horse, with trailing rope and dropped bridle, panted and cropped thankfully of the grass along the steam in the gorge. Bob Tidball opened the sack, and drew out double handfuls of the neat packages of currency and the one sack of gold and chuckled with the glee of a child.

'Say, you old double-decked pirate,' he called joyfully to Dodson, 'you said we could do it – you got a head for financing that knocks the horns off of anything in Arizona.'

'What are we going to do about a hoss for you, Bob? We ain't got long to wait here. They'll be on our trail before daylight in the mornin'.'

'Oh, I guess that cayuse of yourn'll carry double for a while,' answered the sanguine Bob. 'We'll annex the first animal we come across. By jingoes, we made a haul, didn't we? Accordin' to the marks on his money there's $30,000 – $15,000 apiece!'

'It's short of what I expected,' said Shark Dodson, kicking softly at the packages with the toe of his boot. And then he looked pensively at the wet sides of his tired horse.

'Old Bolivar's mighty nigh played out,' he said, slowly. 'I wish that sorrel of yours hadn't got hurt.'

'So do I,' said Bob, heartily, 'but it can't be helped. Bolivar's got plenty of bottom – he'll get us both far enough to get fresh mounts. Dang it, Shark, I can't help thinkin' how funny it is that an Easterner like you can come out here and give us Western fellows cards and spades in the desperado business. What part of the East was you from, anyway?'

'New York State,' said Shark Dodson, sitting down on a boulder and chewing a twig. 'I was born on a farm in Ulster County. I ran away from home when I was seventeen. It was an accident my comin' West. I was walkin' along the road with my clothes in a bundle, makin' for New York City. I had an idea of goin' there and makin' lots of money. I always felt like I could do it. I came to a place one evenin' where the road forked and I didn't know which fork to take. I studied about it for half an hour and then I took the left-hand. That night I run into the camp of a Wild West show that was travelin' among the little towns, and I went West with it. I've often wondered if I wouldn't have turned out different if I'd took the other road.'

'Oh, I reckon you'd have ended up about the same,' said Bob Tidball, cheerfully philosophical. 'It ain't the roads we take; it's what's inside of us that makes us turn out the way we do.'

Shark Dodson got up and leaned against a tree.

'I'd a good deal rather that sorrel of yourn hadn't hurt himself, Bob,' he said again, almost pathetically.

'Same here,' agreed Bob; 'he sure was a first-rate kind of a crowbait. But Bolivar, he'll pull us through all right. Reckon we'd better be movin' on, hadn't we, Shark? I'll bag the boodle ag'in and we'll hit the trail for higher timber.'

Bob Tidball replaced the spoil in the bag and tied the mouth of it tightly with a cord. When he looked up the most prominent object that he saw was the muzzle of Shark Dodson's .45 held upon him without a waver.

'Stop your funnin',' said Bob, with a grin. 'We got to be hittin' the breeze.'

'Set still,' said Shark. 'You ain't goin' to hit no breeze, Bob. I hate to tell you, but there ain't any chance for but one of us. Bolivar, he's plenty tired, and he can't carry double.'

'We been pards, me and you, Shark Dodson, for three years,' Bob said quietly. 'We've risked our lives together time and again. I've always give you a square deal, and I thought you was a man. I've heard some queer stories about you shootin' one or two men in a peculiar way, but I never believed 'em. Now if you're just havin' a little fun with me, Shark, put your gun up, and we'll get on Bolivar and vamoose. If you mean to shoot – shoot, you blackhearted son of a tarantula!'

Shark Dodson's face bore a deeply sorrowful look.

'You don't know how bad I feel, ' he sighed, 'about that sorrel of yourn breakin' his leg, Bob.'

The expression on Dodson's face changed in an instant to one of cold ferocity mingled with inexorable cupidity. The soul of the man showed itself for a moment like an evil face in the window of a reputable house.

Truly Bob Tidball was never to 'hit the breeze' again. The deadly .45 of the false friend cracked and filled the gorge with a roar that the walls hurled back with indignant echoes. And Bolivar, unconscious accomplice, swiftly bore away the last of the holders-up of the 'Sunset Express,' not put to the stress of 'carrying double.'

But as Shark Dodson galloped away the woods seemed to fade from his view; the revolver in his right hand turned to the curved arm of a mahogany chair; his saddle was strangely upholstered, and he opened his eyes and saw his feet, not in stirrups, but resting quietly on the edge of a quartered-oak desk.

I am telling you that Dodson, of the firm of Dodson & Decker, Wall Street brokers, opened his eyes. Peabody, the confidential clerk, was standing by his chair, hesitating to speak. There was a confused hum of wheels below, and the sedative buzz of an electric fan.

'Ahem! Peabody,' said Dodson, blinking. 'I must have fallen asleep. I had a most remarkable dream. What is it, Peabody?'

'Mr. Williams, sir, of Tracy & Williams, is outside. He has come to settle his deal in X. Y. Z. The market caught him short, sir, if you remember.'

'Yes, I remember. What is X. Y. Z. quoted at to-day, Peabody?'

'One eighty-five, sir.'

'Then that's his price.'

'Excuse me,' said Peabody, rather nervously, 'for speaking of it, but I've been talking to Williams. He's an old friend of yours, Mr. Dodson, and you practically have a corner in X. Y. Z. I thought you might – that is, I thought you might not remember that he sold you the stock at 98. If he settles at the market price it will take every cent he has in the world and his home too to deliver the shares.'

The expression on Dodson's face changed in an instant to one of cold ferocity mingled with inexorable cupidity. The soul of the man showed itself for a moment like an evil face in the window of a reputable house.

'He will settle at one eighty-five,' said Dodson. 'Bolivar cannot carry double.'

A BLACKJACK BARGAINER

THE MOST DISREPUTABLE THING in Yancey Goree's law office was Goree himself, sprawled in his creaky old armchair. The rickety little office, built of red brick, was set flush with the street – the main street of the town of Bethel.

Bethel rested upon the foot-hills of the Blue Ridge. Above it the mountains were piled to the sky. Far below it the turbid Catawba gleamed yellow along its disconsolate valley.

The June day was at its sultriest hour. Bethel dozed in the tepid shade. Trade was not. It was so still that Goree, reclining in his chair, distinctly heard the clicking of the chips in the grand-jury room, where the 'court-house gang' was playing poker. From the open back door of the office a well-worn path meandered across the grassy lot to the court-house. The treading out of that path had cost Goree all he ever had – first, inheritance of a few thousand dollars, next the old family home, and latterly, the last shreds of his self-respect and manhood. The 'gang' had cleaned him out. The broken gambler had turned drunkard and parasite; he had lived to see this day come when the men who had stripped him denied him a seat at the game. His word was no longer to be taken. The daily bout at cards had arranged itself accordingly, and to him was assigned the ignoble part of the onlooker. The sheriff, the county clerk, a sportive deputy, a gay attorney, and a chalk-faced man hailing 'from the valley,' sat at table, and the sheared one was thus tacitly advised to go and grow more wool.

Soon wearying of his ostracism, Goree had departed for his office, muttering to himself as he unsteadily traversed the unlucky pathway. After a drink of corn whiskey from a demijohn under the table he had flung himself into the chair, staring, in a sort of maudlin apathy, out at the mountains immersed in the summer haze. The little white patch he saw away up on the side of Blackjack was Laurel, the village near which he had been born and bred. There, also, was the birthplace of the feud between the Gorees and the Coltranes. Now no direct heir of the Gorees survived except this plucked and singed bird of misfortune. To the Coltranes, also, but one male supporter was left – Colonel Abner Coltrane, a man of substance and standing, a member of the State Legislature, and a contemporary with Goree's father.

The feud had been a typical one of the region; it had left a red record of hate, wrong, and slaughter.

But Yancey Goree was not thinking of feuds. His befuddled brain was hopelessly attacking the problem of the future maintenance of himself and his favorite follies. Of late, old friends of the family had seen to it that he had whereof to eat and a place to sleep, but whiskey they would not buy for him, and he must have whiskey. His law business was extinct; no case had been intrusted to him in two years. He had been a borrower and a sponge, and it seemed that if he fell no lower it would be from lack of opportunity. One more chance – he was saying to himself – if he had one more stake at the game, he thought he could win; but he had nothing left to sell, and his credit was more than exhausted.

He could not help smiling, even in his misery, as he thought of the man to whom, six months before, he had sold the old Goree homestead. There had come from 'back yan' ' in the mountains two of the strangest creatures, a man named Pike Garvey and his wife. 'Back yan',' with a wave of the hand towards the hills, was understood among the mountaineers to designate the remotest fastnesses, the unplumbed gorges, the haunts of lawbreakers, the wolf's den, and the boudoir of the bear. In the cabin far up on Blackjack's shoulder, in the wildest part of these retreats, this odd couple had lived for twenty years. They had neither dog nor children to mitigate the heavy silence of the hills. Pike Garvey was little known in the settlements, but all who had dealt with him pronounced him 'crazy as a loon.' He acknowledged no occupation save that of a squirrel hunter, but he 'moonshined' occasionally by way of diversion. Once the 'revenues' had dragged him from his lair, fighting silently and desperately like a terrier, and he had been sent to state's prison for two years. Released, he popped back into his hole like an angry weasel.

Fortune, passing over many anxious wooers, made a freakish flight into Blackjack's bosky pockets to smile upon Pike and his faithful partner.

One a day a party of spectacled, knickerbockered, and altogether absurd prospectors invaded the vicinity of the Garveys' cabin. Pike lifted his squirrel rifle off the hook and took a shot at them at long range on the chance of their being revenues. Happily he missed, and the unconscious agents of good luck drew nearer, disclosing their innocence of anything resembling law or justice. Later on, they offered the Garveys an enormous quantity of ready, green, crisp money for their thirty-acre patch of cleared land, mentioning, as an excuse for such a mad action, some irrelevant and inadequate nonsense about a bed of mica underlying the said property.

When the Garveys became possessed of so many dollars that they faltered in computing them, the deficiencies of life on Blackjack began to grow prominent. Pike began to talk of new shoes, a hogshead of tobacco to set in the corner, a new lock to his rifle; and, leading Martella to a certain spot on the mountainside, he pointed out to her how a small cannon – doubtless a thing not beyond the scope of their fortune in price – might be planted so as to command and defend the sole accessible trail to the cabin, to the confusion of revenues and meddling strangers forever.

But Adam reckoned without his Eve. These things represented to him the applied power of wealth, but there slumbered in his dingy cabin an ambition that soared far above his primitive wants. Somewhere in Mrs. Garvey's bosom still survived a spot of femininity unstarved by twenty years of Blackjack.

For so long a time the sounds in her ears had been the scaly-barks dropping in the woods at noon, and the wolves singing among the rocks at night, and it was enough to have purged her vanities. She had grown fat and sad and yellow and dull. But when the means came, she felt a rekindled desire to assume the perquisites of her sex – to sit at tea tables; to buy inutile things; to whitewash the hideous veracity of life with a little form and ceremony. So she coldly vetoed Pike's proposed system of fortification, and announced that they would descend upon the world, and gyrate socially.

And thus, at length, it was decided, and the thing done. The village of Laurel was their compromise between Mrs. Garvey's preference for one of the large valley towns and Pike's hankering for primeval solitudes. Laurel yielded a halting round of feeble social distractions comportable with Martella's ambitions, and was not entirely without recommendation to Pike, its contiguity to the mountains presenting advantages for sudden retreat in case fashionable society should make it advisable.

Their descent upon Laurel had been coincident with Yancey Goree's feverish desire to convert property into cash, and they bought the old Goree homestead, paying four thousand dollars ready money into the spendthrift's shaking hand.

Thus it happened that while the disreputable last of the Gorees sprawled in his disreputable office, at the end of his row, spurned by the cronies whom he had gorged, strangers dwelt in the halls of his fathers.

A cloud of dust was rolling slowly up the parched street, with something traveling in the midst of it. A little breeze wafted the cloud to one side, and a new, brightly painted carryall, drawn by a slothful gray horse, became visible. The vehicle deflected from the middle of the street as it neared Goree's office, and stopped in the gutter directly in front of his door.

On the front seat sat a gaunt, tall man, dressed in black broadcloth, his rigid hands incarcerated in yellow kid gloves. On the back seat was a lady who triumphed over the June heat. Her stout form was armored in a skintight silk dress of the description known as 'changeable,' being a gorgeous combination of shifting hues. She sat erect, waving a much-ornamented fan, with her eyes fixed stonily far down the street. However Martella Garvey's heart might be rejoicing at the pleasures of her new life, Blackjack had done his work with her exterior. He had carved her countenance to the image of emptiness and inanity; had imbued her with the stolidity of his crags and the reserve of his hushed interiors. She always seemed to hear, whatever her surroundings were, the scaly-barks falling and pattering down the mountainside. She could always hear the awful silence of Blackjack sounding through the stillest of nights.

Goree watched this solemn equipage, as it drove to his door, with only faint interest but when the lank driver wrapped the reins about his whip, and awkwardly descended, and stepped into the office, he rose unsteadily to receive him, recognizing Pike Garvey, the new, the transformed, the recently civilized.

The mountaineer took the chair Goree offered him. They who cast doubts upon Garvey's soundness of mind had a strong witness in the man's countenance. His face was too long, a dull saffron in hue, and immobile as a statue's. Pale-blue, unwinking round eyes without lashes added to the singularity of his gruesome visage. Goree was at a loss to account for the visit.

'Everything all right at Laurel, Mr. Garvey?' he inquired.

'Everything all right, sir, and mighty pleased is Missis Garvey and me with the property. Missis Garvey likes yo' old place, and she likes the neighborhood. Society is what she 'lows she wants, and she is gettin' of it. The Rogerses, the Hapgoods, the Pratts, and the Torys hev been to see Missis Garvey, and she hev et meals to most of thar houses. The best folks hev axed her to differ'nt of doin's. I cyan't say, Mr. Goree, that sech things suits me – fur me, give me them thar.' Garvey's huge yellow-gloved hand flourished in the direction of the mountains. 'That's whar I b'long 'mongst the wild honey bees and the b'ars. But that ain't what I come fur to say, Mr. Goree. Thar's somethin' you got what me and Missis Garvey wants to buy.'

'Buy!' echoed Goree. 'From me?' Then he laughed harshly. 'I reckon you are mistaken about that. I sold out to you, as you yourself expressed it, "lock, stock, and barrel." There isn't even a ramrod left to sell.'

'You've got it; and we 'uns want it. "Take the money," says Missis Garvey, "and buy it fa'r and squar'." '

Goree shook his head. 'The cupboard's bare,' he said.

'We've riz,' pursued the mountaineer, undeflected from his object, 'a heap. We was pore as possums, and now we could hev folks to dinner every day. We been reco'nized, Missis Garvey says, by the best society. But there's somethin' we need we ain't got. She says it ought to been put in the 'ventory ov the sale, but it 'tain't thar. "Take the money, then," she says, "and buy it fa'r and squar'." '

'Out with it,' said Goree, his racked nerves growing impatient.

Garvey threw his slouch hat upon the table, and leaned forward, fixing his unblinking eyes upon Goree's.

'There's a old feud,' he said, distinctly and slowly, "tween you 'uns and the Coltranes.'

Goree frowned ominously. To speak of his feud to a feudist is a serious breach of the mountain etiquette. The man from 'back yan' ' knew it as well as the lawyer did.

'Na offense,' he went on, 'but purely in the way of business. Missis Garvey hev studied all about feuds. Most of the quality folks in the mountains hev 'em. The Settles and the Goforths, The Rankins and the Boyds, the Silers and the Galloways, hev all been cyarin' on feuds f'om twenty to a hundred year. The last man to drap was when yo' uncle, Jedge Paisley Goree, 'journed co't and shot Len Coltrane f'om the bench. Missis Garvey and me, we come f'om the po' white trash. Nobody wouldn't pick a feud with we'uns, no mo'n with a fam'ly of treetoads. Quality people everywhar, says Missis Garvey, has feuds. We 'uns ain't quality, but we're buyin' into it as fur as we can. "Take the money, then," says Missis Garvey, "and buy Mr. Goree's feud, fa'r and squar'." '

The squirrel hunter straightened a leg half across the room, drew a roll of bills from his pocket, and threw them on the table.

'Thar's two hundred dollars, Mr. Goree, what you would call a fa'r price for a feud that's been 'lowed to run down like yourn hev. Thar's only you left to cyar' on yo' side of it, and you'd make mighty po' killin'. I'll take it off yo' hands, and it'll set me and Missis Garvey up among the quality. Thar's the money.'

The little roll of currency on the table slowly untwisted itself, writhing and jumping as its folds relaxed. In the silence that followed Garvey's last speech the rattling of the poker chips in the court-house could/be plainly heard. Goree knew that the sheriff had just won a pot, for the subdued whoop with which he always greeted a victory floated across the square upon the crinkly heat waves. Beads of moisture stood on Goree's brow. Stooping, he drew the wicker-covered demijohn from under the table, and filled a tumble from it.

'A little corn liquor, Mr. Garvey? Of course you are joking about – what you spoke of? Opens quite a new market, doesn't it? Feuds, prime, two-fifty to three. Feuds, slightly damaged – two hundred, I believe you said, Mr. Garvey.'

The mountaineer took the glass Goree handed him, and drank the whiskey without a tremor of the lids of his staring eyes. The lawyer applauded the feat by a look of envious admiration. He poured his own drink, and took it like a drunkard, by gulps, and with shudders at the smell and taste.

'Two hundred,' repeated Garvey. 'Thar's the money.'

A sudden passion flared up in Goree's brain. He struck the table with his fist. One of the bills flipped over and touched his hand. He flinched as if something had stung him.

'Do you come to me,' he shouted, 'seriously with such a ridiculous, insulting, darn-fool proposition?'

'It's fa'r and squar',' said the squirrel hunter, but he reached out his hand as if to take back the money; and then Goree knew that his own flurry of rage had not been from pride or resentment, but from anger at himself, knowing that he would set foot in the deeper depths that were being opened to him. He turned in an instant from an outraged gentleman to an anxious chafferer recommending his goods.

'Don't be in a hurry, Garvey,' he said, his face crimson and his speech thick. 'I accept your p-p-proposition, though it's dirt cheap at two hundred. A t-trade's all right when both p-purchaser and b-buyer are s-satisfied. Shall I w-wrap it up for you, Mr. Garvey?'

Garvey rose, and shook out his broadcloth. 'Missis Garvey will be pleased. You air out of it, and it stands Coltrane and Garvey. Just a scrap ov writin', Mr. Goree, you bein' a lawyer, to show we traded.'

Goree seized a sheet of paper and a pen. The money was clutched in his moist hand. Everything else suddenly seemed to grow trivial and light.

'Bill of sale, by all means. "Right, title, and interest in and to" . . . "forever warrant and—" ' No, Garvey, we'll have to leave out that "defend," ' said Goree with a loud laugh. 'You'll have to defend this title yourself.'

The mountaineer received the amazing screed that the lawyer handed him, folded it with immense labor, and placed it carefully in his pocket.

Goree was standing near the window. 'Step here,' he said, raising his finger, 'and I'll show you your recently purchased enemy. There he goes, down the other side of the street.'

The mountaineer crooked his long frame to look through the window in the direction indicated by the other. Colonel Abner Coltrane, an erect, portly gentleman of about fifty wearing the inevitable long, double-breasted frock coat of the Southern lawmaker, and an old high silk hat, was passing on the opposite sidewalk. As Garvey looked, Goree glanced at his face. If there be such a thing as a yellow wolf, here was its counterpart. Garvey snarled as his unhuman eyes followed the moving figure; disclosing long amber-colored fangs.

'Is that him? Why, that's the man who sent me to the pen'tentiary once!'

'He used to be district attorney,' said Goree, carelessly. 'And by the way, he's a first-class shot.'

'I kin hit a squirrel's eye at a hundred yard,' said Garvey. 'So that thar's Coltrane! I made a better trade than I was thinkin'. I'll take keer of this feud, Mr. Goree, better'n you ever did!'

He moved toward the door, but lingered there, betraying a slight perplexity.

'Anything else to-day?' inquired Goree with frothy sarcasm. 'Any family traditions, ancestral ghosts, or skeletons in the closet? Prices as low as the lowest.'

'That was another thing,' replied the unmoved squirrel hunter, 'that Missis Garvey was thinkin' of. 'Tain't so much in my iine as t'other, but she wanted partic'lar that I should inquire, and ef you was willin', "pay fur it," she says, "fa'r and squar'." Thar's a buryin' groun', as you know, Mr. Goree, in the yard of yo' old place, under the cedars. Them that lies thar is yo' folks what was killed by the Coltranes. The monyments has the names on 'em. Missis Garvey says a fam'ly buryin' groun' is a sho' sign of quality. She says ef we git the feud, thar's somethin' else ought to go with it. The names on them monyments is "Goree," but they can be changed to ourn by—'

'Go! Go!' screamed Goree, his face turning purple. He stretched out both hands toward the mountaineer, his fingers hooked and shaking. 'Go, you ghoul! Even a Ch-Chinaman protects the g-graves of his ancestors – go!'

The squirrel hunter slouched out of the door to his carryall. While he was climbing over the wheel Goree was collecting, with Feverish celerity, the money that had fallen from his hand to the floor. As the vehicle slowly turned about, the sheep with a coat of newly grown wool was hurrying, in indecent haste, along the path to the courthouse.

At three o'clock in the morning they brought him back to his office, shorn and unconscious. The sheriff, the sportive deputy, the county clerk, and the gay attorney carried him, the chalk-faced man 'from the valley' acting as escort.

'On the table,' said one of them, and they deposited him there among the litter of his unprofitable books and papers.

'Yance thinks a lot of a pair of deuces when he's liquored up,' sighed the sheriff, reflectively.

'Too much, ' said the gay attorney. 'A man has no business to play poker who drinks as much as he does. I wonder how much he dropped to-night.'

'Close to two hundred. What I wonder is whar he got it. Yance ain't had a cent fur over a month, I know.'

'Struck a client, maybe. Well, let's get home before daylight. He'll be all right when he wakes up, except for a sort of beehive about the cranium.'

The gang slipped away through the early morning twilight. The next eye to gaze upon the miserable Goree was the orb of day. He peered through the uncurtained window, first deluging the sleeper in a flood of faint gold, but soon pouring upon the mottled red of his flesh a searching, white, summer heat. Goree stirred, half unconsciously, among the table's débris, and turned his face from the window. His movement dislodged a heavy law book, which crashed upon the floor. Opening his eyes, he saw, bending over him, a man in a black frock coat. Looking higher, he discovered a well-worn silk hat, and beneath it the kindly, smooth face of Colonel Abner Coltrane.

A little uncertain of the outcome, the colonel waited for the other to make some sign of recognition. Not in twenty years had male members of these two families faced each other in peace. Goree's eyelids puckered as he strained his blurred sight toward this visitor, and then he smiled serenely.

'Have you brought Stella and Lucy over to play?' he said, calmly.

'Do you know me, Yancey?' asked Coltrane.

'Of course I do. You brought me a whip with a whistle in the end.'

So he had – twenty-four years ago; when Yancey's father was his best friend.

Goree's eyes wandered about the room. The colonel understood. 'Lie still, and I'll bring you some,' said he. There was a pump in the yard at the rear, and Goree closed his eyes, listening with rapture to the click of its handle and the bubbling of the falling stream. Coltrane brought a pitcher of the cool water, and held it for him to drink. Presently Goree sat up – a most forlorn object, his summer suit of flax soiled and crumpled, his discreditable head tousled and unsteady. He tried to wave one of his hands toward the colonel.

'Ex-excuse – everything, will you?' he said. 'I must have drunk too much whiskey last night, and gone to bed on the table.' His brows knitted into a puzzled frown.

'Out with the boys a while?' asked Coltrane, kindly.

'No, I went nowhere. I haven't had a dollar to spend in the last two months. Struck the demijohn too often, I reckon, as usual.'

Colonel Coltrane touched him on the shoulder.

'A little while ago, Yancey,' he began, 'you asked me if I had brought Stella and Lucy over to play. You weren't quite awake then, and must have been dreaming you were a boy again. You are awake now, and I want you to listen to me. I have come from Stella and Lucy to their old playmate, and to my old friend's son. They know that I am going to bring you home with me, and you will find them as ready with a welcome as they were in the old days. I want you to come to my house and stay until you are yourself again, and as much longer as you will. We heard of your being down in the world, and in the midst of temptation, and we agreed that you should come over and play at our house once more. Will you come, my boy? Will you drop our old family trouble and come with me?'

'Trouble!' said Goree, opening his eyes wide. 'There was never any trouble between us that I know of. I'm sure we've always been the best of friends. But, good Lord, Colonel, how could I go to your home as I am – a drunken wretch, a miserable, degraded spendthrift and gambler—'

He lurched from the table to his armchair, and began to weep maudlin tears, mingled with genuine drops of remorse and shame. Coltrane talked to him persistently and reasonably, reminding him of the simple mountain pleasures of which he had once been so fond, and insisting upon the genuineness of the invitation.

Finally he landed Goree by telling him he was counting upon his help in the engineering and transportation of a large amount of felled timber from a high mountainside to a waterway. He knew that Goree had once invented a device for this purpose – a series of slides and chutes – upon which he had justly prided himself. In an instant the poor fellow, delighted at the idea of his being of use to any one, had paper spread upon the table, and was drawing rapid but pitifully shaky lines in demonstration of what he could and would do.

The man was sickened of the husks; his prodigal heart was turning again toward the mountains. His mind was yet strangely clogged, and his thoughts and memories were returning to his brain one by one, like carrier pigeons over a stormy sea. But Coltrane was satisfied with the progress he had made.

Bethel received the surprise of its existence that afternoon when a Coltrane and a Goree rode amicably together through the town. Side by side they rode, out from the dusty streets and gaping townspeople, down across the creek bridge, and up toward the mountain. The prodigal had brushed and washed and combed himself to a more decent figure, but he was unsteady in the saddle, and he seemed to be deep in the contemplation of some vexing problem. Coltrane left him in his mood, relying upon the influence of changed surroundings to restore his equilibrium.

Once Goree was seized with a shaking fit, and almost came to a collapse. He had to dismount and rest at the side of the road. The colonel, foreseeing such a condition, had provided a small flask of whiskey for the journey but when it was offered to him Goree refused it almost with violence, declaring he would never touch it again. By and by he was recovered, and went quietly enough for a mile or two. Then he pulled up his horse suddenly, and said:

'I lost two hundred dollars last night, playing poker. Now, where did I get that money?'

'Take it easy, Yancey. The mountain air will soon clear it up. We'll go fishing, first thing, at the Pinnacle Falls. The trout are jumping there like bullfrogs. We'll take Stella and Lucy along, and have a picnic on Eagle Rock. Have you forgotten how a hickory-cured-ham sandwich tastes, Yancey, to a hungry fisherman?'

Evidently the colonel did not believe the story of his lost wealth; so Goree retired again into brooding silence.

By late afternoon they had traveled ten of the twelve miles between Bethel and Laurel. Half a mile this side of Laurel lay the old Goree place; a mile or two beyond the village lived the Coltranes. The road was now steep and laborious, but the compensations were many. The tilted aisles of the forest were opulent with leaf and bird and bloom. The tonic air put to shame the pharmacopoeia. The glades were dark with mossy shade, and bright with shy rivulets winking from the ferns and laurels. On the lower side they viewed, framed in the near foliage, exquisite sketches of the far valley swooning in its opal haze.

Coltrane was pleased to see that his companion was yielding to the spell of the hills and woods. For now they had but to skirt the base of Painter's Cliff; to cross Elder Branch and mount the hill beyond, and Goree would have to face the squandered home of his fathers. Every rock he passed, every tree, every foot of the roadway, was familiar to him. Though he had forgotten the woods, they thrilled him like the music of 'Home, Sweet Home.'

They rounded the cliff, descended into Elder Branch, and paused there to let the horses drink and splash in the swift water. On the right was a rail fence that cornered there, and followed the road and stream. Inclosed by it was the old apple orchard of the home place; the house was yet concealed by the brow of the steep hill. Inside and along the fence, pokeberries, elders, sassafras, and sumac grew high and dense. At a rustle of their branches, both Goree and Coltrane glanced up, and saw a long, yellow, wolfish face above the fence, staring at them with pale, unwinking eyes. The head quickly disappeared; there was a violent swaying of the bushes, and an ungainly figure ran up through the apple orchard in the direction of the house zigzagging among the trees.

'That's Garvey,' said Coltrane; 'the man you sold out to. There's no doubt but he's considerably cracked. I had to send him up for moonshining once, several years ago, in spite of the fact that I believed him irresponsible. Why, what's the matter, Yancey?'

Goree was wiping his forehead, and his face had lost its color. 'Do I look queer, too?' he asked, trying to smile. 'I'm just remembering a few more things.' Some of the alcohol had evaporated from his brain. 'I recollect now where I got that two hundred dollars.'

'Don't think of it,' said Coltrane, cheerfully. 'Later on we'll figure it all out together.'

They rode out of the branch, and when they reached the foot of the hill Goree stopped again.

'Did you ever suspect I was a very vain kind of fellow, Colonel?' he asked. 'Sort of foolish proud about appearances?'

The colonel's eyes refused to wander to the soiled, sagging suit of flax and the faded slouch hat.

'It seems to me,' he replied, mystified, but humoring him, 'I remember a young buck about twenty, with the tightest coat, the sleekest hair, and the prancingest saddle in the Blue Ridge.'

'Right you are,' said Goree, eagerly. 'And it's in me yet, though it don't show. Oh, I'm as vain as a turkey gobbler, and as proud as Lucifer. I'm going to ask you to indulge this weakness of mine in a little matter.'

'Speak out, Yancey. We'll create you Duke of Laurel and Baron of Blue Ridge, if you choose; and you shall have a feather out of Stella's peacock's tail to wear in your hat.'

'I'm in earnest. In a few minutes we'll pass the house up there on the hill where I was born, and where my people have lived for nearly a century. Strangers live there now – and look at me! I am about to show myself to them ragged and poverty-stricken, a wastrel and a beggar. Colonel Coltrane, I'm ashamed to do it. I want you to let me wear your coat and hat until we are out of sight beyond. I know you think it a foolish pride, but I want to make as good a showing as I can when I pass the old place.'

'Now, what does this mean?' said Coltrane to himself, as he compared his companion's sane looks and quite demeanor with his strange request. But he was already unbuttoning the coat, assenting readily, as if the fancy were in no wise to be considered strange.

The coat and hat fitted Goree well. He buttoned the former about him with a look of satisfaction and dignity. He and Coltrane were nearly the same size – rather tall, portly and erect. Twenty-five years were between them, but in appearance they might have been brothers. Goree looked older than his age; his face was puffy and lined; the colonel had the smooth, fresh complexion of a temperate liver. He put on Goree's disreputable old flax coat and faded slouch hat.

'Now,' said Goree, taking up the reins, 'I'm all right. I want you to ride about ten feet in the rear as we go by, Colonel, so that they can get a good look at me. They'll see I'm no back number yet, by any means. I guess I'll show up pretty well to them once more, anyhow. Let's ride on.'

He set out up the hill at a smart trot, the colonel following, as he had been requested.

Goree sat straight in the saddle, with head erect, but his eyes were turned to the right, sharply scanning every shrub and fence and hiding-place in the old homestead yard. Once he muttered to himself, 'Will the crazy fool try it, or did I dream half of it?'

It was when he came opposite the little family burying ground that he saw what he had been looking for – a puff of white smoke, coming from the thick cedars in one corner. He toppled so slowly to the left that Coltrane had time to urge his horse to that side, and catch him with one arm.

The squirrel hunter had not overpraised his arm. He had sent the bullet where he intended, and where Goree had expected that it would pass – pass – through the breast of Colonel Abner Coltrane's black frock coat.

Goree leaned heavily against Coltrane, but he did not fall. The horses kept pace, side by side, and the colonel's arm kept him steady. The little white houses of Laurel shone through the trees, half a mile away. Goree reached out one hand and groped until it rested upon Coltrane's fingers, which held his bridle.

'Good friend,' he said, and that was all.

Thus did Yancey Goree, as he rode past his old home, make, considering all things, the best showing that was in his power.

THE SONG AND THE SERGEANT

HALF A DOZEN PEOPLE SUPPING at a table in one of the upper-Broadway all-night restaurants were making too much noise. Three times the manager walked past them with a politely warning glance; but their argument had waxed too warm to be quelled by a manager's gaze. It was midnight, and the restaurant was filled with patrons from the theatres of that district. Some among the dispersed audiences must have recognized among the quarrelsome sextet the faces of the players belonging to the Carroll Comedy Company.

Four of the six made up the company. Another was the author of the comedietta, 'A Gay Coquette,' which the quartet of players had been presenting with fair success at several vaudeville houses in the city. The sixth at the table was a person inconsequent to the realm of art, but one at whose bidding many lobsters had perished.

Loudly the six maintained their clamorous debate. But one of the party was silent except when answers were stormed from him by the excited ones. That was the comedian of 'A Gay Coquette.' He was a young man with a face even too melancholy for his profession. The oral warfare of four immorderate tongues was directed at Miss Clarice Carroll, the twinkling star of the small aggregation. Excepting the downcast comedian, all members of the party united in casting upon her with vehemence the blame of some momentous misfortune. Fifty times they told her: 'It is your fault, Clarice – it is you alone who spoilt the scene. It is only of late that you have acted this way. At this rate the sketch will have to be taken off.'

Miss Carroll was a match for any four. Gallic ancestry gave her a variety that could easily mount to fury. Her large eyes flashed a scorching denial at her accusers. Her slender, eloquent arms constantly menaced the tableware. Her high, clear soprano voice rose to what would have been a scream had it not possessed so pure a musical quality. She hurled back at the attacking four their denunciations in tones sweet, but of too great carrying power for a Broadway restaurant.

Finally they exhausted her patience both as a woman and an artist. She sprang up like a panther, managed to smash half a dozen plates and glasses with one royal sweep of her arm, and defined her critics. They rose and wrangled more loudly. The comedian sighed and looked a trifle sadder and disinterested. The manager came tripping and suggested peace. He was told to go to the popular synonym for war so promptly that the affair might have happened at The Hague.

Thus was the manager angered. He made a sign with his hand and a waiter slipped out of the door. In twenty minutes the party of six was in a police station, facing a grizzled and philosophical desk sergeant.

'Disorderly conduct in a restaurant,' said the policeman who had brought the party in.

The author of 'A Gay Coquette' stepped to the front. He wore nose-glasses and evening clothes, even if his shoes had been tans before they met the patent-leather-polish bottle.

'Mr. Sergeant,' said he, out of his throat, like Actor Irving, 'I would like to protest against this arrest. The company of actors who are performing in a little play that I have written, in company with a friend and myself, were having a little supper. We became deeply interested in the discussion as to which one of the cast is responsible for a scene in the sketch that lately has fallen so flat that the piece is about to become a failure. We may have been rather noisy and intolerant of interruption by the restaurant people; but the matter was of considerable importance to all of us. You see that we are sober and are not the kind of people who desire to raise disturbances. I hope that the case will not be pressed and that we may be allowed to go.'

'Who makes the charge?' asked the sergeant.

'Me,' said a white-aproned voice in the rear. 'De restaurant sent me to. De gang was raisin' a dough-house and breakin' dishes.'

'The dishes were paid for,' said the playwright. 'They were not broken purposely. In her anger, because we remonstrated with her for spoiling the scene, Miss—'

'It's not true, sergeant,' cried the clear voice of Miss Clarice Carroll. In a long coat of tan silk and a red-plumed hat, she bounded before the desk.

'Its not my fault, she cried, indignantly. 'How dare they say such a thing! I've played the title rôle ever since it was staged, and if you want to know who made it a success, ask the public – that's all.'

'What Miss Carroll says is true in part,' said the author. 'For five months the comedietta was a drawing card in the best houses. But during the last two weeks it has lost favor. There is one scene in it in which Miss Carroll made a big hit. Now she hardly gets a hand out of it. She spoils it by acting it entirely different from her old way.'

'It is not my fault,' reiterated the actress.

'There are only two of you in the scene,' argued the playwright, hotly, 'you and Delmars, here—'

'Then it's his fault,' declared Miss Carroll, with a lightning glance of scorn from her dark eyes. The comedian caught it, and gazed with increased melancholy at the panels of the sergeant's desk.

The night was a dull one in that particular police station.

The sergeant's long-blunted curiosity awoke a little.

'I've heard you,' he said to the author. And then he addressed the thin-faced and ascetic-looking lady of the company who played 'Aunt Turniptop' in the little comedy.

'Who do you think spoils the scene you are fussing about?' he asked.

'I'm no knocker,' said that lady, 'and everybody knows it. So, when I say that Clarice falls down every time in the scene I'm judging her art and not herself. She was great in it once. She does it something fierce now. I'll dope the show if she keeps it up.'

The sergeant looked at the comedian.

'You and the lady have this scene together, I understand. I suppose there's no use asking you which one of you queers it?'

The comedian avoided the direct rays from the two fixed stars of Miss Carroll's eyes.

'I don't know,' he said, looking down at his patent-leather toes.

'Are you one of the actors?' asked the sergeant of a dwarfish youth with a middle-aged face.

'Why, say!' replied the last Thespian witness, 'you don't notice any tin spear in my hands, do you? You haven't heard me shout: "See, the Emperor comes!" since I've been in here, have you? I guess I'm on the stage long enough for 'em not to start a panic by mistaking me for a thin curl of smoke rising above the footlight.'

'In your opinion, if you've got one,' said the sergeant, 'is the frost that gathers on the scene in question the work of the lady or the gentleman who takes part in it?'

The middle-aged youth looked pained.

'I regret to say,' he answered, 'that Miss Carroll seems to have lost her grip on that scene. She's all right in the rest of the play, but – but I tell you, sergeant, she can do it – she has done it equal to any of 'em – and she can do it again.'

Miss Carroll ran forward, glowing and palpitating.

'Thank you, Jimmy, for the first good word I've had in many a day,' she cried. And then she turned her eager face toward the desk.

'I'll show you, sergeant, whether I am to blame. I'll show them whether I can do that scene. Come, Mr. Delmars, let us begin. You will let us won't you, sergeant?'

'How long will it take?' asked the sergeant, dubiously.

'Eight minutes,' said the playwright. 'The entire play consumes but thirty.'

'You may go ahead,' said the sergeant. 'Most of you seem to side against the little lady. Maybe she had a right to crack up a saucer or two in that restaurant. We'll see how she does the turn before we take that up.'

The matron of the police station had been standing near, listening to the singular argument. She came nigher and stood near the sergeant's chair. Two or three of the reserves strolled in, big and yawning.

'Before beginning the scene,' said the playwright, 'and assuming that you have not seen a production of "A Gay Coquette," I will make a brief but necessary explanation. It is a musical-farce-comedy – burlesque-comedietta. As the title implies, Miss Carroll's rôle is that of a gay, rollicking, mischievous, heartless coquette. She sustains that character throughout the entire comedy part of the production. And I have designed the extravaganza features so that she may preserve and present the same coquettish idea.

'Now, the scene in which we take exception to Miss Carroll's acting is called the "gorilla dance." She is costumed to represent a wood nymph, and there is a great song-and-dance scene with a gorilla – played by Mr. Delmars, the comedian. A tropical-forest stage is set.

'That used to get four and five recalls. The main thing was the acting and the dance – it was the funniest thing in New York for five months. Delmars' song, "I'll Woo Thee to My Sylvan Home," while he and Miss Carroll were cutting hide-and-seek capers among the tropical plants, was a winner.'

'What's the trouble with the scene now?' asked the sergeant.

'Miss Carroll spoils it right in the middle,' said the playwright, wrathfully.

With a wide gesture of her ever-moving arms the actress waved back the little group of spectators, leaving a space in front of the desk for the scene of her vindication or fall. Then she whipped off her long tan cloak and tossed it across the arm of the policeman who still stood officially among them.

Miss Carroll had gone to supper well cloaked, but in the costume of the tropic wood nymph. A skirt of fern leaves touched her knee; she was like a humming bird – green and golden and purple.

And then she danced a fluttering, fantastic dance, as agile and light and mazy in her steps that the other three members of the Carroll Comedy Company broke into applause at the art of it.

And at the proper time Delmars leaped out at her side, mimicking the uncouth, hideous bounds of the gorilla so funnily that the grizzled sergeant himself gave a short laugh like the closing of a padlock. They danced together the gorilla dance, and won a hand from all.

Then began the most fantastic part of the scene – the wooing of the nymph by the gorilla. It was a kind of dance itself – eccentric and prankish, with the nymph in coquettish and seductive retreat, followed by the gorilla as he sang 'I'll Woo Thee to My Sylvan Home.'

The song was a lyric of merit. The words were nonsense, as befitted the play, but the music was worthy of something better. Delmars struck into it in a rich tenor that owned a quality that shamed the flippant words.

During one verse of the song the wood nymph performed the grotesque evolutions designed for the scene. At the middle of the second verse she stood still, with a strange look on her face, seeming to gaze dreamily into the depths of the scenic forest. The gorilla's last leap had brought him to her feet, and there he knelt, holding her hand, until he had finished the haunting lyric that was set in the absurd comedy like a diamond in a piece of putty.

When Delmars ceased Miss Carroll started, and covered a sudden flow of tears with both hands.

'There!' cried the playwright, gesticulating with violence; 'there you have it, sergeant. For two weeks she had spoiled that scene in just that manner at every performance. I have begged her to consider that it is not Ophelia or Juliet that she is playing. Do you wonder now at our impatience? Tears for the gorilla song! The play is lost!'

Out of her bewitchment, whatever it was, the wood nymph flared suddenly, and pointed a desperate finger at Delmars.

'It is you – you have done this,' she cried, wildly. 'You never sang that song that way until lately. It is your doing.'

'I give it up,' said the sergeant.

And then the gray-haired matron of the police station came forward from behind the sergeant's chair.

'Must an old woman teach you all?' she said. She went up to Miss Carroll and took her hand.

'The man's wearing his heart out for you, my dear. Couldn't you tell it the first note you heard him sing? All of his monkey flip-flops wouldn't have kept it from me. Must you be deaf as well as blind? That's why you couldn't act your part, child. Do you love him or must he be a gorilla for the rest of his days?'

Miss Carroll whirled around and caught Delmars with a lightning glance of her eye. He came toward her, melancholy.

'Did you hear, Mr. Delmars?' she asked, with a catching breath.

'I did,' said the comedian. 'It is true. I didn't think there was any use. I tried to let you know with the song.'

'Silly!' said the matron; 'why didn't you speak?'

'No, no,' cried the wood nymph, 'his way was the best. I didn't know, but – it was just what I wanted, Bobby.'

She sprang like a green grasshopper; and the comedian opened his arms, and – smiled.

'Get out of this,' roared the desk sergeant to the waiting waiter from the restaurant. 'There's nothing doing here for you.'

ONE DOLLAR'S WORTH

THE JUDGE OF THE UNITED STATES court of the district lying along the Rio Grande border found the following letter one morning in his mail:

> Judge:
>   When you sent me up for four years you made a talk. Among other hard things, you called me a rattlesnake. Maybe I am one – anyhow, you hear me rattling now. One year after I got to the pen, my daughter died of – well, they said it was poverty and the disgrace together. You've got a daughter, Judge, and I'm going to make you know how it feels to lose one. And I'm going to bite that district attorney that spoke against me. I'm free now, and I guess I've turned to rattlesnake all right. I feel like one. I don't say much, but this is my rattle. Look out what I strike.
>
>   Yours respectfully,
>   Rattlesnake

Judge Derwent threw the letter carelessly aside. It was nothing new to receive such epistles from desperate men whom he had been called up to judge. He felt no alarm. Later on he showed the letter to Littlefield, the young district attorney, for Littlefield's name was included in the threat, and the judge was punctilious in matters between himself and his fellow men.

Littlefield honored the rattle of the writer, as far as it concerned himself, with a smile of contempt; but he frowned a little over the reference to the Judge's daughter, for he and Nancy Derwent were to be married in the fall.

Littlefield went to the clerk of the court and looked over the records with him. They decided that the letter might have been sent by Mexico Sam, a half-breed border desperado who had been imprisoned for manslaughter four years before. Then official duties crowded the matter from his mind, and the rattle of the revengeful serpent was forgotten.

Court was in session at Brownsville. Most of the cases to be tried were charges of smuggling, counterfeiting, post-office robberies, and violations of Federal laws along the border. One case was that of a young Mexican, Rafael Ortiz, who had been rounded up by a clever deputy marshal in the act of passing a counterfeit silver dollar. He had been suspected of many such deviations from rectitude, but this was the first time that anything provable had been fixed upon him. Ortiz languished cozily in jail, smoking brown cigarettes and waiting for trial. Kilpatrick, the deputy, brought the counterfeit dollar and handed it to the district attorney in his office in the court-house. The deputy and a reputable druggist were prepared to swear that Ortiz paid for a bottle of medicine with it. The coin was a poor counterfeit, soft, dull-looking, and made principally of lead. It was the day before the morning on which the docket would reach the case of Ortiz, and the district attorney was preparing himself for the trial.

'Not much need of having in high-priced experts to prove the coin's queer, is there, Kil?' smiled Littlefield, as he thumped the dollar down upon the table, where it fell with no more ring than would have come from a lump of putty.

'I guess the Greaser's as good as behind the bars,' said the deputy, easing up his holsters. 'You've got him dead. If it had been just one time, these Mexicans can't tell good money from bad; but this little yaller rascal belongs to a gang of counterfeiters, I know. This is the first time I've been able to catch him doing the trick. He's got a girl down there in them Mexican jacals on the river bank. I seen her one day when I was watching him. She's as pretty as a red heifer in a flower bed.'

Littlefield shoved the counterfeit dollar into his pocket, and slipped his memoranda of the case into an envelope. Just then a bright, winsome face, as frank and jolly as a boy's, appeared in the doorway, and in walked Nancy Derwent.

'Oh, Bob, didn't court adjourn at twelve to-day until to-morrow?' she asked of Littlefield.

'It did,' said the district attorney, 'and I'm very glad of it. I've got a lot of rulings to look up, and—'

'Now, that's just like you. I wonder you and Father don't turn to law books or rulings or something! I want you to take me out plover-shooting this afternoon. Long Prairie is just alive with them. Don't say no, please! I want to try my new twelve-bore hammerless. I've sent to the livery stable to engage Fly and Bess for the buckboard; they stand fire so nicely. I was sure you would go.'

They were to be married in the fall. The glamour was at its height. The plovers won the day – or, rather, the afternoon – over the calf-bound authorities. Littlefield began to put his papers away.

There was a knock at the door. Kilpatrick answered it. A beautiful, dark-eyed girl with a skin tinged with the faintest lemon color walked into the room. A black shawl was thrown over her head and wound once around her neck.

She began to talk in Spanish, a voluble, mournful stream of melancholy music. Littlefield did not understand Spanish. The deputy did, and he translated her talk by portions, at intervals holding up his hands to check the flow of her words.

'She came to see you, Mr. Littlefield. Her name's Joya Treviñas. She wants to see you about – well, she's mixed up with that Rafael Ortiz. She's his – she's his girl. She says he's innocent. She says she made the money and got him to pass it. Don't you believe her, Mr. Littlefield. That's the way with these Mexican girls; they'll lie, steal, or kill for a fellow when they get stuck on him. Never trust a woman that's in love!'

'Mr. Kilpatrick!'

Nancy Derwent's indignant exclamation caused the deputy to flounder for a moment in attempting to explain that he had misquoted his own sentiments, and then he went on with the translation:

'She says she's willing to take his place in the jail if you'll let him out. She says she was down sick with the fever, and the doctor said she'd die if she didn't have medicine. That's why he passed the lead dollar on the drug store. She says it saved her life. This Rafael seems to be her honey, all right; there's a lot of stuff in her talk about love and such things that you don't want to hear.'

It was an old story to the district attorney.

'Tell her,' said he, 'that I can do nothing. The case comes up in the morning, and he will have to make his fight before the court.'

Nancy Derwent was not so hardened. She was looking with sympathetic interest at Joya Treviñas and at Littlefield alternately. The deputy repeated the district attorney's words to the girl. She spoke a sentence or two in a low voice, pulled her shawl closely about her face, and left the room.

'What did she say then?' asked the district attorney.

'Nothing special,' said the deputy. 'She said: "If the life of the one" – let's see how it went – "Si la vida de ella a quien tu amas – if the life of the girl you love is ever in danger, remember Rafael Ortiz." '

Kilpatrick strolled out through the corridor in the direction of the marshal's office.

'Can't you do anything for them, Bob?' asked Nancy. 'It's such a little thing – just one counterfeit dollar – to ruin the happiness of two lives! She was in danger of death, and he did it to save her. Doesn't the law know the feeling of pity?'

'It hasn't a place in jurisprudence, Nan,' said Littlefield, 'especially in re the district attorney's duty. I'll promise you that the prosecution will not be vindictive; but the man is as good as convicted when the case is called. Witnesses will swear to his passing the bad dollar which I have in my pocket at this moment as "Exhibit A." There are no Mexicans on the jury, and it will vote Mr. Greaser guilty without leaving the box.'

The plover-shooting was fine that afternoon, and in the excitement of the sport the case of Rafael and the grief of Joya Treviñas was forgotten. The district attorney and Nancy Derwent drove out from the town three miles along a smooth, grassy road, and then struck across a rolling prairie toward a heavy line of timber on Piedra Creek. Beyond this creek lay Long Prairie, the favorite haunt of the plover. As they were nearing the creek they heard the galloping of a horse to their right, and saw a man with black hair and a swarthy face riding toward the woods at a tangent, as if he had come up behind them.

'I've seen that fellow somewhere,' said Littlefield, who had a memory for faces, 'but I can't exactly place him. Some ranchman, I suppose, taking a short cut home.'

They spent an hour on Long Prairie, shooting from the buckboard. Nancy Derwent, an active, outdoor Western girl, was pleased with her twelve-bore. She had bagged within two brace of her companion's score.

They started homeward at a gentle trot. When within a hundred yards of Piedra Creek a man rode out of the timber directly toward them.

'It looks like the man we saw coming over,' remarked Miss Derwent.

As the distance between them lessened, the district attorney suddenly pulled up his team sharply, with his eyes fixed upon the advancing horseman. That individual had drawn a Winchester from its scabbard on his saddle and thrown it over his arm.

'Now I know you, Mexico Sam!' muttered Littlefield to himself. 'It *was* you who shook your rattles in that gentle epistle.'

Mexico Sam did not leave things long in doubt. He had a nice eye in a matters relating to firearms, so when he was within good rifle range, but outside of danger from No. 8 shot, he threw up his Winchester and opened fire upon the occupants of the buckboard.

The first shot cracked the back of the seat within the two-inch space between the shoulders of Littlefield and Miss Derwent. The next went through the dashboard and Littlefield's trouser leg.

The district attorney hustled Nancy out of the buckboard to the ground. She was a little pale, but asked no questions. She had the frontier instinct that accepts conditions in an emergency without superfluous argument. They kept their guns in hand, and Littlefield hastily gathered some handfuls of cartridges from the pasteboard box on the seat and crowded them into his pockets.

'Keep behind the horses, Nan,' he commanded. 'That fellow is a ruffian I sent to prison once. He's trying to get even. He knows our shot won't hurt him at that distance.'

'All right, Bob,' said Nancy, steadily. 'I'm not afraid. But you come close, too. Whoa, Bess; stand still, now!'

She stroked Bess's mane. Littlefield stood with his gun ready, praying that the desperado would come within range.

But Mexico Sam was playing his vendetta along safe lines. He was a bird of different feather from the plover. His accurate eye drew an imaginary line of circumference around the area of danger from bird-shot, and upon this line he rode. His horse wheeled to the right, and as his victims rounded to the safe side of their equine breastwork he sent a ball through the district attorney's hat. Once he miscalculated in making a detour, and overstepped his margin. Littlefield's gun flashed, and Mexico Sam ducked his head to the harmless patter of the shot. A few of them stung his horse, which pranced promptly back to the safety line.

The desperado fired again. A little cry came from Nancy Derwent. Littlefield whirled, with blazing eyes, and saw the blood trickling down her cheek.

'I'm not hurt, Bob – only a splinter struck me, I think he hit one of the wheel-spokes.'

'Lord!' groaned Littlefield. 'If I only had a charge of buckshot!'

The ruffian got his horse still, and took careful aim. Fly gave a snort and fell in the harness, struck in the neck. Bess, now disabused of the idea that plover were being fired at, broke her traces and galloped wildly away. Mexican Sam sent a ball neatly through the fullness of Nancy Derwent's shooting jacket.

'Lie down – lie down!' snapped Littlefield. 'Close to the horse – flat on the ground – so.' He almost threw her upon the grass against the back of the recumbent Fly. Oddly enough, at that moment the words of the Mexican girl returned to his mind:

'If the life of the girl you love is ever in danger, remember Rafael Ortiz.' Littlefield uttered an exclamation.

'Open fire on him, Nan, across the horse's back! Fire as fast as you can! You can't hurt him, but keep him dodging shot for one minute while I try to work a little scheme.'

Nancy gave a quick glance at Littlefield, and saw him take out his pocket-knife and open it. Then she turned her face to obey orders, keeping up a rapid fire at the enemy.

Mexico Sam waited patiently until this innocuous fusillade ceased. He had plenty of time, and he did not care to risk the chance of a bird-shot in his eye if it could be avoided by a little caution. He pulled his heavy Stetson low down over his face until the shots ceased. Then he drew a little nearer, and fired with careful aim at what he could see of his victims above the fallen horse.

Neither of them moved. He urged his horse a few steps nearer. He saw the district attorney rise to one knee, and deliberately level his shotgun. He pulled his hat down and awaited the harmless rattle of the tiny pellets.

The shotgun blazed with a heavy report. Mexico Sam sighed, turned limp all over, and slowly fell from his horse – a dead rattlesnake.

At ten o'clock the next morning court opened, and the case of the United States *versus* Rafael Ortiz was called. The district attorney, with his arm in a sling, rose and addressed the court.

'May it please your honor,' he said, 'I desire to enter a *nolle pros*. in this case. Even though the defendant should be guilty, there is not sufficient evidence in the hands of the government to secure a conviction. The piece of counterfeit coin upon the identity of which the case was built is not now available as evidence. I ask, therefore, that the case be stricken off.'

At the noon recess, Kilpatrick strolled into the district attorney's office.

'I've just been down to take a squint at old Mexico Sam,' said the deputy. 'They've got him laid out. Old Mexico was a tough outfit, I reckon. The boys was wonderin' down there what you shot him with. Some said it must have been nails. I never see a gun carry anything to make holes like he had.'

'I shot him,' said the district attorney, 'with Exhibit A of your counterfeiting case. Lucky thing for me – and somebody else – that it was as bad money as it was! It sliced up into slugs very nicely. Say, Kil, can't you go down to the jacals and find where that Mexican girl lives? Miss Derwent wants to know.'

A NEWSPAPER STORY

AT 8 A.M. IT LAY ON GIUSEPPI'S NEWS-STAND, still damp from the presses. Giuseppi, with the cunning of his ilk, philandered on the opposite corner leaving his patrons to help themselves, no doubt on a theory related to the hypothesis of the watched pot.

This particular newspaper was, according to its custom and design, an educator, a guide, a monitor, a champion, and a household counsellor and *vade mecum*.

From its many excellencies might be selected three editorials. One was in simple and chaste but illuminating language directed to parents and teachers, deprecating corporal punishment for children.

Another was an accusive and significant warning addressed to a notorious labor leader who was on the point of instigating his clients to a troublesome strike.

The third was an eloquent demand that the police force be sustained and aided in everything that tended to increase its efficiency as public guardians and servants.

Besides these more important chidings and requisitions upon the store of good citizenship was a wise prescription or form of procedure laid out by the editor of the heart-to-heart column in the specific case of a young man who had complained of the obduracy of his lady love, teaching him how he might win her.

Again, there was, on the beauty page, a complete answer to a young lady inquirer who desired admonition toward the securing of bright tyes, rosy cheeks, and a beautiful countenance.

One other item requiring special cognizance was a brief 'personal,' running thus:

Dear Jack: — Forgive me. You were right. Meet me at corner of Madison and –th at 8.30 this morning. We leave at noon.

Penitent

At 8 o'clock a young man with a haggard look and the feverish gleam of unrest in his eye dropped a penny and picked up the top paper as he passed Giuseppi's stand. A sleepless night had left him a late riser. There was an office to be reached by nine, and a shave and a hasty cup of coffee to be crowded into the interval.

He visited his barber shop and then hurried on his way. He pocketed his paper, meditating a belated perusal of it at the luncheon hour. At the next corner it fell from his pocket, carrying with it his pair of new gloves. Three blocks he walked, missed the gloves and turned back fuming.

Just on the half-hour he reached the corner where lay the gloves and paper. But he strangely ignored that which he had come to seek. He was holding two little hands as tightly as ever he could and looking into two penitent brown eyes, while joy rioted in his heart.

'Dear Jack,' she said, 'I knew you would be here on time.'

'I wonder what she means by that,' he was saying to himself; 'but it's all right, it's all right.'

A big wind puffed out of the west, picked up the paper from the sidewalk, opened it and sent it flying and whirling down a side street. Up that street was driving a skittish bay to a spider-wheel buggy the young man who had written to the heart-to-heart editor for a recipe that he might win her for whom he sighed.

The wind, with a prankish flurry, flapped the flying newspaper against the face of the skittish bay. There was a lengthened streak of bay mingled with the red of running gear that stretched itself out for four blocks. Then a water-hydrant played its part in the cosmogony, the buggy became match wood as foreordained, and the driver rested very quietly where he had been flung on the asphalt in front of a certain brownstone mansion.

They came out and had him inside very promptly. And there was one who made herself a pillow for his head, and cared for no curious eyes, bending over and saying, 'Oh, it was you; it was you all the time, Bobby! Couldn't you see it? And if you die, why, so must I, and—'

But in all this wind we must hurry to keep in touch with our paper.

Policeman O'Brine arrested it as a character dangerous to traffic. Straightening its dishevelled leaves with his big, slow fingers, he stood a few feet from the family entrance of the Shandon Bells Café. One headline he spelled out ponderously. 'The Papers to the Front in a Move to Help the Police.'

But, whist! The voice of Danny, the head bartender, through the crack of the door: 'Here's a nip for ye, Mike, ould man.'

Behind the widespread, amicable columns of the press Policeman O'Brine receives swiftly his nip of the real stuff. He moves away, stalwart, refreshed, fortified, to his duties. Might not the editor man view with pride the early, the spiritual, the literal fruit that had blessed his labors.

Policeman O'Brine folded the paper and poked it playfully under the arm of a small boy that was passing. That boy was named Johnny, and he took the paper home with him. His sister was named Gladys, and she had written to the beauty editor of the paper asking for the practicable touchstone of beauty. That was weeks ago, and she had ceased to look for an answer. Gladys was a pale girl, with dull eyes and a discontented expression. She was dressing to go up to the avenue to get some braid. Beneath her skirt she pinned two leaves of the paper Johnny had brought. When she walked the rustling sound was an exact imitation of the real thing.

On the street she met the Brown girl from the flat below and stopped to talk. The Brown girl turned green. Only silk at $5 a yard could make the sound that she heard when Gladys moved. The Brown girl, consumed by jealousy, said something spiteful and went her way, with pinched lips.

Gladys proceeded towards the avenue. Her eyes now sparked like jager-fonteins. A rosy bloom visited her cheeks; a triumphant, subtle, vivifying smile transfigured her face. She was beautiful. Could the beauty editor have seen her then! There was something in her answer in the paper, I believe, about cultivating a kind feeling towards others in order to make plain features attractive.

The labor leader against whom the paper's solemn and weighty editorial injunction was laid was the father of Gladys and Johnny. He picked up the remains of the journal from which Gladys had ravished a cosmetic of silken sounds. The editorial did not come under his eye, but instead it was greeted by one of those ingenious and specious puzzle problems that enthrall alike the simpleton and the sage.

The labor leader tore off half of the page, provided himself with table, pencil, and paper and glued himself to the puzzle.

Three hours later, after waiting vainly for him at the appointed place, other more conservative leaders declared and ruled in favor of arbitration, and the strike with its attendant dangers was averted. Subsequent editions of the paper referred, in colored inks, to the clarion tone of its successful denunciation of the labor leader's intended designs.

The remaining leaves of the active journal also went loyally to the proving of its potency.

When Johnny returned from school he sought a secluded spot and removed the missing columns from the inside of his clothing, where they had been artfully distributed so as to successfully defend such areas as are generally attacked during scholastic castigations. Johnny attended a private school and had had trouble with his teacher. As has been said, there was an excellent editorial against corporal punishment in that morning's issue, and no doubt it had its effect.

After this can any one doubt the power of the press?

TOMMY'S BURGLAR

AT TEN O'CLOCK P.M. FELICIA, the maid, left the basement door with the policeman to get a raspberry phosphate around the corner. She detested the policeman and objected earnestly to the arrangement. She pointed out, not unreasonably, that she might have been allowed to fall asleep over one of St. George Rathbone's novels on the third floor, but she was overruled. Raspberries and cops were not created for nothing.

The burglar got into the house without much difficulty; because we must have action and not too much description in a 2,000-word story.

In the dining room he opened the slide of his dark lantern. With a brace and centrebit he began to bore into the lock of the silver-closet.

Suddenly a click was heard. The room was flooded with electric light. The dark velvet portières parted to admit a fair-haired boy of eight in pink pajamas, bearing a bottle of olive oil in his hand.

'Are you a burglar?' he asked, in a sweet, childish voice.

'Listen to that,' exclaimed the man, in a hoarse voice. 'Am I a burglar? Wot do you suppose I have a three days' growth of bristly beard on my face for, and a cap with flaps? Give me the oil, quick, and let me grease the bit, so I won't wake up your mamma, who is lying down with a headache, and left you in charge of Felicia who has been faithless to her trust.'

'Oh, dear,' said Tommy, with a sigh. 'I thought you would be more up-to-date. This oil is for the salad when I bring lunch from the pantry for you. And mamma and papa have gone to the Metropolitan to hear De Reszke. But that isn't my fault. It only shows how long the story has been knocking around among the editors. If the author had been wise he'd have changed it to Caruso in the proofs.'

'Be quiet,' hissed the burglar, under his breath. 'If you raise an alarm I'll wring your neck like a rabbit's.'

'Like a chicken's,' corrected Tommy. 'You had that wrong. You don't wring rabbits' necks.'

'Aren't you afraid of me?' asked the burglar.

'You know I'm not,' answered Tommy. 'Don't you suppose I know fact from fiction? If this wasn't a story I'd yell like an Indian when I saw you; and you'd probably tumble downstairs and get pinched on the sidewalk.'

'I see,' said the burglar, 'that you're on to your job. Go on with the peformance.'

Tommy seated himself in an armchair and drew his toes up under him.

'Why do you go around robbing strangers, Mr. Burglar? Have you no friends?'

'I see what you're driving at,' said the burglar, with a dark frown. 'It's the same old story. Your innocence and childish insouciance is going to lead me back into an honest life. Every time I crack a crib where there's a kid around, it happens.'

'Would you mind gazing with wolfish eyes at the plate of cold beef that the butler has left on the dining table?' said Tommy. 'I'm afraid it's growing late.'

The burglar accommodated.

'Poor man,' said Tommy. 'You must be hungry. If you will please stand in a listless attitude I will get you something to eat.'

The boy brought a roast chicken, a jar of marmalade, and a bottle of wine from the pantry. The burglar seized a knife and fork sullenly.

'It's only been an hour,' he grumbled, 'since I had a lobster and a pint of musty ale up on Broadway. I wish these story writers would let a fellow have a pepsin tablet, anyhow, between feeds.'

'My papa writes books,' remarked Tommy.

The burglar jumped to his feet quickly.

'You said he had gone to the opera,' he hissed, hoarsely and with immediate suspicion.

'I ought to have explained,' said Tommy. 'He didn't buy the ticket.' The burglar sat again and toyed with the wishbone.

'Why do you burgle houses?' asked the boy, wonderingly.

'Because,' replied the burglar, with a sudden flow of tears. 'God bless my little brown-haired boy Bessie at home.'

'Ah,' said Tommy, wrinkling his nose, 'you got that answer in the wrong place. You want to tell your hard-luck story before you pull out the child stop.'

'Oh, yes,' said the burglar, 'I forgot. Well, once I lived up in Milwaukee, and—'

'Take the silver,' said Tommy, rising from his chair.

'Hold on,' said the burglar. 'But I moved away. I could find no other employment. For a while I managed to support my wife and child by passing confederate money; but alas! I was forced to give that up because it did not belong to the union. I became desperate and a burglar.'

'Have you ever fallen into the hands of the police?' asked Tommy.

'I said "burglar," not "beggar," ' answered the cracksman.

'After you finish your lunch,' said Tommy, 'and experience the usual change of heart, how shall we wind up the story?'

'Suppose,' said the burglar, thoughtfully, 'that Tony Pastor turns out earlier than usual to-night, and your father gets in from "Parsifal" at 10.30. I am thoroughly repentant because you have made me think of my own little boy Bessie, and—'

'Say,' said Tommy, 'haven't you got that wrong?'

'Not on your colored crayon drawings by B. Cory Kilvert,' said the burglar. 'It's always a Bessie that I have at home, artlessly prattling to the pale-cheeked burglar's bride. As I was saying, your father opens the front door just as I am departing with admonitions and sandwiches that you have wrapped up for me. Upon recognizing me as an old Harvard classmate he starts back in—'

'Not in surprise?' interrupted Tommy, with wide-open eyes.

'He starts back in the doorway,' continued the burglar. And then he rose to his feet and began to shout: 'Rah, rah, rah! rah, rah, rah! rah, rah, rah!'

'Well,' said Tommy, wonderingly, 'that's the first time I ever knew a burglar to give a college yell when he was burglarizing a house, even in a story.'

'That's one on you,' said the burglar, with a laugh. 'I was practising the dramatization. If this is put on the stage that college touch is about the only thing that will make it go.'

Tommy looked his admiration.

'You're on, all right,' he said.

'And there's another mistake you've made,' said the burglar. 'You should have gone some time ago and brought me the $9 gold piece your mother gave you on your birthday to take to Bessie.'

'But she didn't give it to me to take to Bessie,' said Tommy, pouting.

'Come, come!' said the burglar, sternly. 'It's not nice of you to take advantage because the story contains an ambiguous sentence. You know what I mean. It's mighty little I get out of these fictional jobs, anyhow. I lose all the loot, and I have to reform every time; and all the swag I'm allowed is the blamed little fol-de-rols and luck-pieces that you kids hand over. Why in one story, all I got was a kiss from a little girl who came on me when I was opening a safe. And it tasted of molasses candy, too. I've a good notion to tie this table cover over your head and keep on into the silver-closet.'

'Oh, no, you haven't,' said Tommy, wrapping his arms around his knees. 'Because if you did no editor would buy the story. You know you've got to preserve the unities.'

'So've you,' said the burglar, rather glumly. 'Instead of sitting here talking impudence and taking the bread out of a poor man's mouth, what you'd like to be doing is hiding under the bed and screeching at the top of your voice.'

'You're right, old man,' said Tommy, heartily. 'I wonder what they make us do it for? I think the S.P.C.C. ought to interfere. I'm sure it's neither agreeable nor usual for a kid of my age to butt in when a full-grown burglar is at work and offer him a red sled and a pair of skates not to awaken his sick mother. And look how they make the burglars act! You'd think editors would know – but what's the use?'

The burglar wiped his hands on the tablecloth and arose with a yawn.

'Well, let's get through with it,' he said. 'God bless you, my little boy! you have saved a man from committing a crime this night. Bessie shall pray for you as soon as I get home and give her her orders. I shall never burglarize another house – at least not until the June magazines are out. It'll be your little sister's turn then to run in on me while I am abstracting the U.S. 4 per cent. from the tea urn and buy me off with her coral necklace and a falsetto kiss.'

'You haven't got all the kicks coming to you,' sighed Tommy, crawling out of his chair. 'Think of the sleep I'm losing. But it's tough on both of us, old man. I wish you could get out of the story and really rob somebody. Maybe you'll have the chance if they dramatize us.'

'Never!' said the burglar, gloomily. 'Between the box office and my better impulses that your leading juveniles are supposed to awaken and the magazines that pay on publication, I guess I'll always be broke.'

'I'm sorry,' said Tommy, sympathetically. 'But I can't help myself any more than you can. It's one of the canons of household fiction that no burglar shall be successful. The burglar must be foiled by a kid like me, or by a young lady heroine, or at the last moment by his old pal, Red Mike, who recognizes the house as one in which he used to be the coachman. You have got the worst end of it in any kind of a story.'

'Well, I suppose I must be clearing out now,' said the burglar, taking up his lantern and bracebit.

'You have to take the rest of this chicken and the bottle of wine with you' for Bessie and her mother,' said Tommy, calmly.

'But confound it,' exclaimed the burglar, in an annoyed tone, 'they don't want it. I've got five cases of Château de Beychsvelle at home that was bottled in 1853. That claret of yours is corked. And you couldn't get either of them to look at a chicken unless it was stewed in champagne. You know, after I get out of the story I don't have so many limitations. I make a turn now and then.'

'Yes, but you must take them,' said Tommy, loading his arms with the bundles.

'Bless you, young master!' recited the burglar, obedient. 'Second-Story Saul will never forget you. And now hurry and let me out, kid. Our 2,000 words must be nearly up.'

Tommy led the way through the hall toward the front door. Suddenly the burglar stopped and called to him softly: 'Ain't there a cop out there in front somewhere sparking the girl?'

'Yes,' said Tommy, 'but what—'

'I'm afraid he'll catch me,' said the burglar. 'You mustn't forget that this is fiction.'

'Great head!' said Tommy, turning. 'Come out by the back door.'

A CHAPARRAL CHRISTMAS GIFT

THE ORIGINAL CAUSE OF THE TROUBLE was about twenty years in growing.

At the end of that time it was worth it.

Had you lived anywhere within fifty miles of Sundown Ranch you would have heard of it. It possessed a quantity of jet-black hair, a pair of extremely frank, deep-brown eyes, and a laugh that rippled across the prairie like the sound of a hidden brook. The name of it was Rosita McMullen; and she was the daughter of old man McMullen of the Sundown Sheep Ranch.

There came riding on red roan steeds – or, to be more explicit, on a paint and flea-bitten sorrel – two wooers. One was Madison Lane, and the other was the Frio Kid. But at that time they did not call him the Frio Kid, for he had not earned the honors of special nomenclature. His name was simply Johnny McRoy.

It must not be supposed that these two were the sum of the agreeable Rosita's admirers. The bronchos of a dozen others champed their bits at the long hitching rack of the Sundown Ranch. Many were the sheeps'-eyes that were cast in those savannas that did not belong to the flocks of Dan McMullen. But of all the cavaliers, Madison Lane and Johnny McRoy galloped far ahead, wherefore they are to be chronicled.

Madison Lane, a young cattleman from the Nueces country, won the race. He and Rosita were married one Christmas day. Armed, hilarious, vociferous, magnanimous, the cowmen and the sheepmen, laying aside their hereditary hatred, joined forces to celebrate the occasion.

Sundown Ranch was sonorous with the cracking of jokes and six-shooters, the shine of buckles and bright eyes, the outspoken congratulations of the herders of kine.

But while the wedding feast was at its liveliest there descended upon it Johnny McRoy, bitten by jealousy, like one possessed.

'I'll give you a Christmas present,' he yelled, shrilly, at the door, with his .45 in his hand. Even then he had some reputation as an offhand shot.

His first bullet cut a neat underbit in Madison Lane's right ear. The barrel of his gun moved an inch. The next shot would have been the bride's had not Carson, a sheepman, possessed a mind with triggers somewhat well oiled and in repair. The guns of the wedding party had been hung, in their belts, upon nails in the wall when they sat at table, as a concession to good taste. But Carson, with great promptness, hurled his plate of roast venison and frijoles at McRoy, spoiling his aim. The second bullet then, only shattered the white petals of a Spanish dagger flower suspended two feet above Rosita's head.

The guests spurned their chairs and jumped for their weapons. It was considered an improper act to shoot the bride and groom at a wedding. In about six seconds there were twenty or so bullets due to be whizzing in the direction of Mr. McRoy.

'I'll shoot better next time,' yelled Johnny; 'and there'll be a next time.' He backed rapidly out of the door.

Carson, the sheepman, spurred on to attempt further exploits by the success of his plate throwing, was first to reach the door. McRoy's bullet from the darkness laid him low.

The cattlemen then swept out upon him, calling for vengeance, for, while the slaughter of a sheepman has not always lacked condonement, it was a decided misdemeanor in this instance. Carson was innocent; he was no accomplice at the matrimonial proceedings; nor had any one heard him quote the line 'Christmas comes but once a year' to the guests.

But the sortie failed in its vengeance. McRoy was on his horse and away, shouting back curses and threats as he galloped into the concealing chaparral.

That night was the birthnight of the Frio Kid. He became the 'bad man' of that portion of the State. The rejection of his suit by Miss McMullen turned him to a dangerous man. When officers went after him for the shooting of Carson, he killed two of them, and entered upon the life of an outlaw. He became a marvellous shot with either hand. He would turn up in towns and settlements, raise a quarrel at the slightest opportunity, pick off his man, and laugh at the officers of the law. He was so cool, so deadly, so rapid, so inhumanly bloodthirsty that none but faint attempts were ever made to capture him. When he was at last shot and killed by a little one-armed Mexican who was nearly dead himself from fright, the Frio Kid had the deaths of eighteen men on his head. About half of these were killed in fair duels depending upon the quickness of the draw. The other half were men whom he assassinated from absolute wantonness and cruelty.

Many tales are told along the border of his impudent courage and daring. But he was not one of the breed of desperadoes who have seasons of generosity and even of softness. They say he never had mercy on the object of his anger. Yet at this and every Christmastide it is well to give each one credit, if it can be done, for whatever speck of good he may have possessed. If the Frio Kid ever did a kindly act or felt a throb of generosity in his heart it was once at such a time and season, and this is the way it happened.

One who has been crossed in love should never breathe the odor of the blossoms of the ratama tree. It stirs the memory to a dangerous degree.

One December in the Frio country there was a ratama tree in full bloom, for the winter had been as warm as springtime. That way rode the Frio Kid and his satellite and co-murderer, Mexican Frank. The kid reined in his mustang, and sat in his saddle, thoughtful and grim, with dangerously narrowing eyes. The rich, sweet scent touched him somewhere beneath his ice and iron.

'I don't know what I've been thinking about, Mex,' he remarked in his usual mild draw, 'to have forgot all about a Christmas present I got to give. I'm going to ride over to-morrow night and shoot Madison Lane in his own house. He got my girl – Rosita would have had me if he hadn't cut into the game. I wonder why I happened to overlook it up to now?'

'Ah, shucks, Kid,' said Mexican, 'don't talk foolishness. You know you can't get within a mile of Mad Lane's house to-morrow night. I see old man Allen day before yesterday, and he says Mad is going to have Christmas doings at his house. You remember how you shot up the festivities when Mad was married, and about the threats you made? Don't you suppose Mad Lane'll kind of keep his eye open for a certain Mr. Kid? You plumb make me tired, Kid, with such remarks.'

'I'm going,' repeated the Frio Kid, without heat, 'to go to Madison Lane's Christmas doings, and kill him. I ought to have done it a long time ago. Why, Mex, just two weeks ago I dreamed me and Rosita was married instead of her and him; and we was living in a house, and I could see her smiling at me, and – oh! h—l, Mex, he got her; and I'll get him – yes, sir, on Christmas Eve he got her, and then's when I'll get him.'

'There's other ways of committing suicide,' advised Mexican. 'Why don't you go and surrender to the sheriff?'

'I'll get him,' said the Kid.

Christmas Eve fell as balmy as April. Perhaps there was a hint of faraway frostiness in the air, but it tingled like seltzer, perfumed faintly with late prairie blossoms and the mesquite grass.

When night came the five or six rooms of the ranch-house were brightly lit. In one room was a Christmas tree, for the Lanes had a boy of three, and a dozen or more guests were expected from the nearer ranches.

At nightfall Madison Lane called aside Jim Belcher and three other cowboys employed on his ranch.

'Now, boys,' said Lane, 'keep your eyes open. Walk around the house and watch the road well. All of you know the "Frio Kid," as they call him now, and if you see him, open fire on him without asking any questions. I'm not afraid of his coming around, but Rosita is. She's been afraid he'd come in on us every Christmas since we were married.'

The guests had arrived in buckboards and on horseback, and were making themselves comfortable inside.

The evening went along pleasantly. The guests enjoyed and praised Rosita's excellent supper, and afterwards the men scattered in groups about the rooms or on the broad 'gallery,' smoking and chatting.

The Christmas tree, of course, delighted the youngsters, and above all were they pleased when Santa Claus himself in magnificent white beard and furs appeared and began to distribute the toys.

'It's my papa,' announced Billy Sampson, aged six. 'I've seen him wear 'em before.'

Berkly, a sheepman, old friend of Lane, stopped Rosita as she was passing by him on the gallery, where he was sitting smoking.

'Well, Mrs. Lane,' said he, 'I suppose by this Christmas you've gotten over being afraid of that fellow McRoy, haven't you? Madison and I have talked about it, you know.'

'Very nearly,' said Rosita, smiling, 'but I am still nervous sometimes. I shall never forget that awful time when he came so near to killing us.'

'He's the most cold-hearted villain in the world,' said Berkly. 'The citizens all along the border ought to turn out and hunt him down like a wolf.'

'He has committed awful crimes,' said Rosita, 'but – I – don't – know. I think there is a spot of good somewhere in everybody. He was not always bad – that I know.'

Rosita turned into the hallway between the rooms. Santa Claus, in muffling whiskers and furs, was just coming through.

'I heard what you said through the window, Mrs. Lane,' he said. 'I was just going down in my pocket for a Christmas present for your husband. But I've left one for you, instead. It's in the room to your right.'

'Oh, thank you, kind Santa Claus,' said Rosita, brightly.

Rosita went into the room, while Santa Claus stepped into the cooler air of the yard.

She found no one in the room but Madison.

'Where is my present that Santa said he left for me in here?' she asked.

'Haven't seen anything in the way of a present,' said her husband, laughing, 'unless he could have meant me.'

The next day Gabriel Radd, a foreman of the XO Ranch, dropped into the post-office at Loma Alta.

'Well, the Frio Kid's got his dose of lead at last,' he remarked to the postmaster.

'That so? How'd it happen?'

'One of old Sanchez's Mexican sheep herders did it! – think of it! the Frio Kid killed by a sheep herder! The Greaser saw him riding along past his camp about twelve o'clock last night, and was so skeered that he up with a Winchester and let him have it. Funniest part of it was that the Kid was dressed all up with white Angora-skin whiskers and a regular Santy Claus rig-out from head to foot. Think of the Frio Kid playing Santy!'

A LITTLE LOCAL COLOR

I MENTIONED TO RIVINGTON that I was in search of characteristic New York scenes and incidents – something typical, I told him, without necessarily having to spell the first syllable with an 'i.'

'Oh, for your writing business,' said Rivington, 'you couldn't have applied to a better shop. What I don't know about little old New York wouldn't make a sonnet to a sunbonnet. I'll put you right in the middle of so much local color that you won't know whether you are a magazine cover or in the erysipelas ward. When do you want to begin?'

Rivington is a young-man-about-town and a New Yorker by birth, preference, and incommutability.

I told him that I would be glad to accept his escort and guardianship so that I might take notes of Manhattan's grand, gloomy, and peculiar idiosyncrasies, and that the time of so doing would be at his own convenience.

'We'll begin this very evening,' said Rivington, himself interested, like a good fellow. 'Dine with me at seven, and then I'll steer you up against metropolitan phrases so thick you'll have to have a kinetoscope to record 'em.'

So I dined with Rivington pleasantly at his club, in Forty-eleventh Street, and then we set forth in pursuit of the elusive tincture of affairs.

As we came out of the club there stood two men on the sidewalk near the steps in earnest conversation.

'And by what process of ratiocination,' said one of them, 'do you arrive at the conclusion that the division of society into producing and non-possessing classes predicates failure when compared with competitive systems that are monopolizing in tendency and result inimically to industrial evolution?'

'Oh, come off your perch!' said the other man, who wore glasses. 'Your premises won't come out in the wash. You wind-jammers who apply bandy-legged theories to concrete categorical syllogisms and logical conclusions skally-bootin' into the infinitesimal ragbag. You can't pull my leg with an old sophism with whiskers on it. You quote Marx and Hyndman and Kautsky – what are they? – shines! Tolstoi? – his garret is full of rats. I put it to you over the home-plate that the idea of a cooperative commonwealth and an abolishment of competitive systems simply takes the rag off the bush and gives me hyperesthesia of the roopteetoop! The skookum house for yours!'

I stopped a few yards away and took out my little notebook.

'Oh, come ahead,' said Rivington, somewhat nervously; 'you don't want to listen to that.'

'Why, man,' I whispered, 'this is just what I do want to hear. These slang types are among your city's most distinguishing features. Is this the Bowery variety? I really must hear more of it.'

'If I follow you,' said the man who had spoken first, 'you do not believe it possible to reorganize society on the basis of common interest?'

'Shinny on your own side!' said the man with glasses. 'You never heard any such music from my foghorn. What I said was that I did not believe it practicable just now. The guys with wards are not in the frame of mind to slack upon the mazuma, and the man with the portable tin banqueting canister isn't exactly ready to join the Bible class. You can bet your variegated socks that the situation is all spiflicated up from the Battery to breakfast! What the country needs is for some bully old bloke like Cobden or some wise guy like old Ben Franklin to sashay up to the front and biff the nigger's head with the baseball. Do you catch my smoke? What?'

Rivington pulled me by the arm impatiently.

'Please come on,' he said. 'Let's go see something. This isn't what you want.'

'Indeed, it is,' I said resisting. 'This tough talk is the very stuff that counts. There is a picturesqueness about the speech of the lower order of people that is quite unique. Did you say that this is the Bowery variety of slang?'

'Oh, well,' said Rivington, giving it up; 'I'll tell you straight. That's one of our college professors talking. He ran down for a day or two at the club. It's a sort of fad with him lately to use slang in his conversation. He thinks it improves language. The man he is talking to is one of New York's famous social economists. Now will you come on? You can't use that, you know.'

'No,' I agreed; 'I can't use that. Would you call that typical of New York?'

'Of course not,' said Rivington, with a sigh of relief. 'I'm glad you see the difference. But if you want to hear the real old tough Bowery slang I'll take you down where you'll get your fill of it.'

'I would like it,' I said; 'That is, if it's the real thing. I've often read it in books, but I never heard it. Do you think it will be dangerous to go unprotected among those characters?'

'Oh, no,' said Rivington; 'not at this time of night. To tell the truth I haven't been along the Bowery in a long time, but I know it as well as I do Broadway. We'll look up some of the typical Bowery boys and get them to talk. It'll be worth your while. They talk a peculiar dialect that you won't hear anywhere else on earth.'

Rivington and I went east in a Forty-second Street car and then south on the Third Avenue line.

At Houston Street we got off and walked.

'We are now on the famous Bowery,' said Rivington; 'the Bowery celebrated in song and story.'

We passed block after block of 'gents' furnishing stores – the windows full of shirts with prices attached and cuffs inside. In other windows were neckties and no shirts. People walked up and down the sidewalks.

'In some ways,' said I, 'this reminds me of Kokomono, Ind., during the peach-crating season.'

Rivington was nettled.

'Step into one of these saloons or vaudeville shows,' said he, 'with a large roll of money, and see how quickly the Bowery will sustain its reputation.'

'You make impossible conditions,' said I, coldly.

By and by Rivington stopped and said we were in the heart of the Bowery. There was a policeman on the corner whom Rivington knew.

'Hallo, Donahue!' said my guide. 'How goes it? My friend and I are down this way looking up a bit of local color. He's anxious to meet one of the Bowery types. Can't you put us on to something genuine in that line – something that's got the color, you know?'

Policeman Donahue turned himself about ponderously, his florid face full of good-nature. He pointed with his club down the street.

'Sure!' he said, huskily. 'Here comes a lad now that was born on the Bowery and knows every inch of it. If he's ever been above Bleecker Street he's kept it to himself.'

A man about twenty-eight or twenty-nine, with a smooth face, was sauntering toward us with his hands in his coat pockets. Policeman Donahue stopped him with a courteous wave of his club.

'Evening, Kerry,' he said. 'Here's a couple of gents, friends of mine, that want to hear you spiel something about the Bowery. Can you reel 'em off a few yards?'

'Certainly, Donahue,' said the young man, pleasantly. 'Good evening, gentlemen,' he said to us, with a pleasant smile. Donahue walked off on his beat.

'This is the goods,' whispered Rivington, nudging me with his elbow. 'Look at his jaw!'

'Say, cull,' said Rivington, pushing back his hat, 'wot's doin'? Me and my friend's taking a look down de old line – see? De copper tipped us off dat you was wise to de Bowery. Is dat right?'

I could not help admiring Rivington's power of adapting himself to his surroundings.

'Donahue was right,' said the young man, frankly; 'I was brought up on the Bowery. I have been newsboy, teamster, pugilist, member of an organized band of "toughs," bartender, and a "sport" in various meanings of the word. The experience certainly warrants the supposition that I have at least a passing acquaintance with a few phases of Bowery life. I will be pleased to place whatever knowledge and experience I have at the service of my friend Donahue's friends.'

Rivington seemed ill at ease.

'I say,' he said – somewhat entreatingly, 'I thought – you're not stringing us, are you? It isn't just the kind of talk we expected. You haven't even said 'Hully gee!' once. Do you really belong on the Bowery?'

'I am afraid,' said the Bowery boy, smilingly, 'that at some time you have been enticed into one of the dives of literature and had the counterfeit coin of the Bowery passed upon you. The "argot" to which you doubtless refer was the invention of certain of your literary "discoverers" who invaded the unknown wilds below Third Avenue and put strange sounds into the mouths of the inhabitants. Safe in their homes far to the north and west, the credulous readers who were beguiled by this new "dialect" perused and believed. Like Marco Polo and Mungo Park – pioneers indeed, but ambitious souls who could not draw the line of demarcation between discovery and invention – the literary bones of these explorers are dotting the trackless wastes of the subway. While it is true that after the publication of the mythical language attributed to the dwellers along the Bowery certain of its pat phrases and apt metaphors were adopted and, to a limited extent, used in this locality, it was because our people are prompt in assimilating whatever is to their commercial advantage. To the tourists who visited our newly dicovered clime, and who expressed a realization of their literary guide books, they supplied the demands of the market.

'But perhaps I am wandering from the question. In what way can I assist you, gentlemen? I beg you will believe that the hospitality of the streets is extended to all. There are, I regret to say, many catch-penny places of entertainment, but I cannot conceive that they would entice you.'

I felt Rivington lean somewhat heavily against me.

'Say!' he remarked, with uncertain utterance; 'come and have a drink with us.'

'Thank you, but I never drink. I find that alcohol, even in the smallest quantities, alters the perspective. And I must preserve my perspective, for I am studying the Bowery. I have lived in it nearly thirty years, and I am just beginning to understand its heartbeats. It is like a great river fed by a hundred alien streams. Each influx brings strange seeds on its flood, strange silt and weeds, and now and then a flower of rare promise. To construe this river requires a man who can build dykes against the overflow, who is a naturalist, a geologist, a humanitarian, a diver, and a strong swimmer. I love my Bowery. It was my cradle and is my inspiration. I have published one book. The critics have been kind. I put my heart in it. I am writing another, into which I hope to put both heart and brain. Consider me your guide, gentlemen. Is there anything I can take you to see, any place to which I can conduct you?'

I was afraid to look at Rivington except with one eye.

'Thanks,' said Rivington. 'We were looking up ... that is ... my friend ... confound it; it's against all precedent, you know ... awfully obliged ... just the same.'

'In case,' said our friend, 'you would like to meet some of our Bowery young men I would be pleased to have you visit the quarters of our East Side Kappa Delta Phi Society, only two blocks east of here.'

'Awfully sorry,' said Rivington, 'but my friend's got me on the jump to-night. He's a terror when he's out after local color. Now, there's nothing I would like better than to drop in at the Kappa Delta Phi, but – some other time!'

We said our farewells and boarded a home-bound car. We had a rabbit on upper Broadway, and then I parted with Rivington on a street corner.

'Well, anyhow,' said he, braced and recovered, 'it couldn't have happened anywhere but in little old New York.'

Which, to say the least, was typical of Rivington.

GEORGIA'S RULING

IF YOU SHOULD CHANCE TO VISIT the General Land Office, step into the draughts-men's room and ask to be shown the map of Salado County. A leisurely German – possibly old Kampfer himself – will bring it to you. It will be four feet square, on heavy drawing-cloth. The lettering and the figures will be beautifully clear and distinct. The title will be in splendid, undecipherable German text, ornamented with classic Teutonic designs – very likely Ceres or Pomona leaning against the initial letters with cornucopias venting grapes and weiners. You must tell him that this is not the map you wish to see; that he will kindly bring you its official predecessor. He will then say, 'Ach, so!' and bring out a map half the size of the first, dim, old, tattered, and faded.

By looking carefully near its northwest corner you will presently come upon the worn contours of Chiquito River, and, maybe, if your eyes are good, discern the silent witness to this story.

The Commissioner of the Land Office was of the old style; his antique courtesy was too formal for his day. He dressed in fine black, and there was a suggestion of Roman drapery in his long coat-skirts. His collars were 'undetached' (blame haberdashery for the word); his tie was a narrow, funereal strip, tied in the same knot as were his shoe-strings. His gray hair was a trifle too long behind, but he kept it smooth and orderly. His face was clean-shaven, like the old statesmen's. Most people thought it a stern face, but when its official expression was off, a few had seen altogether a different countenance. Especially tender and gentle it had appeared to those who were about him during the last illness of his only child.

The Commissioner had been a widower for years, and his life, outside his official duties, had been so devoted to little Georgia that people spoke of it as a touching and admirable thing. He was a reserved man, and dignified almost to austerity, but the child had come below it all and rested upon his very heart, so that she scarcely missed the mother's love that had been taken away. There was a wonderful companionship between them, for she had many of his own ways, being thoughtful and serious beyond her years.

One day, while she was lying with the fever burning brightly in her cheeks, she said suddenly:

'Papa, I wish I could do something good for a whole lot of children!'

'What would you like to do, dear?' asked the Commissioner. 'Give them a party?'

'Oh, I don't mean those kind. I mean poor children who haven't homes, and aren't loved and cared for as I am. I tell you what, Papa!'

'What, my own child?'

'If I shouldn't get well, I'll leave them you – not *give* you, but just lend you, for you must come to mamma and me when you die too. If you can find time, wouldn't you do something to help them, if I ask you, Papa?'

'Hush, hush dear, dear child,' said the Commissioner, holding her hot little hand against his cheek; 'you get well real soon, and you and I will see what we can do for them together.'

But in whatsoever paths of benevolence, thus vaguely premeditated, the Commissioner might tread, he was not to have the company of his beloved. That night the little frail body grew suddenly too tired to struggle further, and Georgia's exit was made from the great stage when she had scarcely begun to speak her little piece before the footlights. But there must be a stage manager who understands. She had given the cue to the one who was to speak after her.

A week after she was laid away, the Commissioner reappeared at the office, a little more courteous, a little paler and sterner, with the black frock-coat hanging a little more loosely from his tall figure.

His desk was piled with work that had accumulated during the four heart-breaking weeks of his absence. His chief clerk had done what he could, but there were questions of law, of fine judicial decisions to be made concerning the issue of patents, the marketing and leasing of school lands, the classification into grazing, agricultural, watered, and timbered, of new tracts to be opened to settlers.

The Commissioner went to work silently and obstinately, putting back his grief as far as possible, forcing his mind to attack the complicated and important business of his office. On the second day after his return he called the Porter, pointed to a leather-covered chair that stood near his own, and ordered it removed to a lumber-room at the top of the building. In that chair Georgia would always sit when she came to the office for him of afternoons.

As time passed, the Commissioner seemed to grow more silent, solitary, and reserved. A new phase of mind developed in him. He could not endure the presence of a child. Often when a clattering youngster belonging to one of the clerks would come chattering into the big business-room adjoining his little apartment, the Commissioner would steal softly and close the door. He would always cross the street to avoid meeting the school-children when they came dancing along in happy groups upon the side-walk, and his firm mouth would close into a mere line.

It was nearly three months after the rains had washed the last dead flower-petals from the mound above little Georgia when the 'land-shark' firm of Hamlin and Avery filed papers upon what they considered the 'fattest' vacancy of the year.

It should not be supposed that all who were termed 'land-sharks' deserved the name. Many of them were reputable men of good business character. Some of them could walk into the most august councils of the state and say: 'Gentlemen, we would like to have this, and that, and matters go thus.' But, next to a three years' drought and the boll-worm, the Actual Settler hated the land-shark. The land-shark haunted the Land Office, where all the land records were kept, and hunted 'vacancies' – that is, tracts or unappropriated public domain, generally invisible upon the official maps, but actually existing 'upon the ground.' The law entitled any one possessing certain State scrip to file by virtue of same upon any land not previously legally appropriated. Most of the scrip was now in the hands of the land-sharks. Thus, at the cost of a few hundred dollars, they often secured lands worth as many thousands. Naturally, the search for 'vacancies' was lively.

But often – very often – the land they thus secured, though legally 'unappropriated,' would be occupied by happy and contented settlers, who had labored for years to build up their homes, only to discover that their titles were worthless, and to receive peremptory notice to quit. Thus came about the bitter and not unjustifiable hatred felt by the toiling settlers towards the shrewd and seldom merciful speculators who so often turned them forth destitute and homeless from their fruitless labors. The history of the state teems with their antagonism. Mr. Land-shark seldom showed his face on 'locations' from which he should have to eject the unfortunate victims of a monstrously tangled land system, but let his emissaries do the work. There was lead in every cabin, moulded into balls for him; many of his brothers had enriched the grass with their blood. The fault of it all lay far back.

When the state was young, she felt the need of attracting newcomers, and of rewarding those pioneers already within her borders. Year after year she issued land scrip – Headrights, Bounties, Veteran Donations, Confederates; and to railroads, irrigation companies, colonies, and tillers of the soil galore. All required of the grantee was that he or it should have the scrip properly surveyed upon the public domain by the country or district surveyor, and the land thus appropriated became the property of him or it, or his or its heirs and assigns, forever.

In those days – and here is where the trouble began – the state's domain was practically inexhaustible, and the old surveyors, with princely – yes, even Western American – liberality, gave good measure and overflowing. Often the jovial man of metes and bounds would dispense altogether with the tripod and chain. Mounted on a pony that could cover something near a 'vara' at a step, with a pocket compass to direct his course, he would trot out a survey by counting the beat of his pony's hoofs, mark his corners, and write out his field notes with the complacency produced by an act of duty well performed. Sometimes – and who could blame the surveyor? – when the pony was 'feeling his oats,' he might step a little higher and farther, and in that case the beneficiary of the scrip might get a thousand or two more acres in his survey than the scrip called for. But look at the boundless leagues the state had to spare! However, no one ever had to complain of the pony under-stepping. Nearly every old survey in the state contained an excess of land.

In later years, when the state became more populous, and land values increased, this careless work entailed incalculable trouble, endless litigation, a period of riotous land-grabbing, and no little bloodshed. The land-sharks voraciously attack these excesses in the old surveys, and filed upon such portions with new scrip as unappropriated public domain. Wherever the identifications of the old tracts were vague, and the corners were not to be clearly established, the Land Office would recognize the newer locations as valid, and issue title to the locators. Here was the greatest hardship to be found: These old surveys, taken from the pick of the land, were already nearly all occupied by unsuspecting and peaceful settlers, and thus their titles were demolished, and the choice was placed before them either to buy their land over at a double price or to vacate it, with their families and personal belongings, immediately. Land locators sprang up by hundreds. The country was held up and searched for 'vacancies' at the point of a compass. Hundreds of thousands of dollars' worth of splendid acres were wrested from their innocent purchasers and holders. There began a vast hegira of evicted settlers in tattered wagons; going nowhere cursing injustice, stunned, purposeless, homeless, hopeless. Their children began to look up to them for bread, and cry.

It was in consequence of these conditions that Hamlin and Avery had filed upon a strip of land about a mile wide and three miles long, comprising about two thousand acres, it being the excess over complement of the Elias Denny three-league survey on Chiquito River, in one of the middle-western counties. This two-thousand-acre body of land was asserted by them to be vacant land, and improperly considered a part of the Denny survey. They based this assertion and their claim upon the land upon the demonstrated facts that the beginning corner of the Denny survey was plainly identified; that its field notes called to run west 5,760 varas, and then called for Chiquito River; thence it ran south, with the meanders – and so on – and that the Chiquito River was, on the ground, fully a mile farther west from the point reached by course and distance. To sum up: there were two thousand acres of vacant land between the Denny survey proper and Chiquito River.

One sweltering day in July the Commissioner called for the papers in connection with this new location. They were brought, and heaped, a foot deep, upon his desk – field notes, statements, sketches, affidavits, connecting lines – documents of every description that shrewdness and money could call to the aid of Hamlin and Avery.

The firm was pressing the Commissioner to issue a patent upon their location. They possessed inside information concerning a new railroad that would probably pass somewhere near this land.

The General Land Office was very still while the Commissioner was delving into the heart of the mass of evidence. The pigeons could be heard on the roof of the old, castle-like building, cooing and fretting. The clerks were droning everywhere, scarcely pretending to earn their salaries. Each little sound echoed hollow and loud from the bare, stone-flagged floors, the plastered walls, and the iron-joisted ceiling. The impalpable, perpetual lime-stone dust that never settled whitened a long streamer of sunlight that pierced the tattered window-awning.

It seemed that Hamlin and Avery had builded well. The Denny survey was carelessly made, even for a careless period. Its beginning corner was identical with that of a well-defined old Spanish grant, but its other calls were sinfully vague. The field notes contained no other object that survived – no tree, no natural object save Chiquito River, and it was a mile wrong there. According to precedent, the Office would be justified in giving in its complement by course and distance, and considering the remainder vacant instead of a mere excess.

The Actual Settler was besieging the office with wild protests *in re*. Having the nose of a pointer and the eye of a hawk for the land-shark, he had observed his myrmidons running the lines upon his ground. Making inquiries, he learned that the spoiler had attacked his home, and he left the plow in the furrow and took his pen in hand.

One of the protests the Commissioner read twice. It was from a woman, a widow, the granddaughter of Elias Denny himself, She told how her grandfather had sold most of the survey years before at a trivial price – land that was now a principality in extent and value. Her mother had also sold a part, and she herself had succeeded to this western portion, along Chiquito River. Much of it she had been forced to part with in order to live, and now she owned only about three hundred acres, on which she had her home. Her letter wound up rather pathetically:

'I've got eight children, the oldest fifteen years. I work all day and half the night to till what little land I can and keep us in clothes and books. I teach my children too. My neighbors is all poor and has big families. The drought kills the crops every two or three years and then we has hard times to get enough to eat. There is ten families on this land what the land-sharks is trying to rob us of, and all of them got titles from me. I sold to them cheap, and they ain't paid out yet, but part of them is, and if their land should be took from them I would die. My grandfather was an honest man, and he helped to build up this state, and he taught his children to be honest, and how could I make it up to them who bought from me? Mr. Commissioner, if you let them land-sharks take the roof from over my children and the little from them as they has to live on, whoever again calls this state great or its government just will have a lie in their mouths.'

The Commissioner laid this letter aside with a sigh. Many, many such letters he had received. He had never been hurt by them, nor had he ever felt that they appealed to him personally. He was but the state's servant, and must follow its laws. And yet, somehow, this reflection did not always eliminate a certain responsible feeling that hung upon him. Of all the state's officers he was supremest in his department, not even excepting the Governor. Broad, general land laws he followed, it was true, but he had a wide latitude in particular ramifications. Rather than law, what he followed was Rulings: Office Rulings and precedents. In the complicated and new questions that were being engendered by the state's development the Commissioner's ruling was rarely appealed from. Even the courts sustained it when its equity was apparent.

The Commissioner stepped to the door and spoke to a clerk in the other room – spoke as he always did, as if he were addressing a prince of the blood:

'Mr. Weldon, will you be kind enough to ask Mr. Ashe, the state school-land appraiser, to please come to my office as soon as convenient?'

Ashe came quickly from the big table where he was arranging his reports.

'Mr. Ashe,' said the Commissioner, 'you worked along the Chiquito River, in Salado County, during your last trip, I believe. Do you remember anything of the Elias Denny three-league survey?'

'Yes, sir, I do,' the blunt, breezy surveyor answered. 'I crossed it on my way back to Block H, on the north side of it. The road runs with the Chiquito River, along the valley. The Denny survey fronts three miles on the Chiquito.'

'It is claimed,' continued the Commissioner, 'that it fails to reach the river by as much as a mile.'

The appraiser shrugged his shoulder. He was by birth and instinct an Actual Settler, and the natural foe of the land-shark.

'It has always been considered to extend to the river,' he said, dryly.

'But that is not the point I desired to discuss,' said the Commissioner. 'What kind of country is this valley portion of (let us say, then) the Denny tract?'

The spirit of the Actual Settler beamed in Ashe's face.

'Beautiful,' he said, with enthusiasm. 'Valley as level as this floor, with just a little swell on, like the sea, and rich as cream. Just enough brakes to shelter the cattle in winter. Black loamy soil for six feet, and then clay. Holds water. A dozen nice little houses on it, with windmills and gardens. People pretty poor, I guess – too far from market – but comfortable. Never saw so many kids in my life.'

'They raise flocks?' inquired the Commissioner.

'Ho, ho! I mean two-legged kids,' laughed the surveyor; 'two-legged, and bare-legged, and tow-headed.'

'Children! oh, children!' mused the Commissioner, as though a new view had opened to him; 'they raise children!'

'It's a lonesome country, Commissioner,' said the surveyor. 'Can you blame 'em?'

'I suppose,' continued the Commissioner, slowly, as one carefully pursues deductions from a new, stupendous theory, 'not all of them are tow-headed. It would not be unreasonable, Mr. Ashe, I conjecture, to believe that a portion of them have brown, or even black hair.'

'Brown and black sure,' said Ashe; 'also red.'

'No doubt,' said the Commissioner. 'Well, I thank you for your courtesy in informing me, Mr. Ashe. I will not detain you any longer from your duties.'

Later, in the afternoon, came Hamlin and Avery, big, handsome, genial, sauntering men, clothed in white duck and low-cut shoes. They permeated the whole office with an aura of debonair prosperity. They passed among the clerks and left a wake of abbreviated given names and fat brown cigars.

These were the aristocracy of the land-sharks, who went in for big things. Full of serene confidence in themselves, there was no corporation, no syndicate, no railroad company or attorney general too big for them to tackle. The peculiar smoke of their rare, fat brown cigars was to be perceived in the sanctum of every department of state, in every committee-room of the Legislature, in every bank parlor and every private caucus-room in the state capital. Always pleasant, never in a hurry, seeming to possess unlimited leisure, people wondered when they gave their attention to the many audacious enterprises in which they were known to be engaged.

By and by the two dropped carelessly into the Commissioner's room and reclined lazily in the big, leather-upholstered arm-chairs. They drawled a good-natured complaint of the weather, and Hamlin told the Commissioner an excellent story he had amassed that morning from the Secretary of State.

But the Commissioner knew why they were there. He had half promised to render a decision that day upon their location.

The chief clerk now brought in a batch of duplicate certificates for the Commissioner to sign. As he traced his sprawling signature, 'Hollis Summerfield, Comr. Genl. Land Office,' on each one, the chief clerk stood, deftly removing them and applying the blotter.

'I notice,' said the chief clerk, 'you've been going through that Salado County location. Kampfer is making a new map of Salado, and I believe is platting in that section of the country now.'

'I will see it,' said the Commissioner. A few moments later he went to the draughtsmen's room.

As he entered he saw five or six of the draughtsmen grouped about Kampfer's desk, gargling away at each other in pectoral German, and gazing at something thereupon. At the Commissioner's approach they scattered to their several places. Kampfer, a wizened little German, with long, frizzled ringlets and a watery eye, began to stammer forth some sort of an apology, the Commissioner thought, for the congregation of his fellows about his desk.

'Never mind,' said the Commissioner, 'I wish to see the map you are making'; and, passing around the old German, seated himself upon the high draughtsman's stool. Kampfer continued to break English in trying to explain.

'Herr Commissioner, I assure you blenty sat I haf not it bremeditated – sat it wass – sat itself make. Look you! from se field notes wass it blatted please to observe se calls: South, 10 degrees west 1,050 varas; south, 10 degrees each 300 varas; south, 100; south, 9 west, 200; south, 40 degrees west, 400 – and so on. Herr Commissioner, nefer would I have – '

The Commissioner raised one white hand, silently. Kampfer dropped his pipe and fled.

With a hand at each side of his face, and his elbows resting upon the desk, the Commissioner sat staring at the map which was spread and fastened there – staring at the sweet and living profile of little Georgia drawn thereupon – at her face, pensive, delicate, and infantile, outlined in a perfect likeness.

When his mind at length came to inquire into the reason of it, he saw that it must have been, as Kampfer had said, unpremeditated. The old draughtsman had been platting in the Elias Denny survey, and Georgia's likeness, striking though it was, was formed by nothing more than the meanders of Chiquito River. Indeed, Kampfer's blotter, whereon his preliminary work was done, showed the laborious tracings of the calls and the countless pricks of the compasses. Then, over his faint penciling, Kampfer had drawn in India ink with a full, firm pen the similitude of Chiquito River, and forth had blossomed mysteriously the dainty, pathetic profile of the child.

The Commissioner sat for half an hour with his face in his hands, gazing downward, and none dared approach him. Then he arose and walked out. In the business office he paused long enough to ask that the Denny file be brought to his desk.

He found Hamlin and Avery still reclining in their chairs, apparently oblivious of business. They were lazily discussing summer opera, it being their habit – perhaps their pride also – to appear supernaturally indifferent whenever they stood with large interests imperilled. And they stood to win more on this stake than most people knew. They possessed inside information to the effect that a new railroad would, within a year, split this very Chiquito River valley and send land values ballooning all along its route. A dollar under thirty thousand profit on this location, if it should hold good, would be a loss to their expectations. So, while they chatted lightly and waited for the Commissioner to open the subject, there was a quick, side-long sparkle in their eyes, evincing a desire to read their title clear to those fair acres on the Chiquito.

A clerk brought in the file. The Commissioner seated himself and wrote upon it in red ink. Then he rose to his feet and stood for a while looking straight out of the window. The Land Office capped the summit of a bold hill. The eyes of the Commissioner passed over the roofs of many houses set in a packing of deep green, the whole checkered by strips of blinding white streets. The horizon, where his gaze was focussed, swelled to a fair wooded eminence flecked with faint dots of shining white. There was a cemetery, where lay many who were forgotten, and a few who had not lived in vain. And one lay there occupying very small space, whose childish heart had been large enough to desire, while near its last beats, good to others. The Commissioner's lips moved slightly as he whispered to himself: 'It was her last will and testament, and I have neglected it so long!'

The big brown cigars of Hamlin and Avery were fireless, but they still gripped them between their teeth and waited, while they marvelled at the absent expression upon the Commissioner's face.

By and by he spoke suddenly and promptly.

'Gentlemen, I have just endorsed the Elias Denny survey for patenting. This office will not regard your location upon a part of it as legal.' He paused a moment, and then, extending his hand as those dear old-time ones used to do in debate, he enunciated the spirit of that Ruling that subsequently drove the land-sharks to the wall, and placed the seal of peace and security over the doors of ten thousand homes.

'And, furthermore,' he continued, with a clear, soft light upon his face, 'it may interest you to know that from this time on this office will consider that when a survey of land made by virtue of a certificate granted by this state to the men who wrested it from the wilderness and the savage – made in good faith, settled in good faith, and left in good faith to their children or innocent purchasers – when such a survey, although overrunning its complement, shall call for any natural object visible to the eye of man, to that object it shall hold and be good and valid. And the children of this state shall lie down to sleep at night, and rumors of disturbers of title shall not disquiet them. For,' concluded the Commissioner, 'of such is the Kingdom of Heaven.'

In the silence that followed, a laugh floated up from the patent-room below. The man who carried down the Denny file was exhibiting it among the clerks.

'Look here,' he said, delightedly, 'the old man has forgotten his name. He's written "Patent to original grantee," and signed it "Georgia Summerfield, Comr." '

The speech of the Commissioner rebounded lightly from the impregnable Hamlin and Avery. They smiled, rose gracefully, spoke of the baseball team, and argued feelingly that quite a perceptible breeze had arisen from the east. They lit fresh fat brown cigars, and drifted courteously away. But later they made another tiger-spring for their quarry in the courts. But the courts, according to reports in the papers, 'coolly roasted them' (a remarkable performance, suggestive of liquid-air didoes), and sustained the Commissioner's Ruling.

And this Ruling itself grew to be a Precedent, and the Actual Settler framed it, and taught his children to spell from it, and there was sound sleep o' nights from the pines to the sage-brush, and from the chaparral to the great brown river of the north.

But I think, and I am sure the Commissioner never thought otherwise, that whether Kampfer was a snuffy old instrument of destiny, or whether the meanders of the Chiquito accidently platted themselves into that memorable sweet profile or not, there was brought about 'something good for a whole lot of children,' and the result ought to be called 'Georgia's Ruling.'

BLIND MAN'S HOLIDAY

ALAS FOR THE MAN AND FOR THE ARTIST with the shifting point of perspective! Life shall be a confusion of ways to the one; the landscape shall rise up and confound the other. Take the case of Lorison. At one time he appeared to himself to be the feeblest of fools; at another he conceived that he followed ideals so fine that the world was not yet ready to accept them. During one mood he cursed his folly; possessed by the other, he bore himself with a serene grandeur akin to greatness: in neither did he attain the perspective.

Generations before, the name had been 'Larsen.' His race had bequeathed him its fine-strung, melancholy temperament, its saving balance of thrift and industry.

From his point of perspective he saw himself an outcast from society, forever to be a shady skulker along the ragged edge of respectability; a denizen *des trois-quarts de monde*, that pathetic spheroid lying between the *haut* and the *demi*, whose inhabitants envy each of their neighbors, and are scorned by both. He was self-condemned to this opinion, as he was self-exiled, through it, to this quaint Southern city a thousand miles from his former home. Here he had dwelt for longer than a year, knowing but few, keeping in a subjective world of shadows which was invaded at times by the perplexing bulks of jarring realities. Then he fell in love with a girl whom he met in a cheap restaurant, and his story begins.

The Rue Chartres, in New Orleans, is a street of ghosts. It lies in the quarter where the Frenchman, in his prime, set up his translated pride and glory; where, also, the arrogant don had swaggered, and dreamed of gold and grants and ladies' gloves. Every flagstone has its grooves worn by footsteps going royally to the wooing and the fighting. Every house has a princely heartbreak; each doorway its untold tale of gallant promise and slow decay.

By night the Rue Chartres is now but a murky fissure, from which the groping wayfarer sees, flung against the sky, the tangled filigree of Moorish iron balconies. The old houses of monsieur stand yet, indomitable against the century, but their essence is gone. The street is one of ghosts to whosoever can see them.

A faint heartbeat of the street's ancient glory still survives in a corner occupied by the Café Carabine d'Or. Once men gathered there to plot against kings, and to warn presidents. They do so yet, but they are not the same kind of men. A brass button will scatter these; those would have set their faces against an army. Above the door hangs the sign board, upon which has been depicted a vast animal of unfamiliar species. In the act of firing upon this monster is represented an unobtrusive human leveling an obtrusive gun, once the color of bright gold. Now the legend above the picture is faded beyond conjecture; the gun's relation to the title is a matter of faith; the menaced animal, wearied of the long aim of the hunter, has resolved itself into a shapeless blot.

The place is known as 'Antonio's,' as the name, white upon the red-lit transparency, and gilt upon the windows, attests. There is a promise in 'Antonio'; a justifiable expectancy of savory things in oil and pepper and wine, and perhaps an angel's whisper of garlic. But the rest of the name is 'O'Riley.' Antonio O'Riley!

The Carabine d'Or is an ignominious ghost of the Rue Chartres. The Café where Bienville and Conti dined, where a prince has broken bread, is become a 'family ristaurant.'

Its customers are working men and women, almost to a unit. Occasionally you will see chorus girls from the cheaper theatres, and men who follow avocations subject to quick vicissitudes; but at Antonio's – name rich in Bohemian promise, but tame in fulfillment – manners debonair and gay are toned down to the 'family' standard. Should you light a cigarette, mine host will touch you on the 'arrum' and remind you that the proprieties are menaced. 'Antonio' entices and beguiles from fiery legend without, but 'O'Riley' teaches decorum within.

It was at this restaurant that Lorison first saw the girl. A flashy fellow with a predatory eye had followed her in, and had advanced to take the other chair at the little table where she stopped, but Lorison slipped into the seat before him. Their acquaintance began, and grew, and now for two months they had sat at the same table each evening, not meeting by appointment, but as if by a series of fortuitous and happy accidents. After dining, they would take a walk together in one of the little city parks, or among the panoramic markets where exhibits a continuous vaudeville of sights and sounds. Always at eight o'clock their steps led them to a certain street corner, where she prettily but firmly bade him good-night and left him. 'I do not live far from here,' she frequently said, 'and you must let me go the rest of the way alone.'

But now Lorison had discovered that he wanted to go the rest of the way with her, or happiness would depart, leaving him on a very lonely corner of life. And at the same time that he made the discovery, the secret of his banishment from the society of the good laid its fingers in his face and told him it must not be.

Man is too thoroughly an egoist not to be also an egotist; if he love, the object shall know it. During a lifetime he may conceal it through stress of expediency and honor, but it shall bubble from his dying lips, though it disrupt a neighborhood. It is known, however, that most men do not wait so long to disclose their passion. In the case of Lorison, his particular ethics positively forbade him to declare his sentiments, but he must needs dally with the subject, and woo by innuendo at least.

On this night, after the usual meal at the Carabine d'Or, he strolled with his companion down the dim old street toward the river.

The Rue Chartres perishes in the old Place d'Armes. The ancient Cabildo, where Spanish justice fell like hail, faces it, and the Cathedral, another provincial ghost, overlooks it. Its centre is a little, iron-railed park of flowers and immaculate gravelled walks, where citizens take the air of evenings. Pedestalled high above it, the General sits his cavorting steed, with his face turned stonily down the river toward English Turn, whence come no more Britons to bombard his cotton bales.

Often the two sat in this square, but to-night Lorison guided her past the stone-stepped gate, and still riverward. As they walked, he smiled to himself to think that all he knew of her – except that he loved her – was her name, Norah Greenway, and that she lived with her brother. They had talked about everything except themselves. Perhaps her reticence had been caused by his.

They came, at length, upon the levee, and sat upon a great, prostrate beam. The air was pungent with the dust of commerce. The great river slipped yellowly past. Across it Algiers lay, a longitudinous black bulk against a vibrant electric haze sprinkled with exact stars.

The girl was young and of the piquant order. A certain bright melancholy pervaded her; she possessed an untarnished, pale prettiness doomed to please. Her voice, when she spoke, dwarfed her theme. It was the voice capable of investing little subjects with a large interest. She sat at ease, bestowing her skirts with the little womanly touch, serene as if the begrimed pier was a summer garden. Lorison poked the rotting boards with his cane.

He began by telling her that he was in love with some one to whom he durst not speak of it. 'And why not?' she asked, accepting swiftly his fatuous presentation of a third person of straw. 'My place in the world,' he answered, 'is none to ask a woman to share. I am an outcast from honest people; I am wrongly accused of one crime, and am, I believe, guilty of another.'

Thence he plunged into the story of his abdication from society. The story, pruned of his moral philosophy, deserves no more than the slightest touch. It is no new tale, that of the gambler's declension. During one night's sitting he lost, and then had imperilled a certain amount of his employer's money, which, by accident, he carried with him. He continued to lose, to the last wager, and then began to gain, leaving the game winner to a somewhat formidable sum. The same night his employer's safe was robbed. A search was had; the winnings of Lorison were found in his room, their total forming an accusative nearness to the sum purloined. He was taken, tried, and, through incomplete evidence, released, smutched with the sinister *devoirs* of a disagreeing jury.

'It is not in the unjust accusation,' he said to the girl, 'that my burden lies, but in the knowledge that from the moment I staked the first dollar of the firm's money I was a criminal – no matter whether I lost or won. You see why it is impossible for me to speak of love to her.'

'It is a sad thing,' said Norah, after a little pause, 'to think what very good people there are in the world.'

'Good?' said Lorison.

'I was thinking of this superior person whom you say you love. She must be a very poor sort of creature.'

'I do not understand.'

'Nearly,' she continued, 'as poor a sort of creature as yourself.'

'You do not understand,' said Lorison, removing his hat and sweeping back his fine, light hair. 'Suppose she loved me in return, and were willing to marry me. Think, if you can, what would follow. Never a day would pass but she would be reminded of her sacrifice. I would read a condescension in her smile, a pity even in her affection, that would madden me. No. The thing would stand between us forever. Only equals should mate. I could never ask her to come down upon my lower plane.'

An arc light faintly shone upon Lorison's face. An illumination from within also pervaded it. The girl saw the rapt, ascetic look; it was the face either of Sir Galahad or Sir Fool.

'Quite starlike,' she said, 'is this unapproachable angel. Really too high to be grasped.'

'By me, yes.'

She faced him suddenly. 'My dear friend, would you prefer your star fallen?'

Lorison made a wide gesture. 'You push me to the bald fact,' he declared; 'you are not in sympathy with my argument. But I will answer you so. If I could reach my particular star, to drag it down, I would not do it; but if it were fallen, I would pick it up, and thank Heaven for the privilege.'

They were silent for some minutes. Norah shivered, and thrust her hands deep into the pockets of her jacket. Lorison uttered a remorseful exclamation.

'I'm not cold,' she said. 'I was just thinking. I ought to tell you something. You have selected a strange confidante. But you cannot expect a chance acquaintance, picked up in a doubtful restaurant, to be an angel.'

'Norah,' cried Lorison.

'Let me go on. You have told me about yourself. We have been such good friends. I must tell you now what I never wanted you to know. I am – worse than you are. I was on the stage . . . I sang in the chorus . . . I was pretty bad, I guess . . . I stole diamonds from the prima donna . . . they arrested me . . . I gave most of them up, and they let me go . . . I drank wine every night . . . a great deal . . . I was very wicked, but—'

Lorison knelt quickly by her side and took her hands.

'Dear Norah!' he said, exultantly. 'It is you, it is you I love! You never guessed it, did you? 'Tis you I meant all the time. Now I can speak. Let me make you forget the past. We have both suffered; let us shut out the world, and live for each other. Norah, do you hear me say I love you?'

'In spite of—'

'Rather say because of it. You have come out of your past noble and good. Your heart is an angel's. Give it to me.'

'A little while ago you feared the future too much to even speak.'

'But for you; not for myself. Can you love me?'

She cast herself, wildly sobbing, upon his breast.

'Better than life — than truth itself — than everything.'

'And my own past,' said Lorison, with a note of solicitude – 'can you forgive and—'

'I answered you that,' she whispered, 'when I told you I loved you.' She leaned away, and looked thoughtfully at him. 'If I had not told you about myself, would you have — would you—'

'No,' he interrupted; 'I would never have let you know I loved you. I would never have asked you this – Norah, will you be my wife?'

She wept again.

'Oh, believe me; I am good now – I am no longer wicked! I will be the best wife in the world. Don't think I am – bad any more. If you do I shall die, I shall die!'

While he was consoling her, she brightened up eager and impetuous. 'Will you marry me to-night?' she said. 'Will you prove it that way? I have a reason for wishing it to be to-night. Will you?'

Of one of two things was this exceeding frankness the outcome; either of importunate brazenness or of utter innocence. The lover's perspective contained only the one.

'The sooner,' said Lorison, 'the happier I shall be.'

'What is there to do?' she asked. 'What do you have to get? Come! You should know.'

Her energy stirred the dreamer to action.

'A city directory first,' he cried, gayly, 'to find where the man lives who gives licenses to happiness. We will go together and rout him out. Cabs, cars, policemen, telephones, and ministers shall aid us.'

'Father Rogan shall marry us,' said the girl, with ardor. 'I will take you to him.'

An hour later the two stood at the open doorway of an immense, gloomy brick building in a narrow and lonely street. The license was tight in Norah's hand.

'Wait here a moment,' she said, 'till I find Father Rogan.'

She plunged into the black hallway, and the lover was left standing, as it were, on one leg outside. His impatience was not greatly taxed. Gazing curiously into what seemed the hallway to Erebus, he was presently reassured by a stream of light that bisected the darkness, far down the passage. Then he heard her call, and fluttered lampward, like the moth. She beckoned him through a doorway into the room whence emanated the light. The room was bare of nearly everything except books, which had subjugated all its space. Here and there little spots of territory had been reconquered. An elderly, bald man, with a superlatively calm, remote eye, stood by a table with a book in his hand, his finger still marking a page. His dress was sombre and appertained to a religious order. His eyes denoted an acquaintance with the perspective.

'Father Rogan,' said Norah, 'this is he.'

'The two of ye,' said Father Rogan, 'want to get married?'

They did not deny it. He married them. The ceremony was quickly done. One who could have witnessed it, and felt its scope, might have trembled at the terrible inadequacy of it to rise to the dignity of its endless chain of results.

Afterward the priest spake briefly, as if by rote, of certain other civil and legal addenda that either might or should, at a later time, cap the ceremony. Lorison tendered a fee, which was declined, and before the door closed after the departing couple Father Rogan's book popped open again where his finger marked it.

In the dark hall Norah whirled and clung to her companion, tearful.

'Will you never, never be sorry?'

At last she was reassured.

At the first light they reached upon the street, she asked the time, just as she had each night. Lorison looked at his watch. Half-past eight.

Lorison thought it was from habit that she guided their steps toward the corner where they always parted. But, arriving there, she hesitated, and then released his arm. A drug store stood on the corner; its bright, soft light shone upon them.

'Please leave me here as usual to-night,' said Norah, sweetly. 'I must—I would rather you would. You will not object? At six to-morrow evening I will meet you at Antonio's. I want to sit with you there once more. And then—I will go where you say.' She gave him a bewildering, bright smile, and walked swiftly away.

Surely it needed all the strength of her charm to carry off this astounding behaviour. It was no discredit to Lorison's strength of mind that his head began to whirl. Pocketing his hands, he rambled vacuously over to the druggist's windows, and began assiduously to spell over the names of the patent medicines therein displayed.

As soon as he had recovered his wits, he proceeded along the street in an aimless fashion. After drifting for two or three squares, he flowed into a somewhat more pretentious thoroughfare, a way much frequented by him in his solitary ramblings. For here was a row of shops devoted to traffic in goods of the widest range of choice – handiworks of art, skill and fancy, products of nature and labor from every zone.

Here, for a time, he loitered among the conspicuous windows, where was set, emphasized by congested floods of light, the cunningest spoil of the interiors. There were few passers, and of this Lorison was glad. He was not of the world. For a long time he had touched his fellow man only at the gear of a levelled cog-wheel – at right angles, and upon a different axis. He had dropped into a distinctly new orbit. The stroke of ill fortune had acted upon him, in effect, as a blow delivered upon the apex of a certain ingenious toy, the musical top, which, when thus buffeted while spinning, gives forth, with scarcely retarded motion, a complete change of key and chord.

Strolling along the pacific avenue, he experienced a singular, supernatural calm, accompanied by an unusual activity of brain. Reflecting upon recent affairs, he assured himself of his happiness in having won for a bride the one he had so greatly desired, yet he wondered mildly at his dearth of active emotion. Her strange behavior in abandoning him without valid excuse on his bridal eve aroused in him only a vague and curious speculation. Again, he found himself contemplating, with complaisant serenity, the incidents of her somewhat lively career. His perspective seemed to have been queerly shifted.

As he stood before a window near a corner, his ears were assailed by a waxing clamor and commotion. He stood close to the window to allow passage to the cause of the hubbub – a procession of human beings, which rounded the corner and headed in his direction. He perceived a salient hue of blue and a glitter of brass about a central figure of dazzling white and silver, and a ragged wake of black, bobbing figures.

Two ponderous policemen were conducting between them a woman dressed as if for the stage, in a short, white, satiny skirt reaching to the knees, pink stockings, and a sort of sleeveless bodice bright with relucent, armor-like scales. Upon her curly light hair was perched, at a rollicking angle, a shining tin helmet. The costume was to be instantly recognized as one of those amazing conceptions to which competition has harried the inventors of the spectacular ballet. One of the officers bore a long cloak upon his arm, which, doubtless, had been intended to veil the candid attractions of their effulgent prisoner, but, for some reason, it had not been called into use, to the vociferous delight of the tail of the procession.

Compelled by a sudden and vigorous movement of the woman, the parade halted before the window by which Lorison stood. He saw that she was young, and, at the first glance, was deceived by a sophistical prettiness of her face, which waned before a more judicious scrutiny. Her look was bold and reckless, and upon her countenance, where yet the contours of youth survived, were the fingermarks of old age's credentialed courier, Late Hours.

The young woman fixed her unshrinking gaze upon Lorison, and called to him in the voice of the wronged heroine in straits:

'Say! You look like a good fellow; come and put up the bail, won't you? I've done nothing to get pinched for. It's all a mistake. See how they're treating me! You won't be sorry, if you'll help me out of this. Think of your sister or your girl being dragged along the streets this way! I say, come along now, like a good fellow.'

It may be that Lorison, in spite of the unconvincing bathos of this appeal, showed a sympathetic face, for one of the officers left the woman's side, and went over to him.

'It's all right, sir,' he said, in a husky, confidential tone; 'she's the right party. We took her after the first act at the Green Light Theatre, on a wire from the chief of police of Chicago. It's only a square or two to the station. Her rig's pretty bad, but she refused to change clothes – or, rather,' added the officer, with a smile, 'to put on some. I thought I'd explain matters to you so you wouldn't think she was being imposed upon.'

'What is the charge?' asked Lorison.

'Grand larceny. Diamonds. Her husband is a jeweler in Chicago. She cleaned his show case of the sparklers, and skipped with a comic opera troupe.'

The policeman, perceiving that the interest of the entire group of spectators was centred upon himself and Lorison – their conference being regarded as a possible new complication – was fain to prolong the situation – which reflected his own importance – by a little afterpiece of philosophical comment.

'A gentleman like you, sir,' he went on affably, 'would never notice it, but it comes in my line to observe what an immense amount of trouble is made by that combination – I mean the stage, diamonds, and light-headed women who aren't satisfied with good homes. I tell you, sir, a man these days and nights wants to know what his women folks are up to.'

The policeman smiled a good-night, and returned to the side of his charge, who had been intently watching Lorison's face during the conversation, no doubt for some indication of his intention to render succor. Now, at the failure of the sign, and at the movement made to continue the ignominious progress, she abandoned hope, and addressed him, thus, pointedly:

'You damn chalk-faced quitter! You was thinking of giving me a hand, but you let the cop talk you out of it the first word. You're a dandy to tie to. Say, if you ever get a girl, she'll have a picnic. Won't she work you to the queen's taste! Oh, my!' She concluded with a taunting, shrill laugh that rasped Lorison like a saw. The policemen urged her forward; the delighted train of gaping followers closed up the rear; and the captive Amazon, accepting her fate, extended the scope of her maledictions so that none in hearing might seem to be slighted.

Then there came upon Lorison an overwhelming revulsion of his perspective. It may be that he had been ripe for it, that the abnormal condition of mind in which he had for so long existed was already about to revert to its balance; however, it is certain that the events of the last few minutes had furnished the channel, if not the impetus, for the change.

The initial determining influence had been so small a thing as the fact and manner of his having been approached by the officer. That agent had, by the style of his accost, restored the loiterer to his former place in society. In an instant he had been transformed from a somewhat rancid prowler along the fishy side streets of gentility into an honest gentleman, with whom even so lordly a guardian of the peace might agreeably exchange the compliments.

This, then, first broke the spell, and set thrilling in him a resurrected longing for the fellowship of his kind, and the rewards of the virtuous. To what end, he vehemently asked himself, was this fanciful self-accusation, this empty renunciation, this moral squeamishness through which he had been led to abandon what was his heritage in life, and not beyond his deserts? Technically, he was uncondemned; his sole guilty spot was in thought rather than deed, and cognizance of it unshared by others. For what good, moral or sentimental, did he slink, retreating like the hedgehog from his own shadow, to and fro in this musty Bohemia that lacked even the picturesque?

But the thing that struck home and set him raging was the part played by the Amazonian prisoner. To the counterpart of that astounding belligerent – identical, at least, in the way of experience – to one, by her own confession, thus far fallen, had he, not three hours since, been united in marriage. How desirable and natural it had seemed to him then, and how monstrous it seemed now! How the words of diamond thief number two yet burned in his ears: 'If you ever get a girl, she'll have a picnic.' What did that mean but that women instinctly knew him for one they could hoodwink? Still again there reverberated the policeman's sapient contribution to his agony: 'A man these days and nights wants to know what his women folks are up to.' Oh, yes, he had been a fool; he had looked at things from the wrong standpoint.

But the wildest note in all the clamor was struck by pain's forefinger, jealously. Now, at least, he felt that keenest sting – a mounting love unworthily bestowed. Whatever she might be, he loved her; he bore in his own breast his doom. A grating, comic flavor to his predicament struck him suddenly, and he laughed creakingly as he swung down the echoing pavement. An impetuous desire to act, to battle with his fate, seized him. He stopped upon his heel, and smote his palms together triumphantly. His wife was – where? But there was a tangible link; an outlet more or less navigable, through which his derelict ship of matrimony might yet be safely towed – the priest!

Like all imaginative men with pliable natures, Lorison was, when thoroughly stirred, apt to become tempestuous. With a high and stubborn indignation upon him, he retraced his steps to the intersecting street by which he had come. Down this he hurried to the corner where he had parted with – an astringent grimace tinctured the thought – his wife. Thence still back he harked, following through an unfamiliar district his stimulated recollections of the way they had come from that preposterous wedding. Many times he went abroad, and nosed his way back to the trail, furious.

At last, when he reached the dark, calamitous building in which his madness had culminated, and found the black hallway, he dashed down it, perceiving no light or sound. But he raised his voice, hailing loudly; reckless of everything but that he should find the old mischief-maker with the eyes that looked too far away to see the disaster he had wrought. The door opened, and in the stream of light Father Rogan stood, his book in hand, with his finger marking the place.

'Ah!' cried Lorison. 'You are the man I want. I had a wife of you a few hours ago. I would not trouble you, but I neglected to note how it was done. Will you oblige me with the information whether the business is beyond remedy?'

'Come inside,' said the priest; 'there are other lodgers in the house, who might prefer sleep to even a gratified curiosity.'

Lorison entered the room and took the chair offered him. The priest's eyes looked a courteous interrogation.

'I must apologize again,' said the young man, 'for so soon intruding upon you with my marital infelicities, but as my wife has neglected to furnish me with her address, I am deprived of the legitimate recourse of a family row.'

'I am quite a plain man,' said father Rogan, pleasantly; 'but I do not see how I am to ask you questions.'

'Pardon my indirectness,' said Lorison; 'I will ask one. In this room tonight you pronounced me to be a husband. You afterwards spoke of additional rites or performances that either should or could be effected. I paid little attention to your words then, but I am hungry to hear them repeated now. As matters stand, am I married past all help?'

'You are as legally and as firmly bound,' said the priest, 'as though it had been done in a cathedral, in the presence of thousands. The additional observances I referred to are not necessary to the strictest legality of the act, but were advised as a precaution for the future – for convenience of proof in such contingencies as wills, inheritances, and the like.'

Lorison laughed harshly.

'Many thanks,' he said. 'Then there is no mistake, and I am the happy benedict. I suppose I should go stand upon the bridal corner, and when my wife gets through walking the streets she will look me up.'

Father Rogan regarded him calmly.

'My son,' he said, 'when a man and woman come to me to be married I always marry them. I do this for the sake of other people whom they might go away and marry if they did not marry each other. As you see, I do not seek your confidence; but your case seems to me to be one not altogether devoid of interest. Very few marriages that have come to my notice have brought such well-expressed regret within so short a time. I will hazard one question: were you not under the impression that you loved the lady you married, at the time you did so?'

'Loved her!' cried Lorison, wildly. 'Never so well as now, though she told me she deceived and sinned and stole. Never more than now, when, perhaps, she is laughing at the fool she cajoled and left, with scarcely a word, to return to God only knows what particular line of her former folly.'

Father Rogan answered nothing. During the silence that succeeded, he sat with a quiet expectation beaming in his full, lambent eye.

'If you would listen—' began Lorison. The priest held up his hand.

'As I hoped,' he said. 'I thought you would trust me. Wait but a moment.' He brought a long clay pipe, filled and lighted it.

'Now, my son,' he said.

Lorison poured a twelvemonth's accumulated confidence into Father Rogan's ear. He told all; not sparing himself or omitting the facts of his past, the events of the night, or his disturbing conjectures and fears.

'The main point,' said the priest, when he had concluded, 'seems to me to be this – are you reasonably sure that you love this woman whom you have married?'

'Why,' exclaimed Lorison, rising impulsively to his feet— 'why should I deny it? But look at me – am I fish, flesh, or fowl? That is the main point to me, I assure you.'

'I understand you,' said the priest, also rising, and laying down his pipe. 'The situation is one that has taxed the endurance of much older men than you – in fact, especially much older men than you. I will try to relieve you from it, and this night. You shall see for yourself into exactly what predicament you have fallen, and how you shall, possibly, be extricated. There is no evidence so credible as that of the eyesight.'

Father Rogan moved about the room, and donned a soft black hat. Buttoning his coat to his throat, he laid his hand on the doorknob. 'Let us walk,' he said.

The two went out upon the street. The priest turned his face down it, and Lorison walked with him through a squalid district, where the houses loomed, awry and desolate-looking, high above them. Presently they turned into a less dismal side street, where the houses were smaller, and, though hinting of the most meagre comfort, lacked the concentrated wretchedness of the more populous byways.

At a segregated, two-story house Father Rogan halted, and mounted the steps with the confidence of a familiar visitor. He ushered Lorison into a narrow hallway, faintly lighted by a cobwebbed hanging lamp. Almost immediately a door to the right opened and a dingy Irishwoman protruded her head.

'Good evening to ye, Mistress Geehan,' said the priest, unconsciously it seemed, falling into a delicately flavored brogue. 'And is it yourself can tell me if Norah has gone out again, the night, maybe?'

'Oh, it's yer blissid riverence! Sure and I can tell ye the same. The purty darlin' wint out, as usual, but a bit later. And she says: "Mother Geehan," says she, "it's me last noight out, praise the saints, this noight is!" And oh, yer riverence, the swate, beautiful drame of a dress she had this toime! White satin and silk and ribbons, and lace about the neck and arrums – 'twas a sin, yer riverence, the gold was spint upon it.'

The priest heard Lorison catch his breath painfully and a faint smile flickered across his own clean-cut mouth.

'Well, then, Mistress Geehan,' said he, 'I'll just step upstairs and see the bit boy for a minute, and I'll take this gentleman up with me.'

'He's awake, thin,' said the woman. 'I've just come down from sitting wid him the last hour, tilling him fine shtories of ould County Tyrone. 'Tis a greedy gossoon, it is, yer riverence, for me shtories.'

'Small the doubt,' said Father Rogan. 'There's no rocking would put him to slape the quicker, I'm thinking.'

Amid the woman's shrill protest against the retort, the two men ascended the steep stairway. The priest pushed open the door of a room near its top.

'Is that you already, sister?' drawled a sweet, childish voice from the darkness.

'It's only ould Father Denny come to see ye, darlin'; and a foine gintleman I've brought to make ye a gr-r-and call. And ye resaves us fast aslape in bed! Shame on yez manners!'

'Oh, Father Denny, is that you? I'm glad. And will you light the lamp, please? It's on the table by the door. And quit talking like Mother Geehan, Father Denny.'

The priest lit the lamp, and Lorison saw a tiny, tousled-haired boy, with a thin, delicate face, sitting up in a small bed in a corner. Quickly, also, his rapid glance considered the room and its contents. It was furnished with more than comfort, and its adornments plainly indicated a woman's discerning taste. An open door beyond revealed the blackness of an adjoining room's interior.

The boy clutched both of Father Rogan's hands. 'I'm so glad you came,' he said; 'but why did you come in the night? Did sister send you?'

'Off wid ye! Am I to be sint about, at me age, as was Terence McShane of Ballymahone? I come on me own r-r-responsibility.'

Lorison had also advanced to the boy's bedside. He was fond of children; and the wee fellow, laying himself down to sleep alone in that dark room, stirred his heart.

'Aren't you afraid, little man?' he asked, stooping down beside him.

'Sometimes,' answered the boy, with a shy smile, 'when the rats make too much noise. But nearly every night, when sister goes out, Mother Geehan stays a while with me, and tells me funny stories. I'm not often afraid, sir.'

'This brave little gentleman,' said Father Rogan, 'is a scholar of mine. Every day from half-past six to half-past eight – when sister comes for him – he stops in my study, and we find out what's in the inside of books. He knows multiplication, division, and fractions; and he's troubling me to begin wid the chronicles of Ciaran of Clonmacnoise, Corurac McCullenan and Cuan O'Lochain, the gr-r-reat Irish hishtorians.' The boy was evidently accustomed to the priest's Celtic pleasantries. A little, appreciative grin was all the attention the insinuation of pedantry received.

Lorison, to have saved his life, could not have put to the child one of those vital questions that were wildly beating about, unanswered, in his own brain. The little fellow was very like Norah; he had the same shining hair and candid eyes.

'Oh, Father Denny,' cried the boy suddenly, 'I forgot to tell you! Sister is not going away at night any more! She told me so when she kissed me good-night as she was leaving. And she said she was so happy, and then she cried. Wasn't that queer? But I'm glad; aren't you?'

'Yes, lad. And now, ye omadhaun, go to sleep, and say good-night; we must be going.'

'Which shall I do first, Father Denny?'

'Faith, he's caught me again! Wait till I get the sassench into the annals of Tageruach, the hagiographer; I'll give him enough of the Irish idiom to make him more respectful.'

The light was out, and the small, brave voice bidding them good-night from the dark room. They groped downstairs, and tore away from the garrulity of Mother Geehan.

Again the priest steered them through the dim ways, but this time in another direction. His conductor was serenely silent, and Lorison followed his example to the extent of seldom speaking. Serene he could not be. His heart beat suffocatingly in his breast. The following of this blind, menacing trail was pregnant with he knew not what humiliating revelation to be delivered at its end.

They came into a more pretentious street, where trade, it could be surmised, flourished by day. And again the priest paused; this time before a lofty building, whose great doors and windows in the lowest floor were carefully shuttered and barred. Its highest apertures were dark, save in the third story, the windows of which were brilliantly lighted. Lorison's ear caught a distant, regular, pleasing thrumming, as of music above. They stood at an angle of the building. Up, along the side nearest them, mounted an iron stairway. At its top was an upright, illuminated parallelogram. Father Rogan had stopped, and stood, musing.

'I will say this much,' he remarked, thoughtfully. 'I believe you to be a better man than you think yourself to be, and a better man than I thought some hours ago. But do not take this,' he added, with a smile, 'as much praise. I promised you a possible deliverance from an unhappy perplexity. I will have to modify that promise. I can only remove the mystery that enhanced that perplexity. Your deliverance depends upon yourself. Come.'

He led his companion up the stairway. Halfway up, Lorison caught him by the sleeve. 'Remember,' he gasped, 'I love that woman.'

'You desired to know.'

'I— Go on.'

The priest reached the landing at the top of the stairway. Lorison, behind him, saw that the illuminated space was the glass upper half of a door opening into the lighted room. The rhythmic music increased as they neared it; the stairs shook with the mellow vibrations.

Lorison stopped breathing when he set foot upon the highest step, for the priest stood aside, and motioned him to look through the glass of the door.

His eyes, accustomed to the darkness, met first a blinding glare, and then he made out the faces and forms of many people, amid an extravagant display display of splendid robings – billowy laces, brilliant-hued finery, ribbons, silks, and misty drapery. And then he caught the meaning of that jarring hum, and he saw the tired, pale, happy face of his wife, bending, as were a score of others, over her sewing machine – toiling, toiling. Here was the folly she pursued, and the end of his quest.

But not his deliverance, though even then remorse struck him. His shamed soul fluttered once more before it retired to make room for the other and better one. For, to temper his thrill of joy, the shine of the satin and the glimmer of ornaments recalled the disturbing figure of the bespangled

Amazon, and the base duplicate histories lit by the glare of footlights and stolen diamonds. It is past the wisdom of him who only sets the scenes, either to praise or blame the man. But this time his love overcame his scruples. He took a quick step, and reached out his hand for the doorknob. Father Rogan was quicker to arrest it and draw him back.

'You use my trust in you queerly,' said the priest, sternly. 'What are you about to do?'

'I am going to my wife,' said Lorison. 'Let me pass.'

'Listen,' said the priest, holding him firmly by the arm. 'I am about to put you in possession of a piece of knowledge of which, thus far, you have scarcely proved deserving. I do not think you ever will; but I will not dwell upon that. You see in that room the woman you married, working for a frugal living for herself, and a generous comfort for an idolized brother. This building belongs to the chief costumer of the city. For months the advance orders for the coming Mardi Gras festivals have kept the work going day and night. I myself secured employment here for Norah. She toils here each night from nine o'clock until daylight, and, besides, carries home with her some of the finer costumes, requiring more delicate needlework, and works there part of the day. Somehow, you two have remained strangely ignorant of each other's lives. Are you convinced now that your wife is not walking the streets?'

'Let me go to her,' cried Lorison, again struggling, 'and beg her forgiveness!'

'Sir,' said the priest, 'do you owe me nothing? Be quiet. It seems so often that Heaven lets fall its choicest gifts into hands that must be taught to hold them. Listen again. You forgot that repentant sin must not compromise, but look up, for redemption, to the purest and best. You went to her with the fine-spun sophistry that peace could be found in a mutual guilt and she, fearful of losing what her heart so craved, thought it worth the price to buy it with a desperate, pure, beautiful lie. I have known her since the day she was born; she is as innocent and unsullied in life and deed as a holy saint. In that lowly street where she dwells she first saw the light, and she has lived there ever since, spending her days in generous self-sacrifice, for others. Och, ye spalpeen!' continued Father Rogan, raising his finger in kindly anger at Lorison. 'What for, I wonder, could she be after making a fool of hersilf, and shamin' her swate soul with lies, for the like of you!'

'Sir,' said Lorison, trembling, 'say what you please of me. Doubt it as you must, I will yet prove my gratitude to you, and my devotion to her. But let me speak to her once now, let me kneel for just one moment at her feet, and —'

'Tut, tut!' said the priest. 'How many acts of a love drama do you think an old bookworm like me capable of witnessing? Besides, what kind of figures do we cut, spying upon the mysteries of midnight millinery! Go to meet your wife to-morrow, as she ordered you, and obey her thereafter, and maybe some time I shall get forgiveness for the part I have played in this night's work. Off wid yez down the shtairs, now! 'Tis late, and an ould man like me should be takin' his rest.'

MADAME BO-PEEP, OF THE RANCHES

'AUNT ELLEN,' SAID OCTAVIA, cheerfully, as she threw her black kid gloves carefully at the dignified Persian cat on the window-seat, 'I'm a pauper.'

'You are so extreme in your statements, Octavia, dear,' said Aunt Ellen, mildly, looking up from her paper. 'If you find yourself temporarily in need of some small change for bonbons, you will find my purse in the drawer of the writing desk.'

Octavia Beaupree removed her hat and seated herself on a footstool near her aunt's chair, clasping her hands about her knees. Her slim and flexible figure, clad in a modish mourning costume, accommodated itself easily and gracefully to the trying position. Her bright and youthful face, with its pair of sparkling, life-enamored eyes, tried to compose itself to the seriousness that the occasion seemed to demand.

'You good auntie, it isn't a case of bonbons it is abject, staring, unpicturesque poverty, with ready-made clothes, gasolined gloves, and probably one-o'clock dinners all waiting with the traditional wolf at the door. I've just come from my lawyer, Auntie, and, "Please, ma'am, I ain't got nothink 't all. Flowers, lady? Buttonhole, gentleman? Pencils, sir, three for five, to help a poor widow?" Do I do it nicely, Auntie, or, as a bread-winner accomplishment, were my lessons in elocution entirely wasted?'

'Do be serious, my dear,' said Aunt Ellen, letting her paper fall to the floor, 'long enough to tell me what you mean. Colonel Beaupree's estate —'

'Colonel Beaupree's estate,' interrupted Octavia, emphasizing her words with appropriate dramatic gestures, 'is of Spanish castellar architecture. Colonel Beaupree's resources are – wind. Colonel Beaupree's stocks are – water. Colonel Beaupree's income is – all in. The statement lacks the legal technicalities to which I have been listening for an hour, but that is what it means when translated.'

'Octavia!' Aunt Ellen was now visibly possessed by consternation. 'I can hardly believe it. And it was the impression that he was worth a million. And the De Peysters themselves introduced him!'

Octavia rippled out a laugh, and then became properly grave.

'*De mortuis nil*, Auntie – not even the rest of it. The dear old colonel – what a gold brick he was, after all! I paid for my bargain fairly – I'm all here, am I not? – items: eyes, fingers, toes, youth, old family, unquestionable position in society as called for in the contract – no wild-cat stock here.' Octavia picked up the morning paper from the floor. 'But I'm not going to "squeal" – isn't that what they call it when you rail at Fortune because you've lost the game?' She turned the pages of the paper calmly. ' "Stock market" – no use for that. "Society's doings" – that's done. Here is my page – the wish column. A Van Dresser could not be said to "want" for anything, of course. Chambermaids, cooks, canvassers, stenographers —'

'Dear,' said Aunt Ellen, with a little tremor in her voice, 'please do not talk in that way. Even if your affairs are in so unfortunate a condition, there is my three thousand —'

Octavia sprang up lithely, and deposited a smart kiss on the delicate cheek of the prim little elderly maid.

'Blessed auntie, your three thousand is just sufficient to insure your Hyson to be free from willow leaves and keep the Persian in sterilized cream. I know I'd be welcome, but I prefer to strike bottom like Beelzebub rather than hang around like the Peri listening to the music from the side entrance. I'm going to earn my own living. There's nothing else to do. I'm a— Oh, oh, oh! – I had forgotten. There's one thing saved from the wreck. It's a corral – no, a ranch in – let me see – Texas; an asset, dear old Mr. Bannister called it. How pleased he was to show me something he could describe as unencumbered! I've a description of it among those stupid papers he made me bring away with me from his office. I'll try to find it.'

Octavia found her shopping-bag, and drew from it a long envelope filled with typewritten documents.

'A ranch in Texas,' sighed Aunt Ellen. 'It sounds to me more like a liability than an asset. Those are the places where the centipedes are found, and cowboys, and fandangos.'

' "The Rancho de las Sombras," ' read Octavia from a sheet of violently purple typewriting, 'is situated one hundred and ten miles southeast of San Antonio, and thirty-eight miles from its nearest railroad station, Nopal, on the I. and G.N. Ranch consists of 7,680 acres of well-watered land, with title conferred by State patents, and twenty-two sections, or 14,080 acres, partly under yearly running lease and partly bought under State's twenty-year-purchase act. Eight thousand graded merino sheep, with the necessary equipment of horses, vehicles, and general ranch paraphernalia. Ranch-house built of brick, with six rooms comfortably furnished according to the requirements of the climate. All within a strong barbed-wire fence.

' "The present ranch manager seems to be competent and reliable, and is rapidly placing upon a paying basis a business that, in other hands, had been allowed to suffer from neglect and misconduct.

' "This property was secured by Colonel Beaupree in a deal with a Western irrigation syndicate, and the title to it seems to be perfect. With careful management and the natural increase of land values, it ought to be made the foundation for a comfortable fortune for its owner." '

When Octavia ceased reading, Aunt Ellen uttered something as near a sniff as her breeding permitted.

'The prospectus,' she said, with uncompromising metropolitan suspicion, 'doesn't mention the centipedes, or the Indians. And you never did like mutton, Octavia. I don't see what advantage you can derive from this – desert.'

But Octavia was in a trance. Her eyes were steadily regarding something quite beyond their focus. Her lips were parted, and her face was lighted by the kindling furor of the explorer, the ardent, stirring disquiet of the adventurer. Suddenly she clasped her hands together exultantly.

'The problem solves itself, auntie,' she cried. 'I'm going to that ranch. I'm going to live on it. I'm going to learn to like mutton, and even concede the good qualities of centipedes – at a respectful distance. It's just what I need. It's a new life that comes when my old one is just ending. It's a release, auntie; it isn't a narrowing. Think of the gallops over those leagues of prairies, with the wind tugging at the roots of your hair, the coming close to the earth and learning over again the stories of the growing grass and the little wild flowers without names! Glorious is what it will be. Shall I be a shepherdess with a Watteau hat, and a crook to keep the bad wolves from the lambs, or a typical Western ranch girl, with short hair, like the pictures of her in the Sunday papers? I think the latter. And they'll have my picture, too, with the wild-cats I've slain, single-handed, hanging from my saddle horn. "From the Four Hundred to the Flocks" is the way they'll headline it, and they'll print photographs of the old Van Dresser mansion and the church where I was married. They won't have my picture, but they'll get an artist to draw it. I'll be wild and woolly, and I'll grow my own wool.'

'Octavia!' Aunt Ellen condensed into the one word all the protests she was unable to utter.

'Don't say a word, auntie. I'm going. I'll see the sky at night fit down on the world like a big butter-dish cover, and I'll make friends again with the stars that I haven't had a chat with since I was a wee child. I wish to go. I'm tired of all this. I'm glad I haven't any money. I could bless Colonel Beaupree for that ranch, and forgive him for all his bubbles. What if the life will be rough and lonely! I – I deserve it. I shut my heart to everything except that miserable ambition. I – oh, I wish to go away, and forget – forget!'

Octavia swerved suddenly to her knees, laid her flushed face in her aunt's lap, and shook with turbulent sobs.

Aunt Ellen bent over her, and smoothed the coppery-brown hair.

'I didn't know,' she said, gently; 'I didn't know – that. Who was it, dear?'

When Mrs. Octavia Beaupree, née Van Dresser, stepped from the train at Nopal, her manner lost, for the moment, some of that easy certitude which had always marked her movements. The town was of recent establishment, and seemed to have been hastily constructed of undressed lumber and flapping canvas. The element that had congregated about the station, though not offensively demonstrative, was clearly composed of citizens accustomed to and prepared for rude alarms.

Octavia stood on the platform, against the telegraph office, and attempted to choose by intuition from the swaggering, straggling string of loungers, the manager of the Rancho de las Sombras, who had been instructed by Mr. Bannister to meet her there. That tall, serious-looking, elderly man in the blue flannel shirt and white tie she thought must be he. But no, he passed by, removing his gaze from the lady as hers rested on him, according to the Southern custom. The manager, she thought, with some impatience at being kept waiting, should have no difficulty in selecting her. Young women wearing the most recent thing in ash-colored traveling suits were not so plentiful in Nopal!

Thus keeping a speculative watch on all persons of possible managerial aspect, Octavia, with a catching breath and a start of surprise, suddenly became aware of Teddy Westlake hurrying along the platform in the direction of the train – of Teddy Westlake or his sun-browned ghost in cheviot, boots and leather-girdled hat – Theodore Westlake, Jr., amateur polo (almost) champion, all-round butterfly and cucumber of the soil; but a broader, surer, more emphasized and determined Teddy than the one she had known a year ago when last she saw him.

He perceived Octavia at almost the same time, deflected his course, and steered for her in his old, straightforward way. Something like awe came upon her as the strangeness of his metamorphosis was brought into closer range; the rich, red-brown of his complexion brought out so vividly his straw-colored mustache and steel-gray eyes. He seemed more grown-up, and, somehow, farther away. But, when he spoke, the old, boyish Teddy came back again. They had been friends from childhood.

'Why, 'Tave!' he exclaimed, unable to reduce his perplexity to coherence. 'How – what – when – where?'

'Train,' said Octavia; 'necessity; ten minutes ago; home. Your complexion's gone, Teddy. Now, how – what – when – where?'

'I'm working down here,' said Teddy. He cast side glances about the station as one does who tries to combine politeness with duty.

'You didn't notice on the train,' he asked, 'an old lady with gray curls and a poodle, who occupied two seats with her bundles and quarrelled with the conductor, did you?'

'I think not,' answered Octavia, reflecting. 'And you haven't, by any chance, noticed a big, gray-mustached man in a blue shirt and six-shooters, with little flakes of merino wool sticking in his hair, have you?'

'Lots of 'em,' said Teddy, with symptoms of mental delirium under the strain. 'Do you happen to know any such individual?'

'No; the description is imaginary. Is your interest in the old lady whom you describe a personal one?'

'Never saw her in my life. She's painted entirely from fancy. She owns the little piece of property where I earn my bread and butter – the Rancho de las Sombras. I drove up to meet her according to arrangements with her lawyer.'

Octavia leaned against the wall of the telegraph office. Was this possible? And didn't he know?

'Are you the manager of that ranch?' she asked, weakly.

'I am,' said Teddy, with pride.

'I am Mrs. Beaupree,' said Octavia faintly; 'but my hair never would curl, and I was polite to the conductor.'

For a moment that strange, grown-up look came back, and removed Teddy miles away from her.

'I hope you'll excuse me,' he said, rather awkwardly. 'You see, I've been down here in the chaparral a year. I hadn't heard. Give me your checks, please, and I'll have your traps loaded into the wagon. José will follow with them. We travel ahead in the buckboard.'

Seated by Teddy in a feather-weight buckboard, behind a pair of wild, cream-colored Spanish ponies, Octavia abandoned all thought for the exhilaration of the present. They swept out of the little town and down the level road toward the south. Soon the road dwindled and disappeared, and they struck across a world carpeted with an endless reach of curly mesquite grass. The wheels made no sound. The tireless ponies bounded ahead at an unbroken gallop. The temperate wind, made fragrant by thousands of acres of blue and yellow wild flowers, roared gloriously in their ears. The motion was aërial, ecstatic, with a thrilling sense of perpetuity in its effect. Octavia sat silent, possessed by a feeling of elemental, sensual bliss. Teddy seemed to be wrestling with some internal problem.

'I'm going to call you madama,' he announced as the result of his labors. 'That is what the Mexicans will call you – they're nearly all Mexicans on the ranch, you know. That seems to me about the proper thing.'

'Very well, Mr. Westlake,' said Octavia, primly.

'Oh, now,' said Teddy, in some consternation, 'that's carrying the thing too far, isn't it?'

'Don't worry me with your beastly etiquette. I'm just beginning to live. Don't remind me of anything artificial. If only this air could be bottled! This much alone is worth coming for. Oh, look! there goes a deer!'

'Jack-rabbit,' said Teddy, without turning his head.

'Could I – might I drive?' suggested Octavia, panting, with rose-tinted cheeks and the eye of an eager child.

'On one condition. Could I – might I smoke?'

'Forever!' cried Octavia, taking the lines with solemn joy. 'How shall I know which way to drive?'

'Keep her sou' by sou'east, and all sail set. You see that black speck on the horizon under that lowermost Gulf cloud? That's a group of live-oaks and a landmark. Steer halfway between that and the little hill to the left. I'll recite you the whole code of driving rules for the Texas prairies: keep the reins from under the horses' feet, and swear at 'em frequent.'

'I'm too happy to swear, Ted. Oh, why do people buy yachts or travel in palace-cars, when a buckboard and a pair of plugs and a spring morning like this can satisfy all desire?'

'Now, I'll ask you,' protested Teddy, who was futilely striking match after match on the dashboard, 'not to call those denizens of the air plugs. They can kick out a hundred miles between daylight and dark.' At last he succeeded in snatching a light for his cigar from the flame held in the hollow of his hands.

'Room!' said Octavia, intensely. 'That's what produces the effect. I know now what I've wanted – scope – range – room!'

'Smoking-room,' said Teddy, unsentimentally. 'I love to smoke in a buck-board. The wind blows the smoke into you and out again. It saves exertion.'

The two fell so naturally into their old-time goodfellowship that it was only by degrees that a sense of the strangeness of the new relations between them came to be felt.

'Madama,' said Teddy, wonderingly, 'however did you get it into your head to cut the crowd and come down here? Is it a fad now among the upper classes to trot off to sheep ranges instead of to Newport?'

'I was broke, Teddy,' said Octavia, sweetly, with her interest centred upon steering safely between a Spanish dagger plant and a clump of chaparral; 'I haven't a thing in the world but this ranch – not even any other home to go to.'

'Come, now,' said Teddy, anxiously but incredulously, 'you don't mean it?'

'When my husband,' said Octavia, with a shy slurring of the word, 'died three months ago I thought I had a reasonable amount of the world's goods. His lawyer exploded that theory in a sixty-minute fully illustrated lecture. I took to the sheep as a last resort. Do you happen to know of any fashionable caprice among the gilded youth of Manhattan that induces them to abandon polo and club windows to become managers of sheep ranches?'

'It's easily explained in my case,' responded Teddy, promptly. 'I had to go to work. I couldn't have earned my board in New York, so I chummed a while with old Sandford, one of the syndicate that owned the ranch before Colonel Beaupree bought it, and got a place down here. I wasn't manager at first. I jogged around on ponies and studied the business in detail, until I got all the points in my head. I saw where it was losing and what the remedies were, and then Sandford put me in charge. I get a hundred dollars a month, and I earn it.'

'Poor Teddy!' said Octavia, with a smile.

'You needn't. I like it. I save half my wages, and I'm as hard as a water plug. It beats polo.'

'Will it furnish bread and tea and jam for another outcast from civilization?'

'The spring shearing,' said the manager, 'just cleaned up a deficit in last year's business. Wastefulness and inattention have been the rule heretofore. The autumn clip will leave a small profit over all expenses. Next year there will be jam.'

When about four o'clock in the afternoon, the ponies rounded a gentle, brush-covered hill, and then swooped, like a double cream-colored cyclone, upon the Rancho de las Sombras, Octavia gave a little cry of delight. A lordly grove of magnificent live-oaks cast an area of grateful, cool shade, whence the ranch had drawn its name, 'de las Sombras' – of the shadows. The house, of red brick, one story, ran low and long beneath the trees. Through its middle, dividing its six rooms in half, extended a broad, arched passageway, picturesque with flowering cactus and hanging red earthen jars. A 'gallery,' low and broad, encircled the building. Vines climbed about it, and the adjacent ground was, for space, covered with transplanted grass and shrubs. A little lake, long and narrow, glimmered in the sun at the rear. Farther away stood the shacks of the Mexican workers, the corrals, wood sheds and shearing pens. To the right lay the low hills, splattered with dark patches of chaparral; to the left the unbounded green prairie blending against the blue heavens.

'It's a home, Teddy,' said Octavia, breathlessly; 'that's what it is – it's a home.'

'Not so bad for a sheep ranch,' admitted Teddy, with excusable pride. 'I've been tinkering on it at odd times.'

A Mexican youth sprang from somewhere in the grass, and took charge of the creams. The mistress and the manager entered the house.

'Here's Mrs. MacIntyre,' said Teddy, as a placid, neat, elderly lady came out upon the gallery to meet them. 'Mrs. Mac, here's the boss. Very likely she will be wanting a hunk of bacon and a dish of beans after her drive.'

Mrs. MacIntyre, the housekeeper, as much a fixture on the place as the lake or the live-oaks, received the imputation of the ranch's resources of refreshment with mild indignation and was about to give it utterances when Octavia spoke.

'Oh, Mrs. MacIntyre, don't apologize for Teddy. Yes, I call him Teddy. So does every one whom he hasn't duped into taking him seriously. You see, we used to cut paper dolls and play jackstraws together ages ago. No one minds what he says.'

'No,' said Teddy, 'no one minds what he says, just so he doesn't do it again.'

Octavia cast one of those subtle, sidelong glances toward him from beneath her lowered eyelids – a glance that Teddy used to describe as an upper-cut. But there was nothing in his ingenuous, weather-tanned face to warrant a suspicion that he was making an allusion – nothing. Beyond a doubt, thought Octavia, he had forgotten.

'Mr. Westlake likes his fun,' said Mrs. MacIntyre, as she conducted Octavia to her rooms. 'But,' she added, loyally, 'people around here usually pay attention to what he says when he talks in earnest. I don't know what would have become of this place without him.'

Two rooms at the east end of the house had been arranged for the occupancy of the ranch's mistress. When she entered them a slight dismay seized her at their bare appearance and the scantiness of their furniture; but she quickly reflected that the climate was a semi-tropical one, and was moved to appreciation of the well-conceived efforts to conform to it. The sashes had already been removed from the big windows, and white curtains waved in the Gulf breeze that streamed through the wide jalousies. The bare floor was amply strewn with cool rugs; the chairs were inviting, deep, dreamy willows; the walls were papered with a light, cheerful olive. One whole side of her sitting room was covered with books on smooth, unpainted pine shelves. She flew to these at once. Before her was a well-selected library. She caught glimpses of titles of volumes of fiction and travel not yet seasoned from the dampness of the press.

Presently, recollecting that she was now in a wilderness given over to mutton, centipedes, and privations, the incongruity of these luxuries struck her, and, with intuitive feminine suspicion, she began turning to the fly-leaves of volume after volume. Upon each one was inscribed in fluent characters the name of Theodore Westlake, Jr.

Octavia, fatigued by her long journey, retired early that night. Lying upon her white, cool bed, she rested deliciously, but sleep coquetted long with her. She listened to faint noises whose strangeness kept her faculties on the alert – the fractious yelping of the coyotes, the ceaseless, low symphony of the wind, the distant booming of the frogs about the lake, the lamentation of a concertina in the Mexicans' quarters. There were many conflicting feelings in her heart – thankfulness and rebellion, peace and disquietude, loneliness and a sense of protecting care, happiness and an old, haunting pain.

She did what any other woman would have done – sought relief in a wholesome tide of unreasonable tears, and her last words, murmured to herself before slumber, capitulating, come softly to woo her, were, 'He has forgotten.'

The manager of the Rancho de las Sombras was no dilettante. He was a 'hustler.' He was generally up, mounted, and away of mornings before the rest of the household were awake, making the rounds of the flocks and camps. This was the duty of the major-domo, a stately old Mexican with a princely air and manner, but Teddy seemed to have a great deal of confidence in his own eyesight. Except in the busy seasons, he nearly always returned to the ranch to breakfast at eight o'clock, with Octavia and Mrs. MacIntyre, at the little table set in the central hallway, bringing with him a tonic and breezy cheerfulness full of the health and flavor of the prairies.

A few days after Octavia's arrival he made her get out one of her riding skirts, and curtail it to a shortness demanded by the chaparral brakes.

With some misgivings she donned this and the pair of buckskin leggings he prescribed in addition, and mounted upon a dancing pony, rode with him to view her possessions. He showed her everything – the flocks of ewes, muttons and grazing lambs, the dipping vats, the shearing pens, the uncouth merino rams in their little pasture, the water-tanks prepared against the summer drought – giving account of his stewardship with a boyish enthusiasm that never flagged.

Where was the old Teddy that she knew so well? This side of him was the same, and it was a side that pleased her; but this was all she ever saw of him now. Where was his sentimentality – those old, varying moods of impetuous love-making, of fanciful, quixotic devotion, of heart-breaking gloom, of alternating, absurd tenderness and haughty dignity? His nature had been a sensitive one, his temperament bordering closely on the artistic. She knew that, besides being a follower of fashion and its fads and sports, he had cultivated tastes of a finer nature. He had written things, he had tampered with colors, he was something of a student in certain branches of art, and once she had been admitted to all his aspirations and thoughts. But now – and she could not avoid the conclusion – Teddy had barricade against her every side of himself except one – the side that showed the manager of the Rancho de las Sombras and a jolly chum who had forgiven and forgotten. Queerly enough the words of Mr. Bannister's descripton of her property came into her mind – 'all inclosed within a strong barbed-wire fence.'

'Teddy's fenced, too,' said Octavia to herself.

It was not difficult for her to reason out the cause of his fortifications. It had originated one night at the Hammersmiths' ball. It occurred at a time soon after she had decided to accept Colonel Beaupree and his millions, which was no more than her looks and the entrée she held to the inner circles were worth. Teddy had proposed with all his impetuosity and fire, and she looked him straight in the eyes, and said, coldly and finally: 'Never let me hear any such silly nonsense from you again.' 'You won't,' said Teddy, with a new expression around his mouth, and – now Teddy was inclosed within a strong barbed-wire fence.

It was on this first ride of inspection that Teddy was seized by the inspiration that suggested the name of Mother Goose's heroine, and he at once bestowed it upon Octavia. The idea, supported by both a similarity of names and identity of occupations, seemed to strike him as a peculiarly happy one, and he never tired of using it. The Mexicans on the ranch also took up the name, adding another syllable to accommodate their lingual incapacity for the final 'p,' gravely referring to her as 'La Madama Bo-Peepy.' Eventually it spread, and 'Madame Bo-Peep's ranch' was as often mentioned as the 'Rancho de las Sombras.'

Came the long, hot season from May to September, when work is scarce on the ranches. Octavia passed the days in a kind of lotus-eater's dream. Books, hammocks, correspondence with a few intimate friends, a renewed interest in her old water-color box and easel – these disposed of the sultry hours of daylight. The evenings were always sure to bring enjoyment. Best of all were the rapturous horseback rides with Teddy, when the moon gave light over the wind-swept leagues, chaperoned by the wheeling night-hawk and the startled owl. Often the Mexicans would come up from their shacks with their guitars and sing the weirdest of heart-breaking songs. There were long, cosy chats on the breezy gallery, and an interminable warfare of wits between Teddy and Mrs. MacIntyre, whose abundant Scotch shrewdness often more than overmatched the lighter humor in which she was lacking.

And the nights came, one after another, and were filed away by weeks and months – nights soft and languorous and fragrant, that should have driven Strephon to Chloe over wires however barbed, that might have drawn Cupid himself to hunt, lasso in hand, among those amorous pastures – but Teddy kept his fences up.

One July night Madame Bo-Peep and her ranch manager were sitting on the east gallery. Teddy had been exhausting the science of prognostication as to the probabilities of a price of twenty-four cents for the autumn clip, and had then subsided into an anaesthetic cloud of Havana smoke. Only as incompetent a judge as a woman would have failed to note long ago that at least a third of his salary must have gone up in the fumes of those imported Regalias.

'Teddy,' said Octavia, suddenly, and rather sharply, 'what are you working down here on a ranch for?'

'One hundred per,' said Teddy, glibly, 'and found.'

'I've a good mind to discharge you.'

'Can't do it,' said Teddy, with a grin.

'Why not?' demanded Octavia, with argumentative heat.

'Under contract. Terms of sale respect all unexpired contracts. Mine runs until 12 p.m., December thirty-first. You might get up at midnight on that date and fire me. If you try it sooner I'll be in a position to bring legal proceedings.'

Octavia seemed to be considering the prospects of litigation.

'But,' continued Teddy, cheerfully, 'I've been thinking of resigning anyway.'

Octavia's rocking-chair ceased its motion. There were centipedes in this country, she felt sure; and Indians; and vast, lonely, desolate, empty wastes; all within strong barbed-wire fence. There was a Van Dresser pride, but there was also a Van Dresser heart. She must know for certain whether or not he had forgotten.

'Ah, well, Teddy,' she said, with a fine assumption of polite interest, 'it's lonely down here; you're longing to get back to the old life – to polo and lobsters and theatres and balls.'

'Never cared much for balls,' said Teddy, virtuously.

'You're getting old, Teddy. Your memory is failing. Nobody ever knew you to miss a dance, unless it occurred on the same night with another one which you attended. And you showed such shocking bad taste, too, in dancing too often with the same partner. Let me see, what was that Forbes girl's name – the one with wall eyes – Mabel, wasn't it?'

'No; Adèle. Mabel was the one with the bony elbows. That wasn't wall in Adèle's eyes. It was soul. We used to talk sonnets together, and Verlaine. Just then I was trying to run a pipe from the Pierian spring.'

'You were on the floor with her,' said Octavia, undeflected, 'five times at the Hammersmiths.'

'Hammersmiths' what?' questioned Teddy, vacuously.

'Ball – ball,' said Octavia, viciously. 'What were we talking of?'

'Eyes, I thought,' said Teddy, after some reflection; 'and elbows.'

'Those Hammersmiths,' went on Octavia, in her sweetest society prattle, after subduing an intense desire to yank a handful of sunburnt, sandy hair from the head lying back contentedly against the canvas of the steamer chair, 'had too much money. Mines, wasn't it? It was something that paid something to the ton. You couldn't get a glass of plain water in their house. Everything at that ball was dreadfully overdone.'

'It was,' said Teddy.

'Such a crowd there was!' Octavia continued conscious that she was talking the rapid drivel of a school-girl describing her first dance. 'The balconies were as warm as the rooms. I – lost – something at that ball.' The last sentence was uttered in a tone calculated to remove the barbs from miles of wire.

'So did I,' confessed Teddy, in a lower voice.

'A glove,' said Octavia, falling back as the enemy approached her ditches.

'Caste,' said Teddy, halting his firing line without loss. 'I hob-nobbed, half evening, with one of Hammersmith's miners, a fellow who kept his hands in his pockets, and talked like an archangel about reduction plants and drifts and levels and sluice-boxes.'

'A pearl-gray glove, nearly new,' sighed Octavia, mournfully.

'A bang-up chap, that McArdle,' maintained Teddy, approvingly. 'A man who hated olives and elevators; a man who handled mountains as croquettes, and built tunnels in the air; a man who never uttered a word of silly nonsense in his life. Did you sign those lease-renewal applications yet, madama? They've got to be on file in the land office by the thirty-first.'

Teddy turned his head lazily. Octavia's chair was vacant.

A certain centipede, crawling along the lines marked out by fate, expounded the situation. It was early one morning while Octavia and Mrs. MacIntyre were trimming the honeysuckle on the west gallery. Teddy had risen and departed hastily before daylight in response to a word that a flock of ewes had been scattered from their bedding ground during the night by a thunder-storm.

The centipede, driven by destiny, showed himself on the floor of the gallery, and then, the screeches of the two women giving him his cue, he scuttled with all his yellow legs through the open door into the furthermost west room, which was Teddy's. Arming themselves with domestic utensils selected with regard to their length, Octavia and Mrs. MacIntyre, with much clutching of skirts and skirmishing for the position of rear guard in the attacking force, followed.

Once inside, the centipede seemed to have disappeared, and his prospective murderers began a thorough but cautious search for their victim.

Even in the midst of such a dangerous and absorbing adventure Octavia was conscious of an awed curiosity on finding herself in Teddy's sanctum. In that room he sat alone, silently communing with those secret thoughts that he now shared with no one, dreamed there whatever dreams he now called on no one to interpret.

It was the room of a Spartan or a soldier. In one corner stood a wide, canvas-covered cot; in another, a small bookcase; in another, a grim stand of Winchesters and shotguns. An immense table, strewn with letters, papers, and documents and surmounted by a set of pigeon-holes, occupied one side.

The centipede showed genius in concealing himself in such bare quarters. Mrs. MacIntyre was poking a broom-handle behind the bookcase. Octavia approached Teddy's cot. The room was just as the manager had left it in his hurry. The Mexican maid had not yet given it her attention. There was his big pillow with the imprint of his head still in the centre. She thought the horrid beast might have climbed the cot and hidden itself to bite Teddy. Centipedes were thus cruel and vindictive towards managers.

She cautiously overturned the pillow, and then parted her lips to give the signal for reinforcements at sight of a long, slender, dark object lying there. But, repressing it in time, she caught up a glove, a pearl-gray glove, flattened – it might be conceived – by many, many months of nightly pressure beneath the pillow of the man who had forgotten the Hammersmiths' ball. Teddy must have left so hurriedly that morning that he had, for once, forgotten to transfer it to its resting-place by day. Even managers, who are notoriously wily and cunning, are sometimes caught up with.

Octavia slid the gray glove into the bosom of her summery morning gown. It was hers. Men who put themselves within a strong barbed-wire fence, and remember Hammersmith balls only by the talk of miners about sluice boxes, should not be allowed to possess such articles.

After all, what a paradise this prairie country was! How it blossomed like the rose when you found things that were thought to be lost! How delicious was that morning breeze coming in the windows, fresh and sweet with the breath of the yellow ratama blooms! Might one not stand, for a minute, with shining, far-gazing eyes, and dream that mistakes might be corrected?

Why was Mrs. MacIntyre poking about so absurdly with a broom?

'I've found it,' said Mrs. MacIntyre, banging the door. 'Here it is.'

'Did you lose something?' asked Octavia, with sweetly polite non-interest.

'The little devil!' said Mrs. MacIntyre, driven to violence. 'Ye've no forgotten him alretty?'

Between them they slew the centipede. Thus was he rewarded for his agency toward the recovery of things lost at the Hammersmiths' ball.

It seems that Teddy, in due course, remembered the glove, and when he returned to the house at sunset made a secret but exhaustive search for it. Not until evening, upon the moonlit eastern gallery, did he find it. It was upon the hand that he had thought lost to him forever, and so he was moved to repeat certain nonsense that he had been commanded never, never to utter again. Teddy's fences were down.

This time there was no ambition to stand in the way, and the wooing was as natural and successful as should be between ardent shepherd and gentle shepherdess.

The prairies changed to a garden. The Rancho de las Sombras became the Ranch of Light.

A few days later Octavia received a letter from Mr. Bannister, in reply to one she had written to him asking some questions about her business. A portion of the letter ran as follows:

I am at a loss to account for your references to the sheep ranch. Two months after your departure to take up your residence upon it, it was discovered that Colonel Beaupree's title was worthless. A deed came to light showing that he disposed of the property before his death. The matter was reported to your manager, Mr. Westlake, who at once repurchased the property. It is entirely beyond my powers of conjecture to imagine how you have remained in ignorance of this fact. I beg that you will at once confer with that gentleman, who will, at least, corroborate my statement.

Octavia sought Teddy, with battle in her eye.

'What are you working on this ranch for?' she asked once more.

'One hundred—' he began to repeat, but saw in her face that she knew. She held Mr. Bannister's letter in her hand. He knew that the game was up.

'It's my ranch,' said Teddy, like a schoolboy detected in evil. 'It's a mighty poor manager that isn't able to absorb the boss's business if you give him time.'

'Why were you working down here?' pursued Octavia, still struggling after the key to the riddle of Teddy.

'To tell the truth, 'Tave,' said Teddy, with quiet candor, 'it wasn't for the salary. That about kept me in cigars and sunburn lotions. I was sent south by my doctor. 'Twas that right lung that was going to the bad on account of over-exercise and strain at polo and gymnastics. I needed climate and ozone and rest and things of that sort.'

In an instant Octavia was close against the vicinity of the affected organ. Mr. Bannister's letter fluttered to the floor.

'It's – it's well now, isn't it, Teddy?'

'Sound as a mesquite chunk. I deceived you in one thing. I paid fifty thousand for your ranch as soon as I found you had no title. I had just about that much income accumulated at my banker's while I've been herding sheep down here, so it was almost like picking the thing up on a bargain-counter for a penny. There's another little surplus of unearned increment piling up there, 'Tave. I've been thinking of a wedding trip in a yacht with white ribbons tied to the mast, through the Mediterranean, and then up among the Hebrides and down Norway to the Zuyder Zee.'

'And I was thinking,' said Octavia, softly, 'of a wedding gallop with my manager among the flocks of sheep and back to a wedding breakfast with Mrs. MacIntyre on the gallery, with, maybe, a sprig of orange blossom fastened to the red jar above the table.'

Teddy laughed, and began to chant:

'Little Bo-Peep has lost her sheep,
  And doesn't know where to find 'em.
  Let 'em alone, and they'll come home,
  And—'

Octavia drew his head down, and whispered in his ear.
But that is one of the tales they brought behind them.

HEARTS AND CROSSES

BALDY WOODS REACHED FOR THE BOTTLE, and got it. Whenever Baldy went for anything he usually – but this not Baldy's story. He poured out a third drink that was larger by a finger than the first and second. Baldy was in consultation; and the consultee is worthy of his hire.

'I'd be king if I was you,' said Baldy, so positively that his holster creaked and his spurs rattled.

Webb Yeager pushed back his flat-brimmed Stetson, and made further disorder in his straw-colored hair. The tonsorial recourse being without avail, he followed the liquid example of the more resourceful Baldy.

'If a man marries a queen, it oughtn't to make him a two-spot,' declared Webb, epitomizing his grievances.

'Sure not,' said Baldy, sympathetic, still thirsty, and genuinely solicitous concerning the relative value of the cards. 'By rights you're a king. If I was you, I'd call for a new deal. The cards have been stacked on you – I'll tell you what you are, Webb Yeager.'

'What?' asked Webb, with a hopeful look in his pale-blue eyes.

'You're a prince-consort.'

'Go easy,' said Webb. 'I never black-guarded you none.'

'It's a title,' explained Baldy, 'up among the picture-cards; but it don't take no tricks. I'll tell you, Webb. It's a brand they've got for certain animals in Europe. Say that you or me or one of them Dutch dukes marries in a royal family. Well, by and by our wife gets to be queen. Are we king? Not in a million years. At the coronation ceremonies we march between little casino and the Ninth Grand Custodian of the Royal Hall Bedchamber. The only use we are is to appear in photographs, and accept the responsibility for the heir-apparent. That ain't any square deal. Yes, sir, Webb, you're a prince-consort; and if I was you, I'd start a interregnum or a habeas corpus or something'; and I'd be king if I had to turn from the bottom of the deck.'

Baldy emptied his glass to the ratification of his Warwick pose.

'Baldy,' said Webb, solemnly, 'me and you punched cows in the same outfit for years. We been runnin' on the same range, and ridin' the same trails since we was boys. I wouldn't talk about my family affairs to nobody but you. You was line-rider on the Nopalito Ranch when I married Santa McAllister. I was foreman then; but what am I now? I don't amount to a knot in a stake rope.'

'When old McAllister was the cattle king of West Texas,' continued Baldy with Satanic sweetness, 'you was some tallow. You had as much to say on the ranch as he did.'

'I did,' admitted Webb, 'up to the time he found out I was tryin' to get my rope over Santa's head. Then he kept me out on the range as far from the ranch-house as he could. When the old man died they commenced to call Santa the "cattle queen." I'm boss of the cattle – that's all. She 'tends to all the business; she handles all the money; I can't sell even a beef-steer to a party of campers, myself. Santa's the "queen"; and I'm Mr. Nobody.'

'I'd be a king if I was you,' repeated Baldy Woods, the royalist. 'When a man marries a queen he ought to grade up with her – on the hoof – dressed

– dried – corned – any old way from the chaparral to the packing-house. Lots of folks thinks it's funny, Webb, that you don't have the say-so on the Nopalito. I ain't reflectin' none on Miz Yeager – she's the finest little lady between the Rio Grande and next Christmas – but a man ought to be boss of his own camp.'

The smooth, brown face of Yeager lengthened to a mask of wounded melancholy. With that expression, and his rumpled yellow hair and guileless blue eyes, he might have been likened to a schoolboy whose leadership had been usurped by a youngster of superior strength. But his active and sinewy seventy-two inches and his girded revolvers forbade the comparison.

'What was that you called me, Baldy?' he asked. 'What kind of a concert was it?'

'A "consort," ' corrected Baldy – ' "a prince-consort." It's a kind of short-card pseudonym. You come in sort of between Jack-high and a four-card flush.'

Webb Yeager sighed, and gathered the strap of his Winchester scabbard from the floor.

'I'm ridin' back to the ranch to-day,' he said, half-heartedly. 'I've got to start a bunch of beeves for San Antone in the morning.'

'I'm your company as far as Dry Lake,' announced Baldy. 'I've got a round-up camp on the San Marcos cuttin' out two-year-olds.'

The two *compañeros* mounted their ponies and trotted away from the little railroad settlement, where they had foregathered in the thirsty morning.

At Dry Lake, where their routes diverged, they reined up for a party cigarette. For miles they had ridden in silence save for the soft drum of the ponies' hoofs on the matted mesquite grass, and the rattle of the chaparral against their wooden stirrups. But in Texas discourse is seldom continuous. You may fill in a mile, a meal, and a murder between your paragraphs without detriment to your thesis. So, without apology, Webb offered an addendum to the conversation that had begun ten miles away.

'You remember, yourself, Baldy, that there was a time when Santa wasn't quite so independent. You remember the days when old McAllister was keepin' us apart, and how she used to send me the sign that she wanted to see me? Old man Mac promised to make me look like a colander if I ever come in gun-shot of the ranch. You remember the sign she used to send, Baldy – the heart with a cross inside of it?'

'Me?' cried Baldy, with intoxicated archness.

'You old sugar-stealing coyote! Don't I remember! Why, you dadblamed old long-horned turtle-dove, the boys in camp was all cognoscious about them hieroglyphs. The "gizzard-and-crossbones" we used to call it. We used to see 'em on truck that was sent out from the ranch. They was marked in charcoal on the sacks of flour and in lead-pencil on the newspapers. I see one of 'em once chalked on the back of a new cook that old man McAllister sent out from the ranch – danged if I didn't.'

'Santa's father,' exclaimed Webb gently, 'got her to promise that she wouldn't write to me or send me any word. That heart-and-cross sign was her scheme. Whenever she wanted to see me in particular she managed to put that mark on somethin' at the ranch that she knew I'd see. And I never laid eyes on it but when I burnt the wind for the ranch the same night. I used to see her in that coma mott back of the little horse-corral.'

'We knowed it,' chanted Baldy; 'but we never let on. We was all for you.

We knowed why you always kept that fast paint in camp. And when we see that gizzard-and-crossbones figured out on the truck from the ranch we knowed old Pinto was goin' to eat up miles that night instead of grass. You remember Scurry – that educated horse-wrangler we had – the college fellow that tangle-foot drove to the range? Whenever Scurry saw that come-meet-your-honey brand on anything from the ranch, he'd wave his hand like that, and say, "Our friend Lee Andrews will again swim the Hell's point to-night."''

'The last time Santa sent me the sign,' said Webb, 'was once when she was sick. I noticed it as soon as I hit camp, and I galloped Pinto forty mile that night. She wasn't at the coma mott. I went to the house; and old McAllister met me at the door. "Did you come here to get killed?" says he; "I'll disoblige you for once. I just started a Mexican to bring you. Santa wants you. Go in that room and see her. And then come out here and see me."

'Santa was lyin' in bed pretty sick. But she gives out a kind of a smile, and her hand and mine lock horns, and I sets down by the bed – mud and spurs and chaps and all. "I've heard you ridin' across the grass for hours, Webb," she says. "I was sure you'd come. You saw the sign?" she whispers. "The minute I hit camp," says I. "'Twas marked on the bag of potatoes and onions." "They're always together," says she, soft like – "always together in life." "They go well together," I says, "in a stew." "I mean hearts and crosses," says Santa. "Our sign – to love and to suffer – that's what they mean."

'And there was old Doc Musgrove amusin' himself with whisky and a palm-leaf fan. And by and by Santa goes to sleep; and Doc feels her forehead; and he says to me: "You're not such a bad febrifuge. But you'd better slide out now, for the diagnosis don't call for you in regular doses. The little lady'll be all right when she wakes up."

'I seen old McAllister outside. "She's asleep," says I. "And now you can start in with your colander-work. Take your time; for I left my gun on my saddle-horn."

'Old Mac laughs, and he says to me: "Pumpin' lead into the best ranch-boss in West Texas don't seem to me good business policy. I don't know where I could get as good a one. It's the son-in-law idea, Webb, that makes me admire for to use you as a target. You ain't my idea for a member of the family. But I can use you on the Nopalito if you'll keep outside of a radius with the ranch-house in the middle of it. You go upstairs and lay down on a cot, and when you get some sleep we'll talk it over." '

Baldy Woods pulled down his hat, and uncurled his leg from his saddle-horn. Webb shortened his rein, and his pony danced, anxious to be off. The two men shook hands with Western ceremony.

'*Adios*, Baldy,' said Webb. 'I'm glad I seen you and had this talk.'

With a pounding rush that sounded like the rise of a covey of quail, the riders sped away toward different points of the compass. A hundred yards on his route Baldy reined in on the top of a bare knoll and emitted a yell. He swayed on his horse; had he been on foot, the earth would have risen and conquered him; but in the saddle he was a master of equilibrium, and laughed at whisky, and despised the centre of gravity.

Webb turned in his saddle at the signal.

'If I was you,' came Baldy's strident and perverting tones, 'I'd be king!'

At eight o'clock on the following morning Bud Turner rolled from his saddle in front of the Nopalito ranch-house, and stumbled with whizzing rowels toward the gallery. Bud was in charge of the bunch of beef-cattle that was to strike the trail that morning for San Antonio. Mrs. Yeager was on the gallery watering a cluster of hyacinths growing in a red earthenware jar.

'King' McAllister had bequeathed to his daughter many of his strong characteristics – his resolution, his gay courage, his contumacious self-reliance, his pride as a reigning monarch of hoofs and horns. *Allegro* and *fortissimo* had been McAllister's tempo and tone. In Santa they survived, transposed to the feminine key. Substantially, she preserved the image of the mother who had been summoned to wander in other and less finite green pastures long before the waxing herds of kine had conferred royalty upon the house. She had her mother's slim, strong figure and grave, soft prettiness that relieved in her the severity of the imperious McAllister eye and the McAllister air of royal independence.

Webb stood on one end of the gallery giving orders to two or three sub-bosses of various camps and outfits who had ridden in for instructions.

''Morning,' said Bud, briefly. 'Where do you want them beeves to go in town – to Barber's, as usual?'

Now, to answer that had been the prerogative of the queen. All the reins of business – buying, selling, and banking – had been held by her capable fingers. The handling of the cattle had been entrusted fully to her husband. In the days of 'King' McAllister, Santa had been his secretary and helper; and she had continued her work with wisdom and profit. But before she could reply, the prince-consort spake up with calm decision:

'You drive that bunch to Zimmerman and Nesbit's pens. I spoke to Zimmerman about it some time ago.'

Bud turned on his high boot-heels.

'Wait!' called Santa quickly. She looked at her husband with surprise in her steady gray eyes.

'Why, what do you mean, Webb?' she asked, with a small wrinkle gathering between her brows. 'I never deal with Zimmerman and Nesbit. Barber has handled every head of stock from this ranch in that market for five years. I'm not going to take the business out of his hands.' She faced Bud Turner. 'Deliver those cattle to Barber,' she concluded positively.

Bud gazed impartially at the water-jar hanging on the gallery, stood on his other leg, and chewed a mesquite-leaf.

'I want this bunch of beeves to go to Zimmerman and Nesbit,' said Webb, with a frosty light in his blue eyes.

'Nonsense,' said Santa impatiently. 'You'd better start on, Bud, so as to noon at the Little Elm waterhole. Tell Barber we'll have another lot of culls ready in about a month.'

Bud allowed a hesitating eye to steal upward and meet Webb's. Webb saw apology in his look, and fancied he saw commiseration.

'You deliver them cattle,' he said grimly, 'to—'

'Barber,' finished Santa sharply. 'Let that settle it. Is there anything else you are waiting for, Bud?'

'No, m'm,' said Bud. But before going he lingered while a cow's tail could have switched thrice; for a man is man's ally; and even the Philistines must have blushed when they took Samson in the way they did.

'You hear your boss!' cried Webb, sardonically. He took off his hat, and bowed until it touched the floor before his wife.

'Webb,' said Santa rebukingly, 'you're acting mighty foolish to-day.'

'Court fool, your Majesty,' said Webb, in his slow tones, which had changed their quality. 'What else can you expect? Let me tell you. I was a man before I married a cattle-queen. What am I now? The laughing-stock of the camps. I'll be a man again.'

Santa looked at him closely.

'Don't be unreasonable, Webb,' she said calmly. 'You haven't been slighted in any way. Do I ever interfere in your management of the cattle? I know the business side of the ranch much better than you do. I learned it from Dad. Be sensible.'

'Kingdoms and queendoms,' said Webb, 'don't suit me unless I am in the pictures, too. I punch the cattle and you wear the crown. All right. I'd rather be High Lord Chancellor of a cow-camp than the eight-spot in a queen-high flush. It's your ranch; and Barber gets the beeves.'

Webb's horse was tied to the rack. He walked into the house and brought out his roll of blankets that he never took with him except on long rides, and his 'slicker,' and his longest stake-rope of plaited rawhide. These he began to tie deliberately upon his saddle. Santa, a little pale, followed him.

Webb swung up into the saddle. His serious, smooth face was without expression except for a stubborn light that smouldered in his eyes.

'There's a herd of cows and calves,' said he, 'near the Hondo Waterhole on the Frio that ought to be moved away from timber. Lobos have killed three of the calves. I forgot to leave orders. You'd better tell Simms to attend to it.'

Santa laid a hand on the horse's bridle, and looked her husband in the eye.

'Are you going to leave me, Webb?' she asked quietly.

'I am going to be a man again,' he answered.

'I wish you success in a praiseworthy attempt,' she said, with a sudden coldness. She turned and walked directly into the house.

Webb Yeager rode to the southeast as straight as the topography of West Texas permitted. And when he reached the horizon he might have ridden on into blue space as far as knowledge of him on the Nopalito went. And the days, with Sundays at their head, formed into hebdomadal squads; and the weeks, captained by the full moon, close ranks into menstrual companies carrying 'Tempus fugit' on their banners; and the months marched on toward the vast camp-ground of the years; but Webb Yeager came no more to the dominions of his queen.

One day a being named Bartholomew, a sheep-man – and therefore of little account – from the lower Rio Grande country, rode in sight of the Nopalito ranch-house, and felt hunger assail him. *Ex consuetudine* he was soon seated at the mid-day dining-table of that hospitable kingdom. Talk like water gushed from him; he might have been smitten with Aaron's rod – that is your gentle shepherd when an audience is vouchsafed him whose ears are not overgrown with wool.

'Missis Yeager,' he babbled, 'I see a man the other day on the Rancho Seco down in Hidalgo County by your name – Webb Yeager was his. He'd just been engaged as manager. He was a tall, light-haired man, not saying much. Maybe he was some kin of yours, do you think?'

'A husband,' said Santa cordially. 'The Seco has done well. Mr. Yeager is one of the best stockmen in the West.'

The dropping out of a prince-consort rarely disorganizes a monarchy. Queen Santa had appointed as *mayordomo* of the ranch, a trusty subject, named Ramsay, who had been one of her father's faithful vassals. And there was scarcely a ripple on the Nopalito ranch save when the gulf-breeze created undulations in the grass of its wide acres.

For several years the Nopalito had been making experiments with an English breed of cattle that looked down with aristocratic contempt upon the Texas long-horns. The experiments were found satisfactory; and a pasture had been set apart for the blue-bloods. The fame of them had gone forth into the chaparral and pear as far as men ride in saddles. Other ranches woke up, rubbed their eyes, and looked with new dissatisfaction upon the long-horns.

As a consequence, one day a sunburned, capable, silk-kerchiefed nonchalant youth, garnished with revolvers, and attended by three Mexican *vaqueros*, alighted at the Nopalito ranch and presented the following business-like epistle to the queen thereof.

Mrs. Yeager – The Nopalito Ranch:

Dear Madam:

I am instructed by the owners of the Rancho Seco to purchase 100 head of two and three-year-old cows of the Sussex breed owned by you. If you can fill the order please deliver the cattle to the bearer; and a check will be forwarded to you at once.

Respectfully,
Webster Yeager,
Manager of the Rancho Seco.

Business is business, even – very scantily did it escape being written 'especially' – in a kingdom.

That night the 100 head of cattle were driven up from the pasture and penned in a corral near the ranch-house for delivery in the morning.

When night closed down and the house was still, did Santa Yeager throw herself down, clasping that formal note to her bosom, weeping, and calling out a name that pride (either in one or the other) had kept from her lips many a day? Or did she file the letter, in her business way, retaining her royal balance and strength?

Wonder, if you will; but royalty is sacred; and there is a veil. But this much you shall learn.

At midnight Santa slipped softly out of the ranch-house, clothed in something dark and plain. She paused for a moment under the live-oak trees. The prairies were somewhat dim, and the moonlight was pale orange, diluted with particles of an impalpable, flying mist. But the mockbird whistled on every bough of vantage; leagues of flowers scented the air; and a kindergarten of little shadowy rabbits leaped and played in an open space near by. Santa turned her face to the southeast and threw kisses thitherward; for there was none to see.

Then she sped silently to the blacksmith-shop, fifty yards away; and what she did there can only be surmised. But the forge glowed red; and there was a faint hammering such as Cupid might make when he sharpens his arrow-points.

Later she came forth with a queer-shaped, handled thing in one hand, and a portable furnace, such as are seen in branding-camps, in the other. To the corral where the Sussex cattle were penned she sped with these things swiftly in the moonlight.

She opened the gate and slipped inside the corral. The Sussex cattle were mostly a dark red. But among this bunch was one that was milky white – notable among the others.

And now Santa shook from her shoulder something that we had not seen before – a rope lasso. She freed the loop of it, coiling the length in her left hand, and plunged into the thick of the cattle.

The white cow was her object. She swung the lasso, which caught one horn and slipped off. The next throw encircled the forefeet and the animal fell heavily. Santa made for it like a panther; but it scrambled up and dashed against her, knocking her over like a blade of grass.

Again she made the cast, while the aroused cattle milled round the four sides of the corral in a plunging mass. This throw was fair; the white cow came to earth again; and before it could rise Santa had made the lasso fast around a post of the corral with a swift and simple knot, and had leaped upon the cow again with the rawhide hobbles.

In one minute the feet of the animal were tied (no record-breaking deed) and Santa leaned against the corral for the same space of time, panting and lax.

And then she ran swiftly to her furnace at the gate and brought the branding-iron, queerly shaped and white-hot.

The bellow of the outraged white cow, as the iron was applied, should have stirred the slumbering auricular nerves and consciences of the nearby subjects of the Nopalito, but it did not. And it was amid the deepest nocturnal silence that Santa ran like a lapwing back to the ranch-house and there fell upon a cot and sobbed – sobbed as though queens had hearts as simple ranchmen's wives have, and as though she would gladly make kings of prince-consorts, should they ride back again from over the hills and far away.

In the morning the capable, revolvered youth and his *vaqueros* set forth, driving the bunch of Sussex cattle across the prairies to the Rancho Seco. Ninety miles it was; a six days' journey, grazing and watering the animals on the way.

The beasts arrived at Rancho Seco one evening at dusk; and were received and counted by the foreman of the ranch.

The next morning at eight o'clock a horseman loped out of the brush to the Nopalito ranch-house. He dismounted stiffly, and strode, with whizzing spurs, to the house. His horse gave a great sigh and swayed foam-streaked, with down-drooping head and closed eyes.

But waste not your pity upon Belshazzar, the flea-bitten sorrel. Today, in Nopalito horse-pasture he survives, pampered, beloved, unridden, cherished record-holder of long-distance rides.

The horseman stumbled into the house. Two arms fell around his neck and someone cried out in the voice of woman and queen alike: 'Webb – oh, Webb!'

'I was a skunk,' said Webb Yeager.

'Hush,' said Santa, 'did you see it?'

'I saw it,' said Webb.

What they meant God knows; and you shall know, if you rightly read the primer of events.

'Be the cattle-queen,' said Webb; 'and overlook it if you can. I was a mangy, sheep-stealing coyote.'

'Hush!' said Santa again, laying her fingers upon his mouth. 'There's no queen here. Do you know who I am? I am Santa Yeager, First Lady of the Bedchamber. Come here.'

She dragged him from the gallery into the room to the right. There stood a cradle with an infant in it – a red, ribald, unintelligible, babbling, beautiful infant, sputtering at life in an unseemly manner.

'There's no queen on this ranch,' said Santa again. 'Look at the king. He's got your eyes, Webb. Down on your knees and look at his Highness.'

But jingling rowels sounded on the gallery, and Bud Turner stumbled there again with the same query that he had brought, lacking a few days, a year ago.

"Morning. Them beeves is just turned out on the trail. Shall I drive 'em to Barber's, or – '

He saw Webb and stopped, open-mouthed.

'Ba-ba-ba-ba-ba-ba!' shrieked the king in his cradle, beating the air with his fists.

'You hear your boss, Bud,' said Webb Yeager, with a broad grin – just as he had said a year ago.

And that is all, except that when old man Quinn, owner of the Rancho Seco, went out to look over the herd of Sussex cattle that he had bought from the Nopalito ranch, he asked his new manager:

'What's the Nopalito ranch brand, Wilson?'

'X Bar Y,' said Wilson.

'I thought so,' said Quinn. 'But look at that white heifer there; she's got another brand – a heart with a cross inside of it. What brand is that?'

THE RANSOM OF MACK

ME AND OLD MACK LONSBURY, we got out of that Little Hide-and-Seek gold mine affair with about $40,000 apiece. I say 'old' Mack; but he wasn't old. Forty-one, I should say; but he always seemed old.

'Andy,' he says to me, 'I'm tired of hustling. You and me have been working hard together for three years. Say we knock off for a while, and spend some of this idle money we've coaxed our way.'

'The proposition hits me just right,' says I. 'Let's be nabobs a while and see how it feels. What'll we do – take in the Niagara Falls, or buck at faro?'

'For a good many years,' says Mack, 'I've thought that if I ever had extravagant money I'd rent a two-room cabin somewhere, hire a Chinaman to cook, and sit in my stocking feet and read Buckle's History of Civilization.'

'That sounds self-indulgent and gratifying without vulgar ostentation,' says I; 'and I don't see how money could be better invested. Give me a cuckoo clock and a Sep Winner's Self-Instructor for the Banjo, and I'll join you.'

A week afterward me and Mack hits this small town of Piña, about thirty miles out from Denver, and finds an elegant two-room house that just suits us. We deposited half-a-peck of money in the Piña bank and shook hands with every one of the 340 citizens in the town. We brought along the Chinaman and the cuckoo clock and Buckle and the Instructor with us from Denver; and they made the cabin seem like home at once.

Never believe it when they tell you riches don't bring happiness. If you could have seen old Mack sitting in his rocking-chair with his blue-yarn sock feet up in the window and absorbing in that Buckle stuff through his specs you'd have seen a picture of content that would have made Rockefeller jealous. And I was learning to pick out 'Old Zip Coon' on the banjo, and the cuckoo was on time with his remarks, and Ah Sing was messing up the atmosphere with the handsomest smell of ham and eggs that ever laid the honeysuckle in the shade. When it got too dark to make out Buckle's nonsense and the notes in the Instructor, me and Mack would light our pipes and talk about science and pearl diving and sciatica and Egypt and spelling and fish and trade-winds and leather and gratitude and eagles, and a lot of subjects that we'd never had time to explain our sentiments about before.

One evening Mack spoke up and asked me if I was much apprised in the habits and policies of women folks.

'Why, yes,' says I, in a tone of voice; 'I know 'em from Alfred to Omaha. The feminine nature and similitude,' says I, 'is as plain to my sight as the Rocky Mountains is to a blue-eyed burro. I'm onto all their little sidesteps and punctual discrepancies.'

'I tell you, Andy,' says Mack, with a kind of sigh. 'I never had the least amount of intersection with their predispositions. Maybe I might have had a proneness in respect to their vicinity, but I never took the time. I made my own living since I was fourteen; and I never seemed to get my ratiocinations equipped with the sentiments usually depicted toward the sect. I sometimes wish I had,' says old Mack.

'They're an adverse study,' says I, 'and adapted to points of view. Although they vary in rationale, I have found 'em quite often obviously differing from each other in divergences of contrast.'

'It seems to me,' goes on Mack, 'that a man had better take 'em in and secure his inspirations of the sect when he's young and so preordained. I let my chance go by; and I guess I'm too old now to go hopping into the curriculum.'

'Oh, I don't know,' I tells him. 'Maybe you better credit yourself with a barrel of money and a lot of emancipation from a quantity of uncontent. Still, I don't regret my knowledge of 'em,' I says. 'It takes a man who understands the symptoms and by-plays of women-folks to take care of himself in this world.'

We stayed on in Piña because we liked the place. Some folks might enjoy their money with noise and rapture and locomotion; but me and Mack we had had plenty of turmoils and hotel towels. The people were friendly; Ah Sing got the swing of the grub we liked; Mack and Buckle were as thick as two body-snatchers, and I was hitting out a cordial resemblance to 'Buffalo Gals, Can't You Come Out To-night,' on the banjo.

One day I got a telegram from Speight, the man that was working a mine I had an interest in out in New Mexico. I had to go out there; and I was gone two months. I was anxious to get back to Piña and enjoy life once more.

When I struck the cabin I nearly fainted. Mack was standing in the door; and if angels ever wept, I saw no reason why they should be smiling then.

That man was a spectacle. Yes; he was worse; he was a spyglass; he was the great telescope in the Lick Observatory. He had on a coat and shiny shoes and a white vest and a high silk hat; and a geranium as big as an order of spinach was spiked onto his front. And he was smirking and warping his face like an infernal storekeeper or a kid wit colic.

'Hello, Andy,' says Mack, out of his face. 'Glad to see you back. Things have happened since you went away.'

'I know it,' says I, 'and a sacrilegious sight it is. God never made you that way, Mack Lonsbury. Why do you scarify His works with this presumptious kind of ribaldry?'

'Why, Andy,' said he, 'they've elected me justice of the peace since you left.'

I looked at Mack close. He was restless and inspired. A justice of the peace ought to be disconsolate and assuaged.

Just then a young woman passed on the sidewalk; and I saw Mack kind of half snicker and blush, and then he raised up his hat and smiled and bowed, and she smiled and bowed, and went on by.

'No hope for you,' says I, 'if you've got the Mary-Jane infirmity at your age. I thought it wasn't going to take on you. And patent leather shoes! All this in two little short months!'

'I'm going to marry the young lady who just passed to-night,' says Mack, in a kind of a flutter.

'I forgot something at the post-office,' says I, and walked away quick.

I overtook that young woman a hundred yards away. I raised my hat and told her my name. She was about nineteen; and young for her age. She blushed, and then looked at me cool, like I was the snow scene from the 'Two Orphans.'

'I understand you are to be married to-night,' I said.

'Correct,' says she. 'You got any objections?'

'Listen, sissy,' I begins.

'My name is Miss Rebosa Reed,' says she in a pained way.

'I know it,' says I. 'Now, Rebosa, I'm old enough to have owed money to your father. And that old specious, dressed-up, garbled, seasick ptomaine prancing around avidiously like an irremediable turkey gobbler with patent leather shoes on is my best friend. Why did you go and get him invested in this marriage business?'

'Why, he was the only chance there was,' answered Miss Rebosa.

'Nay,' says I, giving a sickening look of admiration at her complexion and style of features; 'with your beauty you might pick any kind of a man. Listen, Rebosa. Old Mack ain't the man you want. He was twenty-two when you was *née* Reed, as the papers say. This bursting into bloom won't last with him. He's all ventilated with oldness and rectitude and decay. Old Mack's down with a case of Indian summer. He overlooked his bet when he was young; and now he's suing Nature for the interest on the promissory note he took from Cupid instead of the cash. Rebosa, are you bent on having this marriage occur?'

'Why, sure I am,' says she, oscillating the pansies on her hat, 'and so is somebody else, I reckon.'

'What time is it to take place?' I asks.

'At six o'clock,' says she.

I made up my mind right away what to do. I'd save old Mack if I could. To have a good, seasoned, ineligible man like that turn chicken for a girl that hadn't quit eating slate pencils and buttoning in the back was more than I could look on with easiness.

'Rebosa,' says I, earnest, drawing upon my display of knowledge concerning the feminine intuitions of reason – 'ain't there a young man in Piña – a nice young man that you think a heap of?'

'Yep,' says Rebosa, nodding her pansies – 'Sure there is! What do you think! Gracious!'

'Does he like you?' I asks. 'How does he stand in the matter?'

'Crazy,' says Rebosa. 'Ma has to wet down the front steps to keep him from sitting there all the time. But I guess that'll be all over after to-night,' she winds up with a sigh.

'Rebosa,' says I, 'you don't really experience any of this adoration called love for old Mack, do you?'

'Lord! no,' says the girl, shaking her head. 'I think he's as dry as a lava bed. The idea!'

'Who is this young man that you like, Rebosa?' I inquires.

'It's Eddie Bayles,' says she. 'He clerks in Crosby's grocery. But he don't make but thirty-five a month. Ella Noakes was wild about him once.'

'Old Mack tells me,' I says, 'that he's going to marry you at six o'clock this evening.'

'That's the time,' says she. 'It's to be at our house.'

'Rebosa,' says I, 'listen to me. If Eddy Bayles had a thousand dollars cash – a thousand dollars, mind you, would buy him a store of his own – if you and Eddie had that much to excuse matrimony on, would you consent to marry him this evening at five o'clock?'

The girl looks at me a minute; and I can see these inaudible cogitations going on inside of her, as women will.

'A thousand dollars?' says she. 'Of course I would.'

'Come on,' says I. 'We'll go and see Eddie.'

We went up to Crosby's store and called Eddie outside. He looked to be estimable and freckled; and he had chills and fever when I made my proposition.

'At five o'clock?' says he, 'for a thousand dollars? Please don't wake me up! Well, you *are* the rich uncle retired from the spice business in India. I'll buy out old Crosby and run the store myself.'

We went inside and got old man Crosby apart and explained it. I wrote my check for a thousand dollars and handed it to him. If Eddie and Rebosa married each other at five he was to turn the money over to them.

And then I gave 'em my blessing, and went to wander in the wild-wood for a season. I sat on a log and made cogitations on life and old age and the zodiac and the ways of women and all the disorder that goes with a lifetime. I passed myself congratulations that I had probably saved my old friend Mack from his attack of Indian summer. I knew when he got well of it and shed his infatuation and his patent leather shoes, he would feel grateful. 'To keep old Mack disinvolved,' thinks I, 'from relapses like this, is worth more than a thousand dollars.' And most of all I was glad that I'd made a study of women, and wasn't to be deceived any by their means of conceit and evolution.

It must have been half-past five when I got back home. I stepped in; and there sat old Mack on the back of his neck in his old clothes with his blue socks on the window and the History of Civilization propped up on his knees.

'This don't look like getting ready for a wedding at six,' I says, to seem innocent.

'Oh,' says Mack, reaching for his tobacco, 'that was postponed back to five o'clock. They sent me a note saying the hour had been changed. It's all over now. What made you stay away so long, Andy?'

'You heard about the wedding?' I asks.

'I operated it,' says he. 'I told you I was justice of the peace. The preacher is off East to visit his folks, and I'm the only one in town that can perform the dispensations of marriage. I promised Eddie and Rebosa a month ago I'd marry 'em. He's a busy lad; and he'll have a grocery of his own some day.'

'He will,' says I.

'There was lots of women at the wedding,' says Mack, smoking up. 'But I didn't seem to get any ideas from 'em. I wish I was informed in the structure of their attainments like you said you was.'

'That was two months ago,' says I, reaching up for the banjo.

TELEMACHUS, FRIEND

RETURNING FROM A HUNTING TRIP, I waited at the little town of Los Piños, in New Mexico, for the south-bound train, which was one hour late. I sat on the porch of the Summit House and discussed the functions of life with Telemachus Hicks, the hotel proprietor.

Perceiving that personalities were not out of order, I asked him what species of beast had long ago twisted and mutilated his left ear. Being a hunter, I was concerned in the evils that may befall one in the pursuit of game.

'That ear,' said Hicks, 'is the relic of true friendship.'

'An accident?' I persisted.

'No friendship is an accident,' said Telemachus; and I was silent.

'The only perfect case of true friendship I ever knew,' went on my host, 'was a cordial intent between a Connecticut man and a monkey. The monkey climbed palms in Barranquilla and threw down cocoanuts to the man. The man sawed them in two and made dippers, which he sold for two *reales* each and bought rum. The monkey drank the milk of the nuts. Through each being satisfied with his own share of the graft, they lived like brothers.

'But in the case of human beings, friendship is a transitory act, subject to discontinuance without further notice.

'I had a friend once, of the entitlement of Paisley Fish, that I imagined was sealed to me for an endless space of time. Side by side for seven years we had mined, ranched, sold patent churns, herded sheep, took photographs and other things, built wire fences, and picked prunes. Thinks I, neither homicide nor flattery nor riches nor sophistry nor drink can make trouble between me and Paisley Fish. We was friends an amount you could hardly guess at. We was friends in business, and we let our amicable qualities lap over and season our hours of recreation and folly. We certainly had days of Damon and nights of Pythias.

'One summer me and Paisley gallops down into these San Andrés mountains for the purpose of a month's surcease and levity, dressed in the natural store habiliments of man. We hit this town Los Piños, which certainly was a roof-garden spot of the world, and flowing with condensed milk and honey. It had a street or two, and air, and hens, and a eating-house; and that was enough for us.

'We strikes the town after supper-time, and we concludes to sample whatever efficacy there is in this eating-house down by the railroad tracks. By the time we had set down and pried up our plates with a knife from the red oil-cloth, along intrudes Widow Jessup with the hot biscuit and fried liver.

'Now, there was a woman that would have tempted an anchovy to forget his vows. She was not so small as she was large; and a kind of welcome air seemed to mitigate her vicinity. The pink of her face was the *in hoc signo* of a culinary temper and a warm disposition, and her smile would have brought out the dogwood blossoms in December.

'Widow Jessup talks to us a lot of garrulousness about the climate and history and Tennyson and prunes and the scarcity of mutton, and finally wants to know where we came from.

' "Spring Valley," says I.

' "Big Spring Valley," chips in Paisley, out of a lot of potatoes and knuckle-bone of ham in his mouth.

'That was the first sign I notices that the old *fidus Diogenes* business between me and Paisley Fish was ended forever. He knew how I hated a talkative person, and yet he stampedes into the conversation with his amendments and addendums of syntax. On the map it was Big Spring Valley; but I had heard Paisley himself call it Spring Valley a thousand times.

'Without saying any more, we went out after supper and set on the railroad track. We had been pardners too long not to know what was going on in each other's mind.

' "I reckon you understand," says Paisley, "that I've made up my mind to accrue that widow woman as part and parcel in and to my hereditaments forever, both domestic, sociable, legal, and otherwise, until death us do part."

' "Why, yes," says I, "I read it between the lines, though you only spoke one. And I suppose you are aware," says I, "that I have a movement on foot that leads up to the widow's changing her name to Hicks, and leaves you writing to the society column to inquire whether the best man wears a japonica or seamless socks at the wedding!"

' "There'll be some hiatuses in your program," says Paisley, chewing up a piece of a railroad tie. "I'd give in to you," says he, "in 'most any respect if it was secular affairs, but this is not so. The smiles of woman," goes on Paisley, "is the whirlpool of Squills and Chalybeates, into which vortex the good ship Friendship is often drawn and dismembered. I'd assault a bear that was annoying you," says Paisley, "or I'd indorse your note, or rub the place between your shoulder-blades with opodeldoc the same as ever; but there my sense of etiquette ceases. In this fracas with Mrs. Jessup we play it alone. I've notified you fair."

'And then I collaborates with myself, and offers the following resolutions and by-laws:

' "Friendship between man and man," says I, "is an ancient historical virtue enacted in the days when men had to protect each other against lizards with eighty-foot tails and flying turtles. And they've kept up the habit to this day, and stand by each other till the bellboy comes up and tells them the animals are not really there. I've often heard," I says, "about ladies stepping in and breaking up a friendship between men. Why should that be? I'll tell you, Paisley, the first sight and hot biscuit of Mrs. Jessup appears to have inserted a oscillation into each of our bosoms. Let the best man of us have her. I'll play you a square game, and won't do any underhanded work. I'll do all of my courting of her in your presence, so you will have an equal opportunity. With that arrangement I don't see why our steamboat of friendship should fall overboard in the medicinal whirlpools you speak of, whichever of us wins out."

' "Good old hoss!" says Paisley, shaking my hand. "And I'll do the same," says he. "We'll court the lady synonymously, and without any of the prudery and bloodshed usual to such occasions. And we'll be friends still, win or lose."

'At one side of Mrs. Jessup's eating-house was a bench under some trees where she used to sit in the breeze after the south-bound had been fed and gone. And there me and Paisley used to congregate after supper and make partial payments on our respects to the lady of our choice. And we was so honorable and circuitous in our calls that if one of us got there first we waited for the other before beginning any gallivantery.

'The first evening that Mrs. Jessup knew about our arrangement I got to the bench before Paisley did. Supper was just over, and Mrs. Jessup was out there with a fresh pink dress on, and almost cool enough to handle.

'I sat down by her and made a few specifications about the moral surface of nature as set forth by the landscape and the contiguous perspective. That evening was surely a case in point. The moon was attending to business in the section of sky where it belonged, and the trees was making shadows on the ground according to science and nature, and there was a kind of conspicuous hullabaloo going on in the bushes between the bull-bats and the orioles and the jack-rabbits and other feathered insects of the forest. And the wind out of the mountains was singing like a jew's-harp in the pile of old tomato-cans by the railroad track.

I felt a kind of sensation in my left side — something like dough rising in a crock by the fire. Mrs. Jessup had moved up closer.

' "Oh, Mr. Hicks," says she, 'when one is alone in the world, don't they feel it more aggravated on a beautiful night like this?"

'I rose up off the bench at once.

' "Excuse me, ma'am," says I, "but I'll have to wait till Paisley comes before I can give a audible hearing to leading questions like that."

'And then I explained to her how we was friends cinctured by years of embarrassment and travel and complicity, and how we had agreed to take no advantage of each other in any of the more mushy walks of life, such as might be fomented by sentiment and proximity. Mrs. Jessup appears to think serious about the matter for a minute, and then she breaks into a species of laughter that makes the wildwood resound.

'In a few minutes Paisley drops around, with oil of bergamot on his hair, and sits on the other side of Mrs. Jessup, and inaugurates a sad tale of adventure in which him and Pieface Lumley has a skinning-match of dead cows in '95 for a silver-mounted saddle in the Santa Rita valley during the nine months' drought.

'Now, from the start of that courtship I had Paisley Fish hobbled and tied to a post. Each one of us had a different system of reaching out for the easy places in the female heart. Paisley's scheme was to petrify 'em with wonderful relations of events that he had either come across personally or in large print. I think he must have got his idea of subjugation from one of Shakespeare's shows I see once called "Othello." There is a colored man in it who acquires a duke's daughter by disbursing to her a mixture of the talk turned out by Rider Haggard, Lew Dockstader, and Dr. Parkhurst. But that style of courting don't work well off the stage.

'Now, I give you my own recipe for inveigling a woman into that state of affairs when she can be referred to as "*née* Jones." Learn how to pick up her hand and hold it, and she's yours. It ain't so easy. Some men grab at it so much like they was going to set a dislocation of the shoulder that you can smell the arnica and hear 'em tearing off bandages. Some take it up like a hot horseshoe, and hold it off at arm's length like a druggist pouring tincture of asafoetida in a bottle. And most of 'em catch hold of it and drag it right out before the lady's eyes like a boy finding a baseball in the grass, without giving her a chance to forget that the hand is growing on the end of her arm. Them ways are all wrong.

'I'll tell you the right way. Did you ever see a man sneak out in the backyard and pick up a rock to throw at a tomcat that was sitting on a fence looking at him? He pretends he hasn't got a thing in his hand, and that the cat don't see him, and that he don't see the cat. That's the idea. Never drag her hand out where she'll have to take notice of it. Don't let her know that you think she knows you have the least idea she is aware you are holding her hand. That was my rule of tactics; and as far as Paisley's serenade about hostilities and misadventure went, he might as well have been reading to her a time-table of the Sunday trains that stop at Ocean Grove, New Jersey.

'One night when I beat Paisley to the bench by one pipeful, my friendship gets subsidized for a minute, and I asks Mrs. Jessup if she didn't think a "H" was easier to write than a "J." In a second her head was mashing the oleander flower in my button-hole, and I learned over and – but I didn't.

' "If you don't mind," says I, standing up "we'll wait for Paisley to come before finishing this. I've never done anything dishonorable yet to our friendship, and this won't be quite fair."

' "Mr. Hicks," says Mrs. Jessup, looking at me peculiar in the dark, "if it wasn't for but one thing, I'd ask you to hike yourself down the gulch and never disresume your visits to my house."

' "And what is that, ma'am?" I asks.

' "You are too good a friend not to make a good husband," says she.

'In five minutes Paisley was on his side of Mrs. Jessup.

' "In Silver City, in the summer of '98," he begins, "I see Jim Batholomew chew off a Chinaman's ear in the Blue Light Saloon on account of a crossbarred muslin shirt that – what was that noise?"

'I had resumed matters again with Mrs. Jessup right where we had left off.

' "Mrs. Jessup," says I, "has promised to make it Hicks. And this is another of the same sort."

'Paisley winds his feet around a leg of the bench and kind of groans.

' "Lem," says he, "we been friends for seven years. Would you mind not kissing Mrs. Jessup quite so loud? I'd do the same for you."

' "All right," says I. "The other kind will do as well."

' "This Chinaman," goes on Paisley, "was the one that shot a man named Mullins in the spring of '97, and that was—"

'Paisley interrupted himself again.

' "Lem," says he, "if you was a true friend you wouldn't hug Mrs. Jessup quite so hard. I felt the bench shake all over just then. You know you told me you would give me an even chance as long as there was any."

' "Mr. Man," says Mrs. Jessup, turning around to Paisley, "if you was to drop in to the celebration of mine and Mr. Hicks's silver wedding, twenty-five years from now, do you think you could get it into that Hubbard squash you call your head that you are *nix cum rous* in this business? I've put up with you a long time because you was Mr. Hicks's friend; but it seems to me it's time for you to wear the willow and trot off down the hill."

' "Mrs. Jessup," says I, without losing my grasp on the situation as fiancé, "Mr. Paisley is my friend, and I offered him a square deal and a equal opportunity as long as there was a chance."

' "A chance!" says she. "Well, he may think he has a chance; but I hope he won't think he's got a cinch, after what he's been next to all the evening."

'Well, a month afterwards me and Mrs. Jessup was married in the Los Piños Methodist Church; and the whole town closed up to see the performance.

'When we lined up in front and the preacher was beginning to sing out his rituals and observances, I looks around and misses Paisley. I calls time on the preacher. "Paisley ain't here," says I. "We've got to wait for Paisley. A friend once, a friend always – that's Telemachus Hicks," says I. Mrs. Jessup's eyes snapped some; but the preacher holds up the incantations according to instructions.

'In a few minutes Paisley gallops up the aisle, putting on a cuff as he comes. He explains that the only dry-goods store in town was closed for the wedding, and he couldn't get the kind of a boiled shirt that his taste called for until he had broke open the back window of the store and helped himself. Then he ranges up on the other side of the bride, and the wedding goes on. I always imagined that Paisley calculated as a last chance that the preacher might marry him to the widow by mistake.

'After the proceedings was over we had tea and jerked antelope and canned apricots, and then the populace hiked itself away. Last of all Paisley shook me by the hand and told me I'd acted square and on the level with him and he was proud to call me a friend.

'The preacher had a small house on the side of the street that he'd fixed up to rent; and he allowed me and Mrs. Hicks to occupy it till the ten-forty train the next morning, when we was going on a bridal tour to El Paso. His wife had decorated it all up with hollyhocks and poison ivy, and it looked real festal and bowery.

'About ten o'clock that night I sets down in the front door and pulls of my boots a while in the cool breeze, while Mrs. Hicks was fixing around in the room. Right soon the light went out inside; and I sat there a while, reverberating over old times and scenes. And then I heard Mrs. Hicks call out, "Ain't you coming in soon, Lem?"

' "Well, well!" says I, kind of rousing up. "Durn me if I wasn't waiting for old Paisley to—"

'But when I got that far,' concluded Telemachus Hicks, 'I thought somebody had shot this left ear of mine off with a forty-five. But it turned out to be only a lick from a broomhandle in the hands of Mrs. Hicks.'

THE HANDBOOK OF HYMEN

'TIS THE OPINION OF MYSELF, Sanderson Pratt, who sets this down, that the educational system of the United States should be in the hands of the weather bureau. I can give you good reasons for it; and you can't tell me why our college professors shouldn't be transferred to the meteorological department. They have been learned to read; and they could very easily glance at the morning papers and then wire in to the main office what kind of weather to expect. But there's the other side of the proposition. I am going on to tell you how the weather furnished me and Idaho Green with an elegant education.

We was up in the Bitter Root Mountains over the Montana line prospecting for gold. A chin-whiskered man in Walla-Walla, carrying a line of hope as excess baggage, grubstaked us; and there we was in the foothills pecking away, with enough grub on hand to last an army through a peace conference.

Along one day comes a mail-rider over the mountains from Carlos, and stops to eat three cans of green-gages, and leave us a newspaper of modern date. This paper prints a system of premonitions of the weather, and the card it dealt Bitter Root Mountains from the bottom of the deck was 'warmer and fair, with light westerly breezes.'

That evening it began to snow, with the wind strong in the east. Me and Idaho moved camp into an old empty cabin higher up the mountain, thinking it was only a November flurry. But after falling three foot on a level it went to work in earnest; and we knew we was snowed in. We got in plenty of firewood before it got deep, and we had grub enough for two months, so we let the elements rage and cut up all they thought proper.

If you want to instigate the art of manslaughter just shut two men up in a eighteen-by-twenty-foot cabin for a month. Human nature won't stand it.

When the first snowflakes fell me and Idaho Green laughed at each other's jokes and praised the stuff we turned out of a skillet and called bread. At the end of three weeks Idaho makes this kind of a edict to me. Says he:

'I never exactly heard sour milk dropping out of a balloon on the bottom of a tin pan, but I have an idea it would be music of the spears compared to this attenuated stream of asphyxiated thought that emanates out of your organs of conversation. The kind of half-masticated noises that you emit every day puts me in mind of a cow's cud, only she's lady enough to keep hers to herself, and you ain't.'

'Mr. Green,' says I, 'you having been friend of mind once, I have some hesitations in confessing to you that if I had my choice for society between you and a common yellow three-legged cur pup, one of the inmates of this here cabin would be wagging a tail just at present.'

This way we goes on for two or three days, and then we quits speaking to one another. We divides up the cooking implements, and Idaho cooks his grub on one side of the fireplace, and me on the other. The snow is up to the windows, and we have to keep a fire all day.

You see me and Idaho never had any education beyond reading and doing 'if John had three apples and James five' on a slate. We never felt any special need for a university degree, though we had acquired a species of intrinsic intelligence in knocking around the world that we could use in emergencies.

But snowbound in that cabin in the Bitter Roots, we felt for the first time that if we had studied Homer or Greek and fractions and the higher branches of information, we'd have had some resources in the line of meditation and private thought. I've seen them Eastern college fellows working in camps all through the West, and I never noticed but what education was less of a drawback to 'em than you would think. Why, once over on Snake River, when Andrew McWilliams' saddle horse got the botts, he sent a buckboard ten miles for one of these strangers that claimed to be a botanist. But that horse died.

One morning Idaho was poking around with a stick on top of a little shelf that was too high to reach. Two books fell down to the floor. I started toward 'em but caught Idaho's eye. He speaks for the first time in a week.

'Don't burn your fingers,' says he. 'In spite of the fact that you're only fit to be the companion of a sleeping mud-turtle, I'll give you a square deal. And that's more than your parents did when they turned you loose in the world with the sociability of a rattlesnake and the bedside manner of a frozen turnip. I'll play you a game of seven-up, the winner to pick up his choice of the book, the loser to take the other.'

We played; and Idaho won. He picked up his book; and I took mine. Then each of us got on his side of the house and went to reading.

I never was as glad to see a ten-ounce nugget as I was that book. And Idaho looked at his like a kid looks at a stick of candy.

Mine was a little book about five by six inches called 'Herkimer's Handbook of Indispensable Information.' I may be wrong, but I think that was the greatest book that ever was written. I've got it to-day; and I can stump you or any man fifty times in five minutes with the information in it. Talk about Solomon or the New York *Tribune!* Herkimer had cases on both of 'em. That man must have put in fifty years and travelled a million miles to find out all that stuff. There was the population of all cities in it, and the way to tell a girl's age, and the number of teeth a camel has. It told you the longest tunnel in the world, the number of the stars, how long it takes for chicken pox to break out, what a lady's neck ought to measure, the veto powers of Governors, the dates of the Roman aqueducts, how many pounds of rice going without three beers a day would buy, the average annual temperature of Augusta, Maine, the quantity of seed required to plant an acre of carrots in drills, antidotes for poisons, the number of hairs on a blond lady's head, how to preserve eggs, the height of all the mountains in the world, and the dates of all wars and battles, and how to restore drowned persons, and sunstroke, and the number of tacks in a pound, and how to make dynamite and flowers and beds, and what to do before the doctor comes – and a hundred times as many things besides. If there was anything Herkimer didn't know I didn't miss it out of the book.

I sat and read that book for four hours. All the wonders of education was compressed in it. I forgot the snow, and I forgot that me and old Idaho was on the outs. He was sitting still on a stool reading away with a kind of partly soft and partly mysterious look shining through his tan-bark whiskers.

'Idaho,' says I, 'what kind of a book is yours?'

Idaho must have forgot, too, for he answered moderate, without any slander or malignity.

'Why,' says he, 'this here seems to be a volume by Homer K. M.'

'Homer K. M. what?' I asked.

'Why, just Homer K. M.,' says he.

'You're a liar,' says I, a little riled that Idaho should try to put me up a tree. 'No man is going 'round signing books with his initials. If it's Homer K. M. Spoopendyke, or Homer K. M. McSweeney, or Homer K. M. Jones, why don't you say so like a man instead of biting off the end of it like a calf chewing off the tail of a shirt on a clothesline?'

'I put it to you straight, Sandy,' says Idaho, quiet. 'It's a poem book,' says he, 'by Homer K. M. I couldn't get color out of it at first, but there's a vein if you follow it up. I wouldn't have missed this book for a pair of red blankets.'

'You're welcome to it,' says I. 'What I want is a disinterested statement of facts for the mind to work on, and that's what I seem to find in the book I've drawn.'

'What you've got,' said Idaho, 'is statistics, the lowest grade of information that exists. They'll poison your mind. Give me old K. M.'s system of surmises. He seems to be a kind of a wine agent. His regular toast is "nothing doing," and he seems to have a grouch, but he keeps it so well lubricated with booze that his worst kicks sound like an invitation to split a quart. But it's poetry,' says Idaho, 'and I have sensations of scorn for that truck of yours that tries to convey sense in feet and inches. When it comes to explaining the instict of philosophy through the art of nature, old K. M. has got your man beat by drills, rows, paragraphs, chest measurement, and average annual rainfall.'

So that's the way me and Idaho had it. Day and night all the excitement we got was studying our books. That snowstorm sure fixed us with a fine lot of attainments apiece. By the time the snow melted, if you had stepped up to me suddenly and said: 'Sanderson Pratt, what would it cost per square foot to lay a roof with twenty by twenty-eight tin at nine dollars and fifty cents per box?' I'd have told you as quick as light could travel the length of a spade handle at the rate of one hundred and ninety-two thousand miles per second. How many can do it? You wake up 'most any man you know in the middle of the night, and ask him quick to tell you the number of bones in the human skeleton exclusive of the teeth, or what percentage of the vote of the Nebraska Legislature overrules a veto. Will he tell you? Try him and see.

About what benefit Idaho got out of his poetry book I didn't exactly know, Idaho boosted the wine-agent every time he opened his mouth; but I wasn't so sure.

This Homer K. M., from what leaked out of his libretto through Idaho, seemed to me to be a kind of a dog who looked at life like it was a tin can tied to his tail. After running himself half to death, he sits down, hangs his tongue out, and looks at the can and says:

'Oh, well, since we can't shake the growler, let's get filled at the corner, and all have a drink on me.'

Besides that, it seems he was a Persian; and I never hear of Persia producing anything worth mentioning unless it was Turkish rugs and Maltese cats.

That spring me and Idaho struck pay ore. It was a habit of ours to sell out quick and keep moving. We unloaded on our grubstaker for eight thousand dollars apiece; and then we drifted down to this little town of Rosa, on the Salmon River, to rest up, and get some human grub, and have our whiskers harvested.

Rosa was no mining-camp. It laid in the valley, and was as free of uproar and pestilence as one of them rural towns in the country. There was a three-mile trolley line champing its bit in the environs, and me and Idaho spent a week riding on one of the cars, dropping off of nights at the Sunset View Hotel. Being now well read as well as travelled, we was soon *pro re nata* with the best society in Rosa, and was invited out to the most dressed-up and high-toned entertainments. It was at a piano recital and quail-eating contest in the city hall, for the benefit of the fire company, that me and Idaho first met Mrs. D. Ormond Sampson, the queen of Rosa society.

Mrs. Sampson was a widow, and owned the only two-story house in town. It was painted yellow, and whichever way you looked from you could see it as plain as egg on the chin of an O'Grady on a Friday. Twenty-two men in Rosa besides me and Idaho was trying to stake a claim on that yellow house.

There was a dance after the song books and quail bones had been raked out of the Hall. Twenty-three of the bunch galloped over to Mrs. Sampson and asked for a dance. I side-stepped the two-step, and asked permission to escort her home. That's where I made a hit.

On the way home says she:

'Ain't the stars lovely and bright to-night, Mr. Pratt?'

'For the chance they've got,' says I, 'they're humping themselves in a mighty creditable way. That big one you see is sixty-six billions of miles distant. It took thirty-six years for light to reach us. With an eighteen-foot telescope you can see forty-three millions of 'em, including them of the thirteenth magnitude, which, if one was to go out now, you would keep on seeing it for twenty-seven hundred years.'

'My!' says Mrs. Sampson. 'I never knew that before. How warm it is! I'm as damp as I can be from dancing so much.'

'That's easy to account for,' says I, 'when you happen to know that you've got two million sweat-glands working all at once. If every one of your perspiratory ducts, which are a quarter of an inch long, was placed end to end, they would reach a distance of seven miles.'

'Lawsy!' says Mrs. Sampson. 'It sounds like an irrigation ditch you was describing, Mr. Pratt. How do you get all this knowledge of information?'

'From observation, Mrs. Sampson,' I tells her. 'I keep my eyes open when I go about the world.'

'Mr. Pratt,' says she, 'I always did admire a man of education. There are so few scholars among the sap-headed plug-uglies of this town that it is a real pleasure to converse with a gentleman of culture. I'd be gratified to have you call at my house whenever you feel so inclined.'

And that was the way I got the goodwill of the lady in the yellow house. Every Tuesday and Friday evenings I used to go there and tell her about the wonders of the universe as discovered, tabulated, and compiled from nature by Herkimer. Idaho and the other gay Lutherans of the town got every minute of the rest of the week that they could.

I never imagined that Idaho was trying to work on Mrs. Sampson with old K. M.'s rules of courtship till one afternoon when I was on my way over to take her a basket of wild hog-plums. I met the lady coming down the lane that led to her house. Her eyes were snapping, and her hat made a dangerous dip over one eye.

'Mr. Pratt,' she opens up, 'this Mr. Green is a friend of yours, I believe.'

'For nine years,' says I.

'Cut him out,' says she. 'He's no gentleman!'

'Why, ma'am,' says I, 'he's a plain incumbent of the mountain, with asperities and the usual failings of a spendthrift and a liar, but I never on the most momentous occasion had the heart to deny that he was a gentleman. It may be that in haberdashery and the sense of arrogance and display Idaho offends the eye, but inside, ma'am, I've found him impervious to the lower grades of crime and obesity. After nine years of Idaho's society, Mrs. Sampson,' I winds up, 'I should hate to impute him, and I should hate to see him imputed.'

'It's right plausible of you, Mr. Pratt,' says Mrs. Sampson, 'to take up the curmudgeons in your friend's behalf; but it don't alter the fact that he has made proposals to me sufficiently obnoxious to ruffle the ignominy of any lady.'

'Why, now, now, now!' says I, 'Old Idaho do that! I could believe it of myself sooner. I never knew but one thing to deride in him; and a blizzard was responsible for that. Once while we was snowbound in the mountains he became a prey to a kind of spurious and uneven poetry, which may have corrupted his demeanor.'

'It has,' says Mrs. Sampson. 'Ever since I knew him he has been reciting to me a lot of irreligious rhymes by some person he calls Ruby Ott, and who is no better than she should be, if you judge by her poetry.'

'Then Idaho has struck a new book,' says I, 'for one he had was by a man who writes under the *nom de plume* of K. M.'

'He'd better have stuck to it,' says Mrs. Sampson, 'whatever it was. And to-day he caps the vortex. I get a bunch of flowers from him, and on 'em is pinned a note. Now, Mr. Pratt, you know a lady when you see her; and you know how I stand in Rosa society. Do you think for a moment that I'd skip out to the woods with a man along with a jug of wine and a loaf of bread, and go singing and cavorting up and down under the trees with him? I take a little claret with my meals, but I'm not in the habit of packing a jug of it into the brush and raising Cain in any such style as that. And of course he'd bring his book of verses along, too. He said so. Let him go on his scandalous picnics alone! Or let him take his Ruby Ott with him. I reckon she wouldn't kick unless it was on account of there being too much bread along. And what do you think of your gentleman friend now, Mr. Pratt?'

'Well, 'm,' says I, 'it may be that Idaho's invitation was a kind of poetry, and meant no harm. Maybe it belonged to the class of rhymes they call figurative. They offend law and order, but they get sent through the mails on the grounds that they mean something that they don't say. I'd be glad on Idaho's account if you'd overlook it,' says I, 'and let us extricate our minds from the low regions of poetry to the higher planes of fact and fancy. On a beautiful afternoon like this, Mrs. Sampson,' I goes on, 'we should let our thoughts dwell accordingly. Though it is warm here, we should remember that at the equator the line of perpetual frost is at an altitude of fifteen thousand feet. Between the latitudes of forty degrees and forty-nine degrees it is from four thousand to nine thousand feet.'

'Oh, Mr. Pratt,' says Mrs. Sampson, 'It's such a comfort to hear you say them beautiful facts after getting such a jar from that minx of a Ruby's poetry!'

'Let us sit on this log at the roadside,' says I, 'and forget the inhumanity and ribaldry of the poets. It is in the glorious columns of ascertained facts and legalized measures that beauty is to be found. In this very log we sit upon, Mrs. Sampson,' says I, 'is statistics more wonderful than any poem. The rings show it was sixty years old. At the depth of two thousand feet it would become coal in three thousand years. The deepest coal mine in the world is at Killingworth, near Newcastle. A box four feet long, three feet wide, and two feet eight inches deep will hold one ton of coal. If an artery is cut, compress it above the wound. A man's leg contains thirty bones. The Tower of London was burned in 1841.'

'Go on, Mr. Pratt,' says Mrs. Sampson. 'Them ideas is so original and soothing. I think statistics are just as lovely as they can be.'

But it wasn't till two weeks later that I got all that was coming to me out of Herkimer.

One night I was waked up by folks hollering 'Fire!' all around. I jumped up and dressed and went out of the hotel to enjoy the scene. When I seen it was Mrs. Sampson's house, I gave forth a kind of yell, and I was there in two minutes.

The whole lower story of the yellow house was in flames, and every masculine, feminine, and canine in Rosa was there, screeching and barking and getting in the way of the firemen. I saw Idaho trying to get away from six firemen who were holding him. They was telling him the whole place was on fire downstairs, and no man could go in it and come out alive.

'Where's Mrs. Sampson?' I asks.

'She hasn't been seen,' says one of the firemen. 'She sleeps upstairs. We've tried to get in, but we can't, and our company hasn't got any ladders yet.'

I runs around to the light of the big blaze, and pulls the Handbook out of my inside pocket. I kind of laughed when I felt it in my hands – I reckon I was some daffy with the sensation of excitement.

'Herky, old boy,' I says to it, as I flipped over the pages, 'you ain't ever lied to me yet, and you ain't ever throwed me down at a scratch yet. Tell me what, old boy, tell me what!' says I.

I turned to 'What to do in Case of Accidents,' on page 117. I run my finger down the page, and struck it. Good old Herkimer, he never overlooked anything! It said:

SUFFOCATION FROM INHALING SMOKE OR GAS. – There is nothing better than flaxseed. Place a few seeds in the corner of the eye.

I shoved the Handbook back in my pocket, and grabbed a boy that was running by.

'Here,' says I, giving him some money, 'run to the drug store and bring a dollar's worth of flaxseed. Hurry, and you'll get another one for yourself. Now,' I sings out to the crowd, 'we'll have Mrs. Sampson!' And I throws away my coat and hat.

Four of the firemen and citizens grabs hold of me. It's sure death, they say, to go in the house, for the floors was beginning to fall through.

'How in blazes,' I sings out, kind of laughing yet, but not feeling like it, 'do you expect me to put flaxseed in a eye without the eye?'

I jabbed each elbow in a fireman's face, kicked the bark off of one citizen's shin, and tripped the other one with a side hold. And then I busted into the house. If I die first I'll write you a letter and tell you if it's any worse down there than the inside of that yellow house was; but don't believe it yet. I was a heap more cooked than the hurry-up orders of broiled chicken that you get in restaurants. The fire and smoke had me down on the floor twice, and was about to shame Herkimer, but the firemen helped me with their little stream of water, and I got to Mrs. Sampson's room. She'd lost conscientiousness from the smoke, so I wrapped her in the bed clothes and got her on my shoulder. Well, the floors wasn't as bad as they said, or I never could have done it – not by no means.

I carried her out fifty yards from the house and laid her on the grass. Then, of course, every one of them other twenty-two plantiffs to the lady's hand crowded around with tin dippers of water ready to save her. And up runs the boy with the flaxseed.

I unwrapped the covers from Mrs. Sampson's head. She opened her eyes and says:

'Is that you, Mr. Pratt?'

'S-s-sh,' says I. 'Don't talk till you've had the remedy.'

I runs my arm around her neck and raises her head, gentle, and breaks the bag of flaxseed with the other hand; and as easy as I could I bends over and slips three or four of the seeds in the outer corner of her eye.

Up gallops the village doc by this time, and snorts around, and grabs at Mrs. Sampson's pulse, and wants to know what I mean by any such sandblasted nonsense.

'Well, old Jalap and Jerusulem oak seed,' says I, 'I'm no regular practitioner, but I'll show you my authority, anyway.'

They fetched my coat, and I gets out the Handbook.

'Look on page 117,' says I, 'at the remedy for suffocation by smoke or gas. Flaxseed in the outer corner of the eye, it says. I don't know whether it works as a smoke consumer or whether it hikes the compound gastro-hippopotamus nerve into action, but Herkimer says it, and he was called to the case first. If you want to make it a consultation, there's no objection.'

Old doc takes the book and looks at it by means of his specs and a fireman's lantern.

'Well, Mr. Pratt,' says he, 'you evidently got on the wrong line in reading your diagnosis. The recipe for suffocation says: "Get the patient into fresh air as quickly as possible, and place in a reclining position." The flaxseed remedy is for "Dust and Cinders in the Eye," on the line above. But, after all—'

'See here,' interrupts Mrs. Sampson, 'I reckon I've got something to say in this consultation. That flaxseed done me more good than anything I ever tried.' And then she raises up her head and lays it back on my arm again, and says: 'Put some in the other eye, Sandy dear.'

And so if you was to stop off at Rosa to-morrow, or any other day, you'd see a fine new yellow house with Mrs. Pratt, that was Mrs. Sampson, embellishing and adorning it. And if you was to step inside you'd see on the marble-top centre table in the parlor, 'Herkimer's Handbook of Indispensable Information,' all rebound in red morocco, and ready to be consulted on any subject pertaining to human happiness and wisdom.

THE PIMIENTA PANCAKES

WHILE WE WERE ROUNDING UP a bunch of the Triangle-O cattle in the Frio bottoms a projecting branch of a dead mesquite caught my wooden stirrup and gave my ankle a wrench that laid me up in camp for a week.

On the third day of my compulsory idleness I crawled out near the grub wagon, and reclined helpless under the conversational fire of Judson Odom, the camp cook. Jud was a monologist by nature, whom Destiny, with customary blundering, had set in a profession wherein he was bereaved, for the greater portion of his time, of an audience.

Therefore, I was manna in the desert of Jud's obmutescence.

Betimes I was stirred by invalid longings for something to eat that did not come under the caption of 'grub.' I had visions of the maternal pantry 'deep as first love, and wild with all regret,' and then I asked:

'Jud, can you make pancakes?'

Jud laid down his sixshooter, with which he was preparing to pound an antelope steak, and stood over me in what I felt to be a menacing attitude. He further indorsed my impression that his pose was resentful by fixing upon me with his light blue eyes a look of cold suspicion.

'Say, you,' he said, with candid, though not excessive, choler, 'did you mean that straight, or was you trying to throw the gaff into me? Some of the boys been telling you about me and that pancake racket?'

'No, Jud,' I said, sincerely, 'I meant it. It seems to me I'd swap my pony and saddle for a stack of buttered brown pancakes with some first crop, open kettle, New Orleans sweetening. Was there a story about pancakes?'

Jud was mollified at once when he saw that I had not been dealing in allusions. He brought some mysterious bags and tin boxes from the grub wagon and set them in the shade of the hackberry where I lay reclined. I watched him as he began to arrange them leisurely and untie their many strings.

'No, not a story,' said Jud, as he worked, 'but just the logical disclosures in the case of me and that pink-eyed snoozer from Mired Mule Cañada and Miss Willella Learight. I don't mind telling you.

'I was punching then for old Bill Toomey, on the San Miguel. One day I gets all ensnared up in aspirations for to eat some canned grub that hasn't even mooed or baaed or grunted or been in peck measures. So, I gets on my bronc and pushed the wind for Uncle Emsley Telfair's store at the Pimienta Crossing on the Neuces.

'About three in the afternoon I throwed my bridle over a mesquite limb and walked the last twenty yards into Uncle Emsley's store. I got up on the counter and told Uncle Emsley that the signs pointed to the devastation of the fruit crop of the world. In a minute I had a bag of crackers and a long-handled spoon, with an open can each of apricots and pineapples and cherries and green-gages beside of me with Uncle Emsley busy chopping away with the hatchet at the yellow clings. I was feeling like Adam before the apple stampede, and was digging my spurs into the side of the counter and working with my twenty-four-inch spoon when I happened to look out of the window into the yard of Uncle Emsley's house, which was next to the store.

'There was a girl standing there – an imported girl with fixings on – philandering with a croquet maul and amusing herself by watching my style of encouraging the fruit canning industry.

'I slid off the counter and delivered up my shovel to Uncle Emsley.

' "That's my niece," says he; "Miss Willella Learight, down from Palestine on a visit. Do you want that I should make you acquainted?"

' "The Holy Land," I says to myself, my thought milling some as I tried to run 'em into the corral. "Why not? There was sure angels in Pales — Why yes, Uncle Emsley," I says out loud, "I'd be awful edified to meet Miss Learight."

'So Uncle Emsley took me out in the yard and gave us each other's entitlements.

'I never was shy about women. I never could understand why some men who can break a mustang before breakfast and shave in the dark, get all left-handed and full of perspiration and excuses when they see a bolt of calico draped around what belongs in it. Inside of eight minutes me and Miss Willella was aggravating the croquet balls around as amiable as second cousins. She gave me a dig about the quantity of canned fruit I had eaten, and I got back at her, flat-footed, about how a certain lady named Eve started the fruit trouble in the first free-grass pasture – "Over in Palestine, wasn't it?" says I, as easy and pat as roping a one-year-old.

'That was how I acquired cordiality for the proximities of Miss Willella Learight; and the disposition grew larger as time passed. She was stopping at Pimienta Crossing for her health, which was very good, and for the climate, which was forty per cent. hotter than Palestine. I rode over to see her once every week for a while; and then I figured it out that if I doubled the number of trips I would see her twice as often.

'One week I slipped in a third trip; and that's where the pancakes and the pink-eyed snoozer busted into the game.

'That evening, while I set on the counter with a peach and two damsons in my mouth, I asked Uncle Emsley how Miss Willella was.

' "Why," says Uncle Emsley, "she's gone riding with Jackson Bird, the sheep man from over at Mired Mule Cañada."

'I swallowed the peach seed and the two damsons seeds. I guess somebody held the counter by the bridle while I got off; and then I walked out straight ahead till I butted against the mesquite where my roan was tied.

' "She's gone riding," I whispered in my bronc's ear, "with Birdstone Jack, the hired mule from Sheep Man's Cañada. Did you get that, old Leather-and-Gallops?"

'That bronc of mine wept, in his way. He'd been raised a cow pony and he didn't care for snoozers.

'I went back and said to Uncle Emsley: "Did you say a sheep man?"

' "I said a sheep man," says Uncle again. "You must have heard tell of Jackson Bird. He's got eight sections of grazing and four thousand head of the finest Merinos south of the Arctic Circle."

'I went out and sat on the ground in the shade of the store and leaned against a prickly pear. I sifted sand into my boots with unthinking hands while I soliloquized a quantity about this bird with the Jackson plumage to his name.

'I never had believed in harming sheep men. I see one, one day, reading a Latin grammar on hossback, and I never touched him! They never irritated me like they do most cowmen. You wouldn't go to work now, and impair and disfigure snoozers, would you, that eat on tables and wear little shoes and speak to you on subjects? I had always let 'em pass, just as you would a jack-rabbit; with a polite word and a guess about the weather, but no stopping to swap canteens. I never thought it was worth while to be hostile with a snoozer. And because I'd been lenient, and let 'em live, here was one going around riding with Miss Willella Learight!

'An hour by sun they come loping back, and stopped at Uncle Emsley's gate. The sheep person helped her off; and they stood throwing each other sentences all sprightful and sagacious for a while. And then this feathered Jackson flies up in his saddle and raises his little stewpot of a hat, and trots off in the direction of his mutton ranch. By this time I had turned the sand out of my boots and unpinned myself from the prickly pear; and by the time he gets half a mile out of Pimienta, I singlefoots up beside him on my bronc.

'I said that snoozer was pink-eyed, but he wasn't. His seeing arrangement was gray enough, but his eye-lashes was pink and his hair was sandy, and that gave you the idea. Sheep man – he wasn't more than a lamb man, anyhow – a little thing with his neck involved in a yellow silk handkerchief, and shoes tied up in bowknots.

' "Afternoon!" says I to him. "You now ride with a equestrian who is commonly called Dead-Moral-Certainty Judson, on account of the way I shoot. When I want a stranger to know me I always introduce myself before the draw, for I never did like to shake hands with ghosts."

' "Ah," says he, just like that – "Ah, I'm glad to know you, Mr. Judson. I'm Jackson Bird, from over at Mired Mule Ranch."

'Just then one of my eyes saw a roadrunner skipping down the hill with a young tarantula in his bill, and the other eye noticed a rabbit-hawk sitting on a dead limb in a water-elm. I popped over one after the other with my forty-five just to show him. "Two out of three," said I. "Birds just naturally seem to draw my fire wherever I go."

' "Nice shooting," says the sheep man, without a flutter. "But don't you sometimes ever miss the third shot? Elegant fine rain that was last week for the young grass, Mr. Judson," says he.

' "Willie," says I, riding over close to his palfrey, "your infatuated parents may have denounced you by the name of Jackson, but you sure moulted into a twittering Willie – let us slough of this here analysis of rain and the elements, and get down to talk that is outside the vocabulary of parrots. That is a bad habit you have got of riding with young ladies over at Pimienta. I've known birds," says I, "to be served on toast for less than that. Miss Willella," says I, "don't ever want any nest made out of sheep's wool by a tomtit of the Jacksonian branch of ornithology. Now, are you going to quit, or do you wish for to gallop up against this Dead-Moral-Certainty attachment to my name, which is good for two hyphens and at least one set of funeral obsequies?"

'Jackson Bird flushed up some, and then he laughed.

' "Why, Mr. Judson," says he, "you've got the wrong idea. I've called on Miss Learight a few times; but not for the purpose you imagine. My object is purely a gastronomical one."

'I reached for my gun.

' "Any coyote," says I, "that would boast of dishonorable—"

' "Wait a minute," says this Bird, "till I explain. What would I do with a wife? If you ever saw that ranch of mine! I do my own cooking and mending. Eating – that's all the pleasure I get out of sheep raising. Mr. Judson, did you ever taste the pancakes that Miss Learight makes?"

' "Me? No," I told him. "I never was advised that she was up to any culinary maneuvers."

' "They're golden sunshine," says he, "honey-browned by the ambrosial fires of Epicurus. I'd give two years of my life to get the recipe for making them pancakes. That's what I went to see Miss Learight for," says Jackson Bird, "but I haven't been able to get it from her. It's an old recipe that's been in the family for seventy-five years. They hand it down from one generation to another, but they don't give it away to outsiders. If I could get that recipe, so I could make them pancakes for myself on my ranch, I'd be a happy man," says Bird.

' "Are you sure," I says to him, "that it ain't the hand that mixes the pancakes that you're after?"

' "Sure," says Jackson. "Miss Learight is a mighty nice girl, but I can assure you my intentions go no further than the gastro—" but he seen my hand going down to my holster and he changed his similitude – "than the desire to procure a copy of the pancake recipe," he finishes.

' "You ain't such a bad little man," says I, trying to be fair. "I was thinking some of making orphans of your sheep, but I'll let you fly away this time. But you stick to pancakes," says I, "as close as the middle one of a stack; and don't go and mistake sentiments for syrup, or there'll be singing at your ranch, and you won't hear it."

' "To convince you that I am sincere," says the sheep man, "I'll ask you to help me. Miss Learight and you being closer friends, maybe she would do for you what she wouldn't for me. If you will get me a copy of that pancake recipe, I give you my word that I'll never call upon her again."

' "That's fair," I says, and I shook hands with Jackson Bird. "I'll get it for you if I can, and glad to oblige." And he turned off down the big pear flat on the Piedra, in the direction of Mired Mule; and I steered north-west for old Bill Toomey's ranch.

'It was five days afterward when I got another chance to ride over to Pimienta. Miss Willella and me passed a gratifying evening at Uncle Emsley's. She sang some, and exasperated the piano quite a lot with quotations from the operas. I gave imitations of a rattlesnake, and told her about Snaky McFee's new way of skinning cows, and described the trip I made to Saint Louis once. We was getting along in one another's estimations fine. Thinks I, if Jackson can now be persuaded to migrate, I win. I recollect his promise about the pancake receipt, and I thinks I will persuade it from Miss Willella and give it to him; and then if I catches Birdie off of Mired Mule again, I'll make him hop the twig.

'So, along about ten o'clock, I put on a wheedling smile and says to Miss Willella: "Now, if there's anything I do like better than the sight of a red steer on green grass it's the taste of a nice hot pancake smothered in sugarhouse molasses."

'Miss Willella gives a little jump on the piano stool, and looked at me curious.

' "Yes," says she, "they're real nice. What did you say was the name of that street in Saint Louis, Mr. Odom, where you lost your hat?"

' "Pancake Avenue," says I, with a wink, to show her that I was on about the family receipt, and couldn't be side-corralled off of the subject. "Come now, Miss Willella," I says; "let's hear how you make 'em. Pancakes is just whirling in my head like wagon wheels. Start her off, now – pound of flour, eight dozen eggs, and so on. How does the catalogue of constituents run?"

' "Excuse me for a moment, please," says Willella, and she gives me a quick kind of sideways look, and slides off the stool. She ambled out into the other room and directly Uncle Emsley comes in in his shirt sleeves, with a pitcher of water. He turns around to get a glass on the table, and I see a forty-five in his hip pocket. "Great post-holes!" thinks I, "but here's a family thinks a heap of cooking receipts, protecting it with firearms. I've known outfits that wouldn't do that much by a family feud."

' "Drink this here down," says Uncle Emsley, handing me the glass of water. "You've rid too far to-day, Jud, and got yourself over-excited. Try to think about something else now."

' "Do you know how to make them pancakes, Uncle Emsley?" I asked.

' "Well, I'm not as apprised in the anatomy of them as some," says Uncle Emsley, "but I reckon you take a sifter of plaster of paris and a little dough and saleratus and corn meal, and mix 'em with eggs and buttermilk as usual. Is old Bill going to ship beeves to Kansas City again this spring, Jud?"

'That was all the pancake specifications I could get that night. I didn't wonder that Jackson Bird found it uphill work. So I dropped the subject and talked with Uncle Emsley a while about hollow-horn and cyclones. And then Miss Willella came and said "Good-night." and I hit the breeze for the ranch.

'About a week afterward I met Jackson Bird riding out of Pimienta as I rode in, and we stopped in the road for a few frivolous remarks.

' "Got the bill of particulars for them flap-jacks yet?" I asked him.

' "Well, no," says Jackson. "I don't seem to have any success in getting hold of it. Did you try?"

' "I did," says I, "and 'twas like trying to dig a prairie dog out of his hole with a peanut hull. That pancake receipt must be a jooka-lorum, the way they hold on to it."

' "I'm 'most ready to give it up," says Jackson, so discouraged in his pronunciations that I felt sorry for him; "but I did want to know how to make them pancakes to eat on my lonely ranch," says he. "I lie awake at nights thinking how good they are."

' "You keep on trying for it," I tells him, "and I'll do the same. One of us is bound to get a rope over its horns before long. Well, so-long, Jacksy."

'You see, by this time we was on the peacefullest of terms. When I saw that he wasn't after Miss Willella I had more endurable contemplations of that sandy-haired snoozer. In order to help out the ambitions of his appetite I kept on trying to get that receipt from Miss Willella. But every time I would say "pancakes" she would get sort of remote and fidgety about the eye, and try to change the subject. If I held her to it she would slide out and round up Uncle Emsley with his pitcher of water and hip-pocket howitzer.

'One day I galloped over to the store with a fine bunch of blue verbenas that I cut out of a herd of wild flowers over on Poisoned Dog Prairie. Uncle Emsley looked at 'em with one eye shut and says:

' "Haven't ye heard the news?"

' "Cattle up?" I asks.

' "Willella and Jackson Bird was married in Palestine yesterday," says he. "Just got a letter this morning."

'I dropped them flowers in a cracker-barrel, and let the news trickle in my ears and down toward my upper left-hand shirt pocket until it got to my feet.

' "Would you mind saying that over again once more, Uncle Emsley?" says I. "Maybe my hearing has got wrong, and you only said that prime heifers was 4.80 on the hoof, or something like that."

' "Married yesterday," says Uncle Emsley, "and gone to Waco and Niagara Falls on a wedding tour. Why, didn't you see none of the signs all along? Jackson Bird has been courting Willella ever since that day he took her out riding."

' "Then," says I, in a kind of a yell, "what was all this zizzaparoola he gives me about pancakes? Tell me *that*."

'When I said "pancakes" Uncle Emsley sort of dodged and stepped back.

' "Somebody's been dealing me pancakes from the bottom of the deck," I says, "and I'll find out. I believe you know. Talk up," says I, "or we'll mix a panful of batter right here."

'I slid over the counter after Uncle Emsley. He grabbed at his gun, but it was in a drawer, and he missed it two inches. I got him by the front of his shirt and shoved him in a corner.

' "Talk pancakes," says I, "or be made into one. Does Miss Willella make 'em?"

' "She never made one in her life and I never saw one," says Uncle Emsley, soothing. "Calm down now, Jud – calm down. You've got excited, and that wound in your head is contaminating your sense of intelligence. Try not to think about pancakes."

' "Uncle Emsley," says I, "I'm not wounded in the head except so far as my natural cogitative instincts run to runts. Jackson Bird told me he was calling on Miss Willella for the purpose of finding out her system of producing pancakes, and he asked me to help him get the bill of lading of the ingredients. I done so, with the results as you see. Have I been sodded down with Johnson grass by a pink-eyed snoozer, or what?"

' "Slack up your grip on my dress shirt," says Uncle Emsley, "and I'll tell you. Yes, it looks like Jackson Bird has gone and humbugged you some. The day after he went riding with Willella he came back and told me and her to watch out for you whenever you go to talking about pancakes. He said you was in camp once where they was cooking flapjacks, and one of the fellows cut you over the head with a frying pan. Jackson said that whenever you got over-hot or excited that wound hurt you and made you kind of crazy, and you went raving about pancakes. He told us to just get you worked off of the subject and soothed down, and you wouldn't be dangerous. So, me and Willella done the best by you we knew how. Well, well," says Uncle Emsley, "that Jackson Bird is sure a seldom kind of a snoozer." '

During the progress of Jud's story he had been slowly but deftly combining certain portions of the contents of his sacks and cans. Toward the close of it he set before me the finished product – a pair of red-hot, rich-hued pancakes on a tin plate. From some secret hoarding place he also brought a lump of excellent butter and a bottle of golden syrup.

'How long ago did these things happen?' I asked him.

'Three years,' said Jud. 'They're living on the Mired Mule Ranch now.

But I haven't seen either of 'em since. They say Jackson Bird was fixing his ranch up fine with rocking chairs and window curtains all the time he was putting me up the pancake tree. Oh, I got over it after a while. But the boys kept the racket up.'

'Did you make these cakes by the famous recipe?' I asked.

'Didn't I tell you there wasn't no receipt?' said Jud. 'The boys hollered pancakes till they got pancake hungry, and I cut this receipt out of a newspaper. How does the truck taste?'

'They're delicious,' I answered. 'Why don't you have some, too, Jud?' I was sure I heard a sigh.

'Me?' said Jud. 'I don't never eat 'em.'

SEATS OF THE HAUGHTY

GOLDEN BY DAY AND SILVER BY NIGHT, a new trail now leads to us across the Indian Ocean. Dusky kings and princes have found out our Bombay of the West; and few be their trails that do not lead down Broadway on their journey for to admire and for to see.

If chance should ever lead you near a hotel that transiently shelters some one of these splendid touring grandees, I counsel you to seek Lucullus Polk among the republican tuft-hunters that besiege its entrances. He will be there. You will know him by his red, alert, Wellington-nosed face, by his manner of nervous caution mingled with determination, by his assumed promoter's or broker's air of busy impatience, and by his bright-red necktie, gallantly redressing the wrongs of his maltreated blue serge suit, like a battle standard, still waving above a lost cause. I found him profitable; and so may you. When you do look for him, look among the light-horse troop of Bedouins that besiege the picket-line of the travelling potentate's guards and secretaries – among the wild-eyed genii of Arabian Afternoons that gather to make astounding and egregious demands upon the prince's coffers.

I first saw Mr. Polk coming down the steps of the hotel at which sojourned His Highness the Gaekwar of Baroda, most enlightened of the Mahratta princes, who, of late, ate bread and salt in our Metropolis of the Occident.

Lucullus moved rapidly, as though propelled by some potent moral force that imminently threatened to become physical. Behind him closely followed the impetus – a hotel detective, if ever white Alpine hat, hawk's nose, implacable watch chain, and loud refinement of manner spoke the truth. A brace of uniformed porters at his heels preserved the smooth decorum of the hotel, repudiating by their air of disengagement any suspicion that they formed a reserve squad of ejectment.

Safe on the sidewalk, Lucullus Polk turned and shook a freckled fist at the caravansary. And, to my joy, he began to breathe deep invective in strange words.

'Rides in howdahs, does he?' he cried loudly and sneeringly. 'Rides on elephants in howdahs and calls himself a prince! Kings – yah! Comes over here and talks horse till you would think he was a president; and then goes home and rides in a private dining-room strapped onto an elephant. Well, well, well!'

The ejecting committee quietly retired. The scorner of princes turned to me and snapped his fingers.

'What do you think of that?' he shouted derisively. 'The Gaekwar of Baroda rides on an elephant in a\howdah! And there's old Bikram Shamsher Jang scorching up and down the pig-paths of Khatmandu on a motor-cycle. Wouldn't that maharajah you? And the Shah of Persia, that ought to have been Muley-on-the-spot for at least three, he's got the palanquin habit. And that funny-hat prince from Korea – wouldn't you think he could afford to amble around on a milk-white palfrey once in a dynasty or two? Nothing doing! His idea of a Balaklava charge is to tuck his skirts under him and do his mile in six days over the hog-wallows of Seoul on a bull-cart. That's the kind of visiting potentates that come to this country now. It's a hard deal, friend.'

I murmured a few words of sympathy. But it was uncomprehending, for I did not know his grievance against the rulers who flash, meteor-like, now and then upon our shores.

'The last one I sold,' continued the displeased one, 'was to that three-horse-tailed Turkish pasha that came over a year ago. Five hundred dollars he paid for it, easy. I says to his executioner or secretary – he was a kind of a Jew or a Chinaman – " 'Tis Turkey Giblets is fond of horses, then?"

' "Him?" says the secretary. "Well, no. He's got a big, fat wife in the harem named Bad Dora that he don't like. I believe he intends to saddle her up and ride her up and down the board-walk in the Bulbul Gardens a few times every day. You haven't got a pair of extra long spurs you could throw in on the deal, have you?" Yes, sir, there's mighty few real rough-riders among the royal sports these days.'

As soon as Lucullus Polk got cool enough I picked him up, and with no greater effort than you would employ in persuading a drowning man to clutch a straw, I inveigled him into accompanying me to a cool corner in a dim café.

And it came to pass that men-servants set before us brewage; and Lucullus Polk spake unto me, relating the wherefores of his beleaguering the ante-chambers of the princes of the earth.

'Did you ever hear of the S. A. & A. P. Railroad in Texas? Well, that don't stand for Samaritan Actor's Aid Philanthropy. I was down that way managing a summer bunch of the gum and syntax-chewers that play the Idlewild Parks in the Western hamlets. Of course, we went to pieces when the soubrette ran away with a prominent barber of Beeville. I don't know what became of the rest of the company. I believe there were some salaries due; and the last I saw of the troupe was when I told them that forty-three cents was all the treasury contained. I say I never saw any of them after that; but I heard them for about twenty minutes. I didn't have time to look back. But after dark I came out of the woods and struck the S. A. & A. P. agent for means of transportation. He at once extended to me the courtesies of the entire railroad, kindly warning me, however, not to get aboard any of the rolling stock.

'About ten the next morning I steps off the ties into a village that calls itself Atascosa City. I bought a thirty-cent breakfast and a ten-cent cigar, and stood on Main Street jingling the three pennies in my pocket – dead broke. A man in Texas with only three cents in his pocket is no better off than a man that has no money and owes two cents.

'One of luck's favorite tricks is to soak a man for his last dollar so quick that he don't have time to look it. There I was in a swell St. Louis tailor-made, blue-and-green plaid suit, and an eighteen-carat sulphate-of-copper scarf pin, with no hope in sight except the two great Texas industries, the cotton fields, and grading new railroads. I never picked cotton, and I never cottoned to a pick, so the outlook had ultramarine edges.

'All of a sudden, while I was standing on the edge of the wooden sidewalk, down out of the sky falls two fine gold watches into the middle of the street. One hits a chunk of mud and sticks. The other falls hard and flies open, making a fine drizzle of little springs and screws and wheels. I looks up for a balloon or an airship; but not seeing any, I steps off the sidewalk to investigate.

'But I hear a couple of yells and see two men running up the street in leather overalls and high-heeled boots and carwheel hats. One man is six or eight feet high, with open-plumbed joints and a heartbroken cast of countenance. He picks up the watch that has stuck in the mud. The other man, who is little, with pink hair and white eyes, goes for the empty case, and says, "I win." Then the elevated pessimist goes down under his leather leg-holsters and hands a handful of twenty-dollar gold pieces to his albino friend. I don't know how much money it was; it looked as big as an earthquake-relief fund to me.

' "I'll have this here case filled up with the works," says Shorty, "and throw you again for five hundred."

' "I'm your company," says the high man. "I'll meet you at the Smoked Dog Saloon an hour from now."

'The little man hustles away with a kind of Swiss movement toward a jewelry store. The heartbroken person stoops over and takes a telescopic view of my haberdashery.

' "Them's a mighty slick outfit of habiliments you have got on, Mr. Man," says he. "I'll bet a hoss you never acquired the right, title, and interest in and to them clothes in Atascosa City."

' "Why no," says I, being ready enough to exchange personalities with this moneyed monument of melancholy. "I had this suit tailored from a special line of coatericks, vestures, and paintings in St. Louis. Would you mind putting me sane," says I, "on this watch-throwing contest? I've been used to seeing timepieces treated with more politeness and esteem – except women's watches, of course, which by nature they abuse by cracking walnuts with 'em and having 'em taken showing in tintype pictures."

' "Me and George," he explains, "are up from the ranch, having a spell of fun. Up to last month we owned four sections of watered grazing down on the San Miguel. But along comes one of these oil prospectors and begins to bore. He strikes a gusher that flows out twenty thousand – or maybe it was twenty million – barrels of oil a day. And me and George gets one hundred and fifty thousand dollars – seventy-five thousand dollars apiece – for the land. So now and then we saddles up and hits the breeze for Atascosa City for a few days of excitement and damage. Here's a little bunch of the *dinero* that I drawed out of the bank this morning," says he, and shows a roll of twenties and fifties as big around as a sleeping-car pillow. The yellowbacks glowed like a sun set on the gable end of Joh D's barn. My knees got weak, and I sat down on the edge of the board sidewalk.

' "You must have knocked around a right smart," goes on this oil Greaseus.

"I shouldn't be surprised if you have saw towns more livelier than what Atascosa City is. Sometimes it seems to me that there ought to be some more ways of having a good time than there is here, 'specially when you've got plenty of money and don't mind spending it."

'Then this Mother Cary's chick of the desert sits down by me and we hold a conversationfest. It seems that he was money-poor. He'd lived in ranch camps all his life; and he confessed to me that his supreme idea of luxury was to ride into camp, tired out from a roundup, eat a peck of Mexican beans, hobble his brains with a pint of raw whisky, and go to sleep with his boots for a pillow. When this bargeload of unexpected money came to him and his pink but perky partner, George, and they hied themselves to this clump of outhouses called Atascosa City, you know what happened to them. They had money to buy anything they wanted; but they didn't know what to want. Their ideas of spendthriftiness were limited to three – whisky, saddles, and gold watches. If there was anything else in the world to throw away fortunes on, they had never heard about it. So, when they wanted to have a hot time, they'd ride into town and get a city directory and stand in front of the principal saloon and call up the population alphabetically for free drinks. Then they would order three or four new California saddles from the storekeeper, and play crackloo on the sidewalk with twenty-dollar gold pieces. Betting who could throw his gold watch the farthest was an inspiration of George's; but even that was getting to be monotonous.

'Was I on to the opportunity? Listen.

'In thirty minutes I had dashed off a word picture of metropolitan joys that made life in Atascosa City look as dull as a trip to Coney Island with your own wife. In ten minutes more we shook hands on an agreement that I was to act as his guide, interpreter and friend in and to the aforesaid wassail and amenity. And Solomon Mills, which was his name, was to pay all expenses for a month. At the end of that time, if I had made good as director-general of the rowdy life, he was to pay me one thousand dollars. And then, to clinch the bargain, we called the roll of Atascosa City and put all of its citizens except the ladies and minors under the table, except one man named Horace Westervelt St. Claire. Just for that we bought a couple hatfuls of cheap silver watches and egged him out of town with 'em. We wound up by dragging the harness-maker out of bed and setting him to work on three new saddles; and then we went to sleep across the railroad track at the depot, just to annoy the S. A. & A. P. Think of having seventy-five thousand dollars and trying to avoid the disgrace of dying rich in a town like that!

'The next day George, who was married or something, started back to the ranch. Me and Solly, as I now called him, prepared to shake off our moth balls and wing our way against the arc-lights of the joyous and tuneful East.

' "No way-stops," says I to Solly, "except long enough to get you barbered and haberdashed. This is no Texas feet shampetter," says I, "where you eat chili-con-carne-con-huevos and then holler 'Whoopee!' across the plaza. We're now going against the real high life. We're going to mingle with the set that carries a Spitz, wears spats, and hits the ground in high spots."

'Solly puts six thousand dollars in century bills in one pocket of his brown ducks, and bills of lading for ten thousand dollars on Eastern banks in another. Then I resume diplomatic relations with the S. A. & A. P., and we hike in a northwesterly direction on our circuitous route to the spice gardens of the Yankee Orient.

'We stopped in San Antonio long enough for Solly to buy some clothes, and eight rounds of drinks for the guests and employees of the Menger Hotel, and order four Mexican saddles with silver trimmings and white Angora *suaderos* to be shipped down to the ranch. From there we made a big jump to St. Louis. We got there in time for dinner; and I put our thumb-prints on the register of the most expensive hotel in the city.

' "Now," says I to Solly, with a wink at myself, "here's the first dinner-station we've struck where we can get a real good plate of beans." And while he was up in his room trying to draw water out of the gas-pipe, I got one finger in the buttonhole of the head waiter's Tuxedo, drew him apart, inserted a two-dollar bill, and closed him up again.

' "Frankoyse," says I, "I have a pal here for dinner that's been subsisting for years on cereals and short stogies. You see the chef and order a dinner for us such as you serve to Dave Francis and the general passenger agent of the Iron Mountain when they eat here. We've got more than Bernhardt's tent full of money; and we want the nosebags crammed with all the Chief Deveries *de cuisine*. Object is no expense. Now, show us."

'At six o'clock me and Solly sat down to dinner. Spread! There's nothing been seen like it since the Cambon snack. It was all served at once. The chef called it *dinnay à la poker*. It's a famous thing among the gormands of the West. The dinner comes in threes of a kind. There was guinea-fowls, guinea-pigs, and Guinness's stout; roast veal, mock turtle soup, and chicken pâté; shad-roe, caviar, and tapioca; canvas-back duck, canvas-back ham, and cottontail rabbit; Philadelphia capon, fried snails, and sloe-gin – and so on, in threes. The idea was that you eat nearly all you can of them, and then the waiter takes away the discard and gives you pears to fill on.

'I was sure Solly would be tickled to death with these hands, after the bob-tail flushes he'd been eating on the ranch; and I was a little anxious that he should, for I didn't remember his having honored my efforts with a smile since we left Atascosa City.

'We were in the main dining room, and there was a fine-dressed crowd there, all talking loud and enjoyable about the two St. Louis topics, the water supply and the color line. They mix the two subjects so fast that strangers often think they are discussing water-colors; and that has given the old town something of a rep as an art centre. And over in the corner was a fine brass band playing; and now, thinks I, Solly will become conscious of the spiritual oats of life nourishing and exhilarating his system. But *nong, mong frang*.

'He gazed across the table at me. There was four square yards of it, looking like the path of a cyclone that has wandered through a stock-yard, a poultry-farm, a vegetable-garden, and an Irish linen mill. Solly gets up and comes around to me.

' "Luke," says he, "I'm pretty hungry after our ride. I thought you said they had some beans here. I'm going out and get something I can eat. You can stay and monkey with this artificial layout of grub if you want to."

' "Wait a minute," says I.

'I called the waiter, and slapped "S. Mills" on the back of the check for thirteen dollars and fifty cents.

' "What do you mean," says I, "by serving gentlemen with a lot of truck only suitable for deck hands on a Mississippi steamboat? We're going out to get something decent to eat."

'I walked up the street with the unhappy plainsman. He saw a saddle-shop open, and some of the sadness faded from his eyes. We went in, and he ordered and paid for two more saddles – one with a solid silver horn and nails and ornaments and a six-inch border of rhinestones and imitation rubies around the flaps. The other one had to have a gold-mounted horn, quadruple-plated stirrups, and the leather inlaid with silver bead-work wherever it would stand it. Eleven hundred dollars the two cost him.

'Then he goes out and heads toward the river, following his nose. In a little side street, where there was no street and no sidewalks and no houses, he finds what he is looking for. We go into a shanty and sit on high stools among stevedores and boatmen, and eat beans with tin spoons. Yes, sir, beans – beans boiled with salt pork.

' "I kind of thought we'd strike some over this way," says Solly.

' "Delightful," says I. "That stylish hotel grub may appeal to some: but for me, give me the husky *table d'goat*."

'When we had succumbed to the beans I leads him out of the tarpaulin-steam under a lamp post and pulls out a daily paper with the amusement column folded out.

' "But now, what ho for a merry round of pleasure," says I. "Here's one of Hall Caine's shows, and a stock-yard company in 'Hamlet,' and skating at the Hollowhorn Rink, and Sara Bernhardt, and the Shapely Syrens Burlesque Company. I should think, now, that the Shapely – '

'But what does this healthy, wealthy, and wise man do but reach his arms up to the second-story windows and gape noisily.

' "Reckon I'll be going to bed," says he, "it's about my time. St. Louis is a kind of quiet place, ain't it?"

' "Oh, yes," says I; "ever since the railroads ran in here the town's been practically ruined. And the building-and-loan associations and the fair have about killed it. Guess we might as well go to bed. Wait till you see Chicago though. Shall we get tickets for the Big Breeze to-morrow?"

' "Mought as well," says Solly. "I reckon all these towns are about alike."

'Well, maybe the wise cicerone and personal conductor didn't fall hard in Chicago; Loolooville-on-the-Lake is supposed to have one or two things in it calculated to keep the rural visitor awake after the curfew rings. But not for the grass-fed man of the pampas! I tried him with theatres, rides in auto-mobiles, sails on the lake, champagne suppers, and all those little inventions that hold the simple life in check; but in vain. Solly grew sadder day by day. And I got fearful about my salary, and knew I must play my trump card. So I mentioned New York to him, and informed him that these Western towns were no more than gateways to the great walled city of the whirling dervishes.

'After I bought the tickets I missed Solly. I knew his habits by then; so in a couple of hours I found him in a saddle-shop. They had some new ideas there in the way of trees and girths that had strayed down from the Canadian mounted police; and Solly was so interested that he almost looked reconciled to live. He invested about nine hundred dollars in there.

'At the depot I telegraphed a cigar-store man I knew in New York to meet me at the Twenty-third Street ferry with a list of all the saddle-stores in the city. I wanted to know where to look for Solly when he got lost.

'Now I'll tell you what happened in New York. I says to myself: "Friend

Heherezade, you want to get busy and make Bagdad look pretty to the sad sultan of the sour countenance, or it'll be the bow string for yours." But I never had any doubt I could do it.

'I began with him like you'd feed a starving man. I showed him the horse-cars on Broadway and the Staten Island ferry-boats. And then I piled up the sensations on him, but always keeping a lot of warmer ones up my sleeve.

'At the end of the third day he looked like a composite picture of five thousand orphans too late to catch a picnic steamboat, and I was wilting down a collar every two hours wondering how I could please him and whether I was going to get my thou. He went to sleep looking at the Brooklyn Bridge; he disregarded the sky-scrapers above the third story; it took three ushers to wake him up at the liveliest vaudeville in town.

'Once I thought I had him. I nailed a pair of cuffs on him one morning before he was awake; and I dragged him that evening to the palm-cage of one of the biggest hotels in the city – to see the Johnnies and the Alice-sit-by-the-hours. They were out in numerous quantities, with the fat of the land showing in their clothes. While we were looking them over, Solly divested himself of a fearful, rusty kind of laugh – like moving a folding bed with one roller broken. It was his first in two weeks, and it gave me hope.

' "Right you are," says I. "They're a funny lot of post-cards, aren't they?"

' "Oh, I wasn't thinking of them dudes and culls on the hoof," says he. "I was thinking of the time me and George put sheep-dip in Horsehead Johnson's whisky. I wish I was back in Atascosa City," says he.

'I felt a cold chill run down my back. "Me to play and mate in one move," says I to myself.

'I made Solly promise to stay in the café for half an hour and I hiked out in a cab to Lolabelle Delatour's flat on Forty-third Street. I knew her well. She was a chorus-girl in a Broadway musical comedy.

' "Jane," says I when I found her, "I've got a friend from Texas here. He's all right, but – well, he carries weight. I'd like to give him a little whirl after the show this evening – bubbles, you know, and a buzz out to a casino for the whitebait and pickled walnuts. Is it a go?"

' "Can he sing?" asks Lolabelle.

' "You know," says I, "that I wouldn't take him away from home unless his notes were good. He's got pots of money – bean-pots full of it."

' "Bring him around after the second act," says Lolabelle, "and I'll examine his credentials and securities."

'So about ten o'clock that evening I led Solly to Miss Delatour's dressing-room, and her maid let us in. In ten minutes in comes Lolabelle, fresh from the stage, looking stunning in the costume she wears when she steps from the ranks of the lady grenadiers and says to the king, "Welcome to our May-day revels." And you can bet it wasn't the way she spoke the lines that got her the part.

'As soon as Solly saw her he got up and walked straight out through the stage entrance into the street. I followed him. Lolabelle wasn't paying my salary. I wondered whether anybody was.

' "Luke," says Solly, outside, "that was an awful mistake. We must have got into the lady's private room. I hope I'm gentleman enough to do anything possible in the way of apologies. Do you reckon she'd ever forgive us?"

' "She may forget it," says I. "Of course it was a mistake. Let's go find some beans."

'That's the way it went. But pretty soon afterward Solly failed to show up at dinner time for several days. I cornered him. He confessed that he had found a restaurant on Third Avenue where they cooked beans in Texas style. I made him take me there. The minute I set foot inside the door I threw up my hands.

'There was a young woman at the desk, and Solly introduced me to her. And then we sat down and had beans.

'Yes, sir, sitting at the desk was the kind of a young woman that can catch any man in the world as easy as lifting a finger. There's a way of doing it. She knew. I saw her working it. She was healthy-looking and plain dressed. She had her hair drawn back from her forehead and face – no curls or frizzes; that's the way she looked. Now I'll tell you the way they work the games; it's simple. When she wants a man, she manages it so that every time he looks at her he finds her looking at him. That's all.

'The next evening Solly was to go to Coney Island with me at seven. At eight o'clock he hadn't showed up. I went out and found a cab. I felt sure there was something wrong.

' "Drive to the Back Home Restaurant on Third Avenue," says I. "And if I don't find what I want there, take in these saddle-shops." I handed him the list.

' "Boss," says the cabby, "I et a steak in that restaurant once. If you're real hungry, I advise you to try the saddle-shops first."

' "I'm a detective," says I, "and I don't eat. Hurry up!"

'As soon as I got to the restaurant I felt in the lines of my palms that I should beware of a tall, red, damfool man, and I was going to lose a sum of money.

'Solly wasn't there. Neither was the smooth-haired lady.

'I waited; and in an hour they came in a cab and got out, hand in hand. I asked Solly to step around the corner for a few words. He was grinning clear across his face; but I had not administered the grin.

' "She's the greatest that ever sniffed the breeze," says he.

' "Congrats," says I. "I'd like to have my thousand now if you please."

' "Well, Luke," says he, "I don't know that I've had such a skyhoodlin' fine time under your tutelage and dispensation. But I'll do the best I can for you – I'll do the best I can," he repeats. "Me and Miss Skinner was married an hour ago. We're leaving for Texas in the morning."

' "Great!" says I. "Consider yourself covered with rice and Congress gaiters. But don't let's tie so many satin bows on our business relations that we lose sight of 'em. How about my honorarium?"

' "Missis Mills," says he, "has taken possession of my money and papers except six bits. I told her what I'd agreed to give you; but she says it's an irreligious and illegal contract, and she won't pay a cent of it. But I ain't going to see you treated unfair," says he. "I've got eighty-seven saddles on the ranch what I've bought on this trip; and when I get back I'm going to pick out the best six in the lot and send 'em to you." '

'And did he?' I asked, when Lucullus ceased talking.

'He did. And they are fit for kings to ride on. The six he sent me must have cost him three thousand dollars. But where is the market for 'em? Who would buy one except one of these rajahs and princes of Asia and Africa? I've got 'em all on the list. I know ever tan royal dub and princerino from Mindanao to the Caspian Sea.'

'It's a long time between customers,' I ventured.

'They're coming faster,' said Polk. 'Nowadays, when one of the murdering mutts gets civilized enough to abolish suttee and quite using his whiskers for a napkin, he calls himself the Roosevelt of the East, and comes over to investigate our Chautauquas and cocktails. I'll place 'em all yet. Now look here.'

From an inside pocket he drew a tightly folded newspaper with much-worn edges, and indicated a paragraph.

'Read that,' said the saddler to royalty. The paragraph ran thus:

His Highness Seyyid Feysal bin Turkee, Imam of Muskat, is one of the most progressive and enlightened rulers of the Old World. His stables contain more than a thousand horses of the purest Persian breeds. It is said that this powerful prince contemplates a visit to the United States at an early date.

'There!' said Mr. Polk triumphantly. 'My best saddle is as good as sold – the one with turquoises set in the rim of the cantle. Have you three dollars that you could loan me for a short time?'

It happened that I had; and I did.

If this should meet the eye of the Imam of Muskat, may it quicken his whim to visit the land of the free! Otherwise I fear that I shall be longer than a short time separated from my dollars three.

HYGEIA AT THE SOLITO

IF YOU ARE KNOWING IN THE CHRONICLES of the ring you will recall to mind an event in the early 'nineties when, for a minute and sundry odd seconds, a champion and a 'would-be' faced each other on the alien side of an international river. So brief a conflict had rarely imposed upon the fair promise of true sport. The reporters made what they could of it, but, divested of padding, the action was sadly fugacious. The champion merely smote his victim, turned his back upon him, remarking, 'I know what I done to dat stiff,' and extended an arm like a ship's mast for his glove to be removed.

Which accounts for a trainload of extremely disgusted gentlemen in uproar of fancy vests and neckwear being spilled from their Pullman in San Antonio in the early morning following the fight. Which also partly accounts for the unhappy predicament in which 'Cricket' McGuire found himself as he tumbled from his car and sat upon the depot platform, torn by a spasm of that hollow, racking cough so familiar to San Antonian ears. At that time, in the uncertain light of dawn, that way passed Curtis Raidler, the Nueces County cattleman – may his shadow never measure under six feet two.

The cattleman, out this early to catch the south-bound for his ranch station, stopped at the side of the distressed patron of sport and spoke in the kindly drawl of his ilk and region, 'Got it pretty bad, bud?'

'Cricket' McGuire, exfeather-weight prize-fighter, tout, jockey, follower of the 'ponies,' all-around sport, and manipulator of the gum balls and walnut shells, looked up pugnaciously at the imputation cast by 'bud.'

'G'wan,' he rasped, 'telegraph pole. I didn't ring for yer.'

Another paroxysm wrung him, and he leaned limply against a convenient baggage truck. Raidler waited patiently, glancing around at the white hats, short overcoats, and big cigars thronging the platform. 'You're from the No'th ain't you, bud?' he asked when the other was partially recovered. 'Come down to see the fight?'

'Fight!' snapped McGuire. 'Puss-in-the-corner. 'Twas a hypodermic injection. Handed him just one like a squirt of dope, and he's asleep, and no tanbark needed in front of his residence. Fight!' He rattled a bit, coughed, and went on, hardly addressing the cattleman, but rather for the relief of voicing his troubles. 'No more dead sure t'ings for me. But Rus Sage himself would have snatched at it. Five to one dat de boy from Cork wouldn't stay t'ree rounds is what I invested in. Put my last cent on, and could already smell the sawdust in dat all-night joint of Jimmy Delaney's on T'irty-seventh Street I was goin' to buy. And den – say, telegraph pole, what a gazaboo a guy is to put his whole roll on one turn of the gaboozlum!'

'You're plenty right,' said the big cattleman; 'more 'specially when you lose. Son, you get up and light out for a hotel. You got a mighty bad cough. Had it long?'

'Lungs,' said McGuire comprehensively. 'I got it. The croaker says I'll come to time for six months longer – maybe a year if I hold my gait. I wanted to settle down and take care of myself. Dat's why I speculated on dat five to one perhaps. I had a t'ousand iron dollars saved up. If I winned I was goin' to buy Delaney's café. Who'd a t'ought dat stiff would take a nap in de foist round – say?'

'It's a hard deal,' commented Raidler, looking down at the diminutive form of McGuire crumpled against the truck. 'But you go to a hotel and rest. There's the Menger and the Maverick, and—'

'And the Fi'th Av'noo, and the Waldorf-Astoria,' mimicked McGuire. 'Told you I went broke. I'm on de bum proper. I've got one dime left. Maybe a trip to Europe or a sail in me private yacht would fix me up – pa'per!'

He flung his dime at a newsboy, got his *Express*, propped his back against the truck, and was at once rapt in the account of his Waterloo, as expanded by the ingenious press.

Custis Raidler interrogated an enormous gold watch, and laid his hand on McGuire's shoulder.

'Come on, bud,' he said. 'We got three minutes to catch the train.'

Sarcasm seemed to be McGuire's vein.

'You ain't seen me cash in any chips or call a turn since I told you I was broke, a minute ago, have you? Friend, chase yourself away.'

'You're going down to my ranch,' said the cattleman, 'and stay till you get well. Six months'll fix you good as new.' He lifted McGuire with one hand, and half-dragged him in the direction of the train.

'What about the money?' said McGuire, struggling weakly to escape.

'Money for what?' asked Raidler, puzzled. They eyed each other, not understanding, for they touched only as at the gear of bevelled cog-wheels – at right angles, and moving upon different axes.

Passengers on the south-bound saw them seated together, and wondered at the conflux of two such antipodes. McGuire was five feet one, with a countenance belonging to either Yokohama or Dublin. Bright-beady of eye, bony of cheek and jaw, scarred, toughened, broken and reknit, indestructible, grisly, gladiatorial as a hornet, he was a type neither new nor unfamiliar. Raidler was the product of a different soil. Six feet two in height, miles broad, and no deeper than a crystal brook, he represented the union of the West and South. Few accurate pictures of his kind have been made, for art galleries are so small and the mutoscope is as yet unknown in Texas. After all, the only possible medium of portrayal of Raidler's kind would be the fresco – something high and simple and cool and unframed.

They were rolling southward on the International. The timber was huddling into little, dense green motts at rare distances before the inundation of the downright, vert prairies. This was the land of the ranches; the domain of the kings of the kine.

McGuire sat, collapsed into his corner of the seat, receiving with acid suspicion the conversation of the cattleman. What was the 'game' of this big 'geezer' who was carrying him off? Altruism would have been McGuire's last guess. 'He ain't no farmer,' thought the captive, 'and he ain't no con man, for sure. W'at's his lay? You trail in, Cricket, and see how many cards he draws. You're up against it, anyhow. You get a nickel and gallopin' consumption, and you better lay low. Lay low and see w'at's his game.'

At Rincon, a hundred miles from San Antonio, they left the train for a buckboard which was waiting there for Raidler. In this they travelled the thirty miles between the station and their destination. If anything could, this drive should have stirred the acrimonious McGuire to a sense of his ransom. They sped upon velvet wheels across an exhilarant savanna. The pair of Spanish ponies struck a nimble, tireless trot, which gait they occasionally relieved by a wild, untrammelled gallop. The air was wine and seltzer, perfumed, as they absorbed it, with the delicate redolence of prairie flowers. The road perished, and the buckboard swam the uncharted billows of the grass itself, steered by the practised hand of Raidler, to whom each tiny distant mott of trees was a signboard, each convolution of the low hills a voucher of course and distance. But McGuire reclined upon his spine, seeing nothing but a desert, and receiving the cattleman's advances with sullen distrust. 'W'at's he up to?' was the burden of his thoughts; 'w'at kind of a gold brick has the big guy got to sell?' McGuire was only applying the measure of the streets he had walked to a range bounded by the horizon and the fourth dimension.

A week before, while riding the prairies, Raidler had come upon a sick and weakling calf deserted and bawling. Without dismounting he had reached and slung the distressed bossy across his saddle, and dropped it at the ranch for the boys to attend to. It was impossible for McGuire to know or comprehend that, in the eyes of the cattleman, his case and that of the calf were identical in interest and demand upon his assistance. A creature was ill and helpless; he had the power to render aid – these were the only postulates required for the cattleman to act. They formed his system of logic and the most of his creed. McGuire was the seventh invalid whom Raidler had picked up thus casually in San Antonio, where so many thousand go for the ozone that is said to linger about its contracted streets. Five of them had been guests of Solito Ranch until they had been able to leave, cured or better, and exhausting the vocabulary of tearful gratitude. One came too late, but rested very comfortably, at last, under a ratama tree in the garden.

So, then, it was no surprise to the ranchhold when the buckboard spun to the door, and Raidler took up his debile *protégé* like a handful of rags and set him down upon the gallery.

McGuire looked upon things strange to him. The ranch-house was the best in the country. It was built of brick hauled one hundred miles by wagon, but it was of but one story, and its four rooms were completely encircled by a mud floor 'gallery.' The miscellaneous setting of horses, dogs, saddles, wagons, guns, and cow-punchers' paraphernalia oppressed the metropolitan eye of the wrecked sportsman.

'Well, here we are at home,' said Raidler, cheeringly.

'It's a h – l of a looking place,' said McGuire promptly, as he rolled upon the gallery floor, in a fit of coughing.

'We'll try to make it comfortable for you, buddy,' said the cattleman, gently. 'It ain't fine inside; but it's the outdoors, anyway, that'll do you the most good. This'll be your room, in here. Anything we got, you ask for it.'

He led McGuire into the east room. The floor was bare and clean. White curtains waved in the gulf breeze through the open windows. A big willow rocker, two straight chairs, a long table covered with newspapers, pipes, tobacco, spurs, and cartridges stood in the centre. Some well-mounted heads of deer and one of an enormous black javeli projected from the walls. A wide, cool cot-bed stood in a corner. Nueces County people regarded this guest chamber as fit for a prince. McGuire showed his eye teeth at it. He took out his nickel and spun it up to the ceiling.

'T'ought I was lyin' about the money, did ye? Well, you can frisk me if you wanter. Dat's the last simoleon in the treasury. Who's goin' to pay?'

The cattleman's clear gray eyes looked steadily from under his grizzly brows into the huckleberry optics of his guest. After a little he said simply, and not ungraciously, 'I'll be much obliged to you, son, if you won't mention money any more. Once was quite a plenty. Folks I ask to my ranch don't have to pay anything, and they very scarcely ever offers it. Supper'll be ready in half an hour. There's water in the pitcher, and some, cooler, to drink in that red jar hanging on the gallery.'

'Where's the bell?' asked McGuire, looking about.

'Bell for what?'

'Bell to ring for things. I can't – see here,' he exploded in a sudden weak fury, 'I never asked you to bring me here. I never held you up for a cent. I never gave you a hard-luck story till you asked me. Here I am fifty mile from a bellboy or a cocktail. I'm sick. I can't hustle. Gee! but I'm up against it!' McGuire fell upon the cot and sobbed shiveringly.

Raidler went to the door and called. A slender, bright-complexioned Mexican youth about twenty came quickly. Raidler spoke to him in Spanish.

'Ylario, it is in my mind that I promised you the position of *vaquero* on the San Carlos range at the fall *rodeo.*'

'*Sí señor*, such was your goodness.'

'Listen. This *señorito* is my friend. He is very sick. Place yourself at his side. Attend to his wants at all times. Have much patience and care with him. And when he is well, or – and when he is well, instead of *vaquero* I will make you *mayordomo* of the Rancho de las Piedras. *Está bueno?*'

'*Sí, sí – mil gracias, señor.*' Ylario tried to kneel upon the floor in his gratitude, but the cattleman kicked at him benevolently, growling, 'None of your opery-house antics, now.'

Ten minutes later Ylario came from McGuire's room and stood before Raidler.

'The little *señor*,' he announced, 'presents his compliments' (Raidler credited Ylario with the preliminary) 'and desires some pounded ice, one hot bath, one gin feez-z, that the windows be all closed, toast, one shave, one Newyorkheral', cigarettes, and to send one telegram.'

Raidler took a quart bottle of whisky from his medicine cabinet. 'Here, take him this,' he said.

Thus was instituted the reign of terror at the Solito Ranch. For a few weeks McGuire blustered and boasted and swaggered before the cow-punchers who rode in for miles around to see this latest importation of Raidler's. He was an absolutely new experience to them. He explained to them all the intricate points of sparring and the tricks of training and defence. He opened to their minds' view all the indecorous life of a tagger after professional sports. His jargon of slang was a continuous joy and surprise to them. His gestures, his strange poses, his frank ribaldry of tongue and principle fascinated them. He was like a being from a new world.

Strange to say, this new world he had entered did not exist to him. He was an utter egoist of bricks and mortar. He had dropped out, he felt, in open space for a time, and all it contained was an audience for his reminiscences. Neither the limitless freedom of the prairie days nor the grand hush of the close-drawn, spangled nights touched him. All the hues of Aurora could not win him from the pink pages of a sporting journal. 'Get something for nothing,' was his mission in life; 'T'irty-seventh' Street was his goal.

Nearly two months after his arrival he began to complain that he felt worse. It was then that he became the ranch's incubus, its harpy, its Old Man of the Sea. He shut himself in his room like some venomous kobold or flibbertigibbet, whining, complaining, cursing, accusing. The keynote of his plaint was that he had been inveigled into a gehenna against his will; that he was dying of neglect and lack of comforts. With all his dire protestations of increasing illness, to the eye of others he remained unchanged. His currant-like eyes were as bright and diabolic as ever; his voice was as rasping; his callous face, with the skin drawn tense as a drum-head, had no flesh to lose. A flush on his prominent cheek bones each afternoon hinted that a clinical thermometer might have revealed a symptom, and percussion might have established the fact that McGuire was breathing with only one lung, but his appearance remained the same.

In constant attendance upon him was Ylario, whom the coming reward of the *mayordomoship* must have greatly stimulated, for McGuire chained him to a bitter existence. The air – the man's only chance for life – he commanded to be kept out by closed windows and drawn curtains. The room was always blue and foul with cigarette smoke; whosoever entered it must sit, suffocating, and listen to the imp's interminable gasconade concerning his scandalous career.

The oddest thing of all was the relation existing between McGuire and his benefactor. The attitude of the invalid toward the cattleman was something like that of a peevish, perverse child toward an indulgent parent. When Raidler would leave the ranch McGuire would fall into a fit of malevolent, silent sullenness. When he returned, he would be met by a string of violent and stinging reproaches. Raidler's attitude toward his charge was quite inexplicable in its way. The cattleman seemed actually to assume and feel the character assigned him by McGuire's intemperate accusations – the character of tyrant and guilty oppressor. He seemed to have adopted the responsibility of the fellow's condition, and he always met his tirades with a pacific, patient, and even remorseful kindness that never altered.

One day Raidler said to him,' 'Try more air, son. You can have the buckboard and a driver every day if you'll go. Try a week or two in one of the cow camps. I'll fix you up plum comfortable. The ground, and the air next to it – them's the things to cure you. I knowed a man from Philadelphy, sicker than you are, got lost on the Guadalupe, and slept on the bare grass in sheep camps for two weeks. Well, sir, it started him getting well, which he done. Close to the ground – that's where the medicine in the air stays. Try a little hossback riding now. There's a gentle pony –'

'What've I done to yer?' screamed McGuire. 'Did I ever double-cross yer? Did I ask you to bring me here? Drive me out to your camps if you wanter; or stick a knife in me and save trouble. Ride! I can't lift my feet. I couldn't sidestep a jar from a five-year-old kid. That's what your d – d ranch has done for me. There's nothing to eat, nothing to see, and nobody to talk to but a lot of Reubens who don't know a punching bag from lobster salad.'

'It's a lonesome place, for certain,' apologized Raidler abashedly. 'We got plenty, but it's rough enough. Anything you think of you want, the boys'll ride up and fetch it down for you.'

It was Chad Murchison, a cow-puncher from the Circle Bar outfit, who first suggested that McGuire's illness was fraudulent. Chad had brought a basket of grapes for him thirty miles, and four out of his way, tied to his saddle-horn. After remaining in the smoke-tainted room for a while, he emerged and bluntly confided his suspicions to Raidler.

'His arm,' said Chad, 'is harder'n a diamond. He interduced me to what he called a shore-perplexus punch, and 'twas like being kicked twice by a mustang. He's playin' it low down on you, Curt. He ain't no sicker'n I am. I hate to say it, but the runt's workin' you for range and shelter.'

The cattleman's ingenuous mind refused to entertain Chad's view of the case, and when, later, he came to apply the test, doubt entered not into his motives.

One day, about noon, two men drove up to the ranch, alighted, hitched, and came in to dinner; standing and general invitations being the custom of the country. One of them was a great San Antonio doctor, whose costly services had been engaged by a wealthy cowman who had been laid low by an accidental bullet. He was now being driven to the station to take the train back to town. After dinner Raidler took him aside, pushed a twenty-dollar bill against his hand, and said:

'Doc, there's a young chap in that room I guess has got a bad case of consumption. I'd like for you to look him over and see just how bad he is, and if we can do anything for him.'

'How much was that dinner I just ate, Mr. Raidler?' said the doctor bluffly, looking over his spectacles. Raidler returned the money to his pocket. The doctor immediately entered McGuire's room, and the cattleman seated himself upon a heap of saddles on the gallery, ready to reproach himself in the event the verdict should be unfavorable.

In ten minutes the doctor came briskly out. 'Your man,' he said promptly, 'is as sound as a new dollar. His lungs are better than mine. Respiration, temperature, and pulse normal. Chest expansion four inches. Not a sign of weakness anywhere. Of course I didn't examine for the bacillus, but it isn't there. You can put my name to the diagnosis. Even cigarettes and a vilely close room haven't hurt him. Coughs, does he? Well, you tell him it isn't necessary. You asked if there is anything we could do for him. Well, I advise you to set him digging post-holes or breaking mustangs. There's our team ready. Good-day, sir.' And like a puff of wholesome, blustery wind the doctor was off.

Raidler reached out and plucked a leaf from a mesquite bush by the railing, and began chewing it thoughtfully.

The branding season was at hand, and the next morning Ross Hargis, foreman of the outfit, was mustering his force of some twenty-five men at the ranch, ready to start for the San Carlos range, where the work was to begin. By six o'clock the horses were all saddled, the grub wagon ready, and the cow-punchers were swinging themselves upon their mounts, when Raidler bade them wait. A boy was bringing up an extra pony, bridled and saddled, to the gate. Raidler walked to McGuire's room and threw open the door. McGuire was lying on his cot, not yet dressed, smoking.

'Get up,' said the cattleman, and his voice was clear and brassy, like a bugle.

'How's that?' asked McGuire, a little startled.

'Get up and dress. I can stand a rattlesnake, but I hate a liar. Do I have to tell you again?' He caught McGuire by the neck and stood him on the floor.

'Say, friend,' cried McGuire wildly, 'are you bug-house? I'm sick – see? I'll croak if I got to hustle. What've I done to yer?' he began his chronic whine – 'I never asked yer to—'

'Put on your clothes,' called Raidler, in a rising tone.

Swearing, stumbling, shivering, keeping his amazed, shiny eyes upon the now menacing form of the aroused cattleman, McGuire managed to tumble into his clothes. Then Raidler took him by the collar and shoved him out and across the yard to the extra pony hitched at the gate. The cow-punchers lolled in their saddles, open-mouthed.

'Take this man,' said Raidler to Ross Hargis, 'and put him to work. Make him work hard, sleep hard, and eat hard. You boys know I done what I could for him, and he was welcome. Yesterday the best doctor in San Antone examined him, and says he's got the lungs of a burro and the constitution of a steer. You know what to do with him, Ross.'

Ross Hargis only smiled grimly.

'Aw,' said McGuire, looking intently at Raidler, with a peculiar expression upon his face, 'the croaker said I was all right, did he? Said I was fakin', did he? You put him onto me. You t'ought I wasn't sick. You said I was a liar. Say, friend, I talked rough, I know, but I didn't mean most of it. If you felt like I did – aw! I forgot – I ain't sick, the croaker says. Well, friend, now I'll go work for yer. Here's where you play even.'

He sprang into the saddle easily as a bird, got the quirt from the horn, and gave his pony a slash with it. 'Cricket,' who once brought in Good Boy by a neck at Hawthorne – and a 10 to 1 shot – had his foot in the stirrups again.

McGuire led the cavalcade as they dashed away from San Carlos, and the cow-punchers gave a yell of applause as they closed in behind his dust.

But in less than a mile he had lagged to the rear, and was last man when they struck the patch of high chaparral below the horse pens. Behind a clump of this he drew rein, and held a handkerchief to his mouth. He took it away drenched with bright, arterial blood, and threw it carefully into a clump of prickly pear. Then he slashed with his quirt again, gasped 'G'wan' to his astonished pony, and galloped after the gang.

That night Raidler received a message from his old home in Alabama. There had been a death in the family; an estate was to divide, and they called for him to come. Daylight found him in the buckboard, skimming the prairies for the station. It was two months before he returned. When he arrived at the ranch-house he found it well-nigh deserted save for Ylario, who acted as a kind of steward during his absence. Little by little the youth made him acquainted with the work done while he was away. The branding camp, he was informed, was still doing business. On account of many severe storms the cattle had been badly scattered, and the branding had been accomplished but slowly. The camp was now in the valley of the Guadalupe, twenty miles away.

'By the way,' said Raidler, suddenly remembering, 'that fellow I sent along with them – McGuire – is he working yet?'

'I do not know,' said Ylario. 'Man's from the camp come verree few times to the ranch. So plentee work with the leetle calves. They no say. Oh, I think that fellow McGuire he dead much time ago.'

'Dead!' said Raidler. 'What you talking about?'

'Verree sick fellow, McGuire,' replied Ylario, with a shrug of his shoulder. 'I theenk he no live one, two month when he go away.'

'Shucks!' said Raidler. 'He humbugged you too, did he? The doctor examined him and said he was sound as a mesquite knot.'

'That doctor,' said Ylario, smiling, 'he tell you so? That doctor no see McGuire.'

'Talk up,' ordered Raidler. 'What the devil do you mean?'

'McGuire,' continued the boy tranquilly, 'he getting drink water outside when that doctor come in room. That doctor take me and pound me all over here with his fingers' – putting his hand to his chest – 'I not know for what. He put his ear here and here and here, and listen – I not know for what. He put his little glass stick in my mouth. He feel my arm here. He make me count like whisper – so – twenty, *treinta, cuarenta*. Who knows,' concluded Ylario, with a deprecating spread of his hands, 'for what that doctor do those verree droll and such-like things?'

'What horses are up?' asked Raidler, shortly.

'Paisano is grazing out behind the little corral, *señor*.'

'Saddle him for me at once.'

Within a very few minutes the cattleman was mounted and away. Paisano, well named after that ungainly but swift-running bird, struck into his long lope that ate up the road like a strip of macaroni. In two hours and a quarter Raidler, from a gentle swell, saw the branding camp by a water hole in the Guadalupe. Sick with expectancy of the news he feared, he rode up, dismounted, and dropped Paisano's reins. So gentle was his heart that at that moment he would have pleaded guilty to the murder of McGuire.

The only being in the camp was the cook, who was just arranging the hunks of barbecued beef, and distributing the tin coffee cups for supper. Raidler evaded a direct question concerning the one subject in his mind.

'Everything all right in camp, Pete?' he managed to inquire.

'So, so,' said Pete, conservatively. 'Grub give out twice. Wind scattered the cattle, and we've had to rake the brush for forty mile. I need a new coffee-pot. And the mosquitoes is some more hellish than common.'

'The boys – all well?'

Pete was no optimist. Besides, inquiries concerning the health of cow-punchers were not only superfluous, but bordered on flaccidity. It was not like the boss to make them.

'What's left of 'em don't miss no calls to grub,' the cook conceded.

'What's left of 'em?' repeated Raidler in a husky voice. Mechanically he began to look around for McGuire's grave. He had in his mind a white slab such as he had seen in the Alabama church-yard. But immediately he knew that was foolish.

'Sure,' said Pete; 'what's left. Cow camps change in two months. Some's gone.'

Raidler nerved himself.

'That – chap – I sent along – McGuire – did – he —'

'Say,' interrupted Pete, rising with a chunk of corn bread in each hand, that was a dirty shame, sending that poor, sick kid to a cow camp. A doctor that couldn't tell he was graveyard meat ought to be skinned with a cinch buckle. Game as he was, too – it's a scandal among snakes – lemme tell you what he done. First night in camp the boys started to initiate him in the leather breeches degree. Ross Hargis busted him one swipe with his chapar-reras, and what do you reckon the poor child did? Got up, the little skeeter, and licked Ross. Licked Ross Hargis. Licked him good. Hit him plenty and everywhere and hard. Ross'd just get up and pick out a fresh place to lay down on agin.

'Then that McGuire goes off there and lays down with his head in the grass and bleeds. A hem'ridge they calls it. He lays there eighteen hours by the watch, and they can't budge him. Then Ross Hargis, who loves any man who can lick him, goes to work and damns the doctors from Greenland to Poland Chiny; and him and Green Branch Johnson they gets McGuire in a tent, and spells each other feedin' him chopped raw meat and whisky.

'But it looks like the kid ain't got no appetite to git well, for they misses him from the tent in the night and finds him rootin' in the grass, and likewise a drizzle fallin'. "Gwan," he says, "lemme go and die like I wanter. He said I was a liar and a fake and I was playin' sick. Lemme alone."

'Two weeks,' went on the cook, 'he laid around, not noticin' nobody, and then —'

A sudden thunder filled the air, and a score of galloping centaurs crashed through the brush into camp.

'Illustrious rattlesnakes!' exclaimed Pete, springing all ways at once: 'here's the boys come, and I'm an assassinated man if supper ain't ready in three minutes.'

But Raidler saw only one thing. A little brown-faced, grinning chap, springing from his saddle in the full light of the fire. McGuire was not like that, and yet —

In another instant the cattleman was holding him by the hand and shoulder.

'Son, son, how goes it?' was all he found to say.

'Close to the ground, says you,' shouted McGuire, crunching Raidler's fingers in a grip of steel; 'and dat's where I found it – healt' and strengt', and tumbled to what a cheap skate I been actin'. T'anks fer kickin' me out, old man. And – say! de joke's on dat croaker, ain't it? I looked t'rough the window and see him playin' tag on dat Dago kid's solar plexus.'

'You son of a tinker,' growled the cattleman, 'whyn't you talk up and say the doctor never examined you?'

'Aw – g'wan!' said McGuire, with a flash of his old asperity, 'no-body can't bluff me. You never ast me. You made your spiel, and you t'rowed me out, and I let it go at dat. And, say, friend, dis chasin' cows is outer sight. Dis is de whitest bunch of sports I ever travelled with. You'll let me stay, won't yer, old man?'

Raidler looked wonderingly toward Ross Hargis.

'That cussed little runt,' remarked Ross tenderly, 'is the Jo-dartin'est hustler – and the hardest hitter in anybody's cow camp.'

AN AFTERNOON MIRACLE

AT THE UNITED STATES END of an international river bridge, four armed rangers sweltered in a little 'dobe hut, keeping a fairly faithful espionage upon the lagging trail of passengers from the Mexican side.

Bud Dawson, proprietor of the Top Notch Saloon, had, on the evening previous, violently ejected from his premises one Leandro Garcia, for alleged violation of the Top Notch code of behavior. Garcia had mentioned twenty-four hours as a limit, by which time he would call and collect plentiful indemnity for personal satisfaction.

This Mexican, although a tremendous braggart, was thoroughly courageous, and each side of the river respected him for one of these attributes. He and a following of similar bravos were addicted to the pastime of retrieving towns from stagnation.

The day designated by Garcia for retribution was to be further signalized on the American side by a cattlemen's convention, a bull fight, and an old settlers' barbecue and picnic. Knowing the avenger to be a man of his word, and believing it prudent to court peace while three such gently social relaxations were in progress, Captain McNulty, of the ranger company stationed there, detailed his lieutenant and three men for duty at the end of the bridge. Their instructions were to prevent the invasion of Garcia, either alone or attended by his gang.

Travel was slight that sultry afternoon, and rangers swore gently, and mopped their brows in their convenient but close quarters. For an hour no one had crossed save an old woman enveloped in a brown wrapper and a black mantilla, driving before her a burro loaded with kindling wood tied in small bundles for peddling. Then three shots were fired down the street, the sound coming clear and snappy through the still air.

The four rangers quickened from sprawling, symbolic figures of indolence to alert life, but only one rose to his feet. Three turned their eyes beseechingly but hopelessly upon the fourth, who had gotten nimbly up and was buckling his cartridge-belt around him. The three knew that Lieutenant Bob Buckley, in command, would allow no man of them the privilege of investigating a row when he himself might go.

The agile, broad-chested lieutenant, without a change of expression in his smooth, yellow-brown, melancholy face, shot the belt strap through the guard of the buckle, hefted his sixes in their holsters as a belle gives the finishing touches to her toilette, caught up his Winchester, and dived for the door. There he paused long enough to caution his comrades to maintain their watch upon the bridge, and then plunged into the broiling highway.

The three relapsed into resigned inertia and plaintive comment.

'I've heard of fellows,' grumbled Broncho Leathers, 'what was wedded to danger, but if Bob Buckley ain't committed bigamy with trouble, I'm a son of a gun.'

'Peculiarness of Bob is,' inserted the Nueces Kid, 'he ain't had proper trainin'. He never learned how to git skeered. Now, a man ought to be skeered enough when he tackles a fuss to hanker after readin' his name on the list of survivors, anyway.'

'Buckley,' commented Ranger No. 3, who was a misguided Eastern man, burdened with an education, 'scraps in such a solemn manner that I have been led to doubt its spontaneity. I'm not quite onto his system, but he fights, like Tybalt, by the book of arithmetic.'

'I never heard,' mentioned Broncho, 'about any of Dibble's ways of mixin' scrappin' and cipherin'.'

'Triggernometry?' suggested the Nueces infant.

'That's rather better than I hoped from you,' nodded the Easterner, approvingly. 'The other meaning is that Buckley never goes into a fight without giving away weight. He seems to dread taking the slightest advantage. That's quite close to foolhardiness when you are dealing with horse-thieves and fence-cutters who would ambush you any night, and shoot you in the back if they could. Buckley's too full of sand. He'll play Horatius, and hold the bridge once too often some day.'

'I'm on there,' drawled the Kid; 'I mind that bridge gang in the reader. Me, I go instructed for the other chap – Spurious Somebody – the one that fought and pulled his freight, to fight 'em on some other date.'

'Anyway,' summed up Broncho, 'Bob's about the gamest man I ever see along the Rio Bravo. Great Sam Houston! If she gets any hotter she'll sizzle!' Broncho whacked at a scorpion with his four-pound Stetson felt, and the three watchers relapsed into comfortless silence.

How well Bob Buckley had kept his secret, since these men, for two years his side comrades in countless border raids and dangers, thus spake of him, not knowing that he was the most arrant physical coward in all that Rio Bravo country! Neither his friends nor his enemies had suspected him of aught else than the finest courage. It was purely a physical cowardice, and only by an extreme, grim effort of will had he forced his craven body to do the bravest deeds. Scourging himself always, as a monk whips his besetting sin, Buckley threw himself with apparent recklessness into every danger, with the hope of some day ridding himself of the despised affliction. But each successive test brought no relief, and the ranger's face by nature adapted to cheerfulness and good humor, became set to the guise of gloomy melancholy. Thus, while the frontier admired his deeds, and his prowess was celebrated in print and by word of mouth in many campfires in the valley of the Bravo, his heart was sick within him. Only himself knew of the horrible tightening of the chest, the dry mouth, the weakening of the spine, the agony of the strung nerves – the never-failing symptoms of his shameful malady.

One mere boy in his company was wont to enter a fray with a leg perched flippantly about the horn of his saddle, a cigarette hanging from his lips, which emitted smoke and original slogans of clever invention. Buckley would have given a year's pay to attain that devil-may-care method. Once the debonair youth said to him: 'Buck, you go into a scrap like it was a funeral. Not,' he added, with a complimentary wave of his tin cup, 'but what it generally is.'

Buckley's conscience was of the New England order with Western adjustments, and he continued to get his rebellious body into as many difficulties as possible; wherefore, on that sultry afternoon he chose to drive his own protesting limbs to investigation of that sudden alarm that had startled the peace and dignity of the State.

Two squares down the street stood the Top Notch Saloon. Here Buckley came upon signs of recent upheaval. A few curious spectators pressed about its front entrance, grinding beneath their heels the fragments of a plate-glass window. Inside, Buckley found Bud Dawson utterly ignoring a bullet wound in his shoulder, while he feelingly wept at having to explain why he failed to drop the 'blamed masquerooter,' who shot him. At the entrance of the ranger Bud turned appealingly to him for confirmation of the devastation he might have dealt.

'You know, Buck, I'd 'a' plum got him, first rattle, if I'd thought a minute. Come in a masquerootin', playin' female till he got the drop, and turned loose. I never reached for a gun, thinkin' it was sure Chihuahua Betty, or Mrs. Atwater, or anyhow one of the Mayfield girls comin' a-gunnin', which they might, liable as not. I never thought of that blamed Garcia until—'

'Garcia!' snapped Buckley. 'How did he get over here?'

Bud's bartender took the ranger by the arm and led him to the side door. There stood a patient gray burro cropping the grass along the gutter, with a load of kindling wood tied across its back. On the ground lay a black shawl and a voluminous brown dress.

'Masquerootin' in them things,' called Bud, still resisting attempted ministrations to his wounds. 'Thought he was a lady till he give a yell and winged me.'

'He went down this side street, ' said the bartender. 'He was alone, and he'll hide out till night when his gang comes over. You ought to find him in that Mexican lay-out below the depot. He's got a girl down there – Pancha Sales.'

'How was he armed?' asked Buckley.

'Two pearl-handled sixes, and a knife.'

'Keep this for me, Billy,' said the ranger, handing over his Winchester. Quixotic, perhaps, but it was Bob Buckley's way. Another man – and a braver one – might have raised a posse to accompany him. It was Buckley's rule to discard all preliminary advantage.

The Mexican had left behind him a wake of closed doors and an empty street, but now people were beginning to emerge from their places of refuge with assumed unconsciousness of anything having happened. Many citizens who knew the ranger pointed out to him with alacrity the course of Garcia's retreat.

As Buckley swung along upon the trail he felt the beginning of the suffocating constriction about his throat, the cold sweat under the brim of his hat, the old, shameful, dreaded sinking of his heart as it went down, down, down in his bosom.

The morning train of the Mexican Central had that day been three hours late, thus failing to connect with the I. & G. N. on the other side of the river. Passengers for *Los Estados Unidos* grumblingly sought entertainment in the little swaggering mongrel town of two nations, for until the morrow, no other train would come to rescue them. Grumblingly, because two days later would begin the great fair and races in San Antone. Consider that at that time San Antone was the hub of the wheel of Fortune, and the names of its spokes were Cattle, Wool, Faro, Running Horses, and Ozone. In those times cattlemen played at crack-loo on the side-walks with double-eagles, and gentlemen backed their conception of the fortuitous card with stacks limited in height only by the interference of gravity. Wherefore, thither journeyed the sowers and the reapers – they who stampeded the dollars, and they who rounded them up. Especially did the caterers to the amusement of the people haste to San Antone. Two greatest shows on earth were already there, and dozens of smallest ones were on the way.

On a side track near the mean little 'dobe depot stood a private car, left there by the Mexican train that morning and doomed by an ineffectual schedule to ignobly await, amid squalid surroundings, connection with the next day's regular.

The car had been once a common day-coach, but those who had sat in it and cringed to the conductor's hatbands slips would never have recognized it in its transformation. Paint and gilding and certain domestic touches had liberated it from any suspicion of public servitude. The whitest of lace curtains judiciously screened its windows. From its fore end dropped in the torrid air the flag of Mexico. From its rear projected the Stars and Stripes and a busy stovepipe, the latter reinforcing in its suggestion of culinary comforts the general suggestion of privacy and ease. The beholder's eye, regarding its gorgeous sides, found interest to culminate in a single name in gold and blue letters extending almost its entire length – a single name, the audacious privilege of royalty and genius. Doubly, then, was this arrogant nomenclature here justified; for the name was that of 'Alvarita, Queen of the Serpent Tribe.' This, her car, was back from a triumphant tour of the principal Mexican cities, and now headed for San Antonio, where, according to promissory advertisement, she would exhibit her 'Marvellous Dominion and Fearless Control over Deadly and Venomous Serpents, Handling them with Ease as they Coil and Hiss to the Terror of Thousands of Tongue-tied Tremblers!'

One hundred in the shade kept the vicinity somewhat depeopled. This quarter of the town was a ragged edge; its denizens the bubbling froth of five nations; its architecture tent, *jacal*, and 'dobe; its distractions the hurdy-gurdy and the informal contribution to the sudden stranger's store of experience. Beyond this dishonorable fringe upon the old town's jowl rose a dense mass of trees, surmounting and filling a little hollow. Through this bickered a small stream that perished down the sheer and disconcerting side of the great cañon of the Rio Bravo del Norte.

In this sordid spot was condemned to remain for certain hours the impotent transport of the Queen of the Serpent Tribe.

The front door of the car was open. Its forward end was curtained off into a small reception room. Here the admiring and propitiatory reporters were wont to sit and transpose the music of Señorita Alvarita's talk into the more florid key of the press. A picture of Abraham Lincoln hung against a wall;

one of a cluster of school-girls grouped upon stone steps was in another place; a third was Easter lilies in a blood-red frame. A neat carpet was under foot. A pitcher, sweating cold drops, and a glass stood upon a fragile stand. In a willow rocker, reading a newspaper, sat Alvarita.

Spanish, you would say, Andalusian, or, better still, Basque; that compound, like a diamond, of darkness and fire. Hair, the shade of purple grapes viewed at midnight. Eyes, long, dusky, and disquieting with their untroubled directness of gaze. Face, haughty and bold, touched with a pretty insolence that gave it life. To hasten conviction of her charm, but glance at the stacks of handbills in the corner, green, and yellow, and white. Upon them you see an incompetent presentment of the señorita in her professional garb and pose. Irresistible, in black lace and yellow ribbons, she faces you; a blue racer is spiralled upon each bare arm; coiled twice about her waist and once about her neck, his horrid head close to hers; you perceive Kuku, the great eleven-foot Asian python.

A hand drew aside the curtain that partitioned the car, and a middle-aged faded woman holding a knife and a half-peeled potato looked in and said:

'Alviry, are you right busy?'

'I'm reading the home paper, ma. What do you think! that pale, tow-headed Matilda Price got the most votes in the *News* for the prettiest girl in Gallipo – *lees*.'

'Shuh! She wouldn't of done it if *you'd* been home, Alviry. Lord knows, I hope we'll be there before fall's over. I'm tired gallopin' round the world playin' we are dagoes, and givin' snake shows. But that ain't what I wanted to say. That there biggest snake's gone again. I've looked all over the car and can't find him. He must have been gone an hour. I remember hearin' somethin' rustlin' along the floor, but I thought it was you.'

'Oh, blame that old rascal!' exclaimed the Queen, throwing down her paper. 'This is the third time he's got away. George never *will* fasten down the lid to his box properly. I do believe he's *afraid* of Kuku. Now I've got to go hunt him.'

'Better hurry; somebody might hurt him.'

The Queen's teeth showed in a gleaming, contemptuous smile. 'No danger. When they see Kuku outside they simply scoot away and buy bromides. There's a crick over between here and the river. That old scamp'd swap his skin any time for a drink of running water. I guess I'll find him there, all right.'

A few minutes later Alvarita stepped upon the forward platform, ready for her quest. Her handsome black skirt was shaped to the most recent proclamation of fashion. Her spotless shirt-waist gladdened the eye in that desert of sunshine, a swelling oasis, cool and fresh. A man's split-straw hat sat firmly upon her coiled abundant hair. Beneath her serene, round, impudent chin a man's four-in-hand tie was jauntily knotted about a man's high, stiff collar. A parasol she carried, of white silk, and its fringe was lace, yellowly genuine.

I will grant Gallipolis as to her costume, but firmly to Seville or Valladolid I am held by her eyes; castanets, balconies, mantillas, serenades, ambuscades, escapades – all these their dark depths guaranteed.

'Ain't you afraid to go out alone, Alviry?' queried the Queen-mother anxiously. 'There's so many rough people about. Mebbe you'd better—'

'I never saw anything I was afraid of yet, ma. 'Specially people. And men in particular. Don't you fret. I'll trot along back as soon as I find that runaway scamp.'

The dust lay thick upon the bare ground near the tracks. Alvarita's eye soon discovered the serrated trail of the escaped python. It led across the depot grounds and away down a smaller street in the direction of the little cañon, as predicted by her. A stillness and lack of excitement in the neighborhood encouraged the hope that, as yet, the inhabitants were unaware that so formidable a guest traversed their highways. The heat had driven them indoors, whence outdrifted occasional shrill laughs, or the depressing whine of a maltreated concertina. In the shade a few Mexican children, like vivified stolid idols in clay, stared from their play, vision-struck and silent, as Alvarita came and went. Here and there a woman peeped from a door and stood dumb, reduced to silence by the aspect of the white silk parasol.

A hundred yards and the limits of the town were passed, scattered chaparral succeeding, and then a noble grove, overflowing the bijou cañon. Through this a small bright stream meandered. Park-like it was, with a kind of cockney ruralness further indorsed by the waste papers and rifled tins of picnickers. Up this stream, and down it, among its pseudo-sylvan glades and depressions, wandered the bright and unruffled Alvarita. Once she saw evidence of the recreant reptile's progress in his distinctive trail across a spread of fine sand in the arroyo. The living water was bound to lure him; he could not be far away.

So sure was she of his immediate proximity that she perched herself to idle for a time in the curve of a great creeper that looped down from a giant water-elm. To reach this she climbed from the pathway a little distance up the side of a steep and rugged incline. Around her chaparral grew thick and high. A late-blooming ratama tree dispensed from its yellow petals a sweet and persistent odor. Adown the ravine rustled a sedative wind, melancholy with the taste of sodden, fallen leaves.

Alvarita removed her hat, and undoing the oppressive convolutions of her hair, began to slowly arrange it in two long, dusky plaits.

From the obscure depths of a thick clump of evergreen shrubs five feet away, two small jewel-bright eyes were steadfastly regarding her. Coiled there lay Kuku, the great python; Kuku, the magnificent, he of the plated muzzle, the grooved lips, the eleven-foot stretch of elegantly and brilliantly mottled skin. The great python was viewing his mistress without a sound or motion to disclose his presence. Perhaps the splendid truant forfeit his capture, but, screened by the foliage, thought to prolong the delight of his escapade. What pleasure it was, after the hot and dusty car, to lie thus, smelling the running water, and feeling the agreeable roughness of the earth and stones against his body! Soon, very soon the Queen would find him, and he, powerless as a worm in her audacious hands, would be returned to the dark chest in the narrow house that ran on wheels.

Alvarita heard a sudden crunching of the gravel below her. Turning her head she saw a big, swarthy Mexican, with a daring and evil expression, contemplating her with an ominous, dull eye.

'What do you want?' she asked as sharply as five hairpins between her lips would permit, continuing to plait her hair, and looking him over with placid contempt. The Mexican continued to gaze at her, and showed his teeth in a white, jagged smile.

'I no hurt-y you, Señorita,' he said.

'You bet you won't,' answered the Queen, shaking back one finished, massive plait. 'But don't you think you'd better move on?'

'Not hurt-y you – no. But maybeso take one *beso* – one li'l kees, you call him.'

The man smiled again, and set his foot to ascend the slope. Alvarita leaned swiftly and picked up a stone the size of a cocoanut.

'Vamoose, quick,' she ordered peremptorily, 'you *coon!*'

The red of insult burned through the Mexican's dark skin.

'*Hidalgo, Yo!*' he shot between his fangs. 'I am not neg-r-ro! *Diabla bonita*, for that you shall pay me.'

He made two quick upward steps this time, but the stone, hurled by no weak arm, struck him square in the chest. He staggered back to the footway, swerved half around, and met another sight that drove all thoughts of the girl from his head. She turned her eyes to see what had diverted his interest. A man with red-brown, curling hair and a melancholy, sunburned, smooth-shaven face was coming up the path, twenty yards away. Around the Mexican's waist was buckled a pistol belt with two empty holsters. He had laid aside his sixes – possibly in the *jacal* of the fair Pancha – and had forgotten them when the passing of -the fairer Alvarita had enticed him to her trail. His hands now flew instinctively to the holsters, but finding the weapons gone, he spread his fingers outward with the eloquent, abjuring, deprecating Latin gesture, and stood like a rock. Seeing his plight, the newcomer unbuckled his own belt containing two revolvers, threw it upon the ground, and continued to advance.

'Splendid!' murmured Alvarita, with flashing eyes .

As Bob Buckley, according to the mad code of bravery that his sensitive conscience imposed upon his cowardly nerves, abandoned his guns and closed in upon his enemy, the old, inevitable nausea of abject fear wrung him. His breath whistled through his constricted air passages. His feet seemed like lumps of lead. His mouth was dry as dust. His heart, congested with blood, hurt his ribs as it thumped against them. The hot June day turned to moist November. And still he advanced, spurred by a mandatory pride that strained its uttermost against his weakling flesh.

The distance between the two men slowly lessened. The Mexican stood, immovable, waiting. When scarce five yards separated them a little shower of loosened gravel rattled down from above to the ranger's feet. He glanced upward with instinctive caution. A pair of dark eyes, brilliantly soft, and fierily tender, encountered and held his own. The most fearful heart and the boldest one in all the Rio Bravo country exchanged a silent and inscrutable communication. Alvarita, still seated within her vine, leaned forward above the breast-high chaparral. One hand was laid across her bosom. One great dark braid curved forward over her shoulder. Her lips were parted; her face was lit with what seemed but wonder – great and absolute wonder. Her eyes lingered upon Buckley's. Let no one ask or presume to tell through what subtle medium the miracle was performed. As by a lightning flash two clouds will accomplish counterpoise and compensation of electric surcharge, so on that eye glance the man received his complement of manhood, and the maid concealed what enriched her womanly grace by its loss.

The Mexican, suddenly stirring, ventilated his attitude of apathetic waiting by conjuring swiftly from his bootleg a long knife. Buckley cast aside his hat, and laughed once aloud, like a happy schoolboy at a frolic. Then, empty-handed, he sprang nimbly, and Garcia met him without default.

So soon was the engagement ended that disappointment imposed upon the ranger's war-like ecstasy. Instead of dealing the traditional downward stroke, the Mexican lunged straight with his knife. Buckley took the precarious chance, and caught his wrist, fair and firm. Then he delivered the good Saxon knock-out blow – always so pathetically disastrous to the fistless Latin races – and Garcia was down and out, with his head under a clump of prickly pears. The ranger looked up again to the Queen of the Serpents.

Alvarita scrambled down to the path.

'I'm mighty glad I happened along when I did,' said the ranger.

'He – he frightened me so,' cooed Alvarita.

They did not hear the long, low hiss of the python under the shrubs. Wiliest of the beasts, no doubt he was expressing the humiliation he felt at having so long dwelt in subjection to this trembling and coloring mistress of his whom he had deemed so strong and potent and fearsome.

Then came galloping to the spot the civic authorities; and to them the ranger awarded the prostrate disturber of the peace, whom they bore away limply across the saddle of one of their mounts. But Buckley and Alvarita lingered.

Slowly, slowly they walked. The ranger regained his belt of weapons. With a fine timidity she begged the indulgence of fingering the great .45's with little 'Ohs' and 'Ahs' of new-born delicious shyness.

The *cañoncito* was growing dusky. Beyond its terminus in the river bluff they could see the outer world yet suffused with the waning glory of sunset.

A scream – a piercing scream of fright from Alvarita. Back she cowered, and the ready, protecting arm of Buckley formed her refuge. What terror so dire as to thus beset the close of the reign of the never-before-daunted Queen?

Across the path there crawled a *caterpillar* – a horrid, fuzzy, two-inch caterpillar! Truly, Kuku, thou wert avenged. Thus abdicated the Queen of the Serpent Tribe – *viva la reina!*

THE HIGHER ABDICATION

CURLY THE TRAMP SIDLED TOWARD the free-lunch counter. He caught a fleeting glance from the bartender's eye, and stood still, trying to look like a business man who had just dined at the Menger and was waiting for a friend who had promised to pick him up in his motor car. Curly's histrionic powers were equal to the impersonation; but his make-up was wanting.

The bartender rounded the bar in a casual way, looking up at the ceiling as though he was pondering some intricate problem of kalsomining, and then fell upon Curly so suddenly that the roadster had no excuses ready. Irresistibly, but so composedly that it seemed almost absentmindedness on his part, the dispenser of drinks pushed Curly to the swinging doors and kicked him out, with a nonchalance that almost amounted to sadness. That was the way of the Southwest.

Curly arose from the gutter leisurely. He felt no anger or resentment toward his ejector. Fifteen years of tramphood spent out of the twenty-two years of his life had hardened the fibres of his spirit. The slings and arrows of outrageous fortune fell blunted from the buckler of his armored pride. With especial resignation did he suffer contumely and injury at the hands of bartenders. Naturally, they were his enemies; and unnaturally, they were often his friends. He had to take his chances with them. But he had not yet learned to estimate these cool, languid, Southwestern knights of the bung-starter, who had the manners of an Earl of Pawtucket, and who, when they disapproved of your presence, moved you with the silence and despatch of a chess automaton advancing a pawn.

Curly stood a few moments in the narrow, mesquite-paved street. San Antonio puzzled and disturbed him. Three days he had been a non-paying guest of the town, having dropped off there from a box car of an I. & G. N. freight, because Greaser Johnny had told him in Des Moines that the Alamo City was manna fallen, gathered, cooked, and served free with cream and sugar. Curly had found the tip partly a good one. There was hospitality in plenty of a careless, liberal, irregular sort. But the town itself was a weight upon his spirits after his experience with the rushing, business-like, system-atized cities of the North and East. Here he was often flung a dollar, but too frequently a good-natured kick would follow it. Once a band of hilarious cowboys had roped him on Military Plaza and dragged him across the black soil until no respectable rag-bag would have stood sponsor for his clothes. The winding, doubling streets, leading nowhere, bewildered him. And then there was a little river, crooked as a pot-hook, that crawled through the middle of the town, crossed by a hundred little bridges so nearly alike that they got on Curly's nerves. And the last bartender wore a number nine shoe.

The saloon stood on a corner. The hour was eight o'clock. Homefarers and outgoers jostled Curly on the narrow stone sidewalk. Between the buildings to his left he looked down a cleft that proclaimed itself another thoroughfare. The alley was dark except for one patch of light. Where there was a light there were sure to be human beings. Where there were human beings after nightfall in San Antonio there might be food, and there was sure to be drink. So Curly headed for the light.

The illumination came from Schwegel's Café. On the sidewalk in front of it Curly picked up an old envelope. It might have contained a check for a million. It was empty; but the wanderer read the address, 'Mr. Otto Schwegel,' and the name of the town and State. The postmark was Detroit.

Curly entered the saloon. And now in the light it could be perceived that he bore the stamp of many years of vagabondage. He had none of the tidiness of the calculating and shrewd professional tramp. His wardrobe represented the cast-off specimens of half a dozen fashions and eras. Two factories had combined their efforts in providing shoes for his feet. As you gazed at him there passed through your mind vague impressions of mummies, wax figures, Russian exiles, and men lost on desert islands. His face was covered almost to his eyes with a curly brown beard that he kept trimmed short with a pocket-knife, and that had furnished him with his *nom de route*. Light-blue eyes, full of sullenness, fear, cunning, impudence, and fawning, witnessed the stress that had been laid upon his soul.

The saloon was small, and in its atmosphere the odors of meat and drink struggled for the ascendency. The pig and the cabbage wrestled with hydrogen and oxygen. Behind the bar Schwegel labored with an assistant whose epidermal pores showed no signs of being obstructed. Hot wiernerwurst and sauerkraut were being served to purchasers of beer. Curly shuffled to the end of the bar, coughed hollowly, and told Schwegel that he was a Detroit cabinet-maker out of a job.

It followed as the night the day that he got his schooner and lunch.

'Was you acquainted maybe mit Heinrich Strauss in Detroit?' asked Schwegel.

'Did I know Heinrich Strauss?' repeated Curly, affectionately. 'Why, say, 'Bo, I wish I had a dollar for every game of pinochle me and Heine has played on Sunday afternoons.'

More beer and a second plate of steaming food was set before the diplomat. And then Curly, knowing to a fluid-drachm how far a 'con' game would go, shuffled out into the unpromising street.

And now he began to perceive the inconveniences of this stony Southern town. There was none of the outdoor gaiety and brilliancy and music that provided distraction even to the poorest in the cities of the North. Here, even so early, the gloomy, rock-walled houses were closed and barred against the murky dampness of the night. The streets were mere fissures through which flowed gray wreaths of river mist. As he walked he heard laughter and the chink of coin and chips behind darkened windows, and music coming from every chink of wood and stone. But the diversions were selfish; the day of popular pastimes had not yet come to San Antonio.

But at length Curly, as he strayed, turned the sharp angle of another lost street and came upon a rollicking band of stockmen from the outlying ranches celebrating in the open in front of an ancient wooden hotel. One great roisterer from the sheep country who had just instigated a movement toward the bar, swept Curly in like a stray goat with the rest of his flock. The princes of kine and wool hailed him as a new zoölogical discovery, and uproariously strove to preserve him in the diluted alcohol of their compliments and regards.

An hour afterward Curly staggered from the hotel barroom, dismissed by his fickle friends, whose interest in him had subsided as quickly as it had risen. Full – stoked with alcoholic fuel and cargoed with food, the only question remaining to disturb him was that of shelter and bed.

A drizzling, cold Texas rain had begun to fall – an endless, lazy, unintermittent downfall that lowered the spirits of men and raised a reluctant steam from the warm stones of the streets and houses. Thus comes the 'norther' dousing gentle spring and amiable autumn with the chilling salutes and adieux of coming and departing winter.

Curly followed his nose down the first tortuous street into which his irresponsible feet conducted him. At the lower end of it, on the bank of the serpentine stream, he perceived an open gate in a cemented rock wall. Inside he saw camp fires and a row of low wooden sheds built against three sides of the enclosing wall. He entered the enclosure. Under the sheds many horses were champing at their oats and corn. Many wagons and buckboards stood about with their teams' harness thrown carelessly upon the shafts and doubletrees. Curly recognized the place as a wagon yard, such as is provided by merchants for their out-of-town friends and customers. No one was in sight. No doubt the drivers of those wagons were scattered about the town 'seeing the elephant and hearing the owl.' In their haste to become patrons of the town's dispensaries of mirth and good cheer the last ones to depart must have left the great wooden gate swinging open.

Curly had satisfied the hunger of an anaconda and the thirst of a camel, so he was neither in the mood nor the condition of an explorer. He zigzagged his way to the first wagon that his eyesight distinguished in the semi-darkness under the shed. It was a two-horse wagon with a top of white canvas. The wagon was half filled with loose piles of wool sacks, two or three great bundles of gray blankets, and a number of bales, bundles, and boxes. A reasoning eye would have estimated the load at once as ranch supplies, bound on the morrow for some outlying hacienda. But to the drowsy intelligence of Curly they represented only warmth and softness and protection against the cold humidity of the night. After several unlucky efforts, at last he conquered gravity so far as to climb over a wheel and pitch forward upon the best and warmest bed he had fallen upon in many a day. Then he became instinctively a burrowing animal, and dug his way like a prairie-dog down among the sacks and blankets, hiding himself from the cold air as snug and safe as a bear in his den. For three nights sleep had visited Curly only in broken and shivering doses. So now, when Morpheus condescended to pay him a call, Curly got such a strangle hold on the mythological old gentleman that it was a wonder that any one else in the whole world got a wink of sleep that night.

Six cow-punchers of the Cibolo Ranch were waiting around the door of the ranch store. Their ponies cropped grass near by, tied in the Texas fashion – which is not tied at all. Their bridle reins had been dropped to the earth, which is a more effectual way of securing them (such is the power of habit and imagination) than you could devise out of a half-inch rope and a live-oak tree.

These guardians of the cow lounged about, each with a brown cigarette paper in his hand, and gently but unceasingly cursed Sam Revell, the storekeeper. Sam stood in the door, snapping the red elastic bands on his pink madras shirtsleeves and looking down affectionately at the only pair of tan shoes within a forty-mile radius. His offence had been serious, and he was divided between humble apology and admiration for the beauty of his raiment. He had allowed the ranch stock of 'smoking' to become exhausted.

'I thought sure there was another case of it under the counter, boys,' he explained. 'But it happened to be catterdges.'

'You've sure got a case of happendicitis,' said Poky Rodgers, fence rider of the Largo Verde *potrero*. 'Somebody ought to happen to give you a knock on the head with the butt end of a quirt. I've rode in nine miles for some tobacco; and it don't appear natural and seemly that you ought to be allowed to live.'

'The boys was smokin' cut plug and dried mesquite leaves mixed when I left,' sighed Mustang Taylor, horse wrangler of the Three Elm camp. 'They'll be lookin' for me back by nine. They'll be settin' up, with their papers ready to roll a whiff of the real thing before bedtime. And I've got to tell 'em that this pink-eyed, sheep-headed, sulphur-footed, shirt-waisted son of a calico broncho, Sam Revell, hasn't got no tobacco on hand.'

Gregorio Falcon, Mexican vaquero and best thrower of the rope on the Cibolo, pushed his heavy, silver-embroidered straw sombrero back upon his thicket of jet-black curls and scraped the bottoms of his pockets for a few crumbs of the precious weed.

'Ah, Don Samuel,' he said, reproachfully, but with his touch of Castilian manners, 'escuse me. Dthey say dthe jackrabbeet and dthe sheep have the most leetle *sesos* – how you call dthem – brain-es? Ah, don't believe dthat, Don Samuel – escuse me. Ah dthink people w'at don't keep esmokin' tobacco, dthey – bot you weel escuse me, Don Samuel.'

'Now, what's the use of chewin' the rag, boys,' said the untroubled Sam, stooping over to rub the toes of his shoes with a red-and-yellow handkerchief. 'Ranse took the order for some more smokin' to San Antone with him Tuesday. Pancho rode Ranse's hoss back yesterday; and Ranse is goin' to drive the wagon back himself. There wa'n't much of a load – just some woolsacks and blankets and nails and canned peaches an a few things we was out of. I look for Ranse to roll in to-day sure. He's a early starter and a hell-to-split driver, and he ought to be here not far from sundown.'

'What plugs is he drivin'?' asked Mustang Taylor, with a smack of hope in his tones.

'The buckboard grays,' said Sam.

'I'll wait a spell, then,' said the wrangler. 'Them plugs eat up a trail like a road-runner swallowin' a whip snake. And you may bust me open a can of green-gage plums, Sam, while I'm waitin' for somethin' better.'

'Open me some yellow clings,' ordered Poky Rodgers. 'I'll wait, too.'

The tobaccoless punchers arranged themselves comfortably on the steps of the store. Inside Sam chopped open with a hatchet the tops of the cans of fruit.

The store, a big, white wooden building like a barn, stood fifty yards from the ranch-house. Beyond it were the horse corrals; and still farther the wool sheds and the brush-topped shearing pens – for the Rancho Cibolo raised both cattle and sheep. Behind the store, at a little distance, were the grass-thatched *jacals* of the Mexicans who bestowed their allegiance upon the Cibolo.

The ranch-house was composed of four large rooms, with plastered adobe walls, and a two-room wooden cell. A twenty-feet-wide 'gallery' circumvented the structure. It was set in a grove of immense live-oaks and water-elms near a lake – a long, not very wide, and tremendously deep lake in which, at nightfall, great gars leaped to the surface and plunged with the noise of hippopotamuses frolicking at their bath. From the trees hung garlands and massive pendants of the melancholy gray moss of the South. Indeed, the Cibolo ranch-house seemed more of the South than of the West. It looked as if old 'Kiowa' Truesdell might have brought it with him from the lowlands of Mississippi when he came to Texas with his rifle in the hollow of his arm in '55.

But, though he did not bring the family mansion, Truesdell did bring something in the way of a family inheritance that was more lasting than brick or stone. He brought one end of the Truesdell-Curtis family feud. And when a Curtis bought the Rancho de los Olmos, sixteen miles from the Cibolo, there were lively times on the pear flats and in the chaparral thickets of the Southwest. In those days Truesdell cleaned the brush of many a wolf and tiger cat and Mexican lion; and one or two Curtises fell heirs to notches on his rifle stock. Also he buried a brother with a Curtis bullet in him on the bank of the lake at Cibolo. And then the Kiowa Indians made their last raid upon the ranches between the Frio and the Rio Grande, and Truesdell at the head of his rangers rid the earth of them to the last brave, earning his sobriquet. Then came prosperity in the form of waxing herds and broadening lands. And then old age and bitterness, when he sat, with his great mane of hair as white as the Spanish-dagger blossoms and his fierce, pale-blue eyes, on the shaded gallery at Cibolo, growling like the pumas that he had slain. He snapped his fingers at old age; the bitter taste of life did not come from that. The cup that stuck at his lips was that his only son Ransom wanted to marry a Curtis, the last youthful survivor of the other end of the feud.

For a while the only sounds to be heard at the store were the rattling of the tin spoons and the gurgling intake of the juicy fruits by the cow-punchers, the stamping of the grazing ponies, and the singing of a doleful song by Sam as he contentedly brushed his stiff auburn hair for the twentieth time that day before a crinkly mirror.

From the door of the store could be seen the irregular, sloping stretch of prairie to the south, with its reaches of light-green, billowing mesquite flats in the lower places, and its rises crowned with nearly black masses of short chaparral. Through the mesquite flat wound the ranch road that, five miles away, flowed into the old government trail to San Antonio. The sun was so low that the gentlest elevation cast its gray shadow miles into the green-gold of sunshine.

That evening ears were quicker than eyes.

The Mexican held up a tawny finger to still the scraping of tin against tin.

'One waggeen,' said he, 'cross dthe Arroyo Hodo. Ah hear dthe wheel. Verree rockee place, dthe Hondo.'

'You've got good ears, Gregorio,' said Mustang Taylor. 'I never heard nothin' but the song-bird in the bush and the zephyr skally-hootin' across the peaceful dell.'

In ten minutes Taylor remarked: 'I see the dust of a wagon risin' right above the fur end of the flat.'

'You have verree good eyes, señor,' said Gregorio smiling.

Two miles away they saw a faint cloud dimming the green ripples of the mesquites. In twenty minutes they heard the clatter of horses' hoofs: in five minutes more the gray plugs dashed out of thicket, whickering for oats and drawing the light wagon behind them like a toy.

From the *jacals* came a cry of: '*El Amo! El Amo!*' Four Mexican youths raced to unharness the grays. The cow-punchers gave a yell of greeting and delight.

Ranse Truesdell, driving, threw the reins to the ground and laughed.

'It's under the wagon sheet, boys,' he said. 'I know what you're waiting for. If Sam lets it run out again we'll use them yellow shoes of his for a target. There's two cases. Pull 'em out and light up. I know you'll want a smoke.'

After striking dry country Ranse had removed the wagon sheet from the bows and thrown it over the goods in the wagon. Six pairs of hasty hands dragged it off and grabbled beneath the sacks and blankets for the cases of tobacco.

Long Collins, tobacco messenger from the San Gabriel outfit, who rode with the longest stirrups west of the Mississippi, delved with an arm like the tongue of a wagon. He caught something harder than a blanket and pulled out a fearful thing – a shapeless, muddy bunch of leather tied together with wire and twine. From its ragged end, like the head and claws of a disturbed turtle, protruded human toes.

'Who-ee!' yelled Long Collins. 'Ranse, are you a-packin' around of corpuses? Here's a – howlin' grasshoppers!'

Up from his long slumber popped Curly, like some vile worm from its burrow. He clawed his way out and sat blinking like a disreputable, drunken owl. His face was as bluish red and puffed and seamed and crosslined as the cheapest round steak of the butcher. His eyes were swollen slits; his nose a pickled beet; his hair would have made the wildest thatch of a Jack-in-the-box look like the satin poll of a Cléo de Mérode. The rest of him was scarecrow done to the life.

Ranse jumped down from his seat and looked at his strange cargo with wide-open eyes.

'Here, you maverick, what are you doing in my wagon? How did you get in there?'

The punchers gathered around in delight. For the time they had forgotten tobacco.

Curly looked around him slowly in every direction. He snarled like a Scotch terrier through his ragged beard.

'Where is this,' he rasped through his parched throat. 'It's a damn farm in an old field. What'd you bring me here for – say? Did I say I wanted to come here? What are you Reubs rubberin' at – hey? G'wan or I'll punch some of your faces.'

'Drag him out, Collins,' said Ranse.

Curly took a slide and felt the ground rise up and collide with his shoulder blades. He got up and sat on the steps of the store shivering from outraged nerves, hugging his knees and sneering. Taylor lifted out a case of tobacco and wrenched off its top. Six cigarettes began to glow, bringing peace and forgiveness to Sam.

'How'd you come in my wagon?' repeated Ranse, this time in a voice that drew a reply.

Curly recognized the tone. He had heard it used by freight brakemen and large persons in blue carrying clubs.

'Me?' he growled. 'Oh, was you talkin' to me? Why, I was on my way to the Menger, but my valet had forgot to pack my pajamas. So I crawled into that wagon in the wagon-yard – see? I never told you to bring me out to this bloomin' farm – see?'

'What is it, Mustang?' asked Poky Rodgers, almost forgetting to smoke in his ecstasy. 'What do it live on?'

'It's a galliwampus, Poky,' said Mustang. 'It's the thing that hollers "williwallo" up in ellum trees in the low grounds of nights. I don't know if it bites.'

'No, it ain't, Mustang,' volunteered Long Collins. 'Them galliwampuses has fins on their backs, and eighteen toes. This here is a hicklesnifter. It lives under the ground and eats cherries. Don't stand so close to it. It wipes out villages with one stroke of its prehensile tail.'

Sam, the cosmopolite, who called bartenders in San Antone by their first name, stood in the door. He was a better zoölogist.

'Well, ain't that a Willie for your whiskers?' he commented. 'Where'd you dig up the hobo, Ranse? Goin' to make an auditorium for inbreviates out of the ranch?'

'Say,' said Curly, from whose panoplied breast all shafts of wit fell blunted.

'Any of you kiddin' guys got a drink on you? Have your fun. Say, I've been hittin' the stuff till I don't know straight up.'

He turned to Ranse. 'Say, you shanghaied me on your d—d old prairie schooner – did I tell you to drive me to a farm? I want a drink. I'm goin' all to little pieces. What's doin'?'

Ranse saw that the tramp's nerves were racking him. He despatched one of the Mexican boys to the ranch-house for a glass of whisky. Curly gulped it down, and into his eyes came a brief, grateful glow – as human as the expression in the eye of a faithful setter dog.

'Thanky, boss,' he said, quietly.

'You're thirty miles from a railroad, and forty miles from a saloon,' said Ranse.

Curly fell back weakly against the steps.

'Since you are here,' continued the ranchman, 'come along with me. We can't turn you out on the prairie. A rabbit might tear you to pieces.'

He conducted Curly to a large shed where the ranch vehicles were kept. There he spread out a canvas cot and brought blankets.

'I don't suppose you can sleep,' said Ranse, 'since you've been pounding your ear for twenty-four hours. But you can camp here till morning. I'll have Pedro fetch you up some grub.'

'Sleep!' said Curly. 'I can sleep a week. Say, sport, have you got a coffin nail on you?'

Fifty miles had Ransom Truesdell driven that day. And yet this is what he did.

Old 'Kiowa' Truesdell sat in his great wicker chair reading by the light of an immense oil lamp. Ranse laid a bundle of newspapers fresh from town at his elbow.

'Back, Ranse?' said the old man, looking up.

'Son,' old 'Kiowa' continued, 'I've been thinking all day about a certain matter that we have talked about. I want you to tell me again. I've lived for you. I've fought wolves and Indians and worse white men to protect you. You never had any mother that you can remember. I've taught you to shoot straight, ride hard, and live clean. Later on I've worked to pile up dollars that'll be yours. You'll be a rich man, Ranse, when my chunk goes out. I've made you. I've licked you into shape like a leopard cat licks its cubs. You don't belong to yourself – you've got to be a Truesdell first. Now, is there to be any more nonsense about this Curtis girl?'

'I'll tell you once more,' said Ranse, slowly. 'As I am a Truesdell and as you are my father, I'll never marry a Curtis.'

'Good boy,' said old 'Kiowa.' 'You'd better go get some supper.'

Ranse went to the kitchen at the rear of the house. Pedro, the Mexican cook, sprang up to bring the food he was keeping warm in the stove.

'Just a cup of coffee, Pedro,' he said, and drank it standing. And then:

'There's a tramp on a cot in the wagon-shed. Take him something to eat. Better make it enough for two.'

Ranse walked out toward the *jacals*. A boy came running.

'Manuel, can you catch Vaminos, in the little pasture, for me?'

'Why not, señor? I saw him near the *puerta* but two hours past. He bears a drag-rope.'

'Get him and saddle him as quick as you can.'

'*Prontito, señor.*'

Soon mounted, on Vaminos, Ranse leaned in the saddle, pressed with his knees, and galloped eastward past the store, where sat Sam trying his guitar in the moonlight.

Vaminos shall have a word – Vaminos the good dun horse. The Mexicans, who have a hundred names for the colors of a horse, called him *gruyo*. He was a mouse-colored, slate-colored, flea-bitten road-dun, if you can conceive it. Down his back from his mane to his tail went a line of black. He would live forever; and surveyors have not laid off as many miles in the world as he could travel in a day.

Eight miles east of the Cibolo ranch-house Ranse loosened the pressure of his knees, and Vaminos stopped under a big ratama tree. The yellow ratama blossoms showered fragrance that would have undone the roses of France. The moon made the earth a great concave bowl with a crystal sky for a lid. In a glade five jack-rabbits leaped and played together like kittens. Eight miles farther east shone a faint star that appeared to have dropped below the horizon. Night riders, who often steered their course by it, knew it to be the light in the Rancho de los Olmos.

In ten minutes Yenna Curtis galloped to the tree on her sorrel pony Dancer. The two leaned and clasped hands heartily.

'I ought to have ridden nearer your home,' said Ranse. 'But you never will let me.'

Yenna laughed. And in the soft light you could see her strong white teeth and fearless eyes. No sentimentality there, in spite of the moonlight, the odor of the ratamas, and the admirable figure of Ranse Truesdell, the lover. But she was there, eight miles from her home, to meet him.

'How often have I told you, Ranse,' she said, 'that I am your half-way girl? Always half-way.'

'Well?' said Ranse, with a question in his tones.

'I did,' said Yenna, with almost a sigh. 'I told him after dinner when I thought he would be in a good humor. Did you ever wake up a lion, Ranse, with the mistaken idea that he would be a kitten? He almost tore the ranch to pieces. It's all up. I love my daddy, Ranse, and I'm afraid – I'm afraid of him, too. He ordered me to promise that I'd never marry a Truesdell. I promised. That's all. What luck did you have?'

'The same,' said Ranse, slowly. 'I promised him that his son would never marry a Curtis. Somehow I couldn't go against him. He's mighty old. I'm sorry, Yenna.'

The girl leaned in her saddle and laid one hand on Ranse's, on the horn of his saddle.

'I never thought I'd like you better for giving me up,' she said ardently, 'but I do. I must ride back now, Ranse. I slipped out of the house and saddled Dancer myself. Good-night, neighbor.'

'Good-night,' said Ranse. 'Ride carefully over them badger holes.'

They wheeled and rode away in opposite directions. Yenna turned in her saddle and called clearly:

'Don't forget I'm your half-way girl, Ranse.'

'Damn all family feuds and inherited scraps,' muttered Ranse vindictively to the breeze as he rode back to the Cibolo.

Ranse turned his horse into the small pasture and went to his own room. He opened the lowest drawer of an old bureau to get out the packet of letters that Yenna had written him one summer when she had gone to Mississippi for a visit. The drawer stuck, and he yanked at it savagely – as a man will. It came out of the bureau, and bruised both his shins – as a drawer will. An old, folded yellow letter without an envelope fell from somewhere – probably from where it had lodged in one of the upper drawers. Ranse took it to the lamp and read it curiously.

Then he took his hat and walked to one of the Mexican *jacals*.

'Tía Juana,' he said, 'I would like to talk with you awhile.'

An old, old Mexican woman, white-haired and wonderfully wrinkled, rose from a stool.

'Sit down,' said Ranse, removing his hat and taking the one chair in the *jacal*. 'Who am I, Tía Juana?' he asked, speaking Spanish.

'Don Ransom, our good friend and employer. Why do you ask?' answered the old woman wonderingly.

'Tía Juana, who am I?' he repeated, with his stern eyes looking into hers.

A frightened look came in the old woman's face. She fumbled with her black shawl.

'Who am I, Tía Juana?' said Ranse once more.

'Thirty-two years I have lived on the Rancho Cibolo,' said Tía Juana. 'I thought to be buried under the coma mott beyond the garden before these things should be known. Close the door, Don Ransom, and I will speak. I see in your face that you know.'

An hour Ranse spent behind Tía Juana's closed door. As he was on his way back to the house Curly called to him from the wagon-shed.

The tramp sat on his cot, swinging his feet and smoking.

'Say, sport,' he grumbled. 'This is no way to treat a man after kidnappin' him. I went up to the store and borrowed a razor from that fresh guy and had a shave. But that ain't all a man needs. Say – can't you loosen up for about three fingers more of that booze? I never asked you to bring me to your d—d farm.'

'Stand up out here in the light,' said Ranse, looking at him closely.

Curly got up sullenly and took a step or two.

His face, now shaven smooth, seemed transformed. His hair had been combed, and it fell back from the right side of his forehead with a peculiar wave. The moonlight charitably softened the ravages of drink; and his aquiline, well-shaped nose and small, square-cleft chin almost gave distinction to his looks.

Ranse sat on the foot of the cot and looked at him curiously.

'Where did you come from – have you got any home or folks anywhere?'

'Me? Why, I'm a dook,' said Curly. 'I'm Sir Reginald – oh, cheese it. No; I don't know anything about my ancestors. I've been a tramp ever since I can remember. Say, old pal, are you going to set 'em up again tonight or not?'

'You answer my questions and maybe I will. How did you come to be a tramp?'

'Me,' answered Curly. 'Why, I adopted that profession when I was an infant. Case of had to. First thing I can remember, I belonged to a big, lazy hobo called Beefsteak Charley. He sent me around to houses to beg. I wasn't hardly big enough to reach the latch of a gate.'

'Did he ever tell you how he got you?' asked Ranse.

'Once when he was sober he said he bought me for an old six-shooter and six bits from a band of drunken Mexican sheep-shearers. But what's the diff? That's all I know.'

'All right,' said Ranse. 'I reckon you're a maverick for certain. I'm going to put the Rancho Cibolo brand on you. I'll start you to work in one of the camps to-morrow.'

'Work!' sniffed Curly, disdainfully. 'What do you take me for? Do you think I'd chase cows, and hop-skip-and-jump around after crazy sheep like that pink-and-yellow guy at the store says these Reubs do? Forget it.'

'Oh, you'll like it when you get used to it,' said Ranse. 'Yes. I'll send you up one more drink by Pedro. I think you'll make a first-class cowpuncher before I get through with you.'

'Me?' said Curly. 'I pity the cows you set me to chaperon. They can go chase themselves. Don't forget my nightcap, please, boss.'

Ranse paid a visit to the store before going to the house. Sam Revell was taking off his tan shoes regretfully and preparing for bed.

'Any of the boys from the San Gabriel camp riding in early in the morning?' asked Ranse.

'Long Collins,' said Sam, briefly. 'For the mail.'

'Tell him,' said Ranse, 'to take that tramp out to camp with him and keep him till I get there.'

Curly was sitting on his blankets in the San Gabriel camp cursing talentedly when Ranse Truesdell rode up and dismounted on the next afternoon. The cow-punchers were ignoring the stray. He was grimy with dust and black dirt. His clothes were making their last stand in favor of the conventions.

Ranse went up to Buck Rabb, the camp boss, and spoke briefly.

'He's a plum buzzard,' said Buck. 'He won't work, and he's the lowdownest passel of inhumanity I ever see. I didn't know what you wanted done with him, Ranse, so I just let him set. That seems to suit him. He's been condemned to death by the boys a dozen times, but I told 'em maybe you was savin' him for torture.'

Ranse took off his coat.

'I've got a hard job before me, Buck, I reckon, but it has to be done. I've got to make a man out of that thing. That's what I've come to camp for.'

He went up to Curly.

'Brother,' he said, 'don't you think if you had a bath it would allow you to take a seat in the company of your fellow-man with less injustice to the atmosphere?'

'Run away, farmer,' said Curly, sardonically. 'Willie will send for nursey when he feels like having his tub.'

The *charco*, or water hole, was twelve yards away. Ranse took one of Curly's ankles and dragged him like a sack of potatoes to the brink. Then with the strength and sleight of a hammer-thrower he hurled the offending member of society far into the lake.

Curly crawled out and up the bank spluttering like a porpoise.

Ranse met him with a piece of soap and a coarse towel in his hands.

'Go to the other end of the lake and use this,' he said. 'Buck will give you some dry clothes at the wagon.'

The tramp obeyed without protest. By the time supper was ready he had returned to camp. He was hardly to be recognized in his new blue shirt and brown duck clothes. Ranse observed him out of the corner of his eye.

'Lordy, I hope he ain't a coward,' he was saying to himself. 'I hope he won't turn out to be a coward.'

His doubts were soon allayed. Curly walked straight to where he stood. His light-blue eyes were blazing.

'Now I'm clean,' he said, meaningly, 'maybe you'll talk to me. Think you've got a picnic here, do you? You clodhoppers think you can run over a man because you know he can't get away. All right. Now, what do you think of that?'

Curly planted a stinging slap against Ranse's left cheek. The print of his hand stood out a dull red against the tan.

Ranse smiled happily.

The cow-punchers talk to this day of the battle that followed.

Somewhere in his restless tour of the cities Curly had acquired the art of self-defence. The ranchman was equipped only with the splendid strength and equilibrium of perfect health and the endurance conferred by decent living. The two attributes nearly matched. There were no formal rounds. At last the fibre of the clean liver prevailed. The last time Curly went down from one of the ranchman's awkward but powerful blows he remained on the grass, but looking up with an unquenched eye.

Ranse went to the water barrel and washed the red from a cut on his chin in the stream from the faucet.

On his face was a grin of satisfaction.

Much benefit might accrue to educators and moralists if they could know the details of the curriculum of reclamation through which Ranse put his waif during the month that he spent in the San Gabriel camp. The ranchman had no fine theories to work out – perhaps his whole stock of pedagogy embraced only a knowledge of horse-breaking and a belief in heredity.

The cow-punchers saw that their boss was trying to make a man out of the strange animal that he had sent among them; and they tacitly organized themselves into a faculty of assistants. But their system was their own.

Curly's first lesson stuck. He became on friendly and then on intimate terms with soap and water. And the thing that pleased Ranse most was that his 'subject' held his ground at each successive higher step. But the steps were sometimes far apart.

Once he got at the quart bottle of whisky kept sacredly in the grub tent for rattlesnake bites, and spent sixteen hours on the grass, magnificently drunk. But when he staggered to his feet his first move was to find his soap and towel and start for the *charco*. And once, when a treat came from the ranch in the form of a basket of fresh tomatoes and young onions, Curly devoured the entire consignment before the punchers reached the camp at supper time.

And then the punchers punished him in their own way. For three days they did not speak to him, except to reply to his own questions or remarks. And they spoke with absolute and unfailing politeness. They played tricks on one another; they pounded one another hurtfully and affectionately; they heaped upon one another's heads friendly curses and obloquy; but they were polite to Curly. He saw it, and it stung him as much as Ranse hoped it would.

Then came a night that brought a cold, wet norther. Wilson, the youngest of the outfit, had lain in camp two days, ill with a fever. When Joe got up at daylight to begin breakfast he found Curly sitting asleep against a wheel of the grub wagon with only a saddle blanket around him, while Curly's blankets were stretched over Wilson to protect him from the rain and wind.

Three nights after that Curly rolled himself in his blanket and went to sleep. Then the other punchers rose up softly and began to make preparations. Ranse saw Long Collins tie a rope to the horn of a saddle. Others were getting out their six-shooters.

'Boys,' said Ranse, 'I'm much obliged. I was hoping you would. But I didn't like to ask.'

Half a dozen six-shooters began to pop – awful yells rent the air – Long Collins galloped wildly across Curly's bed, dragging the saddle after him. That was merely their way of gently awaking their victim. Then they hazed him for an hour, carefully and ridiculously, after the code of cow camps. Whenever he uttered protest they held him stretched over a roll of blankets and thrashed him woefully with a pair of leather leggins.

And all this meant that Curly had won his spurs, that he was receiving the punchers' accolade. Nevermore would they be polite to him. But he would be their 'pardner' and stirrup-brother, foot to foot.

When the fooling was ended all hands made a raid on Joe's big coffeepot by the fire for a Java nightcap. Ranse watched the new knight carefully to see if he understood and was worthy. Curly limped with his cup of coffee to a log and sat upon it. Long Collins followed and sat by his side. Buck Rabb went and sat at the other. Curly – grinned.

And then Ranse furnished Curly with mounts and saddle and equipment, and turned him over to Buck Rabb, instructing him to finish the job.

Three weeks later Ranse rode from the ranch into Rabb's camp, which was then in Snake Valley. The boys were saddling for the day's ride. He sought out Long Collins among them.

'How about that bronco?' he asked.

Long Collins grinned.

'Reach out your hand, Ranse Truesdell,' he said, 'and you'll touch him. And you can shake his'n, too, if you like, for he's plumb white and there's none better in no camp.'

Ranse looked again at the clear-faced, bronzed, smiling cow-puncher who stood at Collins's side. Could that be Curly? He held out his hand, and Curly grasped it with the muscles of a bronco-buster.

'I want you at the ranch,' said Ranse.

'All right, sport,' said Curly, heartily. 'But I want to come back again. Say, pal, this is a dandy farm. And I don't want any better fun than hustlin' cows with this bunch of guys. They're all to the merry merry.'

At the Cibolo ranch-house they dismounted. Ranse bade Curly wait at the door of the living room. He walked inside. Old 'Kiowa' Truesdell was reading at a table.

'Good-morning, Mr. Truesdell,' said Ranse.

The old man turned his white head quickly.

'How is this?' he began. 'Why do you call me "Mr.—"?'

When he looked at Ranse's face he stopped, and the hand that held his newspaper shook slightly.

'Boy,' he said slowly, 'how did you find it out?'

'It's all right,' said Ranse, with a smile. 'I made Tía Juana tell me. It was kind of by accident, but it's all right.'

'You've been like a son to me,' said old 'Kiowa,' trembling.

'Tía Juana told me all about it,' said Ranse. 'She told me how you adopted me when I was knee-high to a puddle duck out of a wagon train of prospectors that was bound West. And she told me how the kid – your own kid, you know – got lost or was run away with. And she said it was the same day that the sheep-shearers got on a bender and left the ranch.'

'Our boy strayed from the house when he was two years old,' said the old man. 'And then along came these emigrant wagons with a youngster they didn't want; and we took you. I never intended you to know, Ranse. We never heard of our boy again.'

'He's right outside, unless I'm mighty mistaken,' said Ranse, opening the door and beckoning.

Curly walked in.

No one could have doubted. The old man and the young had the same sweep of hair, the same nose, chin, line of face, and prominent light-blue eyes.

Old 'Kiowa' rose eagerly.

Curly looked about the room curiously. A puzzled expression came over his face. He pointed to the wall opposite.

'Where's the tick-tock?' he asked, absentmindedly.

'The clock,' cried old 'Kiowa' loudly. 'The eight-day clock used to stand there. Why—'

He turned to Ranse, but Ranse was not there.

Already a hundred yards away, Vaminos, the good flea-bitten dun, was bearing him eastward like a racer through dust and chaparral towards the Rancho de los Olmos.

CUPID À LA CARTE

'THE DISPOSITIONS OF WOMAN,' said Jeff Peters, after various opinions on the subject had been advanced, 'run, regular, to diversions. What a woman wants is what you're out of. She wants more of a thing when it's scarce. She likes to have souvenirs of things she never heard of. A one-sided view of objects is disjointing to the female composition.

''Tis a misfortune of mine, begotten by nature and travel,' continued Jeff, looking thoughtfully between his elevated feet at the grocery stove, 'to look deeper into some subjects than most people do. I've breathed gasoline smoke talking to street crowds in nearly every town in the United States. I've held 'em spellbound with music, oratory, sleight of hand, and prevarications, while I've sold 'em jewelry, medicine, soap, hair tonic, and junk of other nominations. And during my travels, as a matter of recreation and expiation, I've taken cognizance some of women. It takes a man a lifetime to find out about one particular woman; but if he puts in, say, ten years, industrious and curious, he can acquire the general rudiments of the sex. One lesson I picked up was when I was working the West with a line of Brazilian diamonds and a patent fire kindler just after my trip from Savannah down through the cotton belt with Dalby's Anti-explosive Lamp Oil Powder. 'Twas when the Oklahoma country was in first bloom. Guthrie was rising in the middle of it like a lump of self-raising dough. It was a boom town of the regular kind – you stood in line to get a chance to wash your face; if you ate over ten minutes you had a lodging bill added on; if you slept on a plank at night they charged it to you as board the next morning.

'By nature and doctrines I am addicted to the habit of discovering choice places wherein to feed. So I looked around and found a proposition that exactly cut the mustard. I found a restaurant tent just opened up by an outfit that had drifted in on the tail of the boom. They had knocked together a box house, where they lived and did the cooking, and served the meals in a tent pitched against the side. That tent was joyful with placards on it calculated to redeem the world-worn pilgrim from the sinfulness of boarding houses and pick-me-up hotels. "Try Mother's Home-Made Biscuits," "What's the Matter with Our Apple Dumplings and Hard Sauce?" "Hot Cakes and Maple Syrup Like You Ate When a Boy," "Our Fried Chicken Never Was Heard to Crow" – there was literature doomed to please the digestions of man! I said to myself that mother's wandering boy should munch there that night. And so it came to pass. And there is where I contracted my case of Mame Dugan.

'Old Man Dugan was six feet by one of Indiana loafer, and he spent his time sitting on his shoulder blades in a rocking-chair in the shanty memorializing the great corn-crop failure of '86. Ma Dugan did the cooking, and Mame waited on table.

'As soon as I saw Mame I knew there was a mistake in the census reports. There wasn't but one girl in the United States. When you come to specifications it isn't easy. She was about the size of an angel, and she had eyes, and ways about her. When you come to the kind of a girl she was, you'll find a belt of 'em reaching from the Brooklyn Bridge west as far as the courthouse in Council Bluffs, Ia. They earn their own living in stores, restaurants, factories, and offices. They're descended straight from Eve, and they're the crowd that's got woman's rights, and if a man wants to dispute it he's in line to get one of them against his jaw. They're chummy and honest and free and tender and sassy, and they look life straight in the eye. They've met man face to face, and discovered that he's a poor creature. They've dropped to it that the reports in the Seaside Library about his being a fairy prince lack confirmation.

'Mame was that sort. She was full of life and fun, and breezy; she passed the repartee with the boarders quick as a wink; you'd have smothered laughing. I am disinclined to make excavations into the insides of a personal affection. I am glued to the theory that the diversions and discrepancies of the indisposition known as love should be as private a sentiment as a toothbrush. 'Tis my opinion that the biographies of the heart should be confined with the historical romances of the liver to the advertising pages of the magazines. So, you'll excuse the lack of an itemized bill of my feelings toward Mame.

'Pretty soon I got a regular habit of dropping into the tent to eat at irregular times when there wasn't so many around. Mame would sail in with a smile, in a black dress and white apron, and say: "Hello, Jeff – why don't you come at mealtime. Want to see how much trouble you can be, of course. Fried-chickenbeefsteakporkchopshamandeggspotpie" – and so on. She called me Jeff, but there was no significations attached. Designations was all she meant. The front names of any of us she used as they came to hand. I'd eat about two meals before I left, and string 'em out like a society spread where they changed plates and wives, and josh one another festively between bites.

Mame stood for it, pleasant, for it wasn't up to her to take any canvas off the tent by declining dollars just because they were chipped in after meal times.

'It wasn't long until there was another fellow named Ed Collier got the between-meals affliction, and him and me put in bridges between breakfast and dinner, and dinner and supper, that made a three-ringed circus of that tent, and Mame's turn as waiter a continuous performance. That Collier man was saturated with designs and contrivings. He was in well-boring or insurance or claim-jumping or something – I've forgotten which. He was a man well lubricated with gentility and his words were such as recommended you to his point of view. So Collier and me infested the grub tent with care and activity. Mame was level full of impartiality. 'Twas like a casino hand the way she dealt out her favors – one to Collier and one to me and one to the board and not a card up her sleeve.

'Me and Collier naturally got acquainted, and gravitated together some on the outside. Divested of his stratagems, he seemed to be a pleasant chap, full of an amiable sort of hostility.

' "I notice you have an affinity for grubbing in the banquet hall after the guests have fled," says I to him one day, to draw his conclusions.

' "Well, yes," says Collier, reflecting; "the tumult of a crowded board seems to harass my sensitive nerves."

' "It exasperates mine some, too," says I. "Nice little girl, don't you think?"

' "I see," says Collier, laughing. "Well, now that you mention it, I have noticed that she doesn't seem to displease the optic nerve."

' "She's a joy to mine," says I, "and I'm going after her. Notice is hereby served."

' "I'll be as candid as you," admits Collier, "and if the drug stores don't run out of pepsin I'll give you a run for your money that'll leave you a dyspeptic at the wind-up."

'So Collier and me begins the race; the grub department lays in new supplies; Mame waits on us, jolly and kind and agreeable and it looks like an even break, with Cupid and the cook working overtime in Dugan's restaurant.

"Twas one night in September when I got Mame to take a walk after supper when the things were all cleared away. We strolled out a distance and sat on a pile of lumber at the edge of town. Such opportunities was seldom, so I spoke my piece, explaining how the Brazilian diamonds and the fire kindler were laying up sufficient treasure to guarantee the happiness of two, and that both of 'm together couldn't equal the light from somebody's eyes, and that the name of Dugan should be changed to Peters, or reasons why not would be in order.

'Mame didn't say anything right away. Directly she gave a kind of shudder, and I began to learn something.

' "Jeff," she says. "I'm sorry you spoke. I like you as well as any of them, but there isn't the man in the world I'd ever marry, and there never will be. Do you know what a man is in my eye? He's a tomb. He's a sarcophagus for the interment of Beefsteakporkchopsliver'nbaconhamandeggs. He's that and nothing more. For two years I've watched men eat, eat, eat, until they represent nothing on earth to me but ruminant bipeds. They're absolutely nothing but something that goes in front of a knife and fork and plate at the table. They're fixed that way in my mind and memory. I've tried to overcome it, but I can't. I've heard girls rave about their sweethearts, but I never could understand it. A man and a sausage grinder and a pantry awake in me exactly the same sentiments. I went to a matinée once to see an actor the girls were crazy about. I got interested enough to wonder whether he liked his steak rare, medium, or well done, and his eggs over or straight up. That was all. No, Jeff; I'll marry no man and see him set at the breakfast table and eat and come back to dinner and eat, and happen in again at supper to eat, eat, eat."

' "But, Mame," says I, "it'll wear off. You've had too much of it. You'll marry some time, of course. Men don't eat always."

' "As far as my observation goes, they do. No, I'll tell you what I'm going to do." Mame turns, suddenly to animation and bright eyes. "There's a girl named Susie Foster in Terre Haute, a chum of mine. She waits in the railroad eating house there. I worked two years in a restaurant in that town. Susie has it worse than I do, because the men who eat at railroad stations gobble. They try to flirt and gobble at the same time. Whew! Susie and I have it all planned out. We're saving our money, and when we get enough we're going to buy a little cottage and five acres we know of, and live together, and grow violets for the Eastern market. A man better not bring his appetite within a mile of that ranch."

' "Don't girls ever—" I commenced, but Mame heads me off sharp.

' "No, they don't. They nibble a little bit sometimes; that's all."

' "I thought the confect—"

' "For goodness' sake, change the subject." says Mame.

'As I said before, that experience put me wise that the feminine arrangement ever struggles after deceptions and illusions. Take England – beef made her; wieners elevated Germany; Uncle Sam owes his greatness to fried chicken and pie, but the young ladies of the Shetalkyou schools, they'll never believe it. Shakespeare, they allow, and Rubinstein, and the Rough Riders is what did the trick.

"Twas a situation calculated to disturb. I couldn't bear to give up Mame; and yet it pained me to think of abandoning the practice of eating. I had acquired the habit too early. For twenty-seven years I had been blindly rushing upon my fate, yielding to the insidious lures of that deadly monster, food. It was too late. I was a ruminant biped for keeps. It was lobster salad to a doughnut that my life was going to be blighted by it.

'I continued to board at the Dugan tent, hoping that Mame would relent. I had sufficient faith in true love to believe that since it has often outlived the absence of a square meal it might, in time, overcome the presence of one. I went on ministering to my fatal vice, although I felt that each time I shoved a potato into my mouth in Mame's presence I might be burying my fondest hopes.

'I think Collier must have spoken to Mame and got the same answer, for one day he orders a cup of coffee and a cracker, and sits nibbling the corner of it like a girl in the parlor, that's filled up in the kitchen, previous, on cold roast and fried cabbage. I caught on and did the same, and maybe we thought we'd made a hit! The next day we tried it again, and out comes Old Man Dugan fetching in his hands the fairy viands.

' "Kinder off yer feed, ain't ye, gents?" he asks, fatherly and some sardonic. "Thought I'd spell Mame a bit, seein' the work was light, and my rheumatiz can stand the strain."

'So back me and Collier had to drop to the heavy grub again. I noticed about that time that I was seized by a most uncommon and devastating appetite. I ate until Mame must have hated to see me darken the door. Afterward I found out that I had been made the victim of the first dark and irreligious trick played on me by Ed Collier. Him and me had been taking drinks together uptown regular trying to drown our thirst for food. That man had bribed about ten bartenders to always put a big slug of Appletree's Anaconda Appetite Bitters in every one of my drinks. But the last trick he played me was hardest to forget.

'One day Collier failed to show up at the tent. A man told me he left town that morning. My only rival now was the bill of fare. A few days before he left Collier had presented me with a two-gallon jug of fine whisky which he said a cousin had sent him from Kentucky. I now have reason to believe that it contained Appletree's Anaconda Appetite Bitters almost exclusively. I continued to devour tons of provisions. In Mame's eyes I remained a mere biped, more ruminant than ever.

'About a week after Collier pulled his freight there came a kind of sideshow to town, and hoisted a tent near the railroad. I judged it was a sort of fake museum and curiosity business. I called to see Mame one night, and Ma Dugan said she and Thomas, her younger brother, had gone to the show. That same thing happened for three nights that week. Saturday night I caught her on the way coming back, and got to sit on the steps a while and talk to her. I noticed she looked different. Her eyes were softer, and shiny like. Instead of a Mame Dugan to fly from the voracity of man and raise violets, she seemed to be a Mame more in line as God intended her, approachable, and suited to bask in the light of the Brazilians and the Kindler.

' "You seem to be right smart inveigled," says I, "with the Unparalleled Exhibition of the World's Living Curiosities and Wonders."

' "It's a change," says Mame.

' "You'll need another," says I, "if you keep on going every night."

' "Don't be cross Jeff," says she; "it takes my mind off business."

' "Don't the curiosities eat?" I ask.

' "Not all of them. Some of them are wax."

' "Look out, then, that you don't get stuck," says I, kind of flip and foolish.

'Mame blushed. I didn't know what to think about her. My hopes raised some that perhaps my attentions had palliated man's awful crime of visibly introducing nourishment into his system. She talked some about the stars, referring to them with respect and politeness, and I drivelled a quantity about united hearts, homes made bright by true affection, and the Kindler. Mame listened without scorn and I says to myself, "Jeff, old man, you're removing the hoodoo that has clung to the consumer of victuals; you're setting your heel upon the serpent that lurks in the gravy bowl."

'Monday night I drop around. Mame is at the Unparalleled Exhibition with Thomas.

' "Now, may the curse of the forty-one seven-sided sea cooks," says I, "and the bad luck of the nine impenitent grasshoppers rest upon this selfsame sideshow at once and forever. Amen. I'll go to see it myself tomorrow night and investigate its baleful charm. Shall man that was made to inherit the earth be bereft of his sweetheart first by a knife and fork and then by a ten-cent circus?"

'The next night before starting out for the exhibition tent I inquire and find out that Mame is not at home. She is not at the circus with Thomas this time, for Thomas waylays me in the grass outside of the grub tent with a scheme of his own before I had time to eat supper.

' "What'll you give me, Jeff," says he, "if I tell you something?"

' "The value of it, son," I says.

' "Sis is stuck on a freak," says Thomas, "one of the side-show freaks. I don't like him. She does. I overheard 'em talking. Thought maybe you'd like to know. Say, Jeff, does it put you wise two dollars' worth? There's a target rifle up town that—"

'I frisked my pockets and commenced to dribble a stream of halves and quarters into Thomas's hat. The information was of the pile-driver system of news, and it telescoped my intellects for a while. While I was leaking small change and smiling foolish on the outside, and suffering disturbances internally, I was saying, idiotically and pleasantly:

' "Thank you, Thomas – thank you – er – a freak, you said, Thomas. Now, could you make out the monstrosity's entitlements a little clearer if you please, Thomas?"

' "This is the fellow," says Thomas, pulling out a yellow handbill from his pocket and shoving it under my nose. "He's the Champion Faster of the Universe. I guess that's why Sis got soft on him. He don't eat nothing. He's going to fast forty-nine days. This is the sixth. That's him."

'I looked at the name Thomas pointed out – "Professor Eduardo Collieri" "Ah!" says I, in admiration, "that's not so bad, Ed Collier. I give you credit for the trick. But I don't give you the girl until she's Mrs. Freak."

'I hit the sod in the direction of the show. I came up to the rear of the tent, and, as I did so, a man wiggled out like a snake from under the bottom of the canvas, scrambled to his feet, and ran into me like a locoed bronco. I gathered him by the neck and investigated him by the light of the stars. It is Professor Eduardo Collieri, in human habiliments, with a desperate look in one eye and impatience in the other.

' "Hello, Curiosity," says I. "Get still a minute and let's have a look at your freakship. How do you like being the willopus-wallopus or the bimbam from Borneo, or whatever name you are denounced by in the sideshow business?"

' "Jeff Peters," says Collier, in a weak voice. "Turn me loose, or I'll slug you one. I'm in the extremest kind of a large hurry. Hands off!"

' "Tut, tut, Eddie," I answers, holding him hard; "let an old friend gaze on the exhibition of your curiousness. It's an eminent graft you fell onto, my son. But don't speak of assaults and battery, because you're not fit. The best you've got is a lot of nerve and a mighty empty stomach." And so it was. The man was as weak as a vegetarian cat.

' "I'd argue this case with you, Jeff," says he, regretful in his style, "for an unlimited number of rounds if I had half an hour to train in and a slab of beefsteak two feet square to train with. Curse the man, I say, that invented the art of going foodless. May his soul in eternity be chained up within two feet of a bottomless pit of red-hot hash. I'm abandoning the conflict, Jeff; I'm deserting to the enemy. You'll find Miss Dugan inside contemplating the only living mummy and the informed hog. She's a fine girl, Jeff. I'd have beat you out if I could have kept up the grubless habit a little while longer. You'll have to admit that the fasting dodge was aces-up for a while. I figured it out that way. But, say, Jeff, it's said that love makes the world go around. Let me tell you, the announcement lacks verification. It's the wind from the dinner horn that does it. I love that Mame Dugan. I've gone six days without food in order to coincide with her sentiments. Only one bite did I have. That was when I knocked the tattooed man down with a war club and got a sandwich he was gobbling. The manager fined me all my salary; but salary wasn't what I was after. 'Twas that girl. I'd give my life for her, but I'd endanger my immortal soul for a beef stew. Hunger is a horrible thing, Jeff. Love and business and family and religion and art and patriotism are nothing but shadows of words when a man's starving!''

'In such language Ed Collier discoursed to me, pathetic. I gathered the diagnosis that his affections and his digestions had been implicated in a scramble and the commissary had won out. I never disliked Ed Collier. I searched my internal admonitions of suitable etiquette to see if I could find a remark of a consoling nature, but there was none convenient.

' "I'd be glad, now," says Ed, "if you'll let me go. I've been hard hit, but I'll hit the ration supply harder. I'm going to clean out every restaurant in town. I'm going to wade waist deep in sirloins and swim in ham and eggs. It's an awful thing, Jeff Peters, for a man to come to this pass – to give up his girl for something to eat – it's worse than that man Esau, that swapped his copyright for a partridge – but then, hunger's a fierce thing. You'll excuse me, now, Jeff, for I smell a pervasion of ham frying in the distance, and my legs are crying out to stampede in that direction."

' "A hearty meal to you, Ed Collier," I says to him, "and no hard feelings. For myself, I am projected to be an unseldom eater, and I have condolence for your predicaments."

'There was a sudden big whiff of frying ham smell on the breeze; and the Champion Faster gives a snort and gallops off in the dark toward fodder.

'I wish some of the cultured outfit that are always advertising the extenuating circumstances of love and romance had been there to see. There was Ed Collier, a fine man full of contrivances and flirtations, abandoning the girl of his heart and ripping out into the contiguous territory in the pursuit of sordid grub. 'Twas a rebuke to the poets and a slap at the best-paying element of fiction. An empty stomach is a sure antidote to an overfull heart.

'I was naturally anxious to know how far Mame was infatuated with Collier and his stratagems. I went inside the Unparalleled Exhibition, and there she was. She looked surprised to see me, but unguilty.

' "It's an elegant evening outside," says I. "The coolness is quite nice and gratifying, and the stars are lined out, first class, up where they belong. Wouldn't you shake these by-products of the animal kingdom long enough to take a walk with a common human who never was on a programme in his life?"

'Mame gave a sort of sly glance around, and I knew what that meant.

' "Oh," says I, "I hate to tell you; but the curiosity that lives on wind has flew the coop. He just crawled out under the tent. By this time he has amalgamated himself with half the delicatessen truck in town."

' "You mean Ed Collier?" says Mame.

' "I do," I answers; "and a pity it is that he has gone back to crime again. I met him outside the tent, and he exposed his intentions of devastating the food crop of the world. 'Tis enormously sad when one's ideal descends from his pedestal to make a seventeen-year locust of himself."

'Mame looked me straight in the eye until she had corkscrewed my reflections.

' "Jeff," says she, "it isn't quite like you to talk that way. I don't care to hear Ed Collier ridiculed. A man may do ridiculous things, but they don't look ridiculous to the girl he does 'em for. That was the man in a hundred. He stopped eating just to please me. I'd be hardhearted and ungrateful if I didn't feel kindly toward him. Could you do what he did?"

' "I know," says I, seeing the point. "I'm condemned. I can't help it. The brand of the consumer is upon my brow. Mrs. Eve settled that business for me when she made the dicker with the snake. I fell from the fire into the frying-pan. I guess I'm the Champion Feaster of the Universe." I spoke humble, and Mame mollified herself a little.

' "Ed Collier and I are good friends," she said, "the same as me and you. I gave him the same answer I did you – no marrying for me. I liked to be with Ed and talk to him. There was something mighty pleasant to me in the thought that here was a man who never used a knife and fork, and all for my sake."

' "Wasn't you in love with him?" I asks, all injudicious. "Wasn't there a deal on for you to become Mrs. Curiosity?"

'All of us do it sometimes. All of us get jostled out of the line of profitable talk now and then. Mame put on that little lemon *glacé* smile that runs between ice and sugar, and says, much too pleasant: "You're short on credentials for asking that question, Mr. Peters. Suppose you do a forty-nine day fast, just to give you ground to stand on, and then maybe I'll answer it."

'So, even after Collier was kidnapped out of the way by the revolt of his appetite, my own prospects with Mame didn't seem to be improved. And then business played out in Guthrie.

'I had stayed too long there. The Brazilians I had sold commenced to show signs of wear, and the Kindler refused to light up right frequent on wet mornings. There is always a time, in my business, when the star of success says, "Move on to the next town." I was traveling by wagon at that time so as not to miss any of the small towns; so I hitched up a few days later and went down to tell Mame good-bye. I wasn't abandoning the game; I intended running over to Oklahoma City and work it for a week or two. Then I was coming back to institute fresh proceedings against Mame.

'What do I find at the Dugan's but Mame all conspicuous in a blue traveling dress, with her little trunk at the door. It seems that sister Lottie Bell, who is a typewriter in Terre Haute, is going to be married next Thursday, and Mame is off for a week's visit to be an accomplice at the ceremony. Mame is waiting for a freight wagon that is going to take her to Oklahoma, but I condemns the freight wagon with promptness and scorn, and offers to deliver the goods myself. Ma Dugan sees no reason why not, as Mr. Freighter wants pay for the job; so, thirty minutes later Mame and I pull out in my light spring wagon with white canvas cover, and head due south.

'That morning was of a praiseworthy sort. The breeze was lively, and smelled excellent of flowers and grass, and the little cottontail rabbits entertained themselves with skylarking across the road. My two Kentucky bays went for the horizon until it come sailing in so fast you wanted to dodge it like a clothesline. Mame was full of talk and rattled on like a kid about her old home and her school pranks and the things she liked and the hateful ways of those Johnson girls just across the street, 'way up in Indiana. Not a word was said about Ed Collier or victuals or such solemn subjects.

About noon Mame looks and finds that the lunch she had put up in a basket had been left behind. I could have managed quite a collation, but Mame didn't seem to be grieving over nothing to eat, so I made no lamentations. It was a sore subject with me, and I ruled provender in all its branches out of my conversation.

'I am minded to touch light on explanations how I came to lose the way. The road was dim and well grown with grass; and there was Mame by my side confiscating my intellects and attention. The excuses are good or they are not, as they may appear to you. But I lost it, and at dusk that afternoon, when we should have been in Oklahoma City, we were seesawing along the edge of nowhere in some undiscovered river bottom, and the rain was falling in large, wet bunches. Down there in the swamps we saw a little log house on a small knoll of high ground. The bottom grass and the chaparral and the lonesome timber crowded all around it. It seemed to be a melancholy little house, and you felt sorry for it. 'Twas that house for the night, the way I reasoned it. I explained to Mame, and she leaves it to me to decide. She doesn't become galvanic and prosecuting, as most women would, but she says it's all right; she knows I didn't mean to do it.

'We found the house was deserted. It had two empty rooms. There was a little shed in the yard where beasts had once been kept. In a loft of it was a lot of old hay. I put my horses in there and gave them some of it, for which they looked at me sorrowful, expecting apologies. The rest of the hay I carried into the house by armfuls, with a view to accommodations. I also brought in the patent Kindler and the Brazilians, neither of which are guaranteed against the action of water.

'Mame and I sat on the wagon seats on the floor, and I lit a lot of the Kindler on the hearth, for the night was chilly. If I was any judge, that girl enjoyed it. It was a change for her. It gave her a different point of view. She laughed and talked, and the Kindler made a dim light compared to her eyes. I had a pocketful of cigars, and as far as I was concerned there had never been any fall of man. We were at the same old stand in the Garden of Eden. Out there somewhere in the rain and the dark was the river of Zion, and the angel with the flaming sword had not yet put up the keep-off-the-grass sign. I opened up a gross or two of the Brazilians and made Mame put them on – rings, brooches, necklaces, eardrops, bracelets, girdles, and lockets. She flashed and sparkled like a million-dollar princess until she had pink spots in her cheeks and almost cried for a looking-glass.

'When it got late I made a fine bunk on the floor for Mame with the hay and my lap robes and blankets out of the wagon and persuaded her to lie down. I sat in the other room burning tobacco and listening to the pouring rain and meditating on the many vicissitudes that come to a man during the seventy years or so immediately preceding his funeral.

'I must have dozed a little before morning, for my eyes were shut, and when I opened them it was daylight, and there stood Mame with her hair all done up neat and correct, and her eyes bright with admiration of existence.

' "Gee whiz, Jeff!" she exclaims, "but I'm hungry. I could eat a—"

'I looked up and caught her eye. Her smile went back in and she gave me a cold look of suspicion. Then I laughed, and laid down on the floor to laugh easier. It seemed funny to me. By nature and geniality I am a hearty laugher, and I went the limit. When I came to, Mame was sitting with her back to me, all contaminated with dignity.

' "Don't be angry, Mame," I says, "for I couldn't help it. It's the funny way you've done up your hair. If you could only see it!"

' "You needn't tell stories, sir," said Mame, cool and advised. "My hair is all right. I know what you were laughing about. Why, Jeff, look outside," she winds up, peeping through a chink between the logs. I opened the little wooden window and looked out. The entire river bottom was flooded, and the knob of land on which the house stood was an island in the middle of a rushing stream of yellow water a hundred yards wide. And it was still raining hard. All we could do was to stay there till the dove brought in the olive branch.

'I am bound to admit that conversations and amusements languished during the day. I was aware that Mame was getting a too prolonged onesided view of things again, but I had no way to change it. Personally, I was wrapped up in the desire to eat. I had hallucinations of hash and visions of ham, and I kept saying to myself all the time, "What'll you have to eat Jeff? – what'll you order, now, old man, when the waiter comes?" I picks out to myself all sorts of favorites from the bill of fare, and imagines them coming. I guess it's that way with all very hungry men. They can't get their cogitations trained on anything but something to eat. It shows that the little table with the broken-legged caster and the imitation Worcester sauce and the napkin covering up the coffee stains is the paramount issue, after all, instead of the question of immortality or peace between nations.

'I sat there, musing along, arguing with myself quite heated as to how I'd have my steak – with mushrooms or à la créole. Mame was on the other seat, pensive, her head leaning on her hand. "Let the potatoes come home-fried," I states in my mind, "and brown the hash in the pan, with nine poached eggs on the side." I felt, careful, in my own pockets to see if I could find a peanut or a grain or two of popcorn.

'Night came on again with the river still rising and the rain still falling. I looked at Mame and I noticed that desperate look on her face that a girl always wears when she passes an ice-cream lair. I knew that poor girl was hungry – maybe for the first time in her life. There was that anxious look in her eye that a woman has only when she has missed a meal or feels her skirt unfastened in the back.

'It was about eleven o'clock or so on the second night when we sat, gloomy, in our ship-wrecked cabin. I kept jerking my mind away from the subject of food, but it kept flopping back again before I could fasten it. I thought of everything good to eat I had ever heard of. I went away back to my kidhood and remembered the hot biscuit sopped in sorghum and bacon gravy with partiality and respect. Then I trailed along up the years, pausing at green apples and salt, flapjacks and maple, lye hominy, fried chicken Old Virginia style, corn on the cob, spareribs and sweet potato pie, and wound up with Georgia Brunswick stew, which is the top notch of good things to eat, because it comprises 'em all.

'They say a drowning man sees a panorama of his whole life pass before him. Well, when a man's starving he sees the ghost of every meal he ever ate set out before him, and he invents new dishes that would make the fortune of a chef. If somebody would collect the last words of men who starved to death they'd have to sift 'em mighty fine to discover the sentiment, but they'd compile into a cook book that would sell into the millions.

'I guess I must have had my conscience pretty well inflicted with culinary mediations, for, without intending to do so, I says, out loud, to the imaginary waiter, "Cut it thick and have it rare, with the French fried, and six, soft-scrambled, on toast."

'Mame turned her head quick as a wink. Her eyes were sparkling and she smiled sudden.

' "Medium for me," she rattles on, "with the Juliennes, and three, straight up. Draw one, and brown the wheats, double order to come. Oh, Jeff, wouldn't it be glorious! And then I'd like to have a half fry, and a little chicken curried with rice, and a cup custard with ice cream, and—"

' "Go easy," I interrupts, "where's the chicken liver pie, and the kidney *sauté* on toast, and the roast lamb, and—"

' "Oh," cuts in Mame, all excited, "with mint sauce, and the turkey salad, and stuffed olives, and raspberry tarts, and—"

' "Keep it going," says I. "Hurry up with the fried squash, and the hot corn pone with sweet milk, and don't forget the apple dumpling with hard sauce, and the cross-barred dewberry pie—"

'Yes, for ten minutes we kept up that kind of restaurant repartee. We ranges up and down and backward and forward over the main trunk lines and the branches of the victual subject, and Mame leads the game, for she is apprised in the ramifications of grub, and the dishes she nominates aggravates my yearnings. It seems that there is set up a feeling that Mame will line up friendly again with food. It seems that she looks upon the obnoxious science of eating with less contempt than before.

'The next morning we find that the flood has subsided. I geared up the bays, and splashed out through the mud, some precarious, until we found the road again. We were only a few miles wrong, and in two hours we were in Oklahoma City. The first thing we saw was a big restaurant sign, and we piled into there in a hurry. Here I finds myself sitting with Mame at table, with knives and forks and plates between us, and she not scornful, but smiling with starvation and sweetness.

"Twas a new restaurant and well stocked. I designated a list of quotations from the bill of fare that made the waiter look out toward the wagon to see how many more might be coming.

'There we were, and there was the order being served. 'Twas a banquet for a dozen, but we felt like a dozen. I looked across the table at Mame and smiled, for I had recollections. Mame was looking at the table like a boy looks at his first stem-winder. Then she looked at me, straight in the face, and two big tears came in her eyes. The waiter was gone after more grub.

' "Jeff," she says, soft like, "I've been a foolish girl. I've looked at things from the wrong side. I never felt this way before. Men get hungry every day like this, don't they? They're big and strong, and they do the hard work of the world, and they don't eat just to spite silly waiter girls in restaurants, do they, Jeff? You said once – that is, you asked me – you wanted me to – well, Jeff, if you still care – I'd be glad and willing to have you always sitting across the table from me. Now give me something to eat, quick, please."

'So, as I've said, a woman needs to change her point of view now and then. They get tired of the same old sights – the same old dinner table, washtub, and sewing machine. Give 'em a touch of the various – a little travel and a little rest, a little tomfoolery along with the tragedies of keeping house, a little petting after the blowing-up, a little upsetting and jostling around – and everybody in the game will have chips added to their stack by the play.'

THE CABALLERO'S WAY

THE CISCO KID HAD KILLED six men in more or less fair scrimmages, had murdered twice as many (mostly Mexicans), and had winged a larger number whom he modestly forebore to count. Therefore a woman loved him.

The Kid was twenty-five, looked twenty; and a careful insurance company would have estimated the probable time of his demise at, say, twenty-six. His habitat was anywhere between the Frio and the Rio Grande. He killed for the love of it – because he was quick-tempered – to avoid arrest – for his own amusement – any reason that came to his mind would suffice. He had escaped capture because he could shoot five-sixths of a second sooner than any sheriff or ranger in the service, and because he rode a speckled roan horse that knew every cowpath in the mesquite and pear thickets from San Antonio to Matamoras.

Tonia Perez, the girl who loved the Cisco Kid, was half Carmen, half Madonna, and the rest – oh, yes, a woman who is half Carmen and half Madonna can always be something more – the rest, let us say, was humming-bird. She lived in a grass-roofed *jacal* near a little Mexican settlement at the Lone Wolf Crossing of the Frio. With her lived a father or grandfather, a lineal Aztec, somewhat less than a thousand years old, who herded a hundred goats and lived in a continuous drunken dream from drinking *mescal*. Back of the *jacal* a tremendous forest of bristling pear, twenty feet high at its worst, crowded almost to its door. It was along the bewildering maze of this spinous thicket that the speckled roan would bring the Kid to see his girl. And once, clinging like a lizard to the ridge-pole, high up under the peaked grass roof, he had heard Tonia, with her Madonna face and Carmen beauty and humming-bird soul, parley with the sheriff's posse, denying knowledge of her man in her soft *mélange* of Spanish and English.

One day the adjutant-general of the State, who is, *ex officio*, commander of the ranger forces, wrote some sarcastic lines to Captain Duval of Company X, stationed at Laredo, relative to the serene and undisturbed existence led by murderers and desperadoes in the said captain's territory.

The captain turned the color of brick dust under his tan, and forwarded the letter, after adding a few comments, per ranger Private Bill Adamson, to ranger Lieutenant Sandridge, camped at a water hole on the Nueces with a squad of five men in preservation of law and order.

Lieutenant Sandridge turned a beautiful *couleur de rose* through his ordinary strawberry complexion, tucked the letter in his hip pocket, and chewed off the end of his gamboge moustache.

The next morning he saddled his horse and rode alone to the Mexican settlement at the Lone Wolf Crossing of the Frio, twenty miles away.

Six feet two, blond as a Viking, quiet as a deacon, dangerous as a machine gun, Sandridge moved among the *Jacales*, patiently seeking news of the Cisco Kid.

Far more than the law, the Mexicans dreaded the cold and certain vengeance of the lone rider that the ranger sought. It had been one of the Kid's pastimes to shoot Mexicans 'to see them kick': if he demanded from them moribund Terpsichorean feats, simply that he might be entertained, what terrible and extreme penalties would be certain to follow should they anger him! One and all they lounged with upturned palms and shrugging shoulders, filling the air with '*quién sabes*' and denials of the Kid's acquaintance.

But there was a man named Fink who kept a store at the Crossing – a man of many nationalities, tongues, interests, and ways of thinking.

'No use to ask them Mexicans,' he said to Sandridge. 'They're afraid to tell. This *hombre* they call the Kid – Goodall is his name, ain't it? – he's been in my store once or twice. I have an idea you might run across him at – but I guess I don't keer to say, myself. I'm two seconds later in pulling a gun than I used to be and the difference is worth thinking about. But this Kid's got a half-Mexican girl at the Crossing that he comes to see. She lives in that *jacal* a hundred yards down the arroyo at the edge of the pear. Maybe she – no, I don't suppose she would, but that *jacal* would be a good place to watch, anyway.'

Sandridge rode down to the *jacal* of Perez. The sun was low, and the broad shade of the great pear thicket already covered the grass-thatched hut. The goats were enclosed for the night in a brush corral near by. A few kids walked the top of it, nibbling the chaparral leaves. The old Mexican lay upon a blanket on the grass, already in a stupor from his mescal, and dreaming, perhaps, of the nights when he and Pizarro touched glasses to their New World fortunes – so old his wrinkled face seemed to proclaim him to be. And in the door of the *jacal* stood Tonia. And Lieutenant Sandridge sat in his saddle staring at her like a gannet agape at a sailorman.

The Cisco Kid was a vain person, as all eminent and successful assassins are, and his bosom would have been ruffled had he known that at a simple exchange of glances two persons, in whose minds he had been looming large, suddenly abandoned (at least for the time) all thought of him.

Never before had Tonia seen such a man as this. He seemed to be made of sunshine and blood-red tissue and clear weather. He seemed to illuminate the shadow of the pear when he smiled, as though the sun were rising again. The men she had known had been small and dark. Even the Kid, in spite of his achievements, was a stripling no larger than herself, with black straight hair and a cold marble face that chilled the noonday.

As for Tonia, though she sends description to the poorhouse, let her make a millionaire of your fancy. Her blue-black hair, smoothly divided in the middle and bound close to her head, and her large eyes full of the Latin melancholy, gave her the Madonna touch. Her motions and air spoke of the concealed fire and the desire to charm that she inherited from the *gitanas* of the Basque province. As for the humming-bird part of her, that dwelt in her heart; you could not perceive it unless her bright red skirt and dark blue blouse gave you a symbolic hint of the vagarious bird.

The newly lighted sun-god asked for a drink of water. Tonia brought it from the red jar hanging under the brush shelter. Sandridge considered it necessary to dismount so as to lessen the trouble of her ministrations.

I play no spy; nor do I assume to master the thoughts of any human heart; but I assert, by the chronicler's right, that before a quarter of an hour had sped, Sandridge was teaching her how to plait a six-strand rawhide stake-rope, and Tonia had explained to him that were it not for her little English book that the peripatetic *padre* had given her and the little crippled *chivo*, that she fed from a bottle, she would be very, very lonely indeed.

Which leads to a suspicion that the Kid's fences needed repairing, and that the adjutant-general's sarcasm had fallen upon unproductive soil.

In his camp by the water hole Lieutenant Sandridge announced and reiterated his intention of either causing the Cisco Kid to nibble the black loam of the Frio country prairies or of hailing him before a judge and jury. That sounded business-like: Twice a week he rode over to the Lone Wolf Crossing of the Frio, and directed Tonia's slim, slightly lemon-tinted fingers among the intricacies of the slowly growing lariat. A six-strand plait is hard to learn and easy to teach.

The ranger knew that he might find the Kid there at any visit. He kept his armament ready, and had a frequent eye for the pear thicket at the rear of the *jacal*. Thus he might bring down the kite and the humming-bird with one stone.

While the sunny-haired ornithologist was pursuing his studies the Cisco Kid was also attending to his professional duties. He moodily shot up a saloon in a small cow village on Quintana Creek, killed the town marshal (plugging him neatly in the centre of his tin badge), and then rode away, morose and unsatisfied. No true artist is uplifted by shooting an aged man carrying an old-style .38 bulldog.

On his way the Kid suddenly experienced the yearning that all men feel when wrong-doing loses its keen edge of delight. He yearned for the woman he loved to reassure him that she was his in spite of it. He wanted her to call his bloodthirstiness bravery and his cruelty devotion. He wanted Tonia to bring him water from the red jug under the brush shelter, and tell him how the *chivo* was thriving on the bottle.

The Kid turned the speckled roan's head up the ten-mile pear flat that stretches along the Arroyo Hondo until it ends at the Lone Wolf Crossing of the Frio. The roam whickered; for he had a sense of locality and direction equal to that of a belt-line street-car horse; and he knew he would soon be nibbling the rich mesquite grass at the end of a forty-foot stake rope while Ulysses rested his head in Circe's straw-roofed hut.

More weired and lonesome than the journey of an Amazonian explorer is the ride of one through a Texas pear flat. With dismal monotony and startling variety the uncanny and multiform shapes of the cacti lift their twisted trunks and fat, bristly hands to encumber the way. The demon plant, appearing to live without soil or rain, seems to taunt the parched traveler with its lush gray greenness. It warps itself a thousand times about what look to be open and inviting paths, only to lure the rider into blind and impassable spine-defended 'bottoms of the bag,' leaving him to retreat if he can, with the points of the compass whirling in his head.

To be lost in the pear is to die almost the death of the thief on the cross, pierced by nails and with grotesque shapes of all the fiends hovering about.

But it was not so with the Kid and his mount. Winding, twisting, circling, tracing the most fantastic and bewildering trail ever picked out, the good roan lessened the distance to the Lone Wolf Crossing with every coil and turn that he made.

While they fared the Kid sang. He knew but one tune and he sang it, as he knew but one code and lived it, and but one girl and loved her. He was a single-minded man of conventional ideas. He had a voice like a coyote with bronchitis, but whenever he chose to sing his song he sang it. It was a

conventional song of the camps and trail, running at its beginning as near as
may be to these words:

> Don't you monkey with my Lulu girl
> Or I'll tell you what I'll do—

and so on. The roan was inured to it, and did not mind.

But even the poorest singer will, after a certain time, gain his own consent
to refrain from contributing to the world's noises. So the Kid, by the time he
was within a mile or two of Tonia's *jacal*, had reluctantly allowed his song
to die away – not because his vocal performance had become less charming
to his own ears, but because his laryngeal muscles were aweary.

As though he were in a circus ring the speckled roan wheeled and danced
through the labyrinth of pear until at length his rider knew by certain
landmarks that the Lone Wolf Crossing was close at hand. Then, where the
pear was thinner, he caught sight of the grass roof of the *jacal* and the
hackberry tree on the edge of the arroyo. A few yards farther the Kid stopped
the roan and gazed intently through the prickly openings. Then he dismounted, dropped the roan's reins, and proceeded on foot, stooping and silent,
like an Indian. The roan, knowing his part, stood still, making no sound.

The Kid crept noiselessly to the very edge of the pear thicket and
reconnoitered between the leaves of a clump of cactus.

Ten yards from his hiding-place, in the shade of the *jacal*, sat his Tonia
calmly plaiting a raw-hide lariat. So far she might surely escape condemnation;
women have been known, from time to time, to engage in more mischievous
occupations. But if all must be told, there is to be added that her head reposed
against the broad and comfortable chest of a tall red-and-yellow man, and
that his arm was about her, guiding her nimble small fingers that required
so many lessons at the intricate six-strand plait.

Sandridge glanced quickly at the dark mass of pear when he heard a slight
squeaking sound that was not altogether unfamiliar. A gun-scabbard will
make that sound when one grasps the handle of a six-shooter suddenly. But
the sound was not repeated; and Tonia's fingers needed close attention.

And then, in the shadow of death, they began to talk of their love; and in
the still July afternoon every word they uttered reached the ears of the Kid.

'Remember, then,' said Tonia, 'you must not come again until I send for
you. Soon he will be here. A *vaquero* at the *tienda* said to-day he saw him
on the Guadalupe three days ago. When he is that near he always comes. If
he comes and finds you here he will kill you. So, for my sake, you must
come no more until I send you the word.'

'All right,' said the ranger. 'And then what?'

'And then,' said the girl, 'you must bring your men here and kill him. If
not, he will kill you.'

'He ain't a man to surrender, that's sure,' said Sandridge. 'It's kill or be
killed for the officer that goes up against Mr. Cisco Kid.'

'He must die,' said the girl. 'Otherwise there will not be any peace in the
world for thee and me. He has killed many. Let him so die. Bring your men,
and give him no chance to escape.'

'You used to think right much of him,' said Sandridge.

Tonia dropped the lariat, twisted herself around, and curved a lemon-
tinted arm over the ranger's shoulder.

'But then,' she murmured in liquid Spanish, 'I had not beheld thee, thou great, red mountain of a man! And thou art kind and good, as well as strong. Could one choose him, knowing thee? Let him die; for then I will not be filled with fear by day and night lest he hurt thee or me.'

'How can I know when he comes?' asked Sandridge.

'When he comes,' said Tonia, 'he remains two days, sometimes three. Gregorio, the small son of Old Luisa, the *lavandera*, has a swift pony. I will write a letter to thee and send it by him, saying how it will be best to come upon him. By Gregorio will the letter come. And bring many men with thee, and have such care, oh, dear red one, for the rattlesnake is not quicker to strike than is "*El Chivato*," as they call him, to send a ball from his *pistola*.'

'The Kid's handy with his gun, sure enough,' admitted Sandridge, 'but when I come for him I shall come alone. I'll get him by myself or not at all. The Cap wrote one or two things to me that make me want to do the trick without any help. You let me know when Mr. Kid arrives, and I'll do the rest.'

'I will send you the message by the boy Gregorio,' said the girl. 'I knew you were braver than that small slayer of men who never smiles. How could I ever have thought I cared for him?'

It was time for the ranger to ride back to his camp on the water hole. Before he mounted his horse he raised the slight form of Tonia with one arm high from the earth for a parting salute. The drowsy stillness of the torpid summer air still lay thick upon the dreaming afternoon. The smoke from the fire in the *jacal*, where the *frijoles* blubbered in the iron pot, rose straight as a plumb-line above the clay-daubed chimney. No sound or movement disturbed the serenity of the dense pear thicket ten yards away.

When the form of Sandridge had disappeared, loping his big dun down the steep banks of the Frio crossing, the Kid crept back to his own horse, mounted him, and rode back along the tortuous trail he had come.

But not far. He stopped and waited in the silent depths of the pear until half an hour had passed. And then Tonia heard the high, untrue notes of his unmusical singing coming nearer and nearer; and she ran to the edge of the pear to meet him.

The Kid seldom smiled; but he smiled and waved his hat when he saw her. He dismounted, and his girl sprang into his arms. The Kid looked at her fondly. His thick black hair clung to his head like a wrinkled mat. The meeting brought a slight ripple of some undercurrent of feeling to his smooth, dark face that was usually as motionless as a clay mask.

'How's my girl?' he asked, holding her close.

'Sick of waiting so long for you, dear one,' she answered. 'My eyes are dim with always gazing into that devil's pincushion through which you come. And I can see into it such a little way, too. But you are here, beloved one, and I will not scold. Qué mal muchacho! not to come to see your *alma* more often. Go in and rest, and let me water your horse and stake him with the long rope. There is cool water in the jar for you.'

The Kid kissed her affectionately.

'Not if the court knows itself do I let a lady stake my horse for me,' said he. 'But if you'll run in, *chica*, and throw a pot of coffee together while I attend to the *caballo*, I'll be a good deal obliged.'

Besides his marksmanship the Kid had another attribute for which he admired himself greatly. He was *muy caballero*, as the Mexicans express it, where the ladies were concerned. For them he had always gentle words and consideration. He could not have spoken a harsh word to a woman. He might ruthlessly slay their husbands and brothers, but he could not have laid the weight of a finger in anger upon a woman. Wherefore many of that interesting division of humanity who had come under the spell of his politeness declared their disbelief in the stories circulated about Mr. Kid. One shouldn't believe everything one heard, they said. When confronted by their indignant men folk with proof of the *caballero's* deeds of infamy, they said maybe he had been driven to it, and that he knew how to treat a lady, anyhow.

Considering this extremely courteous idiosyncrasy of the Kid and the pride that he took in it, one can perceive that the solution of the problem that was presented to him by what he saw and heard from his hiding-place in the pear that afternoon (at least as to one of the actors) must have been obscured by difficulties. And yet one could not think of the Kid overlooking little matters of that kind.

At the end of the short twilight they gathered around a supper of *frijoles*, goat steaks, canned peaches, and coffee, by the light of a lantern in the *jacal*. Afterward, the ancestor, his flock corralled, smoked a cigarette and became a mummy in a gray blanket. Tonia washed the few dishes while the Kid dried them with the flour-sacking towel. Her eyes shone; she chatted volubly of the inconsequent happenings of her small world since the Kid's last visit; it was as all his other home-comings had been.

Then outside Tonia swung in a grass hammock with her guitar and sang sad *canciones de amor*.

'Do you love me just the same, old girl?' asked the Kid, hunting for his cigarette papers.

'Always the same, little one,' said Tonia, her dark eyes lingering upon him.

'I must go over to Fink's,' said the Kid, rising, 'for some tobacco. I thought I had another sack in my coat. I'll be back in a quarter of an hour.'

'Hasten,' said Tonia, 'and tell me – how long shall I call you my own this time? Will you be gone again to-morrow, leaving me to grieve, or will you be longer with your Tonia?'

'Oh, I might stay two or three days this trip,' said the Kid, yawning. 'I've been on the dodge for a month, and I'd like to rest up.'

He was gone half an hour for his tobacco. When he returned Tonia was still lying in the hammock.

'It's funny,' said the Kid, 'how I feel. I feel like there was somebody lying behind every bush and tree waiting to shoot me. I never had mully-grubs like them before. Maybe it's one of them presumptions. I've got half a notion to light out in the morning before day. The Guadalupe country is burning up about that old Dutchman I plugged down there.'

'You are not afraid – no one could make my brave little one fear.'

'Well, I haven't been usually regarded as a jack-rabbit when it comes to scrapping; but I don't want a posse smoking me out when I'm in your *jacal*. Somebody might get hurt that oughtn't to.'

'Remain with your Tonia; no one will find you here.'

The Kid looked keenly into the shadows up and down the arroyo and toward the dim lights of the Mexican village.

'I'll see how it looks later on,' was his decision.

THE BEST OF O. HENRY

At midnight a horseman rode into the ranger's camp, blazing his way by noisy 'halloes' to indicate a pacific mission. Sandridge and one or two others turned out to investigate the row. The rider announced himself to be Domingo Sales, from the Lone Wolf Crossing. He bore a letter for Señor Sandridge. Old Luisa, the *lavandera*, had persuaded him to bring it, he said, her son Gregorio being too ill of a fever to ride.

Sandridge lighted the camp lantern and read the letter. These were its words:

Dear One: He has come. Hardly had you ridden away when he came out of the pear. When he first talked he said he would stay three days or more. Then as it grew later he was like a wolf or a fox, and walked about without rest, looking and listening. Soon he said he must leave before daylight when it is dark and stillest. And then he seemed to suspect that I be not true to him. He looked at me so strange that I am frightened. I swear to him that I love him, his own Tonia. Last of all he said I must prove to him I am true. He thinks that even now men are waiting to kill him as he rides from my house. To escape he says he will dress in my clothes, my red skirt and the blue waist I wear and the brown mantilla over the head, and thus ride away. But before that he says that I must put on his clothes, his *pantalones* and *camisa* and hat, and ride away on his horse from the *jacal* as far as the big road beyond the crossing and back again. This before he goes, so he can tell if I am true and if men are hidden to shoot him. It is a terrible thing. An hour before daybreak this is to be. Come, my dear one, and kill this man and take me for your Tonia. Do not try to take hold of him alive, but kill him quickly. Knowing all, you should do that. You must come long before the time and hide yourself in the little shed near the *jacal* where the wagon and saddles are kept. It is dark in there. He will wear my red skirt and blue waist and brown mantilla. I send you a hundred kisses. Come surely and shoot quickly and straight.

Thine Own Tonia

Sandridge quickly explained to his men the official part of the missive. The rangers protested against his going alone.

'I'll get him easy enough,' said the lieutenant. 'The girl's got him trapped. And don't even think he'll get the drop on me.'

Sandridge saddled his horse and rode to the Lone Wolf Crossing. He tied his big dun in a clump of brush on the arroyo, took his Winchester from his scabbard, and carefully approached the Perez *jacal*. There was only the half of a high moon drifted over by ragged, milk-white gulf clouds.

The wagon-shed was an excellent place for ambush; and the ranger got inside it safely. In the black shadow of the brush shelter in front of the *jacal* he could see a horse tied and hear him impatiently pawing the hard-trodden earth.

He waited almost an hour before two figures came out of the *jacal*. One, in man's clothes, quickly mounted the horse and galloped past the wagon-shed toward the crossing and village. And then the other figure, in skirt, waist, and mantilla over its head, stepped out into the faint moonlight, gazing after the rider. Sandridge thought he would take his chance then before Tonia rode back. He fancied she might not care to see it.

'Throw up your hands,' he ordered, loudly, stepping out of the wagon-shed with his Winchester at his shoulder.

There was a quick turn of the figure, but no movement to obey, so the ranger pumped in the bullets – one – two – three – and then twice more; for you never could be too sure of bringing down the Cisco Kid. There was no danger of missing at ten paces, even in that half moonlight.

The old ancestor, asleep on his blanket, was awakened by the shots. Listening further, he heard a great cry from some man in mortal distress or anguish, and rose up grumbling at the disturbing ways of moderns.

The tall, red ghost of a man burst into the *jacal*, reaching one hand, shaking like a *tule* reed, for the lantern hanging on its nail. The other spread a letter on the table.

'Look at this letter, Perez,' cried the man. 'Who wrote it?'

'*Ah, Dios*! it is Señor Sandridge,' mumbled the old man, approaching. '*Pues, señor*, that letter was written by "*El Chivata*," as he is called – by the man of Tonia. They say he is a bad man; I do not know. While Tonia slept he wrote the letter and sent it by this old hand of mine to Domingo Sales to be brought to you. Is there anything wrong in the letter? I am very old; and I did not know. *Valgame Dios*! it is a very foolish world; and there is nothing in the house to drink – nothing to drink.'

Just then all that Sandridge could think of to do was to go outside and throw himself face downward in the dust by the side of his humming-bird, of whom not a feather fluttered. He was not a *caballero* by instinct, and he could not understand the niceties of revenge.

A mile away the rider who had ridden past the wagon-shed struck up a harsh, untuneful song, the words of which began:

Don't you monkey with my Lulu girl
Or I'll tell you what I'll do—

THE SPHINX APPLE

TWENTY MILES OUT FROM PARADISE, and fifteen miles short of Sunrise City, Bildad Rose, the stage-driver, stopped his team. A furious snow had been falling all day. Eight inches it measured now, on a level. The remainder of the road was not without peril in daylight, creeping along the ribs of a bijou range of ragged mountains. Now, when both snow and night masked its dangers, further travel was not to be thought of, said Bildad Rose. So he pulled up his four stout horses, and delivered to his five passengers oral deductions of his wisdom.

Judge Menefee, to whom men granted leadership and the initiatory as upon a silver salver, sprang from the coach at once. Four of his fellow-passengers followed, inspired by his example, ready to explore, to objurgate, to resist, to submit, to proceed, according as their prime factor might be inclined to sway them. The fifth passenger, a young woman, remained in the coach.

Bildad had halted upon the shoulder of the first mountain spur. Two rail-fences, ragged-black, hemmed the road. Fifty yards above the upper fence, showing a dark blot in the white drifts, stood a small house. Upon this house descended – or rather ascended – Judge Menefee and his cohorts with boyish whoops born of the snow and stress. They called; they pounded at window and door. At the inhospitable silence they waxed restive; they assaulted and forced the pregnable barriers, and invaded the premises.

The watchers from the coach heard stumblings and shoutings from the interior of the ravaged house. Before long a light within flickered, glowed, flamed high and bright and cheerful. Then came running back through the driving flakes the exuberant explorers. More deeply pitched than the clarion – even orchestral in volume – the voice of Judge Menefee proclaimed the succor that lay in apposition with their state of travail. The one room of the house was uninhabited, he said, and bare of furniture; but it contained a great fireplace; and they had discovered an ample store of chopped wood in a lean-to at the rear. Housing and warmth against the shivering night were thus assured. For the placation of Bildad Rose there was news of a stable, not ruined beyond service, with hay in a loft, near the house.

'Gentlemen,' cried Bildad Rose from his seat, swathed in coats and robes, 'tear me down two panels of that fence, so I can drive in. That is old man Redruth's shanty. I thought we must be nigh it. They took him to the foolish house in August.'

Cheerfully the four passengers sprang at the snow-capped rails. The exhorted team tugged the coach up the slant to the door of the edifice from which a mid-summer madness had ravished its proprietor. The driver and two of the passengers began to unhitch. Judge Menefee opened the door of the coach, and removed his hat.

'I have to announce, Miss Garland,' said he, 'the enforced suspension of our journey. The driver asserts that the risk in traveling the mountain road by night is too great even to consider. It will be necessary to remain in the shelter of this house until morning. I beg that you will feel that there is nothing to fear beyond a temporary inconvenience. I have personally inspected the house, and find that there are means to provide against the rigor of the weather, at least. You shall be made as comfortable as possible. Permit me to assist you to alight.'

To the Judge's side came the passenger whose pursuit in life was the placing of the Little Goliath windmill. His name was Dunwoody; but that matters not much. In traveling merely from Paradise to Sunrise City one needs little or no name. Still, one who would seek to divide honors with Judge Madison L. Menefee deserves a cognominal peg upon which Fame may hang a wreath. Thus spake, loudly and buoyantly, the aërial miller:

'Guess you'll have to climb out of the ark, Mrs. McFarland. This wigwam ain't exactly the Palmer House, but it turns snow, and they won't search your grip for souvenir spoons when you leave. We've got a fire going, and we'll fix you up with dry Trilbys and keep the mice away, anyhow, all right, all right.'

One of the two passengers who were struggling in a mêlée of horses, harness, snow, and the sarcastic injunctions of Bildad Rose, called loudly from the whirl of his volunteer duties: 'Say, some of you fellows get Miss Solomon into the house, will you? Whoa, there! you confounded brute!'

Again must it be gently urged that in traveling from Paradise to Sunrise City an accurate name is prodigality. When Judge Menefee – sanctioned to the act by his grey hair and widespread repute – had introduced himself to the lady passenger, she had, herself, sweetly breathed a name, in response, that the hearing of the male passengers had variously interpreted. In the not unjealous spirit of rivalry that eventuated, each clung stubbornly to his own theory. For the lady passenger to have reasseverated or corrected would have seemed didactic if not unduly solicitous of a specific acquaintance. Therefore the lady passenger permitted herself to be Garlanded and McFarlanded and Solomoned with equal and discreet complacency. It is thirty-five miles from Paradise to Sunrise City. *Compagnon de voyage* is name enough, by the gripsack of the Wandering Jew! for so brief a journey.

Soon the little party of wayfarers were happily seated in a cheerful arc before the roaring fire. The robes, cushions and removable portions of the coach had been brought in and put to service. The lady passenger chose a place near the hearth at one end of the arc. There she graced almost a throne that her subjects had prepared. She sat upon cushions and leaned against an empty box and barrel, robe bespread, which formed a defence from the invading draughts. She extended her feet, delectably shod, to the cordial heat. She ungloved her hands, but retained about her neck her long fur boa. The unstable flames half revealed, while the warding boa half submerged, her face – a youthful face, altogether feminine, clearly moulded and calm with beauty's unchallenged confidence. Chivalry and manhood were here vying to please and comfort her. She seemed to accept their devoirs – not piquantly, as one courted and attended; not preeningly, as many of her sex unworthily reap their honors; nor yet stolidly, as the ox receives his hay; but concordantly with nature's own plan – as the lily ingests the drop of dew foreordained to its refreshment.

Outside the wind roared mightily, the fine snow whizzed through the cracks, the cold besieged the backs of the immolated six; but the elements did not lack a champion that night. Judge Menefee was attorney for the storm. The weather was his client, and he strove by special pleading to convince his companions in that frigid jury-box that they sojourned in a bower of roses, beset only by benignant zephyrs. He drew upon a fund of gaiety, wit, and anecdote, sophistical, but crowned with success. His cheerfulness communicated itself irresistibly. Each one hastened to contribute his quota toward the general optimism. Even the lady passenger was moved to expression.

'I think it is quite charming,' she said, in her slow, crystal tones.

At intervals some one of the passengers would rise and humorously explore the room. There was little evidence to be collected of its habitation by old man Redruth.

Bildad Rose was called upon vivaciously for the ex-hermit's history. Now, since the stage-driver's horses were fairly comfortable and his passengers appeared to be so, peace and comity returned to him.

'The old didapper,' began Bildad, somewhat irreverently, 'infested this here house about twenty year. He never allowed nobody to come nigh him. He'd duck his head inside and slam the door whenever a team drove along. There was spinning-wheels up in his loft, all right. He used to buy his groceries and tobacco at Sam Tilly's store, on the Little Muddy. Last August he went up there dressed in a red bedquilt, and told Sam he was King Solomon, and that the Queen of Sheba was coming to visit him. He fetched along all the money he had – a little bag full of silver – and dropped it in

Sam's well. "She won't come," says old man Redruth to Sam, "if she knows I've got any money."

'As soon as folks heard he had that sort of a theory about women and money they know he was crazy; so they sent down and packed him to the foolish asylum.'

'Was there a romance in his life that drove him to a solitary existence?' asked one of the passengers, a young man who had an Agency.

'No,' said Bildad, 'not that I ever heard spoke of. Just ordinary trouble. They say he had had unfortunateness in the way of love derangements with a young lady when he was young; before he contracted red bedquilts and had his financial conclusions disqualified. I never heard of no romance.'

'Ah!' exclaimed Judge Menefee, impressively; 'a case of unrequited affection, no doubt.'

'No, sir,' returned Bildad, 'not at all. She never married him. Marmaduke Muligan, down at Paradise, seen a man once that come from old Redruth's town. He said Redruth was a fine young man, but when you kicked him on the pocket all you could hear jingle was a cuff-fastener and a bunch of keys. He was engaged to this young lady – Miss Alice – something was her name; I've forgot. This man said she was the kind of a girl you like to have reach across you in a car to pay the fare. Well, there come to the town a young chap all affuent and easy, and fixed up with buggies and mining stock and leisure time. Although she was a staked claim, Miss Alice and the new entry seemed to strike a mutual kind of a clip. They had calls and coincidences of going to the post office and such things as sometimes make a girl send back the engagement ring and other presents – "a rift within the loot," the poetry man calls it.

'One day folks seen Redruth and Miss Alice standing talking at the gate. Then he lifts his hat and walks away, and that was the last anybody in that town seen of him, as far as this man knew.'

'What about the young lady?' asked the young man who had an Agency.

'Never heard,' answered Bildad. 'Right there is where my lode of information turns to an old spavined crowbait, and folds its wings, for I've pumped it dry.'

'A very sad—' began Judge Menefee, but his remark was curtailed by a higher authority.

'What a charming story!' said the lady passenger, in flute-like tones.

A little silence followed, except for the wind and the crackling of the fire.

The men were seated upon the floor, having slightly mitigated its inhospitable surface with wraps and stray pieces of boards. The man who was placing Little Goliath windmills arose and walked about to ease his cramped muscles.

Suddenly a trimphant shout came from him. He hurried back from a dusky corner of the room, bearing aloft something in his hand. It was an apple – a large, red-mottled, firm pippin, pleasing to behold. In a paper bag on a high shelf in that corner he had found it. It could have been no relic of the love-wrecked Redruth, for its glorious soundness repudiated the theory that it had laid on that musty shelf since August. No doubt some recent bivouackers, lunching in the deserted house, had left it there.

Dunwoody – again his exploits demand for him the honors of nomenclature – flaunted his apple in the faces of his fellow-marooners. 'See what I found, Mrs. McFarland!' he cried, vaingloriously. He held the apple high up in the light of the fire, where it glowed a still richer red. The lady passenger smiled calmly – always calmly.

'What a charming apple!' she murmured, clearly.

For a brief space Judge Menefee felt crushed, humiliated, relegated. Second place galled him. Why had this blatant, obtrusive, unpolished man of windmills been selected by Fate instead of himself to discover the sensational apple? He could have made of the act a scene, a function, a setting for some impromptu fanciful discourse or piece of comedy – and have retained the rôle of cynosure. Actually, the lady passenger was regarding this ridiculous Dunboddy or Woodbundy with an admiring smile, as if the fellow had performed a feat! And the windmill man swelled and gyrated like a sample of his own goods, puffed up with the wind that ever blows from the chorus land toward the domain of the star.

While the transported Dunwoody, with his Aladdin's apple, was receiving the fickle attentions of all, the resourceful jurist formed a plan to recover his own laurels.

With his courtliest smile upon his heavy but classic features, Judge Menefee advanced, and took the apple, as if to examine it, from the hand of Dunwoody. In his hand it became Exhibit A.

'A fine apple,' he said, approvingly. 'Really, my dear Mr. Dunwindy, you have eclipsed all of us as a forager. But I have an idea. This apple shall become an emblem, a token, a symbol, a prize bestowed by the mind and heart of beauty upon the most deserving.'

The audience, except one, applauded. 'Good on the stump, ain't he?' commented the passenger who was nobody in particular to the young man who had an Agency.

The unresponsive one was the windmill man. He saw himself reduced to the ranks. Never would the thought have occurred to him to declare his apple an emblem. He had intended after it had been divided and eaten, to create diversion by sticking the seeds against his forehead and naming them for young ladies of his acquaintance. One he was going to name Mrs. McFarland. The seed that fell off first would be – but 'twas too late now.

'The apple,' continued Judge Menefee, charging his jury, 'in modern days occupies, though undeservedly, a lowly place in our esteem. Indeed, it is so constantly associated with the culinary and the commercial that it is hardly to be classed among the polite fruits. But in ancient times this was not so. Biblical, historical, and mythological lore abounds with evidences that the apple was the aristocrat of fruits. We still say "the apple of the eye" when we wish to describe something superlatively precious. We find in Proverbs the comparison to "apples of silver." No other product of tree or vine has been so utilized in figurative speech. Who has not heard of and longed for the "apples of the Hesperides"? I need not call your attention to the most tremendous and significant instance of the apple's ancient prestige when its consumption by our first parents occasioned the fall of man from his state of goodness and perfection.'

'Apples like them,' said the windmill man, lingering with the objective article, 'are worth $3.50 a barrel in the Chicago market.'

'Now, what I have to propose,' said Judge Menefee, conceding an indulgent smile to his interrupter, 'is this: We must remain here, perforce, until morning. We have wood in plenty to keep us warm. Our next need is to entertain ourselves as best we can, in order that the time shall not pass too slowly. I propose that we place this apple in the hands of Miss Garland. It is no longer a fruit, but, as I said, a prize, in award, representing a great human idea. Miss Garland, herself, shall cease to be an individual – but only temporarily, I am happy to add' – (a low bow, full of the old-time grace). 'She shall represent her sex; she shall be the embodiment, the epitome of womankind – the heart and brain, I may say, of God's masterpiece of creation. In this guise she shall judge and decide the question which follows:

'But a few minutes ago our friend, Mr. Rose, favored us with an entertaining but fragmentary sketch of the romance in the life of the former possessor of this habitation. The few facts that we have learned seem to me to open up a fascinating field for conjecture, for the study of human hearts, for the exercise of the imagination – in short, for story-telling. Let us make use of the opportunity. Let each one of us relate his own version of the story of Redruth, the hermit, and his lady-love, beginning where Mr. Rose's narrative ends – at the parting of the lovers at the gate. This much should be assumed and conceded – that the young lady was not necessarily to blame for Redruth's becoming a crazed and world-hating hermit. When we have done, Miss Garland shall render the JUDGMENT OF WOMAN. As the Spirit of her Sex she shall decide which version of the story best and most truly depicts human and love interest, and most faithfully estimates the character and acts of Redruth's betrothed according to the feminine view. The apple shall be bestowed upon him who is awarded the decision. If you are all agreed, we shall be pleased to hear the first story from Mr. Dinwiddie.'

The last sentence captured the windmill man. He was not one to linger in the dumps.

'That's a first-rate scheme, Judge,' he said heartily. 'Be a regular short-story vaudeville, won't it? I used to be correspondent for a paper in Springfield, and when there wasn't any news I faked it. Guess I can do my turn all right.'

'I think the idea is charming,' said the lady passenger, brightly. 'It will be almost like a game.'

Judge Menefee stepped forward and placed the apple in her hand impressively.

'In olden days,' he said, profoundly, 'Paris awarded the golden apple to the most beautiful.'

'I was at the Exposition,' remarked the windmill man, now cheerful again, 'but I never heard of it. And I was on the Midway, too, all the time I wasn't at the machinery exhibit.'

'But now,' continued the Judge, 'the fruit shall translate to us the mystery and wisdom of the feminine heart. Take the apple, Miss Garland. Hear our modest tales of romance, and then award the prize as you may deem it just.'

The lady passenger smiled sweetly. The apple lay in her lap beneath her robes and wraps. She reclined against her protecting bulwark, brightly and cosily at ease. But for the voices and the wind one might have listened hopefully to hear her purr. Someone cast fresh logs upon the fire. Judge Menefee nodded suavely. 'Will you oblige us with the initial story?' he asked.

The windmill man sat as sits a Turk, with his hat well back on his head on account of the draughts.

'Well,' he began, without any embarrassment, 'this is about the way I size up the difficulty: Of course Redruth was jostled a good deal by this duck who had money to play ball with who tried to cut him out of his girl. So he goes

around, naturally, and asks her if the game is still square. Well, nobody
wants a guy cutting in with buggies and gold bonds when he's got an option
on a girl. Well, he goes around to see her. Well, maybe he's hot, and talks
like the proprietor, and forgets that an engagement ain't always a lead-pipe
cinch. Well, I guess that makes Alice warm under the lace yoke. Well, she
answers back sharp. Well, he — '

'Say!' interrupted the passenger who was nobody in particular, 'if you
could put up a windmill on every one of them "wells" you're using, you'd
be able to retire from business, wouldn't you?'

The windmill man grinned good-naturedly.

'Oh, I ain't no *Guy de Mopassong*,' he said, cheerfully. 'I'm giving it to
you in straight American. Well, she says something like this: "Mr. Gold
Bonds is only a friend," says she; "but he takes me riding and buys me theatre
tickets, and that's what you never do. Ain't I to never have any pleasure in
life while I can?" "Pass this chatfield-chatfield thing along," says Redruth;
"hand out the mitt to the Willie with creases in it or you don't put your
slippers under my wardrobe."

'Now that kind of train orders don't go with a girl that's got any spirit. I
bet that girl loved her honey all the time. Maybe she only wanted, as girls
do, to work the good thing for a little fun and caramels before she settled
down to patch George's other pair, and be a good wife. But he is glued to the
high horse, and won't come down. Well, she hands him back the ring, proper
enough; and George goes away and hits the booze. Yep. That's what done it.
I bet that girl fired the cornucopia with the fancy vest two days after her
steady left. George boards a freight and checks his bag of crackers for parts
unknown. He sticks to Old Booze for a number of years; and then the aniline
and aquafortis gets the decision. "Me for the hermit's hut," says George,
"and the long whiskers, and the buried can of money that isn't there."

'But that Alice, in my mind, was on the level. She never married, but took
up typewriting as soon as the wrinkles began to show, and kept a cat that
came when you said "weeny - weeny - weeny!" I got too much faith in
good women to believe they throw down the fellow they're stuck on every
time for the dough.' The windmill man ceased.

'I think,' said the lady passenger, slightly moving upon her lowly throne,
'that that is a char — '

'Oh, Miss Garland!' interposed Judge Menefee, with uplifted hand, 'I beg
of you, no comments! It would not be fair to the other contestants. Mr. – er
– will you take the next turn?' The Judge addressed the young man who had
the Agency.

'My version of the romance,' began the young man, diffidently clasping
his hands, 'would be this: They did not quarrel when they parted. Mr.
Redruth bade her good-bye and went out into the world to seek his fortune.
He knew his love would remain true to him. He scorned the thought that
his rival could make an impression upon a heart so fond and faithful. I would
say that Mr. Redruth went out to the Rocky Mountains in Wyoming to seek
for gold. One day a crew of pirates landed and captured him while at work,
and — '

'Hey! what's that?' sharply called the passenger who was nobody in
particular – 'a crew of pirates landed in the Rocky Mountains! Will you tell
us how they sailed — '

'Landed from a train,' said the narrator, quietly and not without some readiness. 'They kept him prisoner in a cave for months, and then they took him hundreds of miles away to the forests of Alaska. There a beautiful Indian girl fell in love with him, but he remained true to Alice. After another year of wandering in the woods, he set out with the diamonds—'

'What diamonds?' asked the unimportant passenger, almost with acerbity.

'The ones the saddlemaker showed him in the Peruvian temple,' said the other, somewhat obscurely. 'When he reached home, Alice's mother led him, weeping, to a green mound under a willow tree. "Her heart was broken when you left," said her mother. "And what of my rival – of Chester McIntosh?" asked Mr. Redruth, as he knelt sadly by Alice's grave. "When he found out," she answered, "that her heart was yours, he pined away day by day until, at length, he started a furniture store in Grand Rapids. We heard lately that he was bitten to death by an infuriated moose near South Bend, Ind., where he had gone to try to forget scenes of civilization." With which, Mr. Redruth forsook the face of mankind and became a hermit, as we have seen.

'My story,' concluded the young man with an Agency, 'may lack the literary quality; but what I want it to show is that the young lady remained true. She cared nothing for wealth in comparison with true affection. I admire and believe in the fair sex too much to think otherwise.'

The narrator ceased, with a sidelong glance at the corner where reclined the lady passenger.

Bildad Rose was next invited by Judge Menefee to contribute his story in the contest for the apple of judgment. The stage-driver's essay was brief.

'I'm not one of them lobo wolves,' he said, 'who are always blaming on women the calamities of life. My testimony in regards to the fiction story you ask for, Judge, will be about as follows: What ailed Redruth was pure laziness. If he had up and slugged this Percival De Lacey that tried to give him the outside of the road, and had kept Alice in the grape-vine swing with the blind-bridle on, all would have been well. The woman you want is sure worth taking pains for.

' "Send for me if you want me again," says Redruth, and hoists his Stetson, and walks off. He'd have called it pride, but the nixycomlogical name for it is laziness. No woman don't like to run after a man. "Let him come back, hisself," says the girl; and I'll be bound she tells the boy with the pay ore to trot; and then spends her time watching out the window for the man with the empty pocket-book and the tickly moustache.

'I reckon Redruth waits about nine year expecting her to send him a note by a nigger asking him to forgive her. But she don't. "This game won't work," says Redruth; "then so won't I." And he goes in the hermit business and raises whiskers. Yes; laziness and whiskers was what done the trick. They travel together. You ever hear of a man with long whiskers and hair striking a bonanza? No. Look at the Duke of Marlborough and this Standard Oil snooper. Have they got 'em?

'Now, this Alice didn't never marry, I'll bet a hoss. If Redruth had married somebody else she might have done so, too. But he never turns up. She has these here things they call fond memories, and maybe a lock of hair and a corset steel that he broke, treasured up. Them sort of articles is as good as a husband to some women. I'd say she played out a lone hand. I don't blame no woman for old man Redruth's abandonment of barber shops and clean shirts.'

Next in order came the passenger who was nobody in particular. Nameless to us, he travels the road from Paradise to Sunrise City.

But him you shall see, if the firelight be not too dim, as he responds to the Judge's call.

A lean form, in rusty-brown clothing, sitting like a frog, his arms wrapping about his legs, his chin resting upon his knees. Smooth, oakum-colored hair; long nose; mouth like a satyr's, with upturned, tobacco-stained corners. An eye like a fish's; a red necktie with a horseshoe pin. He began with a rasping chuckle that gradually formed itself into words.

'Everybody wrong so far. What! a romance without any orange blossoms! Ho, ho! My money on the lad with the butterfly tie and the certified checks in his trouserings.

'Take 'em as they parted at the gate? All right. "You never loved me," says Redruth, wildly, "or you wouldn't speak to a man who can buy you the ice cream." "I hate him," says she. "I loathe his side-bar buggy; I despise the elegant cream bonbons he sends me in gilt boxes covered with real lace; I feel that I could stab him to the heart when he presents me with a solid medallion locket with turquoises and pearls running in a vine around the border. Away with them! 'Tis only you I love." "Back to the cosy corner!" says Redruth. "Was I bound and lettered in East Aurora? Get platonic, if you please. No jack-pots for mine. Go and hate your friend some more. For me the Nickerson girl on Avenue B, and gum, and a trolley ride."

'Around that night comes John W. Croesus. "What! tears?" says he, arranging his pearl pin. "You have driven my lover away," says little Alice sobbing. "I hate the sight of you." "Marry me, then," says John W., lighting a Henry Clay. "What!" she cries, indignantly, "marry you! Never," she says, "until this blows over, and I can do some shopping, and you see about the license. There's a telephone next door if you want to call up the county clerk." '

The narrator paused to give vent to his cynical chuckle.

'Did they marry?' he continued. 'Did the duck swallow the June-bug? And then I take up the case of Old Boy Redruth. There's where you are all wrong again, according to my theory. What turned him into a hermit? One says laziness; one says remorse; one says booze. I say women did it. How old is the old man now?' asked the speaker, turning to Bildad Rose.

'I should say about sixty-five.'

'All right. He conducted his hermit shop here for twenty years. Say he was twenty-five when he took off his hat at the gate. That leaves twenty years for him to account for, or else be docked. Where did he spend that ten and two fives? I'll give you my idea. Up for bigamy. Say there was the fat blonde in Saint Jo, and the panatela brunette at Skillet Ridge, and the gold tooth down in the Kaw valley. Redruth gets his cases mixed, and they send him up the road. He gets out after they are through with him, and says: "Any line for me except the crinoline. The hermit trade is not overdone, and the stenographers never apply to 'em for work. The jolly hermit's life for me. No more long hairs in the comb or dill pickles lying around in the cigar tray." You tell me they pinched old Redruth for the noodle villa just because he said he was King Solomon? Figs! He *was* Solomon. That's all of mine. I guess it don't call for any apples. Enclosed find stamps. It don't sound much like a prize winner.'

Respecting the stricture laid by Judge Menefee against comments upon the stories, all were silent when the passenger who was nobody in particular had concluded. And then the ingenious originator of the contest cleared his throat to begin the ultimate entry for the prize. Though seated with small comfort upon the floor, you might search in vain for any abatement of dignity in Judge Menefee. The now diminishing firelight played softly upon his face, as clearly chiselled as a Roman emperor's on some old coin, and upon the thick waves of his honorable gray hair.

'A woman's heart!' he began, in even but thrilling tones – 'who can hope to fathom it? The ways and desires of men are various. I think that the hearts of all women beat with the same rhythm, and to the same old tune of love. Love, to a woman, means sacrifice. If she be worthy of the name, no gold or rank will outweigh with her a genuine devotion.

'Gentlemen of the – er – I should say, my friends, the case of Redruth *versus* love and affection has been called. Yet, who is on trial? Not Redruth, for he has been punished. Not those immortal passions that clothe our lives with the joy of the angels. Then who? Each man of us here tonight stands at the bar to answer if chivalry or darkness inhabits his bosom. To judge us sits womankind in the form of one of its fairest flowers. In her hand she holds the prize, intrinsically insignificant, but worthy of our noblest efforts to win as a guerdon of approval from so worthy a representative of feminine judgment and taste.

'In taking up the imaginary history of Redruth and the fair being to whom he gave his heart, I must, in the beginning, raise my voice against the unworthy insinuation that the selfishness or perfidy or love of luxury of any woman drove him to renounce the world. I have not found woman to be so unspiritual or venal. We must seek elsewhere, among man's baser nature and lower motives for the cause.

'There was, in all probability, a lovers' quarrel as they stood at the gate on that memorable day. Tormented by jealousy, young Redruth vanished from his native haunts. But had he just cause to do so? There is no evidence for or against. But there is something higher than evidence: there is the grand, eternal belief in woman's goodness, in her steadfastness against temptation, in her loyalty even in the face of proffered riches.

'I picture to myself the rash lover, wandering, self-tortured, about the world. I picture his gradual descent, and, finally, his complete despair when he realizes that he has lost the most precious gift life had to offer him. Then his withdrawal from the world of sorrow and the subsequent derangement of his faculties becomes intelligible.

'But what do I see on the other hand? A lonely woman fading away as the years roll by; still faithful, still waiting, still watching for a form and listening for a step that will come no more. She is old now. Her hair is white and smoothly banded. Each day she sits at the door and gazes longingly down the dusty road. In spirit she is waiting there at the gate, just as he left her – his forever, but not here below. Yes; my belief in woman paints that picture in my mind. Parted forever on earth, but waiting! She in anticipation of a meeting in Elysium; he in the Slough of Despond.'

'I thought he was in the bughouse,' said the passenger who was nobody in particular.

Judge Menefee stirred, a little impatiently. The men sat, drooping, in grotesque attitudes. The wind had abated its violence; coming now in fitful, virulent puffs. The fire had burned to a mass of red coals which shed but a dim light within the room. The lady passenger in her cosy nook looked to be but a formless dark bulk, crowned by a mass of coiled, sleek hair and showing but a small space of snowy forehead above her clinging boa.

Judge Menefee got stiffly to his feet.

'And now, Miss Garland,' he announced, 'we have concluded. It is for you to award the prize to the one of us whose argument – especially, I may say, in regard to his estimate of true womanhood – approaches nearest to your own conception.'

No answer came from the lady passenger. Judge Menefee bent over solicitously. The passenger who was nobody in particular laughed low and harshly. The lady was sleeping sweetly. The Judge essayed to take her hand to awaken her. In doing so he touched a small, cold, round, irregular something in her lap.

'She has eaten the apple,' announced Judge Menefee, in awed tones, as he held up the core for them to see.

THE MISSING CHORD

I STOPPED OVERNIGHT at the sheep-ranch of Rush Kinney, on the Sandy Fork of the Nueces. Mr. Kinney and I had been strangers up to the time when I called 'Hallo!' at his hitching-rack; but from that moment until my departure on the next morning we were, according to the Texas code, undeniable friends.

After supper the ranchman and I lugged our chairs outside the two-room house, to its floorless gallery roofed with chaparral and sacuista grass. With the rear legs of our chairs sinking deep into the hard-packed loam, each of us reposed against an elm pillar of the structure and smoked El Toro tobacco, while we wrangled amicably concerning the affairs of the rest of the world.

As for conveying adequate conception of the engaging harm of that prairie evening, despair waits upon it. It is a bold chronicler who will undertake the descrption of a Texas night in the early spring. An inventory must suffice.

The ranch rested upon the summit of a lenient slope. The ambient prairie, diversified by arroyos and murky patches of brush and pear, lay around us like a darkened bowl at the bottom of which we reposed as dregs. Like a turquoise cover the sky pinned us there. The miraculous air, heady with ozone and made memorably sweet by leagues of wild flowerets, gave tang and savor to the breath. In the sky was a great, round, mellow searchlight which we knew to be no moon, but the dark lantern of summer, who came to hunt northward the cowering spring. In the nearest corral a flock of sheep lay silent until a groundless panic would send a squad of them huddling together with a drumming rush. For other sounds a shrill family of coyotes yapped beyond the shearing-pen, and whippoorwills twittered in the long grass. But even these dissonances hardly rippled the clear torrent of the mocking-birds' notes that fell from a dozen neighboring shrubs and trees. It would not have been preposterous for one to tiptoe and essay to touch the stars, they hung so bright and imminent.

Mr. Kinney's wife, a young and capable woman, we had left in the house. She remained to busy herself with the domestic round of duties in which I had observed that she seemed to take a buoyant and contented pride. In one room we had supped. Presently, from the other, as Kinney and I sat without, there burst a volume of sudden and brilliant music. If I could justly estimate the art of piano-playing, the construer of that rollicking fantasia had creditably mastered the secrets of the keyboard. A piano, and one so well played, seemed to me to be an unusual thing to find in that small and unpromising ranchhouse. I must have looked my surprise at Rush Kinney, for he laughed in his soft Southern way, and nodded at me through he moonlit haze of our cigarettes.

'You don't often hear as agreeable a noise as that on a sheep-ranch,' he remarked; 'but I never see any reason for not playing up to the arts and graces just because we happen to live out in the brush. It's a lonesome life for a woman; and if a little music can make it any better, why not have it? That's the way I look at it.'

'A wise and generous theory,' I assented. 'And Mrs. Kinney plays well. I am not learned in the science of music, but I should call her an uncommonly good performer. She has technic and more than ordinary power.'

The moon was very bright, you will understand, and I saw upon Kinney's face a sort of amused and pregnant expression, as though there were things behind it that might be expounded.

'You came up the trail from the Double-Elm Fork,' he said, promisingly. 'As you crossed it you must have seen an old deserted *jacal* to your left under a coma mott.'

'I did,' said I. 'There was a drove of *invalis* rooting around it. I could see by the broken corrals that no one lived there.'

'That's where this music proposition started,' said Kinney. 'I don't mind telling you about it while we smoke. That's where old Cal Adams lived. He had about eight hundred graded merinos and a daughter that was solid silk and as handsome as a new stake-rope on a thirty-dollar pony. And I don't mind telling you that I was guilty in the second degree of hanging around old Cal's ranch all the time I could spare away from lambing and shearing. Miss Marilla was her name; and I had figured it out by the rule of two that she was destined to become the chatelaine and lady superior of Rancho Lomito, belonging to R. Kinney, Esq., where you are now a welcome and honored guest.

'I will say that old Cal wasn't distinguished as a sheepman. He was a little, old stoop-shouldered *hombre* about as big as a gun scabbard, with scraggy white whiskers, and condemned to the continuous use of language. Old Cal was so obscure in his chosen profession that he wasn't even hated by the cowmen. And when a sheepman don't get eminent enough to acquire the hostility of the cattlemen, he is mighty apt to die unwept and considerably unsung.

'But that Marilla girl was a benefit to the eye. And she was the most elegant kind of a housekeeper. I was the nearest neighbour, and I used to ride over to the Double-Elm anywhere from nine to sixteen times a week with fresh butter or a quarter of venison or a sample of new sheep-dip just as a frivolous excuse to see Marilla. Marilla and me got to be extensively inveigled with each other, and I was pretty sure I was going to get my rope around her neck and lead her over to the Lomito. Only she was so everlastingly permeated with filial sentiments toward old Cal that I never could get her to talk about serious matters.

'You never saw anybody in your life that was as full of knowledge and had less sense than old Cal. He was advised about all the branches of information contained in learning, and he was up to all the rudiments of doctrines and enlightenment. You couldn't advance him any ideas on any of the parts of speech or lines of thought. You would have thought he was a professor of the weather and politics and chemistry and natural history and the origin of derivations. Any subject you brought up old Cal could give you an abundant synopsis of it from the Greek root up to the time it was sacked and on the market.

'One day just after the fall shearing I rides over to the Double-Elm with a lady's magazine about fashions for Marilla and a scientific paper for old Cal.

'While I was tying my pony to a mesquite, out run Marilla, 'tickled to death' with some news that couldn't wait.

' "Oh, Rush," she says, all flushed up with esteem and gratification, "what do you think! Dad's going to buy me a piano. Ain't it grand? I never dreamed I'd ever have one."

' "It's sure joyful," says I. "I always admired the agreeable uproar of a piano. It'll be lots of company for you. That's mighty good of Uncle Cal to do that."

' "I'm all undecided," says Marilla, "between a piano and a organ. A parlor organ is nice."

' "Either of 'em," says I, "is first-class for mitigating the lack of noise around a sheep-ranch. For my part," I says, "I shouldn't like anything better than to ride home of an evening and listen to a few waltzes and jigs, with somebody about your size sitting on the piano-stool and rounding up the notes."

' "Oh, hush about that," says Marilla, "and go on in the house. Dad hasn't rode out to-day. He's not feeling well."

'Old Cal was inside, lying on a cot. He had a pretty bad cold and cough. I stayed to supper.

' "Going to get Marilla a piano, I hear," says I to him.

' "Why, yes, something of the kind, Rush," says he. "She's been hankering for music for a long spell; and I allow to fix her up with something in that line right away. The sheep sheared six pounds all round this fall; and I'm going to get Marilla an instrument if it takes the price of the whole clip to do it."

' "*Star wayno*," says I. "The little girl deserves it."

' "I'm going to San Antone on the last load of wool," says Uncle Cal, "and select an instrument for her myself."

' "Wouldn't it be better," I suggest, "to take Marilla along and let her pick out one that she likes?"

'I might have known that would set Uncle Cal going. Of course, a man like him, that knew everything about everything, would look at that as a reflection on his attainments.

' "No, sir, it wouldn't," says he, pulling at his white whiskers. "There ain't a better judge of musical instruments in the whole world than what I am. I had an uncle," says he, "that was a partner in a piano-factory, and I've seen thousands of 'em put together. I know all about musical instruments from a pipe-organ to a corn-stalk fiddle. There ain't a man lives, sir, that can tell me any news about any instrument that has to be pounded, blowed, scraped, grinded, picked, or wound with a key."

' "You get me what you like, dad," says Marilla, who couldn't keep her feet on the floor from joy. "Of course you know what to select. I'd just as lief it was a piano or a organ or what."

' "I see in St. Louis once what they call a orchestrion," says Uncle Cal, "that I judged was about the finest thing in the way of music ever invented. But there ain't room in this house for one. Anyway, I imagine they'd cost a thousand dollars. I reckon something in the piano line would suit Marilla the best. She took lessons in that respect for two years over at Birdstail. I wouldn't trust the buying of an instrument to anybody else but myself. I reckon if I hadn't took up sheep-raising I'd have been one of the finest composers or piano-and-organ manufacturers in the world."

'That was Uncle Cal's style. But I never lost any patience with him, on account of his thinking so much of Marilla. And she thought just as much of him. He sent her to the academy over at Birdstail for two years when it took nearly every pound of wool to pay the expenses.

'Along about Tuesday Uncle Cal put out for San Antone on the last wagon-load of wool. Marilla's Uncle Ben, who lived in Birdstail, come over and stayed at the ranch while Uncle Cal was gone.

'It was ninety miles to San Antone, and forty to the nearest railroad-station, so Uncle Cal was gone about four days. I was over at the Double-Elm when he came rolling back one evening about sundown. And up there in the wagon, sure enough, was a piano or a organ – we couldn't tell which – all wrapped up in wool-sacks, with a wagon-sheet tied over it in case of rain. And out skips Marilla, hollering, "Oh, oh!" with her eyes shining and her hair a-flying. "Dad – dad," she sings out, "have you brought it – have you brought it?" – and it right there before her eyes, as women will do.

' "Finest piano in San Antone," says Uncle Cal, waving his hand, proud. "Genuine rosewood, and the finest, loudest tone you ever listened to. I heard the storekeeper play it, and I took it on the spot and paid cash down."

'Me and Ben and Uncle Cal and a Mexican lifted it out of the wagon and carried it in the house and set it in a corner. It was one of them upright instruments, and not very heavy or very big.

'And then all of a sudden Uncle Cal flops over and says he's mighty sick. He's got a high fever, and he complains of his lungs. He gets into bed, while me and Ben goes out to unhitch and put the horses in the pasture, and Marilla flies around to get Uncle Cal something hot to drink. But first she puts both arms on that piano and hugs it with a soft kind of a smile, like you see kids doing with their Christmas toys.

'When I came in from the pasture, Marilla was in the room where the piano was. I could see by the strings and wool-sacks on the floor that she had had it unwrapped. But now she was tying the wagon-sheet over it again, and there was a kind of solemn, whitish look on her face.

' "Ain't wrapping up the music again, are you, Marilla?" I asks. "What's the matter with just a couple of tunes for to see how she goes under the saddle?"

' "Not to-night, Rush," says she. "I don't want to play any to-night. Dad's too sick. Just think, Rush, he paid three hundred dollars for it – nearly a third of what the wool-clip brought!"

' "Well, it ain't anyways in the neighborhood of a third of what you are worth," I told her. "And I don't think Uncle Cal is too sick to hear a little agitation of the piano-keys just to christen the machine."

' "Not to-night, Rush," says Marilla, in a way that she had when she
wanted to settle things.

'But it seems that Uncle Cal was plenty sick, after all. He got so bad that
Ben saddled up and rode over to Birdstail for Doc Simpson. I stayed around
to see if I'd be needed for anything.

'When Uncle Cal's pain let up on him a little he called Marilla and says
to her. "Did you look at your instrument, honey? And do you like it?"

' "It's lovely, dad,' says she, leaning down by his pillow; "I never saw one
so pretty. How dear and good it was of you to buy it for me!"

' "I haven't heard you play on it any yet," says Uncle Cal; "and I've been
listening. My side don't hurt quite so bad now – won't you play a piece,
Marilla?"

'But no; she puts Uncle Cal off and soothes him down like you've seen
women do with a kid. It seems she's made up her mind not to touch that
piano at present.

'When Doc Simpson comes over he tells us that Uncle Cal has pneumonia
the worst kind; and as the old man was past sixty and nearly on the lift
anyhow, the odds was against his walking on grass any more.

'On the fourth day of his sickness he calls for Marilla again and wants to
talk piano. Doc Simpson was there, and so was Ben and Mrs. Ben, trying to
do all they could.

' "I'd have made a wonderful success in anything connected with music,"
says Uncle Cal. "I got the finest instrument for the money in San Antone.
Ain't that piano all right in every respect, Marilla?"

' "It's just perfect, dad," says she. "It's got the finest tone I ever heard. But
don't you think you could sleep a little now, dad?"

' "No, I don't," says Uncle Cal. "I want to hear that piano. I don't believe
you've even tried it yet. I went all the way to San Antone and picked it out
for you myself. It took a third of the fall clip to buy it; but I don't mind that
if it makes any good girl happier. Won't you play a little bit for dad, Marilla?"

'Doc Simpson beckoned Marilla to one side and recommended her to do
what Uncle Cal wanted, so it would get him quieted. And her Uncle ben
and his wife asked her, too.

' "Why not hit out a tune or two with the soft pedal on?" I asks Marilla.
"Uncle Cal has begged you so often. It would please him a good deal to hear
you touch up the piano he's bought for you. Don't you think you might?"

'But Marilla stands there with big tears rolling down from her eyes and
says nothing. And then she runs over and slips her arm under Uncle Cal's
neck and hugs him tight.

' "Why, last night, dad," we heard her say, "I played ever so much. Honest
– I have been playing it. And it's such a splendid instrument, you don't
know how I love it. Last night I played "Bonnie Dundee" and the "Anvil
Polka" and the "Blue Danube" – and lots of pieces. You must surely have
heard me playing a little, didn't you, dad? I didn't like to play loud when
you was so sick."

' "Well, well," says Uncle Cal, "maybe I did. Maybe I did and forgot about
it. My head is a little cranky at times. I heard the man in the store play it
fine. I'm mighty glad you like it, Marilla. Yes, I believe I could go to sleep
a while if you'll stay right beside me till I do."

'There was where Marilla had me guessing. Much as she thought of that
old man, she wouldn't strike a note on that piano that he'd bought her. I

couldn't imagine why she told him she'd been playing it, for the wagon-sheet hadn't even been off of it since she put it back on the same day it come. I knew she could play a little anyhow, for I'd once heard her snatch some pretty fair dance-music out of an old piano at the Charco Largo Ranch.

'Well, in about a week the pneumonia got the best of Uncle Cal. They had the funeral over at Birdstail, and all of us went over. I brought Marilla back home in my buckboard. Her Uncle Ben and his wife were going to stay there a few days with her.

'That night Marilla takes me in the room where the piano was, while the others were out on the gallery.

' "Come here, Rush," says she; "I want you to see this now."

'She unties the rope, and drags off the wagon-sheet.

'If you ever rode a saddle without a horse, or fired off a gun that wasn't loaded, or took a drink out of an empty bottle, why, then you might have been able to scare an opera or two out of the instrument Uncle Cal had bought.

'Instead of a piano, it was one of them machines they've invented to play the piano with. By itself it was about as musical as the holes of a flute without the flute.

'And that was the piano that Uncle Cal had selected; and standing by it was the good, fine, all-wool girl that never let him know it.

'And what you heard playing a while ago,' concluded Mr. Kinney, 'was that same deputy-piano machine; only just at present it's shoved up against a six-hundred-dollar piano that I bought for Marilla as soon as we was married.'

A CALL LOAN

IN THOSE DAYS THE CATTLEMEN were the anointed. They were the grandees of the grass, kings of the kine, lords of the lea, barons of beef and bone. They might have ridden in golden chariots had their tastes so inclined. The cattleman was caught in a stampede of dollars. It seemed to him that he had more money than was decent. But when he had bought a watch with precious stones set in the case so large that they hurt his ribs, and a California saddle with silver nails and Angora skin *suaderos*, and ordered everybody up to the bar for whisky – what else was there for him to spend money for?

Not so circumscribed in expedient for the reduction of surplus wealth were those lairds of the lariat who had womenfolk to their name. In the breast of the rib-sprung sex the genius of purse lightening may slumber through years of inopportunity, but never, my brothers, does it become extinct.

So, out of the chaparral came Long Bill Longley ,from the Bar Circle Ranch on the Frio – a wife-driven man – to taste the urban joys of success. Something like half a million dollars he had, with an income steadily increasing.

Long Bill was a graduate of the camp and trail. Luck and thrift, a cool head, and a telescopic eye for mavericks had raised him from cowboy to be a cowman. Then came the boom in cattle, and Fortune, stepping gingerly among the cactus thorns, came and emptied her cornucopia at the doorstep of the ranch.

In the little frontier city of Chaparosa, Longley built a costly residence. Here he became a captive, bound to the chariot of social existence. He was doomed to become a leading citizen. He struggled for a time like a mustang in his first corral, and then he hung up his quirt and spurs. Time hung heavily on his hands. He organized the First National Bank of Chaparosa, and was elected its president.

One day a dyspeptic man, wearing double-magnifying glasses, inserted an official-looking card between the bars of the cashier's window of the First National Bank. Five minutes later the bank force was dancing at the beck and call of a national bank examiner.

This examiner, Mr. J. Edgar Todd, proved to be a thorough one.

At the end of it all the examiner put on his hat, and called the president, Mr. William R. Longley, into the private office.

'Well, how do you find things?' asked Longley, in his slow, deep tones. 'Any brands in the round-up you didn't like the looks of?'

'The bank checks up all right, Mr. Longley,' said Todd; 'and I find your loans in very good shape – with one exception. You are carrying one very bad bit of paper – one that is so bad that I have been thinking that you surely do not realize the serious position it places you in. I refer to a call loan of $10,000 made to Thomas Merwin. Not only is the amount in excess of the maximum sum the bank can loan any individual legally, but it is absolutely without endorsement or security. Thus you have doubly violated the national banking laws, and have laid yourself open to criminal prosecution by the Government. A report of the matter to the Comptroller of the Currency – which I am bound to make – would, I am sure, result in the matter being turned over to the Department of Justice for action. You see what a serious thing it is.'

Bill Longley was leaning his lengthy, slowly moving frame back in his swivel chair. His hands were clasped behind his head, and he turned a little to look the examiner in the face. The examiner was surprised to see a smile creep about the rugged mouth of the banker, and a kindly twinkle in his light-blue eyes. If he saw the seriousness of the affair, it did not show in his countenance.

'Of course, you don't know Tom Merwin,' said Longley, almost genially. 'Yes, I know about that loan. It hasn't any security except Tom Merwin's word. Somehow, I've always found that when a man's word is good, it's the best security there is. Oh, yes, I know the Government doesn't think so. I guess I'll see Tom about that note.'

Mr. Todd's dyspepsia seemed to grow suddenly worse. He looked at the chaparral banker through his double-magnifying glasses in amazement.

'You see,' said Longley, easily explaining the thing away, 'Tom heard of 2,000 head of two-year-olds down near Rocky Ford on the Rio Grande that could be had for $8 a head. I reckon 'twas one of old Laendro Garcia's outfits that he had smuggled over, and he wanted to make a quick turn on 'em. Those cattle are worth $15 on the hoof in Kansas City. Tom knew it and I knew it. He had $6,000, and I let him have the $10,000 to make the deal with. His brother Ed took 'em on to market three weeks ago. He ought to be back 'most any day now with the money. When he comes Tom'll pay that note.'

The bank examiner was shocked. It was, perhaps, his duty to step out to the telegraph office and wire the situation to the Comptroller. But he did not. He talked pointedly and effectively to Longley for three minutes. He succeeded in making the banker understand that he stood upon the border of a catastrophe. And then he offered a tiny loophole of escape.

'I am going to Hilldale's to-night,' he told Longley, 'to examine a bank there. I will pass through Chaparosa on my way back. At twelve tomorrow I shall call at this bank. If this loan has been cleared out of the way by that time it will not be mentioned in my report. If not – I will have to do my duty.'

With that the examiner bowed and departed.

The President of the First National lounged in his chair half an hour longer, and then he lit a mild cigar, and went over to Tom Merwin's house. Merwin, a ranchman in brown duck, with a contemplative eye, sat with his feet upon a table, plaiting a rawhide quirt.

'Tom,' said Longley, leaning against the table, 'you heard anything from Ed yet?'

'Not yet,' said Merwin, continuing his plaiting. 'I guess Ed'll be along back now in a few days.'

'There was a bank examiner,' said Longley, 'nosing around our place to-day, and he bucked a sight about that note of yours. You know I know it's all right, but the thing *is* against the banking laws. I was pretty sure you'd have paid it off before the bank was examined again, but the son-of-a-gun slipped in on us, Tom. Now, I'm short of cash myself just now, or I'd let you have the money to take it up with. I've got till twelve o'clock to-morrow, and then I've got to show the cash in place of that note or—'

'Or what, Bill?' asked Merwin, as Longley hesitated.

'Well, I suppose it means be jumped on with both of Uncle Sam's feet.'

'I'll try to raise the money for you on time,' said Merwin, interested in his plaiting.

'All right, Tom,' concluded Longley, as he turned toward the door; 'I knew you would if you could.'

Merwin threw down his whip and went to the only other bank in town, a private one, run by Cooper & Craig.

'Cooper,' he said, to the partner by that name, 'I've got to have $10,000 to-day or to-morrow. I've got a house and lot here that's worth about $6,000 and that's all the actual collateral. But I've got a cattle deal on that's sure to bring me in more than that much profit within a few days.'

Cooper began to cough.

'Now, for God's sake don't say no.' said Merwin. 'I owe that much money on a call loan. It's been called, and the man that called it is a man I've laid on the same blanket with in cow-camps and ranger-camps for ten years. He can call anything I've got. He can call the blood out of my veins and it'll come. He's got to have the money. He's in a devil of a— Well, he needs the money, and I've got to get it for him. You know my word's good, Cooper.'

'No doubt of it,' assented Cooper, urbanely, 'but I've a partner, you know. I'm not free in making loans. And even if you had the best security in your hands, Merwin, we couldn't accommodate you in less than a week. We're just making a shipment of $15,000 to Myer Brothers in Rockdell, to buy cotton with. It goes down on the narrow gauge to-night. That leaves our cash quite short at present. Sorry we can't arrange it for you.'

Merwin went back to his little bar office and plaited at his quirt again.

About four o'clock in the afternoon he went to the First National and leaned over the railing of Longley's desk.

'I'll try to get that money for you to-night – I mean to-morrow, Bill.'

'All right, Tom,' said Longley, quietly.

At nine o'clock that night Tom Merwin stepped cautiously out of the small frame house in which he lived. It was near the edge of the little town, and few citizens were in the neighborhood at that hour. Merwin wore two six-shooters in a belt and a slouch hat. He moved swiftly down a lonely street, and then followed the sandy road that ran parallel to the narrow-gauge track until he reached the water-tank, two miles below the town. There Tom Merwin stopped, tied a black silk handkerchief about the lower part of his face, and pulled his hat down low.

In ten minutes the night train for Rockdell pulled up at the tank, having come from Chaparosa.

With a gun in each hand Merwin raised himself from behind a clump of chaparral and started for the engine. But before he had taken three steps, two long, strong arms clasped him from behind, and he was lifted from his feet and thrown, face downward, upon the grass. There was a heavy knee pressing against his back, and an iron hand grasping each of his wrists. He was held thus, like a child, until the engine had taken water, and until the train had moved, with accelerating speed, out of sight. Then he was released, and rose to his feet to face Bill Longley.

'The case never needed to be fixed up this way, Tom,' said Longley. 'I saw Cooper this evening, and he told me what you and him talked about. Then I went down to your house to-night and saw you come out with your guns on, and I followed you. Let's go back, Tom.'

They walked away together, side by side.

' 'Twas the only chance I saw,' said Merwin, presently. 'You called your loan, and I tried to answer you. Now, what'll you do, Bill, if they sock it to you?'

'What would you have done if they'd socked it to you?' was the answer Longley made.

'I never thought I'd lay in a bush to stick up a train,' remarked Merwin; 'but a call loan's different. A call's a call with me. We've got twelve hours yet, Bill, before his spy jumps onto you. We've got to raise them spondulicks somehow. Maybe we can – Great Sam Houston! do you hear that?'

Merwin broke into a run, and Longley kept with him, hearing only a rather pleasing whistle somewhere in the night rendering the lugubrious air of 'The Cowboy's Lament.'

'It's the only tune he knows,' shouted Merwin, as he ran. 'I'll bet—'

They were at the door of Merwin's house. He kicked it open and fell over an old valise lying in the middle of the floor. A sunburned, firmjawed youth, stained by travel, lay upon the bed puffing at a brown cigarette.

'What's the word, Ed?' gasped Merwin.

'So, so,' drawled that capable youngster. 'Just got in on the 9:30. Sold the bunch for fifteen, straight. Now, buddy, you want to quit kickin' a valise around that's got $29,000 in greenbacks in its in'ards.'

THE PRINCESS AND THE PUMA

THERE HAD TO BE A KING AND QUEEN, of course. The king was a terrible old man who wore six-shooters and spurs, and shouted in such a tremendous voice that the rattlers on the prairie would run into their holes under the prickly pear. Before there was a royal family they called the man 'Whispering Ben.' When he came to own 50,000 acres of land and more cattle than he could count, they called him O'Donnell 'the Cattle King.'

The queen had been a Mexican girl from Laredo. She made a good, mild, Coloradoclaro wife, and even succeeded in teaching Ben to modify his voice sufficiently while in the house to keep the dishes from being broken. When Ben got to be king she would sit on the gallery of Espinosa Ranch and weave rush mats. When wealth became so irresistible and oppressive that uphol-stered chairs and a centre table were brought down from San Antone in the wagons, she bowed her smooth, dark head, and shared the fate of the Danaë.

To avoid *lèse-majesté* you have been presented first to the king and queen. They do not enter the story, which might be called 'The Chronicle of the Princess, the Happy Thought, and Lion that Bungled his Job.'

Josefa O'Donnell was the surviving daughter, the princess. From her mother she inherited warmth of nature and a dusky, semi-tropic beauty. From Ben O'Donnell the royal she acquired a store in intrepidity, common sense, and the faculty of ruling. The combination was worth going miles to see. Josefa while riding her pony at a gallop could put five out of six bullets through a tomato-can swinging at the end of a string. She could play for hours with a white kitten she owned, dressing it in all manner of absurd clothes. Scorning a pencil, she could tell you out of her head what 1545 two-year-olds would bring on the hoof, at $8.50 per head. Roughly speaking, the Espinosa Ranch is forty miles long and thirty broad – but mostly leased land. Josefa, on her pony, had prospected over every mile of it. Every cow-puncher on the range knew her by sight and was a loyal vassal. Ripley Givens, foreman of one of the Espinosa outfits, saw her one day, and made up his mind to form a royal matrimonial alliance. Presumptuous? No. In those days in the Nueces country a man was a man. And, after all, the title of cattle king does not presuppose blood royal. Often it only signifies that its owner wears the crown in token of his magnificent qualities in the art of cattle stealing.

One day Ripley Givens rode over to the Double Elm Ranch to inquire about a bunch of strayed yearlings. He was late in setting out on his return trip, and it was sundown when he struck the White Horse Crossing of the Nueces. From there to his own camp it was sixteen miles. To the Espinosa ranch-house it was twelve. Givens was tired. He decided to pass the night at the Crossing.

There was a fine water hole in the river-bed. The banks were thickly covered with great trees, undergrown with brush. Back from the water hole fifty yards was a stretch of curly mesquite grass – supper for his horse and bed for himself. Givens staked his horse, and spread out his saddle blankets to dry. He sat down with his back against a tree and rolled a cigarette. From somewhere in the dense timber along the river came a sudden, rageful, shivering wail. The pony danced at the end of his rope and blew a whistling snort of comprehending fear. Givens puffed at his cigarette, but he reached leisurely for his pistol-belt, which lay on the grass, and twirled the cylinder of his weapon tentatively. A great gar plunged with a loud splash into the water hole. A little brown rabbit skipped around a bunch of catclaw and sat twitching his whiskers and looking humorously at Givens. The pony went on eating grass.

It is well to be reasonably watchful when a Mexican lion sings soprano along the arroyos at sundown. The burden of his song may be that young calves and fat lambs are scarce, and that he has a carnivorous desire for your acquaintance.

In the grass lay an empty fruit can, cast there by some former sojourner. Givens caught sight of it with a grunt of satisfaction. In his coat pocket tied behind his saddle was a handful or two of ground coffee. Black coffee and cigarettes! What ranchero could desire more?

In two minutes he had a little fire going clearly. He started, with his can, for the water hole. When within fifteen yards of its edge he saw, between the bushes, a side-saddled pony with down-dropped reins cropping grass a little distance to his left. Just rising from her hands and knees on the brink of the water hole was Josefa O'Donnell. She had been drinking water, and she brushed the sand from the palms of her hands. Ten yards away, to her right, half concealed by a clump of sacuista, Givens saw the crouching form of the Mexican lion. His amber eyelids glared hungrily; six feet from them was the tip of the tail stretched straight, like a pointer's. His hind-quarters rocked with the motion of the cat tribe preliminary to leaping.

Givens did what he could. His six-shooter was thirty-five yards away lying on the grass. He gave a loud yell, and dashed between the lion and the princess.

The 'rucus,' as Givens called it afterward, was brief and somewhat confused. When he arrived on the line of attack he saw a dim streak in the air, and heard a couple of faint cracks. Then a hundred pounds of Mexican lion plumped down upon his head and flattened him, with a heavy jar, to the ground. He remembered calling out: 'Let up, now – no fair gouging!' and then he crawled from under the lion like a worm, with his mouth full of grass and dirt, and a big lump on the back of his head where it had struck the root of a water-elm. The lion lay motionless. Givens, feeling aggrieved, and suspicious of fouls, shook his fist at the lion, and shouted: 'I'll rastle you again for twenty—' and then he got back to himself.

Josefa was standing in her tracks, quietly reloading her silver-mounted .38. It had not been a difficult shot. The lion's head made an easier mark than a tomato-can swinging at the end of a string. There was a provoking, teasing, maddening smile upon her mouth and in her dark eyes. The would-be-rescuing knight felt the fire of his fiasco burn down to his soul. Here had been his chance, the chance that he had dreamed of; and Momus, and not Cupid, had presided over it. The satyrs in the wood were, no doubt, holding their sides in hilarious, silent laughter. There had been something like vaudeville – say Signor Givens and his funny knockabout act with the stuffed lion.

'Is that you, Mr. Givens?' said Josefa, in her deliberate saccharine contralto. 'You nearly spoiled my shot when you yelled. Did you hurt your head when you fell?'

'Oh, no,' said Givens, quietly; 'that didn't hurt.' He stooped ignominiously and dragged his best Stetson hat from under the beast. It was crushed and wrinkled to a fine comedy effect. Then he knelt down and softly stroked the fierce, open-jawed head of the dead lion.

'Poor old Bill!' he exclaimed, mournfully.

'What's that?' asked Josefa, sharply.

'Of course you didn't know, Miss Josefa,' said Givens, with an air of one allowing magnanimity to triumph over grief. 'Nobody can blame you. I tried to save him, but I couldn't let you know in time.'

'Save who?'

'Why, Bill. I've been looking for him all day. You see, he's been our camp pet for two years. Poor old fellow, he wouldn't have hurt a cotton-tail rabbit. It'll break the boys all up when they hear about it. But you couldn't tell of course, that Bill was just trying to play with you.'

Josefa's black eyes burned steadily upon him. Ripley Givens met the test successfully. He stood rumpling the yellow-brown curls on his head pensively. In his eyes was regret, not unmingled with a gentle reproach. His smooth features were set to a pattern of indisputable sorrow. Josefa wavered.

'What was your pet doing here?' she asked, making a last stand. 'There's no camp near the White Horse Crossing.'

'The old rascal ran away from camp yesterday,' answered Givens, readily. 'It's a wonder the coyotes didn't scare him to death. You see, Jim Webster, our horse wrangler, brought a little terrier pup into camp last week. The pup made life miserable for Bill – he used to chase him around and chew his hind legs for hours at a time. Every night when bedtime came Bill would sneak under one of the boys' blankets and sleep to keep the pup from finding him. I reckon he must have been worried pretty desperate or he wouldn't have run away. He was always afraid to get out of sight of camp.'

Josefa looked at the body of the fierce animal. Givens gently patted one of the formidable paws that could have killed a yearling calf with one blow. Slowly a red flush widened upon the dark olive face of the girl. Was it the signal of shame of the true sportsman who has brought down ignoble quarry? Her eyes grew softer, and the lowered lids drove away all their bright mockery.

'I'm very sorry,' she said, humbly; 'but he looked so big, and jumped so high that –'

'Poor old Bill was hungry,' interrupted Givens, in quick defence of the deceased. 'We always made him jump for his supper in camp. He would lie down and roll over for a piece of meat. When he saw you he thought he was going to get something to eat from you.'

Suddenly Josefa's eyes opened wide.

'I might have shot you!' she exclaimed. 'You ran right in between. You risked your life to save your pet! That was fine, Mr. Givens. I like a man who is kind to animals.'

Yes; there was even admiration in her gaze now. After all, there was a hero rising out of the ruins of the anti-climax. The look on Givens's face would have secured him a high position in the S.P.C.A.

'I always loved 'em,' said he; 'horses, dogs, Mexican lions, cows, alligators –'

'I hate alligators,' instantly demurred Josefa; 'crawly, muddy things!'

'Did I say alligators?' said Givens. 'I meant antelopes, of course.'

Josefa's conscience drove her to make further amends. She held out her hand penitently. There was a bright, unshed drop in each of her eyes.

'Please forgive me. Mr. Givens, won't you? I'm only a girl, you know, and I was frightened at first. I'm very, very sorry I shot Bill. You don't know how ashamed I feel. I wouldn't have done it for anything.'

Givens took the proffered hand. He held it for a time while he allowed the generosity of his nature to overcome his grief at the loss of Bill. At last it was clear that he had forgiven her.

'Please don't speak of it any more, Miss Josefa. 'Twas enough to frighten any young lady the way Bill looked. I'll explain it all right to the boys.'

'Are you really sure you don't hate me?' Josefa came closer to him impulsively. Her eyes were sweet – oh, sweet and pleading with gracious penitence. 'I would hate any one who would kill my kitten. And how daring and kind of you to risk being shot when you tried to save him! How very few men would have done that!' Victory wrested from defeat! Vaudeville turned into drama! Bravo, Ripley Givens!

It was now twilight. Of course Miss Josefa could not be allowed to ride on to the ranch-house alone. Givens resaddled his pony in spite of that animal's reproachful glances, and rode with her. Side by side they galloped across the smooth grass, the princess and the man who was kind to animals. The prairie odors of fruitful earth and delicate bloom were thick and sweet around them. Coyotes yelping over there on the hill! No fear. And yet—

Josefa rode closer. A little hand seemed to grope. Givens found it with his own. The ponies kept an even gait. The hands lingered together, and the owner of one explained.

'I never was frightened before, but just think! How terrible it would be to meet a really wild lion! Poor Bill! I'm so glad you came with me!'

O'Donnell was sitting on the ranch gallery.

'Hello, Rip!' he shouted— 'that you?'

'He rode in with me,' said Josefa. 'I lost my way and was late.'

'Much obliged,' called the cattle king. 'Stop over, Rip, and ride to camp in the morning.'

But Givens would not. He would push on to camp. There was a bunch of steers to start off on the trail at daybreak. He said good-night, and trotted away.

An hour later, when thelights were out, Josefa, in her night-robe, came to her door and called to the king in his own room across the brick-paved hallway:

'Say, Pop, you know that old Mexican lion they call the "Gotch-eared Devil" – the one that killed Gonzales, Mr. Martin's sheep herder, and about fifty calves on the Salada range? Well, I settled his hash this afternoon over at the White Horse Crossing. Put two balls in his head with my .38 while he was on the jump. I knew him by the slice gone from his left ear that old Gonzales cut off with his machete. You couldn't have made a better shot yourself, Daddy.'

'Bully for you!' thundered Whispering Ben from the darkness of the royal chamber.

THE INDIAN SUMMER OF DRY VALLEY JOHNSON

DRY VALLEY JOHNSON SHOOK THE BOTTLE. You have to shake the bottle before using; for sulphur will not dissolve. Then Dry Valley saturated a small sponge with the liquid and rubbed it carefully into the roots of his hair. Besides sulphur there was sugar of lead in it and tincture of nux vomica and bay rum. Dry Valley found the recipe in a Sunday newspaper. You must next be told why a strong man came to fall victim to a Beauty Hint.

Dry Valley had been a sheepman. His real name was Hector, but he had been rechristened after his range to distinguish him from 'Elm Creek' Johnson, who ran sheep further down the Frio.

Many years of living face to face with sheep on their own terms wearied Dry Valley Johnson. So, he sold his ranch for eighteen thousand dollars and moved to Santa Rosa to live a life of gentlemanly ease. Being a silent and melancholy person of thirty-five – or perhaps thirty-eight – he soon became that cursed and earthcumbering thing – an elderlyish bachelor with a hobby. Some one gave him his first strawberry to eat, and he was done for.

Dry Valley bought a four-room cottage in the village, and a library on strawberry culture. Behind the cottage was a garden of which he made a strawberry patch. In his old gray woolen shirt, his brown duck trousers and high-heeled boots he sprawled all day on a canvas cot under a live-oak tree at his back door studying the history of the seductive scarlet berry.

The school teacher, Miss De Witt, spoke of him as 'a fine, presentable man, for all his middle age.' But the focus of Dry Valley's eyes embraced no women. They were merely beings who flew skirts as a signal for him to lift awkwardly his heavy, round-crowned, broad-brimmed felt Stetson whenever he met them, and then hurry past to get back to his beloved berries.

And all this recitative by the chorus is only to bring us to the point where you may be told why Dry Valley shook up the insoluble sulphur in the bottle. So long-drawn and inconsequential a thing is history – the anamorphous shadow of a milestone reaching down the road between us and the setting sun.

When his strawberries were beginning to ripen Dry Valley bought the heaviest buggy whip in the Santa Rosa store. He sat for many hours under the live-oak tree plaiting and weaving in an extension to its lash. When it was done he could snip a leaf from a bush twenty feet away with the cracker. For the bright, predatory eyes of Santa Rosa youth were watching the ripening berries, and Dry Valley was arming himself against their expected raids. No greater care had he taken of his tender lambs during his ranching days than he did of his cherished fruit, warding it from the hungry wolves that whistled and howled and shot their marbles and peered through the fence that surrounded his property.

In the house next to Dry Valley's lived a widow with a pack of children that gave the husbandman frequent anxious misgivings. In the woman there was a strain of the Spanish. She had wedded one of the name of O'Brien. Dry Valley was a connoisseur in cross strains; and he foresaw trouble in the offspring of this union.

Between the two homesteads ran a crazy picket fence overgrown with morning glory and wild gourd vines. Often he could see little heads with mops of black hair and flashing dark eyes dodging in and out between the pickets, keeping tabs on the reddening berries.

Late one afternoon Dry Valley went to the post office. When he came back, like Mother Hubbard he found the deuce to pay. The descendants of Iberian bandits and Hibernian cattle raiders had swooped down upon his strawberry patch. To the outraged vision of Dry Valley there seemed to be a sheep corral full of them; perhaps they numbered five or six. Between the rows of green plants they were stooped, hopping about like toads, gobbling silently and voraciously his finest fruit.

Dry Valley slipped into the house, got his whip, and charged the marauders. The lash curled about the legs of the nearest – a greedy ten-year-old – before they knew they were discovered. His screech gave warning; and the flock scampered for the fence like a drove of *javelis* flushed in the chaparral. Dry Valley's whip drew a toll of two more elfin shrieks before they dived through the vine-clad fence and disappeared.

Dry Valley, less fleet, followed them nearly to the pickets. Checking his useless pursuit, he rounded a bush, dropped his whip and stood, voiceless, motionless, the capacity of his powers consumed by the act of breathing and preserving the perpendicular.

Behind the bush stood Panchita O'Brien, scorning to fly. She was nineteen, the oldest of the raiders. Her night-black hair was gathered back in a wild mass and tied with a scarlet ribbon. She stood, with reluctant feet, yet nearer the brook than to the river; for childhood had environed and detained her.

She looked at Dry Valley Johnson for a moment with magnificent insolence, and before his eyes slowly crunched a luscious berry between her white teeth. Then she turned and walked slowly to the fence with a swaying, conscious motion, such as a duchess might make use of in leading a promenade. There she turned again and grilled Dry Valley Johnson once more in the dark flame of her audacious eyes, laughed a trifle school-girlishly, and twisted herself with pantherish quickness between the pickets to the O'Brien side of the wild gourd vine.

Dry Valley picked up his whip and went into the house. He stumbled as he went up the two wooden steps. The old Mexican woman who cooked his meals and swept his house called him to supper as he went through the rooms. Dry Valley went on, stumbled down the front steps, out the gate and down the road into a mesquite thicket at the edge of town. He sat down in the grass and laboriously plucked the spines from a prickly pear, one by one. This was his attitude of thought, acquired in the days when his problems were only those of wind and wool and water.

A thing had happened to the man – a thing that, if you are eligible, you must pray may pass you by. He had become enveloped in the Indian Summer of the Soul.

Dry Valley had had no youth. Even his childhood had been one of dignity and seriousness. At six he had viewed the frivolous gambols of the lambs on his father's ranch with disapproval. His life as a young man had been wasted. The divine fires and impulses, the glorious exaltations and despairs, the glow and enchantment of youth had passed above his head. Never a thrill of Romeo had he known; he was but a melancholy Jaques of the forest with a rudder philosophy lacking the bitter-sweet flavor of experience that tempered the veteran years of the rugged ranger of Arden. And now in his sere and yellow leaf one scornful look from the eyes of Panchita O'Brien had flooded the autumnal landscape with a tardy and delusive summer heat.

But a sheepman is a hardy animal. Dry Valley Johnson had weathered too many northers to turn his back on a later summer, spiritual or real. Old? He would show them.

By the next mail went an order to San Antonio for an outfit of the latest clothes, colors and styles and prices no object. The next day went the recipe for the hair restorer clipped from a newspaper; for Dry Valley's sunburned auburn hair was beginning to turn silvery above his ears.

Dry Valley kept indoors closely for a week except for frequent sallies after youthful strawberry snatchers. Then, a few days later, he suddenly emerged brilliantly radiant in the hectic glow of his belated midsummer madness.

A jay-bird-blue tennis suit covered him outwardly, almost as far as his wrists and ankles. His shirt was ox-blood; his collar winged and tall; his necktie a floating oriflamme; his shoes a venomous bright tan, pointed and shaped on penitential lasts. A little flat straw hat with a striped band desecrated his weather-beaten head. Lemon-colored kid gloves protected his rough hands from the benignant May sunshine. This sad and optic-smiting creature teetered out of its den, smiling foolishly and smoothing its gloves for men and angels to see. To such a pass had Dry Valley Johnson been brought by Cupid, who always shoots game that is out of season with an arrow from the quiver of Momus. Reconstructing mythology, he had risen, a prismatic macaw, from the ashes of the gray-brown phoenix that had folded its tired wings to roost under the tree of Santa Rosa.

Dry Valley paused in the street to allow Santa Rosans within sight of him to be stunned; and then deliberately and slowly, as his shoes required, entered Mrs. O'Brien's gate.

Not until the eleven months' drought did Santa Rosa cease talking about Dry Valley Johnson's courtship of Panchita O'Brien. It was an unclassifiable procedure; something like a combination of cake-walking, deaf-and-dumb oratory, postage stamp flirtation, and parlor charades. It lasted two weeks and then came to a sudden end.

Of course Mrs. O'Brien favored the match as soon as Dry Valley's intentions were disclosed. Being the mother of a woman child, and therefore a charter member of the Ancient Order of the Rat-trap, she joyfully decked out Panchita for the sacrifice. The girl was temporarily dazzled by having her dresses lengthened and her hair piled up on her head, and came near forgetting that she was only a slice of cheese. It was nice, too, to have as good a match as Mr. Johnson paying you attentions and to see the other girls fluttering the curtains at their windows to see you go by with him.

Dry Valley bought a buggy with yellow wheels and a fine trotter in San Antonio. Every day he drove out with Panchita. He was never seen to speak to her when they were walking or driving. The consciousness of his clothes kept his mind busy; the knowledge that he could say nothing of interest kept him dumb; the feeling that Panchita was there kept him happy.

He took her to parties and dances, and to church. He tried – oh, no man ever tried so hard, to be young as Dry Valley did. He could not dance; but he invented a smile which he wore on these joyous occasions, a smile that, in him, was as great a concession to mirth and gaiety as turning hand-springs would be in another. He began to seek the company of the young men in the town – even of the boys. They accepted him as a decided damper, for his attempts at sportiveness were so forced that they might as well have essayed their games in a cathedral. Neither he nor any other could estimate what progress he had made with Panchita.

The end came suddenly in one day, as often disappears the false afterglow before a November sky and wind.

Dry Valley was to call for the girl one afternoon at six for a walk. An afternoon walk in Santa Rose was a feature of social life that called for the pink of one's wardrobe. So Dry Valley began gorgeously to array himself; and so early that he finished early, and went over to the O'Brien cottage. As he neared the porch on the crooked walk from the gate he heard sounds of revelry within. He stopped and looked through the honeysuckle vines in the open door.

Panchita was amusing her younger brothers and sisters. She wore a man's clothes – no doubt those of the late Mr. O'Brien. On her head was the smallest brother's straw hat decorated with an ink-striped paper band. On her hands were flapping yellow cloth gloves, roughly cut out and sewn for the masquerade. The same material covered her shoes, giving them the semblance of tan leather. High collar and flowing necktie were not omitted.

Panchita was an actress. Dry Valley saw his affectedly youthful gait, his limp where the right shoe hurt him, his forced smile, his awkward simulation of a gallant air, all reproduced with startling fidelity. For the first time a mirror had been held up to him. The corroboration of one of the youngsters calling, 'Mamma, come and see Pancha do like Mr. Johnson,' was not needed.

As softly as the caricatured tans would permit, Dry Valley tiptoed back to the gate and home again.

Twenty minutes after the time appointed for the walk Panchita tripped demurely out her gate in a thin, trim white lawn and sailor hat. She strolled up the sidewalk and slowed her steps at Dry Valley's gate, her manner expressing wonder at his unusual delinquency.

Then out of his door and down the walk strode – not the polychromatic victim of a lost summer time, but the sheepman, rehabilitated. He wore his old gray woolen shirt, open at the throat, his brown duck trousers stuffed into his run-over boots, and his white felt sombrero on the back of his head. Twenty years or fifty he might look; Dry Valley cared not. His light blue eyes met Panchita's dark ones with a cold flash in them. He came as far as the gate. He pointed with his long arm to her house.

'Go home,' said Dry Valley. 'Go home to your mother. I wonder lightnin' don't strike a fool like me. Go home and play in the sand. What business have you got cavortin' around with grown men? I reckon I was locoed to be makin' a he poll-parrot out of myself for a kid like you. Go home and don't let me see you no more. Why I done it, will somebody tell me? Go home, and let me try and forget it.'

Panchita obeyed and walked slowly towards her home, saying nothing. For some distance she kept her head turned and her large eyes fixed intrepidly upon Dry Valley's. At her gate she stood for a moment looking back at him, then ran suddenly and swiftly into the house.

Old Antonia was building a fire in the kitchen stove. Dry Valley stopped at the door and laughed harshly.

'I'm a pretty looking old rhinoceros to be gettin' stuck on a kid ain't I, 'Tonia?' said he.

'Not verree good thing,' agreed Antonia, sagely, 'for too much old man to likee *muchacha*.'

'You bet it ain't,' said Dry Valley, grimly. 'It's dum foolishness; and, besides, it hurts.'

He brought at one armful the regalia of his aberration – the blue tennis suit, shoes, hat, gloves, and all, and threw them in a pile at Antonia's feet.

'Give them to your old man,' said he, 'to hunt antelope in.'

Just as the first star presided palely over the twilight Dry Valley got his biggest strawberry book and sat on the back steps to catch the last of the reading light. He thought he saw the figure of someone in his strawberry patch. He laid aside the book, got his whip, and hurried forth to see.

It was Panchita. She had slipped through the picket fence and was halfway across the patch. She stopped when she saw him and looked at him without wavering.

A sudden rage – a humiliating flush of unreasoning wrath – came over Dry Valley. For this child he had made himself a motley to the view. He had tried to bribe Time to turn backward for himself; he had – been made a fool of. At last he had seen his folly. There was a gulf between him and youth over which he could not build a bridge even with yellow gloves to protect his hands. And the sight of his torment coming to pester him with her elfin pranks – coming to plunder his strawberry vines like a mischievous school-boy – roused all his anger.

'I told you to keep away from here,' said Dry Valley. 'Go back to your home.'

Panchita moved slowly toward him.

Dry Valley cracked his whip.

'Go back home,' said Dry Valley, savagely, 'and play theatricals some more. You'd make a fine man. You've made a fine one of me.'

She came a step nearer, silent, and with that strange, defiant, steady shine in her eye that had always puzzled him. Now it stirred his wrath.

His whiplash whistled through the air. He saw a red streak suddenly come through her white dress above her knee where it had struck.

Without flinching and with the same unchanging dark glow in her eyes, Panchita came steadily toward him through the strawberry vines. Dry Valley's trembling hand released his whip handle. When within a yard of him Panchita stretched out her arms.

'God kid!' stammered Dry Valley, 'do you mean—?'

But the seasons are versatile; and it may have been Springtime after all, instead of Indian Summer, that struck Dry Valley Johnson.

CHRISTMAS BY INJUNCTION

CHEROKEE WAS THE CIVIC FATHER of Yellowhammer. Yellowhammer was a new mining town constructed mainly of canvas and undressed pine. Cherokee was a prospector. One day while his burro was eating quartz and pine burrs Cherokee turned up with his pick a nugget weighing thirty ounces. He staked his claim and then, being a man of breadth and hospitality, sent out invitations to his friends in three states to drop in and share his luck.

Not one of the invited guests sent regrets. They rolled in from the Gila country, from Salt River, from the Pecos, from Albuquerque and Phoenix and Santa Fé, and from the camps intervening.

When a thousand citizens had arrived and taken up claims they named the town Yellowhammer, appointed a vigilance committee, and presented Cherokee with a watch-chain made of nuggets.

Three hours after the presentation ceremonies Cherokee's claim played out. He had located a pocket instead of a vein. He abandoned it and staked others one by one. Luck had kissed her hand to him. Never afterwards did he turn up enough dust in Yellowhammer to pay his bar bill. But his thousand invited guests were mostly prospering, and Cherokee smiled and congratulated them.

Yellowhammer was made up of men who took off their hats to a smiling loser; so they invited Cherokee to say what he wanted.

'Me?' said Cherokee, 'oh, grubstakes will be about the thing. I reckon I'll prospect along up in the Mariposas. If I strike it up there I will most certainly let you all know about the facts. I never was any hand to hold out cards on my friends.'

In May Cherokee packed his burro and turned its thoughtful, mouse-colored forehead to the north. Many citizens escorted him to the undefined limits of Yellowhammer and bestowed upon him shouts of commendation and farewells. Five pocket flasks without an air bubble between contents and cork were forced upon him; and he was bidden to consider Yellowhammer in perpetual commission for his bed, bacon and eggs, and hot water for shaving in the event that luck did not see fit to warm her hands by his campfire of the Mariposas.

The name of the father of Yellowhammer was given him by the gold hunters in accordance with their popular system of nomenclature. It was not necessary for a citizen to exhibit his baptismal certificate in order to acquire a cognomen. A man's name was his personal property. For convenience in calling him up to the bar and in designating him among other blue-shirted bipeds, a temporary appellation, title or epithet was conferred upon him by the public. Personal peculiarities formed the source of the majority of such informal baptisms. Many were easily dubbed geographically from the regions from which they confessed to have hailed. Some announced themselves to be 'Thompsons,' and 'Adamses,' and the like, with a brazenness and loudness that cast a cloud upon their titles. A few vaingloriously and shamelessly uncovered their proper and indisputable names. This was held to be unduly arrogant, and did not win popularity. One man who said he was Chesterton L. C. Belmont, and proved it by letters, was given till sundown to leave the town. Such names as 'Shorty,' 'Bow-legs,' 'Texas,' 'Lazy Bill,' 'Thirsty Rogers,' 'Limping Riley,' 'The Judge,' and 'California Ed' were in favor. Cherokee derived his title from the fact that he claimed to have lived for a time with that tribe in the Indian Nation.

On the twentieth day of December Baldy, the mail rider, brought Yellowhammer a piece of news.

'What do I see in Albuquerque,' said Baldy, to the patrons of the bar, 'but Cherokee all embellished and festooned up like the Czar of Turkey, and lavishin' money in bulk. Him and me seen the elephant and the owl, and we had specimens of this seidlitz powder wine; and Cherokee he audits all the bills, C.O.D. His pockets looked like a pool table's after a fifteen-ball run.'

'Cherokee must have struck pay ore,' remarked California Ed. 'Well, he's white. I'm much obliged to him for his success.'

'Seems like Cherokee would ramble down to Yellowhammer and see his friends,' said another, slightly aggrieved. 'But that's the way. Prosperity is the finest cure there is for lost forgetfulness.'

'You wait,' said Baldy; 'I'm comin' to that. Cherokee strikes a three-foot vein up in the Mariposas that assays a trip to Europe to the ton, and he closes it out to a syndicate outfit for a hundred thousand hasty dollars in cash. Then he buys himself a baby sealskin overcoat and a red sleigh, and what do you think he takes it in his head to do next?'

'Chuck-a-luck,' said Texas, whose ideas of recreation were the gamester's.

'Come and Kiss Me, Ma Honey,' sang Shorty, who carried tintypes in his pocket and wore a red necktie while working on his claim.

'Bought a saloon?' suggested Thirsty Rogers.

'Cherokee took me to a room,' continued Baldy, 'and showed me. He's got that room full of drums and dolls and skates and bags of candy and jumping-jacks and toy lambs and whistles and such infantile truck. And what do you think he's goin' to do with them inefficacious knick-knacks? Don't surmise none – Cherokee told me. He's goin' to load 'em up in his red sleigh and – wait a minute, don't order no drinks yet – he's goin' to drive down here to Yellowhammer and give the kids – the kids of this here town – the biggest Christmas tree and the biggest cryin' doll and Little Giant Boys' Tool Chest blowout that ever seen west of Cape Hatteras.'

Two minutes of absolute silence ticked away in the wake of Baldy's words. It was broken by the House, who, happily conceiving the moment to be ripe for extending hospitality, sent a dozen whisky glasses spinning down the bar, with the slower traveling bottle bringing up the rear.

'Didn't you tell him?' asked the miner called Trinidad.

'Well, no,' answered Baldy, pensively; 'I never exactly seen my way to.

'You see, Cherokee had this Christmas mess already bought and paid for; and he was all flattered up with self-esteem over his idea; and we had in a way flew the flume with that fizzy wine I speak of; so I never let on.'

'I cannot refrain from a certain amount of surprise,' said the Judge, as he hung his ivory-handled cane on the bar, 'that our friend Cherokee should possess such an erroneous conception of – ah – his, as it were, own town.'

'Oh, it ain't the eighth wonder of the terrestrial world,' said Baldy. 'Cherokee's been gone from Yellowhammer over seven months. Lots of things could happen in that time. How's he to know there there ain't a single kid in this town, and so far as emigration is concerned, none expected?'

'Come to think of it,' remarked California Ed, 'it's funny some ain't drifted in. Town ain't settled enough yet for to bring in the rubber-ring brigade, I reckon.'

'To top off this Christmas-tree splurge of Cherokee's,' went on Baldy, 'he's goin' to give an imitation of Santa Claus. He's got a white wig and whiskers that disfigure him up exactly like the pictures of this William Cullen Longfellow in the books, and a red suit of fur-trimmed outside underwear, and eight-ounces gloves, and a stand-up, lay-down croshayed red cap. Ain't it a shame that a outfit like that can't get a chance to connect with a Annie and Willie's prayer layout?'

'When does Cherokee allow to come over with his truck?' inquired Trinidad.

'Mornin' before Christmas,' said Baldy. 'And he wants you folks to have a room fixed up and a tree hauled and ready. And such ladies to assist as can stop breathin' long enough to let it be a surprise for the kids.'

The unblessed condition of Yellowhammer had been truly described. The voice of childhood had never gladdened its flimsy structures; the patter of restless little feet had never consecrated the one rugged highway between the two rows of tents and rough buildings. Later they would come. But now Yellowhammer was but a mountain camp, and nowhere in it were the roguish, expectant eyes, opening wide at dawn of the enchanting day; the eager, small hands to reach for Santa's bewildering hoard; the elated, childish voicings of the season's joy, such as the coming good things of the warm-hearted Cherokee deserved.

Of women there were five in Yellowhammer. The assayer's wife, the proprietress of the Lucky Strike Hotel, and a laundress whose washtub panned out an ounce of dust a day. These were the permanent feminines; the remaining two were the Spangler Sisters, Misses Fanchon and Erma, of the Transcontinental Comedy Company, then playing in the repertoire at the (improvised) Empire Theatre. But of children there were none. Sometimes Miss Fanchon enacted with spirit and address the part of robustious childhood; but between her delineation and the visions of adolescence that the fancy offered as eligible recipients of Cherokee's holiday stores there seemed to be fixed a gulf.

Christmas would come on Thursday. On Tuesday morning Trinidad, instead of going to work, sought the Judge at the Lucky Strike Hotel.

'It'll be a disgrace to Yellowhammer,' said Trinidad, 'if it throws Cherokee down on his Christmas-tree blowout. You might say that that man made this town. For one, I'm goin' to see what can be done to give Santa Claus a square deal.'

'My coöperation,' said the Judge, 'would be gladly forthcoming. I am indebted to Cherokee for past favors. But, I do not see – I have heretofore regarded the absence of children rather as a luxury – but in this instance – still, I do not see — '

'Look at me,' said Trinidad, 'and you'll see old Ways and Means with the fur on. I'm goin' to hitch up a team and rustle a load of kids for Cherokee's Santa Claus act, if I have to rob an orphan asylum.'

'Eureka!' cried the Judge, enthusiastically.

'No, you didn't,' said Trinidad, decidedly. 'I found it myself. I learned about that Latin word at school.'

'I will accompany you,' declared the Judge, waving his cane. 'Perhaps such eloquence and gift of language as I may possess will be of benefit in persuading our young friends to lend themselves to our project.'

Within an hour Yellowhammer was acquainted with the theme of Trinidad and the Judge, and approved it. Citizens who knew of families with offspring within a forty-mile radius of Yellowhammer came forward and contributed their information. Trinidad made careful notes of all such and then hastened to secure a vehicle and team.

The first stop scheduled was at a double loghouse fifteen miles out from Yellowhammer. A man opened the door at Trinidad's hail, and then came down and leaned upon the rickety gate. The doorway was filled with a close mass of youngsters, some ragged, all full of curiosity and health.

'It's this way,' explained Trinidad. 'We're from Yellowhammer, and we come kidnappin' in a gentle kind of a way. One of our leading citizens is stung with the Santa Claus affliction, and he's due in town to-morrow with half the folderols that's painted red and made in Germany. The youngest kid we got in Yellowhammer packs a forty-five and a safety razor. Consequently we're mighty shy on anybody to say 'Oh' and 'Ah' when we light the candles on the Christmas tree. Now, partner, if you'll loan us a few kids we guarantee to return 'em safe and sound on Christmas Day. And they'll come back loaded down with a good time and Swiss Family Robinsons and cornucopias and red drums and similar testimonials. What do you say?'

'In other words,' said the Judge, 'we have discovered for the first time in our embryonic but progressive little city the inconveniences of the absence of adolescence. The season of the year having approximately arrived during which it is a custom to bestow frivolous but often appreciated gifts upon the young and tender—'

'I understand,' said the parent, packing his pipe with a forefinger. 'I guess I needn't detain you gentlemen. Me and the old woman have got seven kids, so to speak; and runnin' my mind over the bunch, I don't appear to hit upon none that we could spare for you to take over to your doin's. The old woman has got some popcorn candy and ragdolls hid in the clothes chest, and we allow to give Christmas a little whirl of our own in a insignificant sort of style. No, I couldn't, with any degree of avidity, seem to fall in with the idea of lettin' none of 'em go. Thank you kindly, gentlemen.'

Down the slope they drove and up another foothill to the ranchhouse of Wiley Wilson. Trinidad recited his appeal and the Judge boomed out his ponderous antiphony. Mrs. Wiley gathered her two rosy-cheeked youngster close to her skirts and did not smile until she had seen Wiley laugh and shake his head. Again a refusal.

Trinidad and the Judge vainly exhausted more than half their list before twilight set in among the hills. They spent the night at a stage road hostelry, and set out again early the next morning. The wagon had not acquired a single passenger.

'It's creepin' upon my faculties,' remarked Trinidad, 'that borrowin' kids at Christmas is somethin' like tryin' to steal butter from a man that's got hot pancakes a-comin'.'

'It is undoubtedly an indisputable fact,' said the Judge, 'that the – ah – family ties seem to be more coherent and assertive at that period of the year.'

On the day before Christmas they drove thirty miles, making four fruitless halts and appeals. Everywhere they found 'kids' at a premium.

The sun was low when the wife of a section boss on a lonely railroad huddled her unavailable progeny behind her and said:

'There's a woman that's just took charge of the railroad eatin' house down at Granite Junction. I hear she's got a little boy. Maybe she might let him go.'

Trinidad pulled up his mules at Granite Junction at five o'clock in the afternoon. The train had just departed with its load of fed and appeased passengers.

On the steps of the eating house they found a thin and glowering boy of ten smoking a cigarette. The dining-room had been left in chaos by the peripatetic appetites. A youngish woman reclined, exhausted, in a chair. Her face wore sharp lines of worry. She had once possessed a certain style of beauty that would never wholly leave her and would never wholly return. Trinidad set forth his mission.

'I'd count it a mercy if you'd take Bobby for a while,' she said, wearily. 'I'm on the go from morning till night, and I don't have time to 'tend to him. He's learning bad habits from the men. It'll be the only chance he'll have to get any Christmas.'

The men went outside and conferred with Bobby. Trinidad pictured the glories of the Christmas tree and presents in lively colors.

'And, moreover, my young friend,' added the Judge, 'Santa Claus himself will personally distribute the offerings that will typify the gifts conveyed by the shepherds of Bethlehem to—'

'Aw, come off,' said the boy, squinting his small eyes. 'I ain't no kid. There ain't any Santa Claus. It's your folks that buys toys and sneaks 'em in when you're asleep. And they make marks in the soot in the chimney with the tongs to look like Santa's sleigh tracks.'

'That might be so,' argued Trinidad, 'but Christmas trees ain't no fairy tale. This one's goin' to look like the ten-cent store in Albuquerque, all strung up in redwood. There's tops and drums and Noah's arks and—'

'Oh, rats!' said Bobby, wearily. 'I cut them out long ago. I'd like to have a rifle – not a target one – a real one, to shoot wildcats with; but I guess you won't have any of them on your old tree.'

'Well, I can't say for sure,' said Trinidad, diplomatically; 'it might be. You go along with us and see.'

The hope thus held out, though faint, won the boy's hesitating consent to go. With this solitary beneficiary for Cherokee's holiday bounty, the canvassers spun along the homeward road.

In Yellowhammer the empty storeroom had been transformed into what might have passed as the bower of an Arizona fairy. The ladies had done their work well. A tall Christmas tree, covered to the topmost branch with candle, spangles, and toys sufficient for more than a score of children, stood in the centre of the floor. Near sunset anxious eyes had begun to scan the street for the returning team of child-providers. At noon that day Cherokee had dashed into town with his new sleigh piled high with bundles and boxes and bales of all sizes and shapes. So intent was he upon the arrangements for his altruistic plans that the dearth of childhood did not receive his notice. No one gave away the humiliating state of Yellowhammer, for the efforts of Trinidad and the Judge were expected to supply the deficiency.

When the sun went down Cherokee, with many winks and arch grins on his seasoned face, went into retirement with the bundle containing the Santa Claus raiment and a package containing special and undisclosed gifts.

'When the kids are rounded up,' he instructed the volunteer arrangement committee, 'light up the candles on the tree and set 'em to playin' "Pussy Wants a Corner" and "King William." When they get good and at it, why – old Santa'll slide in the door. I reckon there'll be plenty of gifts to go 'round.'

The ladies were flitting about the tree, giving it final touches that were never final. The Spangler Sisters were there in costume as Lady Violet de Vere and Marie, the maid, in their new drama, 'The Miner's Bride.' The theatre did not open until nine, and they were welcome assistants of the Christmas-tree committee. Every minute heads would pop out the door to look and listen for the approach of Trinidad's team. And now this became an anxious function, for night had fallen and it would soon be necessary to light the candles on the tree, and Cherokee was apt to make an irruption at any time in his Kriss Kringle garb.

At length the wagon of the child 'rustlers' rattled down the street to the door. The ladies, with little screams of excitement, flew to the lighting of the candles. The men of Yellowhammer passed in and out restlessly or stood about the room in embarrassed groups.

Trinidad and the Judge, bearing the marks of protracted travel, entered, conducting between them a single impish boy, who stared with sullen, pessimistic eyes at the gaudy tree.

'Where are the other children?' asked the assayer's wife, the acknowledged leader of all social functions.

'Ma'am,' said Trinidad with a sigh, 'prospectin' for kids at Christmas time is like huntin' in limestone for silver. This parental business is one that I haven't no chance to comprehend. It seems that fathers and mothers are willin' for their offsprings to be drownded, stole, fed on poison oak, and et by catamounts 364 days in the year; but on Christmas Day they insists on enjoyin' the exclusive mortification of their company. This here young biped, ma'am, is all that washed out of our two days' manoeuvres.'

'Oh, the sweet little boy!' cooed Miss Erma, trailing her De Vere robes to centre of stage.

'Aw, shut up,' said Bobby, with a scowl. 'Who's a kid? You ain't, you bet.'

'Fresh brat!' breathed Miss Erma, beneath her enamelled smile.

'We done the best we could,' said Trinidad. 'It's tough on Cherokee, but it can't be helped.'

Then the door opened and Cherokee entered in the conventional dress of Saint Nick. A white rippling beard and flowing hair covered his face almost to his dark and shining eyes. Over his shoulder he carried a pack.

No one stirred as he came in. Even the Spangler Sisters ceased their coquettish poses and stared curiously at the tall figure. Bobby stood with his hands in his pockets gazing gloomily at the effeminate and childish tree. Cherokee put down his pack and looked wonderingly about the room. Perhaps he fancied that a bevy of eager children were being herded somewhere, to be loosed upon his entrance. He went up to Bobby and extended his red-mittened hand.

'Merry Christmas, little boy,' said Cherokee. 'Anything on the tree you want they'll get it down for you. Won't you shake hands with Santa Claus?'

'There ain't any Santa Claus,' whined the boy. 'You've got old false billy goat's whiskers on your face. I ain't no kid. What do I want with dolls and tin horses? The driver said you'd have a rifle, and you haven't. I want to go home.'

Trinidad stepped into the breach. He shook Cherokee's hand in warm greeting.

'I'm sorry, Cherokee,' he explained. 'There never was a kid in Yellowhammer. We tried to rustle a bunch of 'em for your swaree, but this sardine was all we could catch. He's a atheist, and he don't believe in Santa Claus. It's a shame for you to be out all this truck. But me and the Judge was sure we could round up a wagonful of candidates for your gimcracks.'

'That's all right,' said Cherokee, gravely. 'The expense don't amount to nothin' worth mentionin'. We can dump the stuff down a shaft or throw it away. I don't know what I was thinkin' about; but it never occurred to my cogitations that there wasn't any kids in Yellowhammer.'

Meanwhile the company had relaxed into a hollow but praiseworthy imitation of a pleasure gathering.

Bobby had retreated to a distant chair, and was coldly regarding the scene with ennui plastered thick upon him. Cherokee, lingering with his original idea, went over and sat beside him.

'Where do you live, little boy?' he asked, respectfully.

'Granite Junction,' said Bobby without emphasis.

The room was warm. Cherokee took off his cap, and then removed his beard and wig.

'Say!' exclaimed Bobby, with a show of interest, 'I know your mug, all right.'

'Did you ever see me before?' asked Cherokee.

'I don't know; but I've seen your picture lots of times.'

'Where?'

The boy hesitated. 'On the bureau at home,' he answered.

'Let's have your name, if you please, buddy.'

'Robert Lumsden. The picture belongs to my mother. She puts it under her pillow of nights. And once I saw her kiss it. I wouldn't. But women are that way.'

Cherokee rose and beckoned to Trinidad.

'Keep this boy by you till I come back,' he said. 'I'm going to shed these Christmas duds, and hitch up my sleigh. I'm goin' to take this kid home.'

'Well, infidel,' said Trinidad, taking Cherokee's vacant chair, 'and so you are too superannuated and effete to yearn for such mockeries as candy and toys, it seems.'

'I don't like you,' said Bobby, with acrimony. 'You said there would be a rifle. A fellow can't even smoke. I wish I was at home.'

Cherokee drove his sleigh to the door, and they lifted Bobby in beside him. The team of fine horses sprange away prancingly over the hard snow. Cherokee had his $500 overcoat of baby sealskin. The laprobe that he drew about them was as warm as velvet.

Bobby slipped a cigarette from his pocket and was trying to snap a match.

'Throw that cigarette away,' said Cherokee, in a quiet but new voice.

Bobby hesitated, and then dropped the cylinder overboard.

'Throw the box, too,' commanded the new voice.

More reluctantly the boy obeyed.

'Say,' said Bobby, presently, 'I like you. I don't know why. Nobody never made me do anything I didn't want to do before.'

'Tell me, kid,' said Cherokee, not using his new voice, 'are you sure your mother kissed that picture that looks like me?'

'Dead sure. I seen her do it.'

'Didn't you remark somethin' a while ago about wanting a rifle?'

'You bet I did. Will you get me one?'

'To-morrow – silver-mounted.'

Cherokee took out his watch.

'Half-past nine. We'll hit the Junction plumb on time with Christmas Day. Are you cold? Sit closer, son.'

A CHAPARRAL PRINCE

NINE O'CLOCK AT LAST, and the drudging toil of the day was ended. Lena climbed to her room in the third half-story of the Quarrymen's Hotel. Since daylight she had slaved, doing the work of a full-grown woman, scrubbing the floors, washing the heavy ironstone plates and cups, making the beds, and supplying the insatiate demands for wood and water in that turbulent and depressing hostelry.

The din of the day's quarrying was over – the blasting and drilling, the creaking of the great cranes, the shouts of the foremen, the backing and shifting of the flat-cars hauling the heavy blocks of limestone. Down in the hotel office three or four of the laborers were growling and swearing over a belated game of checkers. Heavy odors of stewed meat, hot grease, and cheap coffee hung like a depressing fog about the house.

Lena lit the stump of a candle and sat limply upon her wooden chair. She was eleven years old, thin and ill-nourished. Her back and limbs were sore and aching. But the ache in her heart made the biggest trouble. The last straw had been added to the burden upon her small shoulders. They had taken away Grimm. Always at night, however tired she might be, she had turned to Grimm for comfort and hope. Each time had Grimm whispered to her that the prince or the fairy would come and deliver her out of the wicked enchantment. Every night she had taken fresh courage and strength from Grimm.

To whatever tale she read she found an analogy in her own condition. The woodcutter's lost child, the unhappy goose girl, the persecuted stepdaughter, the little maiden imprisoned in the witch's hut – all these were but transparent disguises for Lena, the overworked kitchenmaid in the Quarrymen's Hotel. And always when the extremity was direst came the good fairy or the gallant prince to the rescue.

So, here in the ogre's castle, enslaved by a wicked spell, Lena had leaned upon Grimm and waited, longing for the powers of goodness to prevail. But on the day before Mrs. Maloney had found the book in her room and had carried it away, declaring sharply that it would not do for servants to read at night; they lost sleep and did not work briskly the next day. Can one only eleven years old, living away from one's mama, and never having any time to play, live entirely deprived of Grimm? Just try it once and you will see what a difficult thing it is.

Lena's home was in Texas, away up among the little mountains on the Pedernales River, in a little town called Fredericksburg. They are all German people who live in Fredericksburg. Of evenings they sit at little tables along the sidewalk and drink beer and play pinochle and scat. They are very thrifty people.

Thriftiest among them was Peter Hildesmuller, Lena's father. And that is why Lena was sent to work in the hotel at the quarries, thirty miles away. She earned three dollars every week there, and Peter added her wages to his well-guarded store. Peter had an ambition to become as rich as his neighbor, Hugo Heffelbauer, who smoked a meerschaum pipe three feet long and had wiener schnitzel and hassenpfeffer for dinner every day in the week. And now Lena was quite old enough to work and assist in the accumulation of riches. But conjecture, if you can, what it means to be sentenced at eleven years of age from a home in the pleasant little Rhine village to hard labor in the ogre's castle, where you must fly to serve the ogres, while they devour cattle and sheep, growling fiercely as they stamp white limestone dust from their great shoes for you to sweep and scour with your weak, aching fingers. And then – to have Grimm taken away from you!

Lena raised the lid of an old empty case that had once contained canned corn and got out a sheet of paper and a piece of pencil. She was going to write a letter to her mamma. Tommy Ryan was going to post it for her at Ballinger's. Tommy was seventeen, worked in the quarries, went home to Ballinger's every night, and was now waiting in the shadows under Lena's window for her to throw her letter out to him. That was the only way she could send a letter to Fredericksburg. Mrs. Maloney did not like for her to write letters.

The stump of candle was burning low, so Lena hastily bit the wood from around the lead of her pencil and began. This is the letter she wrote:

Dearest Mamma: I want so much to see you. And Gretel and Claus and Heinrich and little Adolf. I am so tired. I want to see you. To-day I was slapped by Mrs. Maloney and had no supper. I could not bring in enough wood, for my hand hurt. She took my book yesterday. I mean 'Grimms's Fairy Tales,' which Uncle Leo gave me. It did not hurt any one for me to read the book. I try to work as well as I can, but there is so much to do. I read only a little bit every night. Dear mamma, I shall tell you what I am going to do. Unless you send for me to-morrow to bring me home I shall go to a deep place I know in the river and drown. It is wicked to drown, I suppose, but I wanted to see you, and there is no one else. I am very tired, and Tommy is waiting for the letter. You will excuse me, mamma, if I do it.

Your respectful and loving daughter,
Lena

Tommy was still waiting faithfully when the letter was concluded, and when Lena dropped it out she saw him pick it up and start up the steep hillside. Without undressing she blew out the candle and curled herself upon the mattress on the floor.

At 10:30 o'clock old man Ballinger came out of the house in his stocking feet and leaned over the gate, smoking his pipe. He looked down the big road, white in the moonshine, and rubbed one ankle with the toe of his other foot. It was time for the Fredericksburg mail to come pattering up the road.

Old man Ballinger had waited only a few minutes when he heard the lively hoofbeats of Fritz's team of little black mules, and very soon afterward his covered spring wagon stood in front of the gate. Fritz's big spectacles flashed in the moonlight and his tremendous voice shouted a greeting to the postmaster of Ballinger's. The mail-carrier jumped out and took the bridles from the mules, for he always fed them oats at Ballinger's.

While the mules were eating from their feed bags old man Ballinger brought out the mail sack and threw it into the wagon.

Fritz Bergmann was a man of three sentiments – or to be more accurate – four, the pair of mules deserving to be reckoned individually. Those mules were the chief interest and joy of his existence. Next came the Emperor of Germany and Lena Hildesmuller.

'Tell me,' said Fritz, when he was ready to start, 'contains the sacks a letter to Frau Hildesmuller from the little Lena at the quarries? One came in the last mail to say that she is a little sick, already. Her mamma is very anxious to hear again.'

'Yes,' said old man Ballinger, 'that's a letter for Mrs. Helterskelter, or some sich name. Tommy Ryan brung it over when he come. Her little gal workin' over thar, you say?'

'In the hotel,' shouted Fritz, as he gathered up the lines; 'eleven years old and not bigger as a frankfurter. The close-fist of a Peter Hildesmuller! – some day shall I with a big club pound that man's dummkopf – all in and out the town. Perhaps in this letter Lena will say that she is yet feeling better. So, her mamma will be glad. *Auf wiedersehen*, Herr Ballinger – your feets will take cold out in the night air.'

'So long, Fritzy,' said old man Ballinger. 'You got a nice cool night for your drive.'

Up the road went the little black mules at their steady trot, while Fritz thundered at them occasional words of endearment and cheer.

These fancies occupied the mind of the mailcarrier until he reached the big post-oak forest, eight miles from Ballinger's. Here his ruminations were scattered by the sudden flash and report of pistols and a whooping as if from a whole tribe of Indians. A band of galloping centaurs closed in around the mail wagon. One of them leaned over the front wheel, covered the driver with his revolver, and ordered him to stop. Others caught at the bridles of Donder and Blitzen.

'Donnerwetter!' shouted Fritz, with all his tremendous voice – 'wass ist? Release your hands from dose mules. Ve vas der United States mail!'

'Hurry up, Dutch!' drawled a melancholy voice. 'Don't you know when you're in a stick-up? Reverse your mules and climb out of the cart.'

It is due to the breadth of Hondo Bill's demerit and the largeness of his achievements to state that the holding up of the Fredericksburg mail was not perpetuated by way of an exploit. As the lion while in the pursuit of prey commensurate to his prowess might set a frivolous foot upon a casual rabbit in his path, so Hondo Bill and his gang had swooped sportively upon the pacific transport of Meinherr Fritz.

The real work of their sinister night ride was over. Fritz and his mail bag and his mules came as a gentle relaxation, grateful after the arduous duties of their profession. Twenty miles to the southeast stood a train with a killed engine, hysterical passengers, and a looted express and mail car. That represented the serious occupation of Hondo Bill and his gang. With a fairly rich prize of currency and silver the robbers were making a wide detour to the west through the less populous country, intending to seek safety in Mexico by means of some fordable spot on the Rio Grande. The booty from the train had melted the desperate bushrangers to jovial and happy skylarkers.

Trembling with outraged dignity and no little personal apprehension, Fritz climbed out to the road after replacing his suddenly removed spectacles. The band had dismounted and were singing, capering, and whooping, thus expressing their satisfied delight in the life of a jolly outlaw. Rattlesnake Rogers, who stood at the heads of the mules, jerked a little too vigorously at the rein of the tender-mouthed Donder, who reared and emitted a loud, protesting snort of pain. Instantly Fritz, with a scream of anger, flew at the bulky Rogers and began assiduously to pommel that surprised free-booter with his fists.

'Villain!' shouted Fritz, 'dog, bigstiff! Dot mule he has a soreness by his mouth. I vill knock off your shoulders mit your head – robber-mans!'

'Yi-yi!' howled Rattlesnake, roaring with laughter and ducking his head, 'somebody git this here sourkrout off'n me!'

One of the band jerked Fritz back by the coat-tail, and the woods rang with Rattlesnake's vociferous comments.

'The dog-goned little wienerwurst,' he yelled, amiably. 'He's not so much of a skunk, for a Dutchman. Took up for his animile plum quick, didn't he? I like to see a man like his hoss, even if it is a mule. The dad-blamed little Limburger he went for me, didn't he! Whoa, now, muley – I ain't a-goin' to hurt your mouth agin any more.'

Perhaps the mail would not have been tampered with had not Ben Moody, the lieutenant, possessed certain wisdom that seemed to promise more spoils.

'Say, Cap,' he said, addressing Hondo Bill, 'there's liable to be good pickings in these mail sacks. I've done some hoss tradin' with these Dutchmen around Fredericksburg, and I know the style of the varmints. There's big money goes through the mails to that town. Them Dutch risk a thousand dollars sent wrapped in a piece of paper before they'd pay the banks to handle the money.'

Hondo Bill, six feet two, gentle of voice and impulsive in action, was dragging the sacks from the rear of the wagon before Moody had finished his speech. A knife shone in his hand, and they heard the ripping sound as it bit through the tough canvas. The outlaws crowded around and began tearing open letters and packages, enlivening their labors by swearing affably at the writers, who seemed to have conspired to confute the prediction of Ben Moody. Not a dollar was found in the Fredericksburg mail.

'You ought to be ashamed of yourself,' said Hondo Bill to the mail-carrier in solemn tones, 'to be packing around such a lot of old, trashy paper as this. What d'you mean by it, anyhow? Where do you Dutchers keep your money at?'

The Ballinger mail sack opened like a cocoon under Hondo's knife. It contained but a handful of mail. Fritz had been fuming with terror and excitement until this sack was reached. He now remembered Lena's letter. He addressed the leader of the band, asking him that particular missive be spared.

'Much obliged, Dutch,' he said to the disturbed carrier. 'I guess that's the letter we want. Got spondulicks in it, ain't it? Here she is. Make a light, boys.'

Hondo found and tore open the letter to Mrs. Hildesmuller. The others stood about, lighting twisted-up letters one from another. Hondo gazed with mute disapproval at the single sheet of paper covered with the angular German script.

'Whatever is this you've humbugged us with, Dutchy? You call this here a valuable letter? That's a mighty low-down trick to play on your friends what come along to help you distribute your mail.'

'That's Chiny writin',' said Sandy Grundy, peering over Hondo's shoulder.

'You're off your kazip,' declared another of the gang, an effective youth, covered with silk handkerchiefs and nickel plating. 'That's shorthand. I seen 'em do it once in court.'

'Ach, no, no, no – dot is German,' said Fritz. 'It is no more as a little girl writing a letter to her mamma. One poor little girl, sick and vorking hard avay from home. Ach! it is a shame. Good Mr. Robber-man, you vill please let me have dot letter?'

'What the devil do you take us for, old Pretzels' said Hondo with sudden and surprising severity. 'You ain't presumin' to insinuate that we gents ain't possessed of sufficient politeness for to take an interest in the miss's health are you? Now, you go on, and you read that scratchin' out loud and in plain United States language to this here company of educated society.'

Hondo twirled his six-shooter by its trigger guard and stood towering above the little German, who at once began to read the letter, translating the simple words into English. The gang of rovers stood in absolute silence, listening intently.

'How old is that kid?' asked Hondo when the letter was done.

'Eleven,' said Fritz.

'And where is she at?'

'At dose rock quarries – working. Ach, mein Gott – little Lena, she speak of drowning. I do not know if she vill do it, but if she shall I schwear I vill dot Peter Hildesmuller shoot mit a gun.'

'You Dutchers,' said Hondo Bill, his voice swelling with fine contempt, 'make me plenty tired. Hirin' out your kids to work when they ought to be playin' dolls in the sand. You're a hell of a sect of people. I reckon we'll fix your clock for a while just to show what we think of your old cheesy nation. Here, boys!'

Hondo Bill parleyed aside briefly with his band, and then they seized Fritz and conveyed him off the road to one side. Here they bound him fast to a tree with a couple of lariats. His team they tied to another tree near by.

'We ain't going to hurt you bad,' said Hondo, reassuringly. ''Twon't hurt you to be tied up for a while. We will now pass you the time of day, as it is up to us to depart. Ausgespielt – nixcumrous, Dutchy. Don't get any more impatience.'

Fritz heard a great squeaking of saddles as the men mounted their horses. Then a loud yell and a great clatter of hoofs as they galloped pell-mell back along the Fredericksburg road.

For more than two hours Fritz sat against his tree, tightly but not painfully bound. Then from the reaction after his exciting adventure he sank into slumber. How long he slept he knew not, but he was at last awakened by a rough shake. Hands were untying his ropes. He was lifted to his feet, dazed, confused in mind, and weary of body. Rubbing his eyes, he looked and saw that he was again in the midst of the same band of terrible bandits. They shoved him up to the seat of his wagon and placed the lines in his hands.

'Hit it out for home, Dutch,' said Hondo Bill's voice, commandingly. 'You've given us lots of trouble and we're pleased to see the back of your neck. Spiel! Zwei bier! Vamoose!'

Hondo reached out and gave Blitzen a smart cut with his quirt.

The little mules sprang ahead, glad to be moving again. Fritz urged them along, himself dizzy and muddled over his fearful adventure.

According to schedule time, he should have reached Fredericksburg at daylight. As it was, he drove down the long street of the town at eleven o'clock a.m. He had to pass Peter Hildesmuller's house on his way to the post-office. He stopped his team at the gate and called. But Frau Hildesmuller was watching for him. Out rushed the whole family of Hildesmullers.

Frau Hildesmuller, fat and flushed, inquired if he had a letter from Lena, and then Fritz raised his voice and told the tale of his adventure. He told the contents of the letter that the robber had made him read, and then Frau Hildesmuller broke into wild weeping. Her little Lena drown herself! Why had they sent her from home? What could be done? Perhaps it would be too late by the time they could send for her now. Peter Hildesmuller dropped his meerschaum on the walk and it shivered into pieces.

'Woman!' he roared at his wife, 'why did you let that child go away? It is your fault if she comes home to us no more.'

Every one knew that it was Peter Hildesmuller's fault, so they paid no attention to his words.

A moment afterward a strange, faint voice was heard to call: 'Mamma!' Frau Hildesmuller at first thought it was Lena's spirit calling, and then she rushed to the rear of Fritz's covered wagon, and, with a loud shriek of joy, caught up Lena herself, covering her pale little face with kisses and smothering her with hugs. Lena's eyes were heavy with the deep slumber of exhaustion but she smiled and lay close to the one she had longed to see. There among the mail sacks, covered in a nest of strange blankets and comforters, she had lain asleep until wakened by the voices around her.

Fritz stared at her with eyes that bulged behind his spectacles.

'Gott in Himmel!' he shouted. 'How did you get in that wagon? Am I going crazy as well as to be murdered and hanged by robbers this day?'

'You brought her to us, Fritz,' cried Frau Hildesmuller. 'How can we ever thank you enough?'

'Tell mamma how you came in Fritz's wagon,' said Frau Hildesmuller.

'I don't know,' said Lena. 'But I know how I got away from the hotel. The Prince brought me.'

'By the Emperor's crown!' shouted Fritz, 'we are all going crazy.'

'I always knew he would come,' said Lena, sitting down on her bundle of bedclothes on the sidewalk. 'Last night he came with his armed knights and captured the ogre's castle. They broke the dishes and kicked down the doors. They pitched Mr. Maloney into a barrel of rain water and threw flour all over Mrs. Maloney. The workmen in the hotel jumped out of the windows and ran into the woods when the knights began firing their guns. They wakened me up and I peeped down the stair. And then the Prince came up and wrapped me in the bedclothes and carried me out. He was so tall and strong and fine. His face was as rough as a scrubbing brush, and he talked soft and kind and smelled of schnapps. He took me on his horse before him and we rode away among the knights. He held me close and I went to sleep that way, and didn't wake up till I got home.'

'Rubbish!' cried Fritz Bergmann. 'Fairy tales! How did you come from the quarries to my wagon?'

'The Prince brought me,' said Lena, confidently.

And to this day the good people of Fredericksburg haven't been able to make her give any other explanation.

THE REFORMATION OF CALLIOPE

CALLIOPE CATESBY WAS IN HIS HUMORS AGAIN. Ennui was upon him. This goodly promontory, the earth – particularly that portion of it known as Quicksand – was to him no more than a pestilent congregation of vapors. Overtaken by the megrims, the philosopher may seek relief in soliloquy; my lady find solace in tears; the flaccid Easterner scold at the millinery bills of his women folk. Such recourse was insufficient to the denizens of Quicksand. Calliope, especially, was wont to express his ennui according to his lights.

Over night Calliope had hung out signals of approaching low spirits. He had kicked his own dog on the porch of the Occidental Hotel, and refused to apologize. He had become capricious and fault-finding in conversation. While strolling about he reached often for twigs of mesquite and chewed the leaves fiercely. That was always an ominous act. Another symptom alarming to those who were familiar with the different stages of his doldrums was his increasing politeness and a tendency to use formal phrases. A husky softness succeeded the usual penetrating drawl in his tones. A dangerous courtesy marked his manners. Later, his smile became crooked, the left side of his mouth slanting upward, and Quicksand got ready to stand from under.

At this stage Calliope generally began to drink. Finally, about midnight, he was seen going homeward, saluting those whom he met with exaggerated but inoffensive courtesy. Not yet was Calliope's melancholy at the danger point. He would seat himself at the window of the room he occupied over Silvester's tonsorial parlors and there chant lugubrious and tuneless ballads until morning, accompanying the noises by appropriate maltreatment of a jingling guitar. More magnanimous than Nero, he would thus give musical warning of the forthcoming municipal upheaval that Quicksand was scheduled to endure.

A quiet, amiable man was Calliope Catesby at other times – quiet to indolence, and amiable to worthlessness. At best he was a loafer and a nuisance; at worst he was the Terror of Quicksand. His ostensible occupation was something subordinate in the real estate line; he drove the beguiled Easterner in buckboards out to look over lots and ranch property. Originally he came from one of the Gulf States, his lank six feet, slurring rhythm of speech, and sectional idioms giving evidence of his birthplace.

And yet, after taking on Western adjustments, this languid pine-box whittler, cracker barrel hugger, shady corner lounger of the cotton fields and sumac hills of the South became famed as a bad man among men who had made a life-long study of the art of truculence.

At nine the next morning Calliope was fit. Inspired by his own barbarous melodies and the contents of his jug, he was ready primed to gather fresh laurels from the diffident brow of Quicksand. Encircled and criss-crossed with cartridge belts, abundantly garnished with revolvers, and copiously drunk, he poured forth into Quicksand's main street. Too chivalrous to surprise and capture a town by silent sortie, he paused at the nearest corner and emitted his slogan – that fearful, brassy yell, so reminiscent of the steam piano, that has gained for him the classic appellation that had superseded his own baptismal name. Following close upon his vociferation came three shots from his forty-five by way of limbering up the guns and testing his aim. A yellow dog, the personal property of Colonel Swazey, the proprietor of the Occidental, fell feet upward in the dust with one farewell yelp. A Mexican who was crossing the street from the Blue Front grocery, carrying in his hand a bottle of kerosene, was stimulated to a sudden and admirable burst of speed, still grasping the neck of the shattered bottle. The new gilt weathercock on Judge Riley's lemon and ultra-marine two-story residence shivered, flapped, and hung by a splinter, the sport of the wanton breezes.

The artillery was in trim. Calliope's hand was steady. The high, calm ecstasy of habitual battle was upon him, though slightly embittered by the sadness of Alexander in that his conquests were limited to the small world of Quicksand.

Down the street went Calliope, shooting right and left. Glass fell like hail; dogs vamosed; chickens flew, squawking; feminine voices shrieked concernedly to youngsters at large. The din was perforated at intervals by the *staccato* of the Terror's guns, and was drowned periodically by the brazen screech that Quicksand knew so well. The occasion of Calliope's low spirits were legal holidays in Quicksand. All along the main street in advance of his coming clerks were putting up shutters and closing doors. Business would languish for a space. The right of way was Calliope's, and as he advanced, observing the dearth of opposition and the few opportunities for distraction, his ennui perceptibly increased.

But some four squares farther down lively preparations were being made to minister to Mr. Catesby's love for interchange of compliments and repartee. On the previous night numerous messengers had hastened to advise Buck Patterson, the city marshal, of Calliope's impending eruption. The patience of that official, often strained in extending leniency toward the disturber's misdeeds, had been overtaxed. In Quicksand some indulgence was accorded the natural ebullition of human nature. Providing that the lives of the more useful citizens were not recklessly squandered, or too much property needlessly laid waste, the community sentiment was against a too strict enforcement of the law. But Calliope had raised the limit. His outbursts had been too frequent and too violent to come within the classification of a normal and sanitary relaxation of spirit.

Buck Patterson had been expecting and awaiting in his little ten-by-twelve frame office that preliminary yell announcing that Calliope was feeling blue. When the signal came the City Marshal rose to his feet and buckled on his guns. Two deputy sheriffs and three citizens who had proven the edible qualities of fire also stood up, ready to bandy with Calliope's leaden jocularities.

'Gather that fellow in,' said Buck Patterson, setting for the lines of the campaign. 'Don't have no talk, but shoot as soon as you can get a show. Keep behind cover and bring him down. He's a nogood 'un. It's up to Calliope to turn up his toes this time, I reckon. Go to him all spraddled out, boys. And don't git too reckless, for what Calliope shoots at he hits.'

Buck Patterson, tall, muscular, and solemn-faced, with his bright 'City Marshal' badge shining on the breast of his blue flannel shirt, gave his posse directions for the onslaught upon Calliope. The plan was to accomplish the downfall of the Quicksand Terror without loss to the attaching party, if possible.

The splenetic Calliope, unconscious of retributive plots, was steaming down the channel, cannonading on either side, when he suddenly became aware of breakers ahead. The City Marshal and one of the deputies rose up behind some dry-goods boxes half a square to the front and opened fire. At the same time the rest of the posse, divided, shelled him from two side streets up which they were cautiously manoeuvring from a well-executed detour.

The first volley broke the lock of one of Calliope's guns, cut a neat underbit in his right ear, and exploded a cartridge in his crossbelt, scorching his ribs as it bursts. Feeling braced up by this unexpected tonic to his spiritual depression, Calliope executed a fortissimo note from his upper registers, and returned the fire like an echo. The upholders of the law dodged at his flash, but a trifle too late to save one of the deputies a bullet just above the elbow, and the marshal a bleeding cheek from a splinter that a ball tore from a box he had ducked behind.

And now Calliope met the enemy's tactics in kind. Choosing with a rapid eye the street from which the weakest and least accurate fire had come, he invaded it a double-quick, abandoning the unprotected middle of the street. With rare cunning the opposing force in that direction – one of the deputies and two of the valorous volunteers – waited, concealed by beer barrels, until Calliope had passed their retreat, and then peppered him from the rear. In another moment they were reinforced by the marshal and his other men, and then Calliope felt that in order to successfully prolong the delights of the controversy he must find some means of reducing the great odds against him. His eye fell upon a structure that seemed to hold out this promise, providing he could reach it.

Not far away was the little railroad station, its building a strong box house, ten by twenty feet, resting upon a platform four feet above ground. Windows were in each of its walls. Something like a fort it might become to a man thus sorely pressed by superior numbers.

Calliope made a bolt and rapid spurt for it, the marshal's crowd 'smoking' him as he ran. He reached the haven in safety, the station agent leaving the building by a window, like a flying squirrel, as the garrison entered the door.

Patterson and his supporters halted under protection of a pile of lumber and held consultations. In the station was an unterrified desperado who was an excellent shot and carried an abundance of ammunition. For thirty yards on each side of the besieged was a stretch of bare, open ground. It was a sure thing that the man who attempted to enter that unprotected area would be stopped by one of Calliope's bullets.

The City Marshal was resolved. He had decided that Calliope Catesby should no more wake the echoes of Quicksand with his strident whoop. He had so announced. Officially and personally he felt imperatively bound to put the soft pedal on that instrument of discord. It played bad tunes.

Standing near was a hand truck used in the manipulation of small freight. It stood by a shed full of sacked wool, a consignment from one of the sheep ranches. On this truck the marshal and his men piled three heavy sacks of wool. Stooping low, Buck Patterson started for Calliope's fort, slowly pushing this loaded truck before him for protection. The posse, scattering broadly, stood ready to nip the besieged in case he should show himself in an effort to repel the juggernaut of justice that was creeping upon him. Only once did Calliope make demonstration. He fired from a window and soft tufts of wool spurted from the marshal's trustworthy bulwark. The return shots from the posse pattered against the window frame of the fort. No loss resulted on either side.

The marshal was too deeply engrossed in steering his protected battleship to be aware of the approach of the morning train until he was within a few feet of the platform. The train was coming up on the other side of it. It stopped only one minute at Quicksand. What an opportunity it would offer to Calliope! He had only to step out the other door, mount the train, and away.

Abandoning his breastworks, Buck, with his gun ready, dashed up the steps and into the room, driving open the closed door with one heave of his weighty shoulder. The members of the posse heard one shot fired inside, and then there was silence.

At length the wounded man opened his eyes. After a blank space he again could see and hear and feel and think. Turning his eyes about, he found himself lying on a wooden bench. A tall man with a perplexed countenance, wearing a big badge with 'City Marshal' engraved upon it, stood over him. A little old woman in black, with a wrinkled face and sparkling black eyes was holding a wet handkerchief against one of his temples. He was trying to get these facts fixed in his mind and connected with past events, when the old woman began to talk.

'There now, great, big, strong man! That bullet never tetched ye! Jest skeeted along the side of your head and sort of paralyzed ye for a spell. I've heerd of sech things afor! con-cussion is what they names it. Abel Wadkins used to kill squirrels that way – barkin' em, Abe called it. You jest been barked, sir, and you'll be all right in a little bit. Feel lots better already, don't ye! You just lay still a while longer and let me bathe your head. You don't know me, I reckon, and 'tain't surprisin' that you shouldn't. I come in on that train from Alabama to see my son. Big son, ain't he? Lands! you wouldn't hardly think he'd ever been a baby, would ye? This is my son, sir.'

Half turning, the old woman looked up at the standing man, her worn face lighting with a proud and wonderful smile. She reached out one veined and calloused hand and took one of her son's. Then smiling cheerily down at the prostrate man, she continued to dip the handkerchief in the waiting-room tin washbasin and gently apply it to his temple. She had the benevolent garrulity of old age.

'I ain't seen my son before,' she continued, 'in eight years. One of my nephews, Elkanah Price, he's a conductor on one of them railroads, and he got me a pass to come out here. I can stay a whole week on it, and then it'll take me back again. Jest think, now, that little boy of mine has got to be a officer – a city marshal of a whole town! That's something like a constable, ain't it? I never knowed he was a officer; he didn't say nothin' about it in his letters. I reckon he thought his old mother'd be skeered about the danger he was in. But, laws! I never was much of a hand to git skeered. 'Tain't no use. I heard them guns a-shootin' while I was gittin' off them cars, and I see smoke a-comin' out of the depot, but I jest walked right along. Then I see son's face lookin' out through the window. I knowed him at oncet. He met me at the door, and squeezed me 'most to death. And there you was, sir, a-lyin' there jest like you was dead, and I 'lowed we'd see what might be done to help sot you up.'

'I think I'll sit up now,' said the concussion patient. 'I'm feeling pretty fair by this time.'

He sat, somewhat weakly yet, leaning against the wall. He was a rugged man, big-boned and straight. His eyes, steady and keen, seemed to linger upon the face of the man standing so still above him. His look wandered often from the face he studied to the marshal's badge upon the other's breast.

'Yes, yes, you'll be all right,' said the old woman, patting his arm, 'if you don't get to cuttin' up agin, and havin' folks shootin' at you. Son told me about you, sir, while you was layin' senseless on the floor. Don't you take it as meddlesome fer an old woman with a son as big as you to talk about it. And you mustn't hold no grudge ag'in my son for havin' to shoot at ye. A officer has got to take up for the law – it's his duty – and them that acts bad and lives wrong has to suffer. Don't blame my son any, sir – 'tain't his fault. He's always been a good boy – good when he was growin' up, and kind and 'bedient and well-behaved. Won't you let me advise you, sir, not to do so no more? Be a good man, and leave liquor alone and live peaceably and godly. Keep away from bad company and work honest and sleep sweet.'

The black-mittened hand of the old pleader gently touched the breast of the man she addressed. Very earnest and candid her old, worn face looked. In her rusty black dress and antique bonnet she sat, near the close of a long life, and epitomized the experience of the world. Still the man to whom she spoke gazed above her head, contemplating the silent son of the old mother.

'What does the marshal say?' he asked. 'Does he believe the advice is good? Suppose the marshal speaks up and says if the talk's right?'

The tall man moved uneasily. He fingered the badge on his breast for a moment, and then he put an arm around the old woman and drew her close to him. She smiled the unchanging mother smile of three-score years, and patted his big brown hand with her crooked, mittened fingers while her son spake.

'I say this,' he said, looking squarely into the eyes of the other man, 'that if I was in your place I'd follow it. If I was a drunken, desp'rate character, without shame or hope, I'd follow it. If I was in your place and you was in mine I'd say: "Marshal, I'm willin' to swear if you'll give me the chance I'll quit the racket. I'll drop the tanglefoot and the gun play, and won't play hoss no more. I'll be a good citizen and go to work and quit my foolishness. So help me God!" That's what I'd say to you if you was marshal and I was in your place.'

'Hear my son talkin',' said the old woman softly. 'Hear him, sir. You promise to be good and he won't do you no harm. Forty-one year ago his heart first beat ag'in mine, and it's beat true ever since.'

The other man rose to his feet, trying his limbs and stretching his muscles.

'Then,' said he, 'if you was in my place and said that, and I was marshal, I'd say: "Go free, and do your best to keep your promise." '

'Lawsy!' exclaimed the old woman, in a sudden flutter, 'ef I didn't clear forget that trunk of mine! I see a man settin' it on the platform jest as I seen son's face in the window, and it went plum out of my head. There's eight jars of home-made quince jam in that trunk that I made myself. I wouldn't have nothin' happen to them jars for a red apple.'

Away to the door she trotted, spry and anxious, and then Calliope Catesby spoke out to Buck Patterson:

'I just couldn't help it, Buck. I seen her through the window a-comin' in.

She had never heard a word 'bout my tough ways. I didn't have the nerve to let her know I was a worthless cuss bein' hunted down by the community. There you was lyin' where my shot laid you, like you was dead. The idea struck me sudden, and I just took your badge off and fastened it onto myself, and I fastened my reputation onto you. I told her I was the marshal and you was a holy terror. You can take your badge back now, Buck.'

With shaking fingers Calliope began to unfasten the disc of metal from his shirt.

'Easy there!' said Buck Patterson. 'You keep that badge right where it is, Calliope Catesby. Don't you dare to take it off till the day your mother leaves this town. You'll be city marshal of Quicksand as long as she's here to know it. After I stir around town a bit and put 'em on I'll guarantee that nobody won't give the thing away to her. And say, you leather-headed, rip-roarin', low-down son of a locoed cyclone, you follow that advice she gave me! I'm goin' to take some of it myself, too.'

'Buck,' said Calliope, feelingly, 'ef I don't I hope I may—'

'Shut up,' said Buck. 'She's a-comin' back.'

TOBIN'S PALM

TOBIN AND ME, THE TWO OF US, went down to Coney one day, for there was four dollars between us, and Tobin had need of distractions. For there was Katie Mahorner, his sweetheart, of County Sligo, lost since she started for America three months before with two hundred dollars, her own savings, and one hundred dollars from the sale of Tobin's inherited estate, a fine cottage and pig on the Bog Shannaugh. And since the letter that Tobin got saying that she had started to come to him not a bit of news had he heard or seen of Katie Mahorner. Tobin advertised in the papers, but nothing could be found of the colleen.

So, to Coney me and Tobin went, thinking that a turn at the chutes and the smell of the popcorn might raise the heart in his bosom. But Tobin was a hard-headed man, and the sadness stuck in his skin. He ground his teeth at the crying balloons; he cursed the moving pictures; and, though he would drink whenever asked, he scorned Punch and Judy, and was for licking the tintype men as they came.

So I gets him down a side way on a board walk where the attractions were some less violent. At a little six by eight stall Tobin halts, with a more human look in his eye.

' 'Tis here,' says he, 'I will be diverted. I'll have the palm of me hand investigated by the wonderful palmist of the Nile, and see if what is to be will be.'

Tobin was a believer in signs and the unnatural in nature. He possessed illegal convictions in his mind along the subjects of black cats, lucky numbers and the weather predictions in the papers.

We went into the enchanted chicken coop, which was fixed, mysterious with red cloth and pictures of hands with lines crossing 'em like a railroad centre. The sign over the door says it is Madame Zozo the Egyptian Palmist. There was a fat woman inside in a red jumper with pothooks and beasties embroidered upon it. Tobin gives her ten cents and extends one of his hands. She lifts Tobin's hand, which is own brother to the hoof of a drayhorse, and examines it to see whether 'tis a stone in the frog or a cast shoe he has come for.

'Man,' says this Madame Zozo, 'the line of your fate shows—'

' 'Tis not me foot at all,' says Tobin, interrupting. 'Sure, 'tis no beauty but ye hold the palm of me hand.'

'The line shows,' says the Madame, 'that ye've not arrived at your time of life without bad luck. And there's more to come. The mount of Venus – or is that a stone bruise? – shows that ye've been in love. There's been trouble in your life on account of your sweetheart.'

' 'Tis Katie Mahorner she has references with,' whispers Tobin to me in a loud voice to one side.

'I see,' says the palmist, 'a great deal of sorrow and tribulation with one whom ye cannot forget. I see the lines of designation point to the letter K and the letter M in her name.'

'Whist!' says Tobin to me; 'do ye hear that?'

'Look out,' goes on the palmist, 'for a dark man and a light woman; for they'll both bring ye trouble. Ye'll make a voyage upon the water very soon, and have a financial loss. I see one line that brings good luck. There's a man coming into your life who will fetch ye good fortune. Ye'll know him when ye see him by his crooked nose.'

'Is his name set down?' asks Tobin. ' 'Twill be convenient in the way of greeting when he backs up to dump off the good luck.'

'His name,' says the palmist, thoughtful looking, 'is not spelled out by the lines, but they indicate 'tis a long one, and the letter "o" should be in it. There's no more to tell. Good-evening. Don't block up the door.'

' 'Tis wonderful how she knows,' says Tobin as we walk to the pier.

As we squeezed through the gates a nigger man sticks his lighted segar against Tobin's ear, and there is trouble. Tobin hammers his neck, and the women squeal, and by presence of mind I drag the little man out of the way before the police comes. Tobin is always in an ugly mood when enjoying himself.

On the boat going back, when the man calls 'Who wants the good-looking waiter?' Tobin tried to plead guilty, feeling the desire to blow the foam off a crock of suds, but when he felt in his pocket he found himself discharged for lack of evidence. Somebody had disturbed his change during the commotion. So we sat, dry, upon the stools, listening to the Dagoes fiddling on deck. If anything, Tobin was lower in spirits and less congenial with his misfortunes than when we started.

On a seat against the railing was a young woman dressed suitable for red automobiles, with hair the color of an unsmoked meerschaum. In passing by Tobin kicks her foot without intentions, and, being polite to ladies when in drink, he tries to give his hat a twist while apologizing. But he knocks it off, and the wind carries it overboard.

Tobin came back and sat down, and I began to look out for him, for the man's adversities were becoming frequent. He was apt, when pushed so close by hard luck, to kick the best dressed man he could see, and try to take command of the boat.

Presently Tobin grabs my arm and says, excited: 'Jawn,' says he, 'do ye know what we're doing? We're taking a voyage upon the water.'

'There now,' says I; 'subdue yeself. The boat'll land in ten minutes more.'

'Look,' says he, 'at the light lady upon the bench. And have ye forgotten the nigger man that burned me ear? And isn't the money I had gone – a dollar sixty-five it was?'

I thought he was no more than summing up his catastrophes so as to get violent with good excuse, as men will do, and I tried to make him understand such things was trifles.

'Listen,' says Tobin. 'Ye've no ear for the gift of prophecy or the miracles of the inspired. What did the palmist lady tell ye out of me hand? 'Tis coming true before your eyes. "Look out," says she, "for a dark man and a light woman; they'll bring ye trouble." Have ye forgot the nigger man, though he got some of it back from me fist? Can ye show me a lighter woman than the blonde lady that was the cause of me hat falling in the water? And where's the dollar sixty-five I had in me vest when we left the shooting gallery?'

The way Tobin put it, it did seem to corroborate the art of prediction, though it looked to me that these accidents could happen to any one at Coney without the implication of palmistry.

Tobin got up and walked around on deck, looking close at the passengers out of his little red eyes. I asked him the interpretation of his movements. Ye never know what Tobin has in his mind until he begins to carry it out.

'Ye should know,' says he, 'I'm working out the salvation promised by the lines in me palm. I'm looking for the crooked-nosed man that's to bring the good luck. 'Tis all that will save us. Jawn, did ye ever see a straighter-nosed gang of hellions in the days of your life?'

'Twas the nine-thirty boat, and we landed and walked up-town through Twenty-second Street, Tobin being without his hat.

On a street corner, standing under a gas-light and looking over the elevated road at the moon, was a man. A long man he was, dressed decent, with a segar between his teeth, and I saw that his nose made two twists from bridge to end, like the wriggle of a snake. Tobin saw it at the same time, and I heard him breathe hard like a horse when you take the saddle off. He went straight up to the man, and I went with him.

'Good-night to ye,' Tobin says to the man. The man takes out a segar and passes the compliments, sociable.

'Would ye hand us your name,' asks Tobin, 'and let us look at the size of it? It may be our duty to become acquainted with ye.'

'My name,' says the man, polite, 'is Friedenhausman – Maximus G. Friedenhausman.'

' 'Tis the right length,' says Tobin. 'Do you spell it with an "o" anywhere down the stretch of it?'

'I do not,' says the man.

'*Can* ye spell it with an "o"?' inquires Tobin, turning anxious.

'If your conscience,' says the man with the nose, 'is indisposed toward foreign idioms ye might, to please yourself, smuggle the letter into the penultimate syllable.'

' 'Tis well,' says Tobin. 'Ye're in the presence of Jawn Malone and Daniel Tobin.'

' 'Tis highly appreciated,' says the man, with a bow. 'And now since I cannot conceive that ye would hold a spelling bee upon the street corner, will ye name some reasonable excuse for being at large?'

'By the two signs,' answers Tobin, trying to explain, 'which ye display according to the reading of the Egyptian palmist from the sole of me hand, ye've been nominated to offset with good luck the lines of trouble leading to the nigger man and the blonde lady with her feet crossed in the boat, besides the financial loss of a dollar sixty-five, all so far fulfilled according to Hoyle.'

The man stopped smoking and looked at me.

'Have ye any amendments,' he asks, 'to offer to that statement, or are ye one too? I thought by the looks of ye ye might have him in charge.'

'None,' says I to him, 'except that as one horsehoe resembles another so are ye the picture of good luck as predicted by the hand of me friend. If not, then the lines of Danny's hand may have been crossed, I don't know.'

'There's two of ye,' says the man with the nose, looking up and down for the sight of a policeman. 'I've enjoyed your company immense. Goodnight.'

With that he shoves his segar in his mouth and moves across the street, stepping fast. But Tobin sticks close to one side of him and me at the other.

'What!' says he, stopping on the opposite sidewalk and pushing back his hat; 'do ye follow me? I tell ye,' he says, very loud, 'I'm proud to have met ye. But it is my desire to be rid of ye. I am off to me home.'

'Do,' says Tobin, leaning against his sleeve. 'Do be off to your home. And I will sit at the door of it till ye come out in the morning. For the dependence is upon ye to obviate the curse of the nigger man and the blonde lady and the financial loss of the one-sixty-five.'

' 'Tis a strange hallucination,' says the man, turning to me as a more reasonable lunatic. 'Hadn't ye better get him home?'

'Listen, man,' says I to him. 'Daniel Tobin is as sensible as he ever was. Maybe he is a bit deranged on account of having drink enough to disturb but not enough to settle his wits, but he is no more than following out the legitimate path of his superstitions and predicaments, which I will explain to you.' With that I relates the facts about the palmist lady and how the finger of suspicion points to him as an instrument of good fortune. 'Now, understand,' I concludes, 'my position in this riot. I am the friend of me friend Tobin, according to me interpretations. 'Tis easy to be a friend to the prosperous, for it pays; 'tis not hard to be friend to the poor, for ye get puffed up by gratitude and have your picture printed standing in front of a tenement with a scuttle of coal and an orphan in each hand. But it strains the art of friendship to be true friend to a born fool. And that's what I'm doing,' says I, 'for, in my opinion, there's no fortune to be read from the palm of me hand that wasn't printed there with the handle of a pick. And, though ye've got the crookedest nose in New York City, I misdoubt that all the fortune-tellers doing business could milk good luck from ye. But the lines of Danny's hand pointed to ye fair, and I'll assist him to experiment with ye until he's convinced ye're dry.'

After that the man turns, sudden, to laughing. He leans against a corner and laughs considerable. Then he claps me and Tobin on the backs of us and takes us by an arm apiece.

' 'Tis my mistake,' says he. 'How could I be expecting anything so fine and wonderful to be turning the corner upon me? I came near being found unworthy. Hard by,' says he, 'is a café, snug and suitable for the entertainment of idiosyncrasies. Let us go there and have a drink while we discuss the unavailability of the categorical.'

So saying, he marched me and Tobin to the back room of a saloon, and ordered the drinks, and laid the money on the table. He looks at me and Tobin like brothers of his, and we have the segars.

'Ye must know,' says the man of destiny, 'that me walk in life is one that is called the literary. I wander abroad be night seeking idiosyncrasies in the masses and truth in the heavens above. When ye came upon me I was in contemplation of the elevated road in conjunction with the chief luminary of night. The rapid transit is poetry and art; the moon but a tedious, dry body, moving by rote. But these are private opinions, for, in the business of literature, the conditions are reversed. 'Tis me hope to be writing a book to explain the strange things I have discovered in life.'

'Ye will put me in a book,' says Tobin, disgusted; 'will ye put me in a book?'

'I will not,' says the man, 'for the covers will not hold ye. Not yet. The best I can do is to enjoy ye meself, for the time is not ripe for destroying the limitations of print. Ye would look fantastic in type. All alone by meself must I drink this cup of joy. But, I thank ye, boys; I am truly grateful.'

'The talk of ye,' says Tobin, blowing through his moustache and pounding the table with his fist, 'is an eyesore to me patience. There was good luck promised out of the crook of your nose, but ye bear fruit like the bag of a drum. Ye resemble, with your noise of books, the wind blowing through a crack. Sure, now, I would be thinking the palm of me hand lied but for the coming true of the nigger man and the blonde lady and—'

'Whist!' says the long man; 'would ye be led astray by physiognomy? Me nose will do what it can within bounds. Let us have these glasses filled again, for 'tis good to keep idiosyncrasies well moistened, they being subject to deterioration in a dry moral atmosphere.'

So, the man of literature makes good, to my notion, for he pays, cheerful, for everything, the capital of me and Tobin being exhausted by prediction. But Tobin is sore, and drinks quiet, with the red showing in his eye.

By and by we moved out, for 'twas eleven o'clock, and stands a bit upon the sidewalk. And then the man says he must be going home, and invites me and Tobin to walk that way. We arrives on a side street two blocks away where there is a stretch of brick houses with high stoops and iron fences. The man stops at one of them and looks up at the top windows which he finds dark.

' 'Tis me humble dwelling,' says he, 'and I begin to perceive by the signs that me wife has retired to slumber. Therefore I will venture a bit in the way of hospitality. 'Tis me wish that ye enter the basement room, where we dine, and partake of a reasonable refreshment. There will be some fine cold fowl and cheese and a bottle or two of ale. Ye will be welcome to enter and eat, for I am indebted to ye for diversions.'

The appetite and conscience of me and Tobin was congenial to the proposition, though 'twas sticking hard in Danny's superstitions to think that a few drinks and a cold lunch should represent the good fortune promised by the palm of his hand.

'Step down the steps,' says the man with the crooked nose, 'and I will enter by the door above and let ye in. I will ask the new girl we have in the kitchen,' says he, 'to make ye a pot of coffee to drink before ye go. 'Tis fine coffee Katie Mahorner makes for a green girl just landed three months. Step in,' says the man, 'and I'll send her down to ye.'

THE GIFT OF THE MAGI

ONE DOLLAR AND EIGHTY-SEVEN CENTS. That was all. And sixty cents of it was in pennies. Pennies saved one and two at a time by bulldozing the grocer and the vegetable man and the butcher until one's cheeks burned with the silent imputation of parsimony that such close dealing implied. Three times Della counted it. One dollar and eighty-seven cents. And the next day would be Christmas.

There was clearly nothing to do but flop down on the shabby little couch and howl. So Della did it. Which instigates the moral reflection that life is made up of sobs, sniffles, and smiles, with sniffles predominating.

While the mistress of the home is gradually subsiding from the first stage to the second, take a look at the home. A furnished flat at $8 per week. It did not exactly beggar description, but it certainly had that word on the lookout for the mendicancy squad.

In the vestibule below was a letter-box into which no letter would go, and an electric button from which no mortal finger could coax a ring. Also appertaining thereunto was a card bearing the name 'Mr. James Dillingham Young.'

The 'Dillingham' had been flung to the breeze during a former period of prosperity when its possessor was being paid $30 per week. Now, when the income was shrunk to $20, the letters of 'Dillingham' looked blurred, as though they were thinking seriously of contracting to a modest and unassuming D. But whenever Mr. James Dillingham Young came home and reached his flat above he was called 'Jim' and greatly hugged by Mrs. James Dillingham Young, already introduced to you as Della. Which is all very good.

Della finished her cry and attended to her cheeks with the powder rag. She stood by the window and looked out dully at a gray cat walking a gray fence in a gray backyard. Tomorrow would be Christmas Day, and she had only $1.87 with which to buy Jim a present. She had been saving every penny she could for months, with this result. Twenty dollars a week doesn't go far. Expenses had been greater than she had calculated. They always are. Only $1.87 to buy a present for Jim. Her Jim. Many a happy hour she had spent planning for something nice for him. Something fine and rare and sterling – something just a little bit near to being worthy of the honor of being owned by Jim.

There was a pier-glass between the windows of the room. Perhaps you have seen a pier-glass in an $8 flat. A very thin and very agile person may, by observing his reflection in a rapid sequence of longitudinal strips, obtain a fairly accurate conception of his looks. Della, being slender, had mastered the art.

Suddenly she whirled from the window and stood before the glass. Her eyes were shining brilliantly, but her face had lost its color within twenty seconds. Rapidly she pulled down her hair and let it fall to its full length.

Now, there were two possessions of the James Dillingham Youngs in which they both took a mighty pride. One was Jim's gold watch that had been his father's and his grandfather's. The other was Della's hair. Had the Queen of Sheba lived in the flat across the airshaft, Della would have let her hair hang out the window some day to dry just to depreciate Her Majesty's jewels and gifts. Had King Solomon been the janitor, with all his treasures piled up in the basement, Jim would have pulled out his watch every time he passed, just to see him pluck at his beard from envy.

So now Della's beautiful hair fell about her rippling and shining like a cascade of brown waters. It reached below her knee and made itself almost a garment for her. And then she did it up again nervously and quickly. Once she faltered for a minute and stood still while a tear or two splashed on the worn red carpet.

On went her old brown jacket; on went her old brown hat. With a whirl of skirts and with the brilliant sparkle still in her eyes, she fluttered out the door and down the stairs to the street.

Where she stopped the sign read: 'Mme. Sofronie. Hair Goods of All Kinds.' One flight up Della ran, and collected herself, panting. Madame, large, too white, chilly, hardly looked the 'Sofronie.'

'Will you buy my hair?' asked Della.

'I buy hair,' said Madame. 'Take yer hat off and let's have a sight at the looks of it.'

Down rippled the brown cascade.

'Twenty dollars,' said Madame, lifting the mass with a practised hand.

'Give it to me quick,' said Della.

Oh, and the next two hours tripped by on rosy wings. Forget the hashed metaphor. She was ransacking the stores for Jim's present.

She found it at last. It surely had been made for Jim and no one else. There was no other like it in any of the stores, and she had turned all of them inside out. It was a platinum fob chain simple and chaste in design, properly proclaiming its value by substance alone and not by meretricious ornamentation – as all good things should do. It was even worthy of The Watch. As soon as she saw it she knew that it must be Jim's. It was like him. Quietness and value – the description applied to both. Twenty-one dollars they took from her for it, and she hurried home with the 87 cents. With that chain on his watch Jim might be properly anxious about the time in any company. Grand as the watch was, he sometimes looked at it on the sly on account of the old leather strap that he used in place of a chain.

When Della reached home her intoxication gave way a little to prudence and reason. She got out her curling irons and lighted the gas and went to work repairing the ravages made by generosity added to love. Which is always a tremendous task, dear friends – a mammoth task.

Within forty minutes her head was covered with tiny, close-lying curls that made her look wonderfully like a truant schoolboy. She looked at her reflection in the mirror long, carefully, and critically.

'If Jim doesn't kill me,' she said to herself, 'before he takes a second look at me, he'll say I look like a Coney Island chorus girl. But what could I do – oh! what could I do with a dollar and eighty-seven cents?'

At 7 o'clock the coffee was made and the frying-pan was on the back of the stove hot and ready to cook the chops.

Jim was never late. Della doubled the fob chain in her hand and sat on the corner of the table near the door that he always entered. Then she heard his step on the stair away down on the first flight, and she turned white for just a moment. She had a habit of saying little silent prayers about the simplest everyday things, and now she whispered: 'Please God, make him think I am still pretty.'

The door opened and Jim stepped in and closed it. He looked thin and very serious. Poor fellow, he was only twenty-two – and to be burdened with a family! He needed a new overcoat and he was without gloves.

Jim stopped inside the door, as immovable as a setter at the scent of quail. His eyes were fixed upon Della, and there was an expression in them that she could not read, and it terrified her. It was not anger, nor surprise, nor disapproval, nor horror, nor any of the sentiments that she had been prepared for. He simply stared at her fixedly with that peculiar expression on his face.

Della wriggled off the table and went for him.

'Jim, darling,' she cried, 'don't look at me that way. I had my hair cut off and sold it because I couldn't have lived through Christmas without giving you a present. It'll grow out again – you won't mind, will you? I just had to do it. My hair grows awfully fast. "Merry Christmas!" Jim, and let's be happy. You don't know what a nice – what a beautiful, nice gift I've got for you.'

'You've cut off your hair?' asked Jim, laboriously, as if he had not arrived at that patent fact yet even after the hardest mental labor.

'Cut it off and sold it,' said Della. 'Don't you like me just as well, anyhow? I'm me without my hair, ain't I?'

Jim looked about the room curiously.

'You say your hair is gone?' he said, with an air almost of idiocy.

'You needn't look for it,' said Della. 'It's sold, I tell you – sold and gone, too. It's Christmas Eve, boy. Be good to me, for it went for you. Maybe the hairs on my head were numbered,' she went on with a sudden serious sweetness, 'but nobody could ever count my love for you. Shall I put the chops on, Jim?'

Out of his trance Jim seemed quickly to wake. He enfolded his Della. For ten seconds let us regard with discreet scrutiny some inconsequential object in the other direction. Eight dollars a week or a million a year – what is the difference? A mathematician or a wit would give you the wrong answer. The magi brought valuable gifts, but that was not among them. This dark assertion will be illuminated later on.

Jim drew a package from his overcoat pocket and threw it upon the table.

'Don't make any mistake, Dell,' he said, 'about me. I don't think there's anything in the way of a haircut or a shave or a shampoo that could make me like my girl any less. But if you'll unwrap that package you may see why you had me going a while at first.'

White fingers and nimble tore at the string and paper. And then an ecstatic scream of joy; and then, alas! a quick feminine charge to hysterical tears and wails, necessitating the immediate employment of all the comforting powers of the lord of the flat.

For there lay The Combs – the set of combs, side and back, that Della had worshipped for long in a Broadway window. Beautiful combs, pure tortoise shell, with jewelled rims – just the shade to wear in the beautiful vanished hair. They were expensive combs, she knew, and her heart had simply craved and yearned over them without the least hope of possession. And now, they were hers, but the tresses that should have adorned the coveted adornments were gone.

But she hugged them to her bosom, and at length she was able to look up with dim eyes and a smile and say: 'My hair grows so fast, Jim!'

And then Della leaped up like a little singed cat and cried, 'Oh, oh!'

Jim had not yet seen his beautiful present. She held it out to him eagerly upon her open palm. The dull precious metal seemed to flash with a reflection of her bright and ardent spirit.

'Isn't it a dandy, Jim? I hunted all over town to find it. You'll have to look at the time a hundred times a day now. Give me your watch. I want to see how it looks on it.'

Instead of obeying, Jim tumbled down on the couch and put his hands under the back of his head and smiled.

'Dell,' said he, 'let's put our Christmas presents away and keep 'em a while. They're too nice to use just at present. I sold the watch to get the money to buy your combs. And now suppose you put the chops on.'

The magi, as you know, were wise men – wonderfully wise men – who brought gifts to the Babe in the manger. They invented the art of giving Christmas presents. Being wise, their gifts were no doubt wise ones, possibly bearing the privilege of exchange in case of duplication. And here I have lamely related to you the uneventful chronicle of two foolish children in a flat who most unwisely sacrificed for each other the greatest treasures of their house. But in a last word to the wise of these days let it be said that of all who give gifts these two were the wisest. Of all who give and receive gifts, such as they are wisest. Everywhere they are wisest. They are the magi.

A COSMOPOLITE IN A CAFÉ

AT MIDNIGHT THE CAFÉ was crowded. By some chance the little table at which I sat had escaped the eye of incomers, and two vacant chairs at it extended their arms with venal hospitality to the influx of patrons.

And then a cosmopolite sat in one of them, and I was glad, for I held a theory that since Adam no true citizen of the world has existed. We hear of them, and we see foreign labels on much luggage, but we find travellers instead of cosmopolites.

I invoke your consideration of the scene – the marble-topped tables, the range of leather-upholstered wall seats, the gay company, the ladies dressed in demi-state toilets, speaking in an exquisite visible chorus of taste, economy, opulence or art; the sedulous and largess-loving *garçons*, the music wisely catering to all with its raids upon the composers; the *mélange* of talk and laughter – and, if you will, the Würzburger in the tall glass cones that bend to your lips as a ripe cherry sways on its branch to the beak of a robber jay. I was told by a sculptor from Mauch Chunk that the scene was truly Parisian.

My cosmopolite was named E. Rushmore Coglan, and he will be heard from next summer at Coney Island. He is to establish a new 'attraction' there, he informed me, offering kingly diversion. And then his conversation rang along parallels of latitude and longitude. He took the great, round world in his hand, so to speak, familiarly, contemptuously, and it seemed no larger than the seed of a Maraschino cherry in a *table d'hôte* grape fruit. He spoke disrespectfully of the equator, he skipped from continent to continent, he derided the zones, he mopped up the high seas with his napkin. With a wave of his hand he would speak of a certain bazaar in Hyderabad. Whiff! He would have you on skis in Lapland. Zip! Now you rode the breakers with the Kanakas at Kealaikahiki. Presto! He dragged you through an Arkansas post-oak swamp, let you dry for a moment on the alkali plains of his Idaho ranch, then whirled you into the society of Viennese archdukes. Anon he would be telling you of a cold he acquired in a Chicago lake breeze and how old Escamila cured it in Buenos Ayres with a hot infusion of the *chuchula* weed. You would have addressed a letter to "E. Rushmore Coglan, Esq., the Earth, Solar System, the Universe,' and mailed it, feeling confident that it would be delivered to him.

I was sure that I had found at least one true cosmopolite since Adam, and I listened to his world-wide discourse fearful lest I should discover in it the local note of the mere globe-trotter. But his opinion never fluttered or drooped; he was as impartial to cities, countries, and continents as the winds or gravitation.

And as E. Rushmore Coglan prattled of this little planet I thought with glee of a great almost-cosmopolite who wrote for the whole world and dedicated himself to Bombay. In a poem he has to say that there is pride and rivalry between the cities of the earth, and that 'the men that breed from them, they traffic up and down, but cling to their cities' hem as a child to the mother's gown.' And whenever they walk 'by roaring streets unknown' they remember their native city 'most faithful, foolish, fond; making her mere-breathed name their bond upon their bond.' And my glee was roused because I had caught Mr. Kipling napping. Here I had found a man not made from dust; one who had no narrow boasts of birthplace or country, one who, if he bragged at all, would brag of his whole round globe against the Martians and the inhabitants of the Moon.

Expression on these subjects was precipitated from E. Rushmore Coglan by the third corner to our table. While Coglan was describing to me the topography along the Siberian Railway the orchestra glided into a medley. The concluding air was 'Dixie,' and as the exhilarating notes tumbled forth they were almost overpowered by a great clapping of hands from almost every table.

It is worth a paragraph to say that this remarkable scene can be witnessed every evening in numerous cafés in the City of New York. Tons of brew have been consumed over theories to account for it. Some have conjectured hastily that all Southerners in town hie themselves to cafés at nightfall. This applause of the 'rebel' air in a Northern city does puzzle a little; but it is not insolvable. The war with Spain, many years' generous mint and watermelon crops, a few long-shot winners at the New Orleans race track, and the brilliant banquets given by the Indiana and Kansas citizens who compose the Night Carolina Society have made the South rather a 'fad' in Manhattan. Your manicure will lisp softly that your left forefinger reminds her so much of a gentleman's in Richmond, Va. Oh, certainly; but many a lady has to work now – the war, you know.

When 'Dixie' was being played a dark-haired young man sprang up from somewhere with a Mosby guerrilla yell and waved frantically his soft-brimmed hat. Then he strayed through the smoke, dropped into the vacant chair at our table and pulled out cigarettes.

The evening was at the period when reserve is thawed. One of us mentioned three Würzburgers to the waiter; the dark-haired young man acknowledged his inclusion in the order by a smile and a nod. I hastened to ask him a question because I wanted to try out a theory I had.

'Would you mind telling me,' I began, 'whether you are from —'

The fist of E. Rushmore Coglan banged the table and I was jarred into silence.

'Excuse me,' said he, 'but that's a question I never like to hear asked. What does it matter where a man is from? Is it fair to judge a man by his post-office address? Why, I've seen Kentuckians who hated whiskey, Virginians who weren't descended from Pocohontas, Indianians who hadn't written a novel, Mexicans who didn't wear velvet trousers with silver dollars sewed along the seams, funny Englishmen, spendthrift Yankees, cold-blooded Southerners, narrow-minded Westerners, and New Yorkers who were too busy to stop for an hour on the street to watch a one-armed grocer's clerk do up cranberries in paper bags. Let a man be a man and don't handicap him with the label of any section.'

'Pardon me,' I said, 'but my curiosity was not altogether an idle one. I know the South, and when the band plays "Dixie" I like to observe. I have formed the belief that the man who applauds that air with special violence and ostensible sectional loyalty is invariably a native of either Secaucus, N. J., or the district between Murray Hill Lyceum and the Harlem River, this city.

I was about to put my opinion to the test by inquiring of this gentleman when you interrupted with your own – larger theory, I must confess.'

And now the dark-haired young man spoke to me, and it became evident that his mind also moved along its own set of grooves.

'I should like to be a periwinkle,' said he, mysteriously, 'on the top of a valley, and sing too-ralloo-ralloo.'

This was clearly too obscure, so I turned again to Coglan.

'I've been around the world twelve times,' said he. 'I know an Esquimau in Upernavik who sends to Cincinnati for his neckties, and I saw a goat-herder in Uruguay who won a prize in a Battle Creek breakfast food puzzle competition. I pay rent on a room in Cairo, Egypt, and another in Yokahama all the year around. I've got slippers waiting for me in a tea-house in Shanghai, and I don't have to tell 'em how to cook my eggs in Rio Janeiro or Seattle. It's a mighty little old world. What's the use of bragging about being from the North, or the South, or the old manor house in the dale, or Euclid Avenue, Cleveland, or Pike's Peak, or Fairfax County, Va., or Hooligan's Flats or any place? It'll be a better world when we quit being fools about some mildewed town or ten acres of swampland just because we happened to be born there.'

'You seem to be a genuine cosmopolite,' I said, admiringly. 'But it also seems that you would decry patriotism.'

'A relic of the stone age,' declared Cogland, warmly. 'We are all brothers – Chinamen, Englishmen, Zulus, Patagonians and the people in the bend of the Kaw River. Some day all this pretty pride in one's city or state or section or country will be wiped out, and we'll all be citizens of the world, as we ought to be.'

'But while you are wandering in foreign lands,' I persisted, 'do not your thoughts revert to some spot – some dear and—'

'Nary a spot,' interrupted E. R. Coglan, flippantly. 'The terrestrial, globular, planetary hunk of matter, slightly flattened at the poles, and known as the Earth, is my abode. I've met a good many object-bound citizens of this country abroad. I've seen men from Chicago sit in a gondola in Venice on a moonlight night and brag about their drainage canal. I've seen a Southerner on being introduced to the King of England hand that monarch, without batting his eyes, the information that his grand-aunt on his mother's side was related by marriage to the Perkinses, of Charleston. I knew a New Yorker who was kidnapped for ransom by some Afghanistan bandits. His people sent over the money and he came back to Kabul with the agent. "Afghanistan?" the natives said to him through an interpreter. "Well, not so slow, do you think?" "Oh, I don't know,' says he, and he begins to tell them about a cab driver at Sixth Avenue and Broadway. Those ideas don't suit me. I'm not tied down to anything that isn't 8,000 miles in diameter. Just put me down as E. Rushmore Coglan, citizen of the terrestrial sphere.'

My cosmopolite made a large adieu and left me, for he thought he saw some one through the chatter and smoke whom he knew. So I was left with the would-be periwinkle, who was reduced to Würzburger without further ability to voice his aspirations to perch, melodious, upon the summit of a valley.

I sat reflecting upon my evident cosmopolite and wondering how the poet had managed to miss him. He was my discovery and I believed in him. How was it? 'The men that breed from them they traffic up and down, but cling to their cities' hem as a child to the mother's gown.'

Not so E. Rushmore Coglan. With the whole world for his —

My meditations were interrupted by a tremendous noise and conflict in another part of the café. I saw above the heads of the seated patrons E. Rushmore Coglan and a stranger to me engaged in terrific battle. They fought between the tables like Titans, and glasses crashed, and men caught their hats up and were knocked down, and a brunette screamed, and a blonde began to sing 'Teasing.'

My cosmopolite was sustaining the pride and reputation of the Earth when the waiters closed in on both combatants with their famous flying wedge formation and bore them outside, still resisting.

I called McCarthy, one of the French *garçons*, and asked him the cause of the conflict.

'The man with the red tie' (that was my cosmopolite), said he, 'got hot on account of things said about the bum sidewalks and water supply of the place he come from by the other guy.'

'Why,' said I, bewildered, 'that man is a citizen of the world – a cosmopolite. He —'

'Originally from Mattawamkeag, Maine, he said,' continued McCarthy, 'and he wouldn't stand for no knockin' the place.'

BETWEEN ROUNDS

THE MAY MOON SHONE BRIGHT upon the private boarding-house of Mrs. Murphy. By reference to the almanac a large amount of territory will be discovered upon which its rays also fell. Spring was in its heyday, with hay fever soon to follow. The parks were green with new leaves and buyers for the Western and Southern trade. Flowers and summer-resort agents were blowing; the air and answers to Lawson were growing milder; hand-organs, fountains and pinochle were playing everywhere.

The windows of Mrs. Murphy's boarding-house were open. A group of boarders were seated on the high stoop upon round, flat mats like German pancakes.

In one of the second-floor front windows Mrs. McCaskey awaited her husband. Supper was cooling on the table. Its heat went into Mrs. McCaskey.

At nine McCaskey came. He carried his coat on his arm and his pipe in his teeth; and he apologized for disturbing the boarders on the steps as he selected spots of stone between them on which to set his size 9, width Ds.

As he opened the door of his room he received a surprise. Instead of the usual stove-lid or potato-masher for him to dodge, came only words.

Mr. McCaskey reckoned that the benign May moon had softened the breast of his spouse.

'I heard ye,' came the oral substitutes for kitchenware. 'Ye can apollygize to riff-raff of the streets for settin' yer unhandy feet on the tails of their frocks, but ye'd walk on the neck of yer wife the length of a clothesline without so much as a "Kiss me fut," and I'm sure it's that long from rubberin' out the windy for ye and the victuals cold such as there's money to buy after drinkin' up yer wages at Gallegher's every Saturday evenin', and the gas man here twice to-day for his.'

'Woman,' said Mr. McCaskey, dashing his coat and hat upon a chair, 'the noise of ye is an insult to me appetite. When ye run down politeness ye take the mortar from between the bricks of the foundations of society. 'Tis no more than exercisin' the acrimony of a gentleman when we ask the dissent of ladies blockin' the way for steppin' between them. Will ye bring the pig's face of ye out of the windy and see to the food?'

Mrs. McCaskey arose heavily and went to the stove. There was something in her manner that warned Mr. McCaskey. When the corners of her mouth went down suddenly like a barometer it usually foretold a fall of crockery and tinware.

'Pig's face, is it?' said Mrs. McCaskey, and hurled a stewpan full of bacon and turnips at her lord.

Mr. McCaskey was no novice at repartee. He knew what should follow the entrée. On the table was a roast sirloin of pork, garnished with shamrocks. He retorted with this, and drew the appropriate return of a bread pudding in an earthen dish. A hunk of Swiss cheese accurately thrown by her husband struck Mrs. McCaskey below one eye. When she replied with a well-aimed coffee-pot full of a hot, black, semi-fragrant liquid the battle, according to courses, should have ended.

But Mr. McCaskey was no 50-cent *table d'hôter*. Let cheap Bohemians consider coffee the end, if they would. Let them make that *faux pas*. He was foxier still. Finger-bowls were not beyond the compass of his experience. They were not to be had in the Pension Murphy; but their equivalent was at hand. Triumphantly he sent the granite-ware wash-basin at the head of his matrimonial adversary. Mrs. McCaskey dodged in time. She reached for a flatiron, with which, as a sort of cordial, she hoped to bring the gastronomical duel to a close. But a loud, wailing scream downstairs caused both her and Mr. McCaskey to pause in a sort of involuntary armistice.

On the sidewalk at the corner of the house Policeman Cleary was standing with one ear upturned, listening to the crash of household utensils.

' 'Tis Jawn McCaskey and his missis at it again,' meditated the policeman. 'I wonder shall I go up and stop the row. I will not. Married folks they are: and few pleasures they have. 'Twill not last long. Sure, they'll have to borrow more dishes to keep it up with.'

And just then came the loud scream below stairs, betokening fear or dire extremity. ' 'Tis probably the cat,' said Policeman Cleary, and walked hastily in the other direction.

The boarders on the steps were fluttered. Mr. Toomey, an insurance solicitor by birth and an investigator by profession, went inside to analyze the scream. He returned with the news that Mrs. Murphy's little boy, Mike, was lost. Following the messenger, out bounced Mrs. Murphy – two hundred pounds in tears and hysterics, clutching the air and howling to the sky for the loss of thirty pounds of freckles and mischief. Bathos, truly; but Mr. Toomey sat down at the side of Miss Purdy, millinery, and their hands came together in sympathy. The two old maids, Misses Walsh, who complained every day about the noise in the halls, inquired immediately if anybody had looked behind the clock.

Major Griggs, who sat by his fat wife on the top step, arose and buttoned his coat. 'The little one lost?' he exclaimed. 'I will scour the city.' His wife never allowed him out after dark. But now she said: 'Go, Ludovic!' in a baritone voice. 'Whoever can look upon that mother's grief without springing to her relief has a heart of stone.' 'Give me some thirty or – sixty cents, my love,' said the Major. 'Lost children sometimes stray far. I may need car-fares.'

Old man Denny, hall room, fourth floor back, who sat on the lowest step, trying to read a paper by the street lamp, turned over a page to follow up the article about the carpenter's strike. Mrs. Murphy shrieked to the moon: 'Oh, ar-r-Mike, f'r Gawd's sake, where is me little bit av a boy?'

'When'd ye see him last?' asked old man Denny, with one eye on the report of the Building Trades League.

'Oh,' wailed Mrs. Murphy, ' 'twas yesterday, or maybe four hours ago! I dunno. But it's lost he is, me little boy Mike. He was playin' on the sidewalk only this mornin' – or was it Wednesday? I'm that busy with work, 'tis hard to keep up with dates. But I've looked the house over from top to cellar, and it's gone he is. Oh, for the love av Hiven—'

Silent, grim, colossal, the big city has ever stood against its revilers. They call it hard as iron; they say that no pulse of pity beats in its bosom; they compare its streets with lonely forests and deserts of lava. But beneath the hard crust of the lobster is found a delectable and luscious food. Perhaps a different simile would have been wiser. Still, nobody should take offence. We would call no one a lobster without good and sufficient claws.

No calamity so touches the common heart of humanity as does the straying of a little child. Their feet are so uncertain and feeble; the ways are so steep and strange.

Major Griggs hurried down to the corner, and up the avenue into Billy's place. 'Gimme a rye-high,' he said to the servitor. 'Haven't seen a bow-legged, dirty-faced little devil of a six-year-old lost kid around here anywhere, have you?'

Mr. Toomey retained Miss Purdy's hand on the steps. 'Think of that dear dear little babe,' said Miss Purdy, 'lost from his mother's side – perhaps already fallen beneath the iron hoofs of galloping steeds – oh, isn't it dreadful?'

'Ain't that right?' agreed Mr. Toomey, squeezing her hand. 'Say I start out and help look for um!'

'Perhaps,' said Miss Purdy, 'you should. But, oh, Mr. Toomey, you are so dashing – so reckless – suppose in your enthusiasm some accident should befall you, then what—'

Old man Denny read on about the arbitration agreement, with one finger on the lines.

In the second floor front Mr. and Mrs. McCaskey came to the window to recover their second wind. Mr. McCaskey was scooping turnips out of his vest with a crooked forefinger, and his lady was wiping an eye that the salt of the roast pork had not benefited. They heard the outcry below, and thrust their heads out of the window.

' 'Tis little Mike is lost,' said Mrs. McCaskey, in a hushed voice, 'the beautiful, little, trouble-making angel of a gossoon!'

'The bit of a boy mislaid?' said Mr. McCaskey, leaning out of the window. 'Why, now, that's bad enough, entirely. The childer, they be different. If 'twas a woman I'd be willin', for they leave peace behind 'em when they go.'

Disregarding the thrust, Mrs. McCaskey caught her husband's arm.

'Jawn,' she said, sentimentally, 'Missis Murphy's little bye is lost. 'Tis a great city for losing little boys. Six years old he was. Jawn, 'tis the same age our little bye would have been if we had had one six years ago.'

'We never did,' said Mr. McCaskey, lingering with the fact.

'But if we had, Jawn, think what sorrow would be in our hearts this night, with out little Phelan run away and stolen in the city nowheres at all.'

'Ye talk foolishness,' said Mr. McCaskey. ' 'Tis Pat he would be named, after me old father in Cantrim.'

'Ye lie!' said Mrs. McCaskey, without anger. 'Me brother was worth tin dozen bog-trotting McCaskeys. After him would the bye be named.' She leaned over the window-sill and looked down at the hurrying and bustle below.

'Jawn,' said Mrs. McCaskey, softly, 'I'm sorry I was hasty wid ye.'

' 'Twas hasty puddin', as ye say,' said her husband, 'and hurry-up turnips and get-a-move-on-ye coffee. 'Twas what ye could call a quick lunch, all right, and tell no lie.'

Mrs. McCaskey slipped her arm inside her husband's and took his rough hand in hers.

'Listen at the cryin' of poor Mrs. Murphy,' she said. ' 'Tis an awful thing for a bit of a bye to be lost in this great big city. If 'twas our little Phelan, Jawn, I'd be breakin' me heart.'

Awkwardly Mr. McCaskey withdrew his hand. But he laid it around the nearing shoulder of his wife.

' 'Tis foolishness, of course,' said he, roughly, 'but I'd be cut up some meself if our little – Pat was kidnapped or anything. But there never was any children for us. Sometimes I've been ugly and hard with ye, Judy. Forget it.'

They leaned together, and looked down at the heart-drama being acted below.

Long they sat thus. People surged along the sidewalk, crowding, questioning, filling the air with rumors, and inconsequent surmises. Mrs. Murphy plowed back and forth in their midst, like a soft mountain down which plunged an audible cataract of tears. Couriers came and went.

Loud voices and a renewed uproar were raised in front of the boarding-house.

'What's up now, Judy?' asked Mr. McCaskey.

' 'Tis Missis Murphy's voice,' said Mrs. McCaskey, harking. 'She says she's after finding little Mike asleep behind the roll of linoleum under the bed in her room.'

Mr. McCaskey laughed loudly.

'That's yer Phelan,' he shouted, sardonically. 'Divil a bit would a Pat have done that trick. If the bye we never had is strayed and stole, by the powers, call him Phelan, and see him hide out under the bed like a mangy pup.'

Mrs. McCaskey arose heavily, and went toward the dish closet, with the corners of her mouth drawn down.

Policeman Cleary came back around the corner as the crowd dispersed. Surprised, he upturned an ear toward the McCaskey apartment, where the crash of irons and chinaware and the ring of hurled kitchen utensils seemed as loud as before. Policeman Cleary took out his timepiece.

'By the deported snakes!' he exclaimed. 'Jawn McCaskey and his lady have been fightin' for an hour and a quarter by the watch. The missis could give him forty pounds weight. Strength to his arm.'

Policeman Cleary strolled back around the corner.

Old man Denny folded his paper and hurried up the steps just as Mrs. Murphy was about to lock the door for the night.

THE SKYLIGHT ROOM

FIRST MRS. PARKER WOULD SHOW you the double parlors. You would not dare to interrupt her description of their advantages and of the merits of the gentleman who had occupied them for eight years. Then you would manage to stammer forth the confession that you were neither a doctor nor a dentist. Mrs. Parker's manner of receiving the admission was such that you could never afterward entertain the same feeling toward your parents, who had neglected to train you up in one of the professions that fitted Mrs. Parker's parlors.

Next you ascended one flight of stairs and looked at the second-floor-back at $8. Convinced by her second-floor manner that it was worth the $12 that Mr. Toosenberry always paid for it until he left to take charge of his brother's orange plantation in Florida near Palm Beach, where Mrs. McIntyre always spent the winters that had the double front room with private bath, you managed to babble that you wanted something still cheaper.

If you survived Mrs. Parker's scorn, you were taken to look at Mr. Skidder's large hall room on the third floor. Mr. Skidder's room was not vacant. He wrote plays and smoked cigarettes in it all day long. But every room-hunter was made to visit his room to admire the lambrequins. After each visit, Mr. Skidder, from the fright caused by possible eviction, would pay something on his rent.

Then – oh, then – if you still stood on one foot, with your hot hand clutching the three moist dollars in your pocket, and hoarsely proclaimed your hideous and culpable poverty, nevermore would Mrs. Parker be cicerone of yours. She would honk loudly the word 'Clara,' she would show you her back, and march downstairs. Then Clara, the colored maid, would escort you up to the carpeted ladder that served for the fourth flight, and show you the Skylight Room. It occupied 7 × 8 feet of floor space in the middle of the hall. On each side of it was a dark lumber closet or storeroom.

In it was an iron cot, a washstand and a chair. A shelf was the dresser. Its four bare walls seemed to close in upon you like the sides of a coffin. Your hand crept to your throat, you gasped, you looked up as from a well – and breathed once more. Through the glass of the little skylight you saw a square of blue infinity.

'Two dollars, suh,' Clara would say in her half-contemptuous, half-Tuskegeenial tones.

One day Miss Leeson came hunting for a room. She carried a typewriter made to be lugged around by a much larger lady. She was a very little girl, with eyes and hair that had kept on growing after she had stopped and that always looked as if they were saying: 'Goodness me! Why didn't you keep up with us?'

Mrs. Parker showed her the double parlors. 'In this closet,' she said, 'one could keep a skeleton or anaesthetic or coal—'

'But I am neither a doctor nor a dentist,' said Miss Leeson, with a shiver.

Mrs. Parker gave her the incredulous, pitying, sneering, icy stare that she kept for those who failed to qualify as doctors or dentists, and led the way to the second-floor-back.

'Eight dollars?' said Miss Leeson. 'Dear me! I'm not Hetty if I do look green. I'm just a poor little working girl. Show me something higher and lower.'

Mr. Skidder jumped and strewed the floor with cigarette stubs at the rap on his door.

'Excuse me, Mr. Skidder,' said Mrs. Parker, with her demon's smile at his pale looks. 'I didn't know you were in. I asked the lady to have a look at your lambrequins.'

'They're too lovely for anything,' said Miss Leeson, smiling in exactly the way the angels do.

After they had gone Mr. Skidder got very busy erasing the tall, black-haired heroine from his latest (unproduced) play and inserted a small, roguish one with heavy, bright hair and vivacious features.

'Anna Held'll jump at it,' said Mr. Skidder to himself, putting his feet up against the lambrequins and disappearing in a cloud of smoke like an aërial cuttlefish.

Presently the tocsin call of 'Clara!' sounded to the world the state of Miss Leeson's purse. A dark goblin seized her, mounted a Stygian stairway, thrust her into a vault with a glimmer of light in its top and muttered the menacing and cabalistic words 'Two dollars!'

'I'll take it!' sighed Miss Leeson, sinking down upon the squeaky iron bed.

Every day Miss Leeson went out to work. At night she brought home papers with handwriting on them and made copies with her typewriter. Sometimes she had no work at night, and then she would sit on the steps of the high stoop with the other roomers. Miss Leeson was not intended for a skylight room when the plans were drawn for her creation. She was gay-hearted and full of tender, whimsical fancies. Once she let Mr. Skidder read to her three acts of his great (unpublished) comedy, 'It's No Kid; or, The Heir of the Subway.'

There was rejoicing among the gentlemen roomers whenever Miss Leeson had time to sit on the steps for an hour or two. But Miss Longnecker, the tall blonde who taught in a public school and said, 'Well, really!' to everything you said, sat on the top step and sniffed. And Miss Dorn, who shot at the moving ducks at Coney every Sunday and worked in a department store, sat on the bottom step and sniffed. Miss Leeson sat on the middle step and the men would quickly group around her.

Especially Mr. Skidder, who had cast her in his mind for the star part in a private, romantic (unspoken) drama in real life. And especially Mr. Hoover, who was forty-five, fat, flush and foolish. And especially very young Mr. Evans, who set up a hollow cough to induce her to ask him to leave off cigarettes. The men voted her 'the funniest and jolliest ever,' but the sniffs on the top step and the lower step were implacable.

I pray you to let the drama halt while Chorus stalks to the footlights and drops an epicedian tear upon the fatness of Mr. Hoover. Tune the pipes to the tragedy of tallow, the bane of bulk, the calamity of corpulence. Tried out, Falstaff might have rendered more romance to the ton than would have Romeo's rickety ribs to the ounce. A lover may sigh, but he must not puff. To the train of Momus are the fat men remanded. In vain beats the faithfullest heart above a 52-inch belt. Avaunt, Hoover! Hoover, forty-five, flush and foolish, might carry off Helen herself; Hoover, forty-five, flush, foolish and fat is meat for perdition. There was never a chance for you, Hoover.

As Mrs. Parker's roomers sat thus one summer's evening, Miss Leeson looked up into the firmament and cried with her little gay laugh:

"Why, there's Billy Jackson! I can see him from down here, too.'

All looked up – some at the windows of skyscrapers, some casting about for an airship, Jackson-guided.

'It's that star,' explained Miss Leeson, pointing with a tiny finger. 'Not the big one that twinkes – the steady blue one near it. I can see it every night through my skylight. I named it Billy Jackson.'

'Well, really!' said Miss Longnecker. 'I didn't know you were an astronomer, Miss Leeson.'

'Oh, yes,' said the small star gazer, 'I know as much as any of them about the style of sleeves they're going to wear next fall in Mars.'

'Well, really!' said Miss Longnecker. 'The star you refer to is Gamma, of the constellation Cassiopeia. It is nearly of the second magnitude, and its meridian passage is—'

'Oh,' said the very young Mr. Evans, 'I think Billy Jackson is a much better name for it.'

'Same here,' said Mr. Hoover, loudly breathing defiance to Miss Longnecker. 'I think Miss Leeson has just as much right to name stars as any of those old astrologers had.'

'Well, really!' said Miss Longnecker.

'I wonder whether it's a shooting star,' remarked Miss Dorn. 'I hit nine ducks and a rabbit out of ten in the gallery at Coney Sunday.'

'He doesn't show up very well from down here,' said Miss Leeson. 'You ought to see him from my room. You know you can see stars even in the daytime from the bottom of a well. At night my room is like the shaft of a coal mine, and it makes Billy Jackson look like the big diamond pin that Night fastens her kimono with.'

There came a time after that when Miss Leeson brought no formidable papers home to copy. And when she went out in the morning, instead of working, she went from office to office and let her heart melt away in the drip of cold refusals transmitted through insolent office boys. This went on.

There came an evening when she wearily climbed Mrs. Parker's stoop at the hour when she always returned from her dinner at the restaurant. But she had had no dinner.

As she stepped into the hall Mr. Hoover met her and seized his chance. He asked her to marry him, and his fatness hovered above her like an avalanche. She dodged, and caught the balustrade. He tried for her hand, and she raised it and smote him weakly in the face. Step by step she went up, dragging herself by the railing. She passed Mr. Skidder's door as he was red-inking a stage direction for Myrtle Delorme (Miss Leeson) in his (unaccepted) comedy, to 'pirouette across the stage from L to the side of the Count.' Up the carpeted ladder she crawled at last and opened the door of the skylight room.

She was too weak to light the lamp or to undress. She fell upon the iron cot, her fragile body scarcely hollowing the worn springs. And in that Erebus of a room she slowly raised her heavy eyelids, and smiled.

For Billy Jackson was shining down on her, calm and bright and constant through the skylight. There was no world about her. She was sunk in a pit of blackness, with but that small square of pallid light framing the star that she had so whimsically and oh, so ineffectually, named. Miss Longnecker must be right: it was Gamma, of the constellation Cassiopeia, and not Billy Jackson. And yet she could not let it be Gamma.

As she lay on her back, she tried twice to raise her arm. The third time she got two thin fingers to her lips and blew a kiss out of the black pit to Billy Jackson. Her arm fell back limply.

'Good-bye, Billy,' she murmured, faintly. 'You're millions of miles away and you won't even twinkle once. But you kept where I could see you most of the time up there when there wasn't anything else but darkness to look at, didn't you? . . . Millions of miles. . . . Good-bye, Billy Jackson.'

Clara, the colored maid, found the door locked at 10 the next day, and they forced it open. Vinegar, and the slapping of wrists and burnt feathers proving of no avail, some one ran to 'phone for an ambulance.

In due time it backed up to the door with much gong-clanging, and the capable young medico, in his white linen coat, ready, active, confident, with his smooth face half debonair, half grim, danced up the steps.

'Ambulance call to 49,' he said, briefly. 'What's the trouble?'

'Oh, yes, doctor,' sniffed Mrs. Parker, as though her trouble that there should be trouble in the house was the greater. 'I can't think what can be the matter with her. Nothing we could do would bring her to. It's a young woman, a Miss Elsie – yes, a Miss Elsie Leeson. Never before in my house—'

'What room?' cried the doctor in a terrible voice, to which Mrs. Parker was a stranger.

'The skylight room. It—'

Evidently the ambulance doctor was familiar with the location of skylight rooms. He was gone up the stairs, four at a time. Mrs. Parker followed slowly, as her dignity demanded.

On the first landing she met him coming back bearing the astronomer in his arms. He stopped and let loose the practised scalpel of his tongue, not loudly. Gradually Mrs. Parker crumpled as a stiff garment that slips down from a nail. Ever afterwards there remained crumples in her mind and body. Sometimes her curious roomers would ask her what the doctor said to her.

'Let that be,' she would answer. 'If I can get forgiveness for having heard it I will be satisfied.'

The ambulance physician strode with his burden through the pack of hounds that follow the curiosity chase, and even they fell back along the sidewalk abashed, for his face was that of one who bears his own dead.

They noticed that he did not lay down upon the bed prepared for it in the ambulance the form that he carried, and all that he said was: 'Drive like h—l, Wilson,' to the driver.

That is all. Is it a story? In the next morning's paper I saw a little news item, and the last sentence of it may help you (as it helped me) to weld the incidents together.

It recounted the reception into Bellevue Hospital of a young woman who had been removed from No. 49 East — Street, suffering from debility induced by starvation. It concluded with these words:

'Dr. William Jackson, the ambulance physician who attended the case, says the patient will recover.'

A SERVICE OF LOVE

WHEN ONE LOVES ONE'S ART no service seems too hard.

That is our premise. This story shall draw a conclusion from it, and show at the same time that the premise is incorrect. That will be a new thing in logic, and a feat in story-telling somewhat older than the great wall of China.

Joe Larrabee came out of the post-oak flats of the Middle West pulsing with a genius for pictorial art. At six he drew a picture of the town pump with a prominent citizen passing it hastily. This effort was framed and hung in the drug-store window by the side of the ear of corn with an uneven number of rows. At twenty he left for New York with a flowing necktie and a capital tied up somewhat closer.

Delia Caruthers did things in six octaves so promisingly in a pine-tree village in the South that her relatives chipped in enough in her chip hat for her to go 'North' and 'finish.' They could not see her f—, but that is our story.

Joe and Delia met in an atelier where a number of art and music students had gathered to discuss chiaroscuro, Wagner, music, Rembrandt's works, pictures, Waldteufel, wall paper, Chopin and Oolong.

Joe and Delia became enamored one of the other, or each of the other, as you please, and in a short time were married – for (see above), when one loves one's Art no service seems too hard.

Mr. and Mrs. Larrabee began housekeeping in a flat. It was a lonesome flat – something like the A sharp way down at the left-hand end of the keyboard. And they were happy; for they had their Art, and they had each other. And my advice to the rich young man would be – sell all thou hast, and give it to the poor – janitor for the privilege of living in a flat with your Art and your Delia.

Flat-dwellers shall indorse my dictum that theirs is the only true happiness. If a home is happy it cannot fit too close – let the dresser collapse and become a billiard table; let the mantel turn to a rowing machine, the escritoire to a spare bedchamber, the washstand to an upright piano; let the four walls come together, if they will, so you and your Delia are between. But if home be the other kind, let it be wide and long – enter you at the Golden Gate, hang your hat on Hatteras, your cape on Cape Horn and go out by the Labrador.

Joe was painting in the class of the great Magister – you know his fame. His fees are high; his lessons are light – his high-lights have brought him renown. Delia was studying under Rosenstock – you know his repute as a disturber of the piano keys.

They were mighty happy as long as their money lasted. So is every – but I will not be cynical. Their aims were very clear and defined. Joe was to become capable very soon of turning out pictures that old gentlemen with thin side-whiskers and thick pocketbooks would sandbag one another in his studio for the privilege of buying. Delia was to become familiar and then contemptuous with Music, so that when she saw the orchestra seats and boxes unsold she could have sore throat and lobster in a private dining-room and refuse to go on the stage.

But the best, in my opinion, was the home life in the little flat – the ardent, voluble chats after the day's study; the cozy dinners and fresh, light breakfasts; the interchange of ambitions – ambitions interwoven each with the other's or else inconsiderable – the mutual help and inspiration; and – overlook my artlessness – stuffed olives and cheese sandwiches at 11 p.m.

But after a while Art flagged. It sometimes does, even if some switchman doesn't flag it. Everything going out and nothing coming in, as the vulgarians say. Money was lacking to pay Mr. Magister and Herr Rosenstock their prices. When one loves one's Art no service seems too hard. So, Delia said she must give music lessons to keep the chafing dish bubbling.

For two or three days she went out canvassing for pupils. One evening she came home elated.

'Joe, dear,' she said, gleefully, 'I've a pupil. And, oh, the loveliest people. General – General A. B. Pinkney's daughter – on Seventy-first Street. Such a splendid house, Joe – you ought to see the front door! Byzantine I think you would call it. And inside! Oh, Joe, I never saw any thing like it before.

'My pupil is his daughter Clementina. I dearly love her already. She's a delicate thing – dresses always in white; and the sweetest, simplest manners! Only eighteen years old. I'm to give three lessons a week; and, just think, Joe! $5 a lesson. I don't mind it a bit; for when I get two or three more pupils I can resume my lessons with Herr Rosenstock. Now, smooth out that wrinkle between your brows, dear, and let's have a nice supper.'

'That's all right for you, Dele,' said Joe, attacking a can of peas with a carving knife and a hatchet, 'but how about me? Do you think I'm going to let you hustle for wages while I philander in the regions of high art? Not by the bones of Benvenuto Cellini! I guess I can sell papers or lay cobblestones, and bring in a dollar or two.'

Delia came and hung about his neck.

'Joe, dear, you are silly. You must keep on at your studies. It is not as if I had quit my music and gone to work at something else. While I teach I learn. I am always with my music. And we can live as happily as millionaires on $15 a week. You mustn't think of leaving Mr. Magister.'

'All right,' said Joe, reaching for the blue scalloped vegetable dish. 'But I hate for you to be giving lessons. It isn't Art. But you're a trump and a dear to do it.'

'When one loves one's Art no service seems too hard,' said Delia.

'Magister praised the sky in that sketch I made in the park,' said Joe. 'And Tinkle gave me permission to hang two of them in his window. I may sell one if the right kind of a moneyed idiot sees them.'

'I'm sure you will,' said Delia, sweetly. 'And now let's be thankful for Gen. Pinkney and this veal roast.'

During all of the next week the Larrabees had an early breakfast. Joe was enthusiastic about some morning-effect sketches he was doing in Central Park, and Delia packed him off breakfasted, coddled, praised and kissed at 7 o'clock. Art is an engaging mistress. It was most times 7 o'clock when he returned in the evening.

At the end of the week Delia, sweetly proud but languid, triumphantly tossed three five-dollar bills on the 8 × 10 (inches) centre table of the 8 × 10 (feet) flat parlor.

'Sometimes,' she said, a little wearily, 'Clementina tries me. I'm afraid she doesn't practise enough, and I have to tell her the same things so often. And then she always dresses entirely in white, and that does get monotonous. But

Gen. Pinkney is the dearest old man! I wish you could know him, Joe. He comes in sometimes when I am with Clementina at the piano – he is a widower, you know – and stands there pulling his white goatee. "And how are the semiquavers and the demisemiquavers progressing?" he always asks.

'I wish you could see the wainscoting in that drawing room, Joe! And those Astrakhan rug portières. And Clementina has such a funny little cough. I hope she is stronger than she looks. Oh, I really am getting attached to her, she is so gentle and high bred. Gen. Pinkney's brother was once Minister to Bolivia.'

And then Joe, with the air of Monte Cristo, drew forth a ten, a five, a two and a one – all legal tender notes – and laid them beside Delia's earnings.

'Sold that watercolor of the obelisk to a man from Peoria,' he announced, overwhelmingly.

'Don't joke with me,' said Delia – 'not from Peoria!'

'All the way. I wish you could see him, Dele. Fat man with a woolen muffler and a quill toothpick. He saw the sketch in Tinkle's window and thought it was a windmill at first. He was game, though, and bought it anyhow. He ordered another – an oil sketch of the Lackawanna freight depot – to take back with him. Music lessons! Oh, I guess Art is still in it.'

'I'm so glad you've kept on,' said Delia, heartily. 'You're bound to win, dear. Thirty-three dollars! We never had so much to spend before. We'll have oysters tonight.'

'And filet mignon with champignons,' said Joe. 'Where is the olive fork?'

On the next Saturday evening Joe reached home first. He spread his $18 on the parlor table and washed what seemed to be a great deal of dark paint from his hands.

Half an hour later Delia arrived, her right hand tied up in a shapeless bundle of wraps and bandages.

'How is this?' asked Joe after the usual greetings. Delia laughed, but not very joyously.

'Clementina,' she explained, 'insisted upon a Welsh rabbit after her lesson. She is such a queer girl. Welsh rabbits at 5 in the afternoon. The General was there. You should have seen him run for the chafing dish, Joe, just as if there wasn't a servant in the house. I know Clementina isn't in good health; she is so nervous. In serving the rabbit she spilled a great lot of it, boiling hot, over my hand and wrist. It hurt awfully, Joe. And the dear girl was so sorry! But Gen. Pinkney! – Joe, that old man nearly went distracted. He rushed downstairs and sent somebody – they said the furnace man or somebody in the basement – out to a drug store for some oil and things to bind it up with. It doesn't hurt so much now.'

'What's this?' asked Joe, taking the hand tenderly and pulling at some white strands beneath the bandages.

'It's something soft,' said Delia, 'that had oil on it. Oh, Joe, did you sell another sketch?' She had seen the money on the table.

'Did I?' said Joe; 'just ask the man from Peoria. He got his depot to-day, and he isn't sure but he thinks he wants another parkscape, and a view on the Hudson. What time this afternoon did you burn your hand, Dele?'

'Five o'clock, I think,' said Dele, plaintively. 'The iron – I mean the rabbit came off the fire about that time. You ought to have seen Gen. Pinkney, Joe, when—'

'Sit down here a moment, Dele,' said Joe. He drew her to the couch, sat beside her and put his arm across her shoulders.

'What have you been doing for the last two weeks, Dele?' he asked.

She braved it for a moment or two with an eye full of love and stubborness, and murmured a phrase or two vaguely of Gen. Pinkney; but at length down went her head and out came the truth and tears.

'I couldn't get any pupils,' she confessed. 'And I couldn't bear to have you give up your lessons; and I got a place ironing shirts in that big Twenty-fourth Street laundry. And I think I did very well to make up both General Pinkney and Clementina, don't you, Joe? And when a girl in the laundry set down a hot iron on my hand this afternoon I was all the way home making up that story about the Welsh rabbit. You're not angry, are you, Joe? And if I hadn't got the work you mightn't have sold your sketches to that man from Peoria.'

'He wasn't from Peoria,' said Joe, slowly.

'Well, it doesn't matter where he was from. How clever you are, Joe – and – kiss me, Joe – and what made you ever suspect that I wasn't giving music lessons to Clementina?'

'I didn't,' said Joe, 'until to-night. And I wouldn't have then, only I sent up this cotton waste and oil from the engine-room this afternoon for a girl upstairs who had her hand burned with a smoothing-iron. I've been firing the engine in that laundry for the last two weeks.'

'And then you didn't—'

'My purchaser from Peoria,' said Joe, 'and Gen. Pinkney are both creations of the same art – but you wouldn't call it either painting or music.'

And then they both laughed, and Joe began:

'When one loves one's Art no service seems—'

But Delia stopped him with her hand on his lips. 'No,' she said – 'just "When one loves."'

THE COMING-OUT OF MAGGIE

EVERY SATURDAY NIGHT the Clover Leaf Social Club gave a hop in the hall of the Give and Take Athletic Association on the East Side. In order to attend one of these dances you must be a member of the Give and Take – or, if you belong to the division that starts off with the right foot in waltzing, you must work in Rhinegold's paper-box factory. Still, any Clover Leaf was privileged to escort or be escorted by an outsider to a single dance. But mostly each Give and Take brought the paper-box girl that he affected; and few strangers could boast of having shaken a foot at the regular hops.

Maggie Toole, on account of her dull eyes, broad mouth and left-handed style of footwork in the two-step, went to the dances with Anna McCarty and her 'fellow.' Anna and Maggie worked side by side in the factory, and were the greatest chums ever. So Anna always made Jimmy Burns take her by Maggie's house every Saturday night so that her friend could go to the dance with them.

The Give and Take Athletic Association lived up to its name. The hall of the association in Orchard Street was fitted out with muscle-making inventions. With the fibres thus builded up the members were wont to engage the police and rival social athletic organizations in joyous combat. Between these more serious occupations the Saturday night hops with the paper-box factory girls came as a refining influence and as an efficient screen. For sometimes the tip went 'round, and if you were among the elect that tiptoed up the dark back stairway you might see as neat and satisfying a little welter-weight affair to a finish as ever happened inside the ropes.

On Saturdays Rhinegold's paper-box factory closed at 3 p.m. On one such afternoon Anna and Maggie walked homeward together. At Maggie's door Anna said, as usual: 'Be ready at seven sharp, Mag, and Jimmy and me'll come by for you.'

But what was this? Instead of the customary humble and grateful thanks from the non-escorted one there was to be perceived a high poised head, a prideful dimpling at the corners of a broad mouth, and almost a sparkle in a dull brown eye.

'Thanks, Anna,' said Maggie; 'but you and Jimmy needn't bother to-night. I've a gentleman friend that's coming round to escort me to the hop.'

The comely Anna pounced upon her friend, shook her, chided and beseeched her. Maggie Toole catch a fellow! Plain, dear, loyal, unattractive Maggie, so sweet as a chum so unsought for a two-step or a moonlit bench in the little park. How was it? When did it happen? Who was it?

'You'll see to-night,' said Maggie, flushed with the wine of the first grapes she had gathered in Cupid's vineyard. 'He's swell all right. He's two inches taller than Jimmy, and an up-to-date dresser. I'll introduce him, Anna, just as soon as we get to the hall.'

Anna and Jimmy were among the first Clover Leafs to arrive that evening. Anna's eyes were brightly fixed upon the door of the hall to catch the first glimpse of her friend's 'catch.'

At 8.30 Miss Toole swept into the hall with the escort. Quickly her triumphant eye discovered her chum under the wing of her faithful Jimmy.

'Oh, gee!' cried Anna, 'Mag ain't made a hit – oh, no! Swell fellow? well, I guess! Style? Look at 'um.'

'Go as far as you like,' said Jimmy, with sandpaper in his voice. 'Cop him out if you want him. These new guys always win out with the push. Don't mind me. He don't squeeze all the lines, I guess. Huh!'

'Shut up, Jimmy. You know what I mean. I'm glad for Mag. First fellow she ever had. Oh, here they come.'

Across the floor Maggie sailed like a coquettish yacht convoyed by a stately cruiser. And truly, her companion justified the encomiums of the faithful chum. He stood two inches taller than the average Give and Take athlete; his dark hair curled; his eyes and his teeth flashed whenever he bestowed his frequent smiles. The young men of the Clover Leaf Club pinned not their faith to the graces of person as much as they did to its prowess, its achievements in hand-to-hand conflicts, and its preservation from the legal duress that constantly menaced it. The member of the association who would bind a paper-box maiden to his conquering chariot scorned to employ Beau Brummell airs. They were not considered honorable methods of warfare. The swelling biceps, the coat straining at its buttons over the chest, the air of conscious conviction of the supereminence of the male in the cosmogony of creation, even a calm display of bow legs as subduing and enchanting agents in the gentle tourneys of Cupid – these were the approved arms and ammunition of the Clover Leaf gallants. They viewed, then, the genuflexions and alluring poses of this visitor with their chins at a new angle.

'A friend of mine, Mr. Terry O'Sullivan,' was Maggie's formula of introduction. She led him around the room, presenting him to each new-arriving Clover Leaf. Almost was she pretty now, with the unique luminosity in her eyes that comes to a girl with her first suitor and a kitten with its first mouse.

'Maggie Toole's got a fellow at last,' was the word that went round among the paper-box girls. 'Pipe Mag's floor-walker' – thus the Give and Takes expressed their indifferent contempt.

Usually at the weekly hops Maggie kept a spot on the wall warm with her back. She felt and showed so much gratitude whenever a self-sacrificing partner invited her to dance that his pleasure was cheapened and diminished. She had even grown used to noticing Anna joggle the reluctant Jimmy with her elbow as a signal for him to invite her chum to walk over his feet through a two-step.

But to-night the pumpkin had turned to a coach and six. Terry O'Sullivan was a victorious Prince Charming, and Maggie Toole winged her first butterfly flight. And though our tropes of fairyland be mixed with those of entomology they shall not spill one drop of ambrosia from the rose-crowned melody of Maggie's one perfect night.

The girls besieged her for introduction to her 'fellow.' The Clover Leaf young men, after two years of blindness, suddenly perceived charms in Miss Toole. They flexed their compelling muscles before her and bespoke her for the dance.

Thus she scored; but to Terry O'Sullivan the honors of the evening fell thick and fast. He shook his curls; he smiled and went easily through the seven motions for acquiring grace in your own room before an open window ten minutes each day. He danced like a faun; he introduced manner and style and atmosphere; his words came trippingly upon his tongue, and – he waltzed twice in succession with the paper-box girl that Dempsey Donovan brought.

Dempsey was the leader of the association. He wore a dress suit, and could chin the bar twice with one hand. He was one of 'Big Mike' O'Sullivan's lieutenants, and was never troubled by trouble. No cop dared to arrest him. Whenever he broke a pushcart man's head or shot a member of the Heinrick B. Sweeney Outing and Literary Association in the kneecap, an officer would drop around and say:

'The Cap'n'd like to see ye a few minutes round to the office whin ye have time, Dempsey, me boy.'

But there would be sundry gentlemen there with large gold fob chains and black cigars; and somebody would tell a funny story, and then Dempsey would go back and work half an hour with the six-pound dumbbells. So, doing a tight-rope act on a wire stretched across Niagara was a safe terpsichorean performance compared with waltzing twice with Dempsey Donovan's paper-box girl. At 10 o'clock the jolly round face of 'Big Mike' O'Sullivan shone at the door for five minutes upon the scene. He always looked in for five minutes, smiled at the girls and handed out real perfectos to the delighted boys.

Dempsey Donovan was at his elbow instantly, talking rapidly. 'Big Mike' looked carefully at the dancers, smiled, shook his head and departed.

The music stopped. The dancers scattered to the chairs along the walls.

Terry O'Sullivan, with his entrancing bow, relinquished a pretty girl in blue to her partner and started back to find Maggie. Dempsey intercepted him in the middle of the floor.

Some fine instinct that Rome must have bequeathed to us caused nearly every one to turn and look at them – there was a subtle feeling that two gladiators had met in the arena. Two or three Give and Takes with tight coat sleeves drew nearer.

'One moment, Mr. O'Sullivan,' said Dempsey. 'I hope you're enjoying yourself. Where did you say you lived?'

The two gladiators were well matched. Dempsey had, perhaps, ten pounds of weight to give away. The O'Sullivan had breadth and quickness. Dempsey had a glacial eye, a dominating slit of mouth, an indestructible jaw, a complexion like a belle's and the coolness of a champion. The visitor showed more fire in his contempt and less control over his conspicuous sneer. They were enemies by the law written when the rocks were molten. They were each too splendid, too mighty, too incomparable to divide pre-eminence. One only must survive.

'I live on Grand,' said O'Sullivan, insolently; 'and no trouble to find me at home. Where do you live?'

Dempsey ignored the question.

'You say your name's O'Sullivan,' he went on. 'Well, "Big Mike" says he never saw you before.'

'Lots of things he never saw,' said the favorite of the hop.

'As a rule,' went on Dempsey, huskily sweet, 'O'Sullivans in this district know one another. You escorted one of our lady members here, and we want a chance to make good. If you've got a family tree let's see a few historical O'Sullivan buds come out on it. Or do you want us to dig it out of you by the roots?'

'Suppose you mind your own business,' suggested O'Sullivan, blandly.

Dempsey's eye brightened. He held up an inspired forefinger as though a brilliant idea had struck him.

'I've got it now,' he said, cordially. 'It was just a little mistake. You ain't no O'Sullivan. You are a ring-tailed monkey. Excuse us for not recognizing you at first.'

O'Sullivan's eye flashed. He made a quick movement, but Andy Geoghan was ready and caught his arm.

Dempsey nodded at Andy and William McMahan, the secretary of the club, and walked rapidly toward a door at the rear of the hall. Two other members of the Give and Take Association swiftly joined the little group. Terry O'Sullivan was now in the hands of the Board of Rules and Social Referees. They spoke to him briefly and softly, and conducted him out through the same door at the rear.

This movement on the part of the Clover Leaf members requires a word of elucidation. Back of the association hall was a small room rented by the club. In this room personal difficulties that arose on the ballroom floor were settled, man to man, with the weapons of nature, under the supervision of the Board. No lady could say that she had witnessed a fight at a Clover Leaf hop in several years. Its gentlemen members guaranteed that.

So easily and smoothly had Dempsey and the Board done their preliminary work that many in the hall had not noticed the checking of the fascinating

O'Sullivan's social triumph. Among these was Maggie. She looked about for her escort.

'Smoke up!' said Rose Cassidy. 'Wasn't you on? Demps Donovan picked a scrap with your Lizzie-boy, and they're waltzed out to the slaughter room with him. How's my hair look done up this way, Mag?'

Maggie laid a hand on the bosom of her cheese-cloth waist.

'Gone to fight with Dempsey!' she said, breathlessly. 'They've got to be stopped. Dempsey Donovan can't fight him. Why, he'll – he'll kill him!'

'Ah, what do you care?' said Rose. 'Don't some of 'em fight every hop?'

But Maggie was off, darting her zig-zag way through the maze of dancers. She burst through the rear door into the dark hall and then threw her solid shoulder against the door of the room of single combat. It gave way, and in the instant that she entered her eye caught the scene – the Board standing about with open watches; Dempsey Donovan in his shirt sleeves dancing light-footed, with the wary grace of the modern pugilist, within easy reach of his adversary; Terry O'Sullivan standing with arms folded and a murderous look in his dark eyes. And without slacking the speed of her entrance she leaped forward with a scream – leaped in time to catch and hang upon the arm of O'Sullivan that was suddenly uplifted, and to whisk from it the long, bright stiletto that he had drawn from his bosom.

The knife fell and rang upon the floor. Cold steel drawn in the rooms of the Give and Take Association! Such a thing had never happened before. Every one stood motionless for a minute. Andy Geoghan kicked the stiletto with the toe of his shoe curiously, like an antiquarian who has come upon some ancient weapon unknown to his learning.

And then O'Sullivan hissed something unintelligible between his teeth. Dempsey and the Board exchanged looks. And then Dempsey looked at O'Sullivan without anger, as one looks at a stray dog, and nodded his head in the direction of the door. 'The back stairs, Giuseppi,' he said, briefly. 'Somebody'll pitch your hat down after you.'

Maggie walked up to Dempsey Donovan. There was a brilliant spot of red in her cheeks, down which slow tears were running. But she looked him bravely in the eye.

'I knew it, Dempsey,' she said, as her eyes grew dull even in their tears. 'I knew he was a Guinea. His name's Tony Spinelli. I hurried in when they told me you and him was scrappin'. Them Guineas always carries knives. But you don't understand, Dempsey. I never had a fellow in my life. I got tired of comin' with Anna and Jimmy every night, so I fixed it with him to call himself O'Sullivan, and brought him along. I knew there'd be nothin' doin' for him if he came as a Dago. I guess I'll resign from the club now.'

Dempsey turned to Andy Geoghan.

'Chuck that cheese slicer out of the window,' he said, 'and tell 'em inside that Mr. O'Sullivan has had a telephone message to go down to Tammany Hall.'

And then he turned back to Maggie.

'Say, Mag,' he said, 'I'll see you home. And how about next Saturday night? Will you come to the hop with me if I call around for you?'

It was remarkable how quickly Maggie's eyes could change from dull to a shining brown.

'With you, Dempsey?' she stammered. 'Say – will a duck swim?'

MAN ABOUT TOWN

THERE ARE TWO OR THREE THINGS that I wanted to know. I do not care about a mystery. So I began to inquire.

It took me two weeks to find out what women carry in dress suit cases. And then I began to ask why a mattress is made in two pieces. This serious query was at first received with suspicion because it sounded like a conundrum. I was at last assured that its double form of construction was designed to make lighter the burden of woman, who make up beds. I was so foolish as to persist, begging to know why, then, they were not made in two equal pieces; whereupon I was shunned.

The third draught that I craved from the fount of knowledge was enlightenment concerning the character known as A Man About Town. He was more vague in my mind than a type should be. We must have a concrete idea of anything, even if it be an imaginary idea, before we can comprehend it. Now, I have a mental picture of John Doe that is as clear as a steel engraving. His eyes are weak blue; he wears a brown vest and a shiny black serge coat. He stands always in the sunshine chewing something; and he keeps half-shutting his pocket knife and opening it again with his thumb. And, if the Man Higher Up is ever found, take my assurance for it, he will be a large, pale man with blue wristlets showing under his cuffs, and he will be sitting to have his shoes polished within sound of a bowling alley, and there will be somewhere about him turquoises.

But the canvas of my imagination, when it came to limning the Man About Town, was blank. I fancied that he had a detachable sneer (like the smile of the Cheshire cat) and attached cuffs; and that was all. Whereupon I asked a newspaper reporter about him.

'Why,' said he, 'a "Man About Town" is something between a "rounder" and a "clubman." He isn't exactly – well, he fits in between Mrs. Fish's receptions and private boxing bouts. He doesn't – well, he doesn't belong either to the Lotos Club or to the Jerry McGeogheghan Galvanized Iron Workers' Apprentices' Left Hook Chowder Association. I don't exactly know how to describe him to you. You'll see him everywhere there's anything doing. Yes, I suppose he's a type. Dress clothes every evening; knows the ropes; calls every policeman and waiter in town by their first names. No; he never travels with the hydrogen derivatives. You generally see him alone or with another man.'

My friend the reporter left me, and I wandered further afield. By this time the 3126 electric lights on the Rialto were alight. People passed, but they held me not. Paphian eyes rayed upon me, and left me unscathed. Diner, heimgangers, shop-girls, confidence men, panhandlers, actors, highwaymen, millionaires, and outlanders hurried, skipped, strolled, sneaked, swaggered, and scurried by me; but I took no note of them. I knew them all; I had read their hearts; they had served. I wanted my Man About Town. He was a type, and to drop him would be an error – a typograph – but no! let us continue.

Let us continue with a moral digression. To see a family reading the Sunday paper gratifies. The sections have been separated. Papa is earnestly scanning the page that pictures the young lady exercising before an open window, and bending – but there, there! Mamma is interested in trying to guess the missing letters in the word N–w Yo–k. The oldest girls are eagerly perusing the financial reports, for a certain young man remarked last Sunday night that he had taken a flyer in Q., X. & Z. Willie, the eighteen-year-old son, who attends the New York public school, is absorbed in the weekly article describing how to make over an old shirt, for he hopes to take a prize in sewing on graduation day.

Grandma is holding to the cosmic supplement with a two-hours', grip; and little Tottie, the baby, is rocking along the best she can with the real estate transfers. This view is intended to be reassuring, for it is desirable that a few lines of this story be skipped. For it introduces strong drink.

I went into a café to – and while it was being mixed I asked the man who grabs up your hot Scotch spoon as soon as you lay it down what he understood by the term, epithet, description, designation, characterization or appellation, viz.: a 'Man about Town.'

'Why,' said he, carefully, 'it means a fly guy that's wise to the all-night push – see? It's a hot sport that you can't bump to the rail anywhere between the Flatirons – see? I guess that's about what it means.'

I thanked him and departed.

On the sidewalk a Salvation lassie shook her contribution receptacle gently against my waistcoat pocket.

'Would you mind telling me,' I asked her, 'if you ever meet with the character commonly denominated as "A Man About Town" during your daily wanderings?'

'I think I know whom you mean,' she answered, with a gentle smile. 'We see them in the same places night after night. They are the devil's body guard, and if the soldiers of any army are as faithful as they are, their commanders are well served. We go among them, diverting a few pennies from their wickedness to the Lord's service.'

She shook the box again and I dropped a dime into it.

In front of a glittering hotel a friend of mine, a critic, was climbing from a cab. He seemed at leisure; and I put my question to him. He answered me conscientiously, as I was sure he would.

'There is a type of "Man About Town" in New York,' he answered. 'The term is quite familiar to me, but I don't think I was ever called upon to define the character before. It would be difficult to point you out an exact specimen. I would say, offhand, that it is a man who had a hopeless case of the peculiar New York disease of wanting to see and know. At 6 o'clock each day life begins with him. He follows rigidly the conventions of dress and manners; but in the business of poking his nose into places where he does not belong he could give pointers to a civet cat or a jackdaw. He is the man who has chased Bohemia about the town from rathskeller to roof garden and from Hester Street to Harlem until you can't find a place in the city where they don't cut their spaghetti with a knife. Your "Man About Town" has done that. He is always on the scent of something new. He is curiosity, impudence, and omnipresence. Hansoms were made for him, and gold-banded cigars; and the curse of music at dinner. There are not so many of him; but his minority report is adopted everywhere.

'I'm glad you brought up the subject; I've felt the influence of this nocturnal blight upon our city, but I never thought to analyze it before. I can see now that your "Man About Town" should have been classified long ago. In his wake spring up wine agents and cloak models; and the orchestra plays "Let's All Go Up to Maud's" for him, by request, instead of Händel. He makes his rounds every evening; while you and I see the elephant once a week. When the cigar store is raided, he winks at the officer, familiar with his ground, and walks away immune, while you and I search among the Presidents for names, and among the stars for addresses to give the desk sergeant.'

My friend, the critic, paused to acquire breath for fresh eloquence. I seized my advantage.

'You have classified him,' I cried with joy. 'You have painted his portrait in the gallery of city types. But I must meet one face to face. I must study the Man About Town at first hand. Where shall I find him? How shall I know him?'

Without seeming to hear me, the critic went on. And his cab-driver was waiting for his fare, too.

'He is the sublimated essence of Butt-in; the refined, intrinsic extract of Rubber; the concentrated, purified, irrefutable, unavoidable spirit of Curiosity and Inquisitiveness. A new sensation is the breath in his nostrils when his experience is exhausted he explores new fields with the indefatigability of a—'

'Excuse me,' I interrupted, 'but can you produce one of this type? It is a new thing to me. I must study it. I will search the town over until I find one. Its habitat must be here on Broadway.'

'I am about to dine here,' said my friend. 'Come inside, and if there is a Man About Town present I will point him out to you. I know most of the regular patrons here.'

'I am not dining yet,' I said to him. 'You will excuse me. I am going to find my Man About Town this night if I have to rake New York from the Battery to Little Coney Island.'

I left the hotel and walked down Broadway. The pursuit of my type gave a pleasant savor of life and interest to the air I breathed. I was glad to be in a city so great, so complex and diversified. Leisurely and with something of an air I strolled along with my heart expanding at the thought that I was a citizen of great Gotham, a sharer in its magnificence and pleasures, a partaker in its glory and prestige.

I turned to cross the street. I heard something buzz like a bee, and then I took a long, pleasant ride with Santos-Dumont.

When I opened my eyes I remembered a smell of gasoline, and I said aloud: 'Hasn't it passed yet?'

A hospital nurse laid a hand that was not particularly soft upon my brow that was not at all fevered. A young doctor came along, grinned, and handed me a morning newspaper.

'Want to see how it happened?' he asked, cheerily. I read the article. Its headlines began where I heard the buzzing leave off the night before. It closed with these lines:

'—Bellevue Hospital, where it was said that his injuries were not serious. He appeared to be a typical Man About Town.'

THE COP AND THE ANTHEM

ON HIS BENCH IN MADISON SQUARE Soapy moved uneasily. When wild geese honk high of nights, and when women without sealskin coats grow kind to their husbands, and when Soapy moves uneasily on his bench in the park, you may know that winter is near at hand.

A dead leaf fell in Soapy's lap. That was Jack Frost's card. Jack is kind to the regular denizens of Madison Square, and gives fair warning of his annual call. At the corners of four streets he hands his pasteboard to the North Wind, footman of the mansion of All Outdoors, so that the inhabitants thereof may make ready.

Soapy's mind became cognizant of the fact that the time had come for him to resolve himself into a singular Committee of Ways and Means to provide against the coming rigor. And therefore he moved uneasily on his bench.

The hibernatorial ambitions of Soapy were not of the highest. In them were no considerations of Mediterranean cruises, of soporific Southern skies or drifting in the Vesuvian Bay. Three months on the Island was what his soul craved. Three months of assured board and bed and congenial company, safe from Boreas and bluecoats, seemed to Soapy the essence of things desirable.

For years the hospitable Blackwell's had been his winter quarters. Just as his more fortunate fellow New Yorkers had bought their tickets to Palm Beach and the Riviera each winter, so Soapy had made his humble arrangements for his annual hegira to the Island. And now the time was come. On the previous night three Sabbath newspapers, distributed beneath his coat, about his ankles and over his lap, had failed to repulse the cold as he slept on his bench near the spurting fountain in the ancient square. So the Island loomed big and timely in Soapy's mind. He scorned the provisions made in the name of charity for the city's dependents. In Soapy's opinion the Law was more benign than Philanthropy. There was an endless round of institutions, municipal and eleemosynary, on which he might set out and receive lodging and food accordant with the simple life. But to one of Soapy's proud spirit the gifts of charity are encumbered. If not in coin you must pay in humiliation of spirit for every benefit received at the hands of philanthropy. As Caesar had his Brutus, every bed of charity must have its toll of a bath, every loaf of bread its compensation of a private and personal inquisition. Wherefore it is better to be a guest of the law, which, though conducted by rules, does not meddle unduly with a gentleman's private affairs.

Soapy, having decided to go to the Island, at once set about accomplishing his desire. There were many easy ways of doing this. The pleasantest was to dine luxuriously at some expensive restaurant; and then, after declaring insolvency, be handed over quietly and without uproar to a policeman. An accommodating magistrate would do the rest.

Soapy left his bench and strolled out of the square and across the level sea of asphalt, where Broadway and Fifth Avenue flow together. Up Broadway he turned, and halted at a glittering café, where are gathered together nightly the choicest products of the grape, the silkworm, and the protoplasm.

Soapy had confidence in himself from the lowest button of his vest upward.

He was shaven, and his coat was decent and his neat black, ready-tied four-in-hand had been presented to him by a lady missionary on Thanksgiving Day. If he could reach a table in the restaurant unsuspected, success would be his. The portion of him that would show above the table would raise no doubt in the waiter's mind. A roasted mallard duck, thought Soapy, would be about the thing – with a bottle of Chablis, and then Camembert, a demi-tasse and a cigar. One dollar for the cigar would be enough. The total would not be so high as to call forth any supreme manifestation of revenge from the café management; and yet the meat would leave him filled and happy for the journey to his winter refuge.

But as Soapy set foot inside the restaurant door the head waiter's eye fell upon his frayed trousers and decadent shoes. Strong and ready hands turned him about and conveyed him in silence and haste to the sidewalk and averted the ignoble fate of the menaced mallard.

Soapy turned off Broadway. It seemed that his route to the coveted Island was not to be an epicurean one. Some other way of entering limbo must be thought of.

At a corner of Sixth Avenue electric lights and cunningly displayed wares behind plate-glass made a shop window conspicuous. Soapy took a cobblestone and dashed it through the glass. People came running around the corner, a policeman in the lead. Soapy stood still, with his hands in his pockets, and smiled at the sight of brass buttons.

'Where's the man that done that?' inquired the officer, excitedly.

'Don't you figure out that I might have had something to do with it?' said Soapy, not without sarcasm, but friendly, as one greets good fortune.

The policeman's mind refused to accept Soapy even as a clue. Men who smash windows do not remain to parley with the law's minions. They take to their heels. The policeman saw a man halfway down the block running to catch a car. With drawn club he joined in the pursuit. Soapy, with disgust in his heart, loafed along, twice unsuccessful.

On the opposite side of the street was a restaurant of no great pretensions. It catered to large appetites and modest purses. Its crockery and atmosphere were thick; its soup and napery thin. Into this place Soapy took his accusive shoes and telltale trousers without challenge. At a table he sat and consumed beefsteak, flapjacks, doughnuts and pie. And then to the waiter he betrayed the fact that the minutest coin and himself were strangers.

'Now, get busy and call a cop,' said Soapy. 'And don't keep a gentleman waiting.'

'No cop for youse,' said the waiter, with a voice like butter cakes and an eye like the cherry in a Manhattan cocktail. 'Hey, Con!'

Neatly upon his left ear on the callous pavement two waiters pitched Soapy. He arose joint by joint, as a carpenter's rule opens, and beat the dust from his clothes. Arrest seemed but a rosy dream. The Island seemed very far away. A policeman who stood before a drug store two doors away laughed and walked down the street.

Five blocks Soapy travelled before his courage permitted him to woo capture again. This time the opportunity presented what he fatuously termed to himself a 'cinch.' A young woman of a modest and pleasing guise was standing before a show window gazing with sprightly interest at its display of shaving mugs and inkstands, and two yards from the window a large policeman of severe demeanor leaned against a water plug.

It was Soapy's design to assume the rôle of the despicable and execrated 'masher.' The refined and elegant appearance of his victim and the contiguity of the conscientious cop encouraged him to believe that he would soon feel the pleasant official clutch upon his arm that would insure his winter quarters on the right little, tight little isle.

Soapy straightened the lady missionary's ready-made tie, dragged his shrinking cuffs into the open, set his hat at a killing cant and sidled toward the young woman. He made eyes at her, was taken with sudden coughs and 'hems,' smiled, smirked and went brazenly through the impudent and contemptible litany of the 'masher.' With half an eye Soapy saw that the policeman was watching him fixedly. The young woman moved away a few steps, and again bestowed her absorbed attention upon the shaving mugs. Soapy followed, boldly stepping to her side, raised his hat and said:

'Ah there, Bedelia! Don't you want to come and play in my yard?'

The policeman was still looking. The persecuted young woman had but to beckon a finger and Soapy would be practically en route for his insular haven. Already he imagined he could feel the cozy warmth of the station-house. The young woman faced him and, stretching out a hand, caught Soapy's coat sleeve.

'Sure, Mike,' she said, joyfully, 'if you'll blow me to a pail of suds. I'd have spoke to you sooner, but the cop was watching.'

With the young woman playing the clinging ivy to his oak Soapy walked past the policeman overcome with gloom. He seemed doomed to liberty.

At the next corner he shook off his companion and ran. He halted in the district where by night are found the lightest streets, hearts, vows and librettos. Women in furs and men in greatcoats moved gaily in the wintry air. A sudden fear seized Soapy that some dreadful enchantment had rendered him immune to arrest. The thought brought a little of panic upon it, and when he came upon another policeman lounging grandly in front of a transplendent theatre he caught at the immediate straw of 'disorderly conduct.'

On the sidewalk Soapy began to yell drunken gibberish at the top of his harsh voice. He danced, howled, raved, and otherwise disturbed the welkin.

The policeman twirled his club, turned his back to Soapy and remarked to a citizen.

' 'Tis one of them Yale lads celebratin' the goose egg they give to the Hartford College. Noisy; but no harm. We've instructions to lave them be.'

Disconsolate, Soapy ceased his unavailing racket. Would never a policeman lay hands on him? In his fancy the Island seemed an unattainable Arcadia. He buttoned his thin coat against the chilling wind.

In a cigar store he saw a well-dressed man lighting a cigar at a swinging light. His silk umbrella he had set by the door on entering. Soapy stepped inside, secured the umbrella and sauntered off with it slowly. The man at the cigar light followed hastily.

'My umbrella,' he said, sternly.

'Oh, is it?' sneered Soapy, adding insult to petit larceny. 'Well, why don't you call a policeman? I took it. Your umbrella! Why don't you call a cop? There stands one on the corner.'

The umbrella owner slowed his steps. Soapy did likewise, with a presentiment that luck would again run against him. The policeman looked at the two curiously.

'Of course,' said the umbrella man – 'that is – well, you know how these mistakes occur – I – if it's your umbrella I hope you'll excuse me – I picked it up this morning in a restaurant – If you recognize it as yours, why – I hope you'll—'

'Of course it's mine,' said Soapy, viciously.

The ex-umbrella man retreated. The policeman hurried to assist a tall blonde in an opera cloak across the street in front of a street car that was approaching two blocks away.

Soapy walked eastward through a street damaged by improvements. He hurled the umbrella wrathfully into an excavation. He muttered against the men who wear helmets and carry clubs. Because he wanted to fall into their clutches, they seemed to regard him as a king who could do no wrong.

At length Soapy reached one of the avenues to the east where the glitter and turmoil was but faint. He set his face down this toward Madison Square, for the homing instinct survives even when the home is a park bench.

But on an unusually quiet corner Soapy came to a standstill. Here was an old church, quaint and rambling and gabled. Through one violet-stained window a soft light glowed, where, no doubt, the organist loitered over the keys, making sure of his mastery of the coming Sabbath anthem. For there drifted out to Soapy's ears sweet music that caught and held him transfixed against the convolutions of the iron fence.

The moon was above, lustrous and serene; vehicles and pedestrians were few; sparrows twittered sleepily in the eaves – for a little while the scene might have been a country churchyard. And the anthem that the organist played cemented Soapy to the iron fence, for he had known it well in the days when his life contained such things as mothers and roses and ambitions and friends and immaculate thoughts and collars.

The conjunction of Soapy's receptive state of mind and the influences about the old church wrought a sudden and wonderful change in his soul. He viewed with swift horror the pit into which he had tumbled, the degraded days, unworthy desires, dead hopes, wrecked faculties and base motives that made up his existence.

And also in a moment his heart responded thrillingly to this novel mood. An instantaneous and strong impulse moved him to battle with his desperate fate. He would pull himself out of the mire; he would make a man of himself again; he would conquer the evil that had taken possession of him. There was time; he was comparatively young yet: he would resurrect his old eager ambitions and pursue them without faltering. Those solemn but sweet organ notes had set up a revolution in him. Tomorrow he would go into the roaring downtown district and find work. A fur importer had once offered him a place as driver. He would find him to-morrow and ask for the position. He would be somebody in the world. He would—

Soapy felt a hand laid on his arm. He looked quickly around into the broad face of a policeman.

'What are you doin' here?' asked the officer.

'Nothin',' said Soapy.

'Then come along,' said the policeman.

'Three months on the Island,' said the Magistrate in the Police Court the next morning.

AN ADJUSTMENT OF NATURE

IN AN ART EXHIBITION the other day I saw a painting that had been sold for $5,000. The painter was a young scrub out of the West named Kraft, who had a favorite food and a pet theory. His pabulum was an unquenchable belief in the Unerring Artistic Adjustment of Nature. His theory was fixed around corned-beef hash with poached egg. There was a story behind the picture, so I went home and let it drip out of a fountain-pen. The idea of Kraft – but that is not the beginning of the story.

Three years ago Kraft, Bill Judkins (a poet), and I took our meals at Cypher's on Eighth Avenue. I say 'took.' When we had money, Cypher got it 'off of' us, as he expressed it. We had no credit; we went in, called for food and ate it. We paid or we did not pay. We had confidence in Cypher's sullenness and smouldering ferocity. Deep down in his sunless soul he was either a prince, a fool, or an artist. He sat at a worm-eaten desk, covered with files of waiter's checks so old that I was sure the bottomest was one for clams that Henry Hudson had eaten and paid for. Cypher had the power, in common with Napoleon III and the goggle-eyed perch, of throwing a film over his eyes, rendering opaque the windows of his soul. Once when we left him unpaid, with egregious excuses, I looked back and saw him shaking with inaudible laughter behind his film. Now and then we paid up back scores.

But the chief thing at Cypher's was Milly. Milly was a waitress. She was a grand example of Kraft's theory of the artistic adjustment of nature. She belonged, largely, to waiting, as Minerva did to the art of scrapping, or Venus to the science of serious flirtation. Pedestalled and in bronze she might have stood with the noblest of her heroic sisters as 'Liver-and-Bacon Enlivening the World.' She belonged to Cypher's. You expected to see her colossal figure loom through that reeking blue cloud of smoke from frying fat just as you expect the Palisades to appear through a drifting Hudson River fog. There amid the steam of vegetables and the vapors of acres of 'ham and,' the crash of crockery, the clatter of steel, the screaming of 'short orders,' the cries of the hungering and all the horrid tumult of feeding man, surrounded by swarms of the buzzing winged beasts bequeathed us by Pharaoh, Milly steered her magnificent way like some great liner cleaving among the canoes of howling savages.

Our Goddess of Grub was built on lines so majestic that they could be followed only with awe. Her sleeves were always rolled above her elbows. She could have taken us three musketeers in her two hands and dropped us out of the window. She had seen fewer years than any of us, but she was of such superb Evehood and simplicity that she mothered us from the beginning. Cypher's store of eatables she poured out upon us with royal indifference to price and quantity, as from a cornucopia that knew no exhaustion. Her voice rang like a great silver bell; her smile was many-toothed and frequent; she seemed like a yellow sunrise on mountain tops. I never saw her but I thought of the Yosemite. And yet, somehow, I could never think of her as existing outside of Cypher's. There nature had placed her and she had taken root and grown mightily. She seemed happy, and took her few poor dollars on Saturday nights with the flushed pleasure of a child that receives an unexpected donation.

It was Kraft who first voiced the fear that each of us must have held latently. It came up apropos, of course, of certain questions of art at which we were hammering. One of us compared the harmony existing between a Haydn symphony and pistache ice cream to the exquisite congruity between Milly and Cypher's.

'There is a certain fate hanging over Milly,' said Kraft, 'and if it overtakes her she is lost to Cypher's and to us.'

'She will grow fat?' asked Judkins, fearsomely.

'She will go to night school and become refined?' I ventured, anxiously.

'It is this,' said Kraft, punctuating in a puddle of spilled coffee with a stiff forefinger. 'Caesar had his Brutus – the cotton has its bollworm, the chorus girl has her Pittsburger, the summer boarder has his poison ivy, the hero has his Carnegie medal, art has its Morgan, the rose has its—'

'Speak,' I interrupted, much perturbed. 'You do not think that Milly will begin to lace?'

'One day,' concluded Kraft, solemnly, 'there will come to Cypher's for a plate of beans a millionaire lumberman from Wisconsin, and he will marry Milly.'

'Never!' exclaimed Judkins and I, in horror.

'A lumberman,' repeated Kraft, hoarsely.

'And a millionaire lumberman!' I sighed, despairingly.

'From Wisconsin!' groaned Judkins.

We agreed that the awful fate seemed to menace her. Few things were less improbable. Milly, like some vast virgin stretch of pine woods, was made to catch the lumberman's eye. And well we knew the habits of the Badgers, once fortune smiled upon them. Straight to New York they hie, and lay their goods at the feet of the girl who serves them beans in a beanery. Why, the alphabet itself connives. The Sunday Newspaper's headliner's work is cut for him.

'Winsome Waitress Wins Wealthy Wisconsin Woodsman.'

For a while we felt that Milly was on the verge of being lost to us.

It was our love of the Unerring Artistic Adjustment of Nature that inspired us. We could not give her over to a lumberman, doubly accursed by wealth and provincialism. We shuddered to think of Milly, with her voice modulated and her elbows covered, pouring tea in the marble teepee of a tree murderer. No! In Cypher's she belonged – in the bacon smoke, the cabbage perfume, the grand, Wagnerian chorus of hurled ironstone china and rattling casters.

Our fears must have been prophetic, for on that same evening the wildwood discharged upon us Milly's preordained confiscator – our fee to adjustment and order. But Alaska and not Wisconsin bore the burden of the visitation.

We were at our supper of beef stew and dried apples when he trotted in as if on the heels of a dog team, and made one of the mess at our table. With the freedom of the camps he assaulted our ears and claimed the fellowship of men lost in the wilds of a hash house. We embraced him as a specimen, and in three minutes we had all but died for one another as friends.

He was rugged and bearded and wind-dried. He had just come off the 'trail,' he said, at one of the North River ferries. I fancied I could see the snow dust of Chilcoot yet powdering his shoulders. And then he strewed the table with the nuggets, stuffed ptarmigans, bead work and seal pelts of the returned Klondiker, and began to prate to us of his millions.

'Bank drafts for two millions,' was his summing up, 'and a thousand a day piling up from my claims. And now I want some beef stew and canned peaches. I never got off the train since I mushed out of Seattle, and I'm hungry. The stuff the niggers feed you on pullmans don't count. You gentlemen order what you want.'

And then Milly loomed up with a thousand dishes on her bare arm – loomed up big and white and pink and awful as Mount Saint Elias – with a smile like day breaking in a gulch. And the Klondiker threw down his pelts and nuggets as dross, and let his jaw fall halfway, and stared at her. You could almost see the diamond tiaras on Milly's brow and the hand-embroidered silk Paris gowns that he meant to buy for her.

At last the bollworm had attacked the cotton – the poison ivy was reaching out its tendrils to entwine the summer boarder – the millionaire lumberman, thinly disguised as the Alaskan miner, was about to engulf our Milly and upset Nature's adjustment.

Kraft was the first to act. He leaped up and pounded the Klondiker's back. 'Come out and drink,' he shouted. 'Drink first and eat afterward.' Judkins seized one arm and I the other. Gaily, roaringly, irresistibly, in jolly-good-fellow style, we dragged him from the restaurant to a café, stuffing his pockets with his embalmed birds and indigestible nuggets.

There he rumbled a roughly good-humored protest. 'That's the girl for my money,' he declared. 'She can eat out of my skillet the rest of her life. Why, I never see such a fine girl. I'm going back there and ask her to marry me. I guess she won't want to sling hash any more when she sees the pile of dust I've got.'

'You'll take another whiskey and milk now,' Kraft persuaded, with Satan's smile. 'I thought you up-country fellows were better sports.'

Kraft spent his puny store of coin at the bar and then gave Judkins and me such an appealing look that we went down to the last dime we had in toasting our guest.

Then, when our ammunition was gone and the Klondiker, still somewhat sober, began to babble again of Milly, Kraft whispered into his ear such a polite, barked insult relating to people who were miserly with their funds, that the miner crashed down handful after handful of silver and notes, calling for all the fluids in the world to drown the imputation.

Thus the work was accomplished. With his own guns we drove him from the field. And then we had him carted to a distant small hotel and put to bed with his nuggets and baby seal-skins stuffed around him.

'He will never find Cypher's again,' said Kraft. 'He will propose to the first white apron he sees in a dairy restaurant to-morrow. And Milly – I mean the Natural Adjustment – is saved!'

And back to Cypher's went we three, and finding customers scarce, we joined hands and did an Indian dance with Milly in the centre.

This, I say, happened three years ago. And about that time a little luck descended upon us three, and we were enabled to buy costlier and less wholesome food than Cypher's. Our paths separated, and I saw Kraft no more and Judkins seldom.

But, as I said, I saw a painting the other day that was sold for $5,000. The title was 'Boadicea,' and the figures seemed to fill all out-of-doors. But of all the picture's admirers who stood before it, I believe I was the only one who longed for Boadicea to stalk from her frame bringing me corned-beef hash with poached egg.

I hurried away to see Kraft. His satanic eyes were the same, his hair was worse tangled, but his clothes had been made by a tailor.

'I didn't know,' I said to him.

'We've bought a cottage in the Bronx with the money,' said he. 'Any evening at 7.'

'Then,' said I, 'when you led us against the lumberman – the – Klondiker – it wasn't altogether on account of the Unerring Artistic Adjustment of Nature?'

'Well, not altogether,' said Kraft, with a grin.

MEMOIRS OF A YELLOW DOG

I DON'T SUPPOSE IT WILL KNOCK any of you people off your perch to read a contribution from an animal. Mr. Kipling and a good many others have demonstrated the fact that animals can express themselves in remunerative English, and no magazine goes to press nowadays without an animal story in it, except the old-style monthlies that are still running pictures of Bryan and the Mont Pelée horror.

But you needn't look for any stuck-up literature in my piece, such as Bearoo, the bear, and Snakoo, the snake, and Tammanoo, the tiger, talk in the jungle books. A yellow dog that's spent most of his life in a cheap New York flat, sleeping in a corner on an old sateen underskirt (the one she spilled port wine on at the Lady Longshoremen's banquet), mustn't be expected to perform any tricks with the art of speech.

I was born a yellow pup; date, locality, pedigree and weight unknown. The first thing I can recollect, an old woman had me in a basket at Broadway and Twenty-third trying to sell me to a fat lady. Old Mother Hubbard was boosting me to beat the band as a genuine Pomeranian-Hambletonian-Red-Irish-Cochin-China-Stoke-Pogis fox terrier. The fat lady chased a V around among the samples of gros grain flannelette in her shopping bag till she cornered it, and gave up. From that moment I was a pet – a mamma's own wootsey quidlums. Say, gentle reader, did you ever have a 200-pound woman breathing a flavor of Camembert cheese and Peau d'Espagne pick you up and wallop her nose all over you, remarking all the time in an Emma Eames tone of voice: 'Oh, oo's um oodlum, doodlum, woodlum, toodlum, bitsy-witsy skoodlums?'

From pedigreed yellow pup I grew up to be an anonymous yellow cur looking like a cross between an Angora cat and a box of lemons. But my mistress never tumbled. She thought that the two primeval pups that Noah chased into the ark were but a collateral branch of my ancestors. It took two policemen to keep her from entering me at the Madison Square Garden for the Siberian bloodhound prize.

I'll tell you about that flat. The house was the ordinary thing in New York, paved with Parian marble in the entrance hall and cobblestones above the first floor. Our flat was three – well, not flights – climbs up. My mistress rented it unfurnished, and put in the regular things – 1903 antique upholstered parlor set, oil chromo of geishas in a Harlem tea house, rubber plant and husband.

By Sirius! there was a biped I felt sorry for. He was a little man with sandy hair and whiskers a good deal like mine. Henpecked? – well, toucans and flamingoes and pelicans all had their bills in him. He wiped the dishes and listened to my mistress tell about the cheap, ragged things the lady with the squirrel-skin coat on the second floor hung out on her line to dry. And every evening while she was getting supper she made him take me out on the end of a string for a walk.

If men knew how women pass the time when they are alone they'd never marry. Laura Lean Jibbey, peanut brittle, a little almond cream on the neck muscles, dishes unwashed, half an hour's talk with the iceman, reading a package of old letters, a couple of pickles and two bottles of malt extract, one hour peeking through a hole in the window shade into the flat across the air-shaft – that's about all there is to it. Twenty minutes before time for him to come home from work she straightens up the house, fixes her rat so it won't show, and gets out a lot of sewing for a ten-minute bluff.

I led a dog's life in that flat. 'Most all day I lay there in my corner watching that fat woman kill time. I slept sometimes and had pipe dreams about being out chasing cats into basements and growling at old ladies with black mittens, as a dog was intended to do. Then she would pounce upon me with a lot of that drivelling poodle palaver and kiss me on the nose – but what could I do? A dog can't chew cloves.

I began to feel sorry for Hubby, dog my cats if I didn't. We looked so much alike that people noticed it when we went out; so we shook the streets that Morgan's cab drives down, and took to climbing the piles of last December's snow on the streets where cheap people live.

One evening when we were thus promenading, and I was trying to look like a prize St. Bernard, and the old man was trying to look like he wouldn't have murdered the first organ-grinder he heard play Mendelssohn's wedding-march, I looked up at him and said, in my way:

'What are you looking so sour about, you oakum trimmed lobster? She don't kiss you. You don't have to sit on her lap and listen to talk that would make the book of a musical comedy sound like the maxims of Epictetus. You ought to be thankful you're not a dog. Brace up, Benedick, and bid the blues begone.'

The matrimonial mishap looked down at me with almost canine intelligence in his face.

'Why, doggie,' says he, 'good doggie. You almost look like you could speak. What is it, doggie – cats.'

Cats! Could speak!

But, of course, he couldn't understand. Humans were denied the speech of animals. The only common ground of communication upon which dogs and men can get together is in fiction.

In the flat across the hall from us lived a lady with a black-and-tan terrier. Her husband strung it and took it out every evening, but he always came home cheerful and whistling. One day I touched noses with the black-and-tan in the hall, and I struck him for an elucidation.

'See here, Wiggle-and-Skip,' I says, 'you know that it ain't the nature of a real man to play dry nurse to a dog in public. I never saw one leashed to a bow-wow yet that didn't look like he'd like to lick every other man that looked at him. But your boss comes in every day as perky and set up as an amateur prestidigitator doing the egg trick. How does he do it? Don't tell me he likes it.'

'Him?' says the black-and-tan. 'Why, he uses Nature's Own Remedy. He gets spifflicated. At first when we go out he's as shy as the man on the steamer who would rather play pedro when they make 'em all jackpots. By the time we've been in eight saloons he don't care whether the thing on the end of his line is a dog or a catfish. I've lost two inches of my tail trying to sidestep those swinging doors.'

The pointer I got from that terrier – Vaudeville please copy – set me to thinking.

One evening about 6 o'clock my mistress ordered him to get busy and do the ozone act for Lovey. I have concealed it until now, but that is what she called me. The black-and-tan was called 'Tweetness.' I consider that I have the bulge on him as far as you could chase a rabbit. Still 'Lovey' is something of a nomenclatural tin can on the tail of one's self-respect.

At a quiet place on a safe street I tightened the line of my custodian in front of an attractive, refined saloon. I made a dead-ahead scramble for the doors, whining like a dog in the press despatches that lets the family know that little Alice is bogged while gathering lilies in the brook.

'Why, darn my eyes,' says the old man, with a grin; 'darn my eyes if the saffron-colored son of a seltzer lemonade ain't asking me in to take a drink. Lemme see – how long's it been since I saved shoe leather by keeping one foot on the foot-rest? I believe I'll—'

I knew I had him. Hot Scotches he took, sitting at a table. For an hour he kept the Campbells coming. I sat by his side rapping for the waiter with my tail, and eating free lunch such as mamma in her flat never equalled with her homemade truck bought at a delicatessen store eight minutes before papa comes home.

When the products of Scotland were all exhausted except the rye bread the old man unwound me from the table leg and played me outside like a fisherman plays a salmon. Out there he took off my collar and threw it into the street.

'Poor doggie,' says he; 'good doggie. She shan't kiss you any more. 'S a darned shame. Good doggie, go away and get run over by a street car and be happy.'

I refused to leave. I leaped and frisked around the old man's legs happy as a pug on a rug.

'You old flea-headed woodchuck-chaser,' I said to him – 'you moon-baying, rabbit-pointing, egg-stealing old beagle, can't you see that I don't want to leave you? Can't you see that we're both Pups in the Wood and the missis is the cruel uncle after you with the dish towel and me with the flea liniment and a pink bow to tie on my tail. Why not cut that all out and be pards forever more?'

Maybe you'll say he didn't understand – maybe he didn't. But he kind of got a grip on the Hot Scotches, and stood still for a minute, thinking.

'Doggie,' says he, finally, 'we don't live more than a dozen lives on this earth, and very few of us live to be more than 300. If I ever see that flat any more I'm a flat, and if you do you're flatter; and that's no flattery. I'm offering 60 to 1 that Westward Ho wins out by the length of a dachshund.'

There was no string, but I frolicked along with my master to the

Twenty-third Street ferry. And the cats on the route saw reason to give thanks that prehensile claws had been given to them.

On the Jersey side my master said to a stranger who stood eating a currant bun:

'Me and my doggie, we are bound for the Rocky Mountains.'

But what pleased me most was when my old man pulled both of my ears until I howled, and said:

'You common, monkey-headed, rat-tailed, sulphur-colored son of a door mat, do you know what I'm going to call you?'

I thought of 'Lovey,' and I whined dolefully.

'I'm going to call you "Pete," ' says my master; and if I'd had five tails I couldn't have done enough wagging to do justice to the occasion.

THE LOVE-PHILTRE OF IKEY SCHOENSTEIN

THE BLUE LIGHT DRUG STORE is downtown, between the Bowery and First Avenue, where the distance between the two streets is the shortest. The Blue Light does not consider that pharmacy is a thing of bric-à-brac, scent and ice-cream soda. If you ask it for pain-killer it will not give you a bonbon.

The Blue Light scorns the labor-saving arts of modern pharmacy. It macerates its opium and percolates its own laudanum and paregoric. To this day pills are made behind its tall prescription desk – pills rolled out on its own pill-tile, divided with a spatula, rolled with the finger and thumb, dusted with calcined magnesia and delivered in little round pasteboard pill-boxes. The store is on a corner about which coveys of ragged-plumed, hilarious children play and become candidates for the cough drops and soothing syrups that wait for them inside.

Ikey Schoenstein was the night clerk of the Blue Light and the friend of his customers. Thus it is on the East Side, where the heart of pharmacy is not glacé. There, as it should be, the druggist is a counsellor, a confessor, an adviser, an able and willing missionary and mentor whose learning is respected, whose occult wisdom is venerated and whose medicine is often poured, untasted, into the gutter. Therefore Ikey's corniform, bespectacled nose and narrow, knowledge-bowed figure was well known in the vicinity of the Blue Light, and his advice and notice were much desired.

Ikey roomed and breakfasted at Mrs. Riddle's two squares away. Mrs. Riddle had a daughter named Rosy. The circumlocution has been in vain – you must have guessed it – Ikey adored Rosy. She tinctured all his thoughts; she was the compound extract of all that was chemically pure and officinal – the dispensatory contained nothing equal to her. But Ikey was timid, and his hopes remained insoluble in the menstruum of his backwardness and fears. Behind his counter he was a superior being, calmly conscious of special knowledge and worth; outside he was a weak-kneed, purblind, motorman-cursed rambler, with ill-fitting clothes stained with chemicals and smelling of socotrine aloes and valerianate of ammonia.

The fly in Ikey's ointment (thrice welcome, pat trope!) was Chunk McGowan.

Mr. McGowan was also striving to catch the bright smiles tossed about by Rosy. But he was no out-fielder as Ikey was; he picked them off the bat. At the same time he was Ikey's friend and customer, and often dropped in at the Blue Light Drug Store to have a bruise painted with iodine or get a cut rubber-plastered after a pleasant evening spent along the bowery.

One afternoon McGowan drifted in in his silent, easy way, and sat, comely, smooth-faced, hard, indomitable, good-natured, upon a stool.

'Ikey,' said he, when his friend had fetched his mortar and sat opposite, grinding gum benzoin to a powder, 'get busy with your ear. It's drugs for me if you've got the line I need.'

Ikey scanned the countenance of Mr. McGowan for the usual evidence of conflict, but found none.

'Take your coat off,' he ordered. 'I guess already that you have been stuck in the ribs with a knife. I have many times told you those Dagoes would do you up.'

Mr. McGowan smiled. 'Not them,' he said. 'Not any Dagoes. But you've located the diagnosis all right enough – it's under my coat, near the ribs. Say! Ikey – Rosy and me are goin' to run away and get married tonight.'

Ikey's left forefinger was doubled over the edge of the mortar, holding it steady. He gave it a wild rap with the pestle, but felt it not. Meanwhile Mr. McGowan's smile faded to a look of perplexed gloom.

'That is,' he continued, 'if she keeps in the notion until the time comes. We've been layin' pipes for the getaway for two weeks. One day she says she will; the same evenin' she says nixy. We've agreed on to-night, and Rosy's stuck to the affirmative this time for two whole days. But it's five hours yet till the time, and I'm afraid she'll stand me up when it comes to the scratch.'

'You said you wanted drugs,' remarked Ikey.

Mr. McGowan looked ill at ease and harassed – a condition opposed to his usual line of demeanor. He made a patent-medicine almanac into a roll and fitted it with unprofitable carefulness about his finger.

'I wouldn't have this double handicap make a false start to-night for a million,' he said. 'I've got a little flat up in Harlem all ready, with chrysanthemums on the table and a kettle ready to boil. And I've engaged a pulpit pounder to be ready at his house for us at 9.30. It's got to come off. And if Rosy don't change her mind again!' – Mr. McGowan ceased, a prey to his doubts.

'I don't see then yet,' said Ikey, shortly, 'what makes it that you talk of drugs, or what I can be doing about it.'

'Old man Riddle don't like me a little bit,' went on the uneasy suitor, bent upon marshalling his arguments. 'For a week he hasn't let Rosy step outside the door with me. If it wasn't for losin' a boarder they'd have bounced me long ago. I'm makin' $20 a week and she'll never regret flyin' the coop with Chunk McGowan.'

'You will excuse me, Chunk,' said Ikey. 'I must make a prescription that is to be called for soon.'

'Say,' said McGowan, looking up suddenly, 'say, Ikey, ain't there a drug of some kind – some kind of powders that'll make a girl like you better if you give 'em to her?'

Ikey's lip beneath his nose curled with the scorn of superior enlightenment; but before he could answer, McGowan continued:

'Tim Lacy told me he got some once from a croaker uptown and fed 'em to his girl in soda water. From the very first dose he was ace-high and everybody else looked like thirty cents to her. They was married in less than two weeks.'

Strong and simple was Chunk McGowan. A better reader of men than Ikey was could have seen that his tough frame was strung upon fine wires. Like a good general who was about to invade the enemy's territory he was seeking to guard every point against possible failure.

'I thought,' went on Chunk, hopefully, 'that if I had one of them powders to give Rosy when I see her at supper to-night it might brace her up and keep her from reneging on the proposition to skip. I guess she don't need a mule team to drag her away, but women are better at coaching than they are at running bases. If the stuff'll work just for a couple of hours it'll do the trick.'

'When is this foolishness of running away to be happening?' asked Ikey.

'Nine o'clock,' said Mr. McGowan. 'Supper's at seven. At eight Rosy goes to bed with a headache, at nine old Parvenzano lets me through to his backyard, where there's a board off Riddle's fence, next door. I go under her window and help her down the fire-escape. We've got to make it early on the preacher's account. It's all dead easy if Rosy don't balk when the flag drops. Can you fix me one of them powders, Ikey?'

Ikey Schoenstein rubbed his nose slowly.

'Chunk,' said he, 'it is of drugs of that nature that pharmaceutists must have much carefulness. To you alone of my acquaintance would I intrust a powder like that. But for you I shall make it, and you shall see how it makes Rosy to think of you.'

Ikey went behind the prescription desk. There he crushed to a powder two soluble tablets, each containing a quarter of a grain of morphia. To them he added a little sugar of milk to increase the bulk, and folded the mixture neatly in a white paper. Taken by an adult this powder would insure several hours of heavy slumber without danger to the sleeper. This he handed to Chunk McGowan, telling him to administer it in a liquid if possible, and received the hearty thanks of the backyard Lochinvar.

The subtlety of Ikey's action becomes apparent upon recital of his subsequent move. He sent a messenger for Mr. Riddle and disclosed the plans of Mr. McGowan for eloping with Rosy. Mr. Riddle was a stout man, brick-dusty of complexion and sudden in action.

'Much obliged,' he said, briefly, to Ikey. 'The lazy Irish loafer! My own room's just above Rosy's. I'll just go up there myself after supper and load the shot-gun and wait. If he comes in my backyard he'll go away in a ambulance instead of a bridal chaise.'

With Rosy held in the clutches of Morpheus for a many-hours deep slumber, and the blood-thirsty parent waiting, armed and forewarned, Ikey felt that his rival was close, indeed, upon discomfiture.

All night in the Blue Light Drug Store he waited at his duties for chance news of the tragedy, but none came.

At eight o'clock in the morning the day clerk arrived and Ikey started hurriedly for Mrs. Riddle's to learn the outcome. And, lo! as he stepped out of the store who but Chunk McGowan sprang from a passing street car and grasped his hand – Chunk McGowan with a victor's smile and flushed with joy.

'Pulled it off,' said Chunk with Elysium in his grin. 'Rosy hit the fire-escape on time to a second, and we was under the wire at the Reverend's at

9.30¼. She's up at the flat – she cooked eggs this mornin' in a blue kimono – Lord! how lucky I am! You must pace up some day, Ikey, and feed with us. I've got a job down near the bridge, and that's where I'm heading for now.'

'The – the – powder?' stammered Ikey.

'Oh, that stuff you gave me!' said Chunk, broadening his grin; 'well, it was this way. I sat down at the supper table last night at Riddle's, and I looked at Rosy, and I says to myself, "Chunk, if you get the girl get her on the square – don't try any hocus-pocus with a thoroughbred like her." And I keeps the paper you give me in my pocket. And then my lamps fall on another party present, who, I says to myself, is failin' in a proper affection toward his comin' son-in-law, so I watches my chance and dumps that powder in old man Riddle's coffee – see?'

MAMMON AND THE ARCHER

OLD ANTHONY ROCKWALL, retired manufacturer and proprietor of Rockwall's Eureka Soap, looked out the library window of his Fifth Avenue mansion and grinned. His neighbor to the right – the aristocratic clubman, G. Van Schuylight Suffolk-Jones – came out to his waiting motor-car, wrinkling a contumelious nostril, as usual, at the Italian renaissance sculpture of the soap palace's front elevation.

'Stuck-up old statuette of nothing doing!' commented the ex-Soap King. 'The Eden Musée'll get that old frozen Nesselrode yet if he don't watch out. I'll have this house painted red, white, and blue next summer and see if that'll make his Dutch nose turn up any higher.'

And then Anthony Rockwall, who never cared for bells, went to the door of his library and shouted 'Mike!' in the same voice that had once chipped off pieces of the welkin on the Kansas prairies.

'Tell my son,' said Anthony to the answering menial, 'to come in here before he leaves the house.'

When young Rockwall entered the library the old man laid aside his newspaper, looked at him with a kindly grimness on his big, smooth, ruddy countenance, rumpled his mop of white hair with one hand and rattled the keys in his pocket with the other.

'Richard,' said Anthony Rockwall, 'what do you pay for the soap that you use?'

Richard, only six months home from college, was startled a little. He had not yet taken the measure of this sire of his, who was as full of unexpectedness as a girl at her first party.

'Six dollars a dozen, I think, dad.'

'And your clothes?'

'I suppose about sixty dollars, as a rule.'

'You're a gentleman,' said Anthony, decidedly. 'I've heard of these young bloods spending $24 a dozen for soap, and going over the hundred mark for clothes. You've got as much money to waste as any of 'em, and yet you stick to what's decent and moderate. Now I use the old Eureka – not only for sentiment, but it's the purest soap made. Whenever you pay more than 10 cents a cake for soap you buy bad perfumes and labels. But 50 cents is doing very well for a young man in your generation, position and condition. As I said, you're a gentleman. They say it takes three generations to make one. They're off. Money'll do it as slick as soap grease. It's made you one. By hokey! it's almost made one of me. I'm nearly as impolite and disagreeable and ill-mannered as these two old knickerbocker gents on each side of me that can't sleep of nights because I bought in between 'em.'

'There are some things that money can't accomplish,' remarked young Rockwall, rather gloomily.

'Now, don't say that,' said old Anthony, shocked. 'I bet my money on money every time. I've been through the encyclopaedia down to Y looking for something you can't buy with it; and I expect to have to take up the appendix next week. I'm for money against the field. Tell me something money won't buy.'

'For one thing,' answered Richard, rankling a little, 'it won't buy one into the exclusive circles of society.'

'Oho! won't it?' thundered the champion of the root of evil. 'You tell me where your exclusive circles would be if the first Astor hadn't had the money to pay for his steerage passage over?'

Richard sighed.

'And that's what I was coming to,' said the old man, less boisterously. 'That's why I asked you to come in. There's something going wrong with you, boy. I've been noticing it for two weeks. Out with it. I guess I could lay my hands on eleven millions within twenty-four hours, besides the real estate. If it's your liver, there's the *Rambler* down in the bay, coaled, and ready to steam down to the Bahamas in two days.'

'Not a bad guess, dad; you haven't missed it far.'

'Ah,' said Anthony, keenly; 'what's her name?'

Richard began to walk up and down the library floor. There was enough comradeship and sympathy in this crude old father of his to draw his confidence.

'Why don't you ask her?' demanded old Anthony. 'She'll jump at you. You've got the money and the looks, and you're a decent boy. Your hands are clean. You've got no Eureka soap on 'em. You've been to college, but she'll overlook that.'

'I haven't had a chance,' said Richard.

'Make one,' said Anthony. 'Take her for a walk in the park, or a straw ride, or walk home with her from church. Chance! Pshaw!'

'You don't know the social mill, dad. She's part of the stream that turns it. Every hour and minute of her time is arranged for days in advance. I must have that girl, dad, or this town is a blackjack swamp forevermore. And I can't write it – I can't do that.'

'Tut!' said the old man. 'Do you mean to tell me that with all the money I've got you can't get an hour or two of a girl's time for yourself?'

'I've put it off too late. She's going to sail for Europe at noon day after to-morrow for a two years' stay. I'm to see her alone to-morrow evening for a few minutes. She's at Larchmont now at her aunt's. I can't go there. But I'm allowed to meet her with a cab at the Grand Central Station to-morrow evening at the 8.30 train. We drive down Broadway to Wallack's at a gallop, where her mother and a box party will be waiting for us in the lobby. Do you think she would listen to a declaration from me during that six or eight minutes under those circumstances. No. And what chance would I have in the theatre or afterward? None. No, dad, this is one tangle that your money can't unravel. We can't buy one minute of time with cash; if we could, rich people would live longer. There's no hope of getting a talk with Miss Lantry before she sails.'

'All right, Richard, my boy,' said old Anthony, cheerfully. 'You may run along down to your club now. I'm glad it ain't your liver. But don't forget to burn a few punk sticks in the joss house to the great god Mazuma from time to time. You say money won't buy time? Well, of course, you can't order eternity wrapped up and delivered at your residence for a price, but I've seen Father Time get pretty bad stone bruises on his heels when he walked through the gold diggings.'

That night came Aunt Ellen, gentle, sentimental, wrinkled, sighing, oppressed by wealth, in to Brother Anthony at his evening paper, and began discourse on the subject of lovers' woes.

'He told me all about it,' said Brother Anthony, yawning. 'I told him my bank account was at his service. And then he began to knock money. Said money couldn't help. Said the rules of society couldn't be bucked for a yard by a team of ten-millionaires.'

'Oh, Anthony,' sighed Aunt Ellen, 'I wish you would not think so much of money. Wealth is nothing where a true affection is concerned. Love is all-powerful. If he only had spoken earlier! She could not have refused our Richard. But now I fear it is too late. He will have no opportunity to address her. All your gold cannot bring happiness to your son.'

At eight o'clock the next evening Aunt Ellen took a quaint old gold ring from a moth-eaten case and gave it to Richard.

'Wear it to-night, nephew,' she begged. 'Your mother gave it to me. Good luck in love she said it brought. She asked me to give it to you when you had found the one you loved.'

Young Rockwall took the ring reverently and tried it on his smallest finger. It slipped as far as the second joint and stopped. He took it off and stuffed it into his vest pocket, after the manner of man. And then he 'phoned for his cab.

At the station he captured Miss Lantry out of the gabbing mob at eight thirty-two.

'We mustn't keep mamma and the others waiting,' said she.

'To Wallack's Theatre as fast as you can drive!' said Richard, loyally.

They whirled up Forty-second to Broadway, and then down the white-starred lane that leads from the soft meadows of sunset to the rocky hills of morning.

At Thirty-fourth Street young Richard quickly thrust up the trap and ordered the cabman to stop.

'I've dropped a ring,' he apologized, as he climbed out. 'It was my mother's, and I'd hate to lose it. I won't detain you a minute – I saw where it fell.'

In less than a minute he was back in the cab with the ring.

But within that minute a crosstown car had stopped directly in front of the cab. The cab-man tried to pass to the left, but a heavy express wagon cut him off. He tried the right and had to back away from a furniture van that had no business to be there. He tried to back out, but dropped his reins and swore dutifully. He was blockaded in a tangled mess of vehicles and horses.

One of those street blockades had occurred that sometimes tie up commerce and movement quite suddenly in the big city.

'Why don't you drive on?' said Miss Lantry impatiently. 'We'll be late.'

Richard stood up in the cab and looked around. He saw a congested flood of wagons, trucks, cabs, vans and street cars filling the vast space where Broadway, Sixth Avenue, and Thirty-fourth Street cross one another as a twenty-six inch maiden fills her twenty-two inch girdle. And still from all the cross streets they were hurrying and rattling toward the converging point at full speed, and hurling themselves into the straggling mass, locking wheels and adding their drivers' imprecations to the clamor. The entire traffic of Manhattan seemed to have jammed itself around them. The oldest New Yorker among the thousands of spectators that lined the sidewalks had not witnessed a street blockade of the proportions of this one.

'I'm very sorry,' said Richard, as he resumed his seat, 'but it looks as if we are stuck. They won't get this jumble loosened up in an hour. It was my fault. If I hadn't dropped the ring we—'

'Let me see the ring,' said Miss Lantry. 'Now that it can't be helped, I don't care. I think theatres are stupid, anyway.'

At 11 o'clock that night somebody tapped lightly on Anthony Rockwall's door.

'Come in,' shouted Anthony, who was in a red dressing-gown, reading a book of piratical adventures.

Somebody was Aunt Ellen, looking like a gray-haired angel that had been left on earth by mistake.

'They're engaged, Anthony,' she said, softly. 'She has promised to marry our Richard. On their way to the theatre there was a street blockade, and it was two hours before their cab could get out of it.

'And oh, Brother Anthony, don't ever boast of the power of money again. A little emblem of true love – a little ring that symbolized unending and unmercenary affection – was the cause of our Richard finding his happiness. He dropped it in the street, and got out to recover it. And before they could continue the blockade occurred. He spoke to his love and won her there while the cab was hemmed in. Money is dross compared with true love, Anthony.'

'All right,' said old Anthony. 'I'm glad the boy has got what he wanted. I told him I wouldn't spare any expense in the matter if—'

'But, Brother Anthony, what good could your money have done?'

'Sister,' said Anthony Rockwall. 'I've got my pirate in a devil of a scrape. His ship has just been scuttled, and he's too good a judge of the value of money to let drown. I wish you would let me go on with this chapter.'

The story should end here. I wish it would as heartily as you who read it wish it did. But we must go to the bottom of the well for truth.

The next day a person with red hands and a blue polka-dot necktie, who called himself Kelly, called at Anthony Rockwall's house, and was at once received in the library.

'Well,' said Anthony, reaching for his check-book, 'it was a good bilin' of soap. Let's see – you had $5,000 in cash.'

'I paid out $300 more of my own,' said Kelly. 'I had to go a little above the estimate. I got the express wagons and cabs mostly for $5; but the trucks and two-horse teams mostly raised me to $10. The motormen wanted $10, and some of the loaded teams $20. The cops struck me hardest – $50 I paid two, and the rest $20 and $25. But didn't it work beautiful, Mr. Rockwall? I'm glad William A. Brady wasn't onto that little outdoor vehicle mob scene. I wouldn't want William to break his heart with jealousy. And never a rehearsal, either! The boys was on time to the fraction of a second. It was two hours before a snake could get below Greeley's statue.'

'Thirteen hundred – there you are, Kelly,' said Anthony, tearing off a check. 'Your thousand, and the $300 you were out. You don't despise money, do you, Kelly?'

'Me?' said Kelly. 'I can lick the man that invented poverty.'

Anthony called Kelly when he was at the door.

'You didn't notice,' said he, 'anywhere in the tie-up, a kind of a fat boy without any clothes on shooting arrows around with a bow, did you?'

'Why, no,' said Kelly, mystified. 'I didn't. If he was like you say, maybe the cops pinched him before I got there.'

'I thought the little rascal wouldn't be on hand,' chuckled Anthony. 'Good-by, Kelly.'

SPRINGTIME À LA CARTE

IT WAS A DAY IN MARCH.

Never, never begin a story this way when you write one. No opening could possibly be worse. It is unimaginative, flat dry, and likely to consist of mere wind. But in this instance it is allowable. For the following paragraph, which should have inaugurated the narrative, is too wildly extravagant and preposterous to be flaunted in the face of the reader without preparation.

Sarah was crying over her bill of fare.

Think of a New York girl shedding tears on the menu card!

To account for this you will be allowed to guess that the lobsters were all out, or that she had sworn ice-cream off during Lent, or that she had ordered onions, or that she had just come from a Hackett matinée. And then, all these theories being wrong, you will please let the story proceed.

The gentleman who announced that the world was an oyster which he with his sword would open made a larger hit than he deserved. It is not difficult to open an oyster with a sword. But did you ever notice any one try to open the terrestrial bivalve with a typewriter? Like to wait for a dozen raw opened that way?

Sarah had managed to pry apart the shells with her unhandy weapon far enough to nibble a wee bit at the cold and clammy world within. She knew no more shorthand than if she had been a graduate in stenography just let slip upon the world by a business college. So, not being able to stenog, she could not enter that bright galaxy of office talent. She was a free-lance typewriter and canvassed for odd jobs of copying.

The most brilliant and crowning feat of Sarah's battle with the world was the deal she made with Schulenberg's Home Restaurant. The restaurant was next door to the old red brick in which she hall-roomed. One evening after dining at Schulenberg's 40-cent, five-course *table d'hôte* (served as fast as you throw the five baseballs at the colored gentleman's head) Sarah took away with her the bill of fare. It was written in an almost unreadable script neither English nor German, and so arranged that if you were not careful you began with a toothpick and rice pudding and ended with soup and the day of the week.

The next day Sarah showed Schulenberg a neat card on which the menu was beautifully typewritten with the viands temptingly marshalled under their right and proper heads from 'hors d'oeuvre' to 'not responsible for over-coats and umbrellas.'

Schulenberg became a naturalized citizen on the spot. Before Sarah left him she had him willingly committed to an agreement. She was to furnish typewritten bills of fare for the twenty-one tables in the restaurant – a new bill for each day's dinner, and new ones for breakfast and lunch as often as changes occurred in the food or as neatness required.

In return for this Schulenberg was to send three meals per diem to Sarah's hall room by a waiter – an obsequious one if possible – and furnish her each afternoon with a pencil draft of what Fate had in store for Schulenberg's customers on the morrow.

Mutual satisfaction resulted from the agreement. Schulenberg's patrons now knew what the food they ate was called even if its nature sometimes puzzled them. And Sarah had food during a cold, dull winter, which was the main thing with her.

And then the almanac lied, and said that spring had come. Spring comes when it comes. The frozen snows of January still lay like adamant in the cross-town streets. The hand-organs still played 'In the Good Old Summertime,' with their December vivacity and expression. Men began to make thirty-day notes to buy Easter dresses. Janitors shut off steam. And when these things happen one may know that the city is still in the clutches of winter.

One afternoon Sarah shivered in her elegant hall bedroom; 'house heated; scrupulously clean; conveniences; seen to be appreciated.' She had no work to do except Schulenberg's menu cards. Sarah sat in her squeaky willow rocker, and looked out the window. The calendar on the wall kept crying to her: 'Springtime is here, Sarah – springtime is here, I tell you. Look at me, Sarah, my figures show it. You've got a neat figure yourself, Sarah – a – nice springtime figure – why do you look out the window so sadly?'

Sarah's room was at the back of the house. Looking out the window she could see the windowless rear brick wall of the box factory on the next street. But the wall was clearest crystal; and Sarah was looking down a grassy lane shaded with cherry trees and elms and bordered with raspberry bushes and Cherokee roses.

Spring's real harbingers are too subtle for the eye and ear. Some must have the flowering crocus, the wood-starring dogwood, the voice of bluebird – even so gross a reminder as the farewell handshake of the retiring buckwheat and oyster before they can welcome the Lady in Green to their dull bosoms. But to old earth's choicest kind there come straight, sweet messages from his newest bride, telling them they shall be no stepchildren unless they choose to be.

On the previous summer Sarah had gone into the country and loved a farmer.

(In writing your story never hark back thus. It is bad art, and cripples interest. Let it march, march.)

Sarah stayed two weeks at Sunnybrook Farm. There she learned to love old Farmer Franklin's son Walter. Farmers have been loved and wedded and turned out to grass in less time. But young Walter Franklin was a modern agriculturist. He had a telephone in his cow house, and he could figure up exactly what effect next year's Canada wheat crop would have on potatoes planted in the dark of the moon.

It was in this shaded and raspberried lane that Walter had wooed and won her. And together they had sat and woven a crown of dandelions for her hair. He had immoderately praised the effect of the yellow blossoms against her brown tresses; and she had left the chaplet there, and walked back to the house swinging her straw sailor in her hands.

They were to marry in the spring – at the very first signs of spring, Walter said. And Sarah came back to the city to pound her typewriter.

A knock at the door dispelled Sarah's visions of that happy day. A waiter had brought the rough pencil draft of the Home Restaurant's next day fare in old Schulenberg's angular hand.

Sarah sat down to her typewriter and slipped a card between the rollers. She was a nimble worker. Generally in an hour and a half the twenty-one menu cards were written and ready.

To-day there were more changes on the bill of fare than usual. The soups were lighter; pork was eliminated from the entrées, figuring only with Russian turnips among the roasts. The gracious spirit of spring pervaded the entire menu. Lamb, that lately capered on the greening hillsides, was becoming exploited with the sauce that commemorated its gambols. The song of the oyster, though not silenced, was *dimuendo con amore*. The frying-pan seemed to be held, inactive, behind the beneficent bars of the broiler. The pie list swelled; the richer puddings had vanished; the sausage, with his drapery wrapped about him, barely lingered in a pleasant thanatopsis with the buckwheats and the sweet but doomed maple.

Sarah's fingers danced like midgets above a summer stream. Down through the courses she worked, giving each item its position according to its length with an accurate eye.

Just above the desserts came the list of vegetables. Carrots and peas, asparagus on toast, the perennial tomatoes and corn and succotash, lima beans, cabbage – and then —

Sarah was crying over her bill of fare. Tears from the depths of some divine despair rose in her heart and gathered to her eyes. Down went her head on the little typewriter stand; and the keyboard rattled a dry accompaniment to her moist sobs.

For she had received no letter from Walter in two weeks, and the next item on the bill of fare was dandelions – dandelions with some kind of egg – but bother the egg! – dandelions, with whose golden blooms Walter had crowned her his queen of love and future bride – dandelions, the harbingers of spring, her sorrow's crown of sorrow – reminder of her happiest days.

Madam, I dare you to smile until you suffer this test: Let the Marechal Niel roses that Percy brought you on the night you gave him your heart be served as a salad with French dressing before your eyes at a Schulenberg *table d'hôte*. Had Juliet so seen her love tokens dishonored the sooner would she have sought the lethean herbs of the good apothecary.

But what witch is Spring! Into the great cold city of stone and iron a message had to be sent. There was none to convey it but the little hardy courier of the fields with his rough green coat and modest air. He is a true soldier of fortune, this *dent-de-lion* – this lion's tooth, as the French chefs call him. Flowered, he will assist at love-making, wreathed in my lady's nut-brown hair; young and callow and unblossomed, he goes into the boiling pot and delivers the word of his sovereign mistress.

By and by Sarah forced back her tears. The cards must be written. But, still in a faint, golden glow from her dandelion dream, she fingered the typewriter keys absently for a little while, with her mind and heart in the meadow lane with her young farmer. But soon she came swiftly back to the rock-bound lanes of Manhattan, and the typewriter began to rattle and jump like a strike-breaker's motor car.

At 6 o'clock the waiter brought her dinner and carried away the typewritten bill of fare. When Sarah ate she set aside, with a sigh, the dish of dandelions with its crowning ovarious accompaniment. As this dark mass had been transformed from a bright and love-indorsed flower to be an ignominious vegetable, so had her summer hopes wilted and perished. Love may, as Shakespeare said, feed on itself: but Sarah could not bring herself to eat the dandelions that had graced, as ornaments, the first spiritual banquet of her heart's true affection.

At 7.30 the couple in the next room began to quarrel: the man in the room above sought for A on his flute; the gas went a little lower; three coal wagons started to unload – the only sound of which the phonograph is jealous; cats on the back fences slowly retreated toward Mukden. By these signs Sarah knew that it was time for her to read. She got out 'The Cloister and the Hearth,' the best non-selling book of the month, settled her feet on her trunk, and began to wander with Gerard.

The front door bell rang. The landlady answered it. Sarah left Gerard and Denys treed by a bear and listened. Oh, yes; you would, just as she did!

And then a strong voice was heard in the hall below, and Sarah jumped for her door, leaving the book on the floor and the first round easily the bear's.

You have guessed it. She reached the top of the stairs just as her farmer came up, three at a jump, and reaped and garnered her, with nothing left for the gleaners.

'Why haven't you written – oh, why?' cried Sarah.

'New York is a pretty large town,' said Walter Franklin. 'I came in a week ago to your old address. I found that you went away on a Thursday. That consoled some; it eliminated the possible Friday bad luck. But it didn't prevent my hunting for you with police and otherwise ever since!'

'I wrote!' said Sarah, vehemently.

'Never got it!'

'Then how did you find me?'

The young farmer smiled a springtime smile.

'I dropped into that Home Restaurant next door this evening,' said he. 'I don't care who knows it; I like a dish of some kind of green at this time of the year. I ran my eye down that nice typewritten bill of fare looking for something in that line. When I got below cabbage I turned my chair over and hollered for the proprietor. He told me where you lived.'

'I remember,' sighed Sarah, happily. 'That was dandelions below cabbage.'

'I'd know that cranky capital W 'way above the line that your typewriter makes anywhere in the world,' said Franklin.

'Why, there's no W in dandelions,' said Sarah in surprise.

The young man drew the bill of fare from his pocket and pointed to a line. Sarah recognised the first card she had typewritten that afternoon. There was still the rayed splotch in the upper right-hand corner where a tear had fallen. But over the spot where one should have read the name of the meadow plant, the clinging memory of their golden blossoms had allowed her fingers to strike strange keys.

Between the red cabbage and the stuffed green peppers was the item:
'DEAREST WALTER, WITH HARD-BOILED EGG.'

THE GREEN DOOR

SUPPOSE YOU SHOULD BE WALKING down Broadway after dinner, with ten minutes allotted to the consummation of your cigar while you are choosing between a diverting tragedy and something serious in the way of vaudeville. Suddenly a hand is laid upon your arm. You turn to look into the thrilling eyes of a beautiful woman, wonderful in diamonds and Russian sables. She thrusts hurriedly into your hand an extremely hot buttered roll, flashes out a tiny pair of scissors, snips off the second button of your overcoat, meaningly ejaculates the one word, 'parallelogram!' and swiftly flies down a cross street, looking back fearfully over her shoulder.

That would be pure adventure. Would you accept it? Not you. You would flush with embarrassment; you would sheepishly drop the roll and continue down Broadway, fumbling feebly for the missing button. This you would do unless you are one of the blessed few in whom the pure spirit of adventure is not dead.

True adventurers have never been plentiful. They who are set down in print as such have been mostly business men with newly invented methods. They have been out after the things they wanted – golden fleeces, holy grails, lady loves, treasure, crowns and fame. The true adventurer goes forth aimless and uncalculating to meet and greet unknown fate. A fine example was the Prodigal Son – when he started back home.

Half-adventurers – brave and splendid figures – have been numerous. From the Crusades to the Palisades they have enriched the arts of history and fiction and the trade of historical fiction. But each of them had a prize to win, a goal to kick, an axe to grind, a race to run, a new thrust in tierce to deliver, a name to carve, a crow to pick – so they were not followers of true adventure.

In the big city the twin spirits Romance and Adventure are always abroad seeking worthy wooers. As we roam the streets they slyly peep at us and challenge us in twenty different guises. Without knowing why, we look up suddenly to see in a window a face that seems to belong to our gallery of intimate portraits; in a sleeping thoroughfare we hear a cry of agony and fear coming from an empty and shuttered house; instead of at our familiar curb a cab-driver deposits us before a strange door, which one, with a smile, opens for us and bids us enter; a slip of paper, written upon, flutters down to our feet from the high lattices of Chance; we exchange glances of instantaneous hate, affection, and fear with hurrying strangers in the passing crowds; a sudden souse of rain – and our umbrella may be sheltering the daughter of the Full Moon and first cousin of the Sidereal System; at every corner handkerchiefs drop, fingers beckon, eyes besiege, and the lost, the lonely, the rapturous, the mysterious, the perilous changing clues of adventure are slipped into our fingers. But few of us are willing to hold and follow them. We are grown stiff with the ramrod of convention down our backs. We pass on; and some day we come, at the end of a very dull life, to reflect that our romance has been a pallid thing of a marriage or two, a satin rosette kept in a safe-deposit drawer, and a lifelong feud with a steam radiator.

Rudolf Steiner was a true adventurer. Few were the evenings on which he did not go forth from his hall bedchamber in search of the unexpected and the egregious. The most interesting thing in life seemed to him to be what might lie just around the next corner. Sometimes his willingness to tempt fate led him into strange paths. Twice he had spent the night in a station-house; again and again he had found himself the dupe of ingenious and mercenary tricksters; his watch and money had been the price of one flattering allurement. But with undiminished ardor he picked up every glove cast before him into the merry lists of adventure.

One evening Rudolf was strolling along a cross-town street in the older central part of the city. Two streams of people filled the sidewalks – the home-hurrying, and that restless contingent that abandons home for the specious welcome of the thousand-candle-power *table d'hôte*.

The young adventurer was of pleasing presence, and moved serenely and watchfully. By daylight he was a salesman in a piano store. He wore his tie drawn through a topaz ring instead of fastened with a stick pin; and once he had written to the editor of a magazine that 'Junie's Love Test,' by Miss Libbey, had been the book that had most influenced his life.

During his walk a violent chattering of teeth in a glass case on the sidewalk seemed at first to draw his attention (with a qualm) to a restaurant before which it was set; but a second glance revealed the electric letters of a dentist's sign high above the next door. A giant negro, fantastically dressed in a red embroidered coat, yellow trousers and a military cap, discreetly distributed cards to those of the passing crowd who consented to take them.

This mode of dentistic advertising was a common sight to Rudolf. Usually he passed the dispenser of the dentist's cards without reducing his store; but to-night the African slipped one into his hand so deftly that he retained it there smiling a little at the successful feat.

When he had travelled a few yards further he glanced at the card indifferently. Surprised, he turned it over and looked again with interest. One side of the card was blank; on the other was written in ink three words, 'The Green Door.' And then Rudolf saw, three steps in front of him, a man throw down the card the negro had given him as he passed. Rudolf picked it up. It was printed with the dentist's name and address and the usual schedule of 'plate work' and 'bridge work' and 'crowns,' and specious promises of 'painless' operations.

The adventurous piano salesman halted at the corner and considered. Then he crossed the street, walked down a block, recrossed and joined the upward current of people again. Without seeming to notice the negro as he passed the second time, he carelessly took the card that was handed him. Ten steps away he inspected it. In the same handwriting that appeared on the first card 'The Green Door' was inscribed upon it. Three or four cards were tossed to the pavement by pedestrians both following and leading him. These fell blank side up. Rudolf turned them over. Every one bore the printed legend of the dental 'parlors.'

Rarely did the arch sprite Adventure need to beckon twice to Rudolf Steiner, his true follower. But twice it had been done, and the quest was on.

Rudolf walked slowly back to where the giant negro stood by the case of rattling teeth. This time as he passed he received no card. In spite of his gaudy and ridiculous garb, the Ethiopian displayed a natural barbaric dignity as he stood, offering the cards suavely to some, allowing others to pass unmolested. Every half minute he chanted a harsh, unintelligible phrase akin to the jabber of car conductors and grand opera. And not only did he withhold a card this time but it seemed to Rudolf that he received from the shining and massive black countenance a look of cold, almost contemptuous disdain.

The look stung the adventurer. He read in it a silent accusation that he had been found wanting. Whatever the mysterious written words on the cards might mean, the black had selected him twice from the throng for their recipient; and now seemed to have condemned him as deficient in the wit and spirit to engage the enigma.

Standing aside from the rush, the young man made a rapid estimate of the building in which he conceived that his adventure must lie. Five stories high it rose. A small restaurant occupied the basement.

The first floor, now closed, seemed to house millinery or furs. The second floor, by the winking electric letters, was the dentist's. Above this a polyglot babel of signs struggled to indicate the abodes of palmists, dressmakers, musicians, and doctors. Still higher up draped curtains and milk bottles white on the window sills proclaimed the regions of domesticity.

After concluding his survey Rudolf walked briskly up the high flight of stone steps into the house. Up two flights of the carpeted stairway he continued; and at its top paused. The hallway there was dimly lighted by two pale jets of gas – one far to his right, the other nearer, to his left. He looked toward the nearer light and saw, within its wan halo, a green door. For one moment he hesitated; then he seemed to see the contumelious sneer of the African juggler of cards; and then he walked straight to the green door and knocked against it.

Moments like those that passed before his knock was answered measure the quick breath of true adventure. What might not be behind those green panels! Gamesters at play; cunning rogues baiting their traps with subtle skill; beauty in love with courage, and thus planning to be sought by it; danger, death, love, disappointment, ridicule – any of these might respond to that temerarious rap.

A faint rustle was heard inside, and the door slowly opened. A girl not yet twenty stood there white-faced and tottering. She loosed the knob and swayed weakly, groping with one hand. Rudolf caught her and laid her on a faded couch that stood against the wall. He closed the door and took a swift glance around the room by the light of a flickering gas jet. Neat, but extreme poverty was the story that he read.

The girl lay still, as if in a faint. Rudolf looked around the room excitedly for a barrel. People must be rolled upon a barrel who – no, no; that was for drowned persons. He began to fan her with his hat. That was successful, for he struck her nose with the brim of his derby and she opened her eyes. And then the young man saw that hers, indeed, was the one missing face from his heart's gallery of intimate portraits. The frank, gray eyes, the little nose, turning pertly outward; the chestnut hair, curling like the tendrils of a pea vine, seemed the right end and reward of all his wonderful adventures. But the face was woefully thin and pale.

The girl looked at him calmly, and then smiled.

'Fainted, didn't I?' she asked, weakly. 'Well, who wouldn't? You try going without anything to eat for three days and see!'

'Himmel!' exclaimed Rudolf, jumping up. 'Wait till I come back.'

He dashed out the green door and down the stairs. In twenty minutes he was back again kicking at the door with his toe for her to open it. With both arms he hugged an array of wares from the grocery and the restaurant. On the table he laid them – bread and butter, cold meats, cakes, pies, pickles, oysters, a roasted chicken, a bottle of milk and one of red-hot tea.

'This is ridiculous,' said Rudolf, blusteringly, 'to go without eating. You must quit making election bets of this kind. Supper is ready.' He helped her to a chair at the table and asked: 'Is there a cup for the tea?' 'On the shelf by the window,' she answered. When he turned again with the cup he saw her, with eyes shining rapturously, beginning upon a huge dill pickle that she had rooted out from the paper bags with a woman's unerring instinct. He took it from her, laughingly, and poured the cup full of milk. 'Drink that first,' he ordered, 'and then you shall have some tea, and then a chicken wing. If you are very good you shall have a pickle to-morrow. And now, if you'll allow me to be your guest we'll have supper.'

He drew up the other chair. The tea brightened the girl's eyes and brought back some of her color. She began to eat with a sort of dainty ferocity like some starved wild animal. She seemed to regard the young man's presence and the aid he had rendered her as a natural thing – not as though she undervalued the conventions; but as one whose great stress gave her the right to put aside the artificial for the human. But gradually, with the return of strength and comfort, came also a sense of the little conventions that belong; and she began to tell him her little story. It was one of a thousand such as the city yawns at every day – the shop girl's story of insufficient wages, further reduced by 'fines' that go to swell the store's profits; of time lost through illness; and then of lost positions, lost hope, and – the knock of the adventurer upon the green door.

But to Rudolf the history sounded as big as the Iliad or the crisis in 'Junie's Love Test.'

'To think of you going through all that,' he exclaimed.

'It was something fierce,' said the girl, solemnly.

'And you have no relatives or friends in the city?'

'None whatever.'

'I am all alone in the world, too,' said Rudolf, after a pause.

'I am glad of that,' said the girl, promptly; and somehow it pleased the young man to hear that she approved of his bereft condition.

Very suddenly her eyelids dropped and she sighed deeply.

'I'm awfully sleepy,' she said, 'and I feel so good.'

Rudolf rose and took his hat.

'Then I'll say good-night. A long night's sleep will be fine for you.'

He held out his hand, and she took it and said 'good-night.' But her eyes asked a question so eloquently, so frankly and pathetically that he answered it with words.

'Oh, I'm coming back to-morrow to see how you are getting along. You can't get rid of me so easily.'

Then, at the door, as though the way of his coming had been so much less important than the fact that he had come, she asked: 'How did you come to knock at my door?'

He looked at her for a moment, remembering the cards, and felt a sudden jealous pain. What if they had fallen into other hands as adventurous as his? Quickly he decided that she must never know the truth. He would never let her know that he was aware of the strange expedient to which she had been driven by her great distress.

'One of our piano tuners lives in this house,' he said. 'I knocked at your door by mistake.'

The last thing he saw in the room before the green door closed was her smile.

At the head of the stairway he paused and looked curiously about him. And then he went along the hallway to its other end; and, coming back, ascended to the floor above and continued his puzzled explorations. Every door that he found in the house was painted green.

Wondering, he descended to the sidewalk. The fantastic African was still there. Rudolf confronted him with his two cards in his hand.

'Will you tell me why you gave me these cards and what they mean?' he asked.

In a broad, good-natured grin the negro exhibited a splendid advertisement of his master's profession.

'Dar it is, boss,' he said, pointing down the street. 'But I 'spect you is a little late for de fust act.'

Looking the way he pointed Rudolf saw above the entrance to a theatre the blazing electric sign of its new play, 'The Green Door.'

'I'm informed dat it's a fust-rate show, sah,' said the negro. 'De agent what represents it pussented me with a dollar, sah, to distribute a few of his cards along with de doctah's. May I offer you one of de doctah's cards, suh?'

At the corner of the block in which he lived Rudolf stopped for a glass of beer and a cigar. When he had come out with his lighted weed he buttoned his coat, pushed back his hat and said, stoutly, to the lamp post on the corner:

'All the same, I believe it was the hand of Fate that doped out the way for me to find her.'

Which conclusion, under the circumstances, certainly admits Rudolf Steiner to the ranks of the true followers of Romance and Adventure.

FROM THE CABBY'S SEAT

THE CABBY HAS HIS POINT OF VIEW. It is more single-minded, perhaps, than that of a follower of any other calling. From the high, swaying seat of his hansom he looks upon his fellow-men as nomadic particles, of no account except when possessed of migratory desires. He is Jehu, and you are goods in transit. Be you President or vagabond, to cabby you are only a Fare. He takes you up, cracks his whip, joggles your vertebrae and sets you down.

When time for payment arrives, if you exhibit a familiarity with legal rates you come to know what contempt is; if you find that you have left your pocketbook behind you are made to realize the mildness of Dante's imagination.

It is not an extravagant theory that the cabby's singleness of purpose and concentrated view of life are the results of the hansom's peculiar construction. The cock-of-the-roost sits aloft like Jupiter on an unsharable seat, holding your fate between two thongs of inconstant leather. Helpless, ridiculous, confined, bobbing like a toy mandarin, you sit like a rat in a trap – you, before whom butlers cringe on solid land – and must squeak upward through a slit in your peripatetic sarcophagus to make your feeble wishes known.

Then, in a cab, you are not even an occupant; you are contents. You are a cargo at sea, and the 'cherub that sits up aloft' has Davy Jones's street and number of heart.

One night there were sounds of revelry in the big brick tenement house next door but one to McGary's Family Café. The sounds seemed to emanate from the apartments of the Walsh family. The sidewalk was obstructed by an assortment of interested neighbors, who opened a lane from time to time for a hurrying messenger bearing from McGary's goods pertinent to festivity and diversion. The sidewalk contingent was engaged in comment and discussion from which it made no effort to eliminate the news that Norah Walsh was being married.

In the fulness of time there was an eruption of the merry-makers to the sidewalk. The uninvited guests enveloped and permeated them, and upon the night air rose joyous cries, congratulations, laughter, and unclassified noises born of McGary's oblations to the hymeneal scene.

Close to the curb stood Jerry O'Donovan's cab. Night-hawk was Jerry called; but no more lustrous or cleaner hansom than his ever closed its doors upon point lace and November violets. And Jerry's horse! I am within bounds when I tell you that he was stuffed with oats until one of those old ladies who leave their dishes unwashed at home and go about having expressmen arrested, would have smiled – yes, smiled – to have seen him.

Among the shifting, sonorous, pulsing crowd glimpses could be had of Jerry's high hat, battered by the winds and rains of many years; of his nose like a carrot, battered by the frolicsome, athletic progeny of millionaires and by contumacious fares; of his brass-buttoned green coat, admired in the vicinity of McGary's. It was plain that Jerry had usurped the functions of his cab, and was carrying a 'load.' Indeed, the figure may be extended and he be likened to a bread-wagon if we admit the testimony of a youthful spectator, who was heard to remark 'Jerry has got a bun.'

From somewhere among the throng in the street or else out of the thin stream of pedestrians a young woman tripped and stood by the cab. The professional hawk's eye of Jerry caught the movement. He made a lurch for the cab, overturning three or four onlookers and himself – no! he caught the cap of a water-plug and kept his feet. Like a sailor shinning up the ratlins during a squall Jerry mounted to his professional seat. Once he was there McGary's liquids were baffled. He seesawed on the mizzenmast of his craft as safe as a Steeple Jack rigged to the flagpole of a skyscraper.

'Step in, lady,' said Jerry, gathering his lines.

The young woman stepped into the cab; the doors shut with a bang; Jerry's whip cracked in the air; the crowd in the gutter scattered, and the fine hansom dashed away 'crosstown.

When the oat-spry horse had hedged a little his first spurt of speed Jerry broke the lid of his cab and called down through the aperture in the voice of a cracked megaphone, trying to please:

'Where, now, will ye be drivin' to?'

'Anywhere you please,' came up the answer, musical and contented.

' 'Tis drivin' for pleasure she is,' thought Jerry. And then he suggested as a matter of course:

'Take a thrip around in the park, lady. 'Twill be ilegant cool and fine.'

'Just as you like,' answered the fare, pleasantly.

The cab headed for Fifth Avenue and sped up that perfect street. Jerry bounced and swayed in his seat. The potent fluids of McGary were disquieted and they sent new fumes to his head. He sang an ancient song of Killisnook and brandished his whip like a baton.

Inside the cab the fare sat up straight on the cushions, looking to right and left at the lights and houses. Even in the shadowed hansom her eyes shone like stars at twilight.

When they reached Fifty-ninth Street Jerry's head was bobbing and his reins were slack. But his horse turned in through the park gate and began the old familiar nocturnal round. And then the fare leaned back, entranced, and breathed deep the clean, wholesome odors of grass and leaf and bloom. And the wise beast in the shafts, knowing his ground, struck into his by-the-hour gait and kept to the right of the road.

Habit also struggled successfully against Jerry's increasing torpor. He raised the hatch of his storm-tossed vessel and made the inquiry that cabbies do make in the park.

'Like shtop at the Cas-sino, lady? Gezzer r'freshm's, 'n lish'n the music. Ev'body shtops.'

'I think that would be nice,' said the fare.

They reined up with a plunge at the Casino entrance. The cab doors flew open. The fare stepped directly upon the floor. At once she was caught in a web of ravishing music and dazzled by a panorama of lights and colors. Some one slipped a little square card into her hand on which was printed a number – 34. She looked around and saw her cab twenty yards away already lining up in its place among the waiting mass of carriages, cabs, and motor cars. And then a man who seemed to be all shirtfront danced backward before her; and next she was seated at a little table by a railing over which climbed a jessamine vine.

There seemed to be a wordless invitation to purchase; she consulted a collection of small coins in a thin purse, and received from them license to order a glass of beer. There she sat, inhaling and absorbing it all – the new-colored, new-shaped life in a fairy palace in an enchanted wood.

At fifty tables sat princes and queens clad in all the silks and gems of the world. And now and then one of them would look curiously at Jerry's fare. They saw a plain figure dressed in a pink silk of the kind that is tempered by the word 'foulard,' and a plain face that wore a look of love of life that the queens envied.

Twice the long hands of the clocks went round. Royalties thinned from their *al fresco* thrones, and buzzed or clattered away in their vehicles of state. The music retired into cases of wood and bags of leather and baize. Waiters removed cloths pointedly near the plain figure sitting almost alone.

Jerry's fare rose, and held out her numbered card simply:

'Is there anything coming on the ticket?' she asked.

A waiter told her it was her cab check, and that she should give it to the man at the entrance. This man took it, and called the number. Only three hansoms stood in line. The driver of one of them went and routed out Jerry asleep in his cab. He swore deeply, climbed to the captain's bridge and steered his craft to the pier. His fare entered, and the cab whirled into the cool fastnesses of the park along the shortest homeward cuts.

At the gate a glimmer of reason in the form of sudden suspicion seized upon Jerry's beclouded mind. One or two things occurred to him. He stopped his horse, raised the trap and dropped his phonographic voice, like a lead plummet, through the aperture:

'I want to see four dollars before goin' any further on th' thrip. Have ye got th' dough?'

'Four dollars!' laughed the fare, softly, 'dear me, no. I've only got a few pennies and a dime or two.

Jerry shut down the trap and slashed his oat-fed horse. The clatter of hoofs strangled but could not drown the sound of his profanity. He shouted choking and gurgling curses at the starry heavens; he cut viciously with his whip at passing vehicles; he scattered fierce and everchanging oaths and imprecations along the streets, so that a late truck driver, crawling homeward, heard and was abashed. But he knew his recourse, and made for it at a gallop.

At the house with the green lights beside the steps he pulled up. He flung wide the cab doors and tumbled heavily to the ground.

'Come on, you,' he said, roughly.

His fare came forth with the Casino dreamy smile still on her plain face. Jerry took her by the arm and led her into the police station. A gray-moustached sergeant looked keenly across the desk. He and the cabby were no strangers.

'Sargeant,' began Jerry in his old raucous, martyred, thunderous tones of complaint. 'I've got a fare here that—'

Jerry paused. He drew a knotted, red hand across his brow. The fog set up by McGary was beginning to clear away.

'A fare, sargeant,' he continued, with a grin, 'that I want to introduce to ye. It's me wife that I married at ould man Walsh's this evening. And a devil of a time we had, 'tis thrue. Shake hands wit th' sargeant, Norah, and we'll be off to home.'

Before stepping into the cab Norah sighed profoundly.

'I've had such a nice time, Jerry,' said she.

AN UNFINISHED STORY

WE NO LONGER GROAN AND HEAP ASHES upon our heads when the flames of Tophet are mentioned. For, even the preachers have begun to tell us that God is radium, or ether or some scientific compound, and that the worst we wicked ones may expect is a chemical reaction. This is a pleasing hypothesis; but there lingers yet some of the old, goodly terror of orthodoxy.

There are but two subjects upon which one may discourse with a free imagination, and without the possibility of being controverted. You may talk of your dreams; and you may tell what you heard a parrot say. Both Morpheus and the bird are incompetent witnesses; and your listener dare not attack your recital. The baseless fabric of a vision, then, shall furnish my theme

– chosen with apologies and regrets instead of the more limited field of pretty Polly's small talk.

I had a dream that was so far removed from the higher criticism that it had to do with the ancient, respectable, and lamented bar-of-judgment theory.

Gabriel had played his trump; and those of us who could not follow suit were arraigned for examination. I noticed at one side a gathering of professional bondsmen in solemn black and collars that buttoned behind; but it seemed there was some trouble about their real estate titles; and they did not appear to be getting any of us out.

A fly cop – an angel policeman – flew over to me and took me by the left wing. Near at hand was a group of very prosperous-looking spirits arraigned for judgment.

'Do you belong with that bunch?' the policeman asked.

'Who are they?' was my answer.

'Why,' said he, 'they are —'

But this irrelevant stuff is taking up space that the story should occupy.

Dulcie worked in a department store. She sold Hamburg edging, or stuffed peppers, or automobiles, or other little trinkets such as they keep in department stores. Of what she earned, Dulcie received six dollars per week. The remainder was credited to her and debited to somebody else's account in the ledger kept by G— Oh, primal energy, you say, Reverend Doctor— Well, then, in the Ledger of Primal Energy.

During her first year in the store, Dulcie was paid five dollars per week. It would be instructive to know how she lived on that amount. Don't care? Very well; probably you are interested in larger amounts. Six dollars is a larger amount. I will tell you how she lived on six dollars per week.

One afternoon at six, when Dulcie was sticking her hat pin within an eighth of an inch of her *medulla oblongata*, she said to her chum, Sadie – the girl that waits on you with her left side:

'Say, Sade, I made a date for dinner this evening with Piggy.'

'You never did!' exclaimed Sadie, admiringly. 'Well, ain't you the lucky one? Piggy's an awful swell; and he always takes a girl to swell places. He took Blanche up to the Hoffman House one evening, where they have swell music, and you see a lot of swells. You'll have a swell time, Dulce.'

Dulcie hurried homeward. Her eyes were shining, and her cheeks showed the delicate pink of life's – real life's – approaching dawn. It was Friday; and she had fifty cents left of her week's wages.

The streets were filled with the rush-hour floods of people. The electric lights of Broadway were glowing – calling moths from miles, from leagues, from hundreds of leagues out of darkness around to come in and attend the singeing school. Men in accurate clothes, with faces like those carved on cherry stones by the old salts in sailors' homes, turned and stared at Dulcie as she sped, unheeding, past them. Manhattan, the night-blooming cereus, was beginning to unfold its dead-white, heavy-odored petals.

Dulcie stopped in a store where goods were cheap and bought an imitation lace collar with her fifty cents. That money was to have been spent otherwise – fifteen cents for supper, ten cents for breakfast, ten cents for lunch. Another dime was to be added to her small store of savings; and five cents was to be squandered for licorice drops – the kind that made your cheek look like the toothache, and last as long. The licorice was an extravagance – almost a carouse – but what is life without pleasures?

Dulcie lived in a furnished room. There is this difference between a furnished room and a boarding-house. In a furnished room, other people do not know it when you go hungry.

Dulcie went up to her room – the third-floor-back in a West Side brownstone-front. She lit the gas. Scientists tell us that the diamond is the hardest substance known. Their mistake. Landladies know of a compound beside which the diamond is as putty. They pack it in the tips of gas-burners; and one may stand on a chair and dig at it in vain until one's fingers are pink and bruised. A hairpin will not remove it; therefore let us call it immovable.

So Dulcie lit the gas. In its one-fourth-candle-power glow we will observe the room.

Couch-bed, dresser, table, washstand, chair – of this much the landlady was guilty. The rest was Dulcie's. On the dresser were her treasures – a gilt china vase presented to her by Sadie, a calendar issued by a pickle works, a book on the divination of dreams, some rice powder in a glass dish, and a cluster of artificial cherries tied with a pink ribbon.

Against the wrinkly mirror stood pictures of General Kitchener, William Muldoon, the Duchess of Marlborough, and Benvenuto Cellini. Against one wall was a plaster of Paris plaque of an O'Callahan in a Roman helmet. Near it was a violent oleograph of a lemon-colored child assaulting an inflammatory butterfly. This was Dulcie's final judgment in art; but it had never been upset. Her rest had never been disturbed by whispers of stolen copes; no critic had elevated his eyebrows at her infantile entomologist.

Piggy was to call for her at seven. While she swiftly makes ready, let us discreetly face the other way and gossip.

For the room, Dulcie paid two dollars per week. On week-days her breakfast cost ten cents; she made coffee and cooked an egg over the gaslight while she was dressing. On Sunday mornings she feasted royally on veal chops and pineapple fritters at 'Billy's' restaurant, at a cost of twenty-five cents – and tipped the waitress ten cents. New York presents so many temptations for one to run into extravagance. She had her lunches in the department-store restaurant at a cost of sixty cents for the week; dinners were $1.05. The evening papers – show me a New Yorker going without his daily paper! – came to six cents; and two Sunday papers – one for the personal column and the other to read – were ten cents. The total amounts to $4.76. Now, one has to buy clothes, and—

I give it up. I hear of wonderful bargains in fabrics, and of miracles performed with needle and thread; but I am in doubt. I hold my pen poised in vain when I would add to Dulcie's life some of those joys that belong to woman by virtue of all the unwritten, sacred, natural, inactive ordinances of the equity of heaven. Twice she had been to Coney Island and had ridden the hobby-horses. 'Tis a weary thing to count your pleasures by summers instead of by hours.

Piggy needs but a word. When the girls named him, an undeserving stigma was cast upon the noble family of swine. The words-of-three-letters lesson in the old blue spelling book begins with Piggy's biography. He was fat; he had the soul of a rat, the habits of a bat, and the magnanimity of a cat. . . . He wore expensive clothes; and was a connoisseur in starvation. He could look at a shop-girl and tell you to an hour how long it had been since she had eaten anything more nourishing than marshmallows and tea. He hung about the shopping districts, and prowled around in department stores with his invitations to dinner. Men who escort dogs upon the streets at the end of a string look down upon him. He is a type; I can dwell upon him no longer; my pen is not the kind intended for him; I am no carpenter.

At ten minutes to seven Dulcie was ready. She looked at herself in the wrinkly mirror. The reflection was satisfactory. The dark blue dress, fitting without a wrinkle, the hat with its jaunty black feather, the but-slightly-soiled gloves – all representing self-denial, even of food itself – were vastly becoming.

Dulcie forgot everything else for a moment except that she was beautiful, and that life was about to lift a corner of its mysterious veil for her to observe its wonders. No gentleman had ever asked her out before. Now she was going for a brief moment into the glitter and exalted show.

The girls said that Piggy was a 'spender.' There would be a grand dinner, and music, and splendidly dressed ladies to look at and things to eat that strangely twisted the girls' jaws when they tried to tell about them. No doubt she would be asked out again.

There was a blue pongee suit in a window that she knew – by saving twenty cents a week instead of ten in – let's see— Oh, it would run into years! But there was a second-hand store in Seventh Avenue where—

Somebody knocked at the door. Dulcie opened it. The landlady stood there with a spurious smile, sniffing for cooking by stolen gas.

'A gentleman's downstairs to see you,' she said. 'Name is Mr. Wiggins.'

By such epithet was Piggy known to unfortunate ones who had to take him seriously.

Dulcie turned to the dresser to get her handkerchief; and then she stopped still, and bit her underlip hard. While looking in her mirror she had seen fairyland and herself, a princess, just awakening from a long slumber. She had forgotten one that was watching her with sad, beautiful, stern eyes – the only one there was to approve or condemn what she did. Straight and slender and tall, with a look of sorrowful reproach on his handsome, melancholy face, General Kitchener fixed his wonderful eyes on her out of his gilt photograph frame on the dresser.

Dulcie turned like an automatic doll to the landlady.

'Tell him I can't go,' she said, dully. 'Tell him I'm sick, or something. Tell him I'm not going out.'

After the door was closed and locked, Dulcie fell upon her bed, crushing her black tip, and cried for ten minutes. General Kitchener was her only friend. He was Dulcie's ideal of a gallant knight. He looked as if he might have a secret sorrow, and his wonderful moustache was a dream, and she was a little afraid of that stern yet tender look in his eyes. She used to have little fancies that he would call at the house sometime, and ask for her, with his sword clanking against his high boots. Once, when a boy was rattling a piece of chain against a lamp post she had opened the window and looked out. But there was no use. She knew that General Kitchener was away over in Japan, leading his army against the savage Turks; and he would never step out of his gilt frame for her. Yet one look from him had vanquished Piggy that night. Yes, for that night.

When her cry was over Dulcie got up and took off her best dress, and put on her old blue kimono. She wanted no dinner. She sang two verses of 'Sammy.' Then she became intensely interested in a little red speck on the side of her nose. And after that was attended to, she drew up a chair to the rickety table, and told her fortune with an old deck of cards.

'The horrid, impudent thing!' she said aloud. 'And I never gave him a word or a look to make him think it!'

At nine o'clock Dulcie took a tin box of crackers and a little pot of raspberry jam out of her trunk and had a feast. She offered General Kitchener some jam on a cracker; but he only looked at her as the sphinx would have looked at a butterfly – if there are butterflies in the desert.

'Don't eat if you don't want to,' said Dulcie. 'And don't put on so many airs and scold so with your eyes. I wonder if you'd be so superior and snippy if you had to live on six dollars a week.'

It was not a good sign for Dulcie to be rude to General Kitchener. And then she turned Benvenuto Cellini face downward with a severe gesture. But that was not inexcusable; for she had always thought he was Henry VIII, and she did not approve of him.

At half-past nine Dulcie took a last look at the pictures on the dresser, turned out the light and skipped into bed. It's an awful thing to go to bed with a good-night look at General Kitchener, William Muldoon, the Duchess of Marlborough, and Benvenuto Cellini.

This story doesn't really get anywhere at all. The rest of it comes later – sometime when Piggy asks Dulcie again to dine with him, and she is feeling lonelier than usual, and General Kitchener happens to be looking the other way; and then—

As I said before, I dreamed that I was standing near a crowd of prosperous-looking angels, and a policeman took me by the wing and asked if I belonged with them.

'Who are they?' I asked.

'Why,' said he, 'they are the men who hired working-girls, and paid 'em five or six dollars a week to live on. Are you one of the bunch?'

'Not on your immortality,' said I. 'I'm only a fellow that set fire to an orphan asylum, and murdered a blind man for his pennies.'

THE CALIPH, CUPID AND THE CLOCK

PRINCE MICHAEL, OF THE ELECTORATE VALLELUNA, sat on his favorite bench in the park. The coolness of the September night quickened the life in him like a rare, tonic wine. The benches were not filled; for park loungers, with their stagnant blood, are prompt to detect and fly home from the crispness of early autumn. The moon was just clearing the roofs of the range of dwellings that bounded the quadrangle on the east. Children laughed and played about the fine-sprayed fountain. In the shadowed spots fauns and hamadryads wooed, unconscious of the gaze of mortal eyes. A hand-organ – Philomel by the grace of our stage carpenter, Fancy – fluted and droned in a side street. Around the enchanted boundaries of the little park street cars spat and mewed and the stilted trains roared like tigers and lions prowling for a place to enter. And above the trees shone the great, round, shining face of an illuminated clock in the tower of an antique public building.

Prince Michael's shoes were wrecked far beyond the skill of the carefullest cobbler. The ragman would have declined any negotiations concerning his clothes. The two weeks' stubble on his face was gray and brown and red and greenish yellow – as if it had been made up from individual contributions from the chorus of a musical comedy. No man existed who had money enough to wear so bad a hat as his.

Prince Michael sat on his favorite bench and smiled. It was a diverting thought to him that he was wealthy enough to buy every one of those closed-ranged, bulky, window-lit mansions that faced him, if he chose. He could have matched gold, equipages, jewels, art treasures, estates and acres with any Croesus in this proud city of Manhattan, and scarcely have entered upon the bulk of his holdings. He could have sat at table with reigning sovereigns. The social world, the world of art, the fellowship of the elect, adulation, imitation, the homage of the fairest, honors from the highest, praise from the wisest, flattery, esteem, credit, pleasure, fame – all the honey of life was waiting in the comb in the hive of the world for Prince Michael, of the Electorate of Valleluna, whenever he might choose to take it. But his choice was to sit in rags and dinginess on a bench in a park. For he had tasted of the fruit of the tree of life, and, finding it bitter in his mouth had stepped out of Eden for a time to seek distraction close to the unarmored, beating heart of the world.

These thoughts strayed dreamily through the mind of Prince Michael, as he smiled under the stubble of his polychromatic beard. Lounging thus, clad as the poorest of mendicants in the parks, he loved to study humanity. He found in altruism more pleasure than his riches, his station and all the grosser sweets of life had given him. It was his chief solace and satisfaction to alleviate individual distress, to confer favors upon worthy ones who had need of succor, to dazzle unfortunates by unexpected and bewildering gifts of truly royal magnificence, bestowed, however, with wisdon and judiciousness.

And as Prince Michael's eye rested upon the glowing face of the great clock in the tower, his smile, altruistic as it was, became slightly tinged with contempt. Big thoughts were the Prince's; and it was always with a shake of his head that he considered the subjugation of the world to the arbitrary measures of Time. The comings and goings of people in hurry and dread, controlled by the little metal moving hands of a clock, always made him sad.

By and by came a young man in evening clothes and sat upon the third bench from the Prince. For half an hour he smoked cigars with nervous haste, and then he fell to watching the face of the illuminated clock above the trees. His perturbation was evident, and the Prince noted, in sorrow, that its cause was connected, in some manner, with the slowly moving hands of the timepiece.

His Highness arose and went to the young man's bench.

'I beg your pardon for addressing you,' he said, 'but I perceive that you are disturbed in mind. If it may serve to mitigate the liberty I have taken I will add that I am Prince Michael, heir to the throne of the Electorate of Valleluna. I appear incognito, of course, as you may gather from my appearance. It is a fancy of mine to render aid to others whom I think worthy of it. Perhaps the matter that seems to distress you is one that would more readily yield to our mutual efforts.'

The young man looked up brightly at the Prince. Brightly, but the perpendicular line of perplexity between his brows was not smoothed away.

He laughed, and even then it did not. But he accepted the momentary diversion.

'Glad to meet you, Prince,' he said, good humoredly. 'Yes, I'd say you were incog. all right. Thanks for your offer of assistance – but I don't see where your butting-in would help things any. It's a kind of private affair, you know – but thanks all the same.'

Prince Michael sat at the young man's side. He was often rebuffed but never offensively. His courteous manner and words forbade that.

'Clocks,' said the Prince, 'are shackles on the feet of mankind. I have observed you looking persistently at that clock. Its face is that of a tyrant, its numbers are false as those on a lottery ticket; its hands are those of a bunco steerer, who makes an appointment with you to your ruin. Let me entreat you to throw off its humiliating bonds and cease to order your affairs by that insensate monitor of brass and steel.'

'I don't usually,' said the young man. 'I carry a watch except when I've got my radiant rags on.'

'I know human nature as I do the trees and grass,' said the Prince, with earnest dignity. 'I am a master of philosophy, a graduate in art, and I hold the purse of a Fortunatus. There are few mortal misfortunes that I cannot alleviate or overcome. I have read your countenance, and found in it honesty and nobility as well as distress. I beg of you to accept my advice or aid. Do not belie the intelligence I see in your face by judging from my appearance of my ability to defeat your troubles.'

The young man glanced at the clock again and frowned darkly. When his gaze strayed from the glowing horologue of time it rested intently upon a four-story red brick house in the row of dwellings opposite to where he sat. The shades were drawn, and the lights in many rooms shone dimly through them.

'Ten minutes to nine!' exclaimed the young man, with an impatient gesture of despair. He turned his back upon the house and took a rapid step or two in a contrary direction.

'Remain!' commanded Prince Michael, in so potent a voice that the disturbed one wheeled around with a somewhat chagrined laugh.

'I'll give her the ten minutes and then I'm off,' he muttered, and then aloud to the Prince: 'I'll join you in confounding all clocks, my friend, and throw in women, too.'

'Sit down,' said the Prince, calmly. 'I do not accept your addition. Women are the natural enemies of clocks, and, therefore, the allies of those who would seek liberation from these monsters that measure our follies and limit our pleasures. If you will so far confide in me I would ask you to relate to me your story.'

The young man threw himself upon the bench with a reckless laugh.

'Your Royal Highness, I will,' he said, in tones of mock deference. 'Do you see yonder house – the one with the three upper windows lighted? Well, at 6 o'clock I stood in that house with the young lady I am – that is, I was – engaged to. I had been doing wrong, my dear Prince – I had been a naughty boy, and she had heard of it. I wanted to be forgiven of course – we are always wanting women to forgive us, aren't we, Prince?

' "I want time to think it over," said she. "There is one thing certain; I will either fully forgive you, or I will never see your face again. There will be no half-way business. At half-past eight," she said, "at exactly half-past

eight you may be watching the middle upper window of the top floor. If I
decide to forgive I will hang out of that window a white silk scarf. You will
know by that that all is as was before, and you may come to me. If you see
no scarf you may consider that everything between us is ended forever.'
That,' concluded the young man, bitterly, 'is why I have been watching that
clock. The time for the signal to appear has passed twenty-three minutes ago.
Do you wonder that I am a little disturbed, my Prince of Rags and Whiskers?'

'Let me repeat to you,' said Prince Michael, in his even, well-modulated
tones, 'that women are the natural enemies of clocks. Clocks are an evil,
women a blessing. The signal may yet appear.'

'Never, on your principality!' exclaimed the young man, hopelessly. 'You
don't know Marian – of course. She's always on time, to the minute. That
was the first thing about her that attracted me. I've got the mitten instead
of the scarf. I ought to have known at 8.31 that my goose was cooked. I'll go
West on the 11.45 to-night with Jack Milburn. The jig's up. I'll try Jack's
ranch awhile and top off with the Klondike and whiskey. Good-night – er
– er – Prince.'

Prince Michael smiled his enigmatic, gentle, comprehending smile and
caught the coat sleeve of the other. The brilliant light in the Prince's eyes
was softening to a dreamier, cloudy translucence.

'Wait,' he said solemnly, 'till the clock strikes. I have wealth and power
and knowledge above most men, but when the clock strikes I am afraid. Stay
by me until then. This woman shall be yours. You have the word of the
hereditary Prince of Valleluna. On the day of your marriage I will give you
$100,000 and a palace on the Hudson. But there must be no clocks in that
palace – they measure our follies and limit our pleasures. Do you agree to
that?'

'Of course,' said the young man, cheerfully, 'they're a nuisance, anyway
– always ticking and striking and getting you late for dinner.'

He glanced again at the clock in the tower. The hands stood at three
minutes to nine.

'I think,' said Prince Michael, that I will sleep a little. The day has been
fatiguing.'

He stretched himself upon a bench with the manner of one who had slept
thus before.

'You will find me in this park on any evening when the weather is
suitable,' said the Prince, sleepily. 'Come to me when your marriage day is
set and I will give you a check for the money.'

'Thanks, Your Highness,' said the young man, seriously. 'It doesn't look
as if I would need that palace on the Hudson, but I appreciate your offer, just
the same.'

Prince Michael sank into deep slumber. His battered hat rolled from the
bench to the ground. The young man lifted it, placed it over the frowsy face
and moved one of the grotesquely relaxed limbs into a more comfortable
position. 'Poor devil!' he said, as he drew the tattered clothes closer about the
Prince's breast.

Sonorous and startling came the stroke of 9 from the clock tower. The
young man sighed again, turned his face for one last look at the house of his
relinquished hopes – and cried aloud profane words of holy rapture.

From the middle upper window blossomed in the dusk a waving, snowy,
fluttering, wonderful, divine emblem of forgiveness and promised joy.

By came a citizen, rotund, comfortable, home-hurrying, unknowing of the delights of waving silken scarfs on the borders of dimly-lit parks.

'Will you oblige me with the time, sir?' asked the young man; and the citizen, shrewdly conjecturing his watch to be safe, dragged it out and announced:

'Twenty-nine and a half minutes past eight, sir.'

And then, from habit, he glanced at the clock in the tower, and made further oration.

'By George! that clock's half an hour fast! First time in ten years I've known it to be off. This watch of mine never varies a —'

But the citizen was talking to vacancy. He turned and saw his hearer a fast receding black shadow flying in the direction of a house with three lighted upper windows.

And in the morning came along two policemen on their way to the beats they owned. The park was deserted save for one dilapidated figure that sprawled, asleep, on a bench. They stopped and gazed upon it.

'It's Dopy Mike,' said one. 'He hits the pipe every night. Park bum for twenty years. On his last legs, I guess.'

The other policeman stooped and looked at something crumpled and crisp in the hand of the sleeper.

'Gee!' he remarked. 'He's doped out a fifty-dollar bill, anyway. Wish I knew the brand of hop that he smokes.'

And then 'Rap, rap, rap!' went the club of realism against the shoe soles of Prince Michael, of the Electorate of Valleluna.

SISTERS OF THE GOLDEN CIRCLE

THE RUBBERNECK AUTO was about ready to start. The merry top-riders had been assigned to their seats by the gentlemanly conductor. The sidewalk was blockaded with sightseers who had gathered to stare at sightseers, justifying the natural law that every creature on earth is preyed upon by some other creature.

The megaphone man raised his instrument of torture; the inside of the great automobile began to thump and throb like the heart of a coffee drinker. The top-riders nervously clung to the seats; the old lady from Valparaiso, Indiana, shrieked to be put ashore. But, before a wheel turns, listen to a brief preamble through the cardiaphone, which shall point out to you an object of interest on life's sightseeing tour.

Swift and comprehensive is the recognition of the white man for white man in African wilds; instant and sure is the spiritual greeting between mother and babe; unhesitatingly do master and dog commune across the slight gulf between animal and man; immeasurably quick and sapient are the brief messages between one and one's beloved. But all these instances set forth only slow and groping interchange of sympathy and thought beside one other instance which the Rubberneck coach shall disclose. You shall learn (if you have not learned already) what two beings of all earth's living inhabitants most quickly look into each other's hearts and souls when they meet face to face.

The gong whirred, and the Glaring-at-Gotham car moved majestically upon its instructive tour.

On the highest, rear seat was James Williams, of Cloverdale, Missouri, and his Bride.

Capitalize it, friend typo – that last word – word of words in the epiphany of life and love. The scent of the flowers, the booty of the bee, the primal drip of spring waters, the overture of the lark, the twist of lemon peel on the cocktail of creation – such is the bride. Holy is the wife; revered the mother; galliptious is the summer girl – but the bride is the certified check among the wedding presents that the gods send in when man is married to mortality.

The car glided up the Golden Way. On the bridge of the great cruiser the captain stood, trumpeting the sights of the big city to his passengers. Wide-mouthed and open-eared they heard the sights of the metropolis thundered forth to their eyes. Confused, delirious with excitement and provincial longings, they tried to make ocular responses to the megaphonic ritual. In the solemn spires of spreading cathedrals they saw the home of the Vander-bilts; in the busy bulk of the Grand Central depot they viewed, wonderingly, the frugal cot of Russell Sage. Bidden to observe the highlands of the Hudson, they gaped, unsuspecting at the upturned mountains of a new-laid sewer.

To many the elevated railroad was the Rialto, on the stations of which uniformed men sat and made chop suey of your tickets. And to this day in the outlying districts many have it that Chuck Connors, with his hand on his heart, leads reform; and that but for the noble municipal efforts of one Parkhurst, a district attorney, the notorious 'Bishop' Potter gang would have destroyed law and order from the Bowery to the Harlem River.

But I beg you to observe Mrs. James Williams – Hattie Chalmers that was – once the belle of Cloverdale. Pale-blue is the bride's, if she will; and this color she had honored. Willingly had the moss rosebud loaned to her cheeks of its pink – and as for the violet! – her eyes will do very well as they are, thank you. A useless strip of white chaf – oh, no, he was guiding the auto car – of white chiffon – or perhaps it was grenadine or tulle – was tied beneath her chin, pretending to hold her bonnet in place. But you know as well as I do that the hat pins did the work.

And on Mrs. James Williams's face was recorded a little library of the world's best thoughts in three volumes. Volume No. 1 contained the belief that James Williams was about the right sort of thing. Volume No. 2 was an essay on the world, declaring it to be a very excellent place. Volume No. 3 disclosed the belief that in occupying the highest seat in a Rubberneck auto they were travelling the pace that passes all understanding.

James Williams, you would have guessed, was about twenty-four. It will gratify you to know that your estimate was so accurate. He was exactly twenty-three years, eleven months and twenty-nine days old. He was well built, active, strong-jawed, good-natured, and rising. He was on his wedding trip.

Dear kind fairy, please cut out those orders for money and 40 H. P. touring cars and fame and a new growth of hair and the presidency of the boat club. Instead of any of them turn backward – oh, turn backward and give us just a teeny-weeny bit of our wedding trip over again. Just an hour, dear fairy, so we can remember how the grass and poplar trees looked and the bow of those bonnet strings tied beneath her chin – even if it was the hat pins that did the work. Can't do it? Very well; hurry up with that touring car and the oil stock, then.

Just in front of Mrs. James Williams sat a girl in a loose tan jacket and a straw hat adorned with grapes and roses. Only in dream and milliners' shops do we, alas! gather grapes and roses at one swipe. This girl gazed with large blue eyes, credulous, when the megaphone man roared his doctrine that millionaires were things about which we should be concerned. Between blasts she resorted to Epictetian philosophy in the form of pepsin chewing gum.

At this girl's right hand sat a young man about twenty-four. He was well built, active, strong-jawed, and good-natured. But if his description seems to follow that of James Williams, divest it of anything Cloverdalian. This man belonged to hard streets and sharp corners. He looked keenly about him, seeming to begrudge the asphalt under the feet of those upon whom he looked down from his perch.

While the megaphone barks at a famous hostelry, let me whisper you through the low-tuned cardiaphone to sit tight; for now things are about to happen, and the great city will close over them again as over a scrap of ticker tape floating down from the den of a Broad Street bear.

The girl in the tan jacket twisted around to view the pilgrims on the last seat. The other passengers she had absorbed; the seat behind her was her Bluebeard's chamber.

Her eyes met those of Mrs. James Williams. Between two ticks of a watch they exchanged their life's experiences, histories, hopes and fancies. And all, mind you, with the eye, before two men could have decided whether to draw steel or borrow a match.

The bride leaned forward low. She and the girl spoke rapidly together, their tongues moving quickly like those of two serpents – a comparison that is not meant to go further. Two smiles and a dozen nods closed the conference.

And now in the broad, quiet avenue in front of the Rubberneck car a man in dark clothes stood with uplifted hand. From the sidewalk another hurried to join him.

The girl in the fruitful hat quickly seized her companion by the arm and whispered in his ear. That young man exhibited proof of ability to act promptly. Crouching low, he slid over the edge of the car, hung lightly for an instant, and then disappeared. Half a dozen of the top-riders observed his feat wonderingly, but made no comment, deeming it prudent not to express surprise at what might be the conventional manner of alighting in this bewildering city. The truant passenger dodged a hansom and then floated past, like a leaf on a stream between a furniture van and a florist's delivery wagon.

The girl in the tan jacket turned again, and looked into the eyes of Mrs. James Williams. Then she faced about and sat still while the Rubberneck auto stopped at the flash of the badge under the coat of the plainclothes man.

'What's eating you?' demanded the megaphonist, abandoning his professional discourse for pure English.

'Keep her at anchor for a minute,' ordered the officer. 'There's a man on board we want – a Philadelphia burglar called "Pinky" McGuire. There he is on the back seat. Look out for the side, Donovan.'

Donovan went to the hind wheel and looked up at James Williams.

'Come down, old sport,' he said pleasantly. 'We've got you. Back to

Sleepytown for yours. It ain't a bad idea, hidin' on a Rubberneck, though. I'll remember that.'

Softly through the megaphone came the advice of the conductor:

'Better step off, sir, and explain. The car must proceed on its tour.'

James Williams belonged among the level heads. With necessary slowness he picked his way through the passengers down to the steps at the front of the car. His wife followed, but she first turned her eyes and saw the escaped tourist glide from behind the furniture van and slip behind a tree on the edge of the little park, not fifty feet away.

Descended to the ground, James Williams faced his captors with a smile. He was thinking what a good story he would have to tell in Cloverdale about having been mistaken for a burglar. The Rubberneck coach lingered, out of respect for its patrons. What could be a more interesting sight than this?

'My name is James Williams, of Cloverdale, Missouri,' he said, kindly, so that they would not be too greatly mortified. 'I have letters here that will show — '

'You'll come with us, please,' announced the plainclothes man. ' "Pinky" McGuire's descriptions fits you like flannel washed in hot suds. A detective saw you on the Rubberneck up at Central Park and 'phoned down to take you in. Do your explaining at the station-house.'

James Williams's wife – his bride of two weeks – looked him in the face with a strange, soft radiance in her eyes and a flush on her cheeks, looked him in the face and said:

'Go with 'em quietly, "Pinky," and maybe it'll be in your favor.'

And then as the Glaring-at-Gotham car rolled away she turned and threw a kiss – his wife threw a kiss – at some one high up on the seats of the Rubberneck.

'Your girl gives you good advice, McGuire,' said Donovan. 'Come on now.'

And then madness descended upon and occupied James Williams. He pushed his hat far upon the back of his head.

'My wife seems to think I am a burglar,' he said, recklessly. 'I never heard of her being crazy; therefore I must be. And if I'm crazy, they can't do anything to me for killing you two fools in my madness.'

Whereupon he resisted so cheerfully and industriously that cops had to be whistled for, and afterwards the reserves, to disperse a few thousand delighted spectators.

At the station-house the desk sergeant asked for his name.

'McDoodle, the Pink, or Pinky the Brute, I forget which,' was James Williams's answer. 'But you can bet I'm a burglar; don't leave that out. And you might add that it took five of 'em to pluck the Pink. I'd especially like to have that in the records.'

In an hour came Mrs. James Williams, with Uncle Thomas, of Madison Avenue, in a respect-compelling motor car and proofs of the hero's innocence – for all the world like the third act of a drama backed by an automobile mfg. co.

After the police had sternly reprimanded James Williams for imitating a copyrighted burglar and given him as honorable a discharge as the department was capable of, Mrs. Williams rearrested him and swept him into an angle of the station-house. James Williams regarded her with one eye. He always said that Donovan closed the other while somebody was holding his good right hand. Never before had he given her a word of reproach or of reproof.

'If you can explain,' he began rather stiffly, 'why you—'

'Dear,' she interrupted, 'listen. It was an hour's pain and trial for you. I did it for her – I mean the girl who spoke to me on the coach. I was so happy, Jim – so happy with you that I didn't dare refuse that happiness to another. Jim, they were married only this morning – those two; and I wanted him to get away. While they were struggling with you I saw him slip from behind his tree and hurry across the park. That's all of it, dear – I had to do it.'

Thus does one sister of the plain gold band know another who stands in the enchanted light that shines but once and briefly for each one. By rice and satin bows does mere man become aware of weddings. But bride knoweth bride at the glance of an eye. And between them swiftly passes comfort and meaning in a language that man and widows wot not of.

THE ROMANCE OF A BUSY BROKER

PITCHER, CONFIDENTIAL CLERK in the office of Harvey Maxwell, broker, allowed a look of mild interest and surprise to visit his usually expressionless countenance when his employer briskly entered at half-past nine in company with his young lady stenographer. With a snappy 'Good-morning, Pitcher,' Maxwell dashed at his desk as though he were intending to leap over it, and then plunged into the great heap of letters and telegrams waiting there for him.

The young lady had been Maxwell's stenographer for a year. She was beautiful in a way that was decidedly unstenographic. She forewent the pomp of the alluring pompadour. She wore no chains, bracelets, or lockets. She had not the air of being about to accept an invitation to luncheon. Her dress was gray and plain, but it fitted her figure with fidelity and discretion. In her neat black turban hat was the gold-green wing of a macaw. On this morning she was softly and shyly radiant. Her eyes were dreamily bright, her cheeks genuine peach-blow, her expression a happy one, tinged with reminiscence.

Pitcher, still mildly curious, noticed a difference in her ways this morning. Instead of going straight into the adjoining room, where her desk was, she lingered, slightly irresolute, in the outer office. Once she moved over by Maxwell's desk, near enough for him to be aware of her presence.

The machine sitting at that desk was no longer a man; it was a busy New York broker, moved by buzzing wheels and uncoiling springs.

'Well – what is it? Anything?' asked Maxwell, sharply. His opened mail lay like a bank of stage snow on his crowded desk. His keen gray eye, impersonal and brusque, flashed upon her half impatiently.

'Nothing,' answered the stenographer, moving away with a little smile.

'Mr. Pitcher,' she said to the confidential clerk, 'did Mr. Maxwell say anything yesterday about engaging another stenographer?'

'He did,' answered Pitcher. 'He told me to get another one. I notified the agency yesterday afternoon to send over a few samples this morning. It's 9.45 o'clock, and not a single picture hat or piece of pineapple chewing gum has showed up yet.'

'I will do the work as usual, then,' said the young lady, 'until some one comes to fill the place.' And she went to her desk at once and hung the black turban hat with the gold-green macaw wing in its accustomed place.

He who has been denied the spectacle of a busy Manhattan broker during a rush of business is handicapped for the profession of anthropology. The poet sings of the 'crowded hour of glorious life.' The broker's hour is not only crowded, but minutes and seconds are hanging to all the straps and packing both front and rear platforms.

And this day was Harvey Maxwell's busy day. The ticker began to reel out jerkily its fitful coils of tape, the desk telephone had a chronic attack of buzzing. Men began to throng into the office and call at him over the railing, jovially, sharply, viciously, excitedly. Messenger boys ran in and out with messages and telegrams. The clerks in the office jumped about like sailors during a storm. Even Pitcher's face relaxed into something resembling animation.

On the Exchange there were hurricanes and landslides and snowstorms and glaciers and volcanoes, and those elemental disturbances were reproduced in miniature in the broker's offices. Maxwell shoved his chair against the wall and transacted business after the manner of a toe dancer. He jumped from ticker to 'phone, from desk to door with the trained agility of a harlequin.

In the midst of this growing and important stress the broker became suddenly aware of a high-rolled fringe of golden hair under a nodding canopy of velvet and ostrich tips, an imitation sealskin sacque and a string of beads as large as hickory nuts, ending near the floor with a silver heart. There was a self-possessed young lady connected with these accessories; and Pitcher was there to construe her.

'Lady from the Stenographer's Agency to see about the position,' said Pitcher.

Maxwell turned half around, with his hands full of papers and ticker tape.

'What position?' he asked, with a frown.

'Position of stenographer,' said Pitcher. 'You told me yesterday to call them up and have one sent over this morning.'

'You are losing your mind, Pitcher,' said Maxwell. 'Why should I have given you any such instructions? Miss Leslie has given perfect satisfaction during the year she has been here. The place is hers as long as she chooses to retain it. There's no place open here, madam. Countermand that order with the agency, Pitcher, and don't bring any more of 'em here.'

The silver heart left the office, swinging and banging itself independently against the office furniture as it indignantly departed. Pitcher seized a moment to remark to the bookkeeper that the 'old man' seemed to get more absent-minded and forgetful every day of the world.

The rush and pace of business grew fiercer and faster. On the floor they were pounding half a dozen stocks in which Maxwell's customers were heavy investors. Orders to buy and sell were coming and going as swift as the flight of swallows. Some of his own holdings were imperilled, and the man was working like some high-geared, delicate, strong machine – strung to full tension, going at full speed, accurate, and never hesitating, with the proper word and decision and act ready and prompt as clockwork. Stocks and bonds, loans and mortgages, margins and securities – here was a world of finance, and there was no room in it for the human world or the world of nature.

When the luncheon hour drew near there came a slight lull in the uproar.

Maxwell stood by his desk with his hands full of telegrams and memoranda, with a fountain pen over his right ear and his hair hanging in disorderly strings over his forehead. His window was open, for the beloved janitress, Spring had turned on a little warmth through the waking registers of the earth.

And through the window came a wandering – perhaps a lost – odor – a delicate, sweet odor of lilac that fixed the broker for a moment immovable. For this odor belonged to Miss Leslie; it was her own, and hers only.

The odor brought her vividly, almost tangibly before him. The world of finance dwindled suddenly to a speck. And she was in the next room – twenty steps away.

'By George, I'll do it now,' said Maxwell, half aloud. 'I'll ask her now. I wonder I didn't do it long ago.'

He dashed into the inner office with the haste of a short trying to cover. He charged upon the desk of the stenographer.

She looked up at him with a smile. A soft pink crept over her cheek, and her eyes were kind and frank. Maxwell leaned one elbow on her desk. He still clutched fluttering papers with both hands and the pen was above his ear.

'Miss Leslie,' he began, hurriedly, 'I have but a moment to spare. I want to say something in that moment. Will you be my wife? I haven't had time to make love to you in the ordinary way, but I really do love you. Talk quick, please – those fellows are clubbing the stuffing out of Union Pacific.'

'Oh, what are you talking about?' exclaimed the young lady. She rose to her feet and gazed upon him, round-eyed.

'Don't you understand?' said Maxwell, restively. 'I want you to marry me. I love you, Miss Leslie. I wanted to tell you, and I snatched a minute when things had slackened up a bit. They're calling me for the 'phone now. Tell 'em to wait a minute, Pitcher. Won't you, Miss Leslie?'

The stenographer acted very queerly. At first she seemed overcome with amazement; then tears flowed from her wondering eyes; and then she smiled sunnily through them, and one of her arms slid tenderly about the broker's neck.

'I know now,' she said, softly. 'It's this old business that has driven everything else out of your head for the time. I was frightened at first. Don't you remember, Harvey? We were married last evening at 8 o'clock in the Little Church around the Corner.'

AFTER TWENTY YEARS

THE POLICEMAN ON THE BEAT moved up the avenue impressively. The impressiveness was habitual and not for show, for spectators were few. The time was barely 10 o'clock at night, but chilly gusts of wind with a taste of rain in them had well nigh depeopled the streets.

Trying doors as he went, twirling his club with many intricate and artful movements, turning now and then to cast his watchful eye adown the pacific thoroughfare, the officer, with his stalwart form and slight swagger, made a fine picture of a guardian of the peace. The vicinity was one that kept early hours. Now and then you might see the lights of a cigar store or of an all-night lunch counter; but the majority of the doors belonged to business places that had long since been closed.

When about midway of a certain block the policeman suddenly slowed his walk. In the doorway of a darkened hardware store a man leaned, with an unlighted cigar in his mouth. As the policeman walked up to him the man spoke up quickly.

'It's all right, officer,' he said, reassuringly. 'I'm just waiting for a friend. It's an appointment made twenty years ago. Sounds a little funny to you, doesn't it? Well, I'll explain if you'd like to make certain it's all straight. About that long ago there used to be a restaurant where this store stands – "Big Joe" Brady's restaurant.'

'Until five years ago,' said the policeman. 'It was torn down then.'

The man in the doorway struck a match and lit his cigar. The light showed a pale, square-jawed face with keen eyes, and a little white scar near his right eyebrow. His scarfpin was a large diamond, oddly set.

'Twenty years ago to-night,' said the man, 'I dined here at "Big Joe" Brady's with Jimmy Wells, my best chum, and the finest chap in the world. He and I were raised here in New York, just like two brothers, together. I was eighteen and Jimmy was twenty. The next morning I was to start for the West to make my fortune. You couldn't have dragged Jimmy out of New York; he thought it was the only place on earth. Well, we agreed that night that we would meet here again exactly twenty years from that date and time, no matter what our conditions might be or from what distance we might have to come. We figured that in twenty years each of us ought to have our destiny worked out and our fortunes made, whatever they were going to be.'

'It sounds pretty interesting,' said the policeman. 'Rather a long time between meets, though, it seems to me. Haven't you heard from your friend since you left?'

'Well, yes, for a time we corresponded,' said the other. 'But after a year or two we lost track of each other. You see, the West is a pretty big proposition, and I kept hustling around over it pretty lively. But I know Jimmy will meet me here if he's alive, for he always was the truest, staunchest old chap in the world. He'll never forget. I came a thousand miles to stand in this door to-night, and it's worth it if my old partner turns up.'

The waiting man pulled out a handsome watch, the lids of it set with small diamonds.

'Three minutes to ten,' he announced. 'It was exactly ten o'clock when we parted here at the restaurant door.'

'Did pretty well out West, didn't you?' asked the policeman.

'You bet! I hope Jimmy has done half as well. He was a kind of plodder, though, good fellow as he was. I've had to compete with some of the sharpest wits going to get my pile. A man gets in a groove in New York. It takes the West to put a razor-edge on him.'

The policeman twirled his club and took a step or two.

'I'll be on my way. Hope your friend comes around all right. Going to call time on him sharp?'

'I should say not!' said the other. 'I'll give him half an hour at least. If Jimmy is alive on earth he'll be here by that time. So long, officer.'

'Good-night, sir,' said the policeman, passing on along his beat, trying doors as he went.

There was now a fine, cold drizzle falling, and the wind had risen from its uncertain puffs into a steady blow. The few foot passengers astir in that quarter hurried dismally and silently along with coat collars turned high and pocketed hands. And in the door of the hardware store the man who had come a thousand miles to fill an appointment, uncertain almost to absurdity, with the friend of his youth, smoked his cigar and waited.

About twenty minutes he waited, and then a tall man in a long overcoat, with collar turned up to his ears, hurried across from the opposite side of the street. He went directly to the waiting man.

'Is that you, Bob?' he asked, doubtfully.

'Is that you, Jimmy Wells?' cried the man in the door.

'Bless my heart!' exclaimed the new arrival, grasping both the other's hands with his own. 'It's Bob, sure as fate. I was certain I'd find you here if you were still in existence. Well, well, well! – twenty years is a long time. The old restaurant's gone, Bob; I wish it had lasted, so we could have had another dinner there. How has the West treated you, old man?'

'Bully; it has given me everything I asked it for. You've changed lots, Jimmy. I never thought you were so tall by two or three inches.'

'Oh, I grew a bit after I was twenty.'

'Doing well in New York, Jimmy?'

'Moderately. I have a position in one of the city departments. Come on, Bob; we'll go around to a place I know of, and have a good long talk about old times.'

The two men started up the street, arm in arm. The man from the West, his egotism enlarged by success, was beginning to outline the history of his career. The other, submerged in his overcoat, listened with interest.

At the corner stood a drug store, brilliant with electric lights. When they came into this glare each of them turned simultaneously to gaze upon the other's face.

The man from the West stopped suddenly and released his arm.

'You're not Jimmy Wells,' he snapped. 'Twenty years is a long time, but not long enough to change a man's nose from a Roman to a pug.'

'It sometimes changes a good man into a bad one,' said the tall man. 'You've been under arrest for ten minutes, 'Silky' Bob. Chicago thinks you may have dropped over our way and wires us she wants to have a chat with you. Going quietly, are you? That's sensible. Now, before we go to the station here's a note I was to hand to you. You may read it here at the window. It's from Patrolman Wells.'

The man from the West unfolded the little piece of paper handed him. His hand was steady when he began to read, but it trembled a little by the time he had finished. The note was rather short.

Bob: I was at the appointed place on time. When you struck the match to light your cigar I saw it was the face of the man wanted in Chicago. Somehow I couldn't do it myself, so I went around and got a plain clothes man to do the job.

                                                                    Jimmy

LOST ON DRESS PARADE

MR. TOWERS CHANDLER WAS PRESSING his evening suit in his hall bedroom. One iron was heating on a small gas stove; the other was being pushed vigorously back and forth to make the desirable crease that would be seen later on extending in straight lines from Mr. Chandler's patent leather shoes to the edge of his low-cut vest. So much of the hero's toilet may be intrusted to our confidence. The remainder may be guessed by those whom genteel poverty has driven to ignoble expedient. Our next view of him shall be as he descends the steps of his lodging-house immaculately and correctly clothed; calm, assured, handsome – in appearance the typical New York young clubman setting out, slightly bored, to inaugurate the pleasures of the evening.

Chandler's honorarium was $18 per week. He was employed in the office of an architect. He was twenty-two years old; he considered architecture to be truly an art; and he honestly believed – though he would not have dared to admit it in New York – that the Faltiron Building was inferior in design to the great cathedral in Milan.

Out of each week's earnings Chandler set aside $1. At the end of each ten weeks with the extra capital thus accumulated, he purchased one gentleman's evening from the bargain counter of stingy old Father Time. He arrayed himself in the regalia of millionaires and presidents; he took himself to the quarter where life is brightest and showiest, and there dined with taste and luxury. With ten dollars a man may, for a few hours, play the wealthy idler to perfection. The sum is ample for a well-considered meal, a bottle bearing a respectable label, commensurate tips, a smoke, cab fare, and the ordinary etceteras.

This one delectable evening culled from each dull seventy was to Chandler a source of renascent bliss. To the society bud comes but one début; it stands alone sweet in her memory when her hair has whitened; but to Chandler each ten weeks brought a joy as keen, as thrilling, as new, as the first had been. To sit among *bon vivants* under palms in the swirl of concealed music, to look upon the *habitués* of such a paradise and to be looked upon by them – what is a girl's first dance and short-sleeved tulle compared with this?

Up Broadway Chandler moved with the vespertine dress parade. For this evening he was an exhibit as well as a gazer. For the next sixty-nine evenings he would be dining in cheviot and worsted at dubious *table d'hôtes*, at whirlwind lunch counters, on sandwiches and beer in his hall bedroom. He was willing to do that, for he was a true son of the great city of razzle-dazzle, and to him one evening in the limelight made up for many dark ones.

Chandler protracted his walk until the forties began to intersect the great and glittering primrose way, for the evening was yet young, and when one is of the *beau monde* only one day in seventy, one loves to protract the pleasure. Eyes bright, sinister, curious, admiring, provocative, alluring were bent upon him, for his garb and air proclaimed him a devotee to the hour of solace and pleasure.

At a certain corner he came to a standstill, proposing to himself the question of turning back toward the showy and fashionable restaurant in which he usually dined on the evenings of his especial luxury. Just then a girl scuddled lightly around the corner, slipped on a patch of icy snow and fell plump upon the sidewalk.

Chandler assisted her to her feet with instant and solicitous courtesy. The girl hobbled to the wall of the building, leaned against it, and thanked him demurely.

'I think my ankle is strained,' she said. 'It twisted when I fell.'

'Does it pain you much?' inquired Chandler.

'Only when I rest my weight upon it. I think I will be able to walk in a minute or two.'

'If I can be of any further service,' suggested the young man, 'I will call a cab, or—'

'Thank you,' said the girl, softly but heartily. 'I am sure you need not trouble yourself any further. It was so awkward of me. And my shoe heels are horridly commonsense; I can't blame them at all.'

Chandler looked at the girl and found her swiftly drawing his interest. She was pretty in a refined way; and her eye was both merry and kind. She was inexpensively clothed in a plain black dress that suggested a sort of uniform such as shop-girls wear. Her glossy dark-brown hair showed its coils beneath a cheap hat of black straw whose only ornament was a velvet ribbon and bow. She could have posed as a model for the self-respecting working girl of the best type.

A sudden idea came into the head of the young architect. He would ask this girl to dine with him. Here was the element that his splendid but solitary periodic feats had lacked. His brief season of elegant luxury would be doubly enjoyable if he could add to it a lady's society. This girl was a lady, he was sure – her manner and speech settled that. And in spite of her extremely plain attire he felt that he would be pleased to sit at table with her.

These thoughts passed swiftly through his mind, and he decided to ask her. It was a breach of etiquette, of course, but oftentimes wage-earning girls waived formalities in matters of this kind. They were generally shrewd judges of men; and thought better of their own judgment than they did of useless conventions. His ten dollars, discreetly expended, would enable the two to dine very well indeed. The dinner would no doubt be a wonderful experience thrown into the dull routine of the girl's life; and her lively appreciation of it would add to his own triumph and pleasure.

'I think,' he said to her, with frank gravity, 'that your foot needs a longer rest than you suppose. Now, I am going to suggest a way in which you can give it that and at the same time do me a favor. I was on my way to dine all by my lonely self when you came tumbling around the corner. You come with me and we'll have a cozy dinner and a pleasant talk together, and by that time your game ankle will carry you home very nicely, I am sure.'

The girl looked quickly up into Chandler's clear, pleasant countenance. Her eyes twinkled once very brightly, and then she smiled ingenuously.

'But we don't know each other – it wouldn't be right, would it?' she said, doubtfully.

'There is nothing wrong about it,' said the young man, candidly. 'I'll introduce myself – permit me – Mr. Towers Chandler. After our dinner, which I will try to make as pleasant as possible, I will bid you good-evening, or attend you safely to your door, whichever you prefer.'

'But, dear me!' said the girl, with a glance at Chandler's faultless attire. 'In this old dress and hat!'

'Never mind that,' said Chandler, cheerfully. 'I'm sure you look more charming in them than any one we shall see in the most elaborate dinner toilette.'

'My ankle does hurt yet,' admitted the girl, attempting a limping step. 'I think I will accept your invitation, Mr. Chandler. You may call me – Miss Marian.'

'Come then, Miss Marian,' said the young architect, gaily, but with perfect courtesy; 'you will not have far to walk. There is a very respectable and good restaurant in the next block. You will have to lean on my arm – so – and walk slowly. It is lonely dining all by one's self. I'm just a little bit glad that you slipped on the ice.'

When the two were established at a well-appointed table, with a promising waiter hovering in attendance, Chandler began to experience the real joy that his regular outing always brought to him.

The restaurant was not so showy or pretentious as the one further down Broadway, which he always preferred, but it was nearly so. The tables were well filled with prosperous-looking diners, there was a good orchestra, playing softly enough to make conversation a possible pleasure, and the cuisine and service were beyond criticism. His companion, even in her cheap hat and dress, held herself with an air that added distinction to the natural beauty of her face and figure. And it is certain that she looked at Chandler, with his animated but self-possessed manner and his kindling and frank blue eyes, with something not far from admiration in her own charming face.

Then it was that the Madness of Manhattan, the Frenzy of Fuss and Feathers, the Bacillus of Brag, the Provincial Plague of Pose seized upon Towers Chandler. He was on Broadway, surrounded by pomp and style, and there were eyes to look at him. On the stage of that comedy he had assumed to play the one-night part of a butterfly of fashion and an idler of means and taste. He was dressed for the part, and all his good angels had not the power to prevent him from acting it.

So he began to prate to Miss Marian of clubs, of teas, of golf and riding and kennels and cotillions and tours abroad and threw out hints of a yacht lying at Larchmont. He could see that she was vastly impressed by this vague talk, so he endorsed his pose by random insinuations concerning great wealth, and mentioned familiarly a few names that are handled reverently by the proletariat. It was Chandler's short little day, and he was wringing from it the best that could be had, as he saw it. And yet once or twice he saw the pure gold of this girl shine through the mist that his egotism had raised between him and all objects.

'This way of living that you speak of,' she said, 'sounds so futile and purposeless. Haven't you any work to do in the world that might interest you more?'

'My dear Miss Marian,' he exclaimed – 'work! Think of dressing every day for dinner, of making half a dozen calls in an afternoon – with a policeman at every corner ready to jump into your auto and take you to the station, if you get up any greater speed than a donkey cart's gait. We do-nothings are the hardest workers in the land.'

The dinner was concluded, the waiter generously feed, and the two walked out to the corner where they had met. Miss Marian walked very well now; her limp was scarcely noticeable.

'Thank you for a nice time,' she said, frankly. 'I must run home now. I liked the dinner very much, Mr. Chandler.'

He shook hands with her, smiling cordially, and said something about a game of bridge at his club. He watched her for a moment, walking rather rapidly eastward, and then he found a cab to drive him slowly homeward.

In his chilly bedroom Chandler laid away his evening clothes for a sixty-nine days' rest. He went about it thoughtfully.

'That was a stunning girl,' he said to himself. 'She's all right, too, I'd be sworn, even if she does have to work. Perhaps if I'd told her the truth instead of all that razzle-dazzle we might – but, confound it! I had to play up to my clothes.'

Thus spoke the brave who was born and reared in the wigwams of the tribe of the Manhattans.

The girl, after leaving her entertainer, sped swiftly cross-town until she arrived at a handsome and sedate mansion two squares to the east, facing on that avenue which is the highway of Mammon and the auxiliary gods. Here she entered hurriedly and ascended to a room where a handsome young lady in an elaborate house dress was looking anxiously out the window.

'Oh, you madcap!' exclaimed the elder girl, when the other entered. 'When will you quit frightening us this way? It's two hours since you ran out in that rag of an old dress and Marie's hat. Mamma has been so alarmed. She sent Louis in the auto to try to find you. You are a bad, thoughtless Puss.'

The elder girl touched a button, and a maid came in a moment.

'Marie, tell mamma that Miss Marian has returned.'

'Don't scold, Sister. I only ran down to Mme. Theo's to tell her to use mauve insertion instead of pink. My costume and Marie's hat were just what I needed. Every one thought I was a shop-girl, I am sure.'

'Dinner is over, dear; you stayed so late.'

'I know. I slipped on the sidewalk and turned my ankle. I could not walk, so I hobbled into a restaurant and sat there until I was better. That is why I was so long.'

The two girls sat in the window seat, looking out at the lights and the stream of hurrying vehicles in the avenue. The younger one cuddled down with her head in her sister's lap.

'We will have to marry some day,' she said, dreamily – 'both of us. We have so much money that we will not be allowed to disappoint the public. Do you want me to tell you the kind of a man I could love, Sis?'

'Go on, you scatterbrain,' smiled the other.

'I could love a man with dark and kind blue eyes, who is gentle and respectful to poor girls, who is handsome and good and does not try to flirt. But I could love him only if he had an ambition, an object, some work to do in the world. I would not care how poor he was if I could help him build his way up. But, Sister dear, the kind of man we always meet – the man who lives an idle life between society and his clubs – I could not love a man like that, even if his eyes were blue and he were so kind to poor girls whom he met in the street.'

BY COURIER

IT WAS NEITHER THE SEASON nor the hour when the Park had frequenters; and it is likely that the young lady, who was seated on one of the benches at the side of the walk, had merely obeyed a sudden impulse to sit for a while and enjoy a foretaste of coming Spring.

She rested there, pensive and still. A certain melancholy that touched her countenance must have been of recent birth, for it had not yet altered the fine and youthful contours of her cheek, nor subdued the arch though resolute curve of her lips.

A tall young man came striding through the park along the path near which she sat. Behind him tagged a boy carrying a suit-case. At sight of the young lady, the man's face changed to red and back to pale again. He watched her countenance as he drew nearer, with hope and anxiety mingled on his own. He passed within a few yards of her, but he saw no evidence that she was aware of his presence or existence.

Some fifty yards further on he suddenly stopped and sat on a bench at one side. The boy dropped the suit-case and stared at him with wondering, shrewd eyes. The young man took out his handkerchief and wiped his brow. It was a good handkerchief, a good brow, and the young man was good to look at. He said to the boy:

'I want you to take a message to that young lady on that bench. Tell her I am on my way to the station, to leave for San Francisco, where I shall join that Alaska moose-hunting expedition. Tell her that, since she has commanded me neither to speak nor to write to her, I take this means of making one last appeal to her sense of justice, for the sake of what has been. Tell her that to condemn and discard one who has not deserved such treatment, without giving him her reasons or a chance to explain is contrary to her nature as I believe it to be. Tell her that I have thus, to a certain degree, disobeyed her injunctions, in the hope that she may yet be inclined to see justice done. Go, and tell her that.'

The young man dropped a half-dollar into the boy's hand. The boy looked at him for a moment with bright, canny eyes out of a dirty, intelligent face and then set off at a run. He approached the lady on the bench a little doubtfully, but unembarrassed. He touched the brim of an old plaid bicycle cap perched on the back of his head. The lady looked at him coolly, without prejudice or favor.

'Lady,' he said, 'dat gent on de oder bench sent yer a song and dance by me. If yer don't know de guy, and he's tryin' to do de Johnny act, say de word, and I'll call a cop in t'ree minutes. If yer does know him, and he's on de square, w'y I'll spiel yer de bunch of hot air he sent yer.'

The young lady betrayed a faint interest.

'A song and dance!' she said, in a deliberate, sweet voice that seemed to clothe her words in a diaphanous garment of impalpable irony. 'A new idea – in the troubadour line, I suppose. I – used to know the gentleman who sent you so I think it will hardly be necessary to call the police. You may execute your song and dance, but do not sing too loudly. It is a little early yet for open-air vaudeville, and we might attract attention.'

'Awe,' said the boy, with a shrug down the length of him, 'yer know what I mean, lady. 'Tain't a turn, it's wind. He told me to tell yer he's got his collars and cuffs in dat grip for a scoot clean out to 'Frisco. Den he's goin' to shoot snow-birds in de Klondike. He says you told him not to send 'round no more pink notes nor come hangin' over de garden gate, and he takes dis means of puttin' yer wise. He says yer refereed him out like a has-been, and never give him no chance to kick at de decision. He says yer swiped him, and never said why.'

The slightly awakened interest in the young lady's eyes did not abate. Perhaps it was caused by either the originality or the audacity of the snow-bird hunter, in thus circumventing her express commands against the ordinary modes of communication. She fixed her eye on a statue standing disconsolate in the dishevelled park, and spoke into the transmitter:

'Tell the gentleman that I need not repeat to him a description of my ideals. He knows what they have been and what they still are. So far as they touch on this case, absolute loyalty and truth are the ones paramount. Tell him that I have studied my own heart as well as one can, and I know its weakness as well as I do its needs. That is why I decline to hear his pleas, whatever they may be. I did not condemn him through hearsay or doubtful evidence, and that is why I made no charge. But, since he persists in hearing what he already well knows, you may convey the matter.

'Tell him that I entered the conservatory that evening from the rear, to cut a rose for my mother. Tell him I saw him and Miss Ashburton beneath the pink oleander. The tableau was pretty, but the pose and juxtaposition were too eloquent and evident to require explanation. I left the conservatory, and, at the same time, the rose and my ideal. You may carry that song and dance to your impressario.'

'I'm shy on one word, lady. Jux – jux – put me wise on that, will yer?'

'Juxtaposition – or you may call it propinquity – or, if you like, being rather too near for one maintaining the position of an ideal.'

The gravel spun from beneath the boy's feet. He stood by the other bench. The man's eyes interrogated him, hungrily. The boy's were shining with the impersonal zeal of the translater.

'De lady says dat she's on to de fact dat gals is dead easy when a feller come spielin' ghost stories and tryin' to make up, and dat's why she won't listen to no soft-soap. She says she caught yer dead to rights, huggin' a bunch o' calico in de hot-house. She side-stepped in to pull some posies and yer was squeezin' der oder gal to beat de band. She says it looked cute, all right all right, but it made her sick. She says yer better git busy, and make a sneak for de train.'

The young man gave a low whistle and his eyes flashed with a sudden thought. His hand flew to the inside pocket of his coat, and drew out a handful of letters. Selecting one, he handed it to the boy, following it with a silver dollar from his vest-pocket.

'Give that letter to the lady,' he said, 'and ask her to read it. Tell her that it should explain the situation. Tell her that, if she had mingled a little trust with her conception of the ideal, much heartache might have been avoided. Tell her that loyalty she prizes so much has never wavered. Tell her I am waiting for an answer.'

The messenger stood before the lady.

'De gent says he's had de ski-bunk put on him widout no cause. He says he's no bum guy; and, lady, yer read dat letter, and I'll bet yer he's a white sport, all right.'

The young lady unfolded the letter, somewhat doubtfully, and read it.

Dear Dr. Arnold: I want to thank you for your most kind and opportune aid to my daughter last Friday evening, when she was overcome by an attack of her old heart-trouble in the conservatory at Mrs. Waldron's reception. Had you not been near to catch her as she fell and to render proper attention, we might have lost her. I would be glad if you would call and undertake the treatment of her case.

Gratefully yours,
Robert Ashburton

The young lady refolded the letter, and handed it to the boy.

'De gent wants an answer,' said the messenger. 'What's de word?'

The lady's eyes suddenly flashed on him, bright, smiling and wet.

'Tell that guy on the other bench,' she said, with a happy, tremulous laugh, 'that his girl wants him.'

THE FURNISHED ROOM

RESTLESS, SHIFTING, FUGACIOUS as time itself is a certain vast bulk of the population of the red brick district of the lower West Side. Homeless they have a hundred homes. They flit from furnished room to furnished room, transients forever – transients in abode, transients in heart and mind. They sing 'Home, Sweet Home' in ragtime; they carry their *lares et penates* in a bandbox; their vine is entwined about a picture hat; a rubber plant is their fig tree.

Hence the houses of this district, having had a thousand dwellers, should have a thousand tales to tell, mostly dull ones, no doubt; but it would be strange if there could not be found a ghost or two in the wake of all these vagrant guests.

One evening after dark a young man prowled among these crumbling red mansions, ringing their bells. At the twelfth he rested his lean hand-baggage upon the step and wiped the dust from his hatband and forehead. The bell sounded faint and far away in some remote, hollow depths.

To the door of this, the twelfth house whose bell he had rung, came a housekeeper who made him think of an unwholesome, surfeited worm that had eaten its nut to a hollow shell and now sought to fill the vacancy with edible lodgers.

He asked if there was a room to let.

'Come in,' said the housekeeper. Her voice came from her throat; her throat seemed lined with fur. 'I have the third-floor back, vacant since a week back. Should you wish to look at it?'

The young man followed her up the stairs. A faint light from no particular source mitigated the shadows of the halls. They trod noiselessly upon a stair carpet that its own loom would have foresworn. It seemed to have become vegetable; to have degenerated in that rank, sunless air to lush lichen or spreading moss that grew in patches to the stair-case and was viscid under the foot like organic matter. At each turn of the stairs were vacant niches in the wall. Perhaps plants had once been set within them. If so they had died in that foul and tainted air. It may be that statues of the saints had stood there, but it was not difficult to conceive that imps and devils had dragged them forth in the darkness and down to the unholy depths of some furnished pit below.

'This is the room,' said the housekpeeper, from her furry throat. 'It's a nice room. It ain't often vacant. I had some most elegant people in it last summer – no trouble at all, and paid in advance to the minute. The water's at the end of the hall. Sprowls and Mooney kept it three months. They done a vaudeville sketch. Miss B'retta Sprowls – you may have heard of her – Oh, that was just the stage names – right there over the dresser is where the marriage certificate hung, framed. The gas is here, and you see there is plenty of closet room. It's a room everybody likes. It never stays idle long.'

'Do you have many theatrical people rooming here?' asked the young man.

'They comes and goes. A good proportion of my lodgers is connected with the theatres. Yes, sir, this is the theatrical district. Actor people never stays long anywhere. I get my share. Yes, they comes and they goes.'

He engaged the room, paying for a week in advance. He was tired, he said, and would take possession at once. He counted out the money. The room had been made ready, she said, even to towels and water. As the housekeeper moved away he put, for the thousandth time, the question that he carried at the end of his tongue.

'A young girl – Miss Vashner – Miss Eloise Vashner – do you remember such a one among your lodgers? She would be singing on the stage, most likely. A fair girl, of medium height and slender, with reddish, gold hair and dark mole near her left eyebrow.'

'No, I don't remember the name. Them stage people has names they change as often as their rooms. They comes and they goes. No, I don't call that one to mind.'

No. Always no. Five months of ceaseless interrogation and the inevitable negative. So much time spent by day in questioning managers, agents, schools and choruses; by night among the audiences of theatres from all-star casts down to music halls so low that he dreaded to find what he most hoped for. He who had loved her best had tried to find her. He was sure that since her disappearance from home this great, water-girt city held her somewhere, but it was like a monstrous quicksand, shifting its particles constantly, with no foundation, its upper granules of to-day buried to-morrow in ooze and slime.

The furnished room received its latest guest with a first glow of pseudo-hospitality, a hectic, haggard, perfunctory welcome like the specious smile of a demirep. The sophistical comfort came in reflected gleams from the decayed furniture, the ragged brocade upholstery of a couch and two chairs, a foot-wide cheap pier glass between the two windows, from one or two gilt picture frames and a brass bedstead in a corner.

The guest reclined, inert, upon a chair, while the room, confused in speech as though it were an apartment in Babel, tried to discourse to him of its divers tenantry.

A polychromatic rug like some brilliant-flowered, rectangular, tropical islet lay surrounded by a billowy sea of soiled matting. Upon the gay.papered wall were those pictures that pursue the homeless one from house to house – The Huguenot Lovers, The First Quarrel, The Wedding Breakfast, Psyche at the Fountain. The mantel's chastely severe outline was ingloriously veiled behind some pert drapery drawn rakishly askew like the sashes of the Amazonian ballet. Upon it was some desolate flotsam cast aside by the room's marooned when a lucky sail had borne them to a fresh port – a trifling vase or two, pictures of actresses, a medicine bottle, some stray cards out of a deck.

One by one, as the characters of a cryptograph became explicit, the little signs left by the furnished rooms' procession of guests developed a significance. The threadbare space in the rug in front of the dresser told that lovely women had marched in the throng. The tiny fingerprints on the wall spoke of little prisoners trying to feel their way to sun and air. A splattered stain, raying like the shadow of a bursting bomb, witnessed where a hurled glass or bottle had splintered with its contents against the wall. Across the pier glass had been scrawled with a diamond in staggering letters the name 'Marie.' It seemed that the succession of dwellers in the furnished room had turned in fury – perhaps tempted beyond forebearance by its garish coldness – and wreaked upon it their passions. The furniture was chipped and bruised; the couch, distorted by bursting springs, seemed a horrible monster that had been slain during the stress of some grotesque convulsion. Some more potent unheaval had cloven a great slice from the marble mantel. Each plank in the floor owned its particular cant and shriek as from a separate and individual agony. It seemed incredible that all this malice and injury had been wrought upon the room by those who had called it for a time their home; and yet it may have been the cheated home instinct surviving blindly, the resentful rage at false household gods that had kindled their wrath. A hut that is our own we can sweep and adorn and cherish.

The young tenant in the chair allowed these thoughts to file, soft-shod, through his mind, while there drifted into the room furnished sounds and furnished scents. He heard in one room a tittering and incontinent, slack laughter; in others the monologue of a scold, the rattling of dice, a lullaby, and one crying dully; above him a banjo tinkled with spirit. Doors banged somewhere; the elevated trains roared intermittently; a cat yowled miserably upon a back fence. And he breathed the breath of the house – a dank savor rather than a smell – a cold, musty effuvium as from underground vaults mingled with the reeking exhalations of linoleum and mildewed and rotten woodwork.

Then suddenly, as he rested there, the room was filled with the strong, sweet odor of mignonette. It came as upon a single buffet of wind with such sureness and fragrance and emphasis that it almost seemed a living visitant. And the man cried aloud: 'What, dear?' as if he had been called, and sprang up and faced about. The rich odor clung to him and wrapped him around. He reached out his arms for it, all his senses for the time confused and commingled. How could one be peremptorily called by an odor? Surely it must have been a sound. But, was it not the sound that had touched, that had caressed him?

'She has been in this room,' he cried, and he sprang to wrest from it a token, for he knew he would recognize the smallest thing that had belonged to her or that she had touched. This enveloping scent of mignonette, the odor that she had loved and made her own – whence came it?

The room had been but carelessly set in order. Scattered upon the flimsy dresser scarf were half a dozen hairpins – those discreet, indistinguishable friends of womankind, feminine of gender, infinite mood and uncommunicative of tense. These he ignored, conscious of their triumphant lack of identity. Ransacking the drawers of the dresser he came upon a discarded, tiny, ragged handkerchief. He pressed it to his face. It was racy and insolent with heliotrope; he hurled it to the floor. In another drawer he found odd buttons, a theatre programme, a pawnbroker's card, two lost marshmallows, a book on the divination of dreams. In the last was a woman's black satin hair bow, which halted him, poised between ice and fire. But the black satin hair bow also is femininity's demure, impersonal common ornament and tells no tales.

And then he traversed the room like a hound on the scent, skimming the walls, considering the corners of the bulging matting on his hands and knees, rummaging mantel and tables, the curtains and hangings, the drunken cabinet in the corner, for a visible sign, unable to perceive that she was there beside, around, against, within, above him, clinging to him, wooing him, calling him so poignantly through the finer senses that even his grosser ones became cognizant of the call. Once again he answered loudly: 'Yes, dear!' and turned, wild-eyed, to gaze on vacancy, for he could not yet discern form and color and love and outstretched arms in the odor of mignonette. Oh, God! whence that odor, and since when have odors had a voice to call? Thus he groped.

He burrowed in crevices and corners, and found corks and cigarettes. These he passed in passive contempt. But once he found in a fold of the matting a half-smoked cigar, and this he ground beneath his heel with a green and trenchant oath. He sifted the room from end to end. He found dreary and ignoble small records of many a peripatetic tenant; but of her whom he sought, and who may have lodged there, and whose spirit seemed to hover there, he found no trace.

And then he thought of the housekeeper.

He ran from the haunted room downstairs and to a door that showed a crack of light. She came out to his knock. He smothered his excitement as best he could.

'Will you tell me, madam,' he besought her, 'who occupied the room I have before I came?'

'Yes, sir. I can tell you again. 'Twas Sprowls and Mooney, as I said. Miss B'retta Sprowls it was in the theatres, but Missis Mooney she was. My house is well known for respectability. The marriage certificate hung, framed, on a nail over—'

'What kind of a lady was Miss Sprowls – in looks, I mean?'

'Why, black-haired, sir, short, and stout, with a comical face. They left a week ago Tuesday.'

'And before they occupied it?'

'Why, there was a single gentleman connected with the draying business. He left owing me a week. Before him was Missis Crowder and her two children, that stayed four months; and back of them was old Mr. Doyle, whose sons paid for him. He kept the room six months. That goes back a year, sir, and further I do not remember.'

He thanked her and crept back to his room. The room was dead. The essence that had vivified it was gone. The perfume of mignonette had departed. In its place was the old, stale odor of mouldy house furniture, of atmosphere in storage.

The ebbing of his hope drained his faith. He sat staring at the yellow, singing gaslight. Soon he walked to the bed and began to tear the sheets into strips. With the blade of his knife he drove them tightly into every crevice around windows and door. When all was snug and taut he turned out the light, turned the gas full on again and laid himself gratefully upon the bed.

It was Mrs. McCool's night to go with the can for beer. So she fetched it and sat with Mrs. Purdy in one of those subterranean retreats where housekeepers foregather and the worm dieth seldom.

'I rented out my third-floor this evening,' said Mrs. Purdy, across a fine circle of foam. 'A young man took it. He went up to bed two hours ago.'

'Now, did ye, Mrs. Purdy, ma'am?' said Mrs. McCool, with intense admiration. 'You do be a wonder for rentin' rooms of that kind. And did ye tell him, then?' she concluded in a husky whisper laden with mystery.

'Rooms,' said Mrs. Purdy, in her furriest tones, 'are furnished for to rent. I did not tell him, Mrs. McCool.'

' 'Tis right ye are, ma'am; 'tis by renting rooms we kape alive. Ye have the rale sense for business, ma'am. There be many people will rayjict the rentin' of a room if they be tould a suicide has been after dyin' in the bed of it.'

'As you say, we has our living to be making,' remarked Mrs. Purdy.

'Yis, ma'am; 'tis true. 'Tis just one wake ago this day I helped ye lay out the third-floor-back. A pretty slip of a colleen she was to be killin' herself wid the gas – a swate little face she had, Mrs. Purdy, ma'am.'

'She'd a-been called handsome, as you say,' said Mrs. Purdy, assenting but critical, 'but for that mole she had a-growin' by her left eyebrow. Do fill up your glass again, Mrs. McCool.'

THE BRIEF DÉBUT OF TILDY

IF YOU DO NOT KNOW BOGLE'S CHOP HOUSE and Family Restaurant it is your loss. For if you are one of the fortunate ones who dine expensively you should be interested to know how the other half consumes provisions. And if you belong to the half to whom waiters' checks are things of moment, you should know Bogle's, for there you get your money's worth – in quantity, at least.

Bogle's is situated in that highway of *bourgeoisie*, that boulevard of Brown-Jones-and-Robinson, Eighth Avenue. There are two rows of tables in the room, six in each row. On each table is a caster-stand, containing cruets of condiments and seasons. From the pepper cruet you may shake a cloud of something tasteless and melancholy, like volcanic dust. From the salt cruet you may expect nothing. Though a man should extract a sanguinary stream from the pallid turnip, yet will his prowess be balked when he comes to wrest salt from Bogle's cruets. Also upon each table stands the counterfeit of that benign sauce made 'from the recipe of a nobleman in India.'

At the cashier's desk sits Bogle, cold, sordid, slow, smouldering, and takes your money. Behind a mountain of toothpicks he makes your change, files your check, and ejects at you, like a toad, a word about the weather. Beyond a corroboration of his meteorological statement you would better not venture. You are not Bogle's friend; you are a fed, transient customer, and you and he may not meet again until the blowing of Gabriel's dinner horn. So take your change and go – to the devil if you like. There you have Bogle's sentiments.

The needs of Bogle's customers were supplied by two waitresses and a Voice. One of the waitresses was named Aileen. She was tall, beautiful, lively, gracious and learned in persiflage. Her other name? There was no more necessity for another name at Bogle's than there was for finger-bowls.

The name of the other waitress was Tildy. Why do you suggest Matilda? Please listen this time – Tildy – Tildy. Tildy was dumpy, plain-faced, and too anxious to please to please. Repeat the last clause to yourself once or twice, and make the acquaintance of the duplicate infinite.

The Voice at Bogle's was invisible. It came from the kitchen, and did not shine in the way of originality. It was a heathen Voice, and contented itself with vain repetitions of exclamations emitted by the waitresses concerning food.

Will it tire you to be told again that Aileen was beautiful? Had she donned a few hundred dollars' worth of clothes and joined the Easter parade, and had you seen her, you would have hastened to say so yourself.

The customers at Bogle's were her slaves. Six tables full she could wait upon at once. They who were in a hurry restrained their impatience for the joy of merely gazing upon her swiftly moving, graceful figure. They who had finished eating ate more that they might continue in the light of her smiles. Every man there – and they were mostly men – tried to make his impression upon her.

Aileen could successfully exchange repartee against a dozen at once. And every smile that she sent forth lodged, like pellets from a scatter-gun, in as many hearts. And all this while she would be performing astounding feats with orders of pork and beans, pot roasts, ham-and, sausage-and-the-wheats, and any quantity of things on the iron and in the pan and straight up and on the side. With all this feasting and flirting and merry exchange of wit Bogle's came mighty near being a salon, with Aileen for its Madame Recamier.

If the transients were entranced by the fascinating Aileen, the regulars were her adorers. There was much rivalry among many of the steady customers. Aileen could have had an engagement every evening. At least twice a week some one took her to a theatre or to a dance. One stout gentleman whom she and Tildy had privately christened 'The Hog' presented her with a turquoise ring. Another one known as 'Freshy,' who rode on the Traction Company's repair wagon, was going to give her a poodle as soon as his brother got the hauling contract in the Ninth. And the man who always ate spareribs and spinach and said he was a stock broker asked her to go to 'Parsifal' with him.

'I don't know where this place is,' said Aileen while talking it over with Tildy, 'but the wedding-ring's got to be on before I put a stitch into a travelling dress – ain't that right? Well, I guess!'

But, Tildy!

In steaming, chattering, cabbage-scented Bogle's there was almost a heart tragedy. Tildy with the blunt nose, the hay-colored hair, the freckled skin, the bag-o'-meal figure, had never had an admirer. Not a man followed her with his eyes when she went to and fro in the restaurant save now and then when they glared with the beast-hunger for food. None of them bantered her gaily to coquettish interchanges of wit. None of them loudly 'jollied' her of mornings as they did Aileen, accusing her, when the eggs were slow in coming, of late hours in the company of envied swains. No one had ever given her a turquoise ring or invited her upon a voyage to mysterious, distant 'Parsifal.'

Tildy was a good waitress, and the men tolerated her. They who sat at her tables spoke to her briefly with quotations from the bill of fare; and then raised their voices in honeyed and otherwise-flavored accents, eloquently addressed to the fair Aileen. They writhed in their chairs to gaze around and over the impending form of Tildy, that Aileen's pulchritude might season and make ambrosia of their bacon and eggs.

And Tildy was content to be the unwooed drudge if Aileen could receive the flattery and the homage. The blunt nose was loyal to the short Grecian. She was Aileen's friend; and she was glad to see her rule hearts and wean the attention of men from smoking pot-pie and lemon meringue. But deep below our freckles and hay-colored hair the unhandsomest of us dream of a prince or a princess, not vicarious, but coming to us alone.

There was a morning when Aileen tripped in to work with a slightly bruised eye; and Tildy's solicitude was almost enough to heal any optic.

'Fresh guy,' explained Aileen, 'last night as I was going home at Twenty-third and Sixth. Sashayed up, so he did, and made a break. I turned him down, cold, and he made a sneak; but followed me down to Eighteenth, and tried his hot air again. Gee! but I slapped him a good one side of the face. Then he give me that eye. Does it look real awful, Til! I should hate that Mr. Nicholson should see it when he comes in for his tea and toast at ten.'

Tildy listened to the adventure with breathless admiration. No man had ever tried to follow her. She was safe abroad at any hour of the twenty-four. What bliss it must have been to have had a man follow one and black one's eye for love!

Among the customers at Bogle's was a young man named Seeders, who worked in a laundry office. Mr. Seeders was thin and had light hair, and appeared to have been recently rough-dried and starched. He was too diffident to aspire to Aileen's notice; so he usually sat at one of Tildy's tables, where he devoted himself to silence and boiled weakfish.

One day when Mr. Seeders came in to dinner he had been drinking beer. There were only two or three customers in the restaurant. When Mr. Seeders had finished his weakfish he got up, put his arm around Tildy's waist, kissed her loudly and impudently, walked out upon the street, snapped his fingers in the direction of the laundry, and hied himself to play pennies in the slot machines at the Amusement Arcade.

For a few moments Tildy stood petrified. Then she was aware of Aileen shaking at her an arch forefinger, and saying:

'Why, Til, you naughty girl! Ain't you getting to be awful, Miss Slyboots. First thing I know you'll be stealing some of my fellows. I must keep an eye on you, my lady.'

Another thing dawned upon Tildy's recovering wits. In a moment she had advanced from a hopeless, lowly admirer to be an Eve-sister of the potent Aileen. She herself was now a man-charmer, a mark for Cupid, a Sabine who must be coy when the Romans were at their banquet boards. Man had found her waist achievable and her lips desirable. The sudden and amatory Seeders had, as it were, performed for her a miraculous piece of one-day laundry work. He had taken the sackcloth of her uncomeliness, had washed, dried, starched and ironed it, and returned it to her sheer embroidered lawn – the robe of Venus herself.

The freckles on Tildy's cheeks merged into a rosy flush. Now both Circe and Psyche peeped from her brightened eyes. Not even Aileen herself had been publicly embraced and kissed in the restaurant.

Tildy could not keep the delightful secret. When trade was slack she went and stood at Bogle's desk. Her eyes were shining; she tried not to let her words sound proud and boastful.

'A gentleman insulted me to-day,' she said. 'He hugged me around the waist and kissed me.'

'That so?' said Bogle, cracking open his business armor. 'After this week you get a dollar a week more.'

At the next regular meal when Tildy set food before customers with whom she had acquaintance she said to each of them modestly, as one whose merit needed no bolstering:

'A gentleman insulted me to-day in the restaurant. He put his arms around my waist and kissed me.'

The diners accepted the revelation in various ways – some incredulously, some with congratulations; others turned upon her the stream of badinage that had hitherto been directed at Aileen alone. And Tildy's heart swelled in her bosom, for she saw at last the towers of Romance rise above the horizon of the gray plain in which she had for so long travelled.

For two days Mr. Seeders came not again. During that time Tildy established herself firmly as a woman to be wooed. She bought ribbons, and arranged her hair like Aileen's and tightened her waist two inches. She had a thrilling but delightful fear that Mr. Seeders would rush in suddenly and shoot her with a pistol. He must have loved her desperately; and impulsive lovers are always blindly jealous.

Even Aileen had not been shot at with a pistol. And then Tildy rather hoped that he would not shoot at her, for she was always loyal to Aileen; and she did not want to over-shadow her friend.

At 4 o'clock on the afternoon of the third day Mr. Seeders came in. There were no customers at the tables. At the back end of the restaurant Tildy was refilling the mustard pots and Aileen was quartering pies. Mr. Seeders walked back to where they stood.

Tildy looked up and saw him, gasped, and pressed the mustard spoon against her heart. A red hair-bow was in her hair; she wore Venus's Eighth Avenue badge, the blue bead necklace with the swinging silver symbolic heart.

Mr. Seeders was flushed and embarrassed. He plunged one hand into his hip pocket and the other into a fresh pumpkin pie.

'Miss Tildy,' said he, 'I want to apologize for what I done the other evenin'. Tell you the truth, I was pretty well tanked up or I wouldn't of done it. I wouldn't do no lady that a-way when I was sober. So I hope, Miss Tildy, you'll accept my 'pology, and believe that I wouldn't of done it if I'd known what I was doin' and hadn't of been drunk.'

With this handsome plea Mr. Seeders backed away, and departed, feeling that reparation had been made.

But behind the convenient screen. Tildy had thrown herself flat upon a table among the butter chips and the coffee cups, and was sobbing her heart out – out and back again to the gray plain wherein travel they with blunt noses and hay-colored hair. From her knot she had torn the red hair-bow and cast it upon the floor. Seeders she despised utterly; she had but taken his kiss as that of a pioneer and prophetic prince who might have set the clocks going and the pages to running in fairyland. But the kiss had been maudlin and unmeant; the court had not stirred at the false alarm; she must forevermore remain the Sleeping Beauty.

Yet not all was lost. Aileen's arm was around her; and Tildy's red hand groped among the butter chips till it found the warm clasp of her friend's.

'Don't you fret, Til,' said Aileen, who did not understand entirely. 'That turnip-faced little clothespin of a Seeders ain't worth it. He ain't anything of a gentleman or he wouldn't ever of apologized.'